Jasmine Haynes

"An erotic, emotional adventure of discovery you won't want to miss."

—Lora Leigh, #1 *New York Times* bestselling author

"A supersexy and wonderfully emotional read from start to finish. I love, love, loved it!"

—Bella Andre, author of *Hot as Sin*

"Delightfully torrid." —*Midwest Book Review*

"More than a fast-paced erotic romance, this is a story of family, filled with memorable characters who will keep you engaged in the plot and the great sex. A good read to warm a winter's night." —*Romantic Times*

"Steamy, sexy, and provocative as well as thought-provoking . . . Not to be missed." —*Night Owl Romance*

"Bursting with sensuality and eroticism."

—*In the Library Reviews*

"The passion is intense, hot, and purely erotic . . . Recommended for any reader who likes their stories realistic, hot, captivating and very, very well written."

—*The Road to Romance*

"Not your typical romance. This one's going to remain one of my favorites." —*The Romance Studio*

"Jasmine Haynes keeps the plot moving and the love scenes very hot." —*Just Erotic Romance Reviews*

"A wonderful novel . . . Try this one—you won't be sorry."

—*The Best Reviews*

THE
FORTUNE
HUNTER

Jasmine Haynes

BERKLEY SENSATION, NEW YORK

THE BERKLEY PUBLISHING GROUP
Published by the Penguin Group
Penguin Group (USA) Inc.
375 Hudson Street, New York, New York 10014, USA
Penguin Group (Canada), 90 Eglinton Avenue East, Suite 700, Toronto, Ontario M4P 2Y3, Canada
(a division of Pearson Penguin Canada Inc.)
Penguin Books Ltd., 80 Strand, London WC2R 0RL, England
Penguin Group Ireland, 25 St. Stephen's Green, Dublin 2, Ireland (a division of Penguin Books Ltd.)
Penguin Group (Australia), 250 Camberwell Road, Camberwell, Victoria 3124, Australia
(a division of Pearson Australia Group Pty. Ltd.)
Penguin Books India Pvt. Ltd., 11 Community Centre, Panchsheel Park, New Delhi—110 017, India
Penguin Group (NZ), 67 Apollo Drive, Rosedale, North Shore 0632, New Zealand
(a division of Pearson New Zealand Ltd.)
Penguin Books (South Africa) (Pty.) Ltd., 24 Sturdee Avenue, Rosebank, Johannesburg 2196,
South Africa

Penguin Books Ltd., Registered Offices: 80 Strand, London WC2R 0RL, England

This is a work of fiction. Names, characters, places, and incidents either are the product of the author's imagination or are used fictitiously, and any resemblance to actual persons, living or dead, business establishments, events, or locales is entirely coincidental. The publisher does not have any control over and does not assume any responsibility for author or third-party websites or their content.

THE FORTUNE HUNTER

A Berkley Sensation Book / published by arrangement with the author

PRINTING HISTORY
Berkley Sensation trade paperback edition / November 2007
Berkley Sensation mass-market edition / November 2010

Copyright © 2007 by Jennifer Skullestad.
Excerpt from *Mine Until Morning* copyright © 2010 by Jennifer Skullestad.
Cover design by George Long.
Cover illustration by Jim Griffin.
Hand lettering by Ron Zinn.
Interior text design by Tiffany Estreicher.

ISBN: 978-0-425-23100-5

BERKLEY® SENSATION
Berkley Sensation Books are published by The Berkley Publishing Group,
a division of Penguin Group (USA) Inc.,
375 Hudson Street, New York, New York 10014.
BERKLEY® SENSATION and the "B" design are trademarks of Penguin Group (USA) Inc.

PRINTED IN THE UNITED STATES OF AMERICA

10 9 8 7 6 5 4 3 2 1

To Terri Schaefer
For always being a straight shooter and
saying it like it is

ACKNOWLEDGMENTS

Thanks to Jenn Cummings, Terri Schaefer, and Rose Lerma, for endless hours of reading. To Nancy Cochran, Elda Minger, and Rose, again, for all their brainstorming when the story was just a germ of an idea. To Christine Zika, for talking me through the rough spots. And to my agent, Lucienne Diver, and my editor, Wendy McCurdy.

1

"FAITH. Over here." Trinity Green waved frantically from the other side of the ballroom, her voice falling into a sudden hush as the dance number ended.

Faith cringed as she suddenly felt every eye on her, the partygoers around her stepping back slightly so that she was in a little circle all her own. The indisputable center of attention.

Trinity would never understand why any woman in her right mind *wouldn't* want to be the center of attention.

Faith, obviously not in her right mind, loathed it. Her friend was now skirting the dance floor, a dark-haired man in tow. Faith smiled. Men loved being towed by Trinity. In addition to her blond hair, Aphrodite looks, and flawless body, she was quite a lovable person.

They'd been best friends since the seventh grade when Trinity had rescued Faith from a spiteful group of girls. Middle school girls could be terrors on anyone different. Though their fathers had known each other for years up to that point, Trinity hadn't seemed to notice Faith existed. Yet Trinity stood by her that day, and Faith would forever love her for it.

"Sweetie, there's someone I'm dying for you to meet." Trinity grabbed Faith's hand, then seized her companion's, and forced their handshake. "This is my best friend in all the world, Faith Castle. And Faith, this is Connor Kingston. He's working with Lance at Daddy's company." Lance was Trinity's brother and heir to the Green company throne.

"It's nice to meet you, Miss Castle."

Out of force of habit due to her short stature, Faith tended to look at hands instead of faces during introductions. But something in Connor Kingston's voice, the husky quality of it, like a rhythm guitar strumming a deep chord, made her look up. And up. She was five foot four in the heels she wore tonight, five foot two without them. Connor was over six.

He had the blackest hair she'd ever seen, so black the chandelier lighting gleamed off it. Charcoal eyes gazed down at her—though charcoal seemed such a boring color. His were the shade of a moonlit midnight.

He and Trinity made a perfect couple.

"And it's nice to meet you, Mr. Kingston."

Trinity snorted. "Give me a break. It's Faith and Connor, okay? No more of that *Mr.* Kingston and *Miss* Castle stuff."

Faith almost laughed hearing the names said so closely together. His king to her castle. Like a chess move. Or a statement on male to female relations.

Introductions done, Trinity stroked his black tuxedo-clad arm. "Connor, would you get us some champagne? I'm parched." Not that Trinity would drink the whole glass. Too many calories.

Connor smiled. A wolf, tamed for the moment, grinning at a cute little bunny. "Of course." He turned the smile on Faith, something flickered in his eyes, then his mouth crooked a little higher on one side.

If she didn't know better, she'd have thought she'd made the wolf comment aloud.

"Isn't he divine?" Trinity whispered as they watched him until he was swallowed up by the crowd at the bar.

"Absolutely."

Then Trinity sighed. "It's too bad he doesn't have a cent to his name other than what Daddy's paying him."

"At least he has a job."

Their small community of Silicon Valley elite, those left after the dot-com crash and the economic downturn a few years ago, could be broken down into two categories: those who had, and those who didn't. Most of the didn't-haves lived off the did-haves, not by working but by being charming and getting their entertainment written off as a tax-deductible business expense by the other half. Or, they married into the class they coveted.

"That's the worst part," Trinity moaned. "Everyone *knows* he works. Daddy would have a hissy fit if I even *mentioned* marrying an employee." She tapped her chin thoughtfully. "But we could have a wild affair." She fluttered her eyelashes. "You know, all that unbridled passion, the fear of being *caught*." She shivered dramatically. "It sounds so intense."

Agreeing completely, Faith wanted to shiver herself. With his dark good looks, Connor Kingston incited many a delicious fantasy. Trinity winked, and they scanned the crowd for him.

Faith spotted the back of his head. My, his shoulders were broad in the tuxedo. "I'll leave you alone to work your magic."

Trinity grabbed her arm. "You can't run off. He wanted to meet you since I talk about you all the time."

Faith gasped. "You do not."

"Close your mouth, sweetie. I told him you're the only one in the whole dissolute lot of us who has a calling."

"What calling?"

Trinity huffed. "As a kindergarten teacher, of course, shaping young minds. You're producing a better next generation."

Faith taught because she loved children. And because she was sometimes terrified she'd never have any of her own. She was twenty-nine years old, thirty by the end of the year, and unless she married one of the didn't-haves looking for a did-have wife, teaching might be the sum total exposure she had to children.

Yet Trinity was right, being a teacher was her calling. Which reminded her. Faith smiled to herself. "Do you know what little Roger Weederman said the other day?"

"That's what I adore about you. You *love* the little monsters. When I have children, you have to quit your job and become their nanny. You'll raise them to be little presidents." Trinity spread her hands. "President of the company, president of the United States, president of the United Nations."

Faith laughed. Heads turned. She sometimes laughed too

boisterously, but when she was with Trinity, she couldn't help herself. Trinity didn't mean half of what she said. She liked to talk, especially at big bashes, saying outrageous things to anyone who would listen. She had, however, graduated from college with honors and would one day make a perfect first lady.

But Faith wasn't going to be anyone's nanny. She wanted children of her own.

Over the crowd, Faith spied Connor fast approaching. She wasn't jealous of Trinity's sleekness when matched against her own relative plumpness, but for some reason, she didn't want to watch *him* do the usual mental comparison. "I really have to go before Mr. Stud-Muffin returns. He's all yours."

"I can't have him. Unbridled passion doesn't outrank one of Daddy's hissy attacks. And Connor got you champagne." Trinity clasped her hands. "Come on, Faith. Pretty please, don't go."

"Ladies' room," Faith whispered as she slipped away.

"Spoilsport," Trinity returned, just before creasing her lips with a smile any man would die for.

Handsome men made Faith nervous. Connor Kingston did worse. For the first time, he made her wish for cosmetic surgery to turn herself into a Trinity clone.

FAITH grimaced. This was a humiliating position to find herself in, sitting in a ladies' room stall, minding her own business, while being forced to listen to mean-spirited gossip.

"Lisa is so dumpy, she deserves to have him cheat. I mean, really, she wore stripes. No one wears stripes to a formal."

"Not only that," the other girl joined in, "they were going the wrong way. Everyone knows stripes make you look fatter when they're horizontal instead of vertical. What possessed her?"

Poor Lisa. Faith commiserated though she was secretly thankful she wasn't the subject of the nasty gossip. She'd chosen a basic black cocktail dress for the evening.

One of them sighed without an ounce of sympathy for the hapless Lisa. "Well, he got exactly what he wanted. A frumpy little heiress and all the afternoon delight he can handle."

Faith couldn't remember the husband's name, only that he was one of the have-nots before he married Lisa. *Afternoon delight.* What a lovely term for adultery. Poor Lisa.

"Do tell. Who's he doing the do with?"

"Kitchum's wife."

Gasp. "That slut. She's twenty years older than him."

"She just had her face done and looks younger than Lisa."

"Well, that's what old man Kitchum gets for marrying a gold digger half his age."

They laughed in unison, then, thank God, their voices faded as the ladies' room door snicked closed behind them.

Faith was now blessedly alone. Which was worse? The cheating, or the humiliation of having it discussed in the restroom? Maybe she was in danger of lumping all those in her own social circle into one neat ziplock Baggie, but gossip did seem to be a favorite pastime amongst them.

What on earth was she doing attending one gala after another? Searching for Mr. Right? That's what her father hoped for her, bless his heart, though he did seem to find something lacking in the few prospects Faith had brought home.

To tell the truth, she didn't need Mr. Right. She only needed children. Her heart ached she wanted them so badly. Yet she grew up without a mother, and she firmly believed kids needed both parents. So, being good potential father material was the only requirement on her list. Amongst her peers, she had serious doubts of finding a man who fit the bill.

Slipping out of the now empty ladies' room, Faith headed into the club's gardens for a respite from the activity. Blooms perfumed the spring night, the garden resplendent with camellias and azaleas, and the crescent moon reflected off the still waters of the man-made lake in the center of the club grounds.

She wandered down the incline through the trees and bushes, and she would have made it to the water's edge if she hadn't suddenly heard a voice on the other side of the hedge.

"Suck it, please, honey. I'm dying here."

Dear Lord, with another few steps, she would have passed the hedge and stumbled right on top of the couple. Faith knew she should find another route to the lake, but something, a devil on her shoulder perhaps, kept her rooted to the spot.

The woman didn't say a word. There was only the rasp of a zipper on the night breeze.

Faith, that devil whispering in her ear, peeked around the end of the hedge. Seated on a stone bench, the woman had a firm grip on her partner's penis, slowly pumping him as his head fell back in total ecstasy.

"Christ, yes. Suck it, sweetheart."

"Don't rush me." The voice was soft with seduction, husky with desire, sultry with power.

The couple cavorted in the shelter of the overhanging trees, and Faith couldn't make out faces. Somehow, their very anonymity fueled her own fantasies.

"Please," he begged.

Faith's nipples beaded against the soft fabric of her dress, and a throb started low in her belly, streaking down between her legs. In an instant, she was damp.

Oh yes, she could almost feel her own hand wrapped around his erection, hard flesh begging her to caress the tip, to suck the tiny drop of come.

She wasn't a virgin. She'd had moments when she'd almost believed she was desirable. Those moments hadn't become anything lasting, and the few men she'd been with had gotten bored quickly. Or they were after her money. Just as her father said.

This, however, was the stuff of her sexually explicit fantasies, where she could have everything done to her and do everything in return. Where she asked for what she wanted without fear of rejection and indulged in all the erotic, sensual acts she'd never done but wanted desperately to experience.

The woman bent her head. Faith could almost taste him, feel him between her lips. Without conscious thought, her hand lifted to her breast, her palm fondling one tight nipple as she watched. Watching was naughty but so incredibly sexy.

Then the woman took his penis all the way, her mouth fusing to him, his fingers tangling in her hair. Whispers, groans, sounds all around her, making Faith almost a participant in what they were doing. Her hand slid down the front of her dress, over her abdomen until her fingers lightly pressed her mound.

She should have walked away. But her feet wouldn't move. Nothing on heaven and earth could make her stop watching.

CONNOR followed Faith Castle into the moonlit gardens, giving her plenty of lead to disguise the fact he was tailing her. When he caught up, the meeting would appear accidental.

Over the past few weeks, as he'd dutifully squired her around town, Trinity Green told him everything there was to know about Faith. She was almost thirty, a schoolteacher, and she loved children beyond anything. She also happened to be the heiress to Castle Heavy Mining. According to the Trinity gospel, Faith was a paragon. Could there actually be such a thing? Trinity had extolled her virtues as if she were putting the woman on the auctioning block. The question was why. What was the benefit in touting Faith?

Whatever her reasons, Trinity had told him everything important about Faith. Or so he thought. She hadn't mentioned Faith's abundant body. Far from a model-thin beauty queen, Faith was round and curvy. A man could hold Faith in his arms and not worry about breaking her. Her breasts were a bounty. Her derriere begged for a man's caress. Her hair, cascading past her shoulders, was the color of an exploding sun, all reds and golds.

Faith lacked the classic aristocratic features revered in

today's world. Her face was round, her nose a tad snub, and her mouth small, but beauty was so much more than bone structure. It was the whole package, inside and out. Trinity had given him a hint of Faith's soft center, but her full impact hit him when she laughed. From across the dance floor, the throaty sound shot straight to his cock. That's when he started imagining her on her knees taking him into her mouth, when he'd envisioned sinking his fingers into her hair and holding her to him as he came.

Yes, Faith Castle was a pleasant surprise. A lush creature begging for him to plumb the depths others casually dismissed. He hadn't imagined that seducing her would be so pleasurable.

Ahead of him, she stopped at a hedge, leaning forward slightly to peer around it.

Connor stole closer. Hushed voices reached him, then indistinguishable sounds. Faith seemed rooted to the spot like a statue hewn in place. She didn't hear him as he circled, coming up on her left. The fingers of her right hand found purchase in the hedge branches, as if to steady herself.

Then he saw what so fascinated her.

Well, well, well, Faith Castle was indeed a bundle of contrasts. Knee-length cocktail dress, well-hidden cleavage, moderate heels on her shoes. One thought prim and proper.

But there she was, standing in the flower-scented garden watching a woman go down on her lover. A breath whispered from Faith's lips as the man drove his cock deep. Her hand left the hedge and skated down the front of her dress, brushing her abdomen, then pressed between her legs.

The sight sucked Connor's breath from his lungs, and his cock surged. Her breasts crested against her dress. Diamond-tipped nipples begged for his mouth. That luscious body was meant for loving, and if Trinity was to be believed, Faith hadn't seen much of that lately. Fucking idiots, the men who passed her over because of a mere body-type fad. She wanted passion. Hell yes, she wanted it badly.

He wanted to give it to her. He'd stumbled onto the perfect supplement to his plan, the ideal stratagem to draw her in.

He hadn't imagined securing his future could be this sweet.

IN her fantasies, Faith felt an arm wrap around her waist, pulling her against hard male thighs and a raging erection. Warm, enticing breath bathed her hair.

"You like watching, don't you?"

"Yes," she murmured.

Her own voice snapped her out of her reverie. Her body stiffened in his embrace. The touch was tangible, his words real, her orgasm on the horizon.

"Let me watch with you."

Smooth and sultry, his pitch seduced her as easily as the tableau in front of them. All she had to do was permit his caress, his nearness. She didn't have to act, simply allow him to do as he would. It was so effortless. He pulled her closer, rubbing his body sinuously against her back, bottom, and thighs.

His hand slipped down her abdomen and covered her own. He moved his fingers over hers, rotating gently, caressing her.

"He's going to blow in her mouth," he murmured.

Faith's breath rasped in her throat. She was dizzy and drunk on sex, on the kinkiness of watching, of letting some stranger take liberties with her body.

Under the trees in front of them, the man groaned louder, his hips pumping frantically. He held his partner's head, taking her mouth with his body rather than the other way around. He clenched, held, then cried out.

Lips dropped to Faith's neck, bit gently. Fingers rolled her nipple, pinched. Between her legs, he guided her hand rhythmically back and forth across her covered pussy.

She almost came when he pressed up and in, hard. Ripples of pleasure shot out from her clitoris. She bit her lip, closed her eyes, and savored the sensation.

Then he yanked her back into hiding on the other side of the hedge just as the male half of the tableau before them spoke.

"Jesus, that was good."

The woman's answer was smug, as was her voice. "I know."

"Let me fuck you."

"You'll get my dress dirty. Tomorrow. Doesn't your wife have tennis lessons or something? Meet me at the usual place."

Behind the hedge, Faith's mystery man held her close in the circle of his arms.

"Shh," he whispered.

As if he knew she was about to twist away and say . . . something. Such as, *How dare you?*

There was the rustle of clothing and what sounded like a belt buckle, then the man's voice again. "You're such a fucking tease."

"You love it. And Lisa doesn't swallow."

"And Kitchum wouldn't be able to fill your mouth with that much come. Don't tell me you don't love it."

God. It was old man Kitchum's wife with the face-lift and Lisa's had-none-of-his-own husband.

And just who was the man holding her?

"Thank you," he whispered, "for letting me join you."

She knew his voice then, the seductive, rough tones she'd first heard not a half hour ago.

Connor Kingston. Trinity's new dish.

She struggled a little in his arms as the lovers drifted off in the opposite direction. They'd part soon and head back to the ballroom. To Lisa with her horizontal stripes, and Kitchum, well, who knew if he was even here? Faith hadn't seen him.

"Let me go."

He shook his head as he once again dropped his lips to her neck. Did he even realize who she was? Or had he merely been turned on by the sight of a woman watching a sex scene played out in the moonlight?

Then he stroked her chin and turned her face to his. For a fraction of a second, his eyes locked with hers. No surprise, no horror. He had known exactly who he was touching. Faith almost drowned in his glittering gaze a moment before he took her lips with his. He tasted of the evening's champagne and something else—hot, hungry male. Greedy, ravenous, his tongue swooped in and stole her breath.

With a kiss like that, he could make a woman do anything.

His touch, then his kiss had her so hot, restless, and bothered, she had to battle her own needs far more than she had to fight him. She tried to wriggle away. "I have to go."

"Not before we make a date."

That made her stop. "A date?"

"Tomorrow evening."

"Why on earth would you want to go out with me?" Screw her, maybe. But a date?

He chuckled, his chest rumbling against her back. "Because I like the way you laugh."

"The way I laugh?" She was repeating like an idiot.

"In the ballroom. Trinity made you laugh."

No one had *ever* thought her laugh was special. She wanted to accept his invitation, but the whole incident was a fluke. And she was the one who'd get hurt. "You think I'm easy because of what just happened. But that was a strange combination of events, and it'll never happen again." Except in her fantasies.

"Not a date, then. Coffee."

"No." She squirmed against him once more.

"I'm not letting you go until you agree."

"Why?" It was the dumbest thing to ask, making it sound as if she couldn't understand why a man like him would want to see a woman like her again. But really, she *didn't* understand.

"I like your laugh, and I like the way you feel in my arms."

He was seducing her with just a few wonderful, tremendous, unbelievable words. He couldn't mean them.

"Meet me. Say yes. Please."

Dammit, the please did it. "Just coffee. And this will be the only time."

He sighed, his breath fluttering her unbound hair.

She said it would be the only time, but she knew without much pressure, she'd do anything he asked. That's how frighteningly hungry *she* was.

HE had a King Kong–sized hard-on for her. She'd been equally affected. He could have made her come with one more touch. A woman hadn't felt that good in his arms since . . . not since he was teenager and still believed in love.

Step one complete. He'd secured the first date. Connor had a plan for Faith Castle, a mutually advantageous plan.

He'd considered Trinity Green for a few short weeks, but while she was beautiful, sweet, and loyal, she was a little too absorbed with outward appearances, not to mention she'd probably freak if she perspired during sex. Besides, he had nothing to offer Trinity in return for what he asked, and he didn't intend making a one-sided deal that benefited only him. But with Faith, he had the one thing she wanted, and, according to Trinity, the thing Faith wasn't sure she'd ever get.

Yet, instead of pulling together a strategy for his campaign, all Connor could think of was the exquisite taste of her on his lips. That was a boon he hadn't anticipated.

Oh yeah, Faith was the one he wanted to marry. The moment he touched her, no other woman would do.

2

"DO you want dessert?" Connor slid her coffee cup over to her.

Faith made a production of adding cream and sugar. "No, thanks. Now, why did you want to meet me?" There, that was businesslike. Not as if this were a real date.

After getting their coffee and snagging a small table in the middle of the café, he'd sat in the chair closest to hers instead of across like a civilized person would do. She was terribly conscious of his thigh only inches from hers. On top of that, she'd been awake all night thinking about what they'd witnessed, what he'd done, the way he'd touched her. That kiss. Oh yes, that delicious, unforgettable kiss.

Faith put up a hand before Connor could answer. "And don't say anything about my laugh or last night."

He chuckled. "How about saying I want to get to know you better?"

At seven on Sunday evening, the little café was bursting at the seams with couples and small groups getting in their last bit of weekend socializing. The place served specialty coffees and tantalizing desserts. The sugary scents unsettled her stomach.

Actually, *he* unsettled her. She'd been jittery all day. Then she'd taken an extraordinary amount of time deciding what to wear, finally choosing a slimming skirt—Trinity wouldn't let her buy any other kind—and a fitted sweater. Spring was definitely here, but the nights could still be cool even in late April.

And the sweater nicely defined her breasts, which were her best feature.

Connor would look good in anything. Jeez, she thought

too much about other people's comparisons. That's why she didn't like going out with good-looking men.

The three young women two tables away stared at him as if he were a chocolate truffle without any calories. Faith dipped her head as they looked at her and started whispering.

"Trinity tells me you're a kindergarten teacher."

Faith realized she hadn't said a word for half a minute. And that Connor hadn't given the gaggle of beauties a single glance since he sat down. Trinity, he was talking about Trinity. "Are you and she dating?" she blurted. Despite Trinity's disclaimer, it was only polite to confirm up front that she wasn't stepping on toes.

"She doesn't like to attend parties alone. So I take her. It's not dating."

She, too, had often attended events with Trinity when an available male couldn't be found at the last minute. Though Trinity usually managed to find one soon after they arrived.

"I haven't seen you at any functions." She almost made it sound like an accusation.

Which didn't seem to bother Connor. "I haven't seen you, either. Must be on different evenings."

What was there about him that made her feel bitchy? Maybe it was that niggling doubt that he could actually be interested in her. "So tell me, why does Trinity talk about me?" She didn't consider herself scintillating party discussion.

Connor looked at her as if she were as cute and silly as her students could sometimes be. "You're the only one of her friends who does anything meaningful, she says. Including herself."

Trinity said things like that to Faith herself, but to tell someone else, especially a hunky guy . . . well, it warmed her heart.

He touched her hand, just a gentle stroke across the back. "It's admirable on your part."

She didn't know what to say. Her skin was warm and her insides gooey like the truffle she'd thought of. "Thanks."

"Why do you do it? Teach, I mean."

"I like children." She loved feeling a part of their lives, knowing she, in some small way, helped mold their futures.

"But you want kids of your own, too, don't you?"

She swirled her spoon in her coffee, the conversation lagging. Talking about herself wasn't easy. "Someday."

Connor pushed his coffee forward and leaned his elbows on the table. His hair glistened blue black under the lights as he focused his smoky gaze on her. "I know this is early in our relationship, but I have a proposition for you."

Her heart did a little lurch. She was sure his leg was closer than it had been. His heat singed her. "What?" She felt trapped by his gaze like a mouse in a cat's paw.

"I have a goal. And I don't want to wait fifteen years or more to achieve it."

That wasn't what she'd thought he'd say. A proposition usually meant something sexual. Didn't it? "What goal?"

He didn't answer that. "You have a goal, too. You want a big family. Together we can achieve our goals faster than we could alone."

Her hands were suddenly numb, cold. The spoon tipped sideways out of her cup, splattering milky coffee across the table. "What's your goal?" She was afraid to hear it.

He sopped her mess up with a couple of napkins. "I want to climb the corporate ladder. Be a CEO. Run the company. Make the important decisions. Your father doesn't have anyone to fill his shoes at Castle Heavy Mining."

Her father. Whose only heir was a kindergarten teacher uninterested in his business. Of course, there was Cousin Preston, but he wouldn't do, according to her father, who'd been looking for an acceptable protégé for a long time and, as Connor correctly stated, had yet to find the perfect candidate.

Trinity had been talking. *A lot.*

"What's that got to do with me?" The words were a painful whisper that hurt her throat. And her heart.

Connor covered her hand with his, giving her back some of the warmth she'd lost. "We can marry; I can help your father. We'll have that big family you want, and I can pass his legacy on to his grandchildren. To *our* children."

His eyes burned with a passion far beyond the physical, but his proposition slammed into her like a huge tree crashing down on a tiny one-room cottage. She yanked her hand away. He needed an heiress. A frumpy heiress barefoot and pregnant at home while he had his afternoon delight with beautiful, sexy women.

Her skin prickled, her eyes ached, and her head started to pound with the need to hold in a vast ocean of tears. "No."

He traced her jaw with the pad of his finger. "Just think about it."

She jerked her head away. "No." She'd have run out of the café if her legs hadn't felt so weak. She thought they'd buckle if she even tried to stand.

He tipped his head, his eyes softening to a light gray. "I've hurt you. That's not what I meant to do."

No way would she let him think that. "You don't have the power to hurt me. Besides, why would I marry a stranger?"

"What do you want to know about me so I'm not a stranger?"

She shook her head so hard her brain seemed to rattle. "Nothing. I'm not interested. I wouldn't even consider marrying you." She leaned forward. "Especially after the way we met."

"We met when Trinity introduced us."

He knew she was talking about the garden, but he just had to go and remind her that wasn't their first meeting. He had to remind her about Trinity's part. "Did Trinity tell you I needed a husband?" That she was desperate for a husband. For children.

"No. She doesn't know anything about what I want."

It was one thing to *be* desperate, quite another to have the fact broadcast. Her best friend wouldn't be that cruel. Except that sometimes Trinity didn't know when she was doing more harm than good. She knew how much Faith wanted to be a mother.

Faith chose indignation over blubbering in front of Connor. "The nerve. I can't believe you'd just come right out and tell me you want to marry me for my money."

"Not your money. And would you prefer I romance you, make you fall in love with me, and *not* tell you my intentions?"

She remembered Lisa and her have-not husband's romance. Starry-eyed Lisa, unsuspecting Lisa. Now unhappy Lisa. No, she didn't want that, either. "I wouldn't fall in love with you if you were the last man on earth." Last night, even fifteen minutes ago, maybe, but now? No way.

Why didn't she just get up and leave?

She noticed he'd stopped touching her, the heat of his leg no longer penetrating her skirt. "Anyway, how do I even know you'd make a good father?"

"Children are a man's most important legacy. I'm an orphan. My mom died when I was seven, and I lost my dad a couple of years later. I know how important a father is."

She felt sorry for him, losing both his parents so young. She almost wanted to know more. Almost. But his proposition was absurd. It would never work. "If you run a company, you'd never be home. Your children wouldn't even know you."

He reached for the cup he'd pushed away earlier. "Was *your* father gone all the time?" The question was a challenge.

"He's special. My mom died when I was young, too. He tried to make up for that by being there when I needed him. Most men with powerful careers think bringing home the bacon is enough."

"I'll be there for my children."

She couldn't shake him, and the way he said it, with an uncompromising glint in his eye, made her believe he meant it. Or maybe she was just blinded by her attraction to him, by what had happened between them last night. She didn't want to admire him, yet she was starting to, for more than his black hair, good looks, and distracting body. Dammit, she was starting to *like* him, and that just couldn't happen.

"Fine. But what kind of husband would you make? If we're not marrying for love, then how do I know you wouldn't be running around behind my back? I won't be a laughingstock whose husband cheats on her." She wouldn't budge on that issue. Ever.

"That won't be a problem." He paused, studied her, his head tipped. "As long as you don't shut me out of the bedroom when you're not trying to get pregnant." Lowering his voice, he moved in on her, his big, wholly male body close, closer, his knee pressing hers. "After the way you reacted last night, I have a feeling great sex won't be an issue."

She didn't move, as if his touch beneath the table had no effect on her. "Do *not* bring up last night. That was an aberration." She mourned the sweet memory. It had been wonderful in a kinky, extraordinary way. His offer tainted it.

Still, he had a way of looking at her, searching her face with his gaze for long, silent moments, his perusal unnerving her. She fidgeted with her coffee cup.

Finishing his assessment, he backed off a few inches. "I'm sorry. I thought you'd prefer honesty right from the get-go. I'd make a good father, a good husband, and a good son-in-law."

"Gee," she quipped. "What more could a girl ask for?"

He gave her face that consuming scrutiny again. "I take it a girl could ask for a lot more."

Like wild declarations of undying love. But Connor was right; she preferred honesty. If love was nothing more than a lie, what good was it in the long run? The lie always came to light in the end and with a lot more pain attached to it. And he wasn't offering love. "Why did you pick me?"

"Why *not* you?" He pulled his chair closer until only a slight bend of his head would bring his cheek to hers.

"Well . . ." She wouldn't say it. She would not mention her weight or her looks. "You met Trinity first." Which got her point across. Why would he choose her over Trinity?

He smoothed flyaway strands behind her ear, his brief touch sending sparks right through her. Her hair was her second-best feature. It wasn't carrottop red, but a rich ginger that shone with blond highlights after she'd been in the summer sun.

"You're sexier than Trinity."

She snorted. It was very inelegant, but really, sexier than Trinity was going too far. She had more in common with Lisa-the-cuckolded-wife. Trinity oozed sex appeal.

His eyes traveled her face, taking in every feature, almost as if he were memorizing. As if . . . of course, he didn't find her beautiful, it was more like . . . well, she didn't know. She'd never had a man look at her that way.

"What about last night? Don't you think I found you sexy?"

She waved a hand, punctuating with an eye roll. "That wasn't me; that was what we were watching."

He shook his head, one corner of his mouth curving. "It was watching you watch them."

"With another woman, you'd have had the same reaction."

He took her chin in his hand and forced her to look at him. "It was *you*. You got hot. And that made *me* hot."

"But—"

He covered her lips with two fingers. "One more *but* and I'll drag you onto my lap to prove it to you."

She almost asked how, but instead managed to say, "I mean really, be serious—why me? There are plenty of heiresses out there to choose from."

He dropped his hand to the top of hers. "I am serious. Besides making me hot, you don't appear to be shallow."

She really should tell him to stop all the touching. But she didn't. "Don't forget that you like the way I laugh."

"I didn't forget that. Or how good you felt pressed up against me last night. You have passion and sensuality, and there's nothing hotter than sex with a passionate woman."

She laughed, a real laugh, not one of horror or disbelief. His compliments warmed her, made her sit straighter in her chair. God. Was he starting to win her over? "I've never met anyone like you. You just say what you're thinking, don't you, without worrying how the other person is going to judge you."

He leaned back in his chair and spread his hands. "What you see is what you get."

The girls at the next table turned saucer-eyed like one of her little kindergartners. He continued to ignore them. Rather, he didn't even appear to notice them.

What you see is what you get. What Faith saw was extremely appealing. Broad chest with nicely defined muscles tapering down to a hard abdomen showcased by a form-fitting polo shirt. She just didn't know that what she saw was the same as what she'd get. With a jolt, she realized she was actually considering his outrageous proposal. "So, I get children and a husband who promises not to wander as long as I have sex with him as often as . . ." She tilted her head. "How often?"

"At least once a day if I'm stressed. It's a good tension reliever." He didn't even crack a smile. "How about you?"

Gee, once a year would be nice. She had low expectations. "I've never really thought about it. But we're talking about the bargain here. Lots of children, no infidelity, as long as there's sex once a day." She started to tingle. "And all you want is to run my father's company."

He didn't address the last comment but went back to the sex issue. "Not just wham-bam sex. Real sex."

She couldn't believe she was having this conversation. She glanced around to see if anyone was listening, but except for the table of young women too far away to eavesdrop, they weren't the center of attention. Far from it, they were just another couple in a crowd talking about sex. "Define *real sex*, please."

His breath whispered across her hair. "Mind-blowing sex. Last night doesn't count since neither of us had an orgasm, but it was a damn good hint of things to come."

She had to swallow and not let her erotic thoughts rule her emotions. "What if you get tired of the same woman every day?"

"We won't get tired if we're willing to try anything. To experiment. To let our inhibitions go and no limits."

His use of "we" was so terribly seductive. She tried to appear unmoved. "Anything? I'm not into bondage or stuff that hurts." She tipped her head one way, then the other. The discussion had become almost a game. Except for the core of heat burgeoning inside her. "Or wife swapping. Or group sex."

"Just the two of us." He stroked her middle finger where her hand lay on the table. "No pain. Only ecstasy."

Her face flushed. "You're too agreeable. I must be missing something here."

He nodded gravely, as if her concerns meant something to him. "Think about it overnight and put any other conditions on it that you want." He was so close, he could have been talking dirty in her ear.

She'd almost lost the ability to think. "I have to give you my answer tomorrow?"

"You can give it to me whenever you're ready." The way he said the word, *it* could mean anything, marriage, an answer.

Or hot, sweaty sex and unbridled passion.

Her throat was completely dry. "You're too accommodating. There's a catch here. I know it."

He picked up her hand and threaded his fingers through hers. "If you think I haven't kept my part of the bargain, divorce me."

"You'd still get half of everything I have. California's a community-property state, remember?" She pulled her hand away, clasping both on her lap. Away from his magnetic pull.

"Draw up a prenuptial agreement. If I violate any of the conditions, I get nothing, not even a part of your father's company, and you get a divorce free and clear. Except for one thing." He put an arm along the back of her chair, casual. His tone, however, was anything but. "If we have children, you can't stop me from seeing them. I'm not going to father a child and walk away as if he or she doesn't exist."

It was the one thing she couldn't have predicted. An alimony payment, part of the company, but not simply that he would want to see his kids. "That's all? No cash settlement?"

He shook his head. "No cash. Will you think about my

proposition?" He uttered the question in a husky tone, just the way he'd sounded last night. He had such a voice, such a way of looking at a woman. He'd get whatever he wanted from her, no strings attached, if she wasn't careful.

She worried her bottom lip. "What if you're planning to bump me off before I get a divorce or have children?" She had to be realistic; she didn't even know the man. Not one bit. Oh, he felt good wrapped around her body, and he was a great kisser, but he wanted something from her that required far more data.

"You can add that to the prenuptial agreement. In the event of your death, under any circumstances, I get nothing."

They were talking about her life, and her demise, as if it were just a mark in her grade book. Or maybe he was merely making a point that she didn't have anything to worry about.

He'd almost given her all the good cards to play with. "You know, I don't think you're getting anything out of this."

"Yes, I will. You're going to get your father to make me his successor at Castle Heavy Mining."

"What if he doesn't step down for years? More than fifteen years." Which was the number Connor had quoted in the beginning.

"He doesn't want to wait that long."

True. But she hadn't told Connor that. "How do you know?"

"I work with Lance Green, and Lance likes to talk."

Lance. She'd forgotten Connor worked at Green Industries. She'd had a marriage offer, from Trinity's brother, one she'd put out of her mind. Lance thought it was a good idea to merge romantically, but Faith suspected marriage wasn't the only merger he wanted. Green was a major contractor for Castle, exclusively providing some of the machined components for the multimillion-dollar mining equipment her father's company manufactured.

If Lance had been as honest about his intentions as Connor, would it have made a difference?

No. Lance oozed false charm. She hadn't liked him even when they were kids. In his marriage attempt, he'd made the moves on her, but she couldn't imagine letting him touch her. Ever. Not to mention having a child by him. She'd never figured out how he and Trinity could have sprung from the same gene pool.

Connor was nothing like Lance. He was certainly charming, but oddly sincere. His every compliment seemed to be genuine, meant especially for her. He made her believe that once he gave his word, he wouldn't break it. Maybe it was the intensity of his gaze. Liars couldn't look you in the eye when they lied.

Yet there was one big problem. "Daddy does want to retire, and he is looking for a trustworthy replacement. But he won't pick you because he'll believe you married me for my money."

"Your part of the bargain is to convince him to choose me."

Only Connor would be able to convince her father. He'd have to prove he was worthy, an impossible task with such a huge strike against him right from the get-go.

She shook her head and murmured to herself, "This just seems so wrong." Yet last night he'd seemed so right.

"Get to know me better before you decide. Have dinner with me tomorrow night."

"I don't know."

"Look at me, Faith."

He reached out to tip her chin when she didn't respond. "I'm not out to hurt you or take advantage of you. This will be good for both of us. All I want you to do is think about it and have dinner with me tomorrow night."

"And what will you do if I decide not to agree to your offer? Scope out another—" She'd almost uttered it. *Scope out another frumpy heiress.*

"I haven't asked anyone else what I'm asking you. And if you say no, I *won't* ask anyone else."

She looked at him, enthralled by his words' allure. "Why?"

"You're not like the rest of the women I've met at all the

parties Trinity's taken me to. I intend to pledge myself to the
woman I marry, even if what I'm proposing sounds more
like a business deal than a marital match. And I wouldn't
pledge myself to any one of them. Not even Trinity."

She felt his pull. That deep gaze taking in her every variation of expression. His eyes were dark and smoky, and his
voice sincere in its urgency. If he was a liar, he was good.

Faith stared at the table, picking out each individual
scratch and mar on the surface.

"Dinner tomorrow night and you can ask me anything
you want," the object of her musings cajoled one more
time.

"Just dinner?"

"Dinner. And questions. And anything else you want."

Another kiss? No. That would further screw up her fac-
ulties. That they *were* screwed up was evident in the fact
that she was seriously considering his proposition. Yet she
owed herself this chance. She wanted no regrets. Twenty
years from now, she didn't want to be alone and childless,
wishing she'd thought it over before she said no. "All right.
Dinner."

She was twenty-nine. Her biological clock was tick-
tick-ticking like a time bomb. She didn't have any viable
marriage prospects on the horizon. She needed to hold her
own children in her arms, carry them in her womb, but
she wouldn't choose the single-mother route. Besides her
own conviction that a child needed two parents, her father
would have heart palpitations.

But how would he react if she told him she wanted to
marry a fortune hunter?

STEP two of his plan had been achieved. Faith would have
dinner with him. And by the end of their evening, step three,
acceptance, would be in effect. He should be triumphant.

Instead, the moisture clouding her eyes had burned
a hole clear through his gut and out the other side. He'd
wanted to gather her close, tease the hair at her nape with

his lips, and *show* her how hot she made him instead of merely murmuring words.

He'd wanted to take her home with him and plead his case with his hands, mouth, and body. For a moment, he'd desired her sweet, succulent pussy more than her father's firm. But sanity returned.

He had a goal. He didn't want to end up like his father, where the only person on the face of the planet who even knew he'd existed was Connor himself. Connor wanted his children to have what he'd never had, a family legacy, bred into them, part of them, something that would live from generation to generation, the glue that bound them all together.

It was the one thing he'd learned to appreciate almost as soon as he started work at Green Industries six months ago, the family atmosphere. He wanted it for himself and his children, his family. At thirty-four it was time to start that family, and he wasn't adverse to marrying into someone else's legacy. In the end, he would make it his own. While he'd first thought of Trinity, he'd soon realized she wasn't the woman for him and Green Industries wasn't the company. Lance Green was next in line to take over the helm, and Connor had quickly discovered that Lance's decision-making abilities sucked. Connor didn't have an ounce of respect for the man. In addition, Green was a stagnant company, with Herman Green unwilling to consider its health or growth potential.

Jarvis Castle was a whole different ball game. Connor had met him several times, found he had a keen mind, and in his tenure as chairman, he'd tripled his company's margins. In Connor's research on the company, which included many a conversation at the country club events to which Trinity dragged him, he came to realize that Jarvis Castle didn't find his pool of relatives to be adequate to handle the job of running the show.

And his daughter needed a husband to start the family she wanted badly. With every word Trinity said about Faith and the company information Connor found on the Internet, he knew Faith was the right woman and Castle Heavy Mining the right legacy.

The prenuptial wouldn't prove a problem. He had no intention of violating their agreement. Besides, after the way she'd reacted last night, he was sure that with encouragement, Faith would give him everything he needed.

Setting her passion completely free would be his pleasure.

3

"TRINITY, can I ask you a really important question?"

The phone crackled with a long pause. "No."

"Tri-in."

"Well, don't *ask* if you can ask me; just ask."

Sitting on the bed, Faith pulled her knees to her chest. She lived with her father, and after leaving Connor an hour ago, she'd snuck upstairs to her own suite of rooms. The house was so big, she barely saw her father if she didn't go looking for him, but tonight, she'd intentionally avoided him as if he might see something of her strange date with Connor written on her face.

Thank God Trinity couldn't see her face, either. "Are you sure you don't want to have an affair with Connor Kingston?"

"I was kidding about that, silly. You know Daddy would have conniptions." Trinity sighed. "Besides, Connor didn't ask."

Oh. "I'm sorry. Do you feel bad about that?"

Trinity laughed with a perfect musical note. Faith wondered how hers compared in Connor's mind.

"Faith, hon, he's not interested. My ego's over it. Plus, he's a total commitment type. He takes his job so *seriously*. I once asked him to escort me to an afternoon gallery showing, and he said he had a report due. I offered to ask Daddy to give him extra time, and he looked at me as if my hair were askew."

Trinity didn't value his dedication. Faith found it another thing to admire about the man. She was finding too many things to appreciate. "Your hair is never askew," was all she said.

"Why all these questions, as if I didn't know?"

Faith bit her lip and said a thank you prayer for the telephone's invention. Trinity wouldn't be able to see the flush on her cheeks. "He took me out for coffee tonight."

"Aha. I knew it." Faith could picture Trinity's happy dance. "I wasn't fibbing when I said he wanted to meet you. And I saw all those sparks flying when you shook hands and your eyes met and angels sang."

"Oh, quit, will you?" She didn't know about angels singing, but sparks had certainly flown later in the garden. She didn't mention that, though. Despite all the glib talk about passion, she and Trinity didn't get into sexual details. Not that Faith had a lot of sexual details to share.

"You weren't matchmaking, were you?" *Matchmaking* was the polite word. She wanted to make sure Trinity hadn't painted her as a hopeless basket case whose friend had to find her a date.

"I didn't have to. He soaked up everything I said like SpongeBob. He's perfect for you. He's so intense, and you're so . . . intense." Obviously, Trinity couldn't find another word. "Ooh," she gushed, "I feel like Cinderella's godmother."

"We just had coffee." And he made a marriage proposal, but she wouldn't tell Trinity about that yet. Not until she made her decision. Even then, the story would be a much-edited version.

"Did he ask you out again?"

"Dinner. Tomorrow."

"Yippee." Trinity clapped her hands in the background and dropped the phone. "Oops. Sorry."

"So I wouldn't be stepping on your toes or hurting your feelings if I went out with him?"

"You know, Faith, you're the only one of my best friends who would even bother to ask."

Faith took that as the highest compliment. "Thank you."

"Hmm. Does this mean he can't squire me around when all my other dates fall through? I mean, he really is so convenient."

"It's just dinner, Trinity. He might not ask me out again."
The white lie bothered her only a bit. Honestly, she hadn't
said yes to anything Connor proposed. Yet.

"Perish the thought. I'll find someone else. There's that
delicious engineer down in Quality Control at the plant.
He's always fiddling with test equipment when I walk
through so I *know* what he can do with his hands." And
Trinity was off making plans for Mr. Quality Control,
though Faith often wondered, despite Trinity's talk of unbridled passion, if her friend was a lot more talk than action. She just never seemed serious about anyone.

Still, Faith offered up a prayer of thanks that her friend
didn't want Connor Kingston, because he might very well
be absolutely perfect for what *Faith* wanted from him.

HE took her to a semicasual Italian place with mood lighting,
candles scenting the air, quiet conversation around them, and
an unobtrusive waiter who seemed to appear only when they
needed something.

The food was good, and she was glad Connor hadn't
tried to impress her with a more showy setting.

"Would you like to go dancing at a club?" Connor
asked.

Their dinner plates had long since been cleared away,
and Faith had run out of questions. "I don't dance."

Connor smiled reassuringly. "Neither do I. But you
don't have to know how to dance at most of these places.
It's just a matter of shuffling your feet."

His arms would be around her, which would completely
muddle her senses.

"Let's just go for a nightcap," he coaxed.

His marriage proposal didn't seem to have a hitch, he
hadn't hesitated answering any of her questions, nor was
she normally a distrusting person. Yet what he proposed
was so . . . out there.

"I'm sure by the time we get to the nightclub, you'll
have another question or two in mind."

She'd asked him everything she could think of. He had

no family, and after his father's death, he'd gone through several foster homes. He'd graduated from high school, supported himself through junior college, then miracle of miracles, he'd won a college scholarship through the fast-food chain he worked for. University, a job in finance at some small manufacturing company in Silicon Valley, then the move to Green Industries.

She felt like she'd gotten a resume for a potential employee. How would he handle something more personal? She thought about asking if he'd ever been in love, but she didn't want to know. Their arrangement didn't involve love. She chose something entirely different. "What about venereal diseases?"

He laughed, as if he could actually trace her thought patterns from his suggestion of a nightcap to her question about STDs. The deep tenor affected her physically, hitting a soft spot around her heart and deep in her belly.

"Not that I know of. But I'll take all the tests you want."

"You're too agreeable."

"I'm determined." He dropped his voice. "I'll make it good for you, Faith."

That could mean a lot of things. Sex. Marriage. Child-bearing. Life. "All right. A drink. But only one." She glanced at her watch. "I have to be up early for school."

He took her to the Bankers Club, which was loud but fairly tame. The music was eighties and nineties. A few dancers swayed on the dance floor, but most of the customers clustered around tables, drinking, laughing, and, Faith was sure, trying to score.

A booth freed up just as they were passing. Connor guided Faith into the seat, and a waitress stopped by promptly. Faith didn't have any illusions. The young woman had made a beeline for Connor, and her gaze never once touched on his "date."

"What do you want, sweetheart?"

Faith almost looked around as if Connor were addressing someone else. He stroked her knuckles with his thumb.

An obvious caress for the waitress's benefit, yet Faith still melted beneath the attention. "White wine is fine."

"What kind?" the waitress asked. "We have—"

Faith cut her off. "Just the house chardonnay." Connor had paid for dinner, and though they hadn't gone to the fanciest place in town, the bill would still have been quite a sum.

Connor ordered the same, then waited for the girl to leave. "I'm not destitute. You don't have to watch pennies for me."

"I wasn't."

He drew her hand to his lips and kissed her fingers lightly. "You were. It's nice. But I don't need your money. When we're married, I don't intend to sponge off you. I'll do a good job, and your father will pay me a decent salary."

"You mean *if* we get married." She shrugged, partly to keep him from assuming too much, partly to prove to herself that his touch didn't have an effect on her. "I'm not even thinking along those lines yet. I'm still getting to know you."

He sidled closer in the booth and put his arm around her.

She'd worn a different yet still slimming skirt, this one a jean-style with snaps down the front, accompanied by another of her formfitting sweaters. She felt good, almost attractive, especially when his gaze caressed her as it did now.

He put his mouth to her hair. "You know I can give you whatever you need." Then he nosed aside the strands and licked the shell of her ear.

A shiver shimmied down her legs. His breath and his lips made her squirm on the seat.

She pushed him away, which didn't amount to more than a few inches. "I can't think when you're doing that."

He opened his mouth, but the waitress's arrival with their drinks interrupted whatever he'd been about to say.

If Faith wasn't careful, he'd seduce her into doing whatever he wanted without any promises. He had charisma that most ordinary women wouldn't be able to withstand. And Faith was very ordinary. She hadn't dated much in the last year. Sex was even longer. Connor touched on all her needs. He knew it, too.

Alone again, he snuggled her into his embrace. "Next question, please. Do you want me to have a sperm count test?"

She couldn't help but smile. He was dogged, while at the same time teasing and putting her at ease. There was something about him that gave her the courage to step beyond her limits. That made her *want* to. What could she say to shock him?

"I'd rather know your measurements. Circumference and length." Her cheeks flamed at her temerity. She shocked herself more than him.

He grinned. When he laughed, he was scrumptious. When he smiled, he stopped her heart. But seeing that devilish grin, she was in danger of falling for his bullshit hook, line, and sinker.

"You want erect length or nonerect?"

She wasn't a sexual banterer for fear of sounding inept, but she liked how he made her feel—free to say or do anything. Being with him was incredibly liberating and unbelievably erotic. She let her fears go. "Erect is the only thing that counts."

"A touch is worth a thousand words." Before she realized his intention, he'd pulled her hand beneath the table and caressed his length with her palm. Up, down, the action hidden from the bar at large by the booth's white tablecloth. He was magnificent, ready to burst through his pants. For her. The touch took forever. Steel against her skin, the scent of male arousal swirling up to fog her mind. Her breath caught in her throat, and his gaze on her darkened to the night sky without a speck of moonlight to soften it.

"Big enough?"

She could only nod. He actually wanted her. The idea was amazing and new. And wonderful.

"I'm glad you approve." He moved his hand to her thigh, stroking up beneath her skirt. One snap popped all on its own.

She felt him throb beneath her hand on his crotch. He pulled her closer still, nuzzling her ear again, driving her absolutely mad even before he whispered, "Go into the bathroom and take off your panties."

She blinked. He robbed her of speech. Which didn't seem to matter one whit, since her thoughts were written on her face.

"I know you're wearing panties. It wouldn't occur to you not to wear them." He pushed gently, steering her out the other side of the booth.

She couldn't. She shouldn't. Yet she wanted to do exactly what he suggested more than anything in her entire life.

In the restroom, she splashed cold water on her face, not caring about her makeup. She dabbed dry, patting away the mascara smudges, and didn't bother to reapply her blusher. Her cheeks were stained with natural color. Embarrassment, but more than that, sexual heat suffused her skin, giving her a sexy glow.

Why, she almost looked beautiful.

In the stall, she rolled her panties down her bare legs and slipped them off over her sandals. As an afterthought, she unfastened her sweater and removed her bra. When she redid the buttons, she left the top two open, revealing ample bare flesh.

She'd been about to shove the utilitarian undies in her purse, but instead, she threw them in the trash, covering the offending articles with a paper towel. Made of too much white cotton, there wasn't a thing alluring about her underwear.

Whether she decided to marry Connor or not, he'd at least released her awareness of her own sensuality. She closed her eyes, remembering the touch of his tongue on her ear.

Maybe she'd have sex with him tonight. Faith had the feeling he'd be more than up to the idea of letting her test out the merchandise before making her decision.

Gazing at herself in the restroom mirror, it seemed like a great idea, but once back in the bar, sliding across the seat to his side, her confidence deserted her. Though her naked sex felt pouty beneath her skirt, and the soft sweater caressed her breasts, she'd lost some essential ingredient she'd felt in the ladies' room. Now, she couldn't utter a single sexual innuendo.

His gaze dropped to her burgeoning nipples. "You take direction well, then you improvise. I like it." His voice was husky and low with sexual intent. Thank God *he* had every intention of seducing *her*.

And Faith would let him.

When he put his hand on her thigh and slid under her skirt, she was powerless to stop him. She didn't even want to try. His touch brought her fantasies to life.

She held her breath as his fingers brushed her curls. Then he stopped.

She didn't realize she'd closed her eyes until he whispered, "Look at me."

He had the most mesmerizing gaze, like the snake oil salesman who got you to buy every last one of his bottles of so-called medicine. Closing his hand around her thigh, Connor guided her leg over the top of his knee, holding her open for his touch.

"Someone will see," she whispered. Protesting seemed the right thing to do, but she prayed he wouldn't stop.

"No one's noticing. Besides, the tablecloth is covering us." He leaned forward to put one elbow on the table and fully hide whatever he planned to do beneath the white cloth.

"It's kinky doing it here, though."

He grinned. "Yeah." Then he nuzzled her hair. "Tell me to stop, and I will. But you'll never know how good it could feel."

If she said yes, she couldn't later claim he'd gone too far. If she said no, he'd remove that exquisite touch from her thigh. Better to say nothing and let him convince her with more action.

"No other people, no wife swapping, no orgies, no pain, no humiliation," he listed. "But everything else goes." He lightly brushed her curls again, then stroked her thigh for a gentle probe against her flesh that didn't quite penetrate inside her cleft to her clitoris. But the promise was there.

She was wet, hot. Her breath seemed trapped in her chest, her nipples ached, and her fingers curled against the seat. Bearing down, she pushed against him, begging him without words, almost trying to force him to touch the hard bead of her clit.

With the hand not occupied beneath the table, he raised her wineglass. "Take a sip."

She did. He turned the glass and drank from the same spot, the wine glistening on his lips. She watched the slight bob of his Adam's apple as he swallowed.

"Say yes, Faith, and I'll give you anything you want." His fingers teased, flirted with her. "Everything you want."

"Not here," she managed to whisper.

While the kinkiness of letting him finger her in a bar raised her temperature to near combustion, she couldn't actually let him. If she did, she'd be under his complete control.

He stilled, cupping her thigh. "Are you starting to see how tantalizing and exciting we can be together?"

Unbearably tantalizing. But was it what they'd bargained for? "This is just supposed to be a business proposition. You give me babies, and I give you my father's company."

"That's before you asked for fidelity, Faith. For that, you have to give me more. All your sensuality and passion. All those kinky fantasies running around in your mind."

"I don't have kinky fantasies."

He backed off a taste and stared at her knowingly. "I saw how you watched that couple in the garden. I felt the heat between your legs. I tasted your mouth. You've got some pretty damn kinky fantasies, Faith, and if you want fidelity, then I want those fantasies."

She shivered at the thought. "Like what?"

"Like my hand surreptitiously up your skirt in a bar. Like taking advantage of a closet at the country club. Or an empty locker room. Like doing anything I suggest wherever we are because you're so fucking hot to get me inside you."

She did burn up then. If he'd had his hand two inches closer, she'd have come all over his fingers.

"I want it hot," he whispered, "I want it fun, and I want it a tad kinky. It'll be the best, Faith. I promise. Lust like you've never known it."

She could barely find her voice. "Lust dies eventually."

"You're wrong." His eyes were deep, dark, mesmerizing pools. "Love is what dies. It's messy and people get hurt. But lust"—he swooped in and took her with a quick hard kiss—"lust can last as long as we're both willing to try anything."

She wasn't so sure about that. Lust was like a drug. You got high, then *bam*, you hit bottom in the morning. Still, she'd never felt *this* with anyone. Ever. He might be right. For them, love would only complicate things. He obviously wasn't going to fall in love with her; she would almost bet he didn't even believe in love. But what he offered . . . maybe, just maybe it was something better. "No wife swapping, no orgies, no pain?"

"I'm the only one who'll touch you, and you're the only one who'll touch me. And I swear you'll love everything I do to you." He squeezed her thigh intimately. "Say yes."

"Yes." She whispered the word, afraid of it, exhilarated by it. And totally surprised by it.

He grabbed her hand, moved so that her leg fell from his, then pulled her out of the booth. She'd forgotten about the popped button of her skirt until she stood, but holding his hand, she couldn't bend down to fasten it.

"Are we going to your place?" He'd make love to her there.

He didn't answer, letting her go long enough to throw a few bills on the table. Sitting next to him, she'd forgotten how tall he was. Standing, the top of her head came to his shoulder. She felt small and engulfed.

God, had she just agreed to marry this man?

He'd parked in the back beneath a burned-out light. Pebbles crunched beneath her feet. The jean skirt roughly caressed her bare bottom, and her breasts bounced freely against her sweater, sweeping her nipples to hard nubs. Heat rushed between her legs. Connor unlocked the car door, helped her inside, then shut her in. If he didn't touch her again soon, she'd hyperventilate.

But he was there, and before he started the engine, he leaned over and took her mouth in a hungry kiss. A kiss even hotter than that night at the country club. His lips and tongue consumed her; the almost brutal taking pushed her head back against the seat. Faith arched into him, rubbed her aching nipples against his chest. Then his hand was between her legs.

He stroked up, parted her expertly, her knees falling open to allow him whatever access he wanted. Then his finger was inside, first one, slipping through all her heat and moisture, then another. She bucked against him, tried to tear her mouth away just so she could breathe. Finally he was on her clitoris, stroking, rubbing, gliding, driving her wild.

He withdrew slowly. Both his mouth and his fingers. "I knew you'd be totally wet, but I had to feel for myself."

She couldn't see his eyes in the darkness of the car's interior, but she could hear the triumph in his voice.

"Take me home with you," she begged.

He slipped loose two more buttons on her sweater, reaching inside to pinch her nipple, then lifted her breast in his hand. "You have gorgeous breasts." He bent, sucked a nipple between his lips, and teased with a soft bite. "And the most succulent nipples. They're like flowers, large and tight and needy."

God, *she* was needy. He didn't need to take her home. He could do her here. In the front seat. Or the back. She didn't care where. She just wanted him between her legs again. Now.

Connor buttoned her sweater, smoothed her skirt, snapping that pesky snap, then straightened in his own seat.

Okay, not here. His apartment. That was a question she'd forgotten to ask—where he lived. "We can go to your place. Now." She felt bold, risky, but she didn't care.

All she could see were his white teeth as he smiled. She felt like a puddle of jelly in the seat, her legs weak.

"Not tonight. We're not going to have sex until we're married." He started the engine.

"What?" She almost shrieked, then put a hand over her mouth when the sound echoed through the car.

"We're waiting for our wedding night."

"You're joking. Right?" *Please say you're joking.* Her body was on fire.

He looked at her, one side of his mouth higher than the other, revealing slightly more teeth. "Back in the bar, you said yes to marrying me when I had my hand between your legs and your thigh on my major hard-on, so it's prudent to wait until you've had a chance to think it over. Just like the three-day law when buying a car. You can change your mind for whatever reason."

"Fine. I can change my mind for whatever reason." She pulled in a deep breath, huffed it back out, and said exactly what she wanted. "But there's no reason you can't take me home and screw the hell out of me."

He chuckled. "Why Miss Castle, I'm shocked."

So was she. "I never say things like that."

"I know you well enough to be aware of that."

"But you've left me very frustrated."

He reached out to stroke a finger down her cheek. "I don't think you have any idea how frustrated *I* am."

"Hah," she puffed out.

He grabbed her hand and pressed her palm against his erection. The front of his slacks was damp.

"I didn't exactly cream in my pants, but I was this close." He gestured with his finger and thumb a half inch apart. "I'd like nothing better than to pull you on top of me right here, sink inside you, and come until I don't even know who I am anymore." He closed his eyes as she pressed her advantage on his pants. "I won't risk starting our child before the wedding."

Our child. It sounded so . . . beautiful on his lips. Faith stopped fighting him. "I don't think I'm going to change my mind. I meant it, even if your hand was up my skirt."

He sighed, a long breath tense with his frustration, yet rife with acceptance. "I'll take you to *your* home. But I'll call you before I go to sleep. We'll see what you think then."

She didn't think her answer would be any different.

She wanted to give Connor all her fantasies.

And she wanted a freaking orgasm, dammit.

*   *   *

HE wanted her so damn badly, he'd almost jacked off in the car on the way home just to relieve the excruciating throb in his balls. Coming inside her would have eased the sexual tension riding him, but he didn't want her accusing him of taking advantage and changing her mind in the morning because her thought processes were messed up when she agreed to his offer.

Problem was his own thinking was screwed up.

In every way, Faith Castle was far more woman than he'd ever imagined. Only time would tell whether that was a good or a bad thing for him.

4

LIGHTS blazed in her father's office as Faith entered the front hall. A crystal chandelier illuminated the marble floor and gleamed on the polished brass handrails of the staircase leading to the second floor. The house was far too large for two people, ostentatious in fact, but it had been in the family since the beginning of the last century.

Since her father hadn't arrived home from the plant by the time she left for her date with Connor, Faith had written him a note so he wouldn't worry. During the drive home, she'd prayed he'd already retired for the evening. She wanted at least one night to phrase in her mind how to tell him about Connor.

"Sweetheart, is that you?"

"Yes, Daddy." Faith stopped on the threshold of his inner sanctum. She wore neither panties nor bra. She *really* wished her father had gone to bed, but now, she'd have to tough it out.

He smiled at her, then waved her in. "So, you had a date. Tell me all about this new young man you've met."

With her desire banked, her brain had begun functioning again. She could view his proposition rationally. She appreciated that Connor was honest about what he wanted. No one else had been. With another man, Lance for instance, she might be lied to, cheated on, and ignored once a baby came. That was another thing. She liked the way Connor thought about children: They weren't just something he'd give her. He actually wanted them. In short, Connor offered everything she could hope for. Except love. She could live without that.

Now, she just had to convince her father.

If she blew the date off tonight as nothing, she couldn't very well come back tomorrow and say she'd found the man she wanted to marry. "He's nice, Daddy. I think you'll like him."

Her father picked up his snifter of brandy, rounded the edge of his desk, and sat in his favorite chair. The fireplace was unlit, but in the wintertime, not that the San Francisco Bay Area had extremely cold winters, he'd get a fire going and sip his usual brandy before going to bed.

"Sit. Tell me all about him."

What was she supposed to say? *He wants to marry me so he can get a foothold in your company, and I'm so desperate for what he offers that I've agreed to everything he wants.*

Settling in the chair opposite him, she took the few spare moments to consider how to answer her father.

"How did you meet him?"

"Trinity introduced us at a country club party." She didn't say that had been on Saturday.

The lamp beside her father gleamed on his white hair. She adored him. She couldn't bear hurting him. He believed she deserved a marriage such as he'd had with her mother. Mutual love and affection. Total happiness and commitment.

But her mother had died. Maybe the best things in life weren't meant to last forever.

"You'll think this is fast and very weird, but he's asked me to marry him." She held her breath a moment, staring at the Persian carpet, then she raised her gaze to his. "I said yes."

Silence. Her father found love later in life with her mother, who was ten years younger than him. He'd been thirty-eight when Faith was born, and this year, he turned sixty-eight. Running Castle Heavy Mining was a monstrous task even for a young man, and her father wasn't young anymore.

In the last few seconds between them, he'd aged another five years. "Is this some sort of joke?"

"I'm not being funny. His name is Connor Kingston, and he wants to marry me. And I want children."

He rose abruptly, droplets of brandy spilling from his

glass. His back to her, he said, "You've got your whole life ahead of you."

"I'm almost thirty."

"This is the first I've heard you mention the man." He turned to her. "How long have you known him?"

"Since Saturday." She sounded timid and hated it. The only way she could convince her father to take Connor into the company was if she remained strong. She mentally firmed up her spine. "That's long enough to know we have the same goals. Family."

He laughed without a single thread of humor in it. "I've never known you to be so stupid, Faith. He's after your money." He stared her down with a hard gaze foreign to his nature.

She winced, but didn't try to deny the truth of it. "Yes. And I don't care. This is more like a business arrangement."

He shook his head, his hair glimmering white and yellow in the different shafts of light. Once tall, he now stooped. Formerly slender, he now appeared gaunt and much too thin. She'd seen the changes, but ignored the implication. She didn't want to think of him as old, but so many creases lined his face, and age spots dotted his forehead, his hands, and his throat.

His usually fond gaze was dark with antagonism. "What's happened? Something must have made you lose your mind."

She set her feet flat on the floor and folded her hands in her lap, like a witness on the stand coming up against the tough questions. "I want a child. I've always wanted children. And I'm not willing to wait until someone comes along with whom I *might* fall in love and who *might* fall in love with me. Connor is willing to give me children now."

Her father narrowed his once-blue eyes, now faded to gray. "And what does he want in return?"

Her natural urge was to stare at the carpet again and whisper. Instead, she met his gaze, and her voice when it came was harder, stronger, and louder. "He wants to work for you. He wants you to teach him the ropes and let him step into your shoes, to be the chairman when you retire."

He slammed his delicate glass down on the sideboard, and splashed more brandy into the dregs of his previous drink.

"No." He didn't even face her when he refused.

"At least talk to Connor about it."

"How the hell could you even tell if this man you've known only *two* days is the right man? If he's any better than the possible replacements I already have?"

"You haven't got anyone."

Oddly enough, Faith didn't know Preston or her other family members well. Her father had never approved much of his cousins. Though the two family branches ran the company jointly, the *Castle* side held controlling interest, and since her father was chairman, he would decide who took over. It might actually be in her favor that he didn't approve of Preston Tybrook or anyone else. Here was his chance to keep the company on his side.

"You don't like Preston," she pushed on, "and you haven't found anyone else. You've told me that over and over."

He didn't bother to argue. "The answer is no."

Her stomach crimped, but she voiced her thoughts anyway. "You're not getting any younger, Daddy."

"Don't you think I know that? Don't you think I worry day and night about how you'll fare when I'm gone? You need someone to take care of you. I've hoped and prayed you'd find a man worthy of you, a man worthy of carrying on Castle for me."

"I don't need anyone to take care of me." It was so like him to treat her as a child. "But I have found a worthy man."

He threw his arm wide, brandy sloshing over the glass rim. "That is the most ridiculous thing I have *ever* heard you say. And you're the least ridiculous person I know." He brushed the droplets from his hand. "Tell me this is a farce, Faith."

"It's not." She rose from her chair. "You haven't approved of anyone I brought home." There hadn't been many. "You're making it impossible for me to get what I want. Children."

"I know you want a family, but I'm trying to protect you from getting hurt later on."

"You scare men off." She felt guilty putting the blame all on him, but she had to convince him. "I'm almost thirty years old. I can make a good decision. You taught me that."

"Honey." He used only that one word, pleading.

"I can't be hurt if I'm only in it for one thing, Daddy. A family. If you won't at least meet him and consider it, for me, then we don't have anything else to say to each other."

He took her arm gently, the way she'd hoped he would.

"There will be someone for you, Faith. I promise."

"What if there isn't? What if this is my last chance?" The thought terrified her. Life without babies would be unbearable.

He trailed a finger down her cheek, smiling at her as if she were ten years old and asking for a pony. "Sweetheart, you have years to find the right man."

From the vantage point of his age, maybe he thought she did. But in childbearing years, she was almost a has-been. "Daddy, please do this for me. I can't wait any longer." She had serious doubts love would happen for her the way he hoped. "Talk to Connor. Give him a chance. Give *me* a chance."

After a long moment, his eyes flicking from her face to the fireplace to somewhere deep inside his own mind, he offered a concession. "Let's talk. Who is he? How old? Is he just some no-good bum who's looking for an easy score?"

She winced but tried to hide it. "No. He went to San Jose State on a scholarship, and he's in his early thirties. He works for Hermie. Why don't you ask him about Connor?"

Something changed on her father's face. Someone who didn't know him as well as she did might have missed the subtle tensing of his jaw. "How long has he worked for Hermie?"

"I'm not sure. He's in the finance department. Budgets."

Wasn't that what Connor had told her? She couldn't remember for sure. His work history had concerned her far less than the fact that he was an orphan with limited opportunity who'd gone on to graduate with an MBA. A pretty impressive feat.

"I think I've met him."

She held her breath. Was that good or bad?

Her father didn't say, staring at the unlit fireplace for a long moment. "Who are his people?" His softened voice lacked a certain amount of attention, as if he asked one thing but his mind was working on something else entirely.

"He doesn't have any people."

"Everyone has people." Still that distracted tone, the faraway look centered on something beyond the andirons.

"His parents died when he was young. He has no relatives. He's alone in the world."

He didn't comment. Faith sometimes saw this preoccupied side of her father when business weighed heavily on him. It wasn't his way to tell her all his problems. She knew little about the actual running of the company. She only knew he worried about keeping it healthy once he was gone. And keeping Castle healthy meant finding someone he could trust to run it.

Faith hoped she'd found that someone for him. But neither of them would know unless her father gave Connor a chance.

"Invite him for dinner tomorrow night. I'll talk to him."

She held in her gasp. "Thank you, Daddy." Something was missing, his change of heart too quick. Faith wanted him to take her hands in his and tell her he'd try his best to like Connor.

Instead, her father continued to stare at the fireplace as if it might spontaneously combust into a brilliant blaze.

"I'm going to bed now." She waited.

He merely raised a hand. "Good night, sweetheart."

"I love you, Daddy."

"Love you, too."

Faith waited a few moments out in the hall. Waited for him to call her back, something, anything.

He didn't. A large hole opened in her chest and engulfed all the euphoria she'd experienced in Connor's arms.

BASTARD. Who the hell did this Connor Kingston think he was? Faith was so naïve, so trusting. She didn't have a clue. No way would Jarvis allow some low-life fortune hunter to use her up, then throw her away like yesterday's garbage. Yet Jarvis had no choice but to agree to talk with the upstart. He had to at least look as if he'd done due diligence in the matter.

Thank God she hadn't said she was in love with the man. There was hope he could get her out of Kingston's scheme emotionally unscathed.

Jarvis set his brandy snifter down and laced his fingers behind his back. Thinking, he rocked back and forth, heel to toe. He'd met the man at a few meetings with Hermie, and while Kingston seemed capable and talked a good line, in the end, he was just another number cruncher. Nothing impressive.

Jarvis had known Hermie since their college days. He'd even loaned the cash to start Green Industries. Castle manufactured custom heavy mining equipment, blasthole drills, excavators, feeder-breakers, loaders, crushers, etc. Green Industries machined, die-cast, and plated many of the component parts. The partnership had worked well for forty-five years.

They'd also shared the grieving when their respective spouses passed on. Faith's mother had died in a car accident almost twenty years ago, and Hermie lost his wife to cancer ten years later. There was nothing that bonded two people together quite so much as a terrible loss.

His dream had been to unite the companies more permanently. He and Hermie had hoped that Lance would one day marry Faith.

Jarvis didn't want Preston Tybrook getting even a ghost of a chance to sell out or bring in outside investors. Castle Heavy Mining had been started by their great-grandfathers, two brothers, one hundred and fifty years ago. Preston's side had bred prodigiously, diluting the family name until there wasn't a real Castle left amongst them. Jarvis's side had kept things more pure, and maintained control of the company with the largest block of voting shares. Since Tybrook's daddy, old Rufus, had died twenty years ago, there wasn't a worthy contributor in the bunch. Jarvis was not letting his company be ruined, but God, he was tired of fighting the daily battles. Faith was right—he wasn't getting any younger.

Lance would be the solution, but despite claiming she wanted children and a family, Faith was the marriage holdout. Now there was hope. Jarvis had seen it the minute she'd said Kingston worked for Herman Green. A little compare and contrast might do the trick. Connor Kingston, who had to *marry* into a family business, versus Lance Green, who'd been born to it as his right.

Faith would soon see who was the more worthy once Jarvis pointed it out to her tomorrow night. Faith was the most important thing in the world. Everything Jarvis Castle did was for his daughter and the company.

If she wanted a family that badly, he'd pay for artificial insemination before he'd give her over to a fortune hunter.

"YOU'RE invited for dinner tomorrow night."

Faith lay in her bed, the lights out, the phone tucked close to her ear. Her suite of rooms was on the opposite end of the house from her father's and overlooked the garden. The conversation in the library had doused her earlier fit of desire, but with moonlight falling through the open curtains, silky sheets against her body, and Connor's voice intimately in her ear, passion sizzled once more through her veins.

"Did your father blow a gasket?"

Faith laughed. Her father was one of the most easygoing men she'd ever met. At least most of the time. "He wasn't terribly pleased, but he's willing to give you a chance." He'd been troubled, but what more had she expected? He needed time to digest Connor's proposal just as she had.

She worried her lip between her teeth. "This part is up to you, you know. If you want me, you'll have to impress him."

If you want me. She'd phrased the words deliberately.

Connor gave her exactly what she'd sought. "Oh, I want you, Faith. You felt that tonight. What are you wearing?"

She smiled, like a woman with a secret she'd been dying to share. "Nothing."

"Is that what you usually wear to bed?"

"My usual nightgown is long and flannel." Actually, she had a pair of soft baby dolls, but she wanted Connor to think she was making even bigger changes for him.

"Are you wet for me, too?"

"Yes." After climbing into bed, she'd relived those minutes in the front seat of his car all over again. She'd been wet and flushed waiting for his call.

"Tell me how wet."

His low voice and probing questions only added to her aroused state. "Very, very wet."

"Put your hand between your legs, and tell me more."

A kernel of unease lodged in her chest. She'd never done anything like this before. Let's face it, no one had been interested enough to have phone sex with her. Connor might want a foot in the door of her father's company, but the husky rasp of his voice over the phone seemed genuine. More than just part of a business deal. She wanted this experience despite her fears. Faith stroked down her abdomen and parted her legs.

"How wet?" he whispered.

"It's all over my fingers." She moaned.

"Where are you touching yourself?"

"My clitoris. And now I've got a finger inside." With her eyes closed and his voice inside her head, she could almost believe it was his touch on her. She stretched on the bed.

"How often do you masturbate, Faith?"

Not if, but how often. "Once a week," she told him.

"That's all?" His voice rose slightly with incredulity.

"How often do *you* do it? Wait, don't tell me, let me guess. At least once a day."

"At the *very* least." He laughed softly. "But not today."

"Oh, you're slipping." Her fingers stopped while they talked, and she rested her hand on her belly.

"I knew it would be better with you." His voice was like honey drizzled over her senses. "Do it with me now."

Yes. She wanted this. If nothing else ever happened between them again, she would have *this*. "Okay."

"That was easy."

"I need to finish what you started tonight," she admitted.

"That's exactly why I started it, so we could do this together." He was so good at seduction, the pure devil of his pitch, the lure in his words.

She wondered if he was as seduced as she. "What should we do?" She wasn't sure exactly how phone sex worked.

He sighed, a long, guttural pleasure sound. "How do you want me to touch myself? How hard? How fast? Tell me what you'd want me to be doing to you if I was there."

She melted on the inside with everything he asked for, but she wasn't good at this. "You tell me first."

"Take a chance," he seduced with a whisper. "You might like the idea of telling me what to do."

She sounded like an insecure teenager, and that wouldn't do. So she began the way he'd started. "What are you wearing?"

"I'm naked."

"Is your cock hard?" Being a kindergarten teacher, she didn't say the word often, and it felt strange on her lips. Naughty yet tempting.

"Yes, my cock is painfully hard."

"Stroke it." The act of telling him what to do intensified the heat between her legs.

"I've been stroking it all along."

The freedom in being on the other end of the phone suffused her. She could say whatever she wanted without embarrassment. She could become the sexy woman she'd always dreamed of being. She puffed out what she hoped sounded like an indignant breath. "You can only touch yourself when I say it's okay."

"I thought you said you weren't into bondage."

"I'm not. Bondage hurts."

"Sometimes it's just about who's in charge. You're going to love having me do your bidding."

She could learn to crave the power in it, though she could never do it face-to-face. "Do it faster."

"Yes, my little dominatrix."

Her hand rested on her belly. For the moment she wanted to savor the rasp of his breath in her ear. She lowered her voice, trying for husky, sultry. "Do it harder."

He groaned.

She gave him another order. "Now move your hand up to the tip of your cock and work just that."

His breath sighed across the phone. "I think you're much more experienced than I imagined."

"I'm not sheltered, if that's what you mean."

"I am so going to enjoy learning everything about you." Then the sound of his breath shivered down her spine. She spread her legs and delved into her pussy.

"Are you touching yourself, Faith?"

"Yes." She pushed her head into the pillow, her body thrusting against her fingers. "God, yes. It's so good."

"Christ, Faith, you're killing me. Pretend it's real. That I'm touching you and you're touching me."

With her eyes closed, the fingers caressing her clit became his. Thrusting deep, she felt *him* inside her. Her body undulated, begging for more.

She was breathing so hard, it was difficult to talk, yet she took command. It was so easy with the phone between them, and with Connor, she figured she'd have to learn to hold her own.

"Yes," she encouraged, "rub me there. Right there. Don't stop." She circled her clitoris, then moaned and squeezed her eyes so tight she saw stars.

"Come with me, Faith. Now." He growled low, then swore in her ear.

She hit her orgasm, hard, her body jerking and tears leaking from her eyes as he groaned with her and said her name as if it were a prayer.

"Christ." Long moments later, his voice was a lazy, satisfied whisper. "That was good."

It was. Incredible. "I'm not usually like that, telling men what to do."

"I want you to do things out of your norm. Like coming with me on the phone. You haven't done that with anyone, have you?"

"No."

"But you've fantasized about it." As if sure of her, he didn't wait for her answer. "There will be more firsts, Faith. A lot of them. And I swear you'll love every one."

She felt his vow, his sincerity, like a stroke of his hand down her breasts, a promise from his lips to hers.

But exactly how kinky would he want her to get? And how would he handle it if she said no?

SHE was so trusting. And so damn hot. Connor had scorched his fingers touching her in the car and blown sky-high on the phone. Even now, his breathing hadn't returned to normal, yet his limbs felt languid and spent. Ah God, the things he wanted to do with her. Desire for her still eddied through his veins. She'd stepped out of her comfort zone on the phone. Her orgasm had been as much a revelation to her as Connor's had been to him. She was perfect for him. She didn't expect love. There'd never be the ugly, messy emotions that went with it.

Could a man have it all? Wealth, family, security, dreams, and a sexy wife willing to do anything he asked waiting for him at home, all night, every night? Connor had never been so lucky. He'd always had to work hard for everything he wanted.

His father's long-ago voice murmured in his ear. "If you don't ask for the moon, Connor, you can't be disappointed when you don't get it." Dad hadn't asked for anything since the day Connor's mother died, and he'd gotten nothing but two years of endless grieving and an early grave.

Connor had learned you couldn't depend on another person for what you needed. You had to go for it yourself.

5

FAITH zipped her navy blue dress, fastened pearls at her throat, and stood before the full-length mirror in her bathroom. Did she look like a frump?

Pots of makeup lay strewn over the pink tile vanity. She'd abandoned two fluffy pink towels on the marble floor outside the shower door. In the bedroom, her walk-in closet looked as though a poltergeist had flown through. She wasn't usually so messy, hating to leave a bunch of crap lying around in her wake for Estelle to clean up. She didn't like anyone to think she expected to be treated as if she were a prima donna. Or the daughter of a rich man. Okay, she had to admit she didn't make her king-sized bed, do her own laundry, or clean her bathroom.

She glanced at her watch. Connor would be here in less than a half hour. Her heartbeat seemed to get louder with each minute that ticked by. Yanking off the navy dress, she threw it on the bed and pulled out the black number she'd worn to the country club on Saturday. Maybe Connor wouldn't notice.

What on earth did her clothes matter? They weren't dating. They were . . . making a pact . . . contemplating parenthood . . . or something. Oh hell, she didn't know what they were doing. She didn't know what *she* was doing. Doubts had assailed her from the moment she woke up this morning. All it took was the light of day to highlight what an idiot she was.

"This is the dumbest thing you have ever done in your entire life," she told her reflection, clothed only in panties, bra, and control-top hosiery. "He doesn't care what you wear; he wants your father's company, and he'll do anything in order to get you to marry him, right down to pretending he finds you attractive."

A huge sigh slipped out, her shoulders sagged, her belly pooched. Oh God. *I can't do this.*

If you don't, you'll never have a baby.

Connor was Mr. Not-Perfect-But-One-Helluva-Good-Bargain. He offered her what she'd always wanted: a family. She liked his honesty. He didn't offer her pretty lies or hopes. He probably had her from the moment he said the only thing he'd never give up was the right to see his children. The statement rang with sincerity. She never imagined she'd fall head over heels with a man head over heels about her, too. Connor promised fidelity, or at the very least, no humiliation. She trusted him simply for the fact that he didn't romance her or offer her the fairy-tale ending. Not to mention that she truly believed he desired her. What more could the woman in the mirror ask for?

She was in the driver's seat. She held all the cards. She pulled all the strings. Gee, how many more clichés could she think of to emphasize that she had the advantage over Connor?

Faith straightened her shoulders, her breasts thrusting up and out, and sucked in her belly. "I want a baby," she told the mirror, "and I'm going to make sure I have one."

The problem was she liked the way Connor made her feel when they were together. What if she started wanting more, some emotion on his part other than lust? She narrowed her eyes at her reflection. *Don't expect anything from him on the emotional front and you'll be fine.*

Pulling the black dress over her head, she slid it down her thighs, smoothing it over her abdomen before she zipped it up. She gave herself a last look in the mirror, and a scolding to stop obsessing about her clothing. It wasn't as if she'd be at the country club.

The doorbell rang just as she started down the stairs from the upper landing. He was early. Butterflies swarmed in her stomach and flew up into her throat. *Come on, Faith, be cool.*

"I'll get it, Archie," she called. She didn't want it to look as though she were making an entrance. And she didn't want to appear to be flaunting their English butler and their money right in Connor's face.

Then again, she and her father lived in a nine thousand square foot house. She had a suite of rooms all to herself. The painting above the long hall table was a genuine Lord Leighton. The pool was Olympic sized, a Jacuzzi on either end, and the guest cottage out back had three bedrooms. Wasn't this ostentation what Connor was buying into with his sperm?

She pulled on the handle, only it wasn't Connor framed in the doorway. "Lance, what are you doing here?"

"Your father invited me for dinner."

Her father? That double-crossing . . . She had to smile. He'd said he'd meet Connor; he never said he'd do it one-on-one. "Where's Trinity? And your dad?"

Lance crooked a half smile. His mustache twitched over his neatly trimmed goatee. "I don't think they were invited. At least, they didn't mention anything to me."

So that's what her father was up to, offering an alternative to Connor. But Lance was . . . Lance. When they were in their young teens, he'd teased her about her weight. Until Trinity gave him a black eye. He'd never taunted Faith again. Instead, he'd become excessively flattering, yet she recognized the glint in his eye that belied his compliments. At thirty-two, he was handsome in a polished, arrogant sort of way. Tonight he wore a casual jacket and pants with the pleat pressed down each leg. He never had a single dark hair out of place, worked out daily, and followed it up with an hour in the tanning booth. Trinity swore she wouldn't go near a tanning booth in case her skin turned to leather the day after she turned thirty.

"Your dress is lovely. New?"

Right. She lifted the waist of the dress away from her body. "This old thing? No. But thank you so much for the compliment." See, she could be sarcastically gracious, too.

"Lance, so glad you could make it." Coming from his study, her father was more elegantly dressed, in a three-piece suit, than Lance in his casual attire. He held out his hand.

"I wouldn't miss a dinner with just you and Faith. This way I don't have to share the limelight with Dad or Trinity."

Now *that* was the truth. Lance didn't like the word *share*. Ah, but he'd have to share dinner tonight with Connor. Faith wondered if her father had told Lance about that ahead of time.

"Let's go into my study for a drink." Jarvis extended an arm. "That whiskey your father loves, direct from Ireland."

"Can't wait, sir." Lance followed.

Once inside, her father poured two shots of the rich Irish whiskey and a glass of Riesling for Faith. She liked the sweeter wines. With an unobtrusive flick of her wrist, she checked the time. Connor would be here in two minutes. She had the feeling he would show up neither unfashionably early nor fashionably late, but right on time.

Her father fully intended to make him appear the outsider in the small, intimate group.

The bell echoed through the hall. This time she'd have to let Archie get it.

"Ah, there's our other guest." Her father raised his glass, looking first to Lance, then sliding his gaze to Faith. "You know him, Lance. He works for you. Connor . . ." He snapped his fingers and groaned. "Faith, what was his last name?"

"Kingston," Lance supplied, a congenial smile on his lips, and a semimalicious sparkle in his eye that confirmed he'd known Connor was also a guest tonight. "Yes, he works for me."

"He works for Green Industries," Faith couldn't help amending.

Lance smiled. "That's what I said."

Okay, so the name of the game for the evening would be "put Connor in his place."

Archie led him in, then departed with an inclination of his head. Unlike her father's, Connor's suit didn't cost a thousand dollars or bear a designer label, but he looked scrumptious.

Faith took his hand as if he were truly a beau she couldn't wait to introduce. Warm fingers closed around her own and squeezed. She looked up, up, up into his smoky eyes, and he gave her a killer smile.

"Daddy, this is Connor."

"Mr. Castle. I believe we've met." They shook hands.

"Please, call me Jarvis. You already know Lance Green."

Lance didn't offer his hand. And when her father poured a drink for Connor, she noticed it wasn't the aged whiskey, but something out of the decanter. He never kept anything good in the decanter in case Archie got into it, at least that's what her father claimed. Then again, Archie knew where the good bottles were. In ways, her father was an anachronism, viewing life and servants with an attitude born in another century.

Clearly, he viewed Connor with the same attitude, and really, Faith couldn't blame him. After all, she'd told him Connor was a fortune hunter. But her father had gone one step further and invited Lance over to help twist the knife.

"So, remind me, what do you do over at Green?" Her father tapped his head. "Getting forgetful, you know." Sure. He wanted to show Connor their previous meetings hadn't made an impression on him.

"Budgets," Lance answered for Connor. "Kingston rides us about wasting pencils and making too many copies of things he doesn't think we need to make copies of in the first place."

She expected Connor to slam Lance down, but Connor merely smiled. "Don't forget about the shredding cost when we have to destroy all those extra copies we don't need."

They went on in that vein for what seemed like an interminable amount of time but was probably only ten minutes, until Archie poked his bald head through the open door and announced dinner. Thank God.

Lance led the way to the dining room, showing that he

knew where it was when obviously Connor didn't. Men. She thought they were supposed to compare the size of their penises, not play table manner games.

Connor took her wrist before she made it out the study door.

"Did you do that on purpose?" he whispered.

"Do what?" Allow her father and Lance to humiliate him?

"Wear that dress."

She didn't even have the urge to dissemble the way she had with Lance. "I know I wore it at the country club, but—"

He put his fingers to her lips and blew her circuits. "And you thought you'd drive me crazy by wearing it again tonight and reminding me how close I was to pulling it to your waist and taking you right there in the garden."

He didn't blow just a few circuits with that; he stole her ability to speak and took her breath away.

"How am I supposed to concentrate on impressing your father when all I want to do is beg you to let me have my way with you?"

He smelled good, some dark, mystical aftershave created by witches over a seething cauldron of love potion number nine. Or lust potion number ninety-nine. Her nipples were beaded tight and stark against the bodice of her dress. He was so good at seducing her. All that vulnerability overwhelming her as she'd dressed came rushing back.

"Don't worry," he murmured. "I'll be a good boy. But be warned, when you call me tonight—"

"Stop it." She didn't realize her whisper was so harsh until he pulled back. "You don't have to flatter me, Connor. You don't have to pretend. We both know what the bargain is. I get a baby, you get Daddy's company."

"Faith—"

She pulled away before he could finish. "We'll have sex. I'll do what you tell me to within the bounds of the agreement we made. But just stop all the false compliments."

Then she turned and followed her father into the dining room, her heart beating in her ears and an ache behind her eyes.

*   *   *

HE'D made a tactical error. Faith had a long way to go before she believed he meant what he said, that he *felt* what he said. She didn't know him well enough yet to understand he never gave a compliment he didn't mean.

She would learn; he could wait. Connor had the patience of a cat watching for a gopher to poke its head out of its hole.

He had little patience, however, for Lance. Connor didn't work for him; as director of Finance and Budgeting, he worked for the CFO, who wasn't a homegrown man, but he might as well have been because he sided with the Greens in every decision he made.

Lance Green had a quality about him that Connor recognized from his youth. There were always the people who'd crawl into your bed at night and take advantage of you if they thought you were weaker than they were and they could get away with it. Connor had learned early on not to show weakness.

"I'm curious, Kingston, if you were able to finish that report my father asked for."

It was an innocuous list of major suppliers, with their contract values, costs, and return rates pie-charted. Busy work designed to make Connor late for his dinner date with Jarvis Castle, he now realized.

"I e-mailed him the data before I left."

"I would have thought pulling together that kind of information would require a bit more effort on your part."

"The data's readily available to anyone who knows how to use the system." Connor couldn't help the cheap shot.

The small group took up one fifth of the twenty-seat dining table, Jarvis at the head, Faith on his right, Lance next to her, and Connor opposite, separated from Jarvis by one chair. The seating arrangements said a bit about the business relationship. Castle Heavy Mining was Green Industries' biggest customer. It was a wonder Jarvis Castle hadn't bought them out years ago. And between them sat Faith. If Lance married her, the two companies would have the familial tie as well as the business.

Is that what Jarvis Castle was angling for? Maybe. Trinity had, in her breezy way, flapped away any possibility of a relationship between Lance and Faith. The fact that Lance was here spoke volumes. He *did* have plans for Faith.

But so did Connor. At Green Industries, he'd learned to appreciate the autonomy in a family-run, family-owned company. *That* was the real legacy for his heirs, to determine their own futures, make their own decisions, without being at the mercy of another's whims, no matter how well-intentioned they were.

The bald butler set another fork by the side of Connor's plate. "For your main course, sir," he stage-whispered.

Connor realized he'd used the dinner fork for his salad.

"Thank you. I don't know what I would have done without it. God forbid I would have had to use my fingers."

The gentleman's lip twitched, and his gray eyes sparkled. Tall and thin-shouldered with a concave belly, he could have done with sitting down for a good meal, too.

Smiling, Faith covered her mouth to hide it. Lance merely looked down his nose.

Connor studied the Castle mogul as Jarvis sliced his greens. His gaze flicked from Faith, to Lance, and finally to Connor. "Tell me more about your experience at Green."

By God, this dinner was a job interview.

"I'm director of Finance. Which means I deal with every aspect of the company from sales to cost, analyzing variable and fixed expenses, ROI, strategic projections." He waved his hand in the air to indicate the on-and-on of his daily activities.

"It's a wonder, given you're *such* an important man, why Jarvis can't quite remember what your exact role is"—Lance did his own sarcastic air wave—"since he is our largest customer."

And so it went. It was almost amusing, figuring out how to raise Lance's hackles. A bit childish, though. He'd never been into one-upmanship before. Yet gazing at Faith across the table from him, watching the way her lips twitched every time he made a direct hit, Connor couldn't help himself. It was like a medieval joust with words instead of lances—pun intended—the winner taking the lady's hand.

He hadn't had so much fun in, well, hell, never. Faith was good for him. He could be good for her, too.

THE whippersnapper would be out of a job tomorrow, that was for sure. Didn't he get it?

Jarvis had to admit Kingston had won the verbal sparring with Lance. Barely needing to interject a word, Jarvis sat back to watch the spectacle, throughout dinner. He'd found it entertaining. He would have admired Kingston if it weren't for Faith. Kingston was smart, articulate, and unemotional. Jarvis liked that in a business associate. Except that the man wanted Faith in the bargain. She couldn't see she was a means to an end. Faced with broad shoulders, handsome features, and a rather earthy quality, women threw logic out the window. What she needed was someone of her own class. Well, not class—Jarvis wasn't classist—but someone who understood the world she lived in. She and Lance were suited. Which is why Jarvis had sent them out into the garden and taken Kingston into his study.

Jarvis poured two generous glasses of brandy, his favorite after-dinner drink. Then he took his customary wing chair before the fireplace without inviting Kingston to sit. Pulling up his pants leg, he crossed his knees.

"Let's not beat around the bush. You want to marry my daughter and take over my company when I retire."

Jarvis expected all sorts of hemming and hawing. What he got was a simple "Yes," which took the wind out of his sails. He'd felt like a grilling. How could you grill the truth?

Kingston then sat, minus the invitation. He, too, crossed one leg over the other. "You need someone to grow the company when you're ready to step down. Faith needs someone to father her children." He took a deliberate sip of brandy before continuing. "I'm offering a solution to both those issues."

"I don't know you," Jarvis said with a pleasant smile, as if they were talking about the wood carving on his mantelpiece. "You might intend to sell off Castle to the highest bidder."

"What I want is a legacy, not money. I want to grow into the future, not make the fast buck in the here and now."

"Yet you're taking the fast climb up the corporate ladder by marrying my daughter. Why not work for it like normal?"

Kingston cocked one brow. "Like you worked your way up?"

"I was in short pants when I started working for my father."

The whippersnapper smiled. So, he saw through the old expression, but Jarvis had damn well earned his chairmanship. And why was he suddenly feeling as if he were on the defensive? "All right, let's agree you're not out to make a fast buck, and you want a legacy"—he allowed a certain amount of disdain to lace the word—"why not marry Trinity Green for it? You've been dating her." He raised a brow, the implication being that Kingston was doing more than date the blond princess.

Kingston smiled. Jarvis was starting to dislike that smile.

"I don't want a woman like Trinity Green."

That started a slow boil in Jarvis's gut. The young asswipe. "No, you want a woman like my daughter. Someone you can manipulate, who'll be so grateful for your attention that she'll jump at the chance to marry you."

Kingston recrossed his legs, took another leisurely sip of too-good-for-him brandy, then leveled a steady gaze on Jarvis. "Actually, I want a wife with more depth than Trinity. A woman like *your* daughter. You undervalue Faith's assets. She's devoted to her students and has an admirable mothering instinct."

Jarvis almost slapped his brandy down on the side table, stopping himself at the last moment. Showing emotion now would indicate weakness. Who the hell was this . . . person to say Jarvis undervalued Faith? He worshiped the ground she walked on. Everything he did was for her. "What would you know about Faith? You met her Saturday night."

Kingston set aside his glass and laced his fingers over his abdomen. "I know a lot. You might call it hearsay, but her friends see her true strengths. She's kind and caring. Right now, she lavishes everything she has on children who don't belong to her. She has a helluva lot more to give to her own children."

"I know that, dammit."

The man raised one dark brow. "Do you?"

Jarvis felt himself splutter but nothing came out. He knew she was kind and generous. Too generous and too trusting. That's why he needed to protect her from fortune hunters.

Ah, finally he could say something. "I make sure no one takes advantage of her."

Quirking a half smile, Kingston slowly shook his head. "Yet you'd give her to Lance Green?"

"I've known Lance since he was a child. They're from the same world; they understand each other." And why the hell was he explaining himself to this upstart?

Kingston uncrossed his legs and leaned his elbows on his knees. "He won't make her happy. You know that."

"And you will?"

"I won't lie to her." He blinked. "I won't lie to you. The question is whether you trust her to make up her own mind."

"Of course I do." Jarvis was beginning to realize how many defensive statements he was throwing out. The truth was he didn't have confidence Faith would choose well. She was a woman and could therefore be blinded by a pretty face. She had a good heart, but kindness and generosity weren't valued these days.

Yet Connor Kingston, a goddamn fortune hunter, was the first man to even mention her inner beauty.

Lance never had. But Lance had known her so long, he didn't need to *say* it. "What about love? You're not offering that."

Kingston drummed two fingers on the armrest. "I've seen love matches. Most of them end up in divorce court or murder."

"That's cynical."

"Maybe. But since we're not going into it expecting romantic perfection, I'm offering Faith better odds at success."

Jarvis had to admit the man had a point. He'd loved Faith's mother to distraction, but their life had been a long series of ups and downs, fights and making up. At times, she'd wanted to leave him; at times, he'd hated her almost as much as he loved her. Yet when she died, he thought he'd never make it. Had it not been for Faith, he might never have survived the grief. He'd always given Faith the picture-perfect version of his life with her mother, but many a time, it had been far from that.

His breath felt heavy in his chest, and the weight of Faith's future sat on his shoulders like sandbags. There would come a time when Jarvis could no longer meet the battles head-on. He was tired of the infighting, the greedy, grabbing fingers of his relatives. He didn't trust a single one to keep Castle Heavy Mining thriving. He had two choices: find her a husband to take care of her or find someone to take care of the company.

Or, he could take a chance on a man who would do both. At least with Kingston, he could control things, ensure a prenuptial that protected Faith in every way. If he left it to the *love* route, he might not be able to protect her at all.

Then again, it was all academic. Right now, if Lance was doing his job out in the garden, Faith would see he was the better choice, and Kingston would be out on his ass. In the meantime, what was the harm in letting the young whippersnapper *think* he'd come out on top? Jarvis had to admit he was curious, and the way to bring out the man's plans was to play along.

"You hurt her in any way, Kingston," he whispered, "and I will break you."

"I wouldn't expect anything different, sir." It was the first time Kingston used the deferential term.

"And you damn well better keep your dick in your pants."

"Would it be feasible," Kingston said with a straight face, "to bring it out in the men's room? When appropriate, of course."

Jarvis couldn't help himself. He laughed. He felt an inkling of like and admiration. The man had a sense of humor. "I'll make sure that exclusion is in the prenuptial." He crossed a leg, his knee creaking. "Let's talk terms."

"You want to keep the company in your direct line. Your daughter wants children. And I want the chairmanship eventually. It seems to me that we can all have our needs met. And let's face it, you've got inbreeding in your management structure. You need fresh blood, fresh ideas."

True. But Jarvis wanted measurable goals for Kingston to meet. "You improve the after-tax bottom line by fifteen percent in three months, a total of twenty-five percent in six months, sign a prenuptial agreement, and impregnate my daughter by her birthday." Which was December fifteenth, seven months away.

Fifteen percent was easy, Jarvis knew. There was always everyday waste that could be eliminated. It was the extra 10 percent that would give Kingston the trouble.

"Twenty-five percent in six months isn't reasonable."

Jarvis almost snickered. "So you're not up to the task?"

"I'm not cutting my own throat before I even start. It'll take that long to know the inner workings of your company in order to figure where the additional cutbacks would come from and probably a year to fully implement."

Jarvis waved a hand. "Fine. You've got one year."

"If I've got the responsibility," Kingston added, "then I want the authority to get it done, which means CEO. And as soon as I achieve the first profitability goal, I get a 2.5 percent share in the company and another 2.5 when I meet the second." He paused, smiling slightly. "And you retire as chairman when I make all my commitments. Including the child your daughter wants more than anything in the world."

What the man didn't know was that Jarvis wanted to hold his grandchild before he died. Yet he also wanted Faith to choose the right father. "You lose it all if Faith divorces you for *any* reason at *any* time. And I want that in writing."

Kingston leaned back, that sardonic smile on his face.

Though maybe it was better described as a shit-eating grin. "Don't forget to add that I get nothing in the event of her death. Just in case you think I plan to murder her."

Jarvis flashed an equally mocking smile. "Good point. I'll make sure you don't get the gum off the bottom of Faith's shoe."

Kingston laughed, then the smile faded to total focus, a deep line bisecting the young man's eyebrows. "I've already told Faith this, but you better know it, too. I want one thing and one thing only that neither you nor she can take away from me." His brows dropped together as he put his head down, spearing Jarvis with his dark gaze. "If there's a divorce, I want the right to see my children. I'm not backing down on that."

An odd request. It made him see the young man in a slightly different light.

Jarvis steepled his fingers and damn near stared cross-eyed at them. Then he raised his gaze and experienced the oddest sensation as he surveyed Kingston's face. *Would* Faith do better with Lance? Would the company do better? Only the Lord knew. Right now, she was probably deciding Lance was the one. Jarvis almost laughed. Wouldn't that frost Kingston's nuts? Hah.

But Lord, what if Jarvis was wrong? What if Lance made her unhappy? What if Kingston here *was* the superior option?

For the moment, Jarvis played the game to the hilt. "Deal." He pointed with his index fingers. "But Faith needs to agree."

"Of course."

Jarvis had the sudden, sickening feeling he was selling his daughter to the highest bidder. He just wasn't sure whether it would be his best friend's son or Kingston.

6

SHE'D led Lance along one of the garden paths. The night air was laden with the scent of blooms. Faith couldn't tell the difference between the perfumes except the lavender. She often picked the lavender, and used it for a sachet in her dresser.

"You need to talk to Trinity about him. He's already tried this whole thing with her."

Naturally. It wasn't as if Lance would even expect Connor to choose Faith first. "Trinity was the one who introduced us."

"She probably didn't expect you to fall for his bullshit lines so easily."

Faith pursed her lips. See, that was the thing about Lance. He could be insulting without even knowing he was. Or maybe he did know and didn't care. Then again, right before dinner, hadn't she accused Connor of using bullshit lines on her?

Obviously, her father and Lance had conspired to get in the way of what she wanted. And who she wanted it with. She folded her arms over her chest. "What did my father tell you about me and Connor when he invited you to dinner?"

"He said that it's my responsibility to make sure you don't get hurt since the guy works for my father's company. I have to agree. I feel responsible for what happens to you."

Right. Lance's caring was laughable. "Hmm." She let the sound hang a moment. "Just what did he *try* with Trinity?"

"I don't know for sure. That's why I want you to talk to her before you let this go any further."

Which meant Lance didn't know a thing about Connor and Trinity, but she was sure Trinity would get an earful when Lance went home tonight. "I really appreciate your concern—"

He put his fingers over her lips, and she recoiled. Lance didn't seem to notice. "We'd be good together, Faith. I've asked you before, you've always said no, but I can give you the same life you're accustomed to. I can take care of you. We're a perfect match in every way. Let's get married."

He sounded like her father's parrot. "Lance, we've been through this before." Except that back then he'd wanted her to believe he had "feelings" for her. "My answer's the same."

"I know you want children, and I want them more than anything in the world, too."

Faith heard Connor's rough voice saying that no matter what happened between them, he wouldn't leave his children behind. Lance didn't have a single note of sincerity.

"I've chosen Connor. You're too late with your offer."

His mustache twitched, and he narrowed his eyes. "I asked you to marry me long before he came on the scene." He sounded like a petulant boy, more a mouse than a man. The moonlight caught his eyes, and the glint there was nasty.

Faith shook her head slowly. "That's the first time you've offered me children."

He snorted, reminiscent of the thirteen-year-old boy who tormented her. Before Trinity blacked his eye. "Children went without saying."

"No, they didn't, Lance. They're very important. And you didn't figure that out."

"So, you were testing me?"

"No. I never intended to marry you." She didn't intend to argue with him or justify her actions. "Let's go inside now."

He took her arm, stopping her. "I hate to see you get hurt, Faith. And he *is* going to hurt you. Connor Kingston isn't like us. He doesn't play by our rules. He'll eat you up and spit you out. He's a liar and a manipulator."

Lance *wasn't*? "He'll sign a prenup guaranteeing everything." She raised her chin. "You never offered that."

"We wouldn't have needed that between us." He leaned in, lowering his voice. "I would have married you for free while Daddy had to *buy* Connor for you with the company."

She wanted to smack him, but that would be stooping to his level. "Did my father tell you that?"

"He didn't have to. A man like Kingston is only after power and money."

And a man like Connor couldn't be interested in a woman like her just for herself. She wouldn't let Lance see a single shred of emotion. "Thanks for the warning. My eyes are open now. You don't need to see me back to the house."

He held on to her arm when she would have walked away. "You're crazy if you think he won't cheat on you every chance he gets. He's a user. You'll find out, Faith. He thinks he knows everything, and everyone else is just a fucking idiot."

So that was it. If she probed deeper, she was sure she'd find a laundry list of things Lance resented Connor for. Lance didn't want *her* so much as he wanted to make sure Connor *didn't* get her. Or her father's company.

She jerked her arm out of his grip. "Go home, Lance."

From the beginning, Connor had told her honestly what he wanted. If her father thought Lance was a better choice either as her husband or chairman of Castle Mining, he was crazy.

SHE didn't knock, and she had the look of a Valkyrie about her as she burst through the double doors to her father's study. God, she was hot. Connor wasn't into dominance or submission in the classic sense of the terms, but he liked a woman who knew her own power. *This* Faith made him completely combustible. It was all he could do to control his rising libido.

"Are you two done talking yet?" she demanded to know.

"Yes," Jarvis said.

Connor let the old man answer without adding a comment.

Faith stood there in the door, a hand on each knob. "Good. Because I have a few things to say."

Damn, how he wanted her right now.

Something had happened during that stroll in the garden with good old Lance. It hadn't been to Lance's liking, he was sure. *You go, baby.* She was his. The company was his. His future lay ahead, bright. He couldn't wait to get inside her two seconds after he slipped his ring on her finger.

"We're getting married, Daddy, so I hope you've worked all the details out while you've been in here."

Jarvis's jaw dropped, and Connor's heart thudded in his chest. Faith's hazel eyes shone with battle light.

"Faith. Are you sure about this?" Jarvis's Adam's apple bobbed as he tried to swallow. Despite all the haggling, he still expected her to change her mind during a few minutes alone in the garden with Lance Green. Connor wouldn't let her.

"I'm absolutely sure, Daddy."

She was amazing. Once Faith Castle—soon to be Faith Kingston—made up her mind, there was no stopping her. Now all Connor had to do was get her to put that level of tenacity to their sex life.

"I want you to agree to the bargain."

"But Faith . . ." Jarvis trailed off. He'd read between the lines of what she said just as Connor had. If he *didn't* agree, Jarvis stood to lose her.

Connor almost put a stop to it. He'd never intended to come between father and daughter.

But Jarvis spoke first. "I hired him."

She didn't smile. "As chief executive officer?"

Jarvis eyed Connor. "Yes." Regaining his equilibrium, he tipped his nose eloquently. "But *I'll* still be chairman."

If that look meant anything, Jarvis could be a problem Connor would have to deal with. But that would come later.

"All right." Faith waved a hand dismissively. "We want the left wing of the house for ourselves."

Jarvis's eyebrow almost met his hairline. "All of it?"

It was time for Connor to add his two cents. "We're not living here. We're getting our own home."

"But—" Faith stopped, her lips slightly parted.

"We'll have our own house." There was something about having sex with a man's daughter in her father's house that was a little too kinky even for Connor. Especially with all the things Connor wanted to teach Faith.

"Can Daddy give us the down payment as a wedding gift?"

How much did he want to be bought and paid for? He intended to give Jarvis his money's worth at Castle Heavy Mining. He intended to give Faith her money's worth in the bedroom.

Things were different for the rich. They got cars for birthday presents and houses for wedding gifts. The last present Connor had gotten was a red fire engine on his seventh birthday. A week later, his mother was dead of a blood clot in her lung; two years later his dad finally managed to drink himself to death out of pure grief. Connor had worked for everything he'd gotten since.

"I have plenty for a down payment," he said.

No matter what anyone else thought, one way or another, he would pay for what Faith and her father gave him.

He rose and held out his hand to her. "Walk me to my car."

"I'll have the papers drawn up tomorrow," Jarvis said.

"I'll be by to sign them. Faith?"

She took his hand, her eyes wide. As if she'd only just realized what she'd committed herself to.

GOOD Lord, she was engaged. Connor's hand wrapped around her cold fingers as he led her out into the garden instead of to his car, following a different path through the flowers and foliage from the one she'd taken with Lance.

Hmm, was that a metaphor or what?

"What's so amusing?"

"I was thinking about Lance."

"You've just agreed to marry me, negotiated my job title, and tried to manage our living arrangements, yet you're thinking about another man?"

Despite the moonlight filtering through the trees, his eyes were dark, but she thought for sure one side of his mouth quirked in a smile. "I'm sorry. I didn't mean to direct things."

He stroked his thumb down her cheek. "I liked it."

"But I treated you like you were one of my students."

"No, you treated me as if you had a stake in the deal I made with your father." He feathered a finger across her lower lip. "You do have a stake."

Now that the *deal* had been made, she had so many questions, she didn't know where to start. And she was afraid. She hadn't thought past convincing her father. Now she had a fiancé.

"What did Lance say that made you charge into your father's study?" He raised one brow. She liked that devilish look.

"I didn't charge."

He tapped her nose. "You did. Like . . . a lioness. Did you know that the lionesses do all the hunting while the male just sits back and enjoys the spoils?"

"Is that how you felt?"

"Yes."

"Is that good or bad?" There were so many things she didn't know about him. Scratch that, she didn't know *anything* about him. Yet she was going to marry him.

"It was good," he whispered. "Very good."

She had the feeling he was telling her something much more. "When are we going to do it? Get married, I mean," she added in case he thought she meant *it* as in sex.

"When's your birthday?"

"I . . . ? My birthday?"

"Your father says I need to have you barefoot and pregnant by then. I don't even know when your birthday is."

He didn't know anything about her at all. "December fifteenth."

"Then we better get married ASAP. As soon as we get a

marriage license, blood tests, whatever else we need. And I have to get that sperm test. You don't want to marry me if my count is too low." He was making fun of her.

"I trust your count," she said before taking a breath and plunging in. "Where are we going to do it? Get married, I mean." She kept feeling the need to explain. Maybe because being so close to him, scenting him as if she were the lioness and he were the lion, *it*, sex, was on her brain.

"We can get the license and go down the hall to the judge's chambers, if you like. Or do you want a church?"

"Daddy and I don't really go to church. Do you?"

"No." He answered quickly, flatly.

"Then we can do it at City Hall. That's fine with me."

"I'll start the arrangements, as soon as your father draws up the prenuptial."

The agreement made her feel uncomfortable. She kept flitting from glowing to uncomfortable to ecstatic to tongue-tied in no particular order. "Tell me why you don't want to live with Daddy. It would save us money. And the house is so big." She fluttered a hand in that general direction.

He encircled her throat with his big hand, his warmth rippling through her body. "If I've got a mind to do you on the dinner table during the dessert course, I don't want to have to ask your father and your butler to vacate the room. And when I make you scream in ecstasy, I don't want you saying"—he raised his voice an octave—"'ooh, Connor, but Daddy might hear.'"

This was when she felt most comfortable with Connor. When they were on a sexual footing. Which was odd because sex had always made her feel uncomfortable with men. What were the expectations? Would she perform well? With Connor, her anxiety seemed to melt away when he touched her, when they talked sex.

"And when I drag you into the backyard on a sultry summer evening to beg for a blow job in the moonlight, I don't want you saying"—he raised his pitch once more—"'ooh, but Connor, Daddy might see us.'"

He set things tingling inside her even as his bad imitation coerced a laugh. The acre and a half surrounding the house didn't qualify as a backyard. It was a garden, paths weaving between flowering bushes and overhanging trees, two lily ponds, one with carp, one without, a gazebo tucked in the corner. A real backyard was a sandbox, a swing set, grass, a picnic table, and a barbecue. A place where children got dirty and the landscaping wouldn't get ruined if they played too hard.

More than anything she wanted Connor to beg for a blow job in her very own backyard. For a moment, she wished hard that he meant every word.

And scared herself half to death. Wanting that from a man who was marrying her for her inheritance was the surest way to drown in her own tears down the road.

She heard Lance's warning all over again. "I don't want you to humiliate me by bagging other women—"

"Bagging?" Connor tipped his face down until his forehead almost rested against hers.

Faith ignored him. "And no phony compliments, either. It'll be just sex, and I'll do it the best I can, but don't say a bunch of other stuff you don't mean." She glanced at him, but his eyes were unreadable.

"Okay." He tucked a lock of her hair behind her ear. "But it's not a lie to say I want you down on your knees right now."

Her heart seemed to fly into her throat, and once again he stole her breath.

"I want your luscious mouth"—he cut himself off— "sorry, that was an adjective. No adjectives because they can sound like phony compliments."

Though he was again teasing her, inside, her heart raced. Heat danced down between her thighs.

"I want you on your knees and your mouth on my cock. I want you to suck me down your throat so hard I explode." He feathered the fine hairs at her temple. "I want that so fucking badly—" He stopped again. "Sorry, that was an adjective *and* an adverb."

She wanted it just as much. "Yes." She tipped her head back to level a steady gaze on him. "What if I'm not good?"

"Haven't you heard the old proverb that the only *bad* blow job is *no* blow job?"

She laughed, and the tension eased from her belly. "I don't think that's exactly a proverb."

"Maybe not, but it's true. Trust me, Faith, you can't do it wrong." Then he pressed her hand to the front of his slacks. He was sweetly hot and hard in her palm. "This isn't a phony compliment. It's my cock hard for you and the thought of your mouth sucking me until I scream."

Connor Kingston was a dangerous man. She could want so many things from him. She could expect him to make her feel like a beautiful woman. That would only get her hurt, yet there was no turning back. She wanted babies. She wanted Connor.

Faith turned and pulled him. "Come into the gazebo."

"Said the spider to the fly," he whispered.

Just who was the spider and who was the fly?

The roof of the gazebo blocked out the moonlight and left them in a pool of darkness. She reached for his belt buckle. He held her hand still.

"Is this coercion? Or do you truly want to?"

She did feel a certain need to prove she was ready to hold up her end of the bargain, sex whenever he asked for it, but there was more to this. "I want it."

He tipped her head back with his thumb beneath her chin. "Remember, when you take me in your mouth, you have the power. In that moment, a woman can make a man do anything she wants."

Was he right? Could little Faith Castle hold all the control? She wanted to try. He made her feel bold and hot and risky. "Well, then, we're going to see if you can actually come for me. In my mouth."

His eyes blazed hot enough to light up the whole gazebo just before he grabbed her and crushed his lips down on hers. It was a kiss to end all kisses, at least any she'd received. Faith's toes curled in her pumps, and her heart raced beneath her breast. She clung to his arms and let him devour her. His tongue swept into her mouth and set her blood thrumming. He tasted of brandy and hot, needy male.

Then he let her go, only one hand remaining on her shoulder to keep her steady on her feet, his breathing harsh. "So far I've been all talk and no action, haven't I? Silly of me to forget I needed to prove to you I can do what I claim I can."

A thin five o'clock shadow darkened his skin. The roughness of his whiskers still shimmered on her skin and lips. His penis was hard against her belly, and she didn't have a doubt he could accomplish what she wanted.

"Unzip me. But leave the belt done."

Her fingers trembled as the rasp of his zipper disrupted the quiet of the night, but she kept his gaze. It wasn't so dark that she couldn't look into his eyes; she just couldn't see where the pupil ended and his iris began. Yet there was the slight reflection of her face, distorted, almost not her at all. Then she slipped inside the opening of his boxers and touched him.

Hot, hard, and pulsing.

"Rub me," he urged, wrapping an arm around her back to hold her in place.

She trailed the back of her fingers from tip to base, nestled his testicles, then rose back up to slide through a generous helping of pre-come at his tip. His nostrils flared.

"Wrap me in your fist and pump." He dropped his voice. "Just a little. I don't want to come yet."

She'd stroked a man before, but never made him come that way. She'd taken a man in her mouth, but darn near suffered lockjaw before she'd gotten him off. She wasn't an innocent by any means. She'd just never felt so powerful as Connor parted his lips to drag in a breath, closed his eyes, put his head back, and groaned from deep in his belly.

No one had ever groaned for her before.

"Too much," he whispered. "Don't make me come now."

She swirled her thumb in the moisture at his crown.

He looked down at her. "Blow me, baby. Now. I'm feeling out of control, and I want your mouth on me. Please, baby."

No one had begged with quite that note of need or called

her baby. If Connor was faking it all, he deserved an Academy Award.

She went down on her knees, her hand still wrapped around him. Pushing his fingers through her hair, he pulled her closer.

"Take me, baby."

She didn't care that she was in her father's garden. She didn't care that she'd just sold her soul for the chance to have a child. All she cared about was the sweet sound of endearments on his tongue, the heady aroma of his sex, the tangy scent of his semen, and the inexorable grip of his fingers in her hair.

"You're so big," she whispered at that first glorious sight of him.

He curled one hand around the back of her head. "When the time comes, I'll be a perfect fit, baby." He guided her to him.

She took him in her mouth, salty and hot, thick and hard. Swirling her tongue around his tip, she delved into the tiny slit and reveled in the involuntary jerk of his body. She licked the rim on the underside of his crown, all around, and shuddered with his growl vibrating against her. He was almost too much to take all the way, but she slid down until her lips met the fist of her hand. With her pinkie, she caressed his sac, then held him in her hand, squeezing lightly.

His hips moved restlessly, forcing him deeper. In clipped words, between a gasp and a groan, he told her how good her mouth felt wrapped around him, how soft her hair was, how smooth her skin. Then he moved urgently, holding her head in his hands.

"Fuck me, Faith, please, fuck me. Make me come, baby."

She held on to his hips with her hands and let him take her mouth. He tightened, throbbed inside her, then said her name softly, almost reverently, and filled her mouth with his essence. So much, so good. He held her until he was done, then draped himself around her, his hands down her back, bunching her dress in his fingers as his body jerked one more time.

"Baby?" he whispered. "You all right?"

He straightened, pulling her to her feet with him as he tucked himself back in his pants, zipped, then finally wrapped her in his arms. "I need a nap," he murmured.

Faith licked her lips. She didn't have to ask if she'd done well. For the first time in her life, she was sure of herself, at least where a man was concerned. In the classroom, she was in control, but men had always made her uneasy.

Connor had given her a special notch on her belt. He'd loved what she'd done. She loved the taste of him still piquant in her mouth. His hands roamed up and down her back. Was it possible? Could she actually satisfy this gorgeous, perfect male specimen? She had. She could keep on doing it.

At least, that's how she felt right now.

Connor tugged gently on her hair until Faith looked up at him. "You've got my come at the corner of your mouth."

Her tongue darted out, and she licked the drop away.

He'd never seen a more beautiful sight in his life. Christ. The long, slow glide of his cock between her lips. The slippery sound of her mouth on him. The fast, hard pump to the finish. Her skin lightly flushed and her lipstick long gone. Her mouth still glistened with his come. Her glorious hair was a tangled mess, falling about her face, her shoulders. He could smell himself on her, a unique sexual musk that was unlike anything else in nature. He loved the scent of sex on a woman, could wallow in the curves of her body drinking it in. He adored the taste of sex, the commingling of flavors. He took her mouth now, still ripe with his come yet tamed with her sweet flavors, remnants of fresh fruit and flavored lip gloss.

She relaxed into him, folding both arms around his shoulders, a sigh falling into his mouth as he kissed her.

They'd do well together. She'd gone to her knees on her own. He hadn't pushed her. She'd swallowed his juice without pulling back, then sucked him dry. He didn't hold any illusions; she'd shy away from some of the things he'd ask her to do, but he would teach her how good sex could be if she let herself go, if she gave herself into his hands.

He would test her limits, push her farther than she'd ever gone. And she would love it. Her insecurities would vanish and her self-esteem would soar.

He'd give her that in addition to the children he'd promised. Their marriage would be so fucking perfect, and all without the messy emotional involvement of so-called love. He should have thought of combining marriage and business years ago.

7

"DO you have a vibrator?" Connor's voice over the cell phone bore a husky edge.

The classroom was empty. In twenty minutes, the school day would begin, and Faith would have twenty screaming, squalling, lovable little five-year-olds each demanding all her attention, but for now, she was alone. Despite the fact that no one could see her, she felt her face heat.

"Because I want to hear you do yourself with your vibrator."

"I don't have one." She was burning up. "This is embarrassing." Her words were barely more than a whisper.

"You gave me the most magnificent orgasm and swallowed my come, Faith." He dropped his voice, almost as if he sank lower into his chair, getting comfy for the long haul. "It's too late to be embarrassed."

She shivered all the way to the center of her bones. God. Last night. She'd lain awake thinking about what she'd done to him in the garden, tasting him in her dreams, reveling in the power of it. "Where are you?"

"In my car in the Green parking lot. I've got a quarterly budget review to attend, but I'm hard just listening to your voice, so I need a few minutes before going in."

How did he know just the right thing to say? He wanted her, desired her. Just the sound of her voice made him hard.

"Here's what you're going to do," he went on. "There's a little shop I know. Lingerie in the front parlor, but in the back, there's exactly what you need. I want you to buy the vibrator that's just right for you. Okay?"

She gasped, the thought horrifying. "I can't do that."

"Faith," he said with mock sternness. "Wasn't it part of our bargain that you were going to do everything I told you to?"

"We aren't married yet."

He clucked his tongue at her. "Picky, picky. Didn't you like sucking me off last night?"

He turned her inside out, and her panties were actually damp. But was she ready for *everything* he wanted? "Connor, I can't walk into a store and ask to look at vibrators."

"You have to own your orgasms, Faith, own your sexuality." His voice dropped to a seductive note. "Do it. A man only enhances a woman's orgasm, but she's the one who creates it. You have to ask for what you want, baby; demand it as your right."

She let the stapler fall to the desk with a thump. Out in the hallway, she heard the slam of a locker, one of the older children. Soon, her students would be racing through the door, demanding, cajoling, screaming, playing.

For now, there was only Connor's voice. He seduced her, yet there was a part of her that balked. He wanted *too* much.

His voice was like that of a mesmerist trying to steal her will. She wanted to believe in what he offered so badly that if she wasn't careful, she wouldn't have a will left to call her own. And they weren't even married.

"SAY yes, Faith. Say you'll buy a new vibrator and let me listen to you. One day I want to watch you with it."

Still she said nothing. Dammit, he should have waited until a private moment together. When he could see her and touch her.

All he could hear was her breath, faster than normal. He made her hot. He knew it. "It'll feel good, Faith. You'll love it. I'm so damn hard just thinking about listening to that little hum over the phone. Say yes, baby, please."

"Yes." Her voice came so softly, he almost didn't hear it. But it was there. Thank God.

Yet she sounded a tad distant, and he disliked the phone

between them. If she was at home in her bed, he could seduce her with words. Jesus, he was starting to sound obsessed. He had to keep the goal in sight. Faith's delectable body was icing on the cake, not the cake itself. If he didn't keep his head straight, he'd screw up what he was working for.

"I'll see you tonight, baby."

She whispered good-bye and cut the connection.

Baby? What's up with that? It had been fine to use the expression last night in the throes of orgasm, but now, the term of endearment was out of sync. As if he were getting possessive.

Connor climbed from his car, his cock still hard in his pants. He closed his eyes, sought the control he needed. It was harder to grab hold of than usual.

Yeah. He was obsessed. But it wasn't a bad thing. Lust was good, and that's all this was, signified by his almost painful erection. He was for damn sure looking forward to the day Faith truly owned her sexuality and started demanding her due as a gorgeous, luscious woman.

MORNING sun streamed across the letter of resignation Connor laid on Herman Green's desk amid a riot of file folders, computer printouts, and cigar ashes. Connor stood; he hadn't been invited to sit in one of Herman's expensive leather chairs.

Herman Green puffed up his chest. His belly was round and his face florid, and right now, his high blood pressure appeared to be getting the better of him.

"If you even think of taking proprietary information over there . . ." His bluster faded off, as if he couldn't come up with an appropriate threat. Herman was generally a jovial man; he didn't do confrontation well.

After Lance appeared at the Castle home last evening, the stage was set for this inevitable scene.

"I have no intention of taking anything over to Castle." Connor didn't have any propriety information to take. Herman Green played his cards close to his chest. Which was why Connor had a devil of a time doing his job. How could you come up with a strategic plan when you weren't given access to the strategy?

If there was one.

Herman shook his finger and the flesh on his arm jiggled. "You've got some scheme up your sleeve, Kingston."

Quite frankly, Connor didn't understand Herman. Green Industries was Castle Heavy Mining's sole supplier of machined, die-cast, and plated parts. Not so bad for Castle—though no company should have *one* source—but for Green, it was disastrous. Castle was *their* primary revenue generator. That wasn't merely unsound business, but a catastrophe waiting to happen.

Herman refused to aggressively search out new markets. Connor had no idea why. Besides Lance being heir apparent, this was another of the reasons he'd discarded Green Industries as a candidate for his legacy building.

He wouldn't broach that subject again, but he did have other advice to offer. "There's no scheme, Herman, but you should take a look at the quality issues." They'd only just managed to reduce costs, and *bam*, quality had gone into the toilet.

Herman's cheeks puffed up like a blowfish. "Are you threatening me?"

Where the hell did he come up with that? "No," Connor said patiently. "But you have mature products yet mysteriously your return rates have risen over the last few months." Yesterday he would have referred to *our* products; today, he was on the other side of the fence. "There's a problem that needs addressing."

Herman settled back into his chair, huffing out a breath, his anger deflating along with the exhale. "Thanks for the consideration, but Lance has a handle on that."

Yeah, sure. Lance was no longer Connor's problem.

"Well." Herman brushed cigar ash from his calendar. "There's no need for you to remain the last weeks." He waved a hand ceremoniously. "Go forth and prepare for the wedding."

A false note rang in Herman's tone that Connor had no

idea how to interpret. Green and Castle had a symbiotic relationship, and he didn't want any burned bridges between them. "We're going to be working together, Herman. I have no ill will."

"Yes, yes, fine, fine." Herman wiped a hand across his mouth, his gaze focused on his desktop. "But it really is pointless for you to stay."

True. Connor had realized weeks ago that his days at Green Industries were numbered. He couldn't work in such a secretive atmosphere. His management philosophy centered around teamwork. The only team at Green Industries was comprised of Herman and Lance. Everyone else was simply an opponent.

He saluted Herman. "It's been a pleasure."

If it did turn out that Green Industries was experiencing irreversible quality issues, Connor's allegiance was now to Castle Heavy Mining. Herman would sink or swim on his own.

Swinging out of Herman's office, he almost ran into Lance in the hall. What, was the guy eavesdropping? Executive row at Green Industries was a wide hallway that dead-ended outside Herman's door. It wasn't what you'd call a normal traffic route, and Lance's office was at the other end.

For the moment, they were alone, and Lance's cologne was overdone in the airless corridor. The man was on the pretty boy side, polished like a new penny. But still a penny. "Lance."

"She's going to regret it."

After the meeting with Herman, Connor felt like rolling his eyes and heaving a great sigh. The Greens were becoming a tiresome lot. Instead he smiled. "Who's going to regret what?"

"Faith. She'll regret marrying you when she sees what a total dick you are."

Lance's antipathy wasn't surprising. Connor'd had several run-ins with him, such as the time Lance signed them into an ill-advised supplier contract that Connor had to negotiate them out of. But that was business. Connor had never cared much about being liked. He cared about doing his job, and he wasn't about to let that deal go through just because the boss's son had made it. Lance, however, took Connor's actions as personal attacks. He'd go so far as to say Lance hated him at this point.

"Thanks for the warning," Connor said without inflection.

"She'll dump you on your ass, and I'll be there to watch."

Connor spread his suit jacket, his hands on his hips. "What's your issue, Lance?" Besides the fact that Connor had gotten the partnership Lance himself wanted with Jarvis Castle.

"I don't have an issue. I just want you to understand that when she tosses you out and Jarvis fires you, you can't slink over here asking for your job back."

Connor was a couple of inches taller and a few pounds heavier, but what was the point in using size to intimidate a buffoon? "Thanks for telling me. I never would have figured that out on my own."

Yeah, he didn't want to burn bridges, but as he walked away, he understood they'd gone up in flames the moment he decided he wanted Faith and Castle Heavy Mining. All that was left was to determine the repercussions and deal with them.

TRINITY picked the walnuts, avocado, and cheese off her salad. Thank God they'd put the dressing on the side or she'd have dipped her lettuce in the water glass to wash it off.

"Why didn't you just ask them to give you greens, carrots, and tomatoes?" Faith remarked. "That would have been easier."

They were seated at a table outside a small sidewalk café, and the midafternoon sun felt good on her arms. A week ago, she'd been a woman hopelessly without a man. Last night, she'd gotten engaged. It still didn't seem real. Not even after the intimate act she'd performed.

"I like the cucumbers," Trinity said defensively.

Faith giggled. Cucumbers and Connor. Oh God, she was losing it.

Trinity frowned. "What's so funny?"

"Nothing." Faith couldn't explain. "Eat your cucumbers."

Trinity wasn't a picky eater. She pretty much liked everything. Just about everything, though, had either fat or added sugar, which converted to fat. At a cocktail party, she treated herself to one glass of champagne that she'd nurse all night long until there wasn't any fizz left, and she'd carry around a plate of carrot sticks so she wouldn't dive on the cheese puffs. Trinity was a perfect size four. Her clothes were labeled size zero, but she claimed that over the last few years clothing manufacturers had been tinkering with women's dress sizes, labeling them as a lower size to make people feel better.

Faith had to admit she might be right. She'd gone down two dress sizes since she was twenty-five, but she could swear she hadn't lost weight. Then again, she rarely stepped on a scale. Weighing yourself could be demoralizing.

Finally, Trinity seemed satisfied with the undressed state of her salad. "Why didn't you tell me about Connor and his marriage proposal?"

That was getting to the point. "Lance has a big mouth."

Trinity flared her nostrils dramatically.

"I didn't want you to talk me out of it."

"*Could* I have talked you out of it, hon?"

"Maybe." Faith shrugged. "In the beginning."

"And"—Trinity arched an already perfectly arched brow—"when exactly was the beginning?"

"Which beginning?"

Trinity tapped the end of her fork on the tabletop. "You owe me the whole story."

Faith realized she did. She'd let her best friend find out from Lance. Faith knew that hurt Trinity's feelings.

She told the whole story, everything, minus the sex stuff. She and Trinity never got into specific sexual details, so how on earth was she supposed to tell Trinity that

Connor wanted her to buy a vibrator so he could listen to her use it, *watch* her use it? Oh God. If she thought too much about all the things he *might* ask her to do, her nerves would snap. *You have to own your sexuality.* What did that really mean?

Trinity held out her hand. "Let me see your ring."

"My ring?" Faith's stomach plummeted.

"Your engagement ring, silly."

Good lord. She hadn't even thought about that. "We haven't picked one out yet."

"Faith." Trinity patted her hand. "I love you oodles and oodles, but you don't have to marry a man who didn't even go down on bended knee and put a ring on your finger."

"But I thought you liked Connor."

"I liked him *before* I knew he was after your father's company. I wouldn't have introduced you if I'd even suspected."

"But I'm glad you did. I want children. And I want to get married in order to have them."

"But you don't have to settle for someone who simply wants your money. There's a man out there who's going to love you for who you are just like there's a man out there who's going to love me just the way I am."

Faith almost laughed. Trinity was gorgeous. "Men drool over you."

"I'm the proverbial dumb blonde, and most of the time I don't mind. But men don't want to just *talk* to me." She leaned forward and shook her fork. "And you're doing that deliberately, trying to push the conversation back on me."

Faith smiled. "Busted."

Trinity speared another bare lettuce leaf. "Hold out for love, Faith. You deserve it. Connor's not good enough for you if he doesn't love you wholeheartedly. I have half a mind to tell him what I think of him, especially since he goaded me into introducing you."

Faith felt the words stick in her throat. Okay, okay. That wasn't really news. Connor said he'd soaked up everything Trinity said about Faith. He'd *chosen* Faith.

"You'll hate me for saying this, but Faith, honey, it's going to kill you the first time someone walks up to you at the country club and tells you what your husband's been up to with some skanky bimbo."

It was worse than a knife thrust. It was a chain saw dismembering her. She didn't expect it from Trinity, everyone else, yes, but not her friend. "Trinity, please."

Moisture glimmered in Trinity's eyes. "I'm sorry," she whispered. "That was mean. I thought he was special, but he's a scumbag like the rest of them. And I gave my best friend to him." She dabbed at the corner of her eye. "It's not fair."

"He's not going to cheat on me, Trinity. He promised."

Trinity gave an unladylike snort. "Men always *promise*."

"No. We're going to put it in a prenuptial agreement. He cheats, he's out. This isn't about sex, Trinity. It's about both of us getting what we want. I want a baby and Connor wants to run Daddy's company. If he cheats, he'll lose that, and it's worth more to him than . . . sex. Some men are like that, you know."

Except that Connor wanted both, the company and sex, with her, whenever he chose. There was a certain buzz in knowing that, and yes, after last night, a thrill in believing it, too.

"It's not as bad as you think, Trin."

"It sounds like a business deal, not a marriage proposal. Your father is *buying* him for you."

Trinity viciously stabbed a cherry tomato, and Faith felt her words stab her own heart. That's what Lance had said. But Daddy wasn't *buying* Connor. He was . . . her chest hurt with a breath she couldn't drag in. Oh yes, he *had* bought her a husband.

"You're the nicest person I know," Trinity went on as if she had no idea of the wound she'd just inflicted, "and you deserve more than that. I can't believe I helped him."

Faith touched her hand. "Trin, I *like* what he's offering." She wouldn't let Lance's words get to her, even if they were out of Trinity's mouth. "Connor didn't lie. He gave me honesty. And I think the whole . . . sex thing will be . . ."

She waved her hand in the air uselessly. Why couldn't she just spit it out?

He makes me so hot I almost cream my panties just listening to his voice on the phone, not to mention how good he tasted in my mouth.

"The whole sex thing," Trinity mimicked. "That's the main problem. You deserve someone who'll make love to you. Mad, passionate love all night long. *That's* what I wanted for you."

"He wants me, Trin. Honest to God, I think he wants me, and it doesn't seem like he's faking it, either."

Trinity stared at her with those gorgeous baby blues men went gaga over, and Faith read every skeptical thought. Trinity couldn't hide a single emotion. "He'd be crazy if he didn't want you," she said softly, a glimmer of moisture in her eyes. "Of the whole sorry lot of us, you're the only one worth having."

For the first time ever, Faith had an inkling that Trinity's life wasn't the perfect scenario she made it out to be. She was still searching for Mr. Future President. She was always smiling, flirting, super confident, and sweetly ditzy. But maybe what she wanted for Faith was what Trinity really wanted for herself. Someone to make mad passionate love to her and mean it.

"I want him, Trinity. I don't love him and he doesn't love me, but together we can make some pretty darn good babies, and that's all I care about. I trust him not to make a fool of me. And I can't say that about a lot of the men we know."

Trinity worried her bottom lip without messing her lipstick. "I support you because you're my best friend." Not *one* of her best friends but her *best* friend. Then she narrowed her eyes. "If he hurts you, I'll torture him with my curling iron. When it's turned on. And where I'll put it, it's gonna hurt badly."

Faith laughed. She could just imagine. "I never knew you had such a sadistic streak."

Trinity waggled her blond brows. "You better let him know he'll have me to deal with."

Faith's chest felt a little tight, and her head throbbed right above her left eye. That's how it always felt when she wanted to cry, but wouldn't allow herself. "Trinity, have I ever told you how much your friendship means to me?"

"A million times, hon"—Trinity waved aside the moment—"and same goes for me."

They didn't talk like this often, but Faith believed Trinity would brand Connor with her curling iron if he misbehaved.

What more could a friend ask for?

8

THE marriage contract, prenuptial, or whatever you called it, had squeezed his balls in a vise. Connor signed away his sperm, his sexual autonomy, and the right to name his first-born child. Jarvis wanted the little tyke called *Jarvis*. Helluva name to saddle a baby with. Despite leaving Green Industries the day after his engagement, Jarvis had refused to take him into Castle. That would happen only after the wedding.

Today, two and a half weeks later, Connor had followed Jarvis's limousine to San Francisco's city hall in Friday afternoon commute traffic because he wasn't allowed to see the bride before the wedding. They didn't have to make the drive to San Francisco; they could have done it down on the Peninsula, but Jarvis had insisted his daughter should be married in the City.

Jarvis Castle controlled every aspect of the nuptials, a not-so-subtle message that he now controlled Connor's life. The old man's actions were almost laughable. He'd probably try to walk into the honeymoon suite and direct things there, too.

Yet Connor Kingston couldn't be happier as he dotted the *i* on the marriage certificate. The civil ceremony was brief, the judge reading the minimalist pitch quickly, with Jarvis and a clerk witnessing. After the ring exchange, the clerk had hustled them into a quaint antechamber for the signatures. The walls were paneled wood, no windows, just a desk, a chair, and a book, like one would find in a church rather than a clerk's office.

Faith was glorious in a cream-colored suit, a prim pale lipstick on her lips, her magnificent hair unbound, and a shell-shocked look in her eyes.

Taking her hand in his, he wrapped her fingers around the ballpoint pen. "Your turn," he murmured.

She licked her lips, her gloss glistening with the light moisture, then Faith signed away her father's company.

Connor had waited almost three weeks for the wedding, yet in many ways, he'd waited a lifetime. Everything he'd told himself he'd get out of life was within his reach.

Not to mention the added bonus. Tonight, he'd finally slide inside his wife's succulent body. He'd been dreaming about that night after night. To date, she hadn't purchased that vibrator as he'd instructed. He hadn't pushed. Yet. Over the phone, he'd coaxed her through multiple orgasms. He'd come with her. But he hadn't touched her again. He wanted her body signed, sealed, and delivered before he took her.

He also wanted to give Faith something special, a real wedding night with a few surprises. He didn't want any question that the child they made wasn't legitimate in every way possible. Faith would get her money's worth. He wasn't a taker. He would make marriage worth everything her father paid for it.

Faith laid down the pen and jutted out her cheek for her father's kiss. Jarvis hugged her hard, his gaze steady over her shoulder. Connor merely smiled. Jarvis Castle had an eye thing going. He'd shot Connor any number of meaningful glares, stares, glances, and steady gazes over the last half hour. And they all held one message. *Hurt my daughter, and I will annihilate you.*

Connor stretched out his hand, palm up, and Jarvis had no choice but to give over his daughter, gently placing her hand in that of her husband's. Connor chastely kissed her forehead. It was the last chaste kiss he'd give her for a long, long time.

"I've booked a table at the Top of the Mark," Jarvis said.

"Daddy, you didn't have to do that."

"I couldn't give you a big wedding, I didn't give you away, you don't want my help with buying a house, but I will give you a memorable send-off."

Any dig the old man could get in, he did. He didn't give

in gracefully, that was for sure. But the restaurant was at the top of the Mark Hopkins Hotel on Nob Hill with a magnificent view, and it was a fitting place for Faith's wedding feast.

The hotel itself was a perfect setting for other things, too, once Connor got rid of Jarvis.

HER father secured a secluded table in the corner right next to the window overlooking San Francisco, and soon, as the sun started to set, the sky would streak with color if the fog didn't roll in. For now, it was still a bright, cloudless blue.

They were early and many of the tables were empty, others occupied by chattering women or couples starting on Happy Hour. While the Top of the Mark was actually a bar, her father had persuaded the staff to have dinner sent up from the restaurant. It was a civilized affair, but Faith couldn't wait for it to be over. Her father talked, about Connor's duties at work, his duty to Faith, the condo they'd rented until they found something to buy—an endless litany that made her want to scream. Yet throughout it all, Connor smiled and nodded, a glint in his eyes. A glint that turned wicked when he fastened his gaze on her.

She went to take a sip of wine, miscalculated the distance, and a drop splashed her cream suit. Her filet mignon tasted like horse meat and the dessert mousse was chalky. All right, it was her. She was so nervous, she felt nauseous.

What have I done?

She'd thought the evening would be dinner for two, but her father had decided it was better if three attended. There was something nerve-racking about sitting next to your father when you knew you were going to give the man right across from you carnal knowledge of your body in a couple of short hours.

She felt her cheeks flush.

Connor's mouth lifted on one side, and the devil winked in his eye.

"If you'll excuse me a moment." He pushed his chair

back and tossed his napkin by the side of his coffee cup. Walking away, he had a flawless rear view in a tailored dark blue suit. A chorus of female gazes followed his progress.

"Thanks for the wonderful dinner, Daddy." *Now it's time for you to go.* "Connor's going to drive me back to our condo." *So there isn't any reason for you to stay.*

"I'll be watching every move he makes, Faith." Her father squeezed her hand. "You'll tell me if he upsets you."

Faith took a belly breath. "No, I won't. I'm married now. If Connor and I have any disagreements, they're between us."

"I'm only looking out for you, sweetheart."

"I know." She squeezed his hand back. She appreciated his concern, but . . . he'd bought Connor for her, and he was still orchestrating everything. If she was ever to let go of that raw nerve, she had to take a stand. "You need to butt out now, Daddy. Go home. If I've made a mistake, it's *my* mistake."

He let go of her, jerking his cup off the saucer and spilling coffee over the side. "It's my mistake, too. He starts work for me on Monday."

She smoothed a couple of crumbs aside on the table-cloth. "Daddy, I want this to work. And the only way it's going to is if you aren't constantly picking apart the things he does."

"I don't pick on him."

She shot him a look from the corner of her eye, then shook her head. "I love you. But I'm married to him, and you hired him. It's done. Now go home, Daddy, and let me run my life."

"But—"

She held up a finger. "No buts. I'm almost thirty."

The waiter arrived with the check, setting it by her father's elbow, then slid an envelope in front of Faith. She tipped her head up at him.

"The gentleman left it for you."

"He's gone?" Her father's voice was a note louder than necessary, and a few heads turned.

"He simply asked me to give this to the lady, sir." The

man backed up two steps, turned on his heel, and walked away.

"I told you, Faith."

She rolled her eyes and yet . . . a tiny tremor ran through her body. Slipping her finger under the flap, she opened the envelope to find a room key in a pocket card. And Connor's neat writing. *Get rid of your father and meet me ASAP.*

She almost hugged the card key to her chest. "He's booked a room at the hotel for tonight."

"You didn't pack clothes." Her father sounded scandalized.

She leaned over and kissed his cheek. "Don't worry about it. I love you. Thanks for dinner. I'll call you tomorrow."

Then she rose from the table, tucked her purse under her arm, and left to meet her husband. When she turned the corner and was out of sight, she ran to the elevators.

She was nervous, afraid of how he'd look at her naked body, terrified she wouldn't measure up, her pulse pounding against her eardrums. What would he ask her to do? How far would he push her? But more than anything, she wanted finally, *finally* to know how Connor felt inside her.

"BUT I didn't pack any clothes."

Faith stood in the middle of a room done in gold tones from the burgundy and gold comforter on the queen-sized bed to the gold-striped wallpaper. The room was all-equipped: antique desk outfitted with the latest Internet hookups, a tallboy disguising the TV and small refrigerator, and a gorgeous view of Alcatraz. A champagne bucket sat on a small table next to an easy chair.

"You're not going to need clothes tonight. But I did get his and hers toothbrushes in the gift shop." Connor pointed to the bathroom. "You wanna see? They're on the counter."

There was something he wanted her to see in the bathroom, and she didn't think it was his and hers toothbrushes.

She stopped on the doorstep and gasped. "It's all mirrors." Two walls were mirrored floor to ceiling, more than enough to show off every crevice. Every bump. Every . . . imperfection. And Connor wasn't the one with the imperfections.

He came up behind her, pushing her inside with his body, his breath at her ear as he whispered, "I can lean you over the counter and watch my cock slide inside you from every angle."

"Pervert." She tried to joke, but her chocolate mousse had curdled in her stomach.

In the mirror, he quirked a smile. "Take your clothes off."

She needed to stall before she collapsed in a quivering heap. "Aren't you going to give me any champagne first?"

"I got the champagne so I could drizzle it all over you and lick it off."

Her nipples puckered against her wedding suit, but her fears and nervousness spiked. "You're rushing me."

He wrapped an arm beneath her breasts and pulled her against him, his erection nudging her spine. "If I don't rush, you'll balk and run. But I can get you drunk on champagne first."

He backed her up, turned, his hand sliding across her midriff, then grabbed her fingers and took her to the champagne. Pouring two glasses, he handed her one, tipped his own against it, and sipped. "Drink up."

He was moving too fast. She wanted to get off the merry-go-round he'd created inside her. "Can't we have some conversation before I take off my clothes?"

"You talk." He nuzzled her neck. "I want to bury my face in your pussy and lick you until you scream."

Oh. Oh. Her body tightened, and moisture gathered between her legs. "You certainly get right to the heart of the matter."

He took her glass, setting both on the table. Then he gathered her lapels in his fingers and drew her closer until her nipples rubbed the backs of his hands. "All I've thought about for the past seventeen days is touching you, tasting you, getting inside you, and coming in you." He undid the buttons on her jacket and dropped his voice. "Do you remember our first date? I rubbed my fingers in you, and later, after I dropped you off, I sucked them. Now I want that taste on my tongue again."

She could barely breathe, let alone answer him. Heat raced through her body, then blazed straight to her clitoris.

He stroked one hard nipple with his thumb. "So tell me, do you still want to have a little conversation first?"

She swallowed and shook her head.

"Good." He undid the buttons on her silk blouse, popped the front clasp of her bra, then bent at the knees and lifted her until her nipple nudged his lips. He sucked her inside, hard, and she felt it in her clitoris and right up into her womb.

Then he tossed her onto the bed. She bounced, squeaked, then laughed. "You're crazy."

"I'm just so fucking horny for you I can't see straight." Grabbing her foot, he raised it, tugged off her high-heeled white pump and threw it over his shoulder, where it hit the wall. Then he did the same with the other. Caressing her instep, he asked, "Are these hose or thigh-highs?"

"Panty hose," she answered.

He grinned, then slid both hands down the outsides of her legs, forcing them apart with his body, and pushed up beneath her skirt. "Lift," he whispered.

She did. Plucking the waistband, he slid everything back down the way he'd come. "Hey. Got the panties, too."

She'd worn black lace, thinking he'd rip them off with his teeth, but now she was just glad they were gone.

Pulling her to the edge of the bed, he went down on his knees between her legs. Her skirt had ridden to her waist, and he pushed her thighs wider to accommodate his body.

She felt exposed and vulnerable.

"Holy Mother," he said on nothing more than a breath.

"What?" What was wrong?

"You are so fucking beautiful."

She felt her brow rise into her hairline. "Down there?"

"All over. But especially down there. It's pink and plump and begging me to suck it." He didn't look up, but simply raised a finger, trailing it down her center. "And you're so wet." Lifting his gaze to hers, he sucked his index finger into his mouth and closed his eyes. "Jesus, you taste good."

Faith swallowed, then bit her lip. No one had ever spoken to her like this. No one had ever said anything like . . . that. She'd never met a man like Connor before. Her previous lovers just . . . did it. Sometimes they made noises of appreciation, but there was nothing like this. No one like Connor.

His head back, his nostrils flared, a slight smile on his lips, he breathed deeply. "I'm going to make you come fast and hard, then we can slow it all down, but I need that first." He opened his eyes. "Okay?"

She wore her jacket, her blouse was halfway undone but still tucked in, and her skirt rode her abdomen. She felt hot and decadent. Wanted. "Yes. Please," she whispered.

"Thank you, baby." Then he shoved his fingers under her hips, took her buttocks in his hands, and set his mouth to her.

Faith almost screamed. His lips were hot, wet. His tongue traced her labia, flicked just under her clitoris, down to her opening, and quickly back up. Then he teased the very center with the pointed tip. Faith was afraid to touch him in case he stopped. His tongue swirled around her one way, then the other. He sucked her hard, then let her go and swirled his tongue all over again. She couldn't stand it. Arching, she pushed herself harder against him. His fingers bit into her butt. She grabbed his head and held him right where she wanted him. Oh, oh, nothing had ever felt like this. He did something miraculous with his tongue and heat shot like a fireball up through her center. Faith cried out his name. Her ears were ringing when she floated back down from the place he'd blasted her to, and his fingers stroked and soothed along her thighs.

"I debauched your wedding outfit."

She covered her eyes. "Do you think anyone heard me?"

"I hope so. I want them to know I'm doing my job properly."

She raised her head. His lips glistened, and his hair was
a spiky mess where she tried to pull it out by the roots.

"Was it good?" he asked with little-boy eagerness.

"You know it was."

"Then come here and give me my wedding kiss." He
pulled her up by the arms, wrapped his across her back, and
stopped, his mouth scant inches from hers.

The scent of hot sex was all over him, the aroma of
musky male and female desire, and she lost herself in his
magician's gaze. Then he closed the last microns between
them and claimed her. It was like the kiss he'd taken that
night in the garden, the mingling of flavors, his and hers,
becoming one. His taste intoxicated her. His scent mesmerized her.

They'd said the words, signed the document, but the kiss
sealed their future. "Make me a baby," she whispered.

Connor laid his wife back on the bed and undid the
rest of her buttons. Reaching beneath her, he unzipped the
skirt and pulled it over her hips. She had glossy red hair
between her thighs with none of the blond streaks. She'd
tasted like sweet aromatic wine. He wanted to bury himself
in her now, without even removing his pants or his shoes. A
swift, hard come shooting inside her, deep enough to take
possession of her womb.

But he wanted to feel her naked skin against him. He
petted the soft skin of her thighs, her belly, rising to the
underside of her breasts. Her eyes followed him, but she
said nothing.

He knew she was unsure of herself. If she had her way,
she would have turned off the lights and covered herself to
the chin with the bedclothes.

The mirrors in the bathroom had terrified her.

He bent to nip the smooth flesh of her hip, tunneling
between her pussy lips for just a moment. She made a small
sound, and heat and wet coated his finger. God, when she
came into her own and let herself loose, she'd be dynamite
in any man's hands. In his, she'd be incomparable.

Raising his head, he gazed up the length of her. She
was naked from the waist down, but still wore her jacket,

blouse, and bra, though everything had been undone and lay askew. Sexy, hot, rumpled, ready for so much more. "No fast, hard fuck for you, Mrs. Kingston." Jesus, he did like the sound of that. "It's going to take all night long."

He hauled her to her feet. "Let's get naked." He divested her of the remains of her wedding outfit, then put her hand on his belt. "Your turn. You know, you've said barely a word."

She arched one brow in a haughty manner so like the *ladies* at the country club. "I do believe I screamed your name," she said. "What more do you want?"

She was exactly the way he wanted her. Sure of herself for that moment. "That'll do for now. Undress me."

"Did you give me this many orders before we married?"

"Yes." He chucked her under the chin. "You did everything I told you to and loved it."

She tugged on the buckle and unzipped his pants, but instead of pushing them off, she pulled at his tie. He'd worn his plain blue interview suit. He'd worn his fucking interview suit to his wedding. Connor smiled. That said it all.

"What's so funny?" She unstrung the tie from his collar and threw it on top of her clothing. When he looked down at her, she pushed his chin back up. "Look straight ahead."

Which meant he was looking over her head, and he suddenly realized she felt uncomfortable in complete nakedness while he still had all his clothes on.

Only Faith was trying to hide it. Putting on a stoic face, so to speak. He was glad he'd asked for a room with mirrors in the bathroom, even if the clerk had looked at him strangely. He'd introduce Faith to her own glory in those mirrors.

"I was laughing that I got married looking like I was going to a job interview. I should have rented a tux."

She smiled at his throat as she finished undoing his buttons and pushed both jacket and shirt off his shoulders. Then she stopped, and her breath was audible in the quiet of the room.

"What?"

"You're beautiful." She played with the light swath of hair on his chest, tickled first one nipple, then the other.

"Suck it," he murmured.

He closed his eyes as he felt the brush of her skin against his abdomen, the lush sweep of her hair across his flesh. Then she took him in her mouth. He didn't know if it was how a woman felt when her nipples were sucked, but it was halfway between pleasure and pain. As if someone tickled you just a little too hard, and he felt the tug of it all the way down in his groin.

And suddenly his cock wanted her mouth's attention, badly.

"Toe off your shoes," she murmured, giving his nipple one last swipe that sent a shiver down to his gut.

He kicked his shoes aside while she pushed his pants and boxers down his legs. He sat on the edge of the bed, yanked everything off the rest of the way, and threw them.

"Should you treat your best suit that way?" She picked up the pants, held them in front of her, smoothing them and covering her own naked body. "You might need it again."

"I'm done interviewing. I got the job."

She moved around the room picking up the bits and pieces of clothing they'd discarded.

"Are you nervous, Faith?" he asked gently.

"Of course not. Don't be silly." She heaved a sigh he felt deep inside. "All right, a little."

He held out his hand. "Come here."

She did, with clothes covering the parts of her body he wanted to touch. He grabbed the whole mess and tossed it.

Taking her by the hips, he reeled her in and put a kiss to her belly. "You're beautiful," he whispered.

Her skin flushed with a pink glow. "We agreed you weren't going to give me a bunch of compliments that aren't true."

He tilted his head back and kissed the sweet bead of a nipple. "I said I wouldn't lie to you. You have gorgeous breasts." He slid over her abdomen to the abundant red hair, and finally inside the jewel between her legs. "And you have the most delicious pussy."

He fingered her clit slowly, lingering while her body softened for him. He eased up inside her, riding her gently, until she gasped and grabbed hold of his shoulders.

"You feel good, you taste good"—he rubbed her belly with his nose—"you smell good." He bit her lightly, then eased back from her opening to caress the sensitive flesh right before her ass. She was close, so close. He nudged between her lips with his tongue and tasted the nectar, stroked her clit until she began the slow, sweet grind of her pussy against his mouth.

Then he pushed her to the carpet and rose over her. Holding his cock in his hand, he grazed the tip up and down her slit. She was so wet, and his own come mingled with hers in a delicious slip-side of bodies. He rode her clit from the base to the tip of his cock and back again, then teased with just his crown.

"Do you like this?"

She nodded, dragged in a breath, then arched off the carpet.

"It's good, but it's not enough to make you come, is it?" It wasn't a question; he knew the answer, but he wanted her to beg for more.

"No, it's not enough."

Pushing the tip of his cock just inside her pussy, he held there with a light pulse of his hips.

"Connor, please." That was all she said.

"Please what?"

"Get inside me."

Ah, that's what he wanted. Her capitulation. Yet he still had so much more to show her before the big moment. "Weren't you afraid it wouldn't fit?"

"It'll fit." She wriggled her intention. "Please."

"No. I think we need to make sure." He pulled out, slid once more over the crest of her clit, then rose to his feet.

"What are you doing?" She didn't bother to cover herself. Good. Her desire was rising, her fears and inhibitions receding.

"I want to watch us. I want to see my cock slide inside you. Just to make sure it fits perfectly."

He grabbed the desk chair, carried it into the bathroom, and set it facing the full mirror along the wall. Then he sat, his gut screaming that he was pushing too hard too fast.

She'd rolled to her stomach, propped herself on her arms and stared through the doorway, first at the hard jut of his cock, then the chair, and finally the mirror.

"Let me show you how we're going to keep our marriage exciting, Faith."

He held out his hand and prayed she'd take it.

9

STANDING in the doorway, her legs were weak, her heart pattered loudly in her chest, and blood buzzed in her ears. The sexual hum hadn't evaporated, yet she'd come down from the high enough to feel self-conscious without her clothes.

"Come to bed," she said. It would be so much easier beneath the covers. She'd welcome anything he wanted to do to her then.

"I want you to watch us. We'll fit, Faith. I promise."

He was so magnificent, smooth, hard chest with a dusting of hair, muscles, firm abdomen, and that mouth-watering penis. It wasn't the fit she worried about. It was seeing herself in the mirror, knowing he saw exactly the same thing. All her flaws.

She did not want to step into that bathroom. Right now, she couldn't see herself, his body in direct line with the mirror.

"Haven't you ever made love with the lights on?" He raised one brow. She loved when he did that; he looked so wicked, and she liked him that way.

She didn't like the mirror. She knew there wasn't a woman on the face of the planet who was happy with the way her body looked. Trinity wanted Faith's breasts, and Faith wanted Trinity's trim waist. All women lusted after the perfect body, and no one quite agreed what that was. Faith did know hers wasn't it. She was Marilyn Monroe on a heavy bloat day.

She wanted to beg. *Please don't make me do this.* But revealing her insecurities aloud would give him too much power.

"Come on, baby."

She closed her eyes, loving the sound of that endearment on his lips. Then she felt his hands at her waist, lifting her, easily, as if she weren't . . . a bloated Marilyn Monroe.

"Wrap your legs around my waist," he urged.

His penis nudged her as she locked her feet behind him and clasped her arms around his neck. Then he carried her back to the chair. "I won't make you watch this time, but I'm going to love seeing every inch of my cock sliding inside you."

He sat once more, pulling her flush up against him as she touched the floor, balancing lightly on the balls of her feet.

His eyes were obsidian dark and devilishly hot. Pushing her back to slip a hand between them, he tested her folds. "You're very wet. Perfect."

She swallowed, biting back a moan when he grazed her clitoris with the tip of his finger.

"Make noise if you want to, Faith. I like it."

"Someone might hear us."

"Fuck 'em." He grinned when her eyes widened. "I'm not a gentleman. I like the words *fuck*, *cock*, *pussy*." He fit a finger inside her, but didn't pump it, letting the warmth of his palm and the feeling of fullness inside her work their magic as he seduced her with dirty talk. "And I'm going to say them. As in, let me fuck you, baby. I want my cock deep inside your sweet, delicious, fuckable pussy. I want to fuck you until you scream."

She felt her breath stop halfway down her throat. "I like it when you talk like that."

He laughed and hitched her closer with an arm across her back. "You're blushing." He pulled her bottom lip between his teeth and sucked lightly. "Fuck me, baby." He swept his tongue along the seam of her lips. "Let me watch my cock while you fuck the hell out of me."

In one fluid movement, he grabbed her butt and raised her over him. "Take me inside you."

Faith closed her hand around him one finger at a time. He was hot, steel hard, and wet with pre-come. Putting her feet on the bottom rungs of the chair to steady herself, she took him.

"Slowly," he murmured, his head bent, his hands holding her, guiding her. "Watch me take you, baby."

There was something wholly erotic, completely seductive about watching his body glide between her lips. Her clitoris was a hard, achy bead, her pussy plump, begging. And the feeling, all that heat, the friction, the sense of being filled. She dug her nails into his shoulders.

"I told you it was beautiful." Then he pulled her down sharply, to the hilt, her clit pushed against his pubic bone, and she almost screamed, almost came.

Her breath came in harsh gasps, and her body seemed to liquefy around him. "Oh God, that's good," she whispered.

"Ride me and it'll get better."

And Faith rode him. He held her close, his chin over her shoulder as he watched in the mirror. When he spread her cheeks, she knew he was exposing the slide of his cock in and out, covered with her moisture, his come. She hung on, let him guide her to a faster pace, the slap of her bottom against his thighs, the sound of slick bodies coming together, the harsh beat of his breath against her ear, and his constant litany of words.

"That's it, baby, fuck me hard, so good. Jesus, Faith, you are so fucking beautiful."

For long glorious moments, he pounded into her, then he slid his fingers into her hair and pulled her head back. "I want you to see this."

Her own reflection flickered in his dark eyes. "Please," she whispered. *Please don't make me* or *please let me*, she couldn't say. She wanted to turn and look in the mirror, yet terror of what she'd see made her clutch harder to his shoulders.

His gaze shifted across her face, then his lips slammed down on hers, sucked her tongue into his mouth. Fast, hard, then he stood. Plopping her on the bathroom counter, he pushed her chest. "Lean back and hold your legs wide."

She was exposed and out of control. And he took her

higher than a man ever had. Curled at the waist, she could see every inch of his cock sweep in and out of her, feel the slap of his testicles on her butt. Her breasts bounced, and Connor reached out to pinch a nipple. Deep inside her, he started to pulse.

"Touch your clit, now."

He closed his eyes, bared his teeth, held her at the joining of her hips and thighs, and thrust home, faster, harder, deeper. Faith put her finger to her clitoris.

The room simply exploded into lights. She half screamed, half moaned and if he said anything, she couldn't hear it over the roar in her ears. Liquid heat filled her, pulsed inside her, then she felt him gather her into his arms and slide down the vanity until he was seated on the floor with her in his lap.

She heard his voice over the drumbeat of her heart. "Hold me inside, baby. As long as you can."

She fell asleep with his body buried deep within her.

SHIT. That was so damn good. He wished he'd stood her on her feet though, bent her over the countertop, and taken her from behind so they could both watch his cock in the mirrored wall.

He'd never seen anything lovelier than the sight of her ass in the reflection, his cock filling her, her pussy devouring him. Why could she not believe how absolutely gorgeous she was?

When she'd agreed to watch, he'd almost lost it right then, deep inside her. Christ. Her guard was down, and she'd wanted, badly. He'd flopped her down on the counter because he couldn't bear to pull out. Not right then. Tight and hot, her body milked the best damn orgasm from him that he'd had in years.

But his ass was falling asleep against the cold tile floor.

She had so much potential. He'd had her, and he wanted her again. He imagined all manner of things he could do to her. A little kink, a lot of hot action. He would please her, and she would please him. He wanted her to surpass him, surprise him, take control, and blow his mind. Yeah, he'd made a good choice.

Lust was so damn good when it wasn't all fucked up by the concept of love. He was well versed in that notion. After his mom died, his dad drank himself to death all because of the loss of *love*. It had taken only two years to accomplish that feat. Connor had had his own brush with the sometimes fatal emotion. She was in his last foster home. He'd loved her for almost a year that felt like a lifetime back then. They'd made momentous plans for the day he turned eighteen. Two weeks before, he found her in bed fucking their foster dad. If it had been molestation, he'd have understood, but she was older than Connor by six months, and she told him "Dad" was getting a divorce to marry her. He'd come out of it with an important lesson. Love sucked. It was just a word. It didn't mean a goddamn thing.

This, Faith sated in his arms, his body on the edge for more, *this* was so much better than love ever could be. When she opened herself completely to him, came into her sexual self-esteem, he'd have perfection in his grasp without fear of crossing the line from love to hate.

FAITH put her hands on her hips and surveyed the living room of their newly rented condo. She didn't mind it being furnished with someone else's seconds, but she did want some of her own things. The load, packed up from her father's house, consisted of her king-sized bed, the dressers, her vanity, a flat-panel TV, an easy chair, and her clothing.

All Connor brought with him were three boxes of clothes, shoes, papers, and his computer. Oh, and his toaster.

They'd gotten married Friday, honeymooned Friday night and Saturday morning up in the City, then in the afternoon, back to the condo for the delivery. Connor had wanted to spend the weekend in the City, but the hotel was much too expensive, and she'd used the furniture as an excuse to come home.

All right, that wasn't the whole truth. When she woke in the morning, she suddenly found the room . . . tiny. Confining. They hadn't an ounce of privacy. That didn't seem to bother Connor, but there were all the little intimate things she hadn't even thought of, something as simple as brushing her teeth before she encountered anyone, let alone exchanged a kiss. And all the other personal needs a woman wanted privacy to attend to.

It was actually easier having sex with him than using the bathroom in front of him. *That* was terrifying. At least in the condo, there were two bathrooms, one upstairs, one down, three small bedrooms on the second floor, and on the first, a combo living room and dining room, and a spacious kitchen.

Space. She could breathe and try to settle her nerves. And think about furniture and what kind of dishes and flatware she needed to buy instead of how she was suddenly living with a man she barely knew except in a carnal way.

Faith puffed out a breath. Three cheesy prints—a sailboat, a vase of flowers, and a forest scene with Bambi in the foreground—graced the living room walls, probably to hide a few holes. The bright, ultrafeminine flower-print sofa and love seat didn't suit Connor in any way, shape, or form.

"We could bring some furniture from your apartment, too."

Connor dismissed the idea with a grunt. "Hand-me-down crap from the Salvation Army. I'm getting rid of it all. If you don't like this sofa, we can buy something else."

"We don't need to spend the money."

He eyed her, shaking his head. "We don't have to watch every penny. I've got a perfectly respectable bank balance."

Except that he hadn't shown her the bank balance. Not that it was any of her business. Theirs wasn't a real marriage; it was a marriage of convenience, which meant they didn't share every single detail with each other.

"Buy what you want this week," he added.

She waited for more. Nothing came. "Don't you want to give me some sort of budget to work with?"

He took her arms, turning her toward him. "What's the big deal about the money?"

She looked down at her toes. Last night—and early this morning—had been wonderful. After she'd gotten over her initial nervousness. Now her stomach churned with all the day-to-day issues of being married to a man her father had bought for her like a prize bull off the auction block. God, why couldn't she get that thought completely out of her head? "I like the sofa. I just thought maybe you didn't."

"I'm fine with the furniture, but if you want something else, I can afford it."

Faith didn't really have a concept of money. She charged what she wanted, and Daddy paid for it. As a teacher, she made a pittance, and it was barely a drop in the bucket to what she spent. She thought nothing of plunking down three hundred for shoes, and that was pretty cheap compared to some of the stuff Trinity bought. She drove a Lexus her father paid cash for; she had her weekly facial and massage. Still, she wasn't extravagant compared to many of the people she knew. Really, paying over two thousand dollars for a dress was ridiculous.

But that wasn't the world Connor came from.

"I need a limit on how much I can spend," she whispered.

He tipped her chin to look at him, his eyes suddenly smoke before the fire. "What did I tell you about limits?"

She swallowed. "There are none."

They hadn't exercised any so far. Faith blushed thinking about the bedroom things he suggested they try. Doing it in front of the mirror was tame as far as Connor was concerned. She didn't know how a man was able to come four times in one night.

He popped the top button on her blouse. "You know, we don't need new stuff until we find our own house." He slipped his hand inside her bra. "There is, however, one thing you need to buy for the condo, and there's no limit on how much you can spend."

Her nipples burgeoned under his attention. How did he do that, talk about getting things for the condo while he played her breasts and rubbed his erection against her belly? She couldn't concentrate at all.

"What?" she managed to say.

With his other hand, he tugged up her skirt and slipped inside the elastic edge of her panties. "You need to get that vibrator." He slid across her clitoris just as he said the word, and she jerked, then clung to his arms.

She closed her eyes and rocked with the slow caress of his hand. "Why don't you get it and give it to me as a present?"

"A vibrator's too personal for someone else to buy." He tapped her chin. "Open your eyes."

She did, drowning in the heat of his gaze. She was so hot and wet, and his face was hazy in her vision.

"You have a parent-teacher day Monday, don't you?"

She nodded, sliding one leg up his to open herself more fully for him. God, the way he made her feel was . . . out of control. Willing to do anything. No limits.

"Buy it at lunch."

"Okay," she murmured, her head falling back. Her body bucked against his hand.

"Good girl. You deserve a reward." Then he picked her up, pulled her legs around his waist. Carrying her into the bedroom, he tossed her on the bed and climbed on top with a predatory, wholly carnal glint in his eyes.

Who cared about a sofa? All they needed was the damn bed.

Faith pulled him down.

THE money might turn out to be an issue. If anything, Connor would have expected Faith to overspend, but the woman was reticent about every dime. As if she didn't trust him to take care of her without digging into Daddy's pockets. Or maybe she thought that without her father, he was incapable of supporting her. He'd been taking care of himself since he was eighteen.

He wouldn't let her fortune stick in his craw. It was enough that *he* knew he could take care of her adequately, even without Daddy's CEO job.

She snuggled against him, her ass cradling his cock,

her breath heating the flesh along his arm. He'd come twice and still he wanted her again. Maybe it was because he hadn't dated in the six months he'd been at Green's. He'd been building his plans, and sex had taken a back seat, nor did he want any tales to make it around the country club circuit. Instead he'd taken care of things himself. But damn, there was nothing like the real thing. Nothing like a full-bodied, glorious woman.

Marrying her wasn't about the money. It was about a legacy, what you left behind, how people remembered you.

Maybe he should have solved the problem by letting her bring the furniture from his apartment. Except that it was a bit ratty, plus he wanted to leave it in the apartment. He said he'd never lie to her, and he hadn't. She just assumed he'd let the apartment go, but it was the last thing in his life that was his. Yes, he wanted Faith and he wanted her father's legacy, but he needed one thing that was his alone. A place he could retreat to if he wanted. It was about choice. He'd probably never set foot in it, but he wanted the option to do so.

She was soft, smooth, and warm against him. He traced the curve of her breast. Her nipple peaked, and she murmured in her sleep. Faith was hot-blooded even if she was shy. He had so many things to show her, so many things to teach her.

He delved between her pussy lips. She made small mewling noises as he stroked. Lifting her leg over his, he nudged the tip of his cock inside her. Flexing his butt muscles, he rocked in and out, slowly, gently. She moaned. Soon she'd wake up.

Oh yeah, he didn't mind how much she spent, but her first purchase better damn well be that vibrator. Staking claim to her own pleasure.

It would be one of many lessons, until his pupil surpassed her teacher.

CONNOR started his campaign to lure his wife to greater heights. He called her on his cell phone as he headed out to the plant on Monday.

She laughed when he said hello. "What, are you nervous on your first day at a new job?"

Her laughter made him hard. He couldn't say why, except that if she was laughing, she wasn't being shy with him. He didn't want to do things *to* his wife. He wanted them to do things to each other. Mutual.

"Yeah, I'm nervous about facing my new boss," he teased. "Tell me what you're wearing so I can get my mind off it."

"You saw me before you left," she said. "My jean skirt and a blouse."

The midcalf skirt pulled tight across her ass and had a slit up the back to just above her knees. Yeah, perfect. "What I want to know is what you're wearing underneath."

She was silent a moment, not even a hint of her earlier smile. "Underneath?"

"Panties or no panties? Bra or no bra?"

"I've got school. Of course I have on a bra and panties."

"You can keep the bra, but ditch the panties."

She gasped. "Connor, I'm going to *school*."

"You've got parent-teacher day. No kids on campus. I want to think of you without panties while all those fathers sit on the opposite side of your desk."

"It's mostly moms."

"Faith." He waited a long moment, then added, "Take off your panties. Because that's how I want to think of you today. All day. I just might have to go into the men's room and whack off because I'll be so damn hard thinking about it."

Her sexual esteem needed building up, and telling her things like that would go a long way. Especially since it was true.

"I'm hard already." He stroked his cock through his pants a couple of times. "Really hard."

"You're insatiable," she whispered, almost in awe. "You came just before we got up this morning."

"So did you. But you're wet again."

Her silence told the story.

"Take off your panties. I'll call you later to make sure."

He disconnected, smiling. She was a hot item under all those inhibitions.

Reaching the monument sign announcing his destination, Connor pulled into Castle Heavy Mining's parking lot. The board meeting, his introduction, was at eight thirty. He smiled to himself. It *was* a bit like a kid's first day at school, and tonight, he'd rush home to his wife to tell her all about it.

Damn. He hadn't realized until this moment how sweet a feeling that would be. Coming home to Faith. He'd make sure she was so damn hot by the time he walked in the door that she'd barely be able to say hello before she had her hand on his cock.

THE manufacturing plant was one long building designed for efficient materials and process flow, and next to it sat the two-story head office. Employees came and went, the lobby a beehive of activity. He caught a few glances and assumed word was out that the new CEO started today. Everyone wondered if it was him.

For his headquarters, Jarvis Castle had spared no expense, creating a world-class lobby of glass and chrome. A long black marble countertop offered coffee, tea, water, or juice, and a mounted TV tuned in to one of the cable financial news networks.

The receptionist was male, with politeness down to an art form as he directed Connor upstairs to the boardroom where his introductory meeting as CEO would be held in— he glanced at his watch—five minutes.

The board consisted of family members with varying percentages of ownership. Jarvis Castle's cousins. They weren't a close-knit bunch, Faith had revealed, and from snippets he'd gleaned from associates at Green Industries, Connor gathered that Jarvis was a bit of a tyrant.

It was all fine for Connor. He wanted to be the glue that brought the family corporation back where it should be. Even if he didn't have the blood relation.

Connor welcomed tough situations.

It was bedlam inside the lushly appointed boardroom. As with the lobby, no expense had been spared. The table was polished mahogany, the chairs leather, and the room out-fitted with state-of-the-art video conferencing equipment. Brewing coffee emitted a rich, luxurious aroma. The board members didn't even notice him, and Connor used the time to take stock of them. Jarvis, in his old-fashioned three-piece suit, was the oldest. The three female board members were clearly outnumbered by the seven men. Though a privately held corporation and not governed by the same rules as publicly traded companies, Castle had done a bang-up job on its annual report, designed primarily for suppliers and customers, including all the requisite facts on its board. He recognized individuals from their pictures.

"You can't just drop a bomb like this on us without some discussion, Jarvis."

That would be Preston Tybrook. At 12 percent, his was the largest family holding next to Jarvis's 48 percent. Gray hair, early fifties, Preston was in gym-toned shape, but his face was far too florid at the moment for his own good. He looked like he might pop a blood vessel.

"Preston's right, Jarvis. This is unacceptable. You can't just foist the man on us like this."

That would be Tybrook's wife, Dora. Like Connor, she'd married into the company. Her hair was dyed jet-black, and she wore it long, which made her white face far too stark and showed the lines of middle age, though she probably thought it made her look younger than her true age of fifty. Upon the birth of their daughter Josie twenty-odd years ago, 3 percent of Preston's original 12 had gone to Dora and guaranteed her board seat.

Though crowded around Jarvis's end of the table, the rest of the assemblage didn't say much beyond a smattering of grumbles. There were the Plumleys, Thomas, Richard, and Alexis, siblings ranging in age from early to midfifties, 5 percent ownership each. Then the Finches, Branson, Gabriel, and Cyril, ages in the forties, 5 percent ownership. And finally, Nina Simon. She was gorgeous, Connor had to admit. Her hair caught his eye, Faith's color, reds and golds, but while Faith's was natural, Nina Simon's looked bottle-born. She stood back from the rest, arms folded beneath ample breasts, a slight curve to her ruby lips. Her short skirt showcased a decent pair of legs and around her ankles, silver bracelets with tiny bells. Close to his own age, she had the look of a man-eater about her, a seductive jut to her hips, her high-heeled shoe tapping on the plush carpet, the anklet bells tinkling. Five percent holding like all the rest, but hers had come by way of her husband's death.

Faith rounded out the ownership with her 5 percent.

"And speak of the devil, here he is."

Jarvis damn near beamed at Connor. Elbowing his way through the combatants, he held out his hand for a good shake.

Connor smiled, pumping his father-in-law's hand. The old man had set him up. He'd set the board up, too. It was obvious Jarvis had sprung the news of Faith's nuptials and Connor's employment contract just before Connor walked in the door.

The board resented him before he'd even gotten started.

Jarvis clapped him on the back with a far firmer slap than Connor would have imagined. "My son-in-law, Connor Kingston."

Preston Tybrook was the next to take his hand. "Welcome to the family." His nostrils flared and something dark swirled in his gray eyes. "My wife, Dora."

Dora shook his hand, her grip firm, actually squeezing his fingers like a man trying to show superior strength. Her blue eyes would have been prettier without the ice chips in them.

Nina Simon was a different kettle of fish. She took his hand and didn't let go. "I can't believe Faith kept *you* a secret." She gave him a sexy, half-lidded once-over.

Oh yeah, his work was cut out for him. Cousin Nina just had an atypical approach from the rest of the family. Getting this group to buy into any cost-cutting measures would be a major challenge.

Earning his 5 percent share wasn't going to be a cakewalk, Connor knew, but the old man had just issued a challenge neither of them would back down from.

"WELL, guess that means Connor is ratified as our new CEO."

"Like it wasn't a forgone conclusion, Jarvis." That grumble came from Thomas Plumley. His bald head gleamed in the overhead lighting, and he slumped slightly in his cushy leather chair.

Thomas was right. Jarvis had it in the bag. He owned 48 percent, so technically, he could be outvoted, but he also had Faith's proxies for her 5 percent. Jarvis ruled.

"Let's give Connor a round of applause." Jarvis was tickled pink with himself. Even his eyes twinkled.

The round of applause was halfhearted. Connor's five-year CEO contract had been confirmed—though it was nullified if he broke the prenup terms—and earning his percentage share of the company upon meeting his cost objectives approved.

"Fifteen-minute break, people, then we've got other business." Jarvis rose, grabbed Connor's arm, and leaned in. "Didn't say I was going to make it easy."

"I have to hand it to you. You outsmarted me."

Jarvis had outsmarted himself, too. This portion of the meeting had lasted an hour and a half, and in that short space of time, Connor witnessed firsthand how Jarvis's family felt about him. He could almost hear their thoughts. *"What's the fucking point in voting on anything?"* It was Jarvis against them. Not a single member of that board voted with Jarvis on anything, even on the authorization to repave the parking lot. Jarvis was a micromanager of the worst order, and his board—his *family*—hated him. It was a wonder they still had a functioning business.

Jarvis walked him halfway down the hallway outside the boardroom. "Didn't you say you enjoyed a challenge?"

"Yes, I did say that somewhere along the way." A bigger challenge than he'd anticipated, but he *would* win in the end.

"Good. When are you going to provide me with those cost-cutting measures?"

"One month," Connor said. He hadn't even toured the plant yet, but Jarvis was push-push-push. He wouldn't let the old man get the better of him. "Now if you'll excuse me, I need to check in with your daughter."

Jarvis rubbed his hands together. "Ooh, she's got you on a tight leash."

He didn't mind giving Jarvis that impression. "Very tight."

Outside, he made his phone call. Faith didn't answer. Probably in with a parent. He left her a brief message. "How wet are you now? I'm so hard thinking about what I'm going to do to you tonight that it's embarrassing in front of your family."

He wanted her thinking about sex, sex, sex all day long. He wanted her wild when he got home to her.

Oddly, *she* was the reward for getting through today rather than the other way round. Connor didn't pause to ponder that thought as he returned to his father-in-law and the lion's den.

SHE'D been married a little over three weeks, but Faith feared she'd spontaneously combust right there in her tiny school office with her cell phone tucked against her ear.

"Are you hot?" Connor murmured.

"Yes," she whispered, as if someone would overhear. She'd closed her office door after her last meeting. There'd been no classes today, just a series of teacher meetings to discuss everything from sixth-grade graduation to summer school to who was bringing the potato salad for the potluck on the last day of the term. All day, Connor left her messages that made her a little insane. He'd told her to go into the bathroom and touch herself. Good Lord, she'd done it, too. Thank God no one had been in the teachers' lounge at the time. Not that she'd made any noise in there, but . . . it was the thought.

And there were so many more messages.

"I want to bend you over your classroom desk, lift your skirt, and slide my cock deep inside."

"I want to slam you up against the chalkboard and do you hard and fast until you beg."

"I need your lips on my cock right this goddamn minute."

With his final message, he'd told her to call him back. Her fingers had trembled punching in his speed-dial number. He'd been number one on speed-dial for three weeks, replacing Trinity.

"Are your nipples hard?" he murmured.

So hard. All morning, all afternoon. "Yes."

"Touch them through your blouse."

"Connor." She hesitated. God, she wanted to touch herself for him, here, now. Secluded in her work office, phone sex had an added thrill over how she'd felt alone in her bed with his voice in her ear. Yet . . . this was risky. "Where are you?"

"I'm in my new office. And right now, I'd like nothing more than for you to walk in, lock the door, spread yourself out on my desk, and beg me to go down on you."

She went up in smoke.

"Pinch your nipples and imagine it's me." He gave the briefest of pauses. "Do it now, Faith."

She did, undoing one button to reach inside her blouse. A tingle streaked down to her pussy. A little moan escaped.

"That's it, baby. You're so hot you could almost come without touching yourself, couldn't you?"

He was such a seducer. She loved how he made her feel—desirable, wanted. She adored the low cadence of his voice, his slightly harsh breath, his words laced with need. She loved it when he came on the phone with her, his rough growl in her ear, the deep groan of satisfaction, and her name on his lips. She wanted him to come now, with her, for her.

She was losing her mind.

After rebuttoning her blouse, she transferred the phone to her other ear. "Connor, we can't do this now."

Yet, he made her want to so badly. Common sense flew out the proverbial window when he talked to her like this.

"Baby." He purred the endearment. "You need to learn that a little risk adds a lot of spice. And really, with the door locked, how big is the risk?"

"It's just that we're both at work."

"That's why it's hot."

"Connor." Someone had to act like the responsible adult.

"You win. But you have to give me something else instead."

Sensation trickled down her spine. "What?"

"Buy the vibrator. Bring it home. You've been stalling me for three weeks. That's long enough."

His request made her feel as she had in front of the hotel room mirror on their brief honeymoon, exposed, vulnerable. Connor just didn't get that buying a vibrator was akin to laying out her sex life for a total stranger. Not to mention what *Connor* would make her do with it.

"What makes you think I didn't buy it at lunch like you told me to?" As he'd told her every day for the past three weeks. And every day, she had another excuse why she hadn't had time.

"Oh, Faith, baby, I know when you're lying. You can't hide anything from me."

It was scary. He was right. Her every emotion was written on her face or in her gaze. All Connor had to do was look, and he knew what she was thinking. Correct that, he didn't have to see. He knew it over the phone. Even her voice was transparent.

"You're a hot-blooded woman, Faith. Act like it." He lowered his voice. "Own it."

She bit her lip, then pursed them together. "Why is it so important to you?"

"Sex is important to me. I want it to be equally important to you. I want an active participant who fearlessly takes what she wants. Because I'm going to take what I want."

"Is this bondage?" Or was he telling her he'd find sex elsewhere if she didn't live up to her end of the bargain? Her sexual desire was rapidly circling the drain.

"No. It's being equals. It's pushing each other farther

than we've ever been. That's what makes sex so fucking good."

He scared her. Not in a physical, life-threatening way. But where she preferred doing it in the dark under the covers, he would force her to do it in front of the mirror, though *force* wasn't the right word. He'd turn her inside out until she was begging to do whatever he wanted.

She was afraid she'd come to crave what he gave her, to the point where she couldn't live without it. That would give him all the power in the world.

10

CRAVING the delicious sexual things he did to her only gave him the power if she allowed him to have it. That fact, which should have been a no-brainer, took Faith an hour to figure out after pressing the end button on her cell phone. When it came to men and sex games, she was a slow learner.

Right now, Connor was in charge, telling her what to do, how to take care of her own needs, yadda yadda. Once *she* took charge, he wouldn't have any power at all.

She parked her car in a lot on the back side of Main Street and sat for a moment in the late afternoon sun. A young mother unloaded her baby from the car seat of her SUV, put the child in a stroller, and hooked a diaper bag over the handles.

Faith wanted a baby, and she didn't want Connor to cheat. She'd made an agreement with him, basically giving him sexual carte blanche. He didn't put the emotion into that, *she* did.

Maybe promising to buy the vibrator, then not doing so was a passive-aggressive attempt at gaining control. She didn't want to be under his thumb, needing him so badly she'd turn a blind eye to whatever he did.

To buy or not to buy, that was the question. Was it giving in to Connor or taking ownership of her sexuality? Come to think of it, was *not* buying the damn toy simply giving in to cowardice? Ooh, she hated all this overanalyzing.

Faith yanked the car door open and marched to Main Street as if she were on a mission. She knew the shop. At Halloween they'd displayed a gorgeous array of feather masks.

Inside, leather, vinyl, and lace abounded, hanging from the walls and racks set about the shop. An assortment of bronze, silver, gold, and black sparkly eye shadows and lip glosses glittered beneath the glass counter. Tittering in the corner, a group of teenage girls fingered through a rack of kilts.

The glimmer of gold caught Faith's eyes. A halter top fashioned of gleaming gold-colored coins dangled from a bust-shaped hanger. Faith ran her palm along the bottom, then gathered the coins in her hand. Heavy and cool to the touch, she imagined how it would feel against her breasts, the metal heating with skin contact. She wanted it, but . . . well . . .

There'd be way too much bare flesh showing below the halter. The thought of trying it on for Connor, then having him say it didn't suit her was demoralizing.

Besides, she was here for a toy, and that room was somewhere in the back. She waded through the rows of skimpy lace teddies, past the crotchless panty rack, and entered a narrow corridor lined along one wall with feather boas of every color imaginable. On the other wall, umm, penises. Gag penises. That didn't sound good, either. They were penis-shaped gag gifts. Penis suckers, penis lipsticks, pencil erasers, swizzle sticks, and highlighters. Next to that were the boobs. Beer mugs with boob handles. Straws with a boob on the top. There was even a child's sippy cup. Now that was in bad taste, no pun intended.

She slipped through the bead curtain at the end of the hall, a million tiny beads clattering to announce her arrival.

"Hi, sweetcheeks, what can we do you for?"

Who was the *we*? The back room was thankfully devoid of customers. Just one giant-sized sales clerk. Of the male variety. With short, spiked pink hair, eyeliner, mascara, and a pair of jeans that hugged his . . . package.

Oh gawd. A man was beyond the pale. Yet she smiled as sweetly as her cheeks would allow. "I'm just looking, thank you." *Please don't follow me. Please don't keep talking to me.*

He merely smiled. "Shout if you have a question."

Faith almost sagged with relief when he squeezed behind the counter and began leafing through . . . yes, it looked like a calculus textbook.

The room was as comparatively pint-sized as the man was giant-sized, but it was jam-packed with sexual accoutrements. Handcuffs, blindfolds, and chains draped one wall. Erotic videos and books filled glass shelves, the covers suggesting something more tasteful than a male porn movie. Stands of varying sizes took up the center floor, individual compartments overflowing with neon condoms, sexual gels, enhancers (for what, she wasn't quite sure), what looked like little plugs (no, she wasn't going to ask). So much . . . stuff. Something for every fetish.

And an entire wall filled with vibrators.

It was an amazing assortment. The John Holmes model was designed for a horse, not a woman. No, the legendary porn star couldn't have been *that* big. Next to "John" was "wet-n-wild," which was plain but more her size. The "pleasure wand," the "swan," the "woman eater." Who came up with these names?

"First time?"

She practically jumped out of her skin. Though, by his liberally applied cologne, she should have known Spike was in the near vicinity. It wasn't a bad smell, something expensive from the men's counter that reminded her of an ocean sail on a hot summer day, nor did it sting her eyes. It was just too *there*.

She knew what he was thinking. He had a pathetic, lonely female on his hands who'd succumbed to the desperate call of the vibrator. All right, that was the third reason she hadn't wanted to come here. Maybe the most important reason.

"Are you looking for hi-tech or low-tech?" he asked when she obviously didn't have a voice to answer with.

Faith shrugged, her mortification growing exponentially. Was it better to stay rooted to the spot or scoot like a mouse?

Pulling a model from the wall, he turned it over to read the back packaging. "This one's programmable." Glancing down at Faith, his blue eyes sparkled. "You can set the speed, the angle of rotation, the level of vibration, changing it all at intervals of thirty seconds. All you have to do is strap it on, then lay back and let it do everything for you."

She couldn't help herself; Faith laughed. "It sounds like one of those treadmills at the health club where you program in the hills and the speed changes."

He slipped it back on the hook. "You're right. Too much like a workout. Now here's a dandy model."

Pink, penis-shaped—obviously—with even a crown and an odd protuberance halfway down the shaft almost near the base.

"This," he said, holding it out for her inspection, "has a clitoral stimulator. And this"—he pointed to the protuberance, a bit like the stalk on a cactus—"works the outside."

Faith's cheeks flamed at the implications. She was talking to a . . . man about . . . vibrators and clitoral stimulators.

Yet he had such a sweet smile and a kind of little boy excitement that was almost infectious. What the heck, she was here, why not have a little fun, too?

She wrinkled her nose. "It's too big."

"Honey, nothing's too big when you're in the right mood, not even John over there." He flapped a dismissive hand at the monster vibrator. "But here's a little secret I tell all the girls," he went on, grabbing a simple "pleasure wand" in zebra stripes. "Nothing fancy, no frills, it just vibrates like the dickens. And the nice thing about it is your man can be doing manual or oral while he's got it inside you or he can be inside and use it for clitoral stimulation."

She should have been a puddle of mortified embarrassment at his feet, yet he'd naturally assumed she had a partner. A man. She wasn't just a pathetic loner.

He rolled his eyes. "With this other stuff, *things* get in the way, if you catch my drift."

It was the right size, simple, no gadgetry, and the zebra stripes would make Connor laugh. She hoped.

"I'll take that one."

"The right choice, sweetie." He tossed it in the air and caught it. "You want to try it out first?"

She felt as if her eyebrows topped out in her hairline. "Try it out?"

"Yeah. It's important to like the feel of it," he said over his shoulder as he headed to the sales counter. "Batteries not included, but I've got some back here."

She watched, terrified, as he popped the plastic packaging. Try it out? They had another back room where she could . . .

"Here we go." He strolled back, grabbed her hand, and plopped the vibrating zebra stripes in her palm. "Nice?" He gazed at her expectantly.

The thing sent vibrations all the way up her arm until she thought her teeth were chattering. Then she started to laugh, biting her lip to keep it in until she could find her voice. "Yes. It's nice."

He sighed belly deep with satisfaction. "You don't have to buy the most expensive to get the best. My S-O *adores* this one."

She had to think. S-O. Oh yeah, duh. Significant Other.

He shook it at her. "So if you and your man don't like it, you bring it back, okay?"

Again, her eyebrows shot to her hair. "If I've *used* it?"

"I can't take it back, but since you bought it on my recommendation, I'll exchange it and toss it." He beamed. "Happy customers are what we're all about." He nipped behind the counter and kachinged on his register. "Oh, and we've got a sale next week on handcuffs. Your man like to restrain you a bit?"

"I don't know. I'll have to ask him."

Connor would die when she told him about this.

It struck her this was the first time she'd thought of running home to tell Connor something, anything. As if he were her man, not just the man she'd married to get a child.

"WHAT the hell is that?" Jarvis stood stock still in the middle of the QC lab, pointing like the grim reaper.

Larry almost tripped over himself, as well he should. Another cousin. They proliferated the work site. This one belonged to Richard, or was it Alexis? One could never tell.

Larry merely stared goggle-eyed at the piece of test equipment sitting in the middle of the linoleum tiles. It was so new it lacked its asset tag and still wore its manufacturer's stickers. The little Asian girl bent over her station, her long, dark hair obscuring her face. Jarvis always forgot her name because she was so silent whenever he entered the lab that he almost forgot she was there. A male QC tech—all Jarvis could see was his white-coated back—rolled a computer cart to the far end of the lab, presumably out of shouting range.

"I didn't authorize this," Jarvis boomed. It was good to use a loud voice to let subordinates know you meant business.

"N-n-no, s-s-sir," Larry stammered. He'd never make it far in this world with that stammer. Hence his being QC supervisor at Castle. Castle was a refuge for family cast-offs.

"Then what the hell is it doing in this lab?"

"I authorized it," Kingston's voice carried into the lab.

"You don't have that much authority for signing CEAs," Jarvis snapped.

Capital expenditure authorizations were the way Jarvis controlled spending, with board approval over ten thousand dollars. And that damn tensile tester was over the mark.

Damn wastrel. Kingston overstepped his bounds left and right. He'd also impugned Jarvis's management skills. He'd actually suggested Jarvis shouldn't yell at his employees. Jarvis never yelled; he simply made his position known in no uncertain terms. In the three weeks since Kingston arrived at Castle, he'd thrown everything into turmoil.

"CEA signing authority for the CEO *is* ten thousand, Jarvis."

Jarvis wanted to snarl. Kingston was all cool, unruffled feathers. The man had no emotion. How could that be good for Faith? And dammit, he was right, too. The signing authority was set when Jarvis was CEO, and he'd forgotten to change the company procedure. Jarvis didn't want to admit he'd forgotten anything.

Connor went on in that calm voice. "We've been spending fifteen thousand a month on outsourcing the analysis." He leaned into Jarvis. "Cost savings, five K per month. That's half a percent toward my first goal."

Bastard. "Once we figure out the problem with the teeth, we won't need it." Recently, the teeth were busting off the shovel buckets when under high stress levels.

"Correction. We've learned it's a test we need to perform on the teeth all the time."

For a moment, Jarvis felt like an idiot. He had a stack of CEAs on his desk, but so much had been happening, he'd pushed that duty to the wayside. It wasn't like him. He almost hated Kingston for making him doubt himself.

"Fine. I approve the purchase. But I want the procedure on my desk to make the necessary change to the signing authorities."

"I'm already working on the procedure," Connor said. He was a smooth one, with that slick smile. "In my opinion, the levels are too low. VPs should have at least twenty-five K."

"They'll bankrupt us!"

Connor didn't say anything, and Jarvis was suddenly aware of the audience. The two QC techs, a receiving boy who'd just entered, and Larry. There was a whole lot of silence going on in that lab, and Jarvis didn't like it. "Don't your people have some testing to do, Larry?"

"Yes, sir." He waved his hand, and everyone pretended they were hard at work.

Jarvis was outmanned and outgunned. For the moment. "You need to check with me on any changes you want to institute."

Connor looked up, gauged the distance between themselves and the lab's occupants, and lowered his voice. "In our agreement, you gave me authority to institute changes and cost reductions."

"With approval." Jarvis felt himself fairly vibrating with

tension. "It's my company, and I'm still chairman of the board."

He thought he saw Kingston's jaw flex. Good. The man needed to learn who was boss. Just because he'd married the chairman's daughter didn't mean he'd become king of *this* Castle.

CONNOR cracked his knuckles, poured a finger of scotch into a glass, and relaxed into the couch. Another long day. After three weeks, he was still getting to know the inner workings of Castle Mining. He'd run late tonight for a meeting with Masters, the head of program management. Instead of dashing home to Faith, he'd stopped by his apartment to unwind. And to think. He didn't think well around Faith. He simply wanted to jump her. He processed the day's events only after she was asleep. This evening, he needed to consider what to do about her father.

Jarvis had humiliated Larry Plumley in front of his work crew. It was an unforgivable thing to do to any subordinate. If you needed to ream them a new asshole, you did it in the privacy of your office, not in full earshot of their workers.

Jarvis Castle was a micromanaging control freak. If he wasn't careful, he'd lose his engineering VP, Don Biddle. And Biddle was too good an asset to lose. Dammit. Connor knew he'd have a fight on his hands, but this wasn't what he'd planned.

The worst was that Jarvis refused to deal with the quality on his purchased parts. Specifically, those from Green Industries. The scope of it had hit Connor the first week at Castle, yet it was still unclear whether the problem originated with Green or if it was something Castle was causing.

His cell rang. Faith. He'd given her a special ring tone.

"I'll be home soon," he said before she even spoke.

"Okay."

That was one of the things he liked about her. She wasn't a nagging wife. "Things ran late here," he explained. He wasn't a loner, but he was better at recharging his batteries alone. Faith, however, was better off with the inference that he was still at the office. "I'll head out in about ten minutes."

"I'll order Chinese. Should be here when you get here."

"Thanks, baby."

Married life was great. Now if only he could fix Castle. It was a challenge. But he thrived on challenge. He'd eventually get Jarvis to see the error in his management style.

Instead of ruminating on his Jarvis problems, though, his mind drifted to Faith. Sipping the last of his scotch, he contemplated all the ways he was going to make her come tonight.

FAITH surveyed the Chinese food bags on the counter. Maybe she should learn how to cook. Sure, she could heat spaghetti; she wasn't useless. But she'd never thought about the domestic thing when she'd agreed to marry Connor. She assumed they'd be living in her suite and eating in Daddy's dining room. Actually, she hadn't thought about it at all until Connor flatly refused to live in her father's house. Just as she hadn't thought about the lack of privacy, though she was starting to get used to it.

And what about the laundry? Or changing the sheets and cleaning the bathroom? To date, she'd borrowed Estelle six times, but she couldn't keep taking her father's household staff.

She hadn't realized she was such a priss. Or so pampered.

"Did you buy it?"

She almost jumped out of her shoes, then her heart stopped beating when she turned.

He was so magnificent. Connor stood in the kitchen doorway, arms akimbo, hands on his hips pushing his suit jacket open, white shirt, striped tie, all that long, lean male body, and a devilish smile on his handsome face.

He stole her breath. He made her legs weak. He heated the blood in her veins. He muddled her brain, and she forgot all about the funny story she'd wanted to tell him. Her marriage was starting to get frightening; or rather her emotions about her husband were getting dangerous.

She knew he wasn't talking about the Chinese food. "I bought it." She tipped her head and tried for saucy to hide the effect he had on her.

He jutted his head forward. "Where is it?"

"Up in my nightstand drawer where it belongs." She turned slightly and flourished her hand. "I've got din—oof—"

Connor had crossed the kitchen without her even seeing, doubled over, and put his shoulder to her stomach for the fireman's carry, his arm across her bottom holding her in place.

Faith squealed. "What are you doing?" She bobbed against his back as he climbed the stairs.

"Dinner can wait. My cock's so hard I could poke a goddamn fire with it. I want you naked now."

He wasn't roses and candlelight and soft music. He wasn't sweet nothings and poetry. But God, he made her insides liquefy.

Setting her on her feet in the bedroom, he took possession of her face with both hands and devoured her lips in a hard, bone-melting kiss. His tongue invaded and owned.

She was halfway to orgasm by the time he stopped. "You taste like . . ." Tipping her head, she considered. "Scotch?"

He grinned. "After five, business meetings go over better with a little alcohol to free the thinking." Stepping back, he tugged off his jacket, tossed it, then yanked his tie. "Take off your clothes," he ordered, a fire in his dark eyes.

Would he be disappointed with the vibrator? It was slim, no bells and whistles. But he could put it in her and use his fingers or his tongue. Or he could climb inside her himself and use the tip of the vibrator on her clitoris.

That's what Spike had recommended. Satisfaction guaranteed or she could bring it back.

"You're lollygagging, Faith."

She started with her shoes, then unbuttoned her blouse. Nervous butterflies fluttered in her stomach. She *still* didn't like undressing in front of him. He was gorgeous; she was . . . not. Naked from the waist up, his body had her salivating.

He tipped her chin with his finger. "You've got the most perfect breasts I've seen in my whole fucking life."

Oh God. He disarmed her with a statement straight from his gut. He didn't say she had the perfect body or that she was beautiful. He chose the one thing she was actually proud of about herself. Or two, as the case may be.

Connor fingered a nipple, his gaze focused, a flush on his cheeks. "Not yet," he whispered as if he were speaking to himself. "Later. I'll take these later."

Then he stepped back once more and unbuckled his belt. She couldn't take her eyes off the hard ridge of his penis bursting from his boxers. The tip glistened.

"It was embarrassing," he said. "I had to keep my suit jacket buttoned so no one saw the come stains. You made me wet all freaking day long."

God, he just *said* things. She'd never known anyone like him. "You were the one who kept calling me."

"You made me call you after you forced me to have sex a million times this weekend."

She laughed. That was another thing Connor did for her—he made sex fun. Someday there would be one too many things Connor did for her, and she'd be lost in needing him.

"Now get the rest of those clothes off and lay on the bed." He pointed as he rounded the end and opened her bedside drawer. Closing her eyes, Faith dropped the blouse, popped the snaps on her skirt, and let it fall to the floor.

He was so comfortable in his nakedness, because he was so beautiful in his skin. She'd never feel that at ease.

"Faith, my darling, I know you can take something much larger than this."

She turned to find him shaking the vibrator at her. He'd

ride right over her if she let him. He might not mean to, but they'd both lose sight of what he wanted versus what she wanted if she didn't draw the line, as hard as that was for her to do.

She shook her finger at him in imitation. "It's *my* vibrator, not yours. So I got what *I* wanted."

He kissed the tip of *her* instrument. "Ooh, baby, that makes me hot. I love it when you take charge."

He would, but only to a point, she feared. Then he'd slam her down. Except that he hadn't gotten annoyed with all her excuses for not buying the darn thing until today. He simply asked her the next day. She'd never actually seen Connor angry.

Faith climbed on the bed and flopped onto her back, trying to appear totally at ease. She fluffed a pillow beneath her head. "Now, surprise me."

"Baby," he whispered from afar, "you're the one who's going to surprise *me*."

Oh Lord. That sounded ominous.

The bed dipped beside her, the vibrator buzzed as he turned it on, and Faith rolled her head on the pillow in time to see him suck the tip. Then he touched it to her nipple. An electric charge shot to her clitoris.

"Do you like that?"

Nodding, she punctuated with a murmured "Mm, yes."

He switched it off and laid the toy between her breasts. "Good, show me everything you like."

She widened her eyes, the momentary lassitude shooting out of her. "Aren't you going to do it for me?"

"No." He wiggled his eyebrows wickedly as he backed off the mattress to grab a chair and pull it to the foot of the bed. "I had it in mind that you'd perform for me."

She'd masturbated with him, but that was on the phone. He couldn't actually *see* her. He'd taken her in front of the mirror, but she'd never turned around and watched. "Why do I always have to be on display?"

She regretted the question the moment it was out of her mouth. She was supposed to test her limits, but letting him know when she'd reached a limit gave him the control.

He crawled up the bed and leaned over her. "Spread your legs and fuck the hell out of yourself with that vibrator." He ran his nose up the side of her cheek and put his lips to her ear. "Because I want to watch you." He licked around the shell. "Because I've been so fucking hard all day imagining it."

But, oh, he knew the right words to make her flush the idea of control down the drain. He took her to 90 percent humidity in less than a second.

"Do it, Faith." It wasn't a demand. It wasn't a plea. It was permission to let herself go; it was his desire to watch.

When she opened her eyes again, he was sitting in the chair, his legs negligently propped on the bed.

"Start with your nipples." He lightly stroked his full, hard cock.

She turned the base, giving it half speed, then rubbed it around her still glistening nipple. "It's not the same as when you do it." There wasn't a jolt, not even a spark.

"Then spread your legs and caress your pussy lips with it. But don't touch your clit yet. And Faith?" He paused until she glanced up. "Look at me while you're doing it."

It was his eyes on her. It was his hand on his cock, slowly pumping. It was his whisper. *Fuck the hell out of yourself with that vibrator because I want to watch you.* Faith couldn't resist him. She couldn't resist the lure of how he made her feel. Wet. Hot. Desired. As if he truly wanted her. *Her.* It was the most powerful aphrodisiac of all.

She turned the vibrator on high, spread her legs, and eased the tip down over her lips. She didn't touch it to her clitoris, yet the sensations hummed through all the nearby erogenous zones. She moaned, because it felt so good and because Connor watched with that intoxicating, hungry light in his eyes. Palming his crown, he smoothed droplets of come over himself.

Faith licked her lips and gave in to him completely.

"Does it feel good, baby?"

"Yes. So good." Her body jerked as she accidentally slid right over her clitoris. Oh, oh, more, but she kept the steady rhythm all around.

"You're so damn wet, I can hear it and it makes me wild." He pumped himself faster. "Touch your clit."

A jolt of lightening streaked through her and she cried out. The vibrations were incredible, setting off mini-explosions, not quite an orgasm, but a sweet prelude. She started to pant.

"That's it, baby. Love yourself with it. Make all the noise you want."

She moaned for him, long, low, then thrashed her head on the pillow. Her body shuddered with need, her breath came in gasps, but drinking in the sight of his hand fisted around his cock, she held off. She wasn't ready to let it end. Sounds rose up from her throat, and she squeezed her eyes shut for a moment, savoring the sensations and the beat of his hand against his own flesh.

"Now dip it inside."

Oh God, yes. With slow, delicious penetration, Faith did what he told her to. The sensations almost too much, she pushed her head back into the pillow as her pussy clenched around the vibrator.

"Fuck yourself with it, baby. Fast."

With his voice urging her on, she pumped in and out, the buzz streaking out to her extremities, along every nerve ending of her skin, and deep, deep inside. She couldn't keep her eyes open. She could only let the scent of sex, the sound of harsh male breath, and the slap of flesh seduce her, drive her higher.

"Pull it out slow this time, baby. And angle it high to hit your G-spot."

She could barely understand, but her body seemed to know. Arching, she dragged the humming toy over a spot that forced a wail from her lips.

Oh, oh, God, so good. So good.

"That's it, baby. You found it." Between her legs, the bed dipped, and he was there, big, hard cock in his hand, hot, avid eyes taking in the sight of her gripping that vibrator.

"Don't stop, baby. We're almost there."

She panted, then Connor set his knee to the end of the

vibrator, holding it deep inside her as he pumped himself fiercely in his hand. A groan rose from his belly, then he hit her clitoris hard with his orgasm, hot come pulsing against her.

And Faith screamed in endless ecstasy.

HOLY Hell. He cradled her damp body in his arms. Tears had leaked from her eyes at the end. She'd screamed his name, and she'd come so hard, he was sure she'd passed out for a moment. Her hair was a tangled mess. He kissed her forehead, then pushed the strands away from her eyes.

"That was beautiful, baby," he whispered in the moist locks.

She muttered, wriggled, then settled once more in his arms.

She had so much passion locked away inside her, it was an honor to help her set it free.

FAITH heard Connor muffling around in the kitchen as she padded downstairs in her robe.

"Hungry?" he said, holding out a fork as she leaned against the doorjamb to watch him.

He was too gorgeous for words, especially since her brain hadn't fully recovered from that orgasm. One unbelievable, stupendous orgasm the like of which she'd never experienced. Yet he hadn't even given it to her. She'd done it herself. Admittedly, it was his gaze on her that made her blow sky-high.

God. She was a closet exhibitionist.

"I'm starving," she said, which she supposed was appropriate after great sex.

Handing her the fork, he unloaded Chinese food containers from the bag. "Your father and I are going to South America next Monday."

It felt like he'd sunk a punch right in her midsection. She couldn't breathe for a moment.

"We'll be gone about two weeks."

Two whole *weeks*? "Why didn't you tell me before?"

He raised a brow. "This is the first chance we've had to talk."

"You could have told me when you walked in the door."

He cocked his head, like a dog that couldn't figure out where the strange noise was coming from. "I didn't feel like telling you then."

"So we had sex beforehand to mollify me." Oh my God, she sounded like . . . a wife.

He opened a container, eased back against the counter, and grabbed a fork. "We had sex before I told you because I've been so fucking hot for you all day, I couldn't wait."

Why did he have to say things like that and totally throw off her equilibrium? She grabbed her own fork and a container, this one full of lukewarm broccoli beef.

He finished his bite of lemon chicken. "It was a given I'd have to go down there sooner or later."

Of course. Her father went down quarterly. But lately, the trips had been wearing on him. He needed a younger man to take over. Why was she being such a bitch? Why did it . . . hurt?

Because, dammit, it felt like Connor was tired of her already, that he didn't even care if he was leaving her for two weeks. And she *hated* the whiny, naggy feeling eating her up inside. She hated sounding like a wife.

Faith squashed her rising emotions. "We shouldn't have wasted the sperm if you're going to be gone that long."

Setting his Chinese box on the counter, he grabbed her chin, held her, forced her to look at him. "It wasn't a waste. It was so goddamn hot, I almost passed out."

She was the one who'd almost passed out. But it was sweet of him to say. He didn't owe her any explanations about the South American trip. Of course he'd be going sometime. She needed to get hold of herself. This—what was it?—this *emotionalism* just wouldn't do. It wasn't part of their bargain.

"Well, you've got almost a week to impregnate me before you go," she quipped, ignoring the hollow feeling in her stomach.

He kissed the tip of her nose. "I'll make it my priority to fuck the hell out of you at least two times per day. And no more coming outside, only deep in your hot, sweet pussy."

God. Things like that just slid so easily off his tongue. And made her so incredibly hot. "Only two times?"

"Twice on weekdays, but weekends, it's four times a day."

Could people actually have *too* much sex?

He considered the horrified expression on her face, then spoke with the most serious of tones. "This baby-making thing is a lot of work, honey. You've got to be totally committed to it."

He was joking; she knew he was. Yet, his words speared straight up inside her. She was committed. She'd traded her father's company for him. She'd given her body over to him.

He was her husband. He was to be the father of her child.

She was suddenly so terrified, she could have thrown up on the floor right there in front of him.

Instead, she gathered plates from the cupboard. "You know, this would be a lot better if we heated it up."

He grabbed her once more, took her mouth, all sweet and zesty. "It would be a lot better," he murmured against her lips, "if we ate off each other's bodies upstairs in bed. I feel my little sperm working up a head of steam again."

Her heart turned over, yet she laughed. "You're voracious."

"There're so many things we haven't done yet."

"Well, we can't do them all tonight." She sounded horribly prim as she dished out the mu shu, rice, beef, and chicken.

"Will you use your vibrator while I'm gone?" He snatched a bit of chicken off the plate before she put it in the microwave.

She shrugged. "Maybe."

"Promise you will."

She shrugged the other shoulder. "How will you know?"

"I'll know. Now promise me."

"I'll think about it and give you my answer before you leave." Okay, that was good. Feisty and sassy.

He crowded her up against the counter and leaned down to whisper in her ear. "You're a hard woman, baby, but I'm a hard man." He punctuated with a roll of his hips. "So do it."

She pushed back. "You know, there's the possibility that I might start liking the vibrator better than you."

"Tease."

She tipped her head back, smiling at him. "That gives me an idea. We can save up your sperm and while you're gone, I'll use a turkey baster to impregnate myself." She let her mouth drop open and gave him an oh-so-innocent gaze. "In fact, with my vibrator and a turkey baster, I might not need you at all."

He pushed aside the boxes, turned her, grabbed her butt, and hoisted her onto the counter. Shoving his hard body between her legs, he growled low and swiped his tongue across her neck. "You need me, baby. Plastic will only go so far. Then you'll be begging me to ram my cock straight up inside you."

"You'll beg first." She shoved him back and put her nose to his. "Because you adore my hot, sweet pussy." She smiled, saucy, a woman totally in control of the banter, and raised one eyebrow. "Isn't that what you said? *Baby?*"

Before she had a chance to move, or even think, he tugged aside her robe and his, and took her sweet, hot pussy high and hard with his cock.

"Yeah, baby, something very close to that."

He rotated his hips. She almost came. Clutching his biceps, she spread her legs to take all of him.

"You've got the sweetest"—he breathed the words against her ear—"hottest"—he slipped a finger between their almost vacuum-packed bodies to caress her clitoris—"most delicious pussy"—then slid inside for dual finger-cock penetration—"and it's all fucking mine." He hammered home one last glorious time.

Faith screamed his name and came apart from the inside out.

Oh God. Her body *was* his.

If she wasn't careful, her heart would be, too.

11

A week later, on a different continent with a long plane ride and a four-hour time change between them, Connor was still amused by her turkey baster comment. Faith had fire. Trinity had portrayed her as sweet but a bit milquetoast, which had been fine with Connor.

Faith was so much more. And no way in hell was she getting herself pregnant off a goddamn turkey baster. Not that he believed she actually could. That was just a myth.

They would make fine children together. She needed him for that at least. Needed him badly.

Didn't she?

He felt the smallest edge of . . . something. He didn't want Faith to *need* him, and he didn't *need* her. The word *need* connoted emotion. This wasn't about emotion; it was about . . . obligation, tit for tat. He got saddled with Jarvis, and she got a baby.

Christ. He had to laugh. In this bargain, she was making out a lot better than he was. The old man was a pain in the ass.

"This damn meeting is a travesty and you're smiling?" Jarvis lowered his voice to a gravel pitch, as if he feared the CEO of Venezuela International Mining had a stoolie standing outside the conference door to eavesdrop on their conversation.

Connor filled a glass with spring water from the carafe and handed it to Jarvis. The meeting in VIM's boardroom at its Caracas headquarters had dispersed for a brief bio break. The room was excellently appointed with comfortable cloth chairs and lateral blinds to shut out the sun as it streamed across the solid wood table. Upon arriving, the

Castle delegation had been plied with coffee, tea, bottled water, and light sandwiches.

VIM's accommodations weren't the problem. Jarvis was.

"Our group is handling the presentation well," Connor said.

"Handling it? What the hell does Biddle think he's doing?" Jarvis was close to sputtering, but though they were alone in the room for the moment, he kept his voice low for propriety's sake.

Connor wouldn't be surprised if Biddle was out looking for a new job the minute he got back to the States. Jarvis had a way of making an extremely capable vice president look like an ass.

They'd arrived in Caracas, Venezuela, late Monday night. In addition to Preston Tybrook, the entourage included Dressert from Sales, Biddle from Engineering, Lukbar from Quality, and Preston's daughter, Josie. She was a pretty little thing but a bit on the butch side. Or maybe her manly attire, consisting of a tailored suit complete with dress shirt and tie, cropped dark hair, and no makeup, was her way of holding her own in a man's world. Josie Tybrook was program manager on several of their South American projects, including two ongoing with Venezuelan International Mining.

The full travel group was rounded out by Dora Tybrook and Nina Simon. Unlike Josie, those two ladies had declined attendance at today's meeting in favor of shopping.

"Jarvis, what the hell are you doing?" Preston, upon re-entering the room, headed for the water bar. He'd removed his jacket in deference to the humidity. His shirt sported underarm rings, and his face was too florid for good health.

Jarvis jutted his chin. "Stepping in where your boy can't get his finger out of his butt."

"*My* boy? I might have brought Biddle in for the first interview but you approved his contract as Engineering VP."

"Only because he falsified his history and said he was a graduate of Cal Tech when obviously he got his degree off the Internet in two weeks."

They were like squirrels chasing each other. They darted this way, then the chasee turned on a dime and became the chaser. Back and forth, an irritated high-pitched natter, like squirrels outside the window at five in the morning.

Connor stepped into the fray. "Excuse me, gentlemen, but the point you're both missing is that Biddle is covering our collective asses by not admitting to our customer that we don't have a clue as to why the shovel teeth keep snapping."

Biddle had actually executed quite good foot play. It would have gone off a lot better if Jarvis hadn't interrupted the man's presentation, breaking the cardinal rule: Don't ream your own player a new asshole in front of the other team; wait till later.

VIM's delegation began to return in dribs and drabs. They'd dressed for the humidity in light cotton. Preston still steamed under his shirt; Jarvis muttered and narrowed his eyes.

Connor took clear stock of the fact that Jarvis Castle needed to step out of his own way.

IT had been an excruciating day. Jarvis had undercut his team no less than four times that Connor observed. It wasn't just his board that Jarvis dictated to; he was in serious danger of alienating his entire management team.

"You meeting us for dinner, Connor?"

Josie smiled at him. She had an eager smile of youthful enthusiasm. A good project manager, she'd be a true asset to the company when she fully matured. He got the impression she and Faith didn't know each other well despite being cousins. The family animosity between Jarvis and his board had affected Faith's relationships, too. That was something he could help with. Faith needed her family. They'd be the most important thing in the world when she got pregnant.

The members of their party had piled into two cabs back to the hotel. Having gotten the riskier cab driver, Jarvis and Preston were already going at it in the bar, and in two hours, VIM's executive group had set up a dinner at a restaurant just down the street. Authentic Venezuelan food.

"Wouldn't miss it." He returned Josie's smile. "I just want to check in with my wife first."

Shit. What was up with that? It made him ridiculously giddy to say it. Maybe it was the word *my*. Connor hadn't been able to say *my* father, mother, brother, sister, family, or whatever since he was nine. He liked the proprietary feeling it gave him. And the sense of belonging.

He punched the elevator button. The hotel was a behemoth. Watching the movies, one got the impression that South America was quaint adobe settings with courtyards, trees, and curlicue railings. The Empress was a modern high-rise with valet parking, luxurious rooms, and secure interior corridors. His suite—with living room, balcony overlooking the Caracas skyline, minibar, and a Jacuzzi tub in the bathroom—was on the eighteenth floor.

Travel would undoubtedly be his next cost-cutting measure. They'd flown first class when business class was adequate, and a room rather than a suite was all one person needed if they weren't entertaining. Which, on this trip, he wasn't.

His door wasn't latched.

There was a trace of perfume, one he recognized, having sat next to it during yesterday's air excursion.

The balcony door was open, and a gentle breeze billowed the see-through drapes. He hadn't ordered it, and it wasn't there this morning when he left, but now a cloth-draped trolley sat in his living room topped with a bottle of Veuve Clicquot in an ice bucket, two brimming glasses, and a tray of chocolate-covered strawberries.

Stepping through the fluttering balcony curtains, Nina Simon snagged a glass and held it out to him, a feline smile on her ruby lips. The shade matched her nail polish.

Connor took the champagne. Hell, he figured it was charged to his room bill, so he might as well indulge.

Yeah, he'd really have to take expense reports in hand, starting with the board of directors.

She tapped her glass to his, then sipped, keeping her eyes on his, lids lowered seductively. Her anklet bells jingled lightly. A droplet of condensation fell from the stem, landing square in her cleavage and sliding down, down, down to disappear between her breasts.

It was too damn perfect to be unplanned.

She had voluptuous breasts on par with Faith's, but less hip. Though her hair was red gold, it lacked the glorious, natural sheen of Faith's.

"I hope the bribe you paid someone to let you into my room doesn't appear on your expense report when we get back."

She smiled. "Would I try to screw the company like that?"

The answer was yes. She'd also try to screw *him*. One way or another. That had been clear the moment she took the first-class seat beside him. She was an expert conversationalist, leaving most men wondering if she'd just made a sexual innuendo, or questioning if he had a dirty mind.

Connor knew he had a genuinely dirty mind. He also knew she was making innuendos.

"To what do I owe the pleasure?" He smiled, sipping. Two could play her game. Maybe it would have been smarter to kick her out on her ass, but he wanted to know if this was a board-ratified setup or if she'd planned it on her own. It was also possible that Jarvis himself had put her up to it.

"I know how those all-day meetings can be. I thought a toast to surviving your first was in order." She'd moved infinitesimally closer, stretching one high-heel–clad foot out so that her toe touched his. She now appeared a tad shorter, her cleavage a tad deeper. Her bells tinkled. She rolled the stem of her glass between her breasts absently, though he was sure Nina never did anything absently. There was always intention.

It was no wonder Faith never wanted a thing to do with the company. She'd have been the baby bunny in the midst of a pack of hyenas. How had she remained fresh and untouched by the decadent, amoral world she'd grown up in? Even Trinity, as sweetly ditzy as she appeared, was more savvy.

"A shame to waste the bottle on just two of us. Why

don't I call Jarvis and Preston?" he suggested. "They're in the bar."

She licked her lips, leaving a glistening trail. She was so damn overtly seductive it was off-putting. He preferred Faith's shyness. He wanted his wife—hell, yeah, he really enjoyed saying that—to be assertive with her needs, but Nina was beyond assertive. She was into the realm of uninteresting.

He smiled. And wasn't that the kiss of death to a woman, to be merely uninteresting.

"I think we should keep it a duo." She punctuated with a little moue.

Ungentlemanly of him, but he wanted to laugh. She'd watched too much film noir and taken the role of femme fatale. Sidling closer, she brushed her hip to his. "Would you like a treat?" she said, fluttering a hand toward the tray of fruit. "Or shall we wait until the main course?"

She sure as hell wasn't talking about food. Connor realized he wasn't going to get a clue one way or another as to whether she and Dora had cooked up this little scheme when they'd made last-minute plans to tag along on the trip or if the scheme was all her own. He truly did have a suspicious mind. Maybe she just wanted to get fucked, and he was the moment's choice.

Gold pants hugged her legs, and the plunging neckline of her jacket didn't appear to harbor anything close to a blouse beneath it. It wasn't shopping expedition attire. It was fuck-me wear.

He wanted to change at least his shirt before dinner. "We're meeting VIM in an hour and a half. I'd like to get a call into Faith before then." Hint, hint. He'd prefer not to make an enemy of her by flatly refusing her offer.

She let the glass stem sway in her hand. "Ah, darling Faith. You know, she really is the smartest of us all, having Daddy buy her such a gorgeous little plaything." She trailed a fingernail down his arm. "Tell me, is she strictly missionary?"

Godammit. It pissed him off that everyone assumed Faith couldn't get a man without Daddy bribing one. He admitted the prenup—which the board knew about due to having ratified his future ownership in the company—didn't help the situation, but the fact was if it weren't for her own fears and insecurities, Faith would have been snapped up a long time ago by a man who was after more than just her father's legacy. Connor didn't like that she was so underrated, especially by her own family.

Suddenly, he didn't give a fuck about making an enemy. Besides, if Nina wasn't before, she would be the minute he disallowed her expense report at the conclusion of this trip. He had her pegged. She'd attend one meeting during the two-week trip, then ask for all her expenses to be reimbursed. *No such luck, sweetheart.*

She didn't give a damn about her position on the board, and the company itself didn't mean a thing to her.

"Are my wife's sexual preferences important at the moment?"

She shook her head slowly, a seductive smile spreading across her lips. "No. Not at all."

"Then I suggest you just blow me. That's all I feel like doing right now. That way we won't have to worry about ruining your delightful outfit. No fuss, no muss."

He'd expected shock, maybe indignation, or even a healthy fit of hysterics. Nina merely lifted one eyebrow in exactly the same manner as Jarvis, despite being related to him only by marriage. "What about *my* orgasm, darling?"

He smiled with equal pleasantry. "I don't care about your orgasm."

It was enough to make her take a step back. The bells on her anklets jangled harshly. "How does Faith deal with that?"

"Her pleasure I care about. Yours, I don't."

There wasn't a woman in the world who would drop to her knees and suck a man's cock after hearing that.

Yet Nina stepped forward and put her hand on his pants, then smiled as if she thought she had him. Ah. So it was a scheme, not just a quick fuck on a business trip.

He put his hand over hers and pulled her fingers back. "I've changed my mind. I'll take care of myself later."

Her nostrils flared. "It's not very nice to tease a lady."

"You're correct. That's why I don't tease *ladies*."

Ice chips gathered in her irises. She was in no doubt as to his meaning. "I don't think you're very nice, Mr. Kingston."

"I'm an asshole. And you don't have to like me any more than I like you."

"Asshole," she mused, her eyes narrowed. "It fits you like a glove."

"One more thing: don't disparage Faith. I don't like it."

"Ooh. You sound so sincere." She tossed her hair, laughed, playing the femme fatale again—badly. "But like all men, you have an Achilles' heel." She smiled and dropped her voice to a seductive pitch. "And I will find it."

"And do what with it?" He raised one brow in query.

Nina merely smiled.

He'd been conciliatory with Preston, complimentary to the man's wife, friendly and nonjudgmental with the other board members, Jarvis's so-called family. He'd kissed ass.

Now he realized he wasn't going to be able to ride the fence, play the diplomat, and make friends, not enemies. It was Jarvis against the rest of the board. If Connor didn't want to be caught in the cross fire, he was going to have to take sides. He'd seen that plainly enough over the past weeks, felt it in his gut during today's meeting. Now, it was a shot between the eyes that couldn't miss. The board would try to bring him down if they could. His best bet was to solidly join forces with Jarvis.

"By the way, before you leave"—he held out his hand—"I'd like the card key you used to get in."

She drew the key from her inside jacket pocket, revealing a great deal of flesh at the same time, and held the slim card out before dropping it to the carpet. After another sip of champagne, the wine glimmering on her lips, she set the glass on the trolley. "Watch your back, Connor," she murmured. "You're not going to know who's holding the knife."

Then she sauntered to the suite door.

Giving her his back, he refilled his glass and sipped

champagne, waiting for the slam of the door. Her grand exit.

It never came. Connor turned.

Jarvis stood in the open doorway. Over his shoulder, Nina smiled and waved her hand.

Busted with a beautiful woman in his room. If there'd been lipstick on his collar, he'd have been a dead man.

JARVIS raised one eyebrow at his son-in-law.

"Do you really think I'd be that stupid, Jarvis?"

Actually, Jarvis didn't. Kingston was smooth, charming, manipulative, and sneaky. But not stupid. Nina, however, was.

If she wanted to trap him, she should have used a little more discretion. Jarvis was sure Kingston could be had for the right inducement. If he thought he could get away with it.

"I'm watching you," Jarvis warned.

Kingston smiled. He had one of those supercilious smiles with a hint of sarcasm that said he was doing nothing more than laughing at an old man. "You won't find anything."

That's what Jarvis was afraid of, that he wouldn't see it until Faith had been hurt. "I love Faith, you know." He couldn't remember actually mentioning that to Kingston.

The young man smiled again. "Yeah. I know." There was something about that smile beyond the usual. The sardonic curve of his eyebrow faded, and his eyes . . . softened. It was almost damn frightening how genuine that tender smile appeared.

Jarvis couldn't afford to contemplate that Kingston might come to care for Faith. If he let his guard down for a second, Faith would pay the price, so he wouldn't believe in the sincerity of that smile. He'd watch the manipulator like a hawk.

But that wouldn't stop him from enjoying it when Kingston brought down the hammer on the board.

"I want sex, and I want it now, so get your cock ready for me." Though she was giddy with her own daring, Faith blushed.

Connor was two thousand miles away in a time zone four hours ahead, but she blushed anyway. She didn't know if she said it for him, because he wanted her assertiveness, or herself, because she craved the feeling of him inside her. He'd only been gone thirty-six hours, but she missed him.

"Now what if your father answered my cell phone for me while I was in heavy negotiations with a customer?"

She loved Connor's voice over the phone, even laced with humor rather than desire. "You wouldn't leave your cell phone lying around for him to answer."

"True. My cock's out, and I'm stroking it."

"Are you in your room?"

"I'm on my balcony. The night is sultry and warm and I can almost feel your mouth sucking the crown of my cock."

She'd been living in a fantasy world for a week. They'd had so much sex, she'd lost six pounds from the workout. She felt deliciously creamy on the inside. After the last student left at the end of the day, she'd stretch languidly, and her nipples would burgeon thinking about Connor. Driving home, she'd catch herself with a ridiculous smile on her face. Last night on the phone, his voice in her ear, she'd come three times. She loved the sound of his deep groan when he climaxed, the hum of her name, like chocolate sauce drizzled over ice cream.

"Spread your legs and shove your vibrator all the way in. Because that's how I'd do you if I were there. Hard and high, no foreplay, just a sweet, fast fuck, baby."

She almost creamed herself right then. God, how she adored his dirty talk. The vibrator slid deep in all her juices.

His voice whispered over the airwaves. "Fuck me, Faith."

It was almost as if he'd asked her to make love to him.

HE'D left the balcony door and the drapes open. The night breeze felt like Faith's fingers on his skin. He stacked his hands beneath his head on the pillow and stared at the ceiling.

Fuck. She was so good. All he had to do was get her to let loose like that when they were together. Recalling her opening demand had him all horny again. Connor figured he'd been ignoring his libido over the past six months. It could be the only explanation for this insatiable . . . lust. He meant every word he'd told Faith about feeding lust with all manner of acts new and exciting, but he hadn't anticipated getting caught up in teaching her. He stroked himself idly, feeling the build in his balls, the quickening of his pulse, the blood rush to his cock.

There'd been nights he'd had her three, four, and once even five times. Yet he wanted her to have *him*. To take *him*. It was nothing so simple as submission versus dominance. It was a need to drive her beyond any place she'd ever dared go. To excite her until her barriers fell, and she'd do anything he wanted. And come up with some things he'd never even dreamed of.

Why did he want these things from her so badly?

She had such a naïveté; perhaps he was simply the type who needed to corrupt. His cock fully hard in his hand, he groaned. He was so fucking lucky compared to the suckers who'd passed her by in search of skinny, vain, high-maintenance beauty queens.

Hell, why ask why? He had Faith. She was all a man needed. Because he knew for sure that one day he'd get her to drop every barrier to her sexuality and send him to the moon.

12

FAITH tried not to be so excited that Connor was coming home in two days. Last week, she'd given her class their summer send-off. Next year, they'd be first graders. How time flew. How her heart had ached watching them. She wanted to watch her own child graduate from kindergarten. While Connor had been away, her fertile time had come and gone, and really, that was why she wanted him home. Honest. Oh God, what a lie—she'd missed him, not just his seed. Badly.

She didn't want to be needy, yet her mind was a jumble of thoughts, her body a riot of emotions. With school out, she didn't have a thing to occupy her mind except Connor. She should have signed on to do summer school. She needed something or she'd go crazy every day waiting for him to come home.

What was that manila envelope stuffed under the front mat? It hadn't been there when she left to have her nails done.

The moment she picked it up, a chill passed over her arms, raising the little hairs. No address or postage, just her name, her new name, *Faith Kingston*, scrawled across the front. She wasn't used to it yet, especially when one of the children actually called her Mrs. Kingston. Seeing it now in block letters on the envelope, her heart tripped all over itself.

Whatever it was, it wasn't good.

Inside, the sun shining through the long bank of windows overlooking the back porch had heated the condo. Faith closed the curtains, not so much to keep out the heat of the June afternoon, but because she felt almost as if someone might be watching her.

The envelope hadn't been sealed except for the metal clasp, which she undid, then pulled out a sheaf of photos. On the top, a note had been clipped on.

What your husband is UP to while he's away.

Faith closed her eyes. The note didn't completely cover the contents of the first picture. A black-and-white. A man standing; a woman on her knees. Her hand wrapped around his penis, the crown slipping between her lips.

Even closing her eyes didn't shut it out.

Connor wouldn't cheat. He promised.

Her blood pounded against her ears. Dizziness swamped her, and the pictures fell to the floor, the note and clip pulling loose, and the photos scattering all over the carpet.

She didn't want to look, but she had to. Sex, so much sex. The woman's lips drawing the nectar from his erection. Her gorgeous body, toned curves, the outline of a voluptuous breast. She was everything Faith wasn't but yearned to be.

She stood there a moment until she realized her body was shaking and the backs of her eyes ached, holding tears at bay.

Her vision swam in the moisture but she could still see those pictures in her mind's eye.

The woman's body, his hands threaded through her long hair, his . . . Faith realized his face never made it into the pictures. She hunkered down and shuffled through the photos. Glossies from a photo printer, all were of him from the neck down. In fact, Faith wouldn't be able to pick out the woman in a room full of long, dark-haired ladies, either. The angle of the camera didn't show her clearly. It looked almost as if the man held the camera himself, up high, and shot pictures of the action.

This didn't *have* to be Connor. It could be . . . anyone.

It could be some nasty prank someone wanted to play on her. Or a malicious lie someone was spreading about Connor.

But who? Faith snorted. Any number of people, from Cousin Preston, who hated Connor taking over, to Lance, who seemed to think he'd been robbed of something, too.

Even her own father could have engineered this. Not that
Daddy would ever stoop this low. Besides, why sabotage
things *after* they'd gotten married?

Faith ripped each photo into pieces, then walked them to
the outside trash. She didn't want a single shred in her house.

"It wasn't him," she whispered aloud. And really, she believed what she was saying. That's why she had absolutely no
intention of telling Connor about it. She wouldn't let him think
she didn't trust him.

FAITH stared at herself in the full-length bedroom mirror.
She wasn't sure she liked the dress Connor had bought her
in South America. The neckline plunged—if she bent over,
the other country club guests would see her nipples—and a
slit rode high, revealing the lace band of the silk stockings
he'd purchased.

Stepping up behind her, he put his hands on her shoulders,
leaned down, and nibbled her ear. "You look gorgeous."

She didn't. She looked . . . well, okay, not frumpy, but
the thigh-highs made her thighs feel chunky. In his new
tux, he looked . . . edible. Completely. Totally.

Every person at the country club tonight would be doing
the compare-and-contrast routine. They'd all be saying that
Daddy bought her a husband, and what a fine specimen,
too. There'd be bets on how long it would take Connor to
cheat and with whom. She so did not want to attend tonight's party. But try as she might, she couldn't tell Connor
that. He wanted to "show her off," as he called it, and she
just could not admit to him how terrified she was. They
lived together, had sex like rabbits, but she couldn't lay out
all her fears for him to dissect.

Looking at their reflections in the mirror, it scared her
how much she'd missed him when he was gone. He smelled
so good, a subtle cologne mixed with his own unique male
scent. Her heart hurt looking at how beautiful he was, but,
as Connor said, this was lust, giddy and overpowering.
That ohmygod-I-have-to-hear-his-voice-or-I'll-die feeling
would fade. It was the newness.

He caressed her bare throat. "I have a present for you. For our one-month anniversary."

God. He'd bought her jewelry like a real husband. She wouldn't dare ask him how much he'd spent.

The box he set on the counter was bigger than a jewelry box. Tissue paper frothed out when she opened it, and Faith poked around until she found black lace panties.

All right, so Connor wasn't the typical husband. On a business trip he'd brought back a sexy evening dress and thigh-high stockings, now this.

"Put them on," he urged.

They were . . . heavy. She peered at the crotch. "What *is* this?" In the center lay a silver cylinder shaped like a bullet but several times larger.

"Loaded panties, and I want you to wear them tonight."

She laughed and gasped at the same time as the thing started to buzz in her hand. Okay, so Connor was the furthest thing from a normal husband. "It's a vibrator."

He held up a flat device in his palm. "The remote."

"You're going to buzz me while we're at the party?"

"If I see you looking bored or giving some hotshot the eye, I'll give you a little warning."

He made her laugh as easily as he got her wet. "You're crazy. And I cannot go to the country club with a vibrator stuck up my—" She stopped. "What if someone hears it?"

"Put it in and we'll check it out."

"Connor." She wasn't so sure about this.

"Faith." He wasn't going to back down.

She sighed, as if there weren't a distinct thrill shooting straight to the heart of her clitoris. "All right, fine." She shimmied the dress high enough to grab the elastic edge of her panties and rolled them down her legs.

Connor held the vibrating panties out for her to step into, and she steadied herself with a hand on his shoulder. Sliding them into place, he dipped inside the panty, slipping over her slick clitoris before he tipped the little bullet vibrator up into her pussy. His palm was warm, the metal cold, the sensations absolutely shivery.

Then he removed his hand, the panty holding the vibrator snugly in place, and pressed the remote. Faith dug her fingers into his shoulder.

"How's it feel?"

It felt like a tongue lapping at her on the inside. Hot, but not enough to make her come. "Nice," she whispered.

"I can't hear a thing. We're safe, sweetheart." He kissed the tip of her nose. "I'll just buzz you when I want you."

"I can't believe you're actually going to do this."

"I told you I like a little excitement."

"This is kinky."

"Believe me, baby, you ain't seen nothing yet." He shoved the remote in his jacket pocket. "We don't want to be late." Raising her hand to his lips, he sucked one finger into his mouth, his gaze steady on her, then he whispered, "Let's see how many times I can make you come without anyone knowing a thing."

He made her crazy, scared, and wet.

But at least for the moment, he made her forget her nervousness about tonight's country club gala.

FUCK. She was hot in the tight dress. It defined her gorgeous curves, her sweet breasts, the roundness of her belly, and the softness of her thighs. The skirt flared at the bottom, accentuating calves toned from her daily lunchtime walks at school. The slit up her thigh made him hard, but her unbound hair flowing over her shoulders and back was the crowning glory. He wanted nothing more than to bury his face between her legs and lick her to a screaming orgasm.

Ah, but he'd have to wait. The club ballroom overflowed with crepe paper decorations in honor of the July fourth holiday and party dresses, anything from short-short to full length, most in red, white, or blue, a few in black like his wife. The women strutted their bright plumage like peacocks. He wondered how much had been spent on face-lifts this past year. Male attire was either black tux or dark three-piece suit. The scents of mouthwatering appetizers overlaid the application of expensive perfume. Laughter and voices drowned out the piped-in music. There'd be fireworks at nine, then dancing.

Faith had gone immediately to say hello to Trinity and her father. Connor's portly former employer reigned over a small table close to the food and the bar. Herman liked his appetizers and his alcohol. Trinity played queen to her father and an impeccably handsome man with roman numerals after his name. Harper Harrington the *Third.* She'd finally found a live one, even if he did look like a cold fish. Good for old Trinity.

Jarvis had joined them eventually, and Connor had done the obligatory glad-handing, bought a round of drinks, then left to make a brief scouting trip for the perfect spot to cop a feel off his wife later. Instead of returning to her side, he'd slipped into an alcove to watch her. She was a mixture of contrasts, shy and hesitant, but with a friend, bubbly and full of laughter.

She'd been nervous about tonight. The party was their debut as a married couple. Connor didn't want the country club circuit espousing the story that he'd married Faith for her money. Faith was a sensitive creature, and the more it was bandied about that he'd hunted her fortune, the less comfortable she'd feel. He wanted Faith . . . comfortable. Willing. He wanted her stepping out of her shell. Just as she'd done every night he was away.

Hence, the micro-vibrator strapped to her panties. He was fucking brilliant with that one. He buzzed her now, just for good measure. Across the room, he saw the slight sexual roll of her shoulders. She turned slowly, jutted her hip, put a hand there, and cocked her head, searching for him in the crowded room. The slit of the dress showcased her luscious thigh in the lacy stocking he'd given her. Connor surveyed her immediate vicinity.

Behind the counter, the bartender sopped up a splotch of fine whiskey he'd accidentally slopped over the side of a glass. He couldn't take his eyes off her, and he wasn't the only one. Several covert glances slid her way. A silver-haired gentleman tapped his male companion's arm, and they exchanged appreciative glances. *Oh, baby, you don't even have a clue, do you?*

Faith noticed the slurs, not the compliments. One day he'd get her to pick up on the latter and ignore the bullshit.

"She's looking for him." The female voice came from beyond the monstrous potted plant outside his little alcove.

"Where'd he go?" Also female. He didn't recognize either.

"He's hiding from her. Wouldn't you if you were him?"

"That's catty." Yet they tittered together.

Connor got a twinge in his gut.

"I heard her father made him CEO to get him to marry her."

Bitches. He glanced at Faith. She put her fingers to her lips, smiled damned seductively, then turned back to pretend attentiveness to Trinity's father.

She knew he was watching her. He liked that she didn't have a doubt about it even if she couldn't see where he was.

Now to deal with the bitchiness outside his alcove.

"I'll bet you a deep tissue massage at Casio's that he's cheating on her by . . . the end of July."

"What makes you think he isn't already?"

Gasp. "With who?"

"Well, he was doing Trinity Green before. A little bird told me he still is."

He was going to murder Trinity Green.

Except . . . he'd swear Trinity actually cared about Faith. She could sometimes be a flighty ditz, but she wasn't a backstabber. More valuable than a deep tissue massage, he'd stake his life on it. Trinity wasn't the one.

He had, however, seen Nina Simon skulking around tonight. When he'd slammed her down in Caracas, he'd known he was making an enemy. Perhaps she was retaliating. Though he didn't quite get the woman. For the remainder of the trip, she'd continued her little flirt, as if she didn't hold the rejection against him. That added to his expectation that she'd bring the hammer down in another, more devious manner.

Right now, he had more immediate things to deal with.

Ready to step out and confront Ms. Cunt One and Ms. Cunt Two, Connor counted to ten. It wouldn't stop the rumors. It would only make them fly. The tale would get around that he was afraid he'd get caught cheating. Making a shitty scene would only hurt Faith.

Besides, actions spoke a lot louder than words. Wasn't that the old saying? He had a better plan than open confrontation.

"ISN'T that right, honey?"

She was hot. And it wasn't the crush of the party crowd. How could Connor expect her to answer, much less pay attention to the conversation, when his touch, even the stroke of one finger along her nape, threatened to send her into orgasmic nirvana? Not to mention the vibrator in her panties. "Yes, dear."

Okay, she had been listening. With half an ear. Connor told Mr. and Mrs. Biddle the story about the Weederman boy verbatim. Just as she'd told it to him at dinner *before* he went to South America. He'd actually listened.

So did the Biddles. Mr. Biddle was tall, angular, and completely bald, yet a five o'clock shadow showed where the fringe of hair used to be. He probably should have left it since his head was shaped rather like an egg.

Connor kissed the tip of Faith's nose. "She'll make the best mom, won't you, sweetheart?"

She wanted to suck his tongue into her mouth.

"Oh goodness, you're pregnant." Mrs. Biddle beamed. Older than her husband by a few years, when she smiled like that she suddenly seemed like a delighted child.

Yet Faith's orgasmic nirvana receded. She felt a jab right up under her rib cage. "Not yet," she murmured, looking at Mrs. Biddle's shoulder instead of meeting her eyes.

"But we're giving it the good old college try." Connor tipped her chin up and made her look at him. "One hundred and fifty percent effort, right, honey?"

He had that devilish glint in his eye, plying her with pet names and a feast of touches. It was sort of scary how he'd made her the center of his attention. He touched her constantly as they talked to people, a kiss on her ear, a squeeze at her waist, a thumb skirting the underside of her breast. Or he'd slide his hand in his pocket, and she'd salivate with anticipation as his mouth creased in a knowing smile just before he buzzed her.

Through it all, he'd introduced her to a number of his new work associates. She'd met most at Daddy's Christmas parties for his employees, but she'd never spent so much time talking to them. She'd moved on the periphery of social events, but Connor dragged her smack-dab into the middle. He complimented her, always included her, actually asked her opinion.

For the first time, she didn't feel like the drab mouse amongst all the beautiful people. God. The things he did. The emotions he evoked. She could almost believe . . . but believing was a slippery slope.

The Biddles moved on. Alone in the crowd, Connor snugged her closer and put his lips to her ear. "I need a bio break, baby. Will you be okay for a few minutes?"

"I've been coming to these things alone for years."

He reeled her in, wrapping both arms around her. "On second thought, come with me and let me do you in the bathroom stall."

She laughed against his shirtfront. "You are so bad." And she loved it.

"But you're hot. I know you are." He nibbled at her earlobe. "Your nipples are damn near poking my eye out and"—he breathed deeply—"your hot, sweet, juicy scent is driving me wild." For good measure, he shifted ever so slightly against her, rubbing her with the hard ridge of his erection.

She wanted to rise on her toes, hug him close with both arms around his neck, and stroke her cleft against his cock.

God, she was even thinking like him and close to letting him drag her into a men's room stall. "Connor, behave." She should give the message to herself.

Sliding a hand down her back, he caressed the base of

her spine in slow circles. "Tell me the truth. One more buzz and you'd come."

She pushed him away with the tips of her fingers on his chest. She wanted that buzz more than anything. But they were in the middle of a crowded ballroom and orgasming right here, right now, would be embarrassing. "Bio break," she said. "Go. I'm fine on my own."

"Don't flirt with anyone while I'm gone."

Yeah, right. She didn't say that, instead giving him a tap on the shoulder to head him in the right direction. Why was he so good to her? She could swear he hadn't once returned any of those longing glances that followed him everywhere he went, even now, as he headed out the double doors.

"I see he's playing his part to the hilt."

She jumped at the touch of a breath against her ear. And turned. "Lance." She backed away, one step.

His gaze pierced Connor's departing back. "He's laying it on a bit thick, though, don't you think?"

"What do you mean?" She regretted the question the moment it was out of her mouth. She *knew* what he meant.

"He's trying too hard to convince everyone this is a great romance when we all know he married you to get Daddy's company."

She swallowed hard and closed her eyes. Long enough to grab some semblance of composure.

Connor had been sweet, and kinky, with the vibrating panties. What more could she want from him? He didn't shame her. He made her laugh. He made her hot, wet, and excited.

He was acting perfectly for her.

She opened her eyes. "Lance." Glancing around, she lowered her voice. "I'll only say this once. I chose him. He chose me. The reason doesn't matter anymore." She leaned forward, tilted her chin. "So butt out. Your comments aren't appreciated."

He backed off, quirking one corner of his mouth. "A bit sensitive, aren't we?"

If he wasn't Trinity's brother, she wouldn't even be talking to him. Then again, he just made her plain mad. Aware of avaricious ears straining to overhear, she didn't care.

"I've found a little backbone." *After all these years.* "Stop trying to push me around or make me think bad things about Connor."

Holding up his hands in surrender, he gave her a sad, woebegone smile. "I cared about you, Faith. I tried to help. But if you want to stick your head in the sand, so be it." Then he put a hand on her bare arm. "But when you need a friend, you can still come to me."

He'd never offered her anything that didn't gain him far more in return. She stepped back, his hand falling away. "I won't need it."

She walked away. Dammit. Lance ruined her buzz. She covered her mouth to hide a bubble of laughter. It was Connor's buzz. He'd been buzzing her all night. But Lance's words had been ice cubes down her back. She melted and not in a good way.

Why had Connor disappeared so many times tonight? The men's room, to get her a drink, to say hello to someone. He always came back, sweet and attentive, but really, where did he go?

She was letting Lance's meanness steal the high she'd been on. Suddenly, the voices were too loud, the laughter around her too shrill, her skin cool and damp, and the thigh-high stockings made her legs feel chubby. Where was Connor, dammit?

Her body started to vibrate. Her clitoris hummed. She put a hand to her stomach and looked up. She couldn't see him, but Connor was playing her on and off with the remote in his pocket.

Putting a hand on the nearby table, she steadied herself. Oh. She tugged her lip between her teeth and breathed deeply. Ooh. When she closed her eyes, the purr of the vibrator, enhanced by the incessant pulse of the on-off switch, felt like flesh throbbing inside her. Her body had warmed the metal bullet, and its sweet little buzz fanned out from her pussy to her clitoris to uncharted territory beyond.

He was here in the room. She scanned the faces, looked for his head above the rest. Her nipples peaked against her bodice.

A hand touched her arm, and a voice broke her husband's spell. "Are you all right?"

Gray eyes, dark hair, and tall. Really tall and handsome in a Harrison Ford kind of way. Where did she know the man from? Oh my God, he was the bartender, out and about gathering dirty glasses. She must look like she was going to faint.

"I'm fine. I was just looking for my husband." Damn. That sounded pathetic, as if she'd been ditched.

The man eyed her, his gaze coming to rest on her chest. Her breasts rose and fell with her agitated breathing. She was afraid to look down because she was sure he could see her hard nipples just below the neckline.

What must the poor man think of her?

"You're flushed. Shall I take you out for some air?"

Well, duh, he thought she'd had too much to drink. "No. Thanks." She fluttered a hand. "I'll just go find my husband."

Then she winced. He was probably going to say he'd seen Connor stepping out onto the dark veranda with some other woman.

A jolt shot straight to her clitoris. Almost as if Connor knew exactly what she'd been thinking. "Yeah," she murmured, stepping back, "I really better look for my husband." With another blast, she almost moaned. Her fingers curled into a fist. "Thanks for your concern, though." She backed up, straight into a broad chest and a pair of strong arms.

"There you are, sweetheart. I lost you in the crush."

She tilted her head back. Connor stared the bartender down, who smiled slightly, picked up a dirty glass, saluted with it, then sauntered back over to the bar.

Connor leaned down and nipped her neck. "He wanted to fuck you, sweetheart."

He was fully aroused, his erection nestled along her spine.

She barely held back rubbing against him. "He did not."

"I watched him. He saw you alone, signaled for a replacement, then came after you." He licked the shell of her ear. "Aren't you glad I rescued you before he dragged you out into the dark and had his way with you?"

She twisted in his arms and steadied herself with both hands on his jacket lapels. Lacing his fingers behind her back, he held her close. She was aware of people around them, the crowd moving out to the lawn for the impending fireworks. Amid the clink of glasses and plates, the musicians began setting up, and the staff cleared the dance floor of tables. Yet there was only Connor's heat and the sweet wetness between her legs.

She didn't care about Lance. Or the bartender. Or what anyone thought. They could say he married her for her money, her father's company. She didn't give a damn, because Connor wanted her. Everything he'd done and said tonight was for her.

"Let's go home," she whispered.

"Let's take a walk," he countered.

"But—"

With a finger to her lips, he cut her off. "I found a place I want to show you." Sliding his fingers down her arm, he took her hand, pulled away, and turned her with him.

In that moment, she'd go anywhere with him. And she knew she was lost.

CONNOR had slipped out of the ballroom several times tonight looking for the perfect spot to take her. He wanted her here, right under their noses, the crowd she was a part of yet the world of people who made her feel less than she truly was. He was hot and hard contemplating it.

They passed a couple of teenagers in the corridor, then the crowd faded out as they entered a new wing of the country club which hadn't officially opened yet.

"Where are we going?"

Her hand was small and warm in his, her head barely topped his shoulder. He adored that she was petite. It made him feel protective. He'd never felt protective of anyone. It was a nice feeling, an appropriate emotion to feel about his wife.

He didn't want to control or dominate her. He simply wanted her to rise to her potential. He wanted her to hold her head high amongst her peers and feel beautiful and powerful no matter what they thought or said.

He squeezed her hand, drew her through a set of heavy wood doors, and pulled them closed behind them.

"Wow." Faith leaned back against the wood. "I didn't even know this was here."

"They'll be opening the piano lounge in a couple of weeks."

The only illumination in the room came from a row of lights along the bar top. The shelves behind the bar were empty but boxes were piled three deep with liquor and glassware. The floor was bare concrete, except for the raised dais on which a grand piano sat and the parquet dance floor in front of it. Black-lacquered tables had been stacked top to top in the corner. The socket in the ceiling over the dance floor, where presumably a chandelier would be hung, was bare wires. Beyond the floor-to-ceiling windows, partygoers gathered on the lawn for the fireworks, but behind the smoked glass, Connor and Faith were virtually invisible.

Dipping forward, he tried to see her face. "Would you like to come for a little dancing once the place is open?"

She stared at the dance floor, and the luscious sexual creature he'd held against his cock in the ballroom vanished. "Connor, you don't have to seduce me. We're married. You've got the job. You don't have to push anymore. All I want is a baby."

She thought as the rest of them did. Once he'd gotten what he wanted, she'd be nothing more than a pussy to stick his dick in and get off. *Just close your eyes, fuck her, and pretend she's someone else.* He'd heard the sentiment in men's locker rooms. He just didn't want Faith to think it.

"I want more than a baby. I want you to blow my mind and rock my world. What's wrong with that?" He tugged her against him, wrapping his arm across her back so she couldn't pull away. "Lust is so hot, Faith. Lust is dreaming about sex at work. It's coming home hard as a fire hydrant, whomping your woman down on the sofa, and doing her hard and fast before you get to dinner, then slow and sweet after dessert."

He could actually hear her swallow. Then she shook her head. "But it's not real. And it doesn't last."

"Fuck real," he whispered. "It's mind over matter. It'll last as long as we make it last." He'd made his decision the minute she said no infidelity, and he wasn't turning back. "If you don't want me to have a mistress, then *you're* my mistress."

She stilled in his arms, her wriggling ceased. He could feel her mind working in the air around them. The soft strains of music drifted beneath the door, and moonlight streaming through the wall of windows stretched its fingers across the concrete floor as far as the bar.

"I'm not the mistress type," she murmured, her gaze fixed on the pleats of his dress shirt.

He chanced letting go long enough to reach inside his pocket for the remote. In the relative quiet of the room, his ear picked up the light buzz only because he knew what it was. She sagged against him, and her heart beat erratically. Her nipples were hard nubs. She reached up, dug her fingers into the shoulders of his jacket, and arched into his cock.

"You're mistress material. Hot, sweet, and tasty, baby."

Backing off, he took her hand in his and pulled her up on the dais. He'd wanted her to take the initiative, to take *him*. It was a slow simmering need in his gut for which he had no explanation. Screw *why* he wanted that so badly; he just did. For now, however, he'd be satisfied with her participation.

Tugging her snug up against him back to front, he gazed down into her magnificent cleavage, and his hands begged to touch and caress. He slid straight down to cup her breast in his palm.

"Connor." She gasped when he flicked her nipple.

"Faith," he mimicked her shocked tone. Finding her sensitive spot, he licked the ridge of her ear, her shiver traveling the length of his body to lodge in the tip of his cock.

She flapped a hand at the wall of windows looking out on the golf course and gardens. "They'll see us," she whispered.

"They'll be watching the fireworks out there, not the ones in here." He covered her eyes. "Let's pretend."

She didn't speak, but neither did she tug his hand away.

He set about seducing her with his voice and his touch. "Let's pretend there's a crowd, and we're the floor show." He circled her tight nipple. "They've come to watch us"— he sucked her earlobe into his mouth, then let it slide slowly away—"fuck," he added on just a breath of air, almost without sound.

She trembled, then squirmed against his cock.

"Yeah, baby, they want to see me bend you over the piano bench and take you from behind." He hated to leave her breasts, but it took both hands to slowly inch up the tight dress. "Pinch your nipples for me."

She caressed herself with her fingernails, then pinched each nipple in tandem. And moaned. He wanted to sink his cock deep inside her so badly his erection surged hot and heavy.

With her dress now to her waist, he slipped a hand down between her legs. "You're drenched, baby. You're so fucking wet, I could drink you."

He wanted her to talk to him, to tell him what she wanted, the way she did on the phone, yet he wasn't sure at what point she'd balk. Cupping her mound, he reached in his pocket for one last buzz, the vibrations passing from her to his palm. She soaked him. Clasping his arm around her waist to steady her, he slipped inside the panty to delve along her slit. While the vibrator worked its magic on the inside, he fondled her clit.

"They want to see you come, baby. Make it a good one."

She moaned and shivered, rolled her head against his shoulder, and undulated with the rhythm of his stroke.

"Please don't stop, please don't stop." She put her hand over his and rocked with him, her legs tightly together, giving him enough room to slide back and forth while her body held the vibrator hard and fast.

"Come for the audience. Christ, you should see them. They're going crazy, they want to see you come so bad." He wanted to feel her detonate in his arms.

She bucked and heaved, and he felt her shudder start from the inside, and just when she opened her mouth to scream out her pleasure, he pulled her head back, took her lips, and swallowed the sound. She moaned as she rode the wave of orgasm.

And before she could come down enough to think, he tore her panties down her legs, rescued the vibrator, then pushed her hands to the piano bench. "Hang on, baby, hang on hard."

His cock was out of his slacks in mere seconds, and he almost came the moment he slid into her sweet depths.

"Oh God, Connor." She arched, her hair sliding down her back and off her shoulders. "You feel so good."

He rolled down over her, chest to back, held her, his cock buried to the hilt. "I want to fuck you so bad." He touched her clit, and her body jerked. "Tell me you want it. Here and now."

"Please, Connor, yes, I want it."

"Put your knee on the bench. I want you wide open for me."

She trembled and panted, but she did what he told her to.

With one last lick to her ear, he whispered a final inducement. "I want them all to see my cock sliding inside you. Remember, baby, they can see everything. It makes them fucking crazy to watch." It would make *him* fucking crazy to see the beauty of his cock riding her.

He straightened, braced her at the waist, and pulled out slowly until only his crown remained. His cock pulsed and felt close to bursting. He punched with short, fast strokes, just the tip, her pussy milking the sensitive ridge. Holy hell, it was too much. He held still a moment, caught his breath, then slowly entered her again, relishing the sight as her body swallowed him. He wanted her to see it. Someday he'd find a way to show her the beauty. "Gorgeous," he murmured.

In, out, he picked up the pace, increased the friction until he almost lost sight of where they were, a dark lounge, the moonlight across the floor like a still pond. All that existed was her sweet pussy, his cock claiming her body for his own.

"Stroke your clit, baby." He wanted her to come when his seed filled her.

She pounded back against him, taking him as much as he took her. Mutual fucking satisfaction. He closed his eyes, the throb building in his balls, yanking them up, squeezing. Outside, the fireworks burst in the air and everything inside him exploded as he lost himself in her completely.

13

OUTSIDE, the fireworks exploded in a crescendo. For a moment there, in the throes of orgasm, she'd thought *they'd* created the fireworks. Actually, they had.

"Jesus." His exclamation was a mere puff of air at her ear. "That was too fucking hot for words," he murmured.

His heart raced against her ear as she lay across his chest. Arms clasped around her, he leaned against a piano leg. Somehow, he'd pulled her dress back down over her hips, tucked his penis back inside his pants, and zipped up.

"Your tux is a mess," she said.

With his finger under her chin, he tipped her head to drop a quick kiss on her nose. "I say that was hot sex, and you worry about my tux?" He nuzzled her hair and lowered his voice to a seductive pitch she felt deep inside. "Screw the tux. Screw the mess. That was the fucking best. Admit it, baby."

It was, and she was fast becoming addicted. To the sex, his arms around her, everything he made her feel. Addicted to *him*. More than lust, her emotions were getting all tied up in him.

"It was good." She could at least give him that without giving away the rest.

He laughed, sucked her bottom lip into his mouth, then finally took her with his tongue, devouring whatever lipstick remained. "Screw good. It was perfect, and you know it."

The boom of the fireworks sounded as if they were in her head. A stab of fear, maybe even terror went through her heart. Why did he insist on that word? Why did he want her to say it?

Please don't lull me into thinking we're perfect, then pull the rug out from under my feet.

Instead of becoming more assured in their marriage, she was less secure than the day she'd agreed to marry him. She pulled away, leaning on her hip, feet tucked beneath her, and tried to restore order to her hair. "It was better than mere *good*." She smiled to lull him into thinking she was teasing.

More than perfect, it was how she'd dreamed of feeling when her knight in shining armor finally came along and rescued her.

"You"—he tapped her nose—"are one hard-edged woman."

Let him think she was hard to get. It kept her safe. "And another thing. You can't say that word all the time. It'll steal into my vocabulary until one day it pops out at school."

He raised a brow. "What word?"

She shot him a stern look. The banter restored her equilibrium. "*That* word."

"*Fuck?*"

He was as mischievous as one of her students. "Yes."

"*Fuck* is a great word." He got right up in her face, his nose to her hair. "As in, that was the best *fuck* I've ever had." He raised his head like a dog and drew in a breath. Eyes closed, a slow groan rose up from his belly as he exhaled, then he impaled her with his dark gaze. "As in, your pussy is so *fucking* hot and juicy that I need to *fuck* you all over again." He pulled back. "See, it's an adjective, a verb, *and* a noun. That's a good lesson for your students."

He was so appealing. She hadn't bargained for this. She didn't want to feel anything, yet she couldn't resist him.

Please don't let me fall in love with him.

But oh, he made her feel wonderful. Never had she felt like this in her life. "No more exhibition sex," she whispered.

"Spoilsport," he murmured.

"I'm a good girl."

He nodded his head slowly. "Oh yeah. You are so fuc—"

She slapped her fingers lightly against his lips. "No more saying that naughty word."

"How about I only say it in the privacy of our own home?" he said against her fingers.

She felt a kernel of fear burgeon inside her. Felt it grow, hot and heavy under her rib cage.

"Or on the phone when we can't be overheard," he went on.

He could hurt her so. He could make her need what he gave her, then take it all away in the blink of an eye when he got tired of her. Despite what he claimed about keeping lust alive, it would evaporate like water in the hot sun.

"Faith."

She blinked. "What?"

"You're thinking, and it's not good things."

He could read her like a book, she was so pathetically obvious and open. And she was going to ruin the best thing that had ever happened to her just by thinking too hard.

"I don't think you do know," she countered.

He tipped his head in a "try-me" gesture.

"I was thinking that when I get you home, I'm going to . . ." She trailed off and fluttered her eyelashes. "No, I think I'll keep that a surprise."

He grabbed her hand and pulled her to her feet. "Then I better get you home right away."

"Patience. You'll have to wait. I want to see the rest of the fireworks." She stepped off the dais and wiggled her butt as she headed to the door.

She'd enjoy what he did for her. She'd take full advantage of the moment instead of worrying about when it would end. She'd relish the pleasant buzz zipping through her body instead of destroying it with a bunch of what-ifs.

Flapping a hand over her shoulder, she added, "Don't forget my panties and the vibrator, dear."

Behind her, he laughed. "Yes, dear."

Then she gasped and stopped and . . . oh my God. "That chair wasn't there when we came in."

He stopped behind her, his body warmth caressing her. "I didn't notice."

"It *wasn't* there." She remembered the stacked folding chairs along the wall when they first walked in. She might have been filled with Connor's irresistible scent and surrounded by his aura, but she'd noticed. And that chair hadn't been next to the door like that. As if someone had unfolded it, set it against the wall, and . . . "Someone was watching us."

"Baby, you're imagining things."

She tipped her head back to look at him. "No. I'm not."

In the dark, a smile grew slowly on his face. His signature devilish grin. "Cool."

"You're bad," she said. She should have been horrified. She *was* horrified.

"Yeah. And you like me that way."

They could have been arrested for . . . indecent exposure, lewd behavior, something. At the very least, they could have been the gossip of the country club. Her father would have had a heart attack. But somehow, Connor turned everything into a sexual fantasy for her. Her heart actually picked up its tempo.

He was so right. She did like him that way. Instead of horror twisting her insides, the most delicious thrill shot straight down to her clitoris at the thought that someone sat in that chair and watched their performance.

Good Lord, she was becoming kinky. Now, if she just kept her emotions in check, she'd be . . . perfect.

CONNOR smiled, totally pleased with himself and his wife. Hell, she hadn't freaked when they realized they'd been seen. Instead, her nipples peaked. And they said women got even hornier when they were pregnant. He'd be in seventh heaven.

He was in fucking seventh heaven now.

"A champagne cocktail, please."

The bartender, the one who'd eyed Connor's *wife*, jumped to do his bidding. The fireworks had ended, and everyone was in line for a refresher. Connor had made it before the rush.

Faith had made a sojourn to the ladies' room to make sure her dress and makeup were properly repaired while

Connor returned to the ballroom to order her a drink. He wanted to show Faith off some more in that dress.

"Where's the wife, darling? Gotten rid of her already?"

Nina wore a red and white top cut low enough to reveal a touch of aureole and silver satin shorts that didn't quite conceal her butt cheeks. She'd switched out the ankle bracelets for a pair of knee-high black boots. He had to admit she looked good in the getup, which couldn't be said of a number of women in their midthirties.

He fished a bill from his wallet and laid it down. "She's powdering her nose," he supplied.

She pursed her lips, smacking them. "Did she miss you while you were gone in South America?"

He grinned. "I missed her more."

"You know, you've got a pretty good act going there. I bet some people actually believe it." She leaned on the bar, swaying her backside and affording him a full view of her nipples. "I think I'm actually starting to like you."

"Thank you."

On the trip, she'd enjoyed baiting him. Sidling up close when Jarvis was in clear view and playing games. It had begun to amuse him. Obviously it amused her, too.

She batted her eyelashes. "Did you sign my expense report?"

"Since you only went to one meeting in the eleven days we were there, I signed off on a ten percent payout."

She tilted her chin and ran a finger from the hollow of her throat to her blouse's neckline. "How about you sign off on all of it and I promise not to tell your wife I was in your suite?"

"How about next time you go to all the meetings and then I'll consider giving you full reimbursement?"

She smiled like Helen of Troy, then pushed away from the bar. "I might have a growing soft spot for you, Connor, but I will make you pay for being such an asshole."

"I'm sure you will, Nina. And I'll enjoy figuring out ways to show you your real place."

She blew him a kiss, whispered "asshole," then turned and wriggled her way back into the crowd.

Connor had thought he had her figured out that first night in Caracas, a man-eater with whom he'd have to watch every step. She'd surprised him. She enjoyed playing men, teasing them, putting them in the one-down position. Even more, she relished the game. She wanted him, mostly because he'd turned her down, and she'd escalate the play until she got what she wanted.

Except in this case. Truthfully, she held no appeal whatsoever. He'd tasted Faith, and she was infinitely a sweeter vintage than Nina Simon could ever be.

"Your drink, sir." The bartender palmed the cash and left the change in one-dollar bills. "There's your lady." He tipped his chin, pointing over Connor's shoulder. "You're a lucky man."

"Yes, I am." He left the bills on the bar and turned to find his lady, sexy Faith in the black dress. *Christ.* She wasn't wearing panties. They were safely tucked in his jacket pocket. He felt a swell beneath his tux.

He wondered if Nina would follow through on her threat. He wondered what Faith would believe. He wasn't completely sure of either of them. And hell if that didn't make life interesting.

IT was all she could do to hold her chin up. The way Nina looked at him. The way he looked at her.

There was a horrible intimacy between them. A hand squeezed her heart. Was it Nina in the piano lounge? Had Connor told her to be there? Was this some sort of game they were playing?

Panic seized her throat, and she almost tripped over an infinitesimal bump in the ballroom carpet. The woman in the photos could have been Nina. The man could have been Connor.

Related only by her marriage to Cousin Lionel, Faith had always felt as though the woman were secretly laughing at her. *Please don't let Connor be doing her.*

They hadn't seen her. She could walk away and pretend she hadn't witnessed their exchange. She could pretend—

"They're married a week, and can you believe it, he leaves on a two-week *business* trip, and *now* he's having nookie at the country club with someone else. Don't you think that's *bold*?"

She almost stopped dead in her tracks. Did they think she was deaf *and* stupid? Only pride kept her moving. It was shades of hearing about Lisa and her cheating husband in the ladies' room that first night she met Connor. Only this time they were talking about Faith. She wanted to throw up.

Nina blew her husband a kiss and melted into the crowd on the other side of the bar.

"I mean, really, he was doing her right in the new piano lounge. You'd think he'd have a little more common sense. Of course, *someone* was going to see him."

This time, Faith did stop, her heart pounding. *I was with him in the piano lounge.* Yet it was as if they couldn't even consider it a possibility that Connor had been doing *her*.

"Oops, God, you don't think she heard us, do you?"

"No way. But I feel kind of sorry for her. She doesn't look like she has a clue."

The bartender slid a champagne flute across the bar to Connor and tipped his chin in her direction. For just a moment, she locked eyes with him. She saw . . . something in the man's gaze. A flicker of interest maybe. Then Connor turned. He smiled, and her heart stopped. He held out his hand, and her bones melted.

She didn't look at her tormentors—she didn't want to know who they were, or to tell them they didn't have to pity her. At least not about the woman with Connor in the piano lounge.

God. She needed a psychiatrist, and maybe some drugs for manic depression. Her emotions had never bounced all over the map before she met Connor, especially not in the space of ten seconds. The elation she felt was the polar opposite of the despair gripping her insides when she'd seen him with Nina.

Maybe she was pregnant, which would explain her mood swings. She closed her eyes and touched her belly. *God, please let there be a baby soon.* She could survive anything if there was a baby.

When she came back to the room once more, he was giving her such a look. If she'd still been wearing the vibrator, she was sure he would have buzzed her.

That look was all she had to hang on to, so she walked to him, took the champagne, and let him fold her beneath his arm.

He nuzzled her ear. "What's wrong?"

"Nothing." God, it was so typically . . . wifely. *I'm fine honey. Which means I'm not fine at all.* Faith didn't want to sound like that. She lowered her voice to a hopefully husky note. "I'm merely in recovery over what you just did to me."

He chuckled. "Don't recover. I want to plow into you the minute we get home, so you better stay wet."

She was aware of eyes on them. Curious, avid gazes. How could she tell him everyone thought he'd been doing someone else? Secretly, she wanted everyone to *know* he'd been with her.

"Drink up," he urged. "We should get out of here soon. Because something's come up. Again."

Trinity—wherever she'd come from because Faith certainly hadn't seen her—put her arms around them both. "Sweetie, can I borrow your husband for a quick dance?"

She glanced at Connor, who raised his shoulders slightly.

Trinity didn't even wait for a yes. "And I want you to go over there and talk to Harper because I absolutely have to know your honest opinion of him. You're the only one I trust, so"—she gave Faith's shoulder a little push—"tell me if he's divine or it's only my imagination because I think I'm totally in love."

Tonight was the first Faith had even heard of Harper Harrington the Third. Connor raised a brow, smiling first at her, then at Trinity, and allowed himself to be dragged away.

Faith wouldn't think about how good they looked on the dance floor. She wouldn't wonder what caused that intense look on Trinity's usually sweet, smiling face. She wouldn't let all sorts of thoughts into her head about what they could possibly be discussing with such concentration. She wouldn't . . .

Oh my God. She was jealous of her best friend. Her emotions about Connor had gone far beyond lust.

DESPITE the slow, seductive tune, Trinity Green danced like a stiff board, holding herself several inches from him and pinching the shoulder of his tux as though that was all she could bear to touch. A pucker marred her forehead. She'd need a shot of Botox to get rid of it if she didn't watch out.

"You are *such* an *ass*hole," she hissed. "I'll murder you."

Interesting. He didn't think Trinity knew the word *asshole*. "I wondered when you'd congratulate Faith and I on our marriage."

She looked as if she could spit pea soup. "Who was she?"

"Who?"

"The woman in the new piano lounge." She raised her hand as if she would dearly love to hit him. "*Everyone* knows. *Everyone.* You humiliated Faith. And I trusted you. I introduced you to her. Like giving a bunny rabbit to a wolf. She told me you promised, but the first chance you get, you—"

"Trinity."

She stopped as if he'd actually put his hand over her mouth.

"I wasn't with another woman in the piano lounge. So who told you I was?" Godammit. A little innocent fun. All right, not so innocent. Hot as hell, in fact. But he hadn't intended *this*, for the club circuit to assume he was with someone else.

"No one had to tell me. It's buzzing in every corner." Trinity groaned and seemed to sag a little in his arms. "This is *all* my fault. I should have *known* you'd cheat on her."

For God's sake. Did no one think he had any integrity? Not one person? Even for Faith, he'd had to sign a prenuptial agreement stating that he got nothing if he committed adultery. Nina finagled her way into his hotel room and was shocked, dammit, *shocked* he didn't take her up on her offer. Jarvis believed he hadn't only because he didn't think Connor was that stupid. And now Trinity, who'd always seemed to see him in a slightly better light than anyone else did, except Faith.

He almost shook her. "I did not cheat." He leaned down and spoke right in her face so she'd *get* it. "And I'm not going to."

"But—"

He gave her a threatening look that quelled insubordination. But what was he supposed to say? Tell her he'd been with Faith?

The song ended, another began. Connor tipped his head. Possibilities started to abound. Ideas clicked on like the proverbial lightbulb. Yeah. He needed something to stop the talk. Something to show the holier-than-thou, jet-setting, hypocritical crowd that Connor Kingston wasn't a cheat and a liar, and that Faith was more woman than they'd ever suspected.

"I *don't* like that look, Connor," Trinity said in her best stern imitation of Faith.

"What happened isn't what you think. Do you believe me?"

She examined his eyes, her feet barely moving to the music. "This time," she murmured. "But if you *ever* hurt Faith, I *will* rip out your innards and hang them from the Golden Gate for the seagulls to peck at."

"I never knew you had such a vicious streak."

"She's my friend."

He'd always thought she was a flighty, vain creature. Maybe Trinity was, but she was also a loyal friend, and for that, he admired her. "And she's my wife. So you just follow along with everything I say."

"Uhh . . . okay."

He could tell she wasn't too sure about it. He didn't

care. Steering her off the dance floor, he headed toward the group knotted around Trinity's new "flame." Faith stood at the edge of the small crowd looking lost. She'd heard the nasty rumors.

As he wrapped his arm around her, she gave the slightest cringe, an almost imperceptible tightening of her body.

"So, baby, what did you think of the new piano lounge?" he said, his voice overloud and attention-grabbing.

Conversation stopped, heads turned. Trinity gaped. She would have hated that look if she could see it in a mirror.

Faith doe-eyed him. The deer, the Mack truck headlights, the whole thing. She was so adorable with that I-can't-believe-you're-bringing-that-up-now expression, he kissed her nose.

"The piano lounge?" she said, her voice barely a squeak.

"Yeah. Great for dancing"—he smiled—"and other things."

Trinity damn near spat out her sip of champagne.

Connor snugged Faith closer and spoke to the crowd around them. Which had grown in size in the past minute. "Faith and I thought we'd check out the new digs. Quite a nice setup." He chucked his wife under the chin. She gazed up in . . . utter shock. "We'll certainly be going back there, won't we, baby?"

Trinity finally found her voice. "*You* were with Connor?"

Except for the ensemble music and the clink of glasses at the bar, there wasn't a single other sound.

Faith locked gazes with him for the longest damn five seconds, and he couldn't read a thing in her eyes. She was usually so transparent. But not now.

Finally, she relaxed, smoothed her hand along his lapel, and turned to Trinity. "Of course Connor showed me the lounge." She tipped her head back to look at him. "We got a very close-up view of it, and it's got the most gorgeous grand piano I've ever seen. Right, honey bunch?"

He wanted to kiss her. Long and deep. "Absolutely the most gorgeous thing I've ever seen."

A man coughed. A woman gasped. Another snickered.

Then whispers filled the air like locusts swarming a fat wheat field.

Faith's heart pounded. "I can't believe you said that," she muttered under cover of the drone around them.

"And let them think I was with someone else?" Connor asked.

She didn't hesitate. "No." Then she bit her lip. "But they all know what we were doing in there."

"Are you embarrassed?" Connor slid a hand beneath the hair at her nape.

"Horrified." At least she *should* have been horrified. Yet she wasn't. Instead she felt warm inside and out.

He smiled that lovely, wicked smile she adored. "You'll get over it."

"Yes, I do believe I will." Then she pursed her lips primly. "But we can't ever do anything like that again."

With both arms around her, Connor pulled her tight against him, his erection hitting her abdomen. "Now that's a promise I have no intention of keeping."

What if the tale got back to her father? Her membership could be revoked. They'd practiced indecent behavior in a public place. So what if they *thought* they were alone. They obviously hadn't been. Instead, they'd created a veritable scandal.

Faith didn't care. Connor had told everyone the woman he wanted was his wife. Looking up into his handsome face, Faith Kingston fell irrevocably in love with her husband.

She loved him. He lusted after her. It was enough, more than she'd ever hoped for.

14

"YOU want to go to *Egypt*?" Faith couldn't keep the utter incredulity out of her voice.

Trinity grabbed her arm and pulled her to the next mummy exhibit for a front-row view. Monday morning at the museum wasn't what one could call busy, and after the busload of summer school students moved on, she and Trinity were alone.

"Harper adores everything Egyptian," Trinity told Faith for the umpteenth time. "He dreams about being the first person to walk into King Tut's tomb."

"Someone walked into King Tut's tomb a hundred years ago."

Trinity flapped her hand. "You *know* what I mean."

Faith didn't. Saturday night at the country club was the first time Faith had even heard of Harper Harrington. Then Trinity had called her at eight this morning and told her they simply *must* go to the museum in San Jose because they had *the* most *marvelous* Egyptian mummies. Faith drove—heavy city traffic scared the heck out of Trinity—to a litany of Harper Harrington the Third's *absolutely magnificent* qualities.

"You know"—Trinity pondered the shriveled unwrapped mummy—"I don't get it. They've got Eva Peron's body mummified under glass down in Argentina. But if that's how she looks"—she fluttered a hand at the almost-unrecognizable-as-a-human remains—"why would she bother?" Trinity made a face. "I mean, *eewwe.*"

Faith laughed. "I don't think it's been on display for years and years. And if I recall, she wasn't mummified either." Maybe she should Google Eva's corpse. "How did you meet Harper?"

Trinity grabbed Faith's arm and looked positively . . . dreamy. "It was at the salon. My manicurist got his manicure slot mixed up with mine, and"—she melted into a sigh—"he let me have it and waited right there talking to me the whole time." She held out her fingers. "He even picked out the polish. Asian orange."

It sounded like something dropped on helpless people during a war. Looked a bit like it, too. Trinity's nails . . . glowed.

"What color did *he* get?"

Trinity laughed. "Don't be silly. He got clear. Then he asked me to lunch afterwards. Come on, I want to see the jewelry." Trinity pulled Faith to the next room.

A couple of tourists strolled through, their reverent whispers rising to the vaulted ceilings with a hiss.

"What does he do for a living?"

"He's an entrepreneur." Leaning just her palms on the metal edge of a glass case, Trinity surveyed the contents. "Hmm, that's pretty unimpressive."

Small trinkets of beaten gold lay on velvet trays. A pendant with a mosaic of tiny intricate pieces forming a woman's face was astounding, but Trinity was into more modern fashions.

"What does an entrepreneur do?" Faith asked.

"You sound like Daddy." Trinity bumped hips with Faith.

She bumped back. "Sorry. I've just never seen you quite so . . ." She couldn't say "bubbly" because Trinity was always bubbly. "You've never gone to a museum for a man before. Not to mention considering a trip to Egypt, where it's dusty and dirty and hot and you'll get all sweaty and your pores will clog."

Trinity laughed. "Don't worry, I'll bring my salon girl with me. And if we start thinking marriage, Daddy will order a background check." She tapped her fingernails on the glass. "Did your father get a background check on Connor?"

As if someone had flipped on a spotlight, Faith saw the real reason for this excursion. "No." She paused. "Do you think I'd have learned something that would have changed my mind?"

Trinity shrugged, her straight blond hair falling over her shoulder. "No. Let's move on. Mummies and their jewelry aren't quite what I'd expected. We should have gone up to the Legion of Honor in San Francisco. They've got a Van Goff."

"You know it's Van *Gogh*," Faith admonished. Trinity had loved art history in school. Faith had never been sure why Trinity felt she had to dumb herself down like that.

Heels clacking on the hardwood floor, Trinity studied her map. "Let's go see the cat mummies down there." She pointed and sidestepped a tour group milling about in the main hall. "What if I did know something? Would you want to hear it?"

Faith's heart plunged to the toes of her sensible walking shoes. "About Connor, you mean?"

"Yes, about Connor." Engrossed in the map, Trinity missed the arrow on the wall indicating the mummified pet exhibit.

Faith didn't point her in the right direction. "That depends on whether it's fact or rumor."

"A bit of both, I guess." Trinity stuffed the map into her bag. After long seconds of looking at everything *but* Faith, she finally met her gaze. "*Was* it you in the lounge with him?"

Trying to wipe all expression off her face, Faith didn't say how much that hurt. "You think I lied to hide my humiliation?"

"I don't know. But doing . . . *that* . . . in a public place . . ." Trinity waved her hands in the air as if that would conjure the right words. "It's just not like you."

Connor gave her the freedom to do things that weren't like her. "It's not like me to lie? Or it's not like me to have a man desperate to make love to me?" Her heart ached merely asking the question.

"I just meant that you've always been so . . . *shy* about stuff like that." Trinity stared at her with limpid blue eyes and blinked back what might have been tears. "Sometimes I don't think I know you, Faith. Especially since Connor."

"We discussed this. I trust him." Even if Daddy had bought him for her. She closed her eyes a fraction of a second.

"But isn't it possible you only trust him because of the agreement he signed?"

She trusted him because she loved him, but she couldn't tell Trinity that. Even Trinity would call her a fool, and her feelings were too new, too tender and uncertain to tell anyone. "It isn't just because of a legal paper. It's the way he treats me, Trin. With respect and caring. It might be a marriage of convenience, but that doesn't mean he thinks I'm a skag."

Trinity yanked her to an unoccupied bench by the wall. "Don't you *ever* say that about yourself." She took a deep breath. "But not all men can play the monogamy game, even when they've got a lot to lose if anyone finds out."

"Just tell me what it is you know. I'm tired of the games."

Trinity bit her lips, heaved a great sigh, then perused her fingernails. Asian orange really wasn't her color. "He had a woman in his room down in South America."

The pictures popped into her mind. *It wasn't him.* And it wasn't Nina. Or at least it wasn't Connor *with* Nina. Except that Trinity wasn't talking about pictures. "Who told you?"

Trinity just came out with it. "Lance."

That sneaky snake. "How would he know? He wasn't there."

"Green talks to Castle and vice versa, and he *heard*."

A child dropped the ice cream off his cone onto the lobby floor and started to wail. Faith felt like wailing with him.

It was those damn photos and that damn agreement making her doubt Connor. The prenuptial was a thorn in her side. She couldn't know for sure he wouldn't stray without it in place.

A fact that hadn't mattered before Saturday night. Before she fell in love with him.

"Why didn't Lance say something on Saturday?"

"He said he couldn't bear to hurt you that way."

That was so much crap. "So he sent you to do it?"

Trinity stroked Faith's arm. "I'm not trying to hurt you, sweetie. I just feel responsible. I don't *want* to believe any of these things I hear, but I can't *not* tell you."

"Why not?" She took Trinity's hand, squeezed it. "Why not just *not* tell me?"

"But Faith—"

"Think about it, Trinity. If it was you, would you want your friends telling you every nasty rumor flying about the man you"—she managed to pull back at the last moment—"married?"

Trinity stared at their clasped hands. "I don't know."

"Wouldn't it put a strain on your marriage if you ran to him every time you heard another story being passed around?"

"But where there's smoke, there's fire."

"Maybe there's people who don't like your husband, who don't like that he took over your father's company. People who have a vested interest in making you believe he's a cheat and a liar."

Trinity gasped. "Lance?"

"Anyone. Who started the rumor about Connor being with another woman in the piano lounge?"

"Well, that wasn't—" Trinity studied her hands sheepishly. "Okay, I heard it in the ladies' room."

Jeez, that was where all the gossip started. She and Connor had an agreement. He wouldn't break it, not when she'd done every kinky, delicious thing he'd told her to. Hadn't she?

Faith resisted rubbing the headache away from her temples.

"You're right, Faith. I'm sorry."

Now Trinity changed her tune?

"That's okay." But was it? A knot of anger lodged in her chest, and she wanted to take it out on her best friend.

"Connor wasn't very happy when I asked him about it."

Faith let her mouth drop open. "You asked Connor?"

Trinity tipped her chin defiantly. For the first time in their relationship, Faith actually felt in the one-up position.

"I told him that if he ever hurt you, I'd hang his guts from the Golden Gate Bridge for the seagulls to eat."

She couldn't help herself—Faith laughed. As usual, heads turned, but this time she didn't feel self-conscious. Connor liked her laugh. "And what did he say to that?"

"That's when he dragged me off the dance floor and told everyone within earshot that he'd *shown* you the piano lounge."

Faith's heart beat furiously all over again, just as it had in the ballroom. He'd done it to protect her from the malicious gossipmongers. The ones Trinity had believed.

"Here's the deal, Trin. Unless you personally see Connor doing something he shouldn't be doing, I don't want to hear it."

"But if I *personally* see it, you want to know. Right?"

It took her forever to think about that. "No." Connor wouldn't break their agreement. But what if there wasn't an agreement between them? Then what would happen?

Trinity let out a long sigh and sagged back against the bench. "Oh, thank you. I so don't want to have to go through the last few days again." She waved her hands. "Should I, shouldn't I? You can't imagine what it's been like." She held Faith's gaze, her blue eyes misty. "Do you still love me, Faith?"

"Yes, Trinity, I still love you."

"Will you be my maid of honor?"

Faith grabbed her hand. "Harper asked you to marry him?"

"Not yet. But he will. So I want to make sure I have all my ducks in a row."

"Are you in love with him?"

"I will be by the time he asks."

"Oh, Trinity. I can't be your maid of honor"—Trinity's lip quivered at Faith's words—"but I can be your matron of honor."

And Trinity beamed.

Forgiveness was that easy. If only she could forget about that damn prenuptial agreement just as readily.

FAITH blinked, and the mascara she'd just applied smudged beneath her eyes. Dammit. She wanted her makeup on before Connor left for work, so she could kiss him good-bye without looking a total fright.

All week, Trinity's questions at the museum had haunted her. Yesterday, Thursday, Faith had gone down to a real estate agent to get the ball rolling on finding their own house. She wanted to be settled in before school started again in the fall, but in addition, she needed to do something, anything, to occupy herself while Connor was gone all day.

When she'd arrived home, another manila envelope had been tucked under the front mat. This time, there was simply a question mark on the outside, and the photos were of a man and woman doing it doggie style on a bed. The camera must have been mounted on a tripod. The pictures were color, the woman had red hair, and once again, the man's head wasn't in the frame.

Nina had red hair, and Connor loved that position. It was the way he'd taken Faith in the piano lounge.

No, no, no. That was *not* Connor in those pictures. Someone was trying to sabotage their marriage. In her office—she and Connor had each taken a spare bedroom—she'd hidden the envelope at the back of the drawer of her new IKEA desk, buried beneath a couple of grade books. Maybe she'd been rash in destroying the first set. She didn't know how she'd prove anything right now, but she was saving these for future evidence. That was the only reason she was keeping them. Really.

She trusted Connor. She *did*. But that damn prenuptial indicated the exact opposite. How could Connor truly come to care for her with that agreement in the way?

All her doubts had been circling like buzzards around her head since her Monday date with Trinity. Connor was right. Lust *was* better than love. She'd been absolutely miserable after she'd fallen in love with him.

She dabbed at the mascara she'd messed up.

She wanted him to care for her. Only he couldn't care for her with the prenuptial like a flashing sign saying, "I trust you only if you've signed on the dotted line and you stand to lose everything if I decide I don't feel like trusting you anymore."

If she told anyone, certainly Trinity, and especially her father, they'd tell her how backwards that logic was, that Connor only toed the line *because* he'd signed away everything.

She was doing it again, her mind going round and round, like water circling the drain. But the question remained: Without the agreement, could their marriage grow to a new level?

"I'm leaving," her husband called.

Faith bounded down the stairs and threw herself at him from the third step.

"What's this in honor of?"

God. That was stupid. He might think she was starting to get all possessive. "Because that *thing* you did in the middle of the night was so good, you deserve an extra hug this morning."

He grinned. "What *thing*?"

"You know, where you had your tongue *there*, then you put your finger back *there*."

"And you went off like a freaking rocket. Now I remember that *thing*." He rubbed her bottom. "What are you going to do today while I'm gone?"

He smelled so good, some manly aftershave and her shampoo because his bottle had run out. She loved smelling her scent on him. *Be bold; ask for what you want.* "I thought I'd drop by and have lunch with you today."

He stroked her arms up beneath the robe sleeves. "I've got a board meeting at one thirty."

Her skin tingled with the glide of his fingers. She was naked and moist beneath the terry cloth. "That's fine. We'll have lunch, and I'll go to the board meeting with you."

"Why the hell would you want to attend a board meeting?"

She felt a tiny pinprick in her bubble. Didn't he want her to go? Maybe he had lunch plans with . . . Nina. "I own shares even if I don't vote them. So I'd like to go."

He wrapped his arms around her, sliding down to cup her butt once more. "It'll be boring, but that's your choice. How about we invite Josie for lunch, too?"

"Josie?"

He interpreted her look and shot an astonished question at her. "Josie Tybrook? Your cousin?"

"Oh." That Josie. "I don't really know her all that well."

"Then maybe it's time you get to know her." He squeezed her bottom lightly. "Family is important. And just because your father doesn't get along with his cousin doesn't mean you won't like Josie. She's nice. Give it a chance."

She felt lots of tingles now, and they weren't a good kind. "Today is special, our first lunch date since you got back from South America. I'll do lunch with Josie another time, okay?"

He nuzzled her robe apart and dropped a kiss on her collarbone. "Fine. Think of somewhere special you'd like to go." He pecked her cheek, grabbed his briefcase, and headed out.

Faith was left staring at the door. *Josie?*

It wasn't Josie in the pictures. Was it? No. Josie had very short hair, at least she did the last time Faith saw her, which was at the company Christmas party.

It wasn't Connor, either. The two people in those photos could have been *anyone*. She was going to stop making herself miserable over everybody else's what-if scenarios about Connor cheating. They weren't even *her* doubts.

She loved him. She trusted him. She wanted to give him proof of that trust. And there really was only one way.

Gathering her robe in her hands, she ran barefoot up the stairs. She had so many things to do before lunch. A new outfit. A trip to Daddy's lawyer. She had to do it today, Friday. When she had the agreement annulled, or whatever it was you did with prenuptials, he'd *know* she trusted him.

They could start being a real wife and husband.

"JOSIE will make a great program manager on this project."

Connor's father-in-law didn't even look up from his *Economist* magazine. "She hasn't the experience for a job the magnitude of the Dominican project."

Connor countered. "How is she supposed to get major project experience if you don't give her the chance?" He was fighting a losing battle. Jarvis had his head stuck in the sand.

Jarvis finally looked up, his eyes narrowed. "Why are you so interested in her anyway?"

"She's a company asset. And as with all assets, if you don't maintain them properly, they stop functioning at the highest capacity." Josie was also the only family member who didn't seem to have an agenda about how and when she could sell shares and get the hell out. She actually cared about the company and about her job.

Jarvis had alienated everyone else.

"The answer is still no. She's not ready."

Connor tapped his fingers on the arm of his chair. He was married to the man's daughter, but he was still on the outside looking in, sitting opposite Jarvis with that huge desk between them while Jarvis threw out edicts. He'd come up with several plans for cost improvement. They all required Jarvis's approval, and the man gave far too many of them a thumbs-down.

"Effectively, you're saying I don't have the authority to implement any of my proposals without your approval."

Jarvis smiled. "I agreed to the new travel policy."

Right, because the new policy stuck it to his family. The fact remained that Connor was merely a figurehead. Jarvis had hosed him. He'd let Connor marry his daughter, but he wasn't about to let him have the company. Maybe he was hoping Connor would just fade away. After he impregnated Faith, of course.

Shit, he couldn't even get that job done, either.

Since when the hell had he been so defeatist? He squashed the thought like a bug under his Italian leather shoe.

"Jarvis, you're making a mistake." He micromanaged his entire staff and drove them crazy with it, but Connor wouldn't even get into that. "Josie will do well for us."

"I still want to know why you're so interested in her."

"Because she loves this company." Connor stopped, realizing he was only digging himself a hole. His father-in-law would soon be asking if Connor was having an affair with the girl. "Fine. Who do you want on the project?"

"Masters."

Masters was the worst choice. Connor looked at his track record when he was making his own list of candidates. The man hadn't come in on budget for two years. Why Jarvis hadn't fired or demoted him, Connor didn't have a clue. Jarvis was the sole decision maker in the company, and he played favorites. Maybe his choice of favorite had to do with history. Masters had been around a long time, and his performance had been better than par until the last couple of years. Maybe it was loyalty as it was with Herman Green. Herman, and by extension Green Industries, could do no wrong despite evidence to the contrary.

Jarvis Castle was an enabler, yet his loyalty didn't extend to his family, except for Faith. The old man had probably been at loggerheads with the rest of his clan since he took over the company from his father thirty-five years ago.

The question was, how to fight Jarvis. Or rather, how to get him to see things Connor's way.

"That might be overloading Masters. He's got Republic going, and they're a tad overbudget. How about Ronson?"

Jarvis seesawed his head side to side. "He might do." He puffed out his cheeks, looked into space a moment, then nodded. "He'll do."

Connor would assign Josie as Ronson's second-in-command. She needed experience, and she'd get it on the Dominican job. "Good." He checked that task off on his day planner. "Now let's talk about the Republic contract." Connor flipped open the file he'd laid on Jarvis's desk. "I've got a few ideas on how to alleviate the cost overruns."

For the next half hour, they dickered back and forth. Jarvis was mostly take and no give, but Connor counted two scores in his own favor.

Yeah, it was a matter of managing Jarvis. But by the time the meeting was over, his temples throbbed. In his office, he downed a couple of ibuprofen. Faith would be here soon.

At least marriage was going in his favor. Every time they came together, he pushed her a little harder, got her to drop one more barrier between her inhibitions and ultimate pleasure.

Last night had been another triumph. But this morning . . .

At the soft shush of shoes on his carpet, he glanced up. She stood in his office doorway. And Christ if she didn't take his breath away for a moment.

Connor couldn't pinpoint what was different about her. Maybe it was when she'd thrown herself in his arms this morning. It was . . . odd. A tad nerve-racking. Faith wasn't demonstrative unless he had her so hot, she lost control. Certainly the new outfit was a change.

What was the neckline called? A cowl, he was pretty sure. Women wore the most amazing fashions. As she leaned forward slightly, bracing herself on the doorjamb, he could see straight down to the lacy half cups of her bra and the dusky outline of her nipples. The filmy skirt was tight across her hips, then flared into a flirty hem that begged him to raise it to the level of her pussy and drink in her hot scent.

Yet it was so much more. It was the way she moved, giving her ass an enticing wriggle, her breasts out, her chin tipped, a sultry cast of her eyelashes. And all so very under-stated. A slight adjustment in attitude he wasn't sure any-one else would notice. But he noted every subtle nuance.

"Have you picked out a place to eat?" He grabbed his suit jacket off the rack.

Faith leaned against his office door, and he heard a deci-sive click of the lock.

"Oh yes, I know exactly where we're going to eat." She sauntered forward. "And what we're going to eat."

He noted the sexy sandals laced up to just above her ankles. For whatever reason, the new footwear made him hard as a hammer. "And where would that be?" He put his jacket back on the rack.

"Right"—she traced a finger along the edge of his desk, round the corner, to his side, stopping next to his chair, her finger in the center of his blotter—"here." She twirled his leather chair, stopping it when it faced him. "Sit, boy."

Holy hell. This was exactly how he wanted her. Demanding laced with a touch of fun.

He sat, faced her, spreading his legs to encompass hers. "So I'm your pet now?"

She smiled, sultry, sexy, her lashes at half mast. Reaching behind, she undid the mass of her hair from its mooring. Her breasts lifted, the jersey material stretching to reveal her peaked nipples.

"Yes, you're my pet. And if you want your reward, you're going to have to perform exactly the way I tell you."

She hoisted herself up on his desk, shoved aside his computer, some paperwork, and his PDA.

"I'm ready to obey any order," he murmured, his fingers itching to ride up her bare legs and under the hem of her skirt.

Putting her sexy sandals on the arms of his chair, she leaned back on her hands and drew him in. Her scent washed over him, hot, wet woman.

Cupping her calf, he kissed her knee. "Love the sandals."

She twisted her foot. "I liked them, too." Then she slid her feet back to the very edge of the armrests, her knees rising until he got a shot of her luscious pussy.

"Bad girl," he whispered. "Where are your panties?"

"In my purse. I'll put them on later. After you're done."

He raised his gaze to hers. "Done with what?"

"Having me for lunch." She smiled, sexy, confident. It was such a goddamn turn-on, he wanted to drive into her right now.

Instead he watched as she pulled her skirt up her thighs, let her knees fall apart and gave him the most gorgeous view of her flaming red bush, the color matching her hair. Her lips were plump and needy, her clitoris already burgeoning.

"Have you been thinking about this all morning?"

"Uh-huh." She punctuated with a nod. "Eat me, baby. Now."

His body damn near went up in smoke. The sultry tone of her demand, the wanton pose as she leaned back on her elbows, her body spread out like a feast on his desk. He slipped his hands under her butt and pulled her to the edge.

She tasted like ambrosia. Running his tongue up her slit, he circled her clit. Yeah, she was hard. And wet. He sucked her, played her, then slid a finger inside to caress the little sweet spot there. She arched, moaned, then squeezed her thighs against his ears.

He worked her inside and out to a litany of soft, sexy sounds that made his balls tighten in his pants. Easing her legs apart, he raised his head to look at her.

She pinched a nipple between her thumb and forefinger, then stared down at him. "Don't stop."

"I won't." But neither was he going to let it be over too soon. Smoothing his hands across her thighs, he pushed her legs as wide as they'd go. He traced a finger down, slipping inside. "You're so wet."

"Lick it up," she urged.

He gathered all her moisture, then slid back up to smear her clitoris with it. "Tell me exactly what you want."

He wanted to hear her say it. He wanted to know what turned her on in her own precise words. He wanted to know what took her to orgasm the fastest.

"Use the tip of your tongue and jab my clitoris."

He did. She arched, fell back, and writhed against the desk top. "Now take it in your mouth and suck, but not too hard."

Her hot arousal burst on his tongue. She tangled her fingers in his hair, directing. Then she pushed up against his mouth, and he knew she wanted it hard.

She groaned when he backed off.

He blew on her. "Tell me how you want it now."

"Your tongue." She gasped as he gave it to her. "All around, really fast."

He circled and plunged, around, over, and under.

"Oh God, yes, baby, yes, just like that." She panted between each word. "Connor, Connor, oh my God."

Her hips rose. She ground against his face.

Then he hit her with his best shot. Thrusting two fingers in her at once, he stabbed his tongue at a spot just below her clitoris. She went off like last Saturday's fireworks, her body contracting around his fingers, squeezing, her pussy flooding his mouth. She rocked and flowed against him. But this time she didn't make a sound. Not a single sound, as if she knew one sound would lead to a scream that would raise the roof.

He didn't give her time to come down off the high. Instead, he yanked out his massively hard cock and drove deep. Ah God. He almost came the moment her soft, warm depths took him.

Curling his body over hers, he inhaled her, steeped himself in her scent, then moved in her. Gentle strokes at first, but his cock couldn't take that for long. With a mind of its own, it demanded. Harder, higher. She wrapped her legs around him, locking her feet at his back, and he fucked her until he couldn't remember who he was and didn't care where they were.

When he came, he filled her. He buried his hands in her hair and took her mouth, staked his claim as her body convulsed around him and tossed him into the sky.

What seemed like hours later, he stirred to look down the length of her body to where they were still joined. Her skin was damp, the cowl neck of her shirt revealing one pink-tipped breast. He licked the nipple, and she jerked against him. Sliding her fingers through his hair, she lifted his head.

"I didn't say you could fuck me. I only said you could eat me. You were a very *bad* boy."

He wanted to laugh. He wanted to shout for . . . something. Joy, maybe. He couldn't be sure.

"You loved it," he whispered. He loved the dirty words on her seemingly innocent lips.

It was the first time she'd used them.

Yet another thing different about her.

A twinge started in his gut. Why had she changed? He wanted her to, but . . .

Connor pulled out slowly. His come filled her, dripped

out of her. Fuck, it was so hot. He pulled a box of tissues from the desk drawer and started to clean her.

"I can do that," she said, holding out her hand.

"I'll do it." He dabbed at his semen. He wanted her to dip her fingers in it and taste him, yet there was something so intimate about cleaning her.

The twinge didn't abate. It got worse. She was different. When she looked at him, her eyes were soft, her smile gentle.

As if she were falling in love with him.

He wanted her abandoned in her sexuality, eager to demand whatever she wanted or needed to please her. Falling in love wasn't part of the plan. That could ruin everything. Love was a messy emotion that turned people into jealous, possessive idiots. Faith knew the rules. She wasn't about to . . .

He wondered if *he* was following his own damn rules. Because he liked everything she did. Hell, he *loved* it. The word itself was enough to strike terror into his heart. The truth was he could count a number of times he used it in reference to something Faith said or did, something he did to her.

Ah hell. He didn't want love to screw with his perfect marriage to his wife. So he wouldn't let it.

15

HER body floating in orgasmic aftermath, Faith could barely pay attention. She wanted to tuck her legs beneath her and fold up into the cushy leather chair. Mmm, she could go to sleep.

Oh, that had been so marvelously, wonderfully . . . perfect.

"Why are you smiling?" Across the table, Nina frowned at her. It puckered her forehead in a most unattractive manner.

Faith almost giggled. Could one get drunk on great sex?

"We had a big lunch," Connor supplied. He touched her hand. "Eating always makes a person tired afterwards."

God. She couldn't believe he'd said that. He was *so* bad. She couldn't help smiling. It might have been Nina in those pictures, but it *wasn't* Connor. "You're absolutely right, honey. Lunch must have made you tired, too. You ate more than I did."

She couldn't believe *she'd* said *that*.

Connor's mouth quivered on the verge of a total guffaw, but he managed to contain himself. Instead, he lightly pinched her arm. She'd pay for her teasing later. Faith really looked forward to the payback.

Preston Tybrook stretched out his arm, pulling back his cuff, and looked at his watch. "Can we get on with it? I've got important things to do."

"What's more important than a board meeting for Castle?" Faith's father glared.

There was so much tension, far beyond what she'd noticed in the past. Her father wasn't fond of Preston, but this was downright antagonistic.

Preston replied to her father's dig with a mutter under his breath. Dora moved her hand under the table and silenced him.

Daddy tapped the table. "Faith, will you vote your shares today since you're here?"

"No, I'm fine with you voting them, Daddy." She wouldn't have any idea how to vote anyway.

Her father smiled and shot Preston a snarky glance. It couldn't be called anything else.

The board members opened their folders containing the agenda and backup. Faith leaned closer to Connor, and he tipped the page so she could see.

And they droned on. Nina Simon studied her fingernails. Cousin Branson Finch slumped in his chair, his hands clasped over his belly, and she could swear he was sleeping with his eyes open. Preston said something about a new venture. Her father snorted and voted it down. Thomas Plumley wanted to appropriate ten thousand dollars for a philanthropic project to save a beetle indigenous to the Santa Cruz mountains. Her father didn't even bother with a snort when he voted no.

Connor didn't get a vote. He was a mere officer.

Then Mr. Biddle was brought in. Technical-schmechnical, his dissertation had to do with Green Industries. Trinity's father provided some of Castle's raw parts, and quality had taken a complete nosedive.

The tension in the room broke loose. "That's bullshit," her father snarled. "We've been using Green for years and never had a single quality problem."

Mr. Biddle scratched the back of his bald egghead as if considering his words. "I realize that, sir, but we've narrowed the issue down to—"

"Your people need to go back to the drawing board."

"Jarvis, at least listen to the man." Connor was the voice of reason in the turmoil her father's outburst created.

Daddy threw out his arm. "He brought this up in South America, in front of our *customer* no less. And who the hell authorized this study?"

"I did," Connor said. "We've got a problem here, Jarvis."

"How *dare* you go behind my back with this, Kingston."

"Let's hear Biddle out." Branson's brother Gabriel pursed his fleshy lips. And waited. Her father simply ignored him.

Mr. Biddle went on to plead his case. "Sir, if you'd just read the report—"

"I don't have to read the report. It's wrong."

Connor held out his hand. "Leave it, Don," he said to Biddle, his hand extended. "We'll go over it."

Mr. Biddle glared at her father as he slid the report across the big table. The door closed behind him with an extra quiet *whoosh* as if he'd tried hard not to slam it.

Connor slipped the report beneath his board folder. "We've got quality issues, and we need to look at every avenue, whether you think it's the right one or not."

"Here-here," someone said under their breath.

For a moment her father looked ready to jump across the table and grab Connor's throat. What on earth was going on? There was serious stress she simply didn't understand.

If she didn't know better, she'd say the board members, his *family*, hated her father. No, that couldn't be, but one thing was for sure: she'd been wrong to ignore this. Connor had a point. She needed to be more involved with her family, and maybe she could bring them closer together. Or at least keep them from tearing one another's throats out.

Instead of continuing the argument, though, her father simply narrowed his eyes. "Fine, we'll bring Herman in on this. Next item on the agenda?" Then he smiled.

It was chilling, like the way a cobra puffed up just before it struck. Faith's heart sank.

"Ah, I see Connor has another excellent expense reduction proposal," he added. "Let's hear it, Mr. CEO."

She couldn't believe her father's tone. Denigrating. And it wasn't just Connor. He spoke that way to everyone. She wished she'd never come to the meeting. She didn't want to know this side of him.

"If you'll turn to exhibit A in the packet," Connor advised, "you'll see a twelve-month analysis of employee expenses."

Papers shuffled.

"Sonuvabitch," Preston muttered.

"Our travel expenses are exorbitant, thirty-two thousand in airfare for that South American trip alone."

"You expect us to travel economy?" Cyril glared. "On these long trips, we'd be basket cases by the time we got to our destination and lose a whole day recovering."

"I suggest business over first class on foreign travel and economy on domestic," Connor said rationally, despite the outburst. "And only one suite per trip. I understand the need for entertaining, but we can restrict a suite to the highest-ranking member of the party." Then he looked from Dora to Nina. "And the business purpose for the trip needs to be approved in advance or the trip isn't reimbursable."

"What are we?" Cousin Richard groused, scratching behind his ear. "Children who have to have our butts wiped?"

"Yes," her father cut in with a certain amount of glee. "If I'd known those airfares were thirty-two K, I never would have approved so many of us making that trip."

"Right. So *you're* going to travel economy, Jarvis," Preston scoffed. "Give me a fat fucking break."

"Watch your language, Preston. This is a business meeting, and there are ladies present." Her father seemed to enjoy the reprimand a little too much. A light danced in his eyes. "I'm voting yes on Connor's proposal."

Preston grumbled and voted no. Dora did the same, without the grumble, but there were extra wrinkles around her lips. Nina, on the other hand, smiled at Connor when she voted no, as if to say he'd taken this round, but the fight wasn't over.

After the exchange she'd witnessed at the club, Faith was a little relieved on that one.

"Then we put it into policy," her father quipped at the end of the vote, which of course, he won because no one else had the votes to counter, not when he voted Faith's 5 percent as well.

She could almost see him rubbing his hands like Scrooge.

"Any other business before we adjourn?"

The strain in the air was thick, oppressive, something she breathed with every inhale. She meant to tell Connor and her father privately about what she'd done this morning, yet when she married, she'd given Connor the company right out from under the noses of her family. Her marriage—and thus the prenuptial agreement—affected everyone in this room. They had as much right as her father to know what she'd done. Didn't they?

"I have something to announce."

Connor tipped his head to regard her.

"I saw Daddy's lawyer this morning." She slid her gaze around the room, landing on her father. His nostrils flared, and his eyes looked almost black as if his pupils had dilated his irises out of existence. Then she came back to Connor. "I had the lawyer tear up our prenuptial agreement."

For a long moment, Connor simply stared at her. Something flickered in his eyes, and she hated that she couldn't always read him. Was he glad? Triumphant? Couldn't care less? *What?*

Then, finally, he took her hand in his and squeezed tightly, a smile on his lips.

She didn't have any idea what the smile meant.

THAT was the last thing he'd expected from Faith.

He wanted to take her in his arms and kiss the soft, fragrant skin at her throat. He wanted to thank her for the trust, though he wasn't sure he'd earned it yet. He wanted to rock his body inside her until she cried out his name.

And he wanted to know why she'd done it. What did Faith want in return? Everything had a price. What was his wife's?

He was semilost in thought, pondering the ramifications, while Faith's family rose and gathered round as if she'd announced their impending marriage rather than the dissolution of the prenuptial agreement.

"How sweet, Faith. I know you two will be terribly happy." Nina air-kissed Faith's cheek, then leaned down to

Connor's ear. "She's a gullible fool tearing up that prenuptial." Retreating several hairsbreadths, she raised her voice and imbued it with syrup. "You are such a *lucky* man." Nina patted his back, lingering too long in the action.

Connor stood to accept the Finch and Plumley obligatory back slaps. Dora Tybrook gave Faith a hug. He wanted them all to get out so he could put his finger on what bothered him.

Finally, he was alone with Faith. And his father-in-law.

"Are you an idiot, Faith?"

A phantom chill rode up the back of his neck. "Don't talk to her like that, Jarvis."

"Butt out, Kingston. This is between my daughter and me."

"Then make it civil." He'd like to smack the old man. But for Faith standing there, he might have. But for Faith, he might have gone for Jarvis's jugular over the whole Green issue. Herman was going to be the downfall of this company if Jarvis didn't get his head out of his ass. But no matter his business differences with Jarvis, he wasn't going to let the old man treat Faith as if she were one of his subordinates.

"It's okay," Faith said, a soft smile gracing her lips.

He wanted to shout at her that it wasn't *okay*. But there were some things she had to figure out for herself. He could help her perceive her sexual beauty, but he couldn't show her that her father had no right to talk to her that way.

She touched her father's arm in appeasement. "Daddy, I—"

But Jarvis was ready to rage. "It wasn't only *your* agreement to dissolve, Faith."

"It was about *my* marriage, and I don't want that agreement. Once I'm pregnant, I don't want that thing hanging over our heads. Connor will be the father of my children."

Connor's insides twisted. Her words humbled him. As much as he wanted to give her, it was nothing compared to the trust she'd just given him.

"Well, you're not pregnant yet." Her father narrowed his eyes to a laser point. "Are you?"

She bowed her head a long moment. Connor's heart suddenly jumped to his throat. *Holy hell.* Was that why she seemed so different? The rush of baby hormones?

He couldn't breathe. Of course, he'd contemplated it, but in an almost clinical manner. Get married, get the company, get her pregnant, create a Kingston dynasty.

He hadn't thought about how it would feel. Like a sucker punch to the kidneys, sudden inexplicable fear gripped him. He hadn't been afraid of anything since he was a teenager. Now he suddenly saw himself holding his tiny newborn in his hands . . . and his guts tensed up. What if he did something wrong? What kind of father would he make? Would they have a son? Or a daughter?

"No, Daddy, I'm not pregnant yet."

Connor's stomach dropped straight to the floor. Down, down, down so fast he almost fell with it. No baby with delicate toes and tiny fingernails and Faith's red hair.

He held on to her hand because it was the only thing that kept him on his feet. *Jesus.* For the space of five seconds, he'd wanted that child more than anything, ever. He'd been scared shitless, but he'd *wanted.*

The old man didn't seem to give a shit. "That damn agreement was about *my* company, too. What he"—Jarvis stabbed a finger in Connor's direction—"has to do to earn it. Cost measurements." He started ticking them off on his fingers. "Goals, forecasts. And getting me a grandson, by God."

Jarvis hadn't even acknowledged her pain that a child wasn't already filling her womb. Connor felt it deep in his gut with her. She was dying for her father's hug, for his approval, his commiseration that she didn't yet have the one thing that would make her world complete. Connor badly needed to knock him upside the head to get him to see. *Look at her,* he wanted to shout.

Jarvis loved her, but Connor didn't believe he'd truly looked at his daughter in years. He didn't even know who she was or understand what she needed.

"The baby will happen in its own time, Daddy."

Connor prayed it had happened today, in his office when he'd shot his seed deep inside her.

Jarvis didn't hear the despair in her voice. "He hasn't done anything he promised, Faith. You've ruined everything. I gave you what *you* wanted, and this is how you repay me."

"I'm sorry." Her hand was limp in Connor's grasp.

Screw that. She didn't have a thing to be sorry about. "*I've* been called an asshole several times over the last weeks, but you, Jarvis, take the cake. You owe Faith an apology."

His father-in-law merely glared at him. "Like hell, I do."

He felt Faith's flinch despite the fact that the only part of her he touched was her hand.

Silence filled the boardroom for several ticks of the clock.

Finally, the old man actually looked at her without wrath blazing in his eyes. A wave of misery washed down his face, pulling his mouth into a grimace. He swallowed hard, as though a lump stuck in his throat. "I'm sorry, sweetheart. I was a little upset and forgot myself. That was no way to speak to you." He held out his arms. "Forgive me?"

She hugged him hard.

But where Faith could forgive, Connor wouldn't forget. Jarvis Castle had crossed a line he couldn't easily brush aside. Working side by side with the old man wasn't going to get any easier. But there was one thing Connor did need. He squeezed Faith's hand. "Baby, I'm taking the rest of the afternoon off, and we'll go for a drive in the mountains. Go powder your nose, and I'll meet you in the lobby."

She left, though by the look she slid over him, she knew full well he had a few things to say to his father-in-law before he took her for that drive.

"Draw up another agreement, Jarvis. I'll still abide by my cost objectives and due dates and all the rules we set forth concerning the business."

"I'll have it on your desk tomorrow," Jarvis said, his glare all maniacally serial killer again.

Without the terms of the prenuptial agreement, Jarvis couldn't easily get rid of him, at least not for the five-year term in his CEO employment contract. But without that agreement, Connor didn't get his five percent share. It wasn't Faith's fault that he'd lost that guarantee when she dissolved the prenuptial. He'd fucked up by not telling her it was there in the first place. He was pretty damn sure Jarvis hadn't, either. She hadn't read everything completely, and she'd signed because she'd trusted her father to take care of her. She'd thrown out the piece of paper because she now trusted Connor.

Yet Connor needed an agreement in place as much as Jarvis did. He didn't trust his father-in-law to give him what he earned. And he would earn every percent despite the roadblocks Jarvis threw in his way.

He wasn't, however, going to let Jarvis disrespect his own daughter in the bargain. That thought brought him full circle to the moment she revealed what she'd done.

What price would Faith try to extract from him? If it was love she wanted, he couldn't pay. But if it was his child she craved? *His* child. God. It hit him all over again. That moment he'd thought his baby grew inside her. *I want that,* his mind whispered.

With or without a physical piece of paper between them, he wanted her body, he wanted to fill her with his cock and his seed. He wanted his child in her belly.

He couldn't give her love, but maybe she'd realize that what he could give her was enough.

THE road Connor chose wound up into the mountains. Faith slouched in her seat, the sun streaming through the side window. Dreamy and warm, she watched Connor's hands on the wheel. He had gorgeous hands, long fingers, large palms. When he touched her, he moved her to ecstasy. When he held her hand and told her father to apologize, he'd chosen her over the company.

She shifted and raised her gaze to his profile, hiding her perusal beneath lowered lashes. Could he be falling in love with her? Why else would he care when her father had gotten so angry?

She shouldn't give herself hopes like that. Not yet.

He'd removed his suit jacket, thrown it across the back seat, then rolled up his shirtsleeves. A dark dusting of hair covered his forearms. With every turn of the wheel, muscles flexed. His scent filled the car, a woodsy aftershave and his unique male aroma. Her body melted on the inside like hot fudge.

He steered the car into another turn, and she allowed the motion to rock her closer, close enough to reach out and touch. Her fingers twitched in her lap.

"You look like Little Red Riding Hood getting ready to eat the Big Bad Wolf." Though relaxed in his seat, seemingly concentrating on his driving, he'd been aware of her scrutiny.

Faith liked that awareness. And she did want to eat the Big Bad Wolf. She'd taken the initiative in his office, and he'd loved it. He seemed to adore having her tell him what she wanted, how fast to lick, how hard, where.

He liked her dirty talk.

"I like your cock." She breathed deeply. "I liked it"—she exhaled, her breath brushing his arm—"when you fucked me on your desk."

He glanced over, not a flicker of movement on his face and his eyes hidden behind dark glasses. Then he shoved his fingers through her hair, caressing her scalp for long sensuous seconds before he pulled her head down to his lap.

"Then fuck me right now with your mouth," he whispered, "because I'm so damn hard, it hurts." The words were Connor's version of sweet nothings.

She unzipped and drew his erection from his shorts. Droplets of semen beckoned. Faith lapped them up. "You taste good," she murmured.

He shifted slightly in his seat, giving her a better fit before the wheel. "I want to be inside you."

She took him inside. Her mouth ringing his crown, she circled the sensitive ridge the way he liked.

"Christ, baby, you make me crazy." He stroked her hair.

Come dripped from the head of his cock, coating her tongue. She thrived on the deep groan that rose up from his belly.

Outside, she heard a car pass on the macadam, the shush of tires and air rushing between the vehicles.

Connor pulled up her skirt and caressed her butt, sliding along the edge of her daring thong panty. She gushed moisture and need and took him as deep as he would go, her lips brushing her fisted hand as she worked him with her tongue and mouth.

A litany of dirty words fell from his mouth. She cupped his balls. They were tight and hard in her palm. Squeezing, she milked him to a stupendous erection.

"Shit, Faith." Over her head, she felt him yank the wheel, step on the brakes, and the car rolled to a stop. Both hands free now, he held her head, guided her with words and motions. "Fuck me, baby, please fuck me. Make me come."

He was close, throbbing in her mouth, and suddenly it wasn't enough just to taste him or swallow him. She wanted all of him.

She let his cock fall from her lips and looked up. Need etched lines into his face.

"I want inside you," he whispered. "Now."

She wanted it just as badly. Pushing him back against the seat, she climbed over him, spread her legs, wedging her body down between his belly and the steering wheel. His cock was hard and heavy against her aching clitoris, and she yanked the edge of her thong aside to slide along the full length of him.

"Jesus, baby." That was all he said, holding her by the arms, arching his cock against her.

Power flowed through her. "Do you want to fuck me, Connor?"

"Jesus, please."

He'd pulled the car to the side on a deep curve, facing the uphill, a long stretch of road bearing down on them. Anyone driving down would see them. So would anyone coming up the hill.

"Right here, Connor? Where anyone can see us?"

"Yes, Jesus, God, Faith, I wanna fuck you here and now."

She plunged down on him hard and almost screamed it was so good. He rammed up to meet her, the friction incredible, unbearable. Then they simply pounded at each other. She couldn't think, only feel, the hard glide of flesh inside her, the bite of his fingers on her upper arms.

She panted and ground and wanted and took as if he were her prisoner. Hers. Sensation built and rocketed to her nerve endings, her body just short of orgasmic contraction. Then a horn honked, and she opened her eyes to a truck headed straight for them, a face, male, through the windshield, and she screamed, long, loud, unstoppable. As unstoppable as the orgasm that rolled through and dragged her under like an ocean wave.

SHE was pregnant. He goddamn knew it. He'd blown so high and so hard, his sperm couldn't help but reach their destination this time. Connor wanted to reach out and touch her stomach, caress the new life that had to be growing inside.

The idea of *his* child inside her didn't scare him the way it had in the boardroom, and this new emotion inside him had nothing to do with falling in love with his wife. Love wasn't something he was capable of. But damn, he would give Faith this, his total commitment to fatherhood.

"Do you think he knew what we were doing?" Faith was safely back in her seat and his cock tucked inside his trousers. He didn't hear any sirens on the road behind them.

Connor laughed. "Hell yes, the guy knew. He was probably unzipping his pants to whack off as he rounded the corner."

They'd been in plain view. He hadn't intended to take her there. He just didn't want to cause an accident when he blew to kingdom come in her mouth.

Je-sus. Somehow, since Saturday night, she'd given herself over to him. Anything he wanted. Anything *she* wanted. She ordered him to go down on her in his office. She blew him while he was driving in broad daylight, then fucked the hell out of him in direct line of sight of oncoming traffic.

Thank God it hadn't been a mom and her underage kids. The truck driver, on the other hand, had given Connor the high five.

She curled up in the passenger seat, sliding her feet beneath her, and smiled at him. "That was very naughty," she said. "Don't do it again."

He had so many things he wanted to do to her. Her willingness to drop her barriers humbled him. Her trust moved him. As if the prenuptial agreement itself were a barrier, once it was gone, she'd released her remaining inhibitions with it.

He wouldn't hurt her. He might not be able to love her, but he would never hurt her. He needed to give her something to seal that unspoken promise, something just for her.

Connor smiled to himself. He knew the perfect thing.

16

FAITH had taken to heart Connor's belief that she should have more of a "relationship" with her relatives. Thus, on Friday, only a week later, here she was at the Bell Tower Café having lunch with Josie *and* Dora. The restaurant was in an old renovated church. One had to reserve a week in advance to dine in the bell tower itself, so instead, they sat in the courtyard beneath some shady trees. Great, except for little seeds (or something—*eewwe*), which kept dropping into her Chinese chicken salad. Faith picked out yet another . . . thing.

"So you like being a project manager at Castle?" Despite having to make small talk every day with parents, teachers, yadda yadda, Faith had never been comfortable with chitchat. The discomfort grew even worse because Josie was her *blood* relative.

"I love it." Josie speared a piece of tomato on her Gorgonzola salad, picked off one of those damn seeds, and glared at her fork. "Maybe we should ask to be moved inside."

"They come off trees and are therefore natural, so they have to be good for you," Dora said. "So just eat them."

They groused more like sisters than mother and daughter. Josie was a year younger than Faith, but with her pixie haircut and boyish figure, she looked barely out of her teens.

"And Connor wants to put me in charge of one of the big projects, like the Dominican job." She rolled her vibrant green eyes beneath long, lush lashes Faith envied. "Except for your dad. He's trying to nix the deal, thinks I can't do it."

Why *was* Connor so interested? First he wanted Faith to be

friends with her, now he advocated putting her in charge of a project Faith's father didn't think she was capable of doing.

"I'm sorry." Faith really didn't know what else to say.

Josie flapped a hand. "Connor'll fix it eventually."

He had one ally at Castle, but Faith felt a twinge.

"How's everything, ladies?" Their waiter tucked a tray beneath his arm.

"These trees suck." Josie beamed at him with a sweet smile.

The man, at least ten years older than her yet obviously captivated, gave a goofy, apologetic grin. "Sorry. I'll put out the umbrella."

He dragged a green canvas sunshade to the side of the table, tilted it on its wood stand, and sheltered them from the trees.

"You're a total doll. Thank you." Josie gave him another of those sunbeam smiles, and he wandered off bemused.

"If you turn some of that charm on Jarvis, he'd let you have the Dominican job." Dora dipped a chicken bite into a side dish of lime juice. That's all she had, greens, grilled chicken, and lime dressing. Her eating habits were more outlandish than Trinity's. "Though why you'd want to travel to godforsaken places to see *gravel trucks*," she went on, "I'll never know."

"Mom, they're not gravel trucks. They're earthmovers and all this really cool stuff."

"But the mines are in the middle of nowhere without modern conveniences."

"They have flush toilets, Mom."

While the headquarters of the companies her father dealt with were in major cities, the mines themselves were often out in the boonies. It *was* kind of cool that Josie got to go to them.

"I think I'm jealous," Faith said, a smile on her lips to let her cousin know it was a good envy. "You get to see so much more than the normal tourist would see."

"But Faith." Dora lowered her voice. "There's *no* shopping. Zippo. Zilch." She added a throat-slashing gesture in case they didn't get the immensity of the issue.

Josie wore blue jeans and a T-shirt emblazoned with "Your village lost their idiot. Shall I let them know we found you?" Faith didn't think Josie cared much about shopping.

Josie leaned forward and studied Faith with a steady gaze. "Faith, this is a very important question. Do you love to shop?"

"Umm." She looked from Dora's sleeveless designer knit to Josie's T-shirt. Was there a right answer? Then she saw the twinkle in Josie's eye. "I'd have to say I hate shopping."

Dora gasped. "You two received the wrong chromosomes. Faith, I was hoping you would be a *good* influence on Josie."

Josie had the eye roll down to an art. "Really, she loves me just the way I am. Don't ya, Mom?"

Dora merely propped her chin on her hand and changed the subject completely. "Did you like the dress Connor brought home for you from our trip?"

"Yes, it was lovely." And totally debauched. Faith couldn't wait to wear it again and relive the memories it evoked.

"I picked it out," Dora announced.

Josie almost snorted her milk out her nose. "You did not, Mom. You just seconded his opinion. And even if you said you hated it, Connor would have bought it anyway. He'd already made up his mind." She tipped her head to Faith. "I have a feeling that man doesn't change his mind easily once it's made up."

Faith couldn't say for sure. She'd only been married to him two months. Josie seemed to know him better than she did.

That fact grated along Faith's nerves.

"Honey, you don't know the man as well as you think you do." Dora snapped her chin up haughtily, and for the first time, all the banter between mother and daughter didn't seem so sweet.

"What's *that* supposed to mean, Mom?"

Yeah, Faith wanted to add, *what does that mean*?

Dora merely zipped her lip, glancing at Faith as she did so. "Nothing. I've said enough."

"No, Mother, you need to finish what you were going to say."

Faith couldn't stand the arguing anymore. "Really, Dora, if you've got something to say about Connor, then say it."

She asked for it, yet her heart was beating far too fast, just as it had when she'd told Trinity to speak up. Trinity had left several messages over the past few days, but Faith kept missing her on the return calls. Maybe that wasn't bad. She hadn't wanted her friend guessing her change in feelings about Connor. A lot of good it did to avoid it with Trinity when she'd somehow fallen into *this* discussion.

Dora put her hand over Faith's. The gesture didn't comfort her. "You shouldn't have gotten rid of the prenuptial. A woman needs protection. Some men"—she punctuated with a meaningful shrug—"have that wandering eye."

"I don't think Connor does." Faith wanted to believe that with all her heart. "Besides, I can still divorce him if I catch him doing something he shouldn't."

"Yes, but California is a community-property state, and he'll still get half of *your* five percent share in the company."

Faith hadn't thought of that. "He knows it doesn't belong to him."

"I hate to bring it home, honey, but that's why he married you. And it will upset the whole balance of power at Castle."

Josie's jaw tensed. "Mom, just drop it, okay?"

Faith couldn't let it go. "Connor's not going to cheat on me. I'll get pregnant, and everything's going to be fine."

Dora gave her such a look, emphasized by a slow, sad shake of her head. *You poor deluded child.* "Faith, if you hadn't dissolved the agreement, I wouldn't *dream* of telling you this."

"Mom, I said stop it."

Dora didn't listen to Josie. "Faith, honey, he had a woman in his room when we were down in South America."

Her stomach burned all the way up into her throat. Trinity had said the same thing.

Josie slapped down her glass, splashing milk over the table. "That is bullshit. You're just spreading rumors."

Dora gave Josie the same sad look. "I saw it, sweets. It was the *wrong* kind of business, if you know what I mean."

This time Josie grabbed Faith's hand and squeezed. She felt as if she were being sucked into a meat grinder.

"Don't you believe it, Faith. Whatever was going on, it wasn't what Mother thinks. At the end of every meeting, he *always* had to rush out to call you. He's not cheating."

Her hands felt numb, her heart seemed heavy in her chest, and she had a piercing pain right above her left eye. Maybe she had an aneurysm that was ready to burst. Why did Josie want to defend Connor? Why did Connor want to promote Josie? Why, why, why? Who was in those goddamn pictures someone kept putting on her doorstep? And what about the times he came home with whiskey on his breath and said he'd been out to drinks with an associate?

All she had to do was ask him, yet she was terrified to. She'd fallen in love and become so insecure about her marriage that she couldn't ask her husband. She could fuck him, but she couldn't talk to him. God. What was she supposed to believe?

Faith didn't realize she'd closed her eyes until she opened them again. That really wasn't the question. What did she truly believe in her heart if she stopped listening to other people's slurs? She thought of him demanding her father's apology on her behalf, his announcement at the club that *she* was a woman worthy of taking in the piano lounge. Connor himself hadn't said or done a single thing to give her doubts about him.

"I believe in Connor."

"But, Faith honey—"

"I'm not saying you're lying, Dora, but you're wrong about what you saw."

Josie beamed that high-wattage smile again. "You're making the right choice, Faith. He's going to be good for Castle, just you wait and see."

"Do you want me to talk to him about making sure

you're in charge of that big project?" Faith couldn't re-member the name.

Josie blushed. "That's not why I'm standing behind him."

"I know." Faith was going to believe in Connor, and part of that was knowing his comments about Josie were be-cause he admired her abilities, nothing more. "I'll lend my support in any way I can." She pressed Josie's hand, then turned to Dora. "Thanks for caring enough to tell me what you thought I should know."

"Faith, I don't want to hurt you."

"I know that, too. And I'm not going to be hurt."

Instead, she was going to believe in her husband. How could she get hurt if she did that?

DAMMIT, he was grinding his teeth to the dentin. Jarvis breathed deeply. His doctor said he needed to avoid stress. With Kingston in his life, he was anything but stress-free.

Jarvis snapped his wrist out despite the crack in his joint and flipped over his watch. Where the hell was the man? One fifty-five PM. Five more minutes, and he'd officially be late.

The dining room was clearing out. Jarvis had specifi-cally chosen a late lunch so they wouldn't be surrounded.

Faith. How could she do that without telling him first? She always consulted him—until Kingston came into their lives. Everything was topsy-turvy. Why, Jarvis yelled at her yesterday. Called her an idiot. It was unforgivable, but he'd done it. That's the havoc Kingston wreaked. Coming between Jarvis and his daughter. But even if he was wrong, how dare Kingston demand an apology? He would pay for that humiliation.

At last Kingston sauntered in and sat in the opposite chair. Their waiter snapped the napkin and handed it to him.

"I've been waiting for fifteen minutes," Jarvis groused.

"Then you shouldn't have gotten here twenty minutes early."

They ordered, Kingston barely looking at the menu and

choosing only a turkey sandwich where Jarvis wanted the filet mignon. Well, dammit, he wasn't going to help the whippersnapper make his cost-reduction goals by cutting down on his lunch expenses. He ordered the filet *and* a side of broccoli, which his doctor would love.

"It's damn lucky I did arrive early," Jarvis went on as if their conversation hadn't been sidetracked for several minutes.

Kingston arched one eyebrow. He really was quite a handsome man. It was no wonder Faith fell for his line of bullshit. Women were so easily taken in by a pretty face. Jarvis almost snorted aloud. So were men. "I've heard a lot about you."

"What," Kingston mocked, "have you taken to skulking in the lobby now?"

Jarvis ignored the insult. "Seems you've been dipping your wick in the wrong places."

"Dipping my wick." The young man sipped his water. "I like that. It's a nice, old-fashioned euphemism. My wick, however, has only burned on the proper occasions with the appropriate"—he smiled broadly—"candleholder in attendance."

Jarvis didn't like the reference. It was unseemly to discuss Faith and . . . wicks. "Davis told me you'd been *seen*."

Davis was his lawyer. The man claimed he tried to talk Faith out of tearing up the agreement, otherwise Jarvis would have fired him. Davis Sr., however, would have called Jarvis first, but he'd give Davis Jr. one more chance for loyalty's sake. Besides, it would be a pain in the ass to change attorneys.

"And Davis actually saw me?"

"He heard it from an acquaintance."

Kingston's eyes darkened to obsidian and the hardness of diamonds. "Who was the acquaintance?"

Jarvis shrugged. "How the hell should I know?"

"I'm not cheating on her." Kingston leaned in. "I will never cheat on her."

Jarvis let his breath hiss through his teeth. "If you do,

you're out." He reached to his inner pocket, pulled out the reason for this friendly lunch, and tossed it on the table.

The *new* agreement. Jarvis was so looking forward to this.

Kingston let it lay there as their meals arrived.

"It guarantees your percentages if you meet your objectives, as we agreed the first time," Jarvis offered, waiting until the boy grabbed for it. Yet he didn't.

"What's the catch this time, Jarvis?"

"What do you mean?"

"You're too pleased with yourself for there not to be a catch." Kingston bit into his sandwich and chewed as if he were unconcerned.

He damn well better be concerned. Since he wasn't going for the bait, Jarvis would have to tell him. "I've thought it over."

"The cost objectives?"

"The agreement. I don't think we need one anymore."

Kingston's jaw tensed. Ah, good, a reaction now. "Why not?" he asked in the same calm tone belied by that muscle tick.

"Because I've decided there's no reason you should have a share in Castle."

His nostrils widened as he let out a breath. He was getting the picture. "Should I remind you that if Faith and I divorce, I get half her shares? Community-property laws and all."

That was all Kingston wanted from the beginning, but Jarvis had a delightful surprise for the man. "You've miscalculated. Faith's shares are in a trust that *isn't* subject to those laws."

The man's obsidian-dark eyes flared with rage, and his cheek muscles rippled. Otherwise, Kingston was perfectly calm. "Touché, Jarvis. Do you expect my resignation now?"

"It would be nice."

"Sorry. I'll be at work tomorrow as usual. We still have Herman Green to discuss."

Jarvis felt his own flare of anger. "I could fire you."

His son-in-law smiled. For some reason, it chilled

Jarvis's bones. "Under the terms of my employment contract, you can only get rid of me for embezzlement, fraud, or negligence."

Jarvis grinned. "Yes. And isn't it the board that defines negligence?" There was an air of legitimacy about that, but they both knew who controlled the board. "Not to worry, you're married to my daughter, and I wouldn't want you unemployed."

He was going to enjoy making the boy's life a living hell. He picked up the agreement and stuffed it back in his pocket.

"This has nothing to do with how I treat Faith, whether I cheat on her or I don't. You simply don't like that I disagree with your management style."

With sudden, inexplicable anger, Jarvis wanted to pound his fist on the table. "My *style* has worked for thirty-five years."

"That's the problem. It's an anachronism."

Asshole. But Jarvis wasn't going to lower himself with insults. "You're free to bring any proposals for cost reduction or productivity improvement to the board for approval." He gave Kingston a beatific smile. "If we deem them worthy, I'm sure you'll get the necessary votes."

"Thank you for your support, Jarvis."

Jarvis studied his fingernails. "It's easy, you know. Make me like you, and perhaps I'll support everything you want to do."

Kingston picked up his sandwich again, but spoke before he took a bite. "If you don't support the things I want to do, Jarvis, your company is going down. It's only a matter of time."

"Is that a threat?"

"No. It's merely a fact. Green Industries and project cost overruns will destroy you. You're already drowning, Jarvis; you just don't know it yet."

Jarvis realized he hadn't touched a bite of his filet, and Kingston was almost done with his lunch. Dammit, the boy had put him off his meal while Jarvis had planned for the whole thing to be the other way round.

*   *   *

PRESTON sipped his neat whiskey and leaned back in his comfy chair, the view of his table obscured by a row of potted plants. Jarvis hadn't even known he was in the dining room. Preston slipped his wallet back in his pocket.

Some waiters were only too happy to report back on interesting conversations, especially when the price was right.

Well, well, well. That was an outstanding bit of drama between the son-in-law and darling daddy.

Preston was sure he could use it to his advantage. Dora, sweetheart that she was, wanted Connor out because he was going to crush poor Faith's heart. Dora also preferred the devil she knew to the devil she didn't. Connor had refused to authorize payment for her spa days, salon trips, and wardrobe costs, which she claimed she needed to maintain the perfect director image.

On the other hand, Preston saw an opportunity. Connor struck him as the take-the-money-and-run type. With him on their side, they might be able to oust Jarvis and sell the company right out from under the old bastard.

Preston would like nothing more than to be rid of his blasted cousin. If Jarvis was a reasonable man, well, things might have been different. Jarvis, however, hadn't seen reason since his wife died over twenty years ago.

Preston smiled. Yes. Very, very interesting possibilities were laid out before him like a feast. All it would take was for Connor to convince his wife to let him vote her shares.

WHO was spreading the talk, dammit? Someone who wanted Connor out of the way? Problem was too many people wanted him gone. Dora Tybrook had gone ballistic when he wouldn't sign her expense voucher for the day spa, though Dora's version of ballistic was silence for five seconds, narrowed eyes, a huffed breath, then the phrase "You'll be sorry." There was Nina, the rest of the board, Lance, Herman Green, even Trinity, if she still believed he'd hurt Faith.

Last but not least, there was Jarvis himself. At lunch today, the old man had screwed him but good. Since there was no longer an agreement, Connor could be fired at any time for negligence, as defined by Jarvis, and he wouldn't be awarded his 5 percent share for any cost reduction goals he met. Connor hadn't seen that one coming; why, he couldn't say. He should have known Jarvis was close to the edge. Faith's dissolution of their agreement had pushed him over. Or maybe it was the business with Green Industries. Connor had plans for correcting that problem he knew damn well and good Jarvis wouldn't approve.

Truth of the matter was he had one real chance against Jarvis now: Faith's proxy votes. He could probably get the rest of the board to go along with his new proposals, but he couldn't beat out Jarvis. The old man was determined to make his life suck even if it meant ignoring problems. Whatever the hell was going on with Green's product, quality was in the crapper, and Castle was sinking under the weight of cost overruns on the major projects. Jarvis had hosed him for sure, but the old man also stood to hose the whole damn company as well.

Unless Connor convinced Faith to let him vote her shares instead of her father. He could turn things around; he *knew* it. Castle would one day belong to his children, and he wasn't going to let Jarvis screw it up for them.

Tonight, however, he wouldn't worry about the company, about her shares, or about Jarvis. Faith was a totally separate issue from Castle Mining. And tonight, he was all hers.

He'd iced the champagne in the bucket that room service provided and chilled the two glasses. When Faith needed sustenance, a plate of fruit and cheese sat on the table beside it. He could have seduced her at home, but he wanted something special. The Fairmont in San Jose was a short drive and presented the elegance he required.

She would arrive in a few minutes.

He laid the video camera in the center of the comforter where she couldn't miss it. Connor wondered how she'd handle it.

17

"WE'RE going to make a movie."

Faith stared at the bed—and the video camera in the middle of it. "What kind of movie?"

He tipped her chin with his index finger. "Of us."

"Oh." She felt queasy. Nerves. Excitement. The need to jump his bones right this minute. But without the camera showing all her flaws.

He'd called her midafternoon and told her to meet him at the Fairmont at seven. When she'd asked what she should wear, he'd simply told her, "Something hot."

Faith took that to mean low-cut and no panties. Choosing a clingy top that showed her pert nipples and a long black skirt, she'd paired demure with brazen. When she didn't see him in the hotel lobby, she'd called his cell phone, and he gave her a room number. She started to pulse deep inside before she even made it on the elevator. He was always coming up with surprises.

But a camera. It made her think too much about the photos on the doorstep. Faith closed her eyes and shoved the thought away. She trusted him. Completely.

"Do you have a script?" she asked.

A lecherous half smile spread across his mouth. Tapping his temple, he said, "It's up here."

Faith badly wanted to take the lead, because she knew that's what Connor loved, but once again, he had her off balance. "And how does it start?"

"You turn around and let me see your outfit."

Closing her eyes, she turned slowly on boots with a four-inch heel. They'd made her hot the day she tried them on in the shoe store, and she'd saved them for just such an occasion.

Stopping, she cocked a hip, resting her hand on it, her head tipped to the side. A marvelous idea came to her. "You were lucky you called when you did. Because there was a man down in the lobby who couldn't take his eyes off my breasts." She cupped herself, then flitted a finger over one tightly beaded nipple.

"Faith, honey, most men can't take their eyes off your breasts." He reached out to caress the other nipple.

It was such a curiously erotic sensation, the two of them touching her at once.

"Most men"—he stepped closer still until his body heated her even through his suit jacket—"want to lay you down on the carpet and ravage you the moment they lay eyes on you."

A flash of worry nailed her insides. How far would he take this whole kinkiness thing? As far as having her sleep with other men? No. He'd promised right in the beginning that it would be only them. This was fantasy, exciting if she let go of all her worries. "Would you want to watch?" she murmured.

He wagged a finger. "Only *I* get to do you." Then he leaned in for a husky whisper. "But they can watch."

He knew exactly what to say, fueling kinky fantasies yet making her feel that she was the only one he wanted. Her breasts ached for his mouth, and she rubbed against him. The scent of aftershave and seductive male hormones rose to tantalize her.

"Strip," he breathed against her ear.

She was oh-so-willing. Until Connor backed off and reached for the camera.

She shook her head. "Not yet."

He pouted like a child. "Why, baby?"

Oh my God, she was really getting to like that little endearment. "Because . . ." She couldn't think of an excuse for almost a second. "Because I want to be naked and spread out on the bed when you turn it on."

He slid an arm across her back and hauled her against him. "Jesus, Faith, you make me crazy saying things like that."

She made herself crazy, too. She wasn't quite sure she could pull it off. "Pour me some champagne while I undress."

There was an art to stripping Faith didn't have, yet Connor was transfixed as she propped a foot on the bed and slid the skirt to her knee to unzip the boot. "Don't spill," she teased.

Connor licked a drop from the flute.

The skirt was a sensuous slide as she raised it a second time to remove the other boot. They both landed with a *thunk* at his feet where she tossed them. Hmm, now what? She wasn't wearing panties, but she was wearing a bra. Turning her back, she tugged the zipper down until warm air brushed her backside.

She hadn't heard him move, but he was suddenly up against her, reaching round to put the glass to her lips. "Drink."

It was fresh and tasted faintly of almonds. He gave her another sip before he backed off. Knowing he watched, she wriggled her hips, then let the skirt glide down her thighs to pool on the carpet.

"You're not wearing panties."

She looked over her shoulder and fluttered her eyelashes. "I don't like panties anymore. I threw all of mine out."

When he got hot, his eyes went dark and his lids lowered. He was burning up now, his slacks stretching over his erection. Faith bent over the bed, lifted one leg, then the other, climbing atop on all fours. Before she had a chance to stop him, he dribbled champagne down her butt cheeks, then swooped in to suck it off, sneaking one finger along her pussy.

"Christ, you're wet."

She could come just from that note of awe in his voice.

Rising fully to her knees, she swiped her top over her head and threw it behind her. Connor laughed. She so wanted to turn around and look at him, but she was putting on a show.

What would turn him on the most? What would make him lose control? She could do anything if she kept that goal in mind, driving Connor mad. She just didn't know how she'd feel when he finally turned the camera on.

Undoing the front clasp of her bra, she held the cups apart. "My breasts are so sensitive," she said as if she were talking to herself. Moving her hands, she traced the aureoles. And moaned. Then she flipped the bra off her shoulders and let it fall. She felt the material drift across her calves as Connor grabbed it.

"Oh, I'm so hot," she whispered, and did exactly what she would have done if she were alone. Sliding both hands down over her abdomen, she reached a finger inside the curls at her apex and stroked herself, arching into her own touch. "Oh yeah."

Then she went down on all fours once again, spread her legs slightly, and reached back to slide a finger inside. In this position, Connor could see everything.

"You're beautiful, baby."

Faith knew she was. "You can turn the camera on, honey."

"Sweetheart, it's already on."

"I knew that." *Not.* She glanced over her shoulder to find him studying the viewfinder. Her heart stuttered in her chest. "Are we going to watch this movie later?"

He gave her such a look, head down, only his eyes rolling up to gaze at her. "What do you think?"

God. Didn't they say the camera added ten pounds? She could do it. She had to since she'd promised him she'd push her limits. Still, her stomach quaked to think about watching her own body. "It can't all be me; you have to be in it, too." She flapped her hand. "Come on. Give me that thing, then strip."

"You're a demanding bitch."

For a moment, the word shocked her, like the first time he talked dirty. He raised that devilish eyebrow, and a smile hovered on his lips. She couldn't resist him. "You love it when I'm demanding," she answered. "You're a closet submissive."

"And you're a closet dominatrix." He gave her the camera and proceeded to strip, just as she told him to.

Her mouth dried up with each layer of clothing he tossed aside until the bare skin of his chest mesmerized her.

"You're not watching the camera, sweetheart. You're probably taking a picture of my navel."

"I like your navel." She centered on his chest, then moved down to his slacks as he unzipped. It was the oddest sensation, like looking at him from afar. "Your cock looks so small."

"Hey, I resent that."

"Don't worry, honey, it still works okay." The enormity of the moment hit her. She was teasing and taking pictures of her naked husband, and she wasn't the least bit self-conscious. It was yet another wonderful thing Connor had done for her.

Yet he was such a magnificent male specimen, she didn't want to think what she'd look like next to him on camera.

Connor grabbed her foot and pulled her to the end of the bed, messing up the covers.

Faith squealed and laughed, and the camera lens went all over the place. "What are you doing?"

"Give me that thing." With him being so much taller, she couldn't hold the camera out of his reach. Stepping between her legs, he aimed straight down. "Now *that* is a beautiful thing. All pink and pretty and wet."

Her face flamed. It was the compliments, not the embarrassment. He always said the most astonishing things.

Parting her, he stroked up, down, and around her clitoris, then dipped inside. Her body filled with moisture, and her hips seemed to move on their own. Watching through the viewfinder, he smiled. "Ah hell, you just flooded my fingers, baby."

"You can't take close-ups of my . . ." She hesitated, searching for a word that made her feel the least uncomfortable.

"Your pussy? Vagina? Honeypot? Sweet little cunt?"

With each word he said, he hit a sensitive spot deep inside. Faith bit her lip to keep from moaning. "Not the last one."

He glanced at her. "There's nothing wrong with calling your beautiful honeypot a cunt. You have the most gorgeous cunt."

"*Eewwe.*" But she writhed on the bed as he adored her *gorgeous cunt*.

"Then pick something you do like," he urged.

Vagina was too clinical, *honeypot* too ridiculous. "*Pussy* works for me." The sentence started on a moan and ended on a gasp as he pushed two fingers inside her.

"I adore your pussy," he whispered to the camera. Pulling his finger back out, he slid along her lips, holding her open, exposing the hard nub of her clitoris. "Touch yourself."

God, she couldn't help doing what he said. She wanted someone's finger right *there*, even if it was her own. They worked her together, Connor dipping inside to gather her juices and caress her pussy lips, her own finger working the bead of her clit. She was wet and hot, her hips rising. Tossing her head back and forth on the bed, she needed to come. Badly.

"Connor, eat me now, please." She bucked and rose against the combined touch. Yet before he could even move, she shot high into orgasm, screaming and clawing her way through it.

When she could open her eyes, he'd set up a tripod and angled the camera to take in the bed. Faith held out a hand. "Give it to me. I want to watch." Just because she came once, didn't mean he got out of making her come with his tongue.

Something deep and blazing flamed in his eyes.

Dragging her down to the end of the bed, he knelt, pushing her thighs wide to accommodate him, then raised her legs to his shoulders. He blew on her and she could barely keep the camera trained on his dark head.

"Suck me, Connor. Hard. Lick every inch of my pussy and make me come." The words were for him, the camera, herself. The dirty talk sent another surge of heat and moisture to her center.

For the camera, he gave a big, white-toothed smile. "Keep talking, baby." Then he spread her with his fingers and sucked her clitoris, tonguing her hard. She almost shot off the bed.

"Oh yeah," she murmured. "Lick me just like that. Right in the center." Telling him what to do was so damn exciting, far beyond merely letting him do it. Words could hold such power.

He cupped her butt and lifted her to his mouth. On the screen, his head bobbed and her body undulated. Powerfully erotic, the physical sensation combined with the sight made her pant and climb to orgasm faster than ever. He opened his eyes to stare in the camera, and it was the oddest feeling, detached, yet as if he were deep inside her with every fiber of his being.

She rose and fell, and finally, when she couldn't stand it anymore, she pushed her head back into the mattress and screamed through her orgasm. The contractions went on and on, mastering her completely, until she came down and realized his fingers were deep inside, her body milking them in the last throes.

And the camera was now in his hands.

"That was good, baby."

God yes. So good she couldn't even manage to speak.

"I wanna watch my cock slide inside you." He stood and pulled her legs to his waist. "Lock your feet behind my back."

Following instructions was the most she could do right now. The camera in one hand, he stroked his cock up and down her slit, coating himself with all her moisture. Then he guided himself into her tender, sensitive pussy. Slowly.

"Christ," he murmured, "that looks so fucking good. As if you're swallowing me whole."

His cock filling her, his words stroking her mind, she almost hit her orgasm right then. Yet he pulled out as slowly as he'd entered until only the tip of his crown breached her, their only connection. "Jesus, Faith, it's so fucking beautiful."

He pulled out, then worked his cock in his hand until a bead of come coated his tip. He rubbed it over his crown. Faith's mouth watered. She reached, but instead of allowing her to touch, he started that slow, inexorable penetration all over again.

"Later," he murmured. "Right now, I want this."

The last millimeter, he slammed home, the camera bobbing. Faith moaned and arched, rubbing herself against his pubic ridge. He repeated the act over and over until she thought she'd gone mad and tears of need leaked from the corners of her eyes.

"Fuck me hard, Connor. I need it. Fast and hard and deep. Please, baby, please."

After planting the camera on the tripod, he pushed her higher on the bed, angling her for the right view through the lens, and finally, finally climbed on top to take her just the way she wanted. Already close, she flew off into outer space, screaming her orgasm against his mouth. She didn't know when he came, all she felt was the pound of his body straight up to her heart, the clean, sweaty smell of maleness, and his voice at her ear driving her over the edge again.

THAT was so fucking perfect, Connor had trouble moving a muscle for long minutes. Faith lay motionless against the comforter, her arms outstretched, her hair fanned about her head, and her eyes closed.

He stroked a few stray strands of her gorgeous red locks back off her forehead, then nuzzled her ear with his nose. "Died and gone to heaven?" he whispered.

"Mmm." She purred in her throat for him, but didn't move.

As he untangled their limbs and climbed off the bed, she whimpered. "Where are you going?"

"I'm plugging the camera in. I want to watch."

That got her undivided attention. Naked and glorious, she rolled onto one elbow, her breasts plump and enticing. Christ, he should have fucked her that way and come all over her throat. She had the perfect breasts for it. Ah, but they had all night.

"We're going to watch it on the TV?"

He almost smiled. She had that squirrel-about-to-be-squashed-by-a-Mack look. "Yeah, baby, we're going to watch on the TV because the viewfinder is too small."

"Oh. Of course." Though she didn't look convinced that it *had* to be done that way.

"Besides, I want to play with you while we watch."

"You mean while you watch yourself go down on me."

He grinned as he plugged in the connector. "Now you've got it. The next orgasm will be even better than the last one."

She made a noise.

"What'd you say, honey?" The endearment amused him. It was so ordinary, as if they'd been married years instead of weeks.

"I said I don't think it could get much better."

He didn't believe that's what she said at all, but glancing up from the TV, he smiled, slow and lecherous. "Wait and see."

By the time he was done, she'd snuggled under the covers. He crawled in, wrapped her in his arms, then pointed the remote.

His dick came to immediate attention during the opening credits, Faith on her hands and knees fingering herself. Hot didn't begin to describe it. He had the sudden urge to roll on top of her and pound her into the mattress all over again.

She laughed during his striptease.

"I'm offended." He clutched his chest in mock affront.

"We could send you out for lessons."

Beneath the covers her nipples rose to hardened peaks as they watched him playing with her sweet pussy. God she'd been wet, so fucking wet. When, on-screen, they both started playing her, he slid a hand down between her legs and tested.

"You're wet, baby." He gently nipped her earlobe. "You love watching yourself play with that hot little cunt of yours."

"Pussy," she whispered.

He stroked her lightly. She opened her legs for him and settled deep against the pillows.

When she came on-screen, he'd raised the camera to her face.

"Look at yourself."

It was the most beautiful thing he'd ever seen, her lips parted, the delicious sound of her orgasm rolling off her tongue. Her skin flushed, her breasts jiggled. He reached up to cup her now, squeezing one nipple.

She gasped and pushed down into the mattress, her fingers crawling between her legs. He toed back the covers to watch. On the TV, she begged him to eat her and took control of the camera.

Holy hell, he'd almost lost it then, but he'd wanted her taste on his tongue more than anything in the world.

He leaned down to lick a nipple just as his face came down between her legs. "Can you feel it all over again, baby?"

Her hips wriggled, her fingers flew. The need to take over simmered, but more, he wanted to watch her excitement rise all over again. On the TV, his head bobbed between her legs.

"Fuck, that's hot." He nuzzled her ear. "Do yourself, baby, fuck yourself. I wanna see you come."

She moaned and writhed, both on-screen and off. Her body undulated, and he could still taste her in his mouth. Whispering in her ear, playing with her nipples, he had a hard-on fit for twenty women. She was so fucking into herself, into watching, into replaying exactly how his tongue felt on her.

She jolted, screamed, and came to the combined sound of her voice on the TV and the real thing filling the room. This was how he wanted her, needed her. Turned on out of her mind.

He held her in his arms as her shudders fell away.

"Oh, Connor, you were right. That was just as good the second time."

"Told you, baby. But damn, I forgot to get you on camera sucking my cock."

"Next time," she murmured, snuggling close as their next scene began.

SHE was so far from finished. Her body was on fire. Connor had barely touched her. She'd done all that herself.

"That felt so . . ." She glanced up at him and let herself go. "So fucking good."

He kissed her hard, taking her mouth as if he were conquering her. Oh Lord, how he made her melt.

"You're a naughty girl." He licked her throat, then rolled to his back. "We're missing the movie. I'll have to rewind."

She put her hand on his arm as he pointed the remote. "No. I want to see this part."

"But I want you to see the way your body sucks my cock inside." He gave her a crooked smile. "And very, very slowly."

She couldn't define how watching made her feel. It was like being a voyeur and an exhibitionist at the same time. It made her so hot, she didn't have time to be self-conscious. When he put his tongue to her clitoris on-screen, she *felt* it.

Connor was right. Their movie was beautiful. Though she'd never believed it before in her life, *she* was beautiful.

Oh God. For a moment, she loved him so damn much for giving this to her that it *hurt*.

"Is that what I really look like?"

Powerful, elemental, his magnificent penis slid slowly inside, stretched her. She was pink, her clitoris hard, her lips plump and full, taking him, all of him.

"That's exactly what you look like." He gathered her close, then wrapped her fingers around his cock, and together they idly stroked him to greater hardness. A bead of come pearled on the tip; he used it to wet the whole length.

He kissed her temple. "That's it, baby."

On-screen, they'd flipped from him standing between her legs to the tripod-mounted shot centered on the bed. She'd been so damn hot, she barely remembered this part.

Her eyes glazed almost the moment he entered her. She started to pant and moan, and her fingers dug firmly into his arms. Hooking a hand under her butt, he angled her and hit deep. She was sure that was the moment she'd started to come.

Connor squeezed her hand around his cock and quickened the pace. "God, baby, you were high then."

She was. High on his voice, his touch, his possession.

"Come on, baby," she could hear him whisper on-screen. "I love it when you come. You do it so good." His hands traveled the length of her, caressing, even as his cock pounded into her. "Come on, baby, hard, do it for me hard. Take me all the way." As if he were crooning a love song to her, he kept up a litany of words. She hadn't heard each individual syllable, but she'd felt the essence deep inside. "Yeah, baby, God, baby, please, baby."

When she cried out, he took her mouth, kissing her into oblivion. When he started his own come, he took her face in his hands and held her, his body pounding into hers, his gaze claiming her. And his words.

"God, Faith, please, Faith." Then her name over and over as he filled her. She could almost feel the throb of his cock in her pussy, the pulse of his semen shooting into her womb.

She hadn't understood it when he took her, but she recognized it now on the TV.

Connor had made love to her. In living color.

Faith slid down his body and took him in her mouth, sucking him, tasting him. He was hers. He thrust up against her, held her head down, begged her with his body to take him.

And she did. Every last drop. Everything he had to give. As she swallowed his essence, Faith knew the camera didn't lie. Connor didn't fuck her. He made love to her.

Yet she knew he wouldn't admit it. And she wasn't sure how long she could live with that.

18

"EVERYONE in favor of Connor's proposal?"

The entire board—except Jarvis—raised their hands.

"All opposed?" Jarvis raised his hand.

Another Monday morning and another great initiative bites the dust. Connor made a tick on his agenda. Meetings had gotten to the point where even minor decisions, such as altering a purchasing policy, had to be approved by the board. Jarvis had called three special meetings. All to mock Connor and exhibit his own omnipotence.

Unfortunately, it merely showed that Jarvis was an ass and not above costing the company money to prove a point.

Connor had married Faith for her father's company, yet over time, especially since that Fairmont trip a week ago, his days at Castle had become hell, while his nights at home with Faith had turned into heaven. Something had changed that night, though he couldn't pinpoint what. He only knew that the transformed Faith was infinitely desirable. She was the only thing that got him through the interminable day.

Yet Connor persisted. "We've got one more proposal on the agenda today."

Jarvis, seated at the head of the table as always, raised an eyebrow and glanced through the bifocals perched on his nose.

Preston made a show of shuffling his papers. Connor couldn't tell if the man had even bothered to read the proposal e-mailed to everyone. One of the Finches cleared his throat. Probably none of them had bothered to read since it was a foregone conclusion that Jarvis would turn down any proposal coming out of Connor's office.

Life at Castle Heavy Mining had gone to shit. He'd actually been better off at Green as a minor manager.

"Any statements before we vote?" Jarvis grinned. But for the glasses, he looked like a smiling death's head.

The so-called statement was a mere formality. Instead of wasting time trying to get buy-in, Connor went for the jugular. "Quality on Green products has now dropped off by 50 percent. Ignoring this problem is detrimental to Castle's health."

"I talked to Herman. He's done the testing *you* required"— meaning Jarvis didn't think it was necessary— "and the issue appears to be in the bonding process once the product gets here."

How would Herman deduce that? "That's bullshit, Jarvis."

"Excuse me?" The old man loved raising that eyebrow. He looked at the three ladies, Nina, Alexis Plumley, and Dora.

Connor was damn sure all three had heard the word before.

"Are you calling Hermie a liar, Kingston?"

Actually, he was calling Jarvis an idiot. Would the old man's hatred for Connor blind him to any threat?

Connor drove his point home. "Customers don't come back to Green when *someone's* bonding fails. They come to us. We're the ones looking like shit. It's on our backs, not Herman's."

Branson stroked his chin. "Are you sure Herman's done his due diligence on this issue, Jarvis?"

For several seconds, you could hear the clock ticking on the wall, then the beep of a car remote outside the window.

And Jarvis finally spoke. "He feels it's too coincidental that all the problems began when Kingston came on the scene."

Was that Herman or Jarvis talking out of his ass? "If Herman isn't willing to provide a better answer than that," Connor countered, "there are only two alternatives: find another source or do it in-house."

"That's bullshit." Spittle flew from Jarvis's mouth. "I will not turn my back on a forty-five-year relationship based on a spurious report by *Preston's* VP of Engineering."

"Biddle is *our* Engineering VP," Preston said, his calm voice in direct opposition to Jarvis's higher-pitched diatribe.

Gabriel Finch cocked his head and stared at Jarvis. Branson pushed slightly back from the table as if distancing himself. Nina tapped her lip with a crimson nail, her glance ping-ponging between Jarvis and Connor. The old man had never endeared himself to his family or his board, but Connor detected something new for the first time. Not only was Jarvis disliked, but his competency was in jeopardy.

"What are the details on the alternatives you've outlined, Connor?" Thomas opened his folder and pulled out the proposal.

"I'm running this meeting," Jarvis raised his voice.

"True," Richard Plumley said, "but we can ask questions."

As a whole, the board shut Jarvis down.

"I've outlined two proposals and the estimated costs of each. First, we find another supplier." They should have had a second supplier all along. You *never* have only one source. "We'll have to have new dies made, and there'll be costs involved with certifying a new contractor. That's all in the report."

"And the second alternative?" Preston asked. He'd been studying the numbers.

"We do it in-house."

"That's a huge capital outlay."

"True, but the return on investment is damn good once we're up and running."

"How quickly can that be accomplished?"

"Worst case, six months; best, we do it in three. The plating line will take the longest to set up and train on."

During the discussion, Jarvis sat silent except for the drum of his fingers. He'd tossed his bifocals on the table and regarded them all with narrowed eyes.

Then he smiled. "We've heard enough. Let's vote. All in favor, raise their hand."

"I make a motion to hold the vote until the next meeting while we do investigation." Preston wore his own evil smile.

"I second the motion," Branson added before Jarvis could say a word, as if the two had somehow rehearsed it.

"I don't ratify that motion," Jarvis snarled.

"Sorry, Jarvis, you don't get a choice." Cyril spoke for the first time. He was a quiet guy, but he was the corporate secretary and knew the bylaws. "A motion was put forward and seconded, and the vote will take place at the next meeting."

They'd outmaneuvered the old man. Amazing.

Of course, he'd vote the proposal down at the next meeting.

Unless Connor got his wife's proxies.

FAITH had called him in the meeting, his cell phone vibrating in its holder on his belt. He needed to call her back, but Christ, his head was pounding. In his office, Connor grabbed a bottle of water and downed three ibuprofen. What he needed was Faith's fingers massaging his temples. Or her mouth sucking his cock.

Funny, it used to be he needed a shot of whiskey and some solitude, but he hadn't been to his apartment in weeks, nor had he missed it. Maybe it was time to let the place go.

In the beginning, he'd imagined that handling Faith day in and day out would be the bigger of his problems when he married. Women could be high maintenance, though he'd done his best to choose a woman at the lowest end of that scale.

Damn if he hadn't chosen well, because it was his wife providing the refuge while the company drove him crazy. His desire for her hadn't waned.

Connor reached to his belt for his cell phone, then hit her speed dial.

"What are you doing?" Faith didn't even say hello.

"Just got out of a meeting."

"Are you in your office?"

"Yes."

"Is the door locked?"

"No." He glanced up. "It's still open."

"Lock it."

"Why?" She made him smile. She'd taken to issuing orders in and out of the bedroom. When she got like that, he knew damn well she had something sweet and sexy planned for him.

"I'm so hot, Connor, and my vibrator keeps calling my name, and I want you to talk me through an orgasm." She gave a plaintive little sigh.

He set the bottled water on his desk, idly turning it under his fingertip. "I'll be home soon."

"But Connor, honey, sweetie, baby, I need it now. I'll take care of you when you get home. Just do me over the phone."

His headache was gone. As easily as that. Her voice or her desire; it certainly wasn't the ibuprofen.

"Talk to me," she whispered, "while I stroke myself with my vibrator and put it inside and ride it . . ."

She trailed off. He wanted to unzip, pull out his dick, and start whacking to the sound of her voice.

The snick of the latch climbed his spine like a chill. Nina leaned against the closed door.

"Someone's just stepped into my office, baby. Why don't you keep it hot for me, and I'll be there pronto."

"Connor—" Faith stopped herself. "Can I give myself an orgasm to take off the edge?"

"No."

"Creep."

He grinned. *This* was how he wanted her. Playful, fun, hot. "I'll be home soon, baby. Promise."

She muttered another curse as he hit the end button.

"The wife?" Nina smiled slyly. "Or someone else?"

He liked Nina. She flirted, and if he'd shown an interest in doing her, she'd have jumped on it, but she didn't hold his vows against him. Odd that, since in South America, he'd feared his goose was cooked, or, at the very least, she'd try to make the job a living hell. But no, Jarvis was the one doing that.

"Faith, of course. There is no one else."

She tipped her head one way, then the other, as if trying to read him. Then a breath puffed out her lips. "My God, you're in love with her."

Her words hit him like a wallop to the solar plexus. For a second. Then the sensation melted away. What he had with Faith was far more sustainable than love. It was painless for both of them, all the upsides of hot sex and no emotional downsides.

However, it would be counterproductive to his plans to deny Nina's statement. In fact, admitting it might work in his favor. "You sound surprised."

"I didn't think you had it in you." She laughed. "I didn't think *Faith* had it in her."

Connor narrowed his eyes. "She's perfect. And I don't like people denigrating her."

Her eyebrows shot up. "Ooh. Said like a besotted man."

He wasn't besotted. He was totally in control. But he liked what he had with Faith. In fact, he'd rather be sliding deep inside her than standing here talking with Nina.

"What can I do for you?" He leaned against the desk.

Nina got down to business. "Is Jarvis getting Alzheimer's?"

Hmm, he hadn't expected that one. Not from Nina anyway.

"I have no idea."

"Are we really in danger over this thing with Green?"

"Yes, I believe we are. Individually, the teeth aren't expensive to fix. But in a customer's point of view, when he keeps having to deal with a piddling problem over and over, he gets pissed and walks."

"Why is Jarvis ignoring it?"

Because he hates my guts. "I have no idea."

He'd been here only months, but he'd never seen her without a twinkle in her eye and a flirty comment rolling off her lips. Her chest, which was already impressive, expanded with her deep breath. Then she tapped the door and opened it. "We'll have to figure out how to take care of the problem, won't we, Connor?"

She was gone. He didn't know what the hell that meant, nor did he care. The only thing he cared about was getting home before his wife exhausted herself with her vibrator and there wasn't anything left for him.

WHAT did that mean?

Jarvis wasn't used to hanging back and making himself invisible, yet he scuttled down the hall before anyone saw him eavesdropping.

Kingston and that bitch Nina were planning something. Figure out how to take care of what problem? Faith?

Jarvis ground his teeth. They were having an affair. Kingston was a cheat, a thief, and a liar. It probably started in South America, right under Jarvis's nose, even as the whippersnapper claimed he'd *never* cheat on Faith.

Thank God he'd hired that private investigator. He'd make sure the man got pictures. Faith would be done with Kingston, and somehow, Jarvis would find a way to buy out his contract and get him out of their lives forever.

"I'M on my way home, Preston."

Damn, his office seemed to have a revolving door. Nina went out, Tybrook came in only a few minutes later. Connor's headache returned.

Didn't these people get it? His wife was waiting at home with her vibrator at the ready. He had a duty to perform.

Connor almost grinned, but managed to keep it to himself.

"This will only take a minute, son."

"I'm not your son."

Preston waved a hand. "Right, sorry, figure of speech."

"What do you want, Preston?" Getting a person out the door as quickly as possible meant no beating around the bush.

"Just a talk, that's all."

Connor pointedly flipped his wrist to look at his watch. "My wife's expecting me."

At that, Preston smiled. "Ah, the little wife. Everything going well in paradise?"

As he'd told Nina, life with Faith was perfect. She was everything he could have hoped for. She didn't nag, and she made no demands. Except for sex. Exactly the way he wanted it.

"Paradise would describe it."

"Well, then, I've a little proposition for you." Without being invited, Preston sat in one of Connor's leather chairs.

Connor didn't make a move to take his own seat. "Preston, this will have to wait till tomorrow."

Again, the man smiled. "It would behoove you to listen to what I have to say now."

Connor crossed his arms. "You have five minutes."

Quirking a half smile, Preston crossed his legs and settled in. "I didn't like you at first."

"And you've changed your mind?"

"Jarvis changed my mind."

"Nice to know. What's the point?"

"Dora and I thought the company would be better off if you went back where you came from, wherever the hell that might be. I even did my share to make sure that happened." When Connor opened his mouth, Preston held up his hand. "A few well-placed rumors at the club about your supposed infidelities."

"So it was you."

Preston grinned. "Yes. But little Faith wouldn't hear a wrong word said against you."

Faith's support warmed his gut and pushed his headache away. Preston didn't seem to have a single compunction about using dirty pool, though. In a way, Connor had to admire him. He wasn't above a little dirty pool himself. "Thanks for the honesty. Now I know who to come to the next time it happens."

"Oh, I'm not the only one. Let's just say there are a few

others in our community who wouldn't mind being rid of you. But me"—Preston tapped his chest—"I've changed my mind. I think you and I can be of great assistance to each other."

Where this was going, Connor didn't have a clue, but he'd hear Preston out. "How?"

"Jarvis is going to run this company into the ground."

Connor shrugged. "He could have an agenda none of us understands." Connor had considered that if he himself were out of the way, Jarvis might very well get things back on track.

It was a big if, though, and project overruns had pre-dated Connor coming on the scene. Jarvis had been showing signs of losing his hold on the company for months.

"Jarvis's agenda has always been making sure he is king at Castle. If it's not his idea, it sucks the big one."

The euphemism didn't fit the dapper man before him, but Preston hit the nail on the head. "And your plan to stop him is . . . ?" Connor spread his hands.

"We vote him out and you in as chairman. We give you the five percent you want so you have equal voting power as everyone else on the board with the exception of Jarvis and myself."

Oh yeah. He knew right where this was going. "One big problem, Preston. With his forty-eight percent and the proxies for Faith's five, none of you can outvote him."

"But if Faith gives you the right to vote her shares . . ." Preston trailed off and quirked that half smile again.

"So you want me to turn my wife against her father."

Preston tut-tutted. "Not *turn against*. That sounds so ruthless and devious." Which is exactly what it was. "We just want to do what's best for all of us. You can solve the few issues we have, then wash your hands of the thing once we sell."

Like Pontius Pilate. He might have been shunted from foster home to foster home, but he had at some point learned his Bible tales from watching TV.

"You'll make a lot of money. You can get out."

"Out of what?" Connor asked. Not that he didn't know.

"The company." Preston paused significantly. "And anything else you want to get out of."

The implication being that he could get out of his marriage.

"Otherwise"—Preston spread his hands—"we all get nothing but the fire sale of the assets."

There was that possibility. If Jarvis went unchecked, the company wouldn't be worth more than the cluster of buildings and the assets, and those would just about cover the liabilities.

Granted, Preston was looking out for his own livelihood, but he had a point.

"I'll let you ponder. Talk it over with Faith. She'll see the logic of it. If you like, I can have Dora speak with her."

"No." He wasn't sure which part he was saying no to. In his gut, he knew Faith would never understand ousting her father.

Yet in the face of his vendetta against everything Connor represented, Jarvis had lost all sense of proportion. The tide couldn't be stemmed forever. Eventually, Castle Heavy Mining would pay the price. So would the family. As would Faith.

Preston was offering them all an alternative.

"The rest of the board will vote with you?" he asked.

Preston nodded. "Talk with each of them, if you'd like."

Of course he would. He wasn't simply taking Preston's word for it. Yet he knew that Nina's questions had been the precursor to this. "And when do you want to do it?"

"We have that meeting scheduled next week."

Connor drew a breath deep into his gut.

"You can walk away with all the money you could need and all the freedom you could ask for," Preston added as inducement.

Why the hell did they all think his only mission was to screw Faith, her father, and the company? *Duh.* Because they all knew he'd married her for her money. Once he had that, what did he really need Faith for?

Except that he did. His goal had never been just the

money. He'd be able to walk away from the company, but he couldn't walk away from the child he *knew* grew inside her even now.

Still, if he was to have a shot at getting it all, he had one week to get Faith's proxies. He told himself it was for the good of the company. For Faith. Even for Jarvis. Connor couldn't let Castle Heavy Mining go down the tubes, and if he left Preston to do his worst, the board might actually sell the company right out from under Jarvis.

He just wasn't sure Faith would understand why he needed to overthrow her father using *her* proxies in order to save it all.

Maybe the only way was not to tell her the real plan.

FAITH had grabbed her keys off the hall table and a coat out of the closet. It was short but covered the bare essentials. *Bare* being the operative word. All she wore was the coat.

She'd wanted to surprise Connor by having him find her lying on the bed with her vibrator. Waiting for him. Instead he'd surprised her with a phone call a half hour after she'd called him. Oddly enough, it was easy to do things like that. She was terrified to tell him she loved him, but she could get all sorts of kinky and sexy now with barely a twinge.

When he'd called her back, he'd given her an address and told her to meet him there, and she hadn't given herself time to dress or even put up her hair. It hung about her shoulders in waves. Connor liked it that way.

Driving in the car, she was hot and shivery. It had nothing to do with the weather and everything to do with the mind-blowing event he had planned this time. He'd promised their sex life would be exciting, and he hadn't let up for a moment.

She'd become obsessed. Trinity had called several times, and Faith still hadn't been able to get hold of her. Was that accidentally on purpose? She just knew she couldn't talk about Connor even with her best friend. As for looking at houses, she hadn't done that, either. Her life had suddenly become all about Connor, and she felt paralyzed when it came to anything else.

She stopped for a red light and imagined the guy in the 4x4 next to her could see she was naked under the coat. She wanted to put her hand between her legs and test how wet she was.

The light changed, and she surged forward, clutching the wheel, dying to get there.

She thought about sex all the time. Hadn't she read in some women's magazine that men thought about it every eight minutes? Or was it eight seconds? Whatever, she had them beat, because she thought about doing Connor *every* second.

Turning the corner onto a residential street, she glanced at the paper she'd written the address and directions on, then at the side of the apartment building. This was it. A cream-colored structure with two levels and parking underneath, it had a row of flowers in boxes along the walkway. Faith parked on the opposite side of the street.

As she climbed out and turned to shut the door, a car drove by and air rushed up her coat, billowing it. She quickly smashed it down, then couldn't resist a giggle.

Sitting in a car by a hydrant, a man glanced up from the newspaper he'd been reading. She wondered if she'd flashed him.

Faith had never done anything like this in her life. Connor had gotten her to go without panties, but without anything at all? Never. She felt like a movie starlet from the forties, draped in mink and nothing else. She couldn't remember the movie or the actress, just the mink pooled on the floor at her feet.

Faith had worn high heels, too.

She crossed the street, glanced at the apartment numbers, and found the one Connor had directed her to on the second floor. Her pulse raced. The beads of her nipples rasped against the coat. Hot, wet, trembling, she put a hand on the railing and climbed the steps.

Could the man in the car see her butt cheeks beneath the

coat? God. It gave her the most delicious thrill to imagine
he could, and she ascended with an extra sway to her hips.

She was turning into an exhibitionist. Wouldn't Connor
be pleased.

The curtains were drawn across the window, yet he
opened the door before she even knocked and grabbed her
arm.

"What took you so long?"

His lips, spiked with the tang of whiskey, crushed hers.
She went up on her toes, wound her arms around his neck,
and kissed him hard. Then she felt the rush of air once
again up her coat as Connor squeezed her butt.

"You're naked under there."

"You told me to get over here now." She smiled. "I didn't
have time to get dressed. My vibrator and I were waiting."

He hitched her closer, using her buns for leverage. "Did
you bring the vibrator?"

Damn. She hadn't even thought of that. "No."

He yanked her inside and closed the door. "You never
cease to amaze me," he said.

Faith pushed him back into the center of the room with
one hand on his chest. She didn't take stock of the room,
other than the fact that it had a couch, a coffee table, and an
entertainment center, and the walls were bare.

Like her. And Faith had the best idea ever.

Though he'd taken off his jacket, he wore his tie. She
pulled on it, bringing his face down to her level.

She licked along the seam of his lips, then locked gazes.
"Fuck me, Connor. Right now."

She loved the blaze in his eyes when she talked dirty,
when she got assertive, when she told him what she wanted
in no uncertain terms.

Then she drew in a deep breath, her breasts rising along
the lapels of her coat, her nipples almost spilling out.
"Fuck me doggie style," she added in barely more than a
whisper.

He pulled her head back by her hair. "Who the hell *are*
you?"

She laughed, deep, throaty, husky. "Whoever I want

to be. Now fuck me." She'd said the word for him three times.

His gaze smoked. He reached for the belt of her jacket and she twisted his fingers back. "No. Do me with it on."

"Jesus, Faith, you're gonna kill me." Then he pushed her to her knees. She went down on her hands beside him and looked up. His erection raged against his slacks. "Better hurry, or I might have to find someone else to do my bidding."

God, she was hot. So hot. The play was fun, exciting, excruciating. She watched as he went to his knees behind her, then slid his hand straight up her center.

"Christ, you're wet."

She was barely able to contain herself. "And you're hard. No preliminaries. Get inside me."

The rasp of his zipper filled the small apartment, then he shoved her coat to her waist, braced her hip with one hand, and slammed home.

Faith cried out. "Oh my God."

"Did I hurt you?"

"No," she said, pushing back on him. "Do it hard and fast."

And he did, pounding her so hard she felt as if she'd lose consciousness. Colors kaleidoscoped all around her. She curled her fingers into the carpet and held on. Oh God, oh God. His cock filled her, drove her to the edge of the world. There was simply his breath, his relentless thrusts, the clench of her pussy every time he withdrew, and a roaring in her ears. She thought she heard him shout her name, then there was only the slap of his testicles, the pulse of his cock, and the heat of his semen, until she melted into orgasmic oblivion.

19

IT could have been one tick of the clock. It could have been hours. Faith couldn't move, and her head felt woozy. But she was oh so deliciously sated and comfy curled up against him, his body still hot against her flesh even through his clothing. Faith couldn't quite remember how they'd fallen like that, a heap on the carpet, his breath at her ear, stirring her hair.

"When's your period due?" Connor idly stroked her belly.

Her cheeks flushed. She did all manner of kinky sexual things with him, let him touch her everywhere he wanted to, yet some things still embarrassed her. The things one took care of behind a locked bathroom door. The first time she'd told him they couldn't have sex because, well—she'd blushed furiously then, too—it was the wrong time, he'd laughed and said there were so many things they could do despite *that*. Only she'd been so crampy and miserable. Connor made her sweet, hot tea, brought her pills to help, and even a heating pad for her stomach. He was so damn good to her, she'd wanted to cry.

"It's supposed to come next week," she said.

He played with her belly button. "I don't think it's going to start this time."

Tipping her head back, she stared up at him. She adored his gorgeous smoky eyes. "And what makes you think that?"

He trailed two fingers along her abdomen, then cupped a breast in his palm. "They're bigger."

"They are not."

Bending his head, he took her nipple in his mouth, only

to let it pop free again. "They are." With his index finger, he circled the beaded nub. "I've sucked them enough to know."

Faith blushed again. How did he make her do that? "I don't think we should get our hopes up, just in case."

"The whole world's ready to crush your hopes under its boot heel, so why the hell should we crush them first? Plenty of time for that later on."

He had the oddest philosophies. They flew in the face of old clichés. "All right." She guided his hand back down to her belly and pressed his warmth to her. "Let's get our hopes up."

God, he really did want to have a baby with her. The thought made her glow inside.

He rubbed his nose against her cheek. "And what gave you the idea to come over naked like this? I almost had to have you out on the landing." He pulled the lapels of her coat together, covering her up again.

So, was that hot and nasty enough for you? That's what she meant to say. Instead, something else entirely came out. "So, was that making love?"

Her stomach tumbled right through the floor.

"Baby, baby, baby," he muffled against her throat. "Everything we do is."

A sigh fell from her lips. At least he hadn't said it was *just* fucking. Her side was starting to ache against the hard floor despite the carpeting. Faith pushed to one elbow. "Whose place is this?"

The couch had seen better days, its beige fabric worn, its springs having lost their bounce in certain spots. Still, it was clean. Nicks and water stains marked the coffee table, and an old TV on a roller stand butted up to the wall in the corner. Not a single picture or painting adorned the walls. No plants, either. The only thing that made it even look lived-in was a single glass of amber liquid on an end table.

Whiskey. She tasted again the pungent smack of whiskey on his lips sometimes when he came home. And Faith started to feel a little sick.

Connor stood, grabbed her hand, and pulled her to her

feet. Attending to his own pants, he zipped as he said, "It's my apartment. The one I lived in before we got married."

"I didn't know you still had it." It sounded so innocuous. It just didn't *feel* that way.

Connor shrugged, then reached up to straighten his tie. "I couldn't get out of the lease."

She thought of the photos hidden under her grade books. Were they taken here? Her jacket suddenly wasn't enough to keep her warm despite the heat of a summer evening. She swallowed, but it sounded loud in the quiet of the room.

"Lease is up, though," he said. "I'm getting rid of it. I don't think there's anything here you'll want; it's just a bunch of Salvation Army stuff, but you can take a look."

For the first time he actually looked at her. She couldn't read a thing in his eyes. She couldn't tell if his concentration on righting his clothes was a significant bit of body language, yet there was something in the way he offered her a chance to look around the place. As if he were giving her a message she couldn't quite grasp.

"Is there anything you want to take to our house?"

Had he put a slight emphasis on *our*? "I don't know," she said. "What's here?" Would she find evidence of secrets she'd be much better off not knowing?

Like the little monkeys, she wanted to close her eyes and cover her ears. She didn't want to see, didn't want to hear.

His fingers were warmer than hers when he led her down the short hallway. Faded brown towels hung on a rack in the bathroom. In the bedroom, the spread was of green chenille. She didn't think they even made things like that anymore.

"Is there anything *you* want to keep?" she asked.

"I don't need this place anymore, Faith. I don't want it, and I don't want anything in it." He put his warm hands to her cold cheeks. "Except you." He smiled. "I'll take you with me."

Okay, okay, he *was* saying something.

"Is the bottle of whiskey empty?"

A tiny light flickered at the back of his eyes. "Yeah. That was the last of it in the glass."

It was all very subliminal and understated, subject to interpretation, but coupled with his talk about her not starting her period, Faith took it to mean what she wanted it to.

Her husband was committing himself to her.

Instead of throwing her arms around him, though, she simply said, "I think we should throw out all the old stuff."

CHRIST, he'd skated through that one. He didn't lie about making love. *Love* was an illusion and *making love* just a term. But she'd delighted the hell out of him, and the moment he realized she'd rushed over naked under her damn coat, he'd wanted nothing more than to bend her over the railing of his apartment building and fuck her for all the world to see.

In the animal kingdom, it was called staking a claim.

Faith was his. It was so much better than love. Been there, done that, gotten screwed, and all the rest of it. What he was creating with Faith was so much better. More solid in that it wasn't based on an illusive emotion that disappeared as quickly as it came.

She got it about the apartment. She understood the sacrifice. He glanced up the stairs of their condo where she'd disappeared only moments ago after arriving home. *Sacrifice* was the wrong word. She understood he was choosing her.

It might have been the appropriate moment to bring up the proxies. Then again, one didn't mix business with pleasure.

Connor smiled to himself. He had the feeling tonight's pleasure was far from over. He'd followed her home, then she'd rushed upstairs, and he didn't think it was to hide her vibrator. He climbed more slowly.

He'd deal with the proxies later. There was plenty of time. He didn't want to ruin tonight. Or tomorrow. Or the week. He had to find the right spiel to get her to accept what needed to be done, but for now he didn't give a goddamn about the company. All he wanted was his cock buried deep inside her again.

He couldn't get enough of her. If she kept creating hot little surprises like she had tonight, he'd never get enough.

She wasn't in the bedroom. He followed the sound of . . . tearing paper? She hadn't quite closed the door of her office. He pushed it open with his fingertip.

"What are you doing, Faith?"

She startled, then jumped to face him, one hand behind her back. Beside her, the desk drawer was open. Looking down, she closed it with her foot, the lower edges of the coat parting to reveal an expanse of delicious thigh he wanted to suck.

After he discovered what she hid behind her back.

"I was just going through some old grade books. Thought I might throw them out."

"You're not a good liar, Faith."

She demonstrated that by looking at the doorjamb over his shoulder. "Why would I lie about a thing like that?"

Three steps into the room brought him to her. "I don't know why. But you and I are far from done tonight, and"— he breathed deeply, loudly—"you still smell like hot, horny woman. So I don't think going through your grade books would be the first thing you'd rush in to do."

She smiled, but he saw through her telltale shifting gaze.

"What are you hiding, Faith?" he whispered in a voice for sweet nothings or dirty talk.

When she didn't move, he slid one hand beneath the jacket to her bare breast while with the other he reached for what she was holding from him.

She clutched tight for a moment, then finally let go.

A manila envelope and a big red question mark on it. And some pictures. For a weird out-of-body moment, he didn't even understand what he was looking at.

"You have porn in your desk?" He smiled lasciviously— until the starkness of her gaze settled in his gut.

She'd already torn one photo to pieces and thrown it in the trash can.

He studied the top picture with a more discerning eye. A couple going at it doggie style. He glanced at Faith but she'd fixed her gaze on the carpet. He turned to another photo, a side view of the couple in action, no faces, just bodies. Red hair, a full breast, a long expanse of flesh from buttocks to thigh to calf spread alongside her partner's leg as he impaled her. And a bracelet around her ankle.

Nina Simon going for the gusto.

"And you think that's my bare ass?" he asked. A knot tied his insides into a not-so-neat little bow.

"No," she whispered, staring at his tie.

"Then why didn't you show me these?"

He heard her swallow.

"Because you didn't trust me," he answered for her.

Godammit. Who? Preston and Nina? Preston admitted to feeding the rumors. But would he send photos? Come to think of it, at his age, would Preston's butt look that toned? Connor grimaced. "When did you get them?"

Faith bit her lip before she answered. "These came three weeks ago or so."

"These?" Hell and damnation. "There are others?"

A nod, still without meeting his gaze. "I tore that first lot up." She pulled her belt tighter at her waist. "They came while you were in South America."

He'd kill that bitch. Nina tried to set him up and when that didn't work, she'd used photos she already had. But something struck him. "Did they come *from* South America?"

"Someone left them under the front mat. Both times."

Sonuvabitch. Nina had *another* accomplice. Obviously her male cohort, which he was pretty damn sure wasn't Preston Tybrook. How many people were out to destroy his marriage?

More important was why Faith had hidden this from him.

"That's not my ass." Shit. He shouldn't have to deny it.

"I know."

But dammit, she was talking to his tie. "Look at me."

Lifting her gaze, she rolled her lips between her teeth and looked at him. A misty sheen filled her eyes.

He felt like howling. "If you didn't think that was me, why didn't you show them to me?"

"I just wanted to rip them up."

"But you didn't." He stepped back from her, raking a hand through his hair.

"That's what I was doing just now."

"After three weeks. What, did you take them out every night with a goddamn magnifying glass and try to figure out if it was me or not? All you had to do was ask."

She didn't answer. He gave her his back, anger seething in his chest. Why the hell was he so angry? With the bastard that left her the pictures, yeah, but with Faith? It didn't make sense, yet it roiled inside him. Finally he turned.

Only to find she'd been waiting for him to look at her. "It's not easy for me to ask."

He felt cold suddenly. "It is if you trust me."

Her breasts rose with a deep breath. "Why did you let me think you'd let your apartment go?"

Her question slammed into his gut. "I never said I had."

"But we talked about you bringing your stuff over and you said you'd rather give it away."

Yes. He'd slyly led her to believe the apartment was gone, yet he'd been sneaking back over sometimes before going home to her. "I didn't take another woman there. I haven't been with another woman since before I met you. I kept it because I needed . . ." He stopped, regarded the wing tips of his shoes. "I wanted a place that wasn't yours or your father's, but mine. Somewhere that I could regroup on my own, recharge." Then he looked at her. "I don't need that anymore."

Her gaze tracked his face, from his mouth to his cheeks and finally to his eyes. "After tonight, I'm not afraid anymore that it's you in the pictures. That's why I was tearing them up."

The knots pulling his chest apart eased. In two strides he was at her side. Slipping his hand beneath the fall of hair at her nape, he pulled her up on her toes until his lips rested on hers. "Come fuck the hell out of me, Faith, and we'll forget about the pictures and the apartment. I'm sorry."

He just wanted to be inside her. He didn't like the lingering taste of bad emotions. So he took her mouth, consumed her with his tongue, his lips, his kiss, and burned away the raw edge of emotion.

Tomorrow, however, someone would pay for sending those photos to his wife.

CONNOR wanted her to have his baby. A child wasn't just part of the bargain they'd made, his payment for giving him her father's company. A baby was something he wanted *with* her.

Faith couldn't sleep. Curled up against her husband's warm body, she could only think of all the good things she'd been blessed with. They'd made love in his apartment, then again here at home. He'd hated those pictures as much as she had. Standing in her office, they'd forged a bond. He didn't need a refuge away from her anymore. Things were going to be okay.

"I love you," she whispered in the dark.

He didn't have to love her as much as she did him, because she had enough love for the two of them.

Her heart froze in her chest. What a pathetic thought.

She wanted him to love her the way she did him. What was it Trinity said the day she heard about the engagement? That Faith deserved a man who would make love to her and cherish her.

Without love, she could never be sure he wouldn't tire of her. She couldn't be sure he wouldn't rent another apartment without her knowledge or that the next set of pictures would show his face in ecstasy while he fucked another woman.

"I love you," she mouthed.

What she had would *have* to be enough. Because it was all she was going to get. And truly, he was more than she'd ever hoped to have.

Still, she could almost hear Trinity's voice telling her she was pathetic.

THE following morning, Connor found Nina seated in a cushy leather chair, the dryer hood propped against the wall. He'd called her assistant—why she needed an assistant to make her hair, nail, and facial appointments, he couldn't say—and Nina was right where she was supposed to be at the appointed time.

Legs spread, he stopped in front of her. "We need to talk."

She raised her head from the fashion magazine she perused. Her ultrachic salon came equipped with space-age hairdryers shaped like huge silver bullets, leather seats, and gilt-edged mirrors. Yet it was ultimately still a beauty parlor where women slathered scary-looking gunk on their heads; the hair products reeked enough to bring tears to a man's eyes, and the blast of dryers and screech of voices trying to be heard *over* the dryers set his ears ringing.

"I'm having my hair highlighted, Connor. Couldn't we discuss what's on your mind later?"

She had a way of looking at a man, starting at his mouth, working her gaze down to his crotch, then lower, punctuating it all with a tilt to her mouth, that spoke of pure boredom. A slow inspection designed to cut a man down to size. He was sure it drove her lovers crazy, made them want to do anything to get her to gaze at them fondly the way she used to.

Connor merely grabbed the magazine, tossed it on the pile beside her chair, and yanked her to her feet. "We'll talk now."

She pulled back when he headed toward the front door. "I am *not* going out there. Look at my hair."

Tinfoil spliced her red locks, and two stripes of dye splotched her forehead where her eyebrows were supposed to be. The contrast turned her skin sallow. He could see why she didn't want to step outside, yet she didn't so much as flinch that he'd discovered her in this state.

"Better find us a back room," he said, "or we'll have our little talk right here."

"Oh my," she cooed, "we do have our panties in a wad, don't we?" She batted her eyelashes at him.

He had to admire the woman. She never lost composure. A man would never cow her. He wondered if she had any chink in her armor at all.

He lifted one brow. "Public or private?" Then he pulled

the sheaf of photos from his inside jacket pocket and fanned them briefly before her like a deck of cards.

She glanced at them. "Well, hell, *that* took Faith ages." She crooked her finger, led him down a hallway, and stepped inside a tanning room. "We only have a couple of minutes before I turn orange." She flicked lightly at a piece of foil.

"Tell me all," he said once the door was closed.

She rolled her eyes and puffed out a breath. "I was pissed. You turned me down. I thought I'd get back at you."

"Bitch." It came out sounding almost friendly. Her answer was typical of the reasons he'd begun to like her. She made no bones about being a malicious bitch. With Nina, you knew what you were up against, an adversary. She didn't hide her machinating personality behind lies and manipulation. It was goddamn refreshing.

"Thank you," she smiled. "When neither of you made a fuss, I figured it didn't matter anyway."

He flapped the photos at her. "Aren't you worried about these things getting on the Internet?"

She shrugged. "Please. Who cares? Look at Paris Hilton."

He preferred not to. Nina didn't care about much, it seemed, certainly not her reputation. "Who did the hand delivery when you were in South America?"

"A . . . friend." She ran a polished nail over his shirt.

He didn't react. His body didn't react. He simply stared her down.

She folded her arms and leaned against the booth wall. "So why did she pick now to tell you?"

The question was really why had Faith picked last night to tear them up. Because he'd earned her trust or because she'd decided to trust him? There was a big difference in the two things, and the answer eluded him. He wanted to earn her confidence, and he didn't like how that desire had somehow morphed into an obsessive need. For Nina, though, he chose a totally innocuous answer. "Because we're a team."

Nina laughed, half mocking, half disbelieving, then she

sucked in a breath of air. "A team? Men and women can't play on the same team, Connor."

"Maybe *you* can't, but Faith isn't anything like you."

"I was thinking more of you." She poked him in the chest. "*You* aren't a team player."

"Hell, yes, I am. Making Castle a *team* is what I've been trying to do since I got there."

"No, it's been you trying to show Jarvis how he's fucked up all these years and you need to come in and save us."

"That's bullshit."

"Is it?" She tapped her fingers on her arm, waiting.

He formulated an answer.

"You took his daughter," she said for him, "you took his company. You told him his best friend was a screwup, and you shoved it down his throat that he's too old to handle it all."

He told Faith what she needed. He told Jarvis what the company needed. Then he'd sought to provide it. He was looking out for their best interests. It wasn't his fault that Green Industries had lost their edge, but did he have to use it like a club on Jarvis's head? Maybe not, but the thought was academic right now. "What the hell does that have to do with your photos on my doorstep?"

She leaned in, her chemical scent wafting up at him.

"It wasn't your doorstep. It was Faith's."

"Same thing."

She shook her head. "No, it's not, Connor."

He suddenly saw himself last night. He'd so magnanimously offered to get rid of his apartment. Then he'd yelled at Faith for keeping the photos from him. He never once asked her how they made her feel. He simply accused her of not trusting him. He'd made the whole episode about *him*.

Just as he'd made the issues at Castle Heavy Mining all about Jarvis's lack of good management.

"Have you told her you love her?" Nina hit him with her best shot.

"I don't." A shard pierced his side. The denial felt shitty. As if he'd said it to Faith herself.

Nina tipped her head, and the smile curving her lips was

neither malicious nor seductive. It was almost encouraging. "You can always tell a little white lie to make someone feel better, you know."

"Faith and I don't lie to each other." He winced again. He'd lied about the apartment. He'd considered lying to her about why he wanted her proxies. And why the hell was he listening to Nina, a self-confessed selfish, conniving bitch?

But was he any better?

She laughed again, this time with her eyes wide and her mouth open in total disbelief. "Oh my God. You really are in love with her. I mean *really* in love."

He didn't believe in love, but he wasn't about to deny it a second time. Faith deserved better than that. "All I want to know is who left the pictures for Faith to find."

"You'll have to beat it out of me." She gave him a twinkling smile.

She knew he wouldn't do a damn thing to her. He arrived fully intending to intimidate the answer from her, yet she'd completely turned the tables on him with her simple talk of love and Faith. She'd known what buttons to push.

He shook his head as if it needed clearing. Only one thing mattered at the moment. "Are you for Jarvis or against him?" he asked. Preston claimed the rest of the board would support Connor if he got Faith's proxies.

"I'm for me," Nina answered. "I don't care whether you're a team player or not as long as I get my money's worth." She leaned in once more. "Get my money for me, Connor, buy me out, whatever. Do that, and I'll support any vote you want me to make." Finally, she pulled at a bit of tinfoil. "I think I'm cooked, Connor-honey. So let me out."

Stepping back, he handed her the photos. "You might as well have these back. Souvenir and all."

She smiled and turned them right side up. After a brief study, she tipped her foiled head to him, all smiles wiped clean. "She got these while I was in South America?"

"No. This set came three weeks ago."

Her mouth dropped open, and she huffed. "That bastard. I never said he could use these."

Connor queried with a raised brow. "What's the difference?"

She raised her chin haughtily. "Because he didn't *ask* if he could use them. And besides, I'd changed my mind about the whole thing anyway before we even took these."

He almost laughed. She had an odd code of conduct. It was all right to harass Faith with them, but only if Nina had given her permission. "And might I ask whose ass that is?"

"Honestly, Connor, you're so dim-witted." She flapped the pictures at him. "Hello? Who's hated you from the moment you asked Faith to marry you?"

Shit. He *was* dim-witted. It was so damn obvious.

"Better get that foil out before you turn orange." Then he stopped her with a hand on her arm. "And don't *ever* try to hurt my wife again. Because I won't forgive a second time."

WHILE the country club dining room was fairly empty at three on a weekday afternoon, the bar area was packed. A round of golf, then a beer or something stronger, and the business took place. Connor had never gotten into golf. It was a slow, boring game. He preferred slamming walls in a racquetball court. Really took care of a man's aggressive instincts.

Lance Green had parked his sorry ass in a cushy chair at the edge of the bar and text messaged with his BlackBerry with one hand. A freshly made iced concoction frothed on the side table.

"That didn't take long," he said, still punching buttons on his handheld.

Ah, Nina had sent out the warning. The woman was good at playing both ends with only one goal in mind—her own best interests. Connor couldn't fault her.

He stuck his hands in his pants pockets and struck an idle stance. "Don't screw with me, Lance. You'll lose."

Lance sipped his piña colada. Connor should have known the guy was into froufrou drinks. "I don't know what you're talking about, Kingston."

Connor smiled. Explanations weren't necessary. He went on in a mild tone. "I can play as dirty as you. Back off Faith, or I will take you down."

"Aren't you already trying to take Green down? Turning Jarvis against us?"

Though there were interested ears all around, the conversation was low-key and imperceptible to even the closest. "All I'm suggesting to Jarvis is that his quality problems will go away with a different supplier." Connor raised a brow. "Or if his current supplier stops using crap material."

Lance tipped his glass and saluted Connor. "We thank you for pointing out that problem. It's under control now."

"Then you don't have anything to worry about, do you?"

"No," Lance said, shaking his head, "I don't. But that doesn't solve all your problems, does it, Kingston?"

"My problems are my concern."

"You and your vendetta against Green made them my concern."

"I don't have a vendetta against you, Lance. But you try poisoning Faith's mind again, and you won't have any doubts about what an asshole I can be."

Lance shivered. "Ooh. I'm so scared." Setting his glass on the table, he rose. "She was mine before you got here, and she'll be mine when you're gone."

For the first time during the interview, Connor struggled for a little calm. "She was never yours, Lance."

Lance smiled with nothing more than his eyes, a bright spark of triumph. "Guess she never told you about how I took her virginity. You know a woman never forgets her first." He straightened his tie. "And she wants it again. Maybe you're the one who has to fear his spouse's infidelity."

Connor wanted to smash his fist into Lance's nose. But he didn't believe the asshole for a moment. Green was a goddamn liar trying to set Connor off in any way he could. Faith would *never* be with this pathetic excuse for a man. Lance just wanted to throw whatever slur he could and see if it stuck in Connor's craw. It would insult Faith even to ask her about it.

His breath harsh in his throat and his heart beating hard in his ears, he wrapped his fist around the knot in Lance's tie, slowly, until his knuckles ached. To their audience, it would look like a mild altercation. "Don't go near her. Ever."

The bastard didn't even try to shake him off. "Or what?"

"Figure that one out for yourself." As slowly as he'd taken hold of Lance, he let go.

"I do have Jarvis on my side," Lance said. He fiddled with the tie knot, putting it back in place.

"Jarvis doesn't matter in this."

"Jarvis will *always* matter in Faith's life." He slipped his BlackBerry into his jacket pocket. "Even if you think you've got her under control right now, today, tomorrow, someday, Jarvis will come between you."

Not if she had Connor's baby.

The thought pounded at him long after he left Lance. Connor's plans at Castle Heavy Mining depended on Faith's proxies. His marriage depended on putting a baby in her womb.

For the first time he wondered what his life in Faith's bed would be like once he screwed over her father.

20

MONDAY'S board meeting had been a disaster. Tuesday, Jarvis had sat at his desk contemplating his navel and possible methods of doing away with Kingston. Today, Hermie had provided an answer, and it wouldn't take murder to accomplish it.

Sitting opposite Hermie in his friend's swank office, Jarvis patted the pocket where he'd stored the damning e-mail printout. "Thank you. It's safe to say, this is enough to terminate him."

Hermie wagged his head, his jowls flopping. "I agree he's an asshole, but I'm sure Kingston thought he was doing a good thing at the time by reducing overall costs." He spread his hands. "After all, he's only an accountant. He wouldn't grasp the implications of using a lower-quality metal."

"Don't make excuses for him. You don't authorize the purchase of material that doesn't meet spec. Even an accountant knows that if he didn't get his college degree off the Internet."

"But—"

Jarvis held up his hand. "And even if he was idiotic *then*, he certainly knows now, and he hasn't owned up to his mistake."

If one read Kingston's e-mails that Herman had had printed off the backups, one discovered the man had deliberately changed a purchase order to bring in substandard materials. He wondered also if perhaps Kingston had gotten a kickback from the vendor. It would explain the irrational act. However, there was no proof. All he had right now was evidence that Kingston himself had caused the whole quality problem.

It wouldn't send him to jail, but it would suffice to vote for his contract termination at next Monday's board meeting.

Hermie tapped a pencil. "How does Faith feel about this?"

He wouldn't tell Faith until it was done. "I know what's best for her."

"But don't you think you should—"

Jarvis slammed his fist on Hermie's desk. "He's a parasite in our midst and needs to be eradicated."

His blood rushed to his ears, and his heart pounded in his chest. For a moment, little spots flitted before his eyes.

Hermie's jowls trembled. "Are you all right, old man?"

He swallowed, his throat parched. "I'm fine."

"You shouldn't get so worked up."

The tips of his fingers tingled. Was it his heart or an anxiety attack? He'd never admit it to a living soul, but recently, he'd experienced a bit of panic. His doctor did the requisite tests and they all came back saying his heart was fine. But his mind . . . He had a lot of worries. With Kingston in his life, they'd gotten worse. The man impugned his intelligence, his managerial skills, and even his love for his own daughter.

He flooded his chest with a deep breath. "He married Faith, and look what he's done to her. Lied to her, cheated on her. A man does what he has to do to save his family regardless of the risks. The end justifies the means."

"And I'm behind you one hundred percent, old man."

Jarvis nodded, deciding to take Hermie's words at face value. The e-mails would rid the company of Kingston. And the photos sitting on his desk at home would rid Faith of him.

Faith wouldn't countenance infidelity, and Jarvis had indisputable proof. Pictures of Kingston in another woman's arms. His tongue down her throat and his hands grabbing her ass couldn't be explained away by simply saying she was a "friend" or some such nonsense.

Even Faith would have to believe those pictures.

He'd terminate Kingston's contract at the next board

meeting, then deliver the coup de grace with Faith right after.

Thank God she wasn't pregnant yet or they might never have gotten rid of the man.

SHE was pregnant. She could *feel* it. Connor had just left for the plant, and Faith stared at herself in the bathroom mirror. Deliriously happy, she giggled at her reflection. Her breasts felt heavy and full, and she was three days late. She was *never* late. She'd started hoping on day one, which had been Wednesday; she'd wanted to burst on day two, but today . . . she wanted to shout but was afraid to. Connor had asked when her period was due, but she'd gotten the exact day wrong. Yet even seeing her mistake, she hadn't told him. He had his hopes up, but she couldn't do the same. It might be Connor's certainty influencing the changes she *thought* she felt in her body.

Every night for the past week, he'd put his hand on her belly and claimed he was touching the baby. He'd kissed her stomach. He'd smile up at her and say he could *feel* a child.

Then he'd make love to her as if he would never get enough of the taste of her in his mouth or the feel of her body milking an orgasm from him. She needed his touch as much as she needed air to breathe, water to drink, or food to eat.

But she wanted to see the doctor first. To make sure she wasn't letting her hopes, *Connor's* hopes, get away with her. Or she could pee on the stick. God, what a euphemism. Couldn't those early pregnancy tests be wrong? She wanted a doctor to tell her. She wanted to be sure. She'd made an appointment for Monday afternoon.

Faith put her fingers to her lips. Okay, okay, she was scared spitless to tell Connor. That was the truth. She wanted him to love her. She was afraid he'd only love the company and the baby, and that what she felt in his arms was an illusion, something she *wanted* to believe rather than reality.

Five nights ago, she'd lain flush against him in bed, his arms wrapped around her, and told herself that he didn't have to love her as much as she loved him.

Now her heart ached for him. She'd been living in Lala-land when she came up with that one.

"Do you realize," she asked the mirror, "that you just went from ecstatically happy to the depths of despair in the space of five seconds?" God. The baby would have a bipolar mother.

In the bedroom, her cell phone rang. Running through the door, she banged her elbow on the jamb, and was out of breath when she answered.

"I told you I'd be busy with my vibrator. What did you forget?" A few short months ago she wouldn't have admitted to anyone she even masturbated, but Connor had helped her lose so many of her silly inhibitions.

Connor was silent a little too long so Faith prompted him. "Hello. Did you hear me?"

"I did, Faith," a female voice answered. "I just don't know how to reply to that."

She almost shrieked as she tore the phone from her ear and looked at the readout. She didn't recognize the number, but the voice . . . the voice . . . "Josie, I didn't realize it was you. I . . . uh, thought it was an obscene phone caller who's been bugging me, so I . . . uh, decided to give him a taste of his own medicine."

"The obscene caller wouldn't be your husband, would it?"

Open mouth, insert foot. She'd have to tough it out. "Busted," she quipped. "I thought you were Connor."

"Well, I'm not, but I do need to talk to you about him."

God. She felt the bipolar disease come over her again as her stomach plunged. "About what?"

"Let's meet, okay? It's easier in person."

Faith didn't like the sound of that. Too many people had been willing to tell her things about Connor. She was getting damn tired of it. "If you're going to bad-mouth him, Josie—"

"I'm not. He's like my favorite guy these days." She

stopped. "Well, not favorite in a sexual way, but favorite in an I-like-working-with-him way."

She should have gotten to know Josie better over the years. The woman was kind of . . . adorable. She came off sounding Valley girl, but she was actually sweet and smart.

"So meet me for coffee, okay? There's this little place in Los Gatos that makes the absolute best white chocolate mochas. They use real shaved chocolate, not syrup or powder. I'll buy."

"Josie, I—"

"I try to live on my salary alone without going to Dad, but I can afford it."

"Josie, that's not what I mean—"

"Meet me, Faith. I don't have my own office here, just a cube, and I can't talk about this over the phone. No one will miss me for an hour or so." Then she gave Faith directions.

It was all so mysterious, but if Josie said one bad word, despite whatever she promised, Faith would slam her down. She wasn't going to put up with this crap anymore.

By the time Faith got to the café, Josie had ordered and picked up their mochas, and found them a table on the sidewalk.

"Okay, I'll get right to it," Josie said before Faith even sat down. She pulled her chair closer, and leaned on the metal table. She wore a tight green tank top with a red Chinese dragon on it and low-waist jeans that revealed a strip of skin above the belt. Dangling dragon earrings matched the shirt.

"Your dad has gone bonkers."

"I don't know how to respond to that," Faith said, imitating Josie's reply to her over the phone.

"He's got it in for Connor. Grapevine has it your dad will vote to terminate his contract at the next board meeting."

Rumors, rumors, rumors. She was sick to death of rumors. "Who is the grapevine?"

"My mom and dad. I heard them talking about it when I had dinner over there last night."

"Why would my father want to do that?"

Josie tipped her head and stared at Faith.

After too many seconds of that, Faith felt her cheeks heat.

"Because Connor wants to get rid of Green as a supplier, and your father hates that Connor questions his managerial judgment all the time. They've been at each other's throats for weeks."

"Why would Connor want to get rid of Green?"

Josie blinked. Faith noticed how long her eyelashes were. She was pretty sure there wasn't a speck of mascara on them, either. *And Connor hasn't talked to you about this?* The question was unspoken, yet Faith felt it roiling inside.

Josie jutted her head forward and dropped her mouth open. "Because quality over at Green has taken a nosedive, and Connor's proven we're better off finding an alternate source or setting up our own in-house shop."

Faith had never been interested in the company. She knew what Castle sold, she knew Green Industries' part in the mining equipment, but she didn't pay attention to the intricacies of it.

"Doesn't Connor talk about work at *all*?"

No. He didn't talk about work. He didn't talk about finances. All he talked about was sex. All they had in common was . . . sex.

And the baby she was almost positive grew inside her. Faith put her hand to her stomach. "He doesn't want to bother me with that stuff."

Josie pursed her lips in a round *O* she held for a couple of seconds before she finally said, "So you don't know that your father has vetoed every good idea that Connor's come up with or that the bottom line has been bottoming out for months or that—" She stopped. "You don't know *anything*."

Josie made it sound like Faith had just committed murder and fed the body parts through a wood chipper.

"No," she whispered. Connor hadn't told her. He hadn't shared it with her. And she hadn't asked.

"Well, your dad's going to ax Connor at the next meeting."

"But won't the board stop him?" She put a finger to her temple, closed her eyes, and rubbed. "Except if he uses my votes to overrule everybody else that sides with Connor."

Josie pointed a finger and shot her. "Bingo. Give the lady a hand. Your dad *hates* Connor, and he *will* use your shares to get rid of him."

Faith wrapped her hands around her coffee cup.

Why hadn't Connor told her any of this?

She thought of all the sweet things he'd done for her in the last week. How wonderful he'd been to her. "How long has everyone known about the meeting on Monday?"

"Since last Monday."

Last Monday. With the weekend left.

Suddenly it all made sense. Connor was buttering her up to get her proxies so her father couldn't fire him.

"WHOA there, Kingston my boy."

Connor didn't have to look to know Preston was on his heels. He was almost to his car, the sun, at its zenith, beating down on his head. Friday afternoon, and he had a blinding headache only a long mountain drive with the windows rolled down could cure.

Or Faith's fingers threading through his hair.

"Just wondering about the mission to secure Faith's votes."

"It's on plan, Preston." He hadn't done shit about it.

The meeting was Monday. He'd never been into avoidance before, but after days of telling himself the moment hadn't come yet, he realized it would never come. The word was out on the company underground. Jarvis had it in for him. Negligence, fraud, whatever, come Monday, the old man planned to rid himself of his son-in-law, at least from the company payroll, and the last thing Connor wanted was Faith in the middle of their fight.

"So she's signed them over to you." Preston beamed a porcelain smile.

"No."

The man's veneers disappeared behind pinched lips. "My boy, we only have two more days."

"No, Preston, *I* have two more days. After Monday, you and Dora will still have your twelve percent share of Castle."

Connor would have nothing. Not even a job. So why hadn't he asked Faith, beyond the fact that he didn't want to involve her in his affairs of business? He kept Faith and her father in two totally separate compartments. He didn't talk about her father with Faith and vice versa.

He just hadn't figured out why that was so.

"It does concern us, Kingston." A tiny foam speck formed at the corner of Preston's mouth. "You're the one who keeps saying Jarvis is going to run us into the ground."

"Perhaps once I'm gone, Jarvis's head will clear."

"That's bullshit, Kingston."

True. Yet he hadn't formulated a palatable lie to tell Faith, nor was he content with telling her the truth. Maybe he was waiting to find out about the baby. He would have fulfilled his part of the bargain.

He should have bought her one of those home pregnancy tests.

But he didn't want the baby to become a pawn. That was his child and the most important thing in the world.

"I haven't known you long, Kingston, but you never struck me as a sit-back-and-take-it-up-the-ass kind of man."

Connor huffed out a chuckle. No, he never had been. The foster system taught him that you never sat back and took it up the ass or you'd be getting reamed for the rest of your life.

He slapped Tybrook on the back. "Preston, my man, everything is under control. Don't worry about Monday."

The older man rubbed his fingers together. "It's a lot of money we're talking about here."

"I'm fully aware of that."

"It's about Faith, too, you know. If Castle goes under, she'll have nothing, either. We're doing this for her, too."

"Right, Preston." Connor beeped his remote, climbed in his car, and took off before Preston could tap on his window.

It was for Faith. He'd been telling himself that for days. It was for the baby. It was the only way to protect them.

Yet another truth had pummeled his guts, one he wanted to ignore. This fight was all about him. He'd created it by mishandling Jarvis, and now, like a child, he was considering asking his wife to fix it for him. He didn't want to go back to being a meaningless middle manager, a grunt, a tiny cog in a huge wheel. A man without a legacy.

Yet to get what he wanted, he had to screw Faith's father, with her help, unwitting or not. She'd never forgive him. Life would be intolerable living with someone who hated you.

At this point, what choice did he have? He either got her votes or he walked away from it all.

A piece of his gut feared walking away from Faith would be so much harder than walking away from that damn legacy.

FAITH'S first thought had been to run to her father and demand an explanation. Her second thought had been to call Connor and ask him why he'd kept all this from her.

Why hadn't he asked for her proxies so that he could vote down her father? Josie had said the board would vote with Connor, not against him.

In the end, she'd done neither of those things.

Instead, she'd gone to the drugstore and gotten a home pregnancy test. Afterward, she'd clutched the tester in her hand for what seemed like hours, until her fingers started to hurt. She'd have to repeat the test in the morning to be sure, but for those few moments, there was only joy. Beautiful, bursting joy.

The problem was she couldn't ignore everything else for long. Connor wanted her proxies. Her father hated Connor. And she was going to have a baby with a man who didn't love her.

When they started out, that hadn't mattered. Now . . . it did. She wanted their child to have the best life, one *with* his or her father right there. Her child would not pay the price for Faith falling in love with her husband. Connor had done everything he claimed he would. He'd stood up for her, treated her well, taught her to appreciate herself as a woman, and gotten her pregnant. He'd fulfilled the bargain to the letter.

Therefore, at the end of a long day filled with so many ups and downs that she *knew* she needed medication, Faith greeted her husband with a big kiss.

"That was nice." He leaned in, sucking her tongue into his mouth for a long, delicious, wet kiss. "That was even nicer."

Her heart ached. Did he mean that? God, she had to stop questioning. "I've got a surprise for you."

He smiled. Her insides melted like cream cheese frosting every time he gave her that smile stamped with his own special brand of sexiness. Her knees felt weak.

Dipping, he pulled on the hem of her skirt. "You're naked and hot and ready under there, right?"

She fought his fingers, pulling her skirt away. "No. I've planned dinner *out* for us. Go get showered and changed."

His eyes twinkled, yet he held her arms with a tight grip that almost bruised. "Do you have something to tell me?"

She pushed him toward the stairs with the other. "Not a word will pass these lips," she bantered, "until we get where we're going." Yet despite the teasing, she couldn't quell the ache around her heart.

His sigh brushed her cheek as he relinquished his hold on her, trailing a long, lingering gaze over her face before he backed up two steps, then turned. It was the oddest look, as if something was going on in his head that she would never fathom. From the top of the stairs, he waved at her before disappearing down the hall. He was such a contrast. Hidden depths, sexy smile, deep emotions flaring in his eyes, yet laughter curving his lips. She wasn't sure who the real Connor was, but God, she loved him. She wanted to be the anchor he came home to, the safe haven, the woman to whom she poured out all his troubles.

Yet she was little more than a bed warmer. Faith closed her eyes and swallowed. She kept remembering Josie's face when she'd said, "You don't know *anything*."

"Get over it," she whispered, "and stop feeling sorry for yourself." Past. Done. They were united now. The positive pregnancy test changed everything. If it truly came down to supporting her father or her husband, she'd choose Connor.

She might want love from him, but she wasn't going to get it. He wanted lust, he wanted hot sex, he wanted her to let down all her barriers. Finally, after all these months, Faith truly understood what the bargain she'd made really meant. It worked both ways. Her heart might be his, but his body was all hers.

It was time she showed him who was in control.

HE'D been going a little crazy the past hour. He wanted to shake the answer out of her. In the bathroom, with the water running in the shower, he'd actually searched the trash can to see if she'd left any pregnancy test evidence.

Why is it so important that she be pregnant, Connor?

If she was, she wouldn't leave him if he lost the battle with Jarvis. He'd gotten used to living with her. He enjoyed their sex. He didn't want to see all that end just because Jarvis had a bug up his ass.

Right. Convenience and comfort. He would have closed his eyes and sighed if she hadn't made him drive.

"Turn left," she said.

"Yes, ma'am."

She'd decked herself out in the very dress she'd worn the night he met her. She looked gorgeous, her hair down, her lips lushly red, her breasts ripe. She was goddamn edible. He wanted her for dinner. She was all the sustenance he needed right now.

With a few more turns, they headed out of town. Into the hills. He thought of the day he'd taken her by the side of the road, and his cock throbbed. She'd probably planned a cozy dinner at one of the restaurants scattered along the mountain summit. He didn't think he could wait to have her until they got home. He wanted her now, under the stars, under the trees, on the hood of the car.

"Right turn at the next little offshoot."

Shit. His mind suddenly focused on exactly where they were. He hooked a right through the gold-etched, wrought iron gates onto her father's long, winding drive.

She wanted to tell them the news together. He felt cheated, jealous. He didn't want to share her.

"Pull over here," she directed.

The main house was visible through the trees, but they were still a quarter mile off. Connor pulled over, shut off the engine and lights, and sat in the darkness.

"We're here to see my father," she said, looking at the house through the leaves.

Daddy would blab about Monday. "Faith, we need to talk."

She put her fingers to his lips. "No talk. I have something else in mind."

Her tongue was sweet with cinnamon toothpaste. Her openmouthed kiss rolled him over and sucked him under. She kissed the way he taught her, with her whole body, her breasts rubbing him, her arms hugging him. Oh yeah, he'd taught her, but Faith added her own unique twist, which was nothing more than the synergy in the sigh of her breath, her sweet flowery scent, and a soft moan in her throat.

She undid him physically in ways he never knew were possible. She wasn't consciously seductive, but sexy from the inside out. She was the genuine article in a place where honesty was just a word in the dictionary. Right here on her father's driveway, the house lights sprinkling through wayward tree branches, he wanted her.

Tunneling his fingers through her hair, he let her retain control. He simply needed to touch the silk. Her hand trailed down his abdomen, and she stroked him through his slacks. He thrust up into her. Reaching further, she cupped his balls, rubbed, caressed.

"You make me nuts," he whispered against her mouth. "So you better stop now or I'm not going to let you stop."

She licked his lips. "I won't stop till you come in my mouth."

His breath snagged in his throat. "Here?"

She laughed, a sexy, cock-grabbing sound. "Of course here."

"Daddy might see," he quipped. It reminded him of the night her father agreed to the contract. That night, Connor had coerced her in the garden. Tonight, she was in charge.

"Daddy won't see." She pulled back, hair mussed, lipstick smudged, nipples hard. "I want you in my mouth now, Connor Kingston. Not later. Not at home. Here. Now." She swiped her tongue along his cheek. "This"—her thumbnail flitted along his cock from base to tip—"is mine," she whispered. "Anyone touches and I'll do serious bodily damage to you both."

Despite the material in the way, he almost came. A shiver coursed across his skin. He truly hadn't belonged to anyone since his father died.

Her gaze locked with his, she unzipped him slowly, the sound racing around the car's interior. Then she reached inside and wrapped her fist around his cock.

"All mine," she whispered.

He'd heard the words before. No, he'd said them. When, he couldn't remember. He simply remembered the need to show her she belonged to him. As he now belonged to her. He couldn't breathe. If he moved, he'd come. She bent her head to him and licked his slit. His body jerked.

"Mine," she said, then her lips closed over his crown.

He arched into her, groaned. Oh Christ, her mouth was good, so sweet and hot and perfect. Her tongue circled the sensitive underside, and he surged up, forcing himself deep.

She sucked hard as he pulled out. Warm, wet woman, that's all he could think. How badly he wanted to come inside her. How hot his come shot would feel.

She circled and swirled and sucked and drove him fucking nuts. He was her prisoner, her victim, her partner, her slave. His body rocked and thrust, his breath rasped in his throat. Squeezing his eyes tightly shut, the colors of the rainbow flashed and sparked.

He thrust deep one last time, shouted her name, and came so hard, his guts tore open and his heart sliced in two. He felt himself fall completely apart and come back together again.

Moments, minutes, hours passed. Or so it seemed. She smelled like come. Delicious. He tasted it on her lips. She'd swallowed it all. She'd taken him. For those few moments, she'd owned him. He wanted to feel that again. Over and over. Despite the terror that threatened to cut off his breath.

"Well, that was nice," she murmured against his throat.

Nice? That was all? His lips couldn't yet form words.

She sighed. "You were right, baby, lust is so much better than all that messy, emotional stuff."

Shit. She was quoting him. And a part of him wasn't so sure anymore that it was true.

Buried in the warm, wet recesses of her mouth, he discovered he didn't want to be just her husband or the father of her child or the CEO of her daddy's company.

He liked belonging to her. He liked being the object of her desire. It wasn't merely *nice*. It was cataclysmic. He wanted her to feel that way, too. He didn't want to be just a cock to her; he wanted more. "Faith, we need to have a serious talk."

She tipped her head back on his shoulder and looked at him. "You're right, we do. I'm going to have your baby, Connor."

A surge of ecstasy rushed through his veins, taking over like a tidal wave. He wanted to grab her, hold her, keep her. Yet a terrible ache around his heart immobilized him. She didn't seem very happy about it. "Faith, are you—"

She put a finger over his lips just as she had the moment before she took his cock in her mouth and his heart in her hand. "I'm going to vote my own shares at the meeting on Monday. And we're here tonight to tell my father that."

He turned, stared at her. She knew about the meeting and the proxies. "Who told you about Monday?"

"Josie bought me coffee."

That little schemer.

"I'm glad she told me, since you weren't going to."

"It didn't concern you."

She glared at him.

He winced. "What I mean is—"

"I know what you meant. There's the part of our bargain that concerned my father and the part that concerned me and never the twain shall meet."

"That was how I thought of it. It's not your problem." He didn't think that explanation was any better.

"The baby changes all that. Whatever happens to you affects the baby. *Everything* concerns *us*."

It was on the tip of his tongue to remind her yet again that he wasn't destitute and that his child wouldn't end up in a workhouse making cheap clothing for twelve cents an hour. But Faith was on a roll.

"My father is using my shares to vote you out, but he and I had an agreement, too. I'm not going to let him back out of it just because he's angry over"—she flapped her hands in the air and shrugged—"over whatever."

"I'll fight my own battles." Hell if he didn't like that she was willing to fight for him, but he couldn't let her do it.

"This *isn't* your battle." She gave him an uncharacteristic glare of total aggression.

"Why not?" He didn't get her logic.

"He's never trusted me to make my own decisions. You heard him after I dissolved our agreement. He called me an idiot."

"I did want to punch his lights out on your behalf."

"Thank you very much, but I won't let *you* fight *my* battle the way you did that day. You're the father of my child, and you're going to run the company that will one day belong to our children. And I won't let my father kick you out."

She was sweet, but a little naïve. Just because she used her shares to save him didn't mean her father would ever work willingly with him.

"Are you with me, Connor?"

He stared at her as if seeing her for the first time all over again. Just as he had the day she stepped into his office and ordered him to go down on her. Sexual confidence energized her then. This time, motherhood turned her into a lioness.

His wife had come into her own. And that wasn't something *he'd* taught her.

He couldn't deny her the right to go up against her father on behalf of her own flesh and blood. Because this was all about the child. Their child.

They'd created a miracle, yet he wanted . . . more.

He wanted a piece of Faith for himself. Asking for it was . . . He couldn't do it. He hadn't asked for anything beyond the physical from a woman since he was eighteen years old. Giving that kind of power to another person could be disastrous.

He might want more, but he wasn't capable of giving anything in return. Except this. Letting her take a stand *she* needed to take no matter how he felt about it. "I'm with you, baby."

She smiled. It tied his stomach in knots.

Wrapping his hand around her nape, her pulled her close. Her lips parted anticipating his kiss. Instead he dropped a hand to her belly.

"For our child," he whispered.

21

ON her father's grand front entrance, flanked by rose-bushes and small marble replicas of famous statues, Faith held her face up for Connor's inspection. "Is my lipstick all messed up?"

Connor laughed. "You just blew me, sweetheart. Yeah, I think it's a little messed up."

She was proud of herself. She'd taken Connor boldly, wrenched a gut-deep orgasm from him, threatened bodily harm if he ever allowed anyone else a touch, and forged a link over the baby they'd made.

It would have been perfect if he'd said he loved her, but she was done living for impossible dreams. Reality and good sex. She would live up to her end of the bargain if it killed her.

Her stomach clenched. It just might kill her if she didn't squash her wayward emotions.

She raised her face. "Fix it," she demanded.

Connor smoothed a finger over her lips. "All fixed."

God. His touch. It simply undid her, made her want to beg.

With him standing on the step below her and she with her heels on, she was so much closer to his height, and Connor misinterpreted her look for worry. "Your father and I will work this out, Faith. You don't have to do this."

It was a tidy little lie to take care of her feelings. She was part of the bargain, and with her father shutting him out of Castle Mining, Connor didn't get a damn thing in return except her love . . . something he'd never asked for and had in fact said he didn't want right from the beginning.

She owed him this battle. Dammit, she owed it to herself.

"Okay, I'm ready then." She was Connor's wife first, her father's daughter second. She rang her father's bell, which was the oddest feeling. She'd never rung the doorbell in her life; she'd simply walked in. In a few short months, everything had changed. When the baby came, they would have to rebuild their lives all over again. She better get used to change now.

Connor came to stand at her side. "Will you tell him about the baby?"

"After I tell him about the shares." It was important to gauge her father's reaction about that first. She'd know his true feelings. Over the past few months, she'd begun to wonder if he even loved her at all.

Connor squeezed her hand. "He loves you."

She shot him a look.

"It's written all over your face."

For a moment, she'd hoped he could read her mind. But it was nothing more than her being incapable of hiding her feelings. She'd have to get better about that in the future. No one must know how she felt about Connor. Not even Trinity. She didn't want anyone's pity.

Archie stooped a little as he opened the massive front door. "Miss Faith?"

Faith thought she heard a question mark on the end of that.

Connor took her hand. "Mrs. Kingston." Then he pulled her inside without being invited.

"Your father's in his study," Archie called as Connor was headed there anyway, "and I don't think he's expecting you."

Faith merely waved over her shoulder.

Oh my God, what do I want to say? She hadn't rehearsed. She only knew that she couldn't let her father walk all over her.

Connor let her enter first. Her father sat behind his leather-top desk. Reading glasses perched on his nose, he flipped a piece of paper. His hair was billowy on top as if he'd been drawing circles in it.

"Father?" Damn, her voice quivered.

He didn't shift his head, merely raised his eyes to gaze over the tops of his glasses. "What's he doing here? I didn't invite him."

"You didn't invite me, either."

"I suppose he's come to you with some sob story about how nasty your old father is."

"No, he didn't say a thing." She stepped away from Connor, closer to her father, looking back over her shoulder, her eyes pleading. *Please let me do this.*

Connor merely blinked his lashes at her.

"Josie told me about the vote on Monday. That you're going to fire Connor." *Take a deep breath,* she told herself. "That wasn't part of our agreement, Father."

As if he recognized the change in his designation, from *Daddy* to *Father,* he simply sat there, his head tipped slightly to the side, his glasses now resting almost on the tip of his nose.

Then he circled his hand, the wind-up motion which meant *Get on with it, girl.* She remembered how many times she'd seen it over the years, as if she were always taking too much of his time. With another step closer to him, she was one step further from Connor.

"I can't let you do that, so I'm voting my shares on Monday."

Her father barked out a laugh, ending it with a sharp cough. "Well, I should have seen *that* coming. Should have known he'd manipulate you. Scumbags always do and women fall for it."

"He's not a scumbag."

Her father crooked his finger. Faith almost shivered, but stopped herself before it shot full-body. She would not revert to a childhood reaction.

On his desk, he turned the piece of paper he'd been staring at, then tapped it with his finger. "He's been cheating on you. I wanted to spare you, but it seems I can't do that anymore."

Connor didn't say a word, but his breath came more harshly.

"He has a hideaway you knew nothing about." Her

father glared over her shoulder at her husband, his eyes narrowed.

In the photograph, Faith recognized the landing of Connor's second-floor apartment. His door was open, he stood in the entry, his hand on the arm of a woman.

"There's more." Her father splayed several photos over the desktop. "I'm sorry, Faith." But the look he leveled on Connor was anything but apologetic.

He didn't seem to care that he was hurting her as well.

The pictures were in a series. Connor grabbing a woman, pulling her to him, kissing her. Connor reaching down to cup her buttocks, her arms around his neck, her coat rising to reveal a bare cheek under the hem. Her long hair flowed down her back like a bloodred waterfall.

Faith pulled the last photo closer. A grainy, badly taken color picture. "I hope you didn't pay a lot for these. I mean, really, with digital photography, you should have been able to get a good close-up."

Her father gave her a woeful gaze. "Honey, I know how hard this must be—"

He didn't. He hadn't even thought about it. He only thought of how he could get rid of her husband. "You were spying on Connor."

"Only to protect you."

This had nothing to do with protecting her. Her eyes stung. He didn't care. He really didn't care.

"And I've never liked Nina," he added.

"Nina?"

"Nina. Married to your cousin Lionel. Nothing but a floozy. If only he hadn't left her his shares. He should have willed them to the family."

Faith pointed to the photo. "You think that's Nina Simon?"

He waved his hand over the display. "Red hair. Flaunting herself. Of course it's her. She was always a hussy."

"I think she looks extremely seductive," Connor said.

Faith hadn't even been aware of him coming to her side.

"In fact," he said, looking right at Faith, "she's a veritable Aphrodite."

"Listen to his audacity, Faith."

Her gaze locked with Connor's, and warmth spread through her. "That's not Nina, Father. It's me."

"Faith, sweetheart, you don't need to lie to protect him." Her father blinked back what might have been tears. Or phony condescending moisture.

She picked up the picture revealing too much bare flesh, flipped first one, then another, and another until they all faced her father. She didn't even feel self-conscious that it was her father looking at the photos.

"That's me. I went to Connor's apartment on Tuesday. Isn't that when your spy took those pictures?"

He looked down, then back at her. And didn't answer.

"*That* is me. I know about Connor's apartment. He's never used it for secret assignations with anyone but me."

"Faith, please don't delude yourself. It's past needing to lie for him."

She stabbed the picture of Connor kissing her. "That's me. You can believe whatever you want, but that's not Nina."

"But Faith, that woman is—" He looked down, up again, shut his mouth.

"Sexy?" Connor supplied. "Gorgeous?" He leaned close. "Perfect?" He kissed her ear. "That woman is my wife."

Her father didn't pay attention. "He's forcing you to lie for him. You could never be so . . . brazen."

"You don't think I could attract a man the way Nina can. That a man like Connor would want to be with me." She tapped her chest. "But I *am* good enough."

"Honey, I didn't mean—"

"Yes, you did. That's exactly what you meant. I'm not good enough to hold a man in my life. I have to buy him with my father's money." God, it hurt. As if he'd reached inside, plucked her heart out, and stomped on it. All those years, he'd chased men away, said they weren't good enough for her, but the truth was, he'd feared she wasn't enough for them, that they'd stray because *she* couldn't hold them.

"You're twisting what I'm saying."

"You were the one spying on us. How twisted is that?" Her blood throbbed in her ears, and a vein ticked at her temple.

"I'm just trying to show you what kind of man he is. There's more, not just these photos." He yanked open his middle desk drawer to pull out another file.

"I don't want to see it."

He spread the folder. "You have to see. It proves what he really planned to do." He grabbed the top piece of paper, crumpling it in his haste. "This. It proves what he was doing at Green and what he's trying to do to us."

Beside her, she felt Connor withdraw behind stone.

"Read it, Faith," her father urged.

She couldn't make sense of it.

"You see?" her father whispered. "He purchased crap material, then laid the blame for all the quality problems at Hermie's door. I think he planned all along to destroy Green Industries because Hermie wouldn't let him marry his daughter."

"Then he married me instead. Is that what you're saying?"

"I'm sorry, Faith." Her father reached out but didn't manage to touch her. "I'm so sorry."

She didn't look at Connor. She didn't want to see the truth on his face. No, she wanted to feel the truth deep inside where her baby grew. *Connor's baby.* Her hand splayed across her abdomen before she even realized it.

Faith closed her eyes and took three deep belly breaths.

JARVIS stared at Faith. His cheeks were gaunt, sunken, his jowls hung heavy, and a five o'clock shadow grizzled his chin.

Her silence was so long and the quiet in the spacious study so intense, Connor felt deafened by it. Waiting for her to speak, he died a thousand excruciating deaths at the hands of his own demons. His knees felt weak. Did she believe the muck her father had raked up?

Jarvis couldn't seem to wait for her answer, either.

"Sweetheart, I just want you to face facts about him. I want you to be happy, and you'll never be happy with him. He's out for numero uno. He's a cancer in our midst."

A chill ran the length of Connor's body, then shot back into his heart, freezing it in his chest. He might not even have been in the room for all the attention Jarvis paid him. The old man's focus was entirely on Faith, as if by concentrating hard enough, he could command her to see what he wanted her to.

Yet Jarvis had just torn him to little pieces and tossed the remains at her feet without a thought. He didn't even care that he'd manufactured some fantastic lie. Maybe by now he'd even convinced himself it was true.

"You're forcing me to choose," she said, her voice low but without inflection, as if Jarvis hadn't even opened his mouth. She leaned both hands on the desk. "I'm voting with Connor, Father. Not you."

Connor didn't realize he'd stopped breathing until she said his name. Then air filled his lungs until he felt high on it.

"You know what that means, don't you?" Jarvis stared at her with suddenly rheumy eyes. The color leached from his face. "He and the rest of the board will sell the company. If he wins, I'm out and that good-for-nothing family of mine will sell to the highest bidder."

She straightened and crossed her arms over her chest. "So be it. I'm going to have his baby, and I'm going stand by him. If you don't like it, then you don't have to see us. Ever."

Jarvis merely stared. He didn't even react to the news of his grandchild.

Connor's momentary relief died.

She was so cold, so unlike the Faith who'd taken him to the moon in his car. She wasn't even the woman who'd told him she needed to stand up to her father for her own mental health. She was an alien.

If he ever wanted the real Faith, for better or for worse, he couldn't allow her to cut her father out of her life on his behalf and live with himself.

Grabbing one damning e-mail page, he flipped it over. "Give me a pen, Jarvis."

Jarvis handed him a felt-tip.

Connor scrawled across the page, dated it, signed it, then shoved it at Jarvis. "My resignation, effectively immediately."

"I knew you were guilty," Jarvis snarled, and Connor wanted to hit him. Didn't he see what he was doing to his daughter?

Faith stood silent, a statue.

"You wanted to steal my company," the old man said, grinding into Connor's wounds.

"No." Connor turned to Faith. "I wanted to buy my way into your family. But I'm not poor, Faith. I have a good 401K. I've worked the stock market to my advantage. I can support you, pay for a child's college education, and buy a house. A nice house in a decent neighborhood with good schools."

"But the company is our bargain." There was no inflection in her voice, no spark in her gaze. "I get a baby, you get my father's company."

Her matter-of-factness stung. "What about you, Faith? Do I get you?"

"Of course." She tipped her head and regarded him as if he were mentally challenged. "We're married."

Godammit, he wanted more than a marriage certificate and Faith in his bed.

As his dad always said, he'd asked for the moon. Problem was he hadn't given his all to get it. He'd wanted a legacy without facing the lean years or spilling the blood, the sweat, and the tears. He wanted a family's acceptance without granting it unconditionally in return. He wanted a wife without opening his heart or risking any pain.

He wanted the one thing he'd turned his back on when he was eighteen. He wanted to be loved. He'd been reaching for the moon when all he really needed was Faith. He wanted *her* love, and there was only one way on God's green earth he could earn it. By loving her.

With so much that needed to be said, he answered Jarvis's accusations first. "I never bought bad material. If I was idiotic enough to compromise the spec, I wouldn't be stupid enough to divulge it in an e-mail."

Jarvis snorted. "Just like you weren't stupid enough to have a woman in your hotel room with your father-in-law's suite right across the hall."

"Yeah, Jarvis, just like that."

Faith scanned his face as if he'd given an answer to a question he didn't even know she had.

Yet believing the scene was all about him, Jarvis wouldn't let go. "Fine. If you're not guilty, then why resign?"

He didn't owe the old man a thing. All he had to give belonged to Faith. He wanted to touch her so badly, his guts ached. "Do you believe I screwed Herman over?"

She shook her head. "I don't believe you did."

He closed his eyes, breathed her in. "But I have been lying to you, baby."

She worried the inside of her lip, perhaps hoping he couldn't see the action. Connor took her hand, clasped it with his, and held them together against his heart.

"I told you that lust beat out love, and that was a lie." His insides quaked, but he bent his forehead to hers. "Lust is nothing compared to what I feel for you," he whispered.

He felt rather than heard her intake of breath.

"I want you for the woman you are, your sweetness, your kindness, your caring, for the way you touch me."

She subsided against him, and he tunneled his hand beneath her hair, caressing her nape lightly with his fingers. "I will never tire of you," he whispered. "Not now, nor when you're eight months pregnant with my baby. I won't tire of you ten years from now or even fifty. Never."

Turning fully into his arms, she burrowed against him.

He held her tightly. "I don't want to push my way into your father's company if it means forcing you to choose between us. So I resign." He lifted her chin and made her look at him. "I will spend the rest of our lives trying to make up to you for how we began and teaching you to love me the way I love you."

Dipping her head, she muffled her laugh against his shirt.

She was laughing?

"You're always trying to teach me things, Connor."

"That's because you're the best student a man ever had." And he wasn't done teaching her all the things he wanted to.

"Well, you don't have to teach me about this. I've been in love with you from the moment you—" She stopped, looking to her father, then rephrased. "From the moment you found me out in the garden at the country club."

In other words, from the first moment he touched her.

"I just didn't know it then," she finished.

This time, Connor laughed with her, then lifted her in his arms. "God, I love you. And I love our baby."

She pushed away, smiled at him, and held his hand to her stomach as she turned to her father. "Daddy, what do you have to say for yourself?"

The old man simply stared. Something had changed during the minutes Connor had concentrated solely on Faith. A single tear had slipped down Jarvis's face and now trembled on his upper lip. In the next instant, it fell to his chin.

"I love you, Faith. I'm sorry I hurt you." He glanced at Connor and blinked away one last tear. "But I have a gut feeling about him—"

Her glare cut him off. His daughter was a tough woman. Jarvis had taught her that. "Don't spy on me ever again, Daddy."

"It wasn't you—"

She held up one finger to stop him. "Connor and I are a team. What you do to him, you do to me."

Her words wrapped around Connor's heart, as if she held it in her hands the way she'd hold their child.

"I know you don't think I trust you to make your own choices, sweetheart, but I do." Jarvis bent his head. "I just lost sight of things for a little while." Then he raised his gaze to hers. "Please forgive me. I love you more than anything."

"I love you, too, Daddy. I never stopped, even if we've hurt each other." Then Faith held Connor's hand to her abdomen. "Except you're still avoiding the issue. What about Connor?"

"I don't want to lose you, sweetheart." Jarvis eyed Connor critically. "But I'm not sure I can love him even for you."

"But will you *accept* him?"

Connor didn't know what the hell that meant, but after a long moment, the old man closed his eyes and nodded.

"What about the baby, Daddy? Will you love our baby?"

"I do already, honey. I swear it. We're family. And if this one"—he pointed a finger at Connor—"has to come with the package, so be it." Then he picked up Connor's resignation and started to tear it in half.

"No." Connor couldn't let the old man do it. "That's over, Jarvis. We've proven we can't work together." There had to be more trust between them. "But I will take care of Faith." He rubbed her belly, nuzzling her hair and breathing in the scent of her. "I promise you that."

"Connor."

Her voice pulled him back from the heaven of her scent. "Yes, dear?" The smile that rose to his lips wasn't even voluntary.

"Castle Heavy Mining is our baby's legacy."

Damn. She was right.

"He'll be running it someday, so you and Daddy need to keep it in good order."

"What if it's a girl?" her father asked.

"Then *she'll* run it," she said, eyes narrowed. "This is the twenty-first century, you know. Women can do anything they set their minds to."

God, he loved her so damn much his insides ached. How had he missed the way she'd become a part of him? Completed him.

"And Connor's going to vote my shares."

"But Faith—" Jarvis stopped at her steely look.

Turning her with a touch to her arm, Connor said, "You can vote your own shares, Faith."

She shook her head. "I've decided I don't want to. I know you probably think that's sacrilege, but while the company will someday belong to our children, I'm a teacher. That's what I do. That's what I *want* to do." She cocked her head and smiled. "And sometime after the baby comes, I'll start my own preschool, giving other children a leg up in life. That's what *I'm* good at." She turned back to her father. "So with Connor voting my shares, neither of you can do anything totally on your own. You're a team now."

Connor wanted to haul her up against him, press her close. He'd never told her what he longed for at Castle, yet she understood. Maybe it was woman's intuition. Motherhood. Love. Damn, he was so proud of her. The woman he'd married a few months ago would never have thought of starting her own school.

"Faith, honey . . ." Jarvis's voice trailed off at another of his daughter's ferocious looks. "Fine. We're a team."

"And I want the authority," Connor stepped in. "No more board votes over mice nuts."

"Define how much authority you want," Jarvis countered, crossing his arms over his chest.

And the negotiations started.

22

THE doorbell rang. Connor had left an hour ago to see her father to "strategize" the Monday board meeting.

He'd made love to her all night long. Real, honest-to-God lovemaking. Then this morning, he'd stood over her as she repeated the EPT. Faith didn't even mind the lack of privacy. Not one bit. When they'd read the positive, he'd swooped her up in his arms and danced around the bedroom with her.

God, how she loved him. She answered the door knowing her joy must be shining on her face. "Trinity!"

Her friend sailed in, long blond hair flying behind her. "I'm sick of playing phone tag. It's been *ages*, and I *had* to see you." She grabbed Faith's hand in hers. "I'm sorry I've been so out of touch. I'm a bad friend, but I love you."

"It's fine, Trin. *I'm* fine."

Trinity stepped back to survey her. "You look beautiful."

Faith smiled and accepted the compliment without question. "I'm going to have a baby."

For just a moment, Trinity's expression was deadpan, absolutely flat, then the look vanished so quickly, Faith was almost sure she'd imagined it.

"Oh my God." Trinity threw her arms around Faith and together they bounced a few steps in the small entry hall. "I'm so happy for you." Then she pulled back. "Are *you* happy?"

"About everything. Trin, I love him. And he really loves me. I know what everyone's been saying—"

Trinity shushed her with a snort. "Who cares what everyone says?" she finished for Faith. "You're the most wonderful person I know and you deserve it. And thank God it all turned out, because I swear, Faith, I really didn't want to have to use my curling iron on him or feed his entrails to the gulls." Trinity beamed a gorgeous smile. "I really do feel like Cinderella's godmother." Then she dipped her head. "Except I should have been around more for you to talk to. I'm sorry."

"I could have tried harder to get hold of you." Faith pulled her into the kitchen. "Sometimes you just have to go through things on your own, Trinity." She set a kettle on the stove to boil. "I love you and I wanted to talk to you, really I did, but I think I really needed to work it out on my own." She held the two mugs she took out of the cupboard to her chest. "Do *you* forgive *me*?"

Just as in the hall, something flitted across Trinity's face, then disappeared. "There's nothing to forgive. You're my best friend. And I love you."

"I love you, too." Trinity was the one to always stand beside her no matter what. "I have to tell you something about your father and Daddy's company."

Then, in the oddest gesture, Trinity put her finger over Faith's lips. "Remember when you said that even if I heard a bad thing about Connor, you didn't want to know about it?"

"Yes, but—"

"This is one of those kinds of things. Daddy was crying last night, and I . . ." Trinity trailed off. "You had to work out your thoughts about Connor on your own and . . . well . . . I think this is something I have to deal with on my own, too."

Faith took her hand. "I'm here if you need me, though. Now tell me how things are going with Harper."

Trinity brightened. "He's absolutely marvelous and do you know where he took me?" And she was off on an enthusiastic tale.

There might be a dark cloud in Trinity's sky, but she was never one to let things get her down for long. And when she was ready for a heart-to-heart, Faith would be there no matter what.

"IF it's a boy, I want him named Jarvis. And if it's a girl, she should be Eleanor after Faith's mother."

"No," Connor said as he opened Jarvis's office door and stepped out into the empty executive hallway.

"Why not?"

"Because Faith and I will choose the name, not be dictated to by you." Baby names. A ghost of emotion whispered through him, and he closed his eyes briefly to savor it.

"You're an asshole, Kingston."

"I know." Connor smiled. "That's why you and I are going to get along so famously. Because you're an asshole, too."

He was sure Jarvis snickered, but the old man tried to cover it with a light sneeze.

Friday night, they'd negotiated a cease-fire. Saturday, they agreed upon the terms of a truce. Sunday, they'd started working together for the first time in months. They'd devised a proposal regarding Green Industries for the Monday board meeting, one they both supported, and in the next few minutes, they'd see how it flew.

"I'm leaving right after the meeting," Connor said. "Faith called a little while ago to say she found a house she wants to show me, then I'm taking her to the doctor."

Jarvis snorted. "In my day, women didn't need so much coddling. Nowadays, the father goes into the damn delivery room with a video camera."

"Welcome to the new millennium, Jarvis."

A hand on Connor's arm, his father-in-law stopped in the middle of the hall. "Take care of her. She's all I have."

"You know, that's your problem. Faith *isn't* the only person you have. You've a whole goddamn family in there." He pointed at the closed double doors of the boardroom.

Jarvis's eyebrows damn near shot to his hairline. "The *cousins*?"

"Yeah, the cousins. Some people have absolutely no one. Maybe you should start valuing what you do have."

Connor had managed that feat. Jesus, he'd even begun to be grateful for his father-in-law. After all, Jarvis had brought him Faith. Without all the shit between him and Jarvis, Connor wasn't sure he'd ever have allowed himself to acknowledge his own feelings for her.

Jarvis shook his head in an absent gesture—whether he'd ever change, who knew?—then grabbed a door handle. Connor did the same, and they entered side by side. A team. Finally. Now, if they could just convince the rest of the board to join.

Preston and Thomas were in various stages of coffee prep at the sideboard. The Finches and Plumleys sat around the table. Dora surveyed herself in the mirror of a small compact. Josie had been invited to join them, too, and perched on the edge of her chair eagerly awaiting the reason why. Nina tapped her crimson nails on the mahogany surface and narrowed her eyes on Lance, who was seated straight across from her.

Yes, Lance and Herman had received invitations also.

"People, let's get down to business." Jarvis shot a pile of agendas to the center of the table, and everyone helped themselves.

Connor sat on Jarvis's right, next to Herman. Interesting. Was it telling that Herman had placed himself on the opposite side of the table from his son? To say that Herman was upset his son had fed him those falsified e-mails would be putting it mildly. He'd been grief-stricken when Jarvis talked with him.

"First on the list," Jarvis began, "we have a new lead project manager."

Josie closed her eyes and bit her lip. Dora, her mouth pursed, looked absolutely horrified.

Pointing his finger at Josie, Jarvis added, "You've got the Dominican job. Don't mess it up."

Connor shook his head sadly. He may *never* change.

"I won't let you down." Josie clutched a fist, shook it lightly, and beamed a high-watt smile at Connor.

"Item number two," Jarvis moved on, "quality issues with Green products." He tapped the folder of proposal copies, but he didn't hand them out.

"Let's all get up to speed here," Lance jumped in. "We've just identified the problem as being in fabrication. Someone"—he turned his gaze on Connor—"purchased substandard materials that didn't meet spec."

Someone had. And if that *someone* wasn't Connor, then that *someone* created bogus e-mails to frame him. At the same time, they'd done Castle Heavy Mining a favor and pinpointed exactly who, what, where, when, and how on the quality issues. It wasn't Herman. He was merely his son's patsy, doing his dirty work without even knowing it.

Connor tapped his mechanical pencil on his agenda. For all the silence in the room, he and Lance might have been the only two present. "That's what we're here to discuss today. Green's responsibilities in regards to the current spate of returns Castle has been experiencing, and how we're both going to remedy the situation."

The corner of Lance's eye twitched. "I think you need to assess your own culpability. My father recently found some e-mails that clearly show where the blame lies."

Next to Connor, Herman huffed out a harsh breath. He'd confirmed yesterday who gave him the printout. His apology to Jarvis had been genuine, his sense of betrayal revealed by the mistiness in his eyes as he'd helped Jarvis and Connor work up the proposal.

For Lance's benefit, Connor smiled. Widely. With lots of teeth. "Let's not talk about *blame*, shall we? It's such an ugly word. Let's look for solutions." He indicated the proposal he and Jarvis had worked out with Herman yesterday afternoon. "I'll give you all a few moments to read."

As he read, Lance's eye problem became a full-fledged tick. Preston tipped his head slightly to regard Connor. When he'd asked about Faith's shares this morning, Connor merely said he had everything under control, including Jarvis.

Lance stabbed the first page of the proposal with his finger. "After all this mumbo jumbo, it's a fucking takeover."

"Please, Lance, watch your language." Jarvis glared. "We have ladies present."

As if making a statement, Nina's anklets jingled.

"Dad?" Lance held both hands in the air. "What the hell?"

Herman shook his head. "We don't have the working capital to cover the returns."

"So you're just going to let them buy us out?"

"Yes." And that was all Herman said. No other explanation.

"Don't worry," Connor added, "your father will run Green, and in addition, he'll get two percent of Castle. It's a fair deal. Let me point you to page three." Papers rustled. "Here, you'll notice it states that you *won't* remain as vice president."

"You *asshole*."

Jarvis clucked his tongue at Lance. "Language, my boy."

Lance didn't seem to hear. "This is all because of Faith."

"This is all because you bought out-of-spec material in order to reduce costs. You took the easy way out, then lied about it when the product started coming back. If you'd been up-front right away, we could have minimized the damage." Connor smiled. All right, it *was* a tad malicious, but really, he hadn't mentioned anything about Lance creating false e-mails or embroiling his unwitting father in the scheme to accuse Connor. "You're just not VP material in our opinion. We have no objection, though, if your father wants to keep you on as, say, a junior buyer with enough authority to purchase"—he waved a hand in the air, thinking—"pencils. And if you prove yourself with that, we might let you start buying small office equipment, such as calculators."

He admitted he was having too much fun. Time to get the show on the road. "Jarvis, if everyone's done reading, and there are no other questions, would you like to call for a vote?"

Lance jutted his head forward. "Dad, are you really going to let them get away with this?"

Herman rose, patting his jacket pocket. "I'm going out for a cigar while you all vote."

"Dad, you can't let them do this to me."

His jaw tense and steel suddenly in his gaze, Herman leaned forward. "*You* did this to yourself." Then he straightened. "You betrayed my trust. You betrayed the company. Then you used *me* to put the blame on someone else." Puffing up his chest with a big breath, Herman walked out the door and left Lance behind.

And thus he punished his son with a public humiliation. Connor wasn't sure they'd needed to go that far, but Lance had killed something when he fed his father the fraudulent e-mails.

Lance jumped to his feet. "You're going to pay for this, Kingston."

"Thanks for the warning. I'll be sure to watch my back."

"OH, sweetie, you are so not an asshole." Faith leaned over, her seat belt tugging across her breasts, and kissed Connor's cheek. "Want me to beat him up for you?"

He shut off the engine and put the car in park two doors down from the storefront. "Thanks, baby, but I have to learn to manage my own playground fights."

She laughed. He made her smile as easily as he made her come. At the doctor's office, he'd wanted to go right into the exam room with her. She figured he'd even change diapers when the time came. He loved the house she showed him, but being that it was a buyer's market right now, he wanted to see a few more before they made an offer. He also forgave her father and Herman for ganging up on him. And he'd spent all weekend showing her just exactly how much he loved her, desired her, and needed her.

What more could a girl ask for? Nothing. Not one thing.

Turning to him, she tucked her feet beneath her. "So then what happened?"

"Lance very dramatically slammed the door. And the board voted in favor of the proposal. Green has now merged with Castle. They'll be a wholly owned subsidiary with Herman still running everything on that end. Even Preston seemed pleased."

Faith sobered. "What does this mean for Trinity?"

"She'll still be able to afford her hair and nails and salon treatments and country club membership and—"

Faith put her hand over his mouth. "Be nice."

"She'll find she's better off than she was before," he said against her fingers before pulling her hand away. "Did you think I was going to screw over her old man?"

"Do *you* think I thought you were going to screw him over?"

He put his forehead to hers. "I love you," he whispered.

Her cell phone chirped. "Oh my God, it's Trinity." Trinity, as well as Connor and her father, had her own special tone. "I *have* to take this. We've been playing phone tag so much, I just can't let it happen again. Do you mind?"

He smiled and nodded his assent.

"Trinity, where are you?"

"Tahoe."

"Tahoe?" Faith felt a tremor of unease. "What are you doing there?"

"Harper and I eloped. We just got married in Dr. Raymond Love's Chapel of Love."

Faith couldn't say a word.

"Are you happy for me?"

She found her voice, but it squeaked a little. "I'm so happy for you." For Connor's benefit, she added, "Trinity just got married to Harper Harrington."

"The Third," Trinity amended. "Okay, I gotta go. Harper got us *the* best room at Harrah's."

"Trinity—"

"Gotta run. Love you, talk to ya later, see ya, bye."

And Trinity was gone. God. This felt just plain *wrong*.

"She married the numerals?" Connor didn't make it sound like a compliment.

And she was terrified Trinity had made this decision too quickly. "Oh my God, this is all my fault. She was over on Saturday and I knew there was something wrong, but I didn't make her talk about it."

"Faith." He held her chin in his fingers. "She's a big girl, and old enough to make her own decisions. The most you can do is be there for her if things go wrong."

She widened her eyes. "That is so *not* a guy thing to say."

"I know, but I'm trying to be sensitive, and sensitivity isn't my strong suit. Now come on, let's go inside and see this present you want me to buy for you."

Her fears about Trinity had taken the joy out of her own moment. Mr. Sensitive was right. Trinity was a big girl, and all Faith could do was be there, just as she'd said she'd be. She needed to be happy for her friend instead of a doomsayer.

So she climbed out of the car and dragged Connor into the toy shop.

"Are we here for handcuffs?" he whispered in her hair.

"No, I want you to buy me something better."

"I do love the idea of buying you naughty gifts," Connor murmured as she pulled him past the counter with all the sparkly makeup into the depths amid the vinyl and leather outfits.

Stopping in front of the bust-shaped hanger, she pointed. "I want that." She'd coveted the halter top that day, but she'd been too afraid to even contemplate trying it on, let alone wearing it for Connor.

Yet he'd given her the confidence to own her sexuality and to ask for what she wanted.

"Holy hell." Connor reached out to touch the gold coins of the bodice, setting them jangling, fingering them, then letting them cascade off his hand to fall back into place on the hanger. "You should have at least warned me. How am I supposed to hide this hard-on, baby, when all I can think about is doing you in all that gold?"

"They're not real," she said as she turned over the price tag and raised an eyebrow. "Though they do cost a small fortune."

"Then we're lucky that I'm a fortune hunter, aren't we?"

"Very lucky." Especially since he was *her* fortune hunter.

He tapped her arm with his elbow. "I'm so hot I'll have to follow you into the dressing room while you try it on."

She buried her face against his shoulder. She was sure he meant it. "I had this fantasy about starring in a movie wearing just the coins." She looked up at him and fluttered her eyelashes. "Don't you think they'd make great sound effects?"

He wrapped both arms around her and hitched her up against his long and very hard body. "Baby, I'm here to make your fantasies come true."

And he had. Every single one of them.

Turn the page for a preview of

MINE UNTIL MORNING

The finale to Jasmine Haynes's
deliciously erotic trilogy
about modern-day courtesans
Coming December 2010 from Berkley Heat!

DANI Dawson was drowning. Every time she thought she had a handle on the bills, she'd find another unexpected statement in the mailbox. The vultures had swooped down on her before Kern was even cold in the ground, and the balance in the checking account was a mere one hundred and forty dollars and change.

The walls of her sunflower yellow kitchen closed in on her. The burn in her belly had risen to her chest. If she'd been a crying person, she would have laid her head on the kitchen table littered with unpaid bills and let loose an ocean of tears; for herself, for Kern, for all his pain, his dying, everything they'd lost. She'd scattered Kern's ashes a week ago, on a September day too bright for mourning. Now she missed him like hell.

But Dani was long over the tears. Instead, she picked up her cell phone. Kern would understand what she had to do. She hit her speed dial.

Isabel answered on the second ring. "How are you doing, kiddo?"

"I'm fine, thanks for asking." Dani forced cheer into her voice. "I could really use a date tonight if you can whip up something fast."

Isabel gave a full five-second pause, an eternity. "You know, Dani, you can give it a little bit more time."

Dani swallowed, her eyes aching, but she gritted her teeth. She had to get through this. She'd cried in the early days, when they'd first learned about Kern's cancer. She'd never let him see her tears. She'd been strong and stoic for him in the ensuing year of treatments that didn't work, mounting medical bills, and the rising fear that he might actually die. Six months ago, when the cancer spread to his kidneys, she'd finally broken down, but not in front of him. No, she'd reserved that mortifying moment for Kern's brother Mac. He'd been kind, comforting, but that was the last time she'd lost a grip on herself. She hadn't cried the day they'd decided to bring hospice into the house—Kern hadn't wanted to die in a hospital—or days ago when he passed away. Not even when she and Mac had flown out over the ocean on that bright and sunny day and let Kern's ashes blow to the four winds.

She would not do it now. If she started, she would never stop.

"Isabel, I appreciate your concern. It's very sweet. But I'm fine. The hard part is over. I'm glad he isn't suffering anymore. Kern would want me to move on." God, that seemed pathetically justifying. "And I need the money." Oddly, the truth sounded better.

"Dani, honey, I can help out—"

"Please, Isabel." God, no. She didn't want charity. She'd never lied. Isabel always knew it was about the money. Sure Dani loved sex, and it was a kick to get paid for it, but she'd only become a courtesan when the money dried up and the medical expenses didn't. When they were doing well financially, they'd occasionally splurged, using Isabel's special agency for a little variety. Dani's sex drive had always burned a few degrees hotter than Kern's, but he loved to watch.

They'd made the decision together that working for Isabel and Courtesans was the perfect solution. Isabel had been more than willing to help, of course.

"Call it a loan, Dani."

Dani snorted. "I owe too much money already." She massaged a temple. "I'm really okay with this. If you can find one of my regulars, great, but someone new, that'll work, too." Yeah, she was getting desperate. She hoped it didn't show in her voice. She would get through this difficult time. And she would do it alone. Kern would have hated anyone knowing how bad things had gotten for them. His biggest fear had been Mac finding out how they'd screwed up. Five years younger than his brother, Kern never felt he measured up.

Aw hell, why not admit the truth? She was not going to lean on Isabel or Mac to get her through. She wouldn't depend on anyone. She'd let Kern make far too many decisions, and look where it had gotten her. She wasn't about to give up her autonomy again.

Besides, this was just sex, and she loved sex. It might be the only way out, but it wasn't such a bad way.

"I don't want to see you push yourself too quickly, sweetie," Isabel said. "You've been through something terribly traumatic."

"I know that." Dani's voice quavered. It was all she could do to stuff the emotion back down. "But I"—suddenly starving for air, she gulped a breath—"I really need this. I—I just need it. Please." It was almost begging. "If it's someone I haven't been with before, could you make sure they're okay with cash?"

Many clients paid in gifts: jewelry, artwork, trips. Dani worked on a strictly cash basis. She had no set price. It depended upon the patron and what they wanted, but Isabel didn't cater to an overly thrifty clientele.

Isabel sighed. "All right, you win. Let me see what we've got going. Will tomorrow night work, too?"

"Yes," Dani answered, feeling a small surge of relief. Tonight, tomorrow night, every night until she could get out from under this weight. "Thanks."

"If you need to talk," Isabel added, "I'm always here for you."

Isabel was one of the few people who knew the true toll Kern's illness had taken on her. "I appreciate it, but I'm fine, honestly. I'll get through this."

"I know you will. You were always the strong one. But you don't have to do it all alone."

Yes, she did. Isabel knew that, too, because she was the same way. "Thanks. I'll wait to hear back."

Hanging up, Dani didn't feel so strong now. In the beginning, getting paid for sex had been a unique thrill. Kern had gotten off on it, too. But the massive financial crisis she found herself in had stolen the fun out of it. Not to mention the fact that she and Kern had always enjoyed talking about it afterward, giving her a second high out of it. It wouldn't be the same doing it all alone, but whatever. Taking care of some of these bills and getting back on her feet was all that mattered for the time being.

She and Kern had made some bad choices. She couldn't blame him; she'd agreed to everything, starting the business, canceling the life insurance, the shitty medical plan. Yeah, when you're in your midthirties, healthy and happy, you don't think about dying. You think you've got years to accomplish anything you want. Until the day some doctor says you've only got a few months left to live.

Water under the bridge. Right now, she needed Isabel to find her a date.

AFTER a long day at the office, McKinley Dawson pulled into the circular driveway of his brother's house. His heart hurt simply looking at the familiar wood siding and manicured bushes. He wondered how long it would be before he stopped seeing Kern's emaciated, ravaged body and could remember him the way he used to be. God, he missed him. They'd lost their parents years ago, their dad to a heart attack and their mom to breast cancer. He'd never expected to lose Kern so soon. At thirty-nine, Kern had been five years younger than Mac, for God's sake. It didn't seem possible. Or fair.

Now Kern had tasked him with taking care of his wife. Dani was tough, amazing, in fact, with the way she'd handled everything. In the eighteen-month battle she and Kern had fought with his cancer, Mac had seen only one crack in her façade. She'd shored it up quickly, and he still saw her as the last woman who would need taking care of. He'd made that deathbed promise, however, and, dammit, he was here to make sure she had whatever she needed.

Standing on the pebbled front stoop, he could hear the doorbell echoing through the house. The two weeks before Kern's death, when things got really bad, he and Dani had shared caring for him, with hospice aides coming in twice a day. He hadn't rung the doorbell then. He'd simply walked in. In the evenings, after a grueling day that had seemed to last forever, while Kern slept, he and Dani had shared a bottle of wine, a talk, or a movie. They'd watched *Young Frankenstein*, and he remembered laughing hysterically, followed by the stab of guilt at being capable of laughter. The last couple of days, after Kern fell into the coma, he'd spent the night so Dani wouldn't be alone if . . . when . . .

For those two weeks, he'd felt closer to her than any other human being, even Kern. He couldn't adequately express how much it meant that she hadn't hesitated to allow him those last few precious days with his brother. Some people never got to say good-bye. Then Kern was gone, his ashes scattered, and she'd slammed the metaphorical door in Mac's face.

Inside, he heard her shoes on the tile entry hall. The door swung open.

"You're early. I'm not quite ready." She glanced up, fastening an earring in her lobe, and stopped, her lips parted as if she'd been about to add something.

Holy hell.

She wore a short black cocktail dress, the deep scoop of the neckline barely covering her nipples. In sheer black stockings and fuck-me high heels, her legs were miles long. Statuesque in bare feet, with the heels and standing a step up from him in the front hall, she was actually taller than his own six two. Her auburn hair curled about her shoulders like a wave, and her lips were painted a deep luscious red.

Christ, she smelled good. Something subtly sweet and exotic like the bottled scent of feminine arousal.

The hall clock started to chime. Behind him, a car pulled into the opposite end of the circular drive, a long black sedan.

She had a date. Kern hadn't been dead a week, and she had a fucking date.

"Sorry. Didn't know you were going out." He couldn't get the hell out fast enough. What the fuck? He needed time to think before he said something he'd regret.

So he left her with the entry light shining down on her burnished hair. She still hadn't said a word. As he pulled away, in his rearview mirror, a man, tall, in a black suit, climbed out of the car.

Had she been cheating on Kern while he lay dying? Mac's head whirled with a load of shitty thoughts. That bitch. His hands tightened on the steering wheel until his knuckles turned white.

She didn't need him to fucking take care of her. She'd already had someone on the side.

His blood raced in his ears, and he wanted to pound something. Passing through a green light, the bright neon of a bar sign flashed from the street corner, and Mac pulled into the parking lot.

He needed a drink.

It felt as if he had to pry his stiff fingers off the steering wheel. All he could hear was Kern's voice in his head.

"I fucked up so bad, man."

In a rare moment of lucidity, before he succumbed to the coma, Kern had gripped Mac's hand. Dani was out buying groceries and to grab a breath of fresh air away from Kern's sickroom. Mac had thought she needed it. While he'd spent as much time as he could with Kern, she'd born the brunt of taking care of his brother.

"You didn't fuck up," Mac had told his brother.

Moisture trickled from Kern's left eye, but not his right. Mac's guts twisted as he wiped it away.

"I did, man, screwed up real bad. You don't know. I was a bad husband. I let her down in so many ways. Now I'm dying on her."

They'd had the storybook marriage, they'd been happy. Until Kern got sick. "It's not your fault. You couldn't help it."

Kern shook his head. "You don't know what she's done for me. You don't know what I've put her through. It's all my fault." He dropped back against the pillow, his face going completely slack, eyelids drooping.

Chest tight, a knot in his throat, Mac put two fingers to Kern's wrist. It seemed like an eternity before he found a pulse.

Kern opened his eyes and spoke as if the moment hadn't happened. "Promise me you'll take care of her."

"Of course." Though Mac knew Dani wouldn't need it. She was strong.

Kern clutched his hand, squeezing with more vigor than Mac would have thought possible.

"Don't tell her I'm saying any of this, okay? She'll kill me if she knew." Kern laughed, then lapsed into a choking cough, his throat rattling. He sucked on the straw Mac held out, his lips dry and cracked despite the Vaseline Mac had rubbed in only a short time ago.

"Joke's on me, I guess." Kern drew in a deep breath. "Where's my cell phone?"

"Right here, buddy." On the bedside table along with Kern's watch, wallet, and keys. As if one of these days he was going to get up out of the hospital bed hospice had brought to the house for him.

"Take it, man. After I'm gone, let her get settled a bit, then call the first number on speed dial."

"Sure. What'll I say?"

"Just say you're my brother, and that you want to help Dani."

"I will." Mac agreed to everything to ease his brother's worry.

"She's gonna hate it when she knows I told you. But don't let that stop you, okay?"

"I won't." Though Kern hadn't told him a damn thing. Mac still didn't know why Kern thought he'd fucked up, what he believed Mac could do for Dani by calling a number, or how the hell long he was supposed to wait to let her "get settled."

That night, Kern lapsed into a coma. He never came out of it. Two days later, he was gone. Dani never asked where his cell phone was.

Sitting in the bar's parking lot, the neon sign flashing on, off, Mac experienced the rush of revelation.

He didn't know where she was going tonight or who the guy driving the car was, but he knew one thing. She'd loved Kern. She'd gone through eighteen months of hell, spent hours at his bedside, soothed his brow, cleaned him, held the tissues as he coughed up phlegm, and so much more. She wouldn't have cheated on him. There had to be another explanation. Something to do with the phone number Kern had wanted Mac to use.

It was time to make that call.

KERN'S phone was burning a hole in his pocket. Mac had been torn, feeling uncomfortable poking around in something he didn't understand, especially when Kern said Dani would hate it. Now, though, between his promise to Kern and Dani's odd behavior, he didn't have a choice. Or maybe that was justification for satisfying his curiosity.

Pulling Kern's phone from his suit jacket, Mac flipped it on. Hitting the first speed dial, the caller ID read Isabel. Jesus. It couldn't have been Kern having the affair. But wait . . . Isabel. She'd been at Kern's memorial. A good-looking blonde. Dani'd hugged her, but didn't introduce her to him, and she hadn't come to the house afterward along with everyone else.

He didn't have time for further analysis as he connected.

"Dani, what are you doing using Kern's phone?" The voice was husky, sexy; the woman obviously knew the number on the caller ID.

"This isn't Dani."

She gasped. "Kern? Oh my God. Kern."

His stomach twisted. "No, Kern's dead. You were at his funeral. This is his brother, McKinley Dawson."

"Oh." She paused. "You scared me." She puffed out a breath. "I thought it was one of those phone calls from the hereafter."

"You've gotten calls from the hereafter before?" Damn. Was she some sort of psychic scam artist that Dani and Kern had gotten involved with?

"No, I've never received a call. But it's always within the realm of possibility." She breathed out a long sigh, as if she were trying to get her heart rate under control. "You sound like him, you know."

Mac had never really thought about that. "Look, Kern gave me his cell phone and said to call you so that I could help Dani."

A phone rang in the background, followed by a low voice, so he knew she was still on the line despite her lengthy silence. "Did he say how you were supposed to help Dani?" she finally asked.

"No."

"Did he tell you who I am?"

"No."

"What did he say?"

"Just to call this number, tell you I was his brother, and that I wanted to help Dani. That's it." He paused to let it sink in. "So what the hell is this all about?"

She growled. "He said he was going to do this, and I warned him not to."

"Well, he didn't listen. I want to know what I have to be worried about here."

"Nothing. Dani can take care of herself."

He'd have agreed until he saw Dani dressed to kill tonight. "I won't know until I hear the story."

"Look, Mr. Dawson, Kern was a very sweet man, but he didn't have the right to reveal Dani's secrets without her permission. I've already stuck my nose into one friend's business, and I realize now that was wrong. So I'm not telling you anything, and I won't mention to her that you called. This is strictly between you and Dani. You figure out how to bring it up with her. Whatever she decides she wants you to know is her call."

"You sure do know how to pique a man's curiosity." Except that what he felt was more than that.

"I most certainly do."

For the first time, he heard a smile in her voice and suspected a double entendre. "Fair enough," he agreed. "I'll talk to Dani about it."

"If she wants your help, feel free to call back. And Mr. Dawson, just so you know, I'm looking out for Dani, too. You really don't have to worry."

Damn. The woman had him going. What the hell was

up with Dani? He'd thought he and Kern were so close, yet his brother had been keeping things from him. Mac was beyond being pissed at a possible affair, and way past mere curiosity. His need to know was fast becoming obsession.

And it was definitely not good to have any kind of obsessive feelings about your brother's widow.

Jasmine Haynes has been penning stories for as long as she's been able to write. Storytelling has always been her passion. With a bachelor degree in accounting from Cal Poly San Luis Obispo, she has worked in the high-tech Silicon Valley for the last twenty years and hasn't met a boring accountant yet! Well, maybe a few. She and her husband live with their cat, Eddie (short for Eddie Munster, get the picture), and Star, the mighty moose-hunting dog (if she weren't afraid of her own shadow). Jasmine's pastimes, when not writing her heart out, are hiking in the Redwoods and taking long walks on the beach.

Jasmine also writes as Jennifer Skully and JB Skully. She loves to hear from readers. Please e-mail her at skully@skullybuzz.com or visit her website, www.jasminehaynes.com. Her newsletter subscription is skullybuzz-subscribe@yahoogroups.com.

*Enter the rich world of
historical romance
with Berkley Books . . .*

Madeline Hunter

Jennifer Ashley

Joanna Bourne

Lynn Kurland

Jodi Thomas

Anne Gracie

Love is timeless.

M9G0610

A FLASH OF LIGHT BLINDED MATRINKA—

As her vision cleared, she gazed at a scene out of some nightmare. Three immense bears towered over the screaming mass of royal children, mouths gaping and claws as long and sharp as daggers. At least one had already claimed a victim; its nails dripped congealing trails of blood. Matrinka took in the other details in an instant; three missing bear statues in a garden, a decapitated body, children screeching and crying from what seemed like a million places.

Their Renshai guardian dodged and hacked at all the bears in turn, his grace belying his age and his sword a silver blur. His tunic hung in tatters, and red lines scored his ribs. Only one bear returned his strikes, the others avoided him, intent on the children. Had the warrior had only himself to defend he might have managed to battle the three effectively or slay the one attacking him. But to limit his cuts to one meant leaving its two fellows free to shred Béarn's young heirs. Instead he bounced from one to the next in an obvious attempt to draw all the danger onto himself. The more the bears separated, the more difficult the strategy became.

Two bears charged the fallen children. A wild chorus of terrified screams filled the air, followed by a haunting shriek of pain that cut off in mid-shrill.

"No," Matrinka whispered, grief aching through her fear. "Do something. Do something. . . . The children," she sobbed.

Mickey Zucker Reichert

BEYOND RAGNAROK

The Renshai Chronicles: Volume One

DAW BOOKS, INC.

DONALD A. WOLLHEIM, FOUNDER

375 Hudson Street, New York, NY 10014

ELIZABETH R. WOLLHEIM

SHEILA E. GILBERT

PUBLISHERS

To D. Allan Drummond
(in lieu of proper payment)
Thanks for . . . a lot.

ACKNOWLEDGMENTS

Many thanks to the following people: Sheila Gilbert, Caroline Oakley, Jonathan Matson, Jody Lee, Mark Moore, Dave Countryman, Jennifer Wingert, Dan Fields, and the Pen-Dragons, each helping in his or her own way to make this a better story.

For patience, support, love, and example: Benjamin, Jonathan, Jacob, and Arianne Moore. Also Sandra Zucker, always interested and always caring.

Contents

Prologue

The valley is called Vigrid
where converge in battle
Surtr and the gracious gods;
a hundred leagues
is it every which way—
yes, that's the appointed place.
                    —*Verse Edda, Vafprudnismal 18*

The battle plain of Vigrid sparkled in Asgard's eternal light, an emerald grassland stretching as far as Colbey Calistinsson's vision. Though half-mortal and raised by human parents, he rode toward the gods' war, *Ragnarok,* honestly. A bastard son of Thor, Colbey had been recruited by the leader of the pantheon, Odin, to change the tide of the ghastly war. Unlike the army of gods around him, he wore no coat of mail or helmet, only a light linen tunic and breeks over an average-sized body honed more for quickness and agility than strength. Golden hair riffled free around a clean-shaven face, his locks short and feathered so as not to obscure sight during battle. His tribe, the Renshai, spurned shields and armor as cowards' tools, though he spoke nothing of his prejudice to the Divine Ones. Even had he not held them in an esteem beyond awe, they already knew.

Colbey's sword, Harval, the Gray Blade, felt only vaguely familiar in his hand. Though it had served him faithfully for years, Odin had recently imbued it with aspects of good and evil, law and chaos, so that Colbey could wield it in the gods' cause of balance after the *Ragnarok*. *After the Ragnarok*. The phrase seemed nonsensical. Fate had decreed that the Heavenly War would spare only two hidden humans and a handful of gods. Yet those survivors included the sons of Thor; and Colbey, Odin assured him, was one. Still, experience had taught Colbey that prophecies could be thwarted. In fact, he had learned that such divine forecasts required champions to fulfill them, at least on man's world of Midgard. Odin's certainty that Colbey would help him kill the Fenris Wolf and elude his own destiny, to die in the wolf's maw, assured Colbey the gods' history was not fully preordained either.

Renshai fought without pattern or strategy, and the rigid, somber procession of gods riding toward Vigrid unnerved Colbey. The mental control Renshai exercised, on and off the battlefield, had strengthened his mind. Later, the title of Western Wizard had been unwittingly forced on him, along with its collective consciousness. His psychic war against millennia of previous Western Wizards had destroyed them and left him with the ability to read minds, though it cost him volumes in concentration and vigor; but he chose not to do so to anyone he respected, finding it a rudeness beyond excuse. Nevertheless, strong thoughts and emotions radiated to him without his intention. Now, he felt bombarded by a wild tumult of fear, excitement, stoicism, faith, doubt, and hope that made his own battle joy seem muddled and weak.

Odin the AllFather rode at the head, light reflecting from his helmet in a multicolored halo, his mail pristine. The one-eyed leader of the gods perched proudly upon his eight-legged steed, his spear raised and ready for combat. Just behind him, Thor and Frey rode at Colbey's either hand. Colbey's birthfather brandished his short-handled hammer, *Mjollnir*. Though fated to die, Thor kept his red-bearded head high; his mood, stance, and attitude defined commitment. Even in the face of imminent death, he would not falter.

Colbey looked longest at his brother-in-law Frey, studying the aristocratic features and honey-blond war braids. The handsomest of the gods affected rain, sunshine, and fortune, but his foremost concern now was the fate of the elves he had created. Colbey sensed a fatherly worry transcending irrefutable legend which stated Frey would die on the sword of the fire giant, Surtr. The events slated to follow his death bothered him more, the inferno Surtr would then live to kindle on the worlds of elves, men, giants, and gods as well. Destiny decreed all Frey's "children" would die in the blaze. And the humans Colbey had pledged to rescue would perish simultaneously.

The rest of the gods followed in steady ranks, including the watchman, Heimdall. He and the traitor god, Loki, would die on one another's swords. One-handed Tyr would slay and be slain by the hound from Hel. Vidar, a son of Odin, was fated to kill the mighty Fenris Wolf only after it swallowed his father. Lesser gods trailed behind, surrounded by the ranks of those brave humans who had died in glorious combat, the *Einherjar* of Valhalla. Those heroes were fated to die in the conflicts against giants and against the souls in Hel, who had died cowards or of disease.

Colbey patted his horse, a mortal, white stallion named Frost Reaver who had served him well and faithfully for years. Like all Renshai, Colbey had dedicated himself since birth to becoming one of the *Einherjar.* He had practiced combat maneuvers with an obsessiveness that made even necessities seem distraction. He had joined every war and skirmish, honing his battle skills until he had become the best, and his dedication had proven his downfall. He had become so competent with swords and horses that an honorable death in battle eluded him. Yet he had achieved his goal in a different way. Though not one of Valhalla's heroes, he would have the distinction of fighting in the *Ragnarok* on the side of the gods. Whether he lived or died in the battle did not matter to Colbey, so long as he gave his all.

Figures became discernible on the plain ahead, distance creating the illusion of smallness though the shortest of their leaders, like the gods, towered to half again or double Colbey's height. Only the hordes of Hel's dead compared to normal men in size; the giants, monsters, and gods overshadowed the others nearly to obscurity. Colbey tried to pick specific enemies from the group. His icy, blue-gray eyes sought out the massive, animal shapes from the others: the Fenris Wolf and its brother, the Midgard Serpent. For now, the man-shapes remained indistinguishable.

The maelstrom of others' emotions bombarding Colbey changed to a mixture of bravado, desperation, and placid acceptance. Colbey attempted to focus in on Odin, but the

AllFather's thoughts had always proven singularly impossible to read. The one time Colbey had attempted to invade Odin's mind, not knowing his identity, the leader of the pantheon had manipulated Colbey's thoughts with a strength and agility that had chilled the Renshai's blood in his veins. The wisdom of the world sat behind that one unreadable eye; nothing seemed to escape him.

Colbey loosened his sword in its scabbard and hoped Odin did not already realize that his chosen savior planned to betray him.

On Alfheim, the world of elves, stars speckled the night sky so densely the darkness seemed penciled between them. Beneath their steady light, Dh'arlo'mé tossed and turned on his bed of spongy *kathkral* leaves, uncertain whether to welcome or curse the rest he needed. Though he'd required it for several months, ever since the Northern Sorceress had taken him as her apprentice, sleep still seemed a new concept to the elf. The Sorceress had explained the strange, human phenomenon as a means to reset body and mind, a condition that sprang out of the need to escape heavy thoughts, injury, and sickness. Until Dh'arlo'mé had willingly embraced the Wizard's cause, championing goodness for the human masses, he had had no need of sleep, no reason to wrest burdens from a mind that knew only joy and a body designed to last millennia.

Dh'arlo'mé ran long fingers over his high, sharp cheekbones and heart-shaped lips. When he chose to become one of the four Cardinal Wizards, he knew he might come to regret the decision. But even the gods could not have predicted the sequence of events that assured the *Ragnarok,* the fated battle that would claim the lives of nearly all mankind, all elves, and most of the gods. The memory would not leave Dh'arlo'mé. Despite his best efforts, the pictures paraded through his mind, accompanied by odors, sounds, and the strangely gentle caress of the wind. Three of the four Cardinal Wizards lay on a moldy carpet of leaves, their life's blood puddling like spilled wine. Each had taken his or her own life, the price for abandoning Odin's laws, for hunting down one of their own like an animal, and for loosing chaos on the world of men, a world that, until that time, knew only order.

The last of the Wizards, Colbey, the Western champion of

Law, had argued for salvation and forgiveness for his peers. But Odin had granted no quarter, and the Wizards apparently agreed with the cruel, gray god. They died by their own hands, permanently, in the manner of humans. At the time, Dh'arlo'mé had appreciated Odin's mercy; he alone of the apprentices had survived the events leading to the coming of the father of gods. Only now, he understood the callousness of leaving him to perish with his brethren in the coming war. The hopelessness haunted every hour, and Odin's decree still echoed in his head:

> *Wizard only in name,*
> *Your Mistress to blame*
> *Her bones rightfully soon entombed.*
> *Go back to the one*
> *Who calls you her son*
> *Alfheim is already doomed.*

Doomed. Dh'arlo'mé rolled, accidentally yanking the fine, red-gold locks trapped beneath his arm. With eyes as glazed and steadfastly colored as emeralds, he studied the open sky, its familiar pattern of stars unchanging and broken by the shadows of broad-leafed trees. Elfin giggling trickled through the branches, the sound more normal than the previous silence yet perpetuating, rather than distracting from, his concerns. Within days, all elves would die in fiery agony, and Dh'arlo'mé seemed helpless to find understanding, let alone a solution. Danger held no meaning to those who lived without weather or individuality. Death came to elves only after centuries or millennia of play, and then it only meant a new beginning as an infant, stripped of memories from the previous lives, though a few always slipped through. Yet, if *Ragnarok* destroyed all, no more babies could be made to re-use those souls. Utter, irrevocable destruction of all elves would result.

Dh'arlo'mé sighed, struck by the irony. He required sleep to escape the worries that now troubled him, the same worries that would not allow him to relax enough to rest. The burden of knowledge had become unbearable, the understanding that the world and elves he loved would vaporize into fiery devastation, leaving nothing, not even a single mind to cherish the memory. And he was helpless to prevent it. *Helpless.* Dh'arlo'mé hated the word like an enemy. What little magic the Northern Sorceress had managed to teach him during his short apprenticeship, all the natural power and chaos of elves, and all the sleepless hours could not spare one life from the holocaust. *Helpless.* Dh'arlo'mé cursed the hours wasted trying to make the other elves understand. To them, imminent meant a decade, and the concept of total annihilation either could not register or did not matter. He had tried to harness their natural power, to combine magic to find salvation. But though their attention spans far exceeded those of humans, their attitudes remained habitually frivolous.

Helpless. An image of Odin filled Dh'arlo'mé's mind, the robust figure and cold, blue eye blurred by a sudden flash of light. The god's magic had opened a gate to the world of elves through which he had returned Dh'arlo'mé to his damned people. The thought sparked insight. Dh'arlo'mé sat up, buoyed with new hope. *Maybe not helpless.*

Dh'arlo'mé rose, rushing to the knobby roots that cradled the texts and tomes the Northern Sorceress had spared him.

Odin's horse leaped for Fenrir, its four forelegs outstretched as if to embrace the massive wolf. Thor's mount, too, sprang for the monster. Frey charged the fire giant destined to slay him, and the other gods and the *Einherjar* took their places in the struggle. Colbey had intended to accompany his brother-in-law; but war rage overtook him, and he sprinted in Odin's wake as if sucked in by momentum. The wolf danced aside, its quickness astounding for its size, its black fur bristling in deadly warning. Odin's spear lunged for a broad head that dodged and reared out of the weapon's path in an instant.

Before Thor could reach his father's side, a monstrous head whipped up, hissing, in front of him. Coils still enwrapping the world, the Midgard Serpent opened its maw, revealing a vast red plain striped with teeth as long as a man's body. The raw stench of its breath blasted Colbey, and each fang dripped clear venom like a hungry dog's spittle. The sight proved too much for the horses. Thor's balked, throwing off the timing of his attack. His sword scraped harmlessly along the bridge of the serpent's nose. Frost Reaver's hooves clawed clouds, and the stallion twisted at the peak of his rear. The mortal beast toppled over backward. Colbey sprang free as his horse struck the ground, glad he habitually used no saddle. He rolled, tucking his limbs as close to his body as the sword allowed. He came up in a ready crouch to the drum of fading hoofbeats. An ax in the hands of a dead man from Hel whipped toward his head.

Colbey blocked as he rose, catching the force of the blow on his sword. The other's strength slammed him into a crouch. He lunged, burying the sword in his enemy's gut. As he jerked it free, three others swarmed upon him at once. Colbey caught one blade on his, raising it to duck beneath the other two. A broad riposte sent the trio into awkward retreat. Colbey sliced down two before they could think to defend. The last slashed furiously. Colbey's sword cut beneath the wild web of attack and gutted the man, now twice dead.

Embroiled in the thick of the battle, Colbey hacked and parried like a mad thing, sending masses of Hel warriors to their final demises. *Einherjar* surged around him, their varied war cries ululating into an echoing frenzy. Though it had been his lifelong dream to battle amid the bravest of slain warriors, Colbey found no joy in the arrangement now. Something unseen prickled and worried at his mind, driving him always toward one goal. For the first time, war became dull routine where always before it had overwhelmed him with excitement, no matter the conflict. The oddity struck him, even as he sliced through or under armor and around foemen's shields. Though it went against honor and training, he allowed long-ingrained habit to take over, trusting eye, reflex, and instinct to protect him while he sought the force that stole joy from his battle and coaxed him toward a goal he could not yet identify.

Then, as if to answer his concern, a pair of black birds circled, then dove, momentarily blotting the sun. Colbey recognized them at once: Hugi and Munin, Thought and Memory, Odin's pets. The crows twined through the tide of dead, those who had perished in glory and those in cowardice or of illness. They rushed Colbey, swirling around his head like inky halos, guiding him toward Odin and the Fenris Wolf. A voice rattled through his head, "It is your task, your destiny, to slay the wolf and rescue the AllFather." A pervading sense of rightness filled him, as if his conception had heralded this moment. All of his past glories paled, and his fate became a bright and beckoning tunnel. Here, he would find the answer to the endless, aching search. Once he'd believed he lived only for the chance to die in glory. Now, truth and reality became an undeniable constant that had eluded him through eternity. He had found his only purpose since birth.

Colbey directed his attacks, hammering and slashing through the ranks of Hel's dead as if possessed. Yet, despite a focus and certainty that should have brought the excitement back into his battle, he felt even more distant. The simple pleasure of war that had spurred him from childhood through old age had disappeared. This purpose, this thing that purported to be all that mattered to him, stole the meaning from all other joys once his.

Forces rose to battle his concern, pounding at his doubts with the strength of his enemies' blades; but the need to combat his natural wonder had the opposite effect. Questions turned to suspicion, and he recognized the feeling of "rightness" and security as foreign. Only one being had managed to influence Colbey's thoughts in the past, the same who would benefit if the old Renshai truly believed in the mission with which the other had charged him. *Odin*. The AllFather's decision to use him, even against his will, raised an ire that no magic or mental skill could quash.

Colbey channeled his rage into controlled sweeps and lunges that sent a dozen dead men back to their pyres and triple that number seeking more evenly matched opponents. The *Einherjar* followed him like a guiding light, hewing and slashing a path of corpses in his wake. Colbey paid them no heed, turning his attention to the crows who cackled, swooped, and pressed him toward the wolf and the father of the gods. Like a sheep or a slave, they herded him, and Colbey would have none of it anymore. Quicker than a heartbeat, his sword cut air, then cleaved a feathered head from its neck. Hugi plummeted. Odin's presence in Colbey's mind flashed in outrage, then faded as closer events commanded its attention. Odin could not afford two battles at once. If the one he fought to save himself killed him, the other no longer mattered.

Colbey savored the clarity of mind that followed the abatement of Odin's will. The character of the mental presence mutated from deceptive to guilt-inspiring, plucking at Colbey's religious foundations, his personal dedication to the gods and their causes throughout his mortal life. But the fueling of long-ingrained loyalties only strengthened Colbey's devotion to his true cause, that of mankind. His allegiance went first to those he championed, the humans whose only means to avert destruction lay in the hands of the *Einherjar*, those who had managed to die in glory prior to the *Ragnarok*. And with Colbey Calistinsson/Thorsson.

Colbey continued to fight Hel's hordes, blood wrath once again a welcome friend. Now properly redirected, he scanned the teeming masses of warriors for the ones he sought, hoping he had not overcome Odin's misdirection too late. The AllFather still raged within him, reduced to making vague, grand promises of rewards, the effort far too late. Colbey could feel Odin groping for the best words and strategy, weakened by his losing battle with the Fenris Wolf. Once, the Renshai might have suffered sympathy for the great, gray god whose long-known doom had come to claim him. Now, Colbey gritted his teeth and strained his vision for a glimpse of the elf-lord and his fiery enemy. Tipping the tide of Frey's conflict had been his goal from the start, allowing his wife's brother to destroy the fire giant and thus rescue mankind from its ruin.

Colbey discovered the whirling blur of combat that was Frey and Surtr. Far to his left, they stabbed and capered like elemental dancers. Surtr's jagged beard swept around his coarse features, the hair as sinuous and red as the force he represented. Sweat sheened every part of Frey that his armor did not hide, pouring in rivulets from his face. Heated by Surtr's presence, the mail surely hampered as much as protected; but the god chose to leave it on. Colbey could not help but suffer a shock of contempt at the display, though he dismissed his aversion as easily as he had avoided disdaining the others their shields and protections. His religious faith and awe of the gods went every bit as deep as the code of the Renshai.

The battle tide surged dizzily around Colbey. *Einherjar* locked with the warriors of Hel. Gods, giants, and the monsters who were Loki's children dodged and attacked repeatedly, the noise of their movements thunderous. The crash of massive weapons and the hollow drumbeat of fists against flesh blended into a frenzied cacophony that dwarfed the normal sounds of battle. The music Colbey knew as warfare had become amplified to a sound that ached painfully in his ears and forced him to strain for the telltale rustle of nearer enemies. Still, he surged toward Frey and Surtr, slaying hundreds who dared delay him, unbalancing the *Einherjar*/Hel horde struggle as he had not done for Odin.

Lightning cleaved the sky in a spreading zigzag, as if the world of gods were cracking like an eggshell. Thor bellowed in triumph, the cry echoing over even the pounding and rattle of unearthly weapons against armor. The head of the Midgard Serpent collapsed, the impact quaking. It writhed, coil looping over coil, stirring clouds and wind into a tempest that shattered many warriors. Some, more distant, lost their footing and fell, turning the tide of several battles. Thor staggered only seven victorious steps before plummeting to the ground, poisoned by his now-dead enemy. Thor's wife dodged through the battles with a dexterity that revealed her own martial training, carrying a cup of antidote. Her cry of grief told Colbey what he did not pause to see; either she arrived too late or the treatment failed. Either way, Asgard's mightiest lay dead.

Finally, Colbey cleaved a clear route to Frey and Surtr. The god panted, mouth wide, nostrils flaring, chest rising and falling in rapid, massive waves. His horse sprawled nearby, the victim of a blow landed early in the combat. Blisters scarred Frey's face in dashes and lines, as if caused by a splashed boiling liquid. Rents marred his mail, the links shattered in places and scratched in others. His notched sword sagged, revealing an exhaustion that might soon prove fatal. Love had driven Frey to buy his wife with his horse that did not shy from magic or flame and his sword that fought giants of its own accord. Now, it seemed, he would pay for his marriage with his life and those of all men, elves, giants, and most of the gods. Nevertheless, Colbey did not disdain his brother-in-law's decision. He would have sacrificed as much or more for his own wife, Freya.

Surtr raised his flaming sword for a killing stroke, eyes glowing red with triumph. Frey tried to dodge, clumsy with fatigue. He tripped over nothing Colbey could see, falling helplessly to the grassy plain of Vigrid. The sword blazed toward Frey's head. Colbey dove between them, hammering his sword against Surtr's forearm. Even with momentum, his strength seemed puny in comparison, but surprise worked as well as power. The point of Surtr's blade plowed into soil a finger's breadth from Frey's chest, igniting the underpadding of the god's mail. The instant it took the giant to free the blade cost him a slash from Colbey's sword that stretched from knee to ankle.

Frey rolled out of range, snuffing his smoldering clothing.

Surtr bellowed in rage and pain, turning his attention to the new danger. The giant towered half again Colbey's height, his sword as long as the Renshai's entire body. Flames leaped and capered along the steel, trailing in the breeze of its every stroke. Apparently mistaking Colbey for one of the *Einherjar,* his expression remained neutral and he swept ponderously, as much to drive Colbey backward as kill him. "Back to your own battle, little manling."

Colbey ducked easily under the attack, not bothering to parry. He had seen the damage the burning sword inflicted upon Frey's blade. Flawlessly, he executed the Renshai triple twist designed to penetrate mail. Harval ruptured the links, biting into underpadding, then falling free. Colbey rushed in for another strike.

Surtr redirected his blade to block; the Renshai's extraordinary competence would not catch him off-guard again. Sword struck sword, launching a wild spray of sparks. Pinpoint burns stung Colbey's limbs, and tiny fires sputtered and died in the grass. Faster, Colbey pulled out of the block first, closing the space between them to accommodate his shorter weapon. Their proximity would also make it more difficult for Surtr to gather momentum for his colossal sword. A single, landed blow from that weapon would sunder or smash Colbey.

Reflexively, Surtr back-stepped. Colbey charged in, plugging the gap, striking for the groin. Surtr twisted with impressive agility. The point of Colbey's sword bit flesh from the giant's thigh, flinging blood that scorched like cinders. Surtr flailed directionlessly. Colbey dodged, lunging for an opening that existed for less than half a second. A lucky kick slammed Colbey's legs, sprawling him. Pain flared through the Renshai's knee, and Surtr raised his sword for a deathblow.

Colbey waited until the blade began its descent, fully committed. He rolled free, feeling the warmth of its approach as he staggered to legs bruised and strained by Surtr's kick. Again, he rushed the monster, diving through the flaming web of offense, the sword's lingering light revealing patterns that would otherwise have remained hidden. He struck for the large artery in the thigh, blade gliding beneath the mail skirt. Surtr jerked, hammering his hilt toward Colbey's skull. Colbey skipped aside, sacrificing attack for defense. His blade skimmed flesh, drawing a superficial line of blood. The giant's hilt clipped the side of his head, screaming past his ear. Though glancing, the blow shot white light through his vision, blinding and dizzying. Had the blow landed squarely, it would have fragmented his skull.

Colbey staggered several steps, blood lust buzzing through him like a living thing. Only once had he faced an opponent as apt and worthy, the day Thor, misreading a situation, had charged him with being an enemy of law. The Renshai tried to clear his head. The blazing sword speeding toward him seemed triple-bladed. No time to dodge. He dropped flat to the ground, hearing the whoosh of its passage overhead, feeling the sting of its loosened sparks. Faster than a heartbeat, he bounded to his feet and launched himself at the giant.

"Modi!" Colbey gasped, calling upon Thor's son who ignited a warrior's battle wrath. He shouted from habit; the Renshai as a tribe had responded to injury this way since long before his birth. Pain provoked rather than daunted them; and he learned to fight not through pain but because of it. Now, amidst the gods, the cry seemed ludicrous. But it spurred Colbey just the same. He became a savage blur of offense, the sword a silver extension of his arm, never still. The blade tore furrows in flesh and armor, rending mail links with maneuvers none but the Renshai knew.

Surtr set to parry and block, weaving a defense with his sword to cover the gaps in his armor. "Who are you?" he demanded. "And from where in the nine worlds do you come?"

Colbey gave no answer. Clever talk could only steal concentration and vigor better spent on battle. When Surtr died, it would not matter who had slain him, only that he would not live to set the worlds on fire, to cause the prophesied destruction. And, if Surtr survived, it did not matter one iota whether Colbey did or not. As a son of Thor, he might outlast the fire giant's conflagration, but the cause to which he dedicated himself would have disappeared. He would have failed to rescue the Renshai and all mankind.

Frey returned to the battle with a wild roar and bold assurance. His sword swept for Surtr's neck, far above the reach of Colbey's blade. Surtr battered it away, then whipped his blade downward to smash Colbey. Too late. The Renshai's sword penetrated mail and tunic and plunged into his abdomen.

Surtr reared back, his expression one of betrayal. Fate had decreed that he would win this battle, that his fires would sweep the nine worlds and nearly all things living would die at his whim. Fuming, he threw back his head and hands, opening his defenses at a time Colbey anticipated the opposite. Words spewed from the giant's mouth, uninterpretable yet as blisteringly hot as his sword. Smoke roiled from his fingertips, twining in the air above him, then thinning to colored streamers that disappeared in the wind. Frey screamed, jabbing for the exposed chest as Colbey slammed his blade home, hilt-deep into the giant's abdomen. Surtr collapsed, arms akimbo, fingers limp; yet, apparently, the damage had already been done.

Frey and Colbey tore their weapons free together, flinging blood now no warmer than their own. Despite the victory, Frey's face went ashen, his blue eyes and demeanor radiating pure agony. He lowered his head, mumbling something unintelligible, fingers thrashing in nervous triangles.

Colbey could not fathom the emergency, though he guessed the actions of giant and god had some basis in magic and felt certain he needed to understand quickly. Terror, rage, and grief poured from Frey, threatening to overwhelm them both with its intensity. "What happened?" Colbey demanded.

Frey gave no answer, only traced an invisible rectangle in the air in front of him. The outline shimmered slightly, almost undetectable, then gradually grew denser and more visible.

"What happened?" Colbey repeated, giving his brother-in-law one last chance to answer before desperation drove him to actions he might regret. He could sense that sorrow and terrible anger were hampering Frey's speed and craft; and Colbey hoped that would delay the god enough so that he could find answers before there were none to find. When Frey gave no response to his question, Colbey violated his own law for the first time. Uninvited, he entered the thoughts of one he considered a friend and ally, did so for the good of mankind and gods alike.

Understanding came in an instant, the details unimportant. Surtr's spell had kindled magical fires on the other worlds, including Alfheim; and Frey was building a gate to transport himself and Colbey to the elves. The Renshai drove perception one step farther. While they battled to save elves, Surtr's flames would incinerate Midgard and all mankind. He would lose the very cause he had rescued Frey and spent Odin's life to protect.

"No!" Colbey seized Frey's arm, shaking.

The rectangular outline wobbled, and Frey hissed in outraged warning. His concentration narrowed to the final sequence of his spell, and he blotted out the physical world, including Colbey's pleas. Nothing external could change what would happen next, so Colbey scrambled for mental control. Helplessly, he watched as each foreign syllable slipped from concept to articulated, as the gestures and intent powered the whole into operative magic. Ignorant of the workings of any magic, he dove ahead, exploring each as yet unspoken sound until he found one he recognized, the last of the sequence: the Northern term for Alfheim.

Alfheim. The chain of idea trickled through Frey's head in a fraction of a second, yet Colbey caught the last before it disappeared. *Midgard* he inserted.

Frey's consciousness bucked against the change. *Alfheim.*

Colbey persisted, *Midgard.*

The spell wavered as Frey's grip on the magical tapestry as a whole weakened.

Midgard! Colbey bullied through the modification, the intensity of concentration draining volumes of physical endurance. Entering minds always cost him dearly, and the effort of wrestling a god, at a time when his strength was already compromised by battle, tired him.

Light flashed, exploding through Colbey's eyes. Vision disappeared, burned away. His orbs felt on fire, and agony urged him to tear out his eyes to stop the pain. Instead, he drew his sword to combat enemies he could not yet see. His face felt flushed and acrid smoke funneled into his lungs, a hot anguish that eclipsed the pain of head and eyes. He managed to pry his lids apart, blinking through a web of rainbow afterimages. Either the world or his vision had washed red. Multihued flames chopped jagged tendrils and spirals across the landscape, all beneath it dead black and gray. Beside him, Frey howled in wordless sorrow.

* * *

One thousand, five hundred and forty-seven of the three thousand elves agreed to assist Dh'arlo'mé's strange tests, though curiosity, kindness, or appeasement seemed the inducements rather than any belief in or concern for the imminence of their destruction. Within a day, he had lost a third of them to boredom. Now, two days later, only six hundred and thirteen remained, melding, concentrating, combining, and experimenting with the natural magic that they and their forefathers had used daily without comprehension of its mechanism. From Dh'arlo'mé's observation, the law/chaos balance was skewed far toward law on man's world, precluding magic for all but the four Cardinal Wizards whom Odin had established and later destroyed. On Alfheim, chaos played a larger role. Magic simply was, as it had always been, a means to enhance love and play that required no explanation.

Dh'arlo'mé oversaw the six hundred-odd elves who had chosen to stay, concentrating most on the twenty-eight his arguments had actually managed to convince. Within hours, their demeanors had gained the ponderous severity of men's. Under ordinary circumstances, the change would have disheartened him; but desperation made the transformation a welcome relief. He kept them together, their seriousness enhancing one another's concentration, and he let most of the others experiment at will. He had caught them doing everything from mutating their appearances to flying in star formations to making love in quads and triads. Elves had always been free with sexuality; the cycle of birth and reincarnation kept their number always at three thousand and pregnancies exactly as rare as deaths.

Suddenly, the eternally cloudless sky darkened to gray then black. The usual pleasant breeze became an unheard of wind that tossed the broad leaves of the *kathkral* trees into a clicking, rattling dance. Their trunks swayed, slightly at first. Then, as the wind rose to a gale, the *kathkral* bent as if to kiss the ground, first one way, then the other. The green-, orange-, and white-striped *yarmshinyin* trees stood firm, though their round, multicolored fruit rolled across the vast blue-green grassland. Soon, the air and land seemed thick with hollow balls, the swarm of colors random and patternless, their diversity a beauty unto itself. Many elves abandoned their work to play "tap," "bounce," or "fling around" with the floating *yarmshinyin* fruit, trading one for another on a whim.

Nameless terror enveloped Dh'arlo'mé. *The Ragnarok has begun.* He knew without comprehending how. The sky quaked and quivered, the movement lost behind the milling *yarmshinyin* fruit. Dh'arlo'mé saw, without normal vision, the world fragmenting around him and imagined seams in the expanse of horizon, in the continuity of ground, in all things once permanent. The boundaries between object and nothingness, between reality and fantasy blurred; and Dh'arlo'mé rushed to the side of those most believing. "Hurry," he shouted, certain of the truth of his warning. "Our time is almost over."

The youngest of the twenty-eight rose, a female of scarcely a century named Baheth'rin. Her hands shook as she traced a rectangle against a background changing by the moment. She stepped back, the outline white, the figure shimmering silver and aqua.

An explosion rocked Alfheim, deafening Dh'arlo'mé and sprawling Baheth'rin along with several of her peers. Distant screams shattered vast millennia of peace, their pain tearing through Dh'arlo'mé as if his own. Baheth'rin's magic disappeared along with her concentration, and the farther horizon glowed red.

Surtr's fires! Hopelessness froze Dh'arlo'mé in place momentarily. Elves scattered in panic, never before having faced a crisis. Others stood rooted, absolutely unable to move in any direction or fashion. A few remained, looking to Dh'arlo'mé for a guidance he felt too weak to give. Then, desperation lent him strength. He assisted Baheth'rin to her feet. "Do your spell!"

Tears dripped from her yellow-pink eyes, glazing them like marbles. Her white hair hung in limp tangles. "But that's all I know. I can't get it to open."

"Try!" Dh'arlo'mé shouted. Already the roar of the fire touched his ears, its acrid stench stung his nose, and the agonized shrieks drew nearer. A small world, Alfheim would not take long to burn.

Baheth'rin started again, chanting and drawing. Her hands fluttered, leaving bumpy outlines in the air. The other seven pressed toward her, lending support, both physical and magical, where they could. They all kept their backs toward the approaching carnage, but Dh'arlo'mé dared a peek. Flames towered from ground to sky, as wide as the great wolf's maw and redder than fresh blood. Colors danced through the conflagration, and Dh'arlo'mé felt a strangeness about the destruction, found himself thinking of it as an entity rather than a force. Living chaos of any kind, he knew, bore the name "demon." He could see figures running ahead of the spreading flames, saw many collapse and disappear beneath the blaze. Surtr's magic moved faster than any elf could fly or run.

Screams erupted amid Dh'arlo'mé's crowd. More elves bolted, fleeing from the approaching mass of flames. Seized with an instinctive urge to join them, Dh'arlo'mé crushed need with understanding. Running would just delay the inevitable. Their only hope lay here.

One of the twenty-eight turned, gasping at the sight, Baheth'rin stiffened, but Dh'arlo'mé grasped her shoulders, preventing her from turning, holding her concentration on the spell. "Don't lose it, girl!"

Baheth'rin gasped, the magic obviously draining energy. "No more. Tried everything. Can't finish."

"Hold what you have." Dh'arlo'mé commanded those who remained, whether by design or paralytic terror. "Help her, damn it! Add whatever you can. There's no escape on Alfheim. This door must open!"

Now the elves rallied in support. Magic crisscrossed and flew, filling the air with a tangible chaos that sent the rectangle flipping through a billion colors. The air grew warm, then hot. Sweat beaded and ran from every brow, and others could no longer contain their fear. More bolted. The rest remained, savagely hurling every trick at their disposal to reinforce what Baheth'rin had started. An elf staggered into their midst from the direction of the fire. Dh'arlo'mé caught the runner before he had a chance to think. Only then, he realized he stared into eyeless sockets in a hairless head. Blisters covered the places that still held skin, most charred away leaving bone exposed. The legs and arms continued to move, though no life remained in the skeletal form.

Dh'arlo'mé recoiled, dropping the corpse, screaming despite every attempt to control the others with his calm. As if it was a signal, the savage heat slammed them. Agony encompassed Dh'arlo'mé, tearing at his insides as if to claim his soul as well as his body. His skin crawled and tingled. He screeched, hearing a chorus of pain resound around him.

A soft voice managed to penetrate his anguish where others had not. "It's open."

Dh'arlo'mé swept forward, shoving as many elves in front of him as he could. He kept his lids closed, certain that to open them meant blindness; his eyes could not survive the heat blistering his flesh. Then, suddenly, the burning disappeared, its absence more soothing than any herb or balm. Grass tickled his ankles. A damp sea breeze tugged at his flesh and the charred tatters of his clothing. He opened his eyes to a pewter sky, green grass, strange trees, and distant mountains. Beside him, Baheth'rin sobbed, eyes locked on the fading rectangle. Other elves stood, lay, or sat around them. He could hear pounding footsteps as some fled to various places on this new world they had discovered.

"Hold the gate!" Dh'arlo'mé shouted, uncertain which of his charges remained responsible for the magic. He shoved both arms through the archway, scrabbling wildly into a world he could no longer see. A heat far beyond mortal fire seared him, and the need to withdraw became overpowering. He managed to grab a wrist with one hand, hair with another, and tug two more coughing, sputtering elves to safety. Then the gate snapped shut, forever closing Alfheim from its creatures.

Dh'arlo'mé stared at his scorched, twisted hands for only a few seconds before unconsciousness claimed him.

On Midgard, Colbey fought the only way he knew. Raising Harval, he charged into the flames, hacking and slashing through a red conflagration that seemed at least as alive as the god at his side. The flames radiated a laughing, mocking sentience, and the land around held an emptiness beyond death. Where chaos touched, it destroyed utterly.

Frey swore, his emanating thoughts turbulent with choices. Though Colbey concentrated elsewhere, he could not miss the myriad thoughts the god unwittingly broadcast, decisions that ranged from allowing Colbey to die and rushing to rescue Alfheim to protecting them both and assisting where he could. All-pervading anger and grief blanketed his mind, making decision-making all the harder.

Colbey's sword cleaved the flames, the hilt like ice in his grip. Above each cut, the crown of each saw-toothed flame dissipated, leaving a stump whose heat withered the Renshai. Within a few seconds, his clothes ignited. Heat blistered his flesh, rising in increments to a crescendo of suffering that stole coordination and, gradually, thought. He staggered, his back striking something solid. Frey's words were senseless over the roar of the blaze. Then, as suddenly as it had begun, the pain disappeared. Frey's magic enfolded him like a sodden blanket, assuaging as well as blocking the intolerable heat.

Colbey did not waste a moment assessing Frey's gift. He charged back into the fray, sword flying with a speed that rendered it all but invisible. The Gray Sword of balance ruptured chaos wherever it struck, slicing through fire as if through flesh. Flames surged, collapsed, and died before him. A swell engulfed him, battering with astounding strength, though its warmth no longer bothered him.

"Alfheim!" Frey screamed above the fire's crackle and rumble, though Colbey could not guess how many times the god spoke before he heard. "Alfheim first, then here!"

"We're here now!" Colbey returned, hating even the minuscule effort speaking claimed from him. "Alfheim next!"

"It'll be too late!"

Colbey did not bother to return the obvious argument. If they did not have the time to destroy chaos in Midgard before Alfheim, how did Frey expect them to transport there, fight the same force, and come back for mankind? The logic self-evident, he gave no response, only continued to wade through the battering fire, slicing as fast as his tired limbs allowed. Exhaustion weighed on him like death, and he doubted he could take much more of chaos' pounding before it crushed him.

"Come to me now!" Frey shouted. "Or I'll leave you, and you'll have no protection from the heat."

Furious, Colbey found a second wind. His arm and sword never slowed. "I saved your worthless hide for this moment! I damned Odin and rescued you instead. Haven't I earned any loyalty?"

"The elves are my people! My creation!"

"Mankind is my charge," Colbey threw back the same point. "And we're already here."

"Come to me!" Frey's voice became a frustrated screech that told Colbey the god wanted his presence not to protect Thor's son but for more selfish reasons. The logical justification filled his thoughts: Frey needed him to battle Alfheim's blaze every bit as much as Colbey relied on Frey's magic. The difference was, they had come to Midgard, no matter the means or reason. Any delay might doom elves and men alike.

"Modi," Colbey said, dredging the last whispers of stamina from his core. He lurched through the closing wall of redness. Fire enclosed him, the roar deafening him to Frey's demands, and he wallowed through, cutting with every advance. It felt like an eternity before he waded to the outer edge of the conflagration, though logic told him he could not have traveled far. The fire encompassed an area no larger than two towns combined, though the number of casualties would depend upon their location. If it actually perched upon a single city, thousands might already have died.

At the boundary, Colbey renewed his battle, hacking and stabbing with rabid determination, yet paradoxically focused on strategy. Spiraling inward, he controlled the spread as well as fought the chaos-entity. He did not see Frey, but his continued imperviousness to the heat told him his companion had chosen the wiser course.

Onward Colbey fought, until his arms went numb and the battle became habit. His head buzzed, emptied of any thought but sleep, and darkness whittled at his consciousness. Frey, too, it seemed, was weakening. The air gradually changed from temperate, to warm, to uncomfortable, and sweat only enhanced the weariness, threatening to steal all reason. The flames continued to assail Colbey, a constant that no longer taunted him. His mind flickered through a series of exhaustion-inspired images: human weapons seemed to thrust at him from all directions, colors swirled into marching blurs, and a lullaby refused to leave his head to the point where he matched his strokes to its beat. Yet, still the fight went on. Whether instinctively or through some knowledge he read from Frey, he knew that to leave a single fire-demon meant losing the battle. He would die, all mankind charred to cinders with him.

Vision left Colbey first. His lids became too heavy to keep open, and he thrashed and stomped in darkness, guided only by the fire's heat. Then, that clue disappeared as well, and he groped desperately, appealing to some higher force to steer his hand. As if in answer to the plea, a voice filled his ear. "Kyndig, stop. It's over." It took Colbey far too long to recognize Frey, and the name "Skilled One" that only gods called him. Then the Renshai dropped to the ground. He drew a rag from his pocket, his only thought to honor his dirty sword before oblivion claimed him.

But Frey would not allow the lapse. "Come on. There may still be time." He sounded as tired as Colbey felt, and the god's dedication spurred Colbey as much as anything could, which was little. Though he did not rise, he allowed Frey to transport him where he would. Spell words sounded thunderous in the hush that followed chaos' destruction. Colbey suspected he had fallen asleep briefly because the gate-creation seemed to span less than a second. The dazzling flash stabbed even through his closed lids. The quality of the air changed, and his lungs sucked in a fragrant, delicate breath riddled with soot.

Frey howled, the sound rich with elemental grief. The inherent sorrow tore at Colbey's soul, rousing an anguish so primal he could not help but cry without truly knowing the reason. *Too late to rescue the elves.* And, though he suffered Frey's anguish as well as his own, he found relief in the void that swallowed him then. On a plain ravaged to nothing by chaos, Colbey mercifully fell asleep.

Chapter 1

King Kohleran's Heirs

The choice between life and honor falls into the hands of the one whose life or honor is at stake.
— Colbey Calistinsson

The sun hovered over the Bellenet Fields in Erythane, glazing the enclosing wooden and wire fence and glittering off its metal hardware. Knight-in-training Ra-khir Kedrin's son continued to review combat tactics on the packed earth of the practice grounds long after his three colleagues had left for the midday meal. Unlike them, Ra-khir had no reason to go home, no one with whom to dine. His knight-captain father had led a troop of Erythane's finest on maneuvers in the high kingdom of Béarn, and his mother had made matters clear on his seventeenth birthday two weeks earlier: Ra-khir could choose to associate with Kedrin or her, not both. His father's unconditional love had made the decision easy, but the consequences still ached within him.

Ra-khir repeated a drill Armsman Edwin had taught, a tricky block/riposte/parry/shield bash combination, working to memorize the maneuver to the point of instinct. His fine red hair swirled around handsome features, and he had finally developed the musculature and power he needed to complete his knight's training, hopefully by his eighteenth birthday.

As the sequence became rote, requiring less of Ra-khir's concentration, his gaze wandered to his dapple-gray steed tethered outside the fence. Its color identified him as an apprentice knight. His imagination transformed the beast into one of the snowy white knight's chargers, its mane braided with ribbons in Béarn's blue and tan, its broad chest and powerful hindquarters giving it a conformation none but another Knight of Erythane's horse could match. In his vision, Ra-khir rode to war at his father's command, his allegiance first to Béarn, then Erythane, and always to his honor.

Ra-khir finished the sequence for the twenty-third time and lowered sword and shield, panting and satisfyingly tired. Sweat plastered errant red strands to his forehead and cheeks. A spring breeze wove through the V-neck of his tunic, refreshingly cool. He flicked back his hair into a tangle, only then noticing a small figure perched on the fence, watching him.

Ra-khir smiled, no stranger to spectators. In the last year, he had gained strength as well as height. The knight's training honed him to a build adolescent girls seemed to find irresistible; and he had always sported his mother's striking green eyes and his father's stately features. At the age of hero worship, about eight to fourteen, most Erythanian boys emulated the knights, often dogging their steps or incorporating their chivalry and style of warfare into their play. The stranger on the fence appeared to be one of the latter, a boy of about twelve years in Ra-khir's estimation.

Ra-khir sheathed his sword and trotted toward the other. Pleased with his self-imposed extra practice, he felt generous. As the gap between them closed, he became more certain of his first impression. The youngster wore a linen tunic and breeks cut in combat style but child-sized. A short sword, obviously borrowed from a father, was thrust through the belt. Soft, white-blond locks dangled to skinny shoulders, and the largeness of the blue eyes made them seem wide with wonder.

"Hello," Ra-khir said.

The stranger nodded a greeting, remarkably calm for a youngster meeting an idol. "Hello."

Ra-khir bowed, hoping formality would make the child feel important. "Ra-khir of Erythane, son of Knight-Captain Kedrin and apprentice knight to the Erythanian and Béarnian kings: His Grace, King Humfreet, and His Majesty, King Kohleran."

More patient than any youngster Ra-khir had ever met, the

stranger allowed him to complete his full title before speaking. "Kevral."

"Kevral," Ra-khir repeated. He had never heard such a name before, but he liked it. He might consider it if he ever had a son of his own. That thought raised a wave of bitterness. His parents' marriage had failed when he was three; and his mother swore his early, happy memories of Kedrin were actually of the man she married later, the one she had insisted was his father. Only later did Ra-khir discover the truth and a brave, gallant father whose love and presence had been banned from his childhood by a domineering mother and a jealous stepfather. *If and when I do have a child, no man or woman will take him from me.* He pushed the thought aside, along with the grief that followed naturally from a decision just beginning to lose its raw edge. "Kevral. A strong name."

"Thank you," Kevral said. "I'll tell my mother you said so."

Ra-khir nodded graciously despite the sarcasm. "If you'd like, I can teach you a move or two." He smiled, stepping back to give Kevral room to enter the ring. He had extended an invitation any Erythanian boy would sacrifice a week of dinners to hear and never doubted Kevral would embrace the opportunity.

"No," Kevral said. "But thank you for the offer."

The response caught Ra-khir off-guard. "No?"

"No," Kevral repeated.

Ra-khir could not believe what he heard. "No?"

Kevral's patience evaporated. "Am I speaking barbarian whistling language? 'No' seems pretty obvious."

Ra-khir's grin wilted. "Wouldn't you like to learn to fight like me?"

Kevral's legs swung, heels alternately thumping against the wooden rail. "Is that what you were doing?"

The question confused Ra-khir. "Is *what* what I was doing?"

"Fighting."

"Practicing, yes. What did you think I was doing?"

Kevral shrugged. "Clambering around like a big, old tortoise. Maybe taking a sword and shield for a walk."

The disrespect struck Ra-khir momentarily dumb. Then rage swept in to displace surprise, "You've insulted my honor."

"I'm sorry," Kevral said, in a voice wholly lacking apology. "I meant to insult *you.*"

Ra-khir knew of only one response to such a challenge, and the realization that he faced a child did not change the obligation, only the choice of end point. "Then I'll have to call you out."

"Call me out?"

Ra-khir explained, believing Kevral ignorant as well as a fool. "Demand a duel."

"Go ahead," Kevral shot back.

"I just did!" Ra-khir shouted, his generous mood utterly spoiled.

"All right." Kevral hopped down from the fence. In a single movement, the short sword swept from its sheath, licked between Ra-khir's fingers, and plucked the hilt from his hand. Ra-khir's sword pinwheeled from his grip, landing at his feet. The short sword completed its cycle, returning to its sheath. Kevral regarded Ra-khir with an insolent, irritating calm. "I win." The young features crinkled, "Or was I supposed to kill you?"

Ra-khir retrieved his sword, clutching it so tightly his fingers blanched. Shaking rage would not allow him to notice the skill inherent in the stroke. Usually, disarming would have left him shy a few fingers, at least. "You won because you cheated. We hadn't even decided place and time yet. Or end point."

"Oh." Kevral looked appropriately chastised, head low and eyes rolled upward to meet Ra-khir's. He was the taller by a full head and nearly double Kevral's weight. "I just assumed here and now."

Ra-khir had no intention of stewing for days. "Fine then. Agreed. Here and now." He balanced his weight, taking a defensive position with sword out and shield in front of him. "End point . . ."

He was still deciding when Kevral's sword rasped free, glided around the shield, and hammered his crosspiece. Impact ached through his fingers, and he lost his grip a second time. His sword thumped to the ground.

"No!" Ra-khir screamed, composure completely lost. "The gods damn you to the pits, you're still cheating. I hadn't finished the particulars. I hadn't even finished my sentence."

"I'm sorry." Another unabashed apology. "Would you like

me to announce my every strike in detail? Or would you like to choose which ones I make. I wouldn't want enemies on the battlefield calling foul."

"Very funny." Ra-khir suffered the first stirrings of hatred for the sarcastic child who had returned nastiness and humiliation for kindness. "Remember, I called the challenge. The law says I get to decide the particulars. I could choose death as an end point." His emerald eyes glared into the softer blue ones, seeking a fear he did not find.

"Death?" Kevral repeated, then shrugged with resignation. "All right, then. Death."

Ra-khir sucked in a deep breath, further irked that his bluff had backfired so badly. Now he either had to back down or slaughter a child. "I only said I *could* choose death, not that I wanted to. It's not my job to butcher a snotty, little boy, only to teach him a lesson."

Kevral grinned with impertinent amusement. "I already said I didn't want your teaching. That's what started this whole thing. Remember?"

Ra-khir remembered. "It's a different lesson I'll be teaching you, bratling. You like disarming so much? Fine. We'll fight until one of us no longer holds a sword." Ra-khir deliberately chose what was probably the child's only maneuver. Besting Kevral at that would make a stronger impression, and his knight's honor would not allow him to suggest an end point that gave him the advantage.

"How 'bout first blood?" Kevral added.

"What?"

"First blood *and* disarming."

Ra-khir studied the youngster in front of him, wondering if he had made a serious mistake. But his eyes assured him he was not facing a small adult. The pudgy face, innocent eyes, and supple hairless cheeks confirmed his first impression. The proportionately big head and short limbs only made him more certain. *Twelve, this boy, no older.* Surely Ra-khir would have heard stories about an Erythanian child with as much talent as this blond had, so far, displayed. He knew of no visiting dignitaries currently in Erythane who might have dragged along a disagreeable child, and Kevral spoke the Western tongue with standard Erythanian/Béarnian dialect and accent. Having never left Erythane himself, Ra-khir could not fathom a youngster traveling from another town to Erythane alone. Only one explanation seemed possible: Kevral knew one good move and had twice caught the knight-in-training unprepared. To refuse the request would make him look weak, so Ra-khir agreed. "First blood and disarming."

This time, Kevral did not charge with the fierce bravado that had won the first two passes but also cost many young warriors their lives in battle.

Ra-khir hated to swing the odds too far in his opponent's favor, but his conscience would not allow him to win a contest unfairly. He removed the shield strap from his arm. "You may use it." He proffered the shield.

Kevral remained in place, making no move to take the offering, studying Ra-khir with mild interest and patting the short sword's hilt. "Thank you, no. I have everything I need."

"Oh." Ra-khir furrowed his brow, frowning. He had not expected the refusal and tried to interpret his duty on the basis of this new development. His mind worried the problem for several moments. *In a dilemma, better to follow the course that works against me. No one could question my honor then.* "Then I won't use it either." He set the shield aside.

Kevral followed Ra-khir's motion, obviously confused by it. "Why not?"

Ra-khir straightened. "It wouldn't be fair."

"To me or to you?"

The question seemed ludicrous. "To you, of course."

Kevral snorted. "Why would it matter to me if you chose to hamper your vision?"

"Hamper my vision?" Ra-khir had never heard of a shield referred to in that manner before. Then again, he had never trained under any man but the knight's armsman or his father. "If that's how you think of a shield, then there's much I could teach you. Perhaps you'll learn to appreciate opportunities for knowledge rather than mocking them."

Kevral dismissed the words with a bored wave. "Use the shield if you're used to it. If we both fight the way we usually do, how can that make it unfair?"

Ra-khir rolled his eyes at the child's simple logic. "Then the fight would go always to the richest, those few who can afford to buy real weapons and metal armor . . . and the lessons to use them."

"Isn't that usually what happens?"

The question stopped Ra-khir cold. More than three centuries had passed since the Great War that had pitted Eastlands against Westlands, and the worst threat to Béarn in his lifetime had been minor skirmishes with pirates on the southern and western coasts. He had never fought a battle or, until now, even a duel. He answered the only way he could, "Not when there're Knights of Erythane involved. Our code of honor won't tolerate injustice."

"No matter," Kevral added, then obviously quoted someone wiser though Ra-khir had never heard the phrase before. "A skilled man needs no weapons or protections but uses those of his enemy against him."

The conversation grated on Ra-khir, who had no wish to defend the way of right without his teachers present to assist. He was still only a knight-in-training. It seemed as if the situation had come full circle, with Kevral now seeking the teaching refused moments earlier; except, where most of the boys begged for sword training, Kevral apparently sought understanding of the tenets. Ra-khir wondered if he should steer the youngster toward becoming a knight but immediately discarded the thought. Kevral's rampant disrespect, constant questioning, and arrogance would make the child a poor candidate indeed.

Kevral raised brows so wispy and blond they seemed nearly invisible. "Are you ready this time?"

"First blood and disarm." Ra-khir settled into a balanced starting stance, left leg leading, body turned to make as small a target as possible. "I'm ready. Let me know when you are."

"You'll know," Kevral said cryptically, not yet drawing. This time, the youngster waited for Ra-khir to strike first.

The knight-in-training lunged in with a low jabbing feint that he turned into a looping drive for Kevral's hilt. Kevral drew and blocked. They disengaged simultaneously, but Kevral riposted before Ra-khir could reposition. The tip scraped skin from Ra-khir's thumb before chopping the haft from his grasp. The blade tumbled toward the dirt. Kevral caught it by the grip before it touched the ground. A sword in each hand, the young stranger smirked, flipped Ra-khir's weapon, and offered it back, hilt leading. "Perhaps you could use it to herd pigs."

The rage that conversation had dispersed returned in a wild rush. Hatred smoldered, and need filled Ra-khir to best the nasty child. If he did not, he feared his head might explode. "Once more!" he shouted through clenched teeth.

Ra-khir did not clarify, and Kevral did not ask. "Fine. This time it's first blood, disarm, and knock the other one on his butt!"

Though far from a standard choice, the end point pleased Ra-khir. Nothing could make him happier than watching Kevral land, backside leading, on the cold, hard ground. Since the child had determined the result, he put aside the guilty realization that his superior size and strength would give him the vast advantage here.

"And you can use the shield," Kevral added.

Despite his fury, Ra-khir stuck with honor. "I don't want to!"

"I want you to," Kevral returned as loudly. "Use it, damn it! I don't want you saying later that the contest wasn't fair."

The implication that he might use the lack as an excuse further enraged Ra-khir. His fists opened and closed spasmodically, and his cheeks felt aflame. Needing to disperse his anger as much as possible and unable to find the words to insist, he snatched up his shield and charged Kevral.

Graceful as a cat, Kevral sidestepped. As Ra-khir barreled past, Kevral's sword slashed a superficial line along his forearm, then cut the hilt from his fingers. At the same time, a small foot cracked against Ra-khir's shin, sweeping his balance out from under him. Ra-khir plummeted. He crashed to his hip on a jutting stone, and pain stoked his temper. He rolled, felt cold steel at his throat, and froze.

Kevral stood over Ra-khir, the points of both blades at his neck, wearing a cocksure grin that Ra-khir would have given his horse to displace. Too bruised and mad to consider the danger, he batted the blades aside.

Kevral laughed, the sound gratingly musical, and tossed Ra-khir his sword. Then, flipping the other to its sheath with an airy toss of white-blond locks, Kevral leaped the fence and headed away.

Glad to see the flippant youngster go, Ra-khir hoped, by all the gods, he would never see Kevral again.

Warped and diluted by glass, sunlight trickled through Béarn's castle window, casting a stripe across the coverlet on King Kohleran's bed. Propped on three fluffy pillows, the old king could breathe without much effort, though the water in his belly hampered full expansion of his lungs. Lying flat took the pressure from his gut; however, the fluid then pooled in his chest, drowning him into fits of choking. Since his illness began two years ago, it had gradually worsened despite the best efforts of every healer in Béarn and its sister city, Erythane, to cure him. His hair had lightened from salt-and-pepper to white, and his dark eyes had developed a film that blurred the world to shapes and colors. His once hearty appetite had disappeared, and his limbs had gone skeletal aside from the bulges of collected fluid.

Yet, despite his illness, Kohleran's mood remained relatively high, as it always did when one of his grandchildren came to his room to visit. His favorite, sixteen-year-old Matrinka, perched on the window seat, stroking the calico cat that was always with her. Now, it curled in her lap. Her smooth, young hands twined paths through the fur, and the cat curled with closed eyes, its purring audible across the room. That he had given her the animal as a bedraggled kitten rescued from a sewage trough three years ago, before his health had failed, only made the association sweeter. Matrinka's long, straight hair framed an oval face and full lips so like her grandmother's. The standard Béarnian dark eyes peered out from under a fringe of black bangs. *Luckily for her,* King Kohleran thought, letting a smile creep onto his features, *she looks nothing like me.*

It was modest self-deprecation. Though never the handsomest of his brothers or peers, Kohleran had sported the classic Béarnian features: a full black beard that met with his hair, mustache, and sideburns to form a mane, shrewd brown eyes, and a whale-boned frame packed with fat and muscle. Like his predecessors, he had carried his mass along with his title, large even for a Béarnide, a race known for its size as well as the craft of its stonemasons.

Matrinka was one of the oldest of his grandchildren, the only child of his second son. Nearly all of his younger grandchildren avoided him, daunted by the odor and appearance of his disease. Kohleran also had three grandchildren older than Matrinka, all the offspring of his firstborn, a son. The twenty-one-year-old visited him occasionally but had his hands full tending a rambunctious four-year-old daughter of his own. The twenty-four-year-old, a girl, rarely concerned herself with matters not involving herself and a mirror. Kohleran had lost his eldest grandson scant months ago to a strange paralytic illness that had taken the life of Matrinka's father months earlier. Oddly, no one else had caught the disease.

Kohleran broke the lull in their conversation, though sitting in silence with his granddaughter pleased him enough. "How are your cousins?"

Matrinka smiled. "Fine, all fine. I'm sure I'll have a crowd to answer to about you when I leave."

Kohleran believed Matrinka spoke from kindness rather than truth, but he did not voice his doubts aloud. It only made sense that his descendants would worry more for their families than over the king's lingering death. Since Kohleran had fallen ill, his four most promising heirs had died under strange circumstances: two of the inexplicable illness and two of accidents. The latter still made him frown. To all appearances, his fourth daughter had fallen from a tree, skewered by a branch on the way down. Yet it made no sense that a thirty-eight-year-old mother of two children would scramble around in a tree like a squirrel. His oldest child, a son, had apparently drowned in a lake just outside their mountain city. The two-year string of bad luck had goaded Béarn's citizens to whisper about a curse on the line of high kings, and Prime Minister Baltraine had even insisted on a silly ceremony led by a priest to try to remove the curse. Within a week after the rite, Kohleran's grandson had died. Kohleran responded to Matrinka's hollow assurance. "You tell all of them I'm doing all right. And I love them."

"I will," Matrinka promised. She rose, dumping the cat to the floor. She closed lacy curtains dyed brilliant sapphire and sporting Béarn's crest: a tan, rearing bear on a blue field. Crossing the room, she gave her deteriorating grandfather a hug that expressed her love better than words ever could. For a moment, the familiar chorus of aches disappeared while he embraced his favorite granddaughter.

"I love you," he said.

"I love you, too," Matrinka whispered, studying his jaundiced, wrinkled features with concern rather than the more familiar revulsion others accorded him. "Get some sleep. I'll be back tomorrow. Is there anything you want me to bring?"

Though sincere, Matrinka's offer seemed senseless. Anything Kohleran wanted, the servants or ministers would get for him. "I'd like to see those flowers I smell on your hair. Could you bring one?"

"I will." Matrinka turned and headed from the room. She held the door while the cat padded out behind her, then closed and latched it softly.

King Kohleran settled back on his pillows, joy dispersing discomfort long enough to allow him to sleep.

Prime Minister Baltraine paced the meeting room floor from the door to the graph-covered slate board to the semicircular table. Béarn's other five ministers watched in silence, allowing him to speak first, as court etiquette demanded. They sat along the rounded side of the table, leaving the flat edge, the head, for their leader. But Baltraine felt too jumpy to sit. Instead, he pinned his chair to the table with his knee, leaned over its back, and tented his fingers on the tabletop. He studied each of the faces before him, reading as much of each expression as he could.

Abran, the aging foreign minister, kept his head cocked to one side, a residual defect from a stroke several years past. He laced his fingers through his gray beard, the movement habit rather than nervousness. Sixty-eight years old, only five years shy of the king, he had held his position since before Kohleran's coronation. In his forty years of service to the kingdom, Abran's loyalty had never fallen into question.

Charletha directed the caretakers of Béarn's livestock, gardens, and food, the youngest of the high kingdom's ministers. Like Abran, she had earned her title honestly, in Baltraine's opinion. She descended from Kohleran's uncle's line, born into her nobility.

The minister of courtroom procedure and affairs, like Baltraine, came from a long line of titled gentry that had lost its link to the king's line in the distant past, if it ever had one. Named Weslin, he had paler features, a lighter bone structure, and browner hair than most Béarnides, suggesting a foreign "contaminant" somewhere in his history.

Limrinial, the minister of local affairs, oversaw relations between Béarn and her closest allies: the Renshai and Erythane, especially the knights. Her wavy hair refused to stay in place longer than a few moments after combing, and a clump always trailed down her forehead. A broad nasal bridge made her eyes seem to never quite look in the same place, as if she could focus each one independently. Baltraine treasured her homely, middle-aged features; she would prove no competition for his daughters as a queen for the next king of Béarn.

Baltraine's gaze swept the internal affairs minister, Fahrthran, last and shortest, as if too long a scrutiny might pollute his eyes. Genealogy traced his ancestry to an Eastern woman and an Erythanian archer, his distant predecessor's title honorary. Although fourteen generations of Béarnides had since married into his family over three hundred years, Baltraine still attributed Fahrthran's dark hair and eyes to his Eastern ancestor. Baltraine knew nothing but disdain for his so-called peer. New blood, and especially foreign blood, tainted Béarn's royalty.

Long reconciled to tolerating King Kohleran's minister of internal affairs, Baltraine kept his aversion well-hidden. Instead, he turned his attention to the matter at hand. "As you all know, our king is dying."

Vague noises of sorrow and resignation greeted the pronouncement. They had lived under the threat of losing their king for two years now. Though muffled and short-lived, their regrets were heartfelt, Baltraine believed. Kohleran was a caring and honest ruler, well liked by the people over his thirty-three-year reign. In fact, history showed that Béarn had not had an unpopular monarch, king or queen, since Morhane the Betrayer got ousted three hundred twenty-one years ago. His successor, Sterrane the Bear, had been in power during the Great Fire that left the northeastern portion of the Westlands a vast wasteland and now the most fertile of farm ground.

Pedigrees had always fascinated Baltraine, especially that of the Béarnian kings, and this was what goaded him to call a special, covert session of Kohleran's ministers. "We need to think about his successor."

Limrinial shook the ever-present forehead curl from her eyes, though it immediately slid back into place. Accustomed to dealing with Renshai, she did everything with a directness that bordered on blunt rudeness. "What's to think about? The order of ascension is a matter of record, and the staff-test assures the proper monarch finds the throne."

Charletha and Abran, youngest and oldest, murmured agreement. Weslin looked confused. Fahrthran studied Baltraine mildly, saying nothing, apparently waiting for the prime minister to speak his piece.

Baltraine addressed Limrinial's point. "True, the order of ascension is a matter of record. I've traced out King

Kohleran's line and numbered all with a potential claim to the throne." He gestured to the drawing on the slate board. "Now, the law states that the title passes only down or across. That means only our king's legitimate progeny, their legitimate progeny, or his siblings have a claim. King Kohleran is the only living descendant of Yvalane, so the sibling option disappears." Baltraine crossed the room, plucked the drawing stone from his pocket, and scratched out all of Kohleran's brothers and sisters. "Unlike most of his predecessors, our beloved liege chose a single wife." He tapped the drawing stone against the figure representing Queen Mildy who had died of old age four years previously. Previous kings had held as many as ten wives and queens up to four husbands. The law did not limit their marriages, except by bloodline.

Always impatient, Limrinial interrupted. "And King Kohleran has four sons and two daughters. We know all this."

Baltraine smiled as the local affairs minister proved his point. "Apparently not. Our king had *six* sons and *three* daughters."

Fahrthran chuckled, without malice. Abran shrugged and nodded simultaneously; he had lived through the birth of each of Kohleran's children.

Limrinial glared, muttering, "Doesn't change anything." However, she went silent, allowing Baltraine to speak his piece.

Baltraine elaborated. "Queen Mildy's fourth pregnancy ended early. Twins, a boy and a girl, and they died within days. His youngest son, Petrostan, left Béarn at the age of about twelve some eighteen or nineteen years ago. Apparently some minor scandal surrounded that exodus." Baltraine looked to Abran for details.

The elder obliged. "As far as I remember, it was pretty innocuous. Non-noble girlfriend or some such. I heard he died a few years later."

Limrinial's left eye pinned Baltraine. "So, for our purposes, King Kohleran had four sons and two daughters."

She had a point that Baltraine refused to concede. "He also has ten grandchildren and four great grandchildren."

Fahrthran performed the math quickly. "That's nineteen heirs. I should think one of them could pass the staff-test."

Baltraine disputed the numbers he had espoused moments

before. "No. One great-granddaughter is illegitimate. We lost one son five years ago when the consumption swept through the city. Two more sons and a daughter fell to the curse."

"If you believe in such things," Limrinial managed to insert.

Baltraine ignored her. "That leaves one daughter, Ethelyn, forty years old, unmarried, and without offspring." The latter details held little import until the time came for her successor, but Baltraine hoped his fellow ministers read his unspoken concern about her ability to pass the staff-test. The populace knew little or nothing of the test that had measured the worthiness of every Béarnian king since Sterrane. Only those who had undergone the test understood its details. From the ministers' standpoint, it involved leaving the heir-apparent alone in a room with two plain-looking wooden sticks called the Staves of Law and Chaos. If the staves found him or her worthy, meaning innocent and "neutral" in affairs of law, chaos, good, and evil, the tested became the new monarch. If not, the next heir in line underwent the same process. No one knew how an heir discovered whether or not he passed, only that, if anyone had lied about the outcome, no punishment had ensued. Undoubtedly, magic suffused the staves. Of those tested, some claimed to have forgotten the events and others gave vague stories of going to an elsewhere or elsewhen and facing moral dilemmas they had handled well or poorly.

Kohleran's last living child, Ethelyn, had never married because no man had yet found the prospect of possibly becoming king enough to overcome an infamously nasty disposition. In turn, Ethelyn had taken no interest in any man. Baltraine believed her marriage or lack did not matter. *Nothing neutral or innocent about her. Surely, the staves would not accept her.*

Baltraine examined the line of Kohleran's grandchildren: six girls and four boys. The odds bothered him in principle. If a woman took the throne, his daughters could not marry into royalty. "The next in line." He tapped the slate board with his finger, indicating the eldest son of Kohleran's eldest son. "Sefraine died last month of illness. Of the others, only four have attained the age of consent." He picked them out individually. "Sefraine's sister and brother. The only child of Kohleran's second son, a girl of sixteen; and the older child of Kohleran's second daughter, a sixteen-year-old boy. The others are all ten years old or younger, as, of course, are the three legitimate great-grandchildren."

Limrinial waved her arms, still missing Baltraine's point. "Age doesn't exclude them. They can still rule with a regent."

"Exactly." Baltraine knew he had to get to the crux of the matter soon or lose any support he might once have gained. "Only five potential heirs of age, the first two of whom are patently unsuited." He touched the figures representing Kohleran's remaining daughter and his oldest living granddaughter, pleased the females seemed most obviously unworthy. The eldest granddaughter had a reputation for vanity and resisting authority. She had even borne a child out of wedlock. "And a curse has already taken the four most promising heirs in the space of a year and a half."

"If you believe in such things," Limrinial repeated.

Baltraine shrugged. The facts spoke for themselves.

Fahrthran drove for the point. "What do you think we should do, Baltraine?"

Baltraine grinned, his moment diminished only by the fact that the lowliest of bloodlines had asked the necessary question. "We should staff-test all the heirs now. That way, we can prime the one who passes, especially if he or she is young, as seems likely. If the heir turns out to be one of those not yet of age, we can get explicit instructions from King Kohleran regarding the line of regents. And we know who to concentrate on protecting from 'the curse.'" Baltraine studied every face for reaction to his unorthodox suggestion. Surely no one could doubt his intentions. As always, he truly believed he had the best interests of Béarn and the Westlands in mind. And, if he wished to curry favor for himself or to kindle friendship between his six daughters and Béarn's king, no one could blame him. Childhood associations often led to trust or romance.

Weslin cleared his throat. "If it's a curse, what makes you think we can safeguard against it?"

Fahrthran raised a more pertinent issue. "I've heard that those who fail the staff-test often become despondent. More than a few went on to suicide."

Baltraine shrugged, seeing little reason to speculate about a test none of them had or could undergo. "Perhaps they would have done so anyway. Maybe that's why the staves failed them."

Fahrthran looked skeptical but had no information with which to argue. Whether the magic of the staves suppressed memory of their testing or the heirs simply chose silence did not matter. No one knew enough about the process or its effects to surmise. Nevertheless, he put forth an opinion. "I see no reason to test now. It only makes sense to safeguard all of our king's heirs, regardless of their chances at the throne. We understand that our next king or queen is likely to be young. That's enough for now."

Limrinial sided with Fahrthran, as usual. "I agree. There's no need to traumatize the children. According to ancient law, the heir to Béarn's throne must be guileless as well as neutral. An experience of this sort could jade them all."

The argument seemed ludicrous to Baltraine. "That's a nonissue. Whether now or later, no one gets crowned without undergoing the test."

Charletha glanced from speaker to speaker without adding her opinion. Apparently, she had not yet made up her mind. Weslin waited for Abran to speak. He had always placed most emphasis on the elder's wisdom and experience.

Abran took the middle ground. "I can see both sides. For now, I say we wait and reconvene in a week. If the king's condition worsens meanwhile, we can discuss the matter again."

He's dying, you old fool. How much worse can it get? Baltraine despised his companions' caution, but he did not allow his feelings to taint his tone. In some ways, delay worked to his advantage. As the prime minister, he would handle affairs of state when Kohleran became too weak or until an heir was coronated. "Consideration for another week, then reconvene? Everyone agree with Abran's plan?"

Each minister nodded agreement, and the meeting came to an end.

Chapter 2

The End of Innocence

What makes a Renshai is not kinship, but a single-minded devotion to swordcraft.
—Colbey Calistinsson

Béarn's courtyard seemed unnaturally bright after the grim interior of King Kohleran's sickroom. Matrinka strolled through tended flower beds aglow with spring sunlight, the multihued blossoms swaying and bowing in the breeze like dancers. Benches carved from whitestone broke the contours in symmetrical patterns. Men in waistcoats and women in dresses of myriad colors and styles dotted the garden at intervals, various nobility seeking solace or enjoyment in the familiar beauty of the courtyard. Matrinka nodded to those she knew as she passed, the calico cat padding in her wake. The mingled perfumes of the flowers made her as giddy as a child, and she acknowledged the many statues in the courtyard with the same silent greeting as she did the sunning lords and ladies. Béarn's stonework had stunned the world for centuries, the city's greatest export aside from the wisdom and grandeur of its high king. In the courtyard, as in citizens' yards, the bear symbol of the kingdom predominated.

Poor Grandpapa Matrinka thought deliberately, knowing the cat would understand. Since the day King Kohleran had given her the grimy, little furball rescued from a sewage trough, Matrinka had believed the cat special. They had bonded in an instant, the bedraggled kitten simultaneously shivering and purring in her arms. An instinct as strong and primal as motherhood had risen, goading Matrinka to protect her tiny charge no matter the cost; and the communication that developed between them seemed as natural as breathing. But only to her and the cat she named Mior. She had tried to explain the connection twice, once to her mother, who "admired her imagination and love for animals," and once to the cousin nearest her age, the closest she had to a brother, who teased her for months afterward.

Poor Grandpapa Mior repeated, as always reading mood as well as words. *No flowers. No warm sunshine on his back. No walks through the pretty garden.*

Matrinka waxed poetic in a way the cat could not. *Senses muddled by sickness. The world seen, heard, tasted, and smelled always through dusty glass and filtering curtains.* She added unnecessarily, *Oh, poor Grandpapa.* This time the words opened a whole new depth of sorrow. *Poor, poor Grandpapa.*

Mior added nothing more, the conversation having reached an intrinsic conclusion. She sprang onto an empty bench, padding across its surface with dexterity, then rolled gleefully across the sun-warmed surface. Belly exposed and paws drawn in, she writhed and rubbed on the whitestone.

Matrinka tipped her head to a deer statue that appeared to be grazing on a rosebush dotted with pink blossoms and buds. In the distance, children screeched and giggled in play, and Matrinka headed toward the sound. She enjoyed overseeing the games of her younger cousins. As much as she cared for animals, she cherished children more. One day, when she found a man she loved who was of proper stature, she would bear as many of her own offspring as the gods blessed her to have. *Someday.*

Matrinka paused to let the dream overtake her, imagining a large bear in the center of a garden as a handsome suitor inviting her to dance. Catching the forepaws in her long-fingered hands, she pranced a graceful circle once around him. Her black hair flowed over her cheeks and shoulders like silk, and she pictured herself in a shimmering betrothal gown. The flower beds became wedding decorations: sculptures carved from butter, ice, and ground meats as well as bouquets. The lounging courtiers turned into servants, winding through the milling guests and the twirling dancers.

Mior's amusement trickled through Matrinka's reverie.
Aren't you getting a bit old for fairy tales?

Never. Matrinka let the images lapse, blushing despite
her negative retort. She glanced about to assure herself no
one had watched her flitter around a stone figure and found
the courtiers involved in their own relaxation and conversations. No one seemed to have noticed. *Someday, I'll find
the one.*

Someday, Mior replied, *you'll discover you've already
found him.*

It was an old argument, not worth discussing now. Mior
had a point. Matrinka already knew all the Béarnian nobility
reasonably within her age, and propriety decreed she must
marry one of them or no one at all. Still, the fantasy persisted, long past the age of magical perceptions and day-
dreams. Sorcery did not exist in the world, at least it hadn't
for the last three hundred years, ever since the tales of Cardinal Wizards had turned from their miraculous abilities to
their destruction. If Wizards had once lived, and few believed they had, they no longer did. Yet, the inexplicable
bond between herself and a cat, a communication no one
seemed capable of believing, convinced Matrinka that magic
had not wholly died with its keepers.

Matrinka left the flower bed for the next, now drawn not
only by the sounds of the children but by a nearer music.
Mandolin strings sang an introduction that seemed to float
on the air like the fragrances of the flowers, chords and runs
as intertwined as the mingled scents. The beauty of the song
left her certain about the identity of the musician, and the
perfect voice that rose above the instrument's harmony
clinched it. *Darris.* Matrinka smiled, as she always did, at
the thought of the bard's heir. She quickened her pace, trailing the mellow wave of sound past a grove of trees pruned
into the shapes of a flock of chickens, through the grape
grove, to the beds of *hacantha,* each patch gorged with blossoms of a specific color, the whole forming a circle around
a thronelike bench. A few lords and ladies clustered around
a familiar central figure.

Darris strummed the mandolin without bothering to un-
sling his favorite lute from his back. The backpack resting
beside him on the bench surely held an assortment of
smaller noisemakers, for Darris lugged sundry instruments
like a portable arsenal. A sword dangled from his belt,

knocked askew by the mandolin. Curly, brown hair swept back from his forehead, unmasking the thin brows that revealed his mostly Pudarian heritage. Though a bit large, his straight nose and broad lips gave him an exotic look that Matrinka appreciated. Though not classically comely, Darris had an attractiveness about his features and bearing that always left her slightly unbalanced in his presence. His gentleness made her discomfort seem foolish, especially since he had no suave lines with which to woo the women Matrinka believed he should need to turn away in droves. An ancient curse passed to the eldest child down through the centuries assured that the bards desperately craved knowledge but could teach what they learned only with song. Having grown up with Darris, who was the same age as she, Matrinka had developed the patience to sit through arias, if necessary. Most people, however, found him tedious—except when he played for their entertainment.

Spotting Matrinka, Darris smiled and winked a hazel eye in greeting. The pause caused a slight stumble in his otherwise flawless song, but no one seemed to notice and Matrinka detected it only because she had heard him perform the piece hundreds of times in the past.

Mior caught up to Matrinka as she stopped to watch the show, winding between her mistress' legs. The instant the cat drew within communication distance, she complained. *Rush, rush, rush. Couldn't wait a moment for me?*

Without taking her eyes from Darris, Matrinka stooped and hefted the calico, scratching beneath the chin and behind the ears until Mior could not help purring. *I'm sorry. I thought you were right behind me.*

Fell off the stupid bench twisting to watch you go, Mior explained sullenly. *Silly seamstress laughed at me, and I don't think I convinced her I did it on purpose.*

Poor, suffering Mior. Matrinka belittled the cat's self-inflicted need to maintain dignity at all times. *What do you care what the seamstress thinks?*

Mior gave no answer beyond satisfied purring, an acceptance of Matrinka's unspoken apology. The question had no logical answer, and the music precluded any need for stale disputes. The song swept princess and cat into a fantasy world peopled with ancient ancestors. Darris sang of twin princes of Béarn in the centuries before the staff-test when birth order alone determined succession. The eldest, Valar, gained the throne. Bitter, the younger, Morhane the Betrayer, slaughtered his brother and all but one of his seven children. The last, a son, escaped with the aid of the Eastern Wizard.

The song painted vivid images so strong the audience seemed to shrink, smashed into a nearly airless, hidden corner with the young heir, Sterrane, while the sounds of slaughter and the odor of blood fouled the castle that once served as all that defined security. The young prince returned as an adult, reclaiming the kingdom from his traitorous uncle, somehow uncorrupted despite the trauma of his family's murder. No death screams haunted his innocent dreams. No desperate need for vengeance burned his heart to a hardened core. No memories of helpless horror made him believe the gods had abandoned him. Simplicity, neutrality, naïveté incarnate, Sterrane had become the template by which all Béarnian kings and queens must rule.

Darris then chanted of a god-mediated mission, one that ended in the suicide of the Cardinal Wizards, sweeping all magic from the world. He sang, too, of Sterrane's traumatic death by a Wizard's hand, instilling a grief that drove tears to Matrinka's eyes though she already knew the story ended happily. The audience became a blur so indistinct she could not tell if the song affected others as strongly as herself, nor did she care. Few truly believed Sterrane had died and returned to life, though the myth abounded; and the joy of his return only made her cry the harder. He had come back to Béarn with tales of gods and with the Staves of Law and Chaos. From that day forth, Renshai, once crazed Northern warriors eager only for battle, became charged with guarding the king's heirs with the same loyalty as the bard protected the king or queen and oversaw the ascension. Their own religion bound them to this task above all others.

As the last notes pealed from the mandolin, a finale that drifted after Darris' last word, the small crowd shuffled restlessly. Several shouted for an encore, only a few suggesting specific pieces. Darris shook his head, replacing the mandolin beside the lute on his back, replying with words Matrinka could not decipher above the noise. As the entreaties became more plaintive, his responses gained a sharper edge. Finally, the group dispersed, leaving the bard's heir a free path to Matrinka. He hefted his pack and walked to her. "Hello."

Matrinka blushed, then felt stupid for being embarrassed

by a perfectly normal greeting. "Hello. That was magnificent."

"Thank you, m'lady." Darris bowed, flicking back his cape, though it barely moved, pinned in place by his instruments. He had learned graciousness from a bard mother ceaselessly barraged with compliments, then later from the mass appreciation of his own growing skill. "How's your grandfather?"

"As well as can be expected." Matrinka relished the question, wishing more of her cousins showed the same interest in their ailing king. Then, realization struck, and she furrowed her brow. "How did you know I was visiting him?"

Darris stiffened, momentarily uncomfortable, then covered awkwardly. "You're often there. Lucky guess." He avoided her dark eyes, rolling his gaze to his feet. "All right, I saw you go in there. Is it a crime to follow the movements of a beautiful woman?"

Matrinka's cheeks felt on fire, and she found herself unable to meet Darris' stare either. She wished she handled praise as well as her peer. "Beautiful? Me?" Suddenly fearing the need to force Darris to insist, possibly cornering him into agreeing with her assessment, she turned to humor. "And, yes, it's a crime. Should I call the guards to haul you to the dungeon?"

"Ach, no." Darris feigned fear. "Will you let me go this time if I promise not to do it again?"

Matrinka pretended to consider. "Maybe this time."

Darris chuckled. He stroked Mior with a finger, following the line from nose to tail. "And 'hello' to you, too, little lady."

Mior rubbed against the bard heir's hand, her purring gaining volume. She swatted lazily at his finger, claws retracted.

"You little flirt." Matrinka nudged the calico, and Mior clambered across her shoulders. Experience told them both she could balance well enough there even to sleep, though Matrinka's muscles would cramp if the cat lay there too long.

Darris ignored the dispersing spectators. To catch their attention would almost certainly lead to another song. "Where are you going? I'll walk you there."

Not wanting to admit she had followed his music, Matrinka hesitated. Then, recalling the other sound that had caught her attention, she used it as an excuse. "I was just going to watch my young cousins play."

Darris brightened, face open beneath curly bangs. Apparently, he enjoyed becoming part of the audience for a change. Instead of words, he offered his arm in reply. Like nobles in a courtroom, they strode toward the giggling, the image ruined only by the peasant's cut of Darris' tunic and the cat draped across Matrinka's shoulders.

As usual, the children frolicked in the statue garden, amidst the most lifelike of Béarn's sculptures: seven rearing bears with every hair intricately detailed, two dogs with haunting eyes, and a family of deer that included a massive stag with antlers that became indistinguishable from tree branches and held an egg-laden nest in a high fork. According to legend, King Aranal had commissioned a statue for the newest garden that every craftsman in Béarn had fought to make. A contest ensued between the seven most competent. The winning bear held the place of honor on a pedestal in the garden's center, but the king insisted on buying the other six exquisite pieces as well. The garden became a statue showcase, the spaces between turned into grassy paths to allow viewing of every detail of every creation. The large open spaces, climbable artwork, and weaving pathways formed a wondrous playground that seemed irresistible to Béarn's children.

More than two dozen children cavorted around the statuary now, most involved in a wild game of "take" that consisted of chasing the person carrying a silver chain and touching him. Once tagged, the carrier would surrender the chain to the toucher who then became the carrier. Matrinka and Darris sat on a bench just outside the garden, watching the action through a gap in the enclosing bushes. Mior leaped from Matrinka's shoulders to her lap, curling contentedly, disinterested in the games.

Matrinka recognized every one of the children. All four of Kohleran's great-grandchildren played "take": the five-year-old twin boys who had lost their father to the same illness as Matrinka's and the two four-year-old, girl cousins. Matrinka's first cousins, a six-year-old boy and his four-year-old sister joined them. Their ten-year-old sister played a quieter game involving dolls with a cousin, a guard's daughter, and a daughter of the prime minister, all of the same age. The last sibling of the four, an eight-year-old girl, pestered the ten-year-olds with a regularity that sent her sister into snapping rages. Matrinka knew the other children as the offspring of various sentries and nobles, identifying each without difficulty. A cluster of nursemaids perched upon or around a pair of benches on the opposite side of the garden. Occasionally one would interrupt the play to guide or chastise a young charge.

An aging Renshai oversaw the activity, lounging against a hedge. Though he did not sit, boredom made his features sag. Inside the courtyard walls, the children had nothing to fear and the Renshai nothing from which to protect them. His graying hair and grizzled features reminded Matrinka that ancient folklore once claimed Renshai drank the blood of enemies to remain eternally young. According to her history lessons, the impression had come from an assortment of facts, some still valid. First, they once had a racial quality that made them look younger than their ages, a tendency that persisted to a lesser degree in those who still carried a significant amount of original Renshai blood. Second, they named their babies for warriors who died in glorious combat, usually before the age of thirty. Though Renshai of both genders still dove into every war and skirmish with an enthusiasm that awed or frightened those of less violent backgrounds, they no longer initiated battles with just anyone when they found no better reason to fight. In ancient days, an old Renshai was an anomaly. Now, though not nearly as common as elderly Béarnides, they drew no strange looks or comments any more.

Unable to think of anything short of inane to say to Darris, Matrinka studied the children's games. She chose silence over the possibility of sounding foolish. Darris seemed content to sit quietly at her side, as he often did. He had explained his apparent shyness once, in song. The bard's curse damned him to constant observation and a fiery longing for knowledge. Only by remaining still and noiseless could he absorb the nuances of every situation. Every moment of every day taught him something new, and he learned from the patterns of breezes, the colors of a mural, and even the crunch of courtiers chewing food. In addition, the need to impart true knowledge only with music limited his conversation.

Somewhat timid and withdrawn herself, Matrinka appreciated Darris' company the way she rarely did others of her

age. She always felt awkward and uncertain, and the need to
guard every word made the ones she chose sound stilted.
Among adults, she had no difficulty expressing herself.
Among peers, she perceived herself as ungainly as a hatch-
ling learning to fly. Yet, with Darris, somehow, she felt comfortable.

Matrinka's gaze strayed to the walls surrounding the
castle and its courtyard. The Renshai had good reason for
apathy. Carved directly from the mountain, castle and wall
held a timelessness that spanned all history. No army had
ever breached its defenses. In tens of thousands of years,
only one man had entered the castle or its grounds uninvited.
More than three hundred years ago, the bards sang, a Western warrior had slipped inside to help Sterrane reclaim the
throne after Morhane the Betrayer had slaughtered his way
to rulership. The intruder had had the assistance of a secret
passage and a Cardinal Wizard, neither of which existed any
longer.

As Matrinka's attention swept the castle, a momentary
light caught the edge of her vision. It seemed more intense
than a glint of sunlight from chips of quartz in the stonework. Curious, she glanced toward it. As she swung her
head to see, another light seized her awareness fully, a brilliant flicker in a fourth-story window that disappeared almost as quickly as she saw it. A third flash blinded her with
its sudden brightness. She closed her eyes reflexively, jerking backward with surprise and pain.

Mior sprang to stiff legs, spitting, fur fluffed into rigid
spikes. Darris leaped from the bench, and Matrinka felt the
warmth of his presence directly in front of her.

Matrinka wrenched open her eyes. Colored aftereffects
scored her vision in spots and squiggles, and she could see
nothing around the patterns except Darris' back. "What's
happening?" she demanded, but screaming children drowned
her question. Terror enfolded her, yet ignorance rooted her
in place. Until she understood the danger, she could not
choose a direction to run in. Desperately, she peeked around
Darris who had spread himself as large as possible to shield
her.

Mior stood with all four legs braced, back tented, and tail
jutting. *Danger!* she shouted mentally, taking stiff backward steps. *Danger!* Panic accompanied the assessment.
One foot came down on empty air, and the cat tumbled from

the bench into a yowling heap. She sped off in the direction from which they had come.

Matrinka's vision cleared enough to reveal a dark, rounded shape flying through the air, trailing splashes of red liquid. Darris choked out a horrified gasp. He stood only a finger's joint taller than Matrinka; and, on tiptoes, she managed to peer around his head. Three immense bears towered over the screaming mass of children, mouths gaping and claws as long and sharp as daggers. At least one had already claimed a victim; its nails dripped congealing trails of blood. Matrinka took in other details in an instant: three missing bear statues in the garden, a decapitated body, children screeching and crying from what seemed like a million places. Some sprawled on the grass, knocked over by others fleeing or their own panicked clumsiness. A few froze in place, as still as the statues had once been. Still others sprinted for the safety of the hedge line or huddled behind sculptures that still stood as proper stone. One grandchild spun in frantic circles.

"Modi!" The Renshai dodged and hacked at all of the bears in turn, his grace belying his age and his sword a silver blur. His tunic hung in tatters, and red lines scored his ribs. Only one bear returned his strikes, the others avoided him, intent on the children. Repeatedly, the bear's jaws fell finger's breadths short of the Renshai's face or limbs. Had the warrior had only himself to defend he might have managed to battle the three effectively or slay the one attacking him; but to limit his cuts to one meant leaving its two fellows free to shred Béarn's young heirs. Instead, he bounced from one to the next in an obvious attempt to draw all the danger onto himself. The more the bears separated, the more difficult the strategy became.

Darris continued to shield Matrinka with his body, gradually forcing her backward with shuffling, smooth steps. Two bears charged the fallen children. A wild chorus of terrified screams filled the air, followed by a haunting shriek of pain that cut off in mid-shrill. "Modi," the Renshai shouted again; this time it sounded more like a curse than a war cry. Matrinka fixed on Darris' back, not daring to look, though droplets of blood sprayed through her peripheral vision. "No," she whispered, grief aching through her fear. "Do something. Do something. Do anything!" She meant the words to spur those who could not hear them, the distant guards who had no reason to suspect danger inside the court-yard. No course of action came to her own mind, and she appreciated Darris' protecting presence, though she felt guilty for it. "The children," she sobbed.

Arrows fluttered down from bowmen on the walls. The Renshai howled, making a final, desperate lunge that precluded defense. His sword glided beneath one bear's rib cage, but the maneuver opened his head. A massive paw slammed against his ear, hooked his neck, and tore. The Renshai went limp as the bear's own momentum impaled it deeper. They collapsed together, the bear on top, the Renshai crushed beneath it.

Another child's pain-scream throbbed through Matrinka's hearing. She buried her eyes in Darris' instruments, shivering and bawling without control. She barely felt the continued backward movement, could not register the battle cries of guards who had finally arrived to assist in the combat. Moments stretched into hours in Matrinka's mind. Then, suddenly, Darris whirled. He hefted her awkwardly, her Béarnian size making her nearly as large as him despite her gender, and hurried toward the safety of the castle.

Matrinka clung, too weak and frightened to do anything more.

Matrinka startled awake to a deeply rooted sensation of terror and dread. She sat up in her own bed, heart pounding, memory returning in a wild, ugly rush that made her wish she had remained asleep. Her mind flashed images of events she would rather forget: bear statues mutated to murderous reality, blood and bodies, one cousin dead at least, the panic that rendered her helpless to rescue herself let alone the child whose slaying would haunt her conscience through eternity. *Was it all a nightmare?* Hope trickled through her, easily staunched by recollection too vivid to deny. *Oh, gods. Let it all be a dream.*

Firmly grounded in reality, her mind would not allow the deception. The events of the previous day had happened, leaving a wake of grief, outrage, and terror that had made her certain sleep would never come. Yet, exhaustion had finally taken her, leaving soldiers, ministers, and the king to sort the events without her assistance. More than a few courtiers, nannies, and children had witnessed the massacre.

Mior marched up Matrinka's leg and settled onto her chest, face close and purring a loud rumble in her ears. Freeing a hand from the coverlet, Matrinka stroked her companion absently. Her thoughts felt lead-weighted and slowed by sorrow, but something still seemed out of place. She concentrated, at first believing the tragedy had sapped her memory of events equally significant, if anything could seem so. Then, she recognized her additional discomfort as a feeling of being watched, an intruder in a familiar place. Her heart rate quickened further, and her lungs felt crushed and suffocated.

Mior responded to the concern and its effects. *Don't blame my weight for your funny breathing. We have guards.* She made it sound like an illness.

Matrinka scanned the darkness. A chink between the curtains admitted an indistinct glaze of moonlight that allowed her to make out contours. Long familiarity helped as well. She followed the vague lumps that represented her desk, dresser, and wardrobe to the door. Someone perched upon the wooden chair near the desk, and the lute-shaped shadow in his hands identified him as the bard's heir. Matrinka smiled, relaxing. If Darris was present and unconcerned, no one else posed a threat. She continued to survey the room, finding two human figures crouched in the blackness near the door. They wore standard tunics and breeks, swords hanging from their belts. Their vigilance but lack of armor or Béarnian tabards suggested Renshai.

Matrinka clutched Mior, stroking the cat with a rapidity that generated static sparks and made the fur stand on end. She had occasionally seen Renshai before, usually distantly overseeing herself and other Béarnian heirs in the courtyard or called to affairs of court. For the most part, they looked like Erythanians: smaller than the Béarnides in height and breadth, their facial hair sparser though some still sported beards. Darris' songs claimed the Renshai had once been Northmen, though they now lived exclusively on a plain near Béarn called the Fields of Wrath. The preponderance of blonds and redheads offered some truth to the story, and many wore the war braids of Northern soldiers. Their worship of Northern gods, however, added little to the impression. Béarn and Erythane also glorified Odin and his pantheon. For the most part, the Renshai kept to themselves,

surfacing only to assure the line of Béarnian rulers proceeded according to some specifications Matrinka did not
fully understand. Based on that knowledge, it made sense
that Renshai would become more prominent now.

The rationalization soothed Matrinka, and her ministrations to the cat grew more normal. She gave Mior a pat, to
indicate she planned to move, and waited until the cat found
a comfortable position against her side. She sat up, modestly
keeping the blankets wrapped over her sleeping gown.
"Good morning."

Darris rose and bowed. "Good morning, m'lady."

The Renshai remained in place, their mumbled respects
lost beneath Darris' more exuberant greeting.

Though glad of his presence, Matrinka dared not smile.
More important matters needed tending. "My cousins? Are
they . . . ?" She left the question open-ended.

"I'm sorry." Darris lowered his head. "We lost Ukrista
and Nylabrin." He named two young girls, aged eight and
four, both daughters of Kohleran's fifth child. He continued,
describing the fate of the ten-year-old daughter of Kohleran's fourth child, an aunt who had, herself, been lost only
months previously to a freak accident, a fall from a tree.
"Fachlaine was badly injured, but is alive. One of your male
cousins suffered minor injuries trying to escape. I'm not sure
which one." He winced, obviously discomforted by what
could be considered inattentiveness. Had Matrinka not loved
children so much and spent so much time with the twin boys
since infancy, she might have been hard-pressed to tell them
apart as well. Darris continued, voice thick with misery, "A
guard's son got trampled. The prime minister's youngest
daughter got scraped up a bit. A Renshai and a Béarnian
guard were killed." He looked up.

Matrinka's eyes burned, spilling tears. She sank back to
the coverlet, sobbing, unable to imagine her younger cousins
dead. She pictured Ukrista, her dark eyes always shining and
black braids flying behind her as she ran. Nylabrin's giggles
would never again fill Béarn's halls, and the statue courtyard
would seem a chill, empty graveyard without them. She
scarcely noticed when Darris enfolded her in a sympathetic
embrace, rocking her like a child. She buried her hands in
Mior's soft fur and let the motion take her back to the innocent days of her own infancy. She clung to Darris, lost in a

dark hole of grief that seemed endless and bottomless. The motion became a necessary foundation for her sense of self and sanity, and it came to an end too soon. Gently, Darris pulled free, raised his lute, and played.

At first, Matrinka felt lost without the merciful, rhythmic swaying that had carried her from the depths of sorrow. Then the music settled over her like a consoling blanket, easing into her heart and mind, soothing the pain. The words of the song glided past her, unheard; but the succor they left behind was real enough. Gradually, she drifted back to sleep.

When Matrinka awakened again, late morning sunlight oozed through the slit between curtains. Mior's warmth and weight felt familiar and pleasant against her leg. She opened her eyes. No longer shapeless blurs, the Renshai crouched in the same positions she had seen them in earlier, like statues. The comparison sent a shiver of revulsion through her, and she could not suppress an image of the bear rearing and slashing at harmless children. Once it, too, had been a monument, unmoving. Somehow someone had replaced it and two others with all too real killers.

Darris sat in the chair, sprawled across its back. His brown curls had fallen across his forehead into his eyes, making him appear childlike. He breathed deeply and regularly, his long vigil over, apparently wrested from him by sleep. She wondered how he had gotten permission to spend the night in a princess' room.

Matrinka managed a smile for her longtime companion, then turned her attention to the Renshai, both women. The taller sported close-cropped, blonde hair and a wiry frame that made her look like a Béarnian adolescent. Her face told a different story, her heavy features those of a woman approaching middle age. Sandy war braids swung around the other's face, and she appeared little older than Matrinka. Both wore serious expressions to match their simple tunics and breeks, clearly cut to allow freest movement in battle. Both studied her as she did them, seeming aware of her awakening even before her lids fluttered open. Their inhuman wariness made her skin crawl.

Despite her discomfort, Matrinka remained polite. "Hello. I'm Matrinka, and this is Mior." She poked the cat in the ribs teasingly.

Mior rolled, catching the finger between paws that allowed just a warning hint of nails.

The blonde rose and bowed. "Kristel Garethsdatter of the Renshai tribe of Modrey."

Her sandy-haired companion waited until Kristel resumed her defensive stance before repeating the gestures of respect. "Nisse Nelsdatter of the Renshai tribe of Rache."

Matrinka had deliberately omitted her own title to keep their relationship on a less formal basis. Clearly the tactic had failed. Both women remained rigidly attentive after reciting their full names as if in court. Matrinka glanced over at Darris to see if their conversation disturbed him, but the bard's heir continued to sleep despite his awkward position. The Renshai returned to their quiet vigil.

Silence left Matrinka's mind too free to mull events she could not affect. Her eyes already felt swollen and painful; more tears would not rescue those already dead nor her injured cousin. She considered the relationship between the flashes of light she had witnessed in the fourth-story window and the bear statues coming to life. Surely ministers and advisers throughout the kingdom already pondered the specifics of the attack while grief stole curiosity from Kohleran and his offspring. Though the wounds remained raw within Matrinka, she rediscovered her concentration and her interest in details. It made no sense that live bears had sneaked into the courtyard and less that they could or would pose as statues prior to the attack. *Magic.* The explanation came to Matrinka instantly, though she doubted others would draw the same conclusion. They would search for a logical explanation they seemed unlikely to find. The facts remained: no one could have penetrated the courtyard unseen and no vicious killer of a bear could have remained unmoving so long.

Matrinka needed nothing more. Her innocence would not allow her to contemplate the possibility of treason, that one of Béarn's trusted had made the switch from inside the courtyard. She did consider the possibility that the creatures that so closely resembled bears were something else altogether. She had heard a bear could rip through hordes of adults in moments. Three of them should have slaughtered all the children in less time than it took her to register their presence, yet this last tangent had an answer. She had seen the guardian Renshai charge from bear to bear, battling with a skill and fury that seemed nearly as inconceivable as the presence of the creatures. Matrinka believed in sorcery, as few did anymore, accepting the whispered tales of Renshai tapping demons for their skill. Her eyes told her she had seen bears, flesh transformed from stone. Whatever its source, the old Renshai's skill and, later, Béarnian archers, guards, and more Renshai warriors had rescued the remaining children.

Matrinka returned her attention to the two Renshai in her room, hoping to ease their tension as well as divert her thoughts. Wiser heads got paid to find the solution she did not have enough information to piece together. She had found an answer that worked for her, and its name was magic. "The tribe of Mowdray? The tribe of Rackee?" She sounded out their titles as carefully as possible. The Renshai's musical accents rendered them difficult to understand, especially when using words not of Western origin. "I thought Renshai was a nationality. Like Béarnide."

Kristel addressed the comment that was not quite a question. "Actually, it's a culture and a style of combat more than a race. Centuries ago, the tribe got whittled down to three couples from whom all current Renshai can trace their roots. The line of Modrey has the most original Renshai blood. The line of Tannin has about half, and the line of Rache descends wholly from Western blood."

Nisse cut in, obviously irritated. The argument, Matrinka guessed, was an old one and the distinction more a point of contention than useful history. "Of course, the lines have interbred so much, the differences have become nonexistent. No matter who your father is, you're considered to belong to the tribe of your mother. And some Renshai do get permission to marry outside the tribe as a whole if the man is worthy and can pass or teach positive features to his offspring."

Nisse glared at Kristel, who could not help adding, "But it's harder for Modreys to get permission."

Nisse nodded once, grudgingly.

Matrinka thought it best to change the subject again. "I guess you were hired to guard me."

Nisse nodded again, sandy war braids bobbing around a face that relaxed noticeably with the diversion.

"Why me?"

Nisse studied Matrinka. "All of the king's heirs have personal guards now. Women got female guards and men males." She shrugged. "We were assigned to you."

Matrinka's gaze strayed to Darris once more.

Apparently interpreting the gesture as a question, Kristel said, "He insisted on staying with you last night. We deemed him harmless so deigned not to kill him this time."

"Kill him?" The words were startled from Matrinka.

Kristel continued, composed, as if discussing nothing more serious than the courtyard flowers. "Anyone who comes too close receives a warning. If they don't heed it, we have no choice but to kill them."

The Renshai's matter-of-fact coldness sent a chill shivering through Matrinka. She imagined her life, boxed in by ruthless demon-soldiers hired to protect her, and the picture made her queasy. She had seen the swarm of guards eternally surrounding King Kohleran and supposed the comparison fit, but she had never expected to hold the title of queen nor sit upon the Béarnian throne. Even now, after the slaughter or accidental death of so many heirs, three Béarnides, an aunt and two cousins, still stood ahead of her in the line of ascension.

Kristel's voice turned contemptuous. "Though an obvious coward, he showed no inclination to harm you during the attack. There is no honor in slaying a craven."

Matrinka's mouth fell open, but she found no response to an insult worsened by the understanding that no curse was crueler or more derisive in the Renshai language than "coward." Matrinka believed Darris uncommonly brave during the attack. He had thrown his body across her own, fearlessly taking whatever punishment the bear might mete in order to give her the opportunity to escape. That the bears had focused their attack elsewhere made the act no less heroic in her estimation. But, apparently, the Renshai saw things otherwise. Before Matrinka could question further or defend her companion, someone knocked on the door.

The Renshai tensed, holding their positions near the door. "Who is it?" Kristel demanded.

A meek voice floated beneath the solid panel. "Just the page again. May I speak with Princess Matrinka now?" His tone suggested he had made the request previously, presumably while Matrinka slept, and had been denied.

Kristel took her cue from Matrinka, who nodded vigorously. She had no intention of spending the rest of her existence locked in her bedroom with Renshai.

Awakened by Kristel's shout through the heavy, wooden panel, Darris yawned and stretched. Then, recognizing his location, he came suddenly alert.

"You're alone?" Kristel called back.

"Alone? Yes," came the reply.

Kristel inclined her head in a silent command, and Nisse pulled the door open. A Béarnian boy of about twelve stood in the hallway, dark eyes darting nervously from Renshai to Renshai beneath a fringe of bangs. When they made no move to leap upon him, he directed his gaze to Matrinka. "Sorry to bother you, m'lady. Your presence is requested at the Room of Staves."

The staff room? Horror clutched Matrinka. If they needed to test her, it could mean only one thing. "Gods, no. Is the king . . . ? I mean, he's not . . ." She could not finish. She had known Kohleran's death was imminent, but that barely cushioned the blow.

The page guessed her obvious, though unfinished, question. "Don't worry, m'lady. King Kohleran is alive. No worse than yesterday."

Relief flooded Matrinka, and she managed a shaky smile that turned into a confused stare. The Room of Staves had only a single purpose, to test for Béarn's next heir. "Then why . . . ?" She stopped herself. A page could not be expected to have the details of such matters.

However, this page had surmised enough and chose to share his opinion. "I don't know for certain, m'lady; but I can tell you I've sent seven heirs there already today. You're number eight. And there hasn't been any particular order to it that I can see."

Matrinka glanced to the Renshai. They remained quietly in place, awaiting her command. She returned her attention to the page. "Give me a moment to change from my sleeping gown, and I'll be right with you."

The page nodded and took a step back, though he had never actually entered the room, apparently intimidated by the guards. Kristel raised a hand, waving for Darris to leave as well.

Darris obeyed without comment, pausing only long enough to nod politely to Matrinka as he left. The Renshai closed the door on his heels, and Matrinka slipped from beneath the covers to dress.

Chapter 3

The Staff-Test

This is going to be the most frustrating, difficult, annoying thing you've ever done in your life. And that's the way it should be.

—Colbey Calistinsson

Matrinka knew the Room of the Staves held a central location on the castle's first floor, tucked between a meditation area and a library. Scarcely larger than a closet, it contained only the Staves of Law and Chaos; nothing about their plain, wooden construction suggested the need for lighting or public display. She threaded through the castle corridors, clutching Mior, preceded and flanked by the two Renshai warriors. Grief still hounded her, and concern for her grandfather's health remained despite the page's reassurance. Other worries crept into her consciousness to join those already aching within her; these new ones involved her ability to pass the test for the crown, with or without her thoughts scattered and distracted by tragedy. Long ago, she had considered and discarded the idea that she might someday need to undergo the staff-test. Too many stood between her and the throne, especially now that her father was dead and could not pass the title.

Mior allowed Matrinka to mull the many problems without her counsel, and the princess appreciated the cat's silence as well as the Renshai's stolid hush. She loved Mior, yet the animal had her limitations when it came to issues requiring deep contemplation. For all her ability to communicate, the calico still had the basic mentality of an animal, tending to divide life into simple slices: avoid the uncomfortable, seek warmth and shelter, eat the tastiest available food whenever possible. Mior would prove of little assistance to Matrinka when it came to composing herself for or undergoing the test. The cat's presence alone proved a solace; no exchange of thoughts was necessary.

As Matrinka and her escort approached the Room of Staves, they discovered only two figures waiting in front of it, both male Béarnides dressed in royal blue and tan. The larger wore the dress silks of Kohleran's ministry while the other sported a servant's tabard. As they drew closer, Matrinka recognized Prime Minister Baltraine and a scribe whose name she could not recall. Remembering Darris' pronouncement that Baltraine's youngest daughter had gotten injured during the bear's attack, Matrinka winced in sympathy.

The Renshai shifted, placing themselves between Matrinka and the men.

As Matrinka approached, the scribe bowed low and Baltraine nodded respectfully. "Good morning, Princess," the minister said.

"Good morning, Baltraine." Matrinka looked around Nisse and Kristel at the kindly featured, middle-aged Béarnide who had been a member of the king's cabinet since her childhood. Years ago, before affairs of state had completely consumed his attention, he used to crouch to her eye level and chat when they passed in the hallways. His eldest girl was Matrinka's age, an occasional playmate in childhood. "I pray your daughter is well."

Baltraine pursed lips lost in a mane of facial hair. "She's fine. Just a few scrapes and bruises." He lowered his head in sorrow. "Unfortunately, some of your cousins did not fare as well."

"I know," Matrinka said softly. Not wishing to hear a repeat of those murdered, she turned the conversation toward the king. "How's Grandpapa?"

"Sad, of course." Baltraine shook his head to imply King Kohleran had suffered more misfortune than any one man should have to endure.

The response addressed Matrinka's concern indirectly. A dead king could feel no sorrow.

Baltraine continued, nudging their talk toward the matter

at hand. "We've lost the king's health and six heirs in less than two years, and another life hangs by a thread. This last incident makes it clear we're not dealing with just bad luck or a curse."

The Renshai remained in place, their postures relaxed but their features alert. Matrinka tightened her hold on Mior. "Murder?"

Baltraine dismissed the one-word question. "Murder definitely. Possibly treason." He spoke freely in front of the scribe and Renshai. The former served the sage, his job to convey details, information, and even the most confidential of the king's judgments only to his master. The Renshai would repeat nothing that might jeopardize the heirs. The core of their religion forbade it.

"Treason?" The idea confused Matrinka. "Why would anyone kill heirs?"

The prime minister tossed his hand in a gesture that implied no explanation.

The staff-test discouraged dissension among the heirs. One who would murder siblings for the throne could never pass the test. An outside force wishing to invade might believe the lack of a king would weaken Béarn, but a troublemaker from within seemed to have nothing to gain. *Unless they could abolish the staff-test.* The thought seemed madness. Surely no one would dare challenge an institution the gods themselves had devised. Matrinka needed one piece of information even to surmise. "What happens if the king dies without a living heir?"

Baltraine shuffled his feet, obviously uncomfortable. "I don't know. No one does." He looked up, his expression deadly earnest. "The law clearly specifies who can and cannot take the throne, and no contingencies exist for such a situation." He let the implication hang.

Kristel spoke scarcely above a whisper, but her words carried for their import. "The Renshai will see an heir in place. The Béarnian ruler is the central balance of the world. Without him or her, Midgard would collapse into Chaos-ruin." Religious faith alone supported her view, yet that seemed enough. They all worshiped in the same temples.

Matrinka felt as if frost speckled her skin, and she shivered. "So the reason for testing me now?"

Baltraine nodded, obviously anticipating a question he had probably answered seven times before. "King Kohleran and

I thought it best to test all the heirs before we lose him or any more of you. Only those most trusted will know who passes. We can focus our security and plans based on the outcome."

The explanation satisfied Matrinka. She tossed back her long, black locks as she mulled the potential consequences. If she passed, she stood a reasonable chance of becoming Béarn's next queen, but she would probably have to spend the remainder of King Kohleran's illness triple guarded like a prisoner. Should she fail, her life could become her own again, without the constant Renshai escort. One thing seemed certain. She would pass or fail on her own merits, and the possible repercussions would not affect her trial by magic. "All right, then. What do I have to do?"

The scribe stepped aside. Baltraine pulled a ring of keys from his belt and unlocked the door to the Room of Staves. The panel swung open to reveal a dark interior, lit only by the light streaming in from the hall torches, bare except for a wooden staff leaning in each far corner. Baltraine gestured at the interior with a flourish. "Take both staves in hand, and the test begins. Once finished, you need only place them properly back and exit."

A flush of fear struck Matrinka, gradually displacing the chilling feeling that Kristel's words had invoked. She willed herself to put Mior down, but her arm would not release the cat. "Can I bring her?" She inclined her head toward the calico.

Baltraine's massive shoulders rose and fell. "I don't see why you can't, unless the staves tell you otherwise. None of the others remained inside longer than a few moments, though they all seemed to believe it had taken hours. I think she'll be fine, in with you or out here." He took a torch from a bracket shaped like a wolf and passed it to Matrinka.

Matrinka managed to set Mior down and accepted the light. "Then I'll let her decide." She headed into the room, the cat scurrying directly at her heels.

Like I'd leave you to handle this alone, Mior chastised.

No offense, but I don't think you can help much. Matrinka heard the door click closed behind them. *In fact, you probably shouldn't even if you can. The staff-test is supposed to measure my appropriateness to rule, not yours.*

Too bad. Think how much better off this world would be if cats controlled it.

Nervous, Matrinka could not think of a gibe to return, though Mior had left her a more than adequate straight line. After placing her torch securely in the room's only wall bracket, she wiped sweating hands on her dress.

Mior turned appropriately serious. *Maybe I can't help directly, but I can be here for you.*

Matrinka hoped Mior could read her gratitude, because she did not waste words. The cat's loyalty lessened her discomfort, but the uneasiness provoked by the staves could not be wholly banished. She dried her hands again, reaching for the first staff with a grip that quivered the more she tried to keep it steady. As her fingers closed over the wood, she braced for a rush of magic that did not come. It felt smooth and cool against her palm, without a single rough grain or knot. She wasted several moments, holding it and waiting for tingling or some other sensation to indicate she clutched something more significant than sanded ash.

Speculation bombarded Matrinka, from the fear that the staff had already judged and found her unworthy to a wonder about whether or not the whole would prove a hoax. Perhaps Béarnian heirs down through history had simply stepped into this booth and made their own decisions, based on self-judgment, about whether or not they should become the next monarch. Her first inclination to expose the test as a sham passed quickly. Whatever the method, the staff-test had resulted in a succession of benevolent and competent kings. The difficult part involved whether or not she found herself worthy of the honor.

Matrinka reached for the second staff, and never knew for certain whether or not she grasped it. Pain shot through her, starting at the fingertips of both hands and exploding through her entire body. Agony stole mastery of movement and senses; she could not even find the control to scream. Something unseen struck her hard enough to send her tumbling, end over end, through a void whose presence she never questioned. The sensation of spinning seemed to last an eternity, gradually becoming more prominent than the suffering. The spasms that racked every part of her body, an instinctive response to pain, became a greater anguish than the pain itself. She forced herself to breathe deeply, relaxing her cramping muscles and opening eyes she never recalled closing.

The twirling stopped. The pain settled into a dull, nagging

discomfort. She lay on a bed, studying blurry surroundings through eyes coated with an irritating, sticky layer of mucus. She rubbed at her eyes, the pressure sparking flashes of light across her retinas, but the beclouding film persisted and a glimpse of her wasted-looking hand made her pause in fear and wonder. She stared at it, trying to recall how she had come to lie here and whether it truly belonged to her. Her mind registered body part and bed as standard, normal situations, assuring her the confusion stemmed from post-sleep amnesia. She was an ancient queen of Béarn, dying of illness and decades past her prime. Now, familiarity defined the vague outlines of richly carved and jeweled furniture, three windows, and Prime Minister Baltraine, who stood patiently near the door.

Matrinka forced a smile, though it took more energy than she would have imagined. She willed away concentration on her own, chronic distress to ease that of her minister. His solemn stance made her certain he had matters of grave importance to discuss. "What can I do for you, Baltraine?"

Once addressed, Baltraine bowed graciously. "Majesty, I deeply apologize for the intrusion. I hope I have not disturbed your sleep."

Matrinka dismissed the possibility, unable to recall whether she had been resting. Time passed in fits and starts. Sometimes pain dragged each second into infinity, and other times sleep and disorientation stole days. "Speak freely, Baltraine."

Baltraine bowed again, though the gesture was unnecessary. It seemed more like nervous habit or delay. "I regret to inform you that a situation occurred in the statue garden. Somehow, three live bears got substituted for sculptures and attacked a group of children."

Grief shocked through Matrinka, then settled to a dull throb that made listening difficult. As if through a thick sheet pulled over her ears, she listened to Baltraine describe casualties, including her grandchildren, with a feeling of twice-hearing, as if she had listened to someone detail the dead and injured before in another context. The sorrow, though genuine, seemed stale. She saw little reason to question him further. The dead would receive proper rest; care of the injured would fall to the royal healers whom Matrinka trusted implicitly. When Baltraine's list finished, she had to force speech. "Where did these bears come from?"

"We don't know, Majesty." Baltraine shook his head sadly and took a step nearer. Now Matrinka could see his eyes had gone red and bloodshot from tears. "We're investigating the details. Every child, nursemaid, and guard has sworn he or she didn't notice the switch until the bears attacked. The bears themselves seemed normal enough, aside from their absolute concentration on killing. We're examining their corpses now. The statues haven't been found. Oh, and there's been some reports of odd things that might have preceded the incident: lights, sounds, movements, color, and so on. Nothing consistent or confirmed."

"Magic?" Matrinka supplied without thinking.

Baltraine shuffled from foot to foot. "Perhaps, Majesty. If we don't find a more . . . um . . ." He searched for the proper word, apparently trying to avoid insulting the suggestion. ". . . mundane possibility." He glanced sidelong, obviously trying to read his queen's face for clues to whether she considered his dispatch of her suggestion an affront.

Matrinka shifted, fluid from her illness settling into the new position. She struggled for breath, hampered by a swollen abdomen and sodden lungs. "Well, yes, of course," she murmured with careful matter-of-factness intended to placate Baltraine as much as to handle the situation. "Logic must always come before mystical considerations." She coughed, tasting blood-tinged froth. "I'm just not certain standard reason will reveal the answer this time."

Baltraine nodded attentively.

If they could not piece together a physical explanation, sorcery would obviously have to fall under consideration. But there would be no precedent for discovering the identity of a wielder of magic. Experience suggested only a god could stand behind any such act. Matrinka shoved aside her speculations about Baltraine's thoughts, certain he had come for more reasons than just delivering information.

Baltraine got to the point. "Majesty, the ministers, including myself, have concerns that we're dealing with assassins."

Matrinka chewed her lower lip, seeing no other way to interpret the current events. She coughed again, the effort sparking pain through her chest. "I would agree with that assessment, though I can't fathom why someone would deliberately disrupt the succession."

"Nor can I, Majesty." Baltraine bowed again. "It's under

consideration now by Béarn's wisest. Once we have a motive, we can start to find a culprit. We're working on that from every side: searching for clues, observation, trying to discover a motive that might direct our search." The set of Baltraine's head made Matrinka believe he had trained his gaze directly on hers. "The one thing we can do now is protect the heirs."

"Agreed."

Baltraine finished his thought. "Majesty, I believe the best interests of the kingdom will be served if we learn just how dangerous the situation has become." He drew himself to his full height as he came to the heart of his intentions. "I think we should have all of Béarn's remaining potential heirs undergo the staff-test. I seek your support in this matter."

For reasons Matrinka could not explain, the unorthodox suggestion did not wholly surprise her. She considered the implications. Historically, the staff-test resulted in the decreed innocent, neutral rulers; but the ones who failed often became despondent. Her father had ruled Béarn into old age, leaving her one of his last surviving children, the youngest of Yvalane's progeny. Her cousin who failed the staff-test drank himself into an oblivion that ended with his death. However, although the sage's records indicated more than one suicide, the vast majority of heirs dealt with their disappointment in less destructive ways. Confronted with the need for a decision, Matrinka frowned. It seemed cruel to inflict the test on anyone unnecessarily. "You sound as if you're suggesting testing every heir, no matter his order in the ascension."

Baltraine did not stir, remaining deadly earnest. "I am, Majesty."

Taken aback, Matrinka squinted, though this pooled the mucus in her eyes, all but blinding her. "Would it not be wiser and kinder to test them in order until one passes?" She returned her eyes to their normal configuration, blinking the film back to its usual arrangement.

"I think not, Majesty." Baltraine contradicted with a respect that did not offend. "For several reasons. First, discretion seems necessary in this instance. Should people learn the identity of the heir, the assassin or his employer may also. If we test only until one passes, the heir will become obvious to too many. Second, it behooves us to know exactly how many appropriate heirs we have in case we lose the first."

"We can guard the first."

"Majesty, Renshai are superior warriors but not invincible. And even the best sentries cannot thwart illness should it choose to take our beloved heir."

The explanation made sense. "Continue," Matrinka encouraged.

"Thank you, Majesty. I've stated my case." Baltraine remained in place, rock steady. "I cannot and will not take action without your support."

Matrinka sensed she had come to a decision somehow even more significant than it already seemed, yet the additional details eluded her. Instinct told her to reject Baltraine's plan since it hinged on inflicting emotional trauma on others. That those others consisted of her children and grandchildren only made the action more onerous. Still, Baltraine had a point she could not deny. The kingdom of Béarn had always served as the Westlands ruling monarchy, taking precedence over all the kings and queens of cities, towns, and villages. According to the tenets, the very foundation of Béarnian, Erythanian, and Northern religion, the monarch in Béarn served as the focal point of balance. She could not last much longer; and, without a ruler, Béarn would topple, dragging the remainder of the world along with it. To staff-test all the heirs might traumatize a few, but to ignore the need to protect the proper heirs at all costs might mean the destruction of the entire world. Matrinka sighed, hating both options. *The greater good lies with preserving the kingdom.* "You have my support," she said. "Proceed."

A feeling of closure washed through her, bringing a pleasant, personal satisfaction though the Staves of Law and Chaos revealed no emotion or sense of passing or failing. Matrinka's identity returned, and she recalled her purpose. Her palms grew warm. King Kohleran's room faded around her. The spinning resumed, whirling her through a soundless, sightless vortex. She considered the events of a moment before in this new context. For all intents and purposes, she had become a duplicate of her grandfather. She had known his illness brought him pain, but never contemplated that the discomfort was a constant that would have made its absence a joy as sweet and primal as the most beautiful stroll through the tended gardens. The simple things she took for granted, such as clear vision, moving, and breathing became wondrous in comparison.

As she continued to tumble, Matrinka pondered the test she had undergone, wishing the staves would give her some indication of whether she had done well or ill. The fact that she had begun the staff-test indicated she had chosen the same course as King Kohleran. Since he had already passed the staff-test, it seemed certain she had performed as a proper innocent, neutral heir should. The success pleased her. *Is that it? Was that the test?* It seemed unlikely. Offered only two possibilities, half of the heirs would pass the tests based only on random guessing. That did not strike Matrinka as likely to constitute a magical task so steeped in religion and mystery. Soon, she imagined, she would undergo another scenario. She clung tightly to her identity and the staves, hoping this time she would not become lost in staff-created delusion.

Suddenly, Matrinka struck solid ground. Terror flashed through her briefly as she naturally imagined the pain that must ensue from landing after falling so far. But she thumped to sand with barely enough impact to notice. Still clutching the staves, she sat up and looked around. She had settled on a tiny island half a dozen paces across. It contained nothing but sand, and a tumultuous ocean pounded every beach. Matrinka knew nothing about land forms in the sea, but she guessed that the waters would eventually claim this tiny scrap of sand. This time, the staves' magic had not thrown her into another persona, at least she did not believe so. *How would I know?* The question defied answer, so Matrinka discarded it. She felt like herself, but she had not questioned her identity as the dying queen of Béarn either.

Matrinka rose, using the staves to assist her, wondering what her task would consist of this time. Her mind told her that escaping the island would not satisfy the staves. The scenario involved something more significant, including other people. *Other people? On this tiny island?* As certain as she felt about forthcoming events involving others, she could see she was alone. From end to end, no one else shared her minuscule piece of the world. She looked out over the ocean, scanning the horizon as she walked the perimeter of the beach. About halfway from her starting point, she found a massive shadow towering through fog and spume kicked up by the waves. Salt burning her eyes, she followed the shadow to its source, far out to sea. Gradually, she made out the form of what appeared to be a giant scale, perfectly balanced, with a person in each tray. Their waving arms made it clear they had seen her and desperately requested her aid.

Matrinka did not challenge the oddity of the situation. Two people hovered over surging ocean, and they needed her help. Whether or not she could assist them remained to be seen, but she could not assess the possibility from such a distance. Neatly setting down the staves in the center of the island, where the waters could not snatch them away, she prepared to dive.

Waves hammered the shore, foaming like a rabid animal. Matrinka hesitated, concerned the ocean might swallow and pound her to oblivion as well. Yet she would not stand back while others lost their lives. Only she could rescue the two people on the scale, so she plunged into the ocean without further deliberation.

The tide gripped her, flinging her back toward the shore. She fought the current, floundering through water that seemed hell-bent on drowning her. A wave flung her into a crazed spiral. She fought it, diving beneath it, and the moment's reprieve allowed her to gain control of her limbs and swim. She clawed to the surface, salt burning her lungs and throat, coughing and sputtering to clear it. The icy waters numbed her joints, making her fight against the current seem futile. Nevertheless, she noted that the island lay some distance behind her. Taking solace from the progress, she pushed onward.

Soon waves no longer closed over her, though the current still dragged at her, towing her toward shore. She gritted her teeth, concentrating on the scale, not daring to check whether she had made any progress. Every three tedious lengths forward seemed accompanied by at least two backward. It felt like an eternity before the scale drew nearer, the people in the trays now obviously a man and a woman, both studying her approach.

As the swimming became easier, facts slipped into Matrinka's mind that her vision could not tell her. Without an iota of doubt, she knew that neither could extract himself or herself from the tray. Something, presumably magic, held them in place so that only an outsider could free them. Furthermore, she realized that the man had a wife and four hungry, young children. He worked as a woodcutter, trading his product for the food his family needed and for cloth so that his wife could patch their clothing. He asked a fair price for his goods and often gave his wood free to cold orphans or other folks living on the street.

The woman, Matrinka understood as she swam, had disowned her parents and never married. She stole what she wanted and killed on occasion. The day before the powers of the staff-test plucked her from her life and spirited her here, she had murdered an elderly couple then robbed their cottage. As Matrinka hauled herself onto the base of the scale, her sympathy for the woodcutter flared nearly as hot as her hatred for the woman and her cruelty. The scale's center had metal handholds for her to climb to the level of the balancing arms. She considered the mechanics. When she added her weight to one side, it would dip toward the ocean. Presuming she could haul the occupant free quickly, she could shove him into the water and dive in afterward to assist him to shore.

Matrinka's mind outlined the events that would follow, though whether from normal logic or the assistance of the staves, she could not tell. Once the pan no longer held a person, the other would fall rapidly, plunging its resident into the depths. Magically trapped, this other would surely drown. *Unless I can get to him or her swiftly.* Matrinka shook her head. Burdened with one of the people, she felt certain she could not rescue the other from the sea's bottom. If she tried, all three of them would probably die.

Matrinka began the climb up the central mast as she continued to outline the situation. To rescue one meant drowning the other. All logic assured her such was the case, and the decision inherent in this scenario seemed obvious now. *I have to choose between them.* It seemed too easy. *Who would ever select a murderer over a kindhearted family man?* She drew herself up to the level of the arms.

The woman shouted to Matrinka. "Please, save me. I can reward you. I can shower you with riches. In addition, I can promise you the heart and soul of a handsome, young man or my own body if such are your proclivities. Whatever you desire, I can see that it becomes yours." Matrinka knew with the same certainty as other details that the woman could deliver on her promises. She glanced toward the man, who shook his head sadly.

"I have nothing," he said. "Nothing but as many warm nights in my family's cottage as you desire. We would share all we have but that would not be much, I'm afraid."

Matrinka pursed her lips, cold wind chilling across her sodden body. She had not braved the ocean to select an option that placed greed over morality. She had made her decision the instant she reached the base of the scale. Without a word to either party, she headed toward the man, the balance of the scale controlled wholly by her movement.

Light sparked through Matrinka's vision, stealing the situation from vision and reality in an instant. Again, she fell into the vortex, body spinning in spirals that seemed infinite. Sharp pains lanced through her head, laced with a guilt she could not fathom. This time, it seemed, the staves had chosen to judge and they deemed her actions unworthy.

The verdict shocked her, and she struggled to discover her mistake. Her own mind called her blameless, yet the staves bombarded her with aspersion until she felt on fire with shame. *What did I do wrong? What was my mistake?* She shot out the same questions a million times, yet no answers came. The magic chose to humiliate without explanation, persuading her that an honorable ruler would know. Tears smeared the blackness of the whirlwind to gray. Self-loathing sparked through her, not only at the obvious low-mindedness of her decision but at her own apparently warped morality that could not fathom the impropriety.

Soon, the rotation stole all of the revulsion in addition to sense of self. Matrinka found herself in the king's high seat of Béarn's court. To her left, the bard, Linndar, wore the proper, stately blue and tan and carried no instrument. To Matrinka's right, Seiryn, the guard captain, oversaw a semicircle of sentries. Courtiers filled the benches, watching a foreign dignitary tread the center aisle toward the dais. The man led a dozen young men and women, chained in a line by collars.

A Béarnian guard introduced the foreigner: "Tichhar, representative of King Shaxchral of LaZar." He named a large city in the Eastlands, one whose relations with Béarn had always been strained at best. The guard stepped aside to allow the Easterner to speak.

Tichhar bowed, and those accompanying him knelt.

Matrinka studied him in silence for several moments. Bard Linndar cleared her throat, politely reminding her queen that she needed to speak first.

Matrinka felt slightly off balance, as if she did not belong to this place or time. She discarded the thought, attributing it to lack of sleep the previous night. "Rise, please, Tichhar of LaZar, and speak your piece."

Tichhar stood, though the chained ones remained in place. He used the common trading tongue. "Your Majesty. I have brought an offering of peace from my country to your own in the hope of long-lasting good relations between us."

The silence became unnerving, reinforcing the significance of such an agreement. Few duties of a ruler seemed more satisfying than turning enemies to advocates, especially in masses. She recalled the conversation Linndar, Baltraine, and she had had before the session, though it seemed faded and distant, a cardboard memory. Eastern law upheld slavery. Their kingdoms sealed alliances with a slave exchange, and the mightier party gave fewer slaves to seal the difference in power. Awarding not enough, or those in poor health, jeopardized the association and had, on more than one occasion, ignited a war.

Matrinka could not understand why her prime minister and bodyguard had not advised her on the details of this situation. Now left to her own devices, she longed for the assistance of wiser heads. Delay, she knew, could also ruin this rare and wonderful opportunity; yet Béarn was opposed to slavery. *How can I uphold Béarnian principles without offending LaZar?* The answer, everyone seemed certain, should rest inside her, as straightforward and basic as breathing.

Matrinka shifted, knowing she could not expect the empty pause to carry her much longer. Soon, she had to speak. "Béarn thanks King Shaxchral for this alliance as well as his generous gift." She spoke slowly, trying to gather her wildly flailing thoughts in the moments this gained her. The difference between peace and war lay in the words she spoke . . . and something more that she could not place, something beyond the confines of the courtroom and a single decision. *Phrase carefully. Don't judge LaZar or apologize for our moratorium.* "It is our wish to return a gift of appropriate merit, but Béarn's only slaves bleat, whinny, and moo."

Matrinka turned her attention to the minister of livestock.

"Charletha, take Tichhar and his party to the royal barns and stables. Let them choose whatever animals they would and in numbers they believe fair." She returned her attention to LaZar's dignitary. "We hope you find this just reconciliation of the differences between our laws and customs." She raised her brows, throwing the burden of rejection or acceptance into LaZar's hands.

Tichhar considered, avoiding Matrinka's stare. Although the East no longer reviled its women, they still believed them secondary to men. That bias would work against Matrinka now. Then, Tichhar looked up, a slight smile bending his dark cheeks. Like many Easterners, he wore a beard without other facial hair, unlike the Béarnides' standard manes. "We accept your offer and would consider this treaty valid." He bowed again, with a different flourish that Matrinka believed indicated farewell.

The exchange of slaves only bound the contract LaZar and Béarn had already written. Although Matrinka did not recall the details of it, she knew she believed the terms fair. Nothing remained but to seal the pact. "Béarn considers the treaty valid also. You may inform King Shaxchral. Dismissed."

The guards led Tichhar from the courtroom amidst the whispered mumbling of the crowd of courtiers on the benches. Matrinka remained in position, unbreathing, until the LaZarian left the room. Only then, she loosed a sigh of relief; and the courtroom erupted into a frenzied chorus of speculation. Bard Linndar placed a hand on Matrinka's arm to indicate a problem averted and a job well-handled. Pride trickled through Matrinka, interrupted only by a question from the one of the guards below. "Excuse me, Majesty."

Matrinka looked down to the speaker and the chained line of slaves waiting on the path.

"Majesty, what would you have us do with these?"

Matrinka froze, so caught up in handling the treaty she had forgotten that her actions had allowed slaves in a free kingdom. *I broke the law.* The thought chilled her, and she could not find words to remedy the matter. *If the queen of Béarn breaks the laws she makes, how can she expect others to follow them?* For several seconds, she stared, speechless, seeking precedent from history. Yet, bargaining with Eastern kingdoms was history-making and she could think of nothing on which to base her next course of action. *Do I apol-*

*ogize to my populace? Do I change the law to allow
temporary slavery in court situations? Do I make amends?*
The latter course made the most sense to her. "Free them.
Then find out where each wishes to be taken, and we will do
everything in our power to see them all safely home."

Agony seized Matrinka with a sudden fury, flinging her
into a darkness that transcended space and time. Once again,
she became Matrinka the tested, the throne and her queen-
ship disappearing into a fantasy something assured her was
unlikely to reach fruition. Once again, the staves proclaimed
her unworthy of sitting upon Béarn's throne. The pride
Matrinka had celebrated for making choices with a skill and
smoothness she never knew she had disappeared in a red
slash of humiliation. *Where did I go wrong this time?* No answers came. Exchanging animals for humans had not only
rescued the treaty but also resulted in happiness for a dozen
slaves who would otherwise have lived only in suffering.
How could I have done any better? Matrinka reviewed every
word, every nuance of the exchange, and her conscience
condoned all that had transpired. Yet a greater power, one
backed by gods, condemned her with a vehemence that
made her own assessments seem foolish. If she had the morality to rule Béarn, she would understand her mistake.

Self-doubt became a lash with which Matrinka punished
herself repeatedly before the third scenario of the staff-test
became the fourth and, she understood, the last. Forever, she
had believed herself a conscientiously ethical person. Always, she had tried to choose the moral path in every aspect
of her existence, doing her best to make life special for everyone around her. Yet, now, she could not help questioning
every action and every decision she'd ever made. No longer
could she trust her judgment alone.

Suddenly, the blackness receded; and Matrinka again
found herself in the court high seat believing herself queen
of Béarn and surrounded by officials and guards. A wiry,
Pudarian man stood before her, making a pitch in earnest
tones, eyes remaining always fixed on her face: "Your Majesty, I'd like to present 'Wonder Tonic,' a concoction of rare
herbs guaranteed to cure even the most advanced case of
lumpy-consumption."

Matrinka sat up straighter at this proclamation. Memory
told her that too many Béarnides had already succumbed to

this disease. The Pudarian promised a miracle, and joy filled her.

The Pudarian shook his mop of brown hair, though it fell back into an equally boyish position. "My aunt put together the mixture, and I found the final root that gives Wonder Tonic its strength." He lowered his head, studying his feet. "Majesty, I'd like to give Wonder Tonic away for free so that it can help as many as possible, but many of the ingredients are rare and expensive and, well, I just need to recoup my costs and, well . . ." He glanced up, eyes soulful. "Majesty, I seek your permission to sell Wonder Tonic to your citizenry without tariff so that I can keep the cost reasonable for those who need it. Majesty, I will, of course, reserve as many bottles as you wish for use by the kingdom, first. I can even give you one free." Despite his generous offer, his tone made it clear that he would need to make up the cost on his other bottles.

Matrinka grinned, scarcely able to contain her excitement. "Of course you may sell this tonic without tariff. As for the kingdom, we can better afford to pay for your product than my citizenry can. How many bottles effect this cure?"

"One, Majesty." The Pudarian bowed.

"Then we'll take six. Thank you for coming to Béarn with your product. It will find good use here, and we appreciate your travel. If you discover Béarnides in need who cannot afford your precious elixir, please send their relatives here."

"Thank you, Majesty. You're too kind."

Too kind? Impossible. Matrinka kept the thought to herself. "Dismissed for now. Return if you encounter any problems at all."

A sense of time passing filled Matrinka, a gray swirl of dreamlike change that brought her to another time within a week of her discussion with the Pudarian healer. Magic filled in the significant events since the courtroom decision: The healer had promised the tonic would heal in four days. He had sold all of his wares the first day and disappeared on the second. By five days, none had recovered; in fact, three died. Natural innocence had driven Matrinka to trust the Pudarian's promises; but, confronted with the facts, she had no choice but to order his arrest. The guards had caught up to and captured the self-proclaimed healer. Now Matrinka sat in the court, deliberating the Pudarian's fate.

No law covered such a situation. No one had ever attempted to defraud the kingdom and its inhabitants before, at least not in such a widespread fashion. Matrinka's judgment would set new precedent, make new law; and she would not do so without careful contemplation.

When Matrinka's silence stretched into an hour, the hissed speculations disappeared, replaced by the more routine, dull roar of conversation. Many thoughts and possibilities underwent her scrutiny and were tucked away or discarded. Finally, she cleared her throat, and the courtiers fell into a startling hush. The Pudarian remained in front of Matrinka, pinioned between Béarnian guards.

"The wrong your deceit inflicted upon my people cannot go unpunished. The false hope you gave and then spirited away caused a pain no man should have the right to inflict on others." Matrinka tried to meet the Pudarian's gaze, but his eyes dodged hers. "In punishment, I sentence you to two years in the dungeon followed by permanent exile from our country." She turned her attention to the guards. "Dismissed."

A buzz swept through the courtiers as each added his or her own personal opinion to the queen's decision. Matrinka wished she could make out individual voices from the crowd, uncertain of her sentence. As the guards escorted their prisoner from the courtroom, another approached and bowed. "Majesty, what would you have us do with moneys confiscated from the guilty?"

Matrinka did not need to consider her answer long. "Return it to those from which it came."

"Yes, Majesty. And what would you have us to with the extra?"

"The extra?"

"Yes, Majesty. We calculated the amount each person paid and the number of bottles. There's a surplus of approximately one hundred coppers."

Matrinka believed the solution should seem as obvious to her as the previous one, yet it did not. She would not return money to a thief, yet she could not see Béarn's kingdom profiting from the Pudarian's deceit either. Only one other possibility came to her. "Divide it equally among those who lost money to the scheme."

The moment she spoke the words, the magical whirlwind claimed her. Matrinka spun, assailed by voices with the strength and power of gods: "Failure. Unworthy failure."

Every sense seemed to leave her. Only the condemnation remained, driving into her head, offering no explanations for how her performance had displeased the gods. The words echoed through her ears, entering her skull, and encompassing the core of her being. *Failure. Unworthy failure.*

Matrinka struck ground with a pain that seemed insignificant compared with the fires of shame inside her. She lay on a stone floor, sobbing. The staves in each hand felt cold and accusatory in her grip. She remained in position for a long time, tears stinging her eyes and guilt slamming her conscience. "Unworthy," she whispered.

Something furry rubbed across her face more than once before she acknowledged its presence. Only then a familiar mind-voice touched her. *I love you.* Mior managed to convey her sympathy and affection at once.

Matrinka sat up, somehow managing a smile. Pulling the cat into her arms, she wept into the clean-smelling fur.

Mior purred, the sound like gentle music.

Chapter 4

The Last Heir

Honor comes not from the method of warfare, but in defeating your enemy with nothing but skill, wits, and, perhaps, a sword.

—Colbey Calistinsson

A light drizzle pattered down on Erythane's Bellenet Fields, and clouds dulled the day to dreary gray. Through armor and underpadding, Ra-khir scarcely noticed the rain, though it had turned the packed earth to mud and glistened in his mount's black mane. For the last time, he charged along the central practice fence under the watchful eye of Armsman Edwin and his three fellow knights-in-training. He clutched his pike in supple gauntlets, supporting it level despite its weight, gaze locked on the hovering ring that was his target.

As always, Ra-khir marveled at how fast he reached the ring yet how long the heavy pull of armor and pike seemed to last in contrast. The sensation of too much time, yet not nearly enough, felt nonsensical. Now, as always, the ring suddenly filled his vision, and every hoof fall made the pike tip bounce, frustratingly beyond his control. Nevertheless, he managed to skewer the ring. Metal rattled down his pike, and his balance wavered. *Great, Stupid. Unhorse yourself.* He flung his weight sideways, instinctively remembering not to overcompensate; the heavy armor made momentum difficult to stop. Managing to keep his seat, he rode back toward Edwin and his peers, holding up lance and ring like a banner.

"Good show!" Edwin clapped twice to display his approval, a moderate gesture. The number of claps usually indicated his degree of pleasure, and the armsman had applauded a spectacularly good maneuver on rare occasions. Usually, though, he limited his tribute to a single clap.

Ra-khir reveled in the praise but showed no outward signs that could be construed as gloating. He had accomplished two successful passes, and only one of the others had speared a single ring. *Another year, and I'm in for sure.* Excitement suffused him, though guilt followed immediately. *I shouldn't feel joy for besting companions.* Training sessions, his father assured him, were not a competition but a chance for knights-in-training to assist one another. Only twenty-six knights existed at any time, a dozen rotating through Béarn, a dozen on duty in Erythane, and two extra to fill spaces left by death or illness. Currently, Erythane had only twenty-five, and Ra-khir hoped to become the twenty-sixth in about a year, when he completed his training. As the son of Knight-Captain Kedrin, he had to prove his competence for the position so obviously that no one credited his lineage as gaining him special favors.

"If that ring had been properly placed, you would have had an easier time of it." Edwin glanced around his students' faces, catching the eye of the eldest, a compact lad of twenty. "Can you tell me the problem with the set of that ring?"

Ra-khir's colleague responded hesitantly. "It was set too . . ." He paused just long enough for Ra-khir to wonder if he was guessing before giving the correct answer. ". . . high."

"Correct." If Edwin noticed the pause, he made no comment on it. "That forced Ra-khir to aim for the head, a notoriously small and mobile target. Better to strike for the torso." Edwin assisted Ra-khir's dismount, then waved him away. "You're done for the day. Everyone else, take one more pass."

Ra-khir retreated to a quiet corner, removed his pack from behind the saddle, and left the gray to graze. Removing his gauntlets, he set to work carefully peeling away armor and padding. The cold sprinkle soothed his hot limbs and sore muscles. He stripped down to the undertunic, letting the spray wash sweat from his face and hair, ignoring the red curl plastered to his cheek. He rose, perspiration and rain forming a foul-smelling adhesive that made his clothes cling with every movement. Doffing his undertunic, he packed his armor in naked comfort, letting the rain wash away the grime and odor.

Caught up in the pleasure of the natural shower and placing each piece of armor into its proper place in the pack, Ra-khir became oblivious to the movement and sounds around him. As he placed the last joint into place, he gradually grew aware of spying eyes. Concerned a young woman might have wandered to the practice area, despite the rain, he looked up quickly.

Kevral perched upon the fence, rocking slightly and studying him with obvious curiosity. Rain sheened the childish face, pasting blond strands in random patterns around forehead, neck, and cheeks. Once again, the child wore loose-fitting combat garb, although a long sword had replaced the short sword in the overlarge belt. "Hello, Ra-khir Kedrin's son. Do knights-in-training always practice in the nude?"

Irritation trickled through Ra-khir, enhanced by the high-pitched, singsong voice that brought back vivid memories of their encounter a week earlier. His honor told him to remain polite, even to one he did not like, so he smiled tolerantly. "Hello, Kevral. I hadn't seen you for a while. I thought maybe you'd gone away." He allowed his tone to imply that he would have preferred such a thing. Even politeness did not seem reason enough to lie, and he did not want to encourage the irksome child to bother him on a regular basis. Taking a rag and clean clothes from his pack, he dried off as well as the continued rain allowed and donned the fresh tunic and britches.

"I've been busy," Kevral said. "Did you miss me?"

Ra-khir could think of several ways to answer that question, none of them kind. Instead, he made a noncommittal grunt and let Kevral interpret it. Finished dressing, he set to lacing his pack. The sooner he finished, the sooner he could make an excuse to leave the practice field. And Kevral.

The youngster continued to watch Ra-khir work, swinging one leg in circular motions from atop the fence. "I thought you might like to spar again. This time we could drop the other on his head instead of his butt, or until the first butt gets severed, the first head gets severed, the first head comes out the first butt." Kevral jumped lightly down onto the muddy field, seeming oblivious to the mud spattered over shoes and pants legs.

Ra-khir took scant satisfaction from the fact that Kevral would probably catch hell at home for the mess. "What is it with you and butts?"

Kevral grabbed the opening. "Me and butts? You were the one parading yours baby-naked."

Ra-khir leaped to his defense. "I wasn't parading. You were spying. Only knights are supposed to come up here." Though true, Ra-khir knew others did watch the knights practice, but rarely in any but the balmiest weather. For years, knights-in-training had used the area to change as well as train, and Ra-khir saw little reason to apologize for long tradition. "Anyway, I'm not interested in sparring with you again. You proved your point. You're pretty damned good for a boy. Someday, you'll make Erythane a great soldier; and so, I hope, will I. I'm not going to challenge you again, especially not to the death." He added so as not to leave it open for later discovery, "If you challenge me, I'll have no choice but to fight. But I believe you're smart enough to see such a battle would not be in your, mine, or Erythane's best interests."

Ra-khir thought he had spoken well, complimenting Kevral and even generously implying that the child was the better warrior. Yet Kevral's hostile expression suggested offense. He could only assume the reaction came of comparing Kevral's skill to that of other boys rather than the man this child apparently attempted to become too quickly.

The accusatory tone of Kevral's response displayed the bitterness Ra-khir had already read from the narrowed eyes and pursed lips. "So what do you knights do in Béarn anyway?"

"Do?" The abrupt switch in topic caught Ra-khir off guard. He finished lacing his pack and hefted it. "First, I'm just an apprentice, remember?"

Kevral made a vague gesture to indicate the detail did not matter. "I just wondered because I noticed Renshai are protecting the heirs and knights aren't. So I wondered about the purpose of the knights at all."

To Ra-khir's relief, Kevral's voice went from condemning to genuine interest.

Ra-khir ignored the issue of how and why a child might have traveled to the king's city. More likely, Kevral had heard stories rather than seen the actual guarding. "The Knights of Erythane perform special missions for the king. And they lead Béarn's military into battle."

"Oh?" Kevral seemed taken aback by the answer, literally shifting a step in reverse. "Well, then. I guess the king's army must be slow to ride behind warriors buried in ... in ..." The youngster pointed at the pack in Ra-khir's hands. "... table wear."

The description sparked an ire that Ra-khir reined in with difficulty. He hoisted the pack, flinging it onto the gray's haunches. At the sudden weight, the horse stiffened, ears flicking backward and left hind leg cocked. It resumed grazing while Ra-khir fastened the pack in place. "This 'table wear,' as you call it, has rescued a lot of heroes otherwise lost to enemies or stray attacks." Believing the child jealous of a shielding only kingdom-supported warriors could afford, Ra-khir attempted to teach though his previous experience told him it would prove futile. "Champions maintain honor no matter the circumstances; weak men revile what they cannot have."

Kevral laughed, returning a different quotation Ra-khir had never heard. "To rely upon any defenses but one's own skill is cowardice of the worst kind. A real warrior needs no props to win the battle or to die with dignity."

Ra-khir continued to tie his pack in place, finding the words ridiculous. "Who said that?"

"A wise prophet named Colbey." Kevral's voice practically dripped admiration, the starry-eyed tone that of an adolescent girl in love.

Colbey. Ra-khir finished affixing the pack, suddenly jarred toward a chain of thought he had once discarded. Until now, he had believed Kevral an Erythanian child, a reasonable thought since travel between Erythane and any city but Béarn occurred rarely; and Kevral lacked any Béarnian features. For reasons lost to obscurity, Béarn and Erythane followed the same religion as the Northmen rather than that of their Western neighbors. All who followed Odin's pantheon knew of the heavenly prophet, Colbey; but Renshai alone revered him like a deity. Renshai also believed the Great Fire had signified *Ragnarok,* while Béarn and Erythane still dreaded the coming of the Great Destruction that would see the end of humanity and nearly all the gods.

Ra-khir studied the child again, seeing nothing different

on this inspection. Moppet features peered at him from beneath shaggy yellow bangs; and the blue eyes seemed more mischievous than cruel. He did not know how to tell a Renshai from an Erythanian, but traveled knights had assured him and his peers it would be obvious. Kevral, Ra-khir decided, was just a young Erythanian boy with a bad disposition, trying to simulate being Renshai to look tough and impress his friends. Given the number of Erythanians who wished to become knights, or feigned the training around companions, it only made sense one might some day choose to emulate Renshai. This child's apparently natural skill granted the tools that might allow the charade to work.

These thoughts raced through Ra-khir's mind in an instant, immediately trailed by others. *Is Kevral an orphan? A street kid? A boy with a bad family life who seeks notoriety when he can't have love?* The train of thought drew Ra-khir to his own family situation, raising sorrow and anger at once. Since the assassination of three Béarnian heirs to the throne, his father had needed to remain in the king's city. Ra-khir understood, but could not stop, the loneliness that crept through him every night of his father's absence, leaving him too much time to contemplate the decision he had made nearly a month ago. He could not regret the choice. His mother's selfish insistence on lying about Ra-khir's father had lost him a lifetime of Kedrin's love. He could not brook the conditions she placed on her devotion to him, not when Kedrin had tried so hard to become a part of his life and loved, even now, without reservations or prerequisites. If only his mother could respect the bond he had with his father, he would have a family again—a broken one, but nevertheless a family.

Ra-khir shook off his considerations. Finished with his pack, he patted the gray's rump then headed around to mount. Though hardly silk, Kevral's garb made it clear this was no poverty-stricken orphan. The sword, though not fancy, could not have belonged to a starving father. More likely, Kevral had a happy home and a stable family. That realization only made the child more irritating. If Ra-khir could choose an honorable path despite his difficult childhood, then he saw no excuse for Kevral. "Thank you for this . . ." Ra-khir searched for the proper word that might end future run-ins without insulting Kevral into a challenge. ". . . interesting discussion. But I need to go now."

Without awaiting a reply, Ra-khir clambered into the saddle and rode toward home.

Prime Minister Baltraine paced a too-familiar course from door to table and back, though he had already called the meeting to order with appropriate ceremony. As he approached the door, his back to the politicians and leaders, he believed he gathered enough composure to discuss a problem no prior prime minister had ever had to handle. He turned to meet the gazes of a dozen somber men and women, and realization crushed him to silence again. Just facing Béarn's other five ministers seemed difficult enough. Abran sat quietly, paper-thin hands twitching through his beard. To his left, the other four ministers formed a line: court attendant Weslin, Charletha who oversaw animals and their caretakers, homely Limrinial with her mismatched eyes and blunt manner, and lowly Fahrthran with his mixed heritage and honorary royal title.

The other side of the table held less commonly assembled leaders: Thialnir, a Renshai chieftain, always met Baltraine's gaze first. Broad-boned and -featured, he sat with a stillness that defined calm, hands resting lightly on his thighs. Blond braids tumbled around placid features and sharp, green eyes. Beside him sat Knight-Captain Kedrin of the Erythanian Knights. His dress uniform and tabard, combining Béarn's blue and tan with Erythane's orange and black, made a glaring contrast to the plain battle garb of the Renshai. Next in line, Béarn's own guard captain, Seiryn, studied his dirt-rimmed fingernails on the tabletop. Though naturally Béarnian large, Seiryn's battle skill stemmed as much from strategy, delegation ability, and physical and mental quickness as from strength. Though of smaller peoples, Thialnir and Kedrin seemed nearly as massive as Béarn's own war leader.

The bard, Linndar, occupied the last seat on the left-hand side of the meeting table. Her mixed heritage made her look frail in the presence of so many Béarnides and warrior officers, yet she seemed the calmest of them all. She practically sprawled in her chair, alert and respectful but comparatively comfortable. In her lap, she cradled a *lonriset,* a ten-stringed lutelike instrument invented by a distant ancestor.

Baltraine headed back toward the table and its eminent array, opening his mouth to speak the piece for which he had called them together. But, once again, discomfort betrayed him. *One more pass,* he promised himself for the third time, emphasizing the finality in his mind. Again he pivoted, delaying his oration though he had already chosen the words. The postponement diffused his tension only slightly as procrastination itself became an increasing worry. This time, for sure, he would speak.

The path to the door had become too routine, the six steps over too quickly. Once more, Baltraine turned, this time resolved to continue the meeting. He had no intention of shirking his responsibility, only of sparing the others bad news that had wrested sleep from him and still kept his heart pounding, his thoughts locked on a tragedy that seemed foregone. He returned to the table, pressed his fists to the smooth surface, and met each and every gaze in turn. Locking last with the soft-eyed bard, he directed his words to her. "As you all know, every heir to the throne of Béarn underwent the staff-test yesterday."

Polite murmurs followed the declaration. They all understood the reason for their meeting.

"Leaders and friends of Béarn, I do not need to remind you that every word spoken here must remain in strictest confidence. More so than usual, we must protect the results and our kingdom. No one other than King Kohleran, too ill to sit among us now, can be privy to a syllable of our discussion today." Baltraine had prepared a long speech to help him ease into the problem, but fancy words seemed unlikely to soften the blow. Politicians alone might have preferred the method he had originally selected. Now, Baltraine thought it best to finish his announcement quickly and spare the warriors the agony of a litany. They liked their news quick, straightforward, and specific. As minister to Renshai, Limrinial also favored directness. Usually, Baltraine did not cater to her whims, but this time forthrightness struck him as the superior course. "No one, no heir to Béarn's throne, passed the staff-test."

A stunned silence followed. Baltraine watched his peers as his lead-weighted words gained meaning in every mind.

Charletha broke the lull. "But that means . . ." She did not finish her sentence, face reddening with obvious embarrassment. The youngest of the ministers, she had not yet totally mastered the art of control.

Baltraine finished the thought to rescue any of lesser intellect too embarrassed to admit their failing. The warriors, he assumed disdainfully, would need his assistance. "It means that when the gods take our king, we have no one to replace him. It means there is no heir to the throne of Béarn."

"No heir," Limrinial repeated, fingers tapping the tabletop nervously. "Is that possible?"

Nearly every head swung toward Linndar for the answer. The bards sought and held the wisdom of the centuries in their songs. Only one other person stored Béarn's knowledge, the ancient sage who dwelt in the westernmost tower with the myriad books and scrolls that chronicled their history through the ages. The sage and his apprentice never left his tower, however; so they could not join the meeting.

Baltraine interrupted before Linndar could answer, wanting to avoid an orchestrated rendition, complete with choruses, of the thirty-seven-page document that detailed nobility, royalty, and ascension. He had studied it long enough to practically memorize it, and the appropriate sections returned verbatim. So many times he had stared at the pages, seeking a loophole that eluded him. "It is possible," Baltraine answered Limrinial's question literally before launching into the explanation. "By decree of King Sterrane, as directed by the word of the gods themselves, the crown passes only downward or across. Only Kohleran's siblings and legitimate children, grandchildren, and great-grandchildren can inherit rulership." Before Baltraine could stop himself, he began to pace again. "Ten living heirs. None found worthy."

"Ten?" Minister Fahrthran seized on the math. "Last I'd heard, we had thirteen in line. We lost two to the bears' attack, but that should still leave eleven."

Baltraine lowered his head, his back to the others, grief still a burden within him. Only two days had passed since the courtyard catastrophe, and the aftereffects throbbed behind this new, inevitable calamity. "I'm sorry to be the bearer of more bad news." He turned to face his peers. "But the healers could not save Princess Fachlaine. Last night, she succumbed to the wounds the bears inflicted. There are ten."

"None found worthy," someone whispered, the voice too soft to recognize.

Thialnir rose suddenly, hands clenched to the hilts of swords at either hip, war braids flying. "There will be an heir to Béarn's throne. My people will see to it!"

All eyes swung from bard to Renshai. Baltraine had expected nothing else from Thialnir, verbalized rage without a solution. The gods had charged his people with seeing to the proper ascension, and any Renshai would rather die than admit defeat.

Knight-Captain Kedrin performed a subtle, archaic gesture, indicating an interest in speaking. Even in a crisis, he would not abandon formality. Baltraine gave over the floor, and the knight spoke his first words of the meeting, attacking the problem with a warrior's eye for detail. "Ten heirs. That includes every child, grandchild, and great-grandchild of King Kohleran?" He looked to Prime Minister Baltraine for confirmation.

Anticipating the next question, Baltraine gave a complete answer. "Everyone. Including the five-year-old twins and the four-year-old girl."

"*The* four-year-old." The eldest, Minister Abran, added his piece. "The king has two four-year-old great-granddaughters."

Fahrthran saved Baltraine the trouble of answering. "One is illegitimate. The law is clear about bastard children. They cannot inherit." He added, clearly to forestall further discussion in this direction. "And marriage now won't change that. Legitimacy is defined and determined at the time of birth." He met Baltraine's gaze, features crinkled in thought. "It seems to me our only option is to encourage the heirs to marry and parent. An infant ruler may not do much good now, but at least we won't lose Béarn's line permanently."

Many nods and mumbles of agreement met this suggestion. The false noble had received the most credit for his idea thus far, and Baltraine suffered a flash of irritation. He had also considered this means of creating new heirs, but details not yet presented made this a less satisfactory solution than it seemed. Baltraine elaborated, placing the plan back into perspective. "Obviously we need to encourage those of Kohleran's blood to reproduce, but the law is clear on this point also. The heir must pass the staff-test within three months of the king's death, and . . ." Baltraine quoted directly from the exemptions section of the document of ascension, ". . . the staff-test must be undertaken willingly with the full consent and understanding of the subject." He returned to paraphrasing. "The law further specifies that only a prodigy could be expected to comprehend the test, even in the most basic sense, before the age of three."

Baltraine returned to the table and sat down. "It should be noted, historically, that the few genius heirs through the centuries have invariably failed the test. Extraordinary brilliance and naïveté don't seem to fit well together."

Thialnir reclaimed his seat. "What's your point?" he asked suspiciously.

Baltraine sighed, realizing he had lapsed into intelligent conversation and believing it natural that the warriors could not follow. *The gods give brains or bulk, never both.* "The point is that our king, all gods keep him safe and happy, is unlikely to last the year. Any child conceived now will be too young to take the staff-test in time to fulfill the law. Remember, too, that only five heirs have come of age, and only one of those is married. The king's last living daughter is past the age of childbearing. That leaves four. His grandson, Xyxthris, has a four-year-old daughter without siblings, not from lack of trying. Of the other three, the eldest has made her position against marriage very clear, with an illegitimate child to seal the point. The other two, male and female cousins, turned sixteen only this year. We can't force them to marry, especially when it seems fruitless anyway."

Knight-Captain Kedrin again gestured formally for a turn to speak that Baltraine granted. Not until the knight sucked in a deep breath did the others notice his appeal and fall into a gloomy, pensive silence.

Baltraine braced himself for typical warrior simplicity, though Kedrin had proven himself skilled with politics as well as tactics in the past. Knight's training included law, honor, and court procedure as much as combat drills. He tossed copper-blond locks from classically handsome features. "My friends, I believe we have elaborated the problem. The consequences, however, are unclear." He trained his gaze on Baltraine, irises so pale a blue they appeared nearly white, and made the rarely used motion that indicated a surrender of the speaking floor.

The prime minister shrugged. "I'm not certain. I couldn't find anything but vague insinuations about horrible consequences should the Béarnian throne remain empty, and those from our religious books. The more ancient tomes refer to the king as the 'central focus of the universe' or the 'mortal keeper of the balance.' " He shivered. The staff-test and the rulers it placed in power formed the core of their faith around which all belief centered. At the least, the lack of a suitable king or queen would destroy the fabric of Western society and probably Northern and Eastern as well. He added carefully, "Most sages feel certain the *Ragnarok* will come. And all mankind and the gods will be destroyed."

Thialnir snorted, green eyes flashing, all semblance of composure disappearing. "The *Ragnarok* has come already. The gods left us the Fertile Oval and the Dead Triangle so that we would never forget that they rescued us from annihilation." He met every gaze in turn, and most looked away from the earnest, angry glare. "How quickly some choose to forget the miracles gods perform for us."

Prime Minister Baltraine seized the floor, fearing the meeting could degenerate into a religious war. Whether the first occurrence or the second, the destruction would prove equally devastating. "Whatever the consequences, we need to find a solution."

Kedrin reclaimed the position as speaker gracefully and with proper formality, his voice soft but commanding. "I believe we can pursue several possibilities. First, we continue to try to save our beloved king, at least prolonging his life as much as possible."

Nods and affirmative platitudes met this most obvious proclamation. Baltraine bobbed his head, keeping the news of Kohleran's most recent deterioration to himself. The death of three grandchildren had hit the old king hard, and the decision to inflict the staff-test on the others had only further shaken his resolve. Occasionally, he slipped into muddled states during which he slept too deeply to awaken, forgot the names of his grandchildren, echoed others' words, or spoke in strings of gibberish. Every breath or movement had become a painful trauma no one should have to suffer. The master healer camped in Kohleran's room. Few besides Baltraine were allowed admittance, and those only during the king's lucid times. Baltraine had not yet told Kohleran the results of the staff-testing, fearing to heap debacle upon catastrophe at a time when the king's life seemed as fragile as a spider's web. The king's long illness had given him more than enough time to delegate his affairs in writing, including naming Baltraine regent to any heir not yet of age and to Kohleran himself as his illness rendered him incompetent. Baltraine appreciated the fact that this had become common knowledge since just before the staff-test. Already, the service staff and minor nobility had begun treating him with the same fawning indulgence and respect as they did their king.

Kedrin continued his list. "Second, we discreetly encourage the three marriageable heirs to marry and the married grandson to continue his reproductive efforts."

More nods. Charletha scribbled furiously to get all the plans in writing. Bard Linndar's lips moved as she memorized the suggestions in song form.

"Third, we protect all of the heirs despite their failing. They deserve our concern and respect. If that is not reason enough, it will allow the younger ones to come of age. Also, it will foil our enemies who cannot know who passed or failed the staff-test."

Baltraine added, "It will also lull Béarn's citizenry. Since they cannot assist, I think it best not to worry them by letting them know about our dilemma." He studied the others, seeking dissension. But, although some seemed to consider the issue at length, no one spoke against it.

Kedrin remained quiet until Baltraine acknowledged him again. Though the prime minister's interruption had not strictly followed the rules of order at such a meeting, the Knight of Erythane would follow each and every detail with maddening distinctness. "Fourth, I believe consulting the sage is in order. We may find historical precedent or a loophole for such a situation."

Baltraine doubted the possibility but allowed the knight to continue. Knights had a tendency to formalize every situation to painful tedium, and he appreciated Kedrin's uncharacteristic clarity. Disturbed too many times, the knight could lapse into trained habit and the meeting could stretch interminably.

"That is all." Kedrin executed the appropriate signal for having spoken his piece.

"I have one more suggestion," Bard Linndar said, placing the *lonriset* into playing position. "If you will indulge me."

Baltraine smiled at the irony. They had escaped the drudgery of knightly liturgy only to fall into the protracted explanations of a woman who could make points only via lengthy song. *Luckily,* he mused, *it will be an ear-pleasing performance.* Though the gravity of the current situation made music inappropriate, the bard's voice and playing could not help but prove a comfort.

"Please," Abran encouraged Linndar, though only

Baltraine could appropriately answer. He nodded his agreement, seeing little reason to press custom or his position. Because of the bardic curse, Linndar rarely spoke more than a sentence or two unless she had something of significance to say.

Linndar played only a single chord by way of introduction:

> Kohleran, our beloved young king,
> Six children our fair land did bring.
> Each hale and good in his own way,
> And only one moved far away.
>
> Petrostan, our king's youngest child,
> The son who later was reviled;
> And Cousin Helana, in the heather
> From infancy they played together.
>
> Their friendship pretty; their friendship pure.
> Marriage one day, their mothers were sure.
> But fate played a role no one could foresee—
> Helana with child by twelve years and three.
>
> For his crime, Petrostan did pay:
> Banished from Béarn far and away
> No family could ever see him;
> No pardon could ever free him.
>
> Helana left with her cousin dear
> No promise or comfort could keep her here
> Took a home near the Dead Triangle.
> Farmed the land, their shame untangled.
>
> Their boy was born, a handsome one;
> And three years later, a second son.
> Father and oldest were killed together,
> An accident in foul plowing weather.
>
> The youngest lives still, as far as I know—
> Healthy and strong, he continues to grow.
> Instead of Béarn into chaos hurled
> This innocent youngster might save our world.

Linndar ended the song on the final syllable, without trailing notes or chords. Clearly, she had ad-libbed the song, the tune simple and the rhyme scheme primitive compared with those she expended effort crafting. Her ability to shape sonnets instantaneously never failed to amaze Baltraine; though, as silence replaced the beauty of the singing, the significance of Linndar's words became all too apparent. *Petrostan married into the proper bloodline and produced a living son. Another heir?* Hope soared, enhanced by the understanding that the missing grandson, if he did indeed exist, was male. Only those of the proper lineage could rule; but a king's marriage to one or more of his daughters might still see Baltraine's descendants on Béarn's throne. Yet doubt tainted the joy, and he kept his emotions in check. He had known of Petrostan's banishment; but if the scandal Linndar described had rocked Béarn, surely he would have heard the details. "This is the truth?"

Linndar frowned, obviously insulted. "Undeniably."

The eldest minister made a thoughtful noise that snapped loudly over the rumble of conversation. As the gathering's attention turned to him, he made his musing audible. "Petrostan would be thirty-three now, which means this must have happened about twenty years ago."

Baltraine did not interrupt. The events had transpired prior to his induction as prime minister, while he was still training for the post.

Abran nodded slowly and repetitively. "So that's what happened."

Baltraine squinted, uncertain whether to trust the description of kingdom events unknown to the minister of foreign affairs who had faithfully served Kohleran for all of his thirty-three-year reign and his father for seven before that. Baltraine knew he needed to handle the situation delicately. Already, he could see hope blazing in warriors and politicians alike as they considered the implications of the bard's revelation. Frustration and crushed faith could cause tempers already high to flare. "Pardon my confusion, but I don't understand how such a thing could occur without the knowledge of the king's ministers."

The only minister in power at the time, Abran, chose to answer. "The king and his then prime minister, your predecessor, kept the details between them. As you know, they made his exile seem relatively insignificant. He was the youngest of six, after all. We all speculated, of course, but it never seemed important enough to concern us." He added carefully, "Until now, of course."

Baltraine studied Linndar, wondering how the bard had acquired the information. Two possibilities presented themselves: as the king's personal bodyguard, the bard at that time, Linndar's mother, may have been privy to the clandestine conversations between king and prime minister. Equally likely, the bard's constant, driving need to travel and learn uncovered information otherwise hidden. With these possibilities in mind, Baltraine did not bother to quiz Linndar. Among other things, the bard's curse made them faithful beyond life to the Béarnian kings. She would do nothing to jeopardize Kohleran or his line.

"All right, then." Baltraine added Linndar's description to the list Knight-Captain Kedrin had made. "Fifth, we enlist the sage for details about a possible missing heir." The elder guarded his writings and knowledge jealously, but Baltraine felt certain he could get the king's order to release the information they needed. The future of the kingdom lay at stake, the very reason the sage chronicled events. "If we can confirm Linndar's findings in any manner, we send a messenger to whoever currently has political jurisdiction in the area in which our heir resides, thus beginning the process of bringing him to Béarn for testing." The meeting wound to an obvious conclusion. "All in favor?"

Kedrin motioned for acknowledgment, and Baltraine yielded the floor to the knight. "Friends, I would like to add just one detail as a reminder. May I proceed prior to the vote?" As per ancient protocol long abandoned by any but knights, he waited for consent from everyone prior to finishing his point. "When it comes to bringing this heir back to Béarn, we need to exercise the utmost caution. Whatever our own feelings and biases, we must remember that simple, guileless folk, such as our king must be, do not always wish to become burdened with the responsibilities of rulership. We cannot coerce this heir. He must come with us willingly and with his innocence intact."

Though Kedrin's pronouncement seemed self-evident to Baltraine, he remained patient. "Thank you, Sir Kedrin. Would anyone else like to add anything prior to the vote?"

A hush ensued, punctuated by shaking heads.

"All in favor of all five points, gesture affirmation." Ordinarily, Baltraine would have allowed a voice vote, interspersed with whatever commentary the politicians wished, but the presence of a Knight of Erythane adhered them to detailed observance of the rules. He did not relish a lecture after the meeting.

The support was unanimous.

Chapter 5

Tae Kahn

Dying young and with honor is part of being Renshai.

—Colbey Calistinsson

Trees punctuated the gray-black film of sky and crisscrossed the rainbow stripes that trailed the sunset at every horizon. Tae Kahn curled on his travel-stained blanket beside the campfire, fatigue pounding him toward stupor even as he tried to instruct his mind to light and wary sleep. Two weeks of hiding in alleys, rat holes, and on rooftops, of dozing always on the razor edge of awakening, had left him exhausted and irritable. Since he had crossed the passes through the Great Frenum Mountains and into the Westlands, he had lost the close-packed, familiar cover of Eastland cities. Western forests seemed as much curse as blessing. He no longer had to compete with waifs and street thugs for shelter, food, and his own belongings; and some of his father's enemies had abandoned their chase at the border. But the forest days seemed strange and forbidding, filled with unidentifiable sounds that sent him diving for cover or tensed to fight at every step. At night, even the summer air turned cold; and the insects descended upon him, leaving him welt-covered and itching.

Until this evening, Tae had not dared to light a fire that might draw enemies far more dangerous than bloodsucking blackflies. Then he had beaten the natural scavengers to a dead squirrel. Having mostly depleted his rations, hunger would not allow him to pass up the feast; yet he refused to eat old meat raw. Once created, the fire produced smoke that kept the insects mostly at bay, and Tae found himself loath to extinguish it even after his meal. Tiredness slowed his thoughts and weighted his usually wiry movements. If the bugs kept him up most of another night, he might not have the strength to face the danger that would catch up to him eventually, with or without the campfire.

Tae Kahn rolled to his back, shaggy black hair falling into eyes nearly as dark. Eighteen years old, he had only just begun to shave; and the thin stubble that had formed since his run began tickled only because he was unaccustomed to it. Traveling light had served him well in the East where he could always find a city in which to steal supplies and clothing. Now, ensconced in forest, he scrounged for food, cast about for water, and his clothing had become a grimy mess inside and out. Though accustomed to handling circumstances as they came, he could not help cursing the father who had condemned him to a life of bluff and bluster, of remaining always one step ahead of the law and the lawless. The men who had killed his mother, who had stabbed him sixteen times and left him for dead were enemies not of his own, but of Weile Kahn, his father.

Despite these disturbing thoughts, sleep overtook Tae, gliding him into the nightmare memories that used to haunt his every slumber and awaken him tremulous, sweaty, and screaming. It all merged into a spinning blur: scarred and filthy strangers, the sharp agony of their knives, the struggle that gained him nothing—his ten-year-old strength no match for adults, the deathly silence that followed his mother's screams, and the stench and drip of his own blood that filled the hours until his father found them. Now, Tae whimpered and kicked in his sleep, drawn toward consciousness; and the sound of movement jerked him suddenly to full awareness.

Instinctively, Tae leaped into a crouch just as a meaty hand closed over his arm. Through a curtain of his own hair, he caught a glimpse of three men in front of him in addition to the one, between him and the campfire, who held him. Tae whipped out his dagger and slashed for the gripping hand as it levered his arm behind him. Before his blow landed, a sword blade flashed silver in the moonlight, tearing the knife from his hand and a furrow of skin from his palm. Agony followed its path. He hesitated for an instant that gave the first stranger the opening he needed to seize Tae's other wrist and pin both arms behind him.

Tae struggled to free his arms, kicking backward at the man who held him. His heels met flesh solid as stone. Lacking momentum, he could do little damage with his feet, but he continued to kick and writhe. The man's fingers tightened to bruising vises. In the hands of one of the other four, the sword tip found the hollow of Tae's throat and its wielder threatened, "Be still."

Tae obeyed, keeping stance and expression defiant. *Show no fear.* The tenet came foremost to his mind, as always. Predators could smell fear; and, he had learned, it drove them to sadistic rages. On the streets, the *"cringers"* became the prey of every rowdy and tough who wanted anything they had. Tae glared up at his captors through the gaps in his leaf-strewn veil of hair, meeting and holding each dark gaze without flinching. The closer warmth of the man holding him blocked that of the fire. Blood trickled from hand to wrist and pattered, drop by drop, to the leaves. With any luck, it would make the other's fingers slippery as well.

"Tae Kahn, Weile's son." A muscled Easterner with a neatly trimmed beard stepped forward now, studying Tae as if purchasing him from a slaver.

Tae remained still, though his heart rate quickened. They knew his name and his father. No bandits, these men; they had clearly hunted him. And they would surely kill him. The fact that he did not recognize them meant nothing. The fringe assassins usually remained outside the politics of organized crime, and Tae had never paid enough attention to the men who visited his father. One thing was certain: if professional killers held him, they would slaughter him swiftly and without much preamble. His only hope lay in making them uncertain they had the right victim, and even that would only gain him time. And, he hoped, an opening.

Tae sagged forward, revealing defeat he did not have to feign. "I've only got a few coppers. They're in my right pocket. Take anything else you want. I won't fight."

The speaker smiled, eyes revealing grim amusement. He inclined his head toward the swordsman. "Kill him."

The killer back-stepped, looping his sword for momentum. Tae slumped further, drawing the holding man with him. The blade sped for his neck.

Abruptly, Tae flung himself over backward. Caught off guard, the man holding him toppled. The sword whisked over Tae's head. The man behind him slammed into the campfire, screaming. Sparks and ash swirled crazily. Tae turned his own fall into a controlled flip. Fire licked at his arms and hands, then he flew free, rolling to snuff stray flames. He lurched to his feet, running, not daring to waste the moments looking back would lose him. Night vision would work to his advantage. The others had been facing the fire's light at Tae's back and would need to adjust to the darkness.

The screeches of the burning man and the speaker's cursing drowned the sounds of pursuit. Tae sprinted down a game trail, clenching his bleeding palm in his other hand, dodging between trunks to foil his pursuers' aim. He had not seen a bow, but desperation had given him little time to take in details. Now, youth and agility would give him advantage where his smaller size and musculature had previously failed him. He raced through the forest, unaccustomed not only to the terrain but to the country. Lost in forest, without even the blanket he had brought, and hunted by assassins, he saw little chance of survival. Yet the boy who had lived through sixteen stab wounds was no stranger to desperate hope. Tae ran on.

Matrinka lay on her bed and stared at the familiar parade of painted animals on the ceiling of her bedroom until they blurred to random blotches of color. Mior sprawled against her side, sleeping. Though Matrinka could not see the two Renshai, she knew they remained alert near the door until her new, single guardian came to replace them, an event scheduled for this day. *I failed.* The thought had obsessed Matrinka in the two weeks since the staff-test had deemed her unworthy of rulership and no logic, rationalization, or self-flagellation had banished it. She felt as if gods had swept down, flayed open her soul, and spat upon what they found inside. Always, she had sought to follow the moral course, proud of the choices she made and the effects that followed naturally from them. Now she discovered she had lived a lie and could no longer trust any action or thought of her own.

The passing week had not proved wholly unproductive. From the depth of depression had come a resolve to change, to find some niche where her faulty judgment could still help the causes of Béarn. Somehow, she could stand behind those who handled the affairs, assisting without becoming involved in the day-to-day decisions that she could not appropriately make. In better moments, becoming more frequent, she considered such positions; but mostly the implications of her failure still haunted her days and dreams.

A knock on the door roused Matrinka, mercifully claiming her attention for a few moments. The Renshai took defensive positions, Nisse moving directly in front of her and Kristel remaining at the door. "Who is it?" the latter demanded.

Matrinka could not hear the reply, but it apparently satisfied Kristel. She glanced toward Matrinka but had obviously learned not to bother to catch her eye. "Our replacement, Princess."

Princess. The title only reminded Matrinka of her failure, and she winced in reply.

Kristel opened the door to reveal a stranger more girl than woman. She wore the simple, tan uniform that Renshai preferred in the service of the king, loose-fitting to allow free movement. A long sword graced each hip. In front, she wore her blonde hair short, parted in a feathered masculine style. Behind, the straight, thin hair fell to her shoulders. She sported the slighter, sinewy build that nearly defined Renshai, lacking the Béarnide's healthy bulk and the curves that made the kingdom's women beautiful. Her large, blue eyes held a hard edge, and she studied the room and its occupants with the same alertness as her two counterparts. She glanced from Kristel to Nisse and said something musical. Apparently, she had spoken Renshai; and, although Matrinka could not understand, she could tell that it contained no trace of a Western accent. It also seemed to annoy the other Renshai, who frowned and exchanged knowing glances before leaving the newcomer to her charge. Matrinka could tell by their attitudes they did not care for her guardian.

The new Renshai said nothing more, diligently exploring the room in a dogged silence whose rudeness irritated Matrinka, especially when the newcomer rearranged a few of her personal belongings. At length, apparently satisfied, the Renshai stopped in front of Matrinka and bowed. She used the Béarnian tongue with surprising fluency and none of the lilt she had adopted to speak Renshai. "Princess

Matrinka, I am your guardian. I will remain at your side and protect you at all times, except when others I trust take my place. Nothing can or will harm you so long as I am with you." She fell silent, stiffly attentive, awaiting a reply.

Matrinka shifted away from Mior, then sat up. The cat yawned and stretched, fixing yellow eyes on the Renshai. *Tight, isn't she?*

Matrinka gave no direct reply to the rhetorical question, though she did acknowledge the cat's presence in her mind. The new guardian disappointed her in many ways. First, her rigid dedication to her job would certainly preclude any privacy, let alone such simple pleasures as a walk in the courtyard. Second, she seemed unlikely to prove any more pleasant company than the pair who had just left. Third, her formality would grow tiresome if not nipped swiftly. Matrinka set her mind to doing just that. "Just call me Matrinka."

The Renshai nodded but said nothing further.

Matrinka asked the obvious question. "What's your name?"

Again, the Renshai bowed, seeming even younger than when she first arrived. Matrinka wondered if her failure at the staff-test had condemned her to become a babysitting service for half-grown Renshai, a testing ground prior to their assigning to a more deserving subject. If so, she and her self-proclaimed guardian had definitely started this relationship with the wrong one in control.

Unaware of the myriad thoughts flooding Matrinka's mind, the Renshai responded to her query alone. "Princess, with all due respect, I think it best that we not exchange names. Such could only risk placing our relationship on a level that might impair my ability to properly perform my duties."

The severity and size of the words issuing from a figure that seemed as small and fragile as a china doll momentarily disarmed Matrinka. "How would that be so?" she finally managed, trying not to sound patronizing.

The Renshai bowed a third time, gaze still fixed on Matrinka, though her stance revealed wariness that went far beyond the focus of her attention. "If we became friends, I might get too relaxed in your presence to properly guard. Worse, you might worry for me, interfere with my efforts, and get yourself hurt or killed." A slight smile crossed features otherwise wholly taut. "If you hate me, you won't do that."

"I'm not going to hate you no matter what." Matrinka lowered her feet over the side of the bed, not yet realizing she had not brooded about her failure since the new Renshai entered. "There's never reason to hate anyone."

In response, the Renshai just shrugged.

Already doubting her own wisdom, Matrinka took the unspoken disagreement hard. *Am I wrong about that, too?*

Nonsense, Mior supplied. *You're not wrong.*

Still bothered by the situation as well as the manner of a guardian who had just sworn to become a constant companion, Matrinka hurled her next observation at the object of her discomfort. "I can't just call you 'You Standing There.' "

"You may call me whatever you wish," the Renshai supplied easily, surprisingly quick for one so young and annoying.

Matrinka refused to create a name for a person who obviously already had one. "What do you *want* to be called?"

The guardian Renshai tensed, turning toward the door and cocking her head to one side. Apparently, she had heard some noise Matrinka had not. It did not concern the Renshai, however, because she relaxed, returned her regard, and responded, "I should be near enough to you always that you don't need to call. I would find neither 'Renshai' nor 'guard' offensive."

Matrinka shrugged, finding the whole business nonsense. "This seems silly."

"To you, perhaps, Princess." The Renshai's careful smile and light tone kept her from sounding insulting. She obviously had experience with bandying words as well as sword strokes. "Please trust me to know the best way to handle the job I was assigned."

Matrinka sighed. Mior's mental touch seemed amused. *I like her. She reminds me of someone.*

Let's see ... a young, female predator. Now, Matrinka smiled inwardly. *Of course you like her. She reminds you of you.*

Mior puzzled that thought in silence while Matrinka turned her attention back to the Renshai. To disengage from conversation meant pondering her inadequacies again. "No offense, um, Renshai, but aren't you a bit young for this job?"

Matrinka's guardian frowned and jerked her head slightly backward, obviously unhappy with the question. "By Renshai law, I'm a woman."

Matrinka called on her lessons regarding Renshai. "You've killed someone already?"

"Blooded?" The Renshai laughed. "My people abandoned that as the measurement for adulthood centuries ago." She sobered, becoming more like Kristel and Nisse in demeanor. "If we hadn't, every young Renshai would be sparking feuds and fights to the death. Now we have to complete a certain level of training. Most don't manage it until they're about eighteen. Some never."

Matrinka studied her guardian, from the wide, twinkling eyes to the child-stout legs. "You don't look eighteen to me." She kept her estimation to herself. *Thirteen maybe.*

"I'm fifteen," the Renshai admitted with a casualness that could not quite hide pride, although she obviously tried.

An idea niggled at the back of Matrinka's mind but could not be called to the foreground yet. She let it simmer while she displayed the knowledge her previous guardians had given. "You must be of the tribe of Modrey."

The Renshai blinked, surprised. "I am. How did you know that?"

Finally having gained the upper hand, Matrinka feigned the same composure the Renshai had moments before. "You look younger than your age. That means you probably have more original Renshai blood than most."

"You're very observant."

"Thank you." The compliment warmed Matrinka. In the past, her tutors had considered her inattentive and under-achieving. When a topic interested her, she could recite lessons back verbatim. However, her mind tended to wander and she missed details when the matter did not enthrall her. She could name every flower, tree, and vegetable in Béarn; but her own lineage eluded her when she tried to remember more than two generations. Mathematics seemed a whole different language.

Matrinka's introspection brought the glimmer of thought to consciousness. *I've been looking for a way to serve the kingdom that doesn't require my judgment. A year younger than me, and this Renshai already found one.* "How hard is it to become a warrior?"

The Renshai blinked, obviously taken aback by the question. "Hard? Compared to what?"

Now it was Matrinka's turn to be surprised. "Well, I mean, just is it. Compared to anything."

The Renshai shrugged. "Compared to being born an heir, it's very hard. Being born's only hard for your mother."

The insult shocked Matrinka, the last thing she expected from one committed to protecting her. Breeding and training held her temper in check, but the weight of her shortcomings seemed even heavier a burden. She returned sarcasm for sarcasm. "Maybe I *could* learn to hate you."

The Renshai smiled without malice.

Matrinka pressed the issue. "So why are you guarding me anyway? It's clearly not from an inherent respect for me."

Matrinka's guardian continued to smile, blue eyes friendly beneath the wild feathers of her hair. "First, I respect any heir to Béarn's throne. Second, it's my job."

Matrinka met the Renshai's gaze earnestly. "Would it make any difference if you knew I failed the staff-test?"

The Renshai did not pause, even long enough to consider the implications of such an admission. "Not at all. It doesn't matter to me if you're a servant, a farmer, or the queen herself. A job is a job. There's nothing honorable about a duty in and of itself; it's the performance of that duty to the best of my ability that gives it virtue. It's my competence and dedication to guarding, not who I guard, that matters."

From the mouth of one so young, the philosophy impressed Matrinka. Even knowing that the girl was nearly her own age did not detract from the Béarnide's amazement. Matrinka could not have come up with words of wisdom so swiftly or with such agility. "You still haven't answered my question. Not really."

The Renshai hesitated. "You mean the one about becoming a warrior?"

"Right."

"Here." The Renshai pulled her left-hand sword from its sheath and offered it to Matrinka, hilt first. "Strike at me."

Matrinka rose, accepting the offering. The grip felt thick in her smooth palm, and the heaviness of the blade surprised her. The tip bowed to the ground, all but touching the floor, which seemed to bother the Renshai. Matrinka managed to

raise the blade into the more normal position she saw the
guards use in spar. Then, the Renshai's words seeped in.
"Strike *at* you? No, I can't do that."

"Why not?" The Renshai took several backward steps to
clear some space in the center of Matrinka's bedroom. She
did not draw the other weapon.

"I might hurt you."

The Renshai snorted.

"You might hurt me," Matrinka corrected.

The Renshai glared. "If you're quite finished insulting
me, as a warrior and as a teacher, you can strike when
ready."

Matrinka shook her head, horrified by the thought of using a weapon against anyone not confirmed as an enemy. "I
can't do that." She drove for the compromise. "I'll just take
a few swings. You can tell me how long you think it'd take
me to learn from that."

The Renshai just stared.

Taking that as an affirmative, Matrinka swung at random.

Before she thought to watch for it, the Renshai's sword
licked out and caught hers at the crossguard. The sword flew
from her hand. The Renshai caught it and sheathed both in
a single, smooth motion. "I think," she said softly, "that being an heir is hard enough for you."

Prime Minister Baltraine whisked through the castle hallways, a brace of Béarnian guards at his back and a sage's
scribe trotting at his side. The morning session in the courtroom had ended; a parade of peasants, merchants, and nobles had presented their various cases and projects. All that
remained was for Baltraine to consult King Kohleran and return with his many judgments. The process had become polite formality, at times even a charade that no longer held
meaning. Nearly as often as not, Baltraine found King
Kohleran unconscious or incomprehensible; and the prime
minister had the obligation to adjudicate in the king's stead.
When lucid, the king always sanctioned the plan Baltraine
presented. Years of relaying the king's decisions had allowed
the prime minister to develop an acutely accurate feel for
Kohleran's settlements and decrees. Although Baltraine did
not always agree with Kohleran's choices, he dictated policies as he believed the king would do. Thus, he hoped, the

kingdom could continue to prosper with the neutrality the gods intended.

Baltraine turned a corner absently, mulling the cases he had seen, the path to the king's door too familiar to require thought. Inattentive, he nearly crashed into Knight-Captain Kedrin, the Erythanian's graceful sidestep all that saved them both from collision. Startled, Baltraine jerked sideways, lost his balance, and flailed to regain it. The scribe scrambled out of the way. Kedrin seized Baltraine's wrist, steadying him before the guards could rush to his rescue. Apparently recognizing the knight, Béarn's guards remained politely at ease behind the prime minister. In the military operations of the kingdom, he far outranked them.

Baltraine balanced himself, glaring into eyes like sapphires encrusted in ice. Their strange white-blue color, trained with frightening sobriety on Baltraine, unnerved him. There could be only one reason why the knight-captain came here alone at this time: he wanted to run into Baltraine. Whether he truly wished to do so literally or just figuratively remained to be seen. "What can I do for you, Sir Kedrin?" he asked with the formality a knight preferred.

"Lord Baltraine, we need to talk." Kedrin's eyes never strayed from Baltraine's face. They seemed not even to blink.

Though requested politely, the audience bothered Baltraine. Never before had Kedrin asked for such a thing, except for the normal discussions regarding the knights' duties and rotations through Béarn and Erythane. "Would you like a slot in the court? For you, we could make an opening today or tomorrow." Even as he spoke, Baltraine cursed himself. Any other noble would have appreciated preferential treatment, but the knights played strictly by the rules.

Kedrin frowned but otherwise showed no reaction to the impropriety. "I wish to speak with you now. In private."

"Now?" Baltraine frowned at the possibility. So many sat awaiting his visit to the king and the judgments that followed. "I'm very busy."

Kedrin made a respectful gesture. "I appreciate the demands on your schedule, Minister, and sympathize with their constancy. I've waited nearly a week to catch you at an open moment, without success. Now, will you meet with me, or should I call an assembly?"

Baltraine's mood jumped from irritation to frank anger.

When an officer called the others to order, it was a grave insult to the prime minister, suggesting that a serious problem existed that he refused to acknowledge.

Kedrin finished, still annoyingly polite in speech and manner despite his threat. "I won't take but a few moments of your time, Lord."

"Very well. Come with me." Waving for the guards and scribe to remain in place, Baltraine headed up the corridor to a position where the Béarnides could still see but could no longer hear them. Procedure dictated that he make the guards move back rather than that he and the knight-captain shift position; but Baltraine knew that such a command would send the guards around the bend in the corridor to where they could no longer follow the conversation visually. The implication that he did not trust Kedrin would be obvious, at least to the knight-captain, an insult at least as grave as the one Kedrin had delivered. Inwardly, Baltraine smiled. There was use to the knight's rigid adherence to rule and honor after all. Subtle affronts could unbalance the knight without outsiders even recognizing that such had occurred. The constant need for self-restraint could blunt the knight's vigilance and give Baltraine the upper hand.

After an initial hesitation, probably due to surprise, Kedrin matched the prime minister pace for pace. He gave no indication that he recognized the insult. "The messenger the council sent has not returned."

This was no news to Baltraine. "I'm aware of that, Captain. We all are."

"It's been two months."

"Yes." Baltraine grew impatient listening to things he already knew, although he believed he understood the knight's eventual point. Normally, the trip from Béarn to Santagithi took a season to travel. However, the messenger lines shortened the trip to just under a month either way. These consisted of a chain of the fastest, calmest horses in existence, all well-provisioned and trained to carry even a sleeping man to the next station. Bound to the saddles, the messengers could travel awake and asleep, without need for camping. Anyone caught tampering with a messenger, or the lines, risked slow execution. Distant messengers sent via the line always received priority when it came to granting audiences, displacing even domestic emergencies except those requiring immediate medical attention.

Undoubtedly, Kedrin felt as foolish as Baltraine stating the obvious, yet he did so dutifully. "The messenger should have returned by now."

"He's barely a week late," Baltraine returned. "Any minor problem could have delayed him."

Kedrin remained relentless, his odd eyes steadfast. "There are provisions for those. The facts remain. The messenger is late. What have you done to further the goals the council set out two months ago?"

Baltraine saw no reason to continue this conversation. "You know we've done as we discussed. Many of the heirs have become despondent, and it's been difficult to instill the importance of marriage and children. We're working on that. The sage confirmed the bard's story of the missing heir, and we sent a messenger immediately. What more would you have me do?"

Kedrin raised his brows as if the whole seemed obvious. "Investigate the missing messenger. That's all I'm asking."

Baltraine sighed. "And I'm only asking for patience. Why waste or risk manpower on an emergency that's only in your head? The messenger may well return tomorrow. Or the day after."

"Or not at all," Kedrin supplied. "This is not a discussion on tariffs. We're talking about the future of Béarn and all the world. We can't sit idly back and wait for a minor delay to worsen the world's most serious crisis. If, gods prevent it, the king should die tomorrow, we would barely have the time to transport the heir here in time to pass the staff-test. It is imperative that the messengers arrive as soon as possible. The messenger was aware that any delay would prove intolerable."

"Aware is not the same as being in a position to prevent one," Baltraine pointed out.

Kedrin did not banter. "So you're going to do nothing about this?"

"I didn't say that." Baltraine abandoned the argument as well, though his face felt flushed. Kedrin's accusations came dangerously close to treason. Had he spoken them directly to the king, there would have been no doubt about the charge. As acting regent, Baltraine deserved the respect and treatment Kohleran would receive in his stead.

"You are going to do something?" The knight continued to press.

"Yes."

"You're going to send an armed party to Santagithi?"

"No." Baltraine believed the captain's suggestion extreme. "But I will dispatch another messenger with the same urgency. I had only planned to wait another couple of days; but, for you, Knight-Captain, I'll send him today. Will that appease you?"

"Yes, Lord," Kedrin said, though his head shook slightly in a negative gesture. "I think a protected party better advised, but I have little choice but to give in to your decision." He bowed stiffly. Then, turning on his heel, he marched away.

Baltraine seethed, all the controlled anger racing to the forefront at once. His fists curled, and he planted them on his hips. *Uppish bastard. Who in Hel does he think he is?* The job of regent had proved difficult enough without an intermittently ineffectual king and a knight questioning not just the content, but the timing, of his every decision. *A troublemaker, that one. Too cocky for his position.* The thought of Kedrin catching plague and dying brought a momentary satisfaction that unconsciously stirred deeper contemplations. Baltraine composed himself briefly, then motioned for the guards to continue. As a unit, they headed for King Kohleran's chamber.

Chapter 6

Subtle Tactics

One's own flaws are the hardest to recognize.
                              —Colbey Calistinsson

Ra-khir followed his father through the iron-bound oak door
into the knight-captain's quarters, mind brimming with images of the king's city. His first visit to Béarn revealed a
town smaller than Erythane or his expectations. Massive
men and women, and children with all the potential size of
their parents, scurried along cobbled streets that put those of
Erythane to shame. Home to the world's most talented ma-
sons, Béarn boasted stonework without peer. From wells to
dwellings, from walls to the myriad statues that decorated
even the poorest of yards, the masonry and granite-craft had
drawn Ra-khir's eye at every turn.

Now Ra-khir glanced around the rooms that would serve
as home for the next weeks or months. A blue carpet, speckled in various shadings, spanned the stone floor nearly from
corner to corner. A desk and matching chair filled most of
one wall, neat stacks of paper and an ink quill on its surface.
Three more chairs, wooden with padded seats, stood in a
rigid line on the opposite side of the desk. A comfortable
looking but faded couch took up most of the remaining
space, and a table at each end held an unlit lantern. Sunlight
from the windows fell across the furnishings, and dust motes
swam through the beams. Three exits opened onto other
rooms that Kedrin identified with distinct gestures: "Wash-

room, pantry, bedroom." He smiled at his son. "Hope you don't mind sharing."

"Not at all," Ra-khir said honestly. He had never seen quarters so large or richly furnished and wondered why his father spent as much time as he did in Erythane with these accommodations waiting in Béarn.

"Sit. We need to talk a moment." Kedrin waved at the couch, waiting for Ra-khir to choose a spot before joining him.

Ra-khir sank into the cushions, pleasantly surprised by the soft support. He had never before lived in a cottage with a real couch. He waited until his father settled beside him before asking the obvious question. "All right. What do you want to talk about?"

"You."

The topic surprised Ra-khir. "Me?" He studied his father's set features, from the firm, square jaw to the attentive eyes. Kedrin seemed quite serious, and his expression revealed concern without anger. Over the last month, Ra-khir had spent most of his free time alone while his father pursued matters in Béarn.

"You," Kedrin confirmed.

Ra-khir nodded, unable to keep his thoughts from running backward to the events of the past few weeks, seeking something he might have done that could upset his father. Dread squeezed him, viselike, at the idea that he might lose the father he had missed for most of his childhood and learned to love more than anyone over the past year. "Is something wrong?"

"Wrong?" Kedrin repeated, then shook his head vigorously. "No, nothing's wrong. I just wanted to make certain I did the right thing uprooting your life in Erythane to bring you here."

"Uprooting? Let me understand this. You give me the chance to spend some time in Béarn, in the high king's city, without even interrupting my training. And you think I might be unhappy about it?"

"Are you?" Now Kedrin held his features in a stony mask, as if afraid any display of emotion from him might influence Ra-khir's personal preference.

"Of course not. I'm thrilled." Ra-khir shook his head to indicate the suggestion was silly. "I've always wanted to come here, and I want to be with you. I couldn't have dreamed a better arrangement."

"I just don't ..." Kedrin started, his pale eyes skittering from his son's bold stare. "I mean, I don't want you to think ..." He sighed, gathering his words and composure so that his final point emerged in his usual commanding voice. "If you'd rather go back to your mother, I won't stop you." He winced, as if just speaking the words pained him.

"Don't be stupid," Ra-khir blurted before he could concoct something more respectful. "My father was stolen from me, and I'm lucky to have him back. I love you, and I want to be with you." A heartfelt rush of emotion accompanied the words, so strong it frightened as well as pleased him. The power and depth of his loyalty was beyond question, but his father's seeming doubt clutched at his mind and clung with a tenacity he could not dispel or quiet without help. "Unless ..." he began, uncertain how to finish. Then, following his father's recent example, he gathered his thoughts into a single, straightforward rush. "Are you politely telling me to go?" Tears accompanied his query, beyond his control.

The horror that opened Kedrin's expression could not have been feigned. "Absolutely not." He gathered Ra-khir into an embrace. "I love you too, son. Not stealing you away from your mother was the hardest thing I ever did."

Head buried against Kedrin's chest, Ra-khir sobbed. Under any other circumstances, he would have felt humiliated for his lapse, but not in his father's arms. "I wish you had," he managed.

"Now, maybe." Kedrin smoothed his son's red locks, so like his own. "But not then. You wouldn't have understood then."

"I would," Ra-khir insisted, voice muffled by Kedrin's tunic.

"Trust me," Kedrin said. "A child could not have understood. It's more complicated even now than I will ever explain."

"Tell me," Ra-khir insisted.

"No." Though soft, Kedrin's tone indicated finality. "Truth or lies, no good could come of me speaking ill of your mother, any more than her having done the same to me. The truth is, you come of good stock; and it shows in everything you do. For all her faults, she raised you well. I'm proud of you, Ra-khir."

I raised me well. Ra-khir refused to forgive as easily as his father. The simple truth was that his mother was a selfish, mean woman who demanded a loyalty she gave to no one else. Over the past year, he'd discovered many things about her he had never suspected: that she had secretly shared her body with other men during both of her marriages, that she had created vicious stories about any who opposed her, that she had threatened his father with harm to Ra-khir should his father dare to reveal the truth. He knew how difficult speaking well of his mother came to Kedrin, the honor he held foremost yet chose to abandon this once to preserve his son's childhood images of his mother. The veil she hid behind, however, had already been ripped away.

Kedrin spoke his final words on the subject. "I just want you to know that if you ever decide to return to her, I'll understand and make any clandestine arrangements you choose so that we can still spend time together."

Ra-khir pulled away, his answer too important to lose to muffling. "The knighthood and my father mean everything to me. By my own choice. I swear upon my honor, death alone will take either away from me." Ra-khir had never meant anything more. He tried to memorize the feelings that enveloped him now, stronger than any he had known before in his life. He believed he finally understood what love meant, a loyalty so strong that he would rather suicide than break it. Someday, he hoped, he would have the same bond with his own son. And no one, *no one* could break it.

The following day, Ra-khir took a stroll through Béarn's courtyard, reveling in the mingled perfumes of greenery and flowers and the light breeze. He had bathed and changed since his morning practice, unusually grueling because he worked with full-fledged knights rather than the apprentices in Erythane. In the afternoon, his father would drive him with at least as much vigor as Armsman Edwin; but, for now, Ra-khir would relish the time he found for relaxation.

Flower beds wove into striking patterns, the colors arranged to form pictures or spell words. Statues accentuated the tended beds without crowding. Apparently, to prevent clutter amid the plants, the statues occasionally were grouped in gardens of their own. Even perfectly sculpted artwork could grow tasteless if overused, but the gardeners clearly had an eye for their work that Ra-khir, at least, could not fault. Each time he believed he'd discovered the most flawless arrangement, he entered a garden that dazzled him all the more.

Ra-khir began noticing other people as well as the statues and shrubbery. Lords and ladies sunned themselves, enjoying the midday warmth as much as he did. Children chased and giggled on the garden pathways, under the watchful eyes of nursemaids or parents. Near one flower bed, Ra-khir discovered a quieter game that involved five children, three nannies, and two somber-eyed, sword-armed guards who could only be Renshai. Apparently, at least one heir played among this group.

Ra-khir watched the interplay for several moments. The Renshai looked little different from Erythanians, but they stood out in a courtyard full of burly Béarnides. They held attentive stances without any apparent cooperation or communication between them. Even when only in pairs, the Knights of Erythane worked as an obvious team, each movement countered, every article of clothing a perfect match down to the angle of sword in sheath. In comparison, the Renshai's actions seemed haphazard. Yet, his scrutiny did not go unnoticed. The first moment of his hesitation brought measuring gazes, and he read violence there should he tarry too long or draw too close. Their gazes did not fixate, moving on, perhaps, to more significant threats.

Thinking it rude to become a concern to guards at their post, Ra-khir continued on to a vegetable garden shaded by a stone ceiling. Many benches lined the area, apparently a place diehard outdoorsmen went when rain made other parts of the courtyard soggy. Though not the first roofed area Ra-khir had seen, this one had an occupant where the others had not. A boy of approximately his own age sat on a central bench staring absently at the wall. Curly brown bangs fell across his forehead, and a mandolin lay on the bench beside him. A sword hung at his belt, and he wore no standard to indicate his identity or station. His size and coloring did not fit Béarn's norm.

Pleased to discover a possible friend with whom he had at least age and foreignness in common, Ra-khir approached. "Hello."

The stranger stiffened with a gasp. Hazel eyes swung from the wall to Ra-khir in an instant, and he grabbed for the instrument though his sudden movement had not dislodged it. "Oh. Hello. You startled me."

Ra-khir agreed. "To the moon, almost."

The dark-haired youth smiled, avoiding the usual adolescent need to defend himself from embarrassment and thus displaying a likable self-confidence. "Almost. I'm afraid you caught me thinking." He laughed ruefully. "I suppose pining would be more accurate."

Though the other had given him the opening, Ra-khir thought it improper to press for personal details prior to introductions. "I'm Ra-khir of Erythane, son of Knight-Captain Kedrin and . . ."

The stranger spoke the rest of the title simultaneously with Ra-khir. ". . . apprentice knight to the Erythanian and Béarnian kings: His Grace, King Humfreet, and His Majesty, King Kohleran."

"Yes," Ra-khir finished, uncertain how to react to the other's recitation. He might have taken umbrage had the musician not used such a friendly tone and looked so inoffensive. "Well. How did you know?"

The dark-haired teen gestured at Ra-khir's uniform, including the standard tabard with Béarn's colors on the front and Erythane's black and orange on the rear. "Pretty obvious really. And I've heard knights speak titles often enough to memorize the words, even if memorizing words wasn't already my job." Realizing the conversation had continued without the necessary exchange, he backtracked. "I'm Darris, by the way . . ."

Ra-khir put the pieces together fast enough to recite Darris' title in another duet. ". . . the bard's heir."

They both laughed.

"You got me," Darris cradled the mandolin in his lap, tapping the bowl-back lightly. "I won't ask what gave *me* away."

Glad to have found a potential friend so quickly in a new place, Ra-khir gestured at the bench across from Darris. "Mind if I sit?"

"Not at all. Please do."

Ra-khir complied, racking his brain for details of the bard and recalling that he or she was charged with acting as the king's personal bodyguard as well as an entertainer. The musical ability was supposed to be some sort of bane passed through the line, though most people saw it as more of a windfall. He had heard no one could come close to matching the talent of Béarn's bards. "Interesting city, Béarn." Realizing "interesting" could have many different meanings and not wishing to sound insulting, Ra-khir added, "I really like it so far."

"This is your first time?" Darris shook the curls from his forehead, though they fell right back into place with the first movement of his head. "I didn't think I'd seen you before. But then again, why would I? The apprentice knights don't usually come here." Though not a question, the last statement left an opening for an answer.

"I'm here with my father."

"Knight-Captain Kedrin."

"Right."

Darris nodded, the topic obviously spent.

When Darris did not open a new matter, Ra-khir did. He had found someone his own age to talk with who seemed reasonably bright and sociable, and he had no pressing needs to attend. "You said you were pining."

"Pining," Darris repeated, as if he had never heard the word before. "Pining. Yes, pining. I suppose I am." He flushed, this time appropriately embarrassed. "I guess that's not something one usually discusses with strangers. I'm sorry. You must have startled me worse than I thought."

"No need for apology. Please." Ra-khir worked hard to save face for his companion. He rather liked the refreshing openness of the bard's heir. It might allow them to become friends where time constraints and personal defenses might otherwise prevent any but the most superficial associations. "What are you pining for?"

"It's not a 'what,' it's a 'who.'" Darris sighed, obviously wrestling with the decision of whether to share his pain with a brand new acquaintance or continue to dismiss his earlier lapse behind social convention. Then he drew the mandolin into playing position. His fingers skipped lightly over the strings, plucking out sounds that seemed too mellow for any instrument of man's making. Usually, it took at least a second playing for Ra-khir to warm to any song; but the beauty of the chords and notes Darris picked drew him to the same quiet awe he knew when he watched the best knights sparring.

But the words that followed the introduction drove all thoughts of warfare and contest from Ra-khir's mind, replacing it with a vision of a Béarnian princess of such beauty, kindness, and grace he could not help adoring this noble woman he had never met. Darris sang, his voice blending so perfectly with the mandolin that Ra-khir could not have separated one from the other even should he have wanted to ruin the listening trying. The bard's heir described a friendship most could only envy, one that spanned childhood and promised to last far beyond. Yet, though the words claimed no love beyond that of siblings, the emotion seeped through the tone of the music. Ra-khir felt as if his new companion had opened his soul to reveal a romantic passion he did not acknowledge, even to himself.

The verse changed, a bitter touch to a sweet song of love long nurtured. Guardians protected the princess, ones to whom Darris felt a debt of gratitude and a hatred at once. For though they kept the object of his passion alive and well, they kept her cloistered from him and every other. And this, he believed, at a time when she most needed his consolation.

As the last notes drifted in wordless epilogue, Ra-khir startled free of the trance Darris created, to discover tears in his own eyes. He rubbed them away, feeling foolish for the lapse. "That was amazing. Truly amazing."

"Thank you," Darris said with routine modesty.

Ra-khir fumbled helplessly for the words he really wanted to speak to express his appreciation for Darris' abundant talent. So much of his knight's training included courtly talk, manners, and protocol; yet, when it came to expressing himself, Ra-khir still felt hopelessly muddled. For now, he spent so much time concentrating on format that little thought remained for content. "Your playing and singing makes everything else I've ever heard called music sound like a herd of sheep."

"Thank you," Darris repeated with less assurance. "Or should I say I'm sorry I ruined others for you. There's music in everything, you know, every sound has its own special associations. Even sheep." To demonstrate, he played a short ditty about a shepherd. The background music simulated bleating in a stylized manner that Ra-khir wished all sheep could emulate. He could smell the clover/manure mixture that practically defined a herd's pasture, could see the lambs capering, and could feel the more ponderous steps of the older sheep.

When Darris finished, Ra-khir laughed. "You *are* good."

"Thank you," Darris said with good-humored finality. "It's my blessing and my curse."

"I'd heard that about the bard." Ra-khir seized the chance to discover the truth about other rumors. "I've also heard you get so good because you sing *everything*. That you'd rather sing than eat." He amended, realizing he addressed the heir, not the actual bard. "Or, rather, your father would."

"Mother," Darris corrected.

"Mother?"

"My mother is the current bard. My father's the head pastry chef."

"Oh." The revelation took Ra-khir aback. An image came instantly to mind, of a meek, flour-speckled man beside a warrior woman whose sword guarded the king of Béarn. Without thinking, he chuckled and was immediately mortified.

Darris took the insult in stride, easily guessing the root of Ra-khir's amusement and smiling to place him at ease. "Weird image, isn't it? But around here, no one thinks much of it. I mean, Renshai women all wield swords, and we see them occasionally, so my mother carrying one doesn't seem so out of place. Besides that, she mostly travels a lot and sings. There really hasn't been much need for her martial training." He shrugged. "And my father makes a vanilla cream cake worth dying for, though it's never killed anyone."

Ra-khir laughed again, this time at Darris' words. "I think you answered my other question, too. Obviously, you don't quite sing everything."

As if to prove Ra-khir wrong, Darris resumed his playing with a heavy, complicated tune. This time, he sang of a young man named Jahiran; and words and music defined an era at least a millennium past. Jahiran, it seemed, had an insatiable curiosity from birth and sought the knowledge of the gods and the universe from the moment he spoke his first words. The song followed this man as he grew and gained understanding, without accompanying common sense and wisdom. From one of the Cardinal Wizards, he was granted the form of an *aristiri,* a hawk that sings with more beauty than any mere songbird. Apparently, in Jahiran's time, the winged predators had been common before men shot them for sport or trophies. Now, only an occasional hunter or woodsman claimed to spot one etched against the sky or to hear its fine, clear voice penetrate the forest.

In *aristiri* form, Jahiran learned much more, hearing the things men and gods do not usually speak of freely. Among so much else, he witnessed the god, Thor, engaged in a tryst with a mortal woman and made the mistake of reporting his observation to Thor's wife, Sif, the goddess of Renshai. Ra-khir cringed as he experienced the quaking rage of Thor in Darris' words and notes. Ra-khir felt mighty Odin, the father of gods, as he hefted the errant man in *aristiri* guise and sliced the bird's tongue into silence, then returned Jahiran to man's form and world. Though unable to speak, Jahiran still had the voice of the *aristiri* whose shape he once held. And he and his line became condemned to an endless curse: to quest desperately for knowledge but reveal it only in song.

Once again, Ra-khir became lost in story and melody, and the return to Béarn's courtyard seemed like a heavy and sorrowful landing. He interpreted what he had heard. "So you can talk about regular things, but when you teach you have to sing."

"Right," Darris confirmed, replacing the mandolin on the seat beside him. "It irritates some people."

"Not me," Ra-khir hastened to place the bard at ease. "I could never get tired of listening to your voice."

Darris smiled, sad knowledge evident. "Not yet, maybe. But it grows tiresome. Sometimes it's easier just to sit quietly with people than to have to keep resorting to music, especially when there's no yet-known song for a certain situation and I have to make one up."

"What happens if you teach without singing?" Ra-khir asked the question that seemed necessary, though it might force Darris to music again. A glance at the sky revealed more time had passed than he would have guessed. He only had a few more moments with his new friend before he had to rush to his afternoon session.

"Oddly, that's one of the few pieces of information no bard has ever managed to gain." Darris shrugged. "Used to be the Wizards would kill him, but there aren't any Wizards anymore. Now, we mostly think Odin might strike us down. Of course, the Renshai believe the *Ragnarok* has come and gone, that Odin's dead, so they just think we're stupid and tedious." Darris shifted restlessly, as if fearing he might find out the correct answer if he said much more without switching to song. "Nowadays, I think it's just tradition and honor. We promised every eldest child would continue to follow the laws Odin set down for Jahiran's descendants. And we stick with that family honor as seriously as the knights to their order."

Ra-khir appreciated the comparison as few could. "Makes perfect sense to me." He rose reluctantly. "I have to go now. I've got a practice. But I'll be around again tomorrow. Where can I find you?"

Darris smiled again, clearly as happy to have made a new friend as Ra-khir. "Here's a pretty good bet these days. I've got some even quieter places outside the walls. I'll show you those sometime."

"Great." Ra-khir smoothed his practice silks then headed from the garden. Behind him, Darris strummed softly, mouthing words to a new song sparked by the conversation.

In the three and a half months since the staff-test, Matrinka's despair had faded from an all-consuming obsession to a dull scar that ached in mind and heart. The need to serve the kingdom in other ways still nagged at her, and she goaded her still-nameless Renshai guard into spar as often as the young blonde would allow. Now, they squared off in the center of Matrinka's room, the Renshai having not yet drawn and Matrinka eyeing her guardian. For the moment, there seemed myriad openings for attack, all of which would close in the instant between when Matrinka committed to her move and before the blade struck. In the last few days, she had at least managed to discard the fear that she might accidentally kill the Renshai, a triumph that seemed to mean far more to the Renshai than to herself.

Mior watched from the bed, silent mentally and physically. She had long ago abandoned trying to assist Matrinka with maneuvers. The instinct that came with owning claws did not translate well into sword strokes, and Matrinka lacked the necessary animal quickness and agility. Mostly, Mior's instructions just made an already difficult, unnatural-feeling task more so.

"All right," the Renshai said, seeming oblivious to Matrinka's menace, an attitude that only fed Matrinka's feelings of inadequacy about her physical skill. "The trick is to commit to each attack enough to give it the power to be-

come a potential killing stroke but still recover quickly
enough that, if you miss, you're not helpless."

Matrinka nodded. In theory, the Renshai made sense. But
translating word into action seemed impossible. The princess
had begun to wonder if she lacked some organ that connected understanding to execution. "I'll try."

"Any time." The Renshai made a gesture that encouraged
Matrinka's attack.

Concentrating hard, Matrinka bit her tongue as she lunged
for the Renshai's chest. Her guardian drew and cut fluidly,
parrying the attack into a harmless circle, then returning a
"killing" strike that sang over Matrinka's head.

"Recovery too slow!" the Renshai shouted. "Are you listening to me at all?"

Matrinka did not reply with words, having long ago
learned her lesson about speaking during combat. She still
had a bruise beside one knee where the side of the Renshai's
sword had slapped to make the point. Matrinka swept low.
The Renshai's sword slammed just above the crosspiece, jarring the hilt from Matrinka's hand.

Once disarmed, Matrinka usually let the Renshai recover
the sword. The young warrior saw serious dishonor in allowing the weapon of one she respected to touch the floor.
Matrinka did not know whether the Renshai's deference was
to the sword's wielder or owner, but the girl instinctively
bore in to snatch the grip just as Matrinka did the same. The
princess' hand bumped the hilt, sending it into an awkward
reverse-spin. The Renshai's hand closed over the blade, and
whetted steel sliced her left index finger to the bone. Nevertheless, she snatched the weapon out of midair, blood splashing a line across the coverlet and wall.

Matrinka gasped, recoiling. The Renshai sheathed both
weapons, growling out a string of words Matrinka could
only guess were curses by their harshness. Before tending
the wound, she studied Matrinka's hands.

Shocked that the Renshai had the presence to worry about
her charge after suffering such an injury, Matrinka stammered. "I–I'm fine."

Assured by that insistence, the Renshai sat on the desk
chair, pulled a rag from her pocket, and clamped it to the
wound.

Pained sympathetically, Matrinka grasped her own finger
in a hold equally tight. She sucked air through her teeth,

guilty for the wound she had accidentally inflicted. "I'm sorry. I'm really sorry."

The previous epithets seemed to completely take away any anger the Renshai might have harbored. "No problem. I know you didn't mean it. It's nothing to get upset about."

"Nothing to get upset about?" Matrinka repeated, stunned. "I cut your finger."

"*I* cut my finger," the Renshai insisted. "And what matters is that I didn't dishonor the sword."

"Dishonor the sword?" Matrinka found herself caught in a pattern of repeating the Renshai's words, stunned. "Who cares about the stupid sword? You almost lost a hand."

The Renshai met Matrinka's gaze coolly, as if trying to teach lofty concepts to a drunkard on Pudar's streets. "Fingers heal. Dishonoring one's sword is intolerable, especially when wielded by one worthy of respect."

"Worthy of respect? Me?" Matrinka shook her head. "I hereby grant you permission to let any sword of mine touch the ground anytime it means taking a chance at injuring yourself to catch it."

The Renshai snorted, twisting her right hand to remove a packet from the pocket on the same side. She opened it one-handed to reveal a standard salve that Matrinka recognized by its color. "Honor is internal. Anyone can give me permission to violate it, but no one can make me do so."

"Don't use that." Matrinka opened the top drawer of her dresser and retrieved a vial of crushed *drilstin* stems that she had picked in the gardens months earlier. "This'll work just as well, but it won't scar."

The Renshai unwrapped the bandage quickly, smearing on her own medication before retightening it. "Scars are a warrior's badge of honor." She smiled, obviously trying not to offend. "But thanks."

This time, Matrinka refused to allow the dismissal. "Is that part of your honor, too? You have to make certain all injuries, no matter how stupid, turn out with the worst possible outcome."

The Renshai raised her brows at the impropriety.

Matrinka did not back down. Two months with various Renshai guardians had taught her that they admired strength and courage above all else, even if it took the form of standing up to Renshai. She remained in place, hands on her hips, gaze directly on the Renshai's face.

"No," the Renshai finally admitted. "If you really wish to tend the wound, you may; but if you ever try to help me at a time when you're in danger . . ." She let the threat hang, there being little she could add without sounding either contrary or foolish. "Just don't. I already warned you what could happen if you learned to like me."

"Fine." The whole seemed ridiculous to Matrinka. Aside from about one day a week when different Renshai relieved this one from her duties, they spent day and night together. It seemed unthinkable to Matrinka that two people could spend so much time side by side without becoming attached. "Does it make you feel any better to know I'd do this for anyone?"

"Much." The Renshai offered her finger, watching curiously while Matrinka gathered soap, scissors, needle, and thread, a clean bowl of water, and several fresh pieces of cloth for bandaging. She watched every movement, even when Matrinka cut away skin edges to make them approximate more evenly and sutured the cut. When she finished, blood stained the water and the desktop, but the end result was a cleanly bandaged injury that would probably heal without infection and with minimal scarring.

Though pleased with her handiwork, Matrinka gathered her tools in silence, not caring whether or not the Renshai appreciated her labor. The joy came from the good feelings it brought her. It was the first time she'd felt positively about herself in a long time.

The Renshai examined the bandage, then tested the use of the hand. Matrinka had deliberately wrapped it so that she could still grip a sword in either hand, and the hilt fit as smoothly as the princess expected. "Nice job," the Renshai admitted grudgingly. "Thanks."

"You're welcome." Matrinka fairly beamed.

The Renshai spoke thoughtfully. "I know a bit about taking care of injuries. It's part of our training. We work with the sick and wounded to assure no one dies of infection or illness rather than in valiant combat." She raised the bandaged hand. "But I'm impressed. Did you ever think about becoming a healer? It might better suit you."

A healer. Matrinka's mouth fell open. *Of course.* Once spoken aloud, the idea that she had never considered it before seemed patently ridiculous. "That's a great idea." She added carefully, "Except . . ."

"Except what?"

"Except it's not enough to have tutors come up here and tell me what plants to use for what. I've read enough books about that. I'd have to get out of this castle to gather herbs."

"So?"

That being the last thing Matrinka expected to hear from her guardian, she stared. "So, I'd have to go outside the castle walls."

"Yes," the Renshai confirmed. "Is that a problem?"

Matrinka blinked, confused. "Well, yes. Since I have a constant guardian Renshai who won't let me go."

"Me?"

"Who else?"

The Renshai shook her head. "Who said I wouldn't let you outside?"

Matrinka froze, not daring to believe she had spent the last three months of her life desperate for a glimpse of the gardens she could have visited any time she wished. "You rarely even let me see my grandpapa."

The Renshai frowned. "That wasn't because of me. The ministers and healers rarely let *anyone* see the king. You're one of the few who has. And when did I ever forbid you going outside?"

"I never asked," Matrinka realized aloud. "The others wouldn't let me, and you seemed . . ." Unable to find a word that would not sound insulting, she followed a different course. "I just assumed—" Again, she broke off, suddenly realizing she might convince her guardian to retract a course of action she had pined after for months. Instead, she channeled her energies to this new pursuit that seemed perfect for her. "I'll need to see the master healer for guidance about books, tutors, and apprenticeship. But first . . ." Matrinka smiled broadly, "a walk in the courtyard, if you please."

Despite her insistence on preventing a friendship, the Renshai's expression and demeanor revealed satisfaction at the change that came over Matrinka in a matter of moments. Despair had finally given way to a realization of self-worth and dignity, despite the deep scars of the gods' judgment. A simple walk outside might do them both good.

Baltraine tromped the castle halls toward the meeting room, his features locked into a scowl and his black hair streaming behind him. Scarcely two months had passed since his confrontation with Kedrin in the hallways, and already the knight-captain had seen fit to undermine his command. Kedrin had initiated the council which Baltraine had needed to hurriedly drop affairs of state to attend. And Kedrin would pay for that mistake.

As Baltraine neared the meeting room, he eased the taut expression from his face to leave the measured mask of a politician. The walk had given him plenty of time to plot his vengeance. The details had not yet fallen into place, but the immediate generalities seemed obvious. He needed to anger Kedrin into doing something stupid, or at least into the appearance of preparing to do so. Though wedded to honor, Kedrin was still a warrior, with a swordsman's temper and approach to problems, not the wiles of a diplomat. *How easily a man's honor can be turned against him.*

That thought buoyed Baltraine's mood, allowing him to cast aside his own rage for the calm detachment he would require to run a meeting, save face, and cast suspicion on the captain. Opening the door, he smiled at those already in place—Kedrin, old Abran, and minister of the court Weslin—then remained standing as the others entered. The usual assortment of ministry and security filled their accustomed seats around the table before Baltraine took the floor. "Friends, I apologize for the prematurity of this meeting." He glanced at Kedrin not-quite casually. The more intentional his jabs, the quicker he might incite the captain, but he needed to appear natural to the others in the room. He had dedicated a lifetime to cultivating trust and hiding disdain.

Kedrin's eyes narrowed, but he showed no other reaction to the insult. He shifted restlessly. Convention demanded that Baltraine immediately give the floor over to him as the one who had called the meeting.

Baltraine deliberately discarded the rules, certain the rest would not notice the difference. Some did not know Kedrin had called the meeting. Others would be ignorant of the rarely invoked protocol; not since long before Baltraine had taken his position had anyone but the prime minister initiated the assembly. Baltraine trusted that the routine of him running the meetings would prove enough to make his doing so seem natural now. He was reasonably certain only Kedrin would take note of his impropriety. Even if any other did, he or she would dismiss it as unimportant. Only the knight would take offense. "As all of you know by now, our first messenger to Santagithi never returned. We sent a second, both to accomplish the same task and to discover the fate of the first. We expect him back within the next two weeks or so."

Kedrin immediately made the subtle gesture that indicated he wished to speak. Baltraine glanced in his direction, smiled briefly and privately, then continued. "Though all seems well, I recommend we form a diplomatic party. If the scout returns with good news, and we have no reason to suspect otherwise, this group could escort our prince back to his kingdom. If the scout does not return, we could send this larger, better armed group to try to deliver the message our scouts could not, as well as to escort the prince to the castle. Does anyone oppose this suggestion?"

No one did. Each man or woman nodded in turn, though Kedrin did signal his need to add his piece. As before, Baltraine ignored the knight. "Very good, then. I'd like to discuss the composition of this group."

Limrinial broke in. "Surely, we need competent warriors. I'd suggest a mixture: a pair of knights, perhaps. Some Béarnian guards. Maybe a Renshai, since there will be an heir along on the return trip." The homely minister of local affairs threw the opening to the military leaders across the table.

Thialnir spoke first. "Of course, a Renshai. Two or three if you feel the need. We would not think of leaving any heir unprotected, especially this one."

Guard-Captain Seiryn raised his brows, offended, though he had become accustomed to the Renshai's blunt manner. "I would hardly call the company of Béarnian guards 'unprotected.' I would send a regiment, if appropriate. What, besides the defense of the kingdom, of course, could compare to this?"

All attention turned naturally to the last military leader, and this time Baltraine acknowledged Kedrin, trusting propriety to hold the knight to the topic. To backtrack or move on would not suit his honor. Like a cornered rat, he would have no choice but to respond to the question on the floor before considering other courses of action. The frustration of claiming the floor only to have to relinquish it before making a long-held point would surely fuel Kedrin's anger. "As you know, a dozen Knights of Erythane directly serve Béarn at any time. In order to continue to maintain the kingdom's defenses and demeanor, I believe not more than six and no fewer than two should become a part of this mission. That is my opinion, of course, and I will bow to the better judgment of this council should they find more or fewer appropriate." He hesitated, lips pursed and pale eyes locked on Baltraine's face; but, yielding to ancient protocol, he sat without adding more.

As the minister of internal affairs, Fahrthran would decide the final division based on the advice of his peers. He cleared his throat carefully and spoke in the clear voice that had come to define the undeserving, newer nobility in Baltraine's mind. "Abran, how do you assess the disappearance of at least one messenger? Do you have any concerns about the kingdom to which we sent them?" Before committing himself, Fahrthran threw the issue to the aging minister of foreign affairs.

Abran took the floor. "Santagithi and Béarn have been at peace for as long as I or history can remember. We can't wholly discard the possibility that their king has designs on Béarn, but it seems distinctly unlikely. They could never hope to win a straight-out war against us, though they do have allies in the north. More probably, our messenger fell prey to accident or footpads ignorant or heedless of the law. Or to whomever harmed our heirs."

A general mutter followed, accompanied by bowed heads. The investigation into responsibility had yielded no answers, and there remained no further leads to follow. No theory grounded in logic could explain how someone had sneaked live bears past dozens of Béarnian guards nor timed their attack so perfectly. No clues remained from probable murders previously attributed to illness, accident, or suicide. Since the staff-test, one heir required constant intervention against taking his own life, and they had lost another child to the paralytic illness the healers had finally learned to treat, if not to explain.

Abran nodded to Fahrthran to indicate he still held the status of speaker. The internal affairs minister laced fingers through his beard, Eastern-dark features thoughtful. "I think we should keep the party reasonably small but strong. We haven't lost any heirs to attack since the Renshai began guarding them. That suggests a limit to the enemy's numbers or power. If we send too many, not only do we increase travel time but also open the way for accidents and delays."

His black eyes squinted as he considered further. "If we send too many, Santagithi may feel threatened, and its king might prove less kindly disposed to talk. We can't afford to make a mistake. Also, the fewer of our people who know about the heir, the less likely the information falls into enemy hands." He glanced about, finding every gaze on him, and continued. "My suggestion: two diplomats fluent in the Western Trading tongue, two servants to attend animals and one for the prince, two Knights of Erythane, three to four guards, and one Renshai should prove enough."

Prime Minister Baltraine took over to turn the suggestion into a motion. "Anyone object to this distribution?"

The question drew no obvious concerns from the ministers. The Renshai sat in stony silence, and Seiryn nodded and shrugged simultaneously. He would do as the ministers decided, trusting their judgment more in such situations. Kedrin mulled the matter, chewing his lip. Apparently, he would have chosen a different composition, yet he gave this one, and its explanation, fair consideration.

Despite protocol, Baltraine did not wait for Kedrin to gesture agreement before considering the motion passed. "All right, then. We continue our investigation. We continue encouraging marriages and births among the heirs. We assemble the envoy party with the hope of good news from the second messenger. Then, if our second messenger has not returned one month from today, we send the envoy anyway."

The knight-captain's features flushed scarlet, and he again made the gesture for acknowledgment, this time with far less subtlety.

Baltraine pretended not to see, beginning the sequence that would adjourn the meeting.

Driven to desperate measures, Kedrin forsook the honor of meeting rules, apparently for one he considered larger. He stood. "Just a moment." He added, as if in afterthought, "Please."

Politely, Baltraine quit, mid-word to emphasize Kedrin's rudeness. Out of spite, he did not make the ancient gesture to indicate the knight held the floor, though everyone studied Kedrin curiously.

The knight-captain's face was a study in rage, the myriad insults by Baltraine now taking their toll at once. "The messenger could have made it back today but didn't. I see no reason to wait another moment before sending the envoy. In fact, we should have done so after the first messenger didn't return, rather than wasting the life of another man."

Baltraine blinked, feigning surprise at the hostility of Kedrin's presentation. "It's a long, difficult journey, especially on the messenger line. It seemed logical to assume our first only got delayed. Since we selected a courier the first time, I assumed it made sense to send another before resorting to armed expeditions. I picked speed over strength. If I chose wrongly, I apologize deeply." He locked a sad, sincere expression on his face. "Knight-Captain, if you had concerns about my decision, why didn't you voice them then?"

Kedrin froze in place, astonished beyond words.

Baltraine seized on the knight's startled pause. "All settled, then. I suggest we meet—"

This time, Kedrin made no attempt to wait for the end of a sentence, obviously aware Baltraine would find a way to make him sound insolent regardless. "First, let the record show I did object to sending a second messenger when an armed group would serve better. Second, I don't believe the matter of time has yet been resolved. I suggest we send the envoy as quickly as we can muster it."

Prime Minister Baltraine glanced sidelong at several of the ministers, silently registering his concern about stress and its effect on Kedrin's manners and sanity. "I apologize for disagreeing, Knight-Captain; but I believe neither the records of our last few meetings, nor of the court, will reveal any evidence that you objected to my plan to send a second messenger. As to the matter of timing ..." He shrugged. "... I see no reason to panic. We don't have aeons, it's true. But even should King Kohleran pass away, may the gods prevent it, we would still have enough time to send an envoy there and back. If we send it prior to the return of the messenger, we have no way to relay any conditions the king in Santagithi might make. Worse, we may violate some tenet he insisted upon. Better to give the messenger another month."

"Excuses." Kedrin caught and held Baltraine's gaze. "The king in Santagithi will see our need and understand. He's never balked on details before. Should we lose the king, we might barely have the time to send an escort there and back in time. Any delay is intolerable."

Baltraine shook his head to indicate he found the argument beneath contempt. He used a patronizing tone, pitched to break the knight's precarious control. "Sir Kedrin, I'm afraid you've let the seriousness of the situation addle you."

Kedrin's fingers balled to fists on the table. "Don't equate taking action with addling. Perhaps the blame lies with the delaying party. What do you gain from holding things back, Baltraine?" He let the words glide in a question that made everyone curious.

Baltraine took a step backward, as if menaced, though a table stood between them. He let the pause hang, hoping Kedrin would prove fool enough to make a witnessed accusation that would pass for treason. When he did not, Baltraine responded. "I gain only the time Kingdom Santagithi needs to state their wishes and for our messenger to find his way home." He gave the only response he could, though the truth dawned more slowly. *Already I'm making many of the king's decisions, and I'm good at it. What's wrong with wanting to rule while I can? It's not like I could ever become king.* Baltraine could see the advantage to making himself and his family an integral part of castle procedure prior to the young heir's arrival. Slightly alarmed by the turn of his own thoughts, Baltraine shoved them aside. He was an excellent regent with a superior eye for justice. Having anticipated and, to some extent, steered Kedrin's words, Baltraine leaped upon the opening to place himself in the position of apparent compromiser. "But if you truly believe that sooner is better, I've always thought highly of your ideas. We can strike a bargain. Two weeks seems a reasonable compromise between one month and no time. Would that suit the council?"

The warriors favored sooner and the ministers the compromise; but, in the end, they came together at the precise two weeks Baltraine had wanted from the start. The prime minister had long ago realized that settlement worked best when he exaggerated his initial demands.

Chapter 7

Reuniting

Battles are won by swordsmen, not swords.
                                        —Colbey Calistinsson

Moonlight drew stripes through the dusty windows of Béarn's tavern, merging with the lantern light at every table. Shadows broke the contour at irregular intervals, and laughter rumbled over the constant buzz of conversation. At a table in the corner, sitting with the master healer and watched over by two guards, Baltraine paid sound and movement little heed. Stale beer and unwashed bodies blended into a familiar, rancid stench that had come to define taverns and seemed pleasant for the association rather than for the smell itself. Nothing Baltraine had ever known came near to matching the distinctive aroma of alcohol in its various formulations.

Baltraine and the healer kept their voices low so that even the hovering pair of guardsmen could not hear them, at least not beneath their own conversation. Baltraine had given them permission to relax, eat, and even to drink a beer or two. In truth, the escort seemed like paranoia. Few knew enough about the prime minister's power to have reason to harm him, and nothing could be gained by doing so. Nevertheless, caution had become the operative word in Castle Béarn. For only the second time in history, Knights of Erythane had been called to permanent station in Béarn and Renshai had become commonplace.

Baltraine anticipated no trouble here. He had come to unwind, to shed the anger he had hidden valiantly during the ministers' meeting. The knight-captain had become an irritation Baltraine could no longer tolerate. In addition, he had needed a private corner to discuss the king's condition without servants or nobles overhearing. Since the suggestion that treason might have played a hand in the deaths of the young heirs, Baltraine felt as if every wall and floor in the castle had sprouted ears. Now, he confirmed what he already suspected. The king's periods of lucidity would only continue to diminish. Eventually, he would slip into permanent coma that could last months, years, or possibly decades with the healer's assistance. Baltraine gave back the only advice he could: the king's life must be prolonged to its utmost, no matter the cost. To prevent a panic or coup, only a handful of Béarn's most trusted and loyal could know how serious the king's condition had become. For now, that consisted only of the master healer and himself. As Baltraine continued his careful assessment of his staff's devotion to their regent, he hoped to invite others into his confidence and designs.

Business settled, Baltraine allowed himself the relaxation he had sought. Concerns of the kingdom had grown into a burden he had not had the time to recognize. In every way but title, he would soon become Béarn's king. The decisions he made affected every aspect of Béarnian politics. Considered in this light for the first time, the implications awed and frightened him. Baltraine knew a brief, guilty pleasure at the recognition of his ruling skill. The survival of a kingdom lay in his capable hands, and those who disrupted the fragile balance he sustained could not be tolerated. Problems like Knight-Captain Kedrin escalated from nuisance to menace if not quickly contained.

"Hey! You there!" A guard's shout yanked Baltraine from his thoughts. He glanced over as a wild-looking teenager scampered deeper into the tavern, the guards thundering after him. "Stop that thief!"

A crowd of Béarnides came to their feet as the boy skittered over their table, sending stoneware crashing to the slate floor. Several lunged for him, mostly managing to entangle themselves as he dodged their attacks with a cat's speed and grace. One guard plowed into the mass of people that suddenly stood between him and his quarry. The other managed to circle the group, closing in on the youngster with an agility that would make a race for the door a close call.

Instinctively, Baltraine checked his pockets. One of his money pouches was missing. He scowled, more annoyed than angry or impressed. Beer and reflection had turned him into a nearly oblivious victim, and his obvious rich dress and demeanor made him the thief's natural target. Still, it had required some skill for the boy to slip unnoticed past the guards, even briefly.

Guard and thief sprinted for the exit. About two running steps from it, the boy abruptly veered back the way he had come. Carried by momentum, the guard slammed into the door, bouncing on his shoulder to deflect his course back in the right direction. Having wrestled through the crowd, the other guard charged the door. The thief sprinted toward another table. The occupants vacated, some grabbing drinks to rescue them from the fate of those on the other table. But the youngster plunged beneath it, scarcely slowed by the need to hunch. The guard scurried for the opposite edge; but the thief darted out from under a side, and the Béarnide's grab fell short. The boy sprang to the window ledge and plunged out into the night.

The guard muttered a harsh oath, then curbed his tongue. He glanced at Baltraine for direction.

"Catch him, if you can. I'll meet you back here." Baltraine gestured at the door, which the second guard had opened. Both hesitated, then headed out after their quarry, shutting the door behind them.

Baltraine excused himself from the healer's company on the pretext of needing to relieve himself. The angle of his seat had shown him something, he believed, no other patron had seen. The thief had not leaped through the window then run, as it appeared. Instead, he had clung to the upper ledge and swung himself to the rooftop. The lack of crashing footfalls overhead suggested he remained quietly in place, watching the guards weave through Béarn's streets in what they hoped was his wake. Baltraine did not yet understand why he had not alerted the guards to his knowledge; but experience told him that, subconsciously, he saw a use for this thief that had not yet reached significance in his own mind.

Baltraine left the tavern, quietly walking to the side without stealth or threat. He wanted to make it clear he knew the other's location without frightening the boy into running or silence. A plan took shape as he moved, one that made the loss of a few silvers seem petty. Careful to skirt the window so the men in the tavern did not notice him, he whispered upward, "Boy."

The chirp and buzz of the night insects was his only reply.

Baltraine wondered whether the thief had crept away while he found the words to explain his own departure. He had assessed the boy's heritage from habit and guessed, by size and conduct, that the thief was no Béarnide. The city's close-knit population precluded orphans, elderly, or the insane living with anyone but family or friends. Pudar, however, held its share of beggars, drunkards, and urchins; and this boy seemed more like a rowdy than any Béarnide ever could. Never having lived on the streets, Baltraine could not know whether hiding or escape seemed the better strategy. Certainly the thief would, however.

"Boy," Baltraine repeated. "You can keep the money. If you help me, I'll see to it the guards leave you alone. And I'll pay you." Baltraine had no intention of giving the thief free rein to steal; but, since it was his purse that had been stolen, he could and would pardon this crime.

More silence followed. Baltraine sighed, dismissing the idea that his plan could not succeed without one such as this boy. He started back toward the entry, arrested by a soft voice from above. "Wait."

Baltraine froze and swiveled his gaze upward, though he saw nothing but the dark silhouette of building and roof.

"How much?" The thief used the trading tongue, as Baltraine had, but with a heavy Eastern accent.

Baltraine paused, surprised. Though more common than Northmen, Easterners came to the West only occasionally and usually specifically to the great trading city of Pudar. Merchants of every type plied their wares in Béarn as well, but none of these seemed likely to leave an adolescent behind. He surmised this boy might have become orphaned by an Eastern family visiting Pudar, then wandered here. Or, perhaps, he had escaped slave service to some Eastern merchant. Baltraine dropped speculation that held no bearing on the matter at hand and returned his thoughts to bargaining. He had no idea how much a theft was worth but guessed he would at least need to supply the value of the item to lower the thief's temptation to keep it, once stolen. "Six silvers."

He left enough doubt in his tone to let the boy know he would haggle.

"What do I have to do?" The voice wafted from the roof, this time accompanied by a shadowed face. Moonlight revealed the straight, shaggy hair Baltraine had seen in the tavern, and a single brown eye glittered beneath the tangles.

Baltraine glanced about to make certain no one could overhear. "Steal a dagger from a knight." He added quickly. "A specific dagger from a specific knight."

"From his person?"

Baltraine considered. Surely, it would prove simpler to sneak the knife from Kedrin's quarters, but that would require allowing the thief inside the castle walls, which would place far more than the knight's possessions at risk. "Yes."

"That will cost you double. Half in advance."

Thoughts raced through Baltraine's mind. His diplomat's training taught him that hesitation killed bargains, raised prices, and drew suspicion where none would otherwise exist. He needed to make decisions swiftly, even in a case where he had no experience from which to speculate. The thief's swift, smooth negotiation suggested familiarity with similar deals and, consequently, with hired thefts. However, his youth and strangeness made such unlikely. An experienced burglar surely would have a standard price for his services or would measure his employer carefully before setting one that maximized profits and minimized dissatisfaction. It seemed more as if this youngster bartered over groceries in an alien market having learned that the natives usually asked for twice as much as they would eventually take in trade. These ideas passed in moments. Baltraine could well afford the twelve silver, and he dared not risk getting caught discussing business with a criminal. "All right. Double. But only a quarter in advance and the rest on delivery. And you have to take the knife without his notice, or the deal's broken."

Darkness swallowed the thief's eyes, leaving only a disembodied voice filtering down from on high. "Agreed. Now exactly what and who?"

Sunlight streamed intermittently through scattered, broken cloud cover, the beams becoming more vertical as the sun snaked higher. Darris sat beneath the stonework canopy that protected his favorite garden from rain in other times. His constant need to be alone had turned his skin sallow, emphasizing the lighter hair and hazel eyes that already set him apart from the full-blooded Béarnides. This day, as the seven before it, approaching midday brought a gladness that had not touched his thoughts for months. Ever since Ra-khir had come to Béarn, Darris had gained a friend to help him forget and to ease the burden of sadness that had poisoned him since overprotective guardians had spirited Matrinka from his sight.

Usually, the loss simply flavored his mood from moment to moment. Now, direct consideration drew his memory to the day of the bears' attack. That night, the two Renshai women had allowed him to stay with Matrinka, with special permission from the king who believed the bard's heir's familiar face might soothe the agony that would follow tragedy and accompany changes. Afterward, the Renshai argued that any frequent presence, no matter how trusted, posed a clear present and future risk to the princess. In addition, they argued, his perceived need to protect Matrinka and his "unorthodox" methods of doing so might interfere with their task. Whether he assisted or not, he would surely get in their way and hamper their guardianship.

Hamper their guardianship. As always, the description left a wake of irritation. Yet Darris understood the need to protect the remaining heirs, had seen the bloody destruction the bears had caused, and knew Matrinka required more than the protection he could accord. She needed Renshai. With that need came a price that made him ill, but he would have it no other way. As a ward of Renshai, Matrinka was safe; and if that meant he could not see her until after an heir took the throne, so be it. Her safety mattered far more than his comfort. He only hoped she did not suffer the misery he did.

Darris had not pressed the boundaries of the Renshai's decision. If guardians trained and indoctrinated from birth believed it best that he not interfere, he would abide by their decision. Nevertheless, his bard's curiosity drove him to glean as much information as he could about a situation of which he was no longer a part. He knew about Matrinka's depression and the push to marry her off as soon as her mood improved. He had studied every possible suitor to assure that she found one who would treat her with the kindness and dignity she deserved. None seemed nearly good enough; but he found a few with whom, he believed, she could find an adequate future.

Lost in his thoughts, Darris scarcely noticed when another entered his private garden. Anticipating Ra-khir's arrival, he raised his head and managed a smile. Instead of friendly green eyes beneath a lengthy snarl of red-blond hair, he found the more familiar Béarnian features that had come to define beauty and compassion in his mind. Startled and thrilled at once, he lurched to his feet while intending only to bow. The result was an awkward stumble that left him on one knee before a princess who detested such formality from friends. Mumbling apologies instead of greetings, he staggered to his feet. The instant he did, Matrinka threw herself into his arms.

The sudden weight in his embrace threw Darris further off-balance. Afraid to let Matrinka fall, he clutched her tightly and stabilized himself with desperate self-control. Eyes closed, Matrinka apparently missed the struggle.

Desire rose within Darris, one he knew he could never satisfy, and it sparked shame. Only as he struggled with his emotions, hoping desperately that Matrinka did not notice his excitement, did he register that she had not come alone. He glanced over her shoulder at a youthful blonde with narrowed, blue eyes that judged every nuance and movement. Her expression held obvious contempt. Apparently, she had measured the inattentiveness that had allowed them to come so close before he noticed them as well as the striking clumsiness he had displayed since their arrival.

Glad for a distraction from inappropriate lust and wishing for a chance to amend the poor impression he had made, Darris pulled free and bowed to the Renshai. "Pleased to meet you. I'm Darris, the bard's heir." He gestured at the pack he had left on the bench, brimming with a lute, a mandolin, and sundry smaller instruments. He paused, awaiting a return introduction that he did not receive.

The Renshai looked beyond or through him, a nasty halfsmile seeming out of place on otherwise cherubic features.

Though put off by the rudeness, Darris maintained his own manners. "You must be Matrinka's bodyguard." His studies and discussions completed the details for him. "Kevralyn Tainharsdatter of the Renshai tribe of Modrey."

The blue eyes glared suddenly and directly at Darris. The Renshai's lips tightened into a grimace, and lines creased the pale forehead. "Don't *ever* call me that! *No one* ever calls me that!"

Apparently startled by the vehemence, Matrinka took a step backward. Darris' mind emptied of amenities. "I—I'm sorry," he stammered. "I—I thought that was your name."

"It is," the Renshai said, her gaze slipping beyond Darris again. "And my title, of which I'm proud. But no one calls me any name but—"

"Kevral." Ra-khir's voice, dripping with distaste, came from behind Darris, the precise location of the Renshai's stare. Ra-khir's tone implied a simple statement of recognition rather than any intention to complete the Renshai's sentence. He had only that moment come within speaking, or hearing, distance.

Darris whirled. Matrinka glanced at Ra-khir, and the Renshai remained in place, the cocksure grin resuming its position on her face. Thrilled to have his two favorite friends together at the same time, Darris launched into introductions. "Ra-khir, this is Princess Matrinka." He returned his gaze to the Béarnide to explain. "Ra-khir's an apprentice knight and the son of their captain."

Ra-khir moved first, as politeness demanded. Removing his cap, he knelt with lowered head, face obscured by a spilled tangle of sweat-matted, copper hair that had obviously spent most of the morning crushed beneath a helmet.

The respect seemed to stun Matrinka who, Darris knew, had always preferred walking the gardens to sitting in the courtroom. Knights' maneuvers rarely brought them into contact with other royalty than the king. While she stared, apparently searching for her tongue, Mior slunk to her side. The cat eased forward, sniffing delicately at the knight apprentice's hair. "Um . . . that's not necessary," Matrinka said softly, face flushed at the grand display. "I'm glad to meet you, Ra-khir. Just treat me as you would anyone else."

Ra-khir rose, tossing back his head to fling hair from his eyes, then replacing his cap. "Princess, I'm honored."

"I'm honored, too," Matrinka said, glancing nervously at Darris who smiled reassuringly. He should have guessed that Matrinka's informality and Ra-khir's training would clash, but the relationship between apprentice knight and Renshai seemed harder to fathom. Ra-khir had stated that he'd never left Erythane before, and honor would not allow him to lie. Yet Renshai remained reclusively on the Fields of Wrath except when duty called them to war or to Béarn. If Ra-khir and Kevral had met in the king's city, he should have known Matrinka as well. Though intrigued by the possibilities, Darris could tell neither would want him to question them.

Darris quelled his burning need for constant understanding and knowledge that cursed him as a birthright and set about creating friendships instead. "Would anyone care for a song?" He asked casually, though it was an offer some Béarnides would pay a day's wages to hear. Although his need to sing knowledge could make normal conversation dull and lengthy, no simple musician could come close to matching the performance of songs rehearsed by bard or heir. Nevertheless, he waited until he received eager affirmation from Ra-khir and Matrinka before commencing. The Renshai stood in stolid silence, her calculating gaze flicking toward every noise or passerby.

Darris played, deliberately choosing a melody and words that inspired friendship and peace among strangers. Though ancient, the song expressed concepts so central to civilization that its tenets held through centuries of advancement, change, and upheaval. The mandolin rang forth in chords and trills designed to lift spirits and to open the trust and hearts of strangers to affection usually shared only by families. The words complemented the tune, a backdrop of harmony that seemed unnecessary, though it required a three-octave range, at times between notes, to complete. More than anything, Darris wished to show his companions, the long-term friend and the new acquaintance, the affection he felt for them both. And he hoped they, too, would learn to care for one another as he did for them.

Matrinka sat, mouthing the words to this song she knew well. Mior sprang onto the bench, then snuggled into her mistress' lap. Kevral remained attentive at the princess' side, arms folded across her abdomen, a hand resting lightly on each sword hilt. Ra-khir stayed on the opposite side of Matrinka, smiling and rocking in place to the beat.

At length, the song wound to a close, the last notes fading into obscurity. Matrinka clapped, her approval evident as always. Ra-khir shook his head with obvious awe. Only the Renshai seemed unmoved. She remained in her place, eyes still tracing sounds and movements. Only then Darris realized a small crowd had begun to gather at the edges of the garden; nobles whose paths had taken them by this area had dawdled to listen. Others came, near enough for the music to draw them even closer. Applause sprinkled through the makeshift gathering, some embarrassedly pretending they had not paused to listen to the private concert. As always, a few requested an encore or a new tune; but Darris waved away their appeals. Within moments of his refusal, they dispersed, leaving Darris, Matrinka, Ra-khir, Mior, and Kevral alone in the garden again.

Darris broke the hush that followed. He set aside his mandolin and leaned across the bench toward Matrinka. Not wishing to antagonize her guardian, he did not attempt to actually move closer. "I've missed you."

Matrinka smiled, hands twining nervously through Mior's fur. She glanced at their two companions, Kevral somber at her left and Ra-khir grinning knowingly at her right. "I've missed you, too," she managed, then added sadly, "And for nothing. Kevral lets me go where I please and see whomever I would."

Darris winced, hating himself for not asking. The hostility of Matrinka's other two guardians had seemed pervasive. Kevral's reputation among her own kind for severity, competence, and self-confidence had made him sure she would control Matrinka's movements even more than Kristel and Nisse had. Only now he realized that the young Renshai's self-assurance might also make her more comfortable about her ability to defend Matrinka under any circumstances. That last heightened his discomfort. Kevral's certainty that she could handle any situation might drive her to place Matrinka into danger, the scope of which she wrongly believed she could manage. Bypassing his thoughts, Darris addressed Matrinka's comment, "You'll see much more of me from now on, then." Realizing concern had made him presumptuous, he amended, "That is, if you wish, of course."

Matrinka chuckled tensely. "Of course I wish." Blushing and obviously uncomfortable, she turned her attention to Ra-khir. "You know my guardian?"

"Yes, Princess," Ra-khir replied, his tone respectful but his glance at Kevral containing evident hostility. "We met in Erythane."

All eyes switched to Kevral then. A Renshai outside the Fields of Wrath or Béarn was a rarity that would pique anyone's curiosity let alone the insatiable need to know that Darris suffered.

Kevral shrugged, obviously quoting. "It is not enough to learn; a student must understand detail and nuance to the depth of instinct. Only experience can bring that level of knowledge." She met Matrinka's gaze, then Darris', and lastly Ra-khir's. The brazen partial smile accompanied her attention to the latter. "I learn maneuvers as their creator intended. I speak languages with proper intonation. How could I truly learn Western-speak without hearing it from the lips of Erythanians?"

Darris accepted the explanation more easily than most, the quest for knowledge a burning passion that no understanding could quench. Though not the only ones who spoke Western as their first language, Erythane had become the largest city to do so anymore. The East spoke its own language, as did the Northmen. The opposite side of the Western lands used the common trading tongue almost exclusively, as did the massive mercantile city of Pudar. Smaller towns, villages, and farms variously preferred the trading tongue, Western, or a combination. Béarn had its own language, though its folk used Western and trading at least as fluently; and the Renshai also spoke a singular, Northern-like tongue.

Ra-khir loosed a soft noise that sounded suspiciously like a snort, but he did not follow it with an explanation. Apparently, something about his meetings with Kevral made him loath to talk about them. Sensing reluctance better broken in male privacy, Darris did not press the matter but turned the conversation back to Matrinka. "I've worried for you. There've been rumors of everything from suicidal depression to impending marriage."

Matrinka laughed, though it sounded strained. Her hands stroked the cat from nose to rump in repetitive cycles while the animal purred with eyes closed. "All false. And all partly true, too." She glanced at Ra-khir. Then, obviously finding him trustworthy for telling personal failings as well as those of the kingdom, she continued. "I flunked the test, as you probably guessed." She caught and held Darris' soft, hazel eyes with an earnestness that implied she would describe her core feelings later, when they could once again speak alone. Their long association allowed her to understand his need for details others could not attain. "The gods found me unworthy." She lowered her head, the thick, black waves that Darris adored falling over her eyes, but not before he noticed moisture blurring them to a smear of brown and white.

Darris crossed half the distance between himself and Matrinka before he remembered his movement might disturb the Renshai guard. But, though Kevral watched his every motion, she allowed him to take a seat at Matrinka's side and gather the princess in his arms. "The gods only found you not the one to sit upon Béarn's throne. What does that signify? You never wanted or expected to do so."

Darris' words broke the floodgates. Matrinka sobbed in his arms, her sorrow an aching burden that precluded the passion her closeness always unwittingly aroused. "I don't care about being queen," Matrinka admitted. "But unworthy . . . ?" She did not bother to finish the thought, her intention obvious. Mior remained in her lap, not bothered by the bard's heir's closeness, though he all but crushed the cat between them.

Darris clutched Matrinka tightly, at once needing to soothe and wishing he never had to let her go. "Matrinka, don't be silly. There's a million reasons why a person wouldn't make the best ruler that have nothing to do with self-worth. The staves judge naïveté, innocence, and neutrality. There's a world of difference between just and merciful, between fair and compassionate. You're a lovely woman, Matrinka. Maybe just *too* kind to be queen. I've traveled a bit, and I know no one more worthy of my loyalty and friendship than you."

Matrinka eased free. "I'm sorry." She tossed back a cascade of Béarnian-dark hair to reveal the oval face and strong features that Darris had memorized, though he usually pictured her without the streaky tears. She wiped those away and raked her hair back in place with delicate, uncallused fingers. "There's something profoundly piercing and unshakable about the staves' disfavor. I thought I'd gotten over it. Now, I'm not sure I ever will." She squeezed Darris' hand with a smile that did not seem forced. "Thanks for your faith in me."

A wave of heat coursed through Darris at her touch, and he feared he might melt into a puddle on the bench. He returned the smile, and listened to himself say words that he didn't recall formulating. "I only spoke truth. Don't berate yourself for being too good to be neutral."

Matrinka nodded a silent promise to try, then changed the subject. "Oh, and I'm not getting married. They want me to, but they can't make me. I'm not ready."

Darris drew back, remaining beside Matrinka on the bench. "Why are they pressuring you?"

Matrinka shrugged. "I'm not sure. Apparently, they want more heirs."

Ra-khir finally joined the conversation, though whether truly out of inquisitiveness or just to remind the others of his presence, Darris did not know. "Why?" Since the question had an obvious answer that could seem insulting if not assumed, he modified, "I mean, why now?"

Matrinka looked at the speaker. "You know, since they started getting persistent about it, I've wondered the same thing." She turned her attention to Darris then. "Can I speak freely?"

Darris knew her well enough to understand the meaning of the question. She wanted to know if Ra-khir and Kevral could be trusted. His own discoveries and research gave him a certain answer. "Absolutely."

Matrinka did not hesitate further. "I've talked with some of my cousins, and I've yet to find anyone who's passed the test. I'm guessing few enough did that we can't afford to lose more, so they want us to make babies just in case."

Darris nodded vigorously. His own efforts had gained him similar information.

For the first time since the conversation had gone beyond introductions, Kevral added her piece. "There's something heir-related going on in the northeast, too."

"What do you mean?" Matrinka pressed for them all. Darris knew about the quiet caravan thrown together for a trip to Santagithi, but those involved had assured him it was a normal diplomatic mission.

"I've got a cousin who got sent there." Kevral paused. "Actually, a bit more distant than a cousin, but a relative in some way. Her name's Rantire." Kevral stopped speaking, as if finished.

Darris waited for the Renshai to continue.

Kevral looked around, pale brows arched in the expectant silence, as if surprised that she needed to say anything more. "If a Renshai goes, then a Béarnian heir has to be involved somehow."

Darris clapped a palm to his chin, irked that he had not made the connection himself. No heir that he knew of had accompanied the entourage. Then again, he had not paid it much heed, its routine nature inspiring little concern.

Ra-khir gave up his share of knowledge, adding to the realization that something more than procedure lay behind this mission. "Two knights got sent there, too." He glanced toward the sky, apparently to check the time, then sighed. "Excuse me. I have to go to practice now."

Darris placed a hand on the knight apprentice's shoulder to delay him. "Just a moment. There's something strange here, and I'd like to know exactly what."

The others mumbled agreement.

"Let's all gather as much information as we can about this and meet again at midday tomorrow."

"Somewhere more private, though," Matrinka added. "Say the Fox-meal Clearing?"

Though not an official name, Darris knew the location. He and Matrinka had many secret hideaways in the forest that they referred to by incidents, imaginings, or formations. They had once found a circle of feathers in a tiny meadow ringed by evergreens where a fox had eaten a pheasant. Though the feathers had long since blown away, they'd referred to the place as Fox-meal ever since. He clarified for Ra-khir. "That's the second woodland place I took you."

Ra-khir nodded, remembering. "I'll meet you there. Tomorrow." He bowed to Matrinka, then waved a formal parting to Darris and a less exuberant one to Kevral.

Darris watched Ra-khir go, concern forming an excited tingle in his chest. Something of import was happening at Béarn Castle. One way or another, he was going to find the details. And solve the problem.

Chapter 8

The Trap Sprung

What god could respect a man who died without a fight?

—Colbey Calistinsson

Twilight caught Béarn's diplomatic party on the Road of Kings, the legendary route by which an ancient Eastern Wizard rescued an infant heir and returned him, as an adult, to his proper place on Béarn's throne. The sun hovered, massive on the horizon, backlighting one of the myriad statues that marked the path. A Wizard's scrawny form etched darkness across the setting sun, the wolf at its heels casting a smaller, stranger shadow. Colors touched the western horizon, a rainbow trail that stalked the last edge of sun.

Antsy for a sword practice after a full day's ride, the Renshai, Rantire, marveled at the beauty nature ascribed to the dying. Each day expired in striking hues that drew poets and songsters irresistibly to its throes. Leaves flashed through sundry colors: their scarlet, ocher, and salmon garish testimony to the plain, green lives they lost. Her death, she vowed, would espouse all the glory that the gods granted its creations. Amid the musical clash of steel, the perfume of enemy blood jelling in her bronze hair, she would find the death in honor that every Renshai sought upon the battlefield.

Inside a coach that rattled along behind the mounted Renshai, the two diplomats discussed when and where to set up camp. Two servants steered the team of bays that hauled the coach, bells in the shape of bears jangling from the harnesses. Behind them, a wagonload of gifts for the king in Santagithi jounced beneath a tarpaulin. A matched pair of chestnut mares pulled this under the even hands of a third servant and whomever of the four Béarnian guardsmen had drawn his chance to rest. The other three rode on various sides of the procession: one in front and two beside. A pair of knights took up the rear, their white steeds like beacons through the greenery. Their horses high-stepped with smooth precision, as composed and somber as their masters. Rantire envied the beasts' responsiveness, conformation, and breeding; but she would not have traded the more natural, less conspicuous coloring of her dark brown gelding even for these near-perfect animals.

Irony tweaked a smile onto Rantire's features. Amid the chiming harnesses and rich-appearing vehicles, the arresting color of the knights' horses seemed trivial. The party's obvious wealth would draw the attention of every highwayman in the Westlands, but the king's writ would surely deter any thief that the vigilant sequence of guards did not. Any foolish enough to ignore both would find a quick death on the point of a Renshai or Béarnian sword.

Rantire's gray eyes missed little as their party traveled the road. Every passing merchant met her scrutiny, and she shifted her position around Béarn's procession to fully study the mercantile entourages. Nontrade related travelers were rare in any part of the Westlands, and they had passed only caravans en route, so far. She had seen no one and nothing that might form a threat to their cargo or their mission, nor did she expect to do so. Thieves bothered the trade routes rarely, finding better pickings within large cities or towns, and few who carried wealth lacked escort. Although Rantire's presence served no specific purpose until they acquired the missing heir, she maintained the wariness trained into her since birth. Despite its intended impression, this mission was anything but routine; and nothing would harm its purpose without slaying her first.

Rantire rode past a statue of a massive Béarnide brandishing an ax and riding a muscled stallion, a representation of the returning king. The Béarnian sculptors had fashioned every detail, from the man's bearing that defined regality, to the horse's shoes, to the individual tendons in its legs, bulging nearly to the point of caricature. Yet upkeep had grown lax in the century since the West had commissioned this spectacular project, a tribute to the restored king and his heroism in the war that had pitted Westlands against Eastlands. Mold limned every crease, and the warrior had sprouted a headful of ivy hair; tiny mushrooms poked red-brown caps through cracks.

A servant's command to the bay team first warned Rantire of their imminent stopping, followed swiftly by a shout from the leading Béarnian guard who rode in her wake. Pulling up her horse, Rantire turned to watch the coach and wagon drawn to the edge of the road. While the servants handled the horses and meals, and the guards and knights tended armor and uniforms, Rantire found a private clearing beyond sight yet near enough that she could hear the others should danger arise.

Rantire launched into her practice with an eager ferocity fueled by a long, boring journey, scarcely begun and already tedious. As if being Renshai did not set her apart enough, she was the party's only female. The Béarnian guards seemed uncomfortable in her presence, guarding their tongues and excluding her from their wagers about passersby or scenery. The Knights of Erythane kept to themselves, their exchanges with Béarnides, when necessary, always clipped and formal. The diplomats remained aloof from the guardsmen's games, and the servants found themselves too busy tending livestock, wagons, and men to pay the Renshai much heed. When their duties did bring them near her, they seemed cowering and fearful in a way they never did around Béarn's nobility. Rantire found it more comfortable for everyone when she handled her own gear and necessities, though she had sent her horse off to graze with the others.

As the *svergelse,* the Renshai name for sword figures practiced alone, progressed and Rantire's maneuvers became more complicated, the rest of the envoy disappeared. All normal sounds of camp-building became lost in the mishmash chorus of insects and frogs. Nothing seemed real but the sword in her hand and the faith in her heart. Like prayer, she dedicated her efforts to the goddess Sif and the goddess' son, Modi, who embodied battle wrath. The sword cut imaginary opponents, a silver blur in her fist. Her feet skimmed over the twisted weeds and grasses that survived in what little sunlight the trees permitted. Activity brought warmth to her limbs, as if the cool night air recoiled from the savagery of a Renshai's practice. The moon struck glittering patches through the branches, shedding light between puddled shadow and creating a million targets for the Renshai's killing strokes.

Yet, though Rantire's concentration on *svergelse* stole meaning from the rattles, laughter, and shouts of her companions, her mind registered sound and movement out of place. A light flickered through the darkness, nearly lost in her peripheral vision, and dispersed as swiftly as it appeared. Alone, Rantire might have dismissed it as a gleam of moonbeam off water on the road, brought to her sight by a motion of her own. Then, unfamiliar voices touched her hearing, whispers she would have lost beneath the rattle of leaves in the wind except for their musical lilt and a language unlike any she had heard. Another flash carved trunks black against tangled masses of foliage, then a grating noise cut the normal woodland fauna to fearful silence.

Sword still drawn, Rantire raced from the clearing as a shout of alarm bounced echoes through the forest. She sprinted for the camp, battle rage like fire in her veins, and something large thrashed toward her. She gathered momentum for a strike as the beast stumbled wildly into sight; a panicked horse floundered through knotted copses, its eyes white rings of terror. She pulled her stroke. The animal charged past, at the lead of a thundering herd she did not try to stop. Let servants chase the horses. She would find and defeat the horror that spooked them. She ran on toward the camp.

A half dozen strides brought her to the scene of the carnage. The wagon lay on its side, its tapestries, silks, and gemstones spilled across the muddy ground. Something had smashed the front of the coach to splinters, and a diplomat hung upside down from the wreckage, his stillness denying life. Nearer the road, the Béarnian guards and the knights swung madly at a densely muscled horse that reared to meet their attacks with hooves and teeth already smeared scarlet. The man on its back swung a battle ax that sent an unarmored Erythanian Knight skidding across the mold, cleaved nearly in half at the waist. A servant screamed, retching in horror, and became lost to sight beneath the flailing hooves.

"Modi!" Rantire charged with all the savagery her people were known for. She had eyes for no one but the enemy, but her scrutiny of man and beast missed nothing in the half a heartbeat between observation and attack. She knew this man and horse, had seen them only an hour before as inanimate stone decorating the Road of Kings.

The horse reeled to avoid a guardsman's sword, then lunged for its attacker with ears flat to its dappled gray head. No life looked out from empty eye sockets, and its hooves thudded to earth with all the power of the quaking stone they had once been. The guard twisted, rescuing his head from steel-shod hooves; but teeth clamped on his wrist with the sickening snap of breaking bone. The man screamed, jerking backward instinctively, wrist still clamped in the beast's flat teeth. The rider's ax sped toward the second knight's neck.

Rantire dove between knight and rider. Sword slammed against ax, and the strength of the king's likeness astounded Rantire. Impact lanced pain through her arms, wrenching tendons to the shoulder and hurling her sideways. The sword snapped, blade slamming the knight she had rescued. He gasped, staggering blindly, sword angled defensively between himself and the aberration. Again, the ax screamed toward him.

Unable to keep her balance, Rantire rolled. Agony pulsed, as yet unlocalized. "Modi!" Training resurfaced like instinct, the need to fight not despite the pain but because of it. She threw down the useless hilt that habit had forced her to cling to even through the fall and the pain. A quick glance found her another weapon near the body of a fallen Béarnide. Snatching it up as she ran, she charged back into the fray.

The knight straggled backward, breathing labored. Rantire crashed into him with her leading shoulder, sprawling him, placing herself into the path of the falling ax. This time she dodged it, not daring to parry. The blade grazed her skull, ringing agony to accompany her other wounds. Seizing the opening, she riposted. But the horse whirled on her then, foiling the opening against its rider. Hooves and teeth filled Rantire's vision, and she met the blank stare that made the creature seem more demon than horse. She felt the knight's leg against the back of hers and knew she had no space to jerk backward. Only one course remained, sure suicide, but she chose it with vicious complaisance. Diving between the stone-gray legs, she assessed in an instant. To kill, she needed to pierce the chest with all the strength that remained in her aching arms. Yet chance assured she would hit rib instead of flesh. Only the quick eye her *torke* had trained could save her and the three warriors still fighting.

One stroke. Rantire did not pause but bonded her will to the training she had embraced since birth. Gaze locked on the slight sag between ribs, she jammed her sword home. The thrust smashed pain through her injured shoulder. Then, the Renshai twists that precluded power parted muscle and lung. Blood frothed from the horse's nostrils, but it lacked even the wind to squeal. Rantire realized, with sudden horror, that she had no space to retreat. The massive gray would surely crush her as it collapsed.

Determination sparked to action. Rantire would die in battle, but not squashed beneath an enemy's death throes. As the animal stumbled, she flung herself against its abdomen, driving. The horse took a frantic step backward, forehooves cleaving air, then toppled rearward. As it fell, Rantire ripped out her sword and dove clear.

The statue horse crumpled, dumping its rider into an awkward heap of shouting madness. The remaining warriors charged the man-once-statue immediately. Three on one, all unmounted, Rantire had faith they could handle the battle. Ignoring the pain that throbbed through her head and shoulder, she turned her focus to other sounds.

Beneath the clang of the final battle and the moans of the dying, she believed she heard soft voices on the roadway. Then, the crash and rattle of brush seized her attention fully. Something huge rushed toward her. The tactics of these enemies and memory of the statues they had passed en route told her what this must be. Rantire turned her head back to the battle for a quick assessment. The knight and two Béarnian guards stabbed and parried the tireless attacks of the king's statue. Judging their skill in an instant, she felt certain they would triumph eventually though not without losses. A diplomat and two servants cowered beyond the coach wreckage, utterly useless. Left alone to face this new threat, Rantire smiled. She would meet the coming bear with courage and dignity or embarrass her heritage and *torke*.

Though it meant leaving the sight of her companions, Rantire charged the approaching animal, hoping to catch a glimpse of the source of the earlier light. There, she surmised, she would find the forces that unleashed statues into violence crueler than vengeance. If she discovered those who worked the magic, she hoped she could end the assassinations fully and finally.

Rantire plunged through the foliage toward rustling that gained volume with every step. Then, suddenly, a gap in the brush fully revealed the road and the figures standing on it. Rantire paused, estimating fifteen in the moment it took to notice them. Her mind registered all as adolescents, the impression coming from disproportionately long arms and legs. They wore robes and cloaks of unfamiliar design that did not distinguish gender. Hair that ranged from elder-white to mahogany flew freely in the breeze. Most stood in a line with lowered heads, their faces obscured and concentration intense. One paced behind the others, step child-light despite the murder he or she surely masterminded. A half dozen at the far end of the grouping carried curved swords thrust through glittering belts, gazes scanning the forest. One knelt in front of a puddle, staring into the depths and talking almost constantly. Rantire could not understand a word of a conversation that sounded more like music.

The transformed bear blustered through a nettled copse of berries, leaving Rantire an instant to decide. Without her to stop it, the bear would devastate the remainder of the party. Yet if she left the sorcerers alive, more statues turned flesh would follow until nothing remained of any of them. Placing her faith in the hope that killing users of magic would disenchant their creations, she plunged toward the people, howling a bloodcurdling cry of battle. Bears, she knew, hated loud noises. She hoped she would draw its attention as well.

The ranks broke instantly, long before she reached them. Several threw themselves backward. Nearly all their heads snapped up, revealing faces that gave an impression of youth and great age at once. Canted eyes held irises like polished gemstones of every hue, their marblelike regularity terrifyingly unnatural. Their sharp cheekbones jutted high in faces that seemed made for smiling, judging by their shape and the set of their creases.

The leader shouted commands that restored the line even before Rantire reached them. The six geared for battle charged in front of the others, meeting Rantire halfway across the moonlit road. Some chanted in a calm cadence that worried at Rantire's courage while it seemed to charge up that of her enemies. Three swords swept for her at once.

She ducked beneath the first, parried the second, and caught the third wielder a kick in the knee that sent him sprawling, sword carving a wild and harmless arc. Rantire's blade opened his throat as he fell.

Rantire recovered instantly, flicking her blade back into position to face the others. Blood splashed, an abnormal pink-red. Yet, to her surprise, the others did not press. They retreated slightly, shock and disbelief traced vividly upon their alien faces. Seizing the opening, Rantire lunged for an unprotected abdomen.

The leader shouted. The chanting changed to a high-pitched keening that hammered Rantire's ears. Her vision blurred, stealing accuracy. Her target scrambled aside, and dizziness crushed down on her. She fought the buzzing in her head that threatened her consciousness, deliberately concentrating on the pounding throb of the ax wound to ground herself in pain. She spun wildly, sword cutting a frantic circle of defense. Again they did not press, but Rantire felt her control slipping, as if plied with one too many drinks. She surged ponderously for an enemy and never knew whether or not that stroke fell. Her mind spiraled into empty darkness.

The hallways between the courtroom and the king's quarters had grown tediously familiar to Baltraine who knew how little sense it made for him to consult with a king as often asleep or unintelligible as lucid. He continued the charade from necessity. Should others learn how near death the king hovered, panic would surely ensue. In the subsequent confusion Baltraine could only guess what courtiers and peasants would demand or what effect that would have on the king-chosen regent and his family. Baltraine had worked too hard to lose everything now. Soon his smooth running of the kingdom and judgments in the courts would please enough to keep any malcontents under control. Once he rid himself of the knight-captain turned nuisance, all of the grumblings about a power-hungry prime minister stalling settlements would end.

Baltraine's routine visits to the king also gave him the opportunity to observe the patterns, cycles, and details of the king's muddled moments. He paid close heed to the herbs the master healer gave and their effects, intended and otherwise, on the king's various states. Books and cautious exper-

imentation taught him more. In addition, the frequent need
to interact with the sage's five scribes as individuals allowed
him to endear himself to them as well as assess their
strengths and weaknesses.

Three guards tromped routinely behind Baltraine and the
scribe as they paced the route they all knew too well. Their
noise masked any other farther up the corridor. Kedrin
would come this time, Baltraine felt certain. The Knight of
Erythane had tried too hard to catch him not to meet him in
the hallway when an invitation was extended. Baltraine
grinned inwardly at the thought. "Invitation" poorly described his insistence that he could spare no time or his
snide suggestion that Kedrin find him en route to the king as
he had once before. Baltraine had taken great pains to ensure
that only Kedrin heard; to the guards, it would appear that
the knight-captain delayed Baltraine's conference with the
king on his own initiative.

Kedrin's recognizable knife, stolen by the hired thief, now
rested in Baltraine's lefthand tunic pocket. The key to his
coming victory, it felt heavy and warm against his thigh.
Compunction prickled at Baltraine's conscience briefly. Still,
the knight had proved himself a dissenting seed that could
sprout at any moment to treason. *Best to dispose of him as
soon as possible.* Baltraine soothed his guilty nerves with rationalizations he only half believed. His bonds and loyalty to
Béarn were real, and anyone who drew them into question
deserved swift judgment.

As Baltraine turned the corner, he found Kedrin waiting,
as he knew he would. The knight-captain wore a grave expression that brooked no further delay or nonsense. The
white-blue eyes seemed as hard and dark as a tempest-
racked ocean. Well-tended red locks accentuated a solid jaw
and straight nose, features any woman might wish upon her
own man even without the majestic bearing and the stately
uniform that outlined sinews muscled for war. Such beauty,
Baltraine lamented, was wasted on inferiors not of noble
lineage. To him, the blue eyes seemed an unforgivable flaw,
the fine, light locks a mockery of Béarn's strong darkness.
The well-defined features should belong to one of royal
breeding.

Baltraine stopped cold at the sight of Kedrin, feigning surprise. "Knight-Captain. I ... um ... did you wish to speak
with me?"

Kedrin scowled, the game wearing thin. "You know I do."

"Yes," Baltraine acknowledged with a hesitation that made it seem as if he humored, not agreed with, the knight. "Well, then. I suppose I have a moment, if you must." He gestured for the scribe and guards to remain in place, as before, then headed up the hallway well within their vision. He kept his voice low so no one but Kedrin could hear. "What do you want this time?"

Baltraine's hostility did not escape Kedrin. The knight scowled, brows creased with irritation; but his tone betrayed no anger. "Lord, I wanted to commend your quick and full response to the needs of Béarn. I appreciate how swiftly you mobilized and sent the envoy."

The prime minister nodded in wary appreciation, uncertain whether true anticipation or only wishful thinking made him believe the other shoe had yet to fall. His hand slid to the knife secreted beneath his cloak, and his fingers massaged the hilt absently. His heart pounded a rapid cadence as understanding of trickery long-planned and -considered dominated his thoughts once more. Sweat trickled down his collar, and he realized the final moment of decision had arrived. One action on his part, whether taken or dismissed, would spark massive repercussions. The certainty with which he had designed the trap melted away now that he stood directly in his victim's presence. Guilt whittled at his confidence. Whatever Kedrin's faults, he had honorably dedicated his service to Béarn and had faithfully executed his duties. One more step and Baltraine would become culpable for the very treason he assigned the knight.

Kedrin cleared his throat, a sure sign he had not yet fully spoken his piece. "This seems the perfect time to call a meeting."

"A meeting?" The suggestion caught Baltraine off guard. "We just had a meeting."

Kedrin adjusted his tabard, though it already hung in perfect symmetry, as if clothes not man determined its position. "Now is the time to determine what we do next. Depending on the results of the expedition, we need to have contingency plans laid."

"You want us to hash out all the possible outcomes and make plans based on each?"

"Indeed."

The idea seemed madness to Baltraine, and all remorse for his vengeance disappeared. "There're endless possibilities."

Kedrin's ghostly eyes fixed on Baltraine's face. "True, if details are taken to extreme." The intimation that the prime minister tended to do so was a subtle insult that did not suit the knight's honor and surely indicated growing impatience otherwise well-hidden. "But there're only a few main categories."

"Is that so?" Baltraine kept his stance light despite his own flaring irritation. The impression he left scribe and guards would fully determine the success or failure of his snare. A mistake would cost him rank, happiness, and leadership of the kingdom. And, possibly, his life.

"Certainly." Kedrin spoke as if the whole should seem obvious. "They could not return. Santagithi could prove hostile. They could return with the heir. They could . . ."

Baltraine did not allow Kedrin to finish, hoping his rudeness would spur the knight-captain to recklessness. "I understand the possibilities, Kedrin." He deliberately avoided the other's title and hoped the persistent calmness that distant observers caused him to adopt provoked as much as his words. "Since when did you become a diplomat? You're paid to guard, parade, and add pomp to ceremonies, not to think. Not *ever* to think."

The nastiness of words and tone, especially without accompanying gesture or manner, momentarily struck the knight dumb, leaving Kedrin standing openmouthed. Warrior instincts drove him a menacing step forward.

Baltraine pounced on the opportunity. "By the way, I believe this is yours." Keeping his back to the guardsmen in the hallway, he drew Kedrin's knife and offered it, hilt first.

Kedrin accepted the weapon without consideration. His mouth clicked shut, and he showed the prime minister a crinkle-faced expression of surprise.

As the knight's hand closed over the hilt, Baltraine skittered sideways with a cry of alarm, fully exposing the blade to the Béarnides' view.

Reacting immediately, the guards charged. Baltraine screamed, a perfect simulation of innocent fear. "No! Don't! Think what you're doing!" Then the guardsmen arrived, easily hammering the knife from Kedrin's fist with the haft of a spear. One placed his person between threat and prime minister, bundling Baltraine to the safety of the hallway. The other two cornered Kedrin against a teak door. The knight surrendered easily, not bothering to speak a word against Baltraine or in his own defense.

Baltraine clung to his "rescuer," forcing a shiver that he hoped would pass for terror. The corners of his mouth started to tug into a triumphant smile, but he quickly schooled his expression to display only sober concern as the guards marched their prisoner toward detainment.

Rantire awoke to damp, spongy ground and the smell of leaf mold. As she did every morning, she achingly flexed muscles overtaxed during *svergelse,* but her left shoulder throbbed and ground beyond all reason. She attempted to switch position to take pressure from her injured shoulder. Her limbs did not obey. Something narrow as a ribbon and cottony soft ringed her wrists and ankles, but it did not bite into her flesh like rope. Then memory flooded back into her awakening senses. She had battled a band of strangers whose racial features fit no description she had ever heard. Worse, she had lost the battle and survived.

Guilt hammered Rantire, followed by self-directed anger. No Renshai worth the title could ever become a prisoner. She had fought with honor and should have died in glory in that battle. Yet, apparently, she had not. *A Renshai a prisoner of war.* The idea left a bitter taste in her mouth that no logic could banish. She had dishonored herself and her tribe. Her only hope lay in escaping her captors, then destroying them or dying in the attempt. For now, though, she needed to understand her predicament. Rantire opened her eyes and cautiously shook aside her yellow-brown hair.

The room was dark, but enough light penetrated a mesh doorway to reveal her surroundings. Vertical stripes on the walls gave the impression of wood paneling. She lay on mulched leaves, like the ground of a forest though evenly spread and patterned like carpet. Through the triangles formed by the bars of the door, she caught glimpses of manlike shadows etched against the light. Although the difference in illumination gave her the advantage of vision, she lay with her back mostly to the only exit or entrance her brief inspection uncovered. To look through, she would need to shift position and reveal her awakening. Eventually, she would do so, but not until her eyes had fully explored what they could without moving.

The ribbons that bound Rantire were white, faintly luminescent in the darkness. Though not tight enough to chafe or cut, they did not allow enough movement for her to explore them with her fingers. Her impressions came from vision and their feel against her wrists and naked ankles. Soft as silk, they seemed unlikely to hold against more than a few moments of struggling. Yet, her inability to loosen them with careful movements revealed a strength far out of proportion to size and composition. The knots seemed equally peculiar, dainty loops that would make sailors jeer in derision.

Having discerned as much as she could from her current position, Rantire dared cautious movement, wriggling to a far corner of her cell. The construction she had, at first, taken for lumber felt smooth, humid, and cold to the touch. *Stone,* she guessed, though she could not fathom why anyone would paint strong granite to appear like flimsy wood. For that matter, it seemed madness to bother to decorate a prison in any manner. Whoever had captured her came of a culture that defied any logic she could fathom. That realization brought a frown of displeasure. How did one escape captors insanely unpredictable?

Rantire recalled her battle on the Road of Kings, certain no weapon stroke had undone her. She had taken, delivered, and witnessed blows to the head before, and any that could have stolen her consciousness would have guaranteed pain, muddled thinking, and vomiting on awakening. But her thoughts were as clear as always. She knew only the agony of her injured shoulder, arm strain, a mild throb she could attribute to the grazing blow of the statue-king's ax, and the ordinary pain of a worthwhile practice.

Voices wafted to Rantire from the hallway, their words rapid, light, and incomprehensible. She twisted her head to the mesh doorway to discover several alien faces studying her through triangles more appropriate for a dog's kennel than a human's cell. Framed against light whose source Rantire could not see, they appeared even stranger than on the road, where urgency had limited scrutiny. Delicate oval faces balanced proportionately on slender necks. High, sharp cheekbones framed timeless features that possessed few wrinkles. Canted eyes, rounder and broader than any Rantire had ever seen, sported a variety of solid colors, without twinkle or blemish. Greens, aquas, reds, ambers, and blues studied her, all lacking variations in hue or the starlike core that many human eyes bore. Experience gave her an impression of blindness; surely no one could see through eyes like marbles. Yet, apparently, these people could.

Rantire stilled, locking her face into an angered pall despite her undignified position, hoping these foreigners would read sobriety as fearlessness. Their power over her did not frighten her, but their ability to steal honor from her death did. One way or another, she would find the glorious end in battle they had stolen from her with powers she could only attribute to magic. She listened while the strangers discussed her in a language that seemed closer to Renshai or Northern than any of the Westland tongues. Eastern, she had heard, sounded harsh and guttural, filled with deep-throated consonants that could not be enunciated without spitting and vowels that randomly varied in pronunciation. The musical tongue of the magic users did not fit the description.

The need to demand answers raged, but Rantire did not succumb. Observation might reveal the same information, accompanied by the advantage of their ignorance of the extent of her knowledge. Every detail that she divined on her own became a tool against them. With that in mind, she focused on their every word, seeking repetition and accompanying action to give clues to meaning. For now, it all seemed gibberish. Over time, she hoped, understanding would come. Every Renshai spoke at least the trading and Renshai tongues. Most, like Rantire, also knew Western and at least rudimentary Northern. Each new language, she had discovered, became easier to learn than the one before.

A louder voice funneled up a corridor, and all but one of the strangers scurried from Rantire's door. The Renshai remained in place, awaiting the speaker who, she believed, would prove a leader of the others.

Rantire listened for the booted footsteps of a soldier on stone, but no such sound wafted to her. Too late, she recalled the spongy floor that cushioned her. The speaker had arrived and was peering at her through the mesh, the same who had issued commands on the road. He sported heart-shaped lips and features similar to the others who had crowded in front of her cell. Alert, green eyes scrutinized her through neighboring triangles of metalwork, their steadfast color reminiscent of glazing. Thin, red-blond hair fell to slender shoulders that seemed more suitable to an adolescent girl. In fact,

Rantire now realized, all of the strangers had features she would normally consider androgynous; yet, for reasons she could not explain, she had no difficulty determining gender. Their line on the Road of Kings had contained equal numbers of males and females, yet only the former had carried weapons. All of those who had analyzed her awakening had been men or boys as well. Their ages, however, eluded her completely.

The newcomer spoke the trading tongue in a melodic singsong that put even the lilting Northern speech to shame. "My name is Dh'arlo'mé'aftris'ter Te'meer Braylth'ryn Amareth Fel-Krin." He seemed to have lapsed back into his native speech. Then he continued in trading, and Rantire realized he simply had an inconceivably long name. "Assuming you share the memory limitations of all humans, you may address me, and the other elves, simply as 'Lordship.' "

Stunned, Rantire lost her stolid mask. As far as any who followed the Northern gods believed, elves existed only in charming fairy stories to draw children to temple and faith. Those who clung to their infantile notions claimed elves existed on a separate world and never interacted with humans. Even the holy tales spoke only of elves alone or facing gods. The odd appearances, unpredictability, and behavioral eccentricities were consistent with the claim of this one of whose name she had caught only Dh'arlo'mé. Yet their ruthlessness and mayhem seemed the furthest thing in the world from the happy-go-lucky, capricious creatures her grandmother had described in bedtime stories.

Dh'arlo'mé continued to study Rantire, as if memorizing everything about her. "What's your name?" he asked.

His scrutiny awakened paranoia, and Rantire picked a Western name. "Call me Brenna." *Or "ladyship" will do.* She kept the last to herself; it seemed a bad time to antagonize him.

The elf accepted the name. "I'm going to ask a series of questions. Answer them fully, honestly, and quickly, and you will not suffer."

The obvious other side to the proposition sparked a frown from Rantire, and she took an instant dislike to the elf. "What happened to my companions?"

The sparse reddish brows rose, leaving a massive gap between eyes and forehead. "Did I choose words too long for a soldier to understand? I will ask the questions. You will answer."

Rantire's face flushed; the word "soldier" instead of "warrior" bothering her as much as the insult. "I understood you. Mutual cooperation will go a long way toward earning your answers." She deliberately chose a complicated way to make her point, thereby putting the insult to rest as well.

The elf's thin shoulders rose and fell in a gesture of grim dismissal. "I have no reason nor need to cooperate. Difficult or easy, I'll get my answers. Your fate is in your own hands. You decide whether or not you suffer along the way."

Rantire lay still, despising the helplessness of her position yet unwilling to give Dh'arlo'mé the satisfaction of watching a graceless struggle to sit. He would get no answers from her. Rantire discovered one light in the dark quagmire of her present situation. Apparently, the elves could not read her mind; otherwise, they would have no use for her responses. Therein lay her greatest strength.

Dh'arlo'mé did not await a retort but launched into her interrogation. "Who is leader of humans?"

The query seemed nonsensical. Each Northern tribe and all of the cities of the Westlands and Eastlands had a king who ruled a section of territory. In turn, every one of these myriad kingdoms answered to a higher power: the superior kingdom of the North in Nordmir, of the East in Stalmize, and of the West in Béarn. Even then, some peoples slipped through, such as the tribal barbarians in the West with their own customs and language that few outsiders had managed to breach. Rantire wondered what plans the elves had for such information, even should she give it, and could think of nothing positive. Obviously, they had designs on the human cities, ones she would never assist or foster in any way.

Rantire let her thoughts roam, as other details slipped to the fore and found their niche: The murders of Béarnian heirs in sloppy ways that made them difficult, then impossible, to pass off as accidents. The illnesses that seemed unlike any other in human history and affected only heirs. The ridiculous constructions of the building that held her prisoner, including stonework painted like paneling, a leafy carpet, and a cell door designed for animals smaller than humans. These latter, she guessed, had to do with elfin misinterpretation of human architecture. So far, the elves had gotten most of their information through glimpses, whether ordinary or magical. Now, apparently, they required direct information, knowledge they would not get from her. Their need, the general nature of the questions, and the cleanliness of her cell suggested they had captured no other human before her. Given the strength of their magic, that discovery surprised as well as pleased her. The elves' magic had caught her off guard on the Road of Kings. Now, she would use every Renshai mind-trick at her disposal to convince the elves that humans could resist their power.

The Renshai grimaced, envious of the quick wit of Colbey Calistinsson and some of her more intellectual cousins. They could concoct a reasonable story that would convince as well as thwart the elves and save themselves the agony. But Rantire knew she would stumble awkwardly should she attempt such a thing, and she worried that her tale might inadvertently endanger rather than rescue the West. Silence seemed the better weapon. At least it might buy her time. She rolled gray eyes to meet her captor's emerald glare and rose to a crouch with far less bumbling than she anticipated. "I choose the hard way."

"Very well." Dh'arlo'mé seemed unaffected by her decision. His expression remained stiff and essentially unreadable. "Bring on the torturer."

Chapter 9

Knight's Honor

Honor comes only of sticking to my own vows and dignity after lesser foemen have abandoned their own.

—Colbey Calistinsson

Courtiers filled every bench of Béarn's courtroom to capacity, leaving peasants to hover in the aisles. Guards threaded amidst them, forcing spectators against walls or seats when necessary, repeatedly clearing the central carpetway for the players in the trial.

Ra-khir sat near the back, squashed between Darris and Matrinka, fighting the restless need for movement. His head pounded, tears spoiled his vision, and a tingling in his chest made him fear for his own life as well as his father's. Shortly before entering the room, he had vomited. That relieved the pain in his gut temporarily, but it was returning in dangerously throbbing increments. Only Matrinka's lulling grip on his hand and Darris' soft voice kept him in place when compulsion prickled at him to batter a path through the crowd and plead his father's innocence in a scream that even the gods could hear. His assurances would prove meaningless. He had not witnessed the incident, had not yet even heard the details. He knew only that his father had been brought up on charges of treason; and, if found guilty, Knight-Captain Kedrin faced execution.

The whole seemed madness. Ra-khir doubted any man would sacrifice more for Béarn and its monarchy. He was outraged at the thought that anyone could accuse his father of such a crime, let alone take the possibility of blame seriously enough to demand a trial. He glanced to the front of the room where Prime Minister Baltraine sat upon his gilded chair on the dais, protected by a semicircle of half a dozen guards. The bard, Linndar, Darris' mother, held an attentive stance to his left while the captain of the Béarnian guards, Seiryn, stood to the right. More guards filled the area between the dais and the first row of spectators, keeping order among the otherwise milling chaos. The ten remaining Knights of Erythane, who had not accompanied the envoy, formed two rigid lines on either side of the dais. They presented a perfectly matched wedge dressed alike down to the set of their tabards and the jaunty angle of their swords in their sheaths.

Baltraine raised his hands to initiate the trial, and conversation gradually faded. As the last unobservant speakers recognized their indiscretion and fell silent, Baltraine spoke. "Friends, cousins, other citizens of Béarn. The time has come to try a man, Sir Kedrin Ramytan's son, for the crime of treason. Your presences here reinforce the severity of this accusation and its consequences should King Kohleran find him guilty. Therefore, I ask that you remain quiet so that I may hear all aspects of the case without missing any detail that might bias the information for or against Sir Kedrin. We cannot suffer traitors, nor the execution of innocents."

Baltraine paused, looking out over the crowd to reinforce his points. Ra-khir fidgeted like a child. His friends' consoling touches became more evident in response.

"Call the primary witness," Baltraine commanded.

The audience shifted, heads turning toward the double doors into the courtroom, directly across the room from the dais.

Linndar stepped forward, clearing her throat loudly, then nodded toward the prime minister. "That would be you, Lord."

"It would indeed," Baltraine accepted the burden as surprised heads snapped back toward the front to witness this unconventional beginning. "I was on my way to King Kohleran's room to discuss the day's business and judgments when Sir Kedrin intercepted me in the hallway. He had done this once before and been reprimanded for the interruption; so, of course, I met him with some impatience.

Nevertheless, he was a respected member of Béarn's entourage, the captain of Erythane's knights, so I agreed to converse with him. We moved up the corridor to speak privately. Once there, he accused me of not assisting strongly enough in decisions about Kohleran's successor. He had made this accusation once before, in front of the other ministers, so it did not catch me wholly by surprise. However, when I denied the accusation, reminding him of the many policies instituted by myself and the council, all of which King Kohleran had approved, he drew his knife and lunged at me. If not for the quick action of my guards, he might have killed me."

Despite Baltraine's insistence on silence, voices rose from every corner, the whole blending into an indecipherable cacophony. Ra-khir appreciated that even the nearest whispers disappeared into the hubbub. One condemnation of his father might send him over the edge, though whether into violent rage or despair, he did not dare to ponder. The prime minister's story defied logic. Ra-khir knew his father would never have disrupted a consultation with the king nor charged any official of Béarn with dishonesty. Those parts he could easily dismiss. Perhaps the prime minister and knight-captain had stumbled upon one another, an accident of location. Words had many interpretations, and Baltraine could have misunderstood or become offended by something innocent. But the drawing of a weapon went beyond believability, especially when Ra-khir alone knew Kedrin had discovered his ceremonial knife missing the previous evening. Ra-khir's mind raced in several directions at once to theories that ranged from lies to impersonation to treason of a different sort. Only one possibility never occurred to him: that his father was guilty of the charge.

The next four witnesses consisted of a scribe and three Béarnian guards, all of whom seemed reluctant to testify. Each told a similar story that confirmed Baltraine's tale, though none could comment on the actual conversation between prime minister and knight-captain. They verified the drawn knife and its unmistakable appearance; Béarn had awarded a similar one to each affirmed knight-captain for as long as any historian could remember. Each knife remained with its wielder, burned in his pyre then buried with his ashes. Ra-khir clung to his imposter theory, discarding the possibility that Baltraine had lied. No threat or payment

could turn three of Béarn's most loyal against a fellow soldier, and their slumped and somber demeanors displayed the
guards' pain vividly.

As the last of the guards departed, Baltraine shouted over
speculation the crowd could not keep to itself. "Call the last
witness."

Linndar complied. "Calling Knight-Captain Kedrin
Ramytan's son as witness."

Conversation vanished instantly, as if choked. Every gaze,
including Ra-khir's, turned to the doorway; and Kedrin's
proud figure strode down the central carpetway accompanied
by four Béarnian guardsmen. A wiry, nervous-looking
Béarnide led the group, wearing gray and purple street
clothes that clashed with the escort's royal blue and tan. Ra-
khir's heart felt as if it sank into his abdomen. No charlatan
this. The thick, red hair, aristocratic features, and piercing
blue-white eyes could not be duplicated. More so, no pre-
tender could simulate the dignity and grace of the knight-
captain's bearing. Every movement and step bespoke duty
and loyalty. No heavy burden of guilt weighted those grand
shoulders. He kept his head high, gaze straight and unwavering, and the stolid expression on his face revealed neither
fear nor smugness. He could have led his knights boldly into
battle in Béarn's defense and looked no different.

No one spoke in the moments it took for Kedrin to reach
the base of the dais. No coughs or sneezes shattered the stillness. Dizziness touched Ra-khir's senses before he realized
he was holding his breath, and the intensity of the silence
around him suggested that everyone had done the same.

Knight-Captain Kedrin executed a respectful bow, filled
with ancient custom and detail. The Béarnide in purple and
gray spoke for him. "Prime Minister Baltraine." He bowed,
then turned. "Gentlemen and ladies." He bowed again, then
spun back to face the dais. "Lord, my client does not wish
to speak in his defense but has agreed to answer questions.
Is that acceptable?"

Baltraine's attention whipped to Kedrin, as if trying to anticipate a trick. The knight returned his scrutiny mildly.
Baltraine shrugged at the peculiarity. "Proceed."

The man in purple and gray smoothed his garb, his face
ashen. Ra-khir whispered to Darris. "Who is he?"

"Lawyer," Darris returned. "He's the one they use for
people who don't request anyone specific to defend them."

Ra-khir nodded his understanding, confused by his father's lack of choice, which had become a decision in and of itself. He hoped Kedrin's replies would reveal his motivation.

The lawyer addressed Kedrin. "State your name and title, please."

The knight's voice rang in reply, filled with stately power and no trace of humiliation or remorse. "Captain Kedrin of Erythane, son of Ramytan and knight to the Erythanian and Béarnian kings: His Grace, King Humfreet, and His Majesty, King Kohleran."

The lawyer hesitated a moment, presumably to allow the length and prestige of the title to sink into the spectators' minds. "Would you please tell the court your version of the events that occurred yesterday afternoon."

Darris sighed, obviously put off by the lawyer's word choices but wisely remaining silent. Ra-khir could almost hear the bard's heir saying, "And they call *me* tedious," and appreciated that Darris kept the thought to himself at a time when Ra-khir had no attention to spare for anything but his father's fate.

"No," Kedrin said. "I will not."

The lawyer knotted his fingers, unnerved but apparently not surprised by his client's refusal to defend himself against accusations that would otherwise assure his death. "Why not?"

A year seemed to tick past while Kedrin drew breath to answer. "Because affirming my innocence would not be in Béarn's best interests."

"How so?" the lawyer pressed.

"Answering that would be equally contrary to Béarn's welfare."

"You would rather die . . ."

"I would."

". . . then say anything that might cause harm to Béarn."

"Yes."

The lawyer sighed, loudly enough to echo in the coiled silence. "You understand that your accuser will adjudicate your guilt or innocence in that he will present the facts to the king and return Kohleran's decision."

"I understand."

"Do you also know that, in such a circumstance, the law

allows for you to insist that a party not directly involved in the proceedings adjudicate in his place?"

A murmur swept through the audience, sounding like a roar after the intensity of the silence. Ra-khir latched his attention onto Baltraine, and because he was watching so closely he realized the prime minister had not known about this legal point. Clearly, the lawyer had evoked an old prerogative lost to obscurity since such a situation probably had not arisen for decades or centuries, if ever.

Kedrin barely moved. "I did not know such law exists. However, I see no reason to invoke it. King Kohleran trusts his prime minister implicitly, so how could I do less? Lord Baltraine, too, would do nothing he believed was outside the best interests of Béarn."

The lawyer stared, surprised, for longer than decorum allowed. Gradually, he awakened from his trance to ask the captain one last question. "Knight-Captain, did you commit an act of treason?"

Kedrin hesitated nearly as long before replying. "That is for King Kohleran to decide."

"Thank you," the lawyer said, though whether to Baltraine, the spectators, or Kedrin was unclear.

Baltraine reclaimed the floor as lawyer and client prepared to leave. "While I am appreciative of Sir Kedrin's faith, I believe it would serve justice better if a scribe accompanied me to the king's chamber and ascertained that I did not inadvertently bias my presentation. He could also witness the king's decision, as the law decrees."

Whispers and a polite smattering of applause met this proclamation.

Ra-khir remained rooted in place as his father and the entourage trod back up the aisle carpet and out the courtroom doors. Kedrin's few words left him little to ponder, yet Ra-khir felt certain he would find the answers if he only studied the situation long enough. Terror, rage, and uncertainty battled within him, making coherent thought difficult; but he concentrated on the story Baltraine had told, the facts he already knew, and his father's taciturn replies.

No flash of insight heralded an answer, but Ra-khir's mind worried the matter even as each knight took the floor to describe Kedrin's long dedication to his post and to his kings. Though honored by his father's deeds of heroism and allegiance, the litanies flowed past Ra-khir, mostly unheard.

He already loved Kedrin, and the long-winded speeches seemed more tedious than helpful. Gradually, though, truth spun a single scenario in Ra-khir's head, based on the kernel of unshakable understanding of Kedrin's innocence. Loyal to Béarn and her king, Kedrin had chosen death over allowing mistrust and disfavor to fall on Kohleran's chosen regent. Apparently, the captain believed that, in all circumstances but this one, Baltraine would act in Béarn's best interests. But Baltraine *was* lying. No other explanation fit. Ra-khir held the final piece to the puzzle, the knowledge that his father did not have the knife in his possession on the day of the so-called act of treason. Now he knew: Baltraine did.

Yet Ra-khir could do nothing with the answer. Even if he convinced the audience of the truth, the final ruling still rested in Baltraine's hands by his father's own decree. The repercussions that would follow Ra-khir's revelation, ones Kedrin had already considered and deemed worse than his own unjust execution, could devastate Béarn. The loss of faith in King Kohleran's regent might lash Béarn's citizens into a froth of civil war from which they would never recover. The weakness and schisms that followed would open the king's city to her enemies. The resulting upheaval was frightening to consider, even in a theoretical way. To undermine Kedrin's decision would besmirch his honor.

Honor meant everything to the Knights of Erythane, to Kedrin more than any other. Ra-khir discovered no action that could display his father's innocence and rescue his honor as well as his life. One without the other meant nothing. No good could come of the selfish desire to win Kedrin back only to have Béarn fall and his father suicide in shame. Still, Ra-khir could not let go, could not surrender his father without a fight.

Baltraine's heart pounded, blood throbbing through his head like a drumbeat as he marched somberly through the hallways toward King Kohleran's room. The lawyer had raised a point of law so archaic that even Baltraine's meticulous studies had missed it. Only Kedrin's fanatical sense of honor had rescued Baltraine's plot from possible disaster. He trusted his presentation and witnesses, as well as the lack of defense, to convince the courtiers, peasants, and king. Still, he dared not allow Kohleran to judge this case with clear-headed justice. His respect for the Knights of Erythane and their captain would interfere.

Four guards and a scribe named Lakorfin accompanied Baltraine as he shuffled past grand, historical scenes, painted and carved by Béarn's finest artists through the centuries. Baltraine saw none of it. His thoughts riveted on the words he had spoken and their consequences at a time when he had expected to focus only on upcoming events. From the start, he had planned to bring a scribe as a witness, though it seemed unnecessary and simpler to work alone. A society based on absolute trust for a single ruler, sanctioned by gods, little understood suspicion; and Kedrin's faith in the king's regent had surely quelled any remaining doubts. Nevertheless, Baltraine insisted on a witness now to avoid future speculation. As knowledge of the king's deterioration and the lack of a suitable heir became more common, the populace would grow more cynical. It only made sense to snuff all possible sparks of mistrust before they could begin to smolder.

Careful preparation, not impulse, had brought Baltraine this far. He had deliberately scheduled the trial on a day Lakorfin held courtroom duty because the young man had proven himself malleable, reverent of Baltraine, and easily daunted. Baltraine had given King Kohleran a dose of a painkiller that dampened his voice to a shaky whisper and awakened him in a slow-witted state. Though alert enough to respond appropriately to questions, the king would prove directable, would parrot formalities or recent conversation, and would forget most of the events when he next awakened—including having taken the herb.

Just before he left King Kohleran to attend court, Baltraine had detailed the events leading up to the trial, substituting a fringe-noble soldier for Kedrin. Under the guise of anticipating his king's need to consider the severity of the crime, and its punishment, Baltraine had left a book for the king to peruse while the painkiller took hold. Now Baltraine had little choice but to trust in the situation he had created and to counter unforeseen details. He drove all thought of the courtroom from his mind, fought the nervousness that unsettled his stomach, and steeled himself for the intense concentration required.

When Baltraine reached the door to King Kohleran's room, he waved the guards aside. The four stationed themselves stiffly along the wall as Baltraine tripped the latch, ushered Lakorfin through, and followed the young scribe. The stench of sickness slammed Baltraine suddenly, intensifying his queasiness. His stomach heaved, and he gasped down a burning mouthful of bile. Desperately, he regained control of his gut. Despising the taste left on his tongue, he managed a thick, "Good morning, Your Majesty."

Baltraine took a position at the king's side, and Lakorfin eased anxiously up beside him. He had to strain to hear Kohleran's breathy reply, "Good morning."

Baltraine and Lakorfin bowed, the boy's head nearly touching the floor. Only then did Baltraine look directly at the sallow, withered features of his king. Kohleran's skin sagged into narrow wrinkles as fine as parchment. "Do you feel well enough to judge, Sire?"

"Well enough to judge," Kohleran sent back in a whisper, the echoing not unexpected.

Believing it safer not to indulge in small talk, Baltraine launched into his story. He substituted "the accused" for Kedrin and interchangeably used "me" and "the accuser" for himself as the situation warranted. He strove to keep his account as accurate as possible, quoting whenever he recalled exact words and summarizing when those failed him or required referral to Kedrin by name or title. He mentioned the Knights of Erythane only once, collectively calling them the "accused's peers." As he spoke, Baltraine glanced occasionally at Lakorfin, as if to ascertain that he was keeping the details impartial. Each time, Lakorfin gave him a shy, encouraging nod.

Finally, Baltraine reached the end. He met Kohleran's watery eyes, the yellowing of the whites and the paling of the irises by mucus blurring the whole into puddled shadow.

The king said nothing, only stared at Baltraine as if waiting for him to continue.

Baltraine did not allow the lapse to grow prolonged. Such would cast suspicion on the king's mental state. "Majesty, it's time for your judgment. Is the accused guilty of the crime of assaulting the king's regent?"

"Guilty," Kohleran repeated carefully. He coughed wetly, though the words that followed emerged equally rattly and thin. "Guilty of the crime."

Though a plain answer for such a lofty decision, it would

serve Baltraine. Lakorfin lowered his head sadly. Though inevitable, the conclusion seemed nonetheless grim.

"Guilty," Baltraine repeated, studying the king as if to reaffirm. He glanced at Lakorfin, who nodded to indicate he had heard the pronouncement.

"And the punishment for high treason?" Baltraine held his breath. Success or failure rode on the king's answer. Béarn's kings and queens were renowned for their mercy. The most famous, Sterrane, had never handed down a death sentence, though traitors nearly destroyed the royal line. The bards sang of a devoted friend who created personal reasons to kill Sterrane's enemies, thereby rescuing the kingdom from its king's compassion. Monarchs since that time had found rare reason for execution. Some had ordered them, and some had not. Until now, no capital offense had occurred during Kohleran's reign.

"The punishment for high treason . . ." King Kohleran repeated, running a hand through his hair as if to physically clear his head. He stiffened, and clarity seemed to burn through the filmy eyes.

Baltraine held his breath, unmoving.

Then King Kohleran gasped in a long breath, and the glassiness returned. As if on cue, he quoted the book Baltraine had given him, ". . . must prove a permanent solution. The guilty party cannot have the opportunity, through intention or accident, to come into the presence of royalty again." The king's brow lapsed into pensive creases, as if he could not understand the origin of the words he had spoken.

"Thank you, Your Majesty." Baltraine did not give the king time for further consideration. "We don't envy your difficult decision, and we will carry out the verdict and sentence you decreed." He herded Lakorfin toward the door, clearing his own throat to cover the soft drawing of breath that indicated the king had more to say.

The scribe had already emerged into the hallway and Baltraine had nearly escaped through the door when the wheeze of Kohleran's voice trickled into his ears like the last fading notes of a song. "I need more time . . ."

Baltraine closed the door, blotting out the words. A glance toward Lakorfin and the guards showed no indication that they had heard that final whisper. Soon, the king would drift off to sleep, his judgment and Baltraine's rudeness forgotten.

An unexpected pang of remorse stabbed through Baltraine

as he, Lakorfin, and the guards headed back to the court-room.

Ra-khir worried the problem during Baltraine's absence. The roar of speculation fell on ears deafened to external sound, and any words spoken by Ra-khir's friends became similarly lost. Hypnotized by his own unwinnable position and the ideas that poked and analyzed every action, he might have become a statue for all the attention he paid the world around him. When Baltraine returned, Ra-khir was still searching for an answer.

The audience's drop into silence broke Ra-khir's trance the way their shouts and comments had not. Baltraine had retaken his position on the chair, surrounded by his guards; and the sage's scribe fidgeted at his right hand near Captain Seiryn. Kedrin and his escort, including the lawyer, had returned to their places at the base of the dais. Baltraine rose, his manner as solemn as a tolling bell. He spoke, tone grave, "It is the feeling of our beloved monarch, King Kohleran, that an act of treason was committed in his castle yesterday afternoon."

The scribe confirmed the verdict with an exaggerated nod.

Baltraine directed his final comment to Kedrin, gaze trained on the knight as if no other in the room existed. "You are sentenced to death by poisoning tomorrow."

Baltraine turned, anything more that he might have said drowned beneath the ensuing tumult. Kedrin was swept from the room. Courtiers rose. Peasants shuffled toward the door. Darris nudged Ra-khir. "Do it," he whispered loudly.

Ra-khir stared into hazel eyes that seemed to pierce his head despite their softness. "Do what?"

"Talk! Say what you need to say, gods damn you, or you'll despise yourself for eternity. Speak your piece before it's too late, Ra-khir Kedrin's son, or I'll do it for you."

The tone of the bard's heir charged Ra-khir with the final impetus he needed. He had planned to shove, swim, and crawl his way to the dais before Baltraine's return, then lost all time in the struggle for words and direction. "It's already too late! I'll never get through this crowd."

"Through it, Hel!" Darris leaped onto his chair, strumming an earsplitting discord on his mandolin that froze every person in his or her tracks and demanded attention.

Ra-khir required no further coaxing. He clambered onto

his own seat as Darris relinquished the position to him. His concern over finding words that would not come disappeared. He spoke from the heart, true to his father's honor . . . and to his own.

Baltraine froze as the musician attracted the crowd's interest and Ra-khir launched into his unexpected and belated litany.

"Béarnides! I am Ra-khir. Sir Kedrin's son."

Though simple and remarkably unadorned compared to diplomats and full-fledged knights, the youngster's pronouncement caught the attention of every man and woman. Among peasants, the straightforward delivery of one unused to public speaking might prove more asset than handicap. "I lost my father today. . . ." The proud voice cracked, reeking of tears withheld and sorrow that touched every heart, Baltraine's included. "Just another judgment to some. To me an agony that will haunt my every thought, every sight, every word, and every action through eternity. I cannot let that go without saying something. Please, hear me out, just this once. Then you can all go home to your own families and do as you always do as if nothing happened here today."

Baltraine listened to Ra-khir's words with an intensity that bordered on dread. He hated tension, though it always heightened his intellect. Common sense told him that interrupting the boy while he held the sympathy of all would turn Béarn against himself. No choice remained but to let the child speak and hope the citizens' trust in their king would carry them beyond the grief Ra-khir shared.

"When I was small, my mother took me away, told horrible lies about Kedrin, and forced another father on me." Unable to hold back any longer, Ra-khir lost control. Though too far to see the tears, Baltraine witnessed cnough to assure him of their presence: sobbing breaths that made speaking more difficult, the occasional need to wipe reddened cheeks, eyes that faded to red blurs of distress. The crowd remained silent, latching onto every word. "My father never denied the evil my mother accused him of. To do so would have done nothing but confused me and tortured me with the constant struggle of wondering who to love and who to hate. He suffered for me, letting her nastiness shred his life and reputation, if it would, to spare me a moment of pain. That's the kind of man my father is."

Ra-khir glanced about wildly, trembling, as if suddenly realizing he addressed hundreds of people. He swallowed hard.

Baltraine remained in place, allowing the youngster to speak, desperately anticipating. Affairs of city and court had occupied him fully, and he had not realized that Kedrin had dragged his child to Béarn. Surely, Ra-khir knew someone had stolen his father's knife. For now, at least, he held the crowd's compassion. Should he mention such an absurdity, they might believe him, turning the tables on Baltraine's plot. The possibility of discovery had not escaped the prime minister in the planning stages, and he had prepared contingencies. Ra-khir, however, he had not foreseen, nor the power of a young man's love for his father.

"I saw my father return from a battle against raiding pirates with a fresh wound that stained through bandages and colored his uniform black. Yet he wept openly for the death of a patriot lost in the battle, a faithful, young Béarnide who had given his life for all of you. His own injuries and pain did not matter. That's the kind of man my father is." Ra-khir lowered his head. "The healers said he refused their aid until all his men got tended first. And that's the kind of man my father is."

"Every day of his young life, my father struggled and practiced until his muscles ached to become the best knight he could. To serve Béarn. And Erythane. In that order. Every day of his adult life, he trained more knights to protect all of us and our families. And everything he did, he did with honor. That's the kind of man my father is." Ra-khir lowered his head and joined the audience's silence.

Baltraine waited with the others, heart hammering but expression betraying nothing but pity. He had come too far to lose control now. He would need to speak next, and he gathered the words needed to evoke the natural loyalty every noble and peasant held for their beloved king. The judgment had already come down from on high. Yet, Baltraine surmised, he would need to find some balm to assuage the guilt of every man and woman who had planned to return home and gossip about the incident in the courtroom this day. So far, Ra-khir had granted no opening for compromise, had presented no contingencies, feasible or otherwise. Baltraine took some comfort from the realization that the child had mentioned nothing of the knife. He hoped that the boy did not know about its disappearance or that the father's grandiose honor would keep the son silent as well.

Apparently, Ra-khir had not finished. He glanced to someone nearby for support, probably whoever had sounded the horrific chord that opened the air for Ra-khir to speak. "Neither my father nor I would question the judgment of our king. If King Kohleran, may he reign forever in happiness and peace, decrees my father guilty of treason, then he is so."

Son like father. Baltraine resorted to an ancient cliché, glad that the knight's overbearing code would work in his favor again.

"I simply wonder if he should give the same punishment to one who has served so faithfully as to some despicable renegade who raises armies to slaughter our innocents in droves." Ra-khir finally turned the floor back to Baltraine. The knight-in-training looked as pale and wobbly as the ailing king.

Baltraine's mind raced, the seriousness of situation and decision legitimately giving him the time to think. Lifelong imprisonment or banishment would serve as the king's "permanent solution" as well as death. Baltraine had trusted rumor, his opening statements, and his pronouncement of execution to keep Lakorfin's thoughts from these other possibilities. Now Ra-khir had offered a settlement the prime minister did not dare to dismiss out of hand. A simple promise against his honor would hold Kedrin to either of those options and keep him out of Baltraine's way. The lighter sentence, and the mercy he would therefore show guiltless Ra-khir, would soothe many consciences, including his own. Something in Ra-khir's words, stance, and manner convinced him that the child could have mentioned the missing knife but did not. It only seemed fair to meet such unspoken compromise partway.

As Baltraine cleared his throat to speak, he discovered the best reason of all to keep Knight-Captain Kedrin alive, one that would enhance his own power even long after the new king took the throne. This thought turned Ra-khir's suggestion to foregone conclusion.

Baltraine rose, forcing a quaver into his voice. "Thank you, Ra-khir Kedrin's son, for rescuing Béarn from a tragic mistake."

Sobs racked the audience, as those most moved by Ra-khir's words loosed pent up breath or tears in hysterical relief. Ra-khir stiffened, the sudden movement nearly knocking him from his chair.

Baltraine's lie came easily, a skill of which he was not proud. "King Kohleran rendered the guilty verdict. When it came to sentencing, he spoke riddles that I now believe I misunderstood. He asked for a permanent penalty. In the name of fairness, I chose the standard punishment for treason; yet now I do not believe our king intended that at all. With your help, the meaning has become manifest." Baltraine cleared his throat again and continued in a loud voice reserved for judgments and proclamations. "Please bring back Sir Kedrin so that I can amend sentencing."

Béarnides clogged the exit, having prepared to leave prior to Ra-khir's speech. Guards opened the pathway with brisk shoves and gruff commands, and one slipped out to relay Baltraine's order.

Gradually, an opening appeared in front of the doors. Moments dragged by, the suspense of Baltraine's new sentencing a strain on all. Finally, the prisoner's guards reappeared, escorting a bewildered Kedrin between them. They traversed the carpet at a mercifully snappy pace, though not quickly enough for some. The roar of the audience rose in cycles as those too impatient clambered to become the first to tell Kedrin he would live. Individual comments got swallowed in the noise, and Kedrin's features still bunched in perplexity as he came directly before the dais again.

"Knight-Captain," Baltraine said.

Kedrin acknowledged Baltraine with a respectful bow.

"Your son, and the people of Béarn, have convinced me that your sentencing was too harsh. Instead, you will spend the rest of your natural life in Béarn's dungeon."

Applause accompanied Baltraine's words, but he remained standing, unfinished. "You will keep your title and position."

Gasps and muttered comments swept the crowd, followed by more vigorous clapping.

Baltraine held his smile. His new plan hinged on keeping Kedrin the knight-captain. That it also made him seem more lenient and compassionate was a bonus he appreciated. "Others will need to assume your day-to-day duties, of course, but will consult with you. Further details will be worked out to the satisfaction of King Kohleran and his ministers. You're dismissed."

With appropriate pomp, the guards again led Kedrin from the room. This time, the knight-captain paused long enough to execute a grand gesture of honor to his son. Only the three of them understood. For all his nervousness and lack of grandiloquence, Ra-khir had managed to rescue his father's life without sacrificing his honor. Kedrin understood and appreciated that effort as few others could.

Baltraine watched the father leave, finally allowing the slight smile to creep onto his face. Similar ones decorated so many countenances now, though those came of relief and, he hoped, renewed trust in and gladness over their king's regent. Only Baltraine's held the joy of personal gain. Kedrin's controlled power turned him into a pawn. Had he been executed, Erythane would have selected his replacement from among the knights. With Kedrin imprisoned, Baltraine could place his own Béarnian choice into power, a man who would relay Kedrin's commands. Baltraine had not yet decided who, but he would select a man of physical strength and unbudgeable loyalty not only to Béarn, but to Baltraine. The arrangement would serve for as long as Kedrin remained alive, just as Baltraine's current power lasted so long as the healers prolonged Kohleran's illness. Yet, where Baltraine would soon need to sacrifice his rulership to the heir for the good of the kingdom he loved, his power over Erythane's knights could last indefinitely. The support of Béarn's citizens, which he now held absolutely, would serve him well.

Baltraine's grin widened.

Chapter 10

The Torturer

A man is as strong as he allows himself to be, and no more.

—*Colbey Calistinsson*

The word "torturer" evoked images of a massive, ugly-faced man with a permanent leer of sadistic pleasure; but the elf who answered Dh'arlo'mé's summons could easily become lost among his peers. He studied Rantire through glossy sapphire eyes, wearing an unfamiliar expression she could only describe as quizzical. White hair fell to his shoulders in thin, soft waves. His dainty features could have adorned a child's beloved doll.

The other elves retreated beyond Rantire's sight, yet she could still hear them exchanging conversation in light, high-pitched bursts of their strange language. When she compared their phrases and accent to Northern rather than the more familiar trading tongue, she found a basis for beginning to interpret their lyrical speech. Yet, for now, she found the torturer's presence too absorbing to concentrate closely on words. She had heard gates click into place as the elves left her presence, but the layout of the prison still eluded her. She found little basis on which to surmise; even the architecture of her cell made little sense to her human-rooted logic.

The torturer said something, glancing over his shoulder as he spoke. After a moment, another elf joined him. Also male, this one seemed cautious to the point of paranoia, keeping the torturer between himself and Rantire's door and flinching at every sound that rumbled or clinked through the corridors. When the torturer came directly up to Rantire's door and spoke in the trading speech, the other elf tensed in a startled crouch.

"We just look at answers for basic questions." The torturer's human speech lacked the fluency of Dh'arlo'mé's, and his musical accent rendered it almost incomprehensible. "You tell to me, we not hurt at you. Stop anytime you tell to me answers. Understand of me?"

Rantire nodded carefully, testing her bonds and anticipating transfer to a room with devices as inscrutable as magic. She guessed communication might prove more difficult than Dh'arlo'mé's articulation had initially suggested, but she understood this elf's speech well enough to catch the gist of his questions. His ability or lack with the trading tongue did not matter. Whatever the question, she would not answer, at least not without assuring that her words would have no adverse effect on anyone but the elves themselves. She had adjusted to the presence of the otherworld ropes that limited movement but did not cause pain. Trial and error revealed she did not have the strength to break them, yet their benign nature allowed experimentation. She could move her arms in a full arc as long as she kept her wrists together. She could stand but not walk, although she believed she might manage a jump.

The torturer checked to his right, as if for reassurance. Rantire could not see if he received it; but, when he returned his attention to her, he seemed more confident. "I do not wish hurt to you. You answer, no hurt to you."

Rantire blinked, bewildered by the preamble. The gentleness with which the other approached inflicting screaming agony seemed impossible, especially after Dh'arlo'mé's intimidation. Already tensed for sudden attack and steeled for punishment, she considered the elves' tactics. *Is he trying to lull me off my guard? Does he think his mercy after threats will make me warm to, even befriend, him? Is this a part of the torture?* No answers came, and Rantire dropped the speculation, seeing no means to prepare for strategy that defied common sense as fully as everything else about the elves. She had little choice but to remain quietly defensive until she learned what she could about elves and their purposes. And to seize whatever openings they left for escape.

Rantire's first came almost immediately. The torturer fitted a bulbous key into the lock of her cell door and twisted. The tumblers gave with a crisp sliding sound that scarcely resembled the anticipated click. The door swung open toward Rantire, and the torturer stepped inside. As he reached to close the door behind him, Rantire sprang, hands clamped and swinging. Her shoulder slammed into his chest, and she met far less mass than she expected. Her hands crashed down on his head. Without a sound, he plummeted, tangled into Rantire's dive for freedom. They hit the ground in a snarl of arms and legs. Rantire rolled free, lumbering awkwardly down the corridor on hands and knees.

The other elf sprinted in the opposite direction, shouting wildly. Rantire saw a closed mesh gate ahead and a sea of elfin legs. She cursed her luck, wasting a moment to look behind her. The elf ran toward a similar barrier, also mobbed by peers. More cells lined the hallway, all but one as clean as her own. She did not pause to study the last, gaining an impression of bloodstains as she sped past. Instead, she trained her gaze on the gateway and the mass of elves beyond it. *Trapped.* Rantire continued to crawl, features fiercely determined and simulating madness. She had two choices now: retire meekly to her cage or battle her way through metal bars and an army of elves. She would not lower herself to the former action, thus committing herself to a blind, futile charge. She hurled herself at the gate.

Elves scurried backward with a quickness and grace that belied their gawky-adolescent appearances. Rantire jarred against metal with a rattle that echoed down the corridor. The gate gave only slightly, then sprang back into position. The elves studied her in a strange silence, broken suddenly by Dh'arlo'mé's command from the back.

At the sound of his voice, the elves snapped to attention, squaring into lines. The crooning Rantire had heard on the Road of Kings began again.

"Magic." Rantire muttered the word like a curse, not even trying to guess what would follow. Instead she channeled her energies into a single action: breaking through before the elves overpowered or killed her. Repeatedly, she threw her body at the mesh. Each time, the gate quivered, more flexible than human-worked steel, then dropped back into perfect alignment. Her efforts accomplished nothing except to aggravate the strained muscles in her arms and the dull buzz of the head injury she had sustained in the battle.

Dh'arlo'mé prattled over the elfin chant, his words harsher in tone and syllable than the melodic elfin-speak. The ropes at Rantire's wrists and ankles grew warm. At first, she believed exertion accounted for the change. Sweat trickled from her brow and stained her tunic in patches. Surely the ropes had grown sodden, though they felt more dryly heated than wet. Rantire continued to fling herself at the gate, even long after she knew it gained her nothing.

Gradually, Rantire's bonds grew hotter until they became a burning agony she could no longer ignore. "Modi!" she growled through gritted teeth, channeling the pain into anger and will to fight. But the enemy held a solidity she could not breach, though she tried even long after agony drove her to mindless motion and, eventually, to unconsciousness.

Rantire awakened to a dull throbbing in her arms that ached beyond the older muscle pain. A restless need to rescue her arms became an obsession, and she tried before awareness fully returned. Her arms would not obey her. She snapped her eyes open. The ceiling consisted of woodlike paneling that, she reminded herself, was actually painted stone. The floor looked similar, and it had warmed to her body heat. To either side, the walls were made of the same striped granite, but the one at her head was wooden and the one at her feet held a carpet that reeked of mildew and damp. The ceiling was composed of the mesh bars she recognized as elfin-work. Rantire's mind registered this arrangement as too odd, and her eyes reoriented to a more logical perspective. She was not lying supine as she'd first assumed but standing, her weight supported by her arms and the rope at her wrists. A hook passed between her hands and beneath the rope, suspending her just high enough that her feet could hardly touch the ground. She shifted her weight to her toes and managed to take some of the pressure from her arms, though they still tingled and throbbed from lack of circulation.

The familiarity of the pain soothed even as its presence charged the need to fight that seemed as much reflex as training. She grew wary, watching through the bars for movement, more angry with herself now than when she discovered she had not died in the battle. She had made a massive and amateur mistake. Always her *torke* had chided her for impatience. Now that fault might well prove the means for her own dishonorable destruction. One of the primary lessons of the Renshai raced through her thoughts: "Be patient. Find the weak point, and use it." Impulsiveness had stolen that option from her. She had acted at first opportunity, without fully exploring her options or the enemy's defenses. She would pay for that, she felt certain, with heightened security that even a Renshai might not breach. The rest of the lesson followed naturally: "If you find no weak point, create it." She would do so, when the time came, by gathering as much information about her captors as possible and finding a way to turn it against them. Renshai prayed with violence for strength and guidance, never mercy or salvation. In her current situation, it never occurred to Rantire to rely on anyone or thing other than her own wits and martial skill.

Shortly after Rantire's awakening, the torturer returned to peer at her through the bars. His presence surprised her. She had not stopped to check how badly her attack injured him. In the heat of escape, it had not mattered to her whether or not one elf lived or died. She had believed she'd hit him hard enough to kill him or, at least, inflict a ringing headache; but, in the scramble, she had apparently not landed as hard a blow as she thought. Either that, or elves handled injuries better than humans. Their youth-lightness suggested just the opposite, but nothing seemed quite right about these creatures from legend.

Meeting her gaze briefly with his canted, sapphire eyes, the torturer tossed a comment over his shoulder that Rantire tucked away in her memory as meaning something on the order of "she's awake." On further consideration, the term *minkelik* seemed inappropriately complicated for a simple pronoun, so she amended her translation to "the human's awake." She waited for the elf to address her directly.

A reply wafted from the sidelines, then the torturer switched to his odd rendition of the trading tongue. "So sudden and violent all humans?"

Several answers came to Rantire's head, most intensely sarcastic. She considered the possibility that what seemed like a personal affront might actually be one of the torturer's questions. She saw advantage in convincing the elves that humans would prove more difficult to confront than they believed. At least, it might make them reconsider any plans to stir war on a grand scale. "Me? Sudden? Violent? I'm just a woman." The self-aspersion proved difficult. Had anyone else referred to her as *"just* a woman," he would not have done so a second time.

"Woman?" the torturer repeated, emphasizing the final syllable.

"Female," Rantire supplied. "Compared to our males, I'm a kitten."

The torturer glanced to his left, apparently assuring himself that someone with a better command of human language was listening. His body shifted, rising and falling at the chest in a gesture that resembled nothing human but somehow suggested resignation. This, she guessed, was the equivalent of a human sigh. "We just want answered simple some questions. None of them require difficult efforts to you. *Like* pain do you?"

Rantire believed the "you" referred to her, not people in general. No matter the nature of elfin society, they would never believe she, or any human, enjoyed being hurt. "No one likes pain."

The elf nodded, his expression suggesting he had meant the question to be rhetorical. Relief softened his alien features. "Talk you now to me?"

Rantire pursed her lips. Her aching arms had become a distraction that made clever thought difficult. "Depends on the question."

"Who is leader of humans?"

Rantire shook her head, saying nothing. The query seemed as ludicrous now as when Dh'arlo'mé had asked, but Rantire believed she could use this gap in elfin understanding to her advantage. As long as they believed a single entity existed who fit this description, and she kept silent, they had reason to keep her alive. But this strategy had a major flaw: the elves need only capture another human and ask him. Luckily, they seemed disinclined to do so, presumably because they did not wish to risk more elfin lives to capture one. Rantire had never heard of elves outside of church tales, which suggested that, for whatever reason, elves did not mingle with mankind often.

"Will you not answer?"

"I will not," Rantire responded, placing the words back into proper sequence.

"Have I to hurt you?" Reluctantly resigned, the torturer

gestured, and the smaller elf that had accompanied him previously edged into view.

"I can't stop you from hurting me," Rantire admitted. "But it'll do you no good. I won't bow to pain. You'll kill me before I give you that answer."

The torturer stiffened at the words, glancing toward someone Rantire could not see. Apparently, she had found a chink in his armor. The dirty cell she had passed during her attempt at escape held the answer, Rantire suspected. Apparently, the elves had killed a human before, by accident; and the torturer's aversion to causing harm suggested his too exuberant ministrations as the cause. Since it seemed to bother him, she filed the knowledge away until the time she could use it against him.

Rantire could no longer feel her arms, though each heartbeat triggered a deep, excruciating pain.

"I have to try," he said.

"I understand." Rantire locked her gaze on him, hoping the sharper pains he inflicted might draw attention from her arms. He carried no paraphernalia and obviously had no intention of moving her, so she could not guess his method. That misinterpretation had undone her before; she had believed he would escort her elsewhere and so never suspected gates would block the way. Clearly, he had not intended to move her that time either.

The torturer unlocked and entered Rantire's cell. Hunched into a wary crouch, the other elf followed, eyes flicking nervously from Rantire to the hallway to the door.

The torturer waved for his companion to approach Rantire. The other did so, moving with slow, shuffling steps that charged Rantire's impatience but did not seem to bother the torturer at all. The smaller elf worked his way to Rantire's side then looked to the torturer for guidance.

The torturer said something in elven, and his companion slid a clammy hand beneath Rantire's tunic, placing his palm flat against her abdomen. His skin felt damp and tremulous, revealing his anxiety.

Rantire waited in silent ignorance, unsure what to expect.

The torturer shouted something, and a low chorus spread outside the cell in both directions down the hallway. *Magic.* Rantire knew but could not speculate further. So far, every spell the elves had thrown had required an assembly and a caster; she hoped it held true for all magic. One-on-one, she believed she would have only their physical abilities to conquer. Without the constant need to anticipate the unpredictable, she could defeat them or die fighting and find Valhalla.

The elf's hand warmed against her skin, and she naturally attributed the change to shared body heat. Then it flared suddenly to a scalding heat. She flinched instinctively. "Ow!"

The elf jerked away from her movement, and his hand lost contact with her skin. The heat diminished instantly, though a painful tingling persisted. Rantire felt like a craven and a fool. She had anticipated some sort of pain, had steeled herself not to scream; but the abruptness of the temperature change had startled as much as hurt her.

"You talk now to me?" the torturer asked.

"No." Rantire met his gaze easily.

The torturer pushed his companion forward again. This time, the smaller elf took a position at her opposite hip, placing his hand flat as before. Rantire knew what to expect now. As the heat scorched her flesh, the agony seared much deeper, but she did not make a sound. Even when tears scored her vision and the need to swear transformed to the desire to scream, she did not move or cry out. Eyes closed, it took her several moments to realize that the heat source, and the chanting, had disappeared. The pain lingered, and nausea accompanied it. The image of vomiting on her captors was the only pleasure she could manage.

"You talk *now* to me?" The torturer's familiar voice penetrated her mental fog.

"No," Rantire said, trying to sound as casual as before, with mixed results.

The torturer accepted the answer more easily than Rantire expected. "I will try for you again later." Turning, he walked back outside the cell, the smaller elf scurrying after him.

The pain receded further, becoming less than the dull ache Rantire's arms still suffered. "There won't be a later. Not if you leave things as they are."

The torturer studied Rantire. "What mean you?"

"I mean," Rantire explained carefully, "that if you leave me hanging like this, I'll lose my arms. Then I'll bleed to death." She did not know if she spoke the truth or not, but the pain in her arms was rapidly growing unbearable. Had the elves known of the discomfort the position caused her, they surely would have left her until the need to move drove her to madness or confession. Rantire did not reveal the level of

her distress, attempting to imply instead that she would succumb to a swift and painless death. "And if you don't tend
that burn, it'll get infected and kill me."

"Infected," the torturer repeated, brows knitted. The word
obviously held no meaning for him. He leaned on the cell
door, calling down the hallway in his native language.

Rantire cycled a battle song through her head to distract
her from the agony throbbing through her arms and hip:

> *Renshai warriors*
> *Swords sharp and gleaming*
> *Allies few and*
> *Enemies streaming*
> *As heroes battle*
> *Honor teeming*
> *Leave our foes*
> *With entrails steaming.*

Eventually, Dh'arlo'mé and three other elves answered the
torturer's summons. They discussed the situation in elven,
Rantire plucking a few more words from their conversation
based on the torturer's need to relay her concern and from
gestures she could only partially interpret. Of the newcomers, one in particular caught Rantire's notice. He bore the
same long-limbed form as the others; yet, where most had a
timelessness that made guessing years impossible, this one
had an aura of great age. Silver wound through red-brown
locks faded from sunlight. His amber eyes held a glaze of
water, though none of the milky whiteness that plagued human elders. Wrinkles scored his face in odd patterns that she
usually associated with smiling, though she had seen little of
that among the elves so far. He watched Rantire with a stu-
diousness the others did not emulate and spoke the least of
the three. His tone contained none of the bitter anger the
others displayed on occasion and Dh'arlo'mé showed all of
the time.

At length they came to an agreement. The elder pulled
something out of his pocket that his fist hid and entered
Rantire's cell. As he approached, he opened his hand, revealing a tiny, round, glass bowl filled with a white cream.
He scooped some of the contents onto his finger, then
smeared a light coating over the burns on Rantire's hip and
abdomen. As he worked, he muttered guttural sounds suspi-

ciously like those she had heard shouted during the casting of magic. No chanting assembly accompanied his work. If he used a spell, her theory lost all significance. Her hopes plummeted at the thought. If some spells or casters did not require an elaborate organization to work their magic, it became that much more difficult to evade or fight them.

Without meeting her gaze, the elder elf continued to work, switching from the harsh syllables to the lilting Northern speech of humans. "Do not judge all elves by our leader."

He glanced at Rantire's face, and she gave a slight nod to indicate she understood him. Her heart slowed as the pain of the burns eased and gradually disappeared, but it quickened anew with eager anticipation. She wondered if she had truly found an ally or just a trick to make her believe so. It seemed impossible that this elf might actually choose loyalty to a human stranger over his own people, but her instincts told her to trust this old elf as she had not the others.

The ancient one returned his gaze to her wounds, though he seemed pleased by her admission of comprehension. "I supported the Golden Prince of Demons when those who claimed kinship turned enemies. The wise become fools when they mistake reasoning for truth." He replaced Rantire's shirt, returned the vial to his pocket, and left the cell as if he had never spoken. He closed the door and stepped aside to allow the torturer to lock it.

The elves padded lightly down the corridor; Dh'arlo'mé the only one who glanced backward. Moments later, the hook supporting Rantire's wrists slid down the stone wall through a groove she had not previously noticed. She snatched back her hands, returning blood flow an agony that usurped all previous pain. Incapacitated, she slid to the floor, mind clotted with a suffering that for a time allowed no coherent thought.

When the pain finally dropped to a tolerable level, Rantire considered the old elf's words: *I supported the Golden Prince of Demons when those who claimed kinship turned enemies.* Mention of Colbey Calistinsson, the Golden Prince of Demons as ancient prophecies once called him, did not escape her. This elf knew about Renshai and that she was one. *How?* Rantire considered. She had said nothing to give herself away, and the days when appearance revealed the Renshai's originally Northern breeding had passed centuries ago. Those from the tribe of Modrey still bore many of the common features: the blond or red hair, pale skin and eyes, and the strange propensity to look younger than chronological age. But Rantire was born of the tribe of Rache, the one that least resembled the old race. *Did he read my mind?* Rantire discarded that possibility, still certain the elves would not bother to question her if they could invade her thoughts. Only one other clue came to mind: her sword and her combat style. Those who knew Renshai well might recognize their distinctive warrior training, riddled with secret maneuvers and ploys only Renshai were allowed to learn.

Apparently, the old elf knew more about humans than his fellows. Yet even his knowledge fell short. He had used the Northern tongue when it made more sense to choose trading or Western; and he had tried to claim kinship with Colbey in the years of the god's mortality. *That would make him more than three centuries old.* The possibility seemed madness, yet it gave Rantire pause. *How long do elves live?* She had no information even to speculate, except for her own inability to gauge age when she stared at the not-quite-human faces. She could not wholly dismiss the possibility that the elder had known Colbey before his ascension, though the ancient's claim to have supported the Golden Prince of Demons seemed more difficult to swallow even than the concept of passing decades like human years. By legend, everyone, including the gods, had turned against Colbey Calistinsson. They had believed him the single-handed bearer of chaos and instigator of the *Ragnarok* when, in fact, he championed balance; and their desperate attempts to slaughter him brought the very war they sought to prevent. No one had sanctioned the Golden Prince. *No one.*

Or could there have been one? Rantire dared to doubt. History tended to condense to absolutes, the details lost in obscurity. Just as no sword technique was entirely effective, and luck could steal victory from the better warrior. Rantire did not trust in "never" or "always." And she began to wonder whether elves did outlive humans in the same ratio that humans outlived horses or dogs or maybe even insects. She could not guess the elfin life span, but the implications of such a thing went far beyond the obvious. And patience became a desperate need.

Chapter 11

The Only Answer

*Through all the battles, killing, and prejudice, the
one thing our people never lost was their code of
laws and their honor.*

—Colbey Calistinsson

The dank darkness of Béarn's dungeon enfolded Ra-khir like
a sodden blanket, and the echo of his footsteps evoked imaginary monsters he had not feared since childhood. "The third
cell on the left," the guard had told him, remaining behind
so the knight-in-training could address his father in private.
They showed no concern over the possibility that Kedrin
might attempt escape. Ra-khir hoped that faith stemmed
from respect for a knight's honor rather than the hopeless,
black maze that stretched beyond the cages and that only a
few of Béarn's most trusted could negotiate. Flight from the
prison meant certain death in lightless, spider-infested bewilderment from slow starvation or madness.

One cell. Ra-khir continued his walk, heart pounding,
envisioning each beat echoing through the cool, stone hallways. Occasionally, a clink or cough broke the stillness,
loud as a drumbeat, the noises of Béarn's prisoners. *Two
cells.* Ra-khir wondered at their crimes: poachers, murderers,
thieves. Outrage flared at the thought of his gallant father
among these.

Three cells. Ra-khir discovered his father sitting calmly
on the stone floor of his cage, head lowered in prayer to the
gods Béarn worshiped. Kedrin had always placed his per-

sonal faith in Thor, law incarnate, a warrior deity who embodied skill, strength, and honor. As Ra-khir drew nearer,
the captain looked up and smiled at his son.

Relief flooded Ra-khir, displacing his anger. His father
looked well. For now, nothing else mattered. He stood in silence, finding no words that would not sound trite after the
events that had transpired. For the first time in his life, he
stood speechless before his father.

Kedrin rose and approached the bars. "Are you well?"

The question seemed every bit the banality Ra-khir was
struggling to avoid. "Me?" he managed, incredulous.

Kedrin's chuckle broke the tense hush that should not exist between a father and son who loved one another as much
as these two. Ra-khir rushed forward, placing his arms between the bars. They accomplished an embrace, metal boring into shoulders and rust smearing otherwise spotless silks.
"I appreciate what you did for me," Kedrin said softly to
avoid the echoes that would publicize their conversation.
"Don't ever think otherwise."

Ra-khir clung, nodding, though the bars scraped his
check. The vision of his proud father moldering in this awful
place would never leave him, and he had already begun to
wonder whether death might not have proved the better
choice. His father did not fear dying or what lay beyond for
men of honor, and Ra-khir could not help worrying that he
had condemned his father to a lifetime of suffering out of his
own selfish need to keep the man he loved alive.

"What really happened?" Ra-khir asked, believing he
knew but needing confirmation.

But Kedrin shook his head. "Perception of truth becomes
truth. What others choose to believe is all that matters. What
you believe is your own personal truth."

The words made no sense to Ra-khir, and the evasiveness
irritated him. He pulled free, though he remained close to
the bars so he could speak as softly as possible and not lose
the one audience he wanted. " 'It's not your affair' would
have sufficed as answer, though you're wrong. I deserve at
least to know whether or not my father committed treason."
He intercepted the response he suspected he would receive
but did not want. "And the king's judgment isn't good
enough. I need the truth." He gazed earnestly into the blue-
white eyes. "I *need* the truth."

"Look to your heart. The truth is there."

"Yes," Ra-khir admitted, tears of frustration welling in his eyes against his will. "I already know the truth, but I need to hear it from my father."

The knight-captain's strange eyes seemed to bore through his son's head to read the extent of that need. "I am innocent of any wrongdoing. I would do nothing to jeopardize Béarn, and neither must you."

Ra-khir breathed a deep sigh. Just as Kedrin had said, Ra-khir had known the truth; but his father's admission freed something primally necessary. He dropped his voice to a whisper, though the low tones they had chosen already protected them from prying ears. "Father, there is no heir to Béarn's throne. Is there?"

Kedrin stiffened, shocked beyond reply. The composure that followed came too late to convince Ra-khir that his question had struck far from the truth. "Why do you ask such a thing?"

Ra-khir glanced behind him to make certain the guard had not come to end his visiting time, though the click of mail and slam of bootfalls would surely have reached his ears long before anyone appeared. "I'm guessing. Based on information my friends and I pieced together."

Kedrin shivered at the implications. "Let's hope others have not come to the same conclusion."

Ra-khir doubted it. Most commoners and nobles had no reason to consider such a thing. Few knew that the staff-tests had occurred, and even most of the Renshai guardians did not know if their charges had passed or failed. "No one has the assortment of friends I've made."

"Like Darris." Kedrin studied his son, obviously remembering earlier talks.

"And a Béarnian heir." Ra-khir added without trying to hide his distaste, "And her Renshai guard."

Ra-khir's aversion did not go unnoticed, though Kedrin misinterpreted it. "I didn't know you disliked Renshai." He frowned. "They lack honor in its pure form, but their loyalty to Béarn's heirs is unquestionable. For that alone, they deserve our support."

Ra-khir dismissed the unnecessary lecture. "I have nothing against Renshai as a race. I just don't like this particular Renshai. He belittled my honor, and I believe he plans to embarrass me in front of my friends."

Kedrin nodded, accepting personal hatred where he had

not tolerated prejudice. "I'm sure you'll deal honorably with the situation, even if *he* does not."

"I will," Ra-khir promised, realizing as he did that Kedrin had neatly circumvented his question. "But I still need to know. Are there any heirs to Béarn's throne? Ones that passed the test?"

The knight-captain kept his voice as low as his son's. "I can tell you only that there may be."

"May be?" Ra-khir glared at his father. "That's not an answer."

"It's the only one I can give you."

"Why?" Ra-khir demanded.

Kedrin smiled. "It is the only answer there is."

Ra-khir mulled over those words. A vast difference existed between the response his father gave and the one he could have. If Kedrin had claimed that castle security forbade an answer, as he had when it came to defending himself from a crime he had not committed, Ra-khir would have learned nothing. Now, however, he knew an heir to Béarn's throne might exist; but his father did not know for certain. Ra-khir tucked that clue away, needing to reconcile it with others he and his friends had accumulated. Understanding that his time with his father was limited, he came to the crux of the matter. "The caravan east. That had something to do with an heir to Béarn, didn't it?"

The grin wilted from Kedrin's face, and he studied his hands, flecked with rust from the bars. "My vows to Béarn and its council forbid me from answering that."

Ra-khir hissed in frustration, then immediately wished he had not. He braced for a lecture about respect and honor, but it never came. Kedrin continued to stare at his hands, and a desperate struggle creased his handsome features. The first stomp of the guard's footsteps carried up the corridor.

Kedrin's hands snaked between the bars, and he seized Ra-khir's wrists in clammy fingers white with strain. He whispered, "Béarn will fall without the proper heir. Someone or something is trying to make that happen, and they will destroy whoever obviously stands in their way. If the caravan doesn't return within the month, act wisely and in secret. Youth may succeed where formal diplomacy fails." He released Ra-khir, who staggered backward, as much from surprise as confusion.

The bootfalls drew closer, accompanied by the jingle of mail.

Ra-khir whispered urgently. "Act? What do you mean act?" He had to know now. Another month would pass before Baltraine allowed him to visit his father again.

Kedrin closed his eyes; obviously torn between his vows to the council and his loyalty to son and kingdom. "Think. I have faith in you. Just keep Béarn safe ..."

The guard drew too close for further privacy.

"... and stay true to your honor."

"Time to go." The Béarnide addressed Ra-khir, avoiding Kedrin's stare. Clearly, he could not reconcile this meek prisoner with the respect for the Knights of Erythane trained into him since infancy. Or, perhaps, he suffered the feelings of betrayal that all guards must feel when they realize even the most slavish devotion to their country cannot assure protection from a fall and its subsequent punishment.

"I will," Ra-khir said earnestly, only partially understanding what his vow entailed. Soon he would meet with Darris and Matrinka again. Together, he believed, they would find answers.

Summer breezes tossed the treetops and branches into playful, rustling dances and rained seedpods on the Foxmeal Clearing. Kevral remained attentive while her companions discussed their various findings, her ears tuned as much to the natural sounds of the forest as to the conversation. In their immediate vicinity, she heard only the rattle of leaves in the wind. A squirrel skittered beyond the clearing, its light step and quick bursts of movement unmistakable. Occasionally, birds alighted on branches that bowed beneath their weight. Otherwise, nothing disturbed their solitude.

A poor sentry lowers his guard for something as fleeting as safety. Mentally, Kevral quoted Colbey Calistinsson as she usually did aloud. Since infancy, she had taken all lessons of the Renshai seriously, but none more so than the teachings about the Renshai hero turned god. In his day, and some said forever, no swordsman had matched his skill or his dedication to his people. From the moment she first heard tales of the great Renshai warrior, at an age younger than she could recall, she had emulated his life, his speech, and his style. Once, she had vowed to become as accomplished as he. That dream had grown. Some day, she swore, she would surpass him.

Darris opened the conversation by addressing Ra-khir, the last to arrive. "How's your father?"

"As well as one could expect from an honorable man imprisoned in a dark, cold hell for a crime he didn't commit." He smiled weakly, apparently realizing that his sarcasm was misdirected. "He's taking it very well. Obviously, better than I am."

Matrinka placed a comforting arm on the knight-in-training's shoulders, and Ra-khir relaxed visibly. Not for the first time, Kevral marveled at her charge's ability to heal with kindness as well as herbs. Mior twined around Ra-khir's legs, rubbing and arching against his sweat-darkened breeks.

Kevral noticed all these things and more. Although she knew logically that Ra-khir could have no designs against the princess, she watched his every movement, seeking the telltale stiffening that would herald violence. *Enemies most dangerous dwell in the least likely places.* She had tested his skill before and found it no match for her own, but it did not require ability to slaughter a princess who so willingly placed her person in harm's way. She wondered if Matrinka realized how unnecessarily difficult she made her guardian's job.

Darris grinned at Ra-khir's halfhearted attempt at a joke. "You're doing fine."

"We'll see how I handle the month that passes before I get to see him again."

A sympathetic silence followed, one that only Ra-khir could break.

"I talked to my father. I put him in a bad position." Then realizing the irony, he added. "Worse, I guess, than the one he's already in. When honor corners him, like at the trial, he tends to speak in riddles. Drives me about insane."

Matrinka drifted away from Ra-khir, to Kevral's relief.

Darris encouraged his friend. "Tell us what he said. Perhaps we can help you interpret."

Ra-khir gestured his thanks, shaking his head simultaneously. "Not necessary. I was up all night thinking about the situation and his words." He added as an aside, "You really had to be there. And know my father." He continued, "I think I've got it reasonably figured out."

Even Kevral eagerly awaited the answer, though she did not show it.

Ra-khir tossed the initiative to the others. "What *you've* learned will help a lot."

Darris obliged, hazel eyes shining beneath the dark curls that obscured his forehead. "To thwart suspicion, Matrinka and I have been working separately on the same sources. All heirs are still in Béarn. No potential king or queen traveled with the envoy, so we can't explain the Renshai who accompanied them that way."

Kevral saw her opening then, but Matrinka spoke first. "Neither of us managed to find a single heir who passed the test. Not everyone would tell us, and some we didn't dare ask; but none of the ones we missed seemed a likely ruler."

Darris nodded vigorously, the lute on his back swaying with the movement.

Kevral could not help smiling. As Darris implied, Matrinka's description was gross understatement. Two of the unquestioned heirs had attempted suicide, a sure sign the staves had found them unworthy. Another had placed the comforts of ale above responsibilities to her husband and children.

Matrinka wrung her hands at the news she had needed to deliver, and the princess' alarm killed Kevral's smile. Ra-khir pursed his lips, green eyes reflecting anger and concern. He glanced at Kevral as if doing so was a chore he would rather forego.

Amused, Kevral gave Ra-khir a brazen grin. "The only Renshai who seems to know anything about this is Chieftain Thialnir who attends the council. He won't tell me anything, though he did pointedly discourage me from asking questions. Of anyone." Another understatement. As she recalled, his precise words were: "Quit stirring up trouble, or I'll hack you into bits for the practice and serve you up as tomorrow night's supper." Had the warning been overheard by the few people who still believed Renshai drank blood to remain eternally young, it would have fueled ancient prejudice properly defunct. Kevral, however, knew the threat was idle, though she did consider taking his challenge just to prove herself the better warrior. In the end, common sense prevailed. Many of her people already considered her too cocky. The younger ones reviled her need for perfection, not only with a sword, which all Renshai strove for, but with such minutiae as languages and history. She had earned the nickname Kevral the Overconfident, unfairly to her mind. Kevral the Confident suited her better, and she refused to make excuses for her self-assurance. *No one ever became the best by hiding behind a mantle of false modesty.*

Kevral finished with a shrug of forbearance. "Rantire went on a mission to Santagithi. An heir has to be directly involved. That's all I can add."

That proved enough for Ra-khir to place the pieces together neatly. "All right. Here's the story as I see it. Stop me if something doesn't fit." He cleared his throat, glancing around to assure their privacy.

Kevral gave an "all clear" signal, though Ra-khir did not bother to glance at her to receive it.

"Someone or some group wants to destroy the line of high kings. I don't know who or why, but bear with me. All of the heirs get tested—"

Matrinka broke in, "—so we know who to protect from the assassin."

"Right," Ra-khir acknowledged. "No heir passes the test, but somewhere east of here—"

"—Santagithi," Matrinka inserted.

"Not necessarily." Ra-khir combed back red hair slick with sweat from his morning practice. Kevral caught herself studying the casually handsome features and hated her lapse. Oblivious, Ra-khir explained. "They might have claimed to be going there since it's a long-allied kingdom. For all we know, they might be headed for the East."

Darris squinted, dubious. "Why east?"

"East. Not east." Ra-khir shrugged. "The location isn't important. What matters is what they're looking for."

Darris spoke the answer just as Kevral drew the obvious conclusion. "An heir."

Ra-khir smiled.

"A missing heir?" Matrinka said thoughtfully, then frowned. "Not very likely. Why would an heir leave Béarn?"

"I don't know," Ra-khir admitted. "But it's the only thing that makes sense. My father's words implied that no one tested by the staves had passed but that there still might be one or more yet to face the test."

Darris' features remained scrunched. "We're making assumptions here. There doesn't seem to be any motivation for any of it. Who would want Béarn to fall? Why? How could they have nearly succeeded? Who is this heir? Why would he or she have left Béarn?"

"I told you I don't have all the explanations," Ra-khir replied. "I'm just putting together the 'whats.' The 'whos' will have to come, and the 'whys' may never be learned."

"You're talking like your father," Kevral said, not caring that her words irritated Ra-khir. "But you're right. Rantire could only have gone to accompany an heir. Since none went with the envoy, it only makes sense that one is supposed to come back with them. Mystery solved. So how does this involve us?"

Ra-khir's green eyes riveted on the Renshai with all the intensity with which they had avoided her in the past. "If I have any say in it, it won't involve *you* at all. As for the rest of us, my father believes the diplomatic party won't survive to return the missing heir, that it'll get waylaid by the same assassin who slaughtered some of our heirs. I don't know why he believes this, but I trust his judgment implicitly and he has information that we don't." He examined Matrinka, Darris, and Mior in turn, "If I'm reading my father right, he believes we might quietly succeed where open diplomacy fails."

"Meaning what?" Darris said before Kevral could spit out the same question using invective.

"Meaning that the three of us working quietly and independently of the kingdom might be better able to find and return this heir than an obvious diplomatic envoy that no assassin could possibly miss seeing."

Ra-khir's words caught Matrinka by surprise, and even Darris seemed stunned by the implications. The Renshai, however, accepted the suggestion easily. The combination of her own stalwart faith in herself and the adolescent belief in one's own immortality made her certain they could succeed. The knight-in-training's assertion that she would not be a part of this was too ridiculous to bother her in the least. She would not leave Matrinka's side.

"Us?" Matrinka asked, shocked.

"Us?" repeated Darris. His lips framed a thoughtful smile, and Kevral doubted this was the first time Darris had considered having a hand in the affair. He relished it, as she did. She guessed his reasons would prove different but did not care. She liked him for the eagerness the others did not share. Ra-khir would act from duty rather than the thirst for adventure that marked a true warrior, at least in Kevral's mind. Matrinka would need to think long and hard about her role in such a thing, and Kevral's involvement would depend wholly on her charge's decision.

"Why not?" Ra-khir said.

"Why not, indeed." Darris took Matrinka's hand, and she smiled at him. The love they shared seemed raw and obvious to Kevral, though neither of them would admit it. Matrinka had called Darris her platonic best friend so many times it seemed more to Kevral as if the princess needed to convince herself. *Silly.* Kevral dismissed the matter. Colbey had turned eighty before finding his wife, and Kevral could wait as long. Until then, relationships could only take away from her sword time.

Matrinka hefted Mior with her free hand, burying her lips in the tricolored fur and giving the animal a gentle kiss. "I've been looking for a way to serve Béarn. I'll do what I can, but I'm no warrior." She glanced sidelong at Kevral who smiled broadly at the understatement.

Ra-khir slumped slightly, relieved by his companions' quick agreement to a difficult task. "Settled, then." He grimaced, abashed "Now all we need to know is who we're looking for. And where to go."

Ra-khir's discomfort became contagious. Even Kevral's expression revealed perplexity. "We look for a Béarnide. Man, woman, or child. I'll bet he or she'd be easy to spot in Santagithi."

Matrinka shook her head in disagreement. "We've been allies for a long time. Surely more than one Béarnide's moved there."

Darris reminded, "And we're not even sure Santagithi's where to go. Easterners have dark hair and eyes, too. Most of them. They don't tend to grow as large ..." He added with a chuckle, "Who does? But I'm sure there're enough big ones to make finding a Béarnide impossible. Not to mention the East's awfully big to search at random."

Mior twined her way to Matrinka's shoulders, then stretched out, forepaws draped on the princess' chest.

Kevral knew nothing about political structure. Renshai had little need for leaders, and "chieftain" mostly served as an honorary title. "Someone has to know who and where. Otherwise, why send the envoy?"

"My mother knows," Darris admitted. "But if I ask, she'll tell me to find out for myself. It's part of a bard's training."

"What if you tell her it's really important?" Matrinka searched for the loophole.

Ra-khir answered for Darris. "She won't tell him. The whole council's sworn to secrecy. If we press too hard, we'll lose the anonymity that might let us succeed where diplomatic parties fail."

Kevral nodded. It certainly explained Thialnir's behavior. Ra-khir confronted Darris directly. "Don't ask your mother. Better no one knows that we've even figured out there's an heir out there."

"If there is," Kevral could not help adding.

"I, for one, believe there is." Matrinka regarded her guardian, who shrugged. If the princess went, Kevral would accompany her, whether she chased heirs or misconceptions. "And there is one other who surely knows the answers we're looking for," Matrinka frowned. "Though getting information from the sage in the tower would be more difficult than trying to extract it from each council member in turn."

"That bad?" Ra-khir sounded incredulous.

Darris nodded, curly bangs bouncing. "He hoards information like misers do silver. Even when the king himself needs to read, the sage hovers over him like an anxious mother placing her infant in a drunkard's care."

A rustle in the brush attracted Kevral's attention, and she whirled toward it, hands falling to her hilts. A young man rose from the undergrowth, black hair snarled and speckled with stems. Dark eyes glimmered, reflecting experience beyond obvious years. He seemed relatively small, though not remarkably so, and was still three finger's breadths taller than her. He moved with a sinuous grace that explained how he had come so close without her noticing him sooner. That made him dangerous.

"I can get what you need." The stranger spoke with an unfamiliar, guttural accent.

At the sound of his voice, Darris, Matrinka, and Ra-khir whirled to face him as well. The men scrambled between the newcomer and Matrinka, though Kevral already had security handled to her satisfaction. As quietly and quickly as he had come, he could never get past her to harm the princess.

"Who are you?" Ra-khir demanded.

The stranger studied the knight-in-training for longer than

decorum allowed. Kevral thought she saw a flicker of recognition, followed by hesitation. Then the dark-haired youth spoke. "I'm Tae." He pronounced it to rhyme with "die," which seemed ironically appropriate.

Kevral continued to study the newcomer's every motion. Nothing about him suggested imminent violence. Faithful to her training, she would not draw a weapon unless and until she chose to kill him.

Tae smiled. "And I can get what you need."

"And what might that be?" Ra-khir's voice became a growl, and he obviously tested Tae. Of them all, the knight's son seemed closest to attacking, and with good cause. Unlike Kevral, whose loyalty was only to Matrinka, Ra-khir had dedicated himself to the kingdom. The details Tae overheard, no matter how few, could harm Béarn.

"Information from a sage's notes," Tae replied. "I can get that."

"How?" Darris demanded, seeming more interested in the process than concerned about Tae's eavesdropping.

"Let's just say I can acquire it."

"Acquire?" Ra-khir's brows lowered until his eyes became slits of condemnation. "You mean steal."

Tae shrugged, accepting the assessment, and the bad will. "You call it stealing; I call it collecting. If you call getting information stealing, then the bard of Béarn should spend his life in prison." He glanced at Darris, then returned his gaze to Ra-khir. At least, it appeared so. Kevral noticed that Tae's eyes never seemed wholly still but flitted from one to another of them, especially in response to movement.

Ra-khir's right hand fell to his sword hilt, and Tae shifted backward, almost imperceptibly. The knight-in-training growled. "I'll not tolerate stealing. You, stranger, have no honor."

Kevral snorted at the obviousness of Ra-khir's assertion, studying Tae more openly, from the rampant mop of too-long black hair to the coiled leg muscles that revealed readiness to fight or flee on an instant's notice. If it came to either, he had best hope he could outmaneuver a Renshai.

Ra-khir finished as if Kevral had never interrupted. "And we can't tolerate your knowledge. I have no choice but to call you out."

"Call me what you want," Tae shot back, "but my name's Tae."

Ra-khir blinked, missing the connection for a moment that allowed Kevral to snicker without reproof. He glared at her, still addressing Tae. "I'll give you the benefit of the doubt and attribute your response to the ignorance of low upbringing rather than malice. I just challenged you to a duel." He glanced knowingly at Matrinka and Darris, unable or unwilling to explain his true motivation aloud. Kevral understood. An untrustworthy foreigner had overheard matters of kingdom security. One way or another, he had to be silenced.

Matrinka clutched Mior, features betraying horror, turning to Darris for the words to diffuse tension that seemed to come wholly of knightly formality. Darris tossed her an "I'll explain later" gesture that obviously only partially mollified her.

Ra-khir continued. "To the death. With knives, since you carry no sword."

"No," Tae said.

"No?" Ra-khir repeated, thoughtfully running back over his words to find the ones to which "no" could possibly apply. "I called the challenge, so I decide the details."

"Fine," Tae returned. "Decide them. But I'm not taking your challenge."

"Refusing the challenge?"

"Right."

"So you have *no* honor."

Kevral snorted. "What clued you first? The silent snooping or the offer to steal?"

Ra-khir glared at Kevral.

Tae did not deny the assertion, though he did fidget less when Ra-khir's scrutiny switched to the Renshai.

Ra-khir turned on Kevral. "You have none either, but I'm forced to tolerate you."

Ra-khir's words inflamed Kevral. As usual, she quoted Colbey, "Don't condemn my honor just because it's different from your own." She added cruelly, "I'll take your challenge any time, Ra-khir. Any time."

The Erythanian tensed, as if to respond to her demand with the violence she requested. But true to his honor, he did not attack in anger. "I'll deal with you later. For now, I have more important matters to handle. I don't appreciate your interference."

Kevral rolled her eyes, annoyed by his formality and feeling vaguely guilty over starting unnecessary conflict. For all his bother, Ra-khir was right this time. "Carry on." She gestured at Tae and closed her mouth.

Tae observed the proceedings, displaying only curiosity, though the set of his stance suggested hidden nervousness to Kevral. Whether that came of threatened battle with Ra-khir or something else, she could not guess. "I don't take your challenge. I don't want to fight. I just want to help."

"Why?" Ra-khir demanded.

"I have my reasons," Tae responded, a worthless answer, yet the only one they would receive.

Ra-khir sighed, then dropped into silence, his work done. If the stranger refused to duel, that decision left Ra-khir little recourse. His honor would not allow him to attack one who would not fight.

But Kevral's honor contained no such rule. She saw an enemy to whom they had unwittingly given information that could destroy Béarn and the one remaining heir. As clearly as Ra-khir, she knew what they must do. Matrinka would never think to kill. Darris would not attack until he gathered the necessary information to prove Tae's motivation. If he killed the Eastlander out of hand, Darris would lose the chance to ever understand or know for certain; and that lapse would haunt him to his grave. Also, he did not seem the type to lead with his sword, preferring songs of peace to those that immortalized heroes or praised warriors. Kevral labored under none of these constraints, yet still she hesitated for reasons of her own. First, though it seemed bluster, Tae might be able to deliver the information he promised and that they so sorely needed, whatever its source. And second, she liked him. *The security of Béarn's heirs must always take precedence.*

These thoughts buzzed through Kevral's mind. In the end, her choice became clear. Without warning, she lunged, drew, and cut; but not fast enough. Her sword cleaved air. Tae disappeared into the woods like an animal, and only a faint rustle of brush revealed his passing. Kevral swore, not bothering to pursue, certain it would prove fruitless.

Ra-khir watched in tacit disapproval, surely torn between condemning her unannounced force against a lesser armed, unwilling opponent and relief that honor did not bind her against such a threat as it had himself.

Matrinka gaped, dropping Mior in her startlement. "Why did you . . . ? Why?" She stopped, deferring to Kevral's better judgment on who or what might prove a threat to her own well-being. "Was he about to harm me?"

"In a manner of speaking," Kevral sheathed her sword, listening for some indication of which direction Tae had fled. She heard only the crackle of leaves in the wind. "He's a stranger, an Eastlander by accent, and he knows Béarn's future rests with a single heir. He also knows where to get details about the heir."

"The sage?" Darris caressed his lute absently. "That was bluster. No one could steal those papers."

Matrinka frowned, while Mior pranced in a disgruntled circle. "He seemed awfully sure he could."

"If he does," Ra-khir groused, "Kevral's virtually assured he sells the sage's notes to our enemies rather than bringing them to us."

"Assuming he isn't already one of them," Darris added.

Kevral stiffened, saying nothing, as enraged at herself as Ra-khir was. Tae's quickness astounded her. Few men, until now she would have said none, could outrun a Renshai draw-cut. The need to concede Tae's agility only fueled her discomfort. If he could escape from her, perhaps he could also do as he claimed. And, though she despised his delivery, Ra-khir was right again.

"Oh, no." Matrinka recognized the threat and shuddered at the potential consequences. "We'd better tell someone. We need to stop him."

"Who are we going to tell?" Darris shook his head. "We can't get to the king. I don't trust Baltraine."

Ra-khir vigorously nodded his agreement. "My father thinks it best for security if the people of Béarn place their faith in Baltraine, but he can't control my feelings about the man."

"Quiet!" Kevral shushed the others in a loud whisper. "Tae, or others like him, may still be listening."

Everyone fell silent, glancing furtively around the clearing. Darris pointed toward the castle and headed for it. They all followed carefully.

No one spoke until they passed through the gates and settled into a private garden in the courtyard. Surrounded by the heady scent of roses, Ra-khir glanced anxiously at the sky. Kevral knew he was already late for practice.

Darris continued as if the interruption had never occurred.

"Anyone we tell is going to report to Baltraine. There's no way to keep this from him."

Kevral remained standing while the others sat. That Tae had managed to draw so close without her knowing it sent chills prickling her back. His inhumanly rapid departure only added to her uneasiness. "There's one way."

All eyes turned to Kevral.

"We don't tell anyone. We handle this ourselves."

"Us?" Matrinka stared. Mior stood on the bench beside her, fur rumpled, apparently on the verge of forgiving Matrinka for her sudden flight. "What can we do?"

"Remember, my father believes we can succeed where diplomats failed." Ra-khir took Kevral's side, to her surprise. "There's no need to risk a panic. We'll just have to find Tae again. And stop him."

Chapter 12

New Information

The Renshai have no need for companions who mistrust us.

—Colbey Calistinsson

For Kevral, the Fox-meal Clearing no longer held the serenity it had prior to Tae's arrival the previous day. Interwoven boughs still formed a leafy umbrella against a drizzle pattering in a steady, regular cadence above their heads. Midday sunlight dribbled through the clouds in patches and through gaps in the foliage in smaller streaks. Matrinka sat with Mior on a weathered stump. Ra-khir perched on a deadfall directly across from her. Kevral remained attentive and standing, holding little faith in Ra-khir's plan to capture Tae. Darris wandered quietly through the woodlands. At Ra-khir's urging, it had become the bard's heir's task to watch for spies while the others conversed. Ra-khir surmised that Tae, or other quiet enemies, would attempt to learn more from them, so they had met here again rather than on the castle grounds. The Erythanian had originally suggested that Kevral skulk around them to kill or, preferably, catch any enemy who tried.

When Kevral refused to leave Matrinka, Ra-khir had dispatched Darris to the task instead. The whole seemed nonsense to the Renshai. Every rattle of brush made her twitchy, and she had to keep reminding herself of Darris' presence. *Tae already learned everything he needed to know from us.* Kevral groused over Ra-khir's plan, finding it useless yet unable to invent a better one of her own. In the first few moments, it had managed only to unnerve her and make any conversation impossible. *It'll never work.*

Kevral scarcely had time to raise the thought before Darris' warning whistle pierced the damp air. All heads swung toward him. Ra-khir scrambled to his feet. They had rehearsed half a dozen similar codes. This one revealed Darris had discovered someone but did not need their assistance. Kevral stiffened, opening a pathway for Darris to haul his captive into camp, remaining near enough to the edge of the clearing that she could handle the spy should he attempt escape or attack. She positioned herself mechanically, while startled thoughts rushed through her mind. She had never expected Darris to find anyone. If he did, she believed he would require their assistance to kill or take even one prisoner. This seemed too simple, and that worried her.

Tae stepped through the trees first, Darris close on his heels, though neither held a drawn weapon. For a hostage, Tae seemed amazingly unconcerned. He smiled as the others came into view. He wore the same tattered shirt and pantaloons as the day before, but they seemed cleaner. He had combed out the stems and tangles from his hair, leaving a glistening mane so black the sun struck blue highlights from it. His face bore a few scratches, and his hands seemed to carry all the dirt that no longer rimed his clothes and head. Kevral studied those hands, work-callused and little larger than her own. They swung loosely, without any indication that Tae intended to brandish a weapon or even to struggle. Kevral did not wholly trust his composure, however. Tae had already shown, by his abrupt disappearance last time, that he did not broadcast his actions as most people did.

Darris followed stiffly, shrugging behind Tae's back, a gesture Kevral took to mean that Tae had come of his own volition. Tae confirmed that impression by stepping unhurriedly but deliberately into the center of the clearing and announcing, "I got it."

Ra-khir glanced at Kevral who shrugged noncommittally, placing the onus back onto the Erythanian. Ra-khir looked at Tae again. "Got what?"

"The information I promised." As if suddenly recalling his manners, Tae nodded a greeting to each of the women in turn. "I know all about the heir."

The group exchanged uncertain gazes. Kevral edged

closer. The clearing left too many openings for evasion, but she hoped proximity would make him easier to grab or kill if either become necessary.

Darris recovered first. "You do?"

"I do."

"How?" Darris asked, his bard-inquisitiveness more fascinated by process than detail. He had tried to acquire the same knowledge and failed.

Tae turned to Darris, his stance growing tenser as he noticed that, intentionally or otherwise, he had become surrounded. "As I said I would."

"From the sage?" Darris persisted.

"Yes." Tae must have read doubt because he continued, describing details to prove his statement. "Twelfth story. South tower."

Matrinka chimed in. "But the only entrance is inside the castle." Her concern for Béarnian security touched Kevral as well. To have done as he claimed, Tae would have had to breach the walls into the courtyard then sneak inside the castle and past a host of guards. That anyone could have done so placed every member of the king's household at risk.

Tae smiled and turned to face Matrinka. "That, my lady, depends upon what you consider an entrance."

Through the window, Kevral surmised, though that course seemed equally difficult. Tae would still have had to work his way past guards and into the courtyard, then undertake a twelve-story climb of Béarnian-smoothed stone. Millennia ago, Béarnides had carved their castle directly from the mountainside; although many structures, such as the south tower, must have been built later. Kevral's knowledge about climbing was paltry at best, but she guessed that anything built from the ground up and from parts had to prove simpler to scale than polished, solid stone.

Apparently tired of having his methods questioned, Tae returned to the matter at hand. "Do you still want the information?"

"Of course." Darris broke in eagerly before Kevral could say anything more demure. Darris' exuberance would cost them dearly. Yet Kevral realized in the next moment, it was all moot. They would get back whatever they paid Tae since they would have no choice but to kill him after he turned over the information. Otherwise, he could sell it to enemies, too. Even that train of thought bowed to one more weighty.

The chances that Tae had really seen the sage's notes were slim. Much more likely, he lied.

Matrinka discovered a specific even Kevral had not considered. "The sage's notes are written in Béarnese."

Tae nodded, offering no explanation until Matrinka pressed further. "You read Béarnese?"

Kevral resisted the obvious, unnecessarily insulting question about whether he could read any language. Even she did not know the obscure language that most of the king's citizens had abandoned for the more common trading tongue. The odds that an Eastern street tough knew even a word of Béarnese seemed remote to the point of inconceivability. For now, however, Kevral played along. They could not afford to do otherwise. "How much is this going to cost?"

"Nothing," Tae said.

It was the last thing Kevral expected to hear. "You risked your life and freedom to give us information for nothing?"

"Not entirely nothing," Tae finally admitted.

Matrinka rose, setting Mior down on the stump. The cat dropped to its haunches, tail flicking in agitation. "What do you want?" Matrinka asked.

"When you go to find the heir, I want to come with you. Just promise I can, and all the information is yours."

The odd request alarmed Kevral. "Why?"

Tae turned his attention to the Renshai, visibly calmer as he grew more accustomed to having to address them from different sides. "I could be useful. And I'm quiet, so I don't think I'll make you any more obvious."

Kevral sighed, certain Tae knew she questioned his motivation not his advantage to them or their task. "I meant why would you *want* to join us?"

Tae dismissed the query. "I have my reasons."

Kevral glared.

Tae relented. "Let's just say I'm used to being part of a group."

"Gang," Kevral inserted, surmising from stories about large Western and Eastern cities.

Tae's dark eyes latched onto Kevral. He neither admitted nor denied the assertion. "I'm not with my group anymore. Haven't been for a while. I've been alone long enough, and I'm ready to join again. Yours is the first one I've found that isn't either a play group or guards. And you've got something important to do that I can help with."

Kevral did not buy the explanation entirely but wondered whether his reasons mattered. If he really had obtained the information they needed, they had little choice but to give in to his demand.

Ra-khir did not see it the same way. "He's not coming with us!" He jabbed a finger at Tae.

Everyone froze, surprised by the outburst.

"And neither is he." Ra-khir pointed at Kevral next.

That broke the tension. Though Matrinka remained politely silent, Darris snickered, and Tae laughed aloud.

Ra-khir's face reddened at the mockery. He drew breath to reinforce his insistence. Then, apparently realizing that the laughter seemed good-natured, he said nothing.

"How long have you all been together?" Tae asked incredulously.

"Not long," Matrinka admitted.

Darris added, still grinning. "But long enough so Ra-khir should know Kevral's female."

Ra-khir froze, breath still held. His eyes slowly widened as he considered the implications of that discovery.

Kevral smiled, her amusement not nearly as inoffensive. Several sarcastic comments came to mind, but she held her tongue. Living with the realization that she could, at any time, humiliate Ra-khir with stories of their meeting would torture the knight-in-training worse than words ever could. She had relished this moment and the embarrassment it would cause Ra-khir. Yet now that it had finally come, she could not explain why she felt nearly as flustered as he did.

Darris seized on Ra-khir's silence. "We need to discuss who goes in private."

Tae inclined his head toward an edge of the clearing far enough away so he could not overhear a quiet conversation.

"You'll wait?" Kevral said. The idea of leaving Tae to wander away bothered her, though he showed no sign of doing so.

"I'm not going anywhere. I'm trying to join you, remember?"

Kevral made no response. Clearly, Tae had come to the clearing specifically to meet with them and not under any compulsion from Darris. She doubted he would run now.

The four gathered in their private corner, Kevral alert to Tae's actions as well as their own. The Easterner crouched and glanced around the clearing while they talked. Mior curled on the stump in a patch of sunlight.

Darris began the discussion. "What do you think about Tae?"

Ra-khir could not help answering first. "He's not coming. I won't travel with a thief."

They all kept their voices low, but Matrinka's sounded unusually soft after Ra-khir's hostility. "We'd hate to lose you."

Kevral bit her cheek to keep from chuckling. Darris and Ra-khir stared at the princess.

Ra-khir lowered his head, offended. "My lady, you'd choose the company of a thief over a future Knight of Erythane?"

"Not usually." Matrinka pulled long, black hair back off her neck with one hand and held it in a ponytail. "But we need the information he's got, and you're not leaving me a choice."

Though Kevral usually liked to make Ra-khir squirm, this time she rescued him from the need to back down and lose face. "Here's how I see it. He either wants to go with us to help us or to work against us. If he's a friend, we might as well have him along. At the least, he's one more target for enemy weapons. If he's an enemy, well, better to have him in sword range than at a distance."

Darris continued along the same lines. "If he's part of the group that's trying to destroy Béarn, they'll probably leave us alone so long as he's with us. That actually makes having him along an advantage. We just need to watch what we say around him."

Ra-khir frowned, but he did listen. "No one could breach the sage's tower. He's lying to send us in the wrong direction, and he wants to join us to make sure we do."

Kevral did not bother to add the more dangerous scenario: that Tae had gathered the information and given it to Béarn's enemies, and now planned to lead the four of them in the wrong direction.

Matrinka released her hair, tossing up her hands in disgust. "You're all so suspicious. Maybe he just wants to become part of a group. Our group. We're a pretty interesting bunch."

Kevral found that possibility the least likely but did not bother to contradict. So long as she remained alert, no harm could come to Matrinka. "I hate it, but he's got us cornered. There's no other way to get that information. So long as he sends us toward Santagithi or the East, and we stay wary, how can it hurt to have him along?" She spoke mostly to placate the others. Once Tae told them all he knew, she had no reason not to kill him.

Ra-khir snorted. "It can hurt our reputation and our honor. Just the thought of being around him for months makes me ill." He sighed deeply. "But if you're all set on having him join us, I won't let you go without me to monitor him."

"Agreed then." Darris summarized, "If he gives us reasonable information, we take him along. We keep watch for him to double-cross us, especially when we get close to finding the heir. If he lies, we're no worse off than before."

They all nodded, Ra-khir grudgingly, then headed back as a group to the opposite edge of the clearing.

Tae remained where they had left him, rising from his crouch as they approached. "Well?"

Mior yawned and stretched each leg stiffly.

Darris spoke for them all. "We want the information. You can come with us once we have it."

Tae nodded blandly. "I want to hear that from Red." He gestured at Ra-khir.

Kevral smiled at Tae's ingenuity. Ra-khir shifted forward and backward without obvious intention, fidgeting. Darris' mouth fell open then closed to a thin line of offense. "You don't trust my word?"

Tae kept his gaze centered on Ra-khir but addressed Darris. "I trust your word just fine when it's only covering you." He continued to stare at Ra-khir, dark brows slowly arching in anticipation.

Ra-khir sighed. "I'm sorry for my hasty hostility." He glanced at Kevral briefly, letting her know the apology applied equally to her. "My friends believe we should bring you along, and I trust my friends' decisions. So long as you pose no threat to us or our cause, I won't harm you."

Kevral almost felt sorry for Ra-khir. Admitting to poor judgment did not come easy to Knights of Erythane; apprentice knights, still uncomfortable with their own integrity, would find it most difficult of all.

Not wholly appeased yet, Tae pressed. "I'll take that as a vow against your honor."

Ra-khir shifted again, this time with obvious impatience.

"Every word I speak and every action I take reflects on my honor."

Tae nodded once, stiffly, to indicate he accepted that explanation.

Matrinka had waited patiently through the preliminaries but now pressed for the information for which they had bargained. "So who is the heir? And where?"

Gently, Tae pulled a scroll from his pocket, its parchment rolled on dowels from both ends. Gripping it by the handholds on one side, he offered it to Matrinka. "Read for yourself."

Matrinka stared, accepting the scroll with shaking hands. She unrolled it from the top only slightly, correctly assuming Tae had left the readings in the proper position. "Gods," she whispered.

Kevral naturally assumed the expletive came in response to something Matrinka read, but Darris understood. He drew to Matrinka's side, studying the parchment over her shoulder. "That's really them, isn't it?"

"The sage's notes." Matrinka looked at Tae, innocently horrified. "You actually *took* the sage's notes?"

Tae threw out his hands, palm up, to indicate such should have been obvious. "Of course. I told you I'd get you the information. How else?"

Matrinka stated what they all had assumed. "I thought you'd read them. Then just bring us the answers."

Tae stared, incredulous. "You would have believed me?"

"No," Kevral answered honestly, before anyone could give a more considerate response. She guessed Tae would prefer simple truth to elaborate lies intended to protect his feelings. Excitement formed a tingle in her chest. Matrinka had seen the sage's writings before in the course of her studies. If she confirmed the handwriting on the scrolls, then it was, at worst, an astounding forgery. That Tae had chosen the proper scroll from hundreds confirmed his claim to read Béarnese.

"You're going to have to take this back." Matrinka's somber tone suggested urgency, but she took the scroll with her as she reclaimed her seat on the stump. She read aloud, though so softly the others shifted closer to hear. Kevral strained to listen, unwilling to give up a position that allowed her to scan for movement in the nearby bush. Tae had once come upon them undetected. That, Kevral assured herself, would never happen again.

Unnecessarily flowery wording described King Kohleran's youngest son, Petrostan, and his indiscretion with a female cousin named Helana. Kevral listened to a story of two exceedingly young lovers not nearly of age and their banishment from Béarn. According to the notes, they fled to a farming community called Dunwoods, outside Santagithi but within the jurisdiction of its king. The cousin bore Petrostan two sons. The elder succumbed to a plowing accident, and the father died trying to rescue him. Mother and youngest lived on, at least to the best knowledge the sage could gather; and she had remarried. The last remaining heir to Béarn's throne was seventeen-year-old Griff, a farm child who had never seen the kingdom he might inherit.

Griff. The name seemed ridiculously plain. *King Griff.* Kevral held back laughter with difficulty. The seriousness of the situation precluded humor. No matter the simplicity of the name, loyalty to the Renshai charged her to see him safely to the staff-test and, eventually, hopefully, to his throne.

Matrinka rerolled the scroll with paranoid caution, as if she feared the sage might notice the tracks of her eyes across the page. "This has to go back. Exactly where you found it. As soon as possible." She shivered. "The sage is so protective, I can't believe you took it. He'll notice it's gone, if he hasn't already. The trouble that could cause. . . ." She trailed off with a shiver of discomfort and glanced nervously at her companions.

Kevral imagined the repercussions without need for clarification. If the sage raised an alarm, it could stir panic about thieves who not only managed to violate archives never before disturbed but the very walls of Béarn's castle. Thoughts would naturally turn to treason, though previous conversation suggested that such had already fallen into consideration. The knowledge that the papers stolen contained the very information they most wished hidden would cause a panic they would have no means of quelling. The group coming forward with their plans might help defuse the apprehension, but it would raise many other concerns.

Kevral hovered while Matrinka returned the scroll to Tae with obvious reluctance. "It'll get back where it belongs," Kevral said, glaring at Tae, though with only token hostility.

He had gotten the information they needed and in the only manner she dared to trust.

"I'll take it back tonight," Tae promised.

Kevral nodded to indicate she would see that he kept his vow. As was often the case, another Renshai had already been assigned to replace her guardianship of Matrinka that night. Overseeing Tae would also give Kevral the opportunity to discover his means of breaching Béarn's defenses undetected. That gap in security needed immediate plugging. She hoped her presence would also thwart any plans Tae might have to meet with enemies of the kingdom.

Under the tightest time constraint, Ra-khir took over. "All right, then. I'll determine the best time for us to leave, when attention is focused elsewhere. Darris, can you work out the supplies?"

The bard's heir nodded.

"And I can get them," Matrinka added.

"Fine." Ra-khir considered further. "Anyone good with towns and deciding routes?"

Kevral suspected no one but Tae had ever gone beyond the immediate vicinity of the West's kingdom and its sister city of Erythane, yet Ra-khir had guarded his phrasing to hide that detail. Tae did not need to know any more of their weaknesses.

Darris paused long enough to let others speak first, though they did not, then launched into a comparatively awkward song, without accompanying instrumentation:

> "The bard's heir must travel
> To learn the world.
> True to every culture,
> He spreads his word.

> "He may sing of peace
> Or of heroes bold;
> But in every language
> His stories are told.

> "I have gone places
> To live and to learn,
> So I can serve Béarn
> When it comes my turn.

"I'll map in my head
And determine our course,
Experience and teachings
Will serve as my source."

Darris finished without apology for his simple tune or irregular rhyme scheme. Ra-khir nodded stiffly, relieved they
were not at Tae's mercy. "Fine," the knight added to close
the matter. Obviously, the next issue could not be so swiftly
or easily handled. "We still need to leave without drawing
attention. How difficult will that prove for all of you?" His
words included everyone, but he studied only Matrinka and
Darris.

The bard deferred to Matrinka. When she remained silent
several moments, he replied first to give her time to think.
"I can ascribe my leaving to learning. The bard's heir tradi-
tionally comes and goes without warning, though I've rarely
done so before."

Kevral believed Darris' song had detailed his bard's training well enough to explain how easy rationalizing travel
would prove for him. When Matrinka still did not answer,
lips pursed and attention focused inward, Kevral added her
piece. "I can justify going anywhere the princess goes. In
fact, my people and family would expect nothing else."

Tae added nothing. His disappearance from Béarn would
go as unnoticed as his presence. Even those who had seen
him would not miss him.

Ra-khir tossed in his own story, gaining Matrinka even
more time for deliberation. "It'll be more difficult than that
for me. I'm not bound here, but I'll have to suspend my
training and delay my knighthood." The pained expression
on his features told Kevral that would prove more discomfort to him than hindrance to their mission. "I don't think it
would raise any wonder if, under the circumstances, I chose
to leave Béarn for a while."

Matrinka clucked sympathetically.

Hyperalert, Kevral noticed a detail even she would otherwise have missed. Tae cringed ever so slightly, as if he, too,
felt some sadness for the plight of Ra-khir's father. *So the
little bastard has a conscience.*

Finally, able to delay no longer, Matrinka spoke her piece.
"I think I know a way."

Kevral listened closely. A flawed plan could pose fully as

much harm to Matrinka as an outside threat. Under the current circumstances, Kevral could not imagine any way to convince the council to allow an heir to leave Béarn. Only Kevral's blatant dismissal of their concern, and her reputation, had rescued her from her lectures about taking Matrinka into the forests and fields to gather herbs. Even so, their trips beyond the castle walls were always closely timed and monitored.

Matrinka explained. "If I abdicated any claim to Béarn's throne, and was therefore no longer an heir, I could go wherever I pleased. It would surprise no one if an heir surrendered nobility for safety, then chose to disappear."

The words stunned Kevral, and the others fell into startled silence. Ra-khir found his voice first. "But you can't do that."

"Why not?" Matrinka shot back.

Ra-khir flushed, stammering a reply. "W—well, I—I suppose you *can* do that, but it seems extreme. Surely, we can find a better way. . . ."

"Better?" Matrinka shook her head doubtfully. "I don't think so. As long as I'm an heir, the council won't let me leave here, not even for a day trip. They'd lock me in my room. Or in the dungeon if it came to that." She spoke matter-of-factly, but Kevral suspected the decision had not come as easily as Matrinka made it seem. Weeks or months of thought had preceded her pronouncement, probably initiated when she first failed the tasks. "If I ran away, it'd trigger a monumental search that would foil any attempts at secrecy. We might just as well announce our departure from the sage's tower."

Ra-khir drummed his fingers on his sword belt, finally recognizing Matrinka's point. "I couldn't let you run either. Not if it would leave the kingdom in turmoil."

Matrinka lowered her head. "It's not like I could ever sit on the throne anyway. Not unless I married the king. . . ."

Darris winced, almost imperceptibly.

"And if I really mean that much to Béarn, they can reinstate me when we return."

Kevral was not sure she followed. "You mean they can disown and reown you?"

Matrinka smiled at the inventive terminology. "The king can do as he pleases. The hard part's going to be talking my grandfather into renouncing me in the first place." She tipped her head, plunged into deeper consideration. "The council or the new king may not be as forgiving, but I'm willing to take that chance. If they held the decision against me after learning the circumstances, I wouldn't want to live among them anyway." She turned her attention to the cat suddenly, though the animal had not made a sound. She nodded, and her features screwed into an uncomfortable knot, as if acknowledging that the process she had so glibly outlined would not prove nearly as straightforward as she had implied.

Knowing Matrinka's expressions well, Kevral guessed that the princess believed her decision would hurt someone; and natural conclusion brought Kevral to King Kohleran. She tried to imagine her own father's reaction should she ever announce that she no longer wished to be Renshai. The idea seemed unfathomable. She would have to abandon every tenet that made her Kevral, and the idea of giving up the training, the honor, and the glory in battle that would become her final reward was a madness beyond plausibility. Her father, indeed the entire tribe, would have no choice but to kill her for such a foolish decision: both to rescue her from derangement and to prevent her from knowing or teaching the sword maneuvers that only Renshai were permitted to learn. She would welcome the execution to escape an insanity strong enough to drive her to such folly.

Kevral frowned, modifying her comparison to a more parallel level. If she only disowned herself from her family, not her tribe, she would scar her parents deeply without risking the knowledge and skill she had developed since the day her infant hand could close around a practice hilt. Having found what she believed to be the source of Matrinka's discomfort, Kevral turned her contemplation to another matter. Once the princess divorced herself from the kingdom, she no longer required a Renshai escort. Kevral believed she could circumvent this problem without much difficulty. Once assigned a task, she would remain rigidly faithful to it. She could convince even those Renshai with the staunchest commitment to semantics by reminding them that Matrinka, or her children, might still sit on the throne if the circumstances changed.

"Settled, then." Ra-khir took over again. "I'll determine the best day to leave." He indicated the bard's heir. "Darris, you plan out our route and gather gear. Matrinka, I think you'll have your hands full. Tae . . ." He turned his attention to the Easterner, unable to entirely keep loathing from his voice.

Tae did not seem to notice the disparaging tone. Unruly black hair dangled over his eyes, and his brows rose in patient expectation.

Ra-khir continued, "You'll need to take those notes back. I'm also betting you can pick the best time and cover for leaving to avoid notice. If anyone sees us leaving together, it'll arouse suspicion. Until we determine who's safe and who isn't, it's best if no one connects our departures."

"Just give me a direction."

"Southeast," Ra-khir supplied.

Tae nodded once.

Ra-khir addressed them all then, and Kevral suspected he left out a job for her deliberately. "Everyone is responsible for getting himself or herself a legitimate reason to disappear, without casting suspicion on oneself or others. If you need help, don't hesitate to ask. Will anyone have trouble getting a horse?"

Tae, Darris, and Matrinka all made fast gestures to indicate no difficulty. "I can get one for Kevral, too," Matrinka added.

"And I've got my own," Ra-khir finished. "Let's meet here in three days and compare information one last time."

Kevral added directly to Tae. "I'll meet you here a little after sundown. We'll get those notes back together." She clung to her promise to see the sage's scroll returned.

Tae shrugged to indicate she could join him if she wished, but her presence would prove unnecessary. And the group adjourned to its separate tasks.

Chapter 13

Oa'si

When you stand on the boundary between war-
ring countries, you become the target of them
both.

—Colbey Calistinsson

Matrinka chewed her lower lip until the skin peeled and the
pressure of her teeth brought pain. Mior sat near her mistress' left foot, tail curled around her paws, waiting with the
patience cats feigned so well. The act did not fool Matrinka.
She knew Mior shared her anxiety and her concern for her
grandfather's well-being. In addition, the animal worried for
Matrinka, which made her burden the heavier one. Matrinka
kept a brave face and fought down the urge to pace, but she
doubted her attempts to appear calm deceived Mior any
more than the cat's did her.

Matrinka glanced down the hallway to where Baltraine,
Kevral, and a scribe waited for her to initiate and complete
her business with the king. Discomforted by their scrutiny,
she turned back to the door to Kohleran's sickroom. Permission to meet with him had proved even more difficult to ob-
tain than Matrinka had expected. Over the past several
months, the king's health had limited her visits to rare occur-
rences closely regulated by Prime Minister Baltraine, but she
thought an issue of this import would earn her swift audience. The council knew, as did she, that her decision would
prove more significant than she had indicated to her companions.

You lied to them, Mior reminded.

Despite the cat's nonjudgmental attitude, Matrinka cringed, suffering enough guilt for them both. *Sometimes it is better to mislead friends than cause them the pain that truth can bring.* The decision had gnawed at her, but in the end, she had chosen compassion over honesty. Ra-khir did not need to bear the burden of knowing she had permanently sacrificed her royalty, and that of her offspring, for this cause. Had Kevral known the irrevocability of Matrinka's decision before they met with Béarn's council, she might not have allowed it at all. She probably would have seen it as her own failure to properly guard an heir. *I'm going to be a part of retrieving the new king. No one will take that from me.* Matrinka could not fully fathom her own unwavering loyalty to the cause, though she knew it came as a direct result of the humiliation she had suffered during the staff-test.

The price is high, Mior reminded.

I'm willing to pay it.

You're not the only one it will cost. The cat had an undeniable point, the very one that held Matrinka frozen in place. She loved her grandfather. This sterling example of humanity had already endured more emotional pain than anyone ever should. He deserved better, yet she had little choice but to proceed with disownment. *I have no other options.* The idea of causing anguish, especially to one she loved, ached through her conscience.

You do have other options.

None that won't jeopardize the mission. Even if I believed we could evade searchers sent to find us. Even if our quest could tolerate everyone in the kingdom knowing and suspicious about my departure, I don't want Béarn wasting time, money, and security tracking me.

Mior lapsed into silence, offering only her presence as consolation.

Matrinka knew she could not afford to stall too long. Initially, the prime minister had denied her request to deliver news that might break the last fragile thread of their beloved king's health. This once, she had not accepted his proclamation meekly. She'd badgered Baltraine, invoking law and convention until he finally agreed to let her present her request to the council. Only after all efforts to convince Matrinka to change her mind had failed did the council finally relent. They would not grant permission for disownment. That decision lay in King Kohleran's hands, and the law decreed she confront him directly.

Baltraine had filled their walk from meeting to waiting rooms with cajoling, chastisement, and appeals that bordered on pleading. He understood that heirs to the throne had rigid and difficult lives now, but that would change, he promised. He knew that watching cousins die hurt, that fearing for one's life every day became as much a sickness as an actual disease, and that failure at the staff-test eroded reason and confidence. He used every argument she could surmise, and several she had never considered, to convince her to stay. Matrinka had listened stoically, answering only when directly questioned and always in the negative. She could not budge from her position. She could not tell him why without endangering their mission, so she gave no explanation at all.

Mior had made a running commentary on Baltraine's arguments in an obvious attempt to keep Matrinka's mind light at a difficult time and keep her from falling prey to the ceaseless desire to confess all to one she trusted. Conversely, Kevral had remained quiet. Even her footfalls made no noise against the polished, wooden floor. Matrinka guessed the confirmation that disownment was the permanent process Kevral had originally assumed had irritated the Renshai. At the least, it would make her excuses for remaining with Matrinka far more difficult to slide past the Renshai chieftains.

Still Matrinka stalled. Baltraine had told her to act quickly as the king needed his sleep. Once he drifted off, Matrinka did not have permission to disturb him. This last thought mobilized her. In his weakened condition, she would not dare awaken him, even if the ministers had allowed her to do so. It seemed too cruel, especially right before shocking him with her news. Steeling herself, Matrinka pushed open the door and stepped inside. Mior slithered in after her, and Matrinka closed the door behind them both.

The rancid odors of old blood and sickness assailed Matrinka's nostrils. Repulsed despite her healer's training, it took strength of will to meet her grandfather's watery stare. He seemed to have aged a decade since her last visit. His familiar features folded into more wrinkles than seemed possible. Cheekbones jutted from a gaunt face that belied its Béarnian heritage. None of the healthy, swarthy hue remained, replaced by a pasty pale yellow. Moisture blurred the once-piercing black eyes, and the whites had dulled to saffron. His silver hair had receded, revealing freckled scalp. Nevertheless, he gave her a broad smile. Life still lingered in the sickly eyes. "Matrinka," he said. "It's always a pleasure to see you. What's happened since I saw you last?"

Mior bounded onto the bed, purring, then curled into the crook of the king's armpit.

"I love you, Grandpapa." Matrinka avoided the question. She shoved aside the lacy curtains, and summer sunlight chased gloom into the farthest corners. She opened the window, admitting a warm breeze pungent with perfume from the courtyard gardens. Memories swept in with the wind, and the fragrance reawakened a happy childhood spent skipping past statues and tended beds of vegetables, braiding flowers into her hair. Her grandfather had spent many hours spinning apocryphal tales of animals or explaining the wonders and history of Béarn. The idea of disclaiming this past brought tears to her eyes.

"I love you, too," Kohleran returned, his adoration for his granddaughter radiating with his words. "You always know what I need."

Not this time. Matrinka bit her lower lip, immediately evoking pain from her previous nervous gnawing at it.

Even through rheumy eyes, Kohleran noticed her pain. "Are you well?"

"I'm well," Matrinka said, crossing the room to sit on the edge of his bed. "I wish you were well, too."

King Kohleran dismissed her concern with a scornful wave. "Bah. I'm old, and it's my time to go. I've missed your grandmother terribly, and soon enough I'll see her again in the Yonderworld." Although the Béarnides believed in the Northern gods, they still clung to the Western concept of a single place where all souls gathered after death. Valhalla and Hel, they believed, existed only for warriors. "Don't feel sorry for me. I've had the happiest life any man could. I wouldn't trade it for anyone's, not even the sickness because it makes me appreciate all I've had. And it makes me appreciate moments like this one." He smiled broadly.

Stricken, Matrinka swallowed hard, able to return only a lopsided grin.

Kohleran picked up on her mood immediately. "What's troubling you?"

His concern proved too much for Matrinka to bear. She

burst into tears, feeling like a lost child. Kohleran raised his hands toward her, though weakness did not allow him to gather her into his arms. Sensing his need, as well as her own, Matrinka settled into his embrace and wrapped her arms around his shoulders. His warmth lodged her firmly in the past, and reality faded around her. With only tactile impression as a guide, her mind conjured images of her grandfather as a robust, gentle man of justice, not yet withered by disease.

For a long time they lay that way, neither speaking, both clinging. Eventually, Matrinka slid free of his grasp and sat near his head. He brushed aside strands of dark hair that clung to drying tears on her cheeks and gave her a sober examination as if to read the pain cloistered inside her. "Times are hard for Béarn now." Misinterpreting the source of her tears, he tried to console. "The world never meant for men to outlive their children. Worse, their grandchildren. That one thing about my life I would change."

Kohleran intended to soothe, to show Matrinka they all shared the same pain. Instead, his words sparked guilt and self-loathing. Matrinka knew her news would strain the worst of her grandfather's sorrow. The yearning to crawl into his lap and beg stories nearly overwhelmed her, yet the urgency of her task forbade it. This might be the last time she saw her grandfather alive. She cleared her throat, speaking before the remnants of her courage crumbled. "Grandpapa, I love you dearly. I'm so sorry for what I have to ask you now."

The king took Matrinka's hand in his withered grip, comforting with a touch as she had done so often for him since his illness started.

Matrinka's voice fell so low, she could scarcely hear herself. "I want you to disown me. I can't be an heir to Béarn any longer."

Though she had spoken barely above a whisper, Kohleran heard. He stared, eyes widening in increments, mouth pursed and still, face a bloodless yellow. Then it was his turn to cry, tears brimming away the mucus coating his eyes and drawing trails along his shrunken cheeks.

Matrinka squeezed his hand, wishing desperately she could make him cease to care about a decision that now seemed like treachery and betrayal. Her chest felt smashed and empty, as if every rib had shattered at once and her lungs could no longer expand.

For several moments, neither spoke. Mior ceased her purring, the only sound the rattle of breath in the old man's tired throat.

Kohleran broke the silence in a painful whisper that scarcely resembled a ghost of his once powerful voice. "No. Oh, no. Not Matrinka. Not my favorite. I can't."

"You have to," Matrinka begged, crying again. "It's the only way."

"Why?" Kohleran wheezed, the question obviously directed at her reasons for asking for renunciation rather than as follow-up to her last statement. "What have I done to drive you away?"

His words jabbed through her like blades. "Nothing, Grandpapa. It's not you."

"Then why?"

Matrinka could not answer, bound by her promises to her companions. "I can't say."

Kohleran studied her through doelike eyes dulled by moisture. "You expect me to disown my granddaughter without explanation?"

"It's the only way." Matrinka looked away, unable to meet his candid gaze.

"I can't do it. I won't." Kohleran twisted his fingers free of her grasp, his weakness now an obvious frustration. "I can deal with losing my grandchildren to illness and even to murder. But I will not willingly let one go."

"Grandpapa," Matrinka whined through her own tears, grabbing for his hand.

Kohleran dodged her attempt, clumsy from illness. "Go away. Leave me to my misery."

Be strong. Mior sent her presence to help buoy Matrinka. The purring resumed, and she rubbed against King Kohleran's hand. He twined his fingers through the soft fur, and a slight smile broke through his sadness for a quarter of a second.

"I will not go, Grandpapa." Matrinka finally managed to meet his gaze again; and, this time, he glanced away. "You can't hold love hostage. You can prevent my becoming a commoner, but I will still leave Béarn. Then my death is assured. Is that what you want?"

"No," Kohleran admitted. "I want my granddaughter to be

proud of her heritage, no matter who threatens it. I want her to be proud of her lineage, whether lowliest gutter stock or kings. I want her to love her grandfather, the memory of her father, and her many cousins enough to remain a part of us and not abandon us in times of trouble." He closed his eyes. "I had thought you among the best. I misjudged."

"I love who and what I am!" Fierce tears and a growing lump in Matrinka's throat rendered the words all but incomprehensible despite volume. "And I love you!" Matrinka turned her attention to Mior. *I have to tell him. I can't leave him like this.*

Not safe.

It's unavoidable.

No one should know. Him least of all. Sick people blather.

Matrinka could never win a battle with her own conscience, and it told her that the truth would soothe the hurt she had inflicted. *He deserves to know.*

Mior did not argue. The cat had an understandable soft spot for King Kohleran and would hate to see him left in inexplicable pain every bit as much as Matrinka.

Matrinka sighed, voice dropping back to a conversational level. "Grandpapa, I don't want to be disowned. I *have* to be."

Finally, their gazes met, and Kohleran waited patiently for explanation.

"My friends and I must be able to travel freely and inconspicuously, without having to fight assassins or evade guards."

"Travel? Travel where? Why?"

"Please, Grandpapa. No one should know about this."

Kohleran looked bewildered. "Not even your grandfather? Not even the king of Béarn?"

"No one," Matrinka insisted.

King Kohleran considered her words somberly for several moments, then shook his head sadly. "I'm sorry. I cannot disown my granddaughter without understanding why."

Matrinka accepted his judgment, trusting his experience and wisdom as well as the worthiness assigned to him by the same test that had condemned her. "Then I have no choice but to tell you. We're going to bring back the last heir. The only one who has not yet undergone the staff-test." She smiled, but it was strained. "In exchange for a granddaughter who can't rule Béarn, you'll get a grandson who just might."

Kohleran frowned, wrinkles deepening. "I don't need my granddaughter to take such a risk. We've sent scouts for him already."

Scouts? The declaration confused Matrinka. "The scouts must have failed, because an envoy was sent. It also has not returned. Knight-Captain Kedrin believes we can succeed where others could not."

"Ah." Kohleran ran clawed fingers through his brittle, white beard thoughtfully. "Kedrin has always been a clever man. A small, secret band of youngsters might go unnoticed." He studied Matrinka through narrowed eyes no longer tear-filled but again filmed with rheum. "Who besides me and Kedrin knows about this?"

"Only my companions."

"Good." Kohleran relaxed visibly. "Baltraine spoke of the possibility of treason. Besides that, even loyal retainers change their behavior when privy to information. To divert attention from you and your friends, we'll need to keep even the prime minister ignorant. That way, Béarn and her council can continue to operate as they would."

Warmth suffused Matrinka at the realization that Béarn's king had faith in an inexperienced, eager band of adolescents that most would dismiss out of hand. "So you'll disown me?"

"No," Kohleran said.

Matrinka froze into shocked silence.

"But I will make it look as if I have. I will proclaim it so, but the sage's notes will reflect the truth. You will always be my granddaughter."

Pleased and frightened at once, Matrinka considered the implications. She had never truly wished to abandon her family, and Kohleran seemed to have solved the problem. But if Tae could steal and read the sage's notes, others might do so also. Kevral had detailed Tae's methods from her observation the previous night. The Renshai claimed that he used self-created tools to climb walls that most believed unscalable. Split second timing had allowed him to slip past the guards; even then, Kevral had needed to distract one to rescue Tae from an otherwise fatal error. Luck had played as strong a hand as skill, especially the first time. For all intents and purposes, the sage's notes were secure. If not, the information Kohleran added scarcely mattered. Anyone with access to the truth about her abdication could also uncover the details about Griff that would prove much more valuable and dangerous.

Seems fair, Mior suggested.

The compromise more than satisfied Matrinka. Her grandfather's ability to settle major dilemmas in a simple fashion that left everyone happy never ceased to amaze her. Herein, she believed, lay the means of passing the staff-test. Though too late for her, she would do everything within her power to ascertain that her children developed this skill. She only hoped her grandfather lived long enough to help instruct them. "I love you, Grandpapa," she said, though the words, even repeated this many times, barely described the depth of her fondness for him.

They embraced one more time, clinging with a desperation neither bothered to conceal. Both knew they would likely never see one another again.

Matrinka remained in place until Kohleran's grip failed and he sank back to the bed. At first, she feared he had fallen asleep. But his gummy eyes peeled open and he spoke in a tired voice scarcely above a whisper. "Go, Matrinka. Please, send in the scribe so I can proceed with what we discussed while it's still strong in my mind." He added sadly, "I forget things sometimes or remember them wrong. But I'll always love you. I wish you and your friends the grace of every god."

From one god-sanctioned, the words meant everything. Matrinka resisted the urge to hold him again. She could say "good-bye" a thousand times, and it would never seem nearly enough. "Thank you," she whispered. Mior rubbed across a withered hand one more time, then hopped down from the bed. The cat and her mistress left the room together.

The elves' torture took a strange tack so subtle Rantire barely recognized it for what it was. One day, she did not eat the peas on her dinner tray. When asked if peas poisoned humans, she admitted that she simply did not care for the taste of them. A week followed during which she received only peas for all her meals: pea paste, pea porridge, even pea cobbler until she sickened of the color green. They supplied her with itchy, woolen blankets, then with nothing but the leafy carpet and its pervading odor of mold. They bombarded her with visitors, elves studying and whispering about her for hours that stretched into days. Other times, they left her in lonely, silent darkness. None of these maneuvers caused anything worse than discomfort; even the indecency of toileting in front of the multicolored, gemlike eyes soon ceased to bother her. Modesty became a luxury she discarded from necessity. She held her silence, practicing combat maneuvers at least once per day whether alone or under scrutiny.

During one of the periods of intensive quiet, a single elf strode boldly to the mesh front of her cave. Though unafraid, he did not radiate the aura of confidence she felt in the presence of Dh'arlo'mé and others. This one seemed more curious, too young or ignorant to fear her. The meager light struck red highlights from black hair that hung to fragile shoulders. Unwinking golden eyes watched from beneath a fringe of bangs. He stood much smaller than any other elf she had seen thus far, and he gave her an impression of childishness much the way the elder had seemed old.

The elf's voice and mannerisms enhanced the image, though he used the human Northern tongue fluently. "Are you a girl-human or a boy-human?"

Rantire could not help smiling, though she did not slip into the high-pitched, simple speech patterns most adults used to address children. In the Renshai culture, skill determined stature far more than age. "I'm a girl-human. A woman."

"Oh." The canted eyes roved up and down, then settled on Rantire's face again. "How can you tell?"

Rantire had no wish to sexually educate someone else's offspring, especially that of an enemy. "The same way you know you're a boy-elf."

"Oh." The elf accepted the answer, though his expression betrayed confusion. "My name is Oa'si-Brahirinth Yozwaran Tril'frawn Ren-whar." He paused for breath. "What's your name?"

Rantire clung to her previous lie. "Brenna."

He waited patiently for her to continue. When she did not, he pressed. "That's all?"

Rantire realized she had said more to this elf than to any other. She found it hard to admit to herself that she preferred his company to solitude. "Humans can't remember long names, and we have more important things to do than worry about such details. Do you mind if I call you Oa'si?" She pronounced it "WAY-see" and did not bother to surmise the spelling. Surely the elfin alphabet bore little resemblance to anything human; and, even if it did, a child might not yet know how to spell.

"All right," he said, face scrunched in confusion. "How come?"

"It's easier," Rantire explained briefly, clinging to the belief that revealing weaknesses might harm her people. Oa'si seemed like a harmless child plying her with questions from natural infantile curiosity, but she could not escape the possibility that the elves had sent him purposely, believing she would open up to a child as she had not to their weak version of torture. She felt comfortable in his presence. As long as she guarded her tongue and did not reveal any major information, she could chat with this youngster. It gave her an outlet other than the madness that accompanied protracted solitude. Better, whether or not the elves had planted Oa'si, she could glean more information from him then he could from her. A child would likely give innocent and honest answers.

"Oh," Oa'si said again, though he still seemed unconvinced. "Oa'si." He tried the name out like a new suit of clothes. "Oa'si's all right, I guess."

"Thank you." Rantire smiled, moving toward the mesh for a more personal discussion. "We use short names so it doesn't take all day to warn someone he's in danger."

Oa'si fidgeted a step backward at her approach, then settled into a nervous crouch. His garnet eyes studied her with guileless fascination. "Danger?"

"Trouble," Rantire explained. "That something might hurt him."

Oa'si mulled her description over for longer than any human child would have. "Why would something hurt someone?"

The concept of threat seemed too integral to life to require explanation, so Rantire did not try. "I don't know. Let's just say something did." She tried another tack, "Or we needed to get someone's attention fast. You can't say long names quickly."

Oa'si remained in place, eyes focused on Rantire, and his discomfort seemed to disappear as he concentrated on their conversation. "You could always call a ..." He hesitated, obviously groping for a translation that didn't exist. "... call a *khohlar*." he tipped his head sideways, examining her reaction with an intensity that made him seem much less childlike.

Rantire shook her head to indicate lack of comprehension.

"It's like a squashing together of a whole lot of words into a ... a ..." He trailed off, at a loss again. "... a magic 'thought' sort of thing," he finished lamely. He brightened suddenly. "Like this." His scrutiny became even more intense, if possible.

A concept caressed the edges of Rantire's mind. She got an image of address, the way Oa'si pictured her; and with it came a barrage of uncertainty and questions. He saw her as an enigma, a puzzle requiring understanding.

The touch finished before Rantire could think to pull away. Startled by the contact, she dropped into a wary crouch that brought her down to Oa'si's level. "How did you do that?"

Oa'si shrugged. Clearly, the skill came naturally to him.

"Can other elves do it, too?"

Oa'si nodded.

"Can I?"

Oa'si blinked, then widened his gemlike eyes incredulously. "Don't you know?"

"No," Rantire admitted. "Can I try?"

"That's up to you." Oa'si's eyes returned to their normal configuration, then narrowed in disbelief. "How could I stop you?"

Rantire had no idea where to begin, nor whether or not the process could be halted or controlled. She did feel certain the information she learned from this child would prove invaluable. "What do I do?"

"Just think at me and draw up magic."

"How?"

"How?" Oa'si shot back.

"Yes, how do I do that?"

"I don't know." Oa'si apparently found the process impossible to describe. "I just do it, and it happens."

Making magic bore no logic Rantire could fathom. Closing her eyes, she riveted on a message of friendship and willed herself to send it to him. After several moments of total concentration, she opened her eyes.

Oa'si still stared at her. "Ready to start now?"

Rantire chuckled, her first laugh in as long as she could remember. "I already tried," she admitted. Only then, concern struck. *Is this a trick? If I attempt to open my thoughts to him, will he then be able to read everything I know?*

But if Oa'si knew anything more about her than before, he showed no sign of it. "Then you probably can't do this either." He lowered his head, flapped his arms once, then rose from the floor to a height at which he could chat comfortably with her had she remained standing. He dropped back down. "Or this." He mumbled a few words and held out a delicate hand with slender, tapering fingers. A colorful lump appeared on his hand, like a solid piece of a rainbow.

Rantire's heart seemed to sink in her chest. Obviously, even the youngest elves could perform magic individually. Oa'si's presentation shattered her hope that she could face them one-on-one in fair combat. She dodged the question of whether or not she or other humans could perform such feats, clinging to the hope that she could learn enough about her captors to find a way to thwart them and escape. "That mind-magic thing is fascinating."

Oa'si shrugged. "Not to me."

Rantire continued questioning despite her companion's loss of interest. Any race that could bandy about eighteen syllable names would not succumb easily to boredom. "Can you tell what I'm thinking?"

"No." Oa'si clenched his hands in his lap and examined the rainbow lump thoughtfully. "We can't tell what anyone's thinking. We can just call a *khohlar.* Like I did." He heaved an elfin sigh. "That means we can say lots of words at someone with a . . ." He borrowed Rantire's description, ". . . mind-magic thing."

"Can you talk that way to more than one person at a time?"

"We can call to one or everyone nearby."

Rantire sought clarification. "So if you had four other elves with you, you could talk to just one or all four but not to just two."

"Uh-huh," Oa'si confirmed. "Can we talk about something else?" Without waiting for an answer, he changed the subject. "Want some . . ." Again he struggled for the word, as he rarely did. ". . . candy?" He broke the multicolored lump into two pieces and offered both to Rantire.

Rantire squeezed her thumb and forefinger through a triangle of the mesh. She plucked a half from the elf's soft, moist palm, as much from politeness and curiosity as hunger. She did not fear poisoning; the elves had already had ample opportunity to place any herb they wished into her food. Nevertheless, natural caution made her wait for Oa'si to take a bite, chew, and swallow before she followed suit.

The candy tasted unlike anything Rantire had eaten before. Her tongue compared it to honey and a mixture of sweet spices, but its flavor resembled these only marginally. "Delicious," she said, hoping her enjoyment of it did not mean she would never have any more. Again, paranoia reared. She had heard of herbs that, eaten too often, created an irresistible craving for more. Stories of men killing for addictions abounded, though she had seen nothing more formidable in that regard than a drunkard pleading for swallows of leftover ale from uncleaned mugs when his money ran short. Rantire did not worry over this possibility long, however. Renshai training included the balancing of spirit and body and the channeling of power between them. Weaker women might fall prey to such a tactic, but Rantire trusted the fortitude of her mind to see her through such a situation. And it would only make her stronger.

Oblivious to Rantire's worries, Oa'si ate in happy silence.

"I wish *I* could create candy from air." Rantire fished for more information about magic that she could use, not only to assist her escape but to take back to humans to help protect them from elves.

"Me, too," Oa'si returned, as if she had fabricated the idea from whole cloth.

Rantire made a noise of amusement. "You just did."

Oa'si's chewing slowed, and he studied the last bit of candy in his hand. The sparse light gleamed from smears of sugar on his palm. "Create? I can't even make it from roots and flowers and sugar. My mama does that."

"But I saw you make it," Rantire insisted, keeping her voice low so elves on the sidelines could not hear. Her ears told her that no elf but Oa'si stood within listening distance, but she could not view the ends of the hallway where she had once become trapped against a gate. "Your hand was empty. Then it was full."

"I didn't make it." Oa'si used a disparaging tone that children reserved for classmates who made stupid comments that all but demanded ridicule. "I *called* it."

"You called it?"

"I told it to come."

"Really?" The applications of that ability seemed incredible and limitless. Rantire felt awash in fascination and apprehension. In the hands of friends, it would prove an invaluable tool. Unfortunately, the same held true for enemies. "Where was it before you called it?"

"In my room."

"Can you call this?" Rantire held out the last piece of her share of the candy, then clamped her fist closed around it.

Oa'si dismissed the possibility with a snort that hinted of derision. "It's not mine anymore. I gave it to you, so I can't call it."

Rantire made the natural connection, that elves, or at least this elf, could only "call" his own possessions. She pressed for more details. "Can all elves call things?"

Oa'si jerked his head in a gesture Rantire already knew to mean a negative response. "Different ones can do different things."

"So some could, maybe, make candy."

"Yeah." Oa'si giggled at the idea. "But not from magic. Magic doesn't have any form. It's like air. You can't make air have shape."

Rantire injected reality and observation into the discussion. "But you could give life to something that already had form but wasn't alive." She saw Oa'si's eyes narrow as he tried to follow the flow of words, and she attempted to make it simpler with an example. "Like a statue."

Oa'si considered much longer than Rantire thought he should have needed. "Someone could do that, I guess, but not by himself. He'd need a ..." Once more, he had no translatable word or phrase. ". . . *jovinay arythanik.*"

Experience gave Rantire the words to attempt the translation Oa'si could not manage. "A joining of magic. A group of elves working together to cast a spell."

"Yes!" Oa'si confirmed triumphantly. "You're not stupid." He obviously intended the last as a compliment, though the implication that he had previously believed her feebleminded transformed it to faint and damning praise. His triangular tongue flicked out, and he polished off the last smear of sugar from his palm with obvious sadness. "Now *you* have to give *me* something."

Rantire smiled. This seemed more like normal child behavior to her. "I have nothing to give. I'm trapped here with only my clothes and blankets. I need those for warmth."

Oa'si's lower lip jutted forward.

Rantire marveled at how much it resembled a human child's pout. She considered other possible presents, finding an easy precedent among Renshai where teaching was the most prized treasure of all. "I could tell you a story."

Oa'si brightened.

Rantire clung to caution and strategy that would further convince the elves of mankind's strength and, hopefully, dissuade them from violence. She searched for a topic that would not reveal weaknesses, and the Renshai's favorite hero came instantly to mind. No story about Colbey could show humans in any way but strong and competent. A tale from Colbey's childhood seemed best for a youngling, though she had not yet established Oa'si's age. "You're a child, aren't you?"

Oa'si nodded, speaking the facts without pride or shame. "I'm the very newest."

That proclamation surprised Rantire. Though obviously immature, Oa'si could walk, run, and communicate in two languages with a skill that assured he had at least eight years behind him. Rantire could not imagine more than two years passing without the birth of a baby among Renshai or Béarnides. "How old are you?"

"A child," Oa'si reconfirmed.

"Yes, I know." Rantire waved away the simple answer. "How many years old?"

"Years?" Oa'si cocked his head and regarded Rantire with his steady, golden eyes.

Rantire believed the concept too common for explanation. His command of the Northern tongue, thus far, had proceeded too smoothly to account for his ignorance. More likely, the long-lived elves saw little need for close reckoning of time. Experience told her they did know how to account in days. "You know how days get longer for a while, then shorter, then longer again?"

Oa'si nodded.

"How many times since you were born have days been short?"

"I don't know," Oa'si's tone suggested the question held no significance for him. "About thirty."

"Goodness." Rantire could not contain the mild expletive.

"Less than you expected?" Oa'si said hopefully.

"More," Rantire admitted. "You're a little older than *me*." She could not help asking. "How old do elves get?"

Oa'si mulled the question, clearly without a scale to measure such a thing. "In short-day times?"

"Years. Right."

"A few thousand, maybe," Oa'si ventured, though Rantire could not begin to guess the accuracy of such a statement. Most children had small grasp of estimation. If he had come close, it validated the elder's claim that he knew Colbey in his mortal years. "How old do humans get?"

It was the natural question. "Not nearly as old," Rantire admitted. "We're old at sixty."

"Years?" Oa'si repeated, incredulous.

"Years," Rantire confirmed.

"Oh." Oa'si sounded sympathetic, though he lost interest quickly. "Where's my story?"

"Right here." Rantire tapped her skull, then smiled. "I'm going to tell you one of a million tales about a human hero named Colbey Calistinsson."

Although Oa'si had pressed for Rantire to begin, he interrupted after only this one sentence. "What's a hero?"

"That's someone we admire for bravery. Someone we all wish we could be like."

"Why?"

The question had no simple answer. The roots of admiration went deeper than any individual could understand or explain. "Do you want me to tell the story or not?"

Oa'si sat back, arms folded across his narrow chest and lips pouting. "Yes."

"All right. This story happened when Colbey was very young, not even two years old yet. That'd be almost half an elfin lifetime ago."

Oa'si opened his mouth. Silenced by a warning glance from Rantire, he closed it again.

"Now it happened Colbey's mother came together with a mother who had borne a child at approximately the same time, also a boy. This mother took to bragging about her son and his brilliance. Already, he could speak half a hundred words, while Colbey, and most boys his age, used only about a dozen. Despite this tendency of the other to boast, the mothers struck up a fast friendship." Rantire glanced at Oa'si to ascertain that he followed the story and had not gotten bored.

Oa'si sat with his hand clamped over his mouth, rocking slightly in place, attention fixed on Rantire.

Encouraged, Rantire continued. "On one occasion, Colbey's mother left her son in this other woman's care for part of a day. Colbey toddled about while the other boy placed and replaced alphabet sticks in sequence."

Oa'si could not contain himself. "Alphabet sticks?" he asked cautiously.

Rantire weathered the interruption without comment. The story would have little meaning if the elf-child did not understand the events. "A set of sticks, about the length of my forearm . . ." She demonstrated the size by holding her hands apart, then dropped them to her sides. ". . . each with a letter of the alphabet on it. You see, the boy could name them and place them in proper order already, a feat most children years older could not accomplish."

Oa'si nodded his understanding, and Rantire continued the tale.

"Colbey watched for some time, but could not yet understand the concept. He would pick up a stick or two and either swing them around or hand them politely to the other boy to put in place. Proud of her son's skill, the mother made many disparaging comments about Colbey's simplicity, calling him dull to her child's genius."

"Why?" Oa'si asked.

Again, Rantire allowed the interference without chastising. The story had much to teach to a child capable of grasping the inherent morality and poetic justice. She wondered if elfin principles gibed closely enough with Western humanity to allow such a thing. Even between different cultures of humans they varied so much. "Why did she insult Colbey?"

"Yes, why?"

"Meanness." Rantire gave the simple answer first. "Insecurity."

Clearly, the explanation did not satisfy the query. "But why did she insult Colbey?"

"Because for some *really* insecure people, the only way to prove they have something better is to belittle others."

Oa'si spouted back what he understood of Rantire's description. "So she wanted to make Colbey look stupider because it would make her son seem even smarter?"

The youngster's insight impressed Rantire. "Right." Inwardly, she realized that, just because elves lived longer did not mean a direct correlation existed between an elfin thirty-year-old and a human nine-year-old. *The extra years have to gain them experience, even if physical maturity occurs more slowly.* No matter the reason, she enjoyed the interaction. Any adult would appreciate an interested, young audience; and she proved no exception.

"Elves don't do that," Oa'si said emphatically.

"Are you sure?"

"Elves don't do that," Oa'si repeated.

Rantire did not have the knowledge to confirm or contradict. "Good. It's not a nice thing."

"Finish the story."

Rantire complied. "While the other boy's mother had the children, a pack of wild dogs came upon them."

"Dogs?" Indulged twice, Oa'si seemed to have forgotten that he was not supposed to interject.

"They're a type of animal that's about a third to half the size of an adult human. They eat meat."

"Meat?"

"The flesh of other animals."

Oa'si screwed his features into a grimace of revulsion and made a noise that Rantire took to indicate disgust.

Understanding dawned. Rantire had noticed that the elves served her no meat, but she attached little significance to it. Many of the foods they served tasted like nothing she had ever eaten and could have come from anywhere. The elves' vegetable diet did not surprise her; the idea that this child had never seen or heard of a carnivore did. "Most wild animals are too afraid of humans to hunt them, but dogs are tamed. We keep them as pets. The ones that become feral, however, are dangerous. They're hungry meat-eaters who don't fear humans." The illustration awoke alarms only after she spoke. Revealing a creature who posed a threat to humans might assist the elves. Rantire returned to her story abruptly and irritably. To abandon it now would only draw attention to her error. "A pack of ravenous dogs charged the mother and the boys, teeth bared and mouths slavering.

"A weakling and a coward, the mother screamed, frozen

in place. Neither of the boys had seen any dog but friendly ones, but the mother's terror cued them to danger. Her son hid behind her. But not Colbey. He snatched up two of the alphabet sticks. Wielding them like swords, he charged the dogs. One attacked first, hungering for the tender meat of a child. Colbey proved a far more difficult target than the animal expected. A few mighty whacks, and the beast fell dead. The others turned tail, seeking a dinner that would not fight back."

Oa'si went right for the heart of the story. "So Colbey had a skill, too. Just a different one."

"Exactly!" Rantire wished all human children could grasp morals so quickly. "Without Colbey's physical skill and courage, the other mother would no longer have had a son to brag about."

"So what happened to them?" Oa'si asked.

"The boys?"

"Yes."

"Colbey became a great warrior hero, so skilled that the gods eventually claimed him as one of their own."

Oa'si's mouth framed an awed circle. "The gods?"

"That's how spectacular he was."

"And the other boy?"

Rantire replied with the answer her mother had told her, though history contradicted the time line. "He became a Cardinal Wizard, one of the very last."

"Oh," Oa'si said, though his voice revealed continued puzzlement.

Apparently, all elves had some magical ability, so it seemed likely that Oa'si would struggle with the concept of Wizards, especially the idea that they would seem special. Yet, he did not question the meaning of the word.

"I have to get home, now," Oa'si said. "My mother will wonder about me." He turned to leave, then glanced over his shoulder. "Can I come by again?"

Rantire shrugged and smiled. "As far as I know, I'm not going anywhere."

Oa'si headed off into the corridor, and was soon lost to Rantire's sight.

Rantire rose and moved deeper into the darkness of her cell. She had known the elf-child less than an hour, yet she missed his soft, musical voice and gentle presence. She con-

sidered the situation for a long time, knowing she would
need to make many decisions and set some limits before
Oa'si returned to her cell. It would be easy to tell him things
about humans that she should not. And dangerous as well.

Chapter 14

Ravn

Me? Start the Ragnarok?

—Colbey Calistinsson

Midgard's trees still looked lanky and emaciated to the eldest of the elves, bearing little resemblance to the bubble-fruited *yarmshinyin* and the broad-leafed *kathkral* that existed only in memories of home. Afternoon sunlight painted shadows through the forest clearing. A breeze stirred the branches, showering the Nine of the elfin council with wing-shaped seeds and collected moisture. The eldest glanced about at the somber faces, their expressions so unlike the eternal smiles that had defined elves throughout his youth and middle years. Only the green seed pods speckling their hair and the runnels of water dribbling along their cheeks took the edge from a solemnity that would once have seemed impossible and had now become the norm.

The meeting had begun at sunup, but Ysh'andra and Vrin'thal'ros had been arguing a point of order until it became tedious even for the most patient among them. Finally, Dh'arlo'mé took command, as he should have done hours ago in the elder's opinion. "Enough. We will do it as Vrin'thal'ros Obtrinéos Pruthrandius Tel'Amorak described and have no further argument. We have matters of import to discuss."

Ysh'andra opened her mouth to protest, caught Dh'arlo'mé's green glare, and, reading the anger there, she said nothing further.

Dh'arlo'mé shook his head, sending seeds and droplets flying from red-blond hair. "And enough of modest persuasion as well. I say we torture the human with vigor. Answers will come only then."

"Or death," Ysh'andra added, and nods circumnavigated the group.

"Or death," Dh'arlo'mé confirmed without remorse. "Then there's one less human. A boon unto itself. We'll get another."

After months of mild and tiresome speculation, the sudden switch to immediate action caught the council off guard. Nothing in elfin society happened quickly, and few knew how to counter such direct decision and strategy.

Only the elder knew humans well enough to take Dh'arlo'mé's abruptness in stride. He had served the Northern Wizard for millennia, transporting all four of the Cardinal Wizards between Midgard and their Meeting Isle on a tiny ship he called the *Sea Seraph*. Thousands of years on the sea had baked his skin and accentuated the wrinkles a constant smile had etched onto his features. Gold highlights wound through mahogany hair crusted with salt and sand. He had used the title "Captain" for so many centuries, it had become his name. Disdaining anything human, the elves now called him Arak'bar Tulamii Dhor: "Oldest among us who has forgotten his name."

"Get another?" One of the younger elves repeated Dh'arlo'mé's claim thoughtfully, lax cheeks revealing he had survived the tragedy that claimed the lives of most of their ilk. Without scarring, magic had healed the hideous agony of scarlet burns and blisters that marred the elves after the *Ragnarok,* but an observant eye could still distinguish those who suffered it from those few born after. Only Captain, who dwelt upon Midgard prior to and during the Gods' War, had avoided the fires completely. "Get another? At what price? The human we have claims to be a gentle example of her species. We cannot afford to lose any more elves."

General gestures of accord swept through the Nine. About this, none would disagree. In the millennia since the world began and Frey created elves, they had lived in harmony and died peacefully after happy lives spanning hundreds or thousands of years. Plucked from its decaying shell, elfin souls were stripped of memory and placed into the body of a newborn. But the elves had discovered a tragedy no one could foresee: Those prematurely lost to The Fires were not re-born. From the time the race established themselves on their island home, the only babies since *Ragnarok* came after the loss of elders to age. Nor had any pregnancy followed the slaughter of an elf by Rantire during her capture. Apparently, the reincarnation they had always taken for granted extended only to elves who died naturally. Diseases, malformations, and infections did not plague elves, so the new could only spring from the old.

"We'll find safer ways to capture humans," Dh'arlo'mé bellowed, his rage superficial and raw. His hands clamped to bloodless fists, and his green eyes flashed. "She murdered one of us. Murdered an immortal soul. A murderer of elves deserves no mercy."

Hri'shan'taé Y'varos Filtanith Adh'taran spoke with the calm, emotionless tone that had become her trademark. Rumor claimed it took her fifty years to shift from one feeling, or opinion, to another. "We have a human. Exchanging it for another seems pointless, though I do agree we need to try different tactics to make her talk."

As usual, the One of Slow Emotions made a strong if obvious argument, and Captain did not point out the fundamental error in her logic. Unlike elves, one human did not represent all humans. Their diversity went beyond current elfin understanding, especially at a time when the elves were only beginning to recognize individuality in themselves. But, unlike the other elves, Captain held no interest in causing the downfall of men and did not fault them with the *Ragnarok*. He had kept his opinion to himself, except for his public disapproval of violence. The vicious bitterness eating at the happy innocence that once characterized elves spared Captain, presumably because he knew so much about humans.

Captain cringed, recalling in painful, vivid detail the agony that had tormented him when Alfheim exploded. Through magically attuned senses, he had heard his people's screams, felt the fiery anguish that stole body and soul alike, and witnessed the colorful cascade of magic as the world of Alfheim crumbled into oblivion. Believing himself the only survivor, he had wandered the oceans, as he always did, but without the Cardinal Wizards to break the monotony. They, too, had fallen. It had taken a century of lonely wandering to discover that some of the elves had escaped to Midgard, to an uninhabited island humans had no cause to suspect or discover.

Dh'arlo'mé and his followers held Midgard's inhabitants responsible for their suffering. Humankind's decay into Chaos had sparked the *Ragnarok:* yet, remarkably, they had been spared the holocaust that all but annihilated the elves. Somehow, Dh'arlo'mé and the others surmised, the humans had diverted the gods' punishment intended for them. Three hundred years of studying humans with magic had failed to reveal understanding of them as a race. One thing seemed certain. The humans carried no remorse for their transgression, and that enraged the elves most of all.

Only Captain knew the truth, but the little he had spoken of it met with scorn. If the elves would not believe him outright, he had no choice but to bide his time and cautiously guide the younger elves. The bitterness of those burned in The Fires could not be quenched, and they refused to listen to one who dismissed their vengeance when he had not endured their agony. Long ago, the elves had considered Captain outcast for his solemnity; now they belittled him for leniency, little realizing that they were daily becoming more like the men they despised.

The remainder of the council spoke his or her piece, most opting for heavier-handed torture of their prisoner with attention to the more fragile constitution of humans. At last, only Captain remained silent, and all attention drifted to him for the words they knew by heart: "Hatred fosters hatred, and violence is what violence begets. Peace reigns so long as humans remain ignorant of our presence. We can accomplish more by making friends than enemies." The speech rang hollow, not only for its repetition. Although "Brenna" had greatly exaggerated it, humans had a propensity toward violence; and peaceful contact by the elves would not necessarily bring amiable resolution. Nevertheless, Captain felt certain that aggression would assure a war resulting in the end of elves or humans, possibly both. It would finish what the *Ragnarok* had left undone.

Captain added, "When making decisions about our captive, we might do well to remember that humans make a distinction between murder and killing; and only the former is considered a crime. Brenna would consider herself a killer, not a murderer. She did not kill from spite or prejudice but to rescue herself from imprisonment, death, or some other fate she felt we might inflict on her."

"Doddering old fool," Dh'arlo'mé muttered, borrowing words from the human Northern tongue where elfin fell short. Their native language held no insults for elders, only terms of respect. Although elves had grown nastier and more resentful with each passing year, Dh'arlo'mé's curse still was met with surprise. Several of the Nine recoiled at the viciousness, though no one made a comment against it. "What the human believes about her own guilt matters not at all. It only proves what we already know. Humans murder without remorse, rationalizing their deeds with terminology or selfish personal justification." The stern green eyes met each gaze in turn, though he held Captain's for only an instant. "The vast majority of the council wishes to apply significant torture, and we will follow those wishes, making every attempt not to lose our victim to human frailty. None of us wants to have to confront another human directly to replace our prisoner. But if she is accidentally killed, we will use that information to increase our understanding of how to slaughter humans. After all, that is the knowledge we're seeking."

Again, nods passed around the circle, sparing only Captain. Their one-dimensional blindness floored him. He could not fathom how Dh'arlo'mé could so viciously denounce the Renshai killing in self-defense then justify slaughtering her, and every other human, in retaliation. Prejudice, alone, could explain the contradiction. An elfin death defined murder. Human life held less significance to Dh'arlo'mé than animals on the dinner table did to mankind. No one but Captain seemed to notice the disparity, and he could not help wondering if he had become as senile as a human drunkard, though such frailties and diseases did not normally affect his kind.

Not that any of it mattered. The council had made its decision, and it would never occur to any elf to act contrary to their leaders' decision.

Summer sunlight glinted from plow, wagon, and windows; and wind riffled the wheat stalks into a green-gold dance. Finished with his morning chores, Griff trotted toward the tiny patch of woodland sheltering the Grove. At seventeen, he had already attained his adult height; at least, he hoped he had. He towered over his stepfather and the few farmers and merchants who called at their farm, and it made him feel awkward and gangly. Despite his height, and the fuzzy growth of beard that required daily shaving, he never considered himself large. He thought of himself as a child, carefree and protected by the love and constant scrutiny of his mother. The adults handled the necessary business that accompanied growing and selling crops. Griff performed his chores without complaint and spent the remainder of the day reading or playing quietly under the watchful eye of his mother. He helped her in the kitchen when she found his assistance useful, and he could not imagine any life happier than his own.

At the edge of the forest, Griff stepped onto the familiar path, its brush matted and smashed from previous passages. The sun warmed the coarse, black hair that fell to his shoulders; and he scanned the surrounding trees with dark eyes sparkling with guileless joy. He had visited this private place since early childhood, yet it never lost its allure. Each trunk seemed a familiar friend, scarcely changed by time. Only the leaves and animals came and went in cycles; the trees held a timeless beauty that comforted Griff at every visit. Here, he passed his special alone-time in thought, the only place beyond sight of the house that his mother allowed him to go. She always watched him disappear into the trees and was always there when he emerged. Her voice wafted easily to him there; she would call if she needed him. But she never physically violated the sanctity of his personal place, intuitively understanding it held special significance to him that her presence might spoil.

Griff's mother granted him that one reprieve where she gave no other. And he understood. She had lost a husband and a son to accident, and that justified her desperate need to protect the last of her blood. Ten years with Griff's stepfather had not resulted in pregnancy, and the midwife had informed her that bearing children before coming of age had permanently harmed her womb. Griff was all she had left of her life with her first love, and logic dictated she shield her son fiercely.

Griff pressed through the tree line into the Grove and a solitude he hoped would prove short-lived. There, in the sanctuary he knew so well, he eagerly anticipated a visit from the only friend his sheltered lifestyle allowed. He sat on his favorite seat, a deadfall near the pathway, and studied the Grove. Grass formed a stubbly carpet, sheltered and nourished by the surrounding trees. Wildflowers burst through at intervals, purple *trithray* and scarlet *perfrans* a welcome change from the emerald stretch of spear-grass. A rabbit munched at a stand of clover, facing Griff and watching his every movement with suspicion. A shallow creek wound across the landscape, either end obscured by trees, the same that fed the watermill and watered the sheep.

Griff dug out a stone from the ground near his foot and flicked it toward the stream. Though a safe distance away, the rabbit leaped and dodged into a copse of thistle, white tail a bobbing beacon against its otherwise mousy gray body. The stone sailed along the creek, skipped twice across the water, then skidded to the opposite bank.

As if from nowhere, a pale hand appeared, snagging the rock before it settled. Griff's gaze traced the extremity from fingers to forearm, partially protected by a supple tunic flapping in the breeze. He took in the rest of his friend, Ravn: slender sinewy limbs, a well-proportioned torso bearing none of the extra weight that plagued Griff even in rigorous times, handsome features haloed by golden hair, and quick blue eyes that missed nothing. He always wore at least one sword at his hip, but the type and position varied. This time, a light scimitar dangled near his right hip, suitable for a left-handed draw. As often, he carried the sword on the left side. Griff had never seen Ravn free any of his weapons, but when he played, he used either hand with equal alacrity.

"Ahh," Ravn said in his pleasantly musical voice, "Only Griff would greet an old friend by stoning him."

Griff laughed, mood buoyed, as always, by Ravn's presence. "Did you think you deserved better?"

"A hello, at least." Ravn sprang gracefully over the creek and toward Griff with a careless agility the farm boy had always admired.

"All right. Hello, then." Griff complied, then playfully tossed a pebble that Ravn caught without changing pace.

"That's better." Ravn stood in front of Griff, one foot balanced on the log. "What's new?"

Griff considered. "Cat had her kittens yesterday."

"Six?" Ravn protected his bet.

"Six." Griff nodded. "You were right."

"Aren't I always?"

"Usually," Griff admitted, without malice. For ten years, he and Ravn had played in this grove; and the blond was seldom wrong. Griff had long ago given up trying to discover his playmate's sources of information. In truth, he had not dared to delve too deeply, just as he had avoided concentrated consideration of Ravn's origins. The boy fit the description of no nearby farmer's kin, the name had triggered no recognition from his mother or stepfather, and Ravn appeared only in the Grove. Direct questions about Ravn's roots had met with vague answers and a change of topics. In the last few years, Griff had finally come to the belief that Ravn was a figment of his own imagination, but he banished that understanding to the farthest corner of his mind. If he concentrated on the thought too long, he feared he might lose his best friend forever. "Four males, two females. You thought it'd be even. You said two calico, and only one is. A female."

"Well, of course a female."

"Why, 'of course'?" Griff pressed, more curious than offended by Ravn's judgmental tone.

"All calicoes are female. Haven't you figured that out yet?"

Since Ravn showed no inclination to sit, Griff rose. "I never thought about it." He considered previous litters, and could not specifically recall any male calicoes. Of the current collection of mousers, the only two calicoes were female. "How come only females are calicoes?"

Ravn shrugged. "You know how there're diseases only men are born with that women don't get?"

Griff had heard stories about a neighbor who had five daughters and no sons. His wife had borne four boys, each of whom bled to death very young from minor injuries. "Like bleeding problems."

"Right." Ravn scraped at the bark with his propped foot. "Well, women have something inside that protects them from certain things. Whatever it is, it also lets cats have an extra color. Only females can have three different colors on them. Rarely, I've seen a male cat that does. His sex organs aren't normal, and he usually can't make kittens."

Griff made a thoughtful noise, though he felt as if they had exhausted the topic. "Anyway, there's just the one calico. You thought the black cat was the father, and I thought it was the gray striped one. There're kittens of all different colors, including ones that look like both toms. So I guess we can't tell who the father is."

"Let's just call it both," Ravn compromised.

"Both, right." Griff chuckled and started collecting flat stones for their usual skipping contest. "Two fathers."

"No, really. It's possible, you know."

"Two fathers?"

"Sure. Happens all the time in animals that have litters. I even once saw a brown cow have twins after being with a black bull and a brown and white one. Each looked exactly like one of the fathers."

"Hmmm." Griff did not challenge the assertion, although he kept a reasonable doubt about everything Ravn taught him. If the knowledge came from his own mind, as he believed it did, it seemed best to maintain some skepticism. Eager to get the contest started, he flung a stone toward the water. It bounced four times from the surface, then sank, leaving five rings slowly widening into obscurity.

Ravn collected a few rocks of his own, flicking one toward the creek. It swept lightly across water, tapping three times, then glided to the far bank.

"Two points for me." Griff flung another stone.

The boys continued playing for several moments, silent except for Griff's announcement of the score. Ravn seemed preoccupied. Usually, he won their contests with ease. This day, concentration proved a problem that left Griff five points ahead after seven tosses. Finally, Ravn paused, a stone clutched between thumb and index fingers. "Change is coming." He tossed the stone, and it skipped four times to Griff's six.

Griff stepped forward but made no attempt to begin the next round. The somberness of Ravn's tone swept a chill through him. Ravn chose to speak in that bizarre fashion only occasionally, but it never ceased to spook Griff when he did. Always, it meant Ravn would discuss serious issues, usually in words which mystified Griff.

"Big changes. And soon."

"What kind of changes?" Griff asked, knowing he would receive no answer he could grasp but still feeling obligated to ask.

"I don't know exactly." Ravn peered out over the creek, avoiding Griff's intensive scrutiny. "But it may mean danger to you."

"Danger?" Griff repeated. Tension squeezed his chest, and he felt more worried for his mother than himself. If something bad happened to him, neither of them could bear the pain it would inflict on her. "What kind of danger?"

Ravn shook his head, still staring at something distant, while the wind tossed his yellow hair. "I don't know exactly." Suddenly, he whirled to Griff, blue eyes frighteningly intense. "Whatever happens, don't let your faith in the world waver. Understand, don't hate your enemies. No matter how dishonorable or ugly their evil, hatred only scars the one who hates."

Griff found no response possible, except a stiff nod. Nausea seethed in his gut, inspired by the obviously sincere concern of a friend who sprang from his own conception.

Ravn seemed satisfied with the humble gesture. "Goodbye, Griff." Turning, he headed into a copse of shrubbery, disappearing from sight long before Griff believed he should.

Daunted by Ravn's ambiguous warning, Griff let the collected stones slide through his fingers and fall quietly to the grass. Logic dictated that he ignore a threat conjured by an imaginary friend seen by no one else and only in his private clearing. But Ravn's distress could not be banished, and his hasty departure unnerved Griff until he worried that his closest companion might never return.

Nervously, full of wary doubts and worry, he headed back toward home.

By the time Béarn's council sent a second envoy to Santagithi, summer had reached its peak. Kevral, Ra-khir, Matrinka, Darris, and Tae Kahn left the following evening under cover of darkness, in the hope that any enemy's attention would focus on the larger, official party and that five adolescents would pass unnoticed.

Tae ranged ahead on his dark brown gelding. No one asked where he had obtained his horse. If he had stolen it, as Kevral surmised, at least he had the intelligence to select one of neutral color. It would prove less easily missed and more difficult to identify. Matrinka rode in the middle on her small, chestnut mare, surrounded by her three companions. Silently, ahead of all but Tae, Ra-khir rode his gray gelding, his head high and his stance proud. Darris and Kevral rode on Matrinka's either flank, the bard on a nervous bay and Kevral riding a calmer bay with a reddish tint to its coat.

Kevral had never left the Béarn/Erythane area before, and conversation with her companions revealed that Darris, Matrinka, and Ra-khir had never done so either. She did not bother asking Tae; his foreign features and accent rendered travel a foregone conclusion. It seemed dangerous to let the untrusted one choose their route, yet they had little choice in the matter. Though they had all studied maps, he alone knew anything about long journeys through forest, and his wary manner suggested he could guide them more safely and unobtrusively than even the most well-traveled merchant.

Early on, they made small talk from horseback, discussing the weather, supplies, and the route. The excitement of trying something new and the danger they had not yet internalized filled them all with excitement. Only Tae seemed immune to it, though whether that came of experience or his hardened nature, Kevral could not guess. As the day dragged on, each became lost in his or her own concerns. Hours on horseback grew tedious, and the constant need to stay in one position irritated Kevral. Others fared worse. Ra-khir held his rigid stance even as the day wore on and exhaustion made posturing difficult, but it took its toll on his temper. Irritation showed clearly in the set of his features, and Kevral did not envy his need to demonstrate exemplary manners at all times. Her own restless annoyance would require venting, and she felt certain she could bring out the worst in the knight apprentice. He did not know it yet, but the explosion her badgering inspired would probably do him good.

Matrinka's cat shifted position from the horse's flank to her mistress' shoulders frequently, the only one with enough leeway to stretch her legs. On occasion, she would leap to the ground, following the horses at an easy lope. Whenever she paused to investigate, she would charge after the horses at an undignified, stiff-legged run. Repeatedly, Kevral believed they would lose Mior among the foliage, but always the cat returned to Matrinka. The princess never seemed concerned about Mior's excursions, so Kevral did not worry for the cat. Matrinka knew her pet better than any of them. If she trusted Mior to return, Kevral could not do otherwise. Darris and Matrinka rode quietly, neither attempting to hide fatigue, though they did not complain of it either. Occasionally, they exchanged glances and smiles; as often, they looked embarrassedly away.

The sky had scarcely grayed, the sun tipping over the western horizon, when Kevral called a halt. Waiting until Tae rejoined them, she announced, "It's time to camp for the night."

Everyone reined up. Ra-khir turned in his saddle to confront Kevral. "We have a long way to go and a task that shouldn't wait any longer than necessary. We can get down and eat if it's hunger that's bothering you, but I think we should ride on as far as possible before sleeping."

"I don't care what you think," Kevral returned more irritably than necessary. "I won't sacrifice sword practice for any cause or reason."

Ra-khir's green eyes narrowed to slits and his nostrils flared, but he reined his temper in admirably. "Not even for the kingdom of Béarn?"

Kevral shrugged, not caring that she had become disrespectful to her charge. "If I let my skills wither, I'm of no use to Béarn at all." She could not help adding, "If you cared about the kingdom, you would worry for your own sword arm."

Ra-khir's fingers blanched around the reins. "A knight's skills endure. They do not wither for want of an evening's practice."

Tae could not resist adding his opinion, in a calm voice that came of having no stake in the argument. "Perhaps that's because knight's skills don't have the refinement of a Renshai's."

Ra-khir whirled on the Easterner, scowling.

The unexpectedness of Tae's involvement shocked Kevral momentarily free of the irritability goading her to bait the knight-apprentice. Clearly, Tae had deliberately fanned the argument, and she wondered if he had joined them specifically to ruin the mission by setting them against one another. She glanced at him; and he winked, mouth curved into a cocky smile that implied he simply enjoyed harassing Ra-khir as much as she did. She remained adamant. "Anyway, I'm stopping here. And I'll fight to see to it Matrinka stays, too. Whatever the circumstances, I still consider her my responsibility."

"I'll camp here," Matrinka said carefully, glancing rapidly from Kevral to Ra-khir, desperate not to offend either one.

Darris winced apologetically. "I have to stay with Matrinka."

Ra-khir's jaw clamped closed as he realized where that left him.

Tae did not allow him to bow out easily, however. "You're on your own, Red."

Ra-khir clung to his remaining dignity, sparing a last disdainful glare for Tae. "Very well, then. I bow to the decision of the party." He dismounted and headed for the side of Matrinka's horse to assist her, nearly colliding with Darris who already waited in position. The bard's heir politely steadied the princess' dismount while Ra-khir instinctively moved to help the only other woman in the party.

"You must be kidding." Ignoring Ra-khir's offer, Kevral leaped lightly from her saddle, accustomed to sore muscles and reveling in the temporary stiffness of her knees. *If you awaken without pain, shame on you. Your practice the night before was slothful and wasted.*

Leaving Matrinka to the care of her companions, with some misgivings, Kevral slipped into the brush and began her practice.

Ra-khir watched Kevral's swaggering walk into the undergrowth, fighting loathing. It did not become a Knight of Erythane to hate, no matter how irritating or detestable the subject. Accepting the irksome Renshai as a female had proven difficult enough; the image of a rude boy had firmly affixed itself in his memory. Her refusal to act as a woman, or even to react pleasantly to his attempts to treat her with common politeness, bothered him. He reconsidered all the comments he had made, all the actions taken that might have offended his companion and realized that he could behave in a less judgmental manner. Yet logic did not leave him all the blame. From the moment they met, Kevral had worked at making their companionship as stormy as possible.

With a sigh of resignation, Ra-khir discarded this line of thought for the more imminent matter of making dinner. They had all eaten well before leaving, and no one had complained about missing the midday meal. Now, Ra-khir's stomach protested the lapse with impatient growls, and he suspected full bellies might put them all in better spirits. Darris gathered and hobbled horses, Matrinka stripped down saddle and pommel packs, and Ra-khir set to the heavier job of removing and arranging tack. Tae seized his own gear, wandered to a deadfall, and sat, presumably finding a good location for a campfire.

Released from their burdens, the horses set calmly to grazing on plentiful brush. Matrinka arranged bedding with Darris' assistance, and Ra-khir headed over to see how Tae was handling the fire. He glanced at the Easterner, only to find no evidence of smoke or kindling. Tae lounged at the base of a log, munching contentedly on jerky, hard rolls, and fruit.

Incensed, Ra-khir approached, his promise to become less presumptuous forgotten in his rage. "What in Hel are you doing?"

Tae drew his food closer to his body, as if protecting it from Ra-khir. Despite this gesture of suspicion, his response was as maddeningly cool as always. "Eating."

"I can see that." Ra-khir managed to swallow some of his anger, reminding himself that Tae had traveled alone a long time and might be as ignorant of cooperation as he was of proper manners. "The rest of us are preparing camp."

"I can see that," Tae returned, without catching the hint. "And a fine job you're doing."

Ra-khir gave up on Tae's sense of fairness. Clearly, it did not exist. Instead, he set to work himself, gathering the kindling Tae had not bothered to collect while the Easterner watched him work in silence. Finally, when Ra-khir had a sizable collection and the others had finished their tasks and sorted enough food for the evening meal, Tae rose, stretched, and casually brushed crumbs from his lap.

Ra-khir mopped his sweat-soaked forehead with the back of his hand.

"What are you doing?" Tae asked.

Ra-khir had hoped labor would distract him from his mood, but the sweat rolling down his cheeks and the time alone to brood only heightened his rage. "Building the fire that you didn't."

"No fire," Tae said.

Ra-khir dropped the last bundle of branches. "What do you mean, no fire?"

"No fire," Tae repeated. "It'll only draw attention."

Ra-khir's mouth fell open, and sweat dragged red hair into his eyes. He flung it away with an abrupt and angry gesture. "How are we going to cook food?"

"We have plenty of dry tack."

"What about wild animals?"

"Our scent will keep them away as well as any fire. In fact, the odor of cooking meat is more apt to draw them."

Ra-khir kicked at the mound of kindling. "Why didn't you say something before I did all this work?"

Tae smiled. "I found you entertaining."

"You ignoble bastard. You have the manners of a pig."

"And the principles of a goat." Tae nodded in agreement. "Yes, I'd say that describes me aptly."

Ra-khir managed a weak grin, but only with effort. It was going to take all of his breeding to survive the week, and only then in the belief that the gods were testing him. Whether or not he passed this trial remained to be seen. Ra-khir would not have laid bets on himself.

C h a p t e r 1 5

The Captain

*Just the fact that my people were Renshai was
considered ample reason for the Northmen to
murder them and Westerners to rejoice in the killing.*

—Colbey Calistinsson

For Matrinka, the first night stretched into an eternity. The
cool night air seemed a pleasure after a long and sweltering
ride, and once she settled into a comfortable position between the blankets, her stiffened muscles did not pain her
much. Though she had never slept outside before, the aro-
mas of mulched leaves and pine delighted her. She enjoyed
and puzzled over animal calls that split the otherwise ceaseless rise and fall of the insect chorus. None of these bothered
her. The torment that wrenched rest from her came from
within, a desperate sorrow triggered by her companions'
bickering.

Don't be sad, Mior sent, curling near her mistress' face
to provide succor as well as warmth.

As always impressed by the cat's ability to read her mood,
Matrinka freed a hand from the blankets and stroked the
spotted fur. *How do you know I'm sad?*

It's in your quietness. Mior began purring softly. *Humans are so easily read.*

Not to other humans, Matrinka returned, realizing she
had just discovered the crux of her concern. *Do you think

*Kevral, Ra-khir, and Tae would quarrel so much if they could read inside each other's minds?**

Mior's purring died away as she considered the mostly rhetorical question. *Depends on how much they could read, I guess.** She paused, then added, *I think it's better this way.**

It was Matrinka's turn to ponder. Mior's smaller brain did not grant her the words or philosophies to explain matters in detail, but often her superficial observations carried a weighty significance. Matrinka never knew whether Mior had a gift for stating consequential ideas in a few words or whether she, herself, simply added profundity the cat never intended. In the end, it did not matter. Mior could communicate with no one but her, so she could not compare her interpretation to others', except in a general way if she chose to quote the calico.

In this instance, Mior had a definite point. Shared too shallowly, her companions' disdain for one another's honor might charge them to violence. However, if they dug to the level of awareness of the differences between their cultures and upbringings, they might find mutual understanding. Read even deeper, their private thoughts violated, they might lapse back into hostility again. A delicate balance existed there, Matrinka surmised; and it made her glad humans could not read one another's thoughts. It would add a whole new dimension to human relationships, and they scarcely seemed capable of handling the superficial ones they already had. *You might be right,** Matrinka conceded. *But if I have to suffer their squabbling all the way to Santagithi, I'll go raving mad.**

Mior commenced purring. *Don't worry about that. They'll come to an understanding one way or another.**

Matrinka had to agree. *I'm concerned about the "another." What if one of them hurts or kills the others?**

*You'll have to choose whether to tolerate the company of a murderer.**

*Funny,** Matrinka shot back without cracking a smile..

*I didn't mean it as a joke.**

The words did not reassure Matrinka. Her stomach churned, gurgling loudly over the jerked meat and bread. *You really think they might kill?** It was a silly question, and Matrinka knew it. Ra-khir had already once challenged

Tae to a duel, and neither Tae nor Kevral seemed to share Ra-khir's need for a willing enemy.

Most cats are smart enough to run when they're losing a fight.

The implication that humans would not necessarily do so did not require verbalizing. Matrinka knew Kevral well enough to realize the Renshai would prefer death in battle to flight. Ra-khir's actions would depend upon the honor of the moment. In Tae's case, comparison to a cat seemed strangely apt.

Having fueled rather than calmed Matrinka's worries, Mior softened her assessment. *I don't think it'll come to killing. I think they'll come to some sort of agreement none of them likes.*

Matrinka sighed, recognizing the hollowness of the assurance and bothered that any compromise might come only after the trauma of murder. Shock had great power for changing human behavior, but anything less might not prove enough. It almost seemed preferable for one to die swiftly so they did not have to endure months of snide comments, challenges, and posturing. She cringed from the thought, conscience battering at her for the selfish disregard for another's life. She recognized her special position as potential arbiter, but she had no idea how to proceed with making peace. The idea of stepping between trained warriors and a twitchy thief seemed at once a madness and a drudgery beyond human endurance.

Darris' voice hissed through the darkness. "Matrinka? Are you still awake?"

Startled by his closeness, Matrinka stiffened, heart pounding. "Yes," she returned. She turned her head toward him, discovering him crouched over her, hazel eyes reflecting concern.

"I heard you tossing," Darris explained, though Matrinka had not asked. "And you look so tense. Are you well?"

Unwilling yet to share the true source of her discomfort, or to burden Darris with a problem he could not alleviate, Matrinka forced a smile. "I'm fine. First night sleeping outside. I'm just a bit nervous."

"Understandable." Darris rested back on his haunches, striking suddenly to the heart of the matter. "Especially with our so-called friends arguing like children."

Stunned beyond reply by Darris' incredible insight, Matrinka simply nodded.

I told you humans are easily read, Mior sent triumphantly. She paused momentarily, then let Matrinka off the hook. *Really, though, he knows you well.*

Matrinka had simultaneously come to the same conclusion. They had spent more than enough time together in deep discussion for Darris to understand few things bothered Béarn's princess more than a dispute, and one of those was her helplessness to defuse it.

Darris drew nearer, keeping their conversation private. "They'll pay for their silliness, though." He winked conspiratorially. "If we do manage to accomplish what we're after, we'll all get immortalized in song. Since I'm along, I'll almost certainly write most or all of what gets sung." He grinned at the obvious implications. "Imagine the embarrassment of having your foibles bellowed out by every would-be minstrel for eternity."

Matrinka managed a real smile for the first time since the trip began.

Moonlight glittered from Darris' features and drew highlights through his curly bangs. The shadows lent the familiar features a mysterious handsomeness. Matrinka wanted to study him for hours: the happy set of his jaw, the glow dancing in adoring eyes that seemed to almost caress her with their attentiveness, and the careless fall of his hair across his forehead. Gradually, their faces drifted closer until she could smell his breath, the odor pleasant and still mildly scented by the fruit from dinner.

Realization dawned on both at once, and they jerked shamefully away from a mistake neither could justify. Only then, Matrinka felt Mior's presence, silent but firmly planted in her mind. *Why didn't you kiss him?* the cat whined.

I wasn't going to kiss him! she denied too vehemently.

You were, Mior would not let go. *You were going to kiss him.*

Maybe I thought about it, Matrinka finally admitted. *But it would have been wrong. I'm still of the royal line, remember? And I have to—*

—marry in the line, Mior finished mockingly. *Humans are absurd when it comes to things like that. You should have—*

It was Matrinka's turn to interrupt. *Leave me alone! And don't talk about it any more.*

You should have, Mior pouted one last time, then fell dutifully silent.

Feigning obliviousness to the near-mistake, Darris sang a quiet lullaby that pacified Matrinka despite embarrassment. Amid the gentle rise and fall of his voice, she drifted into sleep.

Pain became a familiar bed partner to Rantire, and sleep dragged her into nightmares that reawakened the beatings and burnings she suffered by day. No longer did the elves bother with less favorite foods or fabrics. Daily, they drove her to agony with magic, whip, and rod, never bothering to remove her from her cage. She found no means of escape, just endured from one day to the next and hoped death, when it came at last, would find her worthy of a warrior's last rewards. At some point, an elf would slip. Rantire would escape or die nobly in the attempt, and her soul would rise to battle endlessly in Valhalla. She clung to that certainty, and it guided her through the worst of the torture.

Concern for humankind no longer sustained Rantire's silence. Most of the questions the elves asked displayed an ignorance of even the most basic human drives, and she could easily mislead them and forgo the pain. But Rantire would have none of that. Her honor left no place for deception or cowardice. She would endure like a Renshai and tell her captors nothing.

Rantire ate in the evenings, when the torture left her conscious and capable of chewing. Then, unwinking eyes that reflected light would shine from the darkness and watch her every movement. These peeping elves would speak softly to one another while they studied her. At first, Rantire believed they examined her reaction to various forms of torture, discussing malicious plans to cause more hurt the following day. As she grew more accustomed to the patter and pronunciation of the elves' musical, rhythmical language and to their range of emotions, she realized those who came to her by night spoke of matters more curious than cruel. They questioned one another about her and expressed admiration for her stamina. Some even spoke of sympathy, sorrow, and regret; though others chastised those who dared to suffer guilt with reminders that elves must purge any feelings that went against the decisions of their leaders.

Oa'si, too, came in many of Rantire's free moments, chattering like a child and begging story after story about Colbey, though the elf-child clearly understood little of what attracted him, or humans, to heroics.

Over time, Rantire learned much of the fey language that bore slight resemblance to the human, Northern tongue in character, lightness, and timbre. As much from the torturers' questions as through the night whispering and from Oa'si, Rantire learned details of elf behavior and culture. Magic, she discovered, had little pattern; and the elves had less control over their awesome ability than she did of her sword. Most could cast some spells, though these varied between individuals and seemed related as much to luck of birth as to practice and trial. Group spells or *jovinay arythanik* as Oa'si called them, were far more powerful.

The cultural aspects of the elves seemed most astounding to Rantire. Though individuals, they operated as a group, much in the way of ants and bees, though they did not specialize so simplistically as insects. They followed their leaders with a slavish devotion that simulated nothing so closely as religion, yet the group mentality went far beyond faith. It seemed as natural as breathing for all two hundred thirty-seven elves to concur on every action and subject.

Oa'si had supplied the number, and Rantire accepted it since she had no way to ascertain the truth. The relatively small size of elfin society only mildly reassured her. She estimated humans, as a whole, numbered hundreds of thousands but drew little solace from the majority. Humans tended to splinter into tinier groups within groups, in the end driven invariably by self-interest. They rarely agreed on even the most obvious matters, and the elves' magic might prove a weapon more potent than all human swords together. Without her to warn the humans, the elves would certainly catch them off guard, and that alone might seal their fate.

Frequently, an elf was dispatched to cure the worst of Rantire's injuries or provide enough pain relief to allow sleep. Thus far, Rantire had managed to refrain from her natural urge to slaughter the one who tended her. Despite their single-minded association, she considered elves individuals and would not kill the doctor for the wounds inflicted by a torturer. It would gain her nothing anyway but a temporary and incomplete satisfaction. They would butcher her for the crime or, at least, grow too cautious to give her another opportunity to escape or kill. Biding her time seemed the best strategy.

One quiet night, the elder elf returned. Rantire had not seen him since his cryptic message, though she had thought much about him in the interval. He moved with the same grace as the rest of the elves. She still had not reconciled their gawky adolescent appearance with their agility. His hair seemed more brittle than the others, and he wore it in a knot at the nape of his neck. His yellow eyes remained as unreadable as any elf's, but he had adopted some of the facial expressions of humans. Now, she read sympathetic pain in his countenance and saw a determined set to his jaw.

Though battered and aching, she managed a nod of recognition. Seated on the floor of the cell, she did not bother to move.

The elder approached without escort or the usual nervous caution the elves displayed in her presence; neither did he stride with a confidence to suggest he found her a danger unworthy of notice. Rather, he seemed convinced she would not harm him. "May I take away some of your pain?" He used the Northern tongue, the first elf to ask before attending her.

Rantire hoped he did not expect her to beg for his ministrations. She would rather suffer in silence. Instead she found a polite compromise. "You may," she said, then added words she would not have spoken to any other of her captors. "And thank you."

The elder elf cringed. "Please don't thank me for such a small token. I can't atone for the things my people have inflicted on you, but I hope you'll accept my apology for them."

Rantire thought about it while the elder muttered his magical phrases and brought relief to bruises and strains. "I don't hold you accountable for them, and I cannot forgive them."

"Though you condemn me with them, I don't blame you." The elder paused in his work to speak. "You may call me Captain, as the Golden Prince of Demons did before you."

"Captain," Rantire repeated, the human word sounding ridiculous as an elf's appellage. "Surely that's not your name." As soon as she spoke, Rantire wished she had not. Brenna was not her name either.

Captain took the remark in stride, apparently expecting it. "It's the only thing anyone called me for millennia. Whatever name I held before, I have forgotten." He forestalled the obvious skepticism before she voiced it. "Yes, I forgot my name. Even a millennium is a long time to hold on to something without significance. Suffice it to say that a name living on after death is a type of immortality for humans, and we elves live too long to require such devices."

The explanation made enough sense to Rantire that she would not have questioned further. Among Renshai, children were named after heroes who died and found Valhalla; and they believed the hallowed soul guided the hand of the namesake. "I wasn't going to challenge you."

Captain went back to healing. "Colbey did, and I only expected the same from one of his people."

Rantire dismissed the need with a toss of her head. "Colbey did not spend the kind of time I have among elves. At least, stories don't suggest he did." She furrowed her brow, considering further. "In fact, the legends don't mention contact with any elf at all."

Captain ignored the inherent, but unasked, question to continue healing in silence. After several moments, even the grinding aches of the oldest of Rantire's injuries dulled to a tolerable level. Open cuts closed to scabs, and bruises turned from purple-black or blue-yellow to brown. When he finally spoke it was as if no time had passed. "I believe Colbey made his most momentous decision in my presence, the one to champion balance while gods and Wizards dedicated themselves to slaughtering him in the mistaken belief that he advocated chaos." Captain sighed, a surprisingly human gesture. "He gave me more than enough clues to understand that he had no intention of destroying the world, and I believed him. But even my own Wizard would not listen to me." Raw grief entered his voice, and the not-quite-human features screwed into a sorrowful mask that did not suit them.

The words excited Rantire, especially since she no longer felt the distraction of myriad pains. "You mean the Renshai version of religion is true?" She hastened to add for the benefit of any god listening, "Not that I ever doubted it, of course. But you can confirm it?"

Captain tipped his head, and the quizzical position softened the sadness that previously masked his features. "If you mean the Northern gods as the true gods, that is so. I'm not sure how you got that from what I said, however."

"No, no." Rantire brushed aside the suggestion with a broad wave. "Of course the Northern gods are the true gods. There're only a few holdouts in the East and West who believe otherwise anymore." Rantire rushed onward, desperate to confirm the very foundation of her faith since birth. "I mean the part about the Wizards trying to slaughter Colbey because they believed he was spreading chaos when, in fact, they were the ones doing it."

"That's true," Captain affirmed.

"Then they had a big showdown during which Colbey survived and the Wizards died."

"Also true," Captain admitted. "At least according to Dh'arlo'mé, who was there."

"He was *there?*" Rantire asked in amazement.

"True again," Captain confirmed. "As the Northern Sorceress' apprentice."

"I thought all the Wizards died there."

"Dh'arlo'mé was spared."

Rantire made the obvious connection. "Is that why he hates us so much?"

"No."

"Then why?"

Captain hesitated, as if concerned he might violate some elfin confidence. For several moments, he weighed speaking and silence in the balance; then, apparently, he decided to tell her. "Because the *Ragnarok* destroyed most of the elves, but humans survived it."

"That's not *our* fault."

"He believes it is."

Rantire sputtered at the ridiculousness of such an accusation. "But none of us was even alive back then. It happened more than three hundred years ago."

"Humans as an entity existed both then and now. Three hundred years doesn't mean much to an elf."

Warmth suffused Rantire at the realization she had just verified the one religious tenet separating Renshai from every other group, the contention people had argued over for centuries. The *Ragnarok* had, in fact, occurred; and the Great Destruction they now awaited would be the second, and final, destruction of the world. "But it was Colbey's heroic sacrifice that saved mankind, not anything having to do with elves."

Captain's expression opened, and he leaned forward, obviously intensely interested. "What do you mean? What was this sacrifice?"

Rantire hesitated, suspicions aroused in an instant. She had endured too much at the hands of elfin torturers to reveal weaknesses now, even to one she intuitively believed she could trust. Still, Captain had not pressed her for details about current human society. Surely sharing a hotly disputed point of religion could bring no harm upon mankind. "Renshai believe Colbey fought among the gods at the *Ragnarok*. Afterward, when Surtr's fire came to destroy the world, Colbey killed the lord of fire giants then sacrificed his life battling the magical blaze. He spared the world from burning. Most of us also believe our prayers restored life to Colbey Calistinsson, and he lives on among the gods."

"Aaaah." Captain considered this long past the point of politeness.

"Is it true?" Rantire eventually prodded.

"I don't know," Captain admitted. "I would not doubt Colbey fought at the *Ragnarok,* nor that he overcame Surtr." He tapped a long finger on his broad lips. "The return from death seems unlikely. If the gods could raise the dead, surely they would start with their own. We would still have Odin's heavy hand upon us."

Rantire nodded in thoughtful agreement. "I always believed Colbey's resurrection more wishful thinking than truth, though I believe all the rest, of course."

"Of course," Captain said, though without obvious comprehension, as if he found repetition an easy and polite means to avoid conversation. Then he added the last words Rantire expected to hear. "Though, knowing Colbey, I would not put it past him to accomplish all you said and survive the ordeal by stamina and wits alone."

"Thank you," Rantire returned, taking this extreme compliment to Colbey onto her entire tribe.

Captain cheapened his own commendation with faint praise. "No need for gratitude, it is simple truth." He shook his head, as if clearing it, but Rantire doubted this elf elder ever became muddled. "I'll need to go. I've already tarried too long for the job."

"Wait!" Rantire had many questions, more important and immediate than the ancient basis for religion.

Captain headed for the exit, but he did turn around to face Rantire, his reluctance obvious.

"Can you get the others to stop hurting me?"

Captain shook his head, sorrow overtaking his face again. "Dh'arlo'mé is our leader, and I could no more convince him to drop his vendetta than I could the sun not to set."

"Can't you tell him what I told you? That we had nothing to do with the death of the elves."

Captain pursed his wide mouth, searching for words he seemed unlikely to find. "In some ways, humans had everything to do with the *Ragnarok,* though not your generation, of course. Their fall into Chaos made conditions right for it. If left up to me, the elf-human feud would already have ended, if you can truly call hatred a feud when only one side knows of the existence of the other. But the elves are One. I'm in an awkward position. I cannot convince them, and I will not stand against them."

Rantire studied Captain, uncertain whether to appreciate his honesty and presence or despise his unwillingness to halt a battle that might spark into genocide. She sought the phrases to spur him, could not find them in her own limited repertoire, and knew frustration. Then words escaped her lips, her own voice speaking ideas she never crafted: "There may well come a time, Captain, when you need to choose between what's right for your people and your loyalty to them. When that time comes, the world may rest on your decision."

Captain only stared, no reply seeming necessary or reasonable in the wake of such a warning. "That's exactly what ..." he started, then trailed off. Instead, he headed from the cell, the crash of the closing door echoing down the corridor until the sound of his retreating footsteps replaced it.

Rantire sat back, shivering, finishing Captain's statement naturally. ... *exactly what Colbey would have said.* She hoped it was true. Something had inspired her tongue, almost to the point of controlling it, and she could think of no spirit she would rather have guiding her.

The elves found the camped Béarnian envoy precisely where their magic assured them they would. Dh'arlo'mé gathered the three dozen elves under his current command, mentally detailing the strategy to all of them at once. Béarn had nearly tripled the size of its diplomatic group, with particular emphasis on armed guards; but Dh'arlo'mé's plan did not depend on numbers. He kept his followers clustered and silent, awaiting the signal from his half dozen archers to indicate the death of the first of the human party's two sentries.

The call came a moment later, a soft whistle that nearly duplicated the nighthawk's cry. In response, the elves silently fanned out along the edge of the camp, just beyond sight, where the once alert human guard had stood. The archers slipped past, headed to the farther end to make short work of the remaining sentry.

Another human dead. Dh'arlo'mé smiled, though he had had no direct hand in the slaying. Centuries of observation and study had revealed Béarn as the high human kingdom, and he would see to it the ascension remained disrupted and the kingdom cut off from allies. The precise reason for the envoys had not yet come to light, and "Brenna" refused to talk. Eventually, Dh'arlo'mé felt certain, he would understand. In the meantime, he had no choice but to continue slaughtering heirs until no human remained to sit upon the throne and to cut off all communication between the high kingdom and other human lands. That, he believed, would throw mankind into a chaos from which they could not escape. And the elves would destroy them easily, en masse.

A slow chant began as the elves joined minds and magic. Dh'arlo'mé lowered his head, waiting for the meshed talent to reach its peak before tapping power from it. Leadership alone did not grant him the status of caster; his repertoire was more limited than many of his compatriots. This time, however, he alone knew the spell. He had learned it from the last Cardinal Wizards, who had also needed to meld their magic to cast it, a unique occurrence. As champions of opposing forces, they had spurned cooperation of any type until their joint mission against Colbey and his Chaos had finally brought them together. The spell they had created, one of stasis, held everyone in its vicinity to his or her current level of consciousness, including the caster and his minions. Like most elfin magic, he could target it to an individual or an entire group. To affect all of the camped humans, the spell had to envelop the *jovinay arythanik* as well.

This situation seemed perfect for stasis magic, while all of his people remained awake and the enemy asleep.

The archers' birdcall cut above the dull roar of elfin chanting, and Dh'arlo'mé's smile broadened. *Two humans dead, and all of the others locked into unconsciousness.* He had hoped to use a sleep spell since it would have handled the sentries as well as the main body of Béarn's envoy, and a few centuries ago it would not have bothered elves. Now, most bore as many cares as humans and required equal amounts of sleep, and Dh'arlo'mé probably would have fallen first victim to his own casting.

The idea fueled Dh'arlo'mé's rage. The disaster the humans had brought upon the elves had far-reaching consequences. Each month, it seemed, he found another he had not previously considered; and the need for vengeance had become all-consuming, an obsession that time and memory constantly stoked. The screaming agony he and the other survivors had endured, and the destruction of elfin souls otherwise eternal, weighed like lead on his spirit. No amount of human death and suffering could pay for that holocaust, but he would see to it they came as near as possible to reciprocation.

As the elves' chant reached the proper crescendo, Dh'arlo'mé added his voice to the others. The power rose from deep within him, filling him with an aura of weightlessness and eternity. He floated from his shell into the shimmering web of chaos his followers created with their interwoven song. By itself, magic held no solid form, and its colors shifted endlessly and without pattern. But the elves shaped it into ordered strands that quivered, locked into helpless order, flickering through the spectrum to maintain a semblance of its identity. Structured yet formless, it awaited his shaping.

Dh'arlo'mé set to work with practiced skill, fashioning the framework to his will and adding the strokes between that would convert the whole to the stasis spell. Once cast, his followers would need to concentrate only on the skeleton, holding the spell in place while Dh'arlo'mé acted with a free hand and no remorse. Excitement beat through him as he directed the magic and withdrew from the casting. He had never killed a human before, and his blood warmed at the prospect. Alone save for the hidden archers, he headed for the camp.

Dh'arlo'mé first found the sentry, three arrow shafts cleanly through his chest. Blood crusted the wounds, and the blue eyes stared lifelessly at the moon. The sword blade entangled with blond hair and simple clothing. The elf paid the corpse no heed, heading toward the crowd of blankets and gear from which snoring issued. Drawing nearer, he counted seventeen humans huddled in sleep on the ground and three tents that surely held more. Dh'arlo'mé drew his knife as he approached the first, excitement twitching through his chest. He struck for the throat, determined to be the most vulnerable part of a human by examination of the one they had inadvertently killed during torture. He plunged the blade deep, tore as he withdrew, and scarlet spurted from the wound. Splashed, Dh'arlo'mé recoiled, salt stinging his lips. The human's eyes whipped open, and the body bucked once. Then the lids sagged back over the glazing orbs, and the limbs went limp.

Savage joy suffused Dh'arlo'mé, and only the need to concentrate on magic and action at the same time kept him from laughing aloud. *One less human. And soon enough, seventeen less.* He moved to the next, aware his safety lasted only as long as he remained focused and his followers' chant continued, unwavering. Mobilized by this concern, he slaughtered the second more swiftly, not bothering to bask in the triumph before rushing to the next. Sixteen died without a hitch. Dh'arlo'mé left the seventeenth, the smallest, alive and sleeping, a potential hostage to replace the silent one who resisted their torture. Making "Brenna" expendable brought a fierce rush of pleasure nearly as strong as the one that accompanied the easy destruction of an encampment of enemies. Her strong self-restraint irritated him beyond logic or reason.

Cautiously, Dh'arlo'mé peeled aside the tent flap to reveal four humans in various positions of repose. Two huddled beneath silk-soft coverlets of rich design while the others curled under comfortable but modest blankets. A flowery odor wafted from the former, while the others smelled of leather and horses. Decades of observation had revealed hierarchies far more detailed than the simple council/not council arrangement the elves had conformed to over millennia, but Dh'arlo'mé still understood little of human motivation and custom. Currently, magic obsessed him too fully to leave attention for particulars. Without bias or pattern, he killed these four, nostrils so saturated with the odor of blood and death it seemed as much a taste as a smell.

Revolted at last, Dh'arlo'mé hesitated momentarily before time constraints drove him to the second and third tents. Each held four people, and every one succumbed to the quiet danger that magically-enhanced sleep concealed from them. But the effort wore on Dh'arlo'mé as well. Clenched too long around the dagger's hilt, his hand cramped to an agony that begged soothing. The sliminess of blood-soaked leather forced him to tighten an already tiring hold. The long presence of controlled chaos dizzied him, and the sight and stench of human blood stole the last of his reserves. By the time he returned to the remaining human, even the excitement of killing elfin enemies no longer drove him. A swift conclusion and a transport home enticed.

Dh'arlo'mé stood over his last victim, only now realizing exhaustion and mental strain sent him weaving and bobbing in place. Oblivious, the human slept, breathing deeply and silently, the regular, soft whooshes of air lost beneath the rising and falling cadence of night insects and the buzz of magic that washed through Dh'arlo'mé's head. Caution drove him to kill and be finished, but logic intervened. His original decision, to take a new hostage and make the previous one unnecessary, remained too steeped in wisdom to ignore.

The elves' leader drew rope from his pockets, the same slender magic-weave that had held "Brenna" prisoner until they freed her in the cell. He studied the human as he did so. He little trusted his ability to guess a mortal's age or gender, but this one appeared young and male. No wrinkles scored the features, even lax in sleep. Although he lacked the telltale beard or mustache that allowed Dh'arlo'mé to guess sex without error, the roughness of the facial skin suggested shaving. Sandy hair fell haphazardly around his head. Dh'arlo'mé stripped away the blanket to reveal simple, loose clothing that did not bag and a body with tight sinews shorter than any elf's but without the solid bulk of most of the others at the camp. Sleep brought an innocence to the human's countenance, raising a short-lived stab of guilt and tainting the cruel happiness that had made Dh'arlo'mé so eager to kill more humans. Slaughter, for any reason, did not suit elves. Not long ago, the actions he had taken this day would have been inconceivable.

Dh'arlo'mé wound rope around the human's ankles, glancing repeatedly at the features for any response to touch and movement. Spells weakened over time, and lesser manipulations might awaken its victims now where it would have taken gross and foolish mistakes to do so before. The stasis spell had other associated problems. It froze the chanters into a steady, hyperalert state that would eventually wear them into a dangerously deep sleep or into madness. Already, he could feel his support faltering.

Dh'arlo'mé jerked the rope taut, preparing to tie the knot. For a moment, he tore his gaze from the man's face to watch his own fingers at work. That nearly cost him his life.

Dh'arlo'mé'aftris'ter Te'meer Braylth'ryn Amareth Fel-Krin!￼* The mind-shout shot through his head. Blind to the danger, Dh'arlo'mé leaped backward. A sword slashed crookedly across his forehead, the bridge of his nose, and one eye. Shock and pain, as much as impact, toppled him backward, and the world spun in a blur of brown, silver, and green. He rolled and scrambled, visionless. Something whistled through the air near his ear, then voices pounded his hearing and his thoughts, some aloud and others in desperate mind-call.

"Modi!" The human's battle cry rang over the frenzied observations, concerns, and suggestions of the elves. Ducking, protecting his head, Dh'arlo'mé scrambled away from the man. He felt and heard many presences around him, and he slammed into more than one leg before discovering an opening and diving through it. Only then, with elves between himself and the human, did he dare to look.

Dh'arlo'mé's injury allowed vision through only one eye, and dripping blood distorted even that to a flat, red plain. He managed a glimpse of the human he had attempted to capture, cutting and howling like a rabid animal, shouts shattering into distant echoes. Dh'arlo'mé swore, concerned for the reinforcements the noise might bring as well as elfin lives that might already be lost to his decision. The last remnants of guilt fled, never to return. Now, more than ever, hatred boiled inside of Dh'arlo'mé. Elves could never find peace with a species so attuned to murder they could awaken instantly to attack. The speed and effectiveness with which the man had dealt Dh'arlo'mé's wound could come only of a life dedicated to sword and slaughter.

Kill and go!￼* Dh'arlo'mé mind-called, not caring that

his need to generalize the words meant the human would hear them as well. *Kill and go!*

Dh'arlo'mé collapsed to a crouch, vertigo buffeting him and a vast, buzzing wall of whiteness stealing his vision.

Home chant, someone sent, the concept lost in a maelstrom of unrelated thoughts. Magic washed over Dh'arlo'mé, none of it his own, then darkness overtook him.

Chapter 16

A Renshai's Kill

A rousing battle seemed more fun.
—*Colbey Calistinsson*

The insults started earlier on the second day of travel, again ended prematurely by Kevral's insistence on practicing sword forms. Now well into their third day of riding, Ra-khir kept his temper with heroic effort. Kevral's jabs at knight's honor seemed to have run their course, at least until some situation arose to reawaken the barrage. Even Tae's attempts to spur their hostility had fallen flat over the last hour. Biting down on his anger and remaining silent had become a marginally effective strategy. Once Kevral realized how superficially buried Ra-khir's irritation remained, he suspected the cycle would begin again. Daily, he prayed for the control that allowed his father to listen placidly to even the nastiest of affronts before taking swift and calm action, the same that allowed him to accept punishment for a crime he did not commit. But punitive strikes only worked for one whose competence exceeded that of the person he wanted punished. Kevral had already proved herself the better swordsman, but that did not justify the chaos she considered honor.

This thought saw Ra-khir through the afternoon and into a too-familiar dinner of jerked venison and hard bread. He could not help but question the very technique he had admired earlier. Putting a person in his place with agility or violence did not justify one's point of view. It only cowed a disputant into silence. Yet Ra-khir realized, his father never bullied. Usually, he made his points with words as sharp as blades; only when the security of Béarn or Erythane lay at stake did he resort to violence.

While Kevral practiced, Tae deliberately carried on a conversation designed to spark Ra-khir's temper. "So . . ." The Easterner spoke with partially chewed food unswallowed. ". . . we all agree Knights of Erythane have more bluster than talent."

Ra-khir could hold his tongue no longer. He had to tolerate Matrinka's bodyguard, even held grudging respect for her skill; but he would not allow a common street thug to judge a brotherhood he did not have the brains, virtue, or breeding to understand. "We've agreed on nothing," Ra-khir growled, no longer caring that the bickering had driven Matrinka and Darris to the opposite side of camp. Squelched anger expanded to account for hours spent in silent vexation. "And what the Hel kind of name is Tae anyway? T-A-E, pronounced like none of the vowels in it. Why not Tay? Or Tah-*yee?*"

Tae closed his mouth into a tight-lipped smile and swallowed his food before replying. "It's pronounced 'Tie.' Eastern vowels get said different depending on the letters around them. And there're lots of exceptions." His grin became insolent. "That's what makes our language special and yours so incredibly easy to learn."

"And you think that's a *positive* thing?"

Tae shrugged, still grinning. "Sure. I can call you a *gynurith,* and you don't know if I insulted you or not." He pronounced the foreign word "ga-*nar*-ayth."

Ra-khir frowned. His honor would not allow him to affront someone he respected, no matter the tongue, although in this circumstance, respect did not apply. "So, did you insult me?"

"That depends on if you think being called feces is an insult."

Ra-khir pretended to consider. "Only because it would make me *your kin.*"

Tae let the matter drop before it degenerated into childish name-calling. "How's Ra-khir spelled?"

Ra-khir obliged, letter by letter.

Tae snorted. "You worry about how my name's said? Is

that a *silent* hyphen, or does it have some importance I'm not getting from the way you say it?"

Ra-khir flushed, realizing he had gotten caught in his own trap. "Actually, it helps people who read remember to put the accent on the second syllable. Rah-*keer,* not *Rah*-keer." The need to explain defused much of his pent-up anger also. "My father named me Rawlin at birth, and my stepfather tried to change it to Khirwithson, after himself. I was old enough to remember my original name and young enough to keep getting it confused. I called myself Ra-khir, and it finally stuck." Ra-khir had not considered the details of that story for a long time, and he wondered if the mixed name ever bothered his father. If so, Kedrin had given no indication. Unlike mother and stepfather, Ra-khir's father placed more significance on their relationship than on who gave him his name. No matter what they called him, in his heart he had always been Kedrin's son.

For several moments, Tae made no comment about the personal information Ra-khir had volunteered. He seemed lost in distant thoughts of his own, finishing his meal in a silence Ra-khir enjoyed. He wished he had not told such intimate details to one he despised. He did not have to justify his name, or anything else, to a thief.

Only after he'd brushed crumbs from his britches, did Tae finally break the long silence. "You're not the first boy to grow up without his father. A stepfather who claims you as his son is better than no father."

Ra-khir was surprised Tae had sensed the hostility he felt toward Khirwith. Apparently, it had come through in his tone if not his words, but he had never considered Tae the sympathetic or insightful type. Ra-khir's first thought, to change the subject, passed quickly. The pain branded him too deeply to keep silent. He also saw the potential benefit of sharing intimacies with Tae. It might take some of the animosity from their relationship and decrease Tae's incomprehensible need to bait Ra-khir for Kevral's sake. "That may be true if a boy loses his father to death or apathy. But I had a living father who loved and still loves me and wanted more than anything to remain my father in every way. My mother and stepfather denied him and lied to me. There's no justification for that, other than pure nastiness. My mother was willing to hurt me, still is by the way, just to hurt my father. That's not love. It's revenge hiding behind false compassion. And I'm tired of playing her games." A decade of bitter memories finally found an outlet, and Ra-khir felt better for the sharing, even with someone he did not trust. There was truly nothing Tae could do with the information to make the situation any worse.

Tae listened with surprising interest throughout a speech too long considered and withheld. "Some fathers are better than others."

Ra-khir shrugged, not seeing the connection. Recalling his family rerouted his anger, and talking mostly reduced it to a bitterness still raw and painful. Suddenly, he wanted to be alone. "I can't expect a street orphan to understand."

"I never said I was an orphan," Tae returned.

Ra-khir studied the companion he'd never wanted half-heartedly, continuing the conversation only from politeness. Tae had listened to him pour out his heart, and he could do nothing else but return the courtesy. Besides, it seemed safer to have as much personal information on Tae as Tae did on him. "So you're not an orphan?"

"I didn't say that either."

Ra-khir snorted. "So you'll say whatever works to your advantage at the time." Directed at himself, Ra-khir would have found the suggestion offensive, but he knew Tae did not operate under the strict code of honor that he did.

Tae's brows rose, and he gave Ra-khir a scathing look. "No. Just because I choose not to talk about certain things doesn't mean I'd lie about them."

"All right, then," Ra-khir pressed. "Are your parents alive or dead?"

Tae shook his head, the unkempt, black locks flopping into his eyes. "I'm not ready to talk about it."

"I talked about my family. I told you a lot of personal stuff."

"Was I the first?"

"That I told?"

"Yes."

"The second," Ra-khir said. "I told Darris. And I've discussed parts of it with my father. He won't let me say negative things about my mother, though."

"And before Darris?"

Ra-khir grew wise to Tae's strategy. "I wasn't ready to talk about it," he said with a sigh of resignation. "Point taken."

Tae smiled, but this time it seemed genuine rather than one of the smug smirks he usually offered the knight-in-training.

"All right, then," Ra-khir fished for other information while he had Tae in a confiding mood. "So why did you really want to join us?"

Tae stuck with his original story. "I already told you that."

"You wanted company."

"Right."

"There's more to it than that."

"There always is."

Ra-khir fidgeted, gripped by frustration. "And you're not going to tell me."

"No," Tae admitted.

Ra-khir made a disgruntled noise.

"Want me to tell you something you didn't expect about me?"

"I'll settle for that." Ra-khir forced a smile, hoping to spur an honest confession."

Tae leaned closer, dark eyes glittering through greasy bangs. "Those notes were only the second thing I ever stole. Besides food."

"Really?" Ra-khir's skepticism remained high, and he wondered if his irritating companion was setting him up as the butt of some nasty joke.

"Really." Tae seemed sincere. "Only the second time. And as far as I'm concerned, it can stay the last."

"Wait a moment." Not yet convinced, Ra-khir pushed for more information. "Getting those notes seemed awfully easy for someone who claims to have so little experience."

Tae contradicted. "Oh, I didn't say I had little experience. I said it was only the second thing I ever took *besides food.*" He shrugged, shoulders slender as a woman's. "I took a lot of food."

"So you *are* an orphan." Ra-khir believed he had found the hole in Tae's story."

"I didn't say that," Tae reminded.

"And you're not going to."

"No, I'm not going to. Not yet."

Seeing the camaraderie slipping away, Ra-khir changed his tack. He had no interest in becoming close to one so unworthy, yet he believed friendship might make Tae less likely to betray them in the end. *Assuming he has any scru-*

ples at all, which seems unlikely. "So what was the first thing you stole?"

Tae winced, as if he had anticipated that question only after he made his confession. "I can't tell you."

Ra-khir sighed loudly.

Tae shook his head, surprisingly apologetic. "I'm sorry I mentioned it. Believe me. We'll both be much happier if you don't ever know."

Finally driven to exasperation, Ra-khir rose, shaking his head. "I don't tell you this. I won't tell you that." Green eyes met brown, and Ra-khir tried to simulate the piercing quality of his father's glare. "When you finally decide you really want to join us with more than just your physical presence and your insults, let us know." With that, Ra-khir retired to Darris' and Matrinka's side of the camp.

Tae remained in place, performing his normal camp routine with a methodicalness that revealed nothing. Eventually, Kevral finished her practice, ate, and took her place among the blankets. The weary travelers drifted off to sleep in shifts.

Darris' shout jarred Ra-khir awake in a cold sweat. Sleep-fogged, he lurched to his feet, fumbling for his sword in the moonlight. By the time his hand closed around the grip, six strangers were bursting into the camp. All sported dark hair and beards without mustaches. They wore leathers travel-dirty and stained with old blood. One crossed swords with Darris while the others charged past, apparently seeking another victim. *Matrinka,* Ra-khir guessed, racing to her rescue.

A blanket snagged Ra-khir's foot, and he fought desperately for balance. He toppled, half-rolling and half-crawling to Matrinka's defense. His mad dash tumbled him directly into Kevral's path. She hissed, sidestepping with swift agility, a sword gripped lightly in each fist.

Ra-khir did not have a moment to curse his awkwardness. Even as he staggered to his feet, two men closed in on him at once, jabbering words in a language he did not understand. He dodged one's strike, managing to catch the other sword against his own. Spar had not prepared him for the power of the impact. The other man's strength drove his sword arm nearly to the sheath, even as his companion looped for another attack.

Ra-khir damned the night attack that caught him unarmored, befuddled, and slowed by fatigue. Even danger did not seem able to hone his mind to the clarity necessary to modify his defense. He had to keep reminding himself that he had no armor to help fend the blows. As the first man's sword sped for his gut, he leaped backward. The blade swished harmlessly past, and the second lunged for his head before he could riposte. Only their guttural patter delayed their deadly strikes. Ra-khir knew that defense alone would only prolong the inevitable. Somehow, he had to find an opening to attack.

The ringing chime of metal against metal echoed through the forest, and Ra-khir understood he did not fight alone. The need to concentrate on his two enemies left nothing for observation, and he could not know whether or not Matrinka remained safely behind him. He could not protect her from six, but he would handle his two and hope the others could manage as well. For Kevral, at least, he did not worry.

When one of the men looped for momentum, Ra-khir found his opening. He plunged in low, stabbing through the stranger's abdomen. The blade sank deep, the blow jarring Ra-khir's arm to the shoulder. He had never expected flesh to prove so solid, and he realized at once that he could never regain his sword in time to fend the other's offense. Desperate, he dropped to the ground, sacrificing his hilt and rolling free of the battle. Razor-honed steel tore a gash from wrist to shoulder, warm blood trickling from a wound that burned like fire.

Pain momentarily incapacitated Ra-khir, stealing all the attention he needed for defense. Survival instinct warred with shock, and he managed to raise his arms to shield himself from the blow sure to follow. Instead, his blurred gaze showed him two enemies on the ground, one moaning and clutching scarlet entrails, the other prone and limp in the dirt. "Here!" Tae tossed Ra-khir his sword, then whirled with bloody dagger raised.

"Thank you," Ra-khir said, not daring to believe Tae had rescued him. He scanned the clearing for friends needing aid. Darris clutched Matrinka, the man he had fought now lying still in a wine-colored puddle. Another corpse sprawled near Kevral's feet, and the Renshai exchanged blows with the remaining two with an effortlessness Ra-khir could not help but envy. She swept, lunged, and parried with a fierce joy that seemed out of place amidst his own fear and desperation. For their every attack, she returned at least a riposte for each. The bloody rivulets coloring her blade and sleeve told him she had previously faced three men at once.

Ra-khir charged in to even the battle, striking for the nearest enemy. The man shouted something uninterpretable. Both disengaged, then whirled and ran toward the brush.

Glad to see them go, Ra-khir lowered his sword. Kevral cursed. Without hesitation, she pursued, crashing through the vines and copses with a wild war cry that seemed more animal than human. Soon, distance swallowed even that.

Ra-khir stood in indecision, trying to reconcile his honor to the events. War etiquette did not allow him to chase cowards who ran from battle, yet neither could he leave a companion, especially a woman, to handle a threat alone. If the attackers accepted Kevral's relentless challenge, he had little choice but to defend her. That she deserved what she got made no difference. Reluctantly, Ra-khir took a step to follow her.

A hand seized Ra-khir's shoulder and settled there. He turned to Darris, and the bard's heir shook his head vigorously. "Believe me. You don't want to interfere with a kill claimed by a Renshai."

Ra-khir did stop, though he continued to look at the place where Kevral had disappeared into the foliage. "What do you mean?"

"She won't want your help. And if you insist on giving it, she'll as likely kill you as them."

Ra-khir shuddered at the savagery of a people so intent on killing they would slaughter allies to get at enemies. "That's ludicrous."

"That's Renshai."

"It's insane!"

Darris tightened his grip. "I'd explain why I don't judge Renshai, but this doesn't seem the time for a concert." He steered Ra-khir toward Matrinka. "Let's tend that wound first."

Trusting Kevral to secure the area, Ra-khir allowed Darris to lead him to Matrinka where she sat crushing stems into a poultice. Tae perched on a tree branch, scanning the woodlands, though whether from concern about more enemies or from fear, Ra-khir could not tell. Tae had saved his life; at least for now, Ra-khir would not assume the worst of him.

"Take off your shirt," Matrinka said.

Ra-khir did as instructed, pain jabbing his right arm with every movement. The fabric clung to the wound, and it took him several careful tugs to free it, each one claiming its toll in pain. Needing something other than Matrinka's ministrations to occupy his central thoughts, Ra-khir begged the details his own battle did not allow him to observe. "Are you all right?" He addressed Darris.

The eyes of the bard's heir flitted from the corpses to Ra-khir with obvious relief. The need to ascertain their deaths and the natural curiosity of his line should drive him to examine and identify the strangers, yet something held him back. Ra-khir believed he would understand what as soon as the pain lessened. "I'm fine," Darris said. "Just a few strained muscles and a bad bruise." He glanced into the tree above their heads only to find Tae had moved. Ra-khir scanned the clearing, gaze locking on the Easterner where he checked enemies with a swift thoroughness that precluded Darris' need to do so. "It'd be a lot worse if Tae hadn't helped. I didn't even see him coming, then there he was behind the one fighting me. I don't think the bastard even knew what killed him."

Tae glanced over at the mention, then returned to his work.

Ra-khir frowned, reviling Tae's technique and hoping the Easterner had not killed his opponent the same way. An unseen blow from behind was the epitome of dishonor. "I guess I owe him, too."

Tae acknowledged Ra-khir's reluctant and undirected gratitude with a wave.

Matrinka washed and examined the wound, pulling the edges apart to estimate depth. Ra-khir concentrated on allowing the manipulation, discarding his natural instinct to pull away. Pain cut through him, followed by a sweep of light-headedness.

Oblivious to Ra-khir's dizziness, Darris explained the events, his voice thick and the words taking forever to penetrate. "I counted six. We killed four, and Kevral's hunting down the other two."

Still silent, Matrinka smeared salve on Ra-khir's wound then bandaged it in a lengthy spiral. Kevral crashed through a stand of brush at the edge of the clearing, sending sticks and seed pods flying. "Not any more. They got away."

Ra-khir pulled his shirt back on, bandage showing white through the rent left by the blade. As the acute pain subsided into a dull ache, he felt rubber-legged and shaky, and the pervading stench of blood and bowel slammed him with sudden nausea. Acid filled his mouth, and he staggered a step, anchored on the need to keep from vomiting.

Matrinka did not prove as successful. The moment she no longer had a wound on which to concentrate, she collapsed to the ground, limbs visibly trembling and tears glazing her eyes to empty pools of brown. Spasms racked her entire body, and she gagged up her dinner. Darris finally lost his composure as well, face greenish and his struggle to console without collapsing obvious even through Ra-khir's own discomfort. Now he understood Darris' reluctance to touch the corpses.

Only Tae seemed wholly unaffected. He continued to paw through the dead. Kevral ranted, glowering at the corpses, attention always drifting back to Matrinka. Finally, her gaze settled on Ra-khir, and she vented her irritation on this familiar target. "It's your damn fault they got away. If you hadn't meddled, they couldn't have disengaged. I should have just killed you instead of shifting strategy to keep from hurting you. And I could have caught them if I wasn't so worried about no one here to protect Matrinka."

The last was an obvious insult. The words could serve no purpose other than to undermine Ra-khir's ability to guard the princess in Kevral's short absence.

The queasiness brought on as much by the shock of combat as Ra-khir's first view of violent death and his injury did not leave him patience for Kevral's taunts. "I'm sorry if I got in your way. I was trying to help. And I wouldn't have let harm come to any of our companions."

Kevral snorted. "It took all your damn focus just to keep yourself alive." She glared. "Perhaps you could bore Béarn's enemies to death by reciting your rigidly stupid code of honor."

Ra-khir bit his lip, concerned for what might emerge if he opened his mouth now.

"If you practiced half as much with your sword as your mouth, I'd have killed those two and we wouldn't have to watch our backs."

Finally, other emotions displaced nausea and shock. A host of responses rushed to the fore, but Ra-khir could not

concentrate on selecting ones that suited his training. Humiliation and disgust with himself tainted the rage that naturally
grew against Kevral's affronts, making the decision more
difficult. Tears burned in his eyes, and they only added to
his confusion and anger. Afraid she might see how deeply
her tirade affected him, he retreated to a private corner in silence. Defensively curled, face hidden from his companions,
he could not stop himself from crying. He could only muffle
the sighs and gasps.

The crackle of leaves and sticks behind Ra-khir told him
Kevral had pursued, not yet finished eroding his confidence
and insulting his manhood.

Before she reached him, a quiet voice wafted to them.
"Back off, Renshai. You've said enough."

Ra-khir heard Kevral stop, attention diverted. "Should I
take advice from one who hides in a tree?"

Tae did not seem to take offense. "You should take good
advice no matter who offers it."

Ra-khir appreciated the distraction, if not its source. He
concentrated on regaining his composure, allowing Kevral
and Tae to handle their own dispute without his interference.
For the first time, the tough-talking Easterner had taken his
side over Kevral. Though he did not appreciate a thief's defense, he had to believe their personal conversation by the
fire had had a more positive effect than Tae's deadpan responses had revealed.

Morning breezes tossed Ra-khir's sweat-matted hair playfully, as if whispering encouragements in his ear. Music as
beautiful as nature buoyed a mood that seemed beyond despair. At first, he believed the wind itself sang to him. But
as he regained enough inner strength to glance around the
camp, he spied Darris plucking lightly at the strings of his
mandolin, making gentle music that scarcely carried to the
clearing's boundaries. Surely, he sang for Matrinka, attempting to restore the spirit that shock and fear had stolen
from her. His voice blended into soft song, tugging Ra-khir
from beneath the burdensome maelstrom of self-deprecation
and anger directed both inward and out. Matrinka sat, swaying beside the bard's heir, the corners of her lips twitching
into a smile and the color returning to her swarthy face.
Kevral and Tae began piling bodies, ceasing their argument
for the moment.

For the first time since their run-in in Erythane, Ra-khir

studied Kevral while she worked. Debris speckled the thin, blonde locks that framed soft, childlike features. Sweat made her light tunic and breeks cling, and he could see a hint of the feminine curves just beginning to develop. Now aware of her gender, his mind naturally revised every feature. Logically, he knew the masculine cut of her clothing and hair, her slender form, and disproportionately young features had made his earlier assumption understandable. But now that he knew she was a woman, he could not see her as anything else. Had he not fallen prey to her egomaniacal attitudes and insults, he might have found her attractive. Ra-khir shook aside this train of thought, blaming it on some strange effect of Darris' song.

The music finished too soon for Ra-khir's liking, though he knew it best to remain quiet and to move on as soon as they all regained strength and composure. Matrinka rose awkwardly, Darris setting aside his instrument to assist. Without further discussion, everyone gathered packs and horses, preparing for the journey onward. They rode in a tight bunch, with Matrinka at the center, and no one spoke until they had gotten well beyond the clearing. Only then, Tae resumed scouting ahead, and Matrinka spoke the words Ra-khir believed most of them had been considering: "I think we should turn back."

No one responded to the pronouncement, so Matrinka continued. "Obviously, we weren't careful enough."

She had a point even Ra-khir could not deny, and he believed himself the most dedicated to this mission. After all, his jailed father had suggested the need for an inconspicuous group of youngsters to back up the envoys. Once the saboteurs knew of the group's existence, there seemed little reason to continue. Others would attack until they obliterated the adolescent party . . . or themselves. The idea of another battle drove chills through him, yet he discarded that as cowardice and refused to tolerate it in himself. Their task had changed from an interesting and exciting idea to a challenge that might well cost them all their lives. His own death, he could justify. The others did not reconcile so easily. Kevral was a warrior, like himself. But though he had martial training, Darris was more musician and historian than soldier. And Matrinka did not belong in war at all. He found Tae more difficult to categorize. The Easterner's insistence on joining them seemed reason to dismiss him from consideration, but Ra-khir had difficulty separating that from his personal dislike. He would not condemn a man for selfish reasons.

Yet it was Tae himself who rescued the task. "What makes you sure those men had something to do with Béarn?"

It had never occurred to Ra-khir, or apparently to any of them except Tae, to believe otherwise. His brows rose slowly, and he mulled the words several moments before replying. "Who else would attack us?"

"I don't know." Having raised the point, Tae seemed to find no reason to elaborate, though he did make suggestions. "Thieves? Scrappers? Personal enemies of someone else?" He shrugged, twisting on his dark brown gelding to face Ra-khir directly. "They bunched up on Kevral. Maybe they don't like Renshai."

"I herded the three into battle." Kevral denied the possibility of a personal assault on her while leaving the idea of Renshai haters unaddressed. "They weren't after me." She crinkled her brow, lids narrowing around irises the color of the sky. "They didn't exactly make a beeline for Matrinka either."

That information made Tae's suggestion worth pondering. Despite his dislike, Ra-khir trusted Kevral's judgment of action even when embroiled in the thick of battle. If she did not believe the attackers had wanted Matrinka, the party might well have fought enemies without designs against Béarn. Yet the fallacy emerged swiftly. Since Matrinka had divorced herself from the king's line, Béarn's enemies might be after the entire party. In fact, they would tend to single out the obvious warriors: Ra-khir and Darris. And possibly Kevral if they recognized her as Renshai. That seemed more in line with the events, though Ra-khir could not shake the feeling that the men he fought had wanted something or someone beyond him.

Darris kept his eyes on Matrinka as he added his piece to the muddle. "Tae, you checked over the bodies. Did you find anything that might explain who they were or what they were after? Is that why you think they weren't part of the conspiracy against Béarn?"

Tae shook his head with obvious regret. "Regular travel rations, waterskins, knives, and swords of plain design.

Nothing special. The few coins I found were Pudarian mint, but most are nowadays."

Darris tried another tack. "They used a language I don't know. Kevral? Tae? You're the linguists."

Ra-khir rolled his eyes, amused by the term. Tae's rough word choices made him seem the least likely to know even his native tongue well, but the knight-in-training did not interfere. The Easterner had already demonstrated his command of the more obscure Béarnese in addition to trading and Eastern. He obviously read and comprehended a lot more than he spoke.

Kevral answered first. "I didn't understand a word they said. I don't think it was a Western dialect, 'cause those usually overlap one of the ones I know. Enough that I could have picked out a few words." She glanced at each of her companions in turn. "I'd say either Eastern or some weird barbarian speak. And they sure didn't look like barbarians."

All eyes went naturally to Tae. Ra-khir had only heard stories of the wild men who lived at the base of the mountains that separated Westlands and Eastlands, but he doubted they could craft steel weapons.

Tae shook his head. "I couldn't understand them either, and I thought I knew about every tongue." He avoided Ra-khir's gaze, and the young knight did not believe they had received the whole story from Tae. Nor would they. Suspicion grew anew, and Ra-khir tucked it away for future reference.

"Well," Darris sounded resigned. "I guess we've got a decision to make. Do we go on, or do we turn back?"

Ra-khir had an instant answer, one that came from his heart and required little thought. He pictured himself back in Béarn, every moment of the training he had once loved reminding him of the father he could not rescue. He imagined them all meeting in worried huddles and accomplishing nothing while the throne of Béarn lay empty. "I'm going on, even if I go alone."

Kevral, Darris, and Tae said nothing, all tied to Matrinka's decision. Kevral had to remain with her charge, Darris would do so out of loyalty, and Tae had pledged himself to remain with the party. This might well prove a momentous choice for Tae, Ra-khir realized. If he had joined to ruin their success, need would force him to remain with whoever continued the quest. If he had spoken honestly about his motivation, he would stay with the larger group.

Matrinka's words made the test unnecessary. "The cause for which I was willing to give up my family and heritage hasn't changed, only our odds of completing it." She made a bold gesture at Ra-khir to indicate she would stick with him, though her doelike eyes betrayed her fear. She had little choice but to rely on the protection of her companions.

"Onward," Darris said to indicate his support.

Kevral and Tae simply nodded. Despite her soft-spoken manner and quiet apprehension, Matrinka was the party leader. She just did not realize it.

"Onward," Ra-khir repeated, mind immediately returning to memories of the attack. It would occupy him for most of the trip, he felt certain, and probably most of his companions as well.

Kevral interrupted his musings as they continued forward. "You know, if you spent more time practicing and less complaining about my need to stop . . ."

The cycle began again.

Chapter 17

Words in the Dirt

The enemies of my brother are my enemies already.

—Colbey Calistinsson

Books and scrolls lay scattered across the sage's table. The old man hovered over his treasured knowledge, one hand twisting and plucking at his tunic, the other trapped in his pocket as if he feared it might act of its own volition. Prime Minister Baltraine studied laws and lineages until his buttocks ached from the hard, wooden chair and his elbows felt melded into the table. King Kohleran had lapsed into a permanent coma, unresponsive to anything but pain for more than three weeks. Rulership of Béarn had fallen completely into Baltraine's hands; his "conferences" with the king had become nothing more than moments of silence after which he confirmed the actions he wished to take. And while the authority pleased him, it was only a matter of time before the secret of the king's condition leaked or Kohleran died. In either case, Baltraine needed to find a successor soon.

Baltraine sighed, poring desperately over information he already knew by heart. Even the oldest of the sage's notes failed to reveal knowledge Baltraine did not already know. According to the writings of every philosopher and priest through the centuries, Béarn and the Westlands could only thrive beneath the rule of an uncorruptible, neutral heir. He or she had to pass the gods' staff-test, and only direct descendants or siblings of the king qualified as heirs.

Still, Baltraine searched for loopholes, diligent and desperate. Each yellowed, brittle page yielded only dead ends. His own bloodline remained frustratingly outside the broadest definition of the royal line. His daughters could become queens only through marriage to Kohleran's grandson once he took the throne. Aside from Griff, every conceivable living heir had failed the staff-test. The books gave no advice for such a contingency. They did take infertility into account, allowing the line to pass through rulers' nieces and nephews in certain circumstances into which the present problem did not fit. Had Kohleran fathered no children, their heir-base would have become immense, even including Baltraine and his issue. But each book and every paper confirmed what Baltraine already knew: he had to bring Griff back to Béarn swiftly. And the young man had to pass the test.

Baltraine closed the current book, shutting his eyes against the strain of reading for too long. His studies gained him nothing, not even the knowledge of the consequences of allowing the throne to sit empty, only vague, veiled warnings of an anguish that ranged from inexplicable danger to utter destruction of the world. Most historians agreed that the absence of an heir heralded the *Ragnarok*. And still no solution came to Baltraine. Two messengers and a diplomatic envoy sent for Griff had failed to return; and Baltraine finally, reluctantly had to agree that Knight-Captain Kedrin had been right from the start. Baltraine's only chance at permanent power lay in gaining the trust of and marrying one or more of his daughters to Griff.

Weariness crushed down on Baltraine as he rose from the sage's table. The elder brightened, swooping down on the table and gathering his books and papers with the tenderness of a lover. Thoughts of bed and a good night's rest replaced the intense inspection that had filled this day and several prior. Only then, as Baltraine's mind turned to the mundane, his subconscious suggested a last, desperate measure. Nowhere in his readings did it say an heir could only take the staff-test once. Practice enhanced other skills, mental and physical. Why not the ability to pass the gods' test?

Exhaustion retreated before this new idea, and Baltraine's thoughts churned with details. Though unprecedented, he would retest all of the heirs in the hope that one or more might pass on the second try. And this time he would meet no reluctance or resistance from Kohleran. Though temporary, being regent had definite rewards.

Sunlight struggled through the overgrowth to warm the forest in patches, and Kevral became accustomed to the alternating heat and shade that characterized healthy, Western forest. Though not her first, the battle in the clearing had shaken her more than she would dare to admit to her companions. Renshai revered combat, and she would not allow herself to show anything but excitement about the events of the previous night. She worked at trivializing her role in the conflict, though secretly pride gnawed at her self-assured front. She had battled three warriors at once and won. She had always believed herself capable of such a feat; yet this was the first chance she had had, outside of spar, to prove it.

Fresh irritation rose at the realization that the battle had not gone as well as she believed it would. Always before, she'd trusted herself to handle such a minuscule threat with rapidity, dignity, and ease. Yet she had felt hard-pressed battling three, keeping track of six, and guarding Matrinka all at the same time. She had taken no injuries, had never believed herself in personal danger, but two of her opponents had managed to escape to gather allies. And that mistake might cost them dearly.

Tae returned from one of his scouting forays, riding directly to Kevral's side. He spoke an awkward rendition of the Northern tongue, guessing rightly that only she could understand him. "Trouble. Princess should see not."

Kevral's hand fell naturally to a sword hilt, the other remaining on the reins. She stuck with the Northern language, certain Tae would not choose it on a whim, especially when his awkward mastery of it made him sound silly. Always before, he had made painstaking efforts to appear slick and in control. "More enemies?"

Tae apparently understood more than he could speak. "No. Dead." His brow furrowed as he considered his next words. "Our dead."

Kevral tried to piece the message together. "You found dead bodies? Béarnides?"

"Mostly," Tae confirmed. "And allies. Maybe even Renshai." He sighed heavily, realizing he could not find the words he needed in Northern. He lowered his voice, seeking the privacy of a whisper where language failed him. "The envoy, I think."

Kevral huffed out an expletive, then translated the curse into Northern for Tae's future reference.

Tae repeated it, then continued. "Look things over, need. You and me? Princess not." He added in trading, "I don't think she could handle it."

Kevral suspected he deliberately avoided Matrinka's name so as not to make it obvious he spoke about her, although Tae also had a habit of referring to people by features or nationalities for no particular reason. She could see Tae's point. Sweet and relatively innocent, Matrinka might react poorly to seeing friends or kin dead, especially after escaping a similar attack unscathed. The Béarnide had still not recovered from their own struggle. Despite her brave insistence that they continue the mission, she had spent most of the morning ominously quiet, unsuccessfully fighting tears. Darris' comforting had helped, but another shock now might erode her remaining confidence. "So you want to split the party?"

"For moments, yes."

"Women go around and men explore."

Tae gave the suggestion less than a second's consideration. "Better the others go around. You and me explore."

Kevral frowned, immediately dismissing the idea of separating herself from Matrinka, though curiosity prodded her to view the remains of the envoy. She alone could identify a Renshai among them and administer the formal ceremony that would allow the soul to find Valhalla. "I stay with Matrinka," she said with less insistence than she wished to convey.

Tae blew out a heavy breath, as if preparing for a struggle he would rather have avoided. "I understand loyal guarding thing. Sure can Red watch her little time."

"No!" Kevral returned, instantly angry. "I'm not leaving Matrinka in the hands of an incompetent."

Tae sighed again. "One dead man made words in dirt. Can't read. Like Northern. Maybe Renshai." He pulled at his scraggly hair, obviously frustrated by the limitations of his knowledge of the Northern language. "Need you. Princess, no."

Kevral pondered the situation in the light of this new information. "I'm not leaving Matrinka in the hands of an incompetent," she finally repeated, but less emphatically.

Tae motioned Kevral away from the others, obviously loath to continue a disagreement while unequally burdened by a language barrier.

Kevral rode slightly away from the pack, pacing them at a perfect parallel.

Tae blurted in the trading tongue, without preamble. "I think you're being too damned hard on Ra-khir. He held his own pretty well in that fight."

"Not for a Renshai," Kevral shot back.

"He's not a Renshai." Tae pointed out the obvious. "And neither am I. Plus, I'm an Easterner and street slime. You don't judge *me* as tough as you do him, and you don't even know for sure if I'm on your side. Whatever Ra-khir's faults, at least you can trust him."

Tae's self-deprecation distracted Kevral from the brunt of her irritation. She studied him closely for the first time. As always, burrs and twigs twined through his thick, black hair. Though not classically handsome, like Ra-khir, his features bore a strength that made them not wholly unattractive, in a wild sort of way. Her need to guard kept her too suspicious to rely on him, but she had come to enjoy his blunt, sarcastic manner, his confidence, and even the danger he might represent. His easy confession amazed her. "*You* consider yourself street slime?"

"Is that any different than you knowing you're a blonde? Or the princess admitting her best friend is a cat?"

"Yes. It's a lot different." Kevral searched for an analogy. "It's more like me saying I'm a lousy swordsman. And I'm not, so I wouldn't."

Tae denied the comparison. "No, it's more like *Matrinka* saying she's a lousy swordsman. And I've heard her do that, too." He drew the conversation back, point by point. "First, I've been honest with you all. If you choose not to believe that . . ." he paused, considering. ". . . well, I probably wouldn't either in your place. Second, you're still being too hard on Ra-khir."

Just the mention of the Erythanian's name reawakened Kevral's annoyance. "And I don't think I'm being hard enough."

Tae tapped his knee with a finger, several times in rapid succession. "I understand your problem. He didn't take to me either. But I think there's a normal man under all that armor and formality."

"The Knights of Erythane follow a rigid code they call honor. But, since they expect others to abide by their silly, inflexible ideals, they reduce their honor to a set of arbitrary rules. Real honor means sticking to combat morality even after your opponent has abandoned his."

"Ah," Tae said, then laughed. "I suppose you just made that up."

"No," Kevral admitted, irritation increased by Tae's mirth. "I was quoting Colbey Calistinsson. The greatest swordsman who ever lived."

"Fine." Tae shrugged. "I'm not going to argue with a centuries-old dead guy, though I will say that being centuries old and dead don't mean everything you ever said is right."

Kevral opened her mouth to protest, but Tae swiftly and deftly returned to the original subject. "I still think you're being too hard on Ra-khir. I'm sure he didn't write the knight's code. He's just doing what he's taught is right. Just like Renshai do. Just like everyone else does. You think your honor's better. He thinks his is. I think you both limit yourselves too much, but no one bunch of people owns the truth."

Kevral did not agree; her loyalty to the Renshai and devotion to learning within her culture would not allow it. But she conceded Tae's point about that for the moment. "So what's changed? You teased him as much as I did before."

"I'm like that." Tae untwined a stick from his hair. "I still enjoy bugging him, and I'll probably keep doing it. But right now it's getting in the way of our mission and breaking up the group. That's not what's best for any of us."

Matrinka veered, drawing her horse up beside Kevral's and interfering with further private conversation. "What are you two talking about?" she asked with her usual politeness, but her tone revealed annoyance.

Kevral smiled nervously. "Tae found something up ahead he wants me to look over."

"What is it?" Matrinka pressed.

"Um . . ." Kevral did not have a ready answer. "He's not sure yet. He wants me to help him figure things out."

Matrinka raised her brows, obviously not accepting the excuse. The overwhelming newness of travel and anxiety had caused her to take a passive role, just as politeness often did at home. Apparently, the attack had shaken her from her shell, and Kevral saw evidence of the sweet but stable princess she had guarded in Béarn. "You're a bad liar, Kevralyn Tainharsdatter."

Irritation flared at the "lyn," but Kevral suppressed it for the sake of a lame joke. "Lying's not part of my training," she said, uncomfortable hiding the truth from one she served and liked. She glanced at Tae who inclined his head to indicate he had no intention of assisting her.

He followed with an explanation. "Don't expect me to fix what you broke."

Darris and Ra-khir joined the others.

Kevral resorted to truth, preferring not to mislead Matrinka, even for her own good. "He's found the remains of a fight. Thinks it might be the envoy."

Matrinka's mouth closed to a tight line, and color drained from her cheeks. Nevertheless, she maintained her composure. "We need to look."

Kevral glanced again at Tae, who shrugged, throwing the onus back onto her. She met Matrinka's gaze next. "We thought maybe we could spare some of us from seeing the dead."

"Like me?" Matrinka guessed.

That being the case, Kevral nodded.

Matrinka sought confirmation from Tae who gave her a noncommittal gesture.

"Thank you for your concern, but I can handle it. I'm a healer, remember? If there's anyone who needs my help, I should be there."

Tae denied the possibility. "There's no one alive. I'm sure of that."

The argument did not dissuade Matrinka. "Sometimes, it takes a healer to tell. At the least, I can certainly help find final rest for those I can't tend." She added emphatically, "And I don't like the idea of splitting the party for any reason. Especially one as silly as sparing me from ugliness. I'm no innocent, naive heir. The staff-test already determined that."

Kevral sensed bitterness in Matrinka's last point, but she kept the observation to herself.

Tae accepted the change of plans without argument. "Very well, then. This way." He headed into the lead again without looking back. The others followed closely.

Ducking branches, bending spring growth, and trampling young vines and underbrush, the group worked a careful route to a packed earth road. Birds flitted ahead of them in the branches, occasionally calling sour notes to mark their progress. The announcements warned forest animals of human presences, keeping them well beyond sight and sound. The crash of hooves or paws through brush, night or day, made Kevral twitchy, so she appreciated the reprieve. Enemies would head toward them rather than flee, making the discrimination between natural and dangerous easier.

Tae led his companions along the roadway for a time, a relief after nearly a week of breaking trail. Their need to remain unobtrusive had held them away from the more comfortable routes. Kevral had made certain that Tae kept them traveling always in an eastern and southern direction, as they had originally discussed. The sun and stars helped her with this task, though she had no way to determine how far from trade routes he kept them. Now, she suspected, they probably spent most of their time paralleling the roadways.

Tae took the party across the pathway and back into sparser woodlands on the opposite side. Though they had spent only a short time on the road, the switch back to trailblazing drew a sigh from more than Kevral. Then, hooves, wheel ruts, and footprints drew her attention; and her own discomfort lost meaning. She could not mistake the evidence of a large group traveling with conveniences she did not know enough to miss. Surely, this could represent only the envoy or a wealthy merchant's caravan.

Kevral slipped toward the front of the party, immediately behind Tae. If it existed, danger would most likely come from whatever carnage lay ahead.

Tae brushed first through the low branches blocking the deer trail that led to the fateful clearing. Kevral followed, shoving leaf-covered branches from her vision to reveal a mess of blood, bedding, and bodies for which Tae's description had not prepared her. She froze, blocking those behind her from the sight, suddenly wishing she had been more persistent about sparing Matrinka from it.

When Kevral did not move, Matrinka, Darris, and Ra-khir threaded around her, fanning into a quiet semicircle, locked into a silence that covered horror, shock, and rage. Broken, wheelless wagons lay sideways in the dirt, their Béarnian blue and tan unmistakable. Blankets slick with brown gore lay casually wrapped around or carelessly tossed over mottled corpses. No one spoke, but Ra-khir and Tae dismounted first, the former heading to the bodies with a stiff-legged gait that revealed grief and anger and the latter moving aside wreckage without outward emotion. Matrinka slid from her mount, saying something to Darris from which Kevral gleaned only "horses." The bard's heir tended to the animals while Matrinka hurried after Ra-khir.

Steeling herself, Kevral searched for Renshai among the dead, aware two had accompanied Béarn's second envoy. If they died in glorious combat, she would need to honor and celebrate their entrance into Valhalla. Otherwise, her religion allowed her to mourn their descent to icy Hel. Though unafraid, she investigated with trepidation. Her original glimpse had revealed many murdered in their sleep, and she hoped Renshai wariness had spared her people from this worst of all possible fates. Hoped, but dared not anticipate. From the corner of her eyes she watched her companions sort through corpses, identifying people and desperately searching for signs of life. Every one she saw bore evidence of a single, fatal injury delivered without warning or time for defense. And still, she searched for Renshai.

Matrinka cried unabashedly, assigning a name to every Béarnide and reciting a prayer over each body before allowing Ra-khir to haul it away. Soon, Darris secured the horses and joined them in silence, at first consoling Matrinka but soon crushed beneath his own burden of sorrow. Kevral found the first of the Renshai distant from the others, at a corner of the clearing in a sentry position. Three arrow shafts jutted from his chest. On closer examination, she found a fourth in his back, broken beneath his weight as he fell.

A coward's death. Kevral finally succumbed to the tears she had controlled throughout her search, allowing them to flow now that her companions could not see her. With the lapse came comfort as well as shame. She considered herself hard and strong, like Colbey. Though not devoid of the weaker emotions, she could control them, beat them into a deep submission that did not interfere with her mastery of herself and her skills. Yet, too, she felt a secret solace she would not admit, even to herself. The warm tears cleansed a wound discovery of the body and the ghastly means of a friend's death had cut to her core.

Afraid to leave Matrinka too long, Kevral halted the stream of tears, though grief still demanded outlet. She dried her eyes on her sleeve, fighting back need, and hoped she had not cried long enough to leave visible signs. Her temporarily smothered pain remained easily sparked, and she prepared herself for a struggle to keep from humiliating herself in front of the others. They relied on her for fortitude. But the Renshai maneuvers had their basis in quickness and agility rather than strength, and she would need assistance to move the Renshai's corpse among the others. This one needed no pyre. Valhalla could not have him.

Kevral located her companions. Tae paced the edges of the clearing, alert for enemies. Darris was assisting Matrinka, clutching her shuddering body against him. Their closeness struck something primal, and a wistfulness she never knew she possessed passed through her briefly. She wondered how it would feel to share so much with a man, to know him nearly as well as herself, to give and receive love, and to assuage needs she did not even know she had. Yet she did not envy Matrinka and Darris. They could never truly appreciate their bond, each calling the other only friend. And when they finally acknowledged and realized their love, law and propriety would forbid their marriage. *Or would it?* Kevral wondered what effect Matrinka's disinheritance would have on their relationship, then put that contemplation aside for the moment. She had more important matters to attend.

Unwilling to disturb the couple, Kevral looked for Rakhir, though she would have preferred anyone else's assistance. Finding him crouched over one of the corpses, she sighed and headed toward him. For now, they could set aside their differences for the good of the party and their mission. About that, at least, Tae had been right.

Ra-khir looked up as Kevral approached. Tears softened the green eyes and added a gentle, human quality to features otherwise too handsome to seem real. When he recognized Kevral, his expression hardened slightly, but the obvious sorrow defied hiding. He did not apologize for his frailty, though he did draw himself up to face the teasing he had every reason to expect.

But Kevral was in no mood to taunt. Clearly, the man near Ra-khir's feet was one of the four Erythanian Knights who had helped guard the envoy. For the first time, Kevral found a common link, felt bonded in a warrior brotherhood that had not previously allowed the knight-in-training admittance. Blaming too much time with Matrinka for her next action, Kevral placed a comforting hand on his shoulder and squeezed. The muscle felt firm and round beneath her touch, the covering linen supple in her grip. "I'm sorry," she said.

Ra-khir's eyes narrowed uncertainly, squeezing free another pair of tears. Then, apparently realizing the words were heartfelt, he could not help adding, "His life was wasted. There was no honor in this death."

His thoughts mirrored Kevral's. "The *wisule* cowards killed them sleeping." She spoke the worst insults she knew, the word "coward" and comparison to a timid rodent who would abandon its young rather than fight an intruder half its size. "And at least one from a distance with arrows." She spat, and the clearing blurred around her. Only then did she realize she had begun to cry again as well.

Ra-khir apparently recognized the tearful catch in Kevral's voice and rose to face her. He reached for her instinctively, taking a hesitant shuffle-step toward her.

Kevral froze, suddenly knowing he was about to embrace her as Darris did Matrinka. A thrill shivered through her, exactly the opposite of what she expected. To her surprise, her mind welcomed his presence; and she could not pry her gaze from his straight, exquisite features, honed body, and gentle eyes.

But Ra-khir caught himself before he took another step, awkwardly pretending he had had no intention of consoling. He pulled his arms close to his body and rubbed his hands together nervously.

Kevral knew his wariness stemmed from her reaction to his attempt to assist her dismount on their first night of travel. Momentarily, she cursed the trained hardness that made her not just self-reliant, but unnecessarily cold. Then she dismissed the whole as foolish. She despised this man and all he stood for. She could only credit her unrecognized desire to the stress of the situation. Yet even after the rationalization, she could not escape the guilty wish that he would hold her.

"Cowards," Ra-khir repeated after too long a lapse. "Afraid to face real warriors, so they murder without fair challenge." He clung to the overlap between knight's chivalry and Renshai honor.

"Cowards," Kevral said, the moment and the tears gone but not forgotten. She glanced at her companions and found Tae talking with Darris and Matrinka. She hoped the Easterner had not witnessed the recent events on her side of the clearing. She would kill him before suffering his ridicule on this matter. She was having enough trouble sorting her own feelings.

Kevral heard quiet movement through the brush. Instantly alert, she worried for Matrinka, charging across the clearing without wasting breath to shout a warning. She had covered only half the distance when the twang of a bow shot charged her with desperation. Still blind to the enemy, she flung herself at Matrinka, hurling the princess to the ground. Startled, Matrinka shrieked. In a better position to pinpoint abnormal sounds and also trained to guard, Darris reacted more specifically. He drew and cut, stepping in front of Tae and directly into the path of the arrow. Gasping, the bard's heir plummeted. Tae disappeared into the brush.

More arrows followed the first in a wild rain. Kevral cut one from the air. Another stabbed pain through her shoulder with a suddenness that nearly dropped her. Then, dizziness receded behind a burning, red chaos of battle rage. "Modi!" she screamed, vitalized by her own pain-call. She charged the bowmen like a rabid beast, sword slashing through the first before he recognized the danger. She did not bother to count enemies; her mind rejected logic and specifics. Only two things mattered: killing enemies and protecting Matrinka. Thought for all else disappeared beneath the fires of battle wrath.

The seconds it took to drop bows and draw swords cost two more their lives. Kevral pulled her second weapon free without slowing her attack with the first. One of the two she now faced collapsed before her blow fell. Her left-hand sword cleaved the air where he had stood. Directly behind, a man appeared, and she redirected her strike for him. He retreated with a startled cry. Kevral turned her attention to the others, her mind belatedly recognizing Tae.

Kevral's wild strokes ached through her injured shoulder. She concentrated on putting her all into her other blade. Even as the right-hand sword spilled an enemy's entrails, the concept of Tae as a "friend" finally penetrated the savage frenzy that fogged her mind to anything but killing. Only then, she realized another aided her fight. He battled near enough so they could benefit from one another's tactics yet at a distance that kept him from hindering her strokes . . . or accidentally succumbing to them. Unused to strategy, she struck down enemies without pattern, surely hampering her companion's defense even as he worked around her to avoid doing the same.

The shoulder wound sapped Kevral's strength, and the pain throbbed even through a mind otherwise wholly concerned with battle. "Modi!" she said again, desperately tapping flagging reserves. Another man fell to her assault, then someone slipped through her back's defenses and touched her spine.

Kevral whirled, slicing at the intruder in the same motion. Tae ducked beneath the sweep, scuttling beyond reach of the Renshai's sword. "Whoa, Kevral, stop! It's over."

Kevral blinked, gaze sweeping the clearing. Six strangers lay, still and limp, on the forest floor. Ra-khir stood among the bodies, sword dripping, crouched and alert. Matrinka knelt over Darris who remained where he had fallen, as motionless as the corpses scattered just beyond the clearing. Tae stayed in front of Kevral, his attention locked on her hands and awaiting her next move. Kevral saw no more enemies. She relaxed slightly, and excitement ebbed in an instant, followed by a howling rush of pain. She cleaned, inspected, and sheathed her swords, though the agony in her shoulder demanded tending and movement sent waves of dizziness shuddering through her.

Obviously the one who had fought at Kevral's side, Ra-khir cleaned his own sword, less meticulously than Kevral, and returned it to its sheath. Making one last visual sweep for enemies, he rushed to check on Matrinka and Darris.

Tae remained directly in Kevral's path. "You in our world again?"

"I'm fine," Kevral managed, keeping her injured shoulder immobile. Movement might throw her over the edge into uncontrollable pain.

"Why don't I believe that?" Tae stepped closer cautiously, catching Kevral's right upper arm, then answering his own question. "Could it be the gritted teeth? Or the way you tried to kill me twice?"

"Sorry," Kevral gasped, the apology woefully inadequate. She rationalized with a quotation, "Never get in the way of a fighting Renshai."

"I'll keep that in mind." Tae steered Kevral toward Matrinka. "And we'll chat about this later." He shook his head. "What good is saving us from enemies if you kill us along with them?"

It took more concentration than Kevral wanted to devote to talking, but she felt obligated to answer the allegation. "I wouldn't do that."

Tae snorted but did not argue.

At the edge of the clearing, Ra-khir took Kevral's elbow, and Tae released her to his care. The thief headed back to the enemy bodies, presumably to ascertain their deaths as well as search for information about their origin and intentions.

"Is Darris all right?" Kevral managed, braced for the worst.

"He's alive, but he's hurt bad." Ra-khir inclined his head to the bard's heir and the wet-eyed healer who worked over him in silence. Matrinka had removed the blood-soaked shirt. Darris' chest rose and fell rhythmically, in short, shallow breaths. A hole marred the flesh to the right of the midline, and most of a filthy arrow lay at his side. As Kevral watched, Matrinka poured water over the injury, scrubbed at it, added a salve, and started bandaging.

Kevral's legs grew weak as her body responded to an injury her mind had forced it to ignore too long. She slumped against Ra-khir. He tensed, obviously surprised by her sudden lapse, then lowered her gently to the ground. Kevral sat, cross-legged, and awaited her turn. Ra-khir hovered like an anxious father.

Matrinka finished bandaging, covered Darris with blankets, then finally turned to the others. Only then, she wept openly, racked with a grief that need had placed on hold. Kevral could not help comparing the healer's sorrow to her own pain. Each of them had become single-mindedly devoted to a job that could not wait, ignoring personal need until the task had been completed. That hers involved killing and Matrinka's healing did not diminish the analogy. It only added irony.

Understanding Matrinka's need, Ra-khir wrapped her in his arms and held her through the moments when grief overwhelmed understanding. She sobbed into his muscular chest, his height making him more conducive to consoling than Darris, who stood barely taller than she did.

Kevral lowered her head, suffering a pang that felt strangely like jealousy. As such made no sense, she dismissed it as an effect of the injury. Uncomfortable in the position of low-angle spectator, Kevral glanced toward Tae where he worked among the bodies. But the tall grasses stole all detail from her, and she had little choice except to wait for Matrinka's ministrations. Renshai learned healing arts as part of their training, since nothing appalled them more than death by illness or infection after the battle. Yet she did not feel steady enough to attempt her own care at this time. Should she try and pass out, she might cause more damage than she staunched.

At length, Matrinka's undirected sobs turned into explanation. "The arrow broke. The point's still in his lung, and I can't get it. He'll need a more practiced healer, someone who knows surgery."

Ra-khir studied Matrinka's head, still holding her. "Then that's what he'll get." He swiveled his neck toward the battleground. "Tae!"

The Easterner shouted back. "What do you need?"

"What's the nearest large town?"

Tae did not hesitate. "Pudar's only a few day's travel north."

Matrinka drew back, sweeping wet strands of hair from her forehead. "Only a few days?"

Though she spoke much softer, Tae apparently heard. "If we take the road."

Ra-khir faced Matrinka again. "Will that do?"

"It'll have to." The tide of Matrinka's tears slowed. "A town that big'll definitely have someone who can help us." She glanced down at Kevral then and winced. "Here, let me help you."

"Thanks," Kevral said with genuine appreciation, having learned to accept help more graciously since cutting her hand in the princess' room.

Ra-khir released Matrinka, and the healer began work on her second patient.

By the time darkness fell, Ra-khir and Matrinka fashioned a litter for Darris, Kevral had slept long enough to rest her shoulder, and Tae had sorted through as much of the devastated camp as he believed necessary. Kevral awakened to the first stirring of crickets and nighthawks, jerking to awareness with an abrupt need to ascertain Matrinka's safety. She found the princess with Ra-khir, gently transporting Darris from ground to stretcher. She saw no other movement in the clearing.

Where's Tae? The question popped into her head instantly, accompanied by instinctive suspicion. She sat up. In response to her movement, a shadow glided through the darkness to her side, and Tae was with her.

He whispered, "Can you move all right?"

Kevral did not even bother to test. She knew her body, and nothing about it suggested much limitation. Pain, she could handle. "Of course. What do you need?"

"Remember, I told you one of the envoys had written something in the dirt?"

"Right." In the excitement, Kevral had forgotten. "Is it still there?"

"Yeah. Over here."

Kevral rose and followed Tae to a body lying a surprising distance from the remainder of the envoy's corpses. A trail carved through brush marked where he had, apparently, crawled painfully toward the main pathway. As they drew closer, Kevral recognized Randil, a middle-aged Renshai who had accompanied the envoy. Where the others bore single, fatal wounds, clean deaths in dishonor, Randil's body had sustained myriad slashes, stabs, and cuts. The tattered tunic and breeks clung to a mass of wounds. No doubt, he had fought valiantly and against many. His right hand remained tightly clenched around his bloody hilt, even in death. A gash across the tendons left his other gaping open. He had scratched letters in the dirt, the alphabet Northern and the language Renshai. It read: "ELFS," the spelling incorrect but shorter than the proper "elves." And, beneath it, Randil had added: "LEADER: ZHARLOMAY . . ."

Kevral blinked in disbelief.

Tae crowded in. "Can you read it?"

"Yes," Kevral said, though she made no move to do so yet. Randil's proper death, in battle, gave her cause to celebrate not mourn, but the message in the dirt confounded her.

Tae waited for her to continue.

Reluctantly, Kevral obliged.

Tae listened but still said nothing. Finally, he raised his brows. "Elfs? Like creatures from another world?"

"Elves," Kevral confirmed. "Like airy, happy Outworlders."

Tae made a thoughtful noise. "So what does it mean?"

Pain and general irritation at the situation made Kevral curt. "I didn't write it."

Tae shrugged off Kevral's sarcasm. "Must have been trying to tell us something about his attackers."

"Must have been."

"Elves?"

Kevral sighed, hating to attribute anything done by a Renshai as fever-hysteria yet unable to reconcile the writings in the dirt to logical reality. "Doesn't fit with the elves in any of the stories I've ever heard. Even if you assume they're something more than fantasy."

"Ah."

Kevral sighed again. "And there're a billion different descriptions of what they look like." She studied the body, then shook her head. "Tiny, winged creatures couldn't inflict wounds like that."

"I agree. They look like regular sword cuts."

Kevral completed the thought. "And anyone who uses weapons like ours must be built like us. How would you know to call something like us 'elves' even if they were elves?"

Tae had an answer for that. "Maybe they had animal heads. Or three arms."

Kevral had several reasons to dismiss the suggestion. First, she doubted creatures so strange would have escaped human notice for centuries or millennia. And such warped ugliness would have conjured the word "demons" rather than "elves" to any mind steeped in Northern religion. It seemed unlikely they would ever divine Randil's reasons, at least not until they encountered these creatures themselves. For now, it seemed enough to understand the enemies they faced would prove different from any in the past. "Maybe," Kevral said, her tone conveying her doubt and, she hoped, ending further discussion on the matter. Wild speculation could only mislead. Better to anticipate nothing specific and face what they found than chase ungrounded speculation.

Tae apparently caught on to Kevral's unspoken need. "Here. For you." He held out his hand, a round, green gem balanced on his palm.

Kevral blinked, surprised and strangely touched by the gift. She studied Tae's face, trying to read his intentions.

Tae raised his brows, still offering, his expression sober and open.

Kevral reached for the stone, many thoughts and emotions bombarding her at once. She could not help feeling flattered by his attention. Surely one accustomed to living hand to mouth did not surrender such treasures easily or to just anyone. As her fingers closed around its smoothness, she could not keep from blushing at his generosity and the attraction that must lie beneath it. Their time together had taught her he was not demonstrative, and he had kept his fondness for her well hidden. Yet, there could be no mistaking the caring behind such an expensive gift.

Kevral had little choice but to confront her own feelings for Tae. She had come to like him over the last few days, and she had already determined he met her minimum standards for attractiveness. No doubt, their relationship could grow to something stronger than just one between friends, and her eagerness to have Ra-khir hold her earlier in the day made her certain she was ready for a relationship. Maybe, just maybe, Tae was the one.

Kevral took and studied the gemstone. The perfection of its roundness surprised her. No jeweler had carved it; it could only have come from the sea. Yet, Kevral had never heard of a pearl the color of late spring grasses. Embarrassed more than she expected, she found it difficult to look into Tae's eyes a second time. "Is it emerald?"

"No." Tae answered instantly. "And not jade or diamond either." He shrugged, more curious than upset by his ignorance. "I've never seen anything like it."

The obvious question followed. "Where did you get it?"

Tae hesitated, disengaging from Kevral's scrutiny. "He had it." He pointed to the dead Renshai. "That's why I thought you should have it."

"Oh." Disappointment followed the pronouncement, and Kevral could not help feeling mortified. She blamed stress for causing her to place too much emphasis on every gesture her male companions made. For the first time ever, the self-confidence others reviled in her failed. No war or practice could befuddle her, but a tiny conflict of the heart could. Only a few short weeks ago, she had no interest in a relationship at all. She could not fathom the emotions nor the mind-set that allowed her to so readily discard a decision that had so recently seemed so certain.

Sensing Kevral's disappointment, Tae added. "Not that I wouldn't have wanted you to have it anyway." It seemed remarkably lame for one who usually maintained an air of quiet dignity and composure. He drew breath to speak again, then closed his mouth, apparently realizing anything more would only worsen the situation.

Kevral changed the subject but could not wholly deny the irritation that followed misunderstanding. "What else did you find? You know anything the envoy brought as gifts legally belongs to Matrinka."

"Nothing else valuable." Tae's voice had a quiet, resigned timbre that suggested he did not expect to be believed. "Either the killers took it all, or someone cleaned up later. I'd bet on the second."

For now, Kevral set aside the issue of Tae's honesty. Trinkets and money meant little to her, though she would keep the gem for now. Had Tae secretly discovered piles of gold, silk, and jewelry, his pockets and pack would have become noticeably stuffed by now. "What? You don't think the killers robbed them, too?" She could not help but add, "Is it immoral to steal from someone you just murdered?"

Tae ignored the question. "First, it wasn't necessary to kill everyone, maybe not anyone, to steal. So I don't think robbery's the reason they killed. I don't know if they just wanted to kill and didn't care about stealing or they had to leave before they could take everything or they could only carry so much and just left the rest. But the coins I did find all came off those fools we fought. Béarnian gold and silver, all of it. This time, you killed one of those two that got away from you last time, so I figure we fought the same bunch as before. They didn't have any money last time, so they must have gotten it somewhere."

Kevral considered the implications of Tae's words, concentrating as completely as possible to escape other contemplations. If she trusted his assessment, then the killers probably were the same who sought to break the king's line; and it seemed likely all scouts and members of the previous envoy had met the same fate as these. But the men who had twice attacked them must have a different agenda. Hope sprang from the observation. It was possible Béarn's enemies had not discovered their party, just a group of unrelated thieves. That a pack of teens had dispatched one while an envoy's escort had fallen easy prey to the other fit the observation. Hopefully, the very hugeness of Béarn's enemy might blind them to the existence of Kevral and her companions, because she doubted even she could survive an onslaught like the one that killed Randil. Though she would, of course, revel in the challenge.

"Come on. Let's get back to the others. You need your sleep." Smoothly, Tae placed an arm around Kevral, steering her toward the remainder of their companions. The gentle deliberateness of his touch forced her to wonder anew at his feelings for her. The tender smile he gave her and the twinkle in his dark eyes should have dispelled the last of her doubts.

Chapter 18

Breakthrough

*Every time you perform a maneuver, you improve
it. If you don't put your all into your practices,
any warrior with less skill and more dedication
will best you.*

—Colbey Calistinsson

Ra-khir took double sentry duty that night, allowing Kevral
to sleep through the last morning watch. The information
she and Tae had divulged to the party left him much to think
about, and she needed her rest far more than he did. His
wound had already scabbed, while hers was fresh. Herbs and
bandages could only do so much. She required the natural
healing that accompanied sleep.

Ra-khir studied his companions in the red light of dawn.
Darris had finished the day and spent the first half of the
night in a deep, motionless slumber that kept Matrinka constantly at his side. During the latter half of the night Darris
had become restless, shifting repeatedly to escape the pain
of his injury, though he never fully awakened. Ironically,
Matrinka found comfortable sleep when Darris lost all semblance of it. Ra-khir hoped Matrinka's peace stemmed from
an improvement in Darris' condition rather than from personal exhaustion, but he appreciated that she finally found
sleep no matter the cause.

Tae slept with his arms and legs drawn close to his body,
like a newborn baby, though the daggers he clutched in each
fist ruined the comparison. The position granted him the po-

tential for quick defense and movement. He slept on the barest edge of awakening, a trait that seemed ingrained, and it made Ra-khir more certain he had grown up as an orphan on the streets. Surely no child with parents to protect him would acquire a posture so desperate.

Ra-khir studied Kevral last and longest. She lay on her side, blanket falling into folds near her legs. Fine, white-blonde locks fell in loose waves and ringlets around the too-young features. Her sleeping linens sagged, revealing the edge of a breast. Trained to extreme propriety, Ra-khir deliberately avoided looking at the exposed flesh. He was a knight-in-training all the time, not only when others watched his actions or he found it convenient. Sleep exaggerated Kevral's youthful appearance, and she seemed as gentle and innocent as a toddler. The assessment was so far from reality, Ra-khir could not suppress a good-natured smile. She was reasonably attractive, at least to one who appreciated warrior sinewiness, though she lacked the curves that drew the attention of most men, especially ones their own age.

One eye fell open, large and blue. Kevral's sleep-induced calm disappeared abruptly as she assessed the time and realized she had missed her watch. Both eyes snapped open, and she sprang to her feet, a hand falling to each hilt. The blanket flopped into an empty heap. The swift movement must have increased the pain of her injury, but she winced only slightly as she glanced around the campsite.

"It's all right," Ra-khir whispered. "I let you sleep."

Grumbling something unintelligible that sounded like nothing close to thanks, Kevral headed into the woods. They had moved away from the camp the previous evening, far enough they could no longer smell the rotting corpses, the stale blood, or even the smoke of Randil's pyre. Ra-khir wondered where Kevral headed, certain she would not go far from Matrinka. Though curious, he did not follow right away, leaving her plenty of time to relieve herself without compromising modesty. But, when she remained away long enough to defecate three times, he cautiously followed.

Barely on the other side of the trees, Kevral practiced sword forms with the grace of a dancer and a confidence even Kedrin might envy. Her sword cut perfect arcs and lines, leaving silver echoes in its wake. Her legs glided from one balanced stance to another, each movement seeming irreversibly committed yet changing with the speed and whim of fire. Her arms appeared to meld with the steel, and her blades cleaved air with a beautiful patternlessness that held Ra-khir spellbound. He did not know how long he stood in silent wonder before Kevral halted her practice and glared at him.

Ra-khir caught himself stupidly staring back. Whatever ideas he might have entertained about her looks disappeared. Movement added a delicacy and a radiance no other woman could match.

Kevral remained in place, features growing increasingly angry. Blood soaked the sleeve of her tunic, but she did not notice.

Ra-khir said the only words he could think of, heartfelt, though he knew he would pay for them later. "You shouldn't be using that shoulder so hard. It'll never heal if you don't rest it."

Kevral snorted. His words brought her attention to the re-opened injury, and she lost whatever nasty remark she might have made about the differences in their commitment to sword work.

Ra-khir seized on her silence. "Today's practice won't amount to much if you don't have an arm to use tomorrow."

Without modesty or warning, Kevral removed her shirt and examined the wet, scarlet bandage beneath it.

Caught off guard, Ra-khir stared for only a moment before decorum forced him to look away. Now his caution about studying her while she slept seemed ludicrous and misguided. He listened to the sound of tearing as she fashioned another bandage, leaving her time to apply pressure to the wound and replace her clothing.

The lapse also gave Kevral the opportunity to regain her sarcastic manner. "Great. Another knight-stupidity. You'd let an ally bleed to death on the battlefield just because she's a woman."

Ra-khir sighed, pinned into another unwinnable situation. He avoided looking at her as he spoke, politely giving her additional time to cover her nakedness. "You clearly didn't need my assistance, and if I had offered it, you would have condemned me for that. Help, stare, or avert my gaze. Those were my choices. It is not my habit to gawk at a woman's breasts, though I would bare them myself if tending to your injuries required it." Ra-khir tried to speak matter-of-factly, but he could not help picturing her body deliberately opened to him. The unholy thought stabbed at his conscience, and he banished it with effort. The image of Kevral in motion had become a permanent part of his assessment of her, and he would forever see her in that light no matter when he looked upon her.

Kevral paused long enough that Ra-khir felt obligated to glance toward her and ascertain she had not quietly slipped away. She stood in the same place he had last seen her, wearing her garment with the sleeves now torn from it and wrapped as a bandage. Clearly, she considered his words, and the situation she had placed him in; yet she would not verbally concede even this tiny victory. "Why did you follow me?"

Ra-khir shrugged, not wholly certain himself. "I worried about you wandering off alone and injured."

"I can handle myself."

"I know."

"Then why did you worry?"

"I can't control how I feel." Ra-khir found the question nonsensical. "I guess because I care about you."

"Why?" Kevral shot back.

Irritated by her dogged pursuit of unanswerable questions, Ra-khir returned the only reply he could muster. "I don't know! Maybe I'm stupid." He softened his tone, offering her a lopsided grin and hoping to ease the tension between them with gentle self-deprecation. "That, of course, would be in addition to my being rigid and incompetent and bumbling . . ." He tried to remember the other insults Kevral had thrown at him. ". . . and excrement."

For the first time, Kevral returned a smile. "I didn't call you excrement."

Ra-khir mulled the memory. "You're right. Tae said that one." His words sparked a connection he would otherwise have missed, and his grin wilted. The Eastern word Tae had claimed meant feces was *gynurith;* and Ra-khir had heard something remarkably similar shouted by one of their enemies in combat. Now, the phrase came back to Ra-khir easily, indelibly burned into his subconscious: *Ain ya-charth gynurith tykon tee.* If they were speaking Eastern, as Ra-khir now believed, Tae had lied and could no longer be trusted.

Finally, Kevral relented. "I guess I have been a bit hard on you."

"No. No." Ra-khir good-naturedly accepted the near-apology. "Dogs are a bit hard on rabbits. You've been positively brutal."

Kevral's lips pursed, and the hardness entered her eyes again. "Let's just say our honor doesn't mesh."

Ra-khir denied the assertion. "But I don't think that's true."

Kevral shrugged.

Ra-khir pressed the point. "We both agree running from battle is cowardice, and we both revile cowards."

Kevral threw out her hands, conceding. "That's pretty basic."

"All right." Ra-khir did not agree, but he accepted the statement for the sake of diffusing tension. "Do you attack opponents unannounced or from behind?" Although he did not know the details of Renshai strategy or honor, he guessed from their mutual hatred of the means of the envoy's slaughter that she would despise this technique.

"Never!"

"Neither would I. Death in battle?"

"The ultimate honor."

"Right."

Kevral frowned. "Fine. So we have a few things in common. But what about your armor?"

"What about it?" Ra-khir threw the question back to Kevral.

"You use it."

"So."

"It's dishonorable."

"Why?"

Kevral's response was obviously rehearsed. "There's no honor in allowing steel to fend an enemy's blows instead of skill. In personal skill only there is honor."

Ra-khir did not see the connection. "And using armor doesn't require skill?"

Kevral did not need to consider. "No. Armor is for those too lazy to dodge. It takes away the need to learn defense."

"Really?" Ra-khir recalled his hundreds of lessons on the proper use of armor, without fondness. "So you think you could put on my armor and you'd be invincible?"

Kevral avoided the question. "I wouldn't put on any armor."

Foiled without addressing the issue, Ra-khir tried another approach. "You think I'm invincible in armor?"

"Not to me."

"Why, particularly, not to you?"

Kevral smiled wickedly. "Because I'm Renshai. So I know maneuvers to get through armor. And I practice them *every single day.*"

Kevral's refusal to follow an idea through made any attempt at education difficult. He followed her tacks, attributing her style to immaturity. A world of emotional difference existed between her fifteen and his seventeen years. Two years ago, if not for his knight's training, he might have acted the same way. "And I've come to appreciate the skill that gives you. I bow to your ability and admit you're better than I am." He could not help adding, "So far."

Kevral smiled. Few things pleased Renshai more than aggressive competitiveness when it came to combat.

Ra-khir finished with an intended compliment. "Maybe you'll give me some lessons?"

"I can't teach you the Renshai maneuvers if that's what you're after."

That news caught Ra-khir unprepared, but did not surprise him. "I wasn't specifically hoping for those. Maybe just some pointers about how to improve my own technique."

"That might be possible," Kevral said carefully.

Now that Ra-khir had Kevral listening, he eased back onto the subject of honor. "You know, armor's not just a passive defense. In the right hands, it's a weapon. And we have a name for warriors who rely too heavily on armor."

"What's that?"

"Corpses." Ra-khir met Kevral's crystal gaze and could not figure out why he so desperately wanted her to understand. "We've been attacked twice. How many of those times have I worn armor?"

"Neither," Kevral admitted.

"And I'm still alive." Realizing the opening he had just given Kevral, Ra-khir added swiftly, "That may not be a great testimonial to my skill, but it does mean I know how to dodge. It's not like people can go running around all day dressed in armor, so it's mostly only used in war or scheduled challenge."

Kevral remained unconvinced. "So why use it at all?"

"It's there, and it works."

Kevral snorted. "Not much of a reason."

"It gives an edge. It means more warriors alive on your side."

"So does training them competently."

"What's wrong with both?"

"One's dishonorable."

Frustration plied Ra-khir, and he tossed his head, flinging red hair. "And you call *us* rigid and arbitrary? Who decided that a sword's honorable and an ax isn't? That it's fine to use secret maneuvers but not armor?"

"Those things are obvious." Kevral folded her arms across her chest in a gesture Ra-khir took to be resolute and defensive at once.

He pressed the point. So far she had managed to place aside her hostility to listen. "Only to Renshai. That's why Renshai have gone from reviled to reclusive while Knights of Erythane have always been revered."

That struck a nerve. Kevral's large eyes narrowed, and she spat her response. "Just because the masses believe something doesn't make it right."

Even had Ra-khir not agreed, he would have conceded. To do otherwise now would jeopardize any further chance for a friendship. He knew he walked a fine line here. Kevral was listening now, but the wrong words might spark an animosity worse than the one that already existed. Agreeing with her every statement would only make him seem weak and worsen her already low opinion of him. Verbal or physical, warrior tactics would work best with Kevral, challenge followed by a swift and competent offense. "You're right. That's true. A bunch of people believing something doesn't necessarily make it right. But the reverse certainly doesn't make something *obvious*."

Kevral hesitated.

Ra-khir could see he finally won a point. Once he got her to understand that followers of any serious cause believed themselves clearly and morally correct and others wrong, he could begin to delve into the reasons for her nastiness toward him. It came to him in a sudden rush that he was enjoying this conversation despite, or perhaps because of, the care and effort it took. Kevral would prove an invaluable sparring partner, on and off the battlefield. Always, she would keep him guessing. In fact, his own thoughts spurred deeper ones about the common vision of virtue and shook the foundation of chivalry laid for him since birth. *How much does my own upbringing influence what I envision as right? What makes me believe my roots have more validity than hers?* A more frightening idea struck him then. *Or Tae's?* Ra-khir put the whole aside. He had to base his principles on something, and his Western culture currently dominated the world. Like Kevral, he had little choice but to act properly within the scope of his experience and to understand when others followed different paths.

Kevral stiffened, and her head jerked to the right, apparently in response to an unexpected sound. A moment later, Tae stepped through the brush, examining the two with a quizzical expression. Kevral returned to her normal stance, but the moment had been broken.

"Ah, here you are," Tae said. He glanced at Ra-khir next. "And you, too." His gaze roved up and down the Erythanian in exaggerated gestures.

"What are you looking for?" Ra-khir allowed annoyance to seep into his tone, hoping Tae would take the hint and leave.

"Breathing," Tae replied jauntily, ignoring the signals Ra-khir tried to send. "I'd heard interrupting a Renshai's practice was fatal."

All friendliness left Kevral's expression as the words reminded her that Ra-khir had transgressed on something sacred. Ra-khir bit his lip, the urge to throttle Tae almost overwhelming.

"He had a good enough reason," Kevral defended Ra-khir for the first time ever. "At least initially."

"She was bleeding." Ra-khir supplied before Kevral mulled the unnecessary conversation that followed.

To Ra-khir's surprise, Kevral found a way to turn the discussion back on Tae, though she did so without the malice that had colored all of her previous conversations about Ra-khir. "And I thought Easterners hated having their names shortened. I'd heard using a single syllable is a lot like interrupting a Renshai's practice."

"When we're in the East," Tae admitted. "But Westerners shorten everyone's name, so I figured I'd just do it right away, the way I'd want it, before some Westerner picked some weird, annoying little nickname."

"So Tae's not your whole name?" Kevral pieced the detail from the explanation.

"It's Tae Kahn. Two words."

Tae Kahn. Tykon. The puzzle fell into place for Ra-khir, and he did not like what he discovered. Now no longer in doubt about the origin of the enemy who had twice attacked them and might cost Darris his life, Ra-khir knew what he had to do. He only wished he had continued to pursue his first instincts about their newest companion and hoped Tae would not refuse his challenge a second time.

Once everyone but Darris had awakened and eaten, and Kevral finished her practice, they returned to the site of the tragedy for a brief but necessary cleanup and preparation. Matrinka wished to head out as soon as possible, for Darris' sake; but the idea of leaving allies' corpses without proper and full send-off clearly bothered all except Tae. Their Eastern companion's routine nonchalance only increased Ra-khir's distaste. Nevertheless, he bided his time, keeping his irritation appropriately channeled and saving his dispute for the proper moment. Hiding his rage became all the more difficult as circumstances required him to work side by side with the object of his anger, building a rude cart from the shattered remains of an envoy wagon. At first, Tae seemed not to notice his companion's discomfort. Gradually, Ra-khir's irascible silence drove Tae to work in silence, but his mood did not dim. Apparently, he attributed Ra-khir's behavior to one of their many group concerns.

The creaking cart unnerved every horse set to pull it except Kevral's calm bay and Ra-khir's gray, trained to knight maneuvers and battle. The Renshai refused to be burdened, so the responsibility fell to Ra-khir; and he gladly accepted. It only made sense to keep their best warrior unhindered. He never considered asking a princess to work, and he would not have trusted any injured man to Tae.

Midday came and passed before they set out for Pudar again, Darris' cart jouncing and rattling behind him. Tae had little choice but to keep to the roads, and no one complained about the added danger of discovery. Ra-khir enjoyed the easier travel with a guilty pleasure he dared not voice. He would not complain if their route forced them back to brush and forest, but he could not help finding manmade pathways more natural and comfortable. Mostly, he let the others watch and listen for danger, keeping his own attention on Tae and Darris. Kevral could handle Matrinka's security, and her own, without him.

Darris awakened in the early evening. He studied the sky with a look that went from blank to confused in an instant.

"Hold up!" Ra-khir drew rein and dismounted, without waiting to see if his companions complied. Darris needed his assistance now.

Darris shifted, groaning with the movement. His gaze settled on Ra-khir and turned pleading.

Ra-khir knelt beside the cart, resting a hand on Darris' shoulder. It felt warm and dry through the sleeve. "You're going to be all right."

"No," Darris' voice emerged as a croaking whisper. Obviously surprised by the sound, he licked his lips several times. "I'm dying. Let me go. Don't delay for me."

The others had pulled up their horses, and now the women came to Darris' side.

"You're going to be fine," Ra-khir repeated.

"What's wrong?" Matrinka asked, concern breaking her voice. "Is something wrong?"

"He thinks he's dying," Ra-khir explained, wondering how seriously to take the opinion of one in pain. Although trained for war, his only real experience had come within the last few days.

Matrinka stroked Darris' hair, eyes haunted as if she had taken all of his pain onto herself. "We're going to get you to a surgeon in Pudar as quickly as possible. You'll be fine."

"No," Darris rasped. "Don't waste time with me." Each word made him wince, and bloody foam bubbled at his lips. He managed to raise a hand, wiping his face absently, then caught sight of the mess. "Don't waste time."

The urge to cringe and look away nearly overwhelmed Ra-khir, but he controlled it admirably. He had no knowledge with which to contradict Darris' assessment, and Matrinka seemed paralyzed when it came to the necessary reassurance. Her feelings for Darris got in the way.

Kevral suffered from no similar malady. "The only delay you're causing is now, with your irrational talk. If Matrinka says you're going to live, you're going to live! She's the healer, damn it. You're just the stupid patient. I've seen warriors recover from a lot worse than you got." She glared, granting his pain no quarter. "Now hush up and rest." Without further explanation, she turned and headed back to her waiting horse.

Stunned, Matrinka let her mouth fall open.

Ra-khir despised Kevral's harshness, gathering breath to soften her words with gentler ones.

But Darris handled the Renshai's method better than Ra-khir expected. A slight smile touched Darris' features, though Ra-khir could not tell whether her reason, tone, or behavior shaped his mood. Whatever the case, Darris closed his eyes peacefully and remained in a state of quiet composure as they traveled into the night.

Tae was not allowed to take sentry duty alone; the group had determined that the first day of travel. So, the night after Darris' awakening, Ra-khir volunteered for earliest watch with the Easterner. As usual, the initial hour passed in quiet contemplation, allowing the others to drift into sleep before even the lightest of conversation started. This time, Ra-khir had more serious matters on his mind. The long silence did not seem to bother the Easterner. Even during the most enthusiastic conversations, he tended to hold his tongue in a fashion that seemed inexplicable to Ra-khir. Though Tae never acted interested, he always listened, throwing pieces of conversation back verbatim when desired. He chose his words with care, but not in the same way as Ra-khir. While Ra-khir paused for propriety and grammar, Tae seemed more concerned about phrasing his words in a manner that best protected him from ridicule or fit with some strange, low-class pattern Ra-khir could not fathom.

But, for once, Tae broke the hush. "What's fussling you?"

Tae's notice of his quiet agitation further irritated Ra-khir. Tae's and Kevral's discovery of the dying Renshai's message had spurred conversation about Outworlders and magic. Ra-khir had placed little stock in the idea until Matrinka's description of the incident in the courtyard when bears, once statues, devastated young heirs. Apparently, his uncertainty had become a paranoia just beyond conscious thought, reawakened by Tae's understanding. *Can he read my thoughts?* The idea, though ludicrous, could not be wholly banished. Many things about Tae did not fully fit the picture of a street orphan. "*You*'re bothering me," he said at length, substituting the more proper term for Tae's slang. "You lied, Tae. Those men who attacked us were Easterners." He spoke emphatically, leaving Tae no place for denial or explanation. He wanted to convey that he knew the truth, without a shred of doubt.

Tae did not call Ra-khir's bluff. His permanent aura of self-confidence remained, though it seemed more habit than intention. "Yes."

"You said they weren't speaking Eastern."

"As you said, I lied," Tae admitted.

"You told me before you never lied to us."

Tae lowered his head, looking truly shamed. His pretense cracked ever so slightly. "Until then, I hadn't."

"Oh, I see." Ra-khir glared, remembering to keep his voice low despite shaking fury. "Honesty is a matter of convenience for you. Gain our trust with truth, then lie as you please." His hand fell to his hilt. "Well, you did lie before. You didn't join us for the company. You joined us to help you fight your enemies."

Only then, Ra-khir realized the distance between them was gradually increasing as Tae crept almost imperceptibly toward the woods. "You gave your word against your honor. You said I could stay with you." Tae glanced toward the sleeping party, composure visibly shattered now.

"On the condition you posed no threat to us." Ra-khir remembered the promise well, one he should have trusted his instincts not to speak. "You threw us into a war! You may cost a good man his life, a man pledged to become the high king's bodyguard, no less." He took a threatening step forward, without intention, his first realization of the act Tae's sudden, scuttling retreat. "You placed our cause and our lives in danger, and I have no choice but to call you out again."

Tae said nothing, while his long-practiced reserve collapsed around him. "I'm sorry. I really am. Give me a chance to—"

Ra-khir did not allow him to finish. The word "explain" might make him explode. No excuse could account for an action so indefensible. "Do you accept my challenge?"

"No," Tae said softly.

Frustration assailed Ra-khir. At no time in his life did he more wish to abandon the teachings of the Knights of Erythane. Almost, it seemed worth never achieving his life's ambition, worth disavowing his own honor, and worth the shame he would call down upon his life and soul to administer the slow, painful death those of lesser morality might claim Tae deserved. But Ra-khir's virtue ran too deep. Punishing a traitor, even permanently protecting the kingdom from one, did not justify wrongdoing. "Accept my challenge and either live or die a man."

"No," Tae said again, then expanded. "If I follow your rules, I die. And if I do things my way, I kill a friend."

Ra-khir defined the situation differently. "If you surrender honor either way, then you're a craven and a coward. But you need not worry about harming a friend. We are friends no longer."

Tae did not argue semantics, though friendship, as well as animosity, had to run both ways. He brushed hair from his forehead and eyes, gaze subtly measuring escape. "I will not fight you."

Reduced to one option, Ra-khir explained it, as honor demanded. "You still pose a threat to Béarn. I'll give you time to run, if you choose the course of cowardice. But I will pursue. Don't come back. If we meet again under hostile circumstances, I'll kill you without need for challenge. You've been warned."

Tae hesitated.

"Go!" Ra-khir managed to convey command without raising his voice. "Or I'll take your reluctance as acceptance of my challenge. Be glad I, and not Kevral, realized your deceit. She would have killed you by now."

Tae backed into the foliage, then turned abruptly and disappeared.

Ra-khir redoubled his watch, awaiting Tae's retaliation, which never came. Gradually, the night thickened. Matrinka and Kevral took their turns at watch. No one noticed Tae's absence; he wandered off alone so frequently. Although Ra-khir rested, he did not think he fell asleep at all that night. Only Tae's missing pack and horse in the morning told him otherwise.

Chapter 19

Béarn's Betrayal

In some ways, death means everything to me. It depends on whose death it is and when and how that death occurred.

—Colbey Calistinsson

Days ran into nights for Rantire, differentiated only by the torture that accompanied the former and the restless sleep plaguing the latter. Evenings suited her best, the quiet time when the endless charade of questioning and torment had finished. Then she listened to the elves prattle, her growing command of their language yielding more information each time. She appreciated the concentration required to understand them. It took her mind from the pain.

One night, the style of their conversation changed from pitying whispers, curious chatter, and anticipatory guesses to an excited discussion about a battle. She noticed the difference at once, though the details proved more difficult to grasp. Their talk lasted deep into the night, and she followed it with dogged persistence. Gradually, she uncovered a few of the details: a fight between elves and humans resulting in many deaths, though she could not figure out which side had won at first. Numbers came at length. By report, all thirty-one humans had succumbed, and these bore some relation to Béarn. She guessed the dead were not heirs, more by knowledge excluded than addressed, and she finally pieced together that the dead represented a second envoy. Two elves had died, and Dh'arlo'mé lost an eye in the scuffle.

Once she identified the topic, Rantire could not rest. The need for details spurred her far more strongly than the hovering sleep she so desperately needed. Oa'si used the Northern tongue fluently, and she had heard others resort to it for certain concepts that either did not exist in their language or worked better in this human tongue. So far, she had not revealed her knowledge of it, except to Oa'si; but this situation seemed reason enough to try. "Please, I have to know. Did they die in battle?"

Rantire's voice opened a ragged silence. Stunned elves went without speaking for so long she believed they had abandoned her. She wondered if they had all run to tell Dh'arlo'mé or others of the council that she could speak Northern. Oa'si and Captain had figured it out easily enough, and more than one healer or torturer had resorted to Northern in an attempt to communicate. That she had chosen to ignore those questions as completely as ones asked in trading told them nothing about her ability. In comparison to her need to know, the information she revealed by the simple act of speaking held no significance. There would have been Renshai among that envoy, and their fate mattered too much to ignore. She could not build their pyres, but she could properly mourn them. No one else might come upon the carnage who knew the proper ritual.

At length, an elf appeared from the shadows, all arms and legs, and as graceful as his kith. Huge, yellow-white eyes studied her without malice, as unwinking and steady as a statue's gaze. He used the Northern tongue with reasonable fluency, though his word for it little resembled the human. "You speak 'other-speech'?"

"Northern," Rantire corrected absently, then protected her revelation. "Some." She redirected back to the important question. "Did they die in battle?"

Another elf stepped into view, also male. "Who?"

Three more swiftly followed, all huddled at the front of her cage. Eyes that ranged from almost clear to deep violet scrutinized her. Now that a few had dared the contact, others surged closer until a press of elves filled the corridor or peeped through the bars of cells from cross pathways. Before Rantire could respond to the question, another elf said, "Do you speak 'first-speech'?"

Another asked, "What's it like being human?"

Another: "Do they hurt you?"

And another: "How come you didn't talk until now?"

The queries came strangely fast and furious for elves, who normally seemed unhurried to the edge of human endurance. Even their beatings proceeded in a leisurely fashion, one of the few things Rantire appreciated. Finally, Rantire raised a hand. "My questions first. Then I'll answer some of yours." She placed the emphasis on the *some*, having no intention of blurting publicly those responses she had withheld under threat and torture. Their interest in her speech, however, she could and would address. Something had to change soon. She could not endure the suffering much longer.

Other elves began talking even before Rantire finished, their voices loud and their language elfin. She did not understand all of what was said, but she featured prominently in their complaints, along with admonishments about making friends of foes. Dh'arlo'mé's long name got mentioned several times. Gradually, the elves withdrew from Rantire's cell, the first to arrive waiting till last and moving with obvious reluctance.

"Please," Rantire said as they dispersed, desperately needing the information she had sought. "Please, just tell me. I have to know."

But the elves disbanded without another word to her, only whispered exchanges amongst themselves. Then, they disappeared; and Rantire could no longer hear even their quiet movements or exchanges.

Rantire slumped to the floor, hiding her face and its telltale tears. The urge to pound the wall or floor overtook her, but she battered the impulse away. She would not display her frustration, or it might return to haunt her as emotional torture. Now, she suspected, they would hold the knowledge over her head, bait for the answers they sought. And, she realized glumly, the technique might finally work where all else failed. She would not doom the human race, including the Renshai, to spare herself suffering; but she might try lying for the possibility of rescuing warrior souls. Yet even having a decision made failed to soothe. The Renshai death ritual, performed without the bodies, might already be doomed.

Even this burden could not overcome the exhaustion that hammered her after another grueling session of abuse. Mercifully, sleep came to wrest desperate concerns from her. Yet before it fully took hold, the amber-eyed elf returned to her cell, accompanied by some of the others who had plied her with questions. There was a nervousness to their movements that little resembled anything elfin, but the one with the white-yellow stare spoke with a solid sureness that belied the mood. "My name is Haleeyan Sh'borith Nimriel T'mori Na-Kira." He introduced the others, with names equally long and musical, but Rantire's blunted consciousness could not follow.

Rantire waited until he finished, using the time to sharpen her senses, reminding herself that her dealings with them now could become a turning point. Obviously they had chosen to come late at night, at a time they usually stayed away; and their nervousness suggested others would not approve of their visit. This potential split in the elves' usual unanimous behavior boded well. It could be a trick, Rantire knew, yet she had little choice but take a chance sometime. Otherwise, she would die in vain, Valhalla unattainable and mankind left to the whims of fate. "I'm Brenna," she returned.

Several of the elves smiled. She counted close to a dozen of them shifting amid the shadows and knew from experience many more could hide in the dark corridors beyond her sight. The one who had spoken, Hal to Rantire's mind, replied. "We know. It's easy to remember. You're the only human here."

Rantire managed a smile also at the subtle humor. It came naturally, even after so long. Still not fully focused, her mind pursued a tangent, surprised at how humor and its grin could look so similar between creatures so different. She wondered how the gods had determined the details that would separate and link them.

Hal continued, "Oa'si tells me you can't track our names." He did not await confirmation, a good sign to Rantire's mind. "You can call me Halee."

His choice sounded too feminine to Rantire. "How about Hal?"

The elf chuckled. "You humans really do like your names short."

"There's more to it than length," Rantire had no trouble admitting, though she did not explain that her real name had three syllables and Northern peoples rarely shortened. "There's a sound, too. Hal sounds better to humans than Halee. Stronger."

The elves continued to stare.

"Trust me," Rantire finished. "It's true." She glanced at the others, their manners as light as Oa'si's. Though more subtle with expression, the elves seemed to have less control over it. Rantire found this difference interesting as well as useful. Initially, they had seemed blank, devoid of feelings. Now that she had learned their delicate repertoire, however, they would have difficulty hiding their moods from her. She guessed their team approach to everything probably made the need to hide feelings unnecessary. This became particularly understandable in light of the information Oa'si had revealed about sex, pregnancy, and child-rearing. Though astoundingly free with their sexuality, the elves rarely bore babies; and the group raised children with little or no regard to biology.

Now, the elves wore expressions of open-minded interest, and Rantire hoped to seize on their attention. She prayed desperately to Sif that she had made no mistake, no error in judgment that would seal her fate, and that of mankind, to helpless destruction. "We can talk about short forms of other names when I get to know some of you." She noticed now that all the elves in front of her looked male. Apparently elves had gender divisions when it came to jobs, as did every human group Rantire knew of except the Renshai.

"How about mine?" asked a blue-eyed elf with black hair that held a glimmer of red. He repeated his name for the sake of Rantire's human-trained memory. "Dhyano Falkurian L'marithal Gasharyil Domm. Would it be Dhee?" He pronounced it "Jee," with a lingering over the first sound that gave it a strange "zj" sound that did not exist in human languages. Dh'arlo'mé's name started similarly.

"Dhyano. Or maybe Dhyan." Rantire could not easily duplicate the pronunciation, choosing a lazy-sounding but more familiar "Jon" to replace "Dhyan."

"Jon," the elf repeated, laboring as much with the sound as Rantire had, slurring the two together.

Hal interrupted before every other elf in the vicinity insisted on playing the game. "What is this 'die in battle' thing you wanted to know about?"

It never ceased to amaze Rantire how the elves could keep distant conversations going without any apparent notice of the time between sentences. She imagined a dinner conversation during which elves ate entire courses between words. Nevertheless, she appreciated the restoration of the conversation to the problem plaguing her since earlier that evening. "It's important for me to know if the humans died fighting."

"Fighting us?" one chimed in.

Realizing the sensitivity of the situation, Rantire flushed. "Well, yes, I guess so."

"It was us against them," Hal supplied. "Yes. Is that what you wanted to know?"

The answer seemed self-evident to Rantire. "No. I really don't care *who* they fought, just that they were fighting when they died."

The elves glanced around at one another, and the perplexment they shared was inconceivable to Rantire. "Fighting meaning what?" one finally asked.

"Fighting!" Frustration made Rantire a bit curt, and she struggled to keep the whole in perspective. "You know. Swinging swords. Hitting. Trying to kill whoever killed them."

"Oh," the one who had just spoken said, green eyes as pensive and childlike as Oa'si's. "Violently?"

"Exactly."

Attempting to soothe, Hal said exactly the wrong thing. "Oh, no. No. They died peacefully." His lips pursed into an embarrassed line. "All but one."

One? Rantire felt tears sting her eyes and could not help praying. *Oh, please let it be the Renshai. Let it be the only Renshai.* She did not feel guilty for the thought. Most others did not seek Valhalla as their goal, believing only warriors who followed certain philosophies went either to Valhalla or Hel. Béarnides, and the vast majority of the West, felt that those who preferred went to a glorious plain called the Yonderworld after death claimed them. Renshai felt strongly that others deluded themselves; even those Renshai who gave the Yonderworld theory credence would never lower themselves to seek anything but the warrior's afterlife. She clung to the only source of information she had. "Only one died in combat?"

"As you've defined it, yes," Hal admitted.

"Can you describe the one?"

The elves seemed taken aback by the question. "Human," Dhyan finally said. "Humans look much the same to us."

"Yellow hair?" Rantire tried, pointing to her own to demonstrate, though hers was more sandy and many among the elves sported locks of either hue. Aside from a predomi-

nance of extreme colors: black, white, and blond to humans'
more common brown and a tendency for red to accompany
all colors, the elves' hair did not differ much from humans.

Hal confirmed the feature with a nod.

"Blue eyes?"

Another nod.

Rantire's heart began to pound. Those two features alone
excluded all Béarnides and most Erythanians. Not all
Renshai fit the description, but the ones who did made identification easier. "Used a sword as a weapon? Maybe two?"

"A sword," another said. "Yes. And very fast for one
sleeping." He shuddered, and Rantire suspected he had seen
that sword directly in action.

Relief flooded Rantire at the observation. Almost certainly, the one who died in battle was Renshai. "Blessed
Sif," she whispered, unable to fully contain her elation at the
news.

The elves glanced between one another, obviously noticing the significance she placed on the information, enough
to spur her to talk with enemies she had previously ignored
in stoic silence. Yet her motivation confounded them. Hal
finally broke the restless silence. "This is good? To die violently?"

"In battle, yes." Rantire smiled, vicariously basking in
another's glory, only briefly. Her own fate seemed too uncertain to contemplate, and the proper ceremony not yet undertaken for this one either. Summarizing her tribe's entire
existence into a single line did not dilute the goal she had
sought since birth. *Valhalla.* No greater reward awaited any
man, woman, or child. *Valhalla.* If these elves could not
reach it, their immortality and magic became worthless to
Rantire's mind.

The elves buzzed about her answer, their speculation
shared in whispers, as if she could not hear. Only Hal spoke
directly to her. "Two elves died in battle, too."

"That's good," Rantire said emphatically. "Honorable
deaths." She did not voice the second advantage, enemies
dispatched who could kill allies no longer.

"And one lost his eye," Dhyan added. "Is that good, too?"

Rantire shrugged. Once, all Northmen believed a warrior
who lost a major body part was doomed to Hel no matter
how else he lived his life. Half a millennia or longer ago,
Renshai had mutilated dead enemies to demoralize their

comrades. The other Northern tribes had despised Renshai for that reason, eventually using it as an excuse to exile and then slaughter all of them. The tribe had become reborn in the West, through Colbey's diligence, though neither of its two survivors, one Colbey, had added his bloodline to the mix. If not for two men who had remained in the West when the Renshai returned North from their exile, and considered traitors by the rest of the tribe, none of the old blood would remain. Now, the Renshai had split on the matter of losing body parts. Most believed it carried no significance; as long as a warrior died valiantly in combat, he found Valhalla no matter how many of his pieces found his pyre. Others clung to the old doctrine, while some claimed to follow the new system but became despondent if they or loved ones became crippled in any fashion.

Rantire redirected her thoughts to answering the question. It seemed best to cling to the newer belief system, if only because it would not reveal a human weakness to enemies. "Losing an eye isn't necessarily good or bad. The important thing is the battle." As she discussed those matters most important to her, her mind became almost painfully clear, despite aches and exhaustion. She would stay up all night, if necessary. If she fell asleep during torture, she would only look that much stronger.

The elves crowded closer, eager for understanding. Hal voiced the question she suspected they all mulled. "Why?"

That one word encompassed so much. Human ways and motivations baffled the elves at least as much as theirs did her. Apparently, Oa'si's inability to understand honor, heroics, and individual glory had more to do with culture than immaturity. With her mind confused by weeks of torture and pain, it seemed the worst time to switch her strategy, but Rantire believed she had finally found one that might work. If she could get the regular elves to understand, even revere, the fine morality of mankind that their culture did not allow them to experience, she might discover invaluable allies among the common folk.

Calling upon the Renshai techniques of honing mind and thought in battle, she sought the words to enthrall the hardest audience she might ever face. And hoped the words would come.

* * *

Xyxthris, the eldest living male heir to Béarn's throne, dreamed he perched upon a dais in a room so enormous he lost track of walls and ceiling. Wind rushed through the confines, tugging at his curled, black locks, opening his face to the too-bright light. His dark eyes skittered nervously, painfully dry in the empty glare; and no amount of blinking eased their vigil. The dais seemed tiny beneath his Béarnian bulk, for he sported the robust musculature and the girth of most of his predecessors and cousins. Once, the Pudarian circus had traveled to Béarn to entertain the king's grandchildren. Now, Xyxthris felt like the massive elephant balancing on a ball, its foretoes and back heels dangling in midair.

Then, suddenly, the light intensified, like fire against his eyes. Though blinded, he never thought to shut his lids against the agony. It burned through his eyes, spreading wildly to encompass every shred of his being. His skin seemed to sear away, strangely leaving no organs, only the very core of his soul, the spark deep inside that made him himself. Everything he believed moral and right lived there, and it shone with a brilliance greater even than the blaze that burned him. For a moment, he reveled in his victory, the purity of his thought and vision a guiding beacon above reproach.

The figures came, a million shadowy outlines of men and creatures he dared not name. Each brought its own aura of light, and every one turned his into a pale vestige without meaning. They drifted toward him, laughing and pointing, mouthing a single word that, at first, he could not decipher. The air warmed to their presences, stifling, and every breath became an effort. Xyxthris' lungs worked like bellows, sucking furrows beneath and between his ribs. He wore his skin again, enwrapping the usual organs, but he did not notice the change. The dream-state pulled his focus elsewhere, to the beings closing tightly around him. He recognized them now, distantly familiar kings and queens, gods appearing exactly as they did in his picture books. His grandfather floated among them, his features twisted into a sneer of derision, like the others. And now, their chant became clear, so cleanly spoken Xyxthris wondered how he could have missed it before: "Unworthy!" they shouted. "Unworthy!" And each pronouncement twisted through Xyxthris' guts like a thousand knives at once.

"No," Xyxthris whispered.

Those who condemned him circled, laughing horribly. The dais grew until it seemed to stretch into eternity, and Xyxthris became a tiny speck on its expanse. If it grew more, he would disappear entirely, lost in a vast sweep of time that no longer accepted his existence. The word stabbed agony through him repeatedly, until the pain fused into an endless plateau and nothing seemed real but his own self-hatred. He awakened screaming, his guardian Renshai and a healer at his bedside.

Xyxthris sat up, drenched in cold sweat and rigid with remembered pain. Never before in his life had a dream seemed so vivid, and it chased him into his waking moments. He still felt tiny and worthless, tried and convicted of harboring false morality and condemned to nonexistence. Every feat he had ever accomplished became tarnished and ugly, his own four-year-old daughter a shameful testament to his wretchedness.

"Are you ill?" The healer hovered anxiously, face filled with a concern Xyxthris did not deserve.

Xyxthris fought to draw his consciousness fully back into reality. The dream lingered, stealing his last reserves, all that remained to fight the demons that assailed him since the staff-test had rejected him twice. "Just a dream," he managed, not yet able to directly reassure. Then, he gathered the appropriate words for the lie, "I'm fine." But he was not fine. He had reviewed his every action during the first staff-test a million times, certain he had located his mistakes and that his inherent bent toward right and neutrality would carry him through the second. But the gods had swept away his memories of the previous attempt, and the changes he wished to implement left his thoughts the instant the test began. The scenarios had changed only slightly, but his reactions to them remained the same. The personality and morality granted him by right of birth and shaped by environment was flawed, and it drove his actions in the test no matter how much he tried to suppress it. He was not worthy to rule Béarn.

"Prince Xyxthris," the healer continued as the Renshai returned to his post by the door. "May I examine you?"

Xyxthris did not want the poking, staring, and prodding that would accompany the request, but he had not yet gathered the strength to resist. "It was just a dream," he repeated, but he indulged the healer's request.

The healer slipped into his smooth routine while Xyxthris cooperated passively, moving or speaking only when requested to do so. As his thoughts became more firmly grounded in reality, memory swept in. Alcohol had become more crutch than tool, a goal unto itself that no longer blocked consideration of the worthlessness the gods ascribed him. He had turned to stronger drugs: creating aches and ills the healers treated with mind-numbing painkillers. Some of these brought euphoria as well, but their effect did not last. The quest for better formulations became a desperate obsession that ended with his supplier, a Pudarian merchant who hid his illegals beneath the sale of other goods. Always, it seemed, he found something new precisely when Xyxthris needed it, and that man had become the central focus of his universe.

Xyxthris' wife and child had moved to other parts of the castle, horrified by the changes that swept over him in the months following the first staff-test. He rarely missed them. All that mattered was the deep core of agony that burned inside him, the self-hatred it represented, and the cures that masked its pain for moments, hours, or days. Even sleep did not serve him as well. He could live without the wife who already demonstrated her own inferiority by loving one unworthy and the daughter who represented a legacy of futility. As for Xyxthris' bodyguard, either the Renshai did not recognize the drugs' effects or understood their importance to his charge because he accompanied Xyxthris to the clandestine meetings with his supplier and did not interfere with their transactions.

The healer finished his evaluation with a sigh and a gesture that indicated he had found nothing wrong physically, as usual.

"Just a dream," Xyxthris reminded, his voice growing stronger with time. All vestiges of tiredness disappeared, and anger finally swept in to replace the penetrating depression that had directed his life since the first staff-test. Finally, the source of all his problems became clear, and it seemed impossible he had not considered it previously. The latest drug, apparently, clarified the situation in a way reality and previous concoctions never had. The staff-test was to blame, along with all the trappings surrounding it. Had he not been born an heir to Béarn's throne, he could have led a happy, simple life with his wife and child. Béarn and its test for creating kings would not have him; but it was the system's flaws, not his own. At some time, the staff-test had ceased to function properly and began selecting imperfect rulers instead. Xyxthris would not support such a thing. In fact, he would work against it in every manner possible.

The decision, swiftly made, swept a wave of satisfaction through Xyxthris. He would expose the mistake and end a reign of random tyranny, based on some demon's conception of what constituted qualities for kingship. The vengeance this would satisfy only enhanced the decision. He had always known himself to be the most competent of his cousins and siblings. If he could not become Béarn's king, none of his inferiors would either. And the council who had diverted half of his inheritance to his wife and child, who had refused him the additional money he needed to support his only habit, they would pay for their unfairness. Baltraine and the other ministers could never comprehend the flaw in the staff-test and would never listen to his explanation. His only hope lay outside of the current regime, on his own shoulders or . . . elsewhere.

There Xyxthris' thoughts derailed, the final words defying description or category. *Or where?* He shoved aside these contemplations for the moment. He had all the time in the world to think once he dispatched the healer who worried over him like a cat with kittens. "Sleep might do me good, but I don't think I can with that nightmare stalking me."

"I have something for that," the healer said hurriedly, the very answer Xyxthris sought. Though inferior to the herbs the merchant supplied, the healer's medicines would tide him over in times of sparse supply or when, like now, the Pudarian had left to carry on trade and replenish his stock. One day, Xyxthris hoped, he would have enough money to hire the supplier on a full-time basis and obviate the need for him to continue merchanting in other places. It never occurred to him to wonder whether or not the Pudarian would appreciate this idea.

The healer crossed the room to where his bag lay, near the door and the wary Renshai. The guard watched the healer's every movement as he dug through his belongings, making no comment though he judged the idea with a slight shaking of his head so subtle paranoia might better account for it.

The healer laid two vials of clear liquid on the nightstand. "Take one for sleep. The other is for tonight, if you still need it."

"Thank you," Xyxthris said, trying to sound genuinely appreciative though his voice emerged in its routine monotone. He watched the healer head from the room, waiting only until the door closed before guzzling both vials.

The Renshai watched in silence, nothing betraying his opinion of his charge's actions. He moved to the semi-oval window, looking out over the courtyard below, head cocked to catch any noises from the hallway outside the room's only door.

Xyxthris ignored the Renshai, waiting impatiently for the healer's drug to take effect. It would prove a shallow high, though better than none at all. His thoughts returned to the means to destroy Béarn's current methodology, and the idea that had eluded him moments earlier came to him now. He barely had time to smile before the first stirrings of drug-induced euphoria stole over him.

Chapter 20

The Portal

There is always choice. Remember that.
                              —Colbey Calistinsson

Since the tragedy in Béarn's courtyard, something Xyxthris could not define had drawn him to one of the study rooms on the castle's fourth floor. Under usual circumstances, he would have had little reason to approach that particular place, a quiet haven where nobility could spend time in peaceful contemplation or could read one of the tomes from Béarn's sprawling library. Many other rooms served the same purpose; so even had reading or solitude caught his fancy, he would have been unlikely to single out this study. The first time, he had come to explore a flash he had seen in its window moments before the bears attacked and killed his younger cousins. Inexplicable shivers had accompanied that exploration, as if frigid air had suddenly washed in to clutch him like a giant's fist. A wall of trees had saturated his imagination, and a delicate creature with eyes like rubies flitted briefly through his thoughts. He had attributed the visions to stress and would have wondered on them no further except that a tingling swept through him every time he passed this door.

Since that time, Xyxthris had come often. The study was one of the few places his irritatingly ever present Renshai guardian deemed safe enough to leave him alone. Glass sealed the window, thick enough to withstand the strongest of his blows. Even if he should manage to shatter it, it overlooked a pond whose depth would prevent a jump from proving fatal. A padded window seat served as the room's only furniture, an impossible weapon. Not that Xyxthris had tried to kill himself. He had considered the possibility at length, numerous times, when he thought about the gentle innocence of his life before the gods found him unworthy. A swift end to the pain that haunted his waking and sleeping moments seemed the very godsend the staff-test had turned out not to be. Ironically, the wife and daughter he chose to live for had eventually become symbols of his wretchedness, daily reminders of the ruler's life he would never lead and living testimony to his failure.

Now a vague hope added its voice to the cacophony of emotion warring eternally within Xyxthris. In silence, he headed for the fourth floor study, the Renshai dogging his steps, as always. As soon as they arrived at the simple oak door, Xyxthris spoke without meeting the Renshai's gaze. "Some time, please."

The Renshai opened the door and peered inside, shielding Xyxthris with his body as he did so. Seeing nothing to concern him, he stepped aside, taking a wary stance by the door, while Xyxthris entered and pulled it shut behind him.

Hope flared stronger, stoked by the strange fluttering that thrilled through Xyxthris from the moment he approached the room. He wondered how much to attribute to anticipation, for the signal felt more vibrant now than in the past, pulsating through his bones from head to toe like a steady drumbeat. He perched stiffly on the window cushion, studying the courtyard below. The familiar sight of shrubbery cut and coaxed into animal shapes soothed him, and his gaze traced colored lines of flowers forming borders and detailed flourishes. Sunlight flashed from silver fish as they darted for insects or algae on the pond's surface. The single bench lay vacant. He deliberately avoided looking into the more distant gardens, particularly the statue garden where the bears had killed his cousins. The drawback, as well as the fascination, of this room was that it overlooked the site of the murders. That, he guessed, was the reason Béarn's enemies had chosen it.

Months of study had failed to yield a satisfactory explanation for the slaughter. *Magic.* Xyxthris never doubted, though few others embraced his theory. They would turn to the supernatural only after every other possibility had been discarded, if ever. But Xyxthris knew now, and he believed. The sensations he felt in and near this room, unlike anything else in his experience, made him certain.

Scattered reports of a light or noise near this location just before the tragedy had spurred exploration of several rooms immediately after the incident, though the guards had found nothing amiss. Even Xyxthris might have pinned the flashes he saw on the wrong location if not for the aura he felt here. The council had given his description reasonable attention, although he earned more than one odd look when he mentioned the tingling. Yet nothing had come of his claim; and most now dismissed the inexplicable, mildly unpleasant sensation as the result of his drinking or attributed it to post staff-test madness. Xyxthris knew better. He had first experienced it before the testing or the drugs and alcohol. His addictions only enhanced his senses, and where they blunted his pain, they refined his ability to detect what he believed was the aftereffects of magic.

Relaxed by the same courtyard beauty that once sheltered him as a boy and now consumed him with envy, Xyxthris rose and stretched. He explored the room with a thoroughness he had never attempted in the past. Then, he had trusted his eyes to do the work, understanding in an instinctive, human fashion, that nothing existed if he could not see it. Last night, he had finally discovered the basic error in that belief, now as ludicrous to his mind as the atheist who dismisses gods he never personally met and ignores all the wonders beyond man's creation.

Xyxthris concentrated on his talent, for the first time recognizing that its intensity drew him toward the southwest corner of the room. Always before he had considered the signal diffuse, like a distant smell. The analogy continued to work well for him; odors wafted from a source, growing stronger as he moved closer. Why should magic prove any different?

This logic brought Xyxthris toward a corner near the door, rather than by the window as he expected. Once he reached it, wisdom dawned upon him. When he pressed his back against this corner, he gained a perfect view of the entire room and through the window into the courtyard gardens. He shifted to the position that gave him greatest visual access.

Suddenly, Xyxthris' support disappeared. He stumbled

backward, desperately flailing for balance. Brilliant light shattered vision into painful blindness; and he toppled into empty space, screaming with terror. He slammed to the ground, hip crashing into a rock, pawing at eyes that felt burned from their sockets. He managed a desperate scramble to his hands and knees. Lines and squiggles scored his vision. Through the afterimages etched upon his retinas, he saw several figures jostle into a circle around him, studying him through strange, canted eyes.

Concepts touched Xyxthris' mind, a mad jumble of names, questions, and commands he could not begin to sort. At least one sword seeped through the muddle his fragmented eyesight struggled to sort, and he went still. He made a universal symbol of surrender that demonstrated his empty hands and lack of weapons.

Finally, his vision cleared enough to reveal six males surrounding him, their frames adolescent gawky and their features youthful. Their eyes bothered him most, seeming depthless and without normal variation in color and contour. The array included yellow and red. Four wore curved swords at their hips, and the other two had had the presence of mind to draw their weapons and angle them in Xyxthris' general direction. Neither stood close enough to run him through quickly, and he drew solace and courage from this. "Hello," he said carefully in the trading tongue, the most universal of the world's languages and one of the only two he spoke. Again, he made a peaceful gesture of surrender.

The strangers continued to study Xyxthris in verbal silence, their mental communication nearly indecipherable. Gradually, this ceased also, and a concept in a single "voice" touched his mind. He read a need to remain still and a threat of violence should he refuse to heed the warning. There followed a request for his origin and a disdainful air directed against his humanity. The whole came to him in impressions, not words, a single thought encompassing a sentence, a phrase, or more. He could not describe how he understood in such detail, but he tried to answer in the same fashion. He concentrated on the idea of peaceful cooperation, curious about the alienness that had come through so clearly. Whatever he faced was not human.

After longer than any polite conversation, the mind-voice repeated its demands. Again, Xyxthris attempted to radiate his promise, which resulted in another long pause. The mind questions came a third time.

This time, Xyxthris responded aloud. "Can you understand me?"

"Yes," the yellow-eyed one said at length. "Can't you call a *khohlar?*"

"Apparently not." Xyxthris smiled nervously, hoping his captors would take the words to mean he had attempted it and failed rather than a sassy attempt to point out the obvious. The latter interpretation had not occurred to him until after he spoke, and he attempted to lighten the mood with friendly introductions. "My name is Xyxthris. I'm here in peace, and I will cooperate any way I can."

The not-quite-human creatures glanced at one another, obviously surprised by his words and his attitude. Any previous contact with humans must have come under much different circumstances.

Xyxthris' heart pounded as he awaited their reaction, and he wondered if his own fear or an aftereffect of the healer's drug made everything they did seem so maddeningly slow. When he explored the room, he had hoped to find some clue to help him contact those who cast the magic, but he had never considered the possibility he might discover a route directly to them. He seized on their long pauses to study his surroundings. He stood in a forest clearing beneath a fringe of tall trees with long, serrated leaves. The odors of greenery and pollen nearly suffocated him in the close damp, and he could not differentiate the smell of his captors from these. The study room had vanished without a trace. He could still feel the magic that had drawn him, now behind him; and two of the warriors blocked retreat. Only one explanation seemed possible: he had passed through some kind of magical door, one these nonhumans used to secretly enter Béarn's castle. Presumably, he could return the way he had come; but he doubted his captors would allow him to test the theory.

The creatures did not reply in words. Xyxthris felt a sudden blaze of magic, so raw and close it hurt. Then, peace enfolded him. His arms and legs swayed and buckled beneath him. He lay for several moments, staring at ground speckled with dirt and thick with the reek of leaf mold. He struggled for words to remind them of the peace he promised. Then, gradually, he slid into a quiet sleep.

* * *

Captain could not recall the elves ever calling an emergency meeting of the council Nine, and even the oddity of such a thing did not bring them quickly enough, apparently, for Dh'arlo'mé. The leader paced with the heavy tread of the most troubled human while his charges gathered over a matter of hours, an impressive scramble for elves, especially a group of elders. By Dh'arlo'mé's expression, not nearly fast enough. Captain wondered what news would prove so urgent it required such immediacy.

At length, Hri'shan'taé Y'varos Filtanith Adh'taran came, the One of Slow Emotions the last of the Nine to arrive. She took her place beneath the trees without apology, and Dh'arlo'mé led the long ritual of vows and prayer that opened every meeting. His impatience rushed an introduction never before hurried through millennia; and he waited only until the last word was spoken before charging into his point. "We've captured another human." He ceased pacing to glance at every member of the council with his single eye. The empty socket, with its scars partially healed by magic, served as a strong and recent reminder of the violence humans could inflict. It might take two hundred or more years of daily healing sessions before Dh'arlo'mé grew back his missing eye.

Curious expressions drifted across every countenance, though they all remained silent so Dh'arlo'mé could supply details without competing with needless speculation.

"One of Béarn's princes, apparently." Dh'arlo'mé paused at a significant fact the others would surely wish to ponder. Captain could tell by Dh'arlo'mé's manner that he had more to say, and he considered it even more important.

Captain remained quiet while most of his companions bandied comments about what seemed an incredible find. Finally, Vrin'thal'ros questioned Dh'arlo'mé directly. "Are you sure of his identity?"

"Our observers at the gate recognized him as one they previously identified as an heir. The man has confessed his station without duress." Dh'arlo'mé smiled, the expression incongruous with his earlier solemnity. Increasingly, his movements, attitudes, and expressions seemed more human than elfin. "Better yet, he has agreed to give us all the information we could ever want about humans and their culture. He asks only for gold, silver, and gemstones in return."

A stunned hush followed Dh'arlo'mé's pronouncement. Captain alone knew no surprise. He had dreaded this moment for centuries, the day elves discovered humans corrupted by chaos, those who would sell information to enemies, who would place money or power before the good of their species or, ultimately, themselves.

"Is there anyone who sees reason why we should not indulge his request?"

No dissension greeted the words. Even Captain could see how information would benefit elfinkind, no matter the personal baseness of its source.

Dh'arlo'mé's follow-up brought a nearer concern to the fore. "We have no further need of Brenna and her evasiveness. Is there anyone who opposes disposal of this one who has caused so much trouble?"

The words enraged and horrified Captain. He glanced around the assemblage, reading each delicate expression for evidence that someone, anyone, found the situation as deplorable as he did. As usual, he found She of Slow Emotions impossible to fathom; but none of the others greeted Dh'arlo'mé's suggestion with anything short of contemplation.

It suited Captain's nature better to wait before replying, but Dh'arlo'mé's time on man's world had wreaked havoc on his patience. He was unlikely to allow the customary time to pass before considering all in agreement. "I oppose it," Captain said, softly but with solid determination. He looked around the others for support, but no one met his gaze. Undeterred, Captain explained. "We've already determined she can't escape our prison. What need do we have to kill her?"

Dh'arlo'mé glared at Captain, a light in his eyes bespeaking an irritation and disgust rapidly growing into hatred. This threatened to become the last in a long line of disagreements; Dh'arlo'mé's tolerance had worn as thin as Captain's. Though not the most significant issue they had ever faced, it would bring a million others to a head. One way or another, one of them would lose this day, and it would span issues far more significant than the life of a single Renshai.

Dh'arlo'mé addressed Captain's question with appropriate calm, though the answers seemed painfully obvious. "We plan to slaughter all humans eventually. If we kill this one now, we may gain knowledge of the best means to destroy our enemies. Also, we have no concern about possible escape, endangering more elves, or taking care of her needs until the fateful day. If the best reason we have for keeping her alive is having no reason to kill her, our course is clear."

Nods swept the gathering, all except for Hri'shan'taé and Captain. The eldest of the elves took no consolation from the Slow One's quiet stillness. It was her manner, not any particular agreement, that made her act as she did. It told him nothing.

"Our course *is* clear," Captain agreed out of turn. "You just don't see it."

The tension that followed Captain's outburst became tangible. Even Dh'arlo'mé found no immediate reply.

Captain hesitated as well. Once he crossed the fine line between discussion and insubordination, the repercussions might prove more than he could bear. He pictured Rantire, her parting words haunting him, bringing images of an older Renshai to mind. Colbey Calistinsson had said and done much that shocked, at times had fought alone for a morality only he could foresee. Even the gods had become blinded to the proper course, consumed, as all beings, with selfish interest. Colbey had never desired the material things other men did, only to die in glory in battle. He had clung to the basis of his religion the way others hypocritically claimed to do, and it had given him a perspective few had understood until the end. Aside from a handful of gods, only Captain had supported Colbey's need to keep the world in balance and its forces at peace. Now, Rantire's voice seemed to echo in his mind, and he heard those words again, ones that reminded him so much of Colbey: *There may well come a time, Captain, when you need to choose between what's right for your people and your loyalty to them. When that time comes, the world may rest on your decision.* Buoyed by the words, Captain broke the uncomfortable hush. "What's become of us that we place less than no value on a life, especially one most like our own?"

A gasp followed Captain's blasphemy, though he did not attempt to determine its source. Anger drove his words as it never had before, and he could not stop if he wished to do so. "What have we become that we stomp and sleep like humans? That we talk of murder as justice and destruction as a foregone conclusion?" He waved an arm that encompassed the entire forest. "Once, elves played and giggled amidst the trees, living and loving without thought to weighty decisions or the future. Once, we loved life and lived it with joy and vigor, in the manner Our Creator intended."

Dh'arlo'mé found his tongue at last, shouting over Captain's tirade to preserve his control. "Times have changed!" He fingered the empty socket with a gesture that seemed as careless as it surely was deliberate. The hands of others moved naturally to the residual effects from the Fire, Dh'arlo'mé's subtle way of keeping the hatred and bitterness alive. "You always loved humans. That's why you chose to live among them, and you never suffered the agony that changed our people. Once humans are dead and their world our own, we can return to the guileless innocence we once enjoyed if we wish."

"There'll be no possibility for it then," Captain said. "The damage will be done."

"Damage to you," Dh'arlo'mé created sides without the input of any other. "Justice to us."

Dh'arlo'mé had misunderstood Captain's point, so the elder explained. "By damage, I meant the ugly change in the nature of our people, not the evil we inflict upon humans. Once we become impulsive, conniving murderers, we can never return to what we were. Never."

"Maybe, maybe not." Dh'arlo'mé dismissed the speculation. "Perhaps we have no need to become what we used to be, oblivious and naive. We might fall prey to treachery again. The time for change has come, and one who chose to live among men at a time when no other elf would ought to recognize that need."

Captain did not point out that Dh'arlo'mé, too, had lived on man's world by choice prior to the *Ragnarok,* as apprentice to the Northern sorcerer. Such details had little place in this argument. Outcome mattered more, and the elves had to see where violence and cruelty would lead them. They had to see it or suffer consequences the elves as a race could not bear. "Can't you see what vengeance has already turned us into? We argue. We hate. We fester in our own rancor, though hundreds of years and fifteen generations of man have passed. Even if we accept that mankind caused the Fire . . ."

More gasps met those words, the issue settled long ago to

the satisfaction of the unanimity that defined elves. ". . . the humans who live now had no hand in the matter."

The Nine stared at Captain, perplexity clear on seven faces. Elves lived and thought as a unit, and the idea of singular action held no basis for understanding.

"Your words are *treason!*" Dh'arlo'mé sputtered, borrowing a word from the human Northern tongue where elfin failed him. No such entity existed in their society before. "And it is *your* deeds that may doom us." Dh'arlo'mé addressed this one negative action, ignoring the myriad he and those who followed him had already embraced. "Ostracizing is the only answer. Arak'bar Tulamii Dhor, you are no longer welcome among the Nine nor the elves as a whole. Go live in peace, and keep your views for those who ask them."

The confusion turned to horror. Even Hri'shan'taé stiffened visibly at Dh'arlo'mé's proclamation. There was no precedent for such an action. No laws had been needed to govern elfin politics before. Now those rules Dh'arlo'mé had gradually placed into effect and into writing gained true significance. Ideas few imagined any need to invoke had drawn little opposition, and now Captain wondered just how long Dh'arlo'mé had plotted his elder's downfall.

Dh'arlo'mé slipped from rage to deadly composure in an instant, more swiftly than any human Captain had seen and than he would have believed any elf capable. "Are there any among the Council who would oppose such a decision?"

Silence reigned. Fear colored growing uncertainty, and no one wished to speak first. A line had been drawn, and sides needed choosing. To join the one of lesser votes meant sharing the exile. Yet Captain knew the hush would not last as long as such an important choice warranted. In the past, he could not imagine such a situation arising; but if it had, it would stretch out years or decades. Dh'arlo'mé, they all knew, would not allow that. Time would only tear their views further into opposition. This moment, Captain finally realized, had been inevitable. He guessed the others recognized that, too. Soon, his own argument would condemn him. If the elves retained enough of their original makeup to consider his point worthy, they would also feel bound to follow a course of action devised by themselves and the whole of elfinkind over the centuries. Captain's mistake, he realized, was in waiting too long to challenge Dh'arlo'mé's dominance. That, too, he could blame on elfin patience—his own. He should have wrested command from Dh'arlo'mé before three centuries of tradition stood firmly invested behind him. Yet Captain realized he would have had little support then either. Whatever Dh'arlo'mé was now, he had rescued those elves who survived the *Ragnarok*. Dh'arlo'mé would have found a way to exploit the hero worship heretofore unknown to elves.

Vrin'thal'ros responded first, as usual. "I do not oppose. The Council cannot function with disparity." He dodged Captain's studied stare.

Captain saw the wisdom in those words, though he despised them. Even in harmony, things rarely happened fast among elves. So long as Dh'arlo'mé and Captain both remained members of the Nine, few things would ever get decided or accomplished. That realization shoved his thoughts back to Colbey Calistinsson. Like Rantire and the other Renshai, he could learn much from a teacher and friend who had once seemed more like a curse. Colbey had fought against the stasis that had grown out of a world without chaos, insisting that a steady balance between order and disorder would serve mankind better than the slow stagnation into oblivion that came with law alone. Those who opposed him believed as strongly that even a small amount of chaos would bring ruin and the *Ragnarok*. They had all fought for the same goal, preservation of life, yet their battle against one another had taken precedence. It had seemed simpler to blame all the worlds' problems on one man and to hunt him like a criminal than to find a common method or let one another work in opposition.

Captain knew elfin slowness had to do with lifespan rather than law. Magic and nature had more inherent chaos than mankind; Alfheim had always held a balance that mankind and its champions had not understood. Human chaos took a different form, that of lies, theft, and deceit, virtually unknown until the years prior to the *Ragnarok*. Now mankind had found a balance of sorts, and elves seemed destined to find a similar one.

All of these thoughts raced through Captain's mind while the others of the Council deliberated, and his mind channeled all the information into a single focus. Either he or Dh'arlo'mé had to step down, and he doubted Dh'arlo'mé would do so peacefully. Even if the Council sided with Captain, and he doubted they would, Dh'arlo'mé would never let the matter rest. He might even resort to murder, a sin no elf had committed before, and the possible repercussions of such an act terrified Captain worse than those that might come from war against humans.

For the cause of peace, and for the elves, Captain made a desperate choice. "Speak no more, my companions. I will withdraw from the Nine and from elfin society to live out my years peacefully in solitude. I ask only that you proceed cautiously with any plan involving this Béarnian heir. One who would betray his own would not hesitate to betray us as well." He looked around the startled faces and familiar eyes. They would replace him with the next oldest of the elves, as if they had lost him to illness instead of exile. Finally, his gaze came to rest on Dh'arlo'mé's single eye. Glimmers lit red by sunlight danced through it. He recognized his victory and reveled in it, yet Captain read disappointment as well. The eldest of the elves had bowed out too gracefully for the leader's liking. He still itched for a fight.

"You," Captain said softly, "are no longer an elf. You're something I don't recognize, something dark and sinister that frightens me." He shook his head sadly. "Save yourself, or you'll drag all our people into the same darkness." With that, he turned on his heel, but not quickly enough to miss the all-too-human anger burning in Dh'arlo'mé's eye.

Captain headed home to pack, never intending to spy on the Council of which he was no longer a part. But their words wafted to him softly as he departed. He focused on the rattle of leaves in the wind and the trilling birdsong, the more natural sounds that kept his zest for life alive long past even an elf's time. He heard only Hri'shan'taé when she spoke at last, too used to listening to her rare and cautiously chosen words to ignore them now. "Enough of formidable matters for one day. There is no hurry to kill a defenseless prisoner. I say we give that matter the mulling time it deserves."

Captain smiled as he continued through the woods and the follow-up discussion became lost to distance. It was the best he could hope for the Renshai, her fate swallowed into the quagmire of elfin indecisiveness. Eventually, he felt certain, Dh'arlo'mé's wishes would prevail; but Hri'shan'taé had gained her time. Hopefully, it would prove enough for the

Renshai to plan her own escape. She had endured torture that would have killed most men. Once, she had spoken in the words of Colbey. Captain only hoped she would prove as resourceful.

Chapter 21

The Bond Sundered

I have to assume that, for all their divinity and wisdom, the gods don't know everything either.
—*Colbey Calistinsson*

Early in Tae Kahn's travels, the West's thick, lush forests had seemed suffocating and sinister after the wide-open, almost-contiguous cities he had grown accustomed to in the East. The bitterness of his mood had enhanced the feelings of loneliness and discomfort. The trees had looked like the giant bars of a prison cell interspersed with ropy vines like nooses and copses that blocked his passage in every direction. The mingled odors of mold, fungus, greenery, and musk made little sense to him, and his inability to find the source of the various smells kept him always off-balance. Sound traveled strangely. Movement that seemed distant often turned out to be just behind him, and he could not guess how far his own cracks and rustles carried. The brush rattled suddenly, often seemingly without cause, and unseen creatures scurried ahead of him in the impenetrable shadows. The fertile black earth seemed sticky, and his feet left impressions beneath the carpet of leaves.

As rancor faded and he grew more adept at approximating and anticipating his route, the forest's close security became a comfort. All the difficulties to which he had needed to adjust foiled his pursuers as well. The denseness of the brush kept him well-hidden, and he learned to use it to his advantage on occasion. His time with Kevral and the others had turned forest travel from a necessary chore to a pleasure. Planning routes for quickness and secrecy grew into an exciting challenge. Before joining them, he had nearly forgotten how secure it felt to be part of a group. The reason he had given for joining them had been as much truth as the need for their assistance with enemies too strong for him to handle alone.

Now the closeness Tae had felt toward his new friends shattered, like every other relationship since birth. The caring he had developed toward them turned to loathing as he shuffled through leaves and twigs alone. They would pay with their lives for driving him away, Ra-khir most of all. For a moment, all of Tae's hatred focused in on this one source. A thousand ways to dispose of the knight's apprentice filled his mind in an instant, most of them slow and painful, all methods he could accomplish on his own with no outside help or interference. He believed he could divert them with little difficulty, assuring death for Darris, at least. Poisonings, quiet stabbings, crushing, and drowning: with those four, he could assure the end of them all. *Even Kevral.*

Hemmed by deciduous trees, he sat on a deadfall with his chin in his hands. An image of the Renshai rose with the thought: blue eyes as hard as diamonds yet with a hint of mischief dancing behind the danger. Though cropped masculinely short, her blonde hair bounced as she performed katas as beautiful as life. Its color intrigued Tae as much as its cut, strange and special after a childhood of black-haired men and women like himself. He loved her quick, sharp wit, the sarcasm nearly as caustic as his own, and the emotional strength Easterners equated only with men. Though no longer voiceless property legally bound into servitude, women in the East tended toward meek and mousy obedience to their husbands. His mother had been an exception.

Images of the attack in his childhood drained away Tae's anger swiftly. Fear clutched him, as it always did when his thoughts breached the walled defenses he had built to protect him from the memory. His mother's screams exploded through his head, raising a desperate and primitive need to rush to her defense even as she strove to protect him. The pain had followed, the knife blade tearing through him repeatedly, despite his struggle, his own blood warm and sticky on his skin. Pain and terror had heightened his senses at a time when he most needed them blunted. He remembered counting twelve stabs, and the agony that accompanied them, before unconsciousness mercifully claimed him; and the scars told a story of at least four more. His father's enemies had left Tae for dead, and anger alone had seen him through the months of recovery. His father had fueled that rage well with an attitude that left no place for mercy. The father's words remained ingrained as strongly as the memory of his mother's murder: "If you can't survive without coddling, you may as well die now." By luck, the wounds did not fester.

Tae gasped, despising the memory and his own weakness for allowing it to come to the fore again. Situations of intense emotion seemed to awaken it beyond his control. As a child, he had not understood the reason for the seemingly senseless slaughter of a woman and her only child. Now, Tae saw his childhood self as naive beyond belief. Those men had come for his mother and himself because they belonged to Weile Kahn.

A bird trilled in a tree directly overhead, its call answered in spreading lines. It was a cheerful call that attested to the safety of this part of the forest; his still presence no longer bothered them. Tae's inner turmoil contrasted sharply with the serenity of his surroundings. As a child, he had not understood his father's business, though often conducted in front of him. Weile met with a host of strangers, many of whom became familiar to Tae over the years. These ranged from gruff, affluent types to shifty-eyed street scum in rags. Until his mother's murder, Tae never wanted for food, clothing, or attention. Whatever his father did earned him plenty of money.

Only much later Tae broke the code of euphemisms and pieced together the many weird bits of advice his father had given him. The men who visited Weile spoke of deals, murder, and mayhem. They talked often about trust and loyalty, two values his father took great pains to instill, at least verbally. Using every extremity, Tae could not count the number of times Weile Kahn told him to treat allies with generosity, love, and loyalty and enemies with swift justice. "A man who breaks your trust once," Weile always used to say, "does not deserve a second chance." Although he never said it directly, Tae came to know the penalty for a single act of disloyalty must be death.

Tae kicked at the leaves wind had piled against the deadfall, his anger against Ra-khir and the others now fully expended. Tae, not they, had lied. Ra-khir's reaction had been no more severe than his own father's, less so because Weile would have slaughtered him for the deception. Rather, Weile's men would have done so. For all the illegal activities his father supported—contraband sales, murder, theft, and collusion—Weile had never taken a direct hand in any of it. Instead, he had organized criminals into a unit that followed his commands, a feat no one before him had considered or accomplished. On the surface, it seemed ludicrous to expect those who followed chaos to band together, yet they became more effective and secure as a unit. Tae had learned that from the street gang his father had encouraged him to join, while other parents prayed their children would never have to. Occasionally, however, someone within the organization rebelled, attempting to seize Weile's power for their own. Some had even managed to create rough bands of their own. Weile took the revolutions in stride, dealing death and vengeance where necessary and handling every setback calmly—even the death of his wife and the mutilation of his son.

A long time had passed since Tae thought about his childhood in such detail. Now he considered his father's parenting style and judged it, not for the first time. Deep down, Tae believed, Weile loved him. It came out in their private talks, in the time he occasionally took away from directing pursuits and quelling uprisings to walk, talk, or wrestle with his only son. Several times, he had caught his father staring at him while he slept or drawing a blanket over him when the early morning chill filled his bedroom. "I just want you to be tough," Weile had often told him. "I want you to survive." And so, Tae spent months at a time living among orphans and ruffians on the street, sleeping hungry though his father had much more than enough to spare, curled into a shivering ball while his bed and coverlets lay empty, dodging routine predators as well as his father's enemies.

Four years had passed since Tae had last seen his father, four years of living hand to mouth and evading those who would slaughter him for the Kahn name. That, too, had been an invention of his father's, to pass a name to his child other than the standard "son." In the North and West, they also used the suffix "datter" for girls, though the East had not adopted the convention. Women did not need a second name, though Tae felt certain that, had he been born a girl, his mother would have seen to it he still took the name Kahn. When Tae turned fourteen, his father drove him away. "Come back when you're twenty," he had said, his last words to his child. "If you're still alive, all this will become yours." He had waved a hand, the gesture encompassing the city of Stalmize or, perhaps, the world. And four years of running had taught Tae two things: first, survival would prove more difficult than he ever expected; and second, he had no interest at all in taking over his father's business. The wealth and power would prove little reward for a lifetime of sidestepping assassins. Nothing short of eternal agony was severe enough punishment for an enemy who murdered Tae's family, and only then if his grief could bring wife and children back to life.

Thoughts of future family brought Tae full circle. Again, he pictured Kevral, and it frightened him that he could imagine spending the rest of his life with her. Her strength, competence, and outward assurance intrigued him, and he emulated her confidence. He could no longer hide from the truth. He loved her. The realization that he had plotted her downfall, and that of their mutual friends, just moments before horrified him. Guilt tingled through him, quelled by the realization that he was only mentally responding to frustration and anger. He would never have implemented any of his evil thoughts. Not even against Ra-khir. For all his irritatingly high ideals and the billion rules that governed his actions from speech to sleeping to handling enemies, Ra-khir was likable in his own way. He had a human quality about him that, Tae suspected, his manners would someday mask.

Exhausted by consideration of the long, dangerous turmoil he called his life, Tae remained in place, drained of all emotion. His next course of action did not follow naturally, and he found himself unable to make a decision. He hoisted himself from the log, seized the horse's bridle, and led it east, more from habit than intention.

A soft rattle in the brush froze Tae. He had traveled woodlands long enough to recognize the sound as that of a small creature, low to the ground. Ordinarily, he would have dismissed it instantly; but his instincts grew more wary as the sharp edge of his thoughts became dulled by fatigue and emotion. He glanced toward a cluster of dense brush, the ground around speckled with mayapple, and a cat slithered toward him. He recognized Mior at once, the calico's fur peppered with bits of leaves, twigs, and stems. Grass stains smeared long streaks across her sides. As she came upon Tae, she stopped and meowed loudly in complaint. Delicately, she stretched each leg, shook free the most superficial of the dirt, and rubbed against his legs.

The cat's fur tickled through holes in Tae's britches, and he smiled for the first time since Ra-khir had banished him. "What are you doing here, you ugly old cat?" he said, with affection. "Your mistress is probably spinning in circles looking for you."

Mior meowed again, looking up at him with steady yellow eyes. She twined between his legs, purring. Tae sighed, shoving her away with a foot. "Go on, you. You're gonna get me in trouble."

When the cat did not respond to gentle prodding, Tae looped a booted toe beneath her belly and tossed her two arms' lengths further. "Go on, Cat. Don't make me hurt you."

Mior continued to purr, running back to his feet with her tail held high. Again, she twined around him.

"Get out of here, or I'll kill you and eat you." It was an idle threat. Tae knew he had at least a week before he grew desperate enough to feast on the princess' cat. He poked the boot into her ribs. "Come on! Go."

Mior ignored his threats, as well as his increasingly forceful suggestions. Finally, driven past control, he gave her a kick in the ribs with a side of his foot that flung her into a patch of nettles. The cat yelped in surprise as much as pain, the sound sending shivers of remorse through Tae. He had not meant to hurt her.

Even so, the cat returned. Its purring became more intermittent, it rubbed more cautiously, and it watched him more closely. Tae sighed in defeat, its persistence a lesson like everything in his life. The cat's gentleness and easy forgiveness reminded him so much of her kindly mistress. He could not help remembering the happy times he had shared with his one-time companions, one of whom he cherished and all of whom he respected. If his father's lectures, the strength of his mother's love, and the gang security that allowed him to survive the rigors of Stalmize's streets had taught him nothing else, it had ingrained a sense, almost a need, for belonging. Always before, he had considered himself like a stag, a desperate loner who used others as necessary. Now, he realized, group mentality had become a personality trait. Without him, Kevral and the others might not find Pudar, would surely take a too-long route to Santagithi, if they ever found it, and might fall prey to enemies who came upon them undetected.

"I'm sorry, Mior." Tae hefted the cat, stroking her with fond apology, as he would never have done in front of the others. Status, often membership itself, in a gang relied on toughness. He had learned to hide all signs of weakness. Here, alone, however, he could pet a cat and enjoy the calming effect it had on both of them. "Here, you're safe with me." He placed her on the horse's saddle and veered northward, leading his mount.

Tae had come to a decision that surprised even him. He would do all he could to regain the trust he had lost. Whether they wished him to or not, he would see the party safely to Pudar and to Santagithi. He would assure they found food and shelter, and he would divert enemies and passersby who might stumble upon them because they did not understand the best places to camp. And he would see Kevral again.

Nightfall brought a light rain that pattered like drumbeats against the high foliage. Safe beneath a blanket stretched, clipped, and tied between the trees, Matrinka stared into the quiet darkness with Darris' hand clamped between both of hers. His skin felt warm and dry, despite the damp. His fingers hooked around her palm, deliberately holding; and she thrilled to his strength and touch. He sat beside her, enjoying their togetherness as much as she did. Darris' need to impart knowledge only in song had accustomed both of them to long lapses in their conversations. Only his wheezy breathlessness when he spoke more than a few words at a time reminded Matrinka of his injuries.

It seemed easier not to speak at all, to allow their nearness to say all that needed to pass between them. He was recovering well under her ministrations alone, still a half day's travel outside of Pudar; but Matrinka knew it was not the wound itself that placed him in danger. His lung would either heal and reexpand, or he would learn to get by with only one. But the dirty arrowhead embedded in his chest would remain a nidus for infection until someone removed it. For now, she kept him on herbs to prevent the wound from festering, but they would only work temporarily. Patients who took those medications too long not only suffered side effects but eventually developed the most rapid and deadly infections. Until a surgeon removed that foreign body, Darris would surely fall prey to one fever after another, until one claimed him.

The idea winched Matrinka's hands tighter. For a moment, she surrendered to the irrational belief that he could not die so long as she clung. "I love you," she whispered, saying the words to him for the first time, though she did not look at him. "I wish . . ." She let the rest hang, unable to express the concept of the two of them living together, forever committed to one another's arms as well as hearts. The details did not matter. Live or die, they could never marry.

"I love you, too," Darris responded easily, as if they had expressed their feelings for one another a million times. He paused several moments, to gather either words or breath. "Matrinka?" He tightened his grip as well, and she finally turned to meet his gaze. The hazel eyes seemed to grasp hers as solidly as their hands held one another. "I'm going to be with you always. No responsibility to the world, to the king, or to my bardship will ever compromise what we have together. If I cannot have you, I can serve you. And I can serve the lucky man who marries you, as well." Despite the hardship of his words, his voice did not waver.

Tears glazed Matrinka's eyes. "You're the one I love, and I will never marry another."

Darris swallowed hard, shaking his head to the extent dizziness allowed. "You will. You have to. Promise me you will."

Matrinka refused. "I can't make that promise."

"For the good of the kingdom, Matrinka. Especially if I die. You have to promise."

"I can't promise."

Darris grimaced, in as much pain from her words as he had been from the injury. Balms and herbs could not assuage this type of agony. "Would you let the next bard of Béarn live with the guilt of helping destroy the kingdom?" His hold weakened. "I'd rather die now."

Matrinka reconsidered. "I'll relinquish all claims for myself and my family. You mean more to me now even than bonds of blood."

"No," Darris said. Then more loudly. "No! I will not come between you and your family. Don't forsake all that is Matrinka for a dying man. I know surgery is risky. I'd rather die knowing you'll find happiness again and with your honor intact than leave you a grieving widow without ties to your own blood. Knowing you share my love is enough. It is everything."

Matrinka wrapped her arms around Darris, and this time they kissed unabashedly. Years of anticipation added the sweetness that his sickness stole, and Matrinka felt airborne with joy. He fell asleep a moment later, driven to exhaustion by the effort of a lengthy speech and leaving her with an incredible longing she never anticipated. Always, she had seen a kiss as an end, yet now it seemed only a shallow beginning to wonders she would never experience.

Finally! Mior's thought startled Matrinka, and she nearly dropped Darris. *I told you to do that a long time ago.*

Matrinka lowered Darris to the ground, arranging him into a comfortable position, then covering him with a blanket. *You evil beast! Who gave you permission to spy?*

Mior shook water from her fur. *I'm a cat. The gods gave me permission to spy.* She sat delicately. *Besides, I wasn't spying. I just happened to see.* She licked her fur back into place.

Recognizing guilt as the source of her irritation, Matrinka searched for a less emotionally charged topic. *I'll never understand how you dry yourself with a wet tongue.*

Skill, my friend. Great skill.

Skill, indeed. One I've no interest in learning.

You're just jealous.

Matrinka laughed, surprised at how strained the sound emerged. Concern for Darris poisoned her every thought and action. *You're the one who's jealous, my dear. That's why you're so interested in kissing.* She stretched her lips into an exaggerated pucker.

No, thank you. I'd take a good tongue bath over some man's spit in my mouth anytime.

Odd words from one who once stuck her whole kitten face in the king's cup of buttermilk. Matrinka grabbed Mior with playful roughness and drew the animal into her lap. *Odd words from one who drinks from dirty puddles.* Matrinka sensed more than saw Mior wince at the manhandling. All joking disappeared, replaced by worry. *What's wrong?*

He kicked me, Mior admitted with obvious reluctance.
Who?
Tae.
You found him?
Of course.

Matrinka wanted more information on their missing companion, but tending the cat came first. *Are you hurt?*

Not really. Not enough to worry about.

Matrinka stroked Mior, reflexively feeling along the ribs for fractures or swelling and finding neither. *How is Tae? What's he doing?*

Mior leaned into her mistress' touch. *Hey! I'm still in pain here.*

You claimed it was nothing to worry about, Matrinka reminded, smiling at the realization the cat could not be badly injured if she had the presence of mind to demand sympathy.

Well, you could worry a little!

Having found nothing amiss, Matrinka petted Mior with firmer strokes that dislodged twigs, leaf shreds, and shedded hair. *Poor Mior. Poor, poor Mior.*

Too late. You don't sound sincere. The cat lamented, then added quickly, *But keep up the petting. It helps.*

Matrinka studied Darris where he had fallen nearly instantly asleep again. She did not concern herself with the rapidity; he needed rest to heal. She ran her hand along Mior from neck to hindquarters, pausing occasionally to scratch behind the ears and under the chin. The exercise proved therapeutic for both of them, and it stimulated Mior to address the earlier questions.

Tae wasn't ranging ahead the way he usually does, more like dragging behind. He mumbled something about Ra-khir killing him if he caught us together.

Matrinka broke in to clarify. *"Us" meaning you and him?*

I think so.

What else did he say to you?

Nothing much. Except for that, he pretty much didn't talk to me after he told me to go away. And kicked me.

Tae never struck me as the sort to talk to himself. Being

exactly that sort, Matrinka had discussed matters with Mior long before they learned to communicate.

Himself? Hey! That's an insult, isn't it?

Matrinka considered her words, recognizing she had called Mior a nonentity without meaning anything hurtful. *Not an insult, Mior. Most people see talking to a cat the same as they do talking to themselves. Cats don't usually answer back.*

Mior accepted the explanation. *I don't think he thinks he's one of us anymore. Although he did snare some rabbits and put them on the trail just up ahead.*

He did? Matrinka furrowed her brow, though the only logical explanation followed swiftly. *He knows we're getting short on rations. He wanted to feed us. But why didn't he just bring them into camp. And why has he avoided us all day?*

Mior gave no answer, and a long pause followed, finally interrupted by Ra-khir's puzzled voice as he and Kevral drew nearer. "We can't just eat them. Rabbits don't just drop dead in the middle of a trail."

"So maybe they fell off a merchant's wagon," Kevral shot back. "So what? They haven't gone bad. Why throw them away?"

Matrinka hefted Mior and headed toward the discussion. Apparently, Tae wished to give his gifts anonymously, and she would not interfere with that decision, especially since doing so would require an explanation she did not feel ready to give. Discussing her relationship with Mior had gained her enough ridicule for one lifetime, and she did not wish to risk her friendship. Though she had not known them all that long, she felt closer to her current companions than even her many cousins. But she would see to it Tae's labor did not go to waste. "What's going on?"

Kevral rubbed dirt from the back of one hand. "Ra-khir found two dead rabbits on the trail. They're still fresh, but he doesn't want us to eat them."

"Why not?" Matrinka addressed Kevral's words but looked to Ra-khir to supply the answer.

Ra-khir bowed his head, a residual gesture of respect he could never wholly quell in her presence. The knights had trained him well. "The circumstances just seem too strange. Where did they come from? Are we taking food from someone else's mouth?"

Kevral interrupted. "Whose? There's no one else here. By the time someone realized they lost the meat, it won't be worth coming back for."

Matrinka believed she found the perfect compromise, though she refused to think of it in such terms. The gods' staves had already deemed her incapable of competent decision. "So they don't go to waste, why don't we eat them?"

Ra-khir frowned but nodded stiffly.

Matrinka continued, "If someone comes looking for them, we'll give him an equal amount of our supplies to compensate."

Ra-khir's lips twitched upward, into a neutral position then a grudging smile. "That's reasonable. If we can scrape together enough."

"That's why we need these rabbits," Kevral said. "If we can't find enough, we'll catch them something to replace the rabbits." It was an idle promise. Renshai shunned bows as coward's weapons, and knights preferred hand-to-hand combat as well. Matrinka had had no interest in target shooting or weapons of any kind until she met Kevral. Until now, as supplies dwindled, no one had considered the implications of their hunting ignorance. They would need to stock well in Pudar.

Resigned, Ra-khir sat on a deadfall and worked on skinning and gutting. Matrinka suspected he would hold them to resupplying their benefactor, even if it meant chasing down game on foot. Luckily, she knew, it would not matter. "I still don't like the way these just appeared. Like someone wanted us to find them."

Kevral gave Ra-khir's point serious consideration. "Like an enemy," she added. "They could be poisoned."

Ra-khir ceased skinning, features drawn into a mask of horror.

Knowing the source of the offering, Matrinka dismissed the possibility. She offered another reason to her companions. "Cooking deactivates every toxin I know. It'd be silly to poison raw meat. But even if someone did, we just have to make sure we cook it thoroughly, until there's no pink left."

Ra-khir commenced working.

Matrinka considered her next words long and hard before speaking, careful to associate her concerns about Tae with the act of eating dinner rather than tying him to the rabbits.

"Where's Tae? I've never known him to come late for a meal. Nor to stay away quite this long. I hope he's all right."

Ra-khir did not miss a beat. "I sent him away," he answered truthfully, as Matrinka knew he must.

Kevral stiffened, then stared at Ra-khir's back. "You sent him away?"

"I sent him away," Ra-khir confirmed, not bothering to look up from the rabbits.

"What do you mean you sent him away?"

Ra-khir finally glanced directly at Kevral, wiping sweat from his forehead with the back of his arm so as not to smear blood across his face. "I believe the words are self-explanatory." The answer verged on sarcasm, more suited to Tae or Kevral, though the tone softened it to statement with just a hint of defensiveness. Apparently to mellow words ill-suited to his chivalry, he explained. "Those men who attacked us had nothing to do with Béarn. They were Tae's enemies."

"So you sent him away," Kevral accused.

Matrinka sighed, knowing Kevral and Ra-khir perched on the edge of certain argument again. This time, she had too much invested in understanding the situation to walk away. She needed to know what happened to Tae and the danger it posed to the rest of them.

Ra-khir placed the rabbit aside. "He lied to us. He drew threat to us, our mission, and Matrinka. I promised to allow him to accompany us only so long as he posed no danger to the party or our purpose."

"You shouldn't have sent him away." Kevral stared into the forest, lower lip clenched between her teeth and one hand slipping to her hilt. "You should have killed him."

"I did challenge him. My honor doesn't allow—"

"Damn your cursed honor!" Kevral interrupted, so loudly Darris stiffened and opened his eyes. "Now we're worse off than before. We've got a bitter, quiet enemy who knows us in detail as well as our cause and has every reason to work against us."

Matrinka clutched Mior, heading to tend Darris, though she kept an ear to the proceedings.

Ra-khir threw down the rabbit. Though the gesture conveyed his anger, he was obviously composed. He made certain it landed on the deadfall, not the dirty ground. "Look, I can't just kill a man who won't fight back."

Kevral drew closer, within sword range, and therefore a threatening distance from Ra-khir. "But it's fine to place the kingdom . . . nay, the entire world in danger."

"That's not good, either," Ra-khir admitted.

Kevral backed off slightly. "So you made the wrong decision."

"I made the only decision I could." Ra-khir jerked his forehead across his sleeve, obviously bothered by the sweat but frustrated by his inability to use his filthy hands. "I followed my honor. If you find it rigid or stupid, that's your problem. I'm tired of apologizing for acting as I know is right. I'm sick of feeling incompetent and guilty because I don't do things the same way you would."

"Oh, you mean the way a rational person would," Kevral regained her lost ground and more, dangerously violating Ra-khir's space.

"If you wish." Ra-khir did not argue the unwinnable point. "Call it what you will. I'm going to follow my honor, and you have two choices: accept it or leave the party."

"Or I could just kick you to death!"

Matrinka understood the full impact of Kevral's insult as few who did not know Renshai could. It not only implied she could kill Ra-khir, but that she could do so without the effort of drawing a weapon.

"Kick me to death?" Ra-khir remained calm. "I stand corrected. Apparently, you have three choices."

Matrinka suppressed a chuckle, turning her back under the auspices of attending Darris. Her amusement, she feared, would only shame them into escalating the battle.

But Kevral proved insightful enough to see humor in Ra-khir's reaction. She laughed aloud, and Ra-khir carefully joined her. Darris smiled and winked. Matrinka turned to see Ra-khir and Kevral chuckling merrily, a dispersing flush to the Renshai's cheeks all that visibly remained of their dispute.

Though relieved by the sudden break, Matrinka did not allow herself to relax. Surely rage could not disappear so quickly. She suspected it lay shallowly beneath their mirth, waiting for one of them to spark it again.

Mior saw something Matrinka had missed. *Goodness. So that's why they fight all the time.*

Why?

They're in love.

Matrinka could not have been more shocked had Mior proclaimed them brother and sister. *What?*

They're in love, Mior repeated, for emphasis rather than any belief Matrinka had not heard. Their communication worked through empathy and idea, rather than specific word; and it did not rely on volume. *Look at the way he looks at her. It's the exact same way Darris looks at you when he thinks you can't see. And she's dodging his eyes like they might burn her. Just like you do with Darris.*

Embarrassed by the suggestion, Matrinka saw to her own defense first. *I do not.*

You do. Mior would not let the denial pass. *And Kevral does, too.*

Taking her cue from Darris, Matrinka let the unimportant point pass for the more significant one. *You're being ridiculous. Those two hate each other.*

I think they want to hate each other, especially Kevral. I think their attraction really bothers them.

Matrinka took the cat's description seriously, as she always did; but she kept an element of doubt as well. Her instincts told her Mior could not possibly have interpreted the situation correctly. Mior often saw things humans missed, but the cat did not always guess intentions right, either. Matrinka made a mental note to watch the interaction between Kevral and Ra-khir more closely. At best, she might bring the two together as a couple. At worst, she would gain insight into what worsened and what helped break their confrontations. She shifted Mior, turned, and sat down next to Darris, stroking his hair with a tenderness that made him smile and close his eyes again. *When did you get so smart.*

Mior purred gently. *Humans are so easily read.*

Chapter 22

The Keeper of the Balance

*Perhaps if we had balance, (good and evil, Law
and Chaos) we wouldn't have to war against one
another with such a frenzy.*

—Colbey Calistinsson

Grayness filled King Kohleran's room like a presence, and
the rancid odor of disease funneled into Prime Minister
Baltraine's lungs until he could taste it. The richness of the
furnishings no longer distracted him from the hideousness of
the situation. The urge to flee to anywhere else jangled
through him, until the effort of fighting it nearly allowed
him to lose his concentration on holding back the inevitable
need to retch. Twice, he felt his gut heave and choked back
stomach contents that burned his throat and coarsened his
voice.

The master healer, Mikalyn, did not seem to notice the
stench. He addressed Baltraine with a voice filled with pain
and despair. "It's over, Lord. There's nothing left here but a
body kept alive beyond its time by herbs." Tears twined
down his cheeks, almost invisible in the gloom. "Our beloved King Kohleran is dead."

Icy fear clutched at Baltraine. "His heart no longer
beats?"

"It beats," Mikalyn admitted.

"Then he lives."

"In a manner of speaking, Lord. But there's nothing left

here." Mikalyn tapped his own head. "The heart, too, would stop if not for our intervention."

Baltraine sighed, despising the issue he needed to force yet seeing no other way. "How long can you keep him this way?"

Mikalyn shuffled his feet, dodging Baltraine's stare. "It would be cruel to do so a moment longer."

Baltraine did not wish to hear such things. Propriety and the dignity Kohleran deserved drove him to obey the healer's dictum, but the future of all Béarn lay at stake. "That was not the question!" he roared.

Mikalyn stared at his feet. "I don't know, Lord. Days, weeks. It's hard to know. I'm not a god. Eventually, death will claim him no matter what we do." The tears quickened. "There is more to life than a heart beating."

Recognizing the healer's pain and knowing he would ordinarily share it, along with his distaste, Baltraine softened. "For now, a beating heart is all we have. If Kohleran dies now, all of Béarn will die with him. Maybe the world. The *Ragnarok* will consume us all in its fiery agony. I share your concern that our beloved king die with dignity and honor, but I cannot condemn all others to a worse fate. Our king, bless his soul, is not the only one who deserves to live long and die with honor. There are children, Mikalyn. There are kings in other cities. From the moment Kohleran dies, we have only three months to properly replace him. Three months." He sighed loudly. "We've gotten nowhere in years."

"I understand," Mikalyn said softly. His gaze glided upward, as if to finally meet Baltraine's, then skittered away at the last moment. "I hate it, but I understand. And I can make no promises other than to try my best. No matter the herbs, a heart can beat only so long in a rotting body."

"It's all I can ask," Baltraine's voice fell to barely above a whisper. "And the whole world thanks you." Without another word, he slipped from the room and closed the door, pitying Mikalyn's need to remain inside that horrible place indefinitely. Idly, he wondered if, after Kohleran's inevitable death, he could ever return there. No matter how intense the cleaning, the smell would always linger—in his mind if not in the walls themselves.

As Baltraine left Kohleran's tending in Mikalyn's hands, other concerns crowded down upon him. In the last week, chaos had become a loathsome beast, haunting his waking and sleeping hours. No more of the heirs had died mysteriously, but more concrete causes had risen to claim their lives instead. All four of Kohleran's great-grandchildren had died together, victims of a poison they could only have deliberately shared. Though found blameless, their Renshai guardians executed a suicide pact of their own. Kohleran's eldest granddaughter had stabbed her sixteen-year-old cousin, in plain sight of a dozen people. The Renshai had intervened swiftly, but the wound had festered beyond the abilities of Béarn's healers to control. The granddaughter moldered in prison now, safe herself but useless to Béarn. The staves would not have her even if the citizens would. Execution seemed certain, her motives less so. Thus far, those who questioned her found no reason for her action beyond rampant paranoia.

Baltraine shuffled down the familiar corridors, the simple act of moving a struggle that sapped his reserves. Tragedy after tragedy weighted his soul with responsibilities he no longer savored. Béarn's subjects had made his task all the more difficult. Daily, they came in droves, proclaiming the king's line fallen into decadence, offering their own offspring and inheritance as fodder for the staff-test. The more organized of these attempted assassinations that had, so far, proven unsuccessful. They had lost six Renshai and three Béarnian guards to these radicals, however. The heirs had killed self and others because their sentries trusted them. Now, the Renshai had become wary beyond logic, allowing nothing and no one to interfere with their charges. The original enemy, strangely, seemed to have disappeared. Having stirred desperate hysteria among royalty and peasantry alike, they apparently had no further purpose in Béarn.

Baltraine continued moving, despising his situation. The burden temporary rulership placed on him no longer held the appeal it once did. His situation had become desperate enough that the importance of finding the proper heir took precedence even over thoughts of his daughters' security. Once he handled the crisis, he could set his thoughts on the future of himself and his line once more. For now, Béarn and the world had to take precedence. The enemy had concentrated on heirs. The citizenry had taken their disgruntlement one step further. Word had come to him of a faction expressly against him, a gang of angry Béarnides who gathered in the name of Knight-Captain Kedrin, their martyr, and who believed Baltraine sought to steal the kingdom from the rightful heirs.

Nothing, Baltraine thought as he headed toward the room of the staff-testing, *could be further from the truth.* The pride Baltraine felt in himself, because Kohleran had chosen him regent and the wonderful job he believed he had performed in this capacity, had collapsed like rubble beneath the desperate frustration that came with rulership over a realm in hopeless flux. Baltraine had left a trusted page and a guardian Renshai with the last heir to get double tested, Kohleran's only surviving child, Ethelyn. Usually, he remained for the few moments it took for the staves to do their work. This time, he had too many other affairs to manage, and he wanted to delay the heartbreak sure to follow her rejection. An hour had passed since she entered the testing room, and the page had not yet come to inform Baltraine of the results. Maybe, just maybe, this one who seemed least likely had managed to pass.

Baltraine quickened his pace, faith rising despite his attempts to keep it in check. His heart might not weather the inevitable if he allowed hope too large a toehold. Nevertheless, by the time he arrived at the stark room that housed the staves, the page paced restlessly and the Renshai leaned against the wall with obvious boredom. The latter came abruptly to attention as Baltraine's steps clomped through the hallway. The prime minister saw no sign of Ethelyn. "What's happening?"

"Nothing, Lord." The page ceased his pacing and bowed respectfully to the regent. "She's still in there."

Nothing in Baltraine's reading suggested it could take so long, even should the staves find her worthy. He wondered if self-doubt held her prisoner, keeping her from taking the staves from their corners and initiating the trial. He had no idea what effect interrupting the test would have, and the thought of jeopardizing what might prove their last hope sent shivers coursing through his body and paralyzed his vocal cords temporarily. Logic intervened. Eventually, if she did not emerge, they would need to check on Ethelyn.

"Another hour," Baltraine said. "If she's not out by then, we're going in."

The Renshai's mouth snagged into a frown; she was surely as torn by the decision as Baltraine. She could let no harm come to her charge, such as opening the door might cause. Yet, the lengthy, unreasonable period of silence suggested it might already be too late. "Lord," she said. "The princess carried in no weapons. It's not possible to club oneself to death; but even if she could, we would have heard something."

The page bit his lip and swallowed hard, so as not to laugh at the image of the stuffy oldest princess bashing herself over the head with the Staff of Law.

Baltraine considered the words distantly, the idea of suicide not entering his thoughts until that moment, then as easily discarded. Ethelyn's self-confidence went far beyond her abilities or qualities. She seemed the least prone to suicide, and the Renshai's argument was equally compelling. He placed his hand on the doorknob.

The tip of the Renshai's sword cleared its sheath instantly, and the cold steel pressed Baltraine's hand before he could think to move it. Icy gray eyes challenged him from beneath a blonde fringe of bangs. "Lord Baltraine, don't make me chose between my liege and my charge."

Cautiously, Baltraine recoiled, flexing and opening his fingers, though the blade had caused no damage. "I'm sorry," he said sincerely. He had grasped the doorknob absently, without any specific intention of carrying out an action. Yet it had proved an excellent test of the Renshai's competence. Baltraine had no interest in crossing her nor meeting that frosty stare again. "I'm just trying to decide what course of action is most prudent. In every way, we're all on the same side here."

The sword whisked back into its sheath, but the Renshai remained attentive, hands free for any necessary action. Anything Baltraine did without justification that might have an effect upon Ethelyn would meet with reproval at least as severe. He glanced at the page, who nodded his young head indecisively. Baltraine would get no help there.

Baltraine made his decision. "I think we should open the door." He looked askance at the Renshai.

The warrior watched him through narrowed eyes, awaiting explanation. She seemed willing to listen.

"I've read every scrap of information available about the staff-test. Nothing suggested danger, even should the process get interrupted. And, since the task only lasts a few seconds, and she's been in there nearly two hours, it seems unlikely we would happen to open the door at exactly the wrong time anyway."

The Renshai pursed her lips, and a hand dropped casually to her hilt in a gesture more uncertain than threatening.

Baltraine drove the point home. "She might be in danger now. As long as she's there alone, we can't help her."

The Renshai nodded grudging acceptance.

Baltraine returned his hand to the door. Eyes fixed on the Renshai, he turned carefully, making certain the swordswoman did not suddenly change her mind and attack. For her part, the Renshai remained warily at attention, scrutinizing the door as it inched open.

A bar of light from the hallway swept through the crack, playing over Ethelyn lying on the testing room floor. Wide-open and glazed, her brown eyes stared at the ceiling, unseeing. Her mouth twisted into an expression of horror so intense it seemed a parody. One staff lay on the floor, as if it had rolled from her outstretched hand. The other still perched in its corner, untouched.

The Renshai shoved past Baltraine. She knelt at Ethelyn's side, checked a pulse, then sank to her haunches.

Baltraine lowered his head. He did not need such a detail to know she lay dead and for longer than a few moments. The rigidity of the sprawled limbs made it likely she had died not long after her entrance. Hope drained from him in an instant, leaving him feeling ancient and tired. He watched more from inertia than interest as the Renshai pawed over her charge, seeking an explanation.

Baltraine did not need a cause of death. It mattered only that they had lost another heir, the last to undergo the staff-test a second time. The error in judgment was his own. Desperation had driven him to discard Kohleran's wisdom, the simple logic of which the gods approved. The true king would have known the human psyche would prove too fragile to weather the gods' disdain twice. Now, Kohleran's children, grandchildren, and great-grandchildren exactly resembled the weak, unfit rulers much of the populace now proclaimed them to be.

Hopelessness settled over Baltraine, leaving him empty of thought and without energy for action. He could do nothing now except curse his mistakes and pray for the envoy to succeed where messengers and a previous group failed. *Pray.* Béarn's prime minister routinely participated in affirmations and holy days, but he had not set foot in the temple alone for years. Affairs of state and his own agenda had kept him too busy for pious pursuits. Now he saw the castle temple as a sanctuary, a place to escape from the many insurmountable burdens heaped upon him and perhaps, to find some answers.

Once discovered, the need to pray became an obsession. Baltraine spun and took a step before formality took over again. He turned back to the Renshai whose hands had stilled on the corpse. Gray eyes filled with purpose beseeched the heavens, and the crouched posture seemed too tense and painful to hold so long. Baltraine managed reason only in fits and starts, but he knew from experience the Renshai would feel responsible for a death none of them could have anticipated or prevented. If he did not say something to absolve that guilt, they might lose another Renshai to suicide. That thought drove a shiver through his entire body. Renshai suicide involved violence; their desperate need to die in battle and find Valhalla assured it. Vivid images filled his mind's eye, of guards' bodies sprawled through the courtyard and a battle-mad Renshai slashing and howling long after lethal wounds should already have claimed her. More often than not, these fallen Renshai attacked others of their ilk, perhaps believing only other Renshai could stop them or because no one else could understand nor deserved to die for their need.

Either way, Baltraine saw danger. As Béarn became more divided, he desperately needed the Renshai and Béarn's guard force on his side to prevent a coup or his own murder. These ideas only made Baltraine more restless about consulting gods, but he forced himself to speak now. "The stafftest did this." He had no way to confirm whether or not he spoke the truth. "You did the best anyone could have, and you bear no fault in this tragedy." He placed a hand on the Renshai's shoulder, felt her stiffen beneath his touch. He turned his attention to the page. "There will be no investigation against this woman."

Without awaiting a reply, Baltraine turned and whisked down the corridor. No more needed saying. Ultimately, the Renshai's philosophy would determine whether she considered herself innocent or guilty of shirking her duty. She would try herself and determine her own punishment. He had done all he could to convince her she had performed her duty to the satisfaction of the kingdom by demonstrating unconditional trust and nonchalantly absolving her of any blame. Whether or not she followed his lead, she would relay his loyalty back to the other Renshai and they would see him as an ally. Renshai made him nervous, but he could not afford to lose the support of competent swordmasters eager to support Béarn.

Despite their finery, the hallways seemed bleak to Baltraine as he hurried through them to the temple. Torch holders carved into animal shapes held burning brands that seemed incapable of chasing away the darkness. His shadow spiraled, fragmented by the myriad lights, a phenomenon he had never noticed before and now increased his eagerness to find the solace prayer promised. Blue and gold brocade, braided with beads, swung from each holder in the breeze of his passage. Murals sprawled across the walls, broken by doors on both sides of the corridor. Baltraine had long ago ceased to admire art that had become too tedious and familiar. He hastened past, seeing only splotches of color that he did not bother to place into coherent pattern.

At length, Baltraine reached the familiar double doors that led into Béarn's royal temple. Despite his preoccupation, he could not help noticing the rearing bear standing out in bold relief from each door. Blue gemstones glittered from each eye, and shaven pearls lined inner ears and nose leather. Door rings jutted from metalwork intended to simulate the sun and moon, the steel worn smooth by countless hands. He seized the handle embedded in the moon, drawing the heavy oak panel open with a jerk. The hinges protested with a mild squeal. Slipping inside, he let the door glide closed behind him, and the handle crashed back into position like a giant's hand knocking. Though loud, the noise did not bother him. He had grown accustomed to it through the years, and the embarrassment that accompanied the noise all but ascertained no one came late to services.

A carpeted aisle separated rows of benches, and Baltraine trod its length until he reached the altar and dais at the front where the clergy gave their holy day sermons. He found no one else in the temple, and that further soothed Baltraine. He wanted to bellow his prayers until the walls echoed, to relieve himself of some of the tension that ground at him like a deep-seated agony. He headed to the front, rounded the left-side row of benches to seek out one of several niches along the wall that held miniature altars and cushions on which to kneel and offer private prayers. Halfway around, he stopped and turned, his anxiety requiring something larger and more conspicuous to quell it.

Baltraine studied the main dais. No law forbid him from praying there, only a deep-seated awe driven into him since childhood. He had never seen anyone stand there except the berobed, charismatic priests who had terrified him as a child and dumbfounded him as a young adult. Later, he came to know them as people outside the temple as well as priests. They told jokes and stories, suffered from the same minor ailments as he, and lost some of the magic his childhood self imposed upon them. Still, the sanctity of the dais seemed inviolate, and he approached it with caution. At the steps, a brief flurry of fear descended upon him, a carryover from childhood. He battled it with logic, climbed to the dais, and knelt beside the altar.

Words had always come easily to Baltraine, simplifying the task of leading the council meetings and holding court. Now his mouth failed him as it rarely had before. He knelt in silence, head bowed, mind draining of its jumbled problems and replaced by images of gods. He had always preferred Odin. The grim, gray father of the gods symbolized ultimate power in Baltraine's mind, and he coveted the wisdom Odin had won through hardship. Like the priests, images of The Terrible One and his eight-legged horse had scared him as a child, yet his terror had evolved into fascination, and his adult understanding of the AllFather's influence made him all the more appealing.

But though Baltraine easily conjured remembered images of Odin from murals and books, he could not think of a single word to say. He had intended to shout his desperation from the depths of his soul. Now that the time had come, however, he found his tongue unwilling. Instead he demonstrated his weighty concerns with concepts he hoped the gods could read inside his mind. He appealed to them for solutions to problems that seemed insurmountable. He promised daily attendance in church and donation of half his pay should they choose to share their holy guidance. "Please," he finally managed aloud. "Please help me."

Still the proper entreaties would not come, and tears of desperation blurred his vision. To his surprise, that soothed him where all else had failed. Baltraine allowed the tears to fall in an endless stream, the deep sobs clearing away the negative emotions that crowded out all good. He could not recall the last time he cried; he would never have done so had he not found himself so wholly alone. He would have seen it as a sign of weakness, and many would have lost faith in their king's choice of regent. For all its wondrous enormity, power and status seemed as much curse as blessing.

A sound touched Baltraine's ears, the whisk of a hand across stone. Though startled, he remained in place, unobtrusively wiping away the tears before daring to rise and face whoever had intruded on his peace. Crying had helped empty his head of the muddle of overbearing thought, though nothing had yet seeped in to replace it. Logic returned slowly as he stood. He had not heard footsteps in the aisle nor, for that matter, the familiar screech of hinges they could never quite oil enough and the clang of the heavy door ring.

The other who stood upon the temple dais fit the impossible soundlessness of his approach. Blond hair framed a strong, clean-shaven face with parallel scars down one cheek. Cold blue-gray eyes regarded Baltraine with a confidence and composure he could only envy. The stance seemed casual at first glance, though the stranger's left hand rested on the hilt of a sword dangling at his right hip. A matching sword graced his left hip. He kept his weight balanced. Nothing about him suggested strength or bulk. He stood a head shorter and massed half of Baltraine's huge, Béarnian build, yet he carried himself in the manner of an experienced warrior with a long string of triumphs to his name. His coloring, manner, and choice of two long swords seemed most appropriate to Renshai, though Baltraine could not guess what business one of the heirs' guardians could have in Béarn's temple.

Baltraine blinked in silence, gathering his wits. Anyone who belonged in Béarn's castle had the right to worship here, yet this man did not look familiar. Although Baltraine believed he knew everyone in the palace who mattered, many of the servants and ancillary staff could escape his recognition. Surely this warrior was no servant, yet if he had come here, he must belong. Baltraine trusted castle security too much to believe otherwise.

Baltraine's mind touched doubt, and the idea washed into

his mind that this could be an intruder. With it came a desperate terror that dried his mouth to cotton and erased all semblance of tears. Could one of the warring factions have sneaked in an assassin to catch him vulnerable and unguarded? He forced speech, back-stepping to keep the altar between himself and the stranger. "Hello."

"Hello," the blond returned, studying him mildly. He smiled. "Urgent problems need urgent solutions. Have you discussed your situation with men accustomed to dealing with such?"

Baltraine blinked. "Excuse me?"

"Warriors make their decisions on the battlefield, faster than an eye blink; and they rarely get a second chance to be wrong. Perhaps if you sought the advice of generals, you might find the solutions you so desperately seek."

Baltraine trembled, and he nearly lost control of his bladder. This stranger who entered doors without opening them and walked without footfalls also seemed to have read his mind. *A god?* His mind gave no better answer, though logic battered at the thought. *Ridiculous. Gods don't talk to men.* Yet he could not help but doubt. Some faith, deep in his core, had driven him to consult gods. That same part of him believed. "Who . . . who are you?"

"I'm not a god," the blond admitted, again reading Baltraine's thoughts with uncanny accuracy. "But I'm not mortal either." He gave no more specific clues to his identity.

Baltraine did not speculate. He tried to keep his thoughts in check, as much to compose himself as prevent the other from reading the chaos that seemed to have exploded inside him. "You think . . . you think . . ." Baltraine fought to organize his mind and felt as if he fought a frenzied battle underwater. "You think I should talk to Captain Seiryn?" The leader of Béarn's guards already knew the situation.

"A reasonable choice." The blond rested the fingers of one hand directly on the altar, a casual sacrilege. "But there are others to consider."

"Thialnir?" Baltraine referred to the Renshai's representative reluctantly. Although they served the same country, their approach to problems differed to the point of contention. He doubted he could open himself to Thialnir.

"There is one more."

Baltraine fidgeted. No other came immediately to mind,

though he suspected the answer lay, protected, in a deeper portion. Consideration made him desperately uncomfortable, so he did not delve.

The blond waited, impressively patient.

The silence stretched uncomfortably, until Baltraine wondered if he had lost his hearing. Finally, he cleared his throat. The interruption soothed him, though not for long. Words had to follow. "I'm not certain who you mean."

The blond smiled ever so slightly. "I'm referring to the captain of the Knights of Erythane."

"Kedrin," Baltraine said without thinking, and the name tasted bitter in his mouth. "No, not . . ." Unwilling to repeat it, he used the pronoun instead. ". . . him. Not him." He did not explain. "It would be a bad idea."

"I understand your reluctance."

Baltraine doubted that to be the case, but he did not voice his skepticism. The stranger had already twice seemed to read his thoughts. Again, he wondered about the identity of the man in front of him. Baltraine still refused to believe he faced an immortal, despite the blond's claim; but other possibilities seemed equally unlikely. If he accepted the assertion, he also had to admit he faced a god. Other than deities, Béarn's Northern-based religion justified only *Valkyries*, the warrior choosers of the slain, as immortals. And all *Valkyries* were female. Baltraine's mind turned to less likely possibilities, tales from his childhood filled with happy stories of carefree elves and the twisted dwarves who crafted gods' magic. This stranger did not meet the description of either. Therefore, he could not be the immortal, not god, he claimed to be.

If the stranger recognized Baltraine's jumble of thought, he did not directly address it this time. "Your stormy relationship with Knight-Captain Kedrin distresses only you."

Baltraine pounced on the mistake in the other's assumption. "Not only me. There are factions among the citizens of Béarn who use his name to damn me."

"True." The blond spoke as if he knew. "But Kedrin would never sanction their cause. You can no more blame him than the gods when lunatics use their names in wrongful cause. More than one power-mad mortal has called himself a son or messenger of Thor or Odin and used that status to justify his selfish ends. And fools believe and follow him blindly."

Baltraine nodded, understanding the point too well. Men could justify anything they wished to, even murder, in the name of religion.

"Kedrin has given others advice from his prison cell, and never once has he spoken against you. You know that. Your guards have listened and told you."

Baltraine flushed. His eavesdroppers were supposed to be a secret.

"Always, Kedrin puts the cause of Béarn first. He still sees you as the choice of a king whose judgment he would never think to question. You were King Kohleran's chosen regent, and Kedrin will stand behind you no matter the evil you inflicted on him."

Baltraine stared at his clean, supple hands, trying not to reveal the rush of fear that enveloped him. How could this stranger know?

Baltraine could feel the icy gaze upon him though he still kept his own averted. The self-proclaimed immortal continued, "There is much of evil in you, Prime Minister Baltraine. And more chaos than law."

Baltraine shuffled farther backward. His guts felt clenched in sudden knots, and all the anxiety that had dispersed upon the realization he did not face an assassin returned. He met the pale gaze. Though no warrior, he would try to face death bravely.

Yet the stranger made no threatening motions, only studied Baltraine with mild amusement. "But that's all right. The world has room for all four of Odin's forces. In fact, no one could exist without its opposite. But it does exclude you from ruling Béarn." His scrutiny persisted. He remained in place, yet that did not fully pacify Baltraine. This stranger did not broadcast any motions, and he looked quick enough to kill before Baltraine could think to dodge. "Kedrin tried to warn you of that in his own way. Now, I believe, you understand why."

"Who *are* you?" Baltraine demanded again, this time in an awed whisper.

"I am the Keeper of the Balance." Though more full, the answer still did not jibe with Béarnian religion. "I brought the Staves of Law and Chaos to mankind and sanctioned my own beloved people to protect Béarn's balance, no matter the cost. The king or queen of Béarn is mankind's fulcrum, the force that keeps the entire world in balance. Improperly chosen, he assures destruction. You, Baltraine, cannot rule."

"I know that!" Baltraine answered defensively. "I'm just doing the best I can to find the proper heir."

The Keeper acknowledged Baltraine's claim. "True. But you have another agenda as well, one your bent toward self, what we call evil, cannot allow you to forget. Cling to your concern for all of Béarn. Seek Kedrin's advice and follow it. Then, no matter what happens, at least you did all you could."

"I will," Baltraine promised and meant it. Already, his many worries trickled back into his mind, and he added many questions to the boil of desperate thought. Consideration swiftly became an agony he felt little able to contain. He had always considered his loyalties his greatest strength, whether to his family, self, king, or kingdom. Now, those ideals came into conflict, and he urgently needed to place them into proper sequence. "Thank you," he said, looking to the Keeper of the Balance and instead finding empty air between himself and the aisleway. The absence shocked him. He could not recall looking away, only inside himself, yet the other had disappeared without a flash of light or even a slow fade. Neither had he walked away. It seemed more as if he existed one moment and not the next.

Baltraine shivered at the idea that he might have suffered a hallucination. He justified the madness that implied by recalling the stress which had driven him to the temple and to such deep contemplation. Real or imagined, the Keeper had supplied competent advice he had little choice but to try to follow.

Steeling himself for a confrontation he would rather have avoided, Baltraine headed toward Béarn's dungeon.

Chapter 23

Pudar

*In my time, I've seen a lot of friends and loved
ones die. Some of them, I had to kill myself.*
— Colbey Calistinsson

Captain perched on a boulder on the island beach, one knee
tucked to his chest and the other leg dangling comfortably
along the cold, gray surface of the rock. The moon glittered
from the red and gold highlights in his hair like tiny stars in
a brown halo. The lap of the sea soothed him, music to ancient ears that missed the ceaseless roll and crash of break-
ers. He had sailed the Northern Sea for millennia, and it
called him like a distant lover. The sea breeze carried the familiar odor of salt, a friend he had come to miss over the
two centuries he lived on the solid ground of the elves' island. Now, for the first time in longer than a hundred years,
he felt truly free.

Guilt settled over him when his enjoyment grew too great,
a human emotion he had learned to recognize. The freedom
was artificial, the result of ignorance rather than any active
solution to the problem. While he sat on the beach, the other
elves grew more ponderous in their ways, more human, and
their strategies continued unabated. The only thing that had
changed was that he no longer knew what they plotted or
did. As much as he appreciated that lull, he knew he alone
benefited from it. Once, that understanding would not have
entered his mind, let alone bothered him. Elves lived for the
moment, doing whatever brought them joy at the time and

harmed no other. They played, they laughed, they sang, and they coupled without need for or understanding of reason. That which made them happy was all that mattered.

Captain looked out over the sea, watching white water touch the shore, speckled with spindrift. The waves tumbled to the beach and receded, taking and giving in a relentless cycle. One claimed a shell, and the next would return it, sending it tumbling farther up the beach, safe until the tide waxed again. Nearest the water, the sand seemed smooth as glass, while the same sand farther up the beach grated between Captain's toes. Longing filled him, and he dreamed awake of his ship dancing through the sea, foam spirals, lit by dawn light, curling redly in its wake. The clean salt smell tingled through his questing nostrils, and the sun bleached his hair nearly blond. The wrinkles salt and sun etched onto his face had become beloved friends he would not have traded for the supple softness of an infant.

A polite noise interrupted his reverie. Captain stiffened and turned, discovering several elves standing behind his natural seat. Moonlight glazed worried expressions across their faces, and the jerkiness of their movements suggested restlessness and discomfort. He estimated their number between six and a dozen. Most seemed young, though at least one bore scars from the fires of *Ragnarok*.

Captain smiled in greeting, resisting the urge to fret. It did not fit the elves of his youth, the lifestyle to which he wished he, and all of his ilk, could return. Yet he could not keep his mind from thinking, and he guessed Dh'arlo'mé had sent these to worsen his exile. Banning him from society and politics had not proved punishment enough. Perhaps the leader of the elves would not desist until the dissenter was dead.

Egged on by glances from his fellows, Eth'morand Kayhiral No'vahntor El-brinith Tahar stepped to the front to speak. "Arak'bar Tulamii Dhor, we'd like to talk to you."

Captain drew both knees to his chest and clasped his hands together on his calves. He nodded his readiness to engage in conversation, still refusing fear or intimidation. He had lived long, even for an elf; and he had nothing to fear from death. Surely even Dh'arlo'mé would find the patience to wait until an elder died naturally, if only because execution would result in the loss of his soul from the pool of elves. As an infant, with memory mostly scrambled, Captain could easily become as compliant as his peers. It worked in Dh'arlo'mé's best interests to suffer Captain now and wait for old age to take him rather than lose any more elves permanently.

Eth'morand hesitated for a time that tried even elven patience. Captain waited in silence, raising his brows to indicate interest. He would not press. Eth'morand would speak in his own time. Captain called *khohlar*, offering wordless reassurance. Whatever the bad news, he would not hold the messengers responsible.

Finally, Eth'morand gathered his courage. "We've talked to the human, Brenna, many times. Mostly late at night." His blue eyes met Captain's amber, and Captain read need in their depths. "We like her."

A younger elf named Reehanthan Tel'rik Oltanos Leehinith Mir-shanir got straight to the point. "We think we might like humans. We're not completely happy with Dh'arlo'mé'aftris'ter Te'meer Braylth'ryn Amareth Fel-Krin's plans. We find them too . . . dark."

Dark. Captain noted the coincidence. He had described Dh'arlo'mé's ideas using the exact same adjective. *Dark. Svartalf. Dark elves.* The name fit Dh'arlo'mé and his followers perfectly.

Eth'morand furthered the elaboration, the intended speaker from the beginning. "We want to talk with you, to find out or, for some of us, remember how elves used to be."

"We don't believe our lord, Frey, intended us to fight anyone," Reehanthan interrupted again. "We want peace, if we can have it. Will you help us?"

Captain looked over the group like a proud human father, though he did not speak yet. He needed time to consider their request and the possible consequences of any action he or they might take. But first, he had to understand exactly what they expected of him. "What do you want me to do?" Though not a direct answer to their question, he hoped his tone indicated guarded interest.

"Teach us about elves," Eth'morand's statement emerged more like a question. "Teach us about humans. Guide us toward a means to handle the situation without killing anyone."

"To handle it like elves," another added.

Captain studied these elves who had chosen him mentor, moving from one starry-eyed, eager face to the next. Memories rushed down on Captain, confidences shared by millennia of Cardinal Wizards, including the last Western Wizard, Colbey Calistinsson. The Renshai had described the exuberance of those born in the aftermath of war with an uncharacteristic fondness and enthusiasm. Usually hypercritical, especially of all humans not Renshai, Colbey had discovered a cause as significant as his goal, since birth, to die in glory and find Valhalla. He had dedicated himself to rescuing the world's human children from the *Ragnarok*, knowing the very chaos that inspired them also brought the doom upon them. Already pledged to finding and maintaining the balance between the world's forces, Colbey had found a second purpose he had never expected: defending humanity. And, apparently, he had succeeded.

Captain wondered if he could ever prove Colbey's hand, not humans', had rescued mankind from the fiery death that had damned the elves. He wondered if it was even true. As powerful a swordsman as Colbey had become through endless practice and sacrifice, surely he could add little to a fight between gods. *Little, indeed.* Captain shook his head at the thought. Too many had met their doom underestimating the Golden Prince of Demons, and Captain would not fall into that trap. He recalled the glow restored to the jaded, old Renshai's eyes when he spoke of the new vitality of human youth and their honest quest for competence and worth. Nothing, Colbey had insisted, meant more to any teacher than spirited students eager to learn.

Now Captain had his own opportunity to enlighten, and pleasure burned like a fire deep within him. That, in itself, came of his long association with humans. Original elves knew nothing of emotions such as pride, self-regard, and esteem. Frey had created them innocent and happy. On Alfheim, they had frolicked among trees known on no other world, playing and cavorting as the moment's whim pleased them. They knew nothing of sadness or pain, nor of the satisfaction of personal achievement. They knew only joy but gained no specific pleasure from it. Lighthearted play defined what they had all once been.

Yet Captain realized elves could never return to the life they had once exclusively known. They had suffered too much, from the blistering agony of *Ragnarok*'s aftermath to the bitterness spawned by believing in a mortal source for their tragedy. Dh'arlo'mé had ruled too long, pounding hatred, rage, and greed too deeply into the collective elfin psyche to ever fully disperse. The dark elves flourished on the negative. Captain had little choice but to expose his prospective followers to the positive human drives and emotions: honor, glory, accomplishment, generosity, sacrifice, and too many others to consider in the moments Captain had to decide his next course of action. His elves, the light elves or *lysalf* would have to become something other than what they had once been. Millennia on man's world had changed Captain too much for anything else to be the case. And Brenna's conversation had already laid the groundwork for him.

"All right," Captain finally said softly, and the group of elves relaxed visibly. He had not realized the length of his considerations nor the significance to the others of his answer. "I'll teach. But I won't condone any action that tears us apart as a people or fosters violence of any kind."

Accommodating nods traversed the group.

Captain scratched at his sun-bleached hair, missing the salt that used to always crunch beneath his fingers. He loved the sea and mourned the boat, the *Sea Seraph*, he had come to equate with his life. "What's happened since my exile?" He had counted fifteen sunsets since the argument that expelled him from the council, scarcely a moment in the lifetime of an elf. Yet he doubted Dh'arlo'mé had remained idle.

Eth'morand took the lead again. "Too much, I fear. A human sold information for gold and trinkets." The disdain in his voice came through clearly, once outside elfin repertoire. Captain shrugged off the change. Once taught a general dislike of humans, judgment of individuals' behavior—and, eventually of elfin actions—followed naturally. "He told us about how humans don't have a single leader or council. Dh'arlo'mé's already sent elves to stir trouble in other kingdoms, especially the big trading city, Hudan."

"Pudar," Reehanthan corrected, the Western syllables harsh for elfin lips.

"Thank you. Pudar." Eth'morand swayed gently as he continued. "Xyxthris . . ." He mangled the human name, so it emerged in a long hiss. ". . . that's the man who's telling things, he said we could do more damage attacking men at the source of their profit than the source of their morality." His long-lashed lids slid briefly over the gemlike eyes, and mild perplexity creased his features. "I'm not sure what he meant by that."

A chill spiraled through Captain. He knew only too well, and the moment he dreaded had arrived. Dh'arlo'mé had finally learned enough to begin a war in earnest and had already acted to initiate one. He could no longer count on elfin longevity to drag out this foolish cause until hatred stretched into eternity and all reason for vengeance became forgotten. Dh'arlo'mé had grown as impatient as a human, and Captain could only hope, but doubted, it would make him careless as well. The very qualities the Northern Wizard had treasured in him might prove the elves' downfall: intelligence, charisma, and attention to thorough detail. Forbearance, however, could no longer be counted among his virtues. Perhaps he had lost track of others of his strengths as well. Captain could wish, but he would heed the lesson of Colbey Calistinsson to never underestimate an enemy.

As fast as the thought came to Captain's mind, he discarded it like poison. *Dh'arlo'mé is an elf, not an enemy.* Elf, us, and self sounded nearly alike in their language for reasons he dared not ignore. Instead, he concentrated on Eth'morand's words, not quite a question but demanding answer. "Xyxthris meant other humans than himself will work for gold even if it costs others their lives. He meant elves can conquer humans more easily by attacking from more than one front. Humans don't unify as well or completely as we do."

The group discussed Captain's explanation in whispered bursts and *khohlar* concepts. More accustomed to human nature, Captain found their confusion and perceptions refreshingly strange. The strife elves could cause throughout the human kingdoms with a little knowledge and magic had already been aptly demonstrated in Béarn.

"One more thing." A usually timid elf named Ath-tiran Béonwith Bray'onet Ty'maranth Nh'aytemir stepped to Eth'morand's side. "Xyxthris discovered secrets hidden in written notes of his people. First, there's an heir to Béarn's kingdom who lives far away. Dh'arlo'mé's got us all using magic to find him. Apparently, there's a test an heir has to pass to become ruler, and all of them have failed except this one. Including a girl-human who asked not to be an heir anymore but secretly still is."

That arrangement seemed odd even to Captain. "What good is that last secret?"

Eth'morand made a throwaway gesture. "None as far as Xyxthris or we can tell. The human said he included it for completeness."

"And there're other humans, too," Reehanthan added.

Eth'morand elaborated, "Other humans who will sell information. And some who'll do worse things for a price."

"Like kill other people." Reehanthan stepped in again, describing the heinous crime in the fewest possible words. The elfin language held no word for purposeful slaughter of one's own.

"Murder," Captain supplied from the human Northern tongue, the one he had long ago learned to turn to for concepts outside elfin experience. Created by Frey, elves spoke the gods' language in addition to their own. "Unfortunately, it's true. The worst we can do cannot compare with the evil some humans can and will inflict on one another given the right circumstances or the right price. It's an integral part of humanity." Captain glanced at the heavens, silently praying he would have the opportunity to show them examples of the positive parts of humanity, the qualities that made human life, however short, meaningful and special. About this, he suspected, the captured Renshai might prove the better teacher.

Rain pounded the roof of the cottage Kevral and her companions shared in Pudar, and the many streets and alleyways shattered thunder into echoes. Staring out the window, Kevral watched lightning crack open the heavens with the same boredom she suffered whenever she was not directly embroiled in sword work. They had arrived in Pudar two weeks prior, dragging Darris to a surgeon named Harrod that same day. Kevral understood little of the negotiating that followed, noticing only the Pudarian's reluctance and Matrinka's insistence even to the uncharacteristic point of yelling.

In the end, they had agreed to postpone the surgery until Darris regained enough weight and strength to tolerate it. Gradually, Kevral had come to recognize and respect both sides. Harrod needed Darris in the best physical condition possible in order to survive the stress of any surgery, let alone the tricky procedure required to remove the arrow from his lungs. He saw no direct danger in leaving it in place, even for years. Matrinka insisted that the foreignness of the arrow's head would draw infections to Darris' body, thereby weakening him further and making the surgery even more perilous.

Kevral did not have the knowledge to support either view, so she stayed out of the dispute. She trusted Matrinka implicitly and would have pressed the issue to the point of violence had the princess so instructed her. But Matrinka did not consult Kevral nor request her aid. Neither did she seek another surgeon, which told Kevral she held confidence in Harrod regardless of their disagreement. Mostly, Matrinka spent her time hovering over Darris, plying him with herbs at the first hint of fever. Only when he slept did she dare to leave his side. When he awakened, she was there. Their whispered conversations denied prying ears; they seemed oblivious to their companions' presences when they talked. Kevral listened to them profess their friendship and love so many times it made her queasy, and their repetitive "good-byes" and pat phrases meant to hearten and strengthen had lost all charge for her. She preferred to keep her distance.

Ra-khir's heavy tread made the floorboards creak. She waited until the shuffle step that indicated he had stepped around their moldy chest before she turned, blinking away the jagged afterimages the lightning had etched across her retinas. Ra-khir had bashed his shins on that chest so many times it had become a household joke. As obvious as it was, the chest seemed to defy his every effort to notice its presence. On several occasions, he had moved it to one side or another to see if that helped. But if it did, he would never know. Kevral repeatedly inched it back into its original position whenever he left the room. She did not know why she chose that cruel little joke; she simply found it entertaining.

Having avoided the usual pitfall, Ra-khir perched on the chest, leaving the more comfortable barrel seat for Kevral if she chose to relax. "Good afternoon, Kevral."

Kevral leaned against the window frame and made a thoughtful noise she hoped would pass for a greeting. The afternoon seemed anything but good to her.

"What's wrong?" Ra-khir pulled an unfamiliar, oblong fruit from his pocket and used his cloak to shine the skin.

Kevral ignored the question for the moment, more interested in the food. "What's that?"

Ra-khir glanced at Kevral, then followed her gaze to the fruit. He stopped rubbing. "I'm not exactly sure. Fruit merchant said I could pick what I wanted, and this looked interesting. Want some?"

"Sure." Kevral watched Ra-khir's hand retreat. He fumbled briefly in his pocket, emerging with his utility knife. "How much was it?"

"She just gave it to me, like always." Ra-khir cut the fruit in half, exposing pale pink meat and a core of seeds, which he dug out with the point. He offered half to Kevral.

The oddity of the fruit merchant handing away merchandise no longer surprised Kevral. It had begun on their second day in Pudar and persisted. Every day, she insisted Ra-khir take at least a single pomegranate and sometimes a bucketload of fruit so stuffed it fed all of them for a day. She never asked for anything in return, did not even hint that her behavior might seem unusual. If she wanted something personally from Ra-khir, she gave no indication, at least in Kevral's presence. The Renshai would call nothing the fruit merchant said or did flirtatious, though a woman of middle-age surely knew a few subtle tricks for reeling in a man to whom she felt attracted.

The daily allotment of fruit was odd enough even without the windfalls that fell into their lap at the oddest moments. Ever since the dead rabbits they discovered on the trail, they had never gone hungry. Though none of them had a job or any other means to make money, it seemed to find them whenever they needed it. Often, it came in the form of merchants offering to trade goods for minor chores that scarcely seemed worth the bother. How and why they chose Kevral, Ra-khir, or Matrinka over others in the press of people smashed into Pudar's market streets always seemed a mystery.

Kevral accepted Ra-khir's offering.

Ra-khir took a bite of the fruit and returned to his original question. "So, what's wrong?"

Kevral poked at her half of the fruit, avoiding Ra-khir's stare. "Nothing's wrong."

Thunder rolled through Kevral's ears. Ra-khir raised his brows. "So you're moping for no reason?"

"Who said I was moping?"

"I did," Ra-khir returned. "But only because I saw you." Kevral made a noncommittal noise, then took a bite of the fruit. The firm, grainy texture made a pleasant contrast to its sweet taste. She chewed appreciatively and swallowed before continuing. "Good choice." She inclined her head to indicate the fruit.

"Thank you." Ra-khir ate more of his own. "I like it, too." Though Kevral still had not answered his question, he did not press. It was part of his chivalry. He had opened the lines of communication and left it to Kevral to discuss her problem if she wished.

Kevral sighed. Turning away from the window, she headed to the barrel. Like the chest, it had come with the cottage. A previous tenant had cut out part of one side, hollowed it into a chair shape, then added a cushion. Kevral placed one knee on the cushion and leaned on an armrest. She ate the remainder of her fruit and licked juice from her fingers before speaking again. "I'm tired of waiting. I feel for Darris and all, but there's nothing I can do for him. He's got good care. While we're stuck here, who knows what's happening to Béarn or to Griff."

Ra-khir finished his fruit also, politely wiping his mouth and fingers with a handkerchief. "They're fine," he reassured. "A few weeks won't make any difference."

"How do you know that?" Finally, Kevral met his green eyes.

"I don't," Ra-khir admitted. "But it doesn't do any good to assume the opposite. There's no way to know. We'll have to deal with the situation as it comes."

"That's what I mean." Kevral settled uneasily into the chair. "When it comes? It's already here. The longer we waste, the worse things can get."

Ra-khir nodded, acknowledging the truth of Kevral's concern. "But we're stuck here. It doesn't help anyone to have us worrying about something we can't affect."

"There is another solution."

"What's that?"

"Instead of me learning not to worry, we can move on without Darris."

Ra-khir frowned, obviously taken aback by the suggestion. "Leave Darris?"

"Why not?"

"He's a member of the group. It would be wrong."

Kevral heaved a loud sigh. Ra-khir's honor had become

like a brick wall against which she repeatedly banged her head. "Tae was a member of the group, too."

Even Kevral saw the difference, but Ra-khir felt obligated to explain. "Tae betrayed the party. Darris got wounded assisting it."

"And Tae's probably out there now selling information about us and the heir to anyone who'll buy it." Kevral knew she played both sides of the issue, but Ra-khir always brought out the worst in her, and being cooped up in Pudar for two weeks spurred an irritability she seemed unable to shake.

Ra-khir sucked in a deep breath, then released it slowly. "Maybe so. There's nothing we can do about that, either."

Kevral quelled her natural urge to pursue the issue. She had chided Ra-khir enough for his mistake already, and sniping would accomplish nothing more than driving him away. She saw merit to ridding herself of one so incompetent who consistently irritated her, yet she had to work past a gnawing sensation of guilt and a deep realization she did not want him to go. About one thing, Tae had proven definitively right. She *was* too hard on Ra-khir, and she could not figure out why his every tiny fault bothered her so much. "You're right," she admitted grudgingly. "There's not much we could do about Tae now. But we can continue the quest without Darris."

"Matrinka wouldn't leave him." Ra-khir pointed out the obvious. "No matter how good the healers are here."

"We'll leave her, too."

Ra-khir's mouth widened, but nothing emerged for several moments longer than comfortable conversation usually warranted. "You'd leave Matrinka?"

Kevral despised the dilemma, caught between her loyalty to a princess of Béarn who had become her charge and to a prince who was their last hope for salvation. "Probably not," she admitted. "I don't know."

"Don't do anything rash." A slight smile crept across Ra-khir's lips. "I mean rasher than usual. You're good, but enough enemies can kill even a Renshai. Another sword arm can only help you."

"Not if it's incompetent." As soon as Kevral spoke, she rued the curse that drove her to always say the worst possible things in Ra-khir's presence.

Ra-khir's grin wilted, but his voice remained calm and

conversational. "I'm no Kevral, and I thank the gods for that. This world couldn't handle two of you." He winked to show he meant no offense, though she surely deserved it. "I'm not Renshai, but I'm hardly the stumbling dullard you seem intent on calling me. I may not slaughter as many as you, but I won't get in the way of your sword. And I may just take down one or two of my own."

Kevral shrugged, grudgingly conceding the point.

Ra-khir finished, just irritated enough to add his own mild taunt. "You know, Kevral. If I keep practicing, especially with your guidance; and if you learn how to trust a little, we'd make a pretty damn good fighting team."

Kevral smothered a snort, reminding herself of her promise to ease off insulting Ra-khir. "Renshai fight without strategy or pattern."

"I know." Ra-khir held Kevral's gaze again with green eyes that sparkled like diamonds. Even disheveled and sedate, he was strikingly handsome. "That's always been the Renshai's weakness."

Bothered by the passion stirred by Ra-khir's appearance, Kevral looked away. "The Renshai have no weaknesses."

"Ahh," Ra-khir replied, with the tone of one who has just learned a great lesson. "So you're saying skill has a finite limit. One the Renshai have discovered." He shrugged. "I guess you can stop practicing now. You've found perfection."

Kevral sucked air through her teeth. Ra-khir had made his point reasonably well, and it seemed ludicrous to argue that a group of people had discovered the flawlessness an individual could not. Denying the Renshai any failings had been a foolish argument from the start. "All right. You're not a complete toddlebum. I probably couldn't kick you to death."

"Thanks." Ra-khir accepted the backhanded compliment graciously. "That's the nicest thing you've ever said to me."

Finally, Kevral saw the humor in the situation, too. "Enjoy it. I don't give praise freely."

"Really? I hadn't noticed."

"I'm not apologizing for that, mind you," Kevral thought it best to clarify the situation. "Competence is a minimum expectation, not deserving of admiration." Again, she quoted Colbey. "But I should be a little stingier with insults. I *am* sorry for that."

"Accepted." Ra-khir grinned insolently. "You grobian ding-head."

Kevral laughed at Ra-khir's nonsensical insult. "Grobian what?" She twisted into a normal sitting position on the barrel chair. "Should I guess that swear words and insults aren't part of your knight's training?"

"We're taught to flatter, never disparage."

Kevral guessed the meaning of the last word from context and appreciated that Ra-khir avoided mentioning that the Knights of Erythane softened their tone and vocabulary around women. Thinking back, she had never heard a knight curse or blaspheme, even in the company of guards and Renshai. "Yeah, well. A well-aimed sharp word works wonders in certain situations. Maybe I can teach you a few."

"From you?" Ra-khir flicked red hair behind his shoulders. "I'd rather learn sword forms. Better use of my time."

Kevral would never argue that point.

Ra-khir brought the conversation full circle. "Look, I don't know what you're planning to do about waiting for Darris. But if you decide to leave, at least promise me you'll let me know before you go."

The request seemed reasonable. As logic settled into place, Kevral realized she would probably need Darris or Matrinka to recognize Griff. Unless he proved shockingly docile, she doubted she could find the right words to convince him to return with her to Béarn either. "All right."

"Promise."

Kevral sighed. "I promise." She studied Ra-khir, the strong chin and straight nose, the delicate cheekbones, the muscular build, and the red hair with just enough blond to soften the color. Colbey had once said that all redheaded Erythanians carried the blood of Renshai conquerors. The idea of Ra-khir as a distant relative made her smile. She just might come to like Ra-khir despite all he stood for, and that thought raised a pang of alarm. She sensed the avalanche of emotion poised behind such a change in their relationship. The details eluded her, but the intensity did not. Once begun, theirs would not prove a simple friendship. And for all her self-confidence in battle, Kevral felt unprepared for the events that might accompany the simple act of enjoying Ra-khir's company.

Chapter 24

Shattered Peace

Enemies most dangerous dwell in the least likely places.

—Colbey Calistinsson

Clouds enwrapped the crescent moon, turning its scant light into a subtle glaze. Accustomed to the night, Tae Kahn had little difficulty negotiating Pudar's streets, despite the strangeness of a city so unlike the crushed and crowded kingdom of the East. The marketplace had long ago become the central attraction of Pudar. Houses radiated outward from it in concentric semicircles, the confluence broken by Trader's Lake. The farther Tae traveled from the shops and stands, now tarp-covered for the night, the more modern the style of the homes became. Renovated areas interrupted the symmetry of this pattern. An affluent community near the market had sprung from the ruins of a slum, and inns and boarding houses vied for premium space. The fanciest catered to merchants, local royalty, and rare political presences. Yet even poor travelers desperate for the dazzle of Pudar's famed market could find a crumbling dump of a cottage nearby.

Tae Kahn studied the layout more from habit than interest. His life had too long depended on animal alertness and the ability to discern slight movement from shadow. Predators of every type preferred the night, and those who had most to fear from them had little choice but to become nocturnal as well. Under cover of darkness, he also had less chance of discovery by companions turned enemies. Tae bit his lip, hating the weakness that turned his thoughts repeatedly to those who had rejected him. A million times, his father had told him that obsession was synonymous with weakness. In the underground world of violence, invisible to most, preoccupation could prove fatal. Tae had heard of more than one gang lord who opened himself to assassination by coveting money, power, or women. Fixation with any one thing became a blind spot that allowed enemies quiet access.

Yet Tae could not stop picturing Kevral: the short blonde hair that fell into wild feathers, the sinewy body and its competent grace that made her attractively feminine even lacking the usual curves, and the cold blue eyes as sharp as her sarcastic wit. He had too long treasured cleverness and strength not to appreciate both in his women. A thrill shivered through Tae, and he stopped at the mouth of an alley, surrendering to his thoughts. More than his feelings for Kevral kept him in Pudar. He savored the camaraderie he once shared as Ra-khir's distrust had faded. Though Tae had run with gangs before, he had never felt so comfortable with any group. Street orphans knew little of trust. Desperate for the security of a family, they clung to one another; but they betrayed swiftly when circumstance favored self strongly enough. Through death and deception, Tae had lost so many. Even in a group, a child on the streets was always alone.

Tae continued into an alleyway that had become familiar in the two weeks Matrinka and the others had chosen to stay in Pudar. His eyes sought discrepancies even as his mind worried other matters. The patterns of light and shadow were intimately familiar. Though he could not have drawn them for another's inspection, they had become permanently etched on his memory. He would notice even minute changes.

The money Tae had taken off their dead attackers and obtained from selling his horse had nearly run out, spent to feed himself as well as support and shelter his one-time companions. If they remained in Pudar much longer, as Darris' condition suggested they might, Tae would need to resort to other means. He had stolen food on many occasions, but he had not lied to Ra-khir when he claimed he had pilfered other things only twice. He never doubted he had the expertise to part rich men and fools from their money, no matter the technique, but he cared little for petty theft. It made him feel as dirty as the lowest whore-bred scum in his father's operation.

A rustle, too loud for a rat, touched Tae's ears as he reached the end of the alleyway. Street etiquette demanded he not intrude on the operation of another, no matter how nasty or dark the other's work might prove. From habit, he switched directions, heading down a narrow thoroughfare that led toward the richer part of town. Having eaten a reasonable dinner of bread and fruit, with no particular goal in mind, Tae accepted the change in course with graceful ease. At the end of that route, another noise guided him to continue.

Tae moved soundlessly through streets that changed from raunchy, trash-filled dirtways to cobbles scarred by the passage of hooves and steel-soled boots. No matter where he went, the sounds of others working influenced his course, driving him always toward the affluent sector in the northwest corner of town. Warning nagged at the edges of his mind, slipping to conscious thought, then gradually tingling through his body. He analyzed his concern. *Is someone deliberately sending me there?* The thought seemed madness. To do so would require the cooperation of at least twenty people, and he doubted his enemies from the East had that many more to spare. Such a masterful and well-orchestrated feat went beyond the ability of a street gang. More importantly, they would choose a better victim for such a scam. Tae, with his ragged hair and tattered clothes, should not draw the attention of thieves, except as a possible rival.

Rival? Tae mulled that thought a bit longer. He had heard of gangs so possessive of territory, they ritually slaughtered anyone of their ilk who dared step upon it. Tae dismissed this idea, too. He had traveled here before without challenge, and it seemed unlikely hoodlums would set him up by leading him to a prosperous part of the city, that sector most likely to draw patrols and guards. *In fact,* Tae realized as he made another directional change to accommodate a sound and saw the massive, crenellated shadow in the distance, *I'm headed toward the castle.* Tae could not think of any location more heavily protected. Now the whole thing made sense. Fewer thieves would hunt the area near the castle. Therefore, avoiding movement would funnel him directly toward it. That none of his jaunts had ended here in the past scarcely diminished the thought. Perhaps he had simply been lucky before.

The colossal castle of Pudar dwarfed the cottages like a guardian. Towers and guard stations lay black against the glaze, and the holes between seemed lighter for their absence. He heard the distant clomp of footfalls on stone and the clink of mail as the guards paced their watches. Nearer, heavy feet stomped through one of Pudar's streets, intermingled with voices in the delicate, Western tongue. The words blended into an indecipherable rumble, occasionally interspersed with laughter. Tae stopped, recognizing that combination. He heard it twice before. The first time, he had quietly eavesdropped to find the source, a young noble surrounded by an entourage of guardsmen. Discreet questions had yielded an answer: Prince Severin, heir to Pudar's throne, enjoyed surveying his inheritance beneath the stars. Alight with young dreams and plans, he'd promised to end crime in the market city, and part of that vow required him to examine Pudar at dark time and observe the guards at work.

Tae's curiosity dispersed with understanding, and he had found no more reason to study the elder prince of Pudar. The second time, he had quietly avoided the group; and he did so now as well. The detour took him into a strange alleyway, and Tae slowed his pace. All consideration of Kevral disappeared as he set to the intense concentration necessary to accustom himself to this new location. The pattern of the shadows would not help him here, since he had no baseline memory. He had to create one as he already had for so many of Pudar's streets, though still fewer than a third. Though hardly difficult or onerous, he took the task seriously. Given enough time, he would make himself comfortable here.

Tae entered the alley with a slow caution that kept him near the left wall in the shade of a decorative overhang. Buildings of mortared stone hemmed him in on both sides, and he glanced nervously toward the exit. For reasons he could not explain, discomfort settled over him. He felt as if unseen eyes probed him in the darkness. His hand slid to the knife in his pocket, instinctively, before he realized he had moved. The sixth sense trained into him from childhood prickled to life, its source vague and uncentered.

Tae went still, gaze cutting through the darkness and ears attuned for movement. The distant clank of pacing guardsmen, the jumble of voices on the wind, and the cyclic swelling and ebbing of the insects' song made discernment of softer sounds impossible. Herein, Tae guessed, lay the cause for his concern. He believed it came more of the inability to remain fully watchful than because of any specific danger. He continued into the alley.

Inspection revealed two old boards, three rain barrels, and several tufts of weeds growing between the cobbles. Though competent, Tae had never done much climbing. His mind registered that the blocked stone would prove easier to ascend than the sage's tower in Béarn, though difficult enough he would prefer other ways to escape from enemies, should such become necessary. As he studied old stone secured with mortar and slicked by moss, he caught sight of movement at the corner of his eye. Way up on the roof of a two-story dwelling, someone crouched in the shadows.

Tae's heart rate quickened. He continued his slow inspection, battling the urge to tense and crouch for defense. So long as the stranger believed himself unobserved, he might not bother Tae. More likely, the man or woman on the rooftop had more important business, and Tae had simply blundered into his way.

Cued, Tae pretended to study the walls of the building, using peripheral vision to scan the rooftops. The maneuver made his eyes ache, but he discovered another figure on the rooftop. Then another. Within a moment, he had identified five, all small and delicate. *Women,* he guessed. *Or youngsters.* His heart pounded; he could hear the blood hammering in his ears. The need to flee became all-consuming, but he did not. Nothing drew predators faster than terror. Gingerly, without revealing his knowledge or fear, he headed toward the far end of the alley.

Tae managed five steps before a sound at the alley's entrance sent him spinning despite all attempts to remain casual. Three men blocked the way, every one swarthy and bearded. *Easterners.* Tae took a careful back-step. Then, the scrape of fabric against stone sheeted through the alleyway behind him. He turned halfway, reluctantly taking his eyes from the danger to assess more at the opposite end. There, two more large men stood between him and escape.

Tae's thoughts raced, but not quickly enough. The men marched toward him from both directions. Shadows draped their faces, hiding expression; but their stances conveyed the gloating triumph they now had a right to feel. They had him trapped, and Tae saw no way out. Desperately, he measured the alley, vision hawk-acute and heightened by danger. Scaling walls, even could he do so fast enough, would throw him directly into the hands of those stationed above. More likely, they would knock him down as he climbed, and he would plummet to a painful death. The idea of dying in that fashion squeezed at his chest until his breaths became labored. He would rather take a chance on dodging between those who closed around him on the ground.

As his father's enemies drew nearer, Tae found one more hope. The elements had battered a semicircular crack at the base of one of the buildings. Darkness hampered exploration, and his need to not broadcast his next move forced him to study it indirectly. He could not tell how far it extended, but wedging himself inside might gain him a temporary reprieve. With any luck, it would tunnel into the building, and he could escape from inside. If one who lived on the street used it as a sleeping hideout or bolt-hole, it likely led to another exit of some kind.

The men drew nearer. Moonlight revealed identical smirks of pleasure. They would revel in his slaughter, and he would not die quickly.

Tae gauged location and distance, keeping his gaze apparently focused on the walls. He had not revealed his knowledge of those stationed above. Therefore, the Easterners might expect him to climb. He could not stop his mind from pondering where and how they had gotten others to assist them. The beings he had glimpsed on the building roofs did not carry the bulk of grown men.

"What do you want from me?" Tae shouted, hoping to alert the prince and his entourage. If Severin really wished to eliminate crime in Pudar's streets, a distress call should draw him. Tae cursed himself for not thinking of the tactic sooner. In Stalmize, the city watch would as soon victimize him as assist, and calling for help displayed a weakness that would draw predators. He glided to the hole without looking at it, scrutinizing the wall as if seeking handholds.

One of the men growled softly. "We want your life, Tae Kahn Weile's son. And we will have it." The circle tightened, all movement deliberate and unhurried. Many sounds touched Tae's ears, amplified by fear. Beneath the normal night music, he heard a faint chant in dozens of voices in an airy, unfamiliar language. The clomp and click of the guards grew louder, approaching, he believed.

Tae gritted his teeth, bathed in a sweat so cold his skin turned to gooseflesh. He pressed his back against the wall, feeling the jagged edges of the bolt-hole through his britches. Doubt gripped him; it might prove too small. He suppressed the urge to check. He had committed himself to using it. Warning enemies of his intentions would only doom the attempt to failure.

The Easterners hemmed Tae against the wall, never taking their eyes from him. They had, apparently, orchestrated every detail. Their thoroughness shocked him. He had not believed them competent enough to delegate or coordinate so competently. The chanting continued, a distraction and a bother. His head throbbed in rhythm with the sound, and thought became difficult at a time he most needed it clear. One of the men made a sudden grab for Tae. Tae swiveled and dove for the opening.

Laughter chased Tae, muffled to a mocking rumble. Already adjusted to near darkness, Tae's vision showed him a long, straight route trickling into blackness. He could not surmise how far it would go; but it would, at least, take him beyond reach. For now, that was all he could hope for. He scrambled forward, and slammed his head into a clear partition. *Glass?* No other thought followed, as his mind shattered into pain and agony lanced down his neck. Momentarily stunned, he collapsed.

Fingers closed over Tae's ankle. Rough hands dragged him from his hiding place and back into the alley. Stone abraded his face and tore his clothing. Dizzily, he raised his hands to protect his eyes, and a boot toe slammed against his ear. Pain flashed through his head in a white explosion. He scrambled desperately for grounding, but his vision disappeared and his mind worked sluggishly. More boots crashed into his sides and abdomen. His ears rang, the sound a deafening agony that formed a horrible harmony to chanting and laughter.

Tae rolled, whipping his dagger from his pocket. He struck out in blind desperation. A foot hammered his now exposed face. His knife met resistance then came free, and warm blood splashed his hand. Someone cursed. A heel impacted Tae's back, bowling him over. More from instinct than intent, Tae drew his feet under him and tried to stand.

A dribble of vision returned, widening to encompass a blurry view of the alley. Shouts cut above the other sounds, in more than one language. Dazed, Tae could not find the necessary concentration to separate and interpret voices. Only escape mattered. He swung his dagger in desperate arcs, meeting flesh at least one more time. Then, a boot pounded his nose. He heard a crack and felt warm blood cascade down his face. The sensation of falling backward scarcely reached his senses before his head slammed the cobbles with an agony so intense it paralyzed him.

Hands seized him again. Tae cared no longer. The battering lost meaning as the pain passed bearing. More heaped on too much; his body no longer registered any of it. He felt as if he floated through a dark, empty void. Only survival instinct kept him thrusting and sweeping wildly with the dagger. All sound became meaningless noise. At one point, he was aware of the dagger getting jerked from his hand. Then, mercifully, all awareness left him.

As Griff ducked and dodged the branches obscuring the pathway to the Grove, he remembered for the thousandth time this day how much he loved the summer. The leaves gliding past his nose smelled clean, and the damp scent of the creek drew him like his mother's warm berry pie. Sunlight slanted through the trees, highlighting every twig. The foliage seemed alive with missy beetles, their tiny, black carapaces gleaming with every color of the rainbow. As the vibrations of Griff's passage shook her web, a spotted spider raced to the edge.

"Sorry," Griff murmured cheerfully to the spider, gazing around his sanctuary the way a monarch surveys his kingdom. His voice startled a rabbit, and it scampered into the underbrush and was soon lost to sight. Ignoring his usual deadfall seat, Griff headed for the creek.

Singing filled his ears, a gentle melody that rose and fell in steady cadence. The pattern confused him. It seemed too rigid and lengthy for birdsong, and he thought he could discern several different voices, flawlessly merged. He stood for several moments, head cocked, enjoying the distant music, whatever its source. *Aristiri?* Griff had heard of the breed of hawk that sang more beautifully than any songbird, yet he had never seen or heard one of the shy birds of prey.

He made a mental note to ask Ravn about the sound as he continued his walk to the creek.

Sunlight flashed from the water like jewels, and rocks on the bottom chopped its surface into wavelets. Scarcely wider than Griff's arm, the creek twisted through the Grove, burbling its happy song. With a quick glance for Ravn, whom Griff did not see, the heir to Béarn's throne plopped his bulk on the ground. He removed his work boots, then socks darned in several places. Barefoot, he approached the creek, eager to feel the cold water against his ankles and silt squishing between his massive toes. First, however, he knelt and drank from the crystal water. Though tasteless, the cold comfort soothed his throat and palate. He cupped his hands for another sip.

Suddenly, a hand clamped over the back of his head, fingers digging into his scalp. Griff stiffened and tried to pull away, but a second hand joined the first. The intruder drove Griff's face toward the water. "Stop!" Griff shouted, struggling to twist free as his nose breached the surface. Water filled his nostrils, its cold searing. He held his breath, managing to eel his body halfway around. But the hands still gripped his head, their weight more than he could bear. Lines of fire seemed to flow through his neck as his muscles strained to rescue his face.

The intruder's strength shocked Griff. He kicked and writhed as the water numbed his cheeks and eyes. He splashed, hands buried in silt, scrabbling for the purchase he needed to push back harder. Dislodged sand swam before his eyes.

The hands shoved harder, body braced against his back. The thunk and roar of water beat against Griff's ears, the sounds of his own fingers churning. Darkness hovered, threatening consciousness. His chest started to heave and ache, bucking against his control. Logically, he knew he could not breathe water, yet the desperate need to suck something, anything, into his lungs nearly overwhelmed him.

Something cut the air over Griff's head, the breeze of its passage a cold swish over one damp shoulder. The grip on his head went limp, and the body slid awkwardly sideways from his back. No longer opposed, Griff surged free of the creek, throat gasping open too early. He sucked a combination of water and air into his lungs, collapsing to the shore in a desperate fit of choking. Warm liquid splattered his back.

A thump shook the ground, and Griff twisted to look. A body sprawled near his feet, red-pink blood spilling from its throat. Another pinned him. He wriggled from beneath it, and it flopped lifelessly aside. Only then, he noticed the severed head that seemed to stare at him from the creek with glazed, yellow eyes. Griff tried to scream, but only hoarse, gagging noises emerged. Bile bubbled up in his stomach, and he vomited. Steel chimed against steel, shattering the sanctity of his clearing. Still retching, Griff turned his attention to this new sound. A blur of gold and silver fought a desperate battle against four.

Ravn. Griff recognized his benefactor at once. Sick and dizzied, he lurched to his feet. *Ravn?* Mistrusting his own sanity, he charged the battle, scarcely daring to internalize the sight of his "imaginary" friend battling creatures out of nightmare. Even as he covered the distance between them, guts still pinched and heaving, Ravn took down two more with strokes impossibly agile. Griff's eyes could not follow a sword so swift it became invisible, and the enemies, though delicate, seemed cloddish in comparison.

Griff slammed into one of the strangers, his bulk sending the other staggering backward. Ravn pulled a stroke at the last desperate second, barking a profanity. He ran his opponent through before turning his attention to the one Griff had knocked sprawling.

Fast as an animal, the stranger scrambled toward a copse. "Don't let him get away!" Ravn screamed, the command in his voice too driving to ignore.

Griff dove on the last of his enemies, squashing him beneath his tremendous weight. The stranger fought in a panicked frenzy, tiny fists slamming Griff's side with surprising strength, feet kicking air wildly.

Ravn drew up beside Griff. Despite the chaos of battle, his breaths came easily. Dark pink rivulets twined over sword and hand, dripping to the ground. The stranger stopped thrashing, eyes following the drip of his companions' blood. "Let him up."

Griff complied, nausea transforming to dizziness. The water still grated in his airways, and he coughed repeatedly.

Ravn placed his sword at the stranger's throat, waiting for Griff to stand clear. Blood dribbled from the tip, straining pink-red lines across his neck. Smooth eyes, like gems, locked on Ravn's face; and the strangeness of the features finally reached Griff's awareness.

Griff stepped back farther, throat on fire from inhaling gritty water as well as the acid from his vomit. He tasted blood, though he doubted it was his own. His soaked clothes clung to his skin, and strangers' blood matted his hair into sticky clumps.

"Griff, go clean up," Ravn commanded without taking his eyes from his captive.

Griff hesitated, surprised by Ravn's tone as well as his request. "Do you . . . ?" he started, but Ravn waved him silent impatiently.

"Do as I ask. Looking like that, you'll scare your mother to death."

Griff knew Ravn spoke literal truth. Threat against her only remaining child might shock his mother to her grave. Obediently, he headed for the creek. He had gotten only halfway, when a sound like the dying scream of a rabbit pierced his spine. He froze, whirling in time to see Ravn jerk his sword from the still body below him. *No!* Fear, sorrow, and confusion seized Griff at once, and he collapsed to the ground. The intensity of all that had happened battered at his conscience, crippling him into immobility. Ravn looked as ephemeral as always, and the not-quite-human forms and visages added to the illusion. *Was all that had happened real, or a figment of a nasty corner of my imagination?* The idea that such could exist inside his head seemed an insanity he dared not long consider. He forced a shaking hand to his head, feeling the globs of blood, smelling their rancid smell. Real, no doubt. And Ravn, too.

Griff half-crawled and half-dragged himself to the creek to wash. The time for contemplation would come. For now, he needed to do as Ravn said, then leave the beloved Grove that could no longer serve as a sanctuary. Ravn, too, would never seem the same.

Chapter 25

The Lifers' Cell

*There is no law, at least not one Odin enforces,
that says a man always has to act by gods' intentions.*

—Colbey Calistinsson

Tae Kahn awakened to pain grinding and hammering
through his head and body. He gathered his limbs, the movement inflaming the agony to a savage bonfire. He bit his
tongue to keep from screaming and barely noticed the discomfort that seemed so puny in comparison. The metallic
taste of old blood sent bile churning through his stomach.
He managed to hold back the scream, but a tight moan escaped his lips.

A swish of fabric against stone caught his attention, and
a cough echoed through his hearing. Aching, Tae had to
force his thoughts toward his usually instinctive animal
alertness. A thickness befuddled his mind, like too much
drink, though he knew he had tasted nothing alcoholic in
days. He forced his lids open only with conscious effort. His
lashes parted, leaving stripes of gummy discharge tinged red
with blood. Through the gaps, he saw ragged, scrawny men
of varying sizes, all watching him suspiciously. One stood
out from the others. He lounged on a grimy straw pallet
while the others huddled in corners of their mutual cage.
Standing, the stranger would have towered over even Ra-
khir. His flesh sagged, betraying a previously rotund frame;
but his muscles had not withered. His skin bore the neutral

tone of a native Pudarian, marred by the pallor of long captivity. Brown hair covered his head, arms, and torso and
swept into an unkempt beard. His expression was unrevealing, but his eyes measured Tae.

Trained to hide weakness, Tae scurried to a crouch. Movement brutally incited pain, and his consciousness wavered.
He fought the telltale wince or gritted teeth. He was in the
presence of vermin and wolves. Any sign of frailty might
goad them to attack. That they had not done so already,
while he lay unconscious and vulnerable on the floor,
seemed nothing short of miraculous. He guessed it stemmed
more from inertia than mercy.

"Hello," Tae said, trying to sound casual. A hint of pain
sneaked into his tone, minuscule enough that he hoped no
one but him had noticed it.

No one responded to the greeting. Every one of Tae's six
cell mates remained ominously silent. Twelve eyes studied
him with an intensity rarely broken even to blink, eight
brown, two blue, and two gray-green. All bore the hunted,
hungry look of those whose pasts had betrayed them. *Street-
raised, most if not all*, Tae guessed. *Lawless and trustless.*

For a few moments, Tae returned their scrutiny. Despite
dire circumstances, probably lifelong, only one stood shorter
than himself. That one, however, proved a remarkable exception. Tiny, small-boned, and gaunt, he seemed nearly little enough to slip through the bars. They ranged in age from
mid-twenties to late forties, all unshaven and smeared with
filth. The odor of unwashed flesh balled into a stench that
seemed almost solid. Their cautious stances and flat expressions revealed little. Contempt, hatred, and hopelessness radiated from those few eyes that still maintained a spark of
life.

Tae ignored the others to concentrate on the construction
of the cell. Bars composed all four walls, though three lay
recessed against stone. Tae guessed the architect had built
the cage and its crevice separately, sliding the former into
the latter. The remaining barred side left him a clear view of
a dingy, damp room lit by a single torch, inadequate to keep
more than a modest semicircle of darkness at bay. Grooves
held the remains of spent torches and puddles of ancient
wax. Two doors disrupted the cage's face, the first a small,
high one barely within Tae's longest reach and obviously
constructed for passing food or other necessities to the pris-

oners. The other was broad enough for people to pass through. It sported three locks: the first near the ground, the second at a standard height but shielded by jutting plates, and the third well above Tae's reach.

The other prisoners continued to stare. Tae could feel their gazes riveted on his back, but he chose to ignore them. With predators, fearlessness always worked best.

The largest prisoner broke the silence. "You're standing in my place."

Tae continued his examination without glancing toward the other man. He kept each action precise and slow while his mind raced, comparing his brief survey of the other to his voice, his words, and previous experience. Tae knew his life depended on an accurate assessment of his cell mate's power. He chose his reply with caution. "No need to rile yourself. I won't be here long."

The other prisoners shifted restlessly. Tae followed the largest's movements by the rustle of straw and the swish of his tattered pants legs. He seemed unusually quick for a man of his bulk. "You misunderstood me, Eastlander. *You* are standing in *my* place." He lunged.

Instinctively, Tae leaped aside. The other's thick fingers swept the air where he had stood.

The other prisoners shifted out of the way, their motions deliberate with practice. They, too, knew the ways of the streets.

Tae's heart hammered. Consciously, he moderated his breathing to a circular pattern of inhalation through his nose and out his mouth. He knew he could not play the dodging game long in closed quarters. Eventually, the huge Pudarian would catch him; and the consequences after that would depend upon how badly Tae humiliated his opponent prior to that moment. *Play him carefully,* Tae reminded himself. *If I demean him, I force him to kill me.* Locking his gaze on his opponent's hands, Tae suppressed his natural urge to dodge.

The larger man struck, quick and solid. Each hand caught a corner of Tae's collar. Tae remained still, neither flinching nor blinking, even when the other crossed his wrists and effectively closed Tae's windpipe. "Nobody stands in my place, Eastern lizard. Do you understand?"

Though unable to speak, Tae met the man's glare with forced defiance. The cell seemed to spin around him. The words of the prisoner spectators lost meaning, something about life and death and food. He learned the big man's name, Danamelio, though the knowledge could not serve him now. Tae fought rising panic, trusting whatever reason had kept him alive so far to remain valid now.

Gradually, the large man's grip relaxed. Though grateful for air, Tae resisted the urge to gasp and normalized each breath. He remained still until the last wave of dizziness passed and he felt comfortable enough to speak at his regular octave. "Danamelio, if you kill me, I can't help you escape."

Surprise twisted Danamelio's features. For some time, he neither moved nor spoke. Then, his mouth gaped open, and he laughed. "Escape. Escape?" He emitted a second deep rumble of laughter. "I've been here ten years. Me. Danamelio." He released Tae, shoving him away from the disputed position and toward the other prisoners. "Pudar's greatest criminal rots in a cage, and you propose escape?" He laughed again.

Tae caught his balance gracefully, smoothed his clothes with feigned casualness, and shrugged. "Good as you claim, Dano, you can't be Pudar's greatest. He or she is a rogue of such stealth we'd never find him in a prison."

If Danamelio noticed the shortening of his name, the gravest of insults in the East, he took no notice. "And you think you can prove yourself better by escaping?" The anger that flashed through his dark eyes clearly arose from this concern rather than Tae's intentional affront.

"Not at all. I've already proven my clumsiness by getting caught." Tae rubbed crusted blood from his nose and cheeks, and it fell in flakes to the stone floor. "I didn't promise anything. I only mentioned I couldn't help you escape if you killed me." He smiled. "You can't argue with that logic."

Danamelio glared. He made a broad gesture of dismissal to indicate he believed Tae beneath contempt. "You're alive because you mean more food for the rest of us. Don't ever forget that." With that warning, he returned to his pallet, ignoring Tae and the others.

Tae glanced toward his cell mates, and every one avoided his stare. He shrugged and sat in a neutral area, beyond the natural, private circle every person preferred to keep empty. So long as no one violated his space, he could not be bothering theirs either. Except Danamelio, whose territory seemed too broad and arbitrary to attempt definition.

Tae watched the boring routine of the cell, which seemed to consist exclusively of minor movements of its occupants. He attempted to talk with each of his cell mates in turn, without success. Each ignored him with a glare that warned him even words did not and should not cross the boundary. Tae could not suppress a shiver as one bad experience turned into unanimity. His father had warned him about people who lacked even the basic foundation of love they needed to believe in anyone except themselves. Early, then later, experiences converted them into conscienceless automatons lacking all morality but an all-consuming will to perform anything that directly gained them power, wealth, or selfish satisfaction. To them, murder became nothing more difficult than the physical action of raising a weapon. No ethical struggle accompanied it.

Weile Kahn had spent long hours teaching others to distinguish between that type of personality and those more salvageable. A hopeless situation, Tae knew, could create a similar picture. Though he hated giving his father credit for anything, he appreciated the training in subtleties he had learned, both from directed lessons and details overheard. Without it, he would not have found a crack in the defenses of the slender, green-eyed blond among the others. Given reason, Tae believed, that one might talk. Once he did, others might reveal a less vicious, more vulnerable side of themselves as well. Alone in this hell hole, Tae doubted he would last long. He would need allies just to stay alive. And, with assistance, he might make good on the aforementioned escape.

Tae could only guess at the time, when a trio of guards finally wound into the room outside the group cell. They wore the tan shirts and britches of Pudar, a contrastingly simple color for a bustling city of myriad hues. One carried a halberd, another a crossbow, and they all wore short swords at their hips. Tae had noted longer blades on the belts of guards on the streets, and he guessed the prison guards found smaller ones more useful in the dungeon's corridors. The guard without a second weapon wheeled a cart carrying plates of food scraps, apparently left over from a dinner in the palace.

Wordlessly, the prisoners shifted toward the back of the cage as the guards took their positions, and Tae followed their lead. The crossbowman trained his weapon on Danamelio, though whether because he considered the largest most dangerous, from previous difficulties, or simply because he stood nearest the front of the cell, Tae could only surmise. The halberdier crouched near enough to jab for the source of any trouble, but not enough to place himself in danger. Nearly as tall as Danamelio, the third Pudarian guardsman propped the hatch. Dish by dish, he poured the scraps inside, chunks of vegetables and meat pelting the stone floor. Placing the empty plates back in a pile on the cart, he let the door swing shut. Then, he shoved a trough of water through the lower bars with one foot. All three guards left the room.

The prisoners waited only until the crossbowman and halberdier removed their respective threats before launching themselves at the food. Most raked up scattered pieces that had bounced or rolled from the main pile. Danamelio seized the lion's share without challenge, leaving his pile unprotected to snatch a few more choice tidbits. Like Tae, the smallest of the prisoners did not participate in the scramble, though Tae suspected their reasons were different. Tae had not yet reached the stage of hunger where he could stomach other people's cast-offs, some partially-chewed. He noted with quiet satisfaction that the green-eyed one passed near enough to Danamelio's pile to plunder it. Tae did not witness an actual theft, but he guessed such had occurred. Shortly, the green-eyed one's chewing revealed him. Tae smiled at him, rewarded by a mild twitch of the corners of the other's lips before he looked hurriedly away.

Tae noticed one other thing about the dynamics of the feeding frenzy. Danamelio deliberately gave parts of his meal to the smallest of the men, sharing with the tenderness of a parent. Tae wondered if they might not be father and son, although it seemed ludicrous to imagine one so tiny could spring from such a huge man's seed. Their coloring, however, seemed near enough; and Tae wondered if circumstances might have severely stunted the little man.

The smallest took the first drink from the water trough, followed by Danamelio, then the others in pairs. Tae observed the pecking order with a critical eye. The green-eyed one drank third, at the same time as one of the others. The last two took their fill soon after. Though all seemed content, a significant amount of water remained. Tae could drink, but the idea of sharing spit with this bunch repulsed him. At times, he had slurped from muddy livestock tanks and cherished the opportunity. The current situation bothered him more. He watched as the others settled down to sleep, each in his own space.

Tae found an empty edge and settled there, though he could not sleep. The same battering that had thrown him into oblivion now kept him wired and desperately awake. Pain jabbed, jerked, and hammered through every part of him, especially his head. Fear enfolded him like an icy blanket, all the more intense for the long need to hold it at bay. Questions accompanied it. He had awakened here without explanation, left to wonder about location, consequences, and reasons. His cell mates' interactions had become wordless pattern, a sure sign that it had been going on for a lengthy period of time. Despite their suspicious natures and rigid individualism, they worked together better than any of them would have admitted. *What did I do to deserve this?* Tae wondered, forcing his thoughts from contemplation of something far worse: Could he become a part of their horrible routine? Would he have need to do so?

Wonder slipped through despite his best effort, and he appreciated that night stole some of his need to maintain a brave and dangerous front. He followed a mild slope in the floor on hands and knees, correctly guessing it probably led to a drain hole. On occasion, he surmised, the guards dumped water into the cell, and probably over the prisoners, to wash it. As he drew closer, the reek of urine and feces grew stronger over the stink of stale sweat and body odor. The stench threw Tae over the edge. He barely managed to reach the hole before his stomach lurched up its contents. Vomit, stained brown with old blood, spewed forth. The sight and smell of it only worsened the situation, and he threw up repeatedly until his guts heaved dry and his muscles screamed in agony.

Eventually, Tae sank to the floor. The blood, he believed, was swallowed rather than from any deep internal injury. To the credit of his assailants, they had used only blunt weapons, mostly boots and fists. Bruises surely stamped his flesh, inside and out; yet he had no reason to believe they had torn anything vital. He had suffered a broken nose and a possible skull fracture; but, as long as head trauma did not kill him, he doubted any of his other injuries would. Finding it difficult to concentrate around the pain, he pulled himself back toward his sleeping spot, forcing a teeth-gritted look of de-fiancé and pretending his low-crawl position was chosen. No one needed to know he would never willingly drag his body across such filth.

The pain dulled with time, fusing into a throbbing ache, mostly localized to his nose. He clambered back to his position at a steady pace, and nearly placed his hand on another's leg. Someone had shifted into his spot.

Tae looked up swiftly, jerking back his fingers. The green-eyed one studied him in the dank darkness, brows raised in question, body sprawled in the location Tae had chosen.

Tae's mind raced as he measured the situation. The other had caught him in a moment of absolute weakness. Having no strength for confrontation, he wished nothing more than to apologize and move on. Still, doing so might relegate him to a low position in the hierarchy, one for which he might pay for eternity. He gathered breath for bluff.

The green-eyed man saved him the need. "Hello." He shifted to a sitting position.

Tae lowered himself into a crouch, surprised by the civility. He nodded a careful acknowledgment. "I'm Tae."

"Lador," the other said, running a hand through greasy, overgrown curls. "Are you really going to escape?"

Tae shrugged, wishing every movement did not spark so much pain. "What are my options?"

Lador held his hair back from a solemn, blank face used to hiding emotion. As always, the eyes betrayed him, flashing the cautious interest he did not dare let his features assume. "After killing the heir to Pudar's throne?"

Tae stiffened, shocked by the accusation, mind slipping back to the battle in the alleyway. He remembered a pack of Easterners battering him, youngsters on the rooftop, and the prince's entourage nearby. He recalled scrabbling madly with his dagger, desperately fighting for his life. The rest seemed a blur devoid of details. Surely the heir to Pudar would not have joined bullies pummeling a stranger in the street. Tae's knife had struck home at least twice, yet he could not imagine Pudar's guardsmen allowing the prince to draw close enough to die, even should he prove foolish enough to try. Nothing about the situation made sense, and his mind could not separate the details necessary to place any picture, proper or misinterpreted, together.

Oblivious to Tae's introspection, Lador continued. "You'll get kept here for a while, at least. Then, there's no doubt they'll find some horrible death for you." He pursed his lips until they became nearly lost in his beard. "That's why I thought maybe you really meant it when you said you'd escape. A man doesn't commit a doozandazzy of a crime without some plan to get himself out of it." He paused a moment in consideration, then continued in a harsher tone. "Unless he's incredibly stupid."

Tae studied Lador in silence a long time, mostly gathering his wits and his composure.

Lador let go of his hair, and it fell in a wild cascade to his neck. He tensed to rise.

"I'm not stupid," Tae finally said.

Lador remained in place, feet gathered under him to leave but postponing attempts to stand.

"I'll find a way out."

Lador stayed still, waiting for something more concrete that would elevate Tae's claim above idle boasting.

Tae waded through the distractions of agony, desperation, and confusion. No ideas came. Even a single, well-made lock might thwart his expertise; and, what he now knew was Pudar's dungeon would certainly have the finest. The oddness of the locks' positioning and shielding would only add to the problem. Tae settled to his haunches, deep in thought. He glanced around the cell, searching for some object or detail that might help him. He found only the metal water trough and the clothes on his companions' backs. They lay in various stages of repose, from sprawled and snoring to bolt upright and an instant from action.

Desperate situations required desperate answers. *What would my father do?* The need to think like Weile bothered Tae, yet he knew his answer, if it existed, would almost certainly come from that source. His father's strength lay in leadership and the ability to organize those who most people dismissed as the callous damned. Tae's thoughts froze in place. He had categorized his cell mates in a like fashion hours ago, yet one had already approached him. On his own, he could never hope for escape. But if he dared take a lesson from Weile Kahn, he might pool their various talents and find answer where none previously existed.

In his excitement, Tae lost track of his aches and pains. "Lador, I may have the answer. You'll need to tell me about yourself and as much as you know of the others."

Again, Lador stared at Tae. Then, apparently trusting the

newcomer's zeal, he smiled cautiously. "Can't see what that'll do for you, but it'll give us something to talk about, at least. I'm the only one here who seems to care whether he exercises his voice or not."

Tae suspected the reason for Lador's tolerance for company would come out in his story. Weile often said that those who grew up with families made far better allies because they liked people and needed companions of one sort or another. "Exercise away," Tae encouraged. Only then, his own suspicions finally awakened. *Could Pudar have planted an informant among us?* He dismissed the thought instantly. Not even the most devout patriot would condemn himself to such a life. No one forced to do so, by duty or command, could remain loyal long. Besides, Tae reasoned, he had nothing to lose. They already had him for a crime serious enough to punish him in any manner they wished.

"I was a locksmith," Lador began, green-gray eyes distant, as if recounting another person's life. Surely, a long time had passed since history accounted for anything. "A damned good one, too." He did not boast, simply recited what he believed to be the truth.

Tae suspected Kevral could learn from Lador's easy style, ranking himself among the best without disparaging those of lesser skill.

"I could build a lock to thwart almost any thief, then I could find the means to open it if the owner lost his key." Lador chuckled softly so as not to wake the others. "That's the paradox, you see. If I could break into it, surely someone else of skill could do it, too." Lador's expression turned even more grave, if possible. "Obsession with that idea became my downfall." Though unnecessary, he searched for an analogy. "You're an Easterner, right?"

Tae made a gesture of acknowledgment. His accent, if not the darkness of his hair, eyes, and skin, always gave him away.

"I got a few friends from your side of the world. Anyway, every time we'd get down to arguing religion, they'd point out they only needed one god to our bunch. Their god, Sheriva they'd call him, was so powerful he could do anything, including squashing all of ours. So, I'd always ask the stumper question: If he can do anything, can he make a maze so twisty he can't get out of it?"

"And they wouldn't have an answer to that one?" Tae

guessed, having heard the age-old dilemma posed many ways, more often regarding the weight of a created object.

"No, and mostly they'd get mad I asked." A slight smile twitched onto Lador's face at the memory, so mild Tae could not be certain he saw it. "Anyway, I took it as a challenge to create a lock I couldn't open."

"Did you?"

"No. No, I couldn't. I always knew too much about the mechanism. So, then I started working on locks other people made." Lador scratched at his wrist, revealing a rash Tae knew as scabies.

Tae resisted the natural urge to scratch himself. He had lived among companions covered with mites, lice, and fleas too many times to worry. Many people who lived among scabetics all their lives never got the rash, and Tae counted himself among them.

"So I started trying other people's locks, secretly, of course. When I got these open, I started noticing the things people keep behind them. I took some things I shouldn't have, and I wound up here."

"Tossed into a cell with murderers."

Lador glanced around at their cell mates. "Only two murderers. This is the lifer cell—for those they can't rehabilitate but they don't think deserve death. They keep the ones in here who get executed, too. Prior to trial."

"That's where I fit in," Tae guessed.

Lador shrugged. "They're not going to let you live after killing the prince. . . ." He trailed off, a polite request for details that Tae ignored. He could not sort things out in his own mind enough to even attempt explanation to another.

"So you're unrehabilitable?"

"It's an obsession," Lador admitted. "But mostly I think I just took from the wrong people. The most powerful people can afford the best locks."

Tae continued to take the emphasis off of himself. "So how about the others?"

Again, Lador turned his focus to his cell mates, keeping his voice soft under the snores. "You've met Danamelio."

"The other murderer?" Tae guessed.

"Wrong. Child molestation. He'd done it for years out on the streets, but no one worried about it until he snagged one of royal blood. Just a distant cousin of some sort, but that was enough."

Tae had hit the streets too old to fall victim to similar vermin, but a girlfriend had once recounted some of her early experiences. Revolted by the images brought to mind, Tae could not help finally recognizing the relationship that had confounded him until that moment. "That explains the little one." He gestured at the smallest of the prisoners.

Lador nodded. "Sick, isn't it? I don't know his real name, but we call him the Flea. He's no child; he's in his thirties. But I guess you take what you can in a place like this."

Tae squirmed, wishing to talk about anything but the current topic of conversation. "Does the Flea have any talents?"

Lador seemed to enjoy Tae's discomfort. "You mean *other* talents? None that I know of. He's in for big-time vandalism."

"Royal property?" Tae guessed.

"No doubt."

"Hmmm."

Lador moved on. "We call the tall one Stick." He gestured the one who had drank from the trough at the same time as himself. "I've never heard him talk. The guards said he killed someone. Never seen him do anything violent, but he's got a dangerous feel to him if you know what I mean."

Knowing exactly from past experience, Tae nodded.

"Used to have a lot of muscle on him, but now he's mostly just tall and skinny, hence the name. When he stops slouching, he towers over even Danamelio."

Tae made an interested noise.

Lador pointed toward a sandy-haired, nondescript man in a corner. "That's Tadda. He's in for theft. Still protesting his innocence, but he's skilled as hell." Lador lowered his voice to an almost inaudible whisper. "Takes his food from Danamelio's stack and never gets caught."

"I'm impressed," Tae said honestly. "I was watching pretty closely, and I didn't even see him get close."

"I noticed once or twice while I was doing the same thing. Otherwise, I'd have never known it either. Real acrobat, too."

Lador indicated the last of the bunch, a scrawny, dirty bundle of rags. "Street rat. Name Peter. Says he's taking the rap for his buddies, and I think I believe him. No physical skills that I've noticed, but he does have a tremendous eye for direction and detail. From what he says, he used to memorize the routes and locations so the others could do the stealing."

"Do you think he's telling the truth?" Tae could see a use for that talent as well.

"Fits his character all right." Lador turned Tae an evil grin. "That's the lot. So, you got us out of this place yet?"

Ideas stirred through Tae's thoughts, as yet vague and formless, but promising. His father's greatest asset, bringing together those who usually trusted no one, would serve him well now. Resentment became a tense knot in his gut that scarcely grazed the excitement of the challenge. The obvious and necessary comparison to Weile Kahn chafed, but the lessons learned would prove invaluable. He discovered the first glimmer of talent in the most obvious, yet least likely place: his childhood. He would not allow bitterness to taint a strategy necessary to spare his life. Accused of murdering Pudar's crown prince, his slow, agonizing death now held more value than his life. He could not afford mistakes.

His question unanswered, Lador eyeballed Tae, expression demanding.

Tae allowed a smile to creep onto his features. "Have I gotten us out of this place yet? Maybe. I need more information."

Lador lowered and raised his head once, an obvious gesture. He would supply any knowledge at his disposal.

Tae chewed his lower lip, deep in concentration. Without a coherent strategy, he found it difficult to direct his queries. "Locksmith, what do you think about these?"

"These?" Lador indicated the three by pointing, from the lowest to the highest. "Well-made, of course. But not the most complicated I've seen." He amended, truth usurping pride. "Close, though." He rose to demonstrate. "The one near the ground's the only one I've gotten a good look at. This one . . ." He indicated the middle one by inclining his head toward it. ". . . is impossible to feel or see because of the side bars."

Tae nodded, recalling the arrangement from his observation. Metal side walls jutted from the bars, effectively blocking it from view or reach.

"The upper lock's beyond even the Stick's highest reach. The guards use a ladder to get to it. I've never gotten near enough to examine it, though I'd bet it's not much different than the lowest." Lador scratched more deliberately at his arms. The scabies itch always worsened after nightfall. "I've made a crude key I think might work in the low one. Took me months to work a piece of metal loose from the water trough and years of bending and scraping to design it. Mostly, though, it's been an exercise in futility. Fits in all right, and I think it'd turn, too. But when you're working with tools this crude, you can't be sure you can relock what you undo. So, as much as I've wanted to test it, I can't."

Excitement turned Tae's heartbeat to a heavy cadence. "I'm impressed."

"Don't be." Lador dismissed the praise. "It's my job and my obsession, and it's not worth much. One out of three won't get us free." He chuckled at the unintentional rhyme.

"It's a start." Tae refused to deny the usefulness of talent so remarkable. "How often do the guards come?"

"Twice a day. Morning and evening. To check on us and to feed us. There're always three. One does the work and the others threaten. Just like you saw tonight. The only other times they come, and the only time they open the cage, it's to throw someone new in. Then, there're usually a bunch of them."

Tae pressed for details. "A bunch meaning?"

"Anything from seven or eight to a couple dozen. Just depends on whether they anticipate trouble, I guess. I'm not sure whether that's trouble from the prisoner or us, though. You got just a few since you were unconscious. Danamelio got more like a regiment."

Tae did not like those odds. A quiet jailbreak between guard watches seemed far more effective and decidedly safer. "Once we're out, do you know what we'd have to deal with?"

"You mean as far as passageways, doors, locks, guards, and the like?"

"Right."

Lador shrugged. "I've been here six years. Even if I could remember, it's probably changed. You, being the most recent, ought to have the best knowledge."

"I was unconscious," Tae reminded.

"Right."

"Who's next most recent?"

"Isn't it obvious?"

Tae thought the question odd. "Should it be?"

Lador explained. "Once they started giving more food for

more living prisoners, murder became less of a problem down here. But even though no one'll usually kill you outright anymore, you starve to death if you're not either aggressive or quick-handed." He glanced at the Flea. "Or favored by one who is."

Tae considered Lador's description and found a warped logic to it. He also figured out who the second newest cell mate had to be, the only meek one without a penchant for theft. He glanced at the young street tough with a mild pity he had not expected. "Peter." He smiled. The youngster's single confessed talent, knowledge of routes, would serve him well in this situation, if panic had not stripped him of his observational abilities.

Tae asked a few more questions, about the routine in the lifers' cell as well as minor details, including the personalities and foibles of this odd band of criminals with which his lot had become inexorably entwined. He would not have chosen them in any capacity and would not have attempted to talk them into working together on a high-stakes wager or a dare. But now, his life depended on his ability to draw them all together and lead. No doubt, the very talents that condemned them would prove invaluable when it came to escape. A random group of citizens would not have provided him with the many peculiarly useful abilities, but they also would willingly work as a team, without the need to placate egos, threaten, cajole, or coerce. This escape, if it happened, would not come easily.

Once Weile's plans, dreams, and decisions had seemed absurd to the brink of insanity. Now, Tae mulled the potential of his cell mates and found it staggering. Small-time hoods and street rats, disparaged and despised by the populace, were not the worthless, brainless fools common folk and the wealthy proclaimed them. Most believed they fell into crime because they lacked other skills. Now, Tae, realized, they possessed a wide array of underappreciated talents. Alone, they became a nuisance and reviled. Together, they could bind into a community whose capabilities boggled the mind. The man who organized criminals, who could stir loyalty where none seemed to exist, could take down the loftiest of kingdoms. In his own way, Tae finally realized, Weile Kahn ruled the world. And Tae was a crown prince, of a sort, in his own right.

There, the image broke down. Tae frowned as other

thoughts came to shatter the theoretical castle he had built from understanding. Weile was a king plagued by assassins, any or all of whom could usurp his throne without need for bloodline. A king who did not dare to sleep, who spent his life always with his hands beweaponed and his eyes darting over his shoulders was a prisoner in his own castle. For all its power, Tae found little attractive about his father's life. Bitterness swelled into a tidal wave. No matter his lifestyle, his father had treated his own son with unforgivable cruelty. He had failed at protecting his wife and child, those he claimed to love. And the coldness he inflicted upon his only son demonstrated little of the caring he claimed in words. Actions spoke louder.

Tae turned his anger into fuel for a nearer fire. His features set with purpose, he glared into Lador's eyes. "By this time tomorrow," he promised, "I'll have a workable plan."

Chapter 26

Ravn's Lesson

*If you learn to quit when you get tired, you will
die when you get tired.*

—Colbey Calistinsson

Fatigue had claimed Ravn an hour ago, but his father's
sword cuts rained down on him without mercy. The spar had
long outlasted his skill or his patience; but Ravn knew better
than to question Colbey's judgment, even if he could spare
the breath for questions. His lungs gasped for air desperately, scarcely obedient to his mental efforts to regulate
them. Sweat glazed his ivory skin and greased his palms until his grip on both sword hilts threatened to fail with every
blow. He did not know which would give out first, his aching muscles or his hold on a haft that had gone slippery as
a fish; but it seemed certain he could not last much longer.
His air-starved lungs had dried to a rawness that made each
rapid breath agony. Sweat stung blue eyes that remained
open only from urgent need, and his yellow hair flopped into
and out of his eyes with each move. Every lethal trick at his
disposal had fallen prey to Colbey's unbeatable defense.
Ravn had lost enough ground to wonder if they still sparred
within the confines of Asgard.

Still, the relentless assault did not let up. The trained need
to commit to every stroke had worn Ravn to a frazzle, but he
knew better than to slacken, even in spar. Any mistake, no
matter how tiny or how well couched in skill, would never
escape Colbey's notice. The Keeper of the Balance would

find a way to punish his son's slightest hint of laziness with humiliation and effort that made even this seem paltry. Ravn had finally reached the point where he doubted, but did not question, his father's ability to do so. *Is it possible to feel tireder or achier than this?* Ravn's answer came more swiftly than he would have guessed. The spar continued, each movement stretching into a bleak and painful eternity.

Ravn's consciousness stretched and pulled, black dizziness interrupting thought and memory at intervals. Then, just as he felt certain he would collapse, Colbey ceased his assault. His two swords glided into a defensive position, and his blue-gray eyes studied his son coldly.

Ravn avoided his father's gaze; though a sure sign of weakness in itself, it afforded the opportunity to hide others. He closed his mouth, sucking gulps of air through gritted teeth and lowered his head to hide the expression of pain. Sweat ran like blood down his blades.

Colbey remained silent for quite some time. Ravn could feel the eyes upon him and the unseen glower of disapproval. Usually, he enjoyed practice of any kind, disappointed when his father ended sessions to spar his mother or for his own *svergelse*. Hard work gave Ravn a satisfaction few other pleasures could match. Any session ended without pain seemed hollow and worthless, leaving him craving more. He had always believed that to be his father's greatest strength as a *torke,* a teacher of Renshai. Colbey always managed to work his student to a point that left him more knowledgeable but still yearning. The eternity that immortality offered the product of a union between a half-god and a goddess never seemed enough time to learn all his father could teach. In his mortal years, Colbey had dedicated his life to his sword, forgoing eating and sleeping when they interfered with his practice. His responsibilities to the cause of Balance rarely took much of his time, and Colbey would always have three and a half centuries of practice over Ravn no matter how long and consistently he worked himself.

When Ravn felt he could move his head without becoming overpowered by vertigo, he finally looked up. The anger he had imagined in his father's eyes became striking reality.

"Again," Colbey said.

Ravn blinked, unable to internalize the word until Colbey assumed an offensive stance. An eye blink separated Ravn from another grueling session at a time when he could ill afford it. Afraid for his flickering consciousness, he barely raised his sword in time to parry. Sword crashed against sword, the force of the blow staggering. Overbalanced, Ravn barely caught his equilibrium. For a moment, even he believed he had fallen. He twisted out of the path of Colbey's next strike, entertaining thoughts he would never have considered in the past. His father had trained Renshai for centuries. Always, he had insisted that his students attack with the full intention of killing him, often stating that a teacher who could not dodge a student's blows deserved the death they inflicted. Despite that philosophy, no one had managed to give him so much as a scratch during spar. Colbey's own strokes always seemed real, but Ravn knew that could not be the case. Otherwise, no student of the world's best swordsman would live to see his second spar. Ravn wondered what his father would do if he simply stood still and took whatever came his way.

The thought flitted through Ravn's mind only briefly. A sharpened sword could slaughter even a son of gods. Though born centuries after the *Ragnarok,* Ravn had heard the stories, knew gods could die of other things if not of old age. If he made no attempt to protect himself, he doubted his father would find him worthy to do so for him. So Ravn dodged and found another strategy only slightly less abhorrent. Colbey's next attack slammed against his parry. Ravn eeled around his father's second sword, then hurled one of his own blades at his *torke's* feet.

Colbey jerked back, rescuing his toes, surprise etched on his features. Seizing the opening, Ravn retreated beyond sword range. He paused there, gasping and attentive, prepared to run should his father charge.

But Colbey remained in place, blond hair sweat-plastered to his forehead, his expression still open with astonishment. He held a perfect fighting stance; even shock could not dislodge his attention from battle.

Ravn waited for the inevitable explosion.

Gradually, Colbey's gaze rose from the grounded sword to the son who had committed two of the worst sins in Renshai history, second and third only to cowardice. By allowing his sword to strike the ground, Ravn had dishonored it. And the method he chose showed disrespect for his *torke* as well.

Colbey's face settled into angry creases. Methodically, he

polished each of his blades and returned them to their sheaths.

Sweat tickled down Ravn's back. He remained silent, his second sword still freed and his position solid. He would not speak first; that would only worsen the situation.

The pause that followed seemed to span eternity. "Raska Colbeysson," Colbey finally spoke, in a powerful voice, without the unbridled rage Ravn expected. Only the formal use of his full name, rather than his usual nickname, displayed the elder Renshai's dissatisfaction. "Why did you do that?" He indicated the sword with a slow nod that never took his eyes from Ravn.

"I apologize for the indignity I've inflicted on my sword and the affront to my *torke*." In his sixteen years, Ravn had learned to diffuse emotion before delivering a verbal defense. Nothing ignited tempers faster than a desperate denial accompanied by flimsy excuses. He had reason for his actions, ones better accepted after appropriate courtesy and student/teacher balance had been restored. Nevertheless, he refused to assume all of the blame. "There is strategy even against Renshai."

Colbey blinked. "Explain."

"I needed an opening. I created it by using an unexpected maneuver."

"In the process, dishonoring your sword."

Ravn pursed his lips, unable to deny the truth of the assertion. His earliest memories of practice included his father diving for Ravn's sword after disarming maneuvers. A Renshai would rather throw himself in the mud than his weapon. "Considering my opponent, nothing less would have worked."

Colbey could scarcely deny the truth of the statement. He accepted it grudgingly, the matter still open for consideration. "So you were creating an opening."

"Yes." Ravn's breathing finally began to normalize, and he appreciated the long silence that had seemed nerve-racking before. He cleaned his remaining sword and returned it to its sheath. He made no move toward the other.

"Then why did you not press the opening you made?"

Here, Ravn believed, Colbey had found a better reason for lecture. His son's actions bordered on cowardice.

Ravn held his *torke* in too much esteem to lie, even had he not learned its futility long ago. Colbey could read intention as well as word, mood, and, on occasion, actual thoughts. "I did not have the strength left to attack."

Colbey's expression hardened, and his blue-gray eyes glittered with icy disapproval. "So you fled."

Ravn swept soaked hair from his forehead and rubbed sweat from his eyes. "I withdrew from the battle."

"Explain your justification."

Despite respect for his father that bordered on fear, Ravn would not be cowed. "The type of battle allowed it."

Colbey's brows rose gradually, signaling intense interest in a response that seemed unlikely to satisfy. "How so?"

Ravn shifted nervously, but he kept his gaze firmly latched on his father's. "We never likened this to a real battle by defining a fictitious situation. I took it to represent a father so enraged by his son that he attacked in a furious fit. As the son, I took the first opportunity to disengage and used a strategy designed to distract Father long enough from his temper to talk."

Colbey stiffened, a sure sign Ravn had struck something raw. "You are supposed to treat each spar like a real battle."

"I did," Ravn insisted. "This time, I couldn't separate out a style uniquely yours. Had you been an unnamed enemy in wartime, I would have died on the sword of a superior warrior and appreciated the honor of it." Ravn saw no reason to belabor a lesson so basic he had learned it as a toddler. "What did I do wrong?"

"You dishonored your sword!"

Ravn sighed. "I know that. I've apologized, and I'll atone." The latter would consist of driving personal practices with the weapon as well as a thorough cleansing. For mortals, prayers to the goddess Sif would accompany those acts of penance. Often, they would consider themselves unworthy of the blade and would never dare to use it again. "What did I do that got you mad enough to turn me into a soggy bundle of aching muscles?"

"Has it really been that bad?"

"My arms don't work. Mama might have to undress me and put me to bed."

For the first time, Colbey smiled, a small, indulgent grin. "Good."

Good? Ravn dried his hands on britches equally wet. "I'm glad one of us is happy. Now what did I do?"

"Come here." Colbey headed across the grassy plain of

Asgard, each blade a perfect triangle of green-edged blue. He led Ravn on a winding course over the plains, onto a twisting path between perfect evergreens, to the banks of a crystal lake Ravn knew well. Tan and white ducks paddled across the calm waters while water beetles hopped and somersaulted on the surface. Occasionally, a fish flashed silver in the sunlight, nose momentarily visible as it snapped up an insect. Colbey sat on a rock outcropping in a position that appeared relaxed, though it no longer fooled Ravn. He knew his father could rise and cut quicker than Ravn could picture him doing so, no matter how comfortable he appeared. Colbey's hands rested on gray-white boulders, and he stretched his legs in the sunshine.

Ravn remaining standing, confused by what seemed a drastic change in his father's strategy.

"Look," Colbey said.

Ravn continued to study the natural actions of animals on the pond, reveling in stillness after hours of grueling swordplay and the fresh, cool breeze blowing across his sweaty features. The panorama of motion and color never ceased to entertain, though he often feared that eternal life might turn even this pleasure into a dull routine. Freya never seemed to find enjoyment in the simple beauties, but Colbey did. Ravn wondered whether this difference stemmed from his father's relative youth or whether his eight decades as a mortal allowed him to appreciate things Ravn's mother never could. Now, as a thousand times before, Ravn vowed never to lose to boredom the natural loveliness of the world Odin had created. His friendship with Griff had developed that way, as a means to see the world through the eyes of a human mortal his own age.

"You do know that's exactly the problem." Colbey kept his eyes on the lake scene below, as if mesmerized.

Ravn sighed, not bothering to think back on his last spoken words. His father had read his thoughts. Ravn had learned long ago not to accuse Colbey of having done so on purpose. Colbey never invaded minds; things came to him, sometimes against his will. Ravn did not begrudge his father a talent that seemed as much a curse. He worked on his own lessons on mental strength, learning to channel energy from mind to body or in reverse as the situation demanded. Someday, he might become as competent with mind powers, just as he hoped to become Colbey's equal with a sword. "The problem is my friendship with a mortal?"

"Not the friendship by itself." Colbey leaned back slightly while the breeze toyed with the feathers of his hair. "There. That's man's world." Colbey gestured at the pond. "Each player fits into a role and acts in a reasonably predictable way."

Ravn watched the ducks. He could not anticipate every turn they took, but their swimming, splashing, and feeding formed a familiar routine.

"Add man." Colbey tossed a pebble into the water. It struck with a wet, hollow sound, tiny rings widening from its landing. The ducks glanced nervously toward the place the stone had landed, and fish did not feed for several moments. Then, gradually, the cycle returned to normal. "A bit of chaos, but still mostly predictable. Things change, but the world adapts, and man becomes a part of the picture."

"Enter gods." Colbey hefted another stone and threw it. Even as Ravn's eyes followed its course, he realized his father had switched a boulder for the pebble. The hunk of rock slammed the surface hard enough to raise a wild wave of water. The ducks rocketed into the sky, screeching warning. Washed away in the aftermath, the bugs disappeared from sight. Ripples disturbed the surface long after the rock had settled to the bottom. "No matter how hard we try to keep our actions tiny, we cannot. Everything immortals do on man's world gains unexpected momentum and mass. There, the gods can do nothing small." At last, he looked at Ravn directly. "Ravn, you're young now and the son of one raised mortal. You can still interact with humans, mostly with impunity. Over time, however, even the least of your actions will prove too much. You need to learn restraint."

Now the cause of Colbey's wrath became obvious. Ravn turned defensive before he could stop himself. "I had to protect Griff from those elves. They would have killed him."

"Maybe. Maybe not. We'll never know."

Ravn could not contain his temper. "You weren't there, damn it! Griff didn't have a chance without me."

"Then he would have died."

Ravn could not believe the calmness of his father's proclamation. "Griff can't die!"

"All humans die."

"He can't die now. It would mean the end of humankind."

"That remains to be seen."

"But . . ." Ravn started and stopped, realizing he had begun to sputter. Loudness would get him nowhere. He needed strong ammunition to back his argument. "It's the goal of the Renshai to keep a neutral king in Béarn. You've always said Sterrane and his heirs are the central key to mankind's survival. Without Griff, humans will collapse into chaos. And the second war of gods will come, completing the destruction the first did not."

Colbey sat in silence for a long time, displaying a patience he never had during his mortal years. "We're making suppositions based on a source of knowledge I no longer trust. When Odin still lived, no one could surpass his wisdom. But he did not always speak what he knew as truth. In the end, he misled us all. In the long run, his loyalty was only to himself and his own survival."

Ravn bent his points to follow this new tack. "You're committed to balance."

Colbey nodded.

"Without Griff, there can be no balance."

Colbey shrugged. "We don't know that for certain. I believe it to be true, however."

Given that admission, Ravn easily drove home his point. "If I hadn't assisted, he would have died."

"Maybe." Colbey refused to concede. "We'll never know. It's best for gods to let men handle their own affairs."

Ravn could scarcely believe his father's words. He kicked at the outcropping, ignoring the shower of pebbles that tumbled into the lake. "You've interfered. Recently."

Colbey did not deny the assertion.

"And Mama's told me she helped you when you lived on Midgard and the other gods mistakenly believed you worked for chaos."

Colbey smiled and rose gracefully. "Ah, then. Take home the right lessons from that story. First, Freya took the form of a hawk and never spoke directly to me. Second, when I fought Thor, she made no assumptions about who would win that fight. She knew Thor had based his attack on a misconception and that he would cease once he knew the truth. She also realized the destruction would start no matter which of us died. She did not harm either of us, as you did the elves. She merely created a distraction, gaining the time for others to explain the situation to me and to Thor."

Ravn gave the explanation the consideration it deserved. Not yet ready to wholly surrender, he added, "She also watched over you."

"She stayed at my side." Colbey smiled at the memory, gazing at the pond again. "And she gave an occasional warning. But she did not involve herself in the battles nor interfere. Nor did she reveal herself to me."

Ravn nodded. "So I can still watch over Griff?"

"Like all students, I expect you to make mistakes ... and to learn from them. If you do wrong again, I'll let you know."

Ravn rubbed at his aching forearms, never doubting Colbey would do exactly as he promised. For now, the words of wisdom seemed more like a threat.

Footsteps echoed eerily through the damp murk of Béarn's dungeon, and Knight-Captain Kedrin had long ago ceased to speculate abut whose presence they might herald. When a month, then two, had dragged past and Ra-khir had not come, Kedrin ceased to care about the identity of his occasional visitors. He had never worried about other dealings guards might have there. When he asked, a prison sentry had told him Ra-khir had taken a leave of absence from his knight's training, presumably to return to his mother in Erythane. But Kedrin knew better. Surely, Ra-khir had gone to rescue Béarn from its desperate dilemma.

Sound reverberated strangely in Béarn's dungeon, and Kedrin could not tell in which direction the visitor traveled. Journal in his lap, pen poised for more writing, Kedrin tried to ignore the thump of each step, but its peculiarity grasped his attention and stopped the flow of words. Usually, the guards whipped through with a confidence that came from long familiarity. These steps had a faltering, erratic quality that did not suit one accustomed to coming to this place. Whether the new arrival's uncertainty stemmed from fear of the type of men usually found in a prison, from insecurity, indecisiveness, or some more complex reason, Kedrin could not surmise. Unless the other came to him, he would never discover the answer.

Kedrin sighed, saddened that he had spent enough time in Béarn's dungeon to understand routines and interpret noises. But he would not bemoan his fate. He had done as his honor dictated and refused to regret the decision.

The footsteps continued, now definitely headed toward him. Even as he placed his parchment and pen aside, rising to greet the visitor, Baltraine came into view. The Knight of Erythane was surprised, and the hesitancy of Baltraine's approach confused him. Always before, Baltraine had exuded the confidence befitting his rank and title.

Kedrin bowed respectfully to his superior.

Almost imperceptibly, Baltraine cringed. Kedrin took that as a positive sign, an ability to feel guilt for a cruel mistake. Nevertheless, his honor would not allow him to take advantage of the prime minister's emotional state. "How are you, Captain?" Baltraine asked.

"Well enough," Kedrin replied, resisting the temptation to turn to sarcasm. "And you, Minister?"

Baltraine sighed. "Not so good."

"I'm sorry," Kedrin said sincerely. "Is there something I can do?"

Baltraine studied the fallen captain of the Knights of Erythane through dark eyes that betrayed pain. "There's trouble, and I'm not certain where to turn. Spiritually, I was guided here." His eyes widened ever so slightly, requesting support but expecting ridicule.

Kedrin would not judge. Divine guidance came in many forms, and he believed his own honor inspired by gods. Whether it came in the form of heartfelt understanding or the pattern of leaves on a pond, it had brought Baltraine to him. Kedrin refused to lose another chance to strengthen the kingdom and help shape Béarn's failing politics. "Explain the circumstances, my lord, and I will try to help as I can."

Baltraine slumped, tensed, then settled at a level slightly calmer than previously. He had shed a great burden until mistrust drove him to shoulder most of it again. "There are problems in Béarn. I'd like your advice." Though straightforward, the words and tone implied something more.

Again, Kedrin understood. Whatever bothered Baltraine went beyond discussion with ministers in a council room. Baltraine wanted recommendations from one who would not judge previous actions, who would not take credit for his ideas, and who would disappear without complaint should Baltraine choose to ignore some or all of the suggestions. It seemed ironic to the knight that the man jailed for pushing his own ideas too hard could now perfectly fill that niche. Imprisonment had unwittingly turned Kedrin into exactly the sort of adviser Baltraine believed he needed. And, if it meant the prime minister and regent would consider his ideas, Kedrin could find the positive light to his own suffering. "I will always steer anyone who asks toward the best course for Béarn. You need only ask."

Baltraine looked away. If not for the darkness of his mane, Kedrin might have missed the slight blush of pink that touched his cheeks. "King Kohleran has lapsed into permanent coma."

Though inevitable, the news struck hard. Kedrin found himself without words for several moments, glad Baltraine had not yet asked a question. Tears blurred his vision to a shimmering, liquid veil. "I'm sorry," he managed, the words heartfelt but inadequate. The tragedy itself paled in significance compared to its consequences. Death had come for King Kohleran after long illness, but the lack of an heir might herald worse for all mankind.

Baltraine's voice hardened. "Only you, I, and the master healer know this." He glanced around the dungeon to indicate he had made arrangements to keep their conversation private. Whether that entailed moving the other prisoners to places where their conversation did not reach or constructing barriers to block the sound, Kedrin did not try to guess. He had ignored the movements of guards and prisoners except when they related to himself.

Kedrin's white-blue eyes widened in surprise. It seemed impossible to keep such a significant event from the notice of others. "I will not betray your confidence," he said, knowing Baltraine would trust his knight's honor. "How did the envoy fair?" Baltraine's presence gave him part of the answer. Had it done well, the prime minister would have no reason to come here. Yet knowing the envoy failed did not supply Kedrin with the details he needed to speculate about the fate of his son.

"Two envoy parties and three scouts have disappeared without a trace." Baltraine delivered horrible news in a monotone. "We sent the last scout with a note telling anyone who discovered him in whatever state to contact the kingdom. We offered a reward."

Kedrin nodded, the reasoning sound. So long as the scout had gone voluntarily, aware of the dangers of the mission and the uncertainty of his fate, Kedrin condoned the strategy. The lure of gold would encourage footpads to return the scout alive rather than dead. If not, travelers who might otherwise simply burn, bury, or avoid the body might bring it back or, at least, report on the scout's progress. Money might sway assassins to betray one another or could bring one out in the open when he came with false stories and a claim on the money.

"Nothing. Even the last attempt brought no word."

The implications of Baltraine's words hit him hard. In a reckless attempt to rescue the kingdom, Kedrin could well have committed his son to a horrible death. What had once seemed sound strategy now seemed hopeless insanity. Self-loathing flared intolerably; guilt seemed to replace his blood with liquid fire. He had sent six brave knights and his own child into the unknown, a void from which none had returned. A father's instincts hammered him mercilessly for the decision, though leadership training and experience fought the judgment. Given the circumstances, he could have done nothing different. Pain settled to a constant, dull ache in Kedrin's soul, and he forced his concentration back to Baltraine.

"There's more bad news," Baltraine admitted, his voice a barely recognizable ghost of its usual resonance. "Béarn has fallen into disarray. Those heirs still living have mostly succumbed to madness. Citizens have taken sides. Factions have risen, each supporting their own vision of who should become the next king, usually themselves or their relations." Baltraine's lips pursed, lost in his beard; and he shook his head sadly. "Many have forsaken the king's line. Some have condemned me." He glanced sidelong at Kedrin, perhaps believing he had chosen his confidant wrongly.

Horrified by the chaos, Kedrin gaped. "They desert the line of kings? They question King Kohleran's regent? What fools!" Kedrin paced, needing to work off the energy created by his concern for his son and the country he had pledged to serve. An unthinkable urge seized him to collapse into a corner and let tears cleanse his pain, but it did not last long, replaced by rage. His hands balled to impotent, white-knuckled fists.

Baltraine seized on Kedrin's anger to request a favor. "One group has rallied around you. Perhaps if I freed you—"

"No!" Kedrin grasped the bars. He would have none of it. "Regent, bowing to terrorists is always a bad idea, and reversing a decision made by our king would only further erode his support . . . and yours."

Prime Minister Baltraine stared, as if he could not believe Kedrin had spoken. "You want to stay imprisoned?"

Kedrin kneaded the cold steel. "It isn't a matter of what I want. It's a matter of Béarn's security and her future." He released the bars to resume pacing. "Once the populace loses faith in their history and religion, nothing remains."

Baltraine kicked at an irregularity in the floor stones, expression earnest. "Then come and talk to them. Let them know you're here of your own volition."

Again, Kedrin shook his head. "It would convince no one. Those who wish to oppose you would claim torture, drugs, or coercion forced me to speak that way."

Baltraine muttered something unintelligible. "Then what can I do?"

Kedrin tried to make his point without simplifying a complicated situation. "You keep the peace, using the guards as necessary. I will instruct the knights to stand in support of you—their loyalty to the king's regent would not allow them to do otherwise—and also to help unite Béarn's citizens." Kedrin went still, drawing back to the bars to make his next point. Baltraine might well take it as an insult, and Kedrin already knew the danger of affronting the prime minister. Nevertheless, he would speak his mind without faltering, his only compromise to choose his words with care. "Regent, only those who pass the staff-test seem to have the ability to consistently make the right choices for Béarn. It runs in the king's line, a gift from the gods, I believe."

Baltraine tried to anticipate Kedrin. "We need to find and establish the proper heir. I know that."

"Yes," Kedrin confirmed. "And, in the meantime, you'll have to rule as best you can. Our beloved king wanted it that way."

"And the people can't know about his condition. It would cause a panic. Riots."

Kedrin frowned. "I won't condone lying."

Baltraine's brows shot up. "You made a vow."

"Nor will I break my vow," Kedrin added. "I'm just advising, my lord, not threatening."

Baltraine closed his mouth and nodded.

"For the sake of balancing forces, the gods have always seen to it that Béarn remains effectively governed. The most efficient system remains a single king or queen with flawless judgment."

Baltraine nodded again, a grudging agreement. He remained silent, allowing Kedrin to finish.

Kedrin measured Baltraine as he spoke, prepared to revise strategy and words as Baltraine's expressions made it necessary. So far, he had managed to keep his information general. As he narrowed in on specifics, the danger that Baltraine would act in anger grew. Kedrin would do Béarn no good by driving Baltraine into foolishness based on pride. "That only works, though, when the proper heir sits on the throne. Any other, the gods proclaimed, will not have the natural balance to properly rule."

Baltraine's eyes narrowed slightly.

Kedrin attributed the expression to consideration rather than offense and continued. "By King Kohleran's intention, you will rule until a sanctioned heir can be found. Your judgment, though sound, cannot be considered wholly neutral."

Baltraine seemed to handle that well, so Kedrin did not press. To use specific examples, such as Baltraine's personal vendetta against the knight-captain, would prove unnecessarily provocative. He continued, "I think it would behoove you and the kingdom of Béarn not to make any major decisions by yourself."

A frown deeply scored Baltraine's face. Kedrin walked the narrow boundaries between propriety and aspersion. But, to Kedrin's surprise, the prime minister maintained his calm. "What do you suggest?" he asked, a harshness to his tone all that betrayed his irritation.

"A council," Kedrin said. "Not necessarily the ministers, although it could include some of them. If it were up to me, I would choose it this way." He continued to study Baltraine, alert to the moment he overplayed his hand. "Three or five. Odd numbers work better for problem solving. More than five brings in too much dissension and too many approaches. The choosing should be done with caution and certainly should not include only those with opinions similar to your own. Otherwise, you might just as well rule alone. On the other hand, those of extreme opinions might prevent anything from getting decided. Best to find moderates loyal to Béarn."

"That's your advice?" Baltraine spoke softly.

"It is."

"And would you consent to becoming a part of this council?"

Kedrin had not specifically considered such a thing. "Only if you thought it best." A direct answer seemed more appropriate. "If you asked me, I would accept." He added, "Unless conditions placed upon that acceptance went against my honor, of course."

Baltraine smiled, though it was strained. "Of course." He did not go on to actually make the request, however, a detail that Kedrin appreciated. Whether it came of divine guidance or fear, a sudden, dramatic change in Baltraine's attitude could not last. Unless the transition involved long consideration and careful attention, Baltraine would never fully accept his own decision. The prime minister kept his grin pinned in place for longer than convention dictated. "What are you writing?" He inclined his head toward the journal on the floor.

Though acutely aware of its presence, Kedrin followed Baltraine's gesture. He studied the crude book and stylus the guards had allowed him in his solitude. "It's a journal." He tried to sound matter-of-fact. "I started writing it out of boredom. But it's become more of a treatise to my son."

"Your son?" Baltraine repeated.

Surely, Baltraine suspected it would contain information about their run-in that might embarrass him. And it did, although Kedrin had chosen the best words he could find to soften the implications. The book contained much more, the imprisonment and his handling of it only a small part of the whole. It explained his reasons for allowing most of the lies Ra-khir's mother told to go unchallenged. It detailed why he treated the matter the way he did, exposing many of the discrepancies, problems, and approaches Ra-khir could not otherwise understand. Kedrin's journal contained long discussions of honor, including hypothetical situations and explanations for his choices. On the current pages, he was rationalizing his reaction to Baltraine's accusations.

Self-indulgent. Kedrin could think of no other description for his work. Placing his own deepest considerations into words, reawakening the many painful and difficult decisions he had made, forced him to relive agonies he would sooner have forgotten. Still, if his ethical discourses helped one knight to choose the right course, if it assisted Ra-khir's understanding of problems that plagued his young soul, it would prove worth all the pathos.

Finally, after a pause that lasted way too long, Kedrin addressed Baltraine's query. "My son, yes. My honor means everything to me, and I would not forsake it to save my own life. But all the same holds true for my son. What's best for me is not always best for him. Ra-khir may not agree with all the choices I've made, but I want him to understand them. Bitterness has caused more than one good knight to betray his honor. I don't want that to happen to Ra-khir."

Baltraine rocked on his heels, brown eyes wide and mouth twisted. Clearly, he gave full thought to Kedrin's words. The response that followed his consideration could not have surprised Kedrin more. "Whatever happens, I will see to it Ra-khir gets that journal." He met Kedrin's gaze without flinching. "I can't let it endanger Béarn, of course."

"Nor could I," Kedrin added hastily.

Baltraine nodded. "So after you're finished, I might have to hold it until you and I have passed away."

Kedrin lowered his head but nodded also. He could hope for nothing more.

"But eventually Ra-khir will receive it." Baltraine spoke in a strong voice, making his words a promise.

"Thank you," Kedrin said softly, concern rising again. None of this mattered unless Ra-khir lived. If the young knight-in-training had gone to search for Béarn's heir, he may well have fallen prey to the same fate as the scouts and envoys. By now, he could have sent word had his mission succeeded. Kedrin felt the warm sting of tears and fought them down. Baltraine would not understand such a reaction, and Kedrin did not wish to explain. Although he would have liked details about his son, to elicit them meant telling about the task he had suggested to the knight-in-training. Anyone with knowledge of the mission potentially jeopardized it. "Thank you so much."

"It's the very least I can do to make amends." Baltraine seemed to mean words Kedrin never expected to hear. "The very least."

Baltraine left Béarn's prison with a confused muddle of thoughts to sort through and a tiny ray of hope. One thing seemed certain as he trod the corridors to his quarters: more good would come of working with Kedrin than against him.

His divine visitor had, at least, steered him right. But the details still eluded him. He never doubted any suggestion from Kedrin would have Béarn's best interests at its root. Yet, the advice, in a small way, had contradicted itself. The knight-captain had talked about a council made up of moderates and avoiding extremes. He had agreed to become a member, though knights clearly embraced one of the very excesses Kedrin had cautioned him to avoid. Their honor had come to define law, and the small lies necessary to keep things running smoothly would become a point of contention if Kedrin joined the governing body he advocated.

Other ideas plagued Baltraine as he walked the final hallways, noticing none of the finery around him. He had gone to the church, then the dungeon, in a blithering panic. His calm discussion with Kedrin had restored some of his flagging confidence and allowed other crucial issues to come to the fore. Did he dare trust the opinions of inferiors when it came to making policy or decisions that affected the kingdom? As Kedrin pointed out, King Kohleran had chosen Baltraine as his regent. It made no sense to consider the ideas of others as valid as his own. Baltraine clung to the power of his position, the source from which all positive feeling about himself stemmed. Then, too, he had to ponder the best interests of his daughters and, eventually, of their children.

These thoughts haunted Baltraine into the night and the following day, and still he seemed no closer to making a decision. Day after day, Baltraine agonized over his next course of action, weighing his loyalty to self, family, king, world, and kingdom.

While Béarn collapsed all around him.

Chapter 27

Pudar's Audience

There's nothing honorable about a duty in and of itself; it's the performance of that duty to the best of your ability that gives it virtue.

—Colbey Calistinsson

A dank haze filled the city streets of Pudar, as if the mood of the citizenry had tainted the weather. Staring out the cottage window, Kevral knew a desperateness and restless irritation, scarcely worsened by Darris' sudden surgery. Matrinka hovered over his bedside in the only other room, the fear of losing him to infection or the technical aspects of the operation giving way to concerns that he would not recover from the shock.

Kevral did not know why the guards kept the market closed and the citizens off the streets; she could only surmise from rumors. Most agreed a great tragedy had rocked the kingdom, though speculation ranged from threats of war to the death of the king or queen. No matter the reason, it kept them from buying necessities, including food. Their own supplies had run out days ago. If not for the last dregs of their traveling rations, they would not have made it even that far.

With a sigh, Kevral pulled away from the window, drawing her swords with a suddenness that startled Ra-khir from his chair. His scramble for safety did not entertain her as much as she expected, which only added to her annoyance. She threw herself into a practice, her third of the morning.

Her swords sliced arcs through air thick with damp. Imaginary enemies fell before her onslaught while others sprang clear, returning every stroke with the competence and efficiency of Renshai.

Kevral lost herself in the practice, legs skimming over the wooden floor, body twisting lithely to avoid attacks and deal death strokes to fleeing opponents, arms melding with hilts and swords. The grace of the sweeps and patterns simulated dance, but the sharp and deadly blades stole all of the innocent beauty. Swords cleaved air, lines of quicksilver that shifted without pattern. Where her quiet study of the city had failed, the love of battle succeeded. All thought fled Kevral's mind, and no troubles remained in a head filled only with the savage joy of swordplay.

An angry shout from Ra-khir finally interrupted the pleasant world Kevral had temporarily created. Enraged by the interference, she momentarily considered turning her swords against him. Sanity intervened. Kevral let the blades fall lax at her sides, a withering glare the only threat she turned in the Erythanian's direction.

Ra-khir dashed out a quick breath, the only evidence that he felt relieved to have finally caught her attention. Clearly, he had called for her to halt the practice more than once. Before Kevral could huff out a warning about the dangers of disturbing a Renshai practice, or Ra-khir could justify his reasons, a knock hammered through the confines. The volume and intensity indicated impatience. The caller, too, had clearly vied for her attention.

Kevral sheathed her swords even as Matrinka emerged from the sickroom to answer the summons her engrossed companions had ignored.

Matrinka pulled open the door to reveal three men dressed in the tan uniforms of Pudar's guardsmen and a fourth in dirty homespun. The guards appeared robust, muscles defined against linen tunics. One had sandy hair that fell to his shoulders, and the other two had darker locks in shorter cuts. One sported a beard and mustache. The fourth man seemed the piece that jarred. His black hair and swarthy features evoked images of Béarn, but he lacked the usual bulk. He wore a beard but no mustache. "That's them," he said before the door swung fully open.

Kevral smoothed her hair back into place and wiped away

dribbles of sweat from her cheeks with the back of her hand. Ra-khir examined the newcomers.

Matrinka curtsied a polite welcome. "Good day, sirs. What can we do for you?"

The mustached man glanced at Kevral and Ra-khir but addressed Matrinka. "Are you the companions of an Easterner by the name of Tae Kahn?"

"Why, yes. Yes, we are," Matrinka replied before Kevral could think to stop her or say otherwise. A frown deeply scored Ra-khir's face, but he did not contradict Béarn's princess.

The guard made a wordless noise deep in his throat. "Are you relatives?"

"I'm afraid not," Matrinka responded, glancing at her friends.

Ra-khir took over, apparently concerned about the information Matrinka might naively reveal. "Certainly not, good sir. He's an orphan." As politeness demanded, he answered the question before launching into the proper introduction that should have occurred first. "My name is Ra-khir—"

"And I'm Kevral." The Renshai jumped in before Ra-khir could continue his lengthy title. The recognition of a Knight of Erythane in Pudar would spark questions that might jeopardize their mission. "I'm afraid Ra-khir and Tae never got along very well."

Ra-khir opened his mouth again, and Kevral cringed at the thought that his honor might drive him to finish his name regardless of the conversation's turn.

But Ra-khir apparently accepted Kevral's less than subtle hint. "Is Tae in some sort of trouble?"

Kevral pursed her lips, as committed as Ra-khir to making certain Tae's trouble did not become their own.

The guard's features hardened, and his pale eyes flicked from Kevral to Matrinka to Ra-khir. "He killed the heir to Pudar's throne. Is that enough trouble for you?"

Stunned silent, Ra-khir did not answer.

Matrinka's expression went from openly startled to bunched and skeptical in a moment. "Oh, no," she said with amazing calm under the circumstances. "A terrible mistake has been made. Tae would never do such a thing."

Kevral did not feel nearly so certain of their onetime companion's innocence. A chill traversed her. She knew little of Pudar's law, but she guessed she and her companions would need to choose their words and actions with care. Matrinka's candidness and Ra-khir's honor required a monitoring Kevral did not feel qualified to handle, at least not without some prior discussion about control. "As you can see, we've got a mixed group here." Explaining the oddity seemed a better strategy than trying to pretend it did not exist. She looked fair enough to pass for a Northerner, and Ra-khir's features and coloring could come of any Western background. Matrinka typified Béarn. "We decided to travel the world and thought it best to have a well-rounded team. We didn't have an Easterner, so we hitched up with Tae. He didn't work out, though, so we left him behind way back in the woods." She gestured vaguely southwest. "We didn't even know he was here in town." Kevral glanced at her companions for confirmation.

Matrinka said nothing. Ra-khir frowned, presumably to register his disapproval of Kevral's lie, but he did nod once to indicate the appropriateness of her last statement.

One of the guards made a wordless noise, and all three exchanged glances. The Easterner accompanying them shook his head gently to and fro, a glower scoring his features.

Kevral studied the Pudarian who had, thus far, done all of the talking. Impatient and feeling persecuted, she concentrated on keeping her hands away from her swords.

Ra-khir cleared his throat, and Kevral stiffened at what he might say. "Good sir, we're extremely and truly saddened by the news of the crown prince's demise. We're horrified that we might have once known the assassin. We will, of course, assist you in any way possible. But we and Tae parted company some time ago. What exactly can we do for you?"

The onus returned to the guards, and Kevral studied them for evidence of threat. Their tenseness had been apparent from the start, but she saw no specific movements to indicate impending violence. Suddenly, she appreciated Ra-khir's breeding. He had phrased the matter well, better than she could have hoped to do; and he ended with the very question plaguing her.

The mustached guard spoke again. "We thought those who knew him might find a reason for such senseless brutality. And we need to find the killer's relations. There's blood price to pay."

The request seemed reasonable to Kevral, but she still believed it best to discuss the matter privately with her companions before trying to assert their ignorance. She seized on the ensuing silence to find an excuse. "Tae tended to talk more when he was with only one other person. Perhaps Matrinka, Ra-khir, and I can piece together the things he told each of us. Among us, we may find out where he came from and where his relations live. But I don't think we can do that with people standing over us." She raised her brows slowly, giving the others time to digest her words. "Could you come back in a day or so?"

The guards withdrew for discussion. Kevral examined the Easterner in their absence, but he avoided her gaze. Before she could contemplate why, the guards returned. "Be at the castle by sundown, and don't go anywhere else in the meantime. Until such time as the king decides, you may not leave Pudar."

Anger boiled up in Kevral, and she tasted acid. She tensed, prepared to express her opinion of their ultimatum in words she would surely regret.

Sensing Kevral's rage, Ra-khir spoke first. "Thank you, good sirs. We will do as you say." He bowed.

The guards returned the formality, and one opened the door.

Before they could leave, however, Matrinka voiced her concern. "You don't need us all to come to the castle, do you? We have a sick friend who needs tending, so one of us must stay here."

The speaker of the guards bowed again, this time toward Matrinka. "One or two will do. So long as the others don't leave town." Without further exchange, they headed outside. Matrinka closed the door behind them.

Kevral waited only until the latch clicked before releasing pent-up breath in a furious hiss. "How dare they tell me where I can and can't go!"

Ra-khir rolled his eyes. "That's just formality." The words sounded odd from one dedicating his life to similar formalities, equally idiotic to Kevral's thinking. "I knew Tae would get us in trouble." He added thoughtfully, "You don't suppose he did this to get back at us, do you?"

Kevral's laugh shattered the tension that had filled the room since the arrival of the Pudarian guards. "Of course he did. He was mad at us, so he decided to murder someone we don't know and guarantee himself a slow, painful death. That'll teach us a lesson."

"It's not funny!" Matrinka shouted, her voice pained and tearful. Her uncharacteristic loudness silenced both of her companions, and Mior peered into the room from her vigil at Darris' bedside. "A man is dead. A prince. That alone is reason for somberness."

Kevral lowered her head, ashamed.

"Now," Matrinka continued. "I know Tae didn't kill the crown prince of Pudar. I think you both realize it, too."

Kevral considered Matrinka's words. Mior padded to her mistress and rubbed against her legs. Ra-khir gently took Matrinka's hand. "My lady, I know it's hard to imagine someone we once considered a friend doing something so horrible. But we all know Tae is capable of evil."

Matrinka did not back down. "We're all *capable* of evil. But Tae didn't kill the crown prince of Pudar."

Matrinka's resolute certainty intrigued Kevral. "How do you know that?"

"It's not in his nature."

Ra-khir sighed, obviously daunted by the need to demonstrate a bad side invisible to his more innocent companion.

"I think it is," Kevral returned simply.

"That's because you think we parted ways with Tae when Ra-khir sent him away," Matrinka announced cryptically, hefting Mior.

The implications intrigued Kevral. She kept Matrinka too closely under watch for clandestine meetings with an exiled companion. "We didn't?" Kevral asked carefully.

Matrinka stroked Mior, shifting to give the cat access to her shoulders. "Who do you think has been buying our food? Why do you think the fruit-seller has been so generous? Where do you think the money we keep happening upon comes from?"

"Luck?" Ra-khir tried. "Coincidence?"

"Maybe," Kevral said, the amount of both generous for chance but certainly not impossible. Until now, she had accepted good fortune as fact and considered little else.

"Tae." Matrinka answered her own question the way neither of her companions would.

The last of Kevral's anger dispersed, leaving a bitter aftertaste.

Ra-khir furrowed his brow. "I think you're making assumptions here. There are more plausible explanations."

Although engaged in conversation with her companions,

Matrinka kept her attention on Mior. She fidgeted, obviously uncomfortable. She stiffened suddenly, clearly making a difficult decision, and her jaw set. Now, she met Ra-khir's gaze directly. "There *are* other explanations, but they are wrong. Tae has been helping us. It is simply the truth. And a man who anonymously assists those who abandoned him would not murder a prince . . . at least not without just cause."

The sureness of Matrinka's proclamation resisted denial. Not even vague doubt tinged her tone. Only the most devout priests could match the strength of those words, their faith a steady flame that could resist the tempest of uncertainty. A chill invaded Kevral. "You talk as if you saw these things."

"I didn't," Matrinka admitted. "But Mior did."

Kevral froze, torn between pity and laughter. Ra-khir's brows rose, but he covered all other reaction with masterful ease.

"Yes, I know it sounds silly. And, yes, I know you don't believe me. But Mior watches, and she tells me what she sees."

"We believe you," Kevral said carefully.

"No, you don't," Matrinka denied the possibility with an insightfulness that did not suit the absurdity of her previous claim. "You don't believe me, but I can prove it. And I will."

"That's not necessary." Ra-khir looked sidelong at Kevral, his glance suggesting the need for caution. Obviously, he also believed the stress of their mission, combined with Darris' injury and the current situation, had proved too much for Matrinka's sanity.

"It *is* necessary," Matrinka insisted. "Without proof, you may humor me, but you won't truly believe. Tae needs your faith."

"What do you want us to do?" Kevral asked, knowing Matrinka too well to believe her capable of a trick, yet too linked to reality to trust such a story.

"You can test it however you want," Matrinka said. "If you work out the details, you're more likely to believe the results." She scratched Mior's ears and under the chin while the cat purred.

Ra-khir cleared his throat. "Just hearing her say something would be enough for me." He seemed uncomfortable with even acknowledging Matrinka's suggestion.

Kevral nodded agreement.

Matrinka sighed. "She doesn't talk out loud. It's a mental thing. And it's not in exactly specific words, either. It's hard to explain. The best test would be to have me leave the room. You do or say something in front of Mior, and I'll tell you about it."

"Oh," Ra-khir said. "Well." He looked at Kevral.

Kevral obliged. "How about if I whisper a number in your ear and Mior taps out the right amount with her paw?"

"Back paw," Ra-khir added.

"All right," Matrinka said with apparent reticence. "But that's awfully easy. You might be more convinced by something complicated."

"That'll do," Kevral insisted, seeing no reason to humiliate Matrinka in a grand fashion.

"Yes, it will," Ra-khir affirmed.

Matrinka helped the calico down from her shoulder. "Mior, go sit in one of the corners near the door." She resisted the urge to point the way, but Mior still padded to the indicated position.

Though impressed by the cat's obedience, Kevral made no judgments yet. She had seen many dogs who complied with more complex commands, though her limited experience with cats suggested they were not so easily trained. She approached Matrinka and whispered "seven" into her ear.

Matrinka did not bother to face Mior. The cat tapped out seven beats with a hind paw, then calmly sat and cleaned her whiskers.

Kevral stared in silent wonder.

Matrinka turned to Ra-khir. "Want a try?"

"All right," he said slowly and came to Matrinka's side. He hissed something Kevral could not hear.

Again, Matrinka did not bother to look at the animal, though a small smile crept onto her face. Mior delicately raised and lowered the back paw twice then lifted it and kept it dangling. Her yellow eyes fixed directly on Ra-khir, and she wore an almost human expression of impatient questioning.

Ra-khir made a noise to indicate both awe and satisfaction. "Two and a half. Who'd have believed it?" He stepped away from Matrinka to take a stand at Kevral's side. "Tell her she can put it down now."

Mior delicately lowered her foot to the floor, then sat expectantly.

Matrinka frowned. Since she had obviously convinced Ra-khir, Kevral guessed her reaction was aimed at the cat, apparently in response to something unspoken.

"What did she say?" Kevral asked, skepticism turning to curiosity.

"It wasn't polite," Matrinka admitted. "She doesn't understand human needs sometimes, but she's willing to appease them. At least yours. Now, what are we going to do about Tae?"

Mior rose, stretched with dignity, then trotted out of the room, presumably to tend Darris again.

Kevral watched her go, still puzzling over the cat after the subject had changed to more pressing matters. "For one so intelligent, she doesn't even acknowledge us."

Matrinka looked after her pet as she disappeared through the door. "She's a cat, not a four-legged human. She's better with emotions than words. And she can't count well, by the way. I had to help her."

Kevral remained silent, still marveling at a form of communication she had dismissed as nonsense moments ago.

Ra-khir pushed red hair from his forehead and away from his eyes. "From talking to Tae, I'm not sure if he's an orphan or not. He never said for sure. But I'm still not as convinced as you about his innocence."

Kevral sucked air through her nose and let it out slowly through her teeth, an adjunct to a relaxation technique that served as part of her Renshai training. Focusing on Mior, and Matrinka's strange relationship with the cat, had allowed her to shove aside consideration of Tae for a few moments. Dread trickled through her, sending her heart into a wild thumping that pounded in her head. Matrinka's stunt had reestablished a relationship Kevral had forced from her mind for more than a month. The vilified version of Tae that her thoughts had drawn crumbled. She pictured the quick, dark eyes that seemed to catch everything and the black hair worn too long. Unkempt and unruly, it gave him a look of danger reinforced by features full of life and intelligence. "I believe he may be innocent. I want to hear his side of the story. And the other side, for that matter."

Ra-khir's green eyes roved over Kevral's features, as if to read past her words. "Perhaps it would be best, then, if you went to the castle. I will accompany you, if you wish."

Kevral took another deep breath then shook her head. "Matrinka and I will go."

Matrinka opened her mouth as if to protest, then glanced at Kevral and closed it again. Even through the weeks of restless waiting and worry over Darris, Kevral had never allowed Matrinka to go farther alone than into the other room of their rented cottage. "All right," she finally said.

Ra-khir nodded once, without protest. He had long ago learned the futility of arguing with Kevral when it came to matters of Matrinka's welfare. "Be careful," he admonished. "And look to Matrinka for appropriate decorum in the castle."

Kevral shrugged off the insult. She had spent enough time in Béarn's keep with her charge to understand, as well as despise, the formalities of royalty. She retired to Darris' room to change clothes and ready herself, drawing energy together for a discussion that might try her nerves to the point of breaking. She promised herself she would keep her mind open, listen to all the facts, and avoid making judgments based on emotion. If the proof convinced her of Tae's guilt, she would lobby for a painless execution. If she became certain of his innocence, she would fight a desperate battle for his freedom, if necessary. He would not die a silent scapegoat of a tragedy not of his making. Kevral would see to that. And only her need to guard a princess of Béarn would take precedence.

Pudar's cool air and empty streets seemed a pleasure to Kevral after far too much time cooped up in a cottage while Matrinka tended her wounded charge. Curtains shivered aside as they passed, and people tracked their progress down cobbled streets filthy with foot tracks and chipped by the wheels of merchant carts. Pyrite and quartz glimmered like tiny stars in the cobbles, a detail the hordes of shoppers had obliterated in the past. Guards marched along the throughways at intervals, their tan uniforms, weapons, and sharp demeanors unmistakable. These studied the pair of women headed toward the castle, then ignored them or nodded an acknowledgment of their right to traipse the streets at a time all others were held at bay.

Just before they left the house, Kevral had recited a crisp warning to her companions not to reveal their true mission to anyone. At a time when enemies remained hidden and dangerous, they could not afford to have any person other than themselves knowing of Griff's existence. Once outside, however, Kevral had lapsed into silence. After monitoring Ra-khir and Matrinka, the princess alone should prove a simpler matter.

Kevral and Matrinka wound through roadways lined with stands, empty and covered with tarps. Shops, usually cheerful, were now bolted and forbidding. Many concerns flooded Kevral's mind. She had watched Matrinka and Darris over the weeks, had seen their love strengthen as the threat of death hovered over them. So many times, they sat in silence, studying one another with a passion that seemed tangible or whispering conversations Kevral could not politely overhear. The sweet, knowing smiles they exchanged had come to define affection in Kevral's mind. Sometimes it seemed nauseatingly sappy, and Kevral would practice sword maneuvers to rescue herself from the need to watch them. Sometimes, she knew mild pangs of jealousy, wondering. Once or twice, she had passed a moment with Ra-khir that evoked the same feelings. Often these had come during the most innocuous of conversations, spurred more by a glimpse of his eyes, features, or physique in just the right light. From moment to moment, she could not always remember if she cared for Ra-khir or loathed him, if she envied Matrinka and Darris or found them silly and tragic.

Kevral swept these concerns away, appalled by her contemplation of petty matters when Tae's life hung in the balance and their own fate seemed uncertain. Eventually, surely, Pudar would allow citizens and visitors free access to the streets again. She would not allow the grief of a city to keep her from carrying out the mission they had left Béarn to complete. If a kingdom had to fall, she much preferred Pudar to Béarn. The high kingdom of the West served as the central focus of balance and the cause to which Colbey had dedicated the Renshai in perpetuity.

The castle came into view, a vast structure of stone towers and turrets that cut a jagged outline against the gray sky. Thick with damp, the air tasted wet and heavy. The dinginess of the day made the empty shops, stands, and roadways look like moldy bones from a long-dead village. Kevral took Matrinka's hand and gave it a reassuring squeeze. For Tae, they would fight together and, perhaps, without the support of their male friends: one of whom had to follow his honor and the other of whom was recovering from an enemy's arrow.

The castle loomed nearer. Matrinka had chosen a dress she had hauled along and never before had the opportunity to wear. Kevral owned nothing so feminine and had donned the least travel-damaged of her tunics and britches, her wardrobe as practical as her short-cropped hair. The wrought iron gates remained closed as they approached, guarded by two sentries who stood inside the gates. These wore leather armor, broad swords belted at their waists, and had ax-bladed pole arms in hand. They did not speak as the women approached but opened the gates and freely allowed them access.

Matrinka curtsied politely to each. Kevral nodded stiffly, saving her manners for the inner courtroom. Resigning the formalities to Matrinka left her attention and hands free to guard. She did not know how other escorts handled such situations, but no one had reprimanded her for meager shows of respect in Béarn and she doubted they would do so here. The guards gave her no clue as they silently shut and bolted the gates. One led them toward the castle in silence while the other remained in position at the gates. Not one of them betrayed a hint of emotion, their faces locked into somber masks.

The one guard turned them over to two more at the castle entrance, then returned to his partner. These exchanged bows for curtsies from Matrinka before opening the door. Again, one remained at his post while the other guided them to an archway where a man dressed in more formal and colorful attire greeted them. "Welcome to Pudar's castle." His tone did not match his words; his dull monotone fit the dreariness of the day and the mournfulness that had assailed the city.

"Greetings," Matrinka returned. "I am Matrinka, and this is Kevral."

"Yes. That's right," the man replied, as if they might have gotten it wrong. His brown hair contained stray wisps of gray, mostly concentrated at the temples. Creases marred a face just entering middle age, and hazel eyes, much like Darris', studied them from a maze of crow's-feet. "Ladies, come with me."

Matrinka obeyed, Kevral shuffling after. Tapestries lined the walls, a myriad different stories and panels jumbled together without discernible pattern. Unlike the paintings in

Béarn, they told no contiguous story. Shortly, their guide led them into another room, furnished with couches, chairs, and a table that held a bowl of fruit. "Wait here, please. We'll come for you soon." His gaze slid to Kevral's swords, and he frowned. "You'll have to leave the weaponry."

Kevral tensed. Her first instinct, to fight, passed quickly. She made no response for several moments, trying to imagine what Colbey would do in her situation. History told of many times when the greatest of all swordsmen had come into the presence of kings, but none of these addressed the details. A saying attributed to him did, however: "A Renshai is dangerous so long as he shares a room with a sword." In the past, the meaning had escaped Kevral. Now she saw it clearly. So long as the king's court contained a sword, and the presence of guards would assure that it did, she had nothing to fear. More than a hundred Renshai maneuvers involved disarm and recover tactics weaponless against an armed enemy. "Of course," she said, as if no time had passed. "So long as you return them when we leave."

"Certainly." The man gestured the women to the couch and sat on a chair across from it.

Matrinka and Kevral complied.

The man then launched into a dissertation on the proprieties of the king's court that Kevral tuned out after the first sentence. Matrinka leaned forward, showing a proper interest that Kevral attributed to breeding. She had heard a man blather on this long only once before, a Knight of Erythane at a state dinner. And she suddenly remembered where her disdain for knights had shifted from distant understanding to reality. Though alert to sudden movements that might pose a threat to Matrinka, Kevral otherwise let her attention wander where it would. Listening to the minister's litany would surely lull her to sleep.

At last, the lecture ended. Kevral left her sword belt in the minister's care, and guards accompanied them both to the presence of the king.

A dozen guards filled the audience chamber, dressed in mail over the standard tan uniforms. Their tabards bore the wolf symbol of Pudar, silver against a light brown background. A short-hilted, heavy-bladed sword hung at every left hip. The king sat on a padded chair. Inset gemstones in an array of colors glittered and winked in the light of lanterns that hung from rings in every wall. Curly, auburn hair ringed his face, liberally flecked with gray. He appeared old to Kevral, with his cheeks sagging and demeanor slumped. Blue eyes looked out from half-lidded eyes that sparked to life when the two women entered. He waited until they came directly in front of him before speaking. "You are companions of the man who killed my son?"

Matrinka executed an elegant curtsy. Kevral was still trying to copy the movements when the princess addressed the question. "No, Sire."

The king blinked, obviously taken aback. "No?" He glanced at the guard who had accompanied them, seeking confirmation that he attended the right audience. "You did not travel with one called Tae Kahn?"

"Yes, Sire." Matrinka's reply could be taken either way in light of the king's question. It required explanation, and she gave one freely. "We're Tae's friends."

The king's eyes narrowed to slits, and the wrinkles deepened. "Are you playing a game with me?"

"Certainly not, Sire." Matrinka displayed no fear as she returned the king's scrutiny, and her tone contained all the proper strength of a woman trained to court. "I simply wish to convey that we were once companions of Tae, not of the man who caused your son's demise. As to that, Your Majesty, we would like to express our sincerest sympathies regarding your loss and the kingdom's tragedy."

"Hmmm." The king sat back, obviously uncertain how to handle the situation. Matrinka's good wishes certainly sounded earnest to Kevral, but her approach might be considered insolent under the circumstances. No matter how politely, she had questioned the king's judgment.

Kevral remained silent. So far, Matrinka seemed capable of handling the situation. She was in her element now, and Kevral suspected their time spent traveling, and their confrontations with death, had strengthened Matrinka as well. Proud of her charge, who had come a long way since their first meeting, Kevral fought a smile.

The king of Pudar stiffened, leaning forward. The circle of guards tightened. Though subtle, the threat tripled Kevral's wariness. She measured the tiny details that would reveal each man's ability. Colbey had read his enemies' builds and movement, calculating their best maneuvers with a glance. Less experienced, she found the exercise difficult.

A long silence dragged before the king broke it once more. "My guards witnessed the event. An Easterner conclusively identified Tae Kahn and led us to you. I want only the names of his relations, then you may leave without further hardship."

Matrinka curtsied again, though it seemed unnecessary. Kevral attributed the maneuver to delay. "Majesty, we understand your need and again extend our sympathies at your loss. But we have lost someone dear to us as well and cannot stand to do so in ignorance. Knowing the particulars would prove invaluable."

Attentive to the guards, Kevral missed the king's expressive reaction to Matrinka's long-winded demand. The guards grew restless, some hands sliding to rest on hilts and others twitching. Kevral mentally prepared herself for action.

The king's pause grew dramatic. When words came, his voice boomed, displaying waning patience. "So you want to know what happened."

"Yes, Sire," Matrinka's voice sounded like a whisper in the wake of the king's.

"I'll tell you what happened." The king's fists clamped to the edges of his hand rests, blood draining from every finger. Though small, the violence of the movement drew Kevral's notice at once. "The Easterner you call Tae was getting the worst of a battle our informant says he caused by trying to steal. My too kindhearted son and his entourage attempted to rescue Tae, and the nasty little bastard slaughtered my son. The crown prince of Pudar! Killed trying to rescue a filthy, disgusting, thieving, little street rat. Now!" The king's voice became a shout. "All I want from you is the names of his family."

Though unaccustomed to court, Kevral knew they had prolonged the audience past the king's patience. Anything more might cause consequences they could not afford to pay. Surely Matrinka would end the discussion here.

Matrinka maintained all the calm dignity the king had lost. "Sire, forgive my persistence, please, and bear with my need. What does Tae say in his defense?"

The king's lips pursed, but slight motions of his jaw revealed that he ground his teeth. He glared at Matrinka, as if deciding whether to butcher her for steaks or just boil her alive. "Some nonsense about chanting children on rooftops and confusion caused by a blow to the head. He never denied murdering Prince Severin, and he held the dagger wet with my son's blood. Why then . . ." Blue eyes fixed the princess in place. "Why then are you the only one who won't accept the truth?"

Everyone in the room waited for Matrinka's answer. Although some still touched their weapons, no guard seemed poised for imminent battle. Kevral suspected that had more to do with her gender than any particular belief that the king would free them unopposed.

Matrinka's gentle speech seemed misplaced. "Sire, do you truly wish an answer to that question? Or was it purely rhetorical?"

Pudar's king drew in an enormous breath, loosing it slowly through flared nostrils. "An explanation followed by a recitation of relations. Then we are finished here."

"Very well." Matrinka did not flinch, composed despite the king's intensive scrutiny. "Sire, with all possible respect, the event you described has flaws. Why would a prince with an entourage draw near enough to a brawl to fall victim to it? Why would a man slaughter his rescuer? Why would anyone who cared enough for his life to fight for it then kill the prince of Pudar, knowing the obvious penalty? Why would any man kill the prince of Pudar on a whim? If he planned the assassination, doesn't it make sense that those men who attacked him, whose noise drew the prince, must have been a part of the conspiracy? But mostly, I know Tae well enough to believe he would never do such a thing, even in a state of confusion, pain, and fear."

The king stared impassively throughout Matrinka's speech, though Kevral doubted he listened to a single word. The litany did move Kevral to thought. The queries held significance, whether Tae or another was the killer.

"Are you finished?" the king said, manner and tone stiff.

"For the moment, Sire," Matrinka said. "I would need more information to continue."

"Good," the king knotted his fingers in his beard, settling back into the chair. "Now that I have suffered through your rationalizations, your defenses, and your insolence, I return to my question. Give me the names of Tae Kahn's relations, then my guards will escort you home."

"As far as I know, Sire," Matrinka started carefully, back-stepping probably without realizing she was doing it. "Tae has no relations. We believe he's an orphan."

"What?" The king bolted upright in his chair. The guards tensed visibly.

"We believe he's an orphan, Sire." Matrinka repeated.

"Liar!" the king of Pudar shouted. "You're still protecting him, you witch!"

Matrinka blinked several times in rapid succession, obviously taken aback by the king's behavior.

The king waved a hand in dismissal. "Take her to the dungeon until she chooses to talk."

The guards closed in, attentive to their king's command yet approaching as though they expected no trouble from these two. Five interposed themselves between the women and their king, and an equal number retreated toward the door. Kevral had eyes only for the two who headed for Matrinka.

Matrinka cringed, loosing a sharp, short noise of fear. Kevral leaped between her and the oncoming threat. As one guard reached for her, Kevral seized the opening. Her right hand darted to his sword hilt, and the blade rattled from its sheath. The guard grabbed for it, too late. Sharpened steel sliced his palm, and he recoiled beyond sword range. A wild, arcing cut sent the other skittering to safety as well, drawing his sword as he moved.

The five in front of the king closed to a tight wall of defense, weapons springing free at once. Kevral charged her other opponent, sword carving the haft from his hands. His blade flew free. The guard retreated, but Kevral never slowed. Trained to respect steel, she caught the hilt effortlessly in her other hand. The instant it settled into her grip, she sliced a savage web of silver through the air, holding all comers at bay and keeping Matrinka pinned against the wall behind her. Anyone who attempted to take the princess faced deadly, flying steel without discernible pattern. Yet Kevral knew she could not keep up this undirected defense for long. Eventually, even a Renshai must tire.

The first of the disarmed guards crouched, rage purpling his features. The second glanced from hand to Renshai in disbelief. The king said something she did not understand, and one guard broke away from the group at the door, charging Kevral with a bull bellow.

Matrinka screamed. Kevral let the guard come to her, braced for his onslaught. His sword circled, then whipped suddenly down. She deflected it with a deft parry, then hammered his hand with the flat of the other blade. The sword fell from his grasp. Attempting to stop, he skidded into the wall. Dexterously, he bounced and twisted aside, but not before opening his head to Kevral's offense. Instead of pressing her advantage, Kevral snatched up his sword a finger's breadth from the floor. *Better to win this fight by guile than slaughter.* Killing guards in a king's court meant sure execution. Little good came of battling herself, and her charge, free of one room into waiting ranks of soldiers and an angered town. If it came to death strokes, she would deal them; but not before she exhausted other means of escaping first.

Kevral hefted her three swords, two in the left hand and one in the right. Deliberately, she tossed one to the floor and stomped on it, a gesture of eminent disdain probably lost on Pudarians. She went still, eyes measuring the king's guards, waiting for the next move.

For several moments, they remained in stalemate. Five protected their king, four held the door, and the disarmed three stood in wary defense. The urge to battle her way through burned strongly in Kevral. She might even manage to slash a path out of the castle and the city of Pudar. Yet she had other lives than her own to consider. The moment she lost Matrinka, she lost the battle.

The king studied the situation through squinted eyes and beetled brows. "Get bowmen," he finally said.

The tactic seemed an obvious choice. Once the guards had a long-range weapon, they could stand back and pepper Kevral with arrows. One of the guards reached for the knob, prepared to follow his king's bidding.

Kevral could not afford to let him go unchallenged. "Your bowmen will find a roomful of corpses. I won't stand still and wait." She flicked one sword into an offensive position with an agility and skill the king's guards could not hope to match.

"Wait," Pudar's king commanded his guard.

The man obeyed, hand still on the latch.

The king looked at Kevral. "What's your name?"

"Kevral," she answered, without tacking on her lineage and tribal name.

"You're Renshai, aren't you?"

Kevral doubted lying would gain anything. No matter her answer, the king had already recognized the truth. "Yes. I am."

The king of Pudar looked doubtfully at Matrinka hunkered down behind Kevral, then back at the Renshai. Kevral held her breath, hoping he would not make the connection. She did not know how widespread details of Renshai had become, in particular their ties to Béarn's royalty.

"You're a skilled warrior," the king said, his own thick musculature revealing experience with warfare, or at least with training for it.

Kevral accepted the king's words without comment or relaxation of her stance. She took no compliment from them; he simply voiced the obvious. "I'm Renshai," she affirmed.

"So you are." The king glanced away from Kevral and to the first of his disarmed soldiers. The man looked away, cheeks flaming. "You could have killed some of my men, but you spared them. For that, you and your friend may leave my courtroom in peace."

Guards shifted, stiffened, and went wide-eyed at the king's mercy. Kevral lowered the swords.

"I ask only that you answer my original question honestly and that you not leave Pudar until after the execution of the assassin's sentence."

Kevral drew to her full height, meager in the midst of Pudarian guardsmen and a Béarnide woman. Although her swords remained in an inoffensive position, she could defend herself, if need be, more quickly than any of these guards could attack. "To the best of my knowledge, Tae is an orphan. As to the second, that all depends on how quickly the sentence is executed."

A smile crawled onto the king's features, never fully developed. "I won't delay punishment to keep you here, if that's what you fear. Two days hence, Tae Kahn no father's son will be publicly drawn and quartered for the crime of murdering the crown prince of Pudar." He gestured the guards aside as the implication of the words seeped into Kevral's mind. "Is that soon enough?"

"Soon enough," Kevral repeated, discomfort making her voice rasp.

The guardsmen opened a pathway to the door.

"Dismissed," the king said.

Kevral herded a crying Matrinka toward the exit, alert to trickery from the guards. No one tried to block their escape.

Chapter 28

Uniting Predators

*Renshai do not kill the helpless, no matter who
they are. Unless your battle skill took him down,
it's not your right to kill him.*

—Colbey Calistinsson

Without the twice daily feedings, Tae Kahn could not have
kept track of time. The first week had dragged like thirty,
and the stench of the prison and its occupants grew familiar.
His ceaseless patter became routine to them as well. From
the morning after his conversation with Lador, he struggled
to draw those accustomed to trusting no one into a scraggly,
suspicious brotherhood, rallying them around the cause of
freedom. The street punk, Peter, joined them immediately,
the certainty of his death if he remained alone and his experience with gangs allowing him to take a chance where others dared not. Three to four, they stood against those too
paranoid to form alliances with strangers. Three to four they
remained well into the following day when Danamelio fell
sway to Tae's promises, dragging the aptly named Flea into
their ranks. The nondescript thief, Tadda, joined soon after.
Stick remained the only holdout, his pale eyes cold and dangerous and his silence adding to the aura of violence he radiated. Tae smiled. His plan could work with or without the
towering murderer.

Tae explained the details of his idea, working with the
men individually. The more he stressed their specific tasks,
the more comfortable each seemed to feel with the idea of

becoming part of a group. Though the prospect of escape
linked them, the association remained loose and awkward.
Tae would have liked the time to unite them fully, but his
own fate seemed too tenuous. His life, he knew, was measured in days or hours. Each day brought him one step
nearer to an agonizing death whose details he tried not to
fathom. But although he could keep his mind busy during
the day, sleep brought nightmares that kept all rest at bay.
Dull knives and cramping poisons that tore away at his insides filled his dreams. Amputations and gutting possessed
his mind's eye, and red streaks at the corners of his vision
became a symbol of his own blood. Any moment his mind
stole from directed thought became a desperate punishment
he fought to escape. Undirected pain twitched sharply
through him at intervals. Whenever he stiffened in avoidance, he reawakened the throbbing bruises of his beating.

When the trio of guards brought dinner that night, the
prisoners obediently moved to the back of the cell, away
from the threat of crossbow and halberd. All except Tadda.
The sandy-haired thief lay near the bars, hands clamped to
his abdomen and his expression suffering. He fluttered as
the guards approached, a feeble attempt to retreat with the
others that met with little success.

The crossbowman made an insincere noise of sympathy.
"Thieving bastard's finally snottered."

"Never thought he'd make it this long," the halberdier
muttered.

The last of the guards dumped foodstuffs through the
feeding door, much of which landed on Tadda where he lay.
Again, he made a valiant effort to rise before sinking back
down to the floor. The guard ignored him, shoving the water
trough through its slot with a foot. That finished, the
Pudarians marched from the prison room.

The prisoners tensed, accustomed to the desperate, scrambling chaos that always followed feeding yet needing to
know how Tadda had fared first. The thief rose, scraps of
food tumbling from his clothes, then shook his head mourn-
fully. "No keys."

Danamelio growled. Peter made a sharp noise of frustration. The prisoners dove for the food, clawing for scraps in
a frenzy. Excitement usurped Tae's hunger, and he did not
participate, though he had eaten little since his imprisonment. Instead, he stole the first drink from the trough while

the others tussled over rations scarcely fit for the king's dogs. Observation had taught him much, and the differences between this struggle and the ones before did not escape him. They fought less and forgave more. Even scrawny Peter managed to hoard some pieces without incurring the wrath of Danamelio. Tae concealed a smile. His leadership had created the first vague stirrings of loyalty and friendship, but he would not delude himself. These animals in human shape had a long way to go toward learning trust.

Worries descended upon Tae that night, as always. This time a new concern came to the fore. Without gaining the keys to at least the upper two locks, his plan would flop before it got started. He calmed himself with the realization that he had nothing to fear. If his failure upset his cell mates, they would kill him; but they did not have access to the torture devices of a kingdom. Nothing they did to him could prove any worse than the punishment to which the king would sentence him. He had only one thing to fear: that the prisoners would give up on him too soon and a working strategy might crumble because of lack of faith rather than of skill.

Night crawled into morning and breakfast. Again the guards found Tadda near the bars, still moving but, apparently, even weaker than the night before. They paid him little attention, dumping scraps and recovering the water trough with routine efficiency. When they left, Tae could feel every prisoner holding his breath. Even the Stick was affected, blue eyes glancing at Tadda even while he feigned disinterest.

The thief shook his head sadly. "No keys on that one either."

As if it were a signal, the riot of feeding followed amid grumbling and half-whispered comments about Tae's madness. Tae did not eat, instead collapsing into his space, back pressed to the bars and the stone wall seeping cold through the back of his tattered shirt. They might give his tactics one more chance but two seemed unlikely. His life hinged on an event that had now failed twice. Every bruise hammered and gnawed at him, a chorus of pain that shattered his thoughts into a desperate swirl of uncertainty. He scarcely noticed when Lador sat beside him, bolting food with a hastiness that didn't allow speech for several moments.

At last, the locksmith swallowed the last bite. He leaned

against the bars, hands clasped behind his head and his position too close to Tae to be accidentally chosen. "When I'm out of here, the first thing I'm going to do is buy, beg, steal, or borrow enough food to make my stomach explode. That one meal would be worth dying for."

Tae sighed deeply, the point moot.

"What are you going to do?" Lador fixed his green-gray gaze on Tae.

Tae dodged the locksmith's stare. He spoke softly, hoping no one but Lador could hear him beneath the crunch and slurp of eating. "We may not get the keys."

Lador shrugged, undaunted. "So."

The conclusion seemed so obvious, Tae saw no reason to voice it. He did anyway, hoping for the very solace he had interrupted for all of the others. "We may not get out."

"We'll get out," Lador said.

"How do you know?"

"You brought together the nastiest loners in the kingdom. Your idea of combining skills was nothing less than brilliant. Who would ever have thought of doing such a thing?"

My father. Tae did not speak aloud, hating the need to credit Weile Kahn with saving the life that, until now, he seemed bent on destroying. Tae grudgingly admitted that the crime lord's tactics seemed to have worked, at least on this occasion, but he could not escape believing that he could have learned more from gentle example than repeated trials by fire. *If I ever have a son or daughter of my own . . .* The idea seemed impossible and raised a smile where Lador's attempts to comfort had failed. *. . . he or she will never suffer so long as I can prevent it.* "Anyone could have come up with such a plan."

Lador snorted. "Clearly not. Else none of us would have been here for years. If you can plot in such incredible detail, if you can bond these worthless bastards in a cause, you're a leader without equal. Given the right bloodline, you could have made a powerful king."

Or a criminal lord. Tae bit his lip in anger, the idea of following in his father's footsteps abhorrent. Since birth, Weile Kahn had manipulated his son, and it seemed no amount of trying would sway him from his birthright. Tae loved his father . . . and hated him, knew awe and respect for his accomplishments even as he reviled them. *What have you turned me into?*

Lador tossed back snarled blond curls. "Lack of keys won't stop us, you know. Given some time and the help of the others, I can file my creation into shape for each lock."

Tae frowned, considering. It might work, but it all hinged on the amount of time necessary for Lador to work. All three locks would have to open in a space of time between guard visits. If they found one, or even two, sprung, they would not wait for Lador to handle the third. The cooperation necessary to achieve such a goal would likely strain the tenuous alliance past the point of breaking. In any case, it seemed unlikely that any of this would happen before Tae's execution. That he had made it eight days surprised him. The pang that struck Tae at the thought went beyond the sorrow of his own death. To his surprise, he wanted the plan to succeed whether or not he remained to see it do so. He took pride in a leadership skill he had never sought or wanted, and the accomplishments of this ragtag group of would-be fugitives would become his immortality. "If I'm taken away before you work your craft, would you help see it happens?"

"The escape?"

"Yeah."

"Of course." Lador shook his head as if Tae had asked the stupidest question in the world. "Do you think we'll no longer want to escape if you're not with us? I mean you're pleasant enough company, but freedom's a pretty big draw."

Despair retreated, and Tae managed a smile at last.

The evening meal lay on the floor, sickly hunks of gristle, partially chewed meat, and vegetable peels littering the cell. Tae closed his eyes, whispering his first prayer in years to Sheriva, the Eastlands' only god. The guards' footsteps clicked against stone, then gradually faded into obscurity. Tae opened his eyes. Tadda stood, shaking offal from the last scraps of his clothing, his expression hard and unrevealing.

Without sparkle or flicker, the thief's brown eyes gazed into Tae's darker ones. They seemed dead, a stark contrast to the first hint of a smile twitching the corners of his lips upward. The grin grew into an openmouthed smirk. His hand rose. The guard's ring, holding six keys, dangled from his fingers.

Every prisoner remained rooted in place, staring, the daily struggle for the food that spelled survival forgotten in an instant of triumph. No one made a sound. They would not risk whoops or hollers that might bring the guards back to investigate. Much remained of Tae Kahn's plan, and they had only the time it took the guardsman to notice his missing keys.

"Go," Tae said, giving Tadda an encouraging shove. The thief waited while Danamelio moved into position against the bars. Tadda scrambled up the huge man's back, using folds of skin as toeholds, his bare feet no burden to the massive molester. Once perched on Danamelio's neck, Tadda waited for the large man to move into position.

Danamelio drew as close to the bars as he could, and Tadda reached for the highest lock. Everyone, except the Stick, scrambled to a watching position. Tae's heart beat a wild cadence as he watched Tadda's hand fall short. The thief stretched, moving into a precarious standing position on Danamelio's shoulders and maintaining balance with a hand winched around the bars. His fingers touched the lock. He fumbled with the keys, unable to maneuver any of them into the hole. "A little to the left," Tadda instructed Danamelio, trying to gain precious space. When that failed, he tried other directions. "Forward as far as you go."

Limited by his gut, Danamelio grunted. The bars pressed into the flesh of his face and abdomen. "That's it. I don't go no farther."

Tadda hissed in frustration. He twisted, wriggled, and maneuvered; but the key could not quite reach the lock.

Finally, Danamelio had enough. "Get down. I'm not holding you any longer."

Tadda did not hesitate a second. He dropped back to a sitting position on the huge man's shoulders then scrambled to the ground. He looked at Tae for direction.

Slowly, Tae rolled his eyes to the only answer, dreading the need to rely on the one part of the plan that had, thus far, proved unattainable.

The Stick grinned, turning Tae a look that seemed to suggest he never should have believed they could work an elaborate scheme without him. "I'll do it," he said, his voice thick and grating after years of self-imposed silence.

Tae nodded, grinning back at the tall, narrow murderer as Danamelio moved aside. Tadda scurried into position on the Stick. Higher altitude and nearness to the bars gave him the leverage he needed. Three of the keys entered and left the lock. The fourth turned with a satisfying click.

"Yes," Tadda whispered, then jerked the key free. The Stick lowered him to the ground.

The Flea toddled forward now, accepting the keys from Tadda with a gentle squeeze that came as close to conspiratorial congratulations as any of them seemed capable. The Flea sucked in a deep breath, then released it fully. Emptied of air, he winched between the bars. One leg and arm slipped through easily, followed by a narrow hip and his side. His head proved his undoing, too wide to fit through the opening. This surprised no one. Surely, the Flea had attempted escape in this manner before, and something had to have foiled him. He stretched as far as possible, arm wrapped around the bars and the keys clutched tightly in his grip. Blindly, he fumbled around the barriers that hid the middle lock from sight.

Breath held, unable to see the Flea's work, Tae waited for a time that seemed endless. His eyes burned, blurring the scene to a liquid plain. The Flea's face reddened as he strained at his task, careful to maintain his grip on the ring. Should he drop the keys beyond his reach, no one could save them from the guards' wrath. Their lives hung on the competence of the little man's grip.

A click echoed through the confines. Tuned for the sound of dropping keys, Tae jumped and felt the others stiffen around him. Then the Flea pulled back, sweat dripping from his delicate features and the keys mashed into a palm that bore an impression of the ring. He smiled, a spark of light in his eyes. For a few moments seven lives had hinged upon him, and he had won them a third victory. Never again, Tae guessed, would men like Danamelio find this one an easy target.

Lador took the keys in hand next, picking the correct one for the bottom lock in an instant's glance. The last lock fell open. Danamelio slammed the door wide with his shoulder, bellowing victory at a volume that made them all cringe. "This way," Peter shouted, trying to take the lead. But Danamelio had already crashed into the only corridor, charging like a mad thing down the single road to freedom. The others followed in a desperate scramble.

Tae froze, forcing coherent thought through the jumble of excitement that drove him to become a part of the running pack. Words spoken by Kevral swirled through his mind: "Nothing done in panic is done right." Exhilaration, not fear, spurred these prisoners caged too long, but the analogy remained. When he wasted a moment in thought, he realized what his focus on the breakout and freedom did not allow him to consider before. Even if Peter recalled the route out, they would have to negotiate whatever pitfalls Pudarian security placed in their way. At the least, that would consist of locked gates and armed guards. Danamelio's bulk and power would help; but, weaponless, the armed sentries would surely overpower them. Tae shook his head.

As if in answer to his thoughts, shouts wafted down the hallway, followed by the thud of steel against flesh. A pain cry in a deep voice echoed down the corridor. Tae cringed, awakened to action by the ghostly sound. More shouts followed, a haunting mingle of desperation and determination. Footsteps pattered back toward Tae.

Tae's gaze swung left and right, but the only corridor lay ahead. He flinched against the wall, attempting to hide in the dank darkness, irregularities biting into his back. Lador skidded back into the chamber. Blond hair fanned around his face, and fear glared out through his gray-green eyes. "Tae?" he hissed.

"I'm here," Tae admitted as softly.

The locksmith swung around, hands tensing and loosening spasmodically. "Guards," he explained in a word. "Danamelio's down. The others. . . ." He shrugged to show how tenuous their fate remained.

Tae waved him quiet. The details did not matter as much as silence now.

Lador could not stop. "Flea tried to surrender. They chopped him down. They're like wild dogs with a scent of blood."

Tae abandoned subtlety. "Shut up, you idiot," he returned in a hoarse whisper.

Lador fell silent. Something moved in the darkness, too big for a rat.

Tae tried to become one with the wall. Lador glanced frantically about, like a trapped animal.

Tae carved shape and movement from the blackness, identifying the creature as a cat with dark blotches on a white background. *Mior?* Tae dismissed the thought. *Impossible.*

The cat meowed suddenly, a sound eerily like an answer. Lador stiffened, whirling toward the noise.

Tae knelt, and the cat ran to him. A stench like excrement accompanied it.

"Mior?" Tae tried.

It meowed.

Tae hefted the animal. Dirt coarsened the fur, and foul-smelling muck smeared onto his hands. The dim light scarcely allowed him to distinguish slime from pigment, but the patterns looked right.

A scream ripped down the corridor. Lador loosed a startled whimper, and urgency charged through Tae as well. His heart hammered, and his palms went slick. A desperate need for action seized him.

The cat leaped from his arms. She padded into the cell, then turned as if waiting for Tae to follow.

The idea of a cat directing a man seemed ludicrous. Tae considered the wisdom of returning to the cell and pretending to have had no hand in the escape. At least, he and Lador might survive while the guards butchered the others. The insanity of the idea struck a moment later. It would do him little good to escape the guards' slaughter for a painful execution. He stood his ground.

The cat returned, nearly to Tae's feet, then whirled and darted back into the cell.

"Do something," Lador whispered furiously. "You're the leader. You're the smart one. Do something."

When Tae did not follow, the cat jumped up and down hissing, an unfeline gesture that more resembled human frustration.

"Shut up," Tae growled, in as forceful a tone as whispering allowed. He watched the cat.

The cat headed toward the drainage pit, then stopped. It looked back toward Tae. Then, suddenly, it sprang into the hole.

Surprised, Tae edged back into the cell. Lador looked from Tae to the corridor multiple times, completely quiet at last.

Even as Tae approached the hole, the cat scrabbled back out again, nails clicking against stone as it fought its way through the opening. Once more, it stood in the prisoner's cell, but Tae had drawn much closer.

"Meow!"

Tae looked doubtfully through the hole through which he had vomited and excreted over the last few days. Surely, the smell alone down there would kill him, and he could not imagine what possible good could come of trapping himself there. Yet the cat had come from there. If she was Mior, as he believed, she had begun outside. Presumably, she could find her way back to Matrinka.

A crash slammed through the corridor, and more shouts and screams followed. Tae did not waste another moment. Hands on the lip, he wriggled through the hole. Feces smeared his fingers, and the odor of stale urine gagged him. He breathed only through his mouth, tasting something bitter and undefined in the air. Ignoring it, he clawed for toeholds on the sides of the pit. He found them swiftly, then lowered himself into darkness as complete as pitch. Running water splashed and bubbled beneath him, and dampness chilled his limbs.

The cat launched herself into the hole behind him. He felt the breeze of her passage, then the thump of her landing on dry ground. Tae continued to descend carefully, choosing hand and toeholds with swift caution. His bare foot touched water, and he recoiled. Mior mewed softly to his right, and he edged a leg in her direction.

Lador's voice reverberated through the hole. "Tae, wait. Tae!"

"Come down. Hurry up," Tae returned in a low voice.

"I'm not sure I can fit."

Tae did not bother with an answer. If the locksmith could not slide in, it meant leaving someone behind who might tell the guards about the route he took. It also meant certain imprisonment or death for Lador, which bothered Tae more than he expected. He had grown to like his cell mate.

The locksmith's bulk blocked the lit hole far above Tae. He maneuvered for a few moments as Tae located the ledge supporting Mior and shifted carefully onto it. Man-built, it probably served as a way for custodians to clear debris or recover goods that might get thrown or fall through the shafts.

Then, suddenly, Lador plummeted through the opening. Tae jerked back as the locksmith sailed past, landing in the sewage water with a splash that pelted Tae with cold, wet slime.

Water churned and bubbled as Lador fought to the surface, carried downstream even as he did so. Tae cursed the darkness, sound and touch his only usable senses. Mior's fur prickled along his calf, then she headed in the direction

Lador had disappeared. Tae followed. "Hang on," he said, trying to gauge his volume to allow Lador to hear yet not give away their location. He clung to the belief that Mior began her journey outside and he had not simply trapped himself in a hell far worse than the one he had escaped. Quickening his pace, he followed the river, alert to the roughness of the path. He did not want to join Lador in the filth-tainted water.

At length, an anemic glaze of light filtered into the tunnel. Tae pushed on, hope tingling through him though he kept it in check. Too much had gone wrong to trust in miracles now. But the light grew stronger over time, lost only to curves and bends in the deep river. He pushed onward, vision growing stronger as he went. Soon, he could make out Mior's outline. Then, a blond head bobbed near the ledge. "Lador?" Tae rushed over, prepared for the worst. Just as he reached to pull the other toward him, a hand gripped the ledge. He stared directly into green-gray eyes. Tae grabbed the second hand as it flailed for a hold, then helped hoist the locksmith to safety.

Lador lay on the ledge coughing for several moments before managing to speak. "Thank you."

"Sorry it took so long." Tae felt a twinge of guilt, though darkness and circumstance had given him no means to rescue Lador prior to that moment. "Lucky you can swim."

Lador grinned weakly. "Only a true friend could say such a thing to someone who smells like I do."

"Who can smell where the water ends and you start," Tae gave back. "Come on." He extended a hand.

Lador wrapped Tae's hand in his own soggy palm. He rose slowly, careful not to off balance Tae in the process. "Let's go."

They headed onward, around a bend. The light became evening grayness, gleaming over water. A grate covered the exit and, through it, Tae could see the moat surrounding Pudar's castle.

Lador pounded on the grate, then groaned. "So close. So damned close." He hammered a fist on the metal, and it did not so much as shudder beneath the blow.

Tae held back, letting the man more experienced at opening ways perform the examination. "Well?" he asked at length.

"Bolted well. No way for me to get out without tools. What about you?"

Tae shook his head. "If you can't do it, I sure can't." He could not help adding, "I thought you could get through anything."

"Any *lock*," Lador reminded. "I'm a locksmith, not a saw."

Tae crouched, examining the grate though he knew it would prove futile. Mior twined through his legs, fur tickling his skin, then headed back the way they had come. Solid iron spanned the opening. Though rusted and pitted with age, it had not grown weak enough for more than mild flaking. Fourteen steady bolts held it in place, their heads suggesting a span the length of Tae's arm. He sighed. They could spend their lives working on this and accomplish nothing.

The cat returned, rubbing against Tae with an attention-calling sound of impatience. Only then, he realized the holes in the mesh were too small to admit even her. The obvious jerked to understanding. *This isn't the way Mior got in.*

Tae bounded to his feet, watching the calico disappear back into the darkness. "This way." He trotted after, not bothering to see if Lador followed.

Chasing Mior, Tae reluctantly returned to the gloom he had rejoiced to leave. The cat came to him at intervals, which he appreciated. He did not dare stop to wonder how she knew to lead him in this fashion, unable to dispel the silly and superstitious fear that consideration might destroy luck he had never needed more in his difficult life. Then, suddenly, Mior disappeared.

Tae stopped, casting about for Mior and cursing his misfortune. A meow resounded hollowly above his head. *Above?* Tae looked up, seeing nothing in the darkness. Then Mior dropped to the stone at his feet, landing lightly on her paws. She meowed again.

Tae reached upward, feeling the edges of a shaft. The logic of the system finally reached him. All of the sanitary holes would empty into a common sewage area. To do otherwise meant digging a dozen tunnels beneath the castle. Therefore, this shaft must lead to a privy in another room. Tae raised his head instinctively, though his vision failed him completely. Unless this led to another room in the dungeon, it meant a long and treacherous climb to an upper level, one he doubted Mior or Lador could make.

Attention still focused upward, Tae lifted Mior. She settled onto his shoulders, as she so often did for Matrinka. "Can you climb?"

Lador touched Tae's arm to locate himself. "Better than most, I suppose. Nothing spectacular." The truth dawned on him then. "Are we going back up?"

"Further this time, I hope. Can you make it?"

Lador paused, as if inspecting the grade and distance, through the lightless interior. "I doubt it." He sighed. "No. Can you?"

"Yes," Tae responded, not allowing himself to doubt. He had only a vague idea of what such a climb would entail, but he could not afford to fail now. Surely, it would not prove more difficult than the sage's tower; yet, then, he had had spikes, claws, and pitons. This time, he would rely solely on his grip and personal skill. "I'll find a way to get you up when I get to the top."

Lador fell silent. Arguing would prove as fruitless as skepticism; it could only undermine Tae's chances. He squeezed Tae's arm, indicating faith in his ability, though the fear came through as well. Believing Tae would find a way to hoist him out, or take the time to do so, surely strained his trust to its limit. Still, he had little choice but to wait patiently and accept Tae's loyalty.

Without further explanation, Tae gripped the lip of the hole and swung his feet into position on the wall. The crude stone construction afforded him myriad finger and toeholds. He climbed. Accustomed to the stench, he scarcely noticed it. Attentive to balance and grip, he dared not pause to wonder about the slime that slicked the stone. His mind pictured greenish algae, and he allowed the delusion. To ponder long might make him sick or miss a step. He hoped Lador had moved aside so that a fall would not prove fatal for both of them. Tae stole a moment to wonder whose fate would be worse: the climber killed as he struck solid stone or the locksmith stuck wandering the dark sewer until the guards found him.

The image dizzied him, and he forced it away. Instead, he concentrated on each upward movement of hand or foot. The ragged stone bit into the sensitive tips of his fingers and toes. Blood trickled across his right palm, warm and slick.

He concentrated on the concept of "up" until it became a solid picture in his mind. Nothing else mattered but the constant progression of hand over hand, foot over foot.

Tae forgot about the passage of time, about how far below him Lador now was. The weight of the cat on his shoulders ached through the muscles of his back, but he did not waste concentration wondering how Matrinka handled the calico for hours and days at a time. If he reached the top, he lived. If he fell, he died. Nothing else in the world mattered right now.

Gradually, Tae discerned a light above him, closer than he expected. A circle of corresponding brightness appeared as a ring nearly as perfect as the full moon, though far less bright. Indulging a mild smile, Tae dragged himself upward. Three more holds, grabbed more swiftly than in the past, brought him nearly to the top. He lunged for freedom. His hand missed the opening, fingers scraping stone then plowing through muck without substance. For an instant, nothing supported him. He desperately threw his weight onto his remaining limbs. Unable to support the sudden shift, one foot slipped free. Vertigo assailed him. He felt himself spiraling downward in the moment before it almost became a reality. His loose hand scrambled for a hold, catching one just as his other foot failed. Gritting his teeth, he clung with only his hands. Tears mingled with the sweat on his face.

Tae's arms ached, but the pain lost meaning beneath need. Cautiously, he groped for the best toeholds he could find. His fingers trembled, threatening to give out. He worked faster, gradually finding the ledges he needed. More carefully, he pulled himself to the opening and out.

The cat sprang free as Tae lay gasping on the floor. The urge to holler with joy could not have been satisfied physically even could he have risked the noise. For longer than was safe or appropriate, he remained on the floor. Only after several moments of reveling in this temporary safety did it finally occur to him that he had no idea where he was or how to escape. For all he knew, Pudarian nobles might stand surrounding him, waiting for him to move.

Tae managed a quick assessment of the room. He was alone in a small chamber that contained only the hole through which he had climbed and a cushion padding the area around it. A single doorway led into another room, and he could only glimpse its interior. With a deep sigh, he rose and brushed off the worst of the clinging grime. He might need his hands relatively clean, though for what he did not know. He hoped he would not need to fight. Like his father, his power lay in quickness, cleverness, and knowledge, not brute strength. Quietly, he rose, hands no longer shaking. He crept to the entryway and peered into the other room.

A person slept on a canopied bed, features lost beneath the light covers. A robe trimmed with fur hung from one of the posts. A bureau occupied the space along one wall, and a wardrobe stood along another. Beneath an open window lay a long table covered with painted, wooden soldiers in the midst of a fierce battle. A bookshelf held an assortment of texts. A closed door and the entryway through which he had come served as the only exits. Tae slipped into the room, gaze locked on the sleeping figure. By its shape, the other appeared male, and the cut of his robe confirmed the assessment. He breathed deeply and with regularity, definitely asleep.

Keeping an ear tuned toward the sleeper at all times, Tae assessed other parts of the room. Gauzy curtains fluttered in a thin breeze, which, thankfully, blew Tae's stench away from the sleeper. Tae approached cautiously, peering outside. Six stories below him, the courtyard spread like a map, its green blanket of grass interrupted by stone benches and flower gardens at intervals. Moonlight glittered from the distant moat, occasionally catching glints of armor from guards below. Tae studied their movements, defining patterns. For all he and Lador had gone through, freedom still remained beyond their grasp. Thoughts of his companion reminded him of his promise. His eyes swept the miniature battle as he turned to work on a solution to the locksmith's problem. That glimpse registered enough details for him to recognize the Great War, the one the Westerners called the War of Silver Wolves. Longer than three centuries ago, the Eastlands had warred with the West, and Tae's people had nearly lost every man to it.

Tae examined the sleeper once more. But though he stirred a few times, perhaps catching Tae's scent as the breeze momentarily faded, he did not wake but only buried his face deeper in the covers. Tae headed for the bureau. Seizing a drawer, he edged it open, eyes fixed on the owner of the room and fingers testing for resistance, that momentary hesitancy of the wood that might herald a thump or squeak. Well constructed and well oiled, the drawer made no sound. Tae glanced at the contents: britches and breeks dyed in a rainbow of hues. Hurriedly, he knotted them together, passing up silk for more solid materials. Although he did not know how far he had climbed, he estimated, by the distance to the courtyard from the window, making his clothing rope longer than he believed necessary. Seeking ballast, he headed for the bookshelf. He found it before he arrived in the form of boots standing neatly at the foot of the bed. Selecting one, he tied it to the end of the rope and headed back toward the sewer hole.

Tae's eyes swept the titles as he passed. For all of Weile's insistence on Tae learning on the streets, he had placed equal merit on study. He had found tutors and books for most of the world's languages, verbal and written, emphasizing the need for understanding everyone. Much of interest could be learned from those who believed themselves impossible to overhear. The books all held titles in either the Western or common trading tongue. Aside from some general texts on the bottom shelf, every one held some relationship to the Great War. *Some fascination.* Tae looped the farthest end of the clothing chain to the leg of the armoire, knotting it securely.

Tae continued into the small room without dwelling on his observations, but some of the titles registered in his mind even without concentration. One, thinner than most, had borne Colbey Calistinsson's name as part of its title. This held little fascination for Tae personally, but he knew Kevral would find it enthralling and, hopefully, the one who delivered it to her as well. He cared deeply for Kevral, and that was his main reason for assisting the party after they had abandoned him. One way or another, he would win her affection.

Tae stood at the mouth of the hole, glancing in, but he saw nothing. A call down, even soft, might echo intolerably. Hoping Lador had enough sense to stand aside while waiting, Tae tossed down the boot-weighted rope, listening carefully to the hissing sound of the cloth followed by the muffled splash of the boot hitting bottom. Less than a second passed before the line of breeks quivered then shifted. The makeshift rope jerked and swayed as Lador worked his way upward.

Tae waited, attentive to sound from the other room. Assisting Lador would accomplish little. Tae did not have the strength to hoist the locksmith the necessary six to seven stories, nor to lower him when the time came to slither through the window. It occurred to Tae only now that he had lost track of Mior in his need to study the layout, but he knew the cat could look out for herself. He only hoped she would do nothing to awaken the bed's occupant. So far, she had remained quiet except when drawing his attention to some matter he should attend. She had an eerie intelligence about her he could not explain, though he had noticed it long ago. Her comings and goings in the forest, when he traveled otherwise alone, had seemed uncatlike as well.

The tugs on the rope intensified, then Lador's grimy head poked through the hole. He immediately glanced around the room. Seeing only Tae, he relaxed. Tae drew the rope to the edge of the hole, and Lador slid free without difficulty.

Tae made a gesture for silence, then pointed through the doorway. Carefully, Lador headed in the indicated direction and peered through the door, assessing the situation as Tae had already done. Tae hauled the secured boot back to the surface. He wound the makeshift rope around the boot, following its course into the bedroom with every sense alert. He found Mior perched on the window sill while Lador studied the outside, just as Tae had done moments before. Tae untied the breeks from the furniture, then looked at the books again. Lador would need a few moments to decide strategy.

Tae quickly found the book he wanted. The title read, *The Deathseeker, Colbey Calistinsson: His Time as Pudar's General.* Little more than a dozen pages, it could be easily concealed. Tae hefted it, just as Lador turned.

"Take it," the locksmith whispered.

Caught, Tae flushed and returned the volume. He glanced at the figure on the bed, but he had not stirred. "That'd be stealing," he returned carefully.

Lador snorted. "So they'll cut off your hand after they hang you. Take the damned thing and let's go. You can always put it back later."

The argument held no more logic than the suggestion that he could come back at another time and steal it. Still, it convinced Tae. Snatching up the book, he headed toward the window. While they examined the arrangement and movements of the watch, Tae pocketed the wild, blond figure on horseback that represented Colbey in the battle scene and tucked it into his pocket. If he lost the first, he would still have the other.

Lador took no notice of the second theft. After close scrutiny of the courtyard, he made a silent gesture toward the room into which they had first emerged. There, they could plot without so much concern about noise.

Tae did not delude himself as he followed Lador toward the smaller room. Climbing down six stories, even with their knotted chain of britches, would not prove easy. That task barely compared with their need to slip from Pudar's courtyard and between the sentries undetected. Still, the first rush of joy touched Tae's senses. Whatever the hardships, he convinced himself they would make it.

Chapter 29

Rantire's Advice

*No matter the methods of our enemy, the Renshai
will live or die with their honor intact.*

—Colbey Calistinsson

Dh'arlo'mé negotiated the crafted hallways of the imprisonment building with none of the distracting sensations of discomfort and claustrophobia that used to assail him inside
manlike artificial constructs. Centuries of sleeping and playing beneath the bulbous trees of Alfheim had ill-prepared
elves for the enclosed life humans chose. It never ceased to
amaze him that a species so fixated on packing itself into
buildings would use lock-up as a form of punishment.

As he walked, Dh'arlo'mé smiled. At the meeting a few
moments ago, his scouts had returned only good news. In
Béarn, the political structure tottered on the brink of collapse. The elves had withdrawn long ago, spectators without
need for active intervention. They had learned much about
human nature. Given the slightest of reasons, mankind
would annihilate itself with only a few well-placed maneuvers on the part of the elves. Soon, Béarn would fall at the
hands of its own citizenry.

Using Béarn as an example, the elves had already stirred
political unrest in the other large kingdoms. A handful of
thefts and murders had spurred the various Northern tribes
into wars they had, apparently, fought off and on for centuries. According to Xyxthris, border skirmishes had kept the
reclusive Northern warriors honed for as far back as history

recorded. The elves had had little difficulty inciting all of the tribes simultaneously. In the East, the elves chipped at the ruling structure in the largest of its nearly endless parade of cities, especially the high kingdom of Stalmize. Recently, a breakthrough into the criminal element had uncovered a broad, branching hierarchy of men like Xyxthris who would help weaken the Eastlands' infrastructure . . . for a price.

As Dh'arlo'mé traveled deeper into the dank darkness, he passed a few other elves in the corridors. He nodded at each as he passed, pretending not to notice the stares and whispers that followed his passage. He took mental note of all of the ones he passed, however. *Arak'bar Tulamii Dhor's silly band of fools.* Dh'arlo'mé paid the elves' oldest and his followers little heed. They had no momentum or authority, and the power structure of the elves, as well as their own chosen methods, would never allow them to gain it. For now, they were nothing more than nuisance. Should they become more than that, he would find a means to deal with them that did not compromise the elves' population. Imprisonment or banishment until natural death would have to take precedence over the instinctive urge to execute traitors. Their recycled souls would prove invaluable.

Dh'arlo'mé continued through the hallways between cells, his red-blond hair streaming in a wild mane behind him. Only two developments concerned him now. First, he had not yet heard back from the group sent to dispatch Béarn's last heir in Dunwoods. He attributed the delay to elfin difficulty judging time, although he no longer suffered from that malady. Still, their absence worried him, bringing him to the second of his concerns.

At first, they had considered Xyxthris the godsend he appeared to be. Yet, eventually, Dh'arlo'mé began to wonder how far to trust the Béarnian prince. Admittedly, he had brought invaluable information, without which the elves might have progressed no further in the next three hundred years than in the past. But one who chose to stand against his people could not be trusted to stand with their enemies either. Even should his intentions remain pure, he might have flaws in judgment.

The concept of loyalty had little practical application to elves, and Dh'arlo'mé credited his time on man's world as a sorceress' apprentice for the understanding. Wisdom, however, they understood. Though clearly not stupid, Xyxthris might have lapses in common sense. No one could possibly prove correct all of the time, and Dh'arlo'mé dared not plan the future of elfinkind solely on the advice of a single, human traitor. He needed the opinion of another human. He had only Rantire to consult. She had not proved a cooperative source in the past, but times had changed. They had ceased torturing her, and she had befriended many of the elves. He doubted she would give away anything that might harm mankind, but her suggestions to the contrary might prove equally useful. Especially when coupled with Xyxthris' own.

Dh'arlo'mé rounded the final corner and started toward the captive's cell. He had another reason for consulting Rantire about Béarn's last possible heir. Although the elves had killed others of the high king's line without compunction, something felt wrong about the outright murder of this one. It was not the killing of an innocent that bothered him; there was no such thing as an innocent human. Something inexplicable niggled at his consciousness, a concept he once knew but could now no longer pin down. And Xyxthris seemed so adamant about seeing to the last heir's death as soon as possible. His rage seemed almost a separate, living entity. No one acting with so much malice could do so with good judgment.

As Dh'arlo'mé approached, Rantire glanced up. She studied him as he came, eventually recognizing him. Her gaze turned suspicious. She crouched, backing deeper into her cell.

Dh'arlo'mé continued forward, making neither threatening nor peaceful gestures. Either would inflame her understandable mistrust. He stopped in front of her cell.

Rantire watched him, unspeaking.

Dh'arlo'mé cleared his throat, then chose the common trading tongue. "Hello," he said carefully, trying to sound matter-of-fact rather than gloating

"Hello," Rantire returned without warmth. Her time with elves of kinder persuasion had apparently made her more open to talk. Captain's followers had done something in the elves' favor. "Are you going to hurt me again?"

Dh'arlo'mé felt no remorse but thought it better to act as if he did. He lowered his head, wincing slightly, a perfect copy of human discomfort. "I'm sorry about that," he lied.

"I truly am. We still haven't figured out the best way to handle humans, I'm afraid."

Rantire grew bolder as the threat of punishment disappeared. "Well, I can tell you pain doesn't work."

"We see that."

"Cooperation works much better."

"Aah." Dh'arlo'mé tried to sound interested and change the subject at the same time. "We both know it's more complicated than that."

Rantire shrugged. "What do you want, Dh'arlo'mé?"

"Believe it or not, I came for advice."

Rantire looked skeptical.

"Here's what we have. . . ." Dh'arlo'mé detailed the situation of the Béarnian heirs and their staff-test, gauging Rantire's reaction. He could tell she tried to mask her emotions, with some success. But the immensity of human expression, compared to elfin subtlety, allowed him to read her alarm. He did not know whether her concern stemmed from the story he told or from worry that the elves had acquired such knowledge. Whichever its source, her beetled brows, crinkled forehead, and restlessness gave her away.

Dh'arlo'mé's long explanation faded into a silence admirably lengthy for a human. Finally, Rantire spoke. "You can't harm the heir to Béarn's throne."

Dh'arlo'mé had planned to ask exactly that, and the direct answer, prior to the question, startled him. He could only guess whether she anticipated his need or simply addressed the issue she found most crucial. "I believe you are mistaken. We *can* harm the heir to Béarn's throne." He said it mostly to test her, drawing out superstition or religious belief that might state the contrary.

Rantire rose and took a step toward him. She no longer attempted to hide her concern. "I'm not saying you're incapable of it. I'm saying you don't dare do it."

Still anticipating human myth, Dh'arlo'mé allowed a tiny smile. "Why not?"

"Because it would mean the end of all life, including the elves."

The grin wilted. Dh'arlo'mé had not expected anything like this response. "How so?"

"The king of Béarn is the central focus of the universe's balance." Rantire spoke with an elegance she usually lacked. This point, it seemed, had been deeply ingrained and long taught. "The staff-test is a creation of Odin that keeps all of our worlds from collapsing to ruin. Without the proper heir, Béarn would die, it's true. But so would our world and every being on it. The destruction would spiral outward, gaining power as well as size. Eventually, everything on every world would plunge into utter annihilation."

"You seem convinced."

"It's the truth," Rantire asserted.

Dh'arlo'mé had little experience judging sincerity, but Rantire certainly seemed earnest about her pleas. She believed she did not lie, but she was still limited by her own understanding. "Can you prove it?"

Rantire sighed, gaze still intense. "No more than I can prove the sun will rise. I can't prove a pregnant cow will give birth to a calf, but I know these to be true. You can test whether what I said comes to pass, but only after you've set irreversible destruction in motion. If you kill the heir to Béarn, it will happen."

Bluff, truth, or superstition. D'harlo'mé could only speculate. "What do you suggest we do?"

Rantire returned to her defensive position. "I suggest you work with mankind, but I know you won't. Surely, even you see the need to help humans return the rightful center of balance. Even if you won't do that, I beg you not to harm Béarn's heir. Though it pains me to even suggest such a thing, he's worth more to you alive than dead. Even if I'm wrong . . ." She could not help adding, ". . . and I'm not. But even if I were wrong, humans believe what I've told you. She winced and bit her lip, lapsing into another long silence. Obviously, she hated what she was about to say, yet saw it as the lesser of evils. "If you capture the heir alive, you can barter with him. He'd be priceless. Dead, he's worth nothing, and mark my words. Such a murder would herald another Great Destruction that would spare neither elves nor mankind."

"Thank you for your cooperation." Dh'arlo'mé executed a graceful half bow. "I'll heed your words with the seriousness they deserve, and you may well share this prison with Béarn's heir." He did not add that he would need to reach his followers with his decision prior to the murder they had already been charged to commit. "You speak well, and I hope I can count on your advice in the future."

Rantire nodded warily, and a mild spark kindled in her gray eyes.

Dh'arlo'mé headed away, strides typically unhurried. She had proven as useful as he had hoped. And, though she did not know it, she had bought herself a few more months of life.

A pounding on the door awakened Kevral with a jolt that sent her heart racing and her every muscle tensing for action. She sprang from her pallet, hands balled around the two swords she wore even when sleeping. Ra-khir skittered to his feet, tugging his britches and shirt into place. Matrinka struggled groggily to sit up; until recently, her life had never depended on sharp wits and quick responses. Even Darris rolled into a position to rise.

The wild knocking rumbled through the room a second time. Kevral strode for the main chamber without bothering to straighten her hair or clothing. Ra-khir hurried after her. He did not pause to arm himself. Guests, no matter how rude and untimely, did not deserve such a greeting. Matrinka's solid footfalls followed him, but Kevral did not turn to watch her charge. As the third attack on their door resumed, she wrenched it open suddenly.

A guard in Pudar's uniform stumbled, awkwardly dropping his hand as the wood he had been battering disappeared beneath his fist. Seven more hovered behind him. Moonlight funneled into the cottage, broken by the misshapen, black lumps of their shadows. The broad-faced guard with widely spaced eyes responsible for the banging stepped boldly into the cottage.

Kevral did not budge, so his movement brought him uncomfortably close to her, a situation that clearly irritated them both. Ra-khir and Matrinka took positions beside and behind her.

"Where is he?" the guard demanded, glowering down at Kevral. He attempted another forward step. When Kevral did not move, he tried a diagonal, only to find her in his way again. The other guards hung back. A muscular brunet near the front pursed his lips with obvious disapproval. Whether directed against his companion or Kevral, she could not yet tell.

"Where is who?" Kevral shot back, noting how close his hands were to his sword hilt.

"The assassin. The murderer of our beloved crown prince."

"Tae?" Ra-khir supplied. "We thought you had him in custody."

Darris bumped something in the bedroom, and it squeaked and thumped back into place.

The guard pointed toward the noise. "He's in there. Get out of my way." He attempted to shove past Kevral, his superior strength and size creating an opening. Even as he pushed through, Kevral's foot shot abruptly into his way. He tripped, sprawling to the cottage floor.

The brunet in the doorway barely managed to choke back a laugh. The other guards waited uncertainly for a command.

The guard on the floor scrambled to his feet, features reddening and fist blanching on his hilt. "You stupid little bitch." His hand moved suddenly upward.

Even as his sword began to clear its sheath, Kevral drew and cut. The tip of her blade slammed against his crosspiece hard enough to break his grip. As he stared at his tingling hand, Kevral's sword smacked his hilt again, this time returning the blade to its sheath. Completing the arc, she resheathed her own sword and looked at him coolly.

The brunet finally intervened. "What my annoying companion meant to say was, 'Good evening, good people. We're sorry to disturb you. Can we talk?' "

The other six guards said nothing, constant movement revealing restlessness. No one else attempted to draw a weapon. The homely guard inside the cottage turned his glare from Kevral to the brunet. "If you'd backed me as I asked—"

"There'd have been bloodshed. Yours first." The calmer guard turned to Ra-khir and asked, "Would it be all right if we talked?"

"Certainly." Ra-khir indicated the scattered, mismatched furniture. "As long as there're no further threats in our home."

The first guard continued to scowl while the second flushed with genuine embarrassment. "Please accept my apologies. Captain Harltan's promotion was recent, and his methods have always been unorthodox. He does love Pudar and means well. He just doesn't always remember his manners." He bowed slightly. "My name is Captain DeShane."

The one called Harltan grumbled something unintelligible.

Kevral knew little about guards' hierarchies. In Béarn, only one soldier held the title of captain, but the great trading city required a larger army. It only made sense to have more than one commander, and "captain" might have a different meaning here as well. Kevral guessed Harltan had insisted on leading this mission, and DeShane had allowed it rather than bothering to fight, at least until Harltan's actions had forced the issue.

"Come in, Captain." Ra-khir made a broader gesture, actively ushering the guards into the room. As they filed inside, he introduced each of his companions in turn, avoiding the use of titles. He ended as most settled onto the floor. "And our fourth companion is Darris. He's recovering from an injury, so he may not prove good company."

In response to his name, Darris came, looking the best Kevral had seen him since the injury. Still wobbly on his feet, he seemed otherwise well. He nodded at the guards.

DeShane nodded back. Harltan attempted to look around him and into the sleeping room.

While Ra-khir and Matrinka played host and hostess, Kevral took a cautious position between the guards and the bedroom. She remained standing after the others sat, DeShane sacrificing the window seat for Darris. The bard accepted the position with a thankful wave. Harltan continued to look intently into the cottage's other room.

Kevral saw no reason, other than vengeful nastiness, to prevent Harltan from looking. To hide areas of the house might invite unnecessary suspicion. "Before we get started, and before the captain wears his eyes out, you're welcome to search where you please."

"Thank you," said Captain DeShane. "That won't be necessary."

Harltan apparently believed otherwise. He accepted Kevral's invitation with mumbled thanks, which sounded more bitter than appreciative. Giving Kevral a wide berth, he headed into the sleeping room.

With a glance at Kevral to confirm she had no intention of sitting, DeShane took the seat Harltan had vacated, one of only three in the room. Ra-khir sat on the chest, while Matrinka used the barrel seat that Kevral usually chose.

Ra-khir opened the discussion. "So am I to understand you're looking for Tae?"

"I'm afraid so." DeShane turned his attention directly to

Ra-khir, obviously more comfortable conducting his business with a man. So far he had proven reasonable, so Kevral forgave this annoying little quirk. "From what we can gather, he masterminded a prison break of Pudar's most notorious criminals."

Kevral considered, one ear turned toward Harltan. If the guard's rasher captain made a mess of their belongings, she would see to it he suffered for the indiscretion. Tae's motivations eluded her. Her time with him convinced her that his toughness was as much bluff as reality; and Matrinka's descriptions of his actions since Ra-khir had chased him from the group only skewed the picture toward bluster. He had revealed a kindness to her that pulled her toward him in much the way Ra-khir's more open moments made him seem all the more handsome. Although no one seemed to understand Tae well, she did not believe him the type to loose a scourge of killers on innocents in Pudar.

Matrinka asked the obvious question. "Why would Tae do that?" Than a more significant concern struck her. "Are these killers now roaming the streets?"

Though the first query had an obvious answer, DeShane ignored the natural temptation to address the second only. "I can only guess at your friend's motives."

"Previous companion, please," Ra-khir corrected.

"Previous companion," DeShane corrected with an understanding nod. "We're not sure whether he really wanted the others free or only used them as a diversion."

"So they're not roaming the streets," Kevral supplied.

The captain and most of the guards swiveled to look at her. "No. The prison guards killed all but three. We captured one and got the full story from him. Tae Kahn and one other disappeared."

"They're loose somewhere in the castle?" Matrinka sounded worried, perhaps imagining assassins free in Béarn's keep. Surely, that thought brought memories of the heir killings that had haunted her days and nights.

DeShane returned his attention to the princess. "Unlikely. We've scoured the place. They're gone. And in answer to your other question, the one who escaped with Tae was a thief, not a killer."

"Oh." Matrinka relaxed visibly. "And Tae's not a killer either," she assured him.

DeShane made a noncommittal gesture. Obviously, he did not agree, but he would not argue with Matrinka now.

Harltan emerged from the sleeping room. He broke into their discussion even while he continued to search. "It all comes back to this. Are you harboring him? Do you know where he's gone or might have gone? Will you help us catch him?"

A soft meow wafted beneath the front door, followed by a gentle scratch. Kevral walked to the door and opened it a crack. Mior slipped in, as grimy as the day King Kohleran found her, accompanied by the foul odors of ammonia and feces. Heads turned as the smell slowly permeated the room.

With a noise of disgust, Matrinka rose and headed for her cat. "Excuse me," she told the guards, then addressed the animal. "Mior, you dirty cat. Outside."

Kevral stepped aside as the princess herded the calico back toward the door.

Harltan's questions became momentarily lost in these new concerns. When no one answered him, he stopped searching to glance tensely around the room.

DeShane picked up the discussion. "We've had to cordon off Pudar. The gates won't open this morning, so no one can go in or out. No one will enter or leave this city until we have Tae Kahn in custody."

The news seized Kevral like hot iron tongs. Finally, Darris had become nearly well enough to travel. She would not allow a crisis to stall their trip indefinitely. Already, time weighed heavily against their mission. "That's ridiculous!"

Kevral's distress pleased Harltan, who smiled for the first time. Apparently satisfied by his search, he leaned against the wall, across from Kevral, and joined his guards with the same overseeing manner as the Renshai. "Catching an assassin of such danger requires desperate measures."

DeShane shrugged, without apology. "It's the only way, and it's not ideal for Pudar either. We'll lose huge amounts of money in trade. The politics won't please anyone, and we may go without needed goods."

"Tae's probably long gone from Pudar," Kevral insisted as Matrinka returned to her seat, a worried expression creasing her usually gentle features.

"Unlikely." DeShane dismissed Kevral's suggestion. "The wall and gate guards were quadrupled immediately. We called up the wartime army within an hour, and they've reinforced our defenses."

"But he got out of the castle," Kevral reminded.

Harltan responded before DeShane could. "The castle protections are designed to keep danger out, not in. The walls and gates do both."

Kevral glanced at Matrinka, who nodded slow agreement. From that gesture, Kevral guessed Mior had told her Tae had not escaped the city. She huffed in frustration. "Isn't there any other solution?"

"One," Captain DeShane admitted with a warning glance at Harltan, an obvious plea for silence.

To Kevral's surprise, Harltan did defer, amusement replacing his previous surly mask. Clearly, he did not expect a positive response to DeShane's suggestion, and the idea of watching the other captain receive the bulk of their annoyance pleased him.

"There is, apparently, an archaic law, rarely invoked." DeShane shifted uncomfortably and turned his attention back to Ra-khir, although Kevral had asked the question. "No one has done so in my lifetime, at least. It's called the 'One Crime, One Sentence Rule.' Its original intention, I'm guessing now, was to substitute lesser needed individuals for pivotal ones who committed a crime."

Ra-khir asked, "What exactly does this rule state?"

"I don't know the precise words," DeShane admitted. "But it allows transfer of sentencing to a person who claims responsibility for the accused. It's gotten modified a few times, more recently to cover escape since we're long beyond the days when Pudar had only one blacksmith or cooper or healer. Responsibility now falls first onto any person who performs an action that suggests he or she might have aided the escape." His gaze swiveled carefully back to Kevral, but he did not meet her eyes, as if he had done so more to gauge her reaction than to inform her. "Originally, the stand-in had to take the accused's place willingly. The current wording allows the king to demand substitution in a case where someone's behavior makes them suspect."

Darris had remained silent so far. Now, he spoke with more strength than Kevral expected. "Tae could come back and take the substitute's place at any time prior to carrying out the sentencing. Death in this case."

All eyes shifted to Darris in an instant. That Darris knew

Pudarian archaic canon surprised Kevral only for a moment. He had dedicated his life to learning. She worried that he might have to resort to singing if he said much more.

"Correct," DeShane said. "How did you know that?"

Darris shrugged. "Law's an interest of mine." He switched the subject to matters more germane. "But it's all moot, really. What makes you think one of us would die for a renegade rogue we scarcely know?"

DeShane cleared his throat, shifting uncomfortably in his chair. "There's the matter of a fight in the king's audience chamber."

Everything became crystal clear to Kevral in that moment. "Are you saying you're going to force Matrinka or me to take Tae's place?"

Harltan smiled. DeShane shook his head. "I'm not here to do anything but explain the situation and cite the law. Neither I, nor my men, will force anything." His gaze fell to Harltan and paused there several moments in warning.

Kevral did not need the gesture. She already knew neither DeShane nor propriety could fully control the other captain. If he caused more trouble, she would end it swiftly.

"I will give you some advice to do with as you will." Captain DeShane rose, and his men followed suit. "The king will see to it someone dies for a crime as heinous as this. The longer and harder it proves to catch Tae, the worse things will go for him. And we *will* find him. If too long a time passes, the king will almost certainly invoke the ancient law. It will go easier on a volunteer than one forced to comply." He glanced around at the assemblage, his expression betraying a trace of sympathetic misery. The guards headed after him, Harltan moving last.

"Wait," Matrinka started.

Kevral froze, guessing her charge's intention in an instant. Matrinka believed Tae innocent, as did Kevral now. But she would not let the princess die for her loyalty.

"I want—" Matrinka started.

Kevral interrupted, her voice louder. "I'll take Tae's place."

Startled gazes flipped to Kevral in an instant, including Matrinka's.

Ra-khir's expression went from stunned to horrified in an instant. "No," he whispered, the words soft but audible in the silence that followed Kevral's proclamation.

Harltan fairly beamed. DeShane's brows rose, and all of the guards stopped in their places. "Are you sure you want to do that?"

"I'm sure," Kevral said. The hand she raised for a gesture of assurance brushed a bulge in her pocket she had nearly forgotten. She still carried the gem Tae had given her, the gift that had forced her to first ponder the relationship that might develop between them. The consideration that should have come before flashed through her mind now. Their quest was too important to further delay. The party could not spare a princess nor the bard's only heir, and Ra-khir's honor would not allow him to take punishment for a disreputable companion. One other reason surfaced with the touch, one she had not expected and little understood. Like Matrinka, she believed in Tae's innocence. She loved him, she knew that now, apparently enough to die for him. The depth of an emotion she'd scarcely acknowledged she felt surprised her.

"No," Ra-khir said again, this time louder. He rose, clenching his hands to combat the restless need for action. His honor would not allow him to interfere with Pudarian law. Kevral knew he could not offer to substitute for Tae, but the situation had changed. It was no longer Tae's life at stake. "Please, take me in her stead. Please."

The silence intensified, as if everyone in the room held their breath at once. DeShane's attention shifted to Kevral. To save herself, she had to speak. One crime, one punishment. It did not matter who received the sentencing, only that one person did so—not two.

Kevral looked at Ra-khir, his fear and need written plainly in his green eyes. She could no longer deny his love for her nor, she discovered, her own for him. Tae and Ra-khir; so different, yet she cared deeply for them both. The intensity of emotion she had not previously dared to admit frightened her in a way even condemning herself to death did not. "Thank you, Ra-khir, but no. I will take Tae's place for now. He'll come back. I know he will."

Ra-khir opened his mouth, but no words emerged. He tensed, as if to battle through the entire collection of guards at once. But they both knew his honor would prevent it. Tears blurred his gaze to emerald puddles, but he stalwartly refused to look away. Kevral did not envy the war he fought inside himself at that moment.

Kevral turned. "Let's go," she told the guards. They crowded around her, though no one touched her. If she did not go willingly, they could not keep her. "Tae will come." Kevral tossed back one last assurance as she headed peacefully toward execution.

Chapter 30

New Alliances

*I believe in who and what I am. No cause is
worth abandoning my honor.*

—Colbey Calistinsson

Though more than a week had passed since the elves' attack
in the clearing, Ravn had little time to consider his actions
before danger again called him to Griff's side. As always,
the displaced Béarnide found his solace in the Grove. The
shade of many trees coalesced in cool splendor, and wind
ruffled leaves, branches, and stream into beautiful dances.
The odors of living plants and water mingled into a perfume
mankind could never hope to match. The rustle of leaves,
the chop of tiny wavelets, and the irregular skittering of
squirrels seemed more a part of the woodland hush than in-
terruptions of it.

But Ravn saw danger where Griff noticed only the natural
radiance of his sanctuary. Far beyond human sight, elves
crept soundlessly through brush, weeds, and shadows, drawing ever closer to the unsuspecting farm boy.

Ideas flashed through Ravn's mind in a desperate boil.
Suppressing the urge to draw and attack, he charged back toward his home on Asgard. He pounded breathlessly into the
hall only to find his father gone, surely out on the practice
fields or in his own place of privacy. No time to hunt him
down for advice. "Mother! Mother!" Ravn hollered, racing
into his parents' room. He discovered neither of them there.

He could rely on no one but himself, but the solution to his dilemma did not come.

I can't attack and kill in natural form, but it was fine for Mother to protect in hawk guise. The details had no time to settle before Ravn snatched the cloak of feathers from his mother's wardrobe and threw it over his own sinewy shoulders.

Light flashed through the hall of Freya and Colbey, and Ravn burst into flight before he realized he had changed. The cloak's magic transformed his mother into an *aristiri,* one of the beautiful singing hawks that inhabited man's world. But the flashes Ravn caught from the corner of his eyes showed him black feathers befitting his namesake. As a massive raven he soared Asgard's skies, then hurtled down to Midgard in a wild dive. Wind surged and roared around him, drying his eyes to blindness. He caught glimpses of color, the passing of the Bifrost, the rainbow bridge that linked the gods' world with that of mankind. He saw no one as he passed. The Bifrost's guardian, Heimdall, had died in the *Ragnarok,* long before Ravn's birth.

Like a black arrow of vengeance, Ravn rushed to the clearing near Santagithi, the earth flicking past him in streaks of blue, green, and brown. It never occurred to him to wonder how he learned to fly without need to concentrate nor how he moved so quickly. His mind attributed those to the magic of the cloak and focused instead on reaching the Grove. Speed obsessed him, so the trip seemed to take forever, though only a few minutes passed.

The elves closed in on Griff. Now aware of their presence, the Béarnide had risen to meet them, his movements uncharacteristically clumsy. He was saying something Ravn did not bother to decipher. He zipped between the trees in an instant and soared down upon the one nearest Griff.

Before the elf could retreat, Ravn was on him, jabbing his beak into an orange eye. The elf shrieked, driven backward by momentum. The eye popped free, rolling to the ground at Griff's feet. The elf collapsed beneath the buffeting wings.

No killing, Ravn reminded himself. Though rage drove him to hammer the elf to oblivion, he withdrew, turning his attack on another. This one faltered more quickly, throwing his hands over his face to protect his eyes. Ravn slammed his whole body against the shielding arms, sprawling the elf, then he descended on the others.

Another lunged for Griff, diverted by Ravn into a rolling dodge for cover. Ravn screamed a wild battle cry that emerged as a trumpeting squawk. Griff retreated, giving the raven space to maneuver. Ravn set to his task with undiminished fury, poking, pummeling, and hammering to herd the elves into a pack. Occasionally, one broke free, making a desperate move toward Griff that Ravn always countered. Again and again, he redirected them, his blows getting harder as he grew more accustomed to bird form. More like a dog than a raven, he herded the attackers into a defensive bunch and drove them from the clearing. Repeatedly, his beak drove into an ear or for an eye, threatening precious senses as well as causing pain.

Only after he had chased them far from Griff did Ravn pull back long enough to allow a regrouping. Then, the elves drew together for magics of escape. Shortly after he withdrew, they disappeared for other places. *Or Griff.* The thought exploded through Ravn's mind like a panic. He winged his way back, zipping like wind through the clearing.

Griff was gone. Ravn howled, the sound transformed to a squawk his bird larynx could handle. He wove between the trees, searching desperately for the friend his own incaution might have lost. For a moment, he knew a fiery anger for his parents' lecturing. Given his own head, he would have slaughtered this second group of elves as he had the first. His parents had tied his hands, probably costing Griff his life.

Even as the thoughts sprang to life, Ravn spotted Griff running down the final pathway from the Grove to home. The elves had not returned. Apparently, they had fled, leaving Griff to the protection of his own loving family. Not wishing to frighten the Béarnide, Ravn checked his rush, flying directly upward so as not to charge over Griff. For now, the battle had ended, but a worse one had begun. With trepidation, Ravn headed back toward Asgard and the grueling sword practice he knew his father would inflict.

Ravn had done wrong again. And he would pay.

The burden of decision cast upon Baltraine's shoulders felt as if it weighed more than the entire kingdom combined. In one of the private chambers on the fourth floor, he sat and considered his lot, exhaustion a parasite he seemed unable to shake. Repeatedly, the same information paraded through his mind. His research haunted him, and the fate of Béarn hung on a fragile thread that he could reinforce or cut with a single action. Surely, no man before him had ever faced such a desperate and painfully difficult decision. Yet, though all the information lay within his reach, the next course of action would not come.

Though Baltraine would have appreciated the assistance of wise heads and divinity, he consulted neither. He did not know why he avoided advice at a time he most needed it. He did not comprehend his need to explore options alone prior to making what might prove the most fateful decision to affect humankind in centuries, perhaps ever. His own selfish desires eluded understanding. So far, he had not even managed to fully define his choices.

For the millionth time, Baltraine pieced together knowledge he knew better than his own requirements for food and shelter. Béarn required that its ruler embody moral neutrality. So far, it had achieved this goal through a family who carried this ability the way others passed height or birthmarks. But the only heir who might fulfill this requirement lived far away and defied contact. Baltraine reviewed his attempts to reach Griff and felt satisfied that he had done all possible in that regard. Three messengers and two diplomatic groups, including Knights of Erythane and Renshai, had failed. Sending more would only assure more deaths. Somehow he had to find a proper heir, if one existed. *But how?*

The next course of action always eluded Baltraine. He sighed loudly, placing his elbows on the table and resting his heavy head on his palms. His beard trickled through the spaces between his fingers, coarse and curly. His fingers left cold impressions on his cheeks. He backtracked his thinking and began again, dreading the familiar impasse.

A quiet tapping sounded from the other side of the door. Engrossed in his thoughts, Baltraine chose to ignore the intrusion. The knocking continued, gentle but insistent. Despair flared to irritation, then faded to relief in a moment. The interruption pulled him from thoughts pondered too long in helpless circles. He rose, crossed the room, and opened the door.

The master healer stood in the hallway, his sagging features making him look ancient, though he carried fewer than ten years more than Baltraine. Crow's-feet scored the edges of his soft, dark eyes, and moisture coated their surface like rheum. His cheeks drooped in jowly sorrow, and creases marred a face old beyond its years. Gray had replaced the black in his beard, most of it during the last few months.

Baltraine's heart felt as if it was sinking into his abdomen, hammering a wild cadence that made his gut ache. The healer only interrupted his vigil with King Kohleran to inform Baltraine of important changes in the king's condition. The look on the healer's face told all. "Come in, please, Mikalyn." He stepped aside.

The healer obliged, eyes vacant and gait shuffling. Once inside, he turned to face Baltraine again.

Baltraine closed the door and gestured to a seat at the table.

Again, Mikalyn did as his superior bid, collapsing into a seat with a hopelessness too familiar to Baltraine. "My lord, I regret to inform you. King Kohleran is dead."

A new emotion Baltraine could not define filled him in an instant. It was not grief; he had known of the king's imminent demise for too long and the responsibilities the circumstance heaped upon him left no room for sadness. His thoughts exploded like a flock of ducks when a carnivorous turtle emerges suddenly in their midst. His bloodless hands clamped to the ledge of the table, and he sought the same balance and security in his mind that his body found automatically. He did not attempt speech for several moments, nor did the healer seem to expect it.

"Oh, no," Baltraine finally managed, the exclamation far too mild to fit the situation.

The healer nodded.

Baltraine needed to consider the news, to factor it into previous considerations. To do so, he had to be alone, yet he could not dismiss Mikalyn without orders. Until he calculated details, however, he could do little more than maintain the illusion they had thus far managed. "Do what you can to preserve the body and the dignity a beloved king deserves. You must keep up appearances. No one but us must know the king has died."

The healer did not question verbally, but he did study the prime minister with a hint of uncertainty.

"The time is wrong," Baltraine explained. "An announcement like that would throw the populace further into chaos and murder."

Mikalyn nodded, looking even older and more tired, if that was possible. Baltraine wondered if the events of the last few months had taken a similar toll on himself. He felt battered and ancient.

"Dismissed," Baltraine said, his mind already working on this new information.

Mikalyn retreated from the room, and the door clicked closed behind him. Baltraine closed his eyes, trying desperately to compose his thoughts. The finality of the king's death made him at last discard the possibility of ever finding a proper king or queen. The heirs in Béarn had only become more unfit with time and testing. No messenger or envoy could ever reach Santagithi. Once Baltraine accepted the impossibility of the rightful ruler ever sitting upon Béarn's throne, a whole new world of ideas opened to him. In such a situation, it only made sense to fall back on the laws and conventions that existed prior to the staff-test.

Baltraine shifted his thoughts to this new abstraction, his heart rate and breathing quickening. Even before he ran through the sequence of ascension, he knew the older laws no longer eliminated him from becoming king. Right of rulership went first to the king's legitimate children, in order of age. Since Ethelyn's death during the staff-test, none of these remained. Kohleran had no living siblings, so the crown went next to his grandchildren. Murder, suicide, and insanity had claimed all but three. Of these, Griff could not be reached. Matrinka had disappeared, disinherited most believed, though the sage's notes spoke otherwise. The third was Xyxthris.

Thoughts of the twenty-one-year-old son of Kohleran's eldest child made him pause. Once, he had believed the staff-test had plunged the young man into an insanity as deep as that of the six-year-old daughter of Kohleran's sixth child, who sat staring at a wall and had not spoken a word or willingly eaten since the second testing. But, in the last month, Xyxthris seemed to have recovered. He had taken an interest in politics and knowledge for the first time ever. He had attended Baltraine's court daily, despite its tedium, staying after each session to commend Baltraine's decisions. Early on, Baltraine had believed Xyxthris' abrupt change a manifestation of his madness, but time had shown otherwise. The time and effort he put into his studies seemed impossible to feign, and he spoke to Baltraine with increasing logic and insight. More and more, he had worked his way into Baltraine's favor.

Baltraine smiled, hating to admit he had come to like the young man and to trust judgment that nearly always gibed with his own. He could think of far worse rulers than Xyxthris, and he guessed it would prove easy to talk the youngster into marrying at least one of his daughters prior to taking other wives. He had one marriage behind him, but the only offspring of that union was now dead, a victim of the same poison that had taken Kohleran's other great-grandchildren. And the marriage had become as tenuous as Kohleran's life had been until that very morning. Yet Baltraine explored other options. Before the staff-test existed, law had always allowed a king to choose his successor, relative or otherwise. By naming Baltraine regent without specifying an heir, Kohleran had essentially done just that. Baltraine had only to strengthen the wording Kohleran had used to assure his right to the throne in the minds of every citizen.

King Baltraine. The title sounded musical in Baltraine's ears. His chest tingled in apprehension as he considered whether or not he could pull off such a monumental feat. Failure might mean death at the hands of a mob or execution for treason. Still, the reward might prove worth the risk. *King Baltraine.* The image would not leave him. He tried to frame his thoughts into Béarn's need. After all, he surmised, the lack of a neutral ruler could plunge the world into destruction. He did not delude himself into the belief that he could rule better than a proper heir who passed the gods' test. But in the absence of one of those, he felt certain he could do better than anyone else. So long as he considered each judgment and action carefully, perhaps even convened that council Knight-Captain Kedrin had suggested, he could keep Béarn, and the world, on an even keel.

Excitement ran away with Baltraine's thoughts, and he studied the issue from all sides. That he would prove the best king of all of the possibilities did not require deep contemplation. In his heart and mind, he knew no one could best him for honest concern for Béarn and its people. No man or woman could issue more worthy proclamations than himself. Yet the details of how to gain the throne eluded him. No matter the direction of his thoughts, they always returned to a realization that he hated. He could not do this alone. He needed the support of a multitude, and Kohleran's appointment might not prove enough. He needed individual leaders to stand beside him. People like Kedrin and Xyxthris. And, so long as the latter did not wish the throne for himself, Baltraine believed he might curry the very support he needed.

Even as exhilaration built over a fantasy that had never seemed attainable before, reality intruded. Surely Xyxthris worked toward the kingship himself; that would explain his interest in politics and his campaign to win the good graces of Béarn's regent/prime minister. Baltraine knew he could do little to stop the attempt of such a legitimate heir, other than by making the results of the staff-test public. He would have to play the situation carefully. For now, he and Xyxthris needed one another and had much to gain from working together. If it came to a competition for the throne, Baltraine had little choice but to back down. The idea of assassination entered his mind briefly, then fled before the terrible verdict of his conscience. He remained convinced that his bid for Béarn's throne came of reasons wholly altruistic. The gods had reprimanded him for his other lapse in judgment, forcing him to atone by facing and taking advice from the object of his mistake. He would not do such a thing again.

Common sense warred with greed, equally matched despite Baltraine's rationalizations to the contrary. For now, he would enjoy the power given to him by King Kohleran. He would work with Xyxthris toward establishing a new power and hope he could convince the grandson to follow the best course of action rather than the one most beneficial to himself. Otherwise, he would stand loyally by the new king and offer his daughters in marriage.

Simply formulating a course of action lightened Baltraine's burden, and the possibility that he might become king charged him with an energy he had not known in months. That sensation of vigor convinced him he had made the right decision, one supported by the gods. He did not bother to confirm this with a trip to the temple. Something deep inside him knew better. Instead, he headed from the room to begin the process of winning Xyxthris' trust. Experience told him he might find King Kohleran's eldest living heir studying in another room on the same floor. Rising, Baltraine headed for the door.

The prime minister had trod only half the distance from table to door when a firm knock sounded on the panel. Hurrying forward, he grasped the handle and opened.

Xyxthris waited on the other side, unaccompanied as usual. Weeks ago, the council had removed his Renshai guardian, at his insistence. Appearances did not seem reason enough to protect him anymore. His behavior had ruined any trust the populace might once have had in him. A smile on Xyxthris' swarthy features disappeared the moment he caught sight of Baltraine. "Are you well?"

"I'm fine," Baltraine reassured, back-stepping to allow the other entrance and gesturing for him to come inside.

Xyxthris entered, shoving the door closed behind him. He looked at Baltraine. "Oh, dear. He's died, hasn't he?"

"Who?" Baltraine said carefully, not daring to believe news had leaked so quickly. Only he and the master healer knew the truth.

"The king. He's died, hasn't he?"

It seemed fruitless to deny it, the means of Xyxthris' knowledge more important even than secrecy. "How could you possibly know that?"

Xyxthris sighed, the worst confirmed. "It's all over your face. The sorrow. The concern and confusion. The king hovering so near death." Xyxthris shrugged. "What else could do that to you?"

Baltraine studied Xyxthris, seeing more to the heir than he ever had in the past. Sharp brown eyes looked out from wide sockets, nearly round. Pudgy cheekbones rounded the face and softened the otherwise large nose so that he had a look of childlike gentleness about him. For the first time, Baltraine realized how much Kohleran's grandson resembled the king in his youth. It could not hurt to have one who looked so like the ruler the populace had long trusted on his side. Intuition and an ability to read people could prove useful tools to a kingdom in chaos. He suspected Xyxthris had seen the healer come and go, but speculation had also played an impressive role in his knowledge. "I'm sorry," Baltraine said. "He was also your grandfather."

Xyxthris waved off the sentiment. "In that regard, at least, it's for the best. It's hard to watch a loved one suffering."

Baltraine nodded. Concerns of state had made it difficult

to consider the situation in that light. Although he never recalled Xyxthris visiting his grandfather during his illness,
Baltraine could see how the extension of life that had bought
him time also prolonged Kohleran's discomfort.

"The best thing for the king, but it puts you in a bad position."

Baltraine made a thoughtful noise. Anyone with enough
information could have surmised the same.

Xyxthris stared at Baltraine as though attempting to read
his thoughts. Baltraine became uncomfortable under the
scrutiny, but he squelched irritation. He could use, might
even need, Xyxthris' support in the coming days, months, or
years.

"Should we sit down and talk?" Baltraine suggested,
wishing he had had more time to compose his words before
discussing the matter with Xyxthris. But crisis tended to
bring people closer, and he might never get another chance
to talk under similar circumstances.

"Sitting isn't necessary," Xyxthris replied. The steady assurance of his posture and features suggested he had come to
a decision. "We'll need to move anyway."

The words confused Baltraine, but he did not question.
Xyxthris' motivations would become clear soon enough.

"What if I told you," Xyxthris started, gauging Baltraine
with every word, "I had a way to make the people sure the
king still lived?"

Baltraine listened without comment, deliberately holding
his expression neutral.

"But since he really doesn't, you'd stay in command as
long as you want."

Baltraine continued to stare, not daring to believe he had
heard Xyxthris right. He could think of few arrangements
that could please him more, but it seemed impossible that
such could fall into his hands so easily. He knew he needed
to answer Xyxthris, yet he feared the repercussions of what
he might say. He could not exclude the possibility that
Xyxthris baited him into confessing thoughts of treason.
"Well," he responded guardedly, "I think believing their
king still lives might prove best for Béarn and her people.
There's enough violence and confusion out there."

A slight smile formed on Xyxthris' face, so subtle it
seemed more like an impression in his eyes than any change
in his features. "So you'll help?"

Baltraine continued to hedge. "I'll need details first."

"Of course."

"And to understand your motives. What do you get out of such an arrangement?" Baltraine wondered if he had overstepped his boundaries with that question. He did not want to lose Xyxthris' favor when so much lay at stake.

Xyxthris' brow crunched into perplexed furrows. "Béarn is my country, too. And I have as much to lose as anyone if the *Ragnarok* comes. Isn't it obvious?"

"In a general sense, yes." Baltraine saw how the scenario Xyxthris suggested benefited everyone, but he had not expected anyone else to see things as clearly as himself. Some would revile the lying such a strategy required, and others would believe themselves or others more fit to rule than Baltraine. "But don't you want to rule?"

Xyxthris stiffened, and a light flashed in his eyes. Clearly, Baltraine had dredged up something painful, an old wound that had left an ugly scar. "I'm not fit. The staves decreed it so, and I've proved it with my behavior over the past months. I can't even keep a family together. A country would prove too much for me. If I help set you up, at least I'll have a hand in competent rulership."

Baltraine scarcely dared to believe his luck. He kept his breathing deep and even, calming himself. It seemed too good, and that made him suspicious. Yet desire convinced him. "I think you're too hard on yourself," he spoke the necessary words with as much sincerity as he could muster. "Now where do we have to go?"

"Follow me." Xyxthris led the prime minister from the room, across and along the corridor, to the study he regularly chose. They entered. It contained only a chair and table. On its surface lay a book of Béarn's history, apparently Xyxthris' current distraction. Baltraine glanced out the window overlooking the courtyard gardens while Xyxthris closed the door. The young heir came up beside Baltraine and quietly drew the curtains, plunging the room into a dank grayness broken only by sunlight seeping through cracks between the fabric. Having done so, Xyxthris headed for a corner of the room near the door. "Grant me a moment," he said.

Discomfort gnawed at Baltraine, a sensation of profound and supernatural evil. He felt like a toddler desperately trying to sleep while haunted by stories of demons and Loki.

He did not understand the need for darkness, and it took several moments for the obvious to penetrate. More likely, Xyxthris had closed the curtains for privacy rather than to stifle the light. Suddenly, the plan Xyxthris had outlined seemed foolish. No amount of cosmetics could make Baltraine pass for Kohleran. He doubted even Xyxthris could be made up to pass for the grandfather he resembled. The age difference would defy the effort of even the princesses' best handmaidens. But he had little choice except to hear Xyxthris' plan. Maybe the heir had stumbled upon something useful. Or maybe the drugs he had taken had destroyed his mind.

"What do you. . . ?" Baltraine turned from the window, only to find himself alone in the room. He trailed off, startled, and glanced at the door. He had not heard it open or close. The uncomfortable feeling intensified in an instant. He sat in the only chair, feeling out of place, as if he had squeezed into a seat constructed for a child. Obviously, Xyxthris must have slipped quietly away while Baltraine contemplated. Yet Baltraine could not dismiss the image that the younger man had simply disappeared.

Moments stretched into a lengthy pause, while Baltraine's mind conjured everything from Xyxthris returning with a regiment of guards to arrest him to some mystical process that allowed them to read his mind so long as he stayed in this room. He attributed the whole to paranoia, but even logic could not quell his doubts. Something seemed terribly amiss.

Finally, Baltraine had enough. The continued silence and his overactive imagination were quickly driving him to distraction. He rose just as Xyxthris stepped into sight, followed closely by a stranger. Baltraine froze in a position halfway between sitting and standing. The two approached as if through a door, yet through no entrance Baltraine could see. He plopped back down into the chair, uncertain his legs would hold him. Recovering swiftly from that shock, he studied the stranger.

The other stood nearly as tall as himself, with a wild mane of fine red-blond hair. His heart-shaped lips seemed feminine in contour, as did his delicate frame; yet Baltraine unquestionably knew him as a male. One green eye sparkled from between canted, long-lashed lids, its color oddly steady. The other socket lay empty, yet with none of the ugly scarring that drove most with such an abnormality to wear a patch.

Xyxthris gestured from Baltraine to the stranger. "Prime Minister Baltraine, Dh'arlo'mé."

Dh'arlo'mé performed an unfamiliar gesture that seemed respectful. Baltraine copied it with less precision.

"Dh'arlo'mé and his followers can help us. They're elves, and they use magic."

Baltraine swallowed hard, glad he had already chosen to sit. Answers to old questions came to him now, not the least of which was an explanation for the statues come to life in Béarn's courtyard. The belief that he was in the presence of great evil intensified. Xyxthris had intimated that a decision about his involvement in all that came next was imminent. Baltraine suspected the time for choices had ended. He would work with this not-quite-human creature, or he would die.

Baltraine drew breath, desperate to find the words that would make him seem invaluable. To do less, he knew, would translate into suicide.

During the day, crowds filled Pudar's streets from end to end, sweeping past the merchants at a pace few dared to interrupt. Citizens and visitors, trapped too long without necessities, scoured the streets in a mass so tightly packed it resembled a single entity. Therefore, Ra-khir did all of his searching in the quiet darkness that followed the closing of the market. His life became an endless cycle of sleepless days and futile nights. Kevral became an obsession. He heard little of Darris' and Matrinka's discussions. Whenever they talked of any matter but Kevral, they seemed like traitors to him; no topic should take precedence. His own attitude bothered him as much as theirs. He had no right to judge these friends. His honor did not allow it any more than his conscience. It seemed best to ignore them and work on finding Tae. Yet one day followed the next, and he found nothing but gambling houses and empty streets.

By the third day, Ra-khir was becoming desperate. His heart seemed to have tripled in weight, and it burned in his chest like a brand. Food tasted like mud, and the pain swallowing caused drove him to put nothing in his mouth at all. He left the cottage at nightfall, his only hope the kind that accompanies ultimate need.

Cool night air caressed Ra-khir as he wandered the city streets without plan or pattern. The moon seemed to follow him, drawing shadows against the buildings that little resembled the shapes that made them. Tarp-covered stands formed ridges like giants' teeth along the many roadways. Deeper into the city Ra-khir trudged, determined not to quit until he found the key to Kevral's salvation. That her fate lay in Tae's graces only worsened the sense of hopeless distress that plagued Ra-khir.

Ra-khir shied from the opening to an alleyway so narrow and dark he could not see as far as his hand inside it. His instinctive reaction stopped him cold. *I'm looking in the wrong places.* A lifetime of training had kept him on the safer streets, open ones with lighting, guards, and daytime traffic. But a street tough on the run would not follow such a pattern. Ra-khir's mistake was thinking like a knight-in-training instead of an orphan raised on nothing more than his wits and wariness.

A ray of hope trickled through where none had previously existed. Ra-khir reworked the strategy he had not even realized he had, deliberately resisting common sense to pace the scummiest, darkest back alleys Pudar had to offer. Every sense jangled to full alarm as Ra-khir traced roadways he would otherwise not have entered on a dare. Only love could drive him to do such a thing, and he had to believe that such sacrifice would triumph. To think otherwise would undermine the last of his flagging reserves.

Hour flowed into desperate hour. The constant need for caution made him all too aware of every passing second. Though noise might draw unwelcome attention, he called Tae's name softly on occasion. He could not wholly trust the hunted Easterner to find him, especially since they had never cared for one another. Ra-khir clung to Matrinka's explanation and hoped Tae would prove as generous now as he had, apparently, in the past. Kevral could not die.

The image of Kevral sprawled on some torturer's rack, willingly giving herself to the executioner's knife brought tears to his eyes and nausea to his belly. He had eaten little since Kevral's pronouncement, and acid churned through his gut with no food to counterbalance it. His thoughts slid to his father as well and to Kedrin's unjust imprisonment. Loyalty had doomed both of the people he loved: Kevral's to a street punk and Kedrin's to his country. Guilt twitched through Ra-khir then. *I should have stayed in Béarn and worked on freeing my father. If I had, we would still live at home and Kevral would never have sacrificed herself.*

Ra-khir cast the idea aside. Their mission remained sacred, despite the delay; and it was at Kedrin's insistence that he had gone at all. Ra-khir had no way to know the consequences of having chosen this other path, and hating himself for doing what seemed right at the time served no useful purpose. He had no choice but to commit himself to the task at hand.

Even as Ra-khir dismissed the new train of thought plaguing him, something soft slid across the front of his shins. Startled, Ra-khir stiffened, heart rate doubling in an instant. Eyes now adjusted to the darkness, he sorted out patches of white and gray near his feet. *Mior.* The identification swept away fear, and his heart settled back into its regular cadence. "Mior, what are you doing here?" he whispered. "Go back to Matrinka."

In response, the cat meowed and remained in place.

"Go on, Mior. It's not safe for you here." Ra-khir did not know how much Mior understood, but her communication with her mistress suggested it would prove far more than an ordinary cat.

When Mior again did not obey, Ra-khir stepped over her and continued his inspection.

Mior rubbed across the front of his legs twice more, Ra-khir ignoring the animal for the more important matter at hand. Again, Mior twined around his feet, meowing piteously.

The distraction quickly became an annoyance. "Mior," Ra-khir said firmly. "Go away."

Without waiting to see if she obeyed, Ra-khir sidestepped, then edged forward again. The darkness deepened as poorly crafted rooftops overlapped, locking out the light of moon and stars. Ra-khir's vision disappeared, and he became even more wary as his safety depended on fewer, less often used senses. A whisk of movement touched his hearing from ahead, and he paused, uncertain whether to worry or hope. "Tae?" he said softly. He strained his vision, making out a barrier ahead. It appeared he had reached a dead end. Ra-khir sighed, taking one more step to ascertain the impasse. His foot came down on something soft and unstable. *Mior!* Afraid to hurt the animal, Ra-khir twisted. His ankle landed in an unnatural position, and pain shot through his leg. Balance lost, he tumbled to the dirt alleyway. Momentum sent him skidding toward the blockage, tearing skin from his left arm and shin.

"Damn." Ra-khir grabbed at the wall for support, surprised to feel grainy wood rather than the stone construction he expected. Low to the ground, a black square interrupted the otherwise steady surface, hidden by weeds growing in the untended roadway. Curious, he touched the inconsistency, and his hand met no resistance. He had discovered an opening in what had initially seemed a solid wall. *A chute?* It made no sense to have a place to fling laundry or food in the middle of a narrow alley.

Mior paced between Ra-khir and the hole while he tried to ignore the cat. He sat back on his haunches. Whatever its origin, the opening would admit a crawling person. It would prove a tight squeeze for a man as large as Ra-khir, impossible had he worn his armor and sword, but if Tae had stumbled upon the same place, surely he would have taken advantage of it.

Excitement tingled in Ra-khir's chest, and he forced away the hope that accompanied it. His efforts so far had always ended in disappointment. The more faith he placed in having found the right place at last, the worse the fall when he discovered he had made an error. Still, something inexplicable told him he had finally found Tae, a belief as deeply set as his religion. At last, he had uncovered Kevral's liberator, and he could put the situation right. Ra-khir plunged his head and shoulders through the opening, Mior mewing frantically behind him.

Darkness closed around Ra-khir, as tight as the wooden walls. He wriggled forward, the sides pressing the fabric of his tunic against him, rescuing him from scrapes and splinters. For a moment, he stuck, hands scrabbling for purchase on the roadway. Then he fought one shoulder through, and the rest followed as naturally as a baby leaving the womb. He found himself in a short tunnel, a square of light at its end. He crawled through, excitement building despite his best efforts to hold it in check. As he approached the end, he drew breath to call for Tae.

But, before the word left his lips, hands seized his wrists and hair, dragging him through the opening. He twisted, catching a spiraling view of strange, filthy faces studying him with expressions of rage. Six pinned him to an earthen floor, their grips pinching his wrists and ankles like vises. Ra-khir froze, not bothering to struggle yet. The unexpected greeting killed hope and refired desperation. He looked for Tae among the group, noticing details as he did so. He counted nine youths, all in their teens and all male. Those old enough sported scraggly beards that looked more like weeks of stubble. Some wore tattered rags and others newer, cleaner garb; but every one wore red and black with the same fanatical devotion that he had for royal blue and tan. A few cracks in the overlapping rooftops admitted moonlight. Two stone walls from buildings on either side of the alley and two of wood that spanned the roadway formed a room protected from the wind if not the rain. Crates lay stacked in one corner, a few more scattered around the makeshift room, apparently for use as chairs.

Ra-khir attempted to rise, but the hands tightened, holding him in place. "I'm sorry I intruded. I'm looking for someone. I wonder if you've seen—"

"Shut up!" shouted one of the youths who wasn't holding him. Tall and nearly as muscular as Ra-khir, he seemed the leader. Hazel eyes glared at the knight-in-training from beneath uneven, brown bangs. The rest of his hair hung in curtains on either side of his head.

Ra-khir fell silent, more annoyed by the rudeness than afraid. He had no reason to believe these youngsters, many his own age, meant him any harm.

The leader made a gesture Ra-khir could not read. "Pick him up."

The others complied without a word, and Ra-khir made their job easier by rising with them. The ones who had clamped his ankles to the ground withdrew, leaving only two to hold his wrists. He felt the urge to straighten clothes dragged into dirty wrinkles but resisted it. Ra-khir was certain he could wrest his hand free from the child at his left, but it seemed impolite at the moment. He had encroached on their private territory, and they had a right to establish security before releasing him. They had not chosen the politest means of doing so, but Ra-khir expected nothing more from low class youngsters on the streets.

The leader stepped up to Ra-khir, so close the Erythanian could smell the sweeter aroma of fruit on the other's breath, beneath the overpowering odor of beer. "Who are you?"

"I am called Ra-khir." As Kevral had warned, Ra-khir did not complete his title. "Again, I apologize for my intrusion."

"Your intrusion?" The young man snickered, and the others laughed in his wake. "Your in-*troo*-shin." They laughed again, then the leader sobered. He paced a quiet, studying circle around Ra-khir, and came to a halt in front of the prisoner again.

Ra-khir cleared his throat, tiring of the inspection. He had no time to waste. "I'm on important business. May I leave now, please?"

The leader stared at Ra-khir as if he had taken leave of his senses. A few snickers broke the ranks, silenced by a glare from the leader. "I'm not finished with you yet. Not nearly finished. You're going to pay for your mistake."

Ra-khir considered the words and the tone with which they had been spoken. "Pay? Is that a challenge?"

The leader smiled, revealing a mouthful of chipped teeth separated by gaps. "If you wish."

"Fine." Ra-khir could accept that his transgression had earned him a future duel. "You may choose time, place, and weapons then. That's the custom where I come from."

More snickers broke the hush that followed. The leader simply stared. "That's your custom, is it?"

"It is."

"Your custom?"

"Yes," Ra-khir affirmed.

The leader turned his back, hand stroking his stubble as if in consideration. Suddenly, he whirled back. Silver flashed in his hand. Before Ra-khir could consider its origin, a knife tore a fiery path across the skin over his gut. Shock and pain stole his wits momentarily, and he recoiled with enough force to tear his left hand free. He stared in disbelief at the gash in his tunic and the scarlet blood trickling over blue linen.

"That's our custom," the leader stated, sheathing the blood-smeared knife without bothering to clean it. He turned his back again, this time retreating, and spoke to his followers without bothering to look at them. "He's all yours. Do as you please, but be sure he doesn't have the chance to tell anyone about this place."

Ra-khir steeled himself for the worst, gathering breath for a vow of silence and a speech that might earn him a reprieve. A fist crashed into his diaphragm, slamming the air from his lungs. Pain lanced through the depths of his gut, worse than the sharp tear of the knife. He gulped desperately for air, but his lungs refused to function. Kicks, punches, and gouges rained down upon him. The force sent him crashing to the floor, head thumping against the wooden barrier. None of this compared to the agony of needing and not finding air. What little vision the roof gaps allowed disappeared in a wild swirl of dizzying spots.

Ra-khir grappled for his own knife, knowing as he did so that an unexpected slash might gain him an opening to escape. His training resurfaced as naturally as the instinct to breathe. He could not attack unannounced, not and remain a knight-in-training. His diaphragm spasmed, then regained function, and air wheezed through his throat in a trickle. As he gulped hungry breaths, he cursed the very honor he refused to betray. His fingers closed over the hilt even as boots hammered bruises the length of his arm. But he did not whip it free. He used a controlled draw that revealed its presence to his attackers before he could use it.

"Knife!" one yelled, the warning enough for Ra-khir. He plunged it toward one blindly. Then a foot kicked the blade from his grip, and teeth sank into his empty fist. He heard the rasp of steel from several directions at once. He struggled to rise again as short swords and daggers bit rents from his legs. A heavy object cracked against the back of his head, driving his face into the dirt. Consciousness wavered, and the world spun in limping, disjointed circles. Another blow to the side of the head knocked him sprawling. His sight went blank first, then all sensation left him.

Chapter 31

The Black Renshai

Competence is a minimum expectation, not deserving of admiration.

—Colbey Calistinsson

Clutching Mior against her body with her left hand, Matrinka charged through Pudar's night streets, still in slippers and her sleeping gown. Darris managed to keep pace at her side, though he gasped for every breath. He, too, had not changed from his nightclothes, though he had strapped on his sword and belt.

Matrinka's concern for Ra-khir spared nothing for Darris. She knew his chest wound had fully healed. His difficulties came from a process the master healer had called "deconditioning," too much time spent in a sickbed. The run might tax him, but it would not harm him; in fact, the exercise might do his underworked muscles some good.

T.M. here, Mior sent. The concepts of right and left confounded Mior, so they had created a code. "T.M.," or "toward Mior," told Matrinka to turn in the direction of the hand holding the cat. "A.M." meant "away from Mior."

Matrinka paused, nearly missing the thready alleyway. *Here?*

Yes, here. Hurry.

Darris drew up, panting. "Don't you think we should grab a guard or two first?"

"Even if we could spare the time, they wouldn't help us." Matrinka gripped Darris' arm and hauled him into the alley, her mind filled with a story she had once heard in Béarn's courtroom. A Pudarian had come, promising to keep the streets safe for money. He had spoken of the scourge of gangs in Pudar, described the tiny transgressions such rabble punished with bloodshed. As a mob and spurred by the wrong leaders, their private bond of brotherhood allowed them to butcher innocents without conscience. Matrinka kept moving, forcing the memory from her mind. Surely, the Pudarian had exaggerated for the purpose of gaining her grandfather's attention. Similar gangs had never taken root in Béarn. "We may already be too late."

A wall appeared suddenly in front of Matrinka. She skidded to a stop, an abrupt side step all that saved her from a collision. *Now where?*

Down and through. There's an opening. Mior added suddenly, *Be careful. Do you want me to go in first?*

No, go get help. Matrinka cast about for the entrance, finding nothing with her eyes. She ran her hands along the wall, only then identifying it as wood. *Where is it?*

Here. Mior squeezed from Matrinka's grip and guided her hand to the opening. *Wouldn't it be better if I stayed here and you got help? I can't talk.*

Ra-khir may need my ability to talk. A moment could spell the difference between life and death. Without further discussion, Matrinka wriggled into the opening, not knowing whether Mior obeyed her instructions and doubting it mattered.

The fit proved tight, the opening designed for Pudarian youngsters. Matrinka did not hesitate. She had not reached her full growth as Ra-khir had. Anything the muscular Erythanian could fit through, she and Darris could also.

The short tunnel spilled into a room. Matrinka clambered to her feet assessing all she needed to know in an instant. Ra-khir lay still on the far side of the room, surrounded by strangers. Blood stained his familiar blue and tan linens, and bruises stamped the length of his limbs. She did not take the time to study him for evidence of breathing, charging to his aid before Darris could gain his feet to stop her.

"Matrinka, no!" Darris shouted where physical action failed him. Gang members shifted to intercept Matrinka, blocking her view of Ra-khir.

"Get out of my way!" Matrinka shrieked, slamming into

a wall of bodies that barely shifted with the impact. She clawed frantically, shoving for a gap between them.

"To arms!" their leader shouted as Darris lunged to her defense.

Swords clattered to the ready at Matrinka's back, and the line in front of her weakened as gang members turned their attention from her to the new threat. A scrawny blond cursed. His foot cracked against her shin, and he shoved her toward the wall. Equilibrium lost, she crashed against the stone. Her teeth slammed closed on her tongue. She staggered blindly, tasting blood.

"Ra-khir!" Disoriented, Matrinka cast about for her fallen companion. She caught a swirling glimpse of Darris embroiled in combat with too many opponents at once. Then a fist hammered the side of her head, and she collapsed, stars spinning through her vision. She went deliberately limp and hoped they would tire of battering a woman who did not fight back. The Pudarian's description suggested otherwise, but she had no other strategy.

Shouts and the ring of metal told her Darris was still fighting, and she drew some solace from that. Guilt struck as hard as any physical blow. She had dragged them both into danger she knew they could not handle to rescue a friend who might already be dead. Panic had not allowed her to think clearly. Now, strangely, imminent, inescapable death did. Yet, though she regretted what would surely happen next, she could not have handled the situation any differently. As a healer, she would not allow Ra-khir to die. Now, he might still live. Any delay would have brought them too late. She wished Darris had not come, but she knew he would never have let her go alone, not under any circumstances. He had chosen his own fate.

Locating Ra-khir, Matrinka shifted toward him and pulled herself to her hands and knees. Before she could crawl, a foot raced toward her head. She flinched, and it caught her a glancing kick to the ear that sent her sprawling again. This time, she lay still, feigning unconsciousness, tears burning her eyes. Fear became all-consuming. The courage that worry had sparked disappeared in the realization of personal danger. She had made a fatal mistake. It would cost all three of them their lives. Matrinka prayed desperately for help.

The clatter of combat stopped suddenly, and a dull thud followed. *Darris*. Matrinka could not find the strength to look. It would end with Kevral executed for a friend's crime, the three of them killed for trespass, and Tae the only one remaining to restore the high king. *Please don't let him be dead. Please, gods, please, don't let him be dead.*

Mior's "voice" touched her then. *Look up.*

The cat's contact galvanized Matrinka. She twisted to see, just as a body clothed in black plunged through a gap between overhanging rooftops. Silently, it fell. It landed on the leader, bearing him to the ground. Steel flashed in the moonlight. Then, the one who had slipped through a crack that seemed scarcely wide enough for rats rolled to his feet, leaving the leader bleeding from the throat on the earthen floor.

For a moment, no one moved. The newcomer slashed a broad arc through the air in front of him, a maneuver that looked suspiciously Renshai. Dark clothing, hair, and skin all but disappeared into the shadows. He spouted a string of Northern syllables in a voice that made even the musical singsong sound harsh. His eyes measured the group in front of him, and his stance suggested he found them lacking.

A howl sounded above him, an answering battle cry that Matrinka recognized as Mior's.

The newcomer scowled. "Stay out there," he shouted back, as if to an army at his heels. There're only nine of them. Barely worth *my* time. And I'm not sharing." A hint of a harder accent slipped through beneath an adequate rendition of Northern.

If not for her time in Béarn's court, Matrinka might have missed it. Now, it told her conclusively what her eyes refused to believe. *Tae. That's Tae!*

The gang members looked nervously at their leader and the spreading pool of scarlet at his neck. With a healer's detachment, Matrinka noted that it no longer spurted, only trickled. He was dead. The gang looked to the biggest of their members left alive. That one, a sandy-haired, lanky youth studied Tae with a critical eye.

Tae sheathed his sword, glancing fearlessly around the room. The action, the demeanor, the expression were a perfect imitation of Kevral. Tae said nothing, looking bored.

The stalemate continued for several moments as the gang waited for some command from their new leader who silently ogled Tae.

Matrinka moved cautiously toward Ra-khir. Darris sat on the floor, eyes open and alert. She saw no blood on him, and relief filled her. Their lives still hung on the success of Tae's bluff. Previous experience told her that, while tremendously skilled at stalking and attacking unexpectedly, Tae would have difficulty holding his own against even one or two of the gang members. Many of them still held their swords, while Tae would have to draw his again.

Tae motioned to Matrinka, Ra-khir, and Darris in turn, using almost imperceptible head movements. "Those three are mine," he said. "Do I take them now, or do I kill you all and take them?"

The leader's jaw set, and he considered the words. "Who are you?" he finally said.

"I am Tykayrin, the black Renshai." Tae Northernized his name.

"You're Renshai?" the teen interjected, his skepticism evident.

"Yes." Tae's gaze trained unwaveringly on the new leader. "And I'm getting restless. I haven't had a chance to properly blood my sword in a week, not since I slaughtered the crown prince and his fifteen-guard entourage."

Now all of the gang members studied Tae intently. Being the one accused of the crime, he fit the description almost exactly. The sandy-haired leader pointed out the discrepancy. "They said he were an Easterner."

"And don't I look it," Tae replied in his best Northern accent. "That's why they call me the black Renshai. Now, if you've finished your interrogation, I'll take these three and go." He flashed them one of Kevral's toothy, cocksure grins. "Or would you rather attack me? I know I'd prefer that." His hand fell to his hilt.

The leader's fist on his own hilt went bloodless, and his face set with determination. Several of the gang members tensed, as did Matrinka. She tried to study Ra-khir long enough to establish his condition, but her attention kept straying back to the confrontation between Tae and the gang. What happened there decided all else. Better not to ever know whether or not she might have saved Ra-khir.

For several moments, the leader and Tae matched one another, stare for stare. Tears blurred Matrinka's vision, and she trembled uncontrollably. A glance at Darris revealed him frozen in position, watching the proceedings. He looked as pale as he had when the infection nearly claimed him. Matrinka tried to will all of her strength to Tae. He was the one who mattered. If his composure broke for even a millionth of a second, it would doom them all.

But Tae did not falter. His hand on his sword remained relaxed, the other still at his side. His expression revealed only expectation, devoid of self-doubt or fear. For what felt like an hour, Tae flawlessly mimicked Kevral's inhuman confidence and disarming habit of not bothering to draw a weapon until she needed to strike. Finally, the leader backed down. "Take them and go. Don't come back."

Even then, Tae did not concede. "I go where I please, and no man nor army can stop me." He looked from Matrinka to Darris, arrogantly turning his back on the leader as if to show he'd never considered the other a threat. Knowing better, Matrinka watched the sandy-haired youth. Should he attack, she would signal Tae.

But the leader stood aside, not daring to call Tae's bluff. Like Matrinka, he had more than his own life at stake, and Tae's description of street orphans made it clear they saw one another as family.

"Get him, and let's go," Tae said.

Matrinka followed Tae's gaze to Ra-khir, and it took her mind inordinately long to realize he wanted Darris and herself to heft the knight-in-training. Once she understood, she headed for Ra-khir. He felt warm to her touch, obviously alive. As Darris attempted to lift him, he groaned and opened his eyes. Relief flooded her, so intense it washed away the fear. She and Darris hustled Ra-khir toward the tiny exit, while Tae stood guard. As they emerged into the cool night air, Mior joined them. Darris and Matrinka supported Ra-khir, Darris trying to rush him down the alleyway.

Matrinka held back. "We have to wait for Tae."

"He'll catch up," Darris hissed back. "Hurry."

Matrinka assisted Darris. This time, Ra-khir slowed the escape by stopping dead in the roadway. "No. Can't let Tae leave. Have to talk."

"Come on!" Darris dragged at his friends. "He knows what he's doing. If we delay, we may lose our chance."

A moment later, Tae skittered through the opening. "Go. Go!" Tae took over Matrinka's position, and Mior leaped to her shoulders. Together, they moved as quickly as Ra-khir's injuries allowed, winding through Pudar's moonlit streets until they found a quiet place between a cluster of tarp-covered stands.

Ra-khir shifted his weight from his companions. Tae stepped back, but before he could move farther, Ra-khir clutched Tae's wrists in both hands. Earnest green eyes filled with pain pleaded with Tae.

Tae avoided the stare, focused on the fingers clamped around his wrists like shackles.

Ra-khir's voice emerged as a hoarse whisper. "Kevral took your place in the king's custody. If you don't surrender, they'll execute her." He lowered his head, apparently assailed by dizziness. His grip loosened, and he staggered a step backward.

Tae jerked free, into a skittering retreat.

"No," Ra-khir said softly. He scanned the darkness as if he planned to dive on Tae to stop him. But, whatever his intention, his battered body failed him. He sagged to the ground, Matrinka and Darris scarcely managing to grab hold in time to slow his descent.

Matrinka glanced up, seeking Tae in the darkness. At first, she believed he had gone. Then her eyes carved a gray shadow from the blackness. She knew she needed to say something to assist a situation far more complicated than Ra-khir's honor allowed him to understand. Yet the words would not come. She stared helplessly, uncertain who to comfort or what to say. Her healer's instincts drove her to tend Ra-khir, yet she would do him little good treating his body when his mind suffered as well. If she did not talk to Tae now, she might lose the opportunity forever. And still, she found nothing to say.

Accustomed to handling crises with music, Darris launched into a song. His sweet voice filled the roadway with an ancient melody that lacked the wild syncopation of modern ditties. He sang of Sterrane, Béarn's ancient king. In a single, poetic stanza, Darris told the story of the royal slaughter that had left only Sterrane alive of his family and wrested the throne from him and his line. Though Matrinka had heard the story many times, usually with far more detail, the combination of perfect phrases and haunting tune brought tears to her eyes. She knelt at Ra-khir's side, reveling in his living warmth and deep, slow breaths, hiding the sorrow she could not quell though it involved events long before her time.

Darris sang of Sterrane's return as an adult, accompanied by loving friends determined to help restore the title stolen from him by violence. The group met resistance from Sterrane's uncle and his armies, and the idea of a battle daunted Sterrane. Not for its effort; he had demonstrated himself able enough in the biggest of all wars. But peaceful Sterrane could not stomach the idea of innocent deaths for him. When a personal feud placed the outcome into the hands of one friend who agreed to single combat, Sterrane chose to give up his throne rather than allow that friend to risk death for him. Three words, sung in a tune that pierced Matrinka's heart, expressed the bond between friends so strong it transcended a kingship.

The faint shadow that represented Tae shifted but did not disappear. Matrinka's heart pounded, and uncertainty assailed her. The emotion raised by Darris' song lingered. She tried to place herself in Tae's situation, but before she could attempt the mental switch, Darris began another verse.

This time, the bard's heir sang of a cluster of citizens hiding from rampaging Renshai, back in the days when the warrior tribe had devastated the West. Caught up in a stranger's fear, Matrinka found herself incapable of action. She could only listen and pray. Darris sang of a woman and her frightened, hungry baby. The more the mother clutched, the more the infant screamed, threatening the lives of every citizen. Something had to be done, or all of them would perish for the noise of one.

Finally, with tear-filled eyes and a heart like lead, the mother handed the baby to a man among them, an elder she hoped could kill when her own conscience could not allow it. Matrinka's tears quickened, sliding down her face beyond her control. She felt the mother's agony as her own, a fiery pain that seemed to consume her insides. Yet, what good could come of saving this one when all, including the child, would die for its cries.

The elder did not kill. As the baby's wailing turned to frantic shrieks, the elder cuddled it in his arms and ran. Though he had little chance of getting far, he found the choice to try better than the obvious alternative. He left the mother with the hope that her baby survived. For him, that assurance was worth his life.

He did not make it.

Ra-khir moved restlessly beneath Matrinka's fingers, but she could not see him through the blur of tears that followed Darris' verse. The bard's heir crafted another situation, this time a mother sentenced to eternity in the Eastern mines. Her grown son created a disturbance in the courtroom that allowed her escape, though it cost him his life. And the mother lived on, with a guilt that drove her nearly to insanity.

Finally, Darris quit, the last note floating over the sleeping city in judgment. Matrinka wiped the moisture from her eyes in time to watch the shape that represented Tae vanish into the darkness. Only then, Ra-khir sat up, his eyes hollow, though whether from the song, the situation, or both, Matrinka did not know.

"He's gone, isn't he?" Ra-khir managed.

Darris searched the night. "That seems to be the case, though you can never tell with Tae."

Ra-khir stood before Matrinka thought to assist him. "Damn my weakness. I could have stopped him. I could have dragged him to the king." He took a step down the roadway in the direction Tae had taken, as if to chase him. Then, recognizing the futility, he halted. "Damn."

"No, you couldn't have." Darris spoke softly but with authority. "Your honor wouldn't have allowed you to force him to his execution. Especially knowing that he's probably innocent. Even if your honor allowed it, mine wouldn't."

Matrinka looked from Darris to Ra-khir to the place where Tae had stood moments earlier. She no longer saw any sign of the Easterner. She might never see him again; but in her mind, he would remain there until she saw him elsewhere. Mior pressed against her leg, reminding Matrinka of her silent presence. She sent a feeling of sympathy.

Ra-khir turned on Darris. "We can't let Kevral die."

"Well, we certainly can't drag an unwilling man to execution."

Ra-khir defended his position. "There's nothing dishonorable about bringing a guilty man to justice." Matrinka heard the desperation in the knight-in-training's voice, his desire to temper need with principle without rationalizing an unjust decision. She stayed out of the argument, uncertain where she stood. She saw no way to win, only to trade the life of one friend for another. And with Tae's whereabouts once again unknown, the discussion seemed academic anyway. She clutched Mior in a swirl of worry and listened to the men argue over a problem without solution.

"First," Darris asserted, "we haven't established that Tae's guilty. Second, Kevral willingly took Tae's place, without coercion. That frees Tae from any obligation to Pudar." Darris glanced at Matrinka, squirming in a fashion that had become familiar. The bard's laws did not constrain him as tightly as his mother, yet. Still, long discussions outside of song always made him uncomfortable.

Ra-khir lowered his head, conceding the point but obviously unnerved by it. He fidgeted nearly as much as Darris.

"It's Tae's decision." Matrinka finally added her piece. "And I'm not sure there's a right choice."

Ra-khir whirled to face her now, the sudden movement momentarily unbalancing him. He corrected his equilibrium with an irritable side step, but the look he gave Matrinka was harsh with betrayal.

Matrinka defended her words, "You're asking Tae to sacrifice his life for Kevral's."

Ra-khir shrugged. "She agreed to do it for him."

"That was her decision." Matrinka returned. "It's not fair to expect everyone to do what Kevral did. Not any more than you can expect everyone to follow knight's honor."

The last point clearly hit home. Ra-khir's expression became more horrified.

Not meaning to worsen the situation for him, Matrinka reviewed her words. Only then, she realized she had raised the very issue that had kept Kevral at Ra-khir's throat for the first part of their journey: the assumption that knights insisted their enemies follow their honor. Matrinka redirected her point. "I'm just saying Kevral's braver than most. There're many things she does that I wouldn't think to try." She continued with what seemed like a more important detail. "Remember, too, that Kevral put Tae into a difficult situation. He might have evaded Pudar's guards forever. Kevral's the one who created the current dilemma."

Ra-khir stared. "I can't believe you're saying this! Kevral did what she did to save our mission. So we wouldn't get stuck in Pudar. Damn it, Matrinka, she did it for you."

"For the world," Darris corrected. "Our mission reaches far beyond Béarn."

Ra-khir winced. This time, Matrinka believed physical pain responsible.

"Let's go home," Matrinka said, looping an arm through Ra-khir's and inclining her head toward him to cue Darris.

Ra-khir's pride probably would not allow him to request the assistance he needed.

Darris moved into position, his long relationship with Matrinka making words unnecessary. They helped Ra-khir walk toward home; and, though he placed little of his weight on Matrinka, he seemed unusually heavy. Ultimately, they all knew the decision came down to worth, to who mattered more, a young Renshai or a ruffian. And the only man who could make that assessment was the ruffian himself.

Ra-khir threw one last comment, "I'd do it. I'd give myself for Kevral if only she'd let me."

Neither Matrinka nor Darris responded; it was clearly unnecessary. Yet Mior did so in Matrinka's mind. *That's because he loves her. But it still remains to be seen whether Tae loves her enough to do the same.*

The natural movements that accompanied breathing sent waves of pain through Ravn, and he sat as still as possible on the river's shore. Beside his son, Colbey stared at the breeze-ruffled waters, showing no guilt or residual anger for the intensive practice that had left Ravn aching for days. Freya paced with the impatience of a caged animal, her displeasure still unspent. At length, she stopped directly in front of her son, waiting until he met her sapphire gaze before speaking.

"How could you do such a thing after what we told you last time?"

Ravn sighed. Until recently, he had taken his mother's beauty for granted. Now that adolescence had come upon him, he found it painful to look at her, embarrassed by the thoughts her perfect features raised. Her eyes shone from sockets flawlessly set, surrounded by long, thick lashes. Her nose perched straight and strong, and her full lips seemed always to beckon, even when, as now, they were thinned to an angry line. Symmetrical and set at just the right height, her cheeks held a youthful flush.

Yet, for all its radiance, her face scarcely prepared a man for the delicate curves of a body no mortal could ever match. Though a thousand human artists might spend their entire lives trying, they could never capture Freya's loveliness. The gods, themselves, had not managed to do so either. For more than a year, Ravn had wondered whether all sons saw their mothers in such a light. But eventually he had eavesdropped on enough of the gods' conversations to realize his mother was unique. Goddess of fertility, Freya embodied the perfect appearance of a woman, the standard against which all others would always be measured. And he did not know whether to view this as blessing or curse.

Freya's lips pursed still more. "Raska, answer me."

Jarred from his unholy thoughts, Ravn stared, desperately trying to remember the question. Though the words would not come, he guessed it had something to do with his reasons for protecting Griff again. "I didn't attack. I used the same disguise you did when you took care of Father. What did I do wrong?"

Freya's face reddened, and she looked away.

The impression that she had given up on her son hurt worse than any words. Ravn looked toward his father.

"You did better this time than last," Colbey admitted, the concession unusual. When it came to sword work, he expected each practice to exceed the last. Anything less meant a student had not given his all, an insult to his sword and to his teacher. "But you still fought that mortal's battle for him. Neither man's world nor ours can afford the repercussions that might come of such action."

Ravn kicked at a stone. Dislodged, it rolled into the water with a muffled splash, and tiny rings widened from its landing. "So I should have let him die?" He felt certain no words could convince him that such was the case.

"Perhaps." Colbey kept his gaze directly on Ravn. "There are actions between. Subtlety is a virtue all gods and their kith should know and practice, along with patience." For the first time in weeks, he smiled. "And I could use the lesson better than most. At least we know for certain you're my son."

Freya glared. Surely Colbey had meant the comment as an insult to self and son, not to Freya; yet the implication remained. Stories about her wanton nature abounded, mostly exaggerated.

"So what do I do?" Ravn pleaded with his father, but Freya answered.

"Nothing," she said softly. "Until you learn control, you're forbidden from interacting with humans."

Ravn jerked his head toward Freya, dread like a dense cloud in his chest. "But he'll die."

"I have spoken," Freya said. "And I am done." Without

further word, she tossed back her cascade of golden hair and headed toward home.

"Please," Ravn appealed to his father, though his mother usually proved more reasonable. As the Keeper of the Balance, Colbey could allow little leeway. The mistakes of gods had far-reaching repercussions. "He'll die without my help. I'll do better. I promise."

Colbey sighed deeply, his expression thoughtful. "I wouldn't dare gainsay your mother."

Ravn sagged, beaten for the moment.

"However," Colbey continued. "I will teach you the control she mentioned, freeing you to do as you must. Come." He offered his hand.

Eagerly, Ravn accepted it, realizing too late it would prove far less painful to stand at his own pace. As Colbey helped hoist Ravn, every muscle in his body screamed for mercy. Ravn fought to hide the agony. He would not give his father the satisfaction.

Colbey studied Ravn wordlessly, with only mild curiosity. He would punish but never taunt. "Ready?"

"Now?" Ravn could scarcely believe his luck. "Are you going to help that Renshai girl?"

"Yes," Colbey admitted. "With subtlety."

Ravn could scarcely wait to learn.

Chapter 32

Affairs of the Heart

*I've got my sword, my horse, and my trusted
friends. What more could I need?*

—Colbey Calistinsson

Kevral Tainharsdatter looked through the bars of her cell,
watching the three Pudarian guards as they watched her. She
did not bother to test the locks. She had come as a willing
replacement for Tae. Escape would only make fugitives of
them both. Worse, it meant cowardice, and no crime more
violated Renshai tenets and honor. She had made her decision. No matter how foolish it seemed now, she would suffer
the consequences honestly.

Kevral stepped away from the front of the cell to explore
it more fully. Never having been in a dungeon before, she
did not know exactly what to expect. She had, however, anticipated more grime and dankness, as well as other prisoners. Her cage contained a bed and a sewage hole with a
curtain for privacy. A plate of salted pork and vegetables and
a bowl of water lay neatly on the floor. Kevral suspected
they had placed her in a place little used, perhaps reserved
for upper class suspects, foreign dignitaries accused of
wrongdoing, or those who seemed likely to be proved innocent and set free. Or maybe they used it for circumstances
such as her own, in which the prisoner agreed to accept punishment for another. *Like that happens all the time.*

In the cottage, taking Tae's place had seemed natural, a
way to keep Matrinka from doing the same and of rescuing

a mission already delayed too long. The courage such a commitment required had seemed secondary, a small test of a bravery she would never allow to fall into question. Only now, the implications of what she had done were finally beginning to become clear. She would die, outside of battle and without valor. She would never find Valhalla. The goal she had worked toward since birth would elude her, not from cowardice or lack of training, and not because a better foe had bested her in combat. She would die in shame for friendship and Béarn's need.

With a sigh of resignation, Kevral sat on the bed, face clasped in her hands. She did not fear death. As a Renshai, she'd always believed it would find her sooner rather than later. She feared only the means of her death, one that condemned her to the frozen wastes of Hel rather than the eternal war for brave warriors who died giving their all in battle. All of the previous Kevralyns, including the last one, her namesake, would look down from Valhalla in sorrow. The name would die with her. No Renshai would call their baby after one who went to Hel; it would leave the child without a guardian and might doom her to the same fate.

For an instant, panic scattered Kevral's thoughts. She stiffened, calling on the Renshai mind powers she had learned along with her sword work. She reined in pieces of her shattered concentration, stalwartly ejecting fear from her consciousness. She would not let it taint her otherwise pure spirit. Nevertheless, she could not help feeling regrets. She would never fight in a war. She would never have a husband or a family. She would die a virgin.

Kevral sprang to her feet, fighting misgivings. She sought solace in the only thing that could fully occupy her mind. Even without a sword, she could and would practice. Ordinarily, she sought privacy for her training. Now, she had no choice, and the need to work her sword arm had to take precedence over any detail the guards might glean from her. She prided herself on the speed and complexity of her tactics, far beyond her years. Another pang followed the thought. She already knew herself to be one of the greatest swordsmen, but she would never have the chance to prove it to the world.

Kevral launched into a *svergelse*, determined to make it her best ever. She dedicated her effort to Sif, goddess of Renshai, and promised sword work worthy of prayer, though she had no weapon. Imagining a sword in her hand, Kevral leaped, swept, and arced. Her pretend weapon sliced air, hacking through a mass of enemies, one by one. Her limbs never stopped moving, her prayer a wild dance of lethal fury. Like fire, she capered and twisted, consuming every life in her path.

Soon, the bars and stone floor disappeared. She no longer saw the guards who now stared, transfixed. One went to fetch more, and they came in larger numbers, filling the area that contained her cell. Kevral never noticed. They posed her no threat, so her mind dismissed them. Then, suddenly, a presence touched her, a joyful lightness in her mind that quickened an already near-perfect practice. She became a swirling flash of gold hair and blue tunic, her movements unstoppable and all but invisible. The imagined weapon in her hand gained weight, a reality her rational mind could not disprove. Its presence became a reassurance that trebled the significance of the presence in her head. Her goddess, she believed, had come.

Joy exploded through Kevral. She laughed, further quickening her efforts. Every shred of strength, mental and physical, channeled into her practice. Raw power seemed to flow through her veins instead of blood; and fatigue remained at bay. At first, she strained to concentrate on the maneuvers, afraid thinking too hard about the mysterious sword would make it go away. But the more she tried to redirect her attention, the more it settled on the sword. Yet, even when she let her thoughts go where they would, the sword remained, a pressure in her head and an image in her eye. It etched silver lines through air and imaginary opponents. It filled her hand, settling against the calluses as if it belonged to her alone. She could feel its leather against her palm, and its hilt warming to her grip.

And still the guards gathered, each bringing more as the ruthless dance of Kevral's practice showed no sign of abating. And still, she noticed nothing but the sword in her fist, the conjured enemies, the fancied combat. Only if one of the guards attacked could he enter the world she now inhabited, and none of them seemed foolish enough to try.

For hours, Kevral's practice continued, and no one dared to interrupt it. Exhaustion caught up to her, and she fought it. She would rather keep going until all of the water seeped from her body as sweat. Death in this fashion would prove far more satisfying to her. Yet, she knew, it would cheat the executioner and, therefore, might not satisfy the terms of the exchange. She did her companions no good if she killed herself, the king still blocked retreat from the city, and Tae remained hunted. Reluctantly, she quit, lowering her arm to her side and allowing reality to come rushing back. A sea of Pudarians met her gaze, the scene striped by the bars of her cage. Words touched her ears, a brief exchange near the front:

"Wasn't she searched? Where did she get that. . . ?" The voice trailed off as the practice ended.

Yet another answered what must have seemed an obvious query to anyone but her. "It isn't real."

The king of Pudar had joined his men, near the front of the gathering. He studied Kevral, pale eyes full of wonder.

Kevral blinked, surprised by the enormity of her audience. Exhilaration still overwhelmed fatigue, and she looked upon the multitude with shining eyes, her breathing only mildly quickened. Anticipating the rush of shakiness and pain that always followed intense effort, she sat. She balked at showing discomfort to anyone. A good *torke* would chastise her for it with additional lessons. A warrior who revealed weakness to enemies guaranteed her own deserved death.

"Go away," the king commanded softly. "All of you, go away."

For a moment, no one moved, as if replaced by an army of statues. Then, gradually, the guards responded to their king's order. The ones in the back dispersed first, heading off to tend to the duties they had left to watch the show. Others followed in a steady stream, until only the dozen dressed in inner court silks remained.

Kevral watched them impassively, more intent on controlling her breathing than worrying about the guards' obedience. She sucked air through her nose and funnelled it through her mouth without gulping.

Sweat wound a trickle down her forehead, and she cursed even that small show of effort. Casually, she wiped it away with her palm, scratching a pretend itch in the same area.

A frown deeply scored the king's features, and he gestured for the remaining sentries to leave. Some addressed him with a soft meekness that kept their words incomprehensible to Kevral. She guessed they begged the right to stay and protect him.

But the king granted no quarter. Again, he waved them off, this time with an impatient gesture that brooked no ignoring.

The guards dispersed with obvious hesitancy. Only one remained stalwartly at his king's side. He did not look at his monarch, as if he feared he would get sent away as well. So long as he could not see the dismissal, he could ignore it.

The king overlooked this last of his men. Instead, he spoke to Kevral in the same deep baritone she remembered from his court. "Kevral, I presume you understand that by taking a criminal's place you have brought his exact sentence upon yourself."

Kevral's mind felt thick and slow, drained as much as her muscles by the practice. She forgot to curtsy. "Sire, if you're asking if I know I'm going to get killed in Tae's place, I understand."

"You're a brave woman, Kevral."

Kevral shrugged. "I would be an embarrassment to my people if I wasn't."

The king's brow furrowed as he considered the statement. "Yes, I suppose that's true."

Kevral nodded, preferring to stay on track with the conversation. The means of her death held more relevance than any other topic they could discuss.

"You have a great talent."

Kevral ignored her natural inclination to respond with the same phrase as before. Antagonizing the man who determined the means of her death seemed madness.

"My men could well use your expertise. Training from one such as you would prove invaluable."

Kevral fought anger by biting her lip and causing pain instead. "With all respect, Sire. That was not a part of our agreement. Though no enemy of Pudar, I dislike the idea of doing favors for one about to execute me."

The king looked to his one remaining man. Initially, Kevral had assumed him a soldier, like the others. Since all Renshai strove toward the same goal, and every one clutched a sword from the day his or her hand could close around a grip, it seemed a logical mistake. Now she guessed he served as an adviser or confidant. This other Pudarian bowed encouragingly, and the king continued.

"What if I offered you your freedom in exchange for that favor?"

Kevral's heart skipped a beat. She leaned forward, not bothering to hide her interest. "It would depend on the details."

King and adviser whispered back and forth for a few moments, words occasionally audible above Kevral's breathing and the boom of her heartbeat in her ears. She found herself unable to connect these, so she waited for the king to address her again.

Shortly, he did. "You intensively train my men for at least one year. If an obvious improvement results, you're free to go or stay on as you please."

Kevral bit her lip harder to keep from blurting out agreement. Confronted with this new situation, her mind raced. She wanted to ask who determined whether or not this improvement occurred, but she had a more important matter over which to quibble. She had a previous commitment, and seeing that done took precedence over worrying for her later freedom. "If there's no improvement, I have to stay?"

"Until there is," the king said. "Correct."

"And this takes the place of my execution?"

"Exactly," the king agreed.

The other man cut in. "May I add something, Sire?"

The king gestured good-naturedly for him to add his piece.

"We expect you to put real effort into this project. For that one year, or longer if you choose, training Pudar's soldiers must be your primary concern. Under those circumstances, I don't see how improvement could not occur." He answered the question Kevral had chosen not to ask. "Improvement will be determined by a test performed on the guard force before and after your teaching. You will have a hand in determining what that test will entail."

Kevral nodded. It sounded fair. "I have only one condition. I'm already committed to a mission outside Pudar. When it's finished, I'm free to fulfill my obligation to you."

The king squinted, frowning. He looked to his companion for guidance. As if it were contagious, the other frowned, too. Finally, the king spoke. "I appreciate your loyalty to a cause. I'll appreciate it more when your cause is Pudar's guards. But can you assure us you'll return?"

Kevral considered. "I give you my word as a Renshai. I swear to the gods of my people: Sif and Modi. And I promise on the memory of Colbey Calistinsson, our greatest hero.

If there's life left in me by the time my mission ends, I will return to Pudar to train your guards." Kevral did not bother to mention that she could not show Pudar's guards any of the maneuvers uniquely Renshai. Improving their skills would not require it.

Again, the king silently consulted his companion, receiving a definitive nod in answer. "That vow from a Renshai, I would trust."

"Settled, then," the king said, his smile slight but unmissable. "Free her."

Colbey and Ravn shared Odin's vast throne, *Hlidskjalf.* The stone had claimed their body warmth long ago, while they looked out over the entirety of man's world as they pleased. The mansion of the father of gods had changed little since his demise. It had seemed sacred, even to the gods, a shrine no one dared disturb. Rarely did the gods find reason to concern themselves with affairs of mortals. Likely, each had tried the throne, from curiosity at least, then chose to leave it alone inside the silver-roofed palace that had once been the private domain of Odin and his wife, both lost to the *Ragnarok.*

Though embroiled in serious lessons, Colbey reveled in the special time spent with his son. Throughout his mortal life, he had desperately wanted a child to nurture and teach, whether a boy or girl did not matter. His closeness to Ravn now brought back bittersweet memories of a young man named Episte. Though not his by birth, the child had become in every other way his son until tragedy claimed the boy's sanity and forced Colbey to take his life as well. At the time Episte had been close to Ravn's age.

Colbey gave his son a hearty pat on the shoulder, followed by a loving squeeze. This one, he would train right, not just in matters of sword work, but also in matters of logic, love, and understanding. The learning had begun from birth, and Colbey hoped his mortal's impatience would not ruin the need to stretch his lessons over a lifetime. "Well?" he prompted.

Ravn looked at the scene again, while guards released and talked softly with Kevral. "You created the illusion of a sword?"

Colbey shook his head. "I have no such magic. You know that."

"I know that." Ravn shifted to the jeweled arm of the throne, impiously perched like an errant child on a new and expensive couch. Colbey did not chastise his son. Furniture, especially Odin's, held little interest for him, and the expensive construction would prove its own punishment. Soon the inset gemstones would take their toll on Ravn's buttocks. "But I also know what I saw."

"You know what you think you saw."

Ravn's brow crinkled. "All right, then. What I think I saw." The grooves in his forehead deepened. "You're telling me she held no sword."

"Exactly." Colbey smiled at Ravn's quick perception.

Slowly, the creases disappeared, and Ravn's eyes widened with an interest that pleased his father. Ravn had always proved a willing and eager student when it came to battle. Academics, however, he had pursued more to please his parents than himself. "What did you do?"

Colbey continued to smile, pausing to give Ravn more time to consider the possibilities. The lesson would accomplish more if Ravn found the answer on his own.

"You influenced the guards' minds."

"Close," Colbey said. "But remember, I can't enter more than one mind at a time. And you saw it, too."

Again, Ravn's brow knitted. He fidgeted on *Hlidskjalf's* arm. "You influenced . . ." He hesitated, brightening suddenly. ". . . Kevral! You made *her* believe she really held a sword. And she convinced the rest of us by the way she performed her kata."

Colbey beamed. "Exactly! Good job, Ravn."

Ravn looked away, but his face revealed happy pride. He squirmed, seeking a more comfortable position. "It only worked because she's Renshai."

"It only worked," Colbey added, "because she's among the most skilled of Renshai. Not many could have created such an illusion. It requires speed and changes in movement and balance so minute that otherwise imperceptible differences can fool the mind and eye. Nothing magical here. No personal interference. No magnificent suggestions or strategies. Just a spark of an idea."

"That's proper interference?"

"Even that could prove too much for older gods less grounded in mortality."

Ravn sat in silent consideration for a long time, oblivious

to the discomfort of his position. Finally, he shook his yellow mane in frustration. "But that kind of subtlety wouldn't work for Griff."

"Of course not," Colbey admitted. "Every situation calls for different strategy. You only have to find the right action for the moment."

Ravn glanced back at his father, worry straining his young features. "But what if it doesn't work?"

"Then you chose the wrong action."

"And Griff dies."

"And Griff dies," Colbey concurred.

Ravn stared at his father, his aggrieved expression a plea.

"Mortals die," Colbey said, the lesson one he knew only too well. "That's why gods rarely befriend them."

"Gods die, too." Ravn observed astutely as he rose. "Just not of age or illness. If either of those took him, I would understand. If he died in glorious combat, I would celebrate his passing. But I can't stand back while enemies destroy him."

Colbey sighed deeply. "Then you must do as your mother bid. You must stay out of the affairs of mortals until you learn to properly interfere."

Ravn paced, clearly agitated. "You mean interfere as you do."

"With care, yes. Not necessarily using my methods."

Ravn sighed, still moving. "May I continue our friendship? May I watch him?"

Colbey nodded. "You may, if you feel certain you can do so without influencing the course of human events. Have you that much control?" He smiled with kindness. "Few adolescents do. I know I didn't when I was more than your age."

"I do," Ravn said softly, giving the situation the serious attention it deserved. "I'm sure I do."

Colbey did not hold Ravn's faith, yet he also knew it would prove safer for mortals and gods if the youngster made his mistakes now. Over time, the significance of his every action would increase, just as Colbey's had. Soon, he, too, would have to limit appearances and advice even more than he already did. "Then you may go as friend and controlled observer. But don't disappoint me." Colbey added the last as an explicit warning. Should Ravn fail, he would pay with worse than just an exhausting, painful sword practice. If Ravn caused strife between Freya and Colbey, father and son would both suffer her wrath. Colbey feared no enemy, but the punishment Freya could inflict made him shudder. No one could hurt a man as much as a woman he loved. Particularly a goddess. Especially Freya.

King Cymion's court progressed in a whirlwind of excitement that carried into the evening. Buoyed by the newest addition to his supporters, a Renshai of considerable talent who had agreed to train his guards, Cymion tempered his judgments with a mercy that went beyond fairness. The merchants who bartered their taxes that day would brag of their fortune, and permission for every function from parties, to hunting on royal land, to weddings all met the same exuberant agreement. Nothing, it seemed, could sour the king's mood until the nineteenth situation of the afternoon.

A smile felt permanently pasted to the king's face, and his mind kept wandering back to the deal he had made in his prison. No other king could boast a Renshai armsman, not even the high monarchy in Béarn. Kevral-trained, elite guards would become Pudar's equivalent of the Knights of Erythane. And with any luck, Kevral would enjoy her year in Pudar enough to remain forever. If he treated her like royalty, and he would see to it his staff did so, perhaps she would become permanent. She might even bring her Renshai husband, a warrior likely to exceed her in skill; and their offspring might serve his son in turn.

The thought sparked grief at once. Tears sprang to his eyes unbidden, the fires of excitement dampened. An image of Prince Severin filled his mind, the edges frayed. *Have I already begun to forget my firstborn?* Panic spiked through him. He fought it down, calling up the control he needed in the courtroom. Emotional swings did not suit a monarch, even one still grieving for a son lost to an assassin. He would never exact the revenge he once believed he needed to place sadness at rest. But the reward he had gained instead might, poetically, prove more valuable. If he could convince Kevral to remain in Pudar, if he could establish a convention that her offspring became Pudar's armsman, he would give his second son a peerless gift.

"Majesty? Your Majesty?" A cautious nudge roused King Cymion from the depths of thought.

Blinking away tears, the king turned his attention back to Adviser Javonzir beside him. Discreetly, the other man's eyes traced a semicircle to the patch of floor in front of the dais. A man stood there, gaze trained unwaveringly on Cymion, neither bowing nor kneeling despite the guards' weapons leveled around him. The king recognized him in an instant, the way a wolf knows the scent of a rabbit. The tangled black hair and air of defiance were unmistakable. His son's murderer had returned.

Excitement disappeared at once, replaced by a raw hatred Cymion could not banish. He didn't remember moving, but suddenly he was standing, glaring at the Easterner who stood before his throne, uncowed. The brown eyes met his, eyes remarkably hard in an otherwise youthfully innocent face. He read no fear nor remorse in those features, and the lack of the latter further infuriated him. "You," he finally managed.

The Easterner bowed in acknowledgment. "My name is Tae Kahn. I refuse to let a friend die for a crime you believe I committed. I surrendered myself; you may ask your guards if you doubt my word."

Nods bobbed through the ranks, and the distance they kept from Tae added to their sincerity. Had they captured him under duress, they would have bound and dragged him to the court.

Tae finished. "I could not stop you should you choose to execute my friend and myself. I can only trust in the honor of a king and hope you make the just decision. Free Kevral, and you may do as you wish to me." Despite the atrocities Tae's words might have committed him to, he continued to stare at the king. His bravado seemed as permanent a part of him as any limb. Now, however, he had placed even those at risk.

Murmurs swept the courtroom, a steady buzz intensified at intervals. Surely, it had started when Tae first appeared, yet Cymion had not noticed it until this moment. Words formed, hot, hateful epithets that burned his tongue. He recalled the wicked agony of punishments he had conjured once anger had joined grief in his heart. But to speak such words in front of visiting dignitaries and nobles would not suit his station. The necessary control became a curse, but he steeled himself to hide emotion as well as Tae had so far managed. "Lock him up. Take him away. I'll deal with him later."

Javonzir cleared his throat, the sound soft beneath the

hubbub of the dispersing crowd in the courtroom. Yet King Cymion heard it. They had shared the signal for years, Javonzir's way of suggesting Cymion take another look at a judgment without allowing the rest of the court to hear him questioning the king. As the guards led Tae from the courtroom without resistance and the crowd dispersed, King Cymion turned his attention to his adviser again.

"Majesty, you have to let him go."

Rage joined hatred, a wild bonfire King Cymion could scarcely contain. "The murderer of my son? The crown prince's assassin? You would have me free him?"

Javonzir lowered his head. "I'm sorry, Majesty. Justice allows no other course."

"Never!"

"A sentence was already carried out against this charge. The law does not allow us to punish twice for the same infraction."

King Cymion refused to concede the point. "I can do as I please. I'm the king."

Adviser Javonzir bowed. "You're right, Majesty." The look he turned on the king showed savage disappointment. As cousins, the two had shared a childhood, and always before Cymion had given his relation the respect great wisdom and insight earned him.

For a moment, King Cymion dared to believe the issue had another side, and that consideration widened into a wellspring of understanding. Emotion battled logic, and the latter won, as it always must for a king.

Javonzir did not once look back. He twisted the doorknob.

"Wait," Cymion said as the door wrenched open. "Please wait, Javon."

The adviser stiffened, then turned slowly, closing the door. A moment passed in a silence that tore away the many years since their days of sparring for money and honor and their competitions for girls.

"You're right," the king finally said. "Damn you, you're always right."

Javonzir did not smile. "I'll release him. Then I'll recommend he voluntarily exile himself from Pudar."

"Thank you," Cymion said, not daring to sort the specifics of his gratitude. Whether for preventing a travesty of justice, for rescuing his soul, or for handling the matter for the king,

Cymion would rather not even know himself. Right now, he just felt dirty and wanted a long, warm bath.

Once free, Kevral did not waste a moment, packing up her belongings with neat efficiency. Finished, she placed her pack near the cottage door, beside those of Darris, Matrinka, and Ra-khir. The cat, the princess, and the bard's heir waited together in the main room, in plain view of the doorway. They sat in silence, as they often did, sharing one another's company without need for words. Though Darris and Matrinka threw Kevral happy glances at intervals, a deep-rooted sadness always seemed to pervade them. Kevral no longer bothered to pity. The love they could never act upon had become a too-familiar burden.

Ra-khir returned a moment after Kevral finished, leading a string of five horses. She recognized her red bay, Matrinka's chestnut, and Darris' nervous mare. Ra-khir had exchanged his Erythanian Knight's training gray for two dark brown geldings. "I made arrangements for a stable owner to keep and use my horse until we come back." His words reminded Kevral of her promise to Pudar's king, and a catch in Ra-khir's voice revealed sadness at the parting. "He's too light-colored for safety." He did not add the obvious, that hiding would prove more difficult without Tae.

Kevral's hand fell to the strange gem in her pocket, the one Tae had given her. When the king's men had escorted her from the castle, they had told her of the sacrifice Tae had tried to make for her. At the time, he could not have known that she had already bartered her freedom. She had expected him to rejoin the party afterward, but he had not. Apparently, Ra-khir's threat held him as much at bay now as it had when newly spoken in the woods outside Pudar. Kevral guessed, from Ra-khir's decision to buy an extra horse, presumably for Tae, that the knight-in-training felt guilty for his actions.

Matrinka and Darris rose to look over the animals, while Ra-khir moved to Kevral's side. She stiffened at his approach, mind scrambling for the proper words. She owed him a debt of gratitude, yet sentiment did not come easily to her. She tended to forget her manners in polite company, and ceremonies made her giggle. She was already considered an adult by Renshai standards, but she still had the experience and emotional maturity of a fifteen-year-old girl.

Taking her cues from watching Darris and Matrinka, Kevral caught both of Ra-khir's hands and stared into soulful green eyes surrounded by long, dark lashes so rare for a redhead. Her eyes drank in handsome features, scarcely noticing the bruises that marred his face. Unexpected warmth flashed through her lower regions, embarrassing for its newness, and a craving for closeness thrilled through her.

Ra-khir embraced Kevral, and the sensation intensified until it overcame other thought. She reveled in the heat and comfort of his body against her own, the pleasure a guilty one. For the moment she did not care. Recalling her regrets in the prison cell, she promised herself not to let propriety stand in her way. Renshai society encouraged marriage within the tribe, but they made regular exceptions for spouses who could bring new assets into the bloodline. Ra-khir had strength, at least. And he followed his honor loyally, even if it did not fully fit in with her own. Wickeder thoughts followed. So far, everyone who'd attempted their mission had died, including Renshai. Her days of imprisonment had convinced Kevral that, no matter how glorious her death, she did not want to die a virgin. Preventing that did not necessarily require marriage.

Ra-khir released Kevral, and she caught sight of a brief flash of smile as they slid apart. In the past, she would never have allowed him to touch her. Now, she dared not tell him their closeness had brought her as much pleasure as it did him. As the area of contact decreased, the strength of her need diminished, and embarrassment replaced excitement. She flushed, feeling whorish for her previous thoughts. She wanted to slip away and hide, but she fought it away. Matrinka had described the lengths to which Ra-khir had gone to rescue her. Like Tae, he had agreed to die in her place; unlike Tae, he had had no innocence or guilt to dispute. "Thank you for what you did for me."

"I could have done nothing else. I hope to the gods I'm never again placed in the position of choosing between love and honor."

Kevral lowered her head to hide a smile, afraid she might laugh nervously if she met his gaze now. She concentrated on the inherent difficulty of his decision, placing herself in his position. Honor bound him to let her die since she had willingly agreed to the execution. Yet, the agony of watching an innocent friend killed had seemed unbearable. In the reverse situation, Renshai law would have allowed her to rescue him, even should it mean battling Pudar's army. But the knight's code placed its emphasis on laws rather than morality. Usually, the two went together, but as Colbey once said, "Rigid laws do not make allowance for circumstance." So Ra-khir had sought to save her the only way he could, successfully it turned out, though it nearly cost him his life.

What caught Kevral's attention most right now was Ra-khir's mention of love. She did not know for certain whether he meant that in a romantic or a brotherly way, but she suspected it would soon become clear. Only one thing complicated the possibility of a relationship with Ra-khir. She had not yet clarified her feelings for Tae, nor his for her. And she owed him a thank you, too.

Darris interrupted Ra-khir's and Kevral's moment. "We're all loaded and ready to go." He addressed Ra-khir. "Did you have a horse preference?"

Ra-khir stiffened momentarily in response. He missed the gray steed he had ridden through his knight's training. The formality of knights suggested he had undergone an important initiation ceremony during which they had awarded him the horse that would remain a companion until he earned his title. Then he would receive one of the elaborately accomplished and perfectly proportioned white stallions that all the Knights of Erythane rode. Kevral enjoyed horses. Colbey had considered himself an excellent judge of quality as well as a skilled rider. He had actually invented most of the Renshai's mounted maneuvers. Although he valued horses, history stated that he had never tied himself sentimentally to individual animals, not even to the point of giving them names. When Ra-khir finally spoke, his tone revealed no sorrow or bitterness for his loss. "The two are equal. I have no favorite among them." He headed outside with the others.

Kevral followed, closing the cottage behind her. They had lived there long enough to consider it home, yet Kevral felt only relief at leaving. They had delayed their mission far too long.

Darris had fastened all the packs to one of the dark brown horses. He assisted Matrinka to mount before claiming his own horse. Ra-khir hesitated beside Kevral's bay.

Kevral stood a moment, searching her own feelings for an answer.

Ra-khir bowed. "Lady, if I admit that I know you're quite

capable of getting up yourself, would you let me practice the etiquette slammed into my head since birth?"

Kevral returned the smile. "Since you've made it sound so irresistible. . . ." She waited for him to help, though she felt silly. Their dwindling pool of money had forced them to sell saddles and bridles for cruder ones of cracked leather and rope. That made leaping into position less dignified and more difficult.

Ra-khir stabilized Kevral as she clambered onto the horse's back, more concerned about accidentally kicking or gouging him than over mounting. Once she settled into place, Ra-khir climbed onto the remaining horse.

They moved slowly along the cobbled streets, hooves clopping rhythmically against the stones. Though far from the marketplace, Darris still worried about citizens on the streets. Traffic had increased even over Pudar's busy norm since the mourning curfew had lifted. The pace did not matter to Kevral. The simple act of moving excited her. The mild breeze that accompanied motion seemed a welcome friend after weeks cooped up in a cottage and days in a stagnant cell. The promise of romance added an additional tingle to the mix, and her heart relished the possibilities though she did not allow her thoughts to do the same.

Rows of cottages disappeared behind them. They kept to the smaller roadways, avoiding the main thoroughfares and their teeming shops. Occasional shouts of merchants punctuated the dull roar of the masses, drawing potential customers to stands of jewelry, food, spices, and wares of every kind. For centuries, Pudar's central Western location, its land and water access, and its manner of rulership had made it the center of commerce. Its significance and the variety of its products had only increased through generations.

At length, they came to the wall, Darris in the lead. They followed it to the main exit, merging into the stream of patrons. Here, the stands abounded with more luxuries than necessities, merchants attempting to win travelers' last coins, promising treasures and souvenirs for those waiting at home. Travel food replaced the fresher wares sold nearer the entrance. The horses proved as much handicap as asset. They could move more quickly, yet Kevral found herself a magnet for merchants' attention. The sellers assumed people with enough money to purchase mounts had coppers to waste. Also, horsemen usually had farther to travel, suggesting a need for more supplies. On one side, a heavyset salesman in gray shoved salted meats into Kevral's hand, while another regaled her with the merits of spreading a blanket between her backside and the weathered saddle. Kevral ignored both, only to be assaulted a moment later by a woman pushing dried fruit.

Kevral had learned to avoid eye contact while shopping in the market, and she put the knowledge to use now. Matrinka fared far worse. Her fancier, feminine garb attracted the merchants hawking perfumes, silks, and gemstones. Finally, Ra-khir pulled up beside her to stem the tide on one side. Taking the hint, Kevral drew to her other hand. Concentrating on the need to guard, Kevral paid no heed to the merchants. In this manner, they bulled through to the exit with little more delay.

Even after they passed through the gates, the onslaught did not end. Outside, artists, farmers, and others without the money for shops or stands inside hawked crafts, flowers, and vegetables or spoke in grandiose phrases about religions beyond Kevral's knowledge. These, too, they passed with scarcely a glance. They had nearly plowed through the last persistent stragglers, when a familiar voice speared through the crowd. "Kevral! Kevral, wait!"

Tae? Kevral whirled, and Ra-khir did the same in perfect synchrony. Matrinka's horse took a few steps ahead before she stopped it to see what had caught her companions' attention.

Tae perched casually on a boulder, a slight smile on his lips, his black hair wild around a swarthy face that seemed little affected by the events of the past few days. Kevral tossed her reins to Ra-khir and dismounted before he could suggest a different plan. As Kevral headed toward him, Tae climbed down leisurely. She met him at the base of the stone, and they embraced warmly. Again, Kevral found herself embroiled in the fires of longing, more so because Tae practiced none of Ra-khir's manners. The Easterner squished up against her, one hand straying to her buttocks to draw her closer.

Ra-khir cleared his throat.

Tae and Kevral separated. She said, "I heard you gave yourself up for me. Thank you."

Tae raised and lowered his brows, an acknowledgment

that held none of Ra-khir's modesty. "I sure wasn't going to let them kill *you* for something I did."

Kevral froze, only halfway free of Tae's hug. "You did kill the prince?"

"I don't know," Tae admitted. "If I did, I certainly didn't do it on purpose."

The answer confused Kevral.

Tae dismissed the matter with a promise. "I'll explain on the way. And you'll have to tell me exactly what you promised King Kill-me-on." Deliberately twisting the king's name, he looked beyond Kevral to Ra-khir. "That is, if I'm allowed to join up with you again."

Kevral stepped away from Tae, twisting to face Ra-khir. Surely, he understood that he, alone, did not decide who would or would not join them. She did not voice this, however; she could always overrule him later. For now, she was more interested in his response.

Ra-khir closed his eyes, though not before Kevral caught a flash of pain. He had other reasons to keep Tae from the party than trust, yet he would not allow personal desire to determine a course of action better based on fairness. Slowly, he opened his eyes, focusing only on Tae. "Thank you, Tae, for surrendering yourself and for all the good things you did for us, though I did not deserve them. I judged you wrong, and I'm sorry for that mistake. Of course, you may join us again. With my blessing."

Kevral looked back to see Darris and Matrinka already redistributing packs to allow Tae a mount of his own. She headed toward them to help, realized they would finish before she arrived, and stopped. She glanced back to Tae and Ra-khir, only to find both men admiring her from behind. Ra-khir looked away quickly, shamefaced. Tae shrugged off his actions with a brazen grin and a knowing wink. He shifted his attention from her buttocks to her face but made no attempt to apologize or even to acknowledge his conduct as anything but perfectly appropriate.

The men's interest and attention brought warmth and redness to Kevral's cheeks, and she turned back to the horses pretending she had not seen. But she had. And, where nothing in war could fluster her, this did. While she could not help but find their attention flattering, it seemed equally bothersome and confusing. The strange emotions blossoming inside her brought as much pain as pleasure; they made her feel helpless and uncertain, feelings she had learned to despise since birth. Neither served well on the battlefield.

Without another word, Kevral mounted her horse and waited for the others to do the same. She did not meet any of her companions' gazes, instead rechecking the ties of her pack while the others climbed into place.

Discomfort remained with Kevral throughout the rest of the day and into a dinner of travel rations she scarcely tasted and conversation she mostly ignored. Only her sword practice brought reprieve. Then, she concentrated fully on the maneuvers, the mundane worries of the day disappearing into a salvo of thrust and parry, a daily challenge that always seemed fresh and new. She continued her deadly dance well after nightfall when her friends bedded down for sleep. Though not on purpose, she cherished the freedom from talk that working so long gained her.

Kevral sheathed her sword, reveling in the trill of insects, the whirring fox calls, and the chitter of leaves in the late summer breezes. The wind dried sweat from her limbs, prickling her skin into gooseflesh. Glimpses of moon and stars appeared and disappeared as the branches swayed; and a mild, steady glaze bathed the small clearing amid the trees they had chosen for their campsite. Ra-khir slept curled on his side beneath his blanket, breath stirring a leaf near his face. The strawberry-blond locks accentuated features handsome even in sleep. Tae rested at the opposite side of the clearing, leaf- and twig-dirty blanket tumbled around his legs. He lay on his belly, arms and legs drawn beneath him, tangled black hair a curtain that hid his features. Darris formed the last point of a triangle, a comfortable distance from the other men. He, too, slept. Matrinka sat near him, Mior quiet in her lap. As usual, the men had deferred first watch to her just as they often gave the last one to Kevral. Those two times disrupted sleep the least.

Looking at the men brought all of her confusion rushing back. Forgetting about the problem had not in anyway resolved it, nor, she discovered, had it made her thoughts or approach clearer. She glanced at Matrinka with a nod, and the princess returned a cheerful wave. Kevral knew the problem would worry sleep from her. Chatting with Matrinka until she became so tired no amount of mulling could keep sleep at bay seemed preferable. So she inclined her head toward an open area slightly away from the others where they might talk undisturbed.

Matrinka nodded, removing Mior from her lap and moving cautiously away from Darris so as not to awaken him. She joined Kevral, Mior trailing. Matrinka settled onto a rock, Mior lay at her feet, and Kevral chose a cross-legged position in the dirt. For several moments, time seemed to run backward, to the day Kevral had dedicated herself to guarding the Béarnian heir assigned to her. Despite the threat of assassination, those had seemed like more innocent times. Circumstances had changed little, but Kevral felt like a totally different person. Then, she would never have asked the advice of the woman she protected. Now, she relished it, and the words came tumbling forth before she could think to stop them. "I have a problem."

Matrinka touched the Renshai's arm in a soothing manner, and Kevral never doubted the other woman's sincere desire to assist. The princess would not push, allowing Kevral to detail the situation in her own fashion and at her own pace, and their conversation would go no further then the two of them. Kevral saw no need to extract a promise of confidentiality. It would be an insult. Yet, despite the comfort Matrinka offered, Kevral still found it difficult to express her concerns. Unused to sharing and accustomed to hiding imperfections beneath a facade of confidence, she did not know where to start.

Matrinka waited patiently, without pressing. She sat in companionable silence, features gentle, waiting for Kevral to speak.

Kevral debated whether to address the problem. For the moment, it seemed easier to avoid it and let small talk take her mind from it a bit longer. Yet she knew it would return to haunt her as soon as she found herself alone again. Renshai did not avoid matters without better reason than emotion. "I think I'm in love with two men at once."

Matrinka nodded to indicate she had heard, but she did not push for details nor did she assume an expression that suggested she was trying to surmise them or consider the morality of it. Without a word, she allowed Kevral to finish.

But Kevral only looked at her, deliberately placing the burden on Matrinka.

Matrinka accepted the new role. "How do you feel about that?"

"I'm not sure," Kevral admitted, glancing around to make certain none of the men stirred, not wanting them to hear her words or see her display weakness. None of the three moved, all breathing in the deep, steady pattern of sleep. Kevral and Matrinka kept their voices low enough so they had to strain to understand one another, even as close as they sat. "The whole idea of love feels strange enough without having to make a choice, too. I don't know what I want, except not to hurt anyone. I've seen girls tease boys before. I hate the flirting, and I hate the kind of girls who do it. I wouldn't know how to do that even if I wanted to." The idea revolted Kevral. "And I don't."

"How do the men feel about you?" Matrinka asked an important question.

"Well, I can't be sure." Kevral felt the heat returning to her cheeks. "But I think they care about me, too."

"Both?"

"Both," Kevral confirmed. "But I can't really know, can I?" She shrugged. "So what do I do?"

"What do you want to do?"

As not knowing the answer to that was exactly her problem, Kevral turned irritable. "Why do you keep answering my questions with another question?"

Matrinka smiled. "Why not?"

"Because. . . ." Kevral started, then recognized the joke. "Funny."

Matrinka gave a proper reply, "I respond to your questions with other questions because the answers need to come from inside you, not from me."

Kevral frowned, annoyed by Matrinka's words. "So you're saying you can't help me."

Matrinka recoiled, clearly horrified. "That's not what I'm saying at all. I certainly hope I can help you. If in no other way, then by assisting you in finding the right questions."

Kevral just stared.

"I can tell you what I would do in your situation, but that's not really going to help you."

The circular reasoning wore on Kevral. "Just give me some advice, if you would. Believe me, I won't follow it blindly."

Matrinka pursed her lips thoughtfully. She reached over and stroked Mior without taking her gaze from Kevral. "All right, then. Here's what I think: When it comes to affairs of the heart, you should follow your heart."

Kevral knew of highly regarded teachers who spoke in riddles to force students to think. Though it frustrated her, Kevral felt Matrinka stated the truth in that only Kevral could find an answer to this problem. At best, Matrinka could guide, and the simple act of vocalizing had already begun to ease the burden of a difficult decision. Then realization intervened. Kevral's eyes narrowed at the discrepancy. "In affairs of the heart, one should follow one's heart."

"I believe so," Matrinka said emphatically. "Obvious as it sounds, it makes sense."

"So," Kevral said. "I should do precisely as you don't."

Matrinka stared, clearly startled, stricken from her role as psyche healer for the first time. "What do you mean by that?"

"A blind, deaf man could see how much you love Darris, but you still insist you're just friends."

"More like brother and sister," Matrinka clarified.

Kevral snorted. "Brothers and sisters could get arrested for the things you want to do to one another."

Stunned beyond words, Matrinka said nothing.

Kevral waited, guilty about her cruel delivery, yet feeling vindicated. Hypocrisy between word and deed irritated her.

Finally, Matrinka found her tongue. "Is it really that obvious?"

The calm reply to what had, essentially, been an accusation softened Kevral's response. "Remember, I'm the one who can't tell for certain how men feel about *me*. But I have no doubt whatsoever how Darris feels about you."

"That's a different situation," Matrinka defended herself. "I'm an heir to Béarn's throne. The law is strict about who I can or cannot marry."

The explanation seemed moot. "But you're not an heir anymore. You've been disowned. Doesn't that leave you free to marry anyone you want?"

Matrinka sighed. "It's probably better that as few as possible know this, but my grandfather refused my request. I'm still an heir."

Kevral lost her voice momentarily. "But I saw . . . I was there when. . . ." Memory gave her no definitives. "You're still an heir?"

"Not that I could ever sit on the throne, but, yes. I'm still officially an heir."

Kevral's gut twisted with the nausea that accompanied betrayal. "Why didn't you tell me before?"

"Would it have mattered?"

Kevral considered. "No, I suppose not. I've guarded you just the same. I wouldn't stop or anything." She let the matter rest, realizing it had distracted her from a problem that seemed closer to resolution than she would have expected possible. "So what you're telling me is that in matters of the heart I should follow my heart, but you should follow law and logic."

Matrinka fidgeted, eyes restless. "That's not what I'm *trying* to say. I wish I could follow my heart, too. I really do. But I can't do something illegal just because I want to."

The disorientation that had plagued Kevral since Tae returned to the party dispersed, replaced by the familiar overconfidence that had won her enemies even among her own people. Her path seemed clear. She had an inheritance, too. She was Renshai, first and foremost, and Renshai placed one love above any other. Sword work had proved the one essential capable of fully capturing her mind. She doubted any human lover could ever claim her so fully, without distraction. Suddenly her lapse seemed more than preoccupation. It had grown into an evil that nearly affected the most important purpose her life could ever have: her need, her *destiny* to become the world's best swordmaster. From this moment, she would give everything to her sword and to her cause. She would become the most skilled, and the whole world would know it. Ra-khir and Tae would have to find other women to love. "Thank you for talking to me, Matrinka. You've helped a lot."

Matrinka's features returned to their normal, friendly configuration. Then her brows dropped into a squint as she pondered Kevral's gratitude. "You're very welcome, though I don't feel as if I've clarified anything. I feel like I muddled things worse than before."

Kevral placed her hand on her hilt, thoughts on the many battles she would need to fight to win her title. A frenzied whirlwind of excitement eclipsed a deeper sorrow.

Chapter 33

The Last Supper

Battles are won by deeds, not words.
—*Colbey Calistinsson*

The sky stretched like a gray pall over the landscape, and the irregular sunlight burning through clouds scarcely distinguished day from night. Mist tickled Griff's face and glistened like dew in his thick, black mane. More than two weeks had passed since Griff visited the Grove. Concerned about the effect on his overanxious mother, Griff had taken his stepfather, Herwin, aside to discuss the events that had occurred in his special place. Herwin had listened with alarm. Together, they had carefully swept through the area, its sanctity disturbed by the presence of another, even one Griff loved like the father he had lost. They had found nothing, not even a bloodstain or a feather to confirm a story that seemed outlandish even to Griff. It began to seem more logical to question his own sanity than to defend experiences he dared not presume true.

Griff sighed deeply. Fear and confusion had kept him away from his sanctuary; his love for the companion he had so long believed a figment of his imagination brought him back. Real or illusory, he had to know the truth about Ravn. For too long, he had refused to investigate, afraid that knowing would make his best friend disappear. Now, too much lay at stake. Either his life had twice fallen into jeopardy or he had spiraled into a desperate quagmire of madness. Neither option pleased him, but if he could at least distinguish reality, he could address the problem.

Griff pressed forward, courage faltering. Desperately, he wanted his stepfather and mother at his side while he waded back into the shambles. *I've been sheltered too long.* He never doubted his mother's sincere desire and need to keep him safe, but her overprotectiveness had become the framework for his madness. She had walled him into a life of helpless dependence, one he might never have recognized if not for the information mother and stepfather occasionally let slip in their stories. Real or imagined, Griff's near-death experiences had brought a clarity of thought he never knew existed. Details he had packed away since his early childhood emerged to haunt him. As a boy, he had traveled to town with his father and brother. He had buried those memories, now dragged back to the fore. They remained fragmented, faded and interspersed with the sharper images of more recent events. His young mind had been unable to analyze. Now, as a teenager, he saw the events in a new light that frightened him.

Griff reached the edge of the forest, brushing by trees that showered him with collected moisture. Droplets pelted him, icy pinpoints that scarcely punctuated the general coldness that accompanied being damp. Griff recalled a feebleminded adult, past the age when he should have separated from his parents to begin his own life and a farm of his own. The man had drooled and babbled, clinging to his parents like a huge child. Whispers had touched Griff's ears, meaning little to his toddler self yet oddly consequential now. That young man had been eighteen, only a year older than Griff.

Two weeks spent examining the events that had frightened him and finding nothing, two weeks with only the simple, safe chores that had become his lot had left Griff with too much time to think. Every night, he lay awake, realizations rushing down upon him like water held too long by a dam now broken. Whether his insanity had come as a result of his impregnable lifestyle or from the revelations that had assailed him more recently, he needed to face it alone. Were the recent attacks the reason for his mother's excessive caution, or were they fancy that stemmed from the strangeness of his lifestyle? Did she know something about him that she had told no one else, some information that might cause inhuman creatures to hunt him? It seemed unlikely. Griff knew he descended from Béarn's royal family, but he had always believed noble blood a positive feature. Nothing in his past seemed horrible enough to warrant assassins. The deaths of his father and brother, definitely accidental, were reason enough for his mother's paranoia. More likely, his mother sheltered him because of his specialness. Like the teen he had met as a child, Griff had a diseased mind. At the least, his illness took the form of creating friends and monsters. Perhaps he, too, was dull.

Griff's pace slowed as he stepped onto the familiar overgrown path to the Grove. He and Herwin had already searched it minutely. He did not expect to find anything that might prove the veracity of the attacks so vivid in his memory. He came because he missed Ravn like a brother. This day, he would confront Ravn as he had not dared to before. Griff would discover the truth in undeniable detail, even if it lost him the only friend he ever had. If Ravn existed only as a part of Griff, he would make the sacrifices to join his parts together as they belonged. Anything less would only aid the madness.

Griff's walk seemed to last for miles, the usual landmarks appearing strange in his current mind-set. Wet leaves clung to then peeled from his hands and cheeks, tickling. Tiny raindrops obscured his vision, and he wiped away accumulations so like tears. The urge to bring Herwin along became nearly overpowering, but he ignored the childish need. Threat or waking nightmare, it did not matter. He would neither endanger nor rely on his parents. He had to do this himself.

The branches parted to reveal the clearing Griff knew so well. The ordinariness of it promised security yet disappointed at the same time. Somehow, it seemed wrong for him to change so much and his sanctuary turned battleground so impossibly little. His boots left ovoid impressions in the mud, his prints unmistakably large when compared with the stepfather he had already overgrown. Griff perched on a deadfall, his near-drowning too strong a memory for him to go near the creek. He waited with long developed patience, knowing from experience that Ravn would come of his own accord. No amount of calling, coaxing, or wishing would bring him sooner.

A birdcall glided through the Grove, a pretty cry that Griff did not recognize. Others answered, in a chain, growing pro-

gressively more distant. Griff cocked his head, listening.
Only then, with his concentration directed, he noted other
noises so natural his mind had dismissed them. He heard a
squirrel chattering far above his head, followed by the sound
of a nut dropping. It rattled against the leaves in a line, the
sound of its movement soon joined and eclipsed by the tick-
tacking of dislodged droplets falling in a spreading pattern.
Leaves whisked, revealing the motions of animals through
the brush around him. The creek rumbled over the stones, its
song deep and mellow.

Griff could not help smiling. No matter how weighty his
thoughts, the Grove always cheered him. Its sights, odors,
and sounds formed a special world that he happily shared
with every creature and object the gods could devise. Even
as peace lulled him, a song swelled into a surrounding
chorus. For a moment, he listened, caught by its beauty. At
first he attributed it to birds, and he reveled in the joy of
hearing nature at its finest. Then memory reminded him of
its source, and interest prickled into alarm. The ones who
had come to kill him sang like this.

Griff clambered to his feet in an instant, heart rate doubling as he did. The desire to flee did not last long, tempered
by the certainty that Ravn would protect him as he had twice
before, as his mother and stepfather had always done in the
past. Griff knew little of fear, nor the correct response to it.
No one in his parents' stories ever faced firsthand danger;
his mother had seen to that.

Another voice rose above the chorus, strong and lyrical.
Yet its harmony clashed with the tune of the others, a
strange, chaotic discord that jangled at his nerves. Griff
tensed, adrenaline surging through him, uncertain whether to
run or fight. For several moments, he froze in indecision,
waiting for Ravn's arrival. Naïveté, as well as previous experience, stole his opening. Gradually, all concern fled before magic designed to soothe. Curiosity became Griff's
only driving force, and exhaustion fogged his mind. The
song became a lullaby in his mother's voice, one he prayed
would never end.

Griff made no attempt to battle the magic. Trust alone had
served him well for a lifetime. Suspicion and wariness had
no place in an emotional repertoire molded otherwise since
birth, a life fully without pain or struggle. It never occurred

to him to wonder about Ravn's absence. Blissfully, he sat and slid into a quiet sleep.

Baltraine had come to despise his conscience. It burned inside him like a brand, sending heat flashing through his body though autumn was nearly a month old. He sat amid an odd assemblage, guilt tearing at his insides and churning bile through his throat. He had vomited twice since the meal began, unable to eat even had he not known about the poison lacing every plate. He wondered if the toxin would cause pain as horrible as what he suffered, and even dared to fear that the elves had betrayed him. Obviously sick, he shoved aside his dinner, untasted.

Beside Baltraine, the master healer placed a comforting arm around him, features coarse with concern. "Are you well, my lord? Can I help?"

"Just some gut upset," Baltraine explained away his nerves. "Probably something I ate." The lie intensified the pain, all the more discomforting for his knowledge of the truth. "It'll pass."

"I have herbs that might—"

Baltraine dismissed Mikalyn with an irritated wave. Sympathy from one about to succumb to murder only sparked more nausea, and Baltraine worried that he might vomit again.

The healer backed away with a knowing nod, skilled enough to surmise the nervousness that underlay Baltraine's illness, though he would surely wrongly attribute it to the need to reveal King Kohleran's death.

Baltraine glanced around the room, morbid fascination claiming his attention for a time. The familiar faces of Béarn's council swept through his vision as they concentrated on food whose taste gave no hint of its deadliness. Aged, loyal Abran ate in silence, head cocked to the side as always and food drooling from the corner of his mouth as he ate. The old minister of foreign affairs kept to himself, still self-conscious about the lingering effects of the stroke that had claimed some of his facial muscles. For him, death might prove as much blessing as curse, or so Baltraine convinced himself.

Baltraine's gaze shifted to Minister of Courtroom Procedure and Affairs Weslin. The young man assisted Abran cautiously, helping with tasks that the older minister's shaky hands could not successfully perform with a subtlety that did not compromise Abran's dignity. Weslin's light brown hair and eyes, his Pudarian complexion, and his lighter frame stood mute testament to his distance from the line of kings. Again, Baltraine crushed down his guilt, this time with consideration of worth. Béarn could find a far better minister to fill his place.

Internal Affairs Minister Fahrthran sat between the two female ministers, and Baltraine concentrated on him to avoid considering the other two. Fahrthran, he would miss least of all. The minister of internal affairs had never belonged among the council, having descended from honorary nobility, originally with no Béarnian blood. Commoners not only tainted his line but defined it, and he had never deserved to sit among Béarn's ministers. His years of decision-making had already proved far more than he merited.

In addition to Béarn's council, Bard Linndar and the master healer had been asked to join them. The closest of the king's pages sat in the kitchen, rewarded with minister's portions of their own for reasons they did not care to question for fear of losing the bounty. Baltraine continued to fight down guilt with self-righteous, internal struggles that placed him above those who had to die. His own life hinged on how well he cooperated with Dh'arlo'mé and his followers, and his death could only become lost in the purgings. Alive, he could serve Béarn better.

Thoughts of Dh'arlo'mé sent shivers through Baltraine. The single, green eye always seemed to pin him in place, to rip through his every defense to the very core of his being. Emotion evaporated into mist before an onslaught that consisted of nothing more physical than a stare. The elves looked young and frail, but therein lay their power. Unable to rely on appearances, Baltraine found them impossible to read. In their presence, his courage always failed him. His life and sanity hung on a thready balance.

Baltraine buried his head in his hands. Xyxthris and he had directed the elves to those humans who needed destroying. The council required replacing, and those who might insist on frequent close contact with the king must go also. In particular, the bard, who served as the ruler's personal bodyguard, had to die. Baltraine clamped his fingers to his scalp so tightly his nails dug into the flesh. He liked Linndar, her faithfulness and competence as well as her talent with music. The realization that he might have a hand in destroying a god-established institution hurt as well. Linndar would die this day, leaving only an heir who had disappeared months before her, almost certainly a previous victim of the elves. The loss, though painful, paled before a larger one. The Béarnian line of kings had ended. Only magic could rescue Béarn now, and only elves could perform magic. So what choice did Baltraine have but to support them?

A few other options prickled at Baltraine's conscience. He cast them aside. The course that worked best for him required maintaining the status quo, and his thoughts would not allow him to consider anything else. The elves would save Béarn. He would assist them, whatever their methods. And if it furthered the status of himself and his family, no one could begrudge him.

The sickness receded, a pleasant reprieve. Baltraine rose. Dizziness assailed him, and the room seemed to spin into a blur that masked the faces of those soon to be dead. Their features turned skeletal in his mind's eye, empty, round sockets staring helplessly while bony hands shoveled food toward lipless mouths. "Excuse me," Baltraine moaned to no one in particular. He left the room at a fast walk that quickened to a run the moment the door clicked closed behind him. He raced blindly through the castle hallways, the images of dead creatures dripping flesh always just a few steps behind him. He headed for the room with the nearest sewer hole, having already vomited there twice; but fear took him past it, then past the next. Onward he charged through Béarn's corridors, never quite certain where he headed, only noticing that the images grew more faded and the pain less intense the farther he got from the conference room.

Baltraine's feet carried him to the temple, an obvious sanctuary once his mind caught up to his actions. His eyes cleared again, the images of living grave-creatures subsiding. Before him hovered the engraved bears that decorated the temple doors, their sapphire eyes gleaming and their shaven pearl inlay reflecting myriad colors in the scant light of torches. He slowed, panting, uncertain how many servants and nobles might have seen his undignified flight. He had noticed no one.

Baltraine pulled his thoughts together. He needed to act carefully now. Enough people had witnessed his trips to the bathroom and his greenish features to corroborate sickness as the reason why he did not partake of the feast that killed the others. Running away would prove more difficult to explain. He had little choice but to enter and pray. He could later claim that his stomach cramps had become so severe, he worried for his life and required the solace of religion prior to what he believed might prove his last breaths. Surely, most would attribute his distress to the poison, claiming that his greater sensitivity had caused him to react to lower doses before he took in enough to kill him.

Baltraine seized the moon ring. Immediately, other thoughts descended upon him, memories of a previous trip to Béarn's temple. A being who claimed kinship with the gods had come to him. Baltraine's weekly visits to regular services had garnered no more visions of the blond man who had shamed him into consulting Knight-Captain Kedrin. Now the visions returned, vivid in their clarity. He wished for solace but had no interest in seeing the "god" again. Uncertain precisely what sequence of events had brought the one who called himself immortal, Baltraine determined to act in a different fashion. He released the ring held by a carving of the moon and grasped the one of the sun instead.

The difference, though slight, relieved Baltraine immediately. He jerked open the door with more strength then he would have believed possible under the circumstances. He trod up the aisle as the door slammed shut, and he braced instinctively for the solid crash of the door handle against the wood. It did not come. Halfway to the dais, Baltraine froze. The sound had become so familiar since childhood that its absence unbalanced him. Uneasiness prickled through him like a thousand needles stabbing at once. For several moments he paused, wondering if shame had distorted his sense of time. He counted under his breath. When he reached twenty and the sound still did not come, alarm became a ceaseless buzzing in his ears. He felt the presence of unseen eyes, and every muscle tensed into a nervous knot. Carefully, he turned.

The blond stood in the aisle, between Baltraine and the closed double doors. He leaned casually against a pew, his cold blue-gray eyes fixed on the prime minister, his blond hair short and feathered around a face that looked wise beyond its years. The composure seemed extreme, inhuman; and his stance alone intimidated Baltraine. The prime minister took an unintentional backward step.

The blond nodded once. "You have designs against Béarn's throne." It was a statement that left no inflection for question.

Baltraine denied the accusation. "No!" He glanced around to ascertain that no other worshipers knelt amid the aisles and pews. Only the echoes of his denial prevailed; he saw and heard no one. He and the immortal stood alone in the gods' temple. "No," he repeated more softly. "I want only what's best for Béarn."

The immortal's expression hardened. "You've convinced yourself of that, have you? Then I've come too late."

"Too late for what?" Baltraine asked nervously, gaze darting. He suddenly wished the blond had appeared in front of him instead of blocking retreat. The missing bang of the door ring became an obsession.

"Too late to save you from yourself." The blond did not explain further, and Baltraine did not press.

"I'm doing the best I can."

"Indeed?" The blond shrugged. "My condolences, then. You're worth . . . less than I ever expected."

"Worth less?" Baltraine's temper blazed from fearful to furious in an instant. "Worthless. How dare you! I'm in every way noble, a true descendant of kings."

"Ah," the blond said in a tone that trivialized Baltraine's statement. No human would have dared to discount his words in this manner. "First, I did not call you worthless, you did. That says much." The blond straightened. Though he stood a head shorter than Baltraine and was far lighter, he still managed to appear intimidating. "Second, what good is a man whose worth derives from the courage or accomplishments of his ancestors? The deeds of your grandfather's grandfathers might make you a noble, but they don't make you worthy. The worth of a man comes from his own deeds. For those, Prime Minister Baltraine, Fahrthran and Weslin have you beaten by far."

Baltraine's hands clenched at his sides, and his nostrils flared. Rage would accomplish nothing here, and so he contained it. "Everything I've ever done has been for the good of Béarn!"

"Framing her knight-captain? Killing her bard?" The icy eyes fixed on Baltraine's, and the Béarnide felt helpless to evade them. "Your definition of 'for the good' stretches in strange directions."

"I did not come to be judged." The blond had made no physical movements toward Baltraine, and that made the prime minister bolder. "What do you want from me?"

"I ask only that you exercise the judgment my colleagues gave you." The blond lowered his head, disappointment obvious. "You can do nothing for me; I can only advise you. I would tell you to do as Kedrin tells you and to always place the interests of Béarn above your own. But I fear you are already lost." With that, the immortal stepped aside and gestured Baltraine toward the door.

The prime minister hesitated, his conscience driving him to questions and promises he scarcely understood. Then his instinct for self-preservation sent him edging carefully around the immortal, eyes probing the other for any sign of motion, any evidence that the "god" might prevent his exit. Once past the other, Baltraine darted for the door. He reached it in half a dozen rapid strides, then turned to look back.

The blond watched him depart wordlessly, his silence every bit as much a judgment as his words had been. Baltraine opened the door and escaped into the hallway with dignity barely intact. Finding the corridor mercifully empty, he shoved the door. It shut with a bang, followed by the satisfying clap of the massive ring against the wood. Baltraine pressed his back against the oak as his world swirled in crazy circles. A million thoughts converged on him at once, blurring into a sickening war of conscience, a grim self-assessment that alternately found him perfect and desperately wanting.

Baltraine closed his eyes, equalizing his breathing. Gradually, the vertigo grew into a solid wall of darkness that shattered into pinpoints of black and white. That, too, resolved, leaving Baltraine access to more coherent thought. His lids snapped open. The hallway looked as it always did, adorned with torch brackets in animal shapes, gold and blue brocade swaying slightly in an invisible breeze. He glanced longest at a rearing bear. Its granite eyes beckoned, promising all of the power he deserved. Baltraine read it as a sign. Strength flowed back into his shaky limbs, and he raised his head with a pride he had not known in days. Something clicked inside him, and he found the peace he had sought for months.

I am worthy, Baltraine told himself. And believed it. The

situation he had considered from every angle now so obviously had only one solution. The king was dead, without a true heir. Only gods and magic could alter the consequences. If anyone could prevent the Destruction, the elves and their wizardry could. Baltraine would remain as active a part of that as he could. The elves needed his expertise, his position, and his charismatic presence. He needed their magic. A perfect arrangement, and all of it best for Béarn.

The sickness receded, leaving Baltraine's mind clear and his gut devoid of pain. The absence of the nausea and suffering that had ridden him for hours left him feeling powerful and in control. *I am worthy,* he repeated, smiling. He stepped away from the door, finally at peace. He took four steps before an image of the blond, scowling in derision, filled his head. He staggered a single step, recovering his balance and his control an instant later. Head high, he marched through the corridors buoyed by a personal vow. He would not allow the self-proclaimed immortal to bother him. He would not return to the temple again. A more gratifying thought followed. *I will see to it that no one can.*

As Baltraine swept down the last sequence of corridors that would bring him back to the conference room, he cast aside the excitement his decision had created. It would not do for him to leave the room ill and return in high spirits. He ran a hand through his hair and beard, further disheveling them. He sucked in a deep breath, loosing it slowly, forcing away the grin that had settled on his face during the walk. Features sagging, shoulders slumped forward in defiance of his lessons on posture and etiquette, he returned to the condemned.

Everyone looked up as Baltraine entered, most finished with their meals. The master healer greeted him with a firm, "There he is," and every eye watched his entrance.

Baltraine took his seat without ceremony, deliberately ignoring the attention. They all believed he had summoned them here as the senior officer of Béarn. Baltraine needed to convince them otherwise, at least until the poison claimed them. He glanced around the room, surprised to discover he could meet even Linndar's stare without remorse. The war against conscience had been fought, and he could now proclaim himself the victor.

* * *

The meeting ended nearly before it began, as each invited guest denied having arranged it. They all left looking confused, abashed, or suspicious, several already complaining of stomach cramps or vague discomfort. Given the job of tracking down the one who had initiated the gathering, pages scurried along the castle hallways, questioning one another and whichever nobles they dared to accost. Baltraine left them to their own devices, certain they would never piece the source together. They would not question Béarn's ruling regent nor did they know about the elves, and no other course would gain them the correct answers. As the attendees succumbed to poisoned food, tending them would usurp the full attention of every palace servant and healer. Eventually, the hunt would begin again, this time directed toward the citizen factions that opposed Baltraine, the most obvious enemies of himself and his cabinet.

Baltraine gave the scheme no further thought, trusting himself to handle any emergency that might arise. He, the elves, and Xyxthris had plotted the details too carefully to concern themselves with mistakes. Only something completely unforeseen could interfere, and no amount of brooding would anticipate such a thing. Courtroom situations had taught him to deal with the danger of the unexpected in an able and expedient manner.

Baltraine kept his head low as he navigated the corridors and stairs to his own quarters. Any noble or servant who noticed him should attribute his quiet sobriety to the sickness many had directly witnessed. No trace of nausea remained, now replaced by excitement. He appreciated the clarity of thought and movement this left him, though it did not fit his masquerade as well. Though he would not repeat the suffering, he appreciated its timing. He could never have feigned stomach upset as well as the reality he had so vividly demonstrated.

Baltraine passed the familiar carvings and murals with scarcely a glance. The scenes depicted everything from children's stories about the Béarnian bear to graphic depictions of battles. Though exquisitely carved and dramatically painted to the last detail, the art no longer entertained Baltraine. He had examined the same scenes too many times. And now he had more important matters to contemplate.

Baltraine opened the door to his room, comforted by its familiar, personal smell: a combination of his own body odors, his perfume, and the mahogany scent of his furniture. Furniture imported from Pudar lined every wall, the patterns of entwined wolves matching perfectly. Sapphires glimmered from key, tasteful locations around the wood, mostly at seams and handles. He had left the blue and tan silk curtains open, and a panorama of colors played across the glass. At the horizon, a layer of fiery red seemed to draw a circle around the world. Perched atop that was a band of orange, then yellow, followed by green, and royal blue that stretched over the remainder of the sky. Gray-black clouds smeared the beauty of the sunset at intervals.

Taking the pretty picture as an omen of the gods' approval, Baltraine smiled. The glaze of colored light from the sunset scarcely grazed the room's darkness, leaving his bed and the furniture deeper inside as dense shadows. From habit, he reached for the lantern where it hung from a peg, removed a torch from a hallway bracket in the shape of a pig, and lit the wick. Light sputtered to life, condensed into a bright billow. Baltraine returned torch and lantern, then stepped into his room and closed the door.

Something out of place touched Baltraine's consciousness suddenly. He scanned the room again, the lantern sparking blue glimmers from the many decorative sapphires. He watched the glow play over his three dressers, the inset closet, and his writing desk and chair. Papers lay in neat stacks, as he always left them; and shelves above it held his usual collection of books. In the center of his room, the heavy curtains of his bed had been drawn, revealing the double bear symbols, tan against the blue. Baltraine's mind identified this as the change that had raised suspicion, and he shook his head at his own paranoia. The servants who collected his sheets and straightened his bed had likely accidentally left it closed. They could not always satisfy the various preferences of members of the royal household. Probably, his usual maid had taken ill and another had made his bed.

Although Baltraine believed he had solved a simple mystery, caution drove him to open the curtains prior to beginning his nighttime ritual. He gripped the fabric in one hand and jerked it open, the holding clips rattling along the railing. The fabric parted to reveal Dh'arlo'mé lounging atop the blankets, single green eye fixed on Baltraine, expression as unreadable as ever. Another elf sat quietly at the far end of the mattress.

Startled, Baltraine recoiled with a hiss.

Dh'arlo'mé sat up, dark cloak falling into proper alignment with the hood covering his fine, red-blond hair. With his face cast into shadow, his features became even more undecipherable. Baltraine already had difficulty guessing elfin moods, so the hood should not have bothered him. Nevertheless, it did. "I didn't mean to frighten you." The elf's tone made a mockery of his words.

"You didn't," Baltraine returned, leaving Dh'arlo'mé to decide whether he meant he was not frightened or that the elf was lying. The momentary scare had emptied his mind of thought, and now he forced politeness. "What can I do for you?"

"Is the meeting finished?"

"Yes," Baltraine admitted, his gaze flitting from Dh'arlo'mé to the yellow-eyed male elf beside him. This other studied Baltraine with only mild curiosity. At least, Baltraine believed that was the emotion he read.

"And the job done?" Dh'arlo'mé said next, as if continuing the same question.

"The results remain to be seen." Baltraine wanted it clear that the poison had not had time to work yet.

"Good." Still, no emotion entered Dh'arlo'mé's voice or features. The sacrifice of several human lives apparently meant nothing to him. "It's time to train Pree-han." He gestured at the other elf with one long-fingered hand.

Baltraine nodded, glad the elves had finally abandoned using their eighty syllable names, at least around him. He and Xyxthris had taken to shortening them to the most natural-sounding one to four syllables. It had taken several discussions to convince Dh'arlo'mé that the issue went way beyond laziness or disrespect. Humans simply did not have memories capable of processing the tedious alien names.

Xyxthris had spent days through the magical door in the land the elves called Nualfheim, judging elfin voices to find the one closest to King Kohleran's booming bass. Baltraine had not envied the task. He had heard enough of their musical accents and lilting speech to doubt any could approach the necessary harshness and depth of human tones. Their bird-light frames and thin, lengthy proportions seemed appropriate for no human bulkier than an adolescent girl. Yet that had proven less important to Dh'arlo'mé. Apparently, magic could handle concealing appearance, though it could not do the same for speech. "Say something for me, Pree-han."

The elf cleared his throat with a dainty, high-pitched cough. "What would you like me to say?" The voice emerged deeper than Baltraine expected, though still thin for a mature Béarnide. The elf handled the human accent far better than his peers, a good sign.

Baltraine needed more. "Friends, I have gathered you to speak of a matter of utmost urgency."

Pree-han repeated the phrase, this time adding a reasonable facsimile of Baltraine's gruff tenor.

"Not bad," Baltraine admitted, tempering pleasure with doubt. Pree-han still had a long way to go and precious little time. The poisoning of the council would spur retribution from those factions still supporting Baltraine or the rightful heirs to Béarn. They would have to convince the populace that Kohleran had undergone a miraculous recovery soon, before the window for keeping peace disappeared.

"Well?" Dh'arlo'mé demanded an assessment.

"I can work with that." Baltraine inclined his head toward Pree-han. "The right words, a little work on the intonation, some dialect training. I don't think a slightly different voice will bother the populace. One could hardly expect a man awakening from coma to sound precisely the same as before he became ill."

Dh'arlo'mé made a jerky motion with his upper body that Baltraine took to mimic a human shrug. "I wouldn't know."

Baltraine understood that elves did not suffer from sickness of any kind, their hardy constitutions belying their slight builds and delicate movements. He wondered how much of what the elves told them was truth, then decided it really did not matter. So long as he did as they told him, he and his family would come to no harm. That promise from the elves he had little choice but to believe. To do otherwise meant living in constant fear.

Dh'arlo'mé continued, "I'll leave him in your care, then. Work with him every moment. Xyxthris will have your meals brought, carefully so as not to ruin your display of belly sickness nor to make you look unsympathetic as those you worked with die. You'll have to handle the disturbances as they come."

Baltraine sighed, anticipating forthcoming events. Surely, pages would visit as the ministers fell ill, and frequent progress reports would follow. Likely, the healers would insist on plying him with cures despite his insistence that he felt fine and had eaten very little of his share of the council's feast. Many details would come between him and his charge, including the necessities of Béarn's daily routine. At least, the murders of the key officials would disrupt audiences and court proceedings. Nonessentials could wait. No one would expect the prime minister to conduct usual business while those of import died around him and he, too, had been a target of unknown assassins.

Dh'arlo'mé slid to the floor, then straightened fully, his angular face strangely animal within the darkness cast by the hood. "It would prove best, I believe, to feign my arrival tonight or tomorrow. Even a mysterious healer rumored to possess magical powers should not arrive from Pudar without evidence of travel."

"True," Baltraine chimed in quickly. Peasants and nobles would accept Dh'arlo'mé's ability to heal a dying king; their desire for King Kohleran would surely allow them to discard the impossibility of his recovering from his illness. But it seemed prudent to have Dh'arlo'mé seem to arrive from the great trading city in the usual fashion. "I'll make those arrangements now." He considered a moment longer. "It might prove best to arrange for it to happen under cover of darkness. Fewer witnesses if we make a mistake."

Dh'arlo'mé accepted the explanation without comment. "Is there anything else you believe we should do?"

Something niggled at Baltraine's mind, a spark he had not quite stamped out, one that had already twice caught him off guard and stirred guilt he had not believed he harbored. "One thing more. The castle temple serves as a rallying place for humans. Nothing could crush the human spirit more than destroying the very symbol of their faith."

Dh'arlo'mé did not question. For his knowledge of humans, he relied wholly on those few he paid. "Very well, then. Tomorrow, we destroy the temple."

Chapter 34

The Balance Wavers

The first rule of fighting: You always attack! The best defense is to have your opponent bleeding on the ground.

—Colbey Calistinsson

Harval sliced spirals through Asgard's pleasant air, Colbey guiding the blade with such speed that only the occasional glimmer of sun off steel betrayed its presence. As always, he dedicated his practice to his goddess, Sif, though she found the unwavering faith of a colleague ludicrous. Colbey did not care. To allow familiarity to dilute his faith might mean losing the absolute devotion to sword and goddess that had driven him to become his best. Every day, his skills improved; anything less meant failure. Becoming the best swordsman in the world, now all the worlds, never mattered. He would not compare himself to others. Only the betterment of self held significance; and, aside from family, it would remain the only important focus of his universe.

Colbey's mind disappeared into a familiar part of himself as he battled thousands of imaginary enemies at once. Though each thrust would surely have brought down any mortal, he took care to pretend as many of his strokes missed their mark. Since the *Ragnarok*, Colbey had no opponents to battle other than those in his mind. Therefore, he created ones worthy of his greatest efforts. After all, he gave them nothing less. Yet, this time, something felt wrong. The perfect timing of his strokes remained, yet the blade did not land with its usual immediacy. Though subtle, the change disturbed Colbey, prickling at the contentment that had accompanied his practices since his tiny, infant hand could first close around a sword. The sword was only a tool; he was the wielder. Though magic kept its edge eternally sharp and it contained the essences of Law and Chaos, it had never changed or influenced his skill. He had ascertained that prior to agreeing to wield it. No Renshai would allow a lifeless piece of steel to control him or influence his defense or ability. Only a Renshai's own skill would determine death or victory. He would rather die in withering agony than allow armor or helmet to fend a single blow for him.

Immersed in his practice, Colbey no longer felt the eternal sunshine beaming down on his face or the gentle breeze that wound through perfect trees to caress him and dry the sweat nearly as quickly as it formed. The brilliant, uninterrupted blue of Asgard's sky was lost on this swordsman who had eyes for nothing but his own created enemies and his sword. But the presence of another in his practice clearing drew his attention instantly. Nothing, not even a sword practice, could blind Colbey to a potential threat.

Without pausing for an instant, Colbey identified and dismissed the newcomer as Frey's servant, Byggvir. He traveled unarmed, and he meant Colbey no harm. Colbey continued his *svergelse* without so much as a nod of acknowledgment to the other. The gods understood better than anyone the intensity of a Renshai's practice, and their servants should know not to interrupt.

But Byggvir dared a feat no mortal would. He waited in polite silence for what seemed only a few moments to Colbey, though far more had actually passed. Then he called to Colbey. "Lord? Lord Kyndig!"

Still Colbey continued, refusing to allow the voice to upset his concentration. Ordinarily, he could have ignored the servant entirely, but the sudden strangeness of the sword he had wielded for longer than three hundred years made him distractible. By the third call of his name, Colbey lowered his sword, reined his temper, and glared at the young blond who studied him with nervous blue eyes.

"I'm very sorry to bother you, Lord." Byggvir met Colbey's blue-gray stare briefly, then looked away quickly. "Very, very sorry."

Colbey sheathed his sword, saying nothing. He refused to

speculate, only hoped, for Byggvir's sake, that the need justified the transgression.

Byggvir bowed politely. "Lord Vidar called a meeting in the Great Hall. He requests your presence."

"Thank you," Colbey said, not bothering to soften his gaze. His hands balled to fists at his sides, needing a practice now more than before. He needed to work off the aggression that rose naturally at the interruption of a Renshai's *svergelse*. Without awaiting further details, he returned his attention to his sword work, still troubled by the tiny imperfections where none should exist. Something about Harval had changed.

Byggvir remained in place, obviously uncertain about Colbey's plans yet reluctant to disturb him again. For a long moment he stayed, wrestling with the decision. Then, apparently deciding he had performed his duty, he left further action in Colbey's hands and headed from the clearing.

Colbey did not bother to watch Byggvir go. His concentration returned to the world only warriors understood. Too committed to his sword work to let anything disrupt it, he did not contemplate Byggvir's words but let them disappear into memory until such time as he needed them. After his practice.

The blade circled and flew around Colbey, never in one position long enough for the eye to register. The deadly devil dance continued, more graceful than any acrobat and more lethal than fire. But still, the balance felt slightly wrong. The blade always became a steel extension of his arm, but now it seemed as if that limb had sustained an injury.

Colbey wanted to work until the sword felt proper again and the practice lived up to the necessary improvement of the day. But Byggvir's message wormed its way deeper into the conscious portion of his thoughts, displacing concentration at intervals that grew shorter with time. With a sigh of resignation, Colbey sheathed the blade again, straightened his garments, and headed from the clearing. He did not bother to go home to change or to gather his family. His delay would surely make him the latest even of gods whose patience he had learned to tolerate, if not appreciate, over the centuries. Freya and Ravn would already be there, the former making excuses for his tardiness and the latter overwhelmed by his first meeting.

Colbey's long strides took him swiftly across the area between his practice clearing and the Great Hall, though they seemed infantile in the wake of gods more than half again his height. The scenery scarcely changed, Asgard's balmy weather and symmetrical trees flawless but also difficult to differentiate. Colbey paid no attention to his surroundings. His mind sped ahead to the reason for Vidar's concern, and only two possibilities came to mind. Either a situation Colbey knew nothing about had come to light, or Vidar had become worried over the events on Midgard. Either way, it seemed unnecessary to speculate further. Colbey would know the truth soon enough.

Colbey's walk brought him to the squat, massive structure that served as the gods' meeting hall. Walls of silver rose to a ceiling of gold, inlaid with jewels of every hue. These sparkled and glittered in the sunlight. Every movement of Colbey's brought different ones into his view, and they seemed to wink like the thousand eyes of a shimmering monster. Constructed from the wealth given by their followers, it represented every metal, stone, and object valuable on Midgard. Colbey drew open the heavy teak door, and a border of diamonds split light into wild spirals of color. He eased the panel closed behind him, then looked out over the room.

Though once the site of the gods' greatest feasts and merriment, the Great Hall on Asgard now seemed sterile and unwelcoming. Three hundred years had failed to ease the stiffness of every meeting since the *Ragnarok*. In the immediate wake of the Destruction of the Gods, they had gathered frequently, repairing damage, re-creating, and mourning the loss of relatives and friends. The gods and goddesses had taken their accustomed seats, deliberately avoiding those that once belonged to the dead. The arrangement went beyond silly to inconvenient as it forced them, at times, to shout over half a dozen empty chairs.

Now, Colbey noticed, the gods and goddesses had chosen their seats more from convenience than habit. They clustered at one end of the table, sitting on either side, the only remaining sign of deference the head seat that remained unoccupied. They had never dared cross Odin when he lived, and the gods' fear of the Terrible One had, apparently, extended even three centuries beyond his death. Colbey smiled. He had no similar compunction. Although he would have preferred Vidar to take the high seat, the new leader of the gods had chosen not to do so.

Every eye shifted to Colbey as he entered, and the dull rumble of conversation died to silence. As he suspected, he had arrived last. Colbey studied the others as he entered. Vidar and Vali sat together. Though half brothers, sons of Odin, they little resembled one another. Vali, Colbey guessed, favored his giantess mother since Vidar looked much like Odin. However, he lacked the aura of cruel danger and mysterious wisdom that seemed to radiate from Odin like a mantle. Whether one so gentle could prove as strong still remained to be seen.

Opposite Vidar and Vali sat the once-dead god, Balder and blind Hod, the brother tricked into killing him. In his first life, Balder had been the most beautiful of the gods. Time and experience had stolen youth, innocence, and some of his handsomeness. Now, Frey's straight eyes, sculpted jaw, and high cheekbones gave competition where they once could not. That Frey had chosen to sit so close, with only Balder's wife Nanna between them, brought appearances more clearly to light. Colbey did not bother to contrast. The attractiveness of other men meant nothing to him, and no one could compare to the radiance of his own wife, Freya, who sat beside her brother. Colbey could not help grinning. Even after a marriage longer than human comprehension, he still felt like the luckiest man alive.

Freya returned Colbey's smile. Her shapely lips, softly-contoured face, and ivory complexion, that somehow avoided looking sallow, defined loveliness, not only for Colbey, but for all of Midgard. Their very religion designated ultimate beauty by using the name of this goddess. He had seen renditions of her by the finest artists, yet none came close to matching her perfection. The hair that tumbled to her back outshone the roof, and even the pure gold that had come to replace Sif's tresses could not compete. The gods had chosen the impeccable blue of their sky to match the ideal shade of Freya's eyes.

Ravn sat beside Freya and next to Thor's son, Modi. His brother, Magni, had claimed the opposite seat, so that they sat at either hand of the head seat. Idunn and Sigyn, Bragi's widow and Loki's, completed the symmetry.

No chairs remained near his family, so Colbey chose to sit between his half brothers. That this placed him in Odin's seat did not cause so much as a twinge of discomfort—at least not for him. As he settled into Odin's chair, the hush among the other deities grew even more intense, colored by a general restlessness that seemed to seep down the lines of gods and goddesses. Colbey glanced at the others expectantly. He would have looked directly at Vidar, but too many occupied the space between them and every one had placed his or her head in his way. The few whispers he heard remained too distant and garbled to decipher, but his mind powers told him many believed him arrogant or impertinent and in need of discipline. He did not care, seeing himself as a necessary divergence from the oppressive laws and habits that tended to cripple them into inaction. Once, Loki had compared Colbey to himself. The Renshai found it nearly impossible to believe himself akin to the champion of chaos, the gods' enemy, the villain of every story he had heard since birth. Now, however, he saw the comparison. This new age did not require extremes, like those Loki and Odin had personified, not since dishonor, lies, and betrayal had become a regular part of the human repertoire. But Colbey had become the catalyst for change that otherwise might occur way too slowly to benefit anyone.

Vidar cleared his throat, which shifted the attention to him. "We're all here. Now we can commence." He paused, but no one moved or spoke. "I'm concerned about the events taking place on Midgard. The balance is in jeopardy."

"The balance?" Idunn repeated. Attention shifted back to Colbey. They all knew who Odin had designated to guard the delicate symmetry between law and chaos, good and evil.

Colbey weathered the gods' stares without discomfort or comment. Prior to the *Ragnarok*, the gods had seemed frightening and immense, a power that terrified as well as ruled. Odin's single eye pierced games and guises; the shadowed face beneath his broad-brimmed hat had yielded nothing of himself in return. Thor's wild rages could send them all cowering in fear. Though quieter, Heimdall and Tyr had seemed to radiate honor and courage. Loki's sly malevolence came out in his every action; even his voice had conjured images of slimy rocks in putrid streams.

The new order contained little of that directed power. Loki had said extremism would die with the *Ragnarok*, including himself. Colbey had not anticipated how human it would make these others seem in comparison. He tempered his thoughts with consideration, wondering how much of his assessment came of true failing and how much from the contempt familiarity can so swiftly create. Eventually, he guessed, Modi and Magni would demonstrate more of their father's rage. The quest for wisdom and the price he might pay for it would turn Vidar more and more like his father. But if they truly followed in the wake of their parents, might that not cause the need for a second *Ragnarok* to purge the heavens of another wave of fanaticism. *And will I join them? Will I become another Loki?* Colbey spurned the thought. In his mortal years, he had clung to balance even when the greatest forces of the world condemned him for it. His belief in and dedication to balance would never waver, just as his faith in his sword arm would not wither.

Oblivious to Colbey's concerns, Vidar continued. "If Midgard continues on her current course, she will surely flounder. The other worlds will sink with her. Including our own."

Murmured discussions followed the pronouncement, but Colbey did not bother to listen to any of it. Predicted threats could not harm them, only actual ones. Odin had paid with his eye and his mercy for wisdom, including some knowledge of the future. Through him, the gods had gotten advance warning of many events; they had prepared for the inevitability of the *Ragnarok* for aeons. Yet, now that it had come and passed, no prophecies remained. Men and gods had no choice but to live each day as it came, in ignorance. Mankind had adapted quickly, as each succeeding generation had fewer, then no, personal memories of living any other way. The gods clearly found such ignorance a burden.

"You're talking in generalities." Vali did not hesitate to challenge his half brother. "Exactly what will happen if the balance skews too far?"

Vidar gestured at Colbey, deferring to the Keeper of the Balance.

Colbey obliged, his knowledge limited. What he did not know as certainty, he speculated. "It depends on the direction of the imbalance. Toward good, mankind would become too preoccupied with assisting others to attend their own needs. Only the weak would survive, and those not for long. Toward evil, total concern for personal desires would have a similar end, though bloodier, of course. I do not know how that would affect Asgard, but I won't wait to find out."

Colbey made it clear he felt ties to mankind at least as strong. "Toward law, their world, then eventually all worlds, would stagnate into oblivion. Time would cease to pass, and everything would remain locked in position and place. Toward chaos, as now, total destruction of all remaining worlds would ensue."

A polite silence followed, and an array of emotions bombarded Colbey. He did not waste time sorting their sources. He nodded toward Vidar to return the floor.

Modi spoke first. His pale eyes narrowed, and his orange beard seemed to bristle. He placed a hand on the stem of Thor's hammer, *Mjollnir,* where it perched on the table between himself and his brother. "How would that destruction happen? We've defeated the forces of chaos."

Colbey shrugged, ignorant of the details. "I don't know. I can only assume new chaos-creatures would arise. Given the volatility of chaos, one never knows. If any of us could predict chaos, I'd worry." The question deserved serious consideration. The abbreviated version of *Ragnarok* that had occurred had had well-defined causes. Colbey did not have enough information to propose details this time.

Balder spoke next, his musical voice unmistakable. Smiles swept the table as everyone remembered the twice-born god's innocent youth. Beloved child of the gods' matron and the AllFather, he had become the natural target of Loki's venom, hence his death. Even Colbey saw the ironic sadness in the realization that Frigg and Odin had both been lost in the *Ragnarok,* only hours before their most cherished treasure returned from Hel. "How far out of line has the balance gotten? Are we in imminent danger?"

Again the others deferred to Colbey; but, this time, he had no answer. "I don't know."

"You don't know!" Sif shot back. "The Keeper of the Balance doesn't know?"

Having already said exactly that, Colbey did not bother to reply.

"One presumes. . . ." Vidar said carefully, using the generic pronoun when "I" would serve as well. "If such danger existed, the Keeper would know."

"So we're not in danger yet," Vali supplied.

"I don't know," Colbey repeated. "I don't care for assumption, though."

Freya picked up where her husband had left off. "It's not

prudent to presuppose things about a situation that never existed before." Having spoken her defense, she switched to the more important question, one with a specific answer. "Vidar, what made you decide to call a meeting now? What concerned you enough to suspect the balance was in danger?"

Colbey folded his arms across his chest, the pressure diverted from him for the moment.

"I've been watching." Vidar looked at Freya as he spoke as if, having asked the question, she had become the only one interested in his response. "For three centuries, the elves kept to themselves. Then, suddenly, they started moving. Within months, all of the major human kingdoms shifted power. More so, they seem in a state of transition, yet they're not going in any clear direction. And the throne in Béarn lies empty."

Horror wafted to Colbey's senses, accompanied by curiosity and rage. The last of Odin's predictions still haunted them. Midgard's balance hinged on Béarn's structure of power, and if Midgard fell into ruin, one way or another, Asgard would follow.

"How long?" Sif finally asked.

"A month and a half now. Almost two."

The ensuing silence became oppressive. Emotion slammed Colbey with such intensity, he felt suffocated. Snatches of thought cut through the icy burden of fear, in one case panic, the fires of Modi and Magni's anger, and the damp, airless quality of despair. Gods counted birthdays in decades, centuries, or millennia. Few or none might have noticed the events occurring on Midgard over the course of weeks. But Colbey had known. And so, apparently, had Vidar.

"We have a month to fix this problem?" Vali sounded incredulous. To a god, it seemed like moments. "Why didn't you say something sooner?"

Vidar returned the appropriate defense. "Until now, I could not determine whether or not we had a problem. Now I believe we do."

"Then why doesn't the Keeper of the Balance know it?" Idunn spoke her first original words of the meeting, having only echoed Vidar's early words. Like all but Modi and Magni, she sported golden hair; but, unlike the other goddesses, she wore hers short.

No certainty could accompany any answer to Idunn's question, only conjecture. Vidar rose to the occasion. "I suspect it's because the balance has only become fluid. It hasn't tipped yet. Once it does, it may prove too late."

Modi stood, his chiseled features grave. For as long as Colbey knew, the Renshai had called upon this representation of wrath whenever their reserves flagged or they needed to fight through injury. "Then I say we do something now!" Though obvious, the statement rang with power. Thor's sons, like their father, were known more for swift and violent action than for logic.

No one bothered to voice the obvious follow-up. That action needed taking had become evident. The specifics of it defied simplicity. Colbey understood the problem. The gods had learned millennia ago that any action they took on man's world caused massive repercussions that stretched far beyond even the wildest speculation. To give the balance a light tap could mean knocking it over the edge in another direction. Worse, it could spiral off its axis into chaos' deepest void. Anything a god did would likely prove more dangerous than the lack of doing ever could.

Colbey knew this better than anyone. Toward the end of his mortal years, he had championed balance the only way he could, by convincing the other Cardinal Wizards that they sanctioned law and he chaos when the reverse was actually true. His plan had worked too well, convincing gods as well as Wizards. Their attempts to destroy chaos had nearly started the *Ragnarok* early, at a time when chaos would have triumphed. Only Loki, Freya, and Odin had discovered the truth. And only Freya had not used that knowledge to support her own agenda.

"Yes." Vidar responded to Modi's plea for action, though a long time had passed in hushed contemplation. "And only one of us has the absolute commitment to balance to work such a change." His gaze, then every other, shifted back to Colbey.

Doubts assailed Colbey, the concept only vaguely familiar. Confidence had accompanied abilities that grew daily. As a mortal, he had remained close enough to his origins to keep self-assurance from usurping caution. Now, he did not know if he could still maintain the necessary distance. "I've been among you for more than three hundred years."

"A pittance," Vidar supplied. "We've been here tens of thousands."

Colbey looked to Freya, who nodded her support. As always, she believed in him.

Colbey's hands slid naturally to his hilts, though he had no intention of drawing a weapon. In the past, his most stressful moments had always come on the battlefield: swift problems with swifter solutions. "I believe that, if we remove the elves from Midgard, the humans will restore balance on their own."

Frey gasped, half-rising, then freezing in position as he realized he had moved without a plan for completing the action. "Remove the elves? How? Where? Their home was destroyed. . . ." He added, features purpling and volume increasing with each word, ". . . as you well know." His tone laid blame where his words had not.

Only two solutions came to mind. Colbey would not damn any creature to Hel, so that left only Asgard. The *Ragnarok* had obliterated the other six planes of existence.

"Asgard cannot support them," Vidar said, and no one argued. An imbalance on Midgard would likely affect gods. Ruining Asgard's equilibrium would bring more dire consequences.

Whittled to only one possibility, Colbey spoke it. "We may need to destroy them."

"No!" Frey stood fully, blue eyes flashing with rage. His fist crashed to the tabletop, an action better suited to Thor's sons. "I will not allow my people to die." He slammed the table again, and the wood shuddered beneath the blow. The table thrummed, stinging, against Colbey's arm, and many of the assemblage jerked backward. "If you attempt such a thing, I will destroy you."

Colbey remained in place, brows arched, wondering if he had just discovered the enemy of the Second Destruction. At least, he seemed to have uncovered the central conflict. Who got called hero and who enemy depended upon perspective. He understood Frey's determination, as he shared it. Had they reversed their situations, he would not allow Frey to bring ruin upon humans. His own strong sense of poetic justice reminded him that the elves had survived the *Ragnarok* by their own cleverness and will. It went against his deepest faith to punish effort that deserved reward.

Vidar stepped in again to mediate, addressing Colbey. "Are there other solutions?"

Colbey answered without hesitation, ignoring Frey's imposing figure and penetrating glare. "There are always other solutions." He turned his icy eyes on the young leader of the gods. "They're just more difficult and sometimes lead to misinterpretation and misunderstanding."

A collective nod swept gods and goddesses, excluding only Frey and Colbey. Every one remembered Colbey's monumental struggle for balance against humans who believed him mad, Wizards and gods who hunted him down for presuming he sanctioned chaos, and the staff he carried that bludgeoned him toward law.

Vidar raised his hands in a gesture that encompassed all present. "Very well, then. Colbey will restore the balance, the very task he came among us to perform."

Colbey frowned, disliking Vidar's choice of words. He had never believed in destiny. Despite Odin's claim to the contrary, and the One-Eyed One's decision to place law and chaos into Colbey's keeping, Colbey believed, with unshakable faith, that he had chosen to champion balance for himself.

Vidar continued, oblivious to Colbey's displeasure. "None of us will question his methods so long as he does not destroy the elves."

Frey qualified, still standing. "So long as he does not kill *any* elves."

Vidar spoke for Colbey, and the Renshai's scowl deepened. "I'm certain Colbey will resist killing anyone if at all possible, but, when the fate of the gods hangs precariously, it's hardly fair to constrain him too tightly."

Frey's eyes narrowed, and he turned his rage from Colbey to Vidar. "Killing elves is not like killing mortals. Murder destroys an elfin soul, and no other can replace it. Losing only a few could begin their destruction."

Colbey broke in then, tired of others discussing his methods. "I will kill no elves. Or humans, if I can possibly help it."

Now it was Vidar's turn to frown. "You don't have to make such a vow."

Frey's face reddened so deeply it turned purple at the edges.

Colbey shrugged, composed. "I have, though. My brother-in-law deserves the comfort of that knowledge."

The flush drained from Frey's face, and he even managed a small smile.

Colbey finished. "An immortal killing mortals would have an extreme effect on the balance. That's why Odin banned the Wizards from such action." It was not precisely true but near enough. Odin's Laws had not tolerated the slaying of significant mortals, those who might affect the future of man's world. However, since no one could tell precisely who these mortals might be at any time, the Wizards usually interpreted that to mean they could not directly harm mortals at all. Colbey looked around the assemblage, discovering all eyes turned on him. He concentrated on Freya, never tiring of the bright, blue glimmer of her eyes, never taking her beauty for granted. Every day, he recognized anew how lucky her love made him. "I'll handle the balance as long as none of you interfere. And I won't kill anyone."

Vidar rolled his eyes and shrugged sadly but said nothing. His gesture conveyed that he disapproved of Colbey limiting his options before the task had even begun, but he always allowed it to remain Colbey's decision. That fed directly into the Renshai's request to avoid interference. When the leader did speak, he moved on from that point. "Does anyone have anything else to add or discuss?"

Colbey caught a movement from the corner of his eye. He glanced at the source, his own son, Ravn. The boy had stiffened, and his lips parted as if he would speak. But no words emerged. He settled back into his seat with a fitfulness that suggested something unspoken.

Apparently, Vidar missed the signs that indicated one among them wished to add something. "Adjourned, then," he said.

The gods and goddesses rose and filed from the room, Frey giving Colbey a respectful nod that showed his appreciation more than words. The farthest away from the door, Colbey remained in place longest, practicing the patience that so many accused him of never learning.

Finally, as Modi's and Magni's footfalls thundered against the floor's copper tiling, Colbey stood and headed after them. Mild disappointment at his son's timidity disappeared beneath contemplation of the burden the gods had thrust upon him. He felt strongly that no single right way existed to perform the task, and he focused on intruding as little as possible into the affairs of mortals. Certain key figures required visits designed to gently tweak them in the right direction.

Though the method seemed necessary and obvious, doubts descended on Colbey. His experiments into this method thus far had met with as much failure as success: Pudar had freed Kevral, buoyed by his interference; yet now she had become so overconfident she spent more time challenging strangers to combat than attending the companions who needed her and the task to which she had pledged her loyalty. From town to town, she insisted upon facing the finest warrior and demoralizing him in single combat. Colbey's temple meetings with Baltraine had goaded the prime minister to exchange uncertainty and fear for self-assurance. Yet the destruction of Béarn's temple had resulted, and Baltraine now supported the precise opposite of the cause toward which Colbey had tried to steer him. Colbey wrestled with the vexation these earlier attempts raised, wondering whether even he had become too immortal to interfere in the affairs of man.

Still, he trusted no other god to handle such a problem better. One way or another, he would work man's world back to its proper alignment. He simply could not afford to fail.

Colbey's thoughts took him through the long hall, through the great doors, and into Asgard's eternal sunshine. By the time he arrived outside, all of the others had vanished. All, except Ravn. The youngster stood beneath a cluster of the tall, sturdy trees that shaded the gods and bore multicolored fruit as sweet as honey. All of his taciturn reluctance had disappeared. The blue eyes radiated the confidence he had not displayed at the meeting, and his stance revealed strength.

Ravn waited only until Colbey acknowledged his presence. "Father, we need to talk."

It seemed a more than reasonable request. Colbey nodded and approached Ravn, glad for the interruption.

"I did as you and Mother said. I did not interfere when the elves took Griff. Now, I want you to lift my punishment. I have to be with him. He needs me."

Colbey sighed deeply. The last thing he needed was for an overeager, undirected youngster to meddle in a job that already taxed him. In his mortal years, nearly every problem he faced had a violent solution. He had trusted in his ability with a sword, and that had seen him through nearly every crisis. In the end, he had learned to use his intellect as well, but that could fail him in a way his sword arm never did. "I'm sorry, Ravn. No."

"No," Ravn repeated, lips puckering into a thoughtful grimace that showed no sadness or despair. He had heard the word but would not accept it.

"No," Colbey responded, as this seemed necessary. "I have enough problems to deal with on man's world without worrying about you as well."

"You need not worry over me. I'll stand by Griff without harming anyone. I won't free him. I won't crush his enemies. I'll just be there with him to share his pain."

"No," Colbey said.

Ravn continued as if he had not heard, "Without me, he may not maintain the innocence necessary to become Béarn's king. He needs me. And we all know man's world needs him."

Colbey refused to accept anything as certainty. Trusting unproven facts had become the downfall of so many. "We do not *know* man's world needs him."

Ravn shrugged, his point too obvious to dismiss. "Free me from this punishment, and you can inflict as many others as you wish. I can take any other."

"The most effective punishment is the one for which you would trade unlimited others."

Ravn could not possibly deny the truth in Colbey's statement, but he did find an answer. "Effective as punishment, certainly; but only if the mistake warrants it. If you use the most effective punishment on me for this, what can you possibly turn to in the future should I do something worse?"

Colbey laughed, tension broken by the desperation of Ravn's argument. "One hopes that such a strong deterrent will *keep* you from doing anything worse. That's the whole purpose, you know."

"A good point." Ravn smiled back. "But I'm sixteen. I've only just begun doing things that annoy my parents." He raised and lowered his brows once, mischief dancing in his eyes.

Colbey sighed. "I'm creative. Trust me to think of something worse. Eventually."

Ravn dropped a line of conversation that had brought him nowhere. "I know where I belong now. I came to you so I wouldn't have to defy my parents to do as I must. Are you going to force my hand?"

Colbey refrained from the obvious, threatening to keep Ravn under guard. To do so would violate the bond they had created and nurtured since birth. It would only teach Ravn not to come to his father with difficult problems. Instead, he placed an arm around his son's shoulders and discussed the matter conspiratorially. "Look, Ravn. I do know how you feel. I spent a lifetime on man's world, once one of them. But friendships with mortals are doomed from the start. Mortals die in a space of time that still seems long to you and me but becomes an eye blink when the true recognition of immortality arrives. Better not to let such ties arise."

Ravn studied his father with widened, skeptical eyes. No words needed saying. Even after three hundred years, Colbey's tie to man's world remained as strong as the steel of his sword. He followed the deeds and antics of individuals with a father's interest, those of Renshai most of all. For all the gods told him his perspective would broaden, he could not see people only as racial groups or, especially, as a single unit.

"I'm different," Colbey said. "You can't judge by me. I believed myself mortal for too long to change. A man, and apparently even a god, cannot help becoming what he believes himself to be."

"I believe myself to be Griff's friend," Ravn explained softly. Sensing a crack in Colbey's defenses, he bore in like a true Renshai. "At least give me a chance. You would let even the weakest, most despicable enemy battle for his life."

Having been handed the perfect solution, Colbey smiled again. He released Ravn and turned to face the boy who was becoming a man. "Very well, then. We spar. If you win, you get your wish. If I do, you do not raise the issue again."

Ravn paled, mouth poised partway open and unable to speak. Since his mortal youth, Colbey had trained the world's best swordsmen, at times sparring them three and four at once. He drove every student to spar him to the extent of their ability and beyond. He forced them to use live weapons with deadly edges, to battle him as if involved in the greatest war of conscience, and never to pull any strike. Yet, in all his years, no student had ever landed a blow; not one had drawn a single drop of blood. Even Freya, a sword mistress among the gods, had never achieved better against him than a tie.

Colbey watched as his son's anguish turned gradually into resolve. With his mind gift, he felt the emotions switch places, and his gaze tracked the changes that accompanied it. Ravn's jaw set. The color returned to his face, then moved beyond to one shade darker than normal. His hands relaxed at his sides, and his stance become less stiff and more wary. The pale eyes, so like his mother's, met Colbey's directly and held there. So many times, the boy, as most beings did, jerked away from the cold, blue-gray stare. This time, he held firm, revealing a determination that left no room for doubt or fear.

"Have at me!" Ravn used a pet phrase of Colbey's when he tried to spur students to use their rage as a tool against him. "Have at me, then, old Renshai! This spar is mine."

Colbey laughed. All the troubles of the moment disappeared, at least for Colbey, as the concentration required for teaching an able opponent replaced it. Two swords flowed skillfully into Ravn's hands, like water. The left was a straight blade, heavy and ponderous beside the shorter, thinner scimitar in his right. The left lunged for Colbey's gut before the other had fully cleared its sheath. Colbey drew and blocked easily with his right-hand sword, freeing Harval with his left as the scimitar surged for his head. He blocked that strike, too, surprised at the ponderous feel of the movement. Just a split second off, but enough to send alarm jerking through him.

Slowed by his discomfort, Colbey returned only a single attack with each blade. Ravn managed a desperate block/ parry combination that left their swords hopelessly tangled. Both withdrew, Ravn glaring at his father, Colbey bewildered by the difficulties with Harval. *Is it me or the sword?* Experience told him to place blame on himself rather than an inanimate piece of steel.

Ravn's charge left Colbey little time for thought. The youngster came at him like a charging stallion, the swords point first and at chest level. Colbey threw them aside with a simple inner, upward block. Ravn's blades scratched harmlessly down his own, but momentum did not end so simply. Ravn drew in so close Colbey could feel his warm breath. A knee slammed for Colbey's groin. The old Renshai eeled sideways, and Ravn's knee crashed against Colbey's hip instead. Colbey kicked backward, hooking Ravn's ankle. Ravn twisted free awkwardly, retreating beyond sword range before Colbey bothered to riposte.

They faced off again. Under ordinary circumstances, Colbey would have smiled. Ravn was attacking like a Renshai, with a two-sword combination worthy of Colbey and only a few others—all of their race. His boldness pleased his teacher, but Colbey's concern for his own timing distracted him from compliments. Something felt wrong, and he seemed incapable of adjusting to the change. It seemed as if the sword's impeccable balance, forged to his own minute specifications, had become skewed. *Maybe this isn't Harval.* The thought crossed his mind as Ravn bulled toward him again, this time with an unorthodox maneuver called *treved-en* or Loki's cross. Designed for battling three against one, it required the Renshai to pin the central enemy's neck between crossed blades. The opening of the swords would slice open the man's neck and add momentum for each blade to cut foes on either side.

Colbey sprang backward, foiling Ravn's well-aimed attack. The poor choice of maneuver required teaching that Colbey felt too preoccupied to deliver until match's end. A humiliating finish would work as well. So he spiraled in to disarm. Harval lunged for Ravn's right hilt, meant to thread under scimitar and over the hand. But the balance foiled him. Instead, Harval slid on top of both, skewering Ravn's S-shaped crossguard. Colbey's other sword jabbed for Ravn's gut, parried by the broadsword. Ravn twisted. Harval cut a thin gash across his wrist, but the lock untangled, and Ravn recoiled for another pass.

Colbey swore soundlessly. Never in his life had he felt so out of control. Always before, he could take any sword, assess the balance instantly, and use it. Now, a sword he knew as well as his own hand had failed him several times. It seemed more as if the feel was fluid, changing even as he adjusted to the differences. *Hand or sword?* Colbey had to know, and a simple means presented itself in an instant. He switched hilts, Harval now in his right hand and the other sword in his left. For reasons of his own, Ravn sheathed the scimitar and wrapped both hands around the broadsword's longer hilt.

This time, Ravn did not roar in with the bold commitment

that always delighted his father. Colbey often said that he could teach a man maneuvers but never the gall necessary to make a capable warrior. Apparently tiring of the pattern, Ravn turned defensive. He hunched into an in-line stance designed to present the tiniest target possible. He held the sword in a high guard, prepared to counter any attack against him.

Colbey obliged with a few lightning quick sweeps and jabs that Ravn scarcely blocked with simple half circles. It was an easy defense, yet an effective one. A single movement wove a wall in front of him that even Colbey's meteoric jabs could not penetrate. The swords felt better in his hands; and he, once again, seemed in control. Whatever had bothered his left hand or his sword appeared to have disappeared with the switch.

Guarded joy swept through Colbey. He would still need to determine what had thrown off usually impeccable timing. He drove in toward Ravn, trapping the wild half circles of the youngster's sword at a low point, between both of his own. Instantly, Colbey swung back with his right-hand sword for Ravn's head. A certain killing stroke.

Something went wrong. The sword Colbey believed still blocked Ravn's had fallen short. Ravn ripped by it for Colbey's thigh. Too late, Colbey pulled his attack and leaped aside. Ravn's sword creased Colbey's flesh, the contact stinging. Blood wound down his pants leg in a warm trickle, and scarlet colored the tip of Ravn's sword. Howling, as much with surprise as anger, Colbey used his off-blade to lock Ravn's sword against its sheath. A single maneuver cut the hilt from Ravn's hand and sent it spinning like a wounded goose through the air. Colbey caught the haft. To do otherwise would dishonor an opponent who deserved congratulations. Two swords in his left hand and one in his right, Colbey examined the rent in his breeks with disbelief.

Never in his nearly four hundred years of teaching had any student drawn blood from him. He knew from the feel that the injury was superficial, but that made no difference. In battle, he had weathered the slash, stab, and tear of myriad weapons. Axes had cleaved through flesh and bone. Demons had clawed scarring furrows in his hand and face. A sword had once opened his chest horribly enough to make the marks of demons seem trivial. Yet none of those wounds compared to the minuscule scratch a student had inflicted in spar. Loss of control bothered Colbey far more than any accident of war.

Blood colored Ravn's fingers from the nick in his wrist, also superficial. That injury, Colbey dismissed, not because he did not bear it, but because he had not directly inflicted it. Never in his course of teaching with live, steel swords had he accidentally wounded a student, and not this time either. Ravn had made the choice to cut himself and break the sword lock rather than give up his weapon. In battle, Colbey would have made the same decision.

Ravn waited in silence for his teacher's assessment. Ultimately, Colbey had won the battle since he had disarmed his opponent. Yet, though Ravn bled first, he had technically drawn first blood. It was not fair to count self-inflicted injury as a victory.

Colbey clamped a hand to his thigh, placing pressure on the wound more from habit than any real attempt to staunch the flow. He studied his son. The boy waited in an anxious hush. The importance of Colbey's next words became magnified by the eager concern wafting from his son. Ravn would accept whoever his *torke* deemed the winner. It would never occur to the youngster to gainsay such a decision though, once rendered, he might press his father for another chance.

All smiles left Colbey. It had become clear that the problem lay with Harval's stability, not with his own. Suddenly, he understood too well. The sword that held the harmony of the universe had become as unpredictable as the chaos man's world now tipped all of them toward. The delicate balance that distinguished a good sword from a bad one had disappeared, replaced by a clunky asymmetry that shifted along with the world. Vidar had displayed the judgment of his frightening father; he could not have chosen a better time for his counsel. Colbey also knew that he could accomplish his mission far more easily without others in his way. Just as on the battlefield, he would trust his intuition from moment to moment to determine his next course of action. Long-term strategy did not suit Colbey or Renshai; therefore, team efforts befuddled them.

Colbey continued to stare at his son, knowing which decision would prove best for the world. But other things than his own ease and even the disposition of the worlds lay at stake. His son's self-esteem poised on the brink as well. "Go to Griff," he said at length.

Ravn's sudden rush of joy slapped Colbey a staggering blow.

Colbey continued before Ravn could move. "But remember, you're bound by the promise I made. You may not kill elves or humans. The fewer dealings you have with mortals, the less you interfere with my job." He did not bother to stress the importance of his own work on Midgard. Adolescents always responded better to knowledge acquired on their own than to lectures thrust upon them by well-meaning parents. He offered the broadsword, hilt first.

"I understand!" Ravn loosed a wild whoop of excitement as he snatched up the sword, running toward home without bothering with further conversation.

Colbey released the wound, which had already stopped bleeding. He stared at the smear of blood across his hand, shaking his head. A new era had truly begun.

Chapter 35

Griff's Guardian

Never get in the way of a fighting Renshai.
—Colbey Calistinsson

Concentric rings of furrowed bark disrupted the trunks of most of the trees on the elves' island. Flexible, they swayed and bowed in the ocean breezes, their long, serrated leaves drawing massive shadows that danced to the beat of their rattling. The salt air felt strange in Ravn's nostrils. He had spent his only time on man's world in Griff's quiet Grove, and air clotted with rime felt thick and choking in comparison. He guessed the odor came of many sources, blended into a single smell that now defined the sea. Behind him, wavelets chopped white spirals across the fluttering blue-green water. Ahead, sand stretched, heat haze turning the distant horizon to a blur. Ravn's glimpses from Odin's throne indicated a central location for the elves and their few structures, including the angular building in which they kept Griff and another human prisoner.

Sand trickled into Ravn's sandals as he took his first steps, its soft warmth a sensation he did not waste seconds enjoying. He had worried about Griff for too long to allow something as simple and superfluous as pleasure to delay him. Though little taller than his father despite the gods' blood that flowed through him, Ravn had grown accustomed to the tremendous strides of those around him. He stretched his pace to the far side of comfort, without actually running. Eagerness could not wholly displace his need to contemplate strategy. The seemingly unmotivated attacks on Griff had given him reason to despise elves and none at all to care whether they lived or died. Only his father's promise held him to peaceful methods, and that reason had not yet become internalized enough to overcome his natural hatred for them.

At length, a dark spot interrupted the horizon to Ravn's left. Although not likely to represent the elves' town, Ravn steered toward it. He had too little experience reading what he saw from the High Seat to trust his memory of locations. Whatever lay to his left did not look like a natural formation and might represent the very building he sought.

Sand folded over Ravn's sandals in a warm cascade and funneled into each footprint, so they all but disappeared behind him. Ravn did not care about the trail he left. The time for subtlety had passed; it would not assist him in the task sparring skill had won him. He continued toward his goal, soon identifying it as a single, small dwelling holding little promise of being a prison or the home of hundreds of elves. A boat rocked in the waves, sails unfurled and masts like skeletons against the frothy sky. The lone figure perched on the cottage roof and staring out over the sea might give Ravn directions or, at least, an early taste of elfin hostility.

Ravn continued his trek toward the cottage. The figure on the rooftop became clearer as he approached, distinctly recognizable as an elf only as Ravn drew within hailing distance. The fine, angular features grew unmistakable, the frail, long-limbed body only confirming his image. The glimpse gave him an impression of maleness and also of great age, though he could not pick out details that revealed these things to him. Sea breezes ruffled fine red-brown hair over the stranger's lowered hood and twined it into streamers that seemed as soft and flowing as his cloak. The locks contained a trace of silver that little resembled human graying, and the wrinkles creasing the delicate face seemed to come from a combination of salt air and smiling rather than age. Compared to the eyes of humans and gods, the elf's seemed animal, canted and slitted like a cat's but lacking the starlike centers and the variations in tone and color.

Ravn assessed all of this from profile, for the elf continued to stare at the ocean even as Ravn stopped to study him. The cabin's construction looked strange, lacking the supports and details gleaned by humans over millennia. It supported a ceiling tacked and tied in place instead of nailed. The flat roof would shed rain poorly, though it did form an excellent perch for the elf to overlook the ocean.

When the elf paid him no heed, Ravn called out a greeting. Although he expected to meet resistance, he saw no need to begin by antagonizing, so he simply said, "Hello." It held the additional advantage of being nearly universal in every human language.

The elf's eyes crinkled, presumably because he did not recognize the voice. He did not stiffen or jump, suggesting he had known of Ravn's presence but had chosen to ignore him. Unhurriedly, he turned and looked at Ravn, gaze measuring the young god in an instant. His eyes narrowed further, and the scrutiny became intent. "Hello," the elf returned politely, if belatedly, his accent more like Ravn's own than the youth expected. The elf jumped lightly from roof to ledge, then scrambled down a beam with the agility of a squirrel. Many questions surely came to his mind, yet he did not ply Ravn, just waited with an immortal's patience for him to speak again.

More prepared for an attack than conversation, Ravn fidgeted. He chose the Northern language, the one favored by the gods and closest to the elf's intonation. "I'm looking for a prisoner called Griff. Could you tell me where to find him?" Ravn tensed, expecting anything but the civil, matter-of-fact answer he received.

"No, I'm outcast. I only know of one prisoner, and she's female. But if such a prisoner as this Griff exists, you would find him in the compound." The elf gestured toward the center of the island.

"Thank you," Ravn said, and he started to turn in the indicated direction.

But the elf had not finished. "Be careful. You may not find the others as tolerant of humans as myself." He gave a serious but friendly nod. "I am called Captain." He used the trading tongue term.

Although Ravn doubted the elf had used his real name, he did not press. Ravn was a nickname, too, a common one among those of Northern lineage. "And I'm called Ravn."

"Ravn," the elf repeated and paused so long that Ravn believed he had only spoken to confirm he had gotten it right. Ravn had just opened his mouth to affirm it when the elf finally continued, "You resemble a friend, though he would be nearly four centuries old now. And I know humans do not live half that long."

"Nor even a quarter," Ravn asserted honestly. "Perhaps it is only that humans of similar features look alike to one used to living among an entirely different race." Not intending the words as insult, Ravn continued, "I might have the same difficulty distinguishing between elves."

"No." Captain denied the possibility. "I've lived far more of my life among humans than elves. Though I've never moved freely among them, I've seen enough over thousands of years to know the differences."

"Oh," the pronouncement surprised Ravn. He had prepared himself for brief, sarcastic exchanges interspersed with threat. Yet he found himself liking this elf, and it off balanced him.

"It's more than a physical resemblance. Your voices are similar, and your mannerisms. And I've seen few enough humans who wield two swords at once."

It seemed impossible that an elf had known Ravn's father in his mortal years. Surely Colbey would have mentioned such an association. Yet the timetable seemed right. Ravn felt the need to test this elf's knowledge. His *torke* had taught him to know his enemy as well as possible, and not just the maneuvers he chose in combat. "Surely, I'm not the first warrior you've seen carry a spare sword."

"No," Captain admitted. "But you're playing with me now, aren't you? If you carried the second only as a replacement, you would wear both blades on the same side. At either hip, at either hand. Though I've seen warriors use two weapons at once, only Renshai would rather attack twice than defend at all. Only Renshai use two long swords at once, and even few of them master the technique."

"I am Renshai," Ravn admitted, amazed and discomforted by Captain's knowledge.

"And this human you came for. He is Renshai, too?"

Ravn laughed at the image. "No." He chuckled again, unable to think of anyone as un-Renshai as his innocent companion.

"So you did not come to rescue the captured Renshai?"

"There's a captured Renshai?" Ravn asked more from surprise than concern. Colbey had taught that any Renshai would joyfully die in battle before letting an enemy take him hostage.

Captain seemed equally surprised. "Haven't you noticed one missing?"

Ravn shrugged. It was not his way to keep track of such details, except where they affected Griff. He realized now that the elf seemed to be evaluating him with far more accuracy and skill than Ravn could do in the reverse. It made little sense to continue under such conditions. He changed the subject. "Thank you for your assistance. Any suggestions as to how to approach the village?"

Captain accepted the abrupt tack and avoidance of his question without comment, though it surely told him as much as any answer. "Do you go in peace or with intentions of war?"

Ravn appreciated the question. Some would assume the latter for no better reason than the presence of his swords. Too many who reaped the benefits of the lands and freedoms soldiers gained them reviled those same men as having no other skills than killing. "I have no intention of harming anyone." He did not explain his constraints further. Should the elves discover that he could not slay them, any threat he might need would lose significance.

"Even if they refuse you what you seek?"

"Even if they refuse me."

Captain nodded several times. "Then go with my blessing, Human who Travels to Islands Without a Boat. And I'll revel in the understanding that Brenna spoke truth about Colbey. When you return to where you came from, please bear my fondest greetings to your father." With those words, obviously intended as a farewell, he scrambled back onto his roof and again looked out over the sea.

But Ravn could not let the conversation end there. "You know?"

Captain returned his attention to Ravn, his expression slightly disconcerted, probably due to the need to continue after having delivered a strong final line. "I know. But I have access to much that the others would scarcely think to consider."

"You were a friend to my father?"

"At a time when nobody else was, yes."

"He's never mentioned you to me."

Captain smiled. "That doesn't surprise me. Colbey was never the type to dwell on past prowess. His heroics to him were nothing more than proper behavior. He performed more of value day-to-day than most men ever did in a lifetime, and the only thing he believed worth bragging about was his birthright as a Renshai."

"My father?" Ravn repeated, incredulous. "A hero?"

Captain laughed, as if Ravn had uttered the silliest words in the universe. "You are *Colbey's* son?"

"Yes." Ravn saw little reason to hide that now. Besides, the elves might prove more cooperative knowing he was a god.

"Colbey was the consummate hero, the hero heroes envied and desired to become." Captain added, almost reluctantly, "And equally hated for much the same reasons. Humans and elves alike tend to revile and attribute to demons or evil that which seems too special or which they cannot understand."

"My father was a hero."

Captain laughed again. "I can understand he would not boast of his prowess, but surely you noticed no one could best him with a sword." Captain considered a moment. "Or perhaps that's not true in Asgard." He stared intently at Ravn, perhaps to test the veracity of his own observation.

But the words turned Ravn's thoughts to his recent victory, still a red-hot joy within him. It never occurred to him that Captain attempted to affirm that Colbey and Ravn lived among the gods. "It was true," Ravn replied. "Until today."

Captain did not speak, but his brows rose nearly to his hairline in encouragement.

"I bested him in spar," Ravn said, unable to wholly banish pride from his voice. His father taught him to keep his accomplishments to himself, to find satisfaction from within, and to have no need for other's awe. *Vanity is the one sure path to self-destruction,* Colbey had said on more than one occasion. *One does not become the best by degrading others but by hard work and practice.*

"Then you are a skilled swordsman, indeed."

Ravn saw no reason to reply to such a statement. False modesty would prove as demeaning as pride. "You were a friend to my father. Will you help me protect my friend?"

Captain sighed deeply, a sound strangely full of pain. "I could watch your boat for you, if you had one. I can advise you. But I can't assist you. Not so long as the elves oppose you, and we both know they will."

"Even if you tell them to cooperate?"

"That would make them *certain* to oppose you."

Ravn wondered what Captain had done to make him so hated by the others of his ilk, but it did not seem prudent to ask. "You won't help me?"

"I can't," Captain reiterated. "I am always an elf first and foremost, just as Colbey is always Renshai. One elf can never stand against another."

Ravn shrugged. It seemed to him the others had stood against Captain obviously enough. Yet he would not press. He did not need Captain's help, it would only have made the matter easier for all of them. "It's your decision, of course. But don't make invalid comparisons. My father would stand against anyone he felt was doing harm to the world, even me."

Captain did not doubt Ravn aloud, though his expression conveyed it well enough. "Regardless, elves cannot work against one another. I told you the way, and I condone your peaceful intentions. Should they prove otherwise, I will oppose you as strongly as my people, whether I believe them right or wrong. Please, don't put me in that position."

Ravn appreciated the intensity of Captain's loyalty, if not its direction. He also read the sincerity of the warning. "Thank you," he repeated. "You've been very helpful. I wish you well and hope your faith doesn't cause you too much pain before it kills you." Having turned the tables for strong final words, Ravn departed, quickly striding beyond range of Captain's voice.

But that did not deter the elf. His voice touched Ravn's mind, a gentle and mellow good-bye that conveyed several words at once. *Fare well, son of my friend.*

Fare well, Ravn tried to send back, uncertain whether he had communicated his message. His father's lessons had included mind strengthening techniques, but he had not inherited his father's ability to read thoughts, nor to broadcast his own. Colbey claimed the ability, which he named curse as often as gift, had not come to him either at birth. He had worked as hard for it as he had for his skill with a sword.

Captain's cabin swiftly disappeared behind Ravn's ground-eating stride, and the sand became mixed with moist, dark earth in greater quantities. Soon Ravn's path became solid enough that his feet sank only slightly into the ground, and the sand no longer trickled between his toes. Grass dotted the land in intervals, growing denser the farther he went from the shore. He tried to consider strategy, but such thoughts seemed old compared to the new ideas Captain had inspired. *Colbey, a hero.* The consideration did not sit well in his adolescent mind. He recalled how surprised Modi and Magni had seemed upon discovering that most of the deities had considered their father not only moody and powerful, but intellectually slow. Ravn already knew the other gods viewed his father as an arrogant upstart, and most still considered him a mortal granted privileges rather than one of them. Even after longer than three centuries, he remained an oddity among the gods, a renegade with philosophies contrary to gods' logic.

Much of that attitude, Ravn believed, came of Colbey's own tendency to consider himself human. He called himself Colbey Calistinsson, never Thorsson. He accepted others naming Thor his father only because he knew the lord of thunder had never been given the opportunity to act as a father to him. The goddesses had tricked him into knowing nothing of Colbey's birth. Had Thor deliberately broken contact, Ravn guessed, Colbey would deny any connection at all. *But a hero? My father?* Ravn chuckled. In every tale Ravn heard, the humans had despised his father. Yet Captain's words cut deep. *Humans and elves alike tend to revile and attribute to demons or evil that which seems too special or which they cannot understand.*

Many thoughts he would never have considered in the past bombarded Ravn now. Suddenly, he believed he knew why Colbey clung to his humanity so tightly. Those who attributed his skill to his birthright irritated him. Ravn had watched his father's practices for as long as he could remember. Often, they ran from sunup to sundown or beyond; and, always, his intensity exceeded even that most dedicated to survival. If it came to a choice between sword work and breathing, Ravn held no doubts his father would choose the former. Now that he had finally bested Colbey in spar, Ravn believed he understood. The doubts some could raise by attributing his victory to the three quarters of his inheritance that came from gods might rob him of the self-esteem won only by constant practice, effort, and more than a little desperation.

A voice resonating through Ravn's mind broke his train of thought. *A human approaches!*

Where? followed in more than a dozen mental voices.

A detailed description of location followed, mostly in comparison to various positions of creatures, certainly elves, with exceptionally long names. All of this happened in the time it took for Ravn to take a single step. He continued forward amidst a wild flurry of speculation and comment that was cut off suddenly by a single, shouted command. *Fools! Call your khohlars one-on-one. He can hear everything, you know.*

The mental communications broke off suddenly, just as a fenced in compound became visible through the trees. Ravn glimpsed occasional movement as elves flittered into position, though he got no clear look at any of them.

One elf broke the silence, *Jovinay arythanik! I'll cast.*

Ravn guessed they intended to throw some sort of spell. He remained alert but unconcerned, familiar enough with magic to know how to avoid it. Like his parents, he had no specific ability to cast spells, but his father had taught him ways to deflect and ruin the magic of others. While this bothered those gods who did rely more on spells than on force, especially Ravn's Uncle Frey, it seemed likely to prove useful now.

A murmur of sound erupted from ahead and to Ravn's right. Ravn continued walking, tuning his thoughts to the rhythm of their chant, then substituting sounds into the cycle of their repetition. He chose syllables that fit smoothly, naturally, following the pattern without disrupting it. Even as a new voice joined the others, louder and more crisply direct, he inserted his sounds into the composition. Ravn did so aloud, with a gentleness that made his voice a part of the whole. He matched his tone to their alien cadence as well as simulating their timbre and pitch. He also attempted to send the notes telepathically, practicing the mind power and control his father valued nearly as much as combat.

Eventually, the chanting stopped, having had no effect on Ravn that he could fathom. Now behind Ravn, the elves disassembled amid consternated comments and a flurry of abbreviated questions. Ravn heard the rattle of brush as the elves repositioned and regrouped. The buildings came into view, most large and communal in appearance, surrounded by a fence constructed of mesh triangles. They resembled human structures in a general way, but the details defied all logic. Bracing boards often sat in locations more suitable for decoration than stability. Rain gutters were set too high to drain, and the serrated leaves of the native trees replaced the woven thatch that protected many people from the rain. The arrangement of cottages and larger buildings formed no obvious pattern, and hundreds of elves played, relaxed, wrote, or conversed in groups outside. Many perched in nearby trees. Two crude stone statues of bears guarded the arrangement, a mockery of Béarn's statuary.

The chanting started again as Ravn headed toward the buildings, the tempo more hurried and the volume louder. The noise drew the attention of the uninvolved elves, and they scurried in various directions. Most joined the group of chanters, who had drawn too near the structures to hide from Ravn anymore. Many clambered up nearby trees, watching him from the safety of the branches like squirrels. A few entered the buildings, though these seemed more often to be the males, which suggested to Ravn they were calling for reinforcements rather than going inside to hide.

Again, Ravn worked his additions into the elves' song, sliding them gracefully into the pattern so that no one seemed to notice the change. He examined the buildings, trying to select the prison from among the others. Even had he known much about imprisonment, the elves' incomplete reconstruction of human structures would have proved incomprehensible at best. Tired of guessing, he approached the line of elves.

As their magic failed a second time, the elves abandoned it. Those who carried weapons drew them, and a line of wood and steel abruptly confronted Ravn, cutting him off from the compound. Those unarmed retreated behind the others or swung into the trees to watch from a position of safety. Ravn stopped, hands gliding naturally to his own swords. Battle, he knew, and it did not daunt him. But a larger concern did. He not only had to best these elves, he had to do so without fatalities. Combat without killing went against every tenet he had ever learned.

Shortly, a new figure appeared in the uppermost window of the tallest structure, a three-story one composed of mud-chinked logs that directly overlooked the site of conflict. Pale reddish hair curled around somber features with heart-shaped lips and one canted, green eye. Those who noticed the newcomer visibly relaxed. *A leader,* Ravn felt certain.

The leader did not bother with the convention of limiting

conversations to keep Ravn from hearing. His mental voice rang out over the gathering, *Stand where you are!*

Ravn little doubted the leader intended the words for him as well. He remained in position. Cooperation might keep this meeting as peaceful as possible.

The elves, too, froze, their weapons still drawn though they did not attack.

The leader elf switched to verbal communication, using the trading tongue, clearly for Ravn's sake. "Who are you, human? Where do you come from? And what do you want?"

Having been asked three questions, Ravn chose the one he most wished to answer. "I've come to watch over Griff."

"Griff?" the leader repeated. "What is a griff?"

Ravn refused to accept ignorance as an answer. Surely Griff had told his captors his name. "He's a prisoner of yours, and I've come to be with him."

"We have no prisoners," the leader returned, a blatant lie.

Ravn refused to play the game. "You may take me to Griff and lock me up with him. I will go peacefully. Or I can battle my way through your guards and get there myself. Your choice."

The elves tensed, ready. The leader's nostrils flared, though he remained in silent contemplation for several moments before speaking. "Elves, step away." He went quiet again, single eye fixed on Ravn but his mind clearly elsewhere. The elves began a softer, more cautious chant that Ravn dismissed as necessary for opening doors or lowering defenses. Too late, it occurred to him that the elf leader's apparent silence might represent mental communication rather than pondering. By then, the carven bears had already begun their transformation.

The statues shifted. Hair sprouted from every part, and the eyes took on a dull sparkle little more animate than the flat stone. Elves scrambled for trees, corners, and doorways, those involved in the *jovinay arythanik* retreating in a more orderly fashion. Grotesquely misshappen by the artisans who created them, the bears charged Ravn together. Ravn drew and cut. A sword cleaved the air in front of one's nose, a defensive strike to hold it at bay. The other sword wove between the second bear's massive paws and jabbed cleanly through its chest. That one collapsed, bloody froth bubbling from its jowls. Ravn jerked his blade free, still weaving the other in front of the bear to confound it. As the creature reared back, Ravn's upstroke drove a sword through its lower jaw and into its head. He twisted as the bear fell, using momentum to keep his sword from becoming trapped. He took a step back into a defensive posture, both swords raised, one trailing blood.

Prepared for deceit, Ravn refused to become angry. He kept his breathing calm and soundless, and his manner composed. Surely nothing could unnerve these elves more than the quick and easy dispatch of their dirtiest trick. He did not even bother to look at the corpses, their lumpy bodies and narrow heads bizarre compared to the beauty nature had given its own creations. "Interesting," Ravn finally said, "but not part of what I asked for. Take me to Griff. Lock me up with him, and I'll give you no more trouble."

The leader's gaze shifted repeatedly from swords, to bears, to Ravn. "You want us to lock you in the dungeon?"

"With Griff," Ravn repeated. "Yes."

"Why?"

An understandable question, one Ravn refused to answer except as a means to restate his demand. "I want to be with Griff."

"But you don't want him free?"

Ravn shrugged. "His safety, not his freedom, is my concern."

No whispers passed among the elves. Ravn attributed this to their ability to speculate telepathically rather than to any lack of imagination. The leader said, "We don't allow swords in our prison."

No Renshai would willingly sacrifice his sword. "You'll have to make an exception."

The leader made a thoughtful noise. "Am I to understand that you won't attempt to free your friend?"

"That's correct," Ravn affirmed, uncertain whether he would believe such a claim had he stood in the leader's place.

"And what do we get out of giving you what you ask rather than cutting you down where you stand?"

Ravn ignored the fallacy the leader had accepted as truth: that the entire population of elves could kill him. Likely, even Colbey could not stand against all of them; but Ravn would not accept it as fact until as many as he could slaughter lay dead. "You get as many of yours still alive as I would kill if you tried. A fair trade, I think." It was a bluff, but the elves could not know that.

"Very well," the leader agreed, his expression altering only slightly. Ravn believed he read thoughtful confusion there and wondered whether the leader questioned Ravn's sanity or that of all mankind. Likely, many human motivations escaped him, and he might credit Ravn's odd request to his humanity. "But if you lied to me about your intentions, I will see that your friend dies in the most horrible fashion possible. And you, too." He motioned for the weaponed elves to step forward.

They obeyed, with reluctance on their features but no matching hesitation in their actions. Only three led Ravn through the rough-hewn corridors, past a series of locked gates, and to the cell where Griff lay sleeping. A woman occupied the cage next to his, but Ravn had eyes only for his friend. The Béarnide's chest rose and fell normally, and Ravn detected none of the obvious signs of pain. He entered willingly, let the door clang closed behind him, and sacrificed his freedom to hover at the side of his companion.

Griff slept blissfully through the entire transfer.

Chapter 36

Weile Kahn

I've been plunging into every war I could find since I was born. Death has eluded me.
—Colbey Calistinsson

Ravn crouched at Griff's side while elves gathered to watch him in silent curiosity. Refusing to give them a show, he remained in place, unmoving. Their patience proved remarkably godlike. Some remained for hours, waiting for him to do something, anything, to explain his insistence on becoming a prisoner. Ravn outwaited them, his own immortality granting him the same interminable endurance. He could stay in place as long as they deigned to watch him do so. And Griff slept through it all, occasionally rolling to a new position or emitting a dense snore.

The woman in the next cell demonstrated none of the forbearance of the new captive and the elves. She watched for a while, studying Ravn at first with sidelong glances then, as time went on, with unabashed staring. After a while, she must have memorized every detail of him, for she ignored him to practice weaponless combat techniques. She followed those with katas intended for sword, though she could only pretend she held the weapon. Now Ravn gave her the same scrutiny she had accorded him. Half-grown, unkempt hair flopped into her eyes, and her constant shaking of it suggested she had not yet grown accustomed to its length. Her gray eyes remained keen but unfocused, concentrated on enemies he could not see. He recognized too many of the maneuvers of her *svergelse*. Though her hair seemed too dark and her Northern features lost to other breeding, she was clearly Renshai.

Despite this realization, Ravn did not address the woman. He enjoyed watching her. The perfection of his father's lethal practices had become too familiar, too flawless to draw his eye any longer. But he could not resist watching this human Renshai and falling in love again with his own heritage of blood and glory. Day-to-day life among the gods diluted the stories Colbey told of wild warriors wedded to their swords and to the honor of dying in a blaze of savage battle glory. With each practice, Colbey honed his skill one notch closer to the ultimate; but the minuscule gains he could make at his level of ability seemed too small for notice. This woman, however, still had the best of her years ahead. He read the excitement of knowledge gained burning through her eyes. The understanding of a concept that had previously evaded her, the grasp of a movement that had, only the day before, seemed unattainable: her future still held these delights. *And so,* Ravn thought with a smile, *does mine.*

The woman's practice drew to an end nearly the same time the elves finally lost interest and disappeared from sight. The twists of the prison corridor still might hold a few, peeping or listening. Ravn kept that in mind as he addressed the woman in soft tones, using the Renshai tongue. "Hello, my friend. Thank you for the honor of watching your *svergelse.*"

The woman crouched, mouth set and eyes narrowed. She examined him again, though surely she had missed nothing on her previous lengthy inspection.

The hostility surprised Ravn. He had expected a warmer reaction from a fellow Renshai. Colbey had described the intense loyalty trained into every member of the tribe from birth. He studied her again. Movement no longer distracted him from the crisscrossing scars and burns that marred the flesh visible around a war tunic darkened by dirt and sweat and tattered from constant wearing. He saw no fresh injuries, but most appeared less than a few months old. The elves had not treated her well. A warm flush of anger passed through Ravn. He had not given the elves the satisfaction of inspecting Griff for injuries, but he hoped his self-control would prove strong enough to rein his need to kill should he discover Griff as cruelly treated.

Realization accompanied Ravn's rage. The imprisoned Renshai had every reason to doubt his intentions and believe the elves had planted him there to trap her into trusting him.

After several moments, she finally spoke, using Renshai. "Who are you?"

"My name is Raska Colbeysson of the tribe of Renshai." Ravn answered as appropriate for a Northern human, then added, "But I'm called Ravn."

"Colbeysson?" the woman repeated, hope momentarily softening her features before they lapsed into suspicion again.

The woman had defied politeness by not returning her own name and title. Saddened by her ordeal, Ravn concerned himself with making her understand rather than forcing manners. "What can I do to make you believe me?"

The woman shrugged.

Ravn settled to his haunches, suspecting she had placed the burden on him as part of his test. He tried to think like a human, a feat confounded by his limited contact with them and assisted by knowledge of his father. The use of the Renshai language, taught only by Renshai to others of their tribe, had not proved enough. *Why?* Ravn struggled for an answer to his own question and found part of one in his own experience. If some stranger approached claiming to be a god, Ravn would never trust him. The Renshai tribe had remained small enough to allow them all to know one another, at least superficially. She had never seen Ravn before, leading to the natural conclusion he could not be a Renshai. Ravn speculated further. Humans did not use or understand magic. Perhaps she believed elves could learn languages with their spells. *Perhaps they could!* The randomness of magic eluded Ravn at times; even with his superior experiences, he knew little about elves.

Ravn rose, memorized Griff's location, then sprang into a furious kata replete with maneuvers only a Renshai could know. His swords parceled the air into breathable segments, the speed of his cuts funneling dust in a sparkling wake. The prison confined him but it could not cheapen techniques taught by the best of all Renshai swordsmen. He became a twirling tendril of fire, and his blades sliced silver glimmers through the dungeon's dankness, catching the light that glazed through gaps in the elfin construction. At length, he finished, reluctantly stopping far sooner than he wished, mind and body clamoring for more. Ravn had always believed that, if nonmartial humans could only once feel the euphoria that accompanied a well-performed practice, they would burn their drinks and drugs as too inferior.

Ravn glanced at the woman for a reaction and found her kneeling on the floor of her cell, head lowered in deference.

Ravn blinked, uncertain where to go from here. Humans had worshiped the gods in Asgard long before his birth, but no one knew about him so he had never had to deal with such attention. He had always believed it would feel natural, but the actual experience flustered him.

The woman remained in position.

As Ravn realized the onus lay on him, he cleared his throat to gain a few more seconds. "Please, get up." He had to bite his tongue to keep from adding, "You're making me nervous." It would weaken the identity he had finally managed to prove. Instead, as she rose, he returned to his previous question. "Who are you?"

"I am Rantire Ulfinsdatter." She did not bother to add the details of her tribe, since Ravn clearly already knew. "The elves call me Brenna."

"You've been here a long time?"

Rantire shrugged politely. "Even a moment of captivity is too long for a Renshai." Anticipating his question, she explained. "I wasn't expecting magic. I killed some of them," she announced, keeping pride from her tone, "but they got me with some sort of sleeping magic. The most miserable failing of my existence."

"It wasn't your fault." Ravn flipped the fine blond locks from his shoulder.

Rantire sighed. "A Renshai may make a dignified retreat if circumstances allow it; if not, he must fight to his last breath."

"You could hardly be expected to fight unconscious." Ravn did not judge. Rantire needed to handle the humiliation in her own way. He could only keep from intensifying her embarrassment. Dwelling on the incident seemed cruel, and he had more important matters to discuss.

Rantire changed the subject awkwardly. "So, um, Lord, um ... pardon me. I've never met a god before. What should I call you?"

Ravn smiled, forgiving what would pass for rudeness in a king's court. He knew Renshai lived without hierarchy.

When a leader became necessary, they selected the best one for the job: the most competent rallier for battle, the brightest for strategy, or a skilled arbiter for meetings. Therefore, Renshai grew up with sparse knowledge of rank or title. Only their connection to the kingdom of Béarn forced them to learn "sires" and "majesties." Clearly, Rantire had spent little or no time around royalty. Ravn understood his power and ancestry; and, unlike human gentry, needed no reminders. "Ravn will do just fine."

"All right," Rantire said hesitantly, clearly not as comfortable with this as Ravn. "Ravn, did you come to help me?" Her humble tone sapped the hubris from the question.

"No," Ravn admitted. "I came to protect him." He pointed at the sleeping lump of Béarnide.

"Him?" Rantire repeated doubtfully. "But he's so . . ." She trailed off. If a god she admired took an interest in someone, she refused to utter a negative comment about him. Instead, she twisted her comment to a question. "Who is he that he deserves the ultimate honor?"

Ravn glanced at Griff, who stirred, loosed an undignified snore, then lapsed back into unconsciousness, oblivious to the discussion about him. "He is Prince Griff Petrostan's son Kohleran's son, heir to Béarn's throne."

"Ah." Rantire's eyes shifted to the massive Béarnide, even less impressive in sleep. Though not expecting to hear such a thing about one she had, apparently, dismissed as a simpleton, the words did not surprise her either. Any other explanation would make less sense. Her mouth set, and her eyes dodged Ravn's momentarily. Then a hint of scarlet came to her cheeks. Purpose sparked in her eyes, and she met Ravn's gaze directly. "I want to become his guardian."

Stunned, Ravn laughed. "Do you think I'm not guardian enough?"

Rantire's shoulders drifted upward, though she did not complete the shrug. "It does not matter. It's the duty of Renshai to protect Béarn's heirs, to see to it the proper lineage and neutrality are preserved." Her stare grew even more intense, if possible. She glared at Ravn. "I want this, Ravn. I will fight you for it, if I must."

Ravn blinked several times, no reply forthcoming. Finally, he managed words. "You would fight *me* for the right to become Griff's guardian?"

"To the death." Rantire's sincerity shocked Ravn. He had

never faced a certainty so resolute. Even Frey's staunch defense of the elves seemed to pale in significance.

"You would die, you know," Ravn felt compelled to state this fact.

"That remains to be seen. I would enjoy the challenge."

Any Renshai would. Yet Rantire's fierce loyalty to one she had spurned moments before intrigued him. "This is important enough for you to die for?"

"Yes," Rantire admitted, smiling for the first time in his presence. "Isn't it grand?"

"Well . . ." Ravn started, then stopped. "Actually . . . it seems . . . well . . . sort of stupid."

Rantire's grin disappeared instantly.

Ravn realized he had chosen his words poorly. "I mean, you're mortal, right?" That being self-evident, he did not await a reply. "So you don't have that long to live anyway. I'd think every moment would be precious."

"It is," Rantire confirmed. "That's why I'm thrilled to have a cause this important. In their whole lifetimes, few discover a purpose so special they would waste their life for it. But no man or woman truly lives until he does."

Nothing Ravn had ever heard sounded so ridiculous. "So dying makes life worthwhile?"

"Dying for the right reason." Rantire's eyes narrowed. "Like dying in glory and going to Valhalla. What kind of Renshai are you, anyway?"

Ravn grinned, running a finger along the hilt of one sword. "A Renshai who could visit Valhalla anytime, if I wanted to. Without dying." Only at that moment did it occur to Ravn that, to his knowledge, his father had never looked upon Valhalla. Yet he knew Colbey had sought this goal from infancy. For now, however, he tucked the information away.

"Oh. I envy you." But Rantire's expression seemed more pitying than envious.

"Because I can see Valhalla?"

"No. That would only dilute the reward." She gave him another visual once-over. "How old are you?"

"Sixteen."

"Years?"

"No, days. Of course, years."

"Don't get sarcastic with me, Ravn. I just didn't know if gods measure their lives the way we do."

Rantire had a point. In fact, Ravn had never really considered it. Gods did not keep close track of age since it did not affect them. He had only chosen human conventions for time because he knew no others. "Sorry. I'm sixteen years old."

"That's even younger than me."

"So you envy my youth? Or my immortality?"

"Neither," Rantire returned. "And both, in a way. The way I see it, gods can't really experience the ultimate glory, sacrificing their lives for a cause."

Ravn shook his head in disagreement. "We can die."

"All right." Rantire accepted that. "But the only ones who have were thousands of years old."

Ravn failed to see the point. "So."

"So, that's hardly a sacrifice. Like a ninety-year-old human dying so a grandchild can live. That's nothing special. But let the grandchild die for the elder: true sacrifice."

Ravn grudgingly accepted the explanation. "I'm still missing the envy part."

"If you gave your life to a cause now, having only lived sixteen years and having many thousands to go . . ." Rantire closed her eyes, savoring the glory vicariously. "That's a joy I could never have, being human."

Ravn froze, uncertain whether to laugh, shake sense into her, or dismiss her as an idiot. One thing seemed certain, the Renshai tribe was as insane as humans and gods had named them through the centuries. And as brave as Colbey described them. The reasons for their dying young in battle no longer eluded him; their honor hinged upon it. Once, his Uncle Modi stated that Colbey had hated the cycle his skill had created: he wished more than any Renshai to die in glorious combat, but the myriad wars he fought only honed his ability to the point where he could never lose. Ravn had always believed he understood his father's teachings about his heritage, had always thought himself fully Renshai. But the words had never penetrated until this moment. Ironically, it had taken a mortal to allow him to understand the loftiest concepts of Colbey's teachings.

Ravn made a sacrifice of his own, one he would never have believed himself capable of prior to this conversation. "Griff is the only friend I have; yet he clearly matters more to you than to me. I give over my guardianship to you, Rantire, with my blessing. Don't disappoint me."

Rantire's smile seemed to light the dungeon. Every part of

her being radiated joy, making a mockery of what the elves experienced as emotion. Her happiness inspired boldness as well. "Please, I've not held a sword for months. Please." She extended a hand.

Ravn looked at Rantire's callused palm a long time, her brashness bordering on attack. A Renshai protected his sword like a part of his body. To loan one meant a sacrifice as large as the one he had just made. Yet he read her need and understood. She would cherish the weapon he had blithely dishonored during his spar with Colbey.

"Here," Ravn said, studying the mesh triangles that would not admit the weapon whole. Carefully, he removed the pommel, the hilt, then the guard. In four parts, he passed it through the bars. "You may keep it." He added to himself, *You've shown yourself more worthy of it.*

Rantire reassembled the pieces, admiring the sword like a lover and handling it with even more respect. The smile widened, mingling awe with joy. She had received an honor that went far beyond the appearance of a god at her side. Rantire recognized the vastness of that tribute and appreciated it. No sword would ever enter a *svergelse* with more devotion. Had she died at that moment, Rantire would believe her life fulfilled.

The autumn wind carried the damp, green odor of harvest, twined through with acrid wood smoke and the sweet aroma of sap. On the balcony of King Kohleran's room, Prime Minister Baltraine stood to the false king's left, Dh'arlo'mé to his right. Baltraine listened to the gentle patter wafting from the elf he called Pree-han, so like King Kohleran in timbre, thanks to Baltraine's training. The words he had written floated over an appreciative crowd that apparently did not notice the occasional pauses and tiny mispronunciations that blared in Baltraine's ears at intervals. They had little reason to doubt what he knew as deception. Even the most critical skeptic could not explain a duplicate of their beloved king; a world without magic could not suspect its presence. But Baltraine knew; and, to him, Pree-han would always look like Pree-han. The thin cascade of white hair with its fiery highlights could never replace Kohleran's thick, blue-black. The clean-shaven face would never sport the omnipresent Béarnian beard. He would always see static garnets in place of the shrewd, brown eyes that once belonged to King Kohleran. The voice, though close, the words, though well-chosen, could not fool Baltraine even when he closed his eyes and forced time to move backward into memory. It seemed almost as if Pree-han always was and Kohleran had never existed.

Pree-han paused, the gap immediately filled with cheering by the Béarnides below him. Their love for their king remained as strong as at his coronation, though few old enough to remember that day still lived. Baltraine branded them all fools. Even when he forced himself to believe the illusion would beguile him had he not known the truth, he remained farsighted enough to recognize the king's apparent return to health as only a temporary solution. Kohleran could only live so long; when he died, he would still have no heir.

This train of thought jolted Baltraine to a sudden realization. The answer to the problem did lie with the king's return. Soon, the populace might demand that King Kohleran marry again and create another heir. Aged men had sired children before, and it only made sense to procreate in the additional years the gods, and Dh'arlo'mé posing as a Pudarian healer, had granted him. That posed a problem the elves might not recognize, let alone have the wisdom to solve. Baltraine wanted more than just a hand in that solution. A woman kept so near Pree-han would soon see through the illusion. Nor could an elf create a human heir; and, surely, no elfin baby could pass for human. That meant they would need a human sire to handle whichever young noblewoman he chose as queen. In a dark room, in the throes of passion, Baltraine believed he could pass himself off as the king; and that was a project he would relish more than any he could imagine. His line would take over the throne, and ecstasy with a beautiful woman would only sweeten the situation.

Baltraine caught himself smiling and stopped. No one would think anything of his lapse. It was only natural for a caring prime minister to feel joy at the unexpected return to health of his beloved king. Pree-han told Béarn's peasants of his long ascent back from illness. He spoke in reverent tones of the strange-looking healer who had performed miracles using the herbs of his people, reclusive barbarians, called alfen, who lived in the southern woodlands. He spoke with sorrow of his ministers, slaughtered by factions who tortured his heart with their betrayal and treachery. He discussed the need to replace these valuable nobles, at least temporarily, with people more neutral in their views. With Baltraine's careful logic, he told a convincing story about the vast knowledge, wisdom, and goodness of the alfen who would give of themselves to the council as Dh'arlo'mé had done for their king.

Pree-han's voice sounded melodic amid the swelling, happy chant of the peasants beneath the balcony. Knights of Erythane stood ceremonially at attention, leaving Béarnian guardsmen to keep order among the masses. The former remained under Kedrin's command, loyal to regent Baltraine and, of course, to their recovering king. Imprisonment, Baltraine now justified to himself, had done the knight-captain a service. Freed, he would have had to die with the cabinet, his desire to closely serve his king too dangerous to the deception. The current arrangement worked well, allowing Baltraine to relay information to Kedrin with any bias necessary so that the orders given to the Knights of Erythane assisted his cause. Baltraine understood that the elves would eventually see most of the peasants dead. He knew they had designs against much of the royalty as well; but they had assured him that he and his offspring would live out their natural lives. Nothing else mattered. His line would sit upon the throne forever. He felt certain he could convince the elves of that. *Unless Xyxthris tries to weasel himself into the queen's bedroom first.*

Baltraine's hands clenched into fists, and his demeanor became a facade hiding desperation and anger. He calmed himself with the reminder that Xyxthris was an idiot with few ties to family, easily bought with a permanent supply of drugs. There was no doubt in Baltraine's mind that the elves needed him as much as he needed them. And his line would take over the throne of Béarn.

Weile Kahn sat in his favorite chair, a firm pillow nestled between stretched leather and a wooden frame. Though unadorned, its comfort alone bespoke wealth, stark contrast to the dirt-poor childhood he had escaped so long ago. His two burly bodyguards remained attentive at either hand, constant companions he easily ignored. Once castle guards, they had learned their sword skill at the expense of a king whose control and power rapidly crumbled around him, mostly thanks to Weile.

When he had organized the East's petty thugs three decades earlier, Weile had had few concrete ideas of what to do with the loyalty he bought. His intentions were initially altruistic: to bind them in the cause of survival. He had grown up never knowing from where his next meal might come, if he managed to find one. A pickpocket, proud of his abilities, Weile's father had kept them reasonably well fed and clothed until the guards caught up with him and he spent years in prison. The times that followed led to his mother's death and nearly to his own. He learned to despise the pinched agony hunger brought to his gut, the bone-numbing cold of a winter's night in the streets, and the complete inability to plan or control even the tiniest aspects of the future. The street gangs he had joined saved his life on more than one occasion, both by sharing talents and protecting him from others who would take his tiny share of the universe. Weile had always wondered why adults did not have similar organizations to tide them through the leanest times.

Weile ran a muscled hand through his thick, black curls. Every time he had seen a skeletal figure huddled in a corner or a nameless corpse sprawled in the streets, he had vowed to change the plight of others. The filthiest, the meanest, the poorest became his clients. One by one, he took them in, finding use for their unique talents. One by one, he fed them, finding strengths, physical and mental, that their suffering hid. One by one, he bound them into a loyal band, teaching trust to those who otherwise believed in no one, including themselves. And he had formed an organized band of devoted followers who owed their livelihoods, their very lives, and their souls to him. They operated around and under the law, but those who would have died survived and those who would have survived learned how to live.

The others had come later, hoodlums marginally successful on their own who saw organization as a means to riches. The band swelled, requiring hierarchies and records. Weile sighed at the memory. He saw that time as his brightest and darkest. The group multiplied at an astounding rate, but his own hand in its creation and control grew more distant. And weaker. The fierce personal loyalty to him became dispersed. Members weighed their talents against others and ranked themselves, not always accordingly. Some left the group for philosophical differences, and other bands of organized criminals became rivals, much like other gangs of children, but with an important difference. The adults had lost all shreds of decency and innocence. They solved their differences with butchery and mental cruelty, and Weile Kahn had not escaped unscathed.

Weile fingered the scar that ran the length of his left arm, but his thoughts ignited a more painful memory. He had returned to his wife and son in the dark of night, after attending to business he would rather have left undone. The scene at the door remained glaringly, mercilessly vivid even after eight years. The only woman he had ever loved lay naked on the floor, covered with bruises and sprawled in a scarlet puddle. Though glazed in death, the eyes remained wildly staring, and their appearance defined terror ever after. His blameless son, his only child, Tae, lay in a crumpled heap, clothing smeared so red he could not have guessed its original color. Knife wounds tore the fabric in myriad places.

The grief returned in a rush, dulled by time, though it still brought an animal moan to his lips. Then he had screamed until his lungs emptied, at first in desperate sorrow then in violent rage. Only after he had howled himself hoarse had he heard the tiny groan from Tae that told him his son still lived. The rest became a blur that remembrance could never wholly piece together. He knew only that heartache disappeared in the need to save his child. And he had done so, though not without leaving permanent scars, both physical and mental.

Weile put the thought from his mind, though speculation about his son was not so easily banished. He had no way of knowing whether Tae had lived or died in the West. So far, no enemies had come to gloat and sneer about slaughtering his son. He trusted Tae to survive whatever he encountered in any city. It seemed likely the boy still lived, but Weile braced himself daily for a scene as ugly as the one to which his mind had clung all these years.

A knock on the door dispelled Weile's contemplation. Aside from his chair, the one-room dwelling contained three plain wooden seats and a table, nothing more. He used it only as his current private meeting place, and the instant rivals or guards discovered it, he would have to abandon it. Currently, however, he had little to fear from the law. The kingdom had fallen into petty bickering, and the crime lords had grown stronger thanks to the elves. Not only had the disintegration of power aided them, but the elves had hired them to worsen the situation and paid them enough to see it done to the exclusion of all else. Well-paid workers had no reason to steal. "Come in," Weile said.

The bodyguards tensed alertly. The door swung open, and a follower of medium build, with few talents, led a pair of elves into the room. The male was tall and typically elf-willowy with thin red hair and sapphirine eyes that appeared almost faceted. The female sported hair nearly as black as Weile's, though with ruddy highlights where his held a bluish cast. She studied Weile through yellow eyes that discomforted him for their steadiness. Experience told him that eyes should shade and twinkle. Their steady color, though beautiful, seemed inanimate to him, reminding him of stone and also of death. Weile rose and nodded a greeting. He retook his seat, gesturing at the others to do so as well.

Taking the hint, the elves sat. Their strange eyes followed Weile's every movement, and he forced himself to look back. To avoid contact would show weakness that years of dealing with criminals had taught him to hide. Like carnivores, men of their ilk judged frailty as a signal to attack and devour. A leader who did not win every stare down and confrontation did not survive long here.

"What can I do for you?" Weile asked before either of the elves could speak. Long ago, he had struck a delicate balance. To talk too soon demonstrated impulsiveness and lack of composure, but to let another have the first word meant turning the floor and the power over to him.

"We have another job for you," the male elf said. A human voice so musical and high would have made him the butt of every joke.

Weile nodded, indicating the elf should continue.

"We want all travel between kingdoms halted."

Weile caught himself before surprise sent his brows shooting up; instead, he let them arch slowly in question. His flaring nostrils, however, would have revealed his startlement had the elves had any clue how to interpret human emotions. "*All* travel?"

"All travel," the elf confirmed.

Weile's brows knitted now as he considered. "Visitors? Messengers? Trade?"

"All of those things," the elf confirmed. "You may stop them any way you wish and keep anything you find. Naturally, we will triple your pay as well."

"That won't be easy." Weile mapped out the routes in his head. Already, his men occasionally plundered merchants moving from one town to another. In the past, they had kept their thefts to a minimum, afraid to queer their own futures. Boldness would force the merchants to up security to the point where robbery would necessitate violence. The vast majority of theives, Weile knew, were not killers or good swordsmen. Weile saw possibilities where none existed before. As the kingdoms collapsed, their ability to protect merchants and travelers decreased. Perhaps the time had come for his people to take control of the streets.

"We pay as we do *because* of the difficulty." This time, the female addressed Weile. "Are you capable of such a thing, or should we take our money elsewhere?"

Weile visualized the pile of Béarnian silver, gold, and gemstones that would come to his organization if he agreed to the deal. So far the elves had kept their side of every bargain with fanatical detail. Every count had been exact, every payment on time. "We can do it. I just need a clear idea of exactly what you need."

"We need all traffic stopped." The male elf's blue eyes swept Weile's face. "Did I not make that clear enough?"

"I understand that." Weile's mind had already raced well beyond that initial request. "And you're under no obligation to tell me more. However, it would help me to know which result of travel you're trying to stop. For example, if it's trade, that would mean my men could still make money selling information. If it's information, the black market would flourish."

"Are we not paying you enough that your workers still need other sources of income?"

Weile laughed. "You could give my men the sun, and they'd look for ways to make money from the stars and the moon."

The elves did not even smile. Weile came to the conclusion that jokes did not exist in elfin culture. "Then you will need to retrain them. We want it all stopped. Everything. And we will watch. Anyone caught selling information will die. Horribly."

Weile pursed his lips, all humor lost. He considered refusing their offer, the idea of others taking control of his people arousing an ire he subdued from long practice. Yet, should his men get wind of what he gave up, and they surely would, the repercussions would go far beyond elfin threats. Weile glanced around the room, trusting the three of his men who witnessed the event to keep their silence. No one else would ever know about the elf's menacing warning. However, if he let this opportunity go, a rival would grab it; and all of the underground would know of the riches he'd refused. For quite some time, he paused to consider, but the elves sat in calm silence, as if oblivious to the lengthy wait. The bodyguards shifted only to keep themselves limber and ready for action. The man who had escorted the elves fidgeted, stark contrast to the others in the room.

Finally, Weile spoke. "I accept your offer, though I retain the right to reprimand my men in my own fashion. Give us time to set up, and we will halt all human travel except that required by ourselves."

"And elves," the elf added.

"And elves," Weile repeated.

The female elf removed a box from her pocket and set it on the table. At her first movement, the bodyguards shifted between Weile and the object. They all watched as the elf opened the box and dumped its contents. Coins bounced and rolled across the tabletop, some spinning on edge and a few making it over the edge to clang onto the floor. Gemstones of green, burgundy, saffron, and purple poured to the table in a multicolored spray. The meager light in the room sparked a rainbow array from the fortune the elves dumped with a casual and disinterested ease.

And Weile Kahn sold humanity for a pile of wealth and the promise of more.

Chapter 37

The Best

*Vanity is the one sure path to self-destruction.
One does not become the best by degrading others but by hard work and practice.*

— Colbey Calistinsson

Practice finished, Kevral sat, watching the campfire dance
and flicker in the evening breezes. Flames sputtered across
sap that seeped from the wood; occasionally, a jarring pop
rose over the more regular roar of the fire. The familiar
shadows of her companions shifted amid the red-tinged
dusk, their voices comforting as they discussed the evening
meal and their plans for morning travel. Kevral noticed them
only in a distracted sort of way, as always concentrating on
her sword work and the means to improve it. Whenever her
thoughts strayed beyond honing battle techniques or
guarding her charge, she directed them back. At night she
dreamed mostly of steel patterns against backgrounds of
blue or black sky, forest, and rain. During sleep, however,
her mind sometimes managed to drag her back to those considerations she had abandoned. Tae or Ra-khir spoke to her
freely then, and she found herself unable to cut those dream
conversations short.

They had camped in the woods, parallel to the town of
Wynix. Although they kept to the forest as much as possible,
time constraints had driven them back to the open pathways
and trails at intervals. Now an undisputed member of the
group, Tae had become more communicative about their

route. Kevral rarely participated in the discussions, but she did keep careful track of locations. She had challenged the best swordsmen of every town and village to spar, winning with an ease that affirmed her confidence and ability. These matches obsessed her, keeping other thoughts mercifully at bay. Now she faced a greater challenge, or so she hoped. A city the size of Wynix would surely have a warrior who would prove more competent than those she'd faced so far.

"I'll be back," Kevral said, mounting her horse without further explanation. Her forays had become routine. The others would not question.

"Wait," Ra-khir shot back. "I'm going with you." Without awaiting a reply, he headed for his horse.

"You need to stay and guard Matrinka." Kevral did not bother to face him as she spoke but kicked her horse into a walk toward Wynix.

"Tae can handle it." Ra-khir gave the usual response. It had become a game with them. Against her wishes, he had followed her on several other occasions. Objecting would only result in argument and delay. He never interfered with her matches, so Kevral allowed him to follow. She doubted either Ra-khir or Tae could battle a serious threat without her, but she trusted Tae to safely spirit Matrinka away rather than fight. This would surely prove simpler without Ra-khir's glaring presence.

The hooves of Kevral's gelding snapped branches and rattled brush, announcing her presence to any animal or human who cared to listen. She caught occasional glimpses of tiny white tails bobbing off into the distance. The musky odor of a passing fox wound past her nose, though the timid animal never came near enough to spot. A nighthawk shrieked, announcing its kill and warning away scavengers.

At length, Kevral drew up to the portals of the walled city. Swaddled in granite, the city rose in increments, the tallest buildings at the center. Though it bore the same name as an ancient farm town near the Southern Weathered Mountains, it was relatively young, rebuilt long after *Ragnarok*'s fire that had gutted the West centuries earlier. Its modern construction spoke of great wealth, particularly toward the center of town. The poorer folks lived on the outskirts, some in tiny hovels outside the great walls, encroaching on the lush farm fields of the Fertile Oval.

Kevral found the gates open and unguarded. She could see

movement in the streets: people finishing their daily business and heading toward their homes, animals seeking shelter or water, and chickens finding their roosts for the night. A middle-aged man lounged on a stone just outside the city gates. He wore an old tunic and breeks that looked homespun, his blond locks tangled and unkempt. He carried no weapons that she could see. Otherwise, Kevral noticed no one who might oppose her entrance to the city. She drew up her horse beside the stranger. "Excuse me," she said.

The man rose politely and nodded a greeting.

"Are you a guard?" Kevral asked, feeling foolish even as the question left her mouth. In stance, dress, and manner, he seemed anything but official.

"No," the man replied. "Wynix is an open city. Anyone may enter as they please."

"Oh." Kevral tried to fathom why such a policy surprised her. Except for the castle, Béarn had no walls and little need for city sentries. The Renshai's Fields of Wrath required no formal defenses; each citizen could protect him or herself. She attributed her expectations to the time spent in Pudar. The trading city had such a diverse and changing population and so many merchants to support, it required more cautious attention. "Well, then. Do you happen to know where I could find the best warrior in Wynix?"

The man shrugged, pale eyes meeting Kevral's questioningly. He glanced then at Ra-khir, hovering behind her, but the knight-in-training said nothing. The stranger returned his attention to Kevral. "I suppose I do. What need do you have of him?"

Kevral did not believe her interest any of the man's concern, but she saw no reason for rudeness either. He could direct her, so it made sense to indulge him a bit to get the answers she needed. Usually, when she asked that question, people rushed to brag about a beloved officer or a hero they believed the most skilled in the world. "I want to challenge him."

"Do you?" The man nodded sagely. "For what purpose?"

The last question proved one too many. Kevral glared at the stranger, her tense grip on the reins drawing her horse a step backward. It snorted, blasting spit onto the man. "That's my business."

The man seemed to take no notice of the spray. "Of

course. That's why I thought you'd know the answer. But I see you don't, so why don't you go on your way?"

Kevral dismissed the stranger with a wave of annoyance. "I have a reason. I just don't think you need to know it. Now either direct me to this warrior or don't. Stop wasting my time with idle curiosity."

To Kevral's surprise, the man smiled, taking no offense. He studied her with eyes that seemed remarkably old in contrast to unlined features and hair with only a hint of gray. "You think you're good, do you?"

"I'm the best." Kevral stated a simple fact.

"You believe you could triumph over our most capable?"

"I know I could."

"You think highly of yourself."

"I have a right to."

The man placed a hand on Kevral's bridle, a gesture of war in some countries, though she saw nothing hostile about his manner and so forgave the trespass. "Lady, you could not even best me."

Ra-khir drew closer, clearly bothered by the touch as Kevral had not been.

Kevral rolled her eyes, tired of bantering words with an aging townsman. "You're a fool, old man, and you have no intention of telling me what I ask. Get out of my way."

"And you are a coward," the stranger closed his fingers around the leather near the horse's eye, holding the gelding in place. "You call me old and a fool, yet you haven't the courage to fight me."

Kevral's cheeks felt on fire. Any dirty or angry word the stranger might have spoken would not have riled her, except the one he chose. Nothing insulted a Renshai worse than "coward."

"I'm sorry I called you a fool." Kevral leaped from her gelding, tossing the reins to Ra-khir. "I should have called you a *witless* fool. You wish to fight me, and that's what you'll get. Name your end point, and we'll do battle right here."

Ra-khir caught the reins and covered his mouth with a hand. His eyes betrayed the smile manners forced him to hide. Anger did not allow her to recognize the similarity between this encounter and his first run-in with her.

"Death," said the man.

Kevral had never heard the word so calmly spoken. Ra-khir's mirth disappeared instantly, and he cleared his throat to speak. Kevral silenced her companion with a crisp, warning gesture and addressed the man instead. "Are you sure you want to—"

"Yes," the stranger interrupted.

Kevral shrugged. "It's your pyre. Any last affairs you want us to handle for you?"

"That won't be necessary." The man released the horse and stepped away but otherwise made no preparations for battle.

Again noting that the man carried no weapons, Kevral reluctantly reached for hers. The idea of letting another touch one of her swords, perhaps mishandling it, was disturbing, but fairness dictated she not fight an unarmed man. She would reclaim it soon enough. "You may use one of my swords."

"That won't be necessary either."

Doubt eroded the edges of Kevral's confidence. This man's unshakable composure had become irritating to the point of distraction. Surely no one without some trick could remain so utterly unruffled moments before a battle to the death. She judged him in the twilight, seeing nothing she had missed on first inspection. He carried none of the bulk she had come to expect from warriors outside the Fields of Wrath. Though taller than her by a head, his size was unimpressive. Scars on his cheek and hand suggested that he had survived battles in the past, and she believed she noticed a hint of callus on the hand that snagged her bridle. She had seen too little of his movements to guess at style or speed, but his refusal of a weapon suggested he planned to use his limbs alone. Many of the Renshai maneuvers did not require weapons, and much of their proficiency came from using their bodies as well as their swords in combat. "I could put aside my swords, too."

"Unnecessary," he said.

"But I'm not used to—"

The man crouched. "Come on! Use or don't use what you want. Just stop yammering and have at me already!"

"Kevral, I don't think—" Ra-khir started.

Kevral lost the rest of his words beneath her own wild battle cry. She charged the stranger with a looping cut of a single sword, fast as a striking snake. But the man disappeared beneath her cut. She saw only a blur whipping beneath her attack, then the man reappeared behind her, her other blade in his fist.

Kevral gasped, retreating awkwardly as the sword chopped the space where she had stood, twice in an instant. She riposted boldly. Steel rang against steel. Then the other slipped free of the block and cut low. She dodged, but the tip of his sword sliced a painful gash across her thigh. "Modi!" Kevral shouted, the cry slamming her with battle madness. The injury lost meaning as she sprang for her opponent in a furious, weaving assault. He parried three strokes with leisurely ease, then returned another that licked beneath her hand. His blade slapped her guard. Kevral jerked back to protect her hand, but the man bore in. He caught her hilt a blow that ached through her arm, then another that tore away her grip. A moment later, he held both of her swords.

Kevral went still, shocked by the man's agility. Disarmed or not, she would fight to her last breath and face death bravely. She did not even flinch as she settled into a defensive stance.

The man did not attack again. "Here." He tossed her a sword.

Kevral caught it by the hilt, confused. Ra-khir, Tae, and Matrinka had accustomed her to odd forms of honor. Nevertheless, it seemed unlikely this man would allow her to attack him two swords to none but would find it inappropriate to finish the battle when the situation had become reversed by skill alone.

"And here." He tossed Kevral the other sword, which she also caught. She sheathed them both, seeing no reason to continue the battle.

The stranger remained in place, his expression disdainful. "No matter how competent you become, there is always someone better."

Now that Kevral realized he would not kill her, admiration rushed to the fore. A moment ago, he had been her enemy, the personification of every image she created during practice. An instant later, he had become the epitome of her fantasies, the warrior she would struggle for all eternity to become. "Who are you?" she whispered, but she did not need an answer. Only one being could play an accomplished Renshai like a child. The man she had dismissed as an aging Wynixian peasant was Colbey Calistinsson. She tried to kneel, but awe held her rooted in place. All of the emotions she had boxed into a corner flooded through her. The love she had withheld from Ra-khir and Tae filled her like a tidal wave. From infancy, she had dreamed of meeting Colbey face-to-face and sword-to-sword. The moment had passed too swiftly, and she had handled it badly. Her heart pounded, loud and relentless. She felt as if her body might melt, like wax in a flame. Need became a ceaseless ache. Had he asked for her life, she would have given it willingly, though not without a fight. A Renshai who died without glory could never earn his respect.

Colbey dodged her question to ask one of his own. "It remains to be answered: What reason do you have for jeopardizing your quest? What reason do you have for humiliating some of the best warriors of the West? What reason do you have for dashing the faith of young swordsmen as they watch their idols fall in defeat to a girl older, but certainly not wiser, than her appearance?"

Kevral lowered her head. "I was just . . . I wanted to . . ." She gathered her courage and her words. "I want to be the best warrior in the world. I want to be—"

Colbey did not let her finish. "Just because you talk like me and fight like me doesn't mean you're me."

Kevral swallowed the "—like you," she had nearly expressed. "I know that," she said defensively.

"Becoming the best has nothing to do with others."

Kevral lowered her head, too overwhelmed at her hero's presence to dare to argue.

But Colbey read her intentions as if she had spoken them aloud. "If you measure success against yourself instead of others, you will find that you can only strive toward it. If you give your all, you can improve your technique with every stroke. Better becomes certainty, and best unattainable."

"You're the best," Kevral had to speak her mind. "You've always been the best."

"No." Colbey glanced toward Ra-khir, who had not moved since the battle ended. "I've had centuries to improve my skills, and yet I still haven't reached my potential. If I ever do, I'll have no reason left to live."

Kevral conceded, but she wished to make a point of her own. "But I want to fight better than any other human."

"Why?"

"I want to be the best," Kevral amended, frustrated by the need to work around Colbey's definition. "I mean I want to become a swordsman who has no equal." She braced for Colbey's next "why," knowing he would eventually corner her beyond answer. No matter the significance of any conversation, a child could "why" it into oblivion.

This time, however, Colbey changed his tack. "So become that."

"I'm trying to."

Colbey shook his head, his blond hair falling into the classic feathers she had seen in every artist's rendition of him. She could scarcely believe she had not recognized him sooner. "No. You're trying to prove that's what you are to a bunch of strangers whose opinions mean nothing. Becoming a swordsman without equal only requires you to practice."

Kevral felt as if they had talked in circles. Colbey had returned to his original point. "But how would that show people I'm the b . . ." She caught herself. "I'm unequaled."

"Oh." Colbey stretched out the word as if he had just made a brilliant discovery. "It's not that you want to *be* the best. You just want everyone else to *think* you're the best."

"No!" Kevral defended. Then, realizing Colbey's point at last, she closed her eyes and sighed deeply. "You're right, of course. I'm acting like a fool. I'm sorry."

Colbey pursued relentlessly. "It's worse than that. You're running away from a problem. And that, young warrior, is cowardice."

Kevral stiffened, affronted. Ra-khir's horse snorted, and she jumped. She had managed to forget about him waiting there, and now anger drove her to speak despite his presence. "I won't take that from anyone. I've never refused a challenge. I've never run from a battle."

"From a battle, maybe not. Certainly not that I've witnessed. But you have run from a decision. You're still running."

Kevral raked a hand through her short locks, unwittingly aligning them into feathers that closely matched Colbey's own. "All right. I'll make the decision." The words emerged easily; for the moment, she did not consider the enormity of the task. Renshai managed adversity without complaint or timidity. "But what can I do to fix the damage I've done?" Guilt finally trickled through the zealous, burning passion. "Should I go back to those warriors and apologize? Should I tell them what I am? Should I claim I cheated or, maybe, challenge again and let them win?"

Kevral caught a glimpse of Ra-khir shaking his head vigorously before Colbey said, "No. First, you don't have the time. You're on a god-sanctioned mission ..."

God-sanctioned? Excitement supplanted guilt, quickly lost in the raging fires of emotion already overloaded by awe.

"... and anything you tried to do by returning would only further humiliate those warriors. They know you didn't cheat, and they'd recognize an intentional loss for what it was. Most probably believed themselves more competent than a Renshai, and those who didn't already know what you are." Colbey leaned on the rock where Kevral had first found him lounging, one leg propped on its surface. "Strong warriors will use defeat as a tool to spur their practice, and they are the only ones who matter. In time, they will regain the trust of followers. I worry more for those youths who would have emulated their heroes, and I hope they have the courage and strength to work toward your skill instead."

The rationalization did not absolve Kevral, but it did soften discomfort that would bother her more as the elation of meeting Colbey faded. She had so many things she wanted to ask him, details regarding her personal choices, his own, historical facts and myths, and the age-old wonders of the pious. For all her religious zeal, especially for all things Colbey, she had never imagined herself standing directly before a god prior to her own death. She would forever despise herself for missing the chance to ask him everything, yet she doubted he would remain with her long enough to barrage him. Out of a selfish mistake had come an opportunity that arose perhaps once in a million lifetimes. "About my decision," she started. "My sword work comes before anything, like yours did."

"Does," Colbey corrected.

Kevral flushed. "Does. You never let ..." She glanced at Ra-khir, who sat patiently upon his charger, listening but not interfering. "You never got ... um ... that," she finished lamely. She hoped that if he knew about the decision, he could substitute the word "marriage" for her hedging.

Colbey gave Ra-khir an apologetic glance, then placed an arm across Kevral's shoulders and steered her just beyond Ra-khir's hearing.

The touch of her hero, though fatherly, sent desire coursing through Kevral. She shivered, desperate to curl into that embrace and remain there for eternity.

Apparently sensing the effect he had on her, Colbey removed his hand. "For the record, I *am* married. I don't want, and I certainly don't need, any other women. And Freya would rather kill me than share me."

"Freya?" Kevral sputtered, knowing she could never compete with the most beautiful of all goddesses. "But she's so—" Kevral clamped a hand over her mouth before she said something she would regret. She loved the gods too much to disparage any of them, even one most believed a wanton whore. Kevral would far sooner trust that the stories men told about her for millennia were wrong than that Colbey had made a bad choice. "—beautiful," she ended lamely.

Though the switch was blatantly obvious, Colbey accepted Kevral's verbal assessment rather than her original intention. "Though unmatched . . ." Colbey smiled at his word choice. ". . . her beauty is less than half her charm. She gives me a good fight, on and off the practice field." By the latter, Kevral guessed he complimented her wit. "And I think you should know I married once before. I wasn't much older than you." His expression grew wistful, bittersweet. Apparently, even centuries had not swallowed the memory.

Stunned silent, Kevral said nothing, hoping her quiet would encourage him to continue.

Colbey obliged. "She was Renshai, but our marriage died because I couldn't spawn a child."

"What a horrible reason!" Kevral could not contemplate leaving a man she loved.

Colbey shrugged, neither in agreement nor defense. "Times were more violent. Only a rare Renshai reached his or her thirties. Even with our couples fertile, we nearly gloried ourselves into oblivion." He shook his head, as if to erase his own words. "But I understood how she felt. I wanted a family as much as she did. Each month I hoped with a desperation that tore holes as painful as any weapon. Each month, I mourned the death of the baby that could have been but wasn't. I don't fault or begrudge her that decision. She found another, and she had her children."

Kevral lowered her head. Though too young to concern herself with offspring yet, she sympathized with Colbey's anguish. She knew how it felt to pine for one thing above life itself and to know she would never have it. For several moments, she found herself unable to look at him, the object of her desire.

"There were many women after her, all Renshai. Those, I didn't marry."

Kevral tensed, scarcely daring to believe he had admitted such a thing to her. Had her own parents confessed to such behavior, it could not have surprised her more. "You slept with women who weren't your wife?"

"They weren't anyone else's wives either, of course." Colbey inserted that bit of morality hastily, almost defensively. "I'm not particularly proud about that part of my life. I was human, Kevral. In fact, I still consider myself human. I made a lot of mistakes, and I'll make many more." He lowered his voice conspiratorially. "The gods wouldn't want it bandied about, but perfection doesn't exist. Morality is not a constant. Right depends too heavily on personality and perspective."

"Didn't those women worry about the . . . consequences?" Kevral felt her own moral foundation shaking.

"What consequences?" Colbey glanced over Kevral's head at Ra-khir whose honor and manners would not allow him to violate their privacy. "I was safe. Sterile."

Kevral saw other reason for the Renshai women's incaution, one Colbey would never admit even if his modesty allowed him to consider it. The one who bore his child got to marry him, an honor Kevral might have violated her own premarital ethics to attain. She did not bother with the issue of reputation. Colbey, she suspected, would never reveal his partners, even hundreds of years after their deaths. "Did you ever get your child?" History told her that he had not; but, if she had learned nothing else from this encounter, she now knew human chronicling had its failings.

"Two sons whom I loved equally."

Again, Kevral read pain on his features.

"Episte could not have seemed more mine had he sprung from my seed. But his mother hated me and became too obsessed with emphasizing the blood relationship over ours. Others called Episte's Renshai father a hero who died in glory. Episte knew him only as a corpse who abandoned his only child before his birth. I tried to overcome the bitterness his mother instilled; but, in the end, it destroyed him." Colbey's eyes grew moist, and he stared at the distant horizon as if he had forgotten she stood there listening.

Kevral watched him, her heart pounding as another myth was dispelled. So many times, she had held back tears, believing Colbey never cried. Now she wanted nothing more than to seize the opportunity to hold him in her arms and comfort him. But her limbs would not obey her; so she remained in place, driven by longing yet paralyzed by fear of rejection.

Colbey rescued her from the dilemma by recovering his composure and wiping his eyes clean with a hand. "My son in marriage, Raska, our Ravn. He's only a year older than you."

Kevral smiled, glad the story ended happily. "I'm sorry about Episte but happy you got your children." Only then, she realized her problem still confronted her. "How do you feel about Renshai marrying outside the tribe?"

"I never considered it for myself." Colbey laughed. "And yet, in the end, I did it. I think you need to make your own decision. And I think I need to go."

"Wait!" Kevral shouted, immediately embarrassed by her audacity. "Please, just tell me this. Are the quotations attributed to you really yours?"

"Most of them," Colbey admitted.

"Did you say that the Knights of Erythane reduced honor to a rigid bunch of arbitrary rules?"

Colbey cringed. "Not in those precise words. I did once disdain them for expecting enemies to follow the same honor as themselves. I believed it cheapened their honor."

Kevral appreciated the knowledge. At least she had a basis on which to formulate a decision. Colbey's opinion mattered too much to ignore, and he clearly did not think knights fit among Renshai.

"Come here," Colbey said softly. He waved boldly over Kevral's shoulder to indicate Ra-khir should join them. Kevral turned to watch the knight-in-training dismount and lead both horses over to them.

Discomfort jangled through Kevral as Ra-khir joined them. First, she did not wish him to overhear a discussion on coupling and marriage, especially since he played a pivotal role in her choice. And the presence of two men she cared for so near one another made her as anxious as she had felt prior to dedicating herself to sword work and challenges.

Colbey did not lead them far. Just beyond a stand of trees, a white charger cropped quietly at the grass, a pair of long swords in a belt thrust through the wrappings of a pack on its back. "Do you know what this is?" He patted the horse's flank, removed the swords absently, and strapped them around his waist.

Kevral could almost feel the solace that accompanied this action. Any Renshai would feel naked without at least one sword.

"That's an Erythanian Knight's charger, my lord." Ra-khir recognized the stallion at once.

"This is Frost Reaver. He's my horse."

"I'm sorry, my lord. He looks just like one."

Colbey smiled. "He is one. The mount of Sir Colbey Calistinsson, Knight to the Erythanian and Béarnian kings." He executed a bow befitting a knight.

"You?" The incredulous expletive slipped out before Kevral could stop it or Ra-khir could say something more suitable. "A Knight of Erythane? Don't you have to be Erythanian?"

"No," Ra-khir explained for Colbey. "Not if you defeat a knight in fair combat. And you're willing to take and stand by the knight's vow."

Colbey leaped onto the horse's bare back. Drawing a bridle from the pack, he fitted it over the animal's head. The ease of a maneuver Kevral had never seen anyone attempt before suggested horse and rider had grown accustomed to it.

"And you were willing to do these things?" Kevral wished she could drop the skepticism from her voice, but it seemed stuck to her tongue.

"I have no quibble with the actual honor of the knights, only with their interpretation of it and the way most expect enemies to abide by the same rules. Read the vow sometime. It may surprise you."

Kevral determined that she would do so, but curiosity would drive her to question Ra-khir about it first.

"But I didn't come to discuss any of the things we've talked about today."

Kevral wondered if she would ever receive her share of surprises. She had felt so certain Colbey had arrived to chastise her for her behavior, it never occurred to her he might have a higher purpose. Yet surely he must. She had done too many stupid things in her short life without drawing the attention of gods to believe this one thing had brought him.

Colbey patted Frost Reaver's neck as the horse patiently awaited his command without snorting or pawing. History claimed Colbey shared no closeness with animals, never even bothering to name his mounts; but the bond between these two was obvious, proving another fallacy. "As I mentioned, your quest is god-sanctioned. But you will not find the one you seek in Santagithi. Enemies have captured and taken him elsewhere."

"Where?" Kevral and Ra-khir asked, nearly simultaneously.

"I can tell you only that it's a place of this world, though not on any human map. You have an item in your possession. It belongs to one of your enemies and is as sacred to him as your sword arm is to you. It will guide you to him if you let it."

"What is it? How does it work?" Kevral asked.

Colbey's mount started away, without any visible cues from its rider. "Study it carefully. The owner shifts between Béarn and his home. Don't let it lead you to the wrong place." Then he was gone. If he heard Kevral's pleas to stop, he disregarded them.

Kevral slammed her fist against a tree, shaking a spray of moisture down onto their heads. "I don't believe it! He chats with me forever, then gives us only half the clues to perform a mission he calls god-sanctioned."

Ra-khir stared after the retreating figure, still a topic behind. "Colbey Calistinsson a Knight of Erythane. Who'd have believed it?"

Kevral wished Ra-khir had not drawn her back to the choices she had, thus far, avoided. "Who indeed?"

Chapter 38

The Truth Dawns

Scars are a warrior's badge of honor.
                                        —*Colbey Calistinsson*

Kevral's mind felt as swollen as the fullest water skin, and the hopelessness of sorting ideas brought a nervous despair. As she and Ra-khir headed back toward camp, she only half-listened to his attempts at conversation, returning monosyllabic replies intended more to protect her pounding head than to appease him. Overwhelmed by thought and emotion, she did not notice the quiet stillness of the forest, the background harmony of night insects, nor the animal noises that broke melodically through the hush at intervals.

At length, Ra-khir gave up on speaking. He lowered his head in weary surrender, and his straight, solid features disappeared beneath a fiery curtain of hair. Even sorrow could not hide his beauty. His locks fell in a wild cascade that any woman would envy, and the sweeping curves of muscles trained to combat drew her eye after his gentle attempts at conversation failed. Kevral believed Colbey had revealed his knighthood to open her mind rather than directly sway her decision. His insistence that she had to make her own choices seemed far more substantial in her memory. *Ra-khir, Tae, or neither.* Looking upon Ra-khir, it seemed simple now. If they courted, and eventually married, every girl in Erythane would covet her prize. His grace, his manners, and his gentleness would sell them on his charm even without the casual handsomeness he did not even seem to notice.

When Kevral looked deep inside herself, she knew she loved him; but she also realized she needed time to make certain, to consider.

Not wishing to drive Ra-khir away, Kevral shifted her horse nearer and took his hand. Ra-khir's head jerked up. Keen green eyes found Kevral's face. She smiled at him, and he returned the smile. His hand closed over her fingers, firm yet gentle. A flush of passion swept through Kevral, though whether as a result of Ra-khir's attention or a remnant from her meeting with the object of a lifelong crush, she did not try to surmise. For now, it just felt good to be with Ra-khir.

No further words passed between them during the short ride back to camp. Ra-khir sensed her need for nonverbal solace, and he did not speak again. Kevral left her thoughts knotted in place. She had learned long ago how to handle complex katas, and she would use the same techniques on her mind. Taken as a whole, any Renshai maneuver seemed impossible. Broken into manageable pieces, the process became learnable. She would work on her problems and ideas in the same fashion, beginning tonight, until sleep wrested the burden from her, then during her morning practice. Perhaps, when she dedicated her sword work to Colbey, he would bring her the inspiration she needed to make sense of his discussion.

Kevral freed her hand as she and Ra-khir reached the camp. Until she committed herself to a definitive decision, she would not allow circumstance to make it for her.

Kevral and Ra-khir pulled up to a dinner of snared rabbits and bread packed from Pudar. Darris lay propped against a deadfall, strumming his mandolin and humming at the stars. Matrinka leaned against him, eyes half-closed. She opened them the moment the horses entered the clearing, dragging the food farther from the warmth of the fire. Kevral missed Tae completely until she had dismounted and he appeared to assist her with the tack.

"Here, let me do that. You eat." Tae pointed at the food Matrinka had salvaged.

"Thank you." Emotionally battered, Kevral seized the opportunity to loop the reins over her gelding's head and hand them to Tae. She glanced at Ra-khir who had as much right to relax and eat as she did.

"Here." Tae substituted halter for bridle in two deft movements, then offered generously. "You go eat. I'll take care of yours, too."

"Thank you, no." Ra-khir ignored Tae's proffered hand. "It's part of my training."

"Oh." Tae shrugged as he hefted and set aside Kevral's saddle. "Part of your training as what? A stable groom?"

Apparently, Ra-khir had learned to accept Tae's sarcasm, which had gentled greatly since Pudar. "Knight chargers are rare, bought by the kings and trained by the world's best horsemen. They're irreplaceable, and we don't take chances with them." He slipped on a halter, pulled off the bridle, then unbuckled the saddle. "Not that you wouldn't do a good job," Ra-khir added hastily as he apparently realized his words could be taken as insult. "It's just a good habit to get into. For when I have a Knight charger, I mean."

Kevral sat and ate methodically, content with the tough, overcooked meat and warm bread dried to choking consistency by the fire. Many thoughts clamored for attention, and the need to concentrate on nothing wore on her. Pain ached through her thigh, and she examined the wound Colbey had left for the first time since the spar. Superficial, it had clotted without any ministration, yet she hoped it would scar. She had no other physical memento of an experience that had begun to seem more like a dream than reality.

Kevral had eaten and launched into her nightly practice by the time Tae and Ra-khir finished with the horses. Sword work proved invigorating, clearing her mind of all thought while she mastered a technique that had defied her for months. It clarified none of the issues confronting her; yet when Kevral finished and joined her companions beneath blankets near the fire, she came to one swift conclusion. Finding the heir of Béarn took precedence over the personal decision that had plagued her. The dangers of their mission might make the choice for her. Any or all of them might die, and she seemed the most likely first candidate. She needed to focus on the item Colbey had mentioned, the one owned by an enemy.

The breathing of Kevral's companions became a distracting cacophony, and she tried to concentrate on the more regular rhythm of the insects. Four times, her thoughts circled the problem, and each time she returned to the same conclusion. Tae had searched the bodies of the men they had killed. If anyone knew the device to which Colbey referred, Tae would. Yet Kevral kept searching for another route to the answer. She cherished control of herself and her circumstances too much to toss the problem into another's hands. And she questioned her motives as well. Was it possible she just wanted some time alone with Tae after having shared quiet moments with Ra-khir? The possibility shamed her.

Kevral rolled, telling herself she needed sleep too much to worry about the matter any longer. But the realization that someone had crept up on her made her eyes shoot open to meet earnest brown ones in a face attractive only for its familiarity.

"Sorry," Tae whispered. "Didn't mean to startle you. I thought you knew I was there."

"I never know where the hell you are," she returned, equally surprised at having her considerations brought so abruptly to life by Tae's sudden, unexpected presence.

"That's my best feature." Smiling, Tae gave back as good as he got. "Kevral, can we talk?"

"Sure." Kevral rose, barely missing the sleep she would not have gotten anyway.

Tae scrambled backward, out of Kevral's way. His eyes widened, and his mouth formed a small oval.

"Sorry." Kevral repeated Tae's apology. "Didn't mean to startle you."

"It's just that I've been trying to talk to you since Pudar," he hissed. "And you've avoided me every time. This was just too damned easy."

Kevral inclined her head to indicate an area away from their sleeping companions where they could talk without awakening anyone but remain near enough for Tae to continue his watch. Kevral wrapped her blanket tightly around her as they moved beyond the warmth of the fire and into the coldness of forest night. Despite the covering, her hands and feet felt as if they turned instantly to ice, and her shoulders bunched into an aching knot. Tae wore only his regular clothing, seeming to take no notice of the cold.

"Aren't you freezing?" Kevral asked, still keeping her voice low.

Tae shrugged. "I've lived through winter nights with less. A full belly and a nearby campfire make a huge difference."

"And I've had my hand ripped open, but that doesn't mean I slice my fingers because it doesn't hurt as much." Kevral realized she had not addressed Tae's question, and he deserved an answer. "Look, I'm really sorry. I've been acting like a monster."

Tae gave Kevral no leeway. "Yes, you have."

Kevral accepted the words graciously. "I'm not going to argue. I deserve worse."

"And I'm sure you have a good reason."

The moment has come. Kevral drew breath to explain. Anything less than the truth would require the flirting she had promised to avoid.

Tae did not give her the opening to speak. "And I hope you'll tell me sometime. But first, I have some things I've been wanting to give you."

Kevral loosed a long breath, reprieved. "For me?"

Tae pulled a narrow book from beneath his cloak and handed it to Kevral.

She accepted it, studying the cover, running a reverent hand over the binding. Books were rare, usually reserved for nobility; and she could scarcely believe he had brought her such an expensive present. The title *The Deathseeker, Colbey Calistinsson: His Time as Pudar's General,* only made the gift more valuable. She looked at Tae. "Thank you." The words did not seem nearly enough to express her appreciation. "Where did you . . ." she started, then answered her own thought. "It's probably better if I don't know."

Tae dodged the half-asked question. "This goes with it." He balanced a painted wooden figure of a man on horseback on the book in her hands. Though the crafted features did not match recent experience, and the horse was a bay, Kevral knew the artisan intended to depict Colbey. The stance did capture his inhuman confidence, and she could imagine his cold, blue-gray eyes looking out at her. "Thank you," Kevral said again, hoping her tone conveyed the gratitude she could not verbalize. "This is too generous. Thank you." She lowered her head, ashamed. "I really don't deserve these."

Tae did not address the comment. Instead, he gathered a deep breath. "I have something to say to you." He took the book and figurine from Kevral's hand, setting them on the ground beside her. "I know I don't have any right to feel this, but . . ." The pattern of Tae's speech quickened, and his eyes dodged hers. The nervousness caught her wholly by surprise. It was so uncharacteristic of the confident hoodlum she had grown to know that she scarcely recognized him. Yet, oddly, she found the vulnerability a spectacular change. " . . . I love you. There, I said it. I know you don't love me back, but I have to say it anyway and now you know. . . ."

"Whoa," Kevral said. "Stop."

Tae looked at Kevral, finally. His eyes held a sparkle she could not describe and his features a fear that became them. It gave him the appearance of a wild animal cornered, moonlight sheening from hair so dark it was otherwise lost in the night.

"I love you, too." Kevral had to say it. It was true.

Tae did not wait for more. He enfolded her in his arms, drawing her body tight against his. Desire throbbed through Kevral even before his lips touched hers, powerful enough that she knew it was no echo of what she had wanted and missed from Colbey. She relished the taste of his lips, the touch of his tongue, the caress of his fingers along her back and buttocks. For the moment, there was only Tae. He was the one.

"Stop." Kevral had to force the word, breathing it into Tae's mouth.

Though clearly as aroused as she, Tae did as Kevral bade, reluctantly releasing his hold and pulling away from the kiss she had returned as eagerly as he had given it. His hands slid down her arms, and he grasped her fingertips so that he did not have to fully let her go. "What's wrong?"

"I'm not ready for this." Kevral turned away, need still aching through her.

"We were just kissing. Even if I didn't respect you enough not to press you any further than you wanted to go, I could hardly force anything you didn't want. And I know this isn't the right time or place." Tae scattered explanations the way a bowman with poor aim shot random flights in the hope of hitting the target.

"You don't understand." Kevral's eyes stung. For once, she did not fight the tears, taking a lesson from Colbey. "I really do love you. But I love Ra-khir, too."

"Oh."

Kevral braced herself for a clever, if nasty, slur against the knight-in-training.

But Tae proved more sensitive than she ever expected. "Well." He laughed self-deprecatingly. "What kind of silly, beautiful woman would choose a dashing Knight of

Erythane over a punk? I'm sorry. I feel pretty stupid." He tried to pull away, but Kevral closed her fingers tightly over his.

"Stop that."

Tae looked at his feet.

"First, thanks for calling me beautiful. A woman never tires of hearing that, even when it's not true. And second, did I say I had chosen him over you?"

"I don't understand." Tae sneaked a look, a tiny glimmer of hope lighting features more than attractive enough for Kevral's standards.

"I love you both. I'm sorry. I didn't mean for that to happen. I didn't mean to fall in love with anyone. A month ago, I didn't even believe it possible." Kevral sighed to break the patter of her own speech, so like the apprehensive rambling Tae had displayed just a few moments earlier. "I know I have to choose, but this just doesn't seem like the right time or place to do that."

"No," Tae said. "By 'I don't understand' I meant that I don't understand what you mean when you say you're not beautiful. You're the most beautiful woman in the world."

"Gods," Kevral closed her eyes, the tears now leaking from beneath her lids. "Don't make this any harder."

"I have to," Tae said. "Or I might lose you."

Kevral sobbed.

Tae picked up Kevral's presents and led her to a deadfall, resisting the natural urge to hold her in this susceptible moment. "Look. I don't have much to offer, but you deserve to know the details."

Kevral sat and listened to the story of Tae's childhood with sympathy and disbelief. The Eastern streets granted a lifestyle she would never have known existed; though Tae insisted Pudar's did not differ significantly, she had missed it completely. The people of the night shifted silently through darkness and shadow, their survival from moment to moment a tenuous uncertainty. Kevral's internal struggle seemed petty in comparison. While she worried over too much love, they fought for every scrap of sustenance. Yet, Tae assured her, he had not discovered this world until his early teens, after his mother's death when his father had no time for a child.

Kevral heard the tale of a loving mother and a father who had created a covert kingdom from the lawless. Bitterness warped the story. Kevral doubted the mother was quite as perfect as the son remembered or the father so cruel and wooden. Through Tae's tone, and even his choice of words, Kevral found instances where the mother erred and the father demonstrated deep affection for mother and son alike. She cringed at the descriptions of ugliness that a child should never see, the deeds of the father's followers and partners. She shuddered as he detailed the brutal assault in which he watched his mother slaughtered and was himself left for dead. And she listened raptly to the father's final speech after which he sent his son, hunted, into the world to die or return to claim his inheritance.

"So I didn't really lie when I joined the group." Tae made a circular motion to indicate all five of them. "I did want the camaraderie, but Ra-khir was also right about needing the protection. Until Pudar, I thought we'd killed all the enemies chasing me. At twenty, I can go home and claim a valuable business. So, I guess, if you married me, you'd marry the heir to a lot of money and power."

"Which you don't intend to claim," Kevral finished with the obvious.

"All things considered, I'd rather be poor and hunted. I have no reason to go back there. Ever."

"Except to see your father." Kevral latched onto the one positive.

Tae's expression hardened. "I have no reason to go back there," he repeated. "My father can die the horrible death he arranged for himself."

"You don't mean that."

Tae shrugged, leaving Kevral to draw her own conclusions about the sincerity of a statement that certainly sounded emphatic. She did not usually press people to maintain links to family members they detested. Early in their journey, Ra-khir had described the situation with his parents, and she had condoned breaking ties with his mother as categorically as her companions. Even Matrinka, who found good in everyone, believed Ra-khir had made a proper decision.

Yet Kevral had gathered clues throughout Tae's story that proved his situation far different. Beneath the expressed hatred, Kevral thought she heard respect and affection. Although Tae claimed his father had dumped him into a street orphan's life by ignoring him, the remainder of the story did not fit this picture. The father had spent too many quiet nights in the alley with his son, choosing family company over an enterprise that required his full attention. He had explained his purpose for pushing Tae into gangs rather than coddling him in plush, hidden cabins. Kevral did not condone the father's actions, yet she saw a strange logic to them. The man believed he had taken the necessary steps to assure his son's survival. A ruthless love, to be sure, but love nonetheless. Bad decisions well-motivated deserved attention but not necessarily disownment.

However, Kevral refused to take on another problem now. Tae's relationship, or lack of one, with his father could wait. Instead, she latched on to something else Tae had said. "Until Pudar, you thought we had killed the ones chasing you?"

"Right. The prince-murdering incident." Tae grinned wickedly. "You remember that."

"Vividly," Kevral admitted, imprisonment and expectation of dismemberment would remain with her for eternity.

"I didn't kill the prince, you know."

"We all knew you hadn't. Why do you think everyone asked so little about it?"

Tae snorted, staring at Kevral as if she had just appeared from another world. "Where have you been?"

Blushing, Kevral looked away. "Mostly avoiding you and Ra-khir. And the decision." She met his gaze again. "I already apologized for that."

"The Red Knight grilled me into the ground." Tae slipped back into substituting descriptions for names. He had used one of his more complimentary terms for Ra-khir, wise enough to avoid condemning his competitor and subsequently alienating the object of his affection. "You know, it took me up until yesterday to feel sure I hadn't done it."

The words made little sense to Kevral. "I remember you said if you did kill the prince, you didn't mean to. But how could you not know if you'd killed someone?"

"This may sound stupid," Tae warned.

Kevral dismissed his concern with a broad wave. They had shared too many intimate secrets to worry about how something sounded.

"It was like this weird fog covered my memory. The whole thing was a blur anyway. People attacking me from all sides. The prince and his guards rushing in to help. And there were these little people, children I used to think, singing songs from the roofs of buildings."

"You're right," Kevral admitted. "It does sound stupid. But not until the children on the roofs."

"I kept leaving them out, too, thinking I imagined them. But they're getting more definite in my memory, and they're the key to making sense of this." Tae sighed. "A type of sense anyway."

"Go on," Kevral encouraged.

"The prince got closer than he should have under the circumstances, and I was swinging pretty wildly." Knowing Kevral well enough to realize she would hone right in on the battle technique, he defended his actions. "All right. Not the best strategy, but it was the only one I had with a dozen guys all jabbing at me at once."

Kevral listened without judging. Quick, chaotic defenses could buy time while sorting enemies.

"I couldn't concentrate at all. Usually, in a frenzied situation, my sight and thoughts become disturbingly sharp. This time, I couldn't differentiate anything. All I could do was flail and hope. I knew my knife landed more than once. In all that confusion, who knew whether I hit the prince or not?"

"But now you know for sure you didn't do it?" Kevral could not fathom how he could sort out an event so muddily obscured at the time.

"Strange, isn't it? It's like I said. This mist has been dissipating slowly, and the scene keeps getting clearer. I stabbed two of the men who attacked me, but not the prince. Someone pushed him toward me, and another killed him. Very deliberately."

"So what's your idea about the children on the roofs?"

Tae smiled. The expression wilted suddenly into a perplexed look, as if a new idea had just reached him even as he started to answer. He grinned again, this time in triumph. "Elfs," he said.

"What?" Kevral's hand clutched the book.

"Sure. Stay with me." The speed of Tae's speech increased as he worked the problem out for himself as well as her. "First Matrinka tells us about an attack by bears in the courtyard. 'Magic,' she says, but no one believes her. Not even us. But there's no logical explanation found either. Then there're the singing children that confuse an already confusing situation. But they weren't children. They were small adults with animal faces and glazed eyes. Magic."

"Oh, please." Kevral's rational mind refused to accept a supernatural explanation so quickly, even in the wake of having just met a god.

"You weren't there," Tae defended himself fiercely. "I've been in tight situations before, every bit as horrible as the one in Pudar's alley. That lapse of memory doesn't make sense with any other explanation, and its return feels eerie. It's not natural. Add in the message from the dead Renshai. 'Elfs,' he wrote. Remember?"

"I remember." The instant Kevral allowed herself to believe, another answer snapped into her mind. "The gem you gave me. That's the item Colbey was talking about." She prepared to explain. "Last night, I met—"

Tae interrupted. "Ra-khir told me over dinner." He smiled impishly. "Wish I'd been there to see you knocked on your butt for a change."

Excited about her discovery, Kevral let the gibe pass. She rifled through her pockets, uncovering the odd green gem and drawing it from her pocket.

Tae glanced at it for only an instant before loosing a thoughtful noise. "Here, let me see it."

Kevral handed over the gem, and Tae hurried over to the firelight to examine it.

"Ra-khir said that Colbey said it belonged to its owner as surely as your limbs belong to you."

"Something like that." Kevral recalled more eloquent wording, though the details escaped her at the moment. Colbey had said so many things that bore quoting, they had blurred together after a while.

"I think he meant that literally. Kevral, I think it's an eye."

"An eye?" Kevral dismissed the possibility. "I've seen severed eyes. There're muscles and veins, all kinds of guts hanging off them."

"You didn't see this before I licked it clean for you."

Kevral had witnessed enough gore not to let such a comment bother her, especially when she knew he was joking. "That notwithstanding, eyes are soft. And they're white, except for the black part and the colored ring, of course."

"*Human* eyes are soft and the rest of that." Tae tipped the gem up to the light. "See that." His finger encompassed too large an area for Kevral to feel certain of the indicated spot. She studied it from different positions until a dark circle became visible in the center. "I think the Renshai was right. It belongs to an elf. Or a demon. Or whatever you want to call these things."

Uneasiness shivered through Kevral at the sight. Now that she believed it an eye, she could not shake the feeling that it studied her. "Put it away."

Tae went quiet, tightened his hand around it, and closed his eyes.

"You know, if Randil knew the leader's name, he probably had some reason for calling them elves, too."

Tae made no reply. Nor did he move.

"Don't you think?"

More silence.

Kevral seized Tae's arm. "Stop that. You're making me nervous."

Tae opened his eyes. "I'm just concentrating on this thing. If you block everything else out, there is a decided southern pull to it."

"Really?"

"Really." Tae offered the gem back. "Here."

Kevral shook her head, making no attempt to take it. "You hold onto it. We're not done fighting, and you're far more likely to escape enemies than me. It's safer with you."

Tae placed the elf-eye in his pocket without arguing the point. He looked at Kevral, lower lip clenched between his teeth and expression more somber than she had ever seen it. "We've got magical elves and enemies linked together. They've stirred unrest in Pudar, Béarn, and who knows where else. One or both groups has slaughtered at least one, probably at least two of Béarn's envoy parties that included Renshai and Knights of Erythane."

Kevral nodded, the details falling together exactly as Tae described them, and a feeling of doom creeping over her as he verbalized the danger.

"Far be it for a punk, or a Renshai, to call anything hopeless. But . . ." Tae let the topic trail. Nothing more needed saying.

"We have to try."

"I know that," Tae returned. "But Matrinka and Darris have this irritatingly happy view that love will bring them through anything. And Ra-khir . . ." He chose his words carefully, ". . . well, Ra-khir is Ra-khir. All that matters is doing the right thing. I'm not sure the concept of death will really reach them until the first of us actually dies."

Kevral did not bother to contradict him. As a Renshai, she embraced rather than feared death. She would joyfully give her life for the cause of Béarn's heir, though never in vain. If possible, she would see the entire mission through, but she never doubted for a moment that some, more likely all, of them would die. "They'll handle it."

"They'll have to," Tae gave back. "But I hope one of us is there to assist. I need to confess another weakness."

"Proceed." Kevral smiled. In the wake of so many, it would barely make an impact.

"I never thought I could become so attached to people, but you five have become the most important in my life."

The math confused Kevral. "Five?"

Tae raised and lowered his brows. "All right, I admit it. I'm including the damned cat. Without her, I'd never have gotten out of that prison, and she helped me through some rough times when I wondered if I wouldn't rather kill all of you than try to win back your trust."

"That," Kevral insisted, "I want to hear about in detail sometime."

"Of course. Anyway, I think Darris getting hurt gave them a good scare, but they're not as ready as they think for the real thing."

Kevral shrugged. "What happens happens. I admit you're right. We're the only two with enough experience and a dark enough viewpoint to anticipate. But trusting in poetic justice has its positive side."

Tae refused the assessment. "There is no justice, poetic or otherwise."

"Perhaps not. But confidence in the triumph of good over evil is not without its rewards." Although she could never become an optimist, Kevral enjoyed the company of too many to let Tae disparage them. "If faith works best for them, let them believe."

"Fine, I've got no problem with that. I just think that, when their world view shatters, we should both be prepared to pick up the pieces."

"Agreed."

"And, Kevral?" Tae took her hand again.

"Yes."

"If we both survive this, promise me one thing."

At that moment, Kevral would have given him anything. "What?"

"Before you run off to live happily with Ra-khir, you'll act upon our love one time. Just once, and I'll never bother you again."

"You mean sleep with you?"

"Right."

Kevral sighed, preparing a speech about typical men whose minds always leaped to sex no matter the situation. But when she met his gaze, she read desperation in dark eyes that reflected the flickering red of the fire. Nothing lascivious tainted his expression. This was no ploy or game, just a reckless, hopeless plea for one chance at happiness with the woman he loved enough to trade his life for. No bond or vow tied him to Béarn or the kingdom's politics. He was going to fight, probably to die, for Kevral. Once, she would have slapped him, denying the possibility with a vehemence that would not even have brooked the suggestion. But Colbey had coupled with many women outside of marriage. She could do so once with one she loved. And if she chose Tae, as she now believed she would, she would not even violate common morality. "Don't go making decisions for me about whom I'll spend the rest of my life with. If you don't want to wait, I'll understand. I have no right to expect it. But if you do, I'm as likely to run off with you as with him."

"I'll wait," Tae said, "and suffer the anticipation gladly if you choose in my favor." He did not allow this to distract him from his request, "And my promise?"

Kevral squeezed his hand, loving him all the more. "Consider it made."

Chapter 39

Ambush

*If I die, I'll find Valhalla never having fought a
coward. When I lead men, I measure their skills.
I would command no one to do the things I do.*
                              —Colbey Calistinsson

Colbey Calistinsson pounded on the door to Frey's hall,
chest painfully constricted. Over the past week, he had wrestled with Midgard's layout, toying with the leading players
like chessmen in a desperate game of strategy. In Béarn, the
kingdom fell under the rule of elves who planned to system-
atically execute all the humans under their command. The
tribes in the North battled with a ferocity far beyond the border skirmishes which had been routine even back in
Colbey's mortal years. In the East, brothers bickered over
property and rulership while the kingdom and the major cities fell into ruin around them. Criminals swarmed to the
roads and passes, whipped into a spree of murder that
slowed trade and communication toward oblivion. Even the
mighty market city, Pudar, had not escaped the chaos
wrought by Frey's creation. As the first caravans beset by
bandits and assassins failed to arrive, the city prepared for
war and the king frantically trained his younger son for the
throne. Colbey hammered on the door again, the sound
stretching into a deep, metallic echo.

Byggvir, Frey's manservant, opened the door, then started
to speak, "Good—"

Colbey did not pause for amenities. He slipped past

Byggvir and trotted down the hallway to a sitting room surrounded by book-filled shelves and comfortably furnished with six padded chairs. Five doors radiated from the hexagonal room. Colbey hesitated, uncertain which route to take.

Byggvir chased after his master's guest, forced to a sudden, skidding stop at Colbey's heels. The carpet bunched beneath the servant's feet, stealing his balance. Rather than slam into Colbey, Byggvir jerked backward, falling gracelessly to his buttocks.

Colbey whirled, not meeting the gaze he expected. His eyes tracked downward until he found Byggvir on the floor. "Where's your master?"

Byggvir scrambled to his feet and bowed. "Through there, my lord." He indicated the rightmost door. "With your son, lord."

"Ravn?"

"Do you have another son, lord?"

Colbey smiled, enjoying the human invective the gods rarely exchanged. He liked Byggvir and his wife, Beyla, the only other mortals in Asgard. "Thank you."

"Let me announce you, lord." Byggvir galloped ahead, Colbey only half a step behind him. He opened the door to another room much like the first, except that it had windows overlooking a courtyard filled with multihued flowers. Frey sat in an overstuffed chair, and Ravn had settled into another across from the god of fortune, rain/sunshine, and elves. It looked as if the conversation had not yet begun.

"Colbeytoseeyou,m'lord." Byggvir slurred his words together to get them all out before Colbey crossed the threshold.

Frey smiled. "Thanks for the warning," he said with uncharacteristic humor. He turned his attention immediately to Colbey. "Have a seat, if you like."

Colbey obliged, choosing the chair beside Ravn as Frey dismissed his servant. "After all you went through? Why aren't you guarding Griff?"

"I found someone else who wanted the job even more than me."

"Someone who wanted it more than one who challenged me for the honor?"

"Yes." Ravn smiled gleefully. "Someone who challenged the only one who ever bested you."

Colbey nodded good-naturedly, not bothering to mention

the unbalancing sword that had allowed the victory. *Let the boy have his fame.* Yet thoughts of Harval brought him painfully back to the matter at hand. By the moment, his control over the blade had continued to lessen, so that it now sat in his hands like a bar of unworked lead.

Frey waited patiently for a break in their conversation before asking, "So what can I do for the two of you?"

Colbey let Ravn speak first. It seemed only right as he had arrived earlier.

Ravn shifted restlessly in his chair. "Actually, Father, I'm glad you're here. I planned to come to you with this if Uncle Frey agreed."

Colbey nodded understandingly, sorry to break in on his son's initiative. "Would you like me to go until you're done?" It was an idle gesture. Colbey lacked the patience to leave and return.

Luckily, Ravn obviated the need. "No, stay." He cleared his throat, not quite sure how to start. "The heir to Béarn is in the elves' custody. I'd like permission to break him free and his guardian Renshai, Rantire, too."

Colbey had already guessed who Ravn must have found to take his place, but all the pleasure he knew at watching his son realize that he did not belong in human affairs vanished with the request.

Frey shrugged. "That's not something I can grant."

Ravn opened his mouth to explain Frey's role in the affair.

Already guessing that Ravn wanted permission to kill elves in the process, Colbey cut in. The question would only infuriate Frey and make it that much harder for Colbey to make a similar request. "No, Ravn. That's too much interference."

Ravn closed his mouth sullenly. "But I only wanted . . ."

"No." Colbey closed the matter, forcefully enough to send a warning.

"Just let me talk," Ravn insisted. "If Griff doesn't make it to Béarn, there's no way to restore the balance."

"Don't you think I know that!" The urgency of the situation made Colbey curt. "But you can't be the one who gets him free, nor can I. The humans have to do that. I thought you'd realized that when you turned your charge over to one."

"But Rantire can't escape. She's tried."

"I've got good humans on the way to assist." Colbey's argument died there, leading him into his business with Frey. "To get through, they'll need to kill elves."

"No!" shouted Frey.

"No, yourself," Colbey sent back calmly. "You and I can't interfere with what humans and elves do to one another. You know that."

Frey clenched his hands so tightly his nails bit semicircles into his palms. "I can if you assist them. If you give those humans weapons to use against elves, I have a right to get involved."

"Foolishly."

"Calling me names won't change that." Frey shifted his hands to the arms of the chair, gouging fabric instead of flesh.

Colbey gathered a deep breath, then loosed it in a hiss between his teeth. "Help me, here. We're all part of this. I'm just trying to save Asgard from oblivion."

"Find another way. A way that doesn't require murdering elves. Why don't you kill all the humans instead?"

Colbey shook his head, frustrated. Their every disagreement came back to the day he'd forced Frey's magic so that Midgard survived and Alfheim died. "That won't work, and I think you know it."

Frey refused to accept Colbey's assessment. "I believe it would."

Colbey could not argue that point. He did not know for certain, but he refused to allow mankind to die. He had not rescued them for such a sacrifice. "All I'm asking for is a crack in the elves' defenses. Just one tiny opening that might give these humans a chance at an otherwise hopeless mission."

"What about Captain?" Ravn supplied.

Colbey had nearly forgotten his son's presence. Now he gave the boy his full attention. "Captain?" Hope surged. "The old elf, Captain? He's still alive?" He shook his head, dismissing the possibility. "He was thousands of years old when I knew him."

"I'm sure it's the same one," Ravn said. "An exiled old elf on the shore. He told me all about you."

What's a few centuries after millennia? "Good work, Ravn." Colbey did not give praise freely, and he could feel pride emanating from a son more accustomed to his father's criticism. He glanced at Frey. "And thank you for absolutely nothing." With that, he rose to leave, not waiting for Byggvir to assist. His doubts felt nearly as ponderous as the sword he could no longer wield. *Even if he still trusts me after all this time, will he help?* Colbey had no choice but to hope. He had only one tool to bargain with, his speaking ability, and he placed little faith in that. He had dedicated his life to combat. His mouth failed him repeatedly the way his sword never did. Never, at least, until his match with Ravn. Too many things had changed, and he had to change with them.

One other possibility came to Colbey's mind, a long shot but a prospect he could not simply discard. Aegir, the god of oceans and tides, might help him gather the remaining pieces of an ancient boat called the *Sea Seraph*.

Kevral anticipated difficulty convincing those companions who had not witnessed Colbey's visit to veer southward so near the Granite Hills which divided Santagithi, and a few other villages, from the rest of the Westlands. But Matrinka seemed relieved that others finally gave credence to her theories about magical enemies, and Darris accepted the deviation without comment. In the last week, he had grown quiet to the point of invisibility. When he did talk, he nearly always did so in song, as if he had gradually forgotten any other way of speaking. He performed songs so beautiful they conjured images from quiet, windy nights to raging battles. At other times, he hastily threw together rhymes scarcely better than an amateur poet's that seemed a mockery of his range and fluency.

Kevral enjoyed Darris' songs, especially the soft, poignant love ballads he crooned to Matrinka when he thought no one else could hear. The two had stopped trying to pretend nothing but friendship existed between them. Yet as far as Kevral could tell, their relationship went no further than moon-eyed stares and smiles. A law they respected too much to violate kept them apart. For now, however, their relationship mattered little more than Kevral's pending decision. Rescuing Griff had to take precedence.

As Colbey had warned, the direction the elf-eye sent them in switched intermittently from directly south to diagonally south and west, toward Béarn. Since Ra-khir and Kevral had described their meeting with Colbey, Darris insisted on riding beside the Renshai, periodically plying her with questions about the encounter, the only times he spoke normally. Then he would withdraw, mumbling rhyme schemes under his breath, experimenting with chords and tunes, then returning for more. At first, Kevral delighted in the opportunity to relive a meeting she had dreamed about nearly from birth, but never truly expected to have. Ra-khir filled in enough of the blanks to help her recall direct quotations, her only regret that she had not insisted the spar continue until her arms gave out from fatigue. She could have learned so much.

After most of a day's ride, Kevral believed she had recounted the episode fully, and the boundless interest of the bard's heir became more like petty badgering. "Please," he begged, in a heartrending tone she could not ignore. "When he spoke with you alone, what did you discuss?"

Kevral shook her head, unwilling to admit her man problems to Darris. "It was private. I don't want to talk about it."

"Please."

"No."

"Please."

"No!"

"Please." Darris wore at Kevral's resistance until the urge to kill him became almost overwhelming.

"Look, I don't want my personal life immortalized in some song. First, it isn't that interesting to anyone but me and a handful of others. Second, it would humiliate me. And, third, it's not something I'm willing to share with everyone in this group yet, let alone the entire world." Kevral could not help adding, "Now leave me alone."

Darris waited until the tirade finished, riding alongside Kevral for several moments of blissful silence. Then he added facetiously. "So you're saying it was a private conversation?"

Kevral growled, no longer tempering her reply with politeness. But before she could speak, Tae's horse skidded back to them from the path ahead. His sudden appearance surprised Kevral. Usually, he remained hidden, scouting ahead, then quietly returning to guide them to the quickest route or the best camping site. Now he directed them off the road with crisp jerks of his hands. His horse pranced, expending the nervous energy of its rider.

"Off. Over," Tae commanded softly. "Ambush ahead. Go!"

Kevral whirled her horse to obey. It took one plunging

step toward the brush, then halted as two men appeared directly in front of her. One brandished a spear, the other an arrow nocked and drawn on his bow. "Be still," the spearman commanded. Wicked, dark eyes glared at the party from a scarred face beneath a tangled mop of black hair. "Get off your horses, give us everything you have, then start walking back the way you came."

Kevral weighed options in the instant it took for the man's words to register. Obedience was not a possibility she considered. Running away would invite weapons in their backs. Charging ahead not only equally opened their defenses, it would only plow them into the rest of the ambush. Kevral did not hesitate. "Go! Protect Matrinka!" she shouted as she slammed her heels into the horse's flanks. The beast sprang directly for the two men at the woodside.

The spearman braced his weapon, barb aimed for the horse's chest. The bowman fired. Rallied by tales of Colbey cutting shafts from the air, she sliced for the speeding arrow. But the need to anticipate her next stroke ruined her timing. Her blade nicked the feathers. The tip plowed through the hole between hand and hilt, tearing a furrow of flesh from her palm. Diverted, the arrow plummeted. The horse rushed within a handbreadth of the spear before Kevral made her move. Her sword severed the tip from the spear, the pole bobbing harmlessly beneath her mount's chest. A reverse stroke with the blade carved a fatal wound in the spearman's side. He collapsed. The horse sidled to avoid him, hip crashing into the archer as he hastily dropped his bow in favor of a belt ax. This weapon, too, slipped from his grasp, and Kevral's downcut ended his life as well.

Only then, pain howled through Kevral's wound. She passed the sword to her other hand, hilt slick with blood, both hers and theirs. The injury hurt worse than experience told her it should, as if someone had rubbed stinging nettles into it. A musty, mouselike odor rose above the more familiar tang of fresh blood.

Kevral hauled a rag from her pocket to staunch the bleeding as she turned back to her companions. Nearly a dozen men stretched across the path ahead, brandishing a mismatched conglomerate of weapons, mostly belt axes and curved swords. Between the trees, she saw others, tossing aside bows, aim foiled by the shifting positions of their allies.

Ra-khir did not hesitate. He rode low, his mount's stride closing the distance between him and the enemy in a moment, red hair streaming like fire behind him. Darris hung back, horse turned sideways to guard Matrinka with its body and his own. Tae, as usual, was nowhere Kevral could see. An arrow arched through the trees, a desperate shot from an archer either confident of his skills or uncaring for his companions' safety. It speared Ra-khir's hood and struck his light mail shirt hard enough to jar him forward in his seat. Tangled in his cloak, it bounced with every movement of his horse.

Without time to properly bandage, Kevral wadded the rag into her injured hand. Soon, they would all become engaged in combat, and she would trust Matrinka in no hands but her own. Sheathing her sword temporarily, Kevral hauled the princess up behind her, leaving a yowling cat and a sputtering bard guarding an empty saddle. "Hang on!" she shouted to Matrinka. Using her injured arm to help steady her charge, Kevral again drew her sword. She spurred her horse into a wild lunge toward the enemy line.

Ra-khir's horse bit and kicked. As it kept enemies at bay on one side, Ra-khir concentrated on the other, slashing at dark heads with the ferocity of a Renshai. Grasping the pommel, he leaned out over the air, keeping his seat with impressive dexterity and catching an Easterner a clouting blow that left him lying in a lifeless heap. Ra-khir's horse overran the enemies' line. He reined in abruptly, momentum spinning his mount into a frantic half circle. Ra-khir loosed a mild expletive as he realized he had charged alone, and the ambush now separated him from his friends.

Then Kevral charged into the fray. No longer needed to tend Matrinka, Darris joined them. Swords seemed to fly for Kevral from every direction. She made a broad sweep, to separate enemies into a logical sequence, weaving defensive loops between Matrinka and danger while the Béarnide clung desperately to the saddle. Kevral cut down three, the last requiring a broad reach to her unweaponed side. In the same situation, she knew Colbey would either draw two swords to protect all sides or would launch into the flying maneuvers he had created especially for horseback combat. Wounded and burdened with a passenger, Kevral relied only on her own reflexes and skill, attentive to danger on all sides but especially at the back.

Darris claimed a position just off Kevral's right flank, his sword skill impressive now that he had chosen to join the battle. Ra-khir waded through enemies, guarding his off-side with his shield as well as his horse. Kevral struck down two more, hampered nearly as much by Darris' presence as by Matrinka. At length, the Easterners around Kevral fell dead. One engaged Ra-khir, and Darris finished his last with a wide sweep. The last broke suddenly, fleeing a losing battle.

"Hold on!" Kevral slammed her gelding's sides with her heels, and it pitched forward after the escaping ambusher. Before she reached him, however, Tae appeared so suddenly that the Easterner jerked backward with a gasp to keep from running into him. Tae and Kevral both lunged for him. Matrinka screamed, agony in Kevral's ears. Tae's eyes widened as he realized Kevral would not pull her charge, or her strike. He threw himself flat to the ground, rolling. Kevral's sword hammered the Easterner, the cut sending his body flying, and the gelding's hooves thundered past Tae.

Tae scrambled to his feet and halfway up the nearest tree before Kevral managed to turn her mount around and walk calmly to him. "I'm sorry," she said, not meaning a word of it and hoping her tone conveyed that.

Tae clung to the bark. "Are you safe now? I mean, as safe as you get. Not quite so deadly to people on your side."

Darris rode up, assisting Matrinka from the rump of Kevral's horse, a maneuver the young Renshai allowed without comment.

Tae started down the tree. "Because I don't think my heart can last through a lifetime of near misses. Forgive my criticism, but I only think it can stop and restart beating so many times." He dropped the jokes for a moment. "I've seen you fight. You could have pulled that attack."

"Of course, I could have." Kevral would not deny the truth, especially when doing so might disparage her sword work and her control. "I was trying to teach you a lesson."

"What," Tae demanded. "A critical analysis of the moments prior to death?"

"Not to disappear when we need you." Kevral used the bandage still stuffed in her injured fist to thoroughly clean her blade. The gentle pressure of steel against her hand shot fiery pangs through the wound. Nevertheless, she managed to finish the job and sheathe the sword.

Oblivious to Kevral's agony, Tae defended his actions. "Is that what you think I do? Scurry off to another dimension to hide while my friends risk their lives?"

The pain grew unbearable. Tae's words flowed around her like an Erythanian drum chant.

"I killed two Easterners in their camp in the woods and scattered their horses to even the fight. I'm not a Renshai or a knight or a bard. I'm not good enough with a weapon to plunge willy-nilly into combat and trust my sword to keep me alive. If I catch them by surprise, that usually gains me enough of an edge to make up for not having a lifetime of . . ." He trailed off, apparently cued by Kevral's demeanor. "Are you all right?"

Tae's voice seemed to come through a tunnel, from a long distance. Kevral nodded, answering more from habit than honesty. "I'm fine." Suddenly, staying on her horse seemed more chore than she could manage. She gripped the pommel with her uninjured hand while the world spun in lazy circles around her.

"Matrinka!" Tae hollered, the worry in his voice penetrating Kevral's fog. He turned his attention to the Renshai. "Here, let me help you down."

"I don't need help," Kevral responded mechanically, shifting her weight to the left for a dismount and overbalancing. She tumbled from the saddle with a suddenness that caught even Tae off his guard. He slowed her descent but failed to catch her. She flopped to the ground, unhurt but unsupported.

Ra-khir's face appeared above her. "Kevral, are you well?"

"She just slid right off," Tae explained.

"I'm fine," Kevral could not stop herself from answering, feeling as if she had drunk too much wine. "Are you all right?" She rolled to her hands and knees, but before she could stand, Ra-khir hefted her in strong arms.

"Are you all right?" Kevral repeated. "I saw them shoot you." A stomach cramp rammed through her abdomen, and she stiffened in his grip.

"Didn't make it through the mail," Ra-khir responded absently, allaying her concerns in order to redirect the discussion. "Where does it hurt?"

"My hand. My stomach." Kevral glanced about for Tae, who seemed to have disappeared again. Restlessness assailed her, and she found herself unable to focus. Her eyes shifted of their own accord, and the forest jumped overhead.

Ra-khir set Kevral down on a bed of blankets and leaves that Matrinka must have arranged. The Béarnide uncurled Kevral's fingers and studied the wound while Ra-khir paced in frantic circles that only worsened her vertigo. "Something caught her right across here," Matrinka drew a line parallel to the injury on Kevral's palm, then dumped icy water over it.

Pain ached from the wound, through Kevral's fingers, and up her arm in a rush. "Ow!" The immediacy of the agony momentarily cleared the fog, and she followed the first expletive with a swear word she had never used in her life. The cramp passed, dispersing as if the water's pressure had driven shards through the cut.

Matrinka shrank from Kevral's reaction. "Sorry," she said meekly. "No matter what else I do, I have to clean it."

Kevral managed to quip through a dry mouth and a tongue that felt swollen, "But do you have to clean it with broken glass?"

Matrinka dabbed at the wound more gently, then applied a salve, each faint touch sparking suffering that set Kevral sucking air through her teeth. The stress of trying to work under those conditions reached even Matrinka. She turned on Ra-khir suddenly. "Would you sit still! You're getting in my light, and your pacing is making me crazy!"

"Sorry," Ra-khir said contritely. "Can I help?"

"No," Matrinka said, then changed her answer instantly. "Yes. Do something to calm her, could you?"

Ra-khir carefully took Kevral's other hand, staying out of Matrinka's way and squeezing the Renshai's fingers with an affection that did manage to distract Kevral from the pain. Darris launched into a low, sweet song that seeped into Kevral's muscles and seemed to physically loosen them one by one.

Tae returned as Matrinka finished with the wound. "Here's your culprit!" He dropped an empty vial at Matrinka's feet, followed by one filled with purple-black berries.

Matrinka's brows twitched as she stared dumbly at the berries.

"What is it?" Ra-khir finally asked, his tone conveying that it must be something horrible, judging from Matrinka's expression.

Kevral shook her head, trying to clear it. She could scarcely contain the agitation that made her want to surge to her feet and do something, anything, to expend it.

"I have absolutely no idea," Matrinka admitted.

Darris continued playing, his words becoming entwined with the music so that Kevral could no longer distinguish individual sounds. She concentrated on his playing, the diversion allowing her to maintain control she would otherwise have lost.

"Isn't this what you do?" Tae pressed. "You studied healing. You know herbs."

"I studied healing in Béarn." Matrinka's voice gained the breathy quality that accompanied tears. "That's all the way on the other side of the world. I've never seen anything like this."

Tae glanced at Ra-khir. Kevral watched their faces whirl and blur together. "You better check yourself, Red. Make sure that arrow didn't nick you."

"It didn't touch me. I'm fine." Ra-khir shook off the question brusquely, unwilling to claim attention from one who needed it. Then, apparently recognizing the concern behind such a warning, he softened his tone. "Thank you for thinking of it and worrying for me. I really am fine."

Finally, Matrinka spoke directly to Kevral. "Kevral?"

Kevral's mind conjured a vortex through which Matrinka's words spun before they reached her ears. She managed to croak out a "yes."

"You've been poisoned, and we're trying to help you. Drink this."

Kevral wanted to tell Matrinka that her stomach seethed, and the idea of placing anything inside it seemed madness. But the healer poured a cold liquid down her throat before she could protest. Kevral forced herself to swallow.

"What is it?" someone asked. Kevral did not waste concentration identifying the speaker.

Kevral's limbs twitched, beyond her control.

"A universal antidote," Matrinka returned. "It may or may not help, but it certainly won't hurt."

Kevral's guts pitched and rolled, then lurched. She tried to twist her head, her only thought to protect the blankets, then vomited. The warm acid set off an elaborate reaction. She felt every muscle twitch into a violent convulsion, then all awareness left her.

Chapter 40

Frost Reaver's Charge

There can be no skill without pain.
—*Colbey Calistinsson*

Kevral awakened to nausea and stabbing pains in her injured hand. She shifted, the movement sending agony tearing through every muscle. It also brought Ra-khir instantly to her side. "Kevral," he whispered.

Kevral placed a hand on his, not quite ready to attempt speech but wanting to let him know she understood him. She likened the discomfort to the soreness she suffered daily, after proper practices; only this seemed more generalized, affecting some parts she rarely worked so hard. She opened her eyes. Moonlight glared down, seeming too bright through the branches. She squinted, blinking to protect her vision. Her stomach felt knotted, twisting and writhing within her. "What happened," she finally said.

"Poison," Ra-khir explained in a word, his green eyes sharp with rage, presumably against the immoral bowman who dared to use it. "You had a seizure."

"Oh." That explained the muscle pains.

"Several," he added.

"Oh," Kevral said again. "Am I done?" Her hand did not throb as much as it had the previous day, and she seemed to have more control over her mind and body.

"You seem to be. Do you feel better?"

"Mostly," Kevral dismissed the soreness. With time, that would pass. "What does Matrinka say?"

"She said . . ." Ra-khir winced, but honor forced him to tell the truth. "She said there're two parts to surviving any poisoning."

"The part I made it through."

"Right," Ra-khir gazed off into the distance and kissed her hand with an absent fondness, as if he did not realize he had done it. "When you fell asleep, we didn't know if you'd lapsed into a coma. Or if you'd awaken with your mind intact."

"Is that the second part?" Kevral ventured.

"No." Ra-khir clasped her hand in both of his and returned his attention directly to her. The moon lit blond highlights in his hair, softening its otherwise vibrant color. He looked like a Béarnian carving, an artist's rendition of the male ideal. "There could be damage to a vital organ. Matrinka says poisons that do that usually target one system."

If it's vital, one is all it takes. Kevral did not bother to speak the words aloud.

"Kevral Tainharsdatter, there's something I have to say to you."

Kevral closed her eyes again. *Here it comes.* She tried to steel herself from the inevitable flood of emotion his words would bring.

"I love you, Kevral." Ra-khir's tone captured the depth of feeling words could never fully express.

Despite preparation, Kevral could not stop the quickening of her heart. The previous day, she had believed Tae the one with whom she wanted to spend the rest of her life. Now, that idea seemed strange. The man who sat vigil by her bedside through the night suited her far better. The maneuver she had seen him execute from horseback was worthy of the master warrior horseman, Colbey himself. She needed a man who could surprise and challenge her with his weapon work, one who took his lessons with sword as seriously, or nearly so, as she did. And their upbringings matched more closely as well. "I love you, too," she admitted, speaking truth but feeling like a traitor to both men.

Kevral had expected Ra-khir's pronouncement. His next words caught her fully off her guard. "I'd like you to marry me."

Shocked, Kevral lost her voice.

Ra-khir lowered his head, waiting patiently for some reply.

"Now?" Kevral quipped, resorting to humor to dispel the tension.

"Not necessarily right now." Ra-khir laughed. "We've got other problems to deal with first."

"Like whether or not I live till tomorrow."

Ra-khir bit his lip. "So, the answer to my question. That's a maybe?"

"Yes." Kevral caught herself. "I mean, yes, that's a maybe not 'yes'...."

"I knew what you meant," Ra-khir reassured her. He huffed out a short sigh, caught her gaze with his, and delivered an insight Kevral never expected. "You love Tae, too, don't you?"

Kevral drew a deep breath, preparing for the long explanation Ra-khir deserved. But the words would not come, so she had to content herself with a simple, "Yes."

An uncomfortable silence followed. Finally, Ra-khir spoke, "What are you going to do?" His tone conveyed hope and curiosity rather than the demand she expected and he had every right to exercise.

"First, I'm going to survive."

Ra-khir nodded at the obvious. "That goes without saying. Your death would clearly preclude any other action."

"Second, I'm going to help rescue the heir to Béarn's throne."

"Of course."

Kevral paused while Ra-khir waited for the all-important third. "Then, I'm going to reassess how I feel and make a choice. Following that, I'll gladly take whichever of you is still waiting for an obnoxious, young warrior to make a decision she had no right to expect either of you to tolerate. Or, if you've both had the sense to leave me for someone more deserving, I'll die alone."

"Love comes when and where it does. I can't just throw it away like a sword too chipped to keep an edge. I'll wait," Ra-khir promised.

Kevral snuggled back into her blanket while Ra-khir prepared to watch over her again. "Somehow," she said through a yawn. "Though I have no right to expect it, I knew that's what you'd say."

* * *

Ra-khir kept a close watch over Kevral through a day of travel and into the next. Her attitude told him that her morning practice did not go as well as she hoped. That she had only just recovered from the acute effects of poison apparently did not factor into her expectations, or else not fully enough. Thinking back, Ra-khir remembered she had accepted the news about her convulsions so easily, leaving him to wonder if she truly understood how near she had come to dying or that she was not yet out of danger.

Losing Kevral to the delayed consequences of poison was only one of the many hazards plaguing the day's travel. Tae rode ahead most of the day, returning at intervals to drag them deeper into the woodlands. Their progress suffered, and, with it, their tempers. Easterners like the ones they fought blocked the trails at widespread intervals, and no one seemed eager to face their swords or toxic arrows again.

As day darkened into night, the trees became more foreboding. In daylight, the cheerful chorus of birds accompanied them through the trees, brush, and tangles; at night, they disappeared. The jerky rustle of squirrels collecting nuts and berries was replaced by unidentifiable swishing and the occasional whiff of musk where a fox had once passed. They chose not to light a fire, though no one dared to admit this caution stemmed from fear of whom the light or smoke might attract. To do so might mean forcing Kevral into a battle they could not win.

After the evening meal, Matrinka took a seat beside Kevral and asked the questions a healer needed to know while Darris, Ra-khir, and Tae listened in silence. Although Kevral seemed embarrassed to discuss personal details in front of an audience, even one of close friends, she replied promptly to all of Matrinka's queries. Only two abnormalities emerged: Kevral felt more fatigue than usual, and she had not urinated since the seizures.

Ra-khir slept fitfully until his watch, worried throughout his time awake, then woke Matrinka for hers with relief. No matter how bad Kevral's prognosis, it could prove no worse than the horrors his mind created from ignorance. Plucking at Matrinka's arm, he let her know he wanted to talk to her beyond earshot of their sleeping companions, and Matrinka followed him a short distance away. "What do you think?" he asked.

Matrinka looked at him sleepily. "I'm tired, but I can handle it."

Ra-khir was taken aback until he realized she had answered a different question than he'd asked. Concern had caused him to make assumptions. "I meant about Kevral. Do you think she'll be all right?"

Matrinka mulled this over longer than necessary. Surely, she already had an opinion. "She seems reasonably well." The tone suggested worries left unsaid.

"You'd expect her to be tired, wouldn't you?"

"Yes."

"That's only natural after poisoning, isn't it?"

"Yes, it is."

The assurances only partially relieved Ra-khir's tension. "And the urine?"

Matrinka took a deep breath through her nose and released it suddenly through her mouth. "I'm sorry, Ra-khir. It's a bad sign." She looked away, unable to meet his gaze. "A very bad sign."

Although Ra-khir had expected it, the truth still struck him a blow that took the strength from all the muscles in his limbs at once. He staggered a step, then caught his balance, which surprised him. His mind had prepared him for collapsing into a helpless heap. "Can you help her?" he asked meekly, feeling desperately useless.

"I can try." Matrinka took Ra-khir's hand, the touch warm and comforting. "But I can only guess. I don't know the poison, and I don't know how it works."

"But you know how the body works, right?"

"Actually, Ra-khir, all the healers in the world together only know a little bit about how the body works."

The news stunned Ra-khir. Healers had always seemed so knowledgeable. "But someone must know what to do for people who don't . . ." Even the euphemism came hard. ". . . pass water."

"I do know that," Matrinka admitted, though her voice conveyed nothing more positive. "But it depends on the cause. Some of the cures for one could be disastrous for others."

"Oh," Ra-khir said, uncertain where to take the conversation. He suspected details would only confuse him, and he could now see where inexactness could take far more study than distinct facts. If every malady had a simple answer, becoming a healer would not require so much schooling. "So what do we do now?"

"All I can do is support her and hope."

"And her chances?"

Matrinka shrugged, the moisture suddenly blurring her dark eyes all the answer he needed.

Ra-khir remained in place, listening to the rising and falling trill of insects and desperately trying not to imagine the world continuing without Kevral. He felt as if sorrow was carving a hole in his chest. Soon, it would leave nothing but a dark emptiness and pain where his heart had once beat. "What if I gathered some details about the poison?"

"What do you mean?"

"Well, Tae said he thought he'd seen those berries in some of the clearings we passed recently. If it's common in these parts, someone might know how to treat it."

Matrinka looked up, her expression momentarily hopeful. Then she shook her head. "We don't know where to find people here. And even if we did, we'd have to deal with killers on the road. And then, what would be the likelihood that you'd find a healer?"

"I'll find one." Ra-khir steeled himself, determined to locate a healer or die in the attempt. He could not stand by helplessly while Kevral died. Neither love nor honor would allow it, and the guilt would haunt him to the end of his own life. "I'm leaving in the morning."

Matrinka's grip tightened on his hand. "No, Ra-khir. It's too dangerous."

"I'm leaving in the morning," Ra-khir affirmed, surrendering no opening for argument. "Thank you for—"

"Don't thank me!" Matrinka interrupted. "I won't take responsibility for a bad decision." Her attitude changed from assertive to pleading. "Please don't go. Kevral may recover on her own. I don't want to lose you both to a bleak quest without much chance for success."

"I'm going," Ra-khir finished emphatically. "It's for the best."

Matrinka clearly did not agree, but she did not voice her opposition again. "We could all go."

"No." The idea rankled. "First, we don't have the time to spare. Second, I can move faster by myself. And third, one man alone is far less likely to draw the hostility or interest of highwaymen."

"And far less likely to survive an attack," Matrinka reasoned.

"I can avoid them."

"Not as well as Tae can."

The words sent a stab of irritation through Ra-khir. Unwilling to consider the matter carefully enough to decide whether his discomfort stemmed from jealousy over Kevral or annoyance at the intimation that Tae could perform the job better, Ra-khir shoved his feelings aside. Either emotion was negative, and a Knight of Erythane did not allow such things to interfere with thought or action. "Tae could get there easier, but he looks too much like the people who ambushed us. Western townsfolk won't talk to an Easterner, especially if he comes demanding information about a local poison. An Erythanian knight-in-training, they'll trust."

Matrinka nodded, the words undeniably true. The valor of the Knights of Erythane had long been legend throughout the West.

"You keep moving south. I'll catch up."

"If I can't talk you out of it, I can only wish you good luck."

"Thank you."

"Please," Matrinka said, finally letting go of Ra-khir's hand. "Don't thank me."

The day dawned bright, sunlight warm and blinding through the branches. Ra-khir waited only long enough to ascertain that Kevral still had not urinated before heading for the horses. Matrinka could explain his mission after he left. He did not want the others to interfere.

When Ra-khir reached the horses, however, he immediately noticed a new one among them. A familiar white charger grazed placidly beside Kevral's gelding. *Frost Reaver?* Ra-khir glanced around quickly, seeing no sign of the old Renshai who had spoken with Kevral such a short time ago. The stallion looked up as Ra-khir approached, whinnying a greeting. He trotted to Ra-khir's side, nuzzling his arm.

"Hello, handsome." Ra-khir greeted the animal with gentle strokes across the muzzle and down to the velvety nose. He glanced over the graceful arch of its neck, seeking his own mount, which seemed to have disappeared. Ra-khir's brow furrowed as he glanced from Tae's dark brown to

Darris' nervous bay to Kevral's bay and Matrinka's chestnut. Ra-khir's horse was not among them.

Ra-khir attempted to walk around Frost Reaver, but the stallion followed his movement, looping back into his path. He called for his mount, a long, high-pitched whistle that used to bring his gray running. The heads of all four brown horses rose, but the fifth did not appear. Concern arose, beaten back by a force in Ra-khir's mind that he could not name. Somehow, he knew his horse was well and would not come to any call. He studied Frost Reaver. The wide nostrils and the broad depth of chest promised stamina, while the muscular legs and rump guaranteed speed. The arching neck and delicate head added a beauty that seemed too much to expect from an animal with so many practical virtues. Sunlight slanted through the treetops, and all the rays seemed to converge in rainbow patterns around the great stallion. Though he knew it a trick of the light, Ra-khir caught his breath. The knowledge that he would someday own a horse like this one sparked joy and a little pride. He suppressed the latter, still believing himself one of the luckiest men in the world.

Hoping he read Colbey's intentions correctly, Ra-khir slipped his bridle over the white's head. Reaver stood still, accepting leather and bit without complaint. Encouraged, Ra-khir added his saddle. The stallion remained in place through all the adjustments and tugging. Finally, Ra-khir prepared to mount. Here, he hesitated. It seemed sacrilege to clamber onto the back of a god's horse without his express permission; yet, clearly, the god had intended him to do exactly that. Ra-khir took the stallion's presence as a sign Colbey had sanctioned a mission that Matrinka believed madness. Whether the god actually supported his idea or had simply found a way to make him faster, Ra-khir did not speculate. Riding up on a white charger, he would have no difficulty convincing any Westerner that he was, already, a Knight of Erythane.

Ra-khir considered the deceit inherent in such an action. Guilt trickled through him at the thought of misleading others into believing him a full-fledged knight before his testing, yet he saw the need for such an innocent and subtle ruse. He would never consider calling himself anything more than a knight apprentice, but townsfolk would likely not know or be interested in such details. He would not be tricking them, merely allowing them their expectations.

Having convinced himself, Ra-khir placed a foot in the stirrup. Before he could swing aboard, a hand clasped his shoulder.

Surprised by the sudden contact, Ra-khir tensed and hurriedly returned his foot to the ground. He spun, expecting to confront an enraged Renshai. Instead, he met all too familiar features.

"Head southeast," Tae suggested. "There're farms that way and maybe a small village or two. That'll keep you partially on the same course as us, so you'll only have to make a triangle instead of covering the same ground. You're more likely to catch up sooner that way. And we're likely to need you." Tae raised his brows slightly to emphasize the dependence he would not have admitted scant weeks ago. "Do you want me to go with you?"

Ra-khir started a "no" that he stifled. A swift and negative response would offend a man with whom he had spent far too long developing a friendship both had initially resisted. "Someone has to keep the others out of trouble."

"Right." Tae glanced back to the camp. "I'll be watching for your return, you know, so don't go killing everything that startles you."

Ra-khir smiled. "I'm not Kevral."

Tae chuckled, though it sounded strained. "Good luck, Red. I mean that."

"I know you do." Ra-khir pitched his words to reassure. Tae had as much resting on his success as he did, though he could scarcely have blamed the young Easterner for hoping Ra-khir died and Kevral survived the poison without him.

Frost Reaver took off at a ground-eating lope so smooth it scarcely felt like movement. Tae had mentioned nothing about the horse, but Ra-khir was certain the wily Easterner had noticed. Though he rarely revealed his knowledge, those quick, brown eyes missed nothing.

Soon, all thoughts of Tae left Ra-khir's mind as he concentrated on the sights around him. The trees whipped past. Any lesser horse would have balked at racing through virgin territory, but Frost Reaver continued his rapid, quick-footed movement without protest. It seemed more as if he chose their way, though he responded instantly to Ra-khir's commands and shifts in direction. Uncertain whether the animal had some divine means of avoiding bad terrain or just total trust in his rider, Ra-khir paid close attention to the footing. He would not let any animal come to harm under his care, especially not one belonging to a god and that also represented every facet on which he based his honor and his life. So he steered, with or without need, protecting the pink hooves from jutting roots, holes, and irregularities. When he dared to take his eyes from their path, he scanned the horizon for any sight of habitation. In the East, he could never have ridden a few horse lengths without running into a crowded city or a farmer's field. In the more sparsely populated West, however, he knew he could ride for a day without seeing land belonging to anyone. Once they crossed the divide onto the barren salt flats called the Western Plains, he knew he could never find help.

Within a few hours, the forest thinned to locusts, poplar, and spindly *binyal* trees. Frost Reaver dodged a copse of thistle and emerged abruptly into full daylight glistening from straight rows of wilting vines. The harvest had come and gone, and the vines still clung tenaciously to stakes and one another. The distant, mellow lowing of cows reached Ra-khir's ears like music. He headed toward the sound, trusting Frost Reaver to remain on the paths between the crops, though nothing remained to salvage.

The noise became more distinct with every step. The short, contented moos seemed out of place after the sudden and brutal violence that had torn their party. Soon, the animals became visible as brown and white mounds shifting amidst scanty trees in an otherwise open pasture. Beyond them, he saw a gray barn so faded it seemed to disappear against the horizon and, beside it, a small cottage.

Ra-khir shifted direction to skirt the pasture. The cows ignored Frost Reaver as thoroughly as he did them; only four of the two dozen odd animals even raised their heads. Ra-khir kept his attention fixed on the little house. His heart pounded a loud, slow cadence that quickened the nearer he drew to the buildings. Shortly, he would discover the distance and difficulty of his course to the nearest healer.

As Ra-khir rode past the barn, a clatter inside stopped him. Turning Frost Reaver, he headed back toward its broad opening. Massive hinges supported a heavy, open door probably closed only in the worst weather. The sweet odor of straw and the fresher, greener smell of hay wafted cleanly to his nose.

Inside, beams supported a peaked roof, and wooden ledges around the walls held tools of myriad shapes and sizes. A plump, gray-haired woman hauled piles of empty buckets, shooing away four mewling cats with her free hand. The animals ignored her gestures, twining around her ankles. Despite the obvious weight of the buckets, she seemed to have no difficulty carrying them, aside from the presence of the cats hampering every step.

"Hello, good lady," Ra-khir called cheerfully.

The woman glanced up, sun-wrinkled face peering through stray strands of hair that had escaped from her bun. "Well, hello." She studied him. A polite smile grew gradually, as if she wanted to welcome him but wrestled suspicion.

Ra-khir believed it best to ease her concerns as swiftly as possible. "I am Ra-khir of Erythane, son of Knight-Captain Kedrin and apprentice knight to the Erythanian and Béarnian kings: His Grace, King Humfreet, and His Majesty, King Kohleran."

"A knight?" The woman did not wait for confirmation. "Oh, dear. It's worse than I thought."

"What's worse?" Ra-khir asked with growing alarm.

"I isn't exactly sure." The woman set down her buckets and wiped grimy hands on the hem of her shift. "First, there was them stories of people what disappeared or got chased away while travelin'. Then, people stopped comin'. Even the youngster what delivers my milk to the village isn't been here in more'n a week."

Though relieved to find it a problem he already knew about, Ra-khir worried for the far-reaching consequences he had not yet considered. With a field of crops and a herd of cows, this farm family seemed unlikely to starve. But he grew alarmed for all the people cut off from necessities by the halt in trade. Although he hated to be blunt, Ra-khir did not have time for small talk. "I'm looking for a healer, good lady. Where can I find one?"

"Pudar?" the woman suggested unhelpfully, then laughed. "When you live so far from your neighbors, there isn't no time to haul folks around when they's sick or hurt. You got to know some basic remedies at least." Her eyes narrowed slightly, from thoughtful concern not suspicion. "One of yours get cut up by those hoodlums?"

"Yes," Ra-khir returned, seeing no need to supply details about the actual injury. "But we can handle that. It's this we don't know how to fix." He removed the vial of berries from his pocket, dismounted, and headed toward the woman with his arm extended.

The woman waited patiently for his approach, without a touch of fear. Ra-khir attributed her courage to his status as a knight and blessed the reputation for kindness and heroism they had gained over the centuries. It rescued him from the need to convince while Kevral slipped nearer to death. Frost Reaver remained quietly in place. Ra-khir trusted the horse not to stray.

Eventually, Ra-khir drew near enough for the woman to take the vial from him. She reached out a hand, and Ra-khir dropped it into her palm. She studied the berries, first the warped image the glass allowed. Then she removed the cork and examined the contents through the top. She nodded sagely, then dumped two of the purple berries into her hand.

Ra-khir stiffened, uncertain how the poison took effect. It seemed unlikely that simply touching a berry would harm her, yet he dared not allow her to take such a chance. "Careful," he warned. "They're poisonous."

The woman looked up from the berries to meet Ra-khir's gaze. Soft, blue eyes danced with a surprising amount of life, and she giggled like an adolescent. "Did you think I was going to eat them?"

"No. Of course not." Ra-khir hoped he had not offended her. "I'm just not sure how poisonous they are. Our healer never saw anything like them."

"Pissweed." She dumped the berries back into their container. "Least that's what we call it. I'm sure it's got a fancy name, too. Grows 'round here occasional. Least once a year, one of the cows gets a few mouthfuls."

Excitement flashed through Ra-khir. "What happens to them?" He winced, afraid to hear the reply.

"Oh, their mouths swell up pretty bad, and it hurts them, too, by the way they act. If they get enough, their whole neck swells, and they strangulate." She studied Ra-khir and the effect her words were having on him before continuing. "Most of the time, though, that don't happen. Then, they stagger around, maybe fall down. Maybe die. If they lives through that then, about a day or so later . . ."

Ra-khir hung on every word.

". . . one of a few things happens. Can be nothin'. Or they starts pissin' constantly or not at all. Or they gets blood in their water. That's why we calls it pissweed."

"What do you do for them?" Ra-khir asked through a mouth that had gone painfully dry. Though he feared the answer, he desperately needed it.

"Depends. If they's goin' all the time, you gots to make sure they's got water all the time. They goes through bucket after bucket, and you can't let it get dry. Seems obvious now, but it tooked me a long time to figure that one out. If you don't keep up, they dies. The ones what bleed, I isn't figured out how to help them yet, 'cept they seems to do better with grass than grain, and if you salt the hay, you always lose them. They seems to do better with lots of water, too. Their piss either gets clearer till they gets better or bloodier till they dies."

Ra-khir refrained from rushing the woman, letting her come to the cows in Kevral's situation in her own time. He nodded vigorously to indicate that he was listening.

"The ones what stops pissin', they's the hardest."

Ra-khir choked back a groan.

"Took me forever to get this figured out. Lost several good ones to not knowing."

Come on. Come on. Ra-khir resisted any words or gestures that would demonstrate the impatience that made every instant a torment.

"Those ones you don't let drink even though they wants to. Water's like more poison to them. Grain hurts them, too. I either don't feed them at all or sticks to grass."

"What usually happens to them?"

"With that treatment? 'bout half live. I loses the others within a day or two."

A day or two? Desperation exploded through Ra-khir, and the realization that he had given Kevral a drink from his own supply only worsened the terror. "And there's no antidote?"

"None that I knows of," the woman admitted. "But I isn't a healer."

"Thank you, good lady," Ra-khir said, scrambling back to Frost Reaver with a haste that grazed the edges of rudeness.

He did not bother to waste time taking back the vial. "You've helped immensely."

The woman's reply disappeared into the rustle of movement as Ra-khir swung Frost Reaver around and pounded back the way he had come. He believed he heard a "good luck" beneath the clamor. *Luck may not prove enough this time.* Frantic worry kept him low over Frost Reaver's neck as they passed around the pasture, through the field, to the woods; and he resisted the urge to quicken the charger's pace. The steady lope was already too fast for the terrain, but Ra-khir knew he needed to return before Kevral drank too much. Kevral's life hinged on Frost Reaver's speed.

With this in mind, Ra-khir hauled back on the reins. Obediently, the horse stopped, the knight-in-training leaping from the saddle before the hooves came fully still. Tearing a young locust the width of his wrist from the soil by the roots, he carved off branches and roots with brisk flicks of his knife blade. Remounting, he carved a point on his crude spear while Frost Reaver continued his smooth, rolling gait. Once finished, Ra-khir redirected the white charger toward the road.

The horse complied without hesitation, whisking in an arc toward the means of open travel. Once on the packed earth, he stretched his long legs into a level run that seemed more like flight. The pace lanced a shock of fear through Ra-khir, emptying his mind of other purpose; and he did nothing but cling to saddle and spear for several moments. The white mane whipped into his face, stinging; and air thundered through his ears. Then, gradually, he shed his apprehension. Excitement torrented in to fill the gap. As a child, he had wondered how a bird might feel, arrowing through the clouds at a speed he could only imagine. Now, he felt certain he knew. Wind funneled through mail and lashed his cloak into a wild dance. The feeling seemed to define a freedom he never realized existed.

Then reality intruded in the form of three Easterners who stepped into the path in front of him. Determination hardened Ra-khir's thoughts. He did not have to hear them speak threats to know they meant him harm. He lowered his spear until it jutted ahead of Frost Reaver's nose. The charger jerked slightly as the pole appeared suddenly in his right-side vision, the discrepancy a barely discernible bump in the stallion's movement. Reaver lowered his head, his pace quickening to a rocketing gallop that shocked Ra-khir who believed the horse had already been racing at its topmost speed. He crouched, low and tight to Reaver's neck.

The Easterners scurried aside, and the horse charged harmlessly through the opening. Ra-khir dared not revel in this minor victory. More would surely come, but he would not let them slow him. His mission was too vital to interrupt, and anyone who deliberately stepped into his way deserved the suicide they chose. This time, he would let no one stop him.

The next attempt came sooner than Ra-khir expected. Within a dozen strides, he came upon another ambush. Bowmen lined one side of the road, so as not to risk companions on the opposite side, and swordsmen formed a line directly across the path. Frost Reaver did not slow. Ra-khir took a deep breath, expecting death to come in the form of bolts and arrows, yet he refused to falter. If he paused to fight, he had no chance at all. "Go! Go! Go!" Ra-khir shouted to his mount unnecessarily. He jerked on the right rein, veering the white charger to the edge of the woods and the waiting archers. Suddenly menaced, the bowmen scrambled out of the way. A few loosed shafts, their aim foiled by the abrupt movement as well as the unexpected need for defense. A bolt rattled off Ra-khir's mail. Another skimmed Reaver's flank, leaving a bloody furrow that marred the sleek hide but did not slow his charge.

Then horse and rider sprang into the ambush line. Ra-khir's spear slammed home, the impact sickening. Having never actually struck a human target with a spear before, Ra-khir was caught unprepared. Impact tore the weapon from his hands. Frost Reaver rocked, hooves trampling a body. Ra-khir fumbled for his sword, drawing it just as the enemy's line shattered. Men scurried from their path, and Frost Reaver sprinted ahead.

Ra-khir knew only relief. Battle grunts and bellows of triumph had no place in a knight's repertoire, and a lusty shout of honor seemed out of place after such a brutal maneuver. Desperation, determination, and luck had won the moment, not skill, but Ra-khir did not care. Soon he would reach Kevral and his companions. Anyone else who stood in his way would pay.

Frost Reaver galloped onward.

Chapter 41

The Southern Weathered Range

*Warriors make their decisions on the battlefield,
faster than an eye blink; and they rarely get a
second chance to be wrong.*

—Colbey Calistinsson

The road disappeared beneath Frost Reaver's ground-eating
strides, and the trees lining either side seemed to funnel Ra-
khir through the forest. The sun drew higher, then sank toward gray evening. Ra-khir never slowed until a dark horse
and rider appeared suddenly in his path. Weary rage built
within Ra-khir again, and he lowered his newest spear for
another charge. The strangeness of finding a lone Easterner
after massed ambushes raised his suspicions. He reined in
Frost Reaver for a cautious and better look.

"Finally," the rider said, the voice unmistakably Tae's.

Still careful, Ra-khir couched his makeshift weapon and
sent Frost Reaver forward at a walk. Within a few steps, he
recognized Tae definitively. Froth bubbled from his mount's
lips, and foam streaked its dark hide. Head sagging, it
waited with an uncharacteristic stillness, not wasting a single
movement.

Tae made an unreadable gesture then glided his horse into
the brush on the right side of the pathway. Ra-khir followed
wordlessly. They wound through the trunks, vines clutching
at Reaver's muddy hooves. Only after he had led them two
man lengths from the road did Tae turn his head to speak.
The horse remained in place, neck low and head wilting. It

cropped lazily at the overgrowth, as if the effort of eating cost too much energy. "You overran us, you know."

"Oh," Ra-khir returned sheepishly. "I didn't know."

Tae turned his mount so that they now traveled in the exact opposite direction, at a parallel. "Didn't think I'd ever catch you. Fast horse you got there."

Ra-khir read the unasked question beneath Tae's observation. "It's Colbey's."

"Colbey's?" Tae repeated, not demanding explanation, though Ra-khir felt obliged to give it.

"He substituted it for mine. Apparently, he had a stake in getting Kevral better."

Tae mumbled something scarcely intelligible. Ra-khir considered the garbled words for several seconds before interpreting them as, "Don't we all." Then Tae spoke more clearly, "Or else he has a stake in our mission."

"That does seem a little more likely," Ra-khir admitted. The timing of Colbey's return for Frost Reaver would set that question to rest. If he took the horse back that night, he would clearly have lent it for Kevral. Ra-khir never doubted Colbey would come for the stallion; the bond between knight and charger was like a kinship.

"Did you find a cure?" Tae asked hopefully, the obvious question.

"Not exactly," Ra-khir admitted. "But I learned some treatment ideas that might make more sense to Matrinka."

Tae went silent, and Ra-khir followed suit, trusting the Easterner's judgment when it came to avoiding enemies. He wanted to tell Tae everything would turn out all right, to soothe the fires of fear and doubt that raged within them both. But Ra-khir did not have the antidote that could restore sure faith, and he refused to lie. It occurred to him that Tae had worked himself and his horse into a lather to see to it Ra-khir did not become lost. Tae could have let Ra-khir ride past without repercussions; eventually, enemies would have overpowered a lone knight-in-training on the cold, unfamiliar roadways through these Western woods. That Tae had gone to so much effort to keep a rival alive impressed Ra-khir. He would never have given the street urchin that much credit. Apparently, they both intended to fight an honest war for Kevral's hand. Either that, or Tae trusted him to have found an antidote.

Brush rattled, crackled, and snapped beneath the horses'

feet. Birds twittered and trilled in the upper branches. Otherwise, Ra-khir heard no sounds until garbled speech sifted to his hearing. He recognized Matrinka's gentle voice. Almost the moment he did, she went quiet, and she and Darris peered toward him and Tae as they crashed nearer. Darris' horse whinnied a greeting.

Ra-khir winced at the loud sound that might draw enemies and noticed several of his companions did the same. He and Tae joined the others, fitting smoothly into the pattern. Tae headed directly for a position near Kevral. Though Ra-khir would have liked to do the same, he drew up beside Matrinka instead, to discuss the information he had gleaned about the poison. She listened intently as he described the conversation with the woman on the farmstead. Darris, too, listened raptly. He had long ago grown accustomed to the accursed bard-curiosity that forced him to learn from every word, movement, sound, and nuance. The details that appeared in Darris' songs attested to the thoroughness of his observation skills.

Matrinka remained silent for a long time after Ra-khir finished. Curled on the rump of her horse, Mior did not move except for the gentle stirring of her fur by the wind.

Ra-khir waited anxiously for what seemed like far longer than politeness or propriety demanded. "Has she been drinking?"

Matrinka nodded sadly. "As the day went on, I started limiting her more and more. I've given her a few herbs to try to slow the damage, and they seem to be helping. At least, she seems to be doing all right so far."

Matrinka's words told only half the story. Ra-khir fished for the rest. "Is she getting better?"

"No," Matrinka admitted.

Ra-khir glanced over to make certain Kevral could not overhear them. Tae had her deep in conversation, a situation Ra-khir found both merciful and painful. "What happens if she doesn't start . . ." Embarrassed about discussing a function usually kept private, he stumbled over the words. ". . . doesn't start—"

Matrinka obviated his need to finish. "Then things stay in the body that are supposed to come out."

"Water," Ra-khir suggested, returning his attention to Matrinka. "If we just don't give her any, won't she be all right?"

"It's not that simple." Matrinka sighed, again placed into the position of trying to explain months of training in a few sentences. "Urine isn't the same as water. And there're other ways the body loses water besides urine."

"Like sweat."

"Right. And spit. So you can't just take a person completely off water. It would kill them. Just because someone isn't putting out urine doesn't mean they have too much water. More often, they have too little."

"I see," Ra-khir said graciously, though he did not. He withdrew from the conversation, certain he could never understand and glad Matrinka did. He had always believed himself intelligent. The strategic and historical parts of his knight training had come easily to him. Healing, however, seemed like a foreign language. "So what do we do?"

"I'm still deciding that." Now, Matrinka glanced at her other companions. "If the woman says stopping the water works, I don't think we have much choice but to try it. If it gains us a day, that's a long time."

Ra-khir froze, horror overtaking him again, though the farm woman's description had prepared him for this. "A day is a long time?"

Matrinka met his gaze, her eyes soft as a puppy's. "There's a reason why we pass urine every day, Ra-khir. It needs to go out."

Ra-khir glanced at Kevral again. The round features and huge eyes that had once belonged to an irritating child he had mistaken for a boy now defined the emotion love. The wispy white brows and short blonde locks drew him like a beacon. He wanted to enfold her in an embrace that bound not just their souls but their bodies as well. If he held her tightly enough, they could entwine into one and then, perhaps, he could take over the functions her body no longer performed. Logically, he knew it was impossible, yet he held the image of hope as long as his mind allowed the illusion. It carried him into the evening and another night camped in the woods.

As usual, Kevral practiced while the others built the camp. Ra-khir performed his share of the work as swiftly as possible, ministering to the horses while Matrinka and Darris spread blankets and divided rations for the evening meal and Tae attended to the tack. Ra-khir fussed over Frost Reaver with the same dedication as he would his gray, and he treated every horse as if it were his own. He tried to focus on his work, but his thoughts always slipped back to Kevral and the fate awaiting her in days. At the time, the farm woman's suggestions had seemed vital. Now they became little more than a waste of the last precious moments he could have shared with the woman he loved.

Ra-khir finished his work and hurried to the heavily wooded site Kevral had chosen for her practice. She swung and capered amid the trunks, her confident slashes missing the trees by no margin Ra-khir could see or fathom. Yet, though he could not match her skill, he noticed the differences in her technique. Her movements seemed slower than he recalled, though still quicker than his own. Her strikes lacked the agility so familiar it remained vividly etched upon his memory. And Kevral's pinched expression revealed a frustration that validated Ra-khir's observations. For several moments, he watched her from between the branches, reveling in radiance magnified a hundredfold by action. Yet, as wondrous as the sight seemed to him, Kevral's obvious tension riddled his joy with painful holes. At length, aching from empathy and knowing his observation of both her Renshai practice and her weakness would wound her, he withdrew.

At Matrinka's suggestion, Kevral drank no water, even to replace the sweat that streamed down her forehead after a grueling practice that had lasted far longer than usual. Enraged by her new limitations, Kevral spoke only in monosyllables through dinner and retired early, mumbling something about a mouth so dry the blacksmith could use it to forge his swords.

Ra-khir murmured a short prayer to Thor and Odin. *Please, gods. Let her live. But if you must take her, let her last moments be filled with happiness and peace, not bitterness. Send me the necessary words to comfort her in her time of need. Please, gods, just let Kevral live.* Despite the sorrow and need plaguing his every thought and action, exhaustion brought merciful sleep to Ra-khir.

The next morning brought no improvement in Kevral's condition. The remainder of the party drank surreptitiously, making no mention of Kevral's puffy face and swollen ankles. But Ra-khir found himself unable to take a sip of water. He rode Frost Reaver and tried not to feel too much pride at Kevral's awe. For the first time, she truly seemed to respect his presence, a goal that had eluded Ra-khir since their first humiliating meeting. It appeared she had finally learned to approve of him, too late. It bothered Ra-khir that an action of Colbey's, rather than his own, was the source of that appreciation.

As the morning wore on, the forest thinned enough to reveal mountains on the horizon. The gray magnificence of the Southern Weathered Range was familiar; Béarn's castle had been carved from its crags. Yet Ra-khir had gone so long without sight of the familiar rocky cliffs rising into cloudy obscurity. Surely, they could have seen the mountains weeks ago had the trees not intertwined so densely overhead. Even now, the close-packed trunks admitted only glimpses of dull rock, revealing little of the shimmering, breathtaking grandeur that delighted him throughout his childhood.

Shortly, Tae redirected his companions to the road. "It's clear to the pass, and there's only one way through the mountains, at least only one nearby."

No one complained about the shift in course. One by one, they emerged from the dimness of the forest and onto a crude path, once rarely used and now speckled with boot tracks. Ra-khir needed no explanation. Passage through the mountains led to the Western Plains, a vast, sandy wasteland too harsh for habitation. The tracks came from Easterners who had crossed through the only fordable route through the Great Frenum Mountains to the plains and on into the Westlands.

The transition from forest dankness to open sunlight dazzled Ra-khir's eyes more than he expected after the previous day's ride. The mountains loomed, filling the southern skyline like a craggy wall built to support the clouds and sun. To the East, more forest obscured near vision, but now Ra-khir could see mountains filling the spaces between treetops and horizon.

"Careful," Tae cautioned. "I've crossed the passes before. We should be able to get the horses through them, but there're places where it gets too narrow to safely ride two abreast. There're twists and switchbacks, so we can't go fast. We need to take it slow and keep a constant eye for enemies. Better to make up the lost time on the plains than take any chances on the rocks. We should make it through in a day or two, regardless."

Had the knight's training not included a study of terrain, Ra-khir would not have known about switchbacks, trails through mountains that ascended or descended in a sawtooth fashion. It surprised him that no one asked for a description until he realized that the other three had spent at least a little time in Béarn's castle. Reportedly, some of the tower staircases were once mountain switchbacks.

"Let's go," Kevral took the lead suddenly, an uncharacteristic action. Usually, she let Darris or Tae lead, hanging back to protect Matrinka.

Ra-khir could not help speculating about Kevral's motivation. Though rarely used, the pass through the mountains would probably be well marked, if not with paint and flags, then because of the volume of recent traffic. Trouble now seemed more likely to come from ahead than behind, and Kevral likely wanted to face any enemies they encountered first. A natural instinct rose inside Ra-khir, to slip ahead and protect the woman he loved. Honor, too, drove him to take the burden of enemies onto himself. He struggled with both, battling them back into perspective. Had he journeyed with only Knights of Erythane, he would have automatically seen the wisdom in placing the strongest warrior in the front.

Tae rode up beside Kevral, a logical location for the only party member who had previously traversed the route. Ra-khir suffered a pang of jealousy that made him feel weak and petty as he took the rear position, behind Matrinka and Darris. The party had evaded rather than defeated the enemies behind them, leaving a threat he would not allow the bard's heir to face alone. In that formation, they headed toward the pass.

At first, the horses tripped over the uneven ground and stumbled on loose hunks of shale, except Frost Reaver who seemed as surefooted here as on the roadways. Over time, the animals adjusted to the change, and their shoes rang against stone in even rhythms. Pathways so wide the enclosing walls disappeared into fog narrowed abruptly to chasms that admitted only one horse at a time. As they rose higher, ledges jutted over dizzying heights, a fall to the crags below meaning certain death. The horses huddled against the solid side of the mountain at these times, sometimes so closely their riders had to hover sideways in the saddle to protect their ankles from banging against the crags.

Concentrating on the terrain, the party spoke little. Darris and Matrinka seemed content to ride side by side in silence when the pathways allowed it. Darris' bard curse had accustomed them to a quiet that would have seemed awkward to other couples. Tae and Kevral occasionally made gestures that indicated they chatted, but Tae clearly held up more than his share of the conversation. Trusting his mount, Ra-khir did not require the intensity of attention to each step that the others did. He kept his ears tuned to sounds around and behind them, listening to the trickle and soft patter of water running along the rocks in rivulets. Rare bird calls cut through the mountain stillness, in songs Ra-khir did not recognize from home or their months of travel through wilderness. Tiny brown lizards skittered from patches of sunlight, and insects chittered deep inside crevices so that the mountains seemed to vibrate with the sound.

The party did not stop for the midday meal, and each ate and drank in his own time, without fanfare. Kevral did not eat. Once, she pulled her waterskin from her pack, the gesture thoughtless habit. A moment later, she returned it without drinking.

They approached the highest point of the pass in midafternoon, still leagues from the mountain's summit. Its peak disappeared among the clouds, a distant blur that seemed endlessly high. The path ascended in a long, zigzagging switchback that kept Ra-khir always one level below Kevral. Tae dropped back on the narrower parts of the passes. Sunlight sheened from the granite, reflecting glimmers from the shoes of Kevral's and Tae's horses with every step.

Suddenly, Frost Reaver tensed, shying several steps forward. A moment later, a rumble ground through Ra-khir's hearing, seeming to come from all directions. The charger surged forward, crashing into the rump of Darris' horse and sending it dancing ahead in a wild scramble. Rubble bounced from the ledge above Kevral, ricocheted over her head, and crashed down the mountainside with a deafening roar. The ground shook, jerking Ra-khir into helpless tremors and threatening to tear him from the road like so much flotsam. Matrinka's mount stumbled. Darris fought his horse as it reared wildly and tried to run. Frost Reaver braced his feet and held steady, even as tons of rock slammed the path at his heels. A stone hammered Ra-khir's shoulder, and agony shot through his arm. The impact sent him spinning from Frost Reaver's back. He tumbled wildly, stabbed abruptly with a certainty of doom. He crashed to the path and rolled beneath Frost Reaver's sheltering form. His arm ached, and he gasped for air. Suddenly, the quaking stopped. A few small rocks trickled down the cliff face in the wake of the avalanche, then all went still. The silence seemed as deafening as the quake.

Ra-khir scrambled to his feet to assess the damage. Rubble blocked the path behind him, preventing retreat. All of the horses remained standing, and only he had fallen from his mount. The other mounts pranced directionlessly. Their eyes rolled white, and their ears twitched frantically. Kevral's horse jerked forward and back, alternately attempting to bolt and being jerked under control.

Relieved to find his friends well, Ra-khir scrambled into Frost Reaver's saddle, nursing his injured arm. His mail had broken much of the impact. The shoulder would bruise, but nothing felt broken or dislocated. He drew breath to inform anyone who had seen him fall that he was well. Only then, he realized his friends had naturally turned their attention in the direction from which the rock slide had come. He glanced up, spying half a dozen figures poised on a higher ledge. Another seven raced down the roadway to finish the task their avalanche had begun.

Kevral's war cry echoed hauntingly between the mountains. She vaulted over her horse's flailing head, even as it spun into a panicked run. It crashed into Tae's mount, sending the dark brown into a rear that foiled any plans the Easterner might have had to assist. Darris threaded between oblivion and Matrinka, planting his mount directly in front of hers to shield her from Tae's horse as well as enemies. Trapped behind them, Ra-khir watched with frustrated need as Kevral's swords flew from their sheaths and cut separate arcs so different in direction and timing it seemed impossible for one person to control them both.

Kevral waded into battle like a rabid creature, slashing and jabbing without attention to defense. The first two Easterners fell dead before they could return a strike, and the others pressed forward in a mass even Kevral could not hope to defeat.

The arrangement of ledges placed the battle beside Ra-

khir, and his inability to reach enemies with his sword became a boiling frustration. Unable to control his horse, Tae
also dismounted, charging toward the fray to assist Kevral;
but the Renshai swung with broad, frenzied sweeps, keeping
Tae as much at bay as the other Easterners. He retreated,
swearing, violently jamming his useless sword back into its
sheath. He scrambled for something in his pocket.

Three swords sped for Kevral at once, and Ra-khir knew
she could block only two. Snatching up his makeshift spear,
he jabbed wildly at the battle above and beside him, vision
hampered and aim all but impossible. Kevral parried and returned two attacks. "MO—" she started, biting off her triumphant death cry as Ra-khir's spear pierced the third man's
thigh. Tae's thrown dagger sped between the savage blur of
swordplay and sent another staggering backward.

Kevral plunged ahead, howling wordlessly. Ra-khir withdrew his spear, then lunged in for a second attack. One of
Kevral's swords hacked an Easterner's neck, and blood
fountained from the wound. Warm droplets pattered over
Ra-khir as his spear grazed an Easterner's head. A looping
cut of Kevral's other sword severed the shaft of Ra-khir's
spear, dangerously near his fingers.

Ra-khir jerked back, disbelief displacing thought. No
doubt, she had removed him from the combat on purpose,
wasting a stroke better used to dispatch enemies. Effectively
cut off from the battle, he watched as another Tae-thrown
dagger whizzed over Kevral's head and buried itself in an
Easterner's face. The man staggered backward, screaming
and clawing mindlessly at his mangled nose. Only two enemies remained alive, one down and bleeding from Ra-khir's
spear. Kevral skewered the one left up with an animal sound
more tortured than victorious. Then, she whirled, lunging for
Tae with a bloodcurdling shout of rage.

Tae skittered into desperate retreat, tripping over a loose
boulder. He fell, twisting, shielding his face. Kevral surged
over him before he could move, sword raised for a killing
blow.

Horror stole over Ra-khir. Even if he could fight his way
past the others, he could not rescue Tae in time. The bravado
that had seemed so steadfastly Tae shattered in an instant,
revealing terror. Closest, Darris sprang from his horse, leaping between their grounded colleague and the sword that
could have descended but had not yet done so.

Kevral's arm jerked backward. For a terrible moment, Ra-khir felt certain the crazed Renshai would kill them both. Then, her focus shifted. She pivoted, slaughtering the last of the Easterners instead. Tae scrambled to safety.

Only then, Ra-khir turned his attention to the enemies who had caused the avalanche, expecting them to charge down upon them in a second wave. But the Easterners had gone, apparently frightened by the speed and ease with which the party had dispatched their companions. He dismounted, threading through the horses to assist.

"Come back, you cowards!" Kevral hollered at the cliffs. A last shadowy figure disappeared into the fog. Her challenge reverberated, unanswered.

Darris seized Kevral's forearms before she could clean or sheathe her swords. Blood dripped down the tip of one blade, pooling on the rocks. "What in Hel is wrong with you?" he demanded, the curse and tone so unlike Darris, Ra-khir had to look twice to make certain he was the one who spoke.

Tae held Matrinka's reins, peeking around Darris' horse. His unflappable expression had returned, but Ra-khir would never forget the set of his features in that one moment of weakness. "She wanted to die, and we wouldn't let her."

Ra-khir looked at his hand where he still clutched the remains of his broken spear. He knew Tae spoke the truth. Their interference had bothered Kevral not because she refused to share the fight but because she had hoped to die in it. His spear thrust had simultaneously saved her life and betrayed her. Her last chance to die in battle had come and gone, and now she could never find Valhalla. He dropped the shattered pole, the hollow thunk of wood against stone amplified by the enclosing mountains.

The words released the torrent Kevral had held inside for too long. She collapsed to the ground, sobbing, but too dry to form tears.

Ra-khir held himself back and let Tae comfort her. After what he had just suffered, he deserved that minor solace. Returning to Frost Reaver, Ra-khir watched the path ahead to ascertain that their enemies did not return. He did not fear another rock slide; it would take too long for them to gather that much loose stone again. Boulders rolled down the mountainside, however, might prove dangerous if the party did not reach the high point soon. Once there, they need battle only those lower on the cliff face.

The dilemma seemed both unsolvable and unbearable. Torn in two directions, Ra-khir found himself glad he had acted and simultaneously wishing he had not. Love had driven him to protect Kevral at all costs, the same love that told him it was time to let her go. Forcing her to die from poison when she had dedicated her entire life to a glorious death in battle was a torment she did not deserve. What good had it done him to learn to respect her honor when he did not allow her to follow it in the most crucial situation of all? The pain of Ra-khir's shoulder disappeared beneath an anguish that racked mind and body together. "We have to keep going," he finally whispered.

Matrinka nodded, her expression pained and her movements restless. Even after many months with Kevral and himself, warrior honor made little sense to her. Ra-khir hoped Darris would have a soft song about Renshai that could bring the message home without inflicting the same distress the knight-in-training suffered now. He watched Darris climb reluctantly back into his saddle. Then his eyes tracked Kevral as she accepted Tae's assistance for the first time, wriggling into place on her gelding with an awkwardness that pained Ra-khir. The battle had taken far more from her than it should have.

They rode on, Ra-khir tensed for more interference from the Easterners who had triggered the avalanche. Though no one voiced it aloud, he knew they all longed for the safety of the open plains. If the gem continued to draw them straight south, they would soon veer from the route of Easterners jamming into the Westlands to damage travel. No one should bother them on empty plains, no one except for he or she whom the strange green jewel tracked. Aloud, they had speculated little about the gem's owner, and concerns about Kevral had exclusively held Ra-khir's attention for the past several days. Now, as they approached the Western wasteland, new wonder crept into the knight-in-training's mind.

The party pushed on into the night, despite the danger of navigating mountain terrain in darkness and the need for torches that might draw undesirable notice. They did not stop until their descent became level movement and granite turned to shattered flagstone and sand beneath their feet. Only then, they swerved westward, beneath a sheltering overhang and beyond sight of anyone headed toward the pass from the East. Here, they should find safety from all but the most persistent enemies.

Clouds bunched, gathering into dense clusters as the night wore onward. Moonlight spilled through a gap in the clouds, sparkling from chips of quartz in the sand. Accustomed to their nightly camps, Ra-khir had no difficulty performing his part of the routine in the dark. He groomed horses with brisk, efficient strokes and released them to graze on the scrubby mountain grasses and the rare weed patch poking through flagstone.

Tae talked more than usual as he cleaned and arranged the sweat-soaked tack. He told stories of a flagstone quarry, not far from their camp. There, the finest general in Eastern history had made his only mistake, one so heinous it had turned the tide of the Great War against the best-trained and biggest army ever assembled. Ra-khir had heard the centuries-old story from the opposite perspective: how the East's forces had massed to slaughter all the peoples of the West but were thwarted, about the many heroes still glorified in song and story. No Western child's upbringing was complete without tales of King Sterrane and Arduwyn the archer. The former was the only Béarnian and the latter the only Erythanian to fight in the war, and both had proven their mettle repeatedly on the battlefield. So many others had won permanent fame in that war, including Colbey Calistinsson the Deathseeker, the charismatic yet rabid general of the Pudarian army.

For the first time, Ra-khir listened to the other side of the story, hearing about Eastern heroes with names omitted from his West-skewed books. The Eastern general had hidden his army with the expectation of catching the Westerners by surprise. Yet, the tide turned when enemy scouts discovered them, and the flagstone quarry turned into a flagstone tomb.

Darris waited only until the story concluded. Brushing the ever-present curl from his forehead, he announced softly, "I have to see it, you know."

Ra-khir smiled. The bardic curiosity never died, and Darris was informing, not asking. "If we survive the quest, we'll stop on the way back." Rescuing Béarn's only heir, the man Darris would eventually dedicate his life to guarding, had to take precedence over side trips. Yet he also knew that learning, for Darris, was a god-inspired compulsion.

Kevral remained quiet. Forgoing her practice for the first

time ever, she dropped into sleep before the others had finished eating. No one mentioned the oddity, though they did exchange worried glances as they stretched out on their own blankets.

"I'll take first watch," Ra-khir volunteered, knowing even exhaustion could not lull him to sleep now. Kevral seemed unlikely to make it through the night. He would spend her last moments at her side.

No one argued, though Matrinka did tousle his hair with a sympathy beyond any he could have conveyed with a gesture. After keeping a weeks-long vigil at Darris' side, she understood. Ra-khir sat with his legs in front of him, staring out over the vast wasteland. Even at night, his vision seemed to extend forever. Faraway sand dunes broke the contour; and, from his reading, he knew they would have to slog through a narrow salt marsh to reach the ocean. The final battles of the Great War had taken place in the shallows that lapped the beach.

Ra-khir continued to study the view in front of him long after his companions had drifted into their own quiet worlds. He listened to the cacophony of deep regular breathing, punctuated by snores whose source he did not isolate, feeling it rude. He did sort Kevral's breathing from the others, regulating his own to its pattern, as if he could continue for her should her life slip away in the night. He watched the horses, some lying down, some standing with lowered heads, and one still seeking scant mouthfuls of vegetation. Near Frost Reaver, something moved.

Ra-khir stiffened, preparing to awaken the others. As recognition dawned, he froze in place. Colbey had come, stroking the nose of his stallion in a silent greeting. Less careful, the horse whickered a soft welcome that sent Tae rolling into a wary crouch. Ra-khir scurried to his light-sleeping companion's side and gripped an arm in a plea for silence. Together, they watched the immortal Renshai reunite with his horse, moonlight flinging gold and silver highlights with the slightest of their movements.

"Colbey?" Tae whispered.

Ra-khir tightened his hold and nodded, hoping Tae could read his meaning in the darkness.

"Impressive, isn't he?" the Easterner hissed.

Colbey turned toward them, answering the question for Ra-khir. "You should see me fight."

It was the most insolent answer Ra-khir had ever heard, yet Colbey's attitude and tone made it seem proper. He marveled at how Colbey could speak such a line without raising an iota of irritation or malice. Now, Ra-khir believed he understood Kevral's arrogance and the verbal delivery to which she aspired.

"I think," Tae said carefully, "I would be happier and healthier if I didn't."

Colbey laughed. "Good answer. And don't worry. You won't see me fight. But you will see me ride. I'm going with you to the shore."

"Really?" Ra-khir's hopes soared, then plummeted an instant later. "My lord, is that because . . ." he sought a euphemism that would not immediately drive him to tears. ". . . because we need a Renshai with us?" He left the implication obvious, that Kevral would not survive the night.

"No." Colbey patted Frost Reaver's neck. "You don't need a Renshai with you, and if you did, you already have one."

Ra-khir kept his emotions in check, though he felt as if poison gnawed through his own belly. "So Kevral isn't going to die?"

"Of course, Kevral's going to die." Colbey's matter-of-fact delivery seemed cruel until he added, "Like every mortal. But whether she dies tonight depends on her."

"Forgive my ignorance," Tae said, voice revealing all the negativism Colbey had managed to avoid. "But doesn't it depend on the poison?"

"The poison has already done its damage. The healing has to come from Kevral."

Ra-khir knew it was wrong to expect assistance from gods, though he had prayed for it. Nevertheless, he had to ask. "Lord Colbey, can you help her?"

"Not directly, no. Even if I had such power, the balance would not tolerate straightforward interference by an immortal. That's why you won't see me fight either. No matter the circumstances."

Ra-khir quelled a sigh and accepted the answer, even as Colbey qualified.

"I can remind her of the skills she has. And I will once we've finished talking."

"We're done!" Tae said quickly.

Ra-khir nodded vigorous agreement.

"Very well, then." Colbey gave Frost Reaver's forelock one last playful toss, then headed toward them. Ra-khir and Tae shifted, allowing Colbey a clear path to Kevral. The immortal crouched at Kevral's side in a defensive position that would allow him to rise and strike in an instant. It seemed more routine than intentionally chosen; surely, Colbey had nothing to fear on man's world.

Ra-khir and Tae hovered, anticipating a mystical, educational process they might remember as a pivotal moment in their lives. Yet Colbey did nothing more sensational than remain far too long in a position that should have cramped every muscle in his body. After a few moments, the god ceased to hold Ra-khir's attention, and his mind and eyes wandered to other things. First, Ra-khir noticed that his horse had returned and grazed among the others. Its coat gleamed in the narrow ribbon of moonlight that struggled through the clouds. Ra-khir resisted the urge to examine the animal more closely. To imply that Colbey had not supplied the finest care would be an insult.

Ra-khir expected to pace in endless worry while the old Renshai worked. To his surprise, however, he found himself calmer than he had felt in days. Tension seemed to glide from him the moment Colbey shifted his attention to Kevral. He could not fathom how he planned to teach her in silence, yet Kevral's constant quotations, her unfailing faith in this man turned immortal, would drive her to learn, in explicit detail, whatever he chose to teach. This night, Kevral would live or die on her own merits.

And the words of Colbey Calistinsson would guide her.

Chapter 42

The Battle Within

> *United against a common enemy and death, the changes in your life and the differences between people may not seem so large.*
>
> —Colbey Calistinsson

Agony gnawed at Kevral's body, and her head pounded a ceaseless cadence that made thought all but impossible. In her dreams, enemies struck from all directions, their hammers battering flesh despite her best defenses. Darkness hemmed her in, and she swung blindly. Her blades cleaved only air, nothing solid. Frustration added its grinding anguish to the relentless pain that dogged every part and every movement. Among a press of so many, it seemed impossible to miss. Even a wild swing should hit something, and she jabbed and hewed with the skill and logic trained into her since birth.

At her back, a dark, cool void beckoned, promising permanent solace from the pain. She considered its sanctuary for less than a heartbeat. Renshai never fled from suffering or enemies; they fought not despite, but because of, pain. *Modi!* The war cry barely spurred her against an invisible, soundless enemy that pelted inexorably but never with a killing blow.

Tendrils extended from the quiet place at her back, caressing her skin with an icy tenderness that soothed her. *Come,* it called. *Comfort,* it promised. *An end to the pain. I am your answer and your friend.*

Kevral never doubted the goodness of its intentions, yet she ignored its call. Slowly, she could feel it drawing her. She resisted, leaping forward, though the effort slammed misery through every fiber of her being. The battle gained her nothing. Each movement scarcely countered the vacuum that dragged her backward. The agony sparked by each footstep became all-consuming. No rational thought could seep beyond that fiery anguish. Reduced to instinct, she continued to fight, unwilling, even in madness, to end the suffering and let death claim her. Hel would not have her, yet, despite efforts she considered her best, she gained no ground in the battle. Though she labored valiantly, she slipped gradually nearer the void.

Kevral refused to surrender the fight. Her strokes became frantic, agility lost to exhaustion. She tapped mental strength, dragging it into her body, transforming it to physical power. But little enough remained there either. Her thoughts moved in slowed motion, and she gained only a trickle of fortitude where she had expected a torrent. A whisper touched the battered remains of rationality, a voice she recognized and could not place. Her head throbbed, and she could make no sense of the words, only heard them as random sounds without meaning.

Kevral's thoughts crawled, mercilessly slowly, as if through mud. She gathered the scattered pieces of idea, dragging them toward her at a pace that seemed impossibly sluggish. She pieced logic back together with meticulous care, finally managing to make sense of the noise: "This enemy you cannot fight with swords. It is within you."

Within me. Within me. The words pulsed with Kevral's heart, a dull steady drumbeat that left her still with uncertainty. The void loomed larger. She could feel its frigid presence on her back, like a snowman's breath. Hel's respite was true and permanent, yet it was Hel. *Within me.* Kevral's eyes stung first, then pain stabbed another round through every part. Again, she channeled her mental energy, thrusting it to her body, but this time she explored rather than exhausting it in a moment of physical combat.

A tearing sound grated through Kevral's hearing, accompanied by an agony that dwarfed all previous experience. For a moment, she lost everything; even identity eluded her. She felt as if some massive force had ripped her open, exposing her insides to air. Then, abruptly, the pain disappeared. She glided to another world that consisted of only her own inner workings. Nothing seemed quite right. Every part moaned in anguish, needing her assistance. Toxins battered her organs, these not from the Easterner's arrow, but by-products of her body's needs and actions.

Kevral threw herself into the work with all the vigor of a sword practice. She scanned her body, discovering details she never knew existed. Muddled thought gave way to a shining clarity. All the maneuvers she had performed gained a sense beyond understanding, related to the attachments and arrangements of muscles. Lessons, once only words, blossomed into perfect comprehension. Once a confused uncertainty, body systems and functions became a simple schematic. She saw her brain nestled safely in her skull, and the ropelike spinal cord she aimed for when she wished to paralyze an enemy. Her ribs enclosed the all-important lungs and heart, and seeing them gave her the basis for finally understanding the intricacies of the Renshai triple twist that penetrated armor. Now, fluid soaked into her lungs, choking. The heart beat a steady rhythm, still strong despite the venom eating away at its foundation.

Kevral's concentration dropped further, to the tangle of intestines. She had seen enemies disemboweled before, a tedious, agonizing death she would not wish on anyone. Still lower, her attention became riveted on the kidneys. She had never known their function and did not believe the healers did either. Experience taught her that a stab there delivered a swift and bloody death. That was all she ever needed to understand—until now. Kevral's new connection with her own body told her that here lay the source of her problems.

Kevral drew a deep breath, feeling the air channeling through her lungs and gliding into her blood. She drove all thought and feeling there, becoming one with an organ she had before considered only a place that needed defending from cnemy weapons. Now, she prodded. She pounded, squeezed, and stretched. She opened tubules and stroked tiny clusters of cells. She drew the little vigor remaining to her and channeled it to them. She delivered speeches and threats, tenderness and promises. An eternity skulked past before she finally felt a tiny, quivering response. Gradually, a pinpoint of seemingly lifeless kidney responded. A single filter, not enough. Kevral fanned the flame with all the vigor she usually reserved for sword practices. Desperate hope alone stayed her from collapse. The fire grew, consuming a tiny circle around the spark, then bursting into a bonfire that roared to encompass the whole. Kevral managed a cry of triumph that emerged more like a breathless moan. Then, all understanding left her.

Ra-khir's fierce whoop of joy awakened Kevral, soaked in a puddle of urine. The absence of pain struck her first. She had grown accustomed to the throbbing and to moving and thinking thickly. The lucidity that followed seemed frighteningly impossible. The realization that she had escaped Hel and still had a chance for Valhalla thrilled through her. When she opened her eyes, she found all of her friends standing over her, excited smiles on every face; and she felt undeservedly lucky.

Sunshine beamed beyond the row of happy faces, broken by the shadow of the sheltering overhang. Morning dew sparkled in rainbow colors, captured into crevices, on moss, and dribbling from the spiny leaves of those few hardy weeds that managed to poke through rock. The light spread like a halo at her companions' backs, and Kevral half expected them to break into a bright, Valkyrie chorus. Needing to break a silence rapidly growing awkward, Kevral quipped, "When I wet my bed as a child, I used to get a spanking, not an ovation."

Nervous laughter followed.

"A spanking?" Tae repeated carefully. "Come here, then. I think I can handle that."

Tae's words earned him a heated glare from Ra-khir.

Memory returned in a rush, and Kevral winced with honest discomfort. "I deserve one, and not for this." She indicated her soaked bedclothes with a casual wave. "I'm sorry, Tae. I shouldn't have attacked you. The poison affected my mind, and I just couldn't think." She did not bother to differentiate between the archer's poison and the toxins left by her failed kidneys. It would only complicate the matter. "All I knew was that I had one last chance to die in battle." She met his gaze earnestly. "It won't happen again. I promise."

"Yes, it will." Tae shook back his shaggy, black locks without even a shade of doubt in his voice. "And next time you try to kill me, I'll deal with it again."

"No," Kevral insisted. "I won't do it again." Honor forced

her to clarify. "And I never really tried to kill you. You're alive, aren't you?"

Tae's brows shot up. "That's a testament to my skill and Darris', not yours."

"If I wanted you dead, you would be dead. That's the Renshai way."

Colbey stepped into view from around the overhang. "If you're going to quote me, at least give me credit."

Startled, Kevral bounded to her feet, wet britches clinging to her legs. "*You*'re here?" The words were shocked from her, not at all the ones she would ordinarily have chosen.

"Obviously."

"A great honor, indeed." Kevral attempted to make up for her previous lapse.

"Colbey's agreed to ride with us to the beach," Darris explained. "And I'm working real hard to find out why."

To Kevral's surprise, Colbey grimaced. Apparently, the bards tried even an immortal's patience, although she had never found Darris particularly wearisome. In fact, more often then not, he had remained a quiet, passive observer.

"We've got everything packed and ready to go." Matrinka smoothed the fur near Mior's tail as the calico perched on her shoulders. "As soon as you clean up—"

"—and practice," Kevral added, glancing carefully at Colbey in the hope he would volunteer to teach.

Matrinka sighed. Long ago, they had all learned not to interfere with Kevral's *svergelse*. "And practice. Then, we'll go."

The party dispersed, leaving Kevral alone to change in private. She did so swiftly, excited to charge into her first practice since the archer's poison had unbalanced her. Once dressed, she remained in place. Without trees to screen her, she would soon be forced to practice in open sight on the Western Plains; but, for now, the overhang and the cut of the mountains allowed her one last chance for seclusion.

As Kevral launched into her sword work, her friends' voices wafted to her on the wind. More than just Darris plied Colbey with questions to which he gave short, clipped answers that often seemed unrelated. He vehemently denied assisting in her healing, although Kevral believed him the author of the whispered sentence that caused her to turn her attention inward. From there, she had relied on the mental training her *torke* had emphasized; the Renshai's unique methods of combat and their daily mind-set hinged heavily on those teachings.

Kevral's timing remained frustratingly off. Her long illness had weakened her just enough to make her new clarity of thought a curse. She heard the barrage of questions regarding their bearing and destination and Colbey's evasive replies. From these, she learned only that they would need to travel all the way to the shore of the Southern Sea. Then, all details not directly related to her sword work disappeared. She channeled every part of her concentration to her practice, hacking arcs, jabs, and S-curves through the morning air. Her limbs responded to her commands with an edge of sluggishness that spurred irritation. In tiny increments, the deadly speed and agility returned. Nothing in the world existed but her body and her sword, not even the Renshai-turned-immortal she had worshiped as her ideal since infancy. The one who would lead them to the Southern Sea.

The sage hovered over his table, scribbling notes on parchment in the smooth hand that defined Béarn's history. Sunlight streamed through the tower's single window, casting a glare across the crisp paper. The sage blinked his dark eyes, tapping his quill in the ink, and tolerating the too bright light for several moments. Then, with a sigh, he set the pen aside and rose. The familiar voice of the castle rang through his head, providing information his fingers desperately needed to write.

"Can I get you something, Master?" His apprentice's voice shattered a long silence.

The sage stiffened, startled. He had become so engrossed in his work, he had forgotten the young man's presence. He glanced over to the smaller of the two tables. The apprentice leaned over a practice scroll filled with flowery letters that closely approximated the sage's penmanship. It always amazed him that the apprentice heard none of the shouts that rolled through the walls of the castle and seemed to quake the room. Yet when he managed to remember back to his own learning years, he recalled that he had been equally oblivious. He could not explain the voice, nor its source; but his master had heard it and his master before him. "Thank you, no. You keep working."

Obediently, the apprentice lowered his head, his close-cropped, black hair scarcely dipping with the movement.

Like his master, he would not tolerate anything near his eyes that might foil the perfection of the most wondrous of sights: words properly lettered on parchment. He clasped his meaty, Béarnian hands behind his thick neck, stretching each finger delicately. Then he returned to his work.

The sage shuffled to one of the bookshelves lining the walls, his gait stiff and his back permanently hunched. Selecting a tome at random, he walked back to his chair and sat. The castle's voice reviled his lapse, but he ignored it. He had learned long ago that he could work neither to its approval nor its pace, and he had given up trying. Eventually, all of the important details would find their way onto his scrolls, even if it meant working far into the night.

The sage knew the truth of Béarn's current situation, but his job did not allow him to act upon or judge the information. He could not leave his tower. He could only pen down the events as the voices told him. The castle gave him an account honest to the most intricate detail while the descriptions Baltraine delivered bore little resemblance to the reality. Still, the sage did not lay blame. He simply chronicled the prime minister's accounts and properly credited them.

The voice raged on, its honesty strangely as bothersome as Baltraine's obvious lies. The sage wrote, desperate not to criticize, to keep his opinion from his mind as well as his pen. The sage's job left no place for subjectivity. Yet though he would not judge the words or story, he could not help being made edgy by the castle's voice. It spoke only truth, but he knew a discomfort in its presence that had not lessened even over the four decades he had held his position. In fact, it seemed to intensify. His mind conjured images of a creature crouched beneath the castle's foundation, a beast who used integrity and order as a weapon and would one day burst free. The thought seemed madness but the sage had never managed to banish it.

Setting the book on its edge on the table, the sage carefully ruffled the pages until it stood upright on its own. He shifted it until it blocked the glare from the window, then he took his pen back into his hand. The writing began anew, tales of elves who gradually purged the castle and plotted to end all humanity in a sudden sweep, stories of elfin meetings during which they detailed the havoc they had wreaked on other countries and kingdoms. In the North, the tribal wars had sparked back into killing frenzies. In the East, order floundered beneath a new wave of corruption and greed. Pudar, New Lovén, and Santagithi all wavered as death struck the royal heirs and blame ignited wars of ideology and race.

The voice filled the sage's head each day. Every night, he fell into bed too exhausted to contemplate solutions or details: knowledge without power, understanding without the ability to act or delegate. He fell asleep to his own sobs and awakened with eyes sore and nose clogged. Helpless, he watched Béarn sink—and did nothing more than chronicle the details and hope future generations would live to see them.

Three days of fast-paced travel over blistering sand, slogging through tidal marshes, and weaving over dunes that showered mounds of sand to the beach below brought Kevral and her companions to the edge of the Southern Sea. Blue-green water seemed to stretch to eternity, and only the extent of her vision limited how far she could see. Waves rose in towering curls, then whipped open, crashing against the shore and spreading into a thin spray that scarcely coated the sand. Foam engulfed the sand, hiding shells, stones, and crabs. The water receded, sticks tumbling through it, and the beach returned, with more or less flotsam dotting its shore.

Darris locked his eyes on a process he had never seen before, but his mouth continued to form the many questions he could not resist asking their immortal companion. "Does Asgard have oceans?"

Kevral sighed. Colbey had bluntly stated on their first day that anyone who wished details of the gods and their world would have to divine them or find a way to visit. This time, he simply ignored Darris' query. He stood with a booted foot on a large rock. His eyes sought something far into the ocean. The sea breezes tore down his hood, spilling golden hair; and his cloak peeled back from a warrior-sinewy body. Though he lacked Ra-khir's massive musculature, Kevral stole the moment when his attention was fixed elsewhere to caress every part of him with her gaze. And envy Freya.

At length, he stepped down, shaking his head without explaining the cause of his discomfort. He turned to Darris, as if to answer his hovering question. "Play something loud and magnificent."

"Me?" Darris seemed taken aback by the sudden command.

Kevral smiled but managed to keep from laughing. She glanced at Matrinka who studied Darris with the same intensity Kevral had focused on the object of her lifelong crush. Mior sprang from her shoulders, stalking the receding water of the latest wave. Ra-khir looked out over the water, expression unreadable. Tae clutched the gemstone, thoughtful.

"Of course, me," Darris leaped in before anyone else could make a sarcastic comment. He went to his horse, opened his pack of instruments, and drew out his favorite lute. Closing the pack, he sat cross-legged on the sand. "Why am I playing?"

Colbey turned an annoyed gaze to the bard.

"I know a million songs, and I can create anything my repertoire is missing. How can I know what to choose unless you give me some idea of why I'm choosing?"

Colbey smiled at an argument he could not counter. "Sing a poignant song for nostalgic sailors. Sing a stirring melody of the sea. And play loudly. Your sound must carry."

Kevral could not help wondering about Colbey's purpose as well. According to Tae, the gem still pulled intermittently toward Béarn or directly southward. Whoever they followed must spend time on the sea, apparently on a ship. Her hands slid naturally to the hilts of her swords. If Colbey intended to draw enemies to them, but not to assist in the fight, she had best prepare herself for combat.

Mellow notes sprang from the strings of Darris' lute, blending into rushing chords that emulated the roar and slap of the sea near the shore. Then the music gentled, though the volume remained the same. The slam of waves striking sand softened to the swish of a hull through water, and notes spiraled from the lute like foam from a ship's bow. Kevral believed she heard the gentle patter of droplets trickling from oars and the whistle of wind through canvas. Darris added his voice and words, the whole blending into a magnificent tapestry that added four more senses to the sound.

Individual words slipped by Kevral, unheard. Need kept her tensed and watchful, fighting the sweetness of sound that beckoned her to escape beyond the confines of her world. She felt the icy sting of spray on her face, and months in sun that glared from sky and sea tanned her skin to leather and faded her hair. She tasted salt on her lips, felt ropes grind through her callused hands, and heard the hiss of their movement against her flesh. Nautical terms she had never heard made sense within the context of Darris' song. Unlike the others, she had some scant experience with sailing. Renshai shipped boats from mountain crags the way their ancestors once did from fjords and islands.

Kevral had never cared much for the ocean-faring aspects of her people. Yet, suddenly, the rocking deck became an old and welcome friend. The rattle of sheet clamps and the flutter of sail in heavy winds grew into a lullaby. The feel of the ship lurching into a run beneath her, with its sails outspread and its lines taut, became a pleasure that precluded any other. The camaraderie of fellow sailors, sharing songs, promised an irresistible bond of brotherhood.

Then the whole died back to the ripple of waves, and the song wound to a sweet conclusion that left her aching for more of Darris' talent. Only then did she realize the morning had glided into midday without her knowledge. She had stood attentively throughout a song that had lasted far longer than she would have otherwise believed.

"More," Colbey said as the gurgle of the ocean sucking back its waters replaced the sweet perfection of Darris' music.

Darris looked stricken. He flexed the fingers of his left hand, their heavy calluses striped with indentations from the stings. Surely, his hands had begun to ache, but he obeyed without question. Again, the pure tones rang from his instrument, dragging Kevral back to a world where wave and weather formed the central focus upon which all decisions rested. Though wholly different in form and melody, Darris' new song conjured many of the same images. The hull of a ship sliced the water into frothy spirals, spume coloring its sides and wake. Seagulls wheeled and shrilled overhead, occasionally daring to perch in the riggings. The odors of salt and fish became overpowering, and the sweet, fresh aroma of the sea breeze scarcely trickled through it. The ship tossed, a toy in waves that started calm and built to a crescendo so gradually that Kevral could not distinguish the stepwise changes in tempo and volume. The whole reached a stormy discord that sent the ship into a rollicking dance. The bow reared like an unbroken stallion, slamming back down onto the dark water, swirled into a vortex of windy fury. Rain lashed the deck, and the gale shredded sails like old parchment.

The sailors clung in wet misery, repairing as the storm allowed, praying to every deity with any relation to the ocean. Most pleaded with Aegir, Northern god of the sea. Others begged the mercy of Weese, the Western god of wind. As the storm raged on, kicking salt spume in sheets over the gunwales, lesser gods found their moment amid the hopes and promises of sailors facing death. They called on Sheriva, the Eastlands' one god; on Ciacera, the goddess of sea life who took the form of an octopus; on Mahaj the dolphin god; and on Morista, the god of swimming creatures. Kevral had heard of none of these except Aegir, yet the desperation of their prayers raised wonder. At least for the duration of the song, they all existed.

A dark spot sneaked into Kevral's vision, far out in the Southern Sea. She found herself staring at it through squinted lids, protecting her eyes from the gale that raged only in song yet seemed so real.

The discord unwound from Darris' music, replaced by the smooth harmonics that gave his work its unsurpassable beauty. The storm huffed its last against the tattered sails and thrashed timbers. The boat groaned, bruised and battered but whole; the sailors rushed to the task of repair. For hours they patched and replaced the ruined sails, rewound and retied lines, bailed, and caulked. The waves lightened, in power and color. Sunlight struggled through thinning clouds that gradually faded from black to pale gray. Warmth touched the deck, and rays glimmered from cleats and clamps. The sailors rested, singing ditties of their love for the sea, the storm shoved into the inner depths of memory.

As Darris sang, Kevral watched the dot on the horizon glide closer. Soon, it became discernible as a boat, its single sail heeling leftward and its prow parting water at a swift pace. As it drew nearer to the shore, she nudged Ra-khir and inclined her head toward it. Glancing out to sea, Ra-khir nodded; and Kevral turned her attention to her other companions. Tae had already noticed the boat, his eyes intermittently fixed on it and measuring the terrain around them. Darris, too, saw the boat. His fingers twined across the lute, and his voice never missed cue or note, but his gaze revealed the object of his attention. Colbey sat watching the boat's approach with a contented half-smile. Only Matrinka seemed completely oblivious. She sat in front of Darris with her eyes closed, allowing the song to fully enfold her. Mior lay beside her, ears and tail damp from sea air.

The last notes of Darris' song hovered, becoming a part of the ocean's rumble and hiss. He set the instrument lovingly aside, sheltering it from blowing sand beneath the rock he had used as a seat. Climbing atop the boulder, he watched the approaching ship. Kevral shifted position so that she now waited between Matrinka and the ocean. The boat wound nearer, too small for her to consider a ship. Kevral's sharp eyes found only a single sailor on the deck. She saw no cabin nor hatch, and it did not look thick enough to have a below deck area.

"My lord, were you expecting company?" Ra-khir put forth the question on every mind.

This time, Colbey deigned to answer directly. "It was my intention to call out Captain, yes. Whether he proves friend, foe, or neither remains to be seen; but no violence will be necessary." He headed toward the ocean, ignoring the water sloshing over the toes of his boots. "By the way, he's an elf."

Kevral glanced at Tae, who returned a wary nod. The sea breeze whipped his black hair into tangles, and he had gone one more day without shaving than his youth allowed. The dark stubble added a danger to his already wild appearance. "He's not the one." He opened his hand to reveal the green gem, then returned it to his pocket. "It still wants south."

The boat rasped on sand, and the sailor leaped over the gunwale to the beach with impressive agility. Kevral studied him in the shadow cast by the sail. Wrinkled features and faded red-brown hair belied the long limbs that made him appear adolescent. Sockets slanted like a cat's held amber eyes like round, unfaceted topaz. One glimpse told Kevral the origin of the gem Tae carried, and she whirled to whisper her discovery to him. As soon as her attention shifted to him, he bobbed his head to indicate he had already made the connection. Kevral returned to her scrutiny as Colbey caught the front of the boat and the two hauled it to shore together. High, arching cheekbones completed the face above a broad mouth and full lips. He wore his hair knotted at the nape of his neck.

Only after they finished the task of grounding the boat did the elf bother to speak. "Colbey Calistinsson." He executed a graceful gesture, a combination of bow and wave. His wrinkles deepened, etched by a simple smile. "So the stories are true."

"That all depends," Colbey returned carefully, "on which stories you're listening to."

"You're living among the gods now."

"True."

"No doubt causing them as much trouble as every other whose life you've touched."

Colbey smiled good-naturedly. "No doubt."

"I met your son."

"A handsome lad, isn't he?"

"He looks like you."

Colbey laughed. "I'll take that as a compliment, undeserved as it is. When one has a dolphin for a mother and an octopus for a father, it seems absurd to compare one's beauty to the octopus."

"You only wish yourself an octopus." The elf's smile did not budge, even when he spoke. "Imagine eight arms to hold eight swords at once."

Kevral saw a thoughtful expression cross Colbey's face and experienced a mild thrill of her own at the idea. The chance and challenge would prove irresistible to any Renshai.

Colbey and the elf stopped in front of the party, and the old Renshai made the first introduction. "This is Captain. Trust his sailing; he's the best. I've placed my life in his hands, and I would do so again."

Kevral accepted the ultimate praise with the seriousness it deserved. Renshai lived or died by their own skill, and the method of their dying wholly determined the value of their life.

The captain executed another of his dancelike bows, then glanced at each of the humans in turn. His eyes lingered longest over Darris, and he addressed the bard's heir first. "Mar Lon's great-grandson, I presume."

Darris bowed respectfully in return. "Add another dozen or so 'greats' to your list, but, yes. I'm the bard's heir. My name is Darris."

Colbey gently corrected him. "Actually, Darris, you are the bard."

"Bard's heir," Darris responded instinctively. "My mother—" He broke off, as if suddenly realizing who he addressed. His head whipped to Colbey. "My mother is . . ." He started again. "My mother?"

"You've been gone a long time. There have been many changes in Béarn, few of them good."

"My mother?" Darris repeated. "My mother." He seemed incapable of other speech. Matrinka took him in her arms and whispered comforts to him.

Ra-khir fidgeted, awaiting his turn, caught between the need to console a friend and concerns about his own relations.

Captain looked at Matrinka then. "A Béarnide. I only know of one by name, so I have little choice in this guess. A descendant of Sterrane?"

Captain addressed Colbey, but he received no answer there. Matrinka's biology was her own business, and only she had a right to share it. Matrinka, too, stayed silent on the matter. Either Darris' distress engrossed her fully or she pretended such was the case to avoid the question. Kevral believed it better. No matter the faith Colbey held in Captain, the fewer who knew Matrinka a princess, the safer she remained.

"Her name is Matrinka," Kevral explained. "And I'm Kevral."

"Pleased to meet you, Renshai," Captain said in fluent Northern. "If you are a descendant of Rache or Mitrian, then I knew your family, too."

"I'm neither," Kevral returned in trading, quashing irritation for Colbey's sake. She had to assume Captain had placed her in the lesser tribes because of his personal associations rather than because he believed her Renshai blood diluted.

"Ahh." Captain accepted his mistake easily. "What were the odds I would know the origin of more than one? And I'll lose this one, too." He turned to Tae. "I've never known any Easterners."

"Tae Kahn." Tae offered nothing more than his name, in word or gesture.

Finally, Ra-khir got his turn. He executed a grandiose flourish that rattled his mail. "Ra-khir of Erythane, son of Knight-Captain Kedrin and apprentice knight to the Erythanian and Béarnian kings: His Grace, King Humfreet, and His Majesty, King Kohleran."

"A Knight of Erythane, of course." Captain glanced from

Kevral to Ra-khir, then from Ra-khir to Tae. "A stranger association, I could not imagine." He laughed. "But what more could I expect from Colbey?"

Colbey made a broad sweep with his arm that included every member of the oddly matched party. "This was none of my doing. I don't interfere with the affairs of mortals, and you know why."

Captain's brows rose, and he nodded gravely. "But you're here now."

"That's how desperate matters have become."

"You brought them here," Captain said.

"Yes."

"And you called me here, too."

"I told Darris to do so. Yes."

Captain asked the obvious question. "Why?"

It was an answer they all sought. Even Darris pulled away from Matrinka, dabbing at his eyes, so he could hear Colbey's response.

"Because these five have business with the elves. They've come to rescue the heir to Béarn's throne, whom Dh'arlo'mé has taken prisoner."

Kevral recognized the name Randil had penned phonetically in the dirt. Apparently, Tae did also because he turned her a knowing glance.

When Captain said nothing, Colbey continued. "And you have a boat that can get them there."

The elf studied the five, all of whom now returned the scrutiny. "I'm sorry. I can't help you."

"You mean you won't." A hard edge entered Colbey's tone, and all amusement left him.

"I mean I can't." Captain back-stepped cautiously toward his boat. "I'm an elf, Colbey. I can't defy my own."

"Your loyalty is foolish," Colbey returned, ice-blue eyes flashing.

"My loyalty is what it is." Captain gave physical ground, but no other. "Elves aren't like humans. We have no individuality, no personal honor. We're united into a single entity. No one elf can defy that."

"You can."

"I can't."

"You can. And if you don't, nothing will remain for you to stand by. The destruction of the universe will not spare elves. If you remain a single entity, you will die a single entity."

"So be it."

Kevral watched in fascination as the elf returned Colbey's advice with defiance. As a devout follower of Colbey, she could not imagine anyone wishing to discount him. Yet, as a Renshai, she could not help respecting the elf's courage.

Colbey took another tack. "Transporting humans may not please the other elves, but it won't harm them either. Surely, you can take them to the island so long as you don't work against your own."

Captain drew a lengthy breath, closed his eyes, and exhaled slowly. He gathered more air and opened his eyes. "It's not as simple as it once was. When Ravn arrived, he met no resistance. My people learned a lesson from his coming. They will not be caught unprepared a second time."

"I trust these young warriors to handle the matter."

Captain's canted lids narrowed, and his gemstone eyes found Kevral among the others. "I know how Renshai handle threats. I will not let her harm my people."

"Even if some of your people are wrong?"

"Even though." Captain shrugged with a resignation that suggested he doubted he would ever make his point clear. Nevertheless, he tried. "I know my people have abandoned everything elves once represented. I spoke against this stance more than once, and my disagreement with their current policies is how I became outcast. I know humans can't understand the elfin racial union that once bound us all to common belief and policy and still holds us together in spirit while our thoughts begin to diverge. But that unbreakable trust is the very reason my views were tolerated and I was not executed even long after I ceased to agree with any of the council's decisions."

Colbey accepted Captain's explanation. "But you're not alone in your struggles."

"No." Captain lowered his head. "I know Brenna meant well. She taught them the qualities of mankind that allowed me to befriend the likes of you. Honor, morality, heroism. But along with those lessons must come the vices, if only as contrast. Treason is a concept unknown to elves. I've seen the effect of chaos on mankind. I will not bring down my own. I would rather the universe destruct."

"Now that," Colbey said softly, "I understand. You place

your personal honor above the future of mankind, gods, and elves. Your refusal to become the instrument of change will damn your people to far worse than any schism between them could. I can appreciate that stance, but do not mistake it for something other than what it is: your personal refusal to do what one elf must do to save his own. Your personal honor."

Captain paused to consider, and Colbey seized on this hesitation. "Here." He headed toward the beach, giving the elf a wide berth as he waded deeper into the waters. He plucked an object from his pocket that looked to Kevral like a tiny boat very like the ones Béarnian carvers made from wood and sold as children's toys. He placed it onto the sand beside the boat Captain had brought. For several moments, it tossed in the swells. Then, light sparked to life around it, outlining hull and sail in a vague brilliance that turned it to a blinding, shapeless blur. As Kevral watched, it grew.

The mast stretched upward, reaching for the sky. The two sails unfurled, rolling down the lanyards and flapping aimlessly in the breeze. A figurehead became discernible, a dolphin; and the words *"Sea Seraph"* were written in Western Trading tongue on the bow. Planks ran flawlessly from stem to stern, interrupted only by the masts and the square set of cracks that defined a hatchway.

"The *Seraph*," Captain whispered. A moment later, he was charging toward the ship as if to a long lost lover. Without a change in stride, he sprang over the gunwale to the deck, examining every stripe and knothole as if to memorize them. Tenderly, he secured the sails with a speed and ease that betrayed tireless practice. His feet made no sound on the deck as he trotted aft and clung to the tiller.

Matrinka and Darris watched, hand in hand. The bard had slung his lute across his back. Mior batted at a crab washed up by the waves. Tae slipped up quietly to examine the ship, and Ra-khir waited with straining patience. He remained in place, but he straightened his well-aligned tabard and smoothed unwrinkled britches at frequent intervals.

Finally, Captain whispered something to the tiny ship, then jumped back to the sand with a splash that darkened the hull with small circles. He walked over to Colbey and wrapped him in an embrace the old Renshai tolerated. Then, suddenly, the elf pulled away. "This is meant as a trade, isn't it?" His voice became breathy and hesitant, a prelude to tears.

"No." Colbey ran a finger over the hilt of his left-hand sword, a gesture more wistful than threatening. "It's a gift." He cast his gaze from the sword to the ship to the elf. He understood the bond. "Long ago, I made a decision that every being I respected believed to be wrong, including the gods I had worshiped since birth. I told you a time would come when loyalties clashed and the boundaries between opposites blurred. For me, that time came and went; you were the only one who understood the course I chose." Colbey waded deeper, looking out over the placid sea without meeting Captain's gaze again. "There's only so much I can do these days before my power overwhelms its mission and I cause the very problems I try to avert. Now I truly understand the frustrations of the Wizards I once worked against: to know what must be done, to have the ability to do it, yet to understand that my hand has become too large to move the pieces without knocking all others askew. I brought these five to you, and I did my best to convince you to make the right choice. The world and its creatures are in your hands . . . and in theirs." He pointed toward the shore. "The choices are no longer mine."

Colbey turned suddenly then, striding northward. His boots disrupted the water's surface in lines and ovals, then left footprints in the sodden sand. He headed toward Frost Reaver, his last words a desperate farewell. Yet Ra-khir could not allow him to leave without asking the question that had plagued him since Colbey mentioned the fate of Bard Linndar.

"Lord, it deeply aggrieves me to bother you—"

Ra-khir got no further. Colbey passed him as if blind and deaf, placing a hand on Frost Reaver's saddle. For a moment, he remained in place, as if preparing to mount. At last, he swiveled his head and addressed Ra-khir. "Your father still lives, last I knew. But time runs short. Your mission must take precedence. If you fail, the world dies with you." Without awaiting comment, Colbey sprang into his saddle. Frost Reaver galloped across the sand and was soon lost to sight.

Kevral watched until the white horse and its golden rider disappeared, feeling empty and alone. Colbey had placed the fate of the world in the hands of five adolescents scarcely beyond childhood. She would not disappoint him, no matter the cost. Her gaze—and all of her companions'—turned to Captain.

To his credit, the elf met every gaze in turn. Kevral believed she could read the struggle taking place behind eyes like marbles, though his expression revealed little. He turned one last look in the direction Colbey had taken, then locked his gaze directly on the *Sea Seraph*. "All right," he said to no one in particular. "I'll take you where you need to go. But, from there, you're on your own. No matter what I think of their politics, I won't raise a hand against my own. And I won't condone your doing so either."

Ra-khir took command. "Matrinka, Darris, Kevral." He indicated the tiny ship with a high, arching gesture. "Tae and I will handle the horses."

Kevral waited while Matrinka scooped up Mior and Darris assisted her onto the *Sea Seraph*. Captain remained in place while Kevral hopped up to keep guard at Matrinka's side. Tae and Ra-khir hauled the gear shipside, and Darris lugged pack after pack to the deck. Finally, nothing remained but the horses' saddles and bridles. "I guess we won't be needing these anymore," Ra-khir said, his matter-of-fact tone scarcely hiding his concern for the animals. "And there's not enough room anyway."

"Don't worry about space," the elf said, his voice revealing the melancholia his expression hid. "My lady's bigger than she looks."

Kevral did not doubt the claim, having already seen it grow. She lifted the hatch, discovering a cabin far larger than she would have believed possible. Bookshelves lined three walls, filled with myriad texts in every language she knew and several others besides. Cots surrounded a table and chair in a semicircle, and a narwhal horn hung on the wall over it. Darris headed inside, and Kevral passed the packs to him one by one.

"You will have to leave the horses, though. She's not *that* big."

Tae consoled Ra-khir. "Horses are pretty smart. They'll head toward fresh water."

"Bandits will probably wind up with them," Ra-khir said sadly.

"Better than starving."

When Ra-khir made no reply, Tae continued. "If it means

that much to you, we'll come back and rescue them. I'm not afraid of bandits, and I know damn well you're not. But one crisis at a time, Red. All right?"

"All right," Ra-khir finally agreed.

The two approached the *Sea Seraph* just as Kevral and Darris finished loading. Captain gestured for them to climb aboard. Tae scrambled inside, but Ra-khir hesitated. "I'll help you launch."

Captain shook his head. "You'll get your mail rusted for nothing. I pushed her out to sea for millennia, I think I know how to do it."

"She'll be heavier with people aboard."

Captain dismissed the concern. "It's been centuries since I've held her timbers in my hands. Give me my moment."

"As you wish." Ra-khir climbed the ladder steps and hopped over the rail.

Captain shoved the *Sea Seraph* backward. The hull rasped over sand, then glided delicately into the ocean as the old elf sprang onto the foredeck. He trotted backward with a grace impressive even for a young warrior, then settled himself at the tiller. A wind seemed to rise from nowhere, filling the sails. And the *Sea Seraph* swung out on a broad reach for the open sea.

Chapter 43

A Renshai's Promise

There comes a time when every man, and perhaps every god, needs to redefine his honor and his faith.

—Colbey Calistinsson

The ocean reflected the deep blue of the autumn sky like a mirror, interrupted by floating seaweed and patches of white water chopped by the wind. Kevral stood on the aft deck, watching foam streamers trail in the *Sea Seraph*'s wake. She had chosen her position to guard the elf at the tiller. Until they reached the elves' island, any danger they faced could only come from him, whether it took the form of a direct attack, a poisoning, or steering them into submerged rocks. The fact that none of these seemed likely did not deter Kevral from her vigil. She knew Darris had taken a position at the forerail, drawing tactile impressions from the feel of wind streaming through his hair and the slap of spray against the bow. Their other companions had descended into the cabin, accepting the elf's suggestion that they rest, wash up, and eat freely from his larder.

Captain smiled as he manned the tiller, clutching the polished wood in a light grip that seemed never to move, though the ship changed course at intervals. It seemed as if the craft responded to his thought rather than to his touch. He took no obvious notice of Kevral's hovering, constant presence. He sang songs of the sea in a lyrical voice that might have seemed pretty had Darris' recent concert not so overshadowed his efforts. Sometimes, he switched to a whistle or a hum to the rhythmical beat of water rushing around the sleek hull.

For hours, they continued this way: the elf joyfully steering and the Renshai guarding in sullen silence. Then, as the sun looped its arc across the sky, beginning its descent to starboard, Captain released the tiller and rose. Turning his back to Kevral, he groped beneath his bench, unhinging a compartment she had not previously noticed. In Renshai culture, leaving one's unshielded back exposed to a warrior was a clear sign of contempt, indicating no need to worry for the other's skill. In this case, Kevral suspected, the elf's incaution stemmed from ignorance rather than any deliberate wish to antagonize her. In a moment, he laughed. "Who would have thought. . . ?" He pulled out two crystal goblets and a vial half-full of yellow wine. "It's still here."

He glanced at Kevral, still smiling. She blinked back at him without returning the silent greeting. She watched as he filled each of the goblets then gestured for her to choose, his first acknowledgment that she had selected her position because of mistrust. By allowing her to select the glass, he could demonstrate that he had not tainted her drink.

Kevral shook her head, not fully reassured, still paranoid from her recent poisoning.

Captain shrugged, selecting one at random and taking a careful sip. "Colbey and I once shared this very drink in this precise location." He swallowed, and his face assumed an expression of delight. "Three hundred years has done my wine well."

Though Kevral had watched him in stolid silence for a long time, she saw no reason for rudeness. "I'm glad you're enjoying it."

"You're sure you won't join me?"

"No."

The elf shrugged, balancing a foot on the bench and staring over the starboard rail toward the dolphin-headed prow. "Colbey didn't trust me at first either." He took a long pull at the wine.

"Why was that? Did you tell someone in front of him that you would support Colbey's enemies?"

Captain looked at Kevral and gave an answer she never expected. "Something like that. He knew I served a force in opposition to his own. I assured him Odin's laws forbade my harming him, or losing him, or taking him to a destination other than the one I promised. Back then, man's world held only a trickle of chaos. When a man made a promise, he did not break it. Lies simply did not exist on a world built solely on order."

"Times change." Kevral found his assertion difficult to believe.

"They do indeed." Captain considered that simple statement longer than it warranted. "And Colbey had the biggest role in that change. More than three hundred years ago, we stood on this deck, riding a different sea. He told me that, to avoid the *Ragnarok,* the world had to change, but I was the one who talked him into becoming the one to effect that change."

Kevral had little choice but to consider the likelihood that Captain spoke the truth. Colbey had deliberately delivered the party into the elf's hands. If Colbey trusted Captain, Kevral would at least hear him out. "So, because of a conversation between Colbey and yourself, our world now has lies and broken promises?"

Captain continued the sentence as if Kevral had not finished. ". . . lies, broken promises, betrayal, and dishonor. But it also has creativity, genius, and compromise. Once, humans lived their lives in absolutes. All Easterners were evil, all Northerners good, and all Westerners neutral. You knew a man's beliefs at a glance, without need to ask. Honor was as straightforward as the difference between mountain and valley. Laws varied from place to place, yet mankind's adherence to them did not. Colbey brought balance, the shades of gray."

Kevral imagined a world based on the simplicity Captain had described, weighing limitations and opportunities. If Colbey had supported the current system, she would not do otherwise. Yet she could not banish the idea of never needing to doubt promises or motivations. If people spoke their minds directly, it might result in ruffled feathers; but it would obviate the constant need to sort fact from fabrication. Knowing friend from enemy at a glance surely had its merits.

Captain set down his goblet on the gunwale, the rocking ship sending the wine sloshing. Kevral had seen little enough crystal to worry for its safety, but she did not admonish the elf. If he had truly sailed the seas for thousands of years, he could judge the precariousness of its position better than she.

Captain hefted the goblet again, just as the bow bumped a rough spot in the water and crashed back to the surface, tossing spray. He finished the wine in a gulp, set it down beside the other, then poured the liquid from the second glass to his own. "Colbey's enemies saw only the danger chaos represented, the immoralities, like those you named. But Colbey knew that without change man's world would stagnate into oblivion. Chaos represented the deeds of humiliation and disgrace, but it promised art and creativity. Chaos was the plan to law's creation, the genius behind law's greatest architecture. And I believe chaos brought one thing more, something even Colbey never considered."

Kevral appreciated Captain's subtle reinforcement of his harmlessness, drinking her share of the wine without comment. Now she regretted the insult of refusing his hospitality. She studied the carafe and the empty goblet, seeking a polite way to atone for her mistake. "What was that thing?"

Captain grinned, tossing his knotted hair from his right shoulder to his back. "Tolerance." Setting down his glass, he refilled Kevral's and returned to his position behind the bench. "No longer forced to adhere to rigid codes, humans suddenly had choices. Choice of honor. Choice of religion. Choice of morality. The understanding that these are no longer determined solely by location of birth. The self-realization that you can become whatever you wish, that you can change your opinion over time, opens your mind to the differences of others."

Now Kevral hefted her goblet and sipped. The wine tasted sweet, with a pleasant salt tang. Only then, it occurred to her that Captain could have tainted it with something that affected humans and spared elves. His words had sparked guilt, and her paranoia added a modicum of self-irritation. Deliberately, to spite her suspicions, she took a large swallow of the wine. "I guess," she started, uncertain of her point and allowing her mind to run freely with it. "I guess it's still possible to close your mind."

"You mean never see the choices?"

"I mean make your own choices, then assume every sane person should reach the exact same conclusions. I mean intolerance." Kevral tapped her fingers on the railing, understanding the allure this elf had for Colbey. Captain made her think. "And I'm as guilty of it as anyone. More than most."

The elf finished and refilled his goblet, then topped off Kevral's though she had taken only the two swallows. "Renshai honor runs high."

Kevral felt the same joyous rush of certainty that thrilled her every time she considered the honor of her people. "It means everything to me. My mistake has been expecting everyone else to view it as the ultimate way of life, as I do. I've been as rigid as I once accused Ra-khir of being."

Captain delivered the coup de grâce. "Then you understand my position, too. Why I must do as I must."

"That depends on what you plan to do with us."

"A fair question." Captain replaced his foot on the bench. "I'll do as I promised. I'll take you to my people's island. Once there, you're on your own. I will neither assist nor will I interfere unless it becomes necessary." He sighed deeply, clearly realizing, as she did, that "necessity" required some definition. "Colbey trusted you to handle the problem. Implicit in that trust was the promise that you would not kill unnecessarily. There are other ways to deal with impasse besides violence." Captain drew himself up to his full height, placing both feet firmly on the deck. Sunlight sheened from steadfast, amber eyes. "You are the one who worries me."

"Because I'm Renshai," Kevral guessed.

"Yes," Captain admitted easily. "No other people learn to clutch a sword before a rattle. No others base the passage to adulthood on killing."

"Nor do Renshai anymore." Kevral refused to condemn the history of her people. "Now a Renshai becomes a man or woman when he reaches a certain level of competence through teaching and testing. First kill is no longer the measure."

Captain's brows lifted slowly. His point remained valid.

"All right," Kevral admitted. "We're still a violent people. But we're not the same Renshai you knew centuries ago. Colbey saw to that, and you claim to trust his judgment."

"I do trust his judgment. I did even when all others forsook him."

"No one has studied his teachings more thoroughly than I. He once accused me of trying to become him. He was right. Until recently, given the chance, I would have allowed the powers of the universe to transform me into him and considered it the greatest moment of my existence."

"What changed that?"

Kevral swirled the wine in her cup and studied the golden sparkles the sun drew in their wake. "Tolerance. I let understanding of others in, and I learned to love them. I still want his skill and insight—better! Over time, I'll surpass him; and I'll revel in the effort and the challenge. But I want to live my life and get to know the people in it."

Captain grinned again, his smiles so frequent Kevral did not know how to interpret them. But this time, his stance revealed genuine delight. "I'm as pleased to have talked with you as I was with Colbey. And nearly as surprised by the outcome."

The compliment warmed Kevral, and she returned his smile. Encouraged by the exchange, she took it one step farther. "With Colbey's help, and yours, I've faced my blind spots. Now, I hope I can lead you to your own."

"Mine?" Captain laughed. "I'm many thousands of years old, and I've spent whole millennia more alone than in company. Do you not think I've had more time than I can stand exploring my thoughts?"

"I know only what I've heard and seen: an elf staunchly defending change as a savior for humans yet discarding it for the elves he claims to love. I've listened to you embrace the cause of personal freedom yet deny individuality for your own."

Captain smoothed his tunic and britches against the wind. "Elves are different than humans. The same rules do not apply." He opened his mouth to say more, then shook his head sadly. "I can't explain in an evening what it took me centuries to understand."

Kevral quoted Colbey, "Age, by itself, doesn't make a man clever. Elders only become wiser if they seek experience and wisdom."

"What are you saying?" Captain set his goblet down, clearly offended.

"I'm saying that if you've truly explored a matter to its finest details, you should be able to sort the significant from the extraneous. An expert *can* teach in an evening what it took him years of study and experience to learn."

"You're tough," Captain admitted.

"I modeled myself after a competent Renshai."

"And quite effectively."

"You're avoiding the topic." Kevral remained relentless. The lives of all mankind might depend on it.

"I hope it will suffice for me to say that change has brought only harm to the elves. They fell prey to human bitterness, and it may destroy them. Had the elves remained as they were, we could have lived happily on our own, with or without interaction with humans."

"So elves have already changed." Kevral set her goblet beside his.

"Unfortunately, yes."

"And you want them to revert back."

"Not necessarily," Captain defended his position. "Change isn't always bad, of course. I just don't agree with the direction our race is taking now."

"But you won't stand against those currently in power, the ones dragging your people in a dangerous direction."

"I can't."

"You mean you won't."

"I can't," Captain reaffirmed. And there, at the same impasse, the conversation ended.

Through the long night, the party sat on the aft deck discussing strategy while Captain manned the tiller. The ocean became a flat black expanse, and the *Sea Seraph* bobbed on otherwise invisible swells. Moonlight glittered off the water churned up by the ship's movement, leaving a long spray, like diamonds, in their wake. Captain answered questions and entered comments about how the elves would respond to various approaches. Kevral established that they lived on an island undiscovered by humans, probably because of its location. Those with enough money for ships would have no cause to search off the coast of a barren wasteland. Captain claimed two hundred and thirty elves inhabited the island, of which, strangely, only six were children.

Captain described the general layout of the village. The elves lived in three communal buildings of flimsy and temporary construction. They had learned architecture from spying on human dwellings with magic, which gave them little understanding of basic framework and structuring. Before they came to man's world, elves had lived without weather, insects, or violence. They had needed no shelters on

Alfheim. The prison stood in the center of the triangle formed by the dwellings, and a fence surrounded all four.

Having learned all of that, the party discussed methods for dealing with the elves and their magic. Captain's clarity disappeared when he detailed the latter. "There are no specific things they can or cannot do with magic. It comes of shaping chaos, and elfin society leans farther toward chaos than humans' anyway. We act as a unit, so there is no need for laws. Since long before my birth, magic simply was a part of us. We never used it in a structured manner, only to enhance our play. We never tried to control it."

Captain's marblelike eyes gleamed in the moonlight. "I worked for the Cardinal Wizards. They fashioned spells only rarely, turning chaos into a power for law. Using chaos in this manner always created unintentional side effects, some of which proved more dangerous than the reason for casting. That's why the Wizards rarely used any but the most basic powers, those magics their bodies tuned to naturally. The elves have taken to casting as a unit, a *jovinay arythanik*. As the magic channels through the group, each controls that part of the spell most closely attuned to him. The use of an assemblage adds size and power, too. It allows us to work more difficult spells without those side effects that so limited the Wizards. A single elf may or may not be able to cast spells, and power varies with the individual. The danger lies in their collective chanting."

Tae stood with a hand on the aft rail, his face hidden by dark hair and shadow. "I've experienced their magic and their chant. It's not pleasant."

Kevral recalled Tae's description of the incident on Pudar's streets. "How can we fight magic if we have none of our own?"

No answers followed. Even Captain offered no solution. Kevral's mind conjured one. She needed to stop the chanting before the casting. She imagined her sword dancing through lines of elves, and the image soothed frustration momentarily. A solution that seemed best to her would serve only as last resort. She had promised Captain and, ultimately, Colbey Calistinsson.

Matrinka finally broke the hush. She sat on the deck, Mior in her lap, and stroked the cat until its hair stood on end. "If we parlay well, we'll have no need to counter magic."

To Kevral it seemed a naive answer, but Ra-khir and

Darris nodded thoughtfully in response. From there, the conversation turned to approaches. Each time a party member proposed a method of bargaining, Captain described the effect it would have on the elves. He returned possible replies that ranged from polite refusal to attack, but not one of the possibilities suggested seemed adequate.

Kevral disappeared from the discussion after the first two recommendations. Her mind turned to the violence the others avoided. No matter how hard they tried to find a peaceful solution, they failed. The elves would not compromise, and they could not afford to do so. Eventually, she felt certain, it would all come to war.

As the night wore on, first fatigue, then total exhaustion, overtook the party. Matrinka surrendered first, excusing herself politely to go below decks and sleep. Tae followed shortly after, and even Darris could not keep his eyes open. After falling asleep twice on the deck, and with obvious reluctance, he sacrificed the chance to learn more and dragged himself to the cabin. Ra-khir's stamina impressed Kevral. His knight's training had included formal bargaining and negotiation, but even his flowery words proved no match for the hostility of the elves Captain imitated. Soon, Ra-khir, too, fell prey to weariness and went below.

Gradually, through the night, Kevral had channeled energy from body to mind. Even so, the edges of her thoughts dulled, and the image of the cots in the *Sea Seraph*'s impossibly large cabin beckoned. She yawned. "Elves don't sleep, do they?"

"Some do now," Captain returned softly. "But I don't."

Kevral yawned again, trying desperately to remain awake and cursing herself for not leaving with Matrinka. She had added little to the exchange, and exhaustion tended to deepen sleep, making guarding more difficult. "Well, I do. Thanks for all your help, but I have to go now."

"Wait," Captain said softly.

Kevral let her eyes sink closed, but she remained in place.

"I'm going to tell you something in strict confidence. Can you keep it that way?"

"Yes," Kevral managed, too tired to speculate.

"Imagine for a moment that Renshai glory came from dying of age rather than in battle."

Kevral shook her head, forcing her eyes open a crack. "You're asking the impossible."

"All right." Captain changed tack as easily with words as he did with his ship. "Imagine then that the Renshai were keeping a man hostage, not realizing that doing so heralded their own doom. You, alone, of the Renshai understand, but the others won't listen to you."

Though difficult, Kevral believed she could handle that rhetorical situation. "Imagined."

"You agree to bring a group of elves to your people in the hope that they can free the prisoner."

Without opening her eyes, Kevral snorted. "I'm not that tired. I see the resemblance to your situation."

"Bear with me. I'm not finished." Captain hesitated a moment, presumably gathering his thoughts to build the proper analogy. "Time is running short. Exploration of all possibilities reveals two effective methods: Either the elves can wade in and battle Renshai to the death."

Kevral smiled.

"Or they can cast a spell that puts all the Renshai to sleep, then kill them one by one."

That last sparked an anger that lent Kevral a second wind. Her eyes shot open, and the wreckage of the envoy filled her memory. She relived the grief and the fiery hatred against the cowards who had killed Renshai, knights, and Béarnides in their sleep, without a chance for Valhalla. "I would tell them that that choice is no choice. Renshai must die in combat."

"And if they chose the latter method?"

Kevral's eyes narrowed again, this time due to emotion, not exhaustion. "I would have no choice but to attack the elves. And kill them all, if I could."

Captain took a stride that placed him directly in front of Kevral. No joy touched his features anymore. Even the smile wrinkles seemed to disappear. "That is the position you may place me into."

Alarm flashed through Kevral, dampened into a shiver by fatigue. "I don't understand."

"This is the part you are not to repeat to anyone. For, if humans know it, they may use it against my people. Swear by Colbey it goes no further than you."

Kevral would not allow the conversation to end there. "So sworn."

"When an elf dies of age, his soul is free to be reused, and an elfin child is born to replace him. If he dies violently, his soul dies with him. Kevral, *every elf who dies at your hand brings us one step nearer to extinction.* In all my millennia, I have never killed for any reason. Not humans. Not animals. Not insects. I've lived on man's world most of my life, as a servant to Wizards. I don't need chants to work my magic. If you force my hand against you, believe me, you'll die in neither glory nor battle. A cause that so needs you, the one Colbey placed into the hands of you and your friends, will die with you."

Kevral blinked in thoughtful silence, separating emotion from fatigue. She could not help prizing his spirit as well as his honor, though it vastly differed from her own. Few had the courage to stand within a sword stroke of a Renshai and threaten her life, and most of those were spurred by stupidity rather than boldness. Respect for the elf blossomed in an instant. Colbey had always admired boldness, in his students, his friends, and his enemies. Kevral found herself as pleased by it as her hero. She could not help quoting him, "There is more to Renshai than killing."

"That's true," Captain said. "But diplomacy isn't one of those other skills."

Kevral shrugged. "I've got friends with me better trained in parlay, but I don't believe words will convince the elves." She added deliberately, "And you don't believe it either."

"I believe," Captain said slowly, "that you'll have to find those words. The fate of the world, including that of elves, hangs on freeing Béarn's heir. But saving the rest of the world means nothing if the elves are already dead."

Kevral tried to think, struggling through the thick blanket of weariness. Discovering a loophole, she clung to it. "You left out one option in your imagined scenario. I might have allowed the elves to put the Renshai to sleep if it meant they slipped past, did their work, and left my people alive."

"I thought of that." Captain returned to the tiller, making a minor adjustment. "It's not a perfect analogy."

Kevral found a near equivalent. "If words fail and if we're forced to face off with the elves ..."

Captain shook his head.

"Hear me out," Kevral persisted. "If I could get the elves out of commission without killing them, would you allow that?"

Captain went still, wind ruffling strands of mahogany hair,

revealing glimmers of gold and silver among the fine locks. "You could do that?" It was as much statement as question.

Kevral did not know for certain. Knocking humans unconscious required a finesse most could not achieve. Differences in human constitution foiled even the most skilled. A head blow that enraged one man might kill another. She felt confident of her ability to disarm, but surrounded by enemies, the instinct to dispatch them might thwart her attempts to harmlessly keep them at bay. It might not prove beyond her patience to parry killing strokes and not return any of her own, but it might prove beyond her ability to fight two hundred and thirty without a single fatality. "I can try." She studied the elf's delicate frame and features doubtfully. "I don't suppose there's much room for error when it comes to sapping without killing elves."

Captain laughed. "Elfin fortitude might surprise you. We don't get sick, we don't grow feeble with age, and we don't die by accident. I've seen elves fall from trees onto their heads, then sit up and join the laughter. Brenna gave Dh'arlo'mé's torturer a hit that would have fractured a human's skull."

Excitement helped Kevral hold hovering exhaustion at bay. "Then we're agreed. If words don't work, we'll try nonlethal attacks." She met Captain's strange, amber eyes. "If I promise to do my Renshai best to kill no elves, will you accept it if one or two die?"

Captain stiffened. "Not well, but it won't be automatic grounds for slaughtering all of you."

Kevral suspected she would get no better compromise. Sleep beckoned urgently, but one detail still bothered her. "Who is this Brenna you've mentioned twice?"

Captain's fingers tightened on the tiller, and he looked taken aback. "Are there so many Renshai you no longer know one another by name?"

"Brenna is a Renshai?" Kevral did not bother to address the query directly.

"And a prisoner. About this tall." Captain indicated the level of his nose. "Yellow-brown hair. Gray eyes." He considered, probably seeking other details that might differentiate her from other Renshai rather than other humans. "Taken from amidst a group of Béarnides just outside the city on the Road of Kings."

Kevral put the whole together. "That's Rantire! She's

alive?" She cringed, sharing Rantire's shame. No Renshai would allow herself to become a living prisoner, although the elves' magic surely explained the lapse better than cowardice.

"Last I knew. I'm not exactly sure how much time's passed since my banishment. Weeks to my reckoning which usually corresponds to months in yours."

Someday, Kevral hoped she would have the time and alertness for an explanation of that oddity. "Are there other prisoners?"

"Not that I know of."

Kevral yawned. "I'm sorry. I'd love to talk all night. But if I don't get some sleep, I'll be worthless tomorrow."

Captain's blank mask revealed nothing of his thoughts, though having placed herself in his position once that night, she guessed at the ideas taking shape in his head. Likely, he saw the positive side to her exhaustion. It meant security for his people. With that in mind, his words amazed her. "Sleep, then. If promises mean as much to you as they do to Colbey, and I believe they do, I'll trust my loved ones to your judgment."

Kevral stood, rooted in place. She recognized a compliment as significant as an "excellent swordsmanship" from Colbey. Yet fatigue blocked her ability to appropriately acknowledge his charity. "I won't betray you," she promised.

And meant it.

Chapter 44

Nualfheim

The victor is the one left standing after the battle.
—Colbey Calistinsson

Tae Kahn awakened to darkness. The lantern in the *Sea Seraph*'s cabin had burned out, but his internal clock told him midday approached. He listened for his companions, identifying them from the familiar patterns of their breathing. They all slept.

Tae lay still on the floor, seeking seams of light and adjusting his vision to them. Gradually, he gained enough sight to distinguish shapes. Matrinka and Kevral used cots, Mior curled at her mistress' feet. Darris and Ra-khir had settled on the floor, leaving the last of the cots free rather than appear impolite. Tae stretched muscles cramped by the hard, wooden floorboards and rubbed at the impressions the wadded blanket had left on his face. He had chosen his place on the floor, believing himself most accustomed to the discomfort of sleeping without a bed. Had he known they would waste his generosity, he would have spent the night in comfort.

Quietly, Tae rose and dressed, without awakening his companions. He climbed the steps to the hatch and pushed it open. Sunlight funneled through the gap and struck his eyes, blinding him. Blinking rapidly to clear his vision, he clambered onto the deck and replaced the hatch. The sun had drifted almost overhead, sheening from the handrails and illuminating sheet clamps among the riggings. Tae glanced upward. The mast would prove an easy climb, barely worth his effort, but he felt safer in high places. People tended to look down or at eye level. Few bothered to learn to scale anything more challenging than a ladder. Treetops and roofs had occasionally proved a haven for Tae in his youth.

Something scratched at the inner side of the hatch. The sound startled Tae until logic intervened. *Mior.* He lifted the door, and the cat squeezed through the crack, purring a welcome.

Tae smiled, patting the calico. His gaze trailed to the bow where a dark shape formed on the horizon. He squinted, studying it through the glare until he felt certain about what he saw. *Land.* He glanced aft, around the main sail to where Captain still stood at the tiller. "Is that the island?"

Mior meandered beneath one hand, around Tae's hip, to his other hand, rubbing on every part of him as she moved.

The captain trotted forward. "That's Nualfheim," he confirmed. "You'd better get the others up."

Tae gave Captain the benefit of the doubt, that the elf would have awakened them soon had Tae not ascended. "How soon till we get there?"

"We're an hour outside of shouting distance."

"Thanks." Tae opened the hatch fully, and it gaped, braced against the deck. "Good morning, everyone. Island's in view." Several shifted, and Darris yawned loudly. Certain he had awakened at least two of them, Tae closed the hatch and left them their privacy. He studied the elf who looked exactly as he had when he arrived on the shore. "Don't you ever sleep?"

"No. Does that bother you?"

"Me? Hell, no. Wish I didn't have to either. Dangerous waste of time. Can you teach me?"

Captain smiled, gaze still fixed on the island. "No."

"Damn." Tae glanced at the mast again, watching the main sail billow. They were about to come face-to-face with an enemy they could only begin to fathom. The idea of challenging undefined weapons, dependent upon the graces of a turncoat who could drown them at will, made him fretful. He fidgeted. His foot came down on something cylindrical, and Mior yowled, clamping her claws on his ankle. Tae danced aside. "Sorry."

Mior sat, fur fluffed, lashing her tail in indignation.

"Sorry, Mior," Tae repeated. He hefted the cat, and she

squirmed in his grip. Apparently still angry, she leaped from his arms and padded aft. She dropped to her haunches, and began to clean herself, giving special attention to her tail.

Shortly, Tae heard the sound of footsteps on the stair. He stepped aside, giving his companions plenty of room to exit. The hatch banged open, and Darris clambered up on deck, followed quickly by Ra-khir. The knight-in-training wore his usual blue and tan, black and orange, though he sported no mail yet. The two glanced out in the direction of Captain's stare.

They'd been above deck only a few moments before Kevral's voice wafted up the stairs. "We're decent now. How soon till the parlay starts?"

Tae responded. "About an hour, Captain says."

"Well, come on down and eat, then," Matrinka called up. "While we can."

Anxiety balled Tae's stomach into a tense knot, but he still saw the wisdom. A heavy meal might make them torpid, but starvation did little to stimulate thought or action. A light breakfast would do them all good. "We're coming," he called, herding the others back down before anyone could protest.

They ate a swift, modest meal from their own rations, too polite to bother the elf's stores, which consisted mostly of water plants they could not identify. Ra-khir added mail and a tabard to his costume, and Darris wore his sword belt as well as a mandolin. Kevral kept her disdain to herself, though Tae caught her rolling her eyes at the way the bard chose to hamper his sword arm with an instrument. Aside from Kevral, who remained ready at the ship's bow, they broke into constantly changing pairs, each saying his or her "good-byes" in their own way. Matrinka hugged each of her companions in turn, then left to share a private moment with Darris in the cabin. That left Ra-khir and Tae alone on the aft deck.

For several moments, the two said nothing, sharing a companionable silence amid the flap of canvas and the creak of timbers. Spray dampened their faces, and the air smelled thick with salt. Finally, Ra-khir broke the hush. His attention swung directly to the Easterner. Sunlight glittered from distinctive, green eyes; and, for the first time, Tae felt a flash of jealousy for the chiseled features and broad muscles. The idea that he could compete with this man for a woman's affection seemed madness. If they all survived, he would content himself with the one night of passion Kevral had promised. "You're a good man in your own way, Tae Kahn. I'm sorry I mistrusted you."

The praise embarrassed Tae. "This is unnecessary, Ra-khir."

"No, let me finish." Ra-khir raised a gauntleted hand and set it firmly on Tae's shoulder. "I couldn't go to my pyre in peace without letting you know I was wrong."

Tae closed his eyes, then opened them, anything but peaceful himself. "Look, Ra-khir. As long as we're realizing we might die here, there's something I have to tell you, too." He looked past the knight-in-training, gaze measuring the distance to the mast.

Ra-khir removed his hand, waiting patiently.

"Before I knew who you were . . ." Tae stopped, releasing his breath through his nose and gathering another before starting again. "Before I knew anything about you." He paused again, knowing he needed to blurt it out quickly or risk never telling at all. "I stole your father's knife for money." Tae did not wait for a reaction. He ducked beneath Ra-khir's grip, skidded across the deck, and skittered up the mast. Only then, among the ropes and pullies, did he dare to look below him.

At that moment, the sky darkened suddenly to slate, and a bolt of lightning split the heavens. A blast of wind slammed the *Sea Seraph* like a god's fist. The blow dipped the bow underwater. Waves surged over the gunwale to the deck, flinging Kevral overboard and jarring Tae from the mast. He plummeted, clawing desperately for a hold. His forehead hit a rope, snapping his neck backward. One frantic hand slammed timbers, and he closed his fingers reflexively. He jerked to a sudden stop, impact tearing fiery pain through his shoulder. Then the gale struck from the opposite side. The boat lurched aft, breaking Tae's grip. Air screamed past his ears. He crashed to the deck, breath dashed from his lungs and head ringing.

Dazed, Tae clung to the planks, gasping desperately for air. His lungs failed him, locked by the fall. He heaved and sucked like a beached fish, the deck bucking wildly beneath him. A tearing sound thundered through his ears. From the corner of his vision, a shape hurtled toward him. Torn from its riggings, the sodden sail plunged. Tae scrambled out of the way, scuttling helplessly on the wet deck. The sail caught him across the spine. A clamp smashed his fingers with a pain that tore a scream from his lips. A waterlogged rope hammered the back of his head, and all consciousness left him.

Tae awakened to throbbing pain in his right hand and lesser aches in his head and shoulder. He lay upon a gently rocking cot. A weight pinned down the blankets near his feet, and a bandage enwrapped his injured hand. A large, gentle hand smoothed the bangs from his forehead; and the touch startled him. He jerked open his eyes, tensing for movement. Matrinka's nurturing gaze looked down at him, the expression on her face one of motherly concern. "Do you remember what happened?" she asked.

"I fell off the mast," Tae replied before he could actually consider the question. They had exchanged these words before, at least once, though Tae could not recall having done so. This time, however, memory came flooding back. "No, that's not right. I got thrown from the mast by an impossible storm that came from nowhere."

Matrinka smiled. "That's right."

"So what happened?"

Matrinka's grin wilted. "You fell off the mast," she returned mechanically.

"No. No, I got that part." Tae examined the bandage that made his hand look three times its normal size. "Did the elves attack us?"

"Apparently. And long before we ever got near enough to parlay."

Tae flushed at the idiocy of placing himself in such a vulnerable position while preparing for a confrontation. Yet embarrassment evaporated as quickly as it came. He had chosen the climb for vantage and security. From on high, he could have seen details the others missed about the elves; and, if physical combat ensued, he might have gained the advantages of momentum and surprise. Furthermore, it had kept him safe from the repercussions of admitting the horrible truth to Ra-khir. That last thought brought a sorrow he never expected. He had intended the revelation as a last needed confession, yet even as he had spoken it, he wished he had let the secret die with him. He had distracted Ra-khir, and ultimately himself, by raising the issue of Kedrin's imprisonment at a time when they most needed their wits about them. Worse, he had shattered a friendship that had once seemed impossible, one a shared love already made tenuous. Tae knew the onus lay on him to try to reassemble the pieces of their companionship, to rebuild a trust that might have flung Ra-khir back to depending only on first impressions. But first, Tae had to understand the immediate dangers to all of them.

Tae gathered his thoughts around the pounding in his skull. "Are we safe now?"

"We retreated just beyond sight of the island. We're anchored now. Darris and Kevral are with Captain, discussing strategy."

Tae threw a sideways glance around the cabin. Mior lay curled against one of his legs. The hatch was closed. "Can we trust Captain, do you think?"

Matrinka pursed her lips, her expression solemn and sincere. "Tae, if you had seen the way he rescued this ship, and us, you wouldn't ask. By all rights, we should lie on the bottom of the ocean, and timbers like toothpicks should litter the beaches. When he claimed he'd sailed these seas for thousands of years, I thought it was exaggeration. Not any more."

Tae accepted Matrinka's evaluation without question. He knew nothing about sailing, while she had the experience of her studies of Béarn's navy. He looked at his hand again, raising it for a closer look. The bandage extended halfway to his elbow, and his inability to move his wrist suggested a splint.

"Broken." Matrinka did not wait for a direct question. "Some fingers. Maybe the hand, too. The shoulder was a dislocation. I put it back, but it'll probably hurt for a while. You hit your head, too."

"Believe me, I know." Tae rubbed the back of his head with his uninjured hand, though the pain seemed vague and unlocalized. "How long have I been out?"

"You've been up and down. We've had several brief conversations. Do you remember the others?"

"Vaguely." Tae recalled only that the "falling from the mast" line seemed too familiar. "Will I go out again, do you think?"

"Not likely. Not if you're clear enough to ask that question."

Purring, Mior worked her way up Tae's body to lie on his chest. He petted her, using steady pressure to shift her slightly out of the way of his view of Matrinka. "So how long *has* it been?"

"It's evening. Captain's put the ship mostly back together. As much as he can do at sea."

"What's the plan?" Tae finally sifted out information left unspoken. "And you said Darris and Kevral are talking strategy. Where's Ra-khir?"

Matrinka handled the questions in order. "We'll stay beyond magic range until we come up with a workable plan. And Ra-khir is right there." She pointed to the far corner of the cabin.

Tae struggled into a sitting position, dumping Mior to his lap. At the same time, Ra-khir rose and came toward him. Despite the hatred he surely felt toward Tae, trained politeness still drove him to save an injured man the pain of movement.

Matrinka stood. "I need to get some air." It was a shallow excuse. "If you have any more questions, Ra-khir can answer them."

A sudden urge seized Tae to find reason for Matrinka to stay. He had dedicated too much of his life to survival to face a man with reason to kill him while alone and wounded. A sense of fairness he never knew he had welled up to stop him. He had created the situation, and he would handle it. Ra-khir's honor would not allow him to slaughter a defenseless man, no matter his crime. "Thank you," Tae said simply.

Mior rose and stretched, measuring the ground as if to leap down and follow her mistress. Instead, she paced a circle and lay back down on Tae's lap.

"Now we know," Tae said. "Her loyalty is to the petter, not the feeder."

Matrinka stopped halfway to the ladder and turned, incredulous. "That's pretty much what *she* told me."

Tae managed a smile, stroking Mior with enough force to dislodge a pile of loose hair in three colors. "I always knew I would have made a good cat . . ." He waited until Matrinka disappeared through the hatch and the door banged shut behind her before finishing the sentence for Ra-khir's benefit. ". . . but not a very good human." He met the Erythanian's gaze. "There's nothing I can say that'll make up for what I did. So if we both survive this, and if that 'calling out' challenge thing you talked about when we first met is still good, I'll fight you till I'm dead." The words went against everything Tae had struggled for since childhood, yet he meant them.

"No," Ra-khir said.

Tae blinked, uncertain. "No what?"

" 'No,' my challenge isn't good anymore. And 'no,' I'm refusing yours."

"You're refusing a duel?"

"Yes."

"Doesn't that mean you have no honor?" Tae threw Ra-khir's words back in his face before he could think to stop himself.

"It's just a different kind of honor. The honor that tells me I don't want to kill a friend."

Tae could scarcely believe what he'd just heard. "We're still friends? After what I did to your father? How could you not want to kill me? How could you not hate me?" Amazement took him one step farther. "Gods! Even *I* hate me."

"Tae, I already knew."

Tae stared. No words could have caught him more by surprise. "You knew? How could you know?"

Ra-khir took the seat Matrinka had used for her vigil. "That first day we talked. I mean, really talked. You said the sage's notes were only the second thing you ever stole. Then you said we'd both be much happier if I didn't know the first."

"You figured it out from that?" Tae gained a new appreciation for Ra-khir's intellect. More than once, he suspected, he had mistaken formality for ignorance. *Just because a man relies on sword more than wits doesn't mean he has none.*

"Not then, no," Ra-khir admitted. "But you gave me a few more clues along the way. I think you wanted me to figure it out."

"No. No, please. Don't give me that much credit."

"Not consciously, perhaps. But you've got more morality than you think."

"You say that like it's a good thing." Tae smiled.

"Isn't it?" Ra-khir did not wait for a reply before continuing. "Anyway, it's obvious you were suffering guilt for your part in the crime. That's more punishment than I could have meted. I don't think you'll steal for money again—

something good came out of something bad. Perhaps most importantly, *you* didn't get my father imprisoned. Baltraine did. If you had not assisted, he would have simply used a different method, with the same results. In the end, it was my father's own honor that condemned him."

Tae accepted the explanation, still ashamed for his hand in the proceedings. "Are we working on any sort of a time limit? I mean other than the obvious danger the elves pose to a captive whose presence draws enemies."

Ra-khir shifted topics easily. "There's a three-month safe opening between the death of the king of Béarn and the passing of a suitability test by his heir." Ra-khir winced, and his head drooped. "Even I make mistakes, Tae. I had one last chance to have Colbey answer a question for me before he left, and I selfishly asked about my father's life when I should have asked about the king."

"You hoodlum," Tae returned with obvious sarcasm. "Selfishly worrying about your father. Stop it, Ra-khir. You're being silly."

Now the knight-in-training took offense where he had not before. "Don't belittle my honor."

It did not seem worth arguing over at the moment, so Tae ended the exchange. "I'm sorry. Do you think the king is dead?"

"Colbey's presence makes that almost a certainty. I don't believe immortals would involve themselves in our affairs until the danger became imminent."

"And we can assume it's a serious enough threat that the gods worry for their own security."

Ra-khir nodded with a thoughtfulness that suggested he had not looked at the problem in that light. "We'll work on strategy and try something new in the morning."

"Right," Tae returned with an enthusiasm he did not feel. The situation looked hopeless. The party had no weapons or defenses for distance attacks. So long as the elves disallowed discussion, nothing but delay could come of any plan. A ship could not slip past them without detection, but a swimming individual might. Someone would have to make the supreme sacrifice, and Tae knew only one among them had learned the ways of stealth and subtlety well enough to have a chance. The others would not allow him to risk himself, so he could not give them a choice in the matter. "Something new in the morning," he mumbled, closing his eyes. He was going to need sleep now, while he could still get it.

Mior's mental call startled Matrinka from the depths of sleep. *Wake up! Quickly!*

Matrinka jerked up from her cot, tangled in blankets. A lantern swung from a gimbal ring, rolling semicircles of light across the interior. Ra-khir and Darris curled on the floor, and Kevral lay still on her cot. Tae's bed was empty, the covers in a rumpled heap. Mior perched on the upper step of the ladder, scratching desperately at the hatch. *What's wrong?*

It's Tae. He went above.

Matrinka sighed, dizzy from fatigue and craving more sleep. *Dearest Mior, he probably went to relieve himself.*

He was fully dressed. I saw him studying knives as the hatch closed. I think he's going to try something dangerous and heroic.

Matrinka rose, for Mior's sake. *Dangerous and heroic? This is Tae we're talking about.*

Let me out, Mior demanded with an urgency Matrinka could not ignore. *Let me just make sure.*

Matrinka padded quietly to the hatch, despising every sound she made. Kevral slept lightly. Tae might be able to dress and leave without her knowledge, but Matrinka did not share that skill. Balancing speed against silence, she pushed at the hatch. It had barely opened a crack when Mior slipped out and galloped onto the deck. Moonlight spilled through the hole, and Matrinka soon lost Mior to the darkness beyond it.

Matrinka waited until Mior returned. *I knew it! He's swimming for the island.*

Alarm swept Matrinka, and she cursed herself for not responding more swiftly. Apparently, her mood slipped through to Mior.

Don't blame yourself. He was out before I even knew it, and no human sleeps lighter than me. Mior added determinedly, *I'm going after him.* She headed back out into the night, her white patches visible long after the other parts of her disappeared.

No, wait! Mior, cats can't swim.

Yes, we can. The contact faded as Mior drew beyond range. Matrinka felt the calico's anticipation as her own, heard the almost inaudible splash of her landing. *We just don't like to.* Then, the last shred of the mind-link pulled away.

"Wait!" Matrinka shouted, not caring who she awakened. "Mior!" She clattered out onto the deck, racing for the rail. The ocean stretched in front of her, the water like ink except where the moonlight touched droplets rebounding from the hull.

Captain and Kevral reached her simultaneously, the Renshai instinctively skidding between elf and princess. "What happened?" the Renshai demanded.

"Tae, it's Tae." Matrinka sobbed. "He swam for the island. And Mior followed him."

Kevral swore with the violence of a warrior. "We'll go after them."

"No," Ra-khir said softly from the hatchway. "Let him go."

Kevral whirled on the knight-in-training. "Are you crazy? You'd let him face two hundred enemies alone?"

Ra-khir threw up his hands. "If it was you, I'd worry about such a thing. Tae won't face them, he'll evade them. I wish he'd told us he was going, but I don't think it's a bad idea."

Matrinka held her breath, frantically trying to catch a glimpse of Mior through the darkness. *What if Mior drowns? What if she drowns?* Tears raced down Matrinka's cheeks, and she hated herself for worrying more for a cat than a human companion. She could not imagine her life without the greatest gift King Kohleran had ever given her. The sleek calico that had grown from the grimy little furball had become a symbol of Matrinka's love for a grandfather she would never see again.

Kevral drew a breath, but Ra-khir did not let her speak. "If you accuse me of wanting Tae to die, we'll duel right here on this ship. No woman is worth killing a friend for. Not even you."

Kevral choked, obviously taken aback by the vehemence of Ra-khir's words. "Calm yourself, Ra-khir. I was just going to volunteer to go after him."

"Bad idea." Darris' voice preceded him up the ladder, though obviously he had heard the gist of the conversation. "Tae's faster, and he has a head start. Anything we try to do to help will only draw attention. And foil what he just risked his life to do."

"I think," Ra-khir said carefully, the anger leaving his voice, "Tae needs this to feel good about himself. More importantly, I think he has a chance to succeed. Right now, that might be more than we have, with or without him."

The urge seized Matrinka to plunge overboard and search for a cat she could never hope to locate in the vastness of the Southern Sea. No lack of courage stopped her, but rather the knowledge that her friends would follow and she would risk other lives on a hopeless mission. Instead, Matrinka slid to the deck and wept.

Despite the hampering bandage, Tae made good time, dragging himself to an empty part of the shore beneath the cover of night. He had found the gathered elves simple to avoid, their locations brilliantly lit with a steady glow that seemed unlike any campfire. Night breezes cut through Tae's sodden clothing, chilling him to the bone. His shoulder throbbed a relentless cadence, and the agony of his hand wound resisted the nagging familiarity that could allow him to ignore its presence. Tae lay still for several moments, trusting the tight black breeks and tunic to conceal him. He kept his breathing to a shallow pant, afraid larger movements might reveal him. As soon as he caught his breath, he rose to a crouch, then skittered into a grove of narrow-leafed trees.

Again Tae waited, ears filled with the natural scrape of leaves in the wind and the high-pitched shrilling of night insects. He appreciated their music which would obscure the rustle of his movements. He trusted his ability to move in silence, but not without sacrificing the speed required to finish before he lost the sheltering darkness. So he moved swiftly through the brush, cursing every misplaced footfall, though it brought him one step closer to Griff.

Then, suddenly, the fence Captain had described appeared in front of Tae. Composed of a mesh he did not recognize, it appeared more like a pen to hem in animals than a means to guard a fortress from invaders. He peered through the closely spaced triangles, locating the central structure with ease. Its rough walls made a stark contrast to obvious attempts at decoration. Fancy columns interrupted its surface at intervals, yet moss cluttered the rooftop. Accustomed to

Eastern cities, placed so close they had all nearly merged into one, Tae could not fathom why builders would take such care to construct artistic touches yet leave one of the most important parts to corrode. He found the answer in Captain's explanation of elfin architecture, then drove it from his mind. All that mattered now was the success or failure of his mission.

Tae seized the meshwork in his left hand and wedged his toes into the tiny spaces the triangles allowed. Though it appeared delicate, its sturdiness surprised him. Where it touched flesh, it seemed to vibrate. Concerned for the magic imbued into the lattice, Tae climbed swiftly and jumped from the top. He rolled into the compound, the jar of the fall aching through his shoulder. His left hand tingled from the contact but seemed uninjured. Suddenly, light caught the corner of his vision, and he took another look at the fence. It glowed. The mesh etched vivid, crisscrossing lines against the night.

Alarm! Tae raced for the prison, desperate to complete his job before the light drew every elf on the island. *Magical alarm!* Time became too precious to waste on caution. He darted across the open ground, surveying as he went. He would not have expected a prison to have windows, yet he searched frantically for any opening but the door. Elfin construction might allow for such a thing.

Tae's split-second exploration revealed nothing useful. He ran for the front, drawing his daggers, hoping the door would shield his mistake from guards inside and taking some solace from the alarm's soundlessness. A noise crunched through his hearing, movement near the outer gate. *Too late.* Tae faded into the building's shadow, praying for a miracle.

The gate clanged open. Tae held his breath, just as a volley of unspoken conversation burst into his head.

Do you see anything? he understood in at least three different mind-voices.

No. Not me. Nothing here. More than a dozen answers followed.

Something triggered the defenses. Keep looking.

Several manlike figures appeared in the compound, many carrying light sources that glowed with a strange steadiness. It seemed to Tae as if they repelled the darkness in patches rather than actively disrupting it like torches or lanterns. He flattened to the ground at the base of the prison, choosing concealment over preparedness.

The elves continued their search, their footsteps a delicate shuffle over grass and sand. Their conversation disappeared. The lights floated in chaotic patterns. Tae remained still and silent in the darkness.

Suddenly, a howl rent the hush. Tae stiffened, glancing up, afraid it was an elfin cry of detection. An animal skittered through the darkness, white patches tracing its movement. Gradually, his mind registered the familiarity of the sound, so much like Mior's protest when he had stomped on her tail. *A cat?*

The elves clustered toward the noise. *What is it?*
An animal of some kind.

A jumble of speculation followed. None could identify the animal, but most blamed it for sparking the alarm. A few demanded a more thorough search. Others had already abandoned their hunt for the more interesting task of befriending and studying the creature they found.

That couldn't be Mior. Tae dared not believe the calico had followed him here. Impossible as it seemed, no other explanation fit. He had never heard of wild cats, and the elves' curiosity suggested they had not found others on their island. He had caught only a brief glimpse of the creature, but its hopping run, feline shape, and mewling complaint suited no other animal. The elves had shown no malice toward the creature, despite their belief that it set off their alarm. Mior or another, Tae had little choice but to use the distraction to his advantage.

Tae took another glance at the closed stone door, then turned his attention to the moss-covered roof. He could never have scaled Béarn-smoothed walls with one hand, but he believed the rough-hewn elfin work might prove easier. Without further consideration, trusting the cat to keep the elves occupied, he sprang for the wall. It offered no ledges, but its irregular surface provided enough friction to cling. He floundered gracelessly, his progress unsteady. At length, in twice the time it should have taken, he flung himself over the edge and onto a low-pitched rooftop.

The moss gave spongily beneath him, sticky and moist against his cheek. It reeked of damp and mildew, a thick odor that all but choked him. He maintained control with difficulty, holding his breath and remaining in position for several moments. No shout, mental or verbal, wafted from below. Tae loosed a pent-up breath, shifted to the side of the building furthest from the door, and dug through the moss with the tip of a dagger.

Dirt and greenery peeled from the rooftop, revealing rotted timbers below. Tae chose a board that appeared particularly eroded, slivering away at the wood. Hammering strokes would enlarge the hole more rapidly, but it would also make more noise. Tae contented himself with slow, steady progress. The board thinned rapidly, the moist layer of decay making his job easier. Soon, a scattering of dark brown wood chips surrounded Tae, and the aroma of oak replaced the musky, moldy stench.

At length, Tae carved a small hole that opened on an area darker than the rooftop. He cursed the lack of inside light that made the moon glow at his back a handicap. Nevertheless, he continued, widening the hole in tiny increments. At length, he risked a peek, poking his head through the opening to examine the support system below. The trussed rafters he expected were missing. The elves had taken advantage of the low slope of the roof to eliminate half the support system usually found on a peaked roof.

Tae jerked backward, his sudden movement more than the tenuous construction could bear. Beneath him, beams folded toward the opening. He made a wild dive as his footing disappeared beneath him, but the impact of his landing proved too much for his new location. The boards crumbled beneath his weight, and he plummeted through the hole amid a shower of shattered wood. The roar of snapping braces and the thunk of wood against the ground hammered in his ears.

Tae landed on his feet, bent his knees, and rolled. Hunks of wood imprinted bruises across his back and shoulder, and he tumbled down a loose pile of broken boards. He staggered to his feet, ears ringing, vision fighting the gloom. Rhythmical music filled the air, a single voice piercing its beat. His consciousness wavered, lost beneath a steady whirring and a wheeling shield of black and white spots. He took another forward step, teetered, and crashed to the floor. *Not again*, he managed to think before oblivion overtook him.

Chapter 45

Division

Soon, there will be another battle. One or more of us will almost certainly die. But, no matter the methods of our enemy, the Renshai will live or die with their honor intact.

—Colbey Calistinsson

The dramatic arrival, capture, and torture of the Easterner drew Rantire's attention from her pinched and aching gut. For more than a week, she and her charge had survived on nothing but the condensation licked from prison walls and handfuls of leaf mold and moss that had once formed their patterned carpets. Rantire's cell had precious little of the vegetation; she had torn it aside months ago, seeking a place to dig free of her prison. Beneath it, she had discovered a layer of stone that had resisted her best efforts. The elves had made no formal mention of their decision to starve their prisoners to death. The food had simply stopped coming, along with the visitors who once came in the night to hear her stories.

Weakened by neglect, Rantire remained seated in the far corner of her cell, as near to Griff as possible. She had cautioned him to remain still and quiet. If the elves believed them nearly dead, they might grow incautious and create the opening Rantire had awaited since her imprisonment. But the elves paid them no heed. They stripped the magically sleeping Easterner of everything but his clothes, set him inside the cage beside Rantire's, and left him in the torturer's care. The partial collapse of the roof left a pile of rubble that had dented or smashed the cells beneath it and knocked one of the hallway gates from its hinges. The elves ignored the mess, leaving the building together, exchanging verbal and mental questions and concerns. The shared thoughts required no understanding of language and consisted mostly of speculation about the man's arrival and methods. Rantire had learned enough of the elves' language to also sift concern about an approaching threat from their conversation.

The Easterner awakened, and a session of brutality followed. Every sound roused Rantire's memories of her own torture, and she alternately suffered sympathy and outrage. She talked to Griff incessantly, directing his concentration so that he could not focus on the events taking place in the cell beyond her. She kept her body always between him and the scene, more a symbolic gesture than a necessity. The darkness hid the Easterner. Occasional screams punctuated the torturer's melodic but distorted trading tongue as pain overwhelmed the stranger.

Griff twitched, losing his train of thought with every gasp or shriek. Moisture filled the Béarnide's dry eyes, and he pleaded with Rantire to let him beg the elf to stop the pain. Rantire found her own vision blurry, more from sympathy for Griff's pain than the stranger's. Once, she would have disdained the man as weak; she had survived the same torment without giving the elves the satisfaction of a whimper. Now she discarded that attitude as callous. She had no right to expect silent courage from a *ganim,* a non-Renshai.

After the first two screams, no conversation could distract Béarn's heir. He curled into a ball of misery, wasting his insufficient water on tears. Rantire kept a consoling hand on her charge, her attention freed to listen to the Easterner's confession. Once he started speaking, voice breathy and gasping, the torturer stilled and the sounds of magic and pounding disappeared. He told a tale of humans who came in peace to discuss a compromise and how, if those people did not get their discussion, they would return with reinforcements and destroy the island. He warned that if he, or any other human prisoner, got harmed, the humans would retaliate with ten elves' lives for every human life. If he gave more detail than that, Rantire missed it. The distraction of her sobbing charge and the dips in volume of the Easterner's voice stole many of his words.

At length, the Easterner sagged to the floor, apparently unconscious. The torturer left carefully, banging the cell door closed behind him. His sweeping steps carried through the prison.

Griff uncurled as the elf departed, dark eyes probing Rantire's earnestly. "Please. Make sure he's all right."

Rantire nodded, skittering to the opposite side of her cage to check on the stranger. He lay curled on his stomach, eyes closed and limbs still. Blood seeped through a filthy bandage on his right hand, and red patches that would become blisters and bruises mottled his flesh. Shaggy tangles of hair hung around his face, hiding his features. His breathing, though regular, remained shallow and a little too rapid for sleep. "Are you awake?" she whispered.

The Easterner made no reply or movement that Rantire noticed. She started to walk away, suddenly realizing his eyes had come open and he studied her in the darkness.

Rantire kept her voice pitched low enough that hovering elves could not hear. "How much of what you said was true?"

"Some," the man admitted, moving nothing but his lips. "Are you Brenna?"

The use of her alias raised alarm. Rantire had learned that some humans had joined the elves' cause for money. "Where did you hear my name?"

"The captain of the ship my friends are on mentioned you to Colbey."

"Colbey?" Rantire could not believe what she was hearing. "You met Colbey?" Her eyes narrowed as the story grew impossible. "Who are you? And what kind of game are you playing with me?"

"Look, I'll satisfy your curiosity in a bit. Right now, I'm in a lot of pain and I'm working on a tight schedule. I'll ask the questions. You answer, all right?"

Rantire's defenses rose immediately. The demand sounded too much like her first conversation with Dh'arlo'mé. *Paranoia, nothing more.* Elfin strategy still confounded her, but she doubted anyone would stage a fall through a ceiling, especially for the benefit of prisoners starved half to death. *You've got to trust someone sometime.* "All right," she agreed reluctantly.

"Is Griff here?" the man whispered.

"In the next cell."

"Is he well?"

"As well as can be expected for a man who hasn't eaten in a week."

"Gods," the Easterner said, spitting it like a curse. He added suddenly, "Are we being watched?"

"It's possible," Rantire admitted. "Sometimes they listen around the corners. Can't hear us if we whisper, and the vast majority don't know the trading tongue. They don't seem to see any farther than we do in the dark. So, if you don't see any of them, they probably can't see us."

The Easterner pulled himself to his hands and knees, crawling to the mesh door and its lock. He examined it briefly.

"Don't underestimate those bars," Rantire whispered. "They're a lot stronger than they look."

"The lock's bizarre."

"You're a locksmith?"

"No. But I've known a few." He added with a look that suggested the words should have proved unnecessary, "Self-taught."

"Is he well?" Griff asked, his voice booming over the whispering.

The Easterner stiffened suddenly, then grimaced. Leaning on the mesh, he worked his way to a stand, still examining the lock.

"Just a moment," Rantire whispered. She headed back to the opposite side of her cell and addressed Griff. "He'll be fine. He seems to think he might be able to get us free." Rantire did not share the newcomer's enthusiasm, but she saw no reason to dash Griff's hopes, too. "Right now, I'm giving him as much information as I can."

"Good luck." Griff stood, grasping the mesh and peering through the darkness at the stranger.

Rantire skittered back to the Easterner who had dropped to his haunches, a pensive look on his scratched, abraded cheeks. Rantire suspected those injuries had come from his fall rather than any affliction of the torturer, who had always spared her face. "What do you think?"

The Easterner shook his head, obviously annoyed. "With the proper tools and ten fingers." He raised and shook his bandaged hand. "I could probably get this thing open."

Griff's voice floated through the darkness. "Here, kitty. Here, kitty. Here, kitty."

The man's head jerked toward the sound.

"If you want to get even more bothered, they keep the key just around that corner." Rantire gestured to a corridor that ended, as far as she could tell, in a rest area.

The Easterner glanced in the indicated direction, pensive. "The guards don't carry the keys?"

"Nice kitty. Good kitty." Griff's happy voice made him sound childlike.

Rantire glanced at Griff. He crouched at the front of his cell, attentive to something in the hallway she could not see. "As far as I can tell, there's only one key and they share it. It opens all three of our cells, at least."

"They've let you see where they keep it?" The Easterner sounded incredulous.

"I don't remember if I saw them or just deduced it. They don't think I know any of their language, but I've figured out quite a bit. Anyway, I was the only prisoner here for a long time. What did it matter where they put the key. If I was free to steal it, why would I need it?"

The Easterner craned his neck toward Griff. "Is that a calico he's playing with?"

"You mean a cat?"

"Yes."

Rantire sidled toward Griff, curious. She had seen no animals of any kind in the prison, and her discussions with Oa'si had revealed that the elves did not keep pets. They lived in harmony with animals, neither eating nor, as Oa'si put it, enslaving them. "You're right. He's a calico."

"*She*'s a calico," Griff corrected. "All calicoes are female."

"Mior, come here." The Easterner beckoned from his cell.

The cat mewed, then trotted past Rantire's cell to the Easterner.

He knelt, as close to the mesh as he could get without touching it. "I don't know why you followed me, girl, but thanks. I owe you a thousand pets." He glanced at Rantire. "This is going to sound insane, but this cat's real smart." He returned his attention to Mior. "I need you to bring me the key. Do you understand?"

Mior sat, twitching her tail. She spoke a soft meow.

"All right, Brenna. Explain where the key is. Keep your description as short and simple as possible. She's a bright cat, but she's still a cat."

Rantire looked at the Easterner, reading sincerity in every line of his face. Agony and exhaustion made him appear nearly as old as she, though she guessed he was closer to Griff's age. Feeling like an idiot, she started talking to the cat.

On the aft deck, Darris coaxed music from his mandolin that perfectly matched the slosh of water against the hull and the gentle whistle of wind in the sail. The rhythm of the swaying ship became a silent drumbeat to the song. Beside Darris, Captain whispered suggestions that the bard gradually incorporated into his playing. The concepts turned alien, and Kevral found herself in wild woodlands unmarred by path or ax. Animals twined freely through the brush, fearing nothing, and laughter wafted from the branches like tiny bells.

A nudge drew Kevral reluctantly from the image. Ra-khir held up two wax-impregnated wads of cloth, then wedged them securely into his ears. Kevral glanced toward the horizon. The island seemed to grow as they drifted nearer. She clutched the fore rail in fists white with strain. In a moment, they would draw up to the spot where the elves had pounded them with magic, and she was not going to be jolted overboard again. It had taken the combined strength of Ra-khir and herself to hoist her back on deck. Soon they would discover whether or not Darris' talent could disrupt the train of concentration necessary for chanting.

Kevral shoved her own earplugs in place, turning Darris' song to muffled noise. Drowning out his talent freed her to concentrate fully on combat. A moment before, she would have believed the precaution unnecessary. Only after she blocked the music did she recognize the significance. The bard's playing controlled her mood while she listened, drawing her to faraway places, granting them an impossible familiarity. She turned her attention to her swords and cycled Renshai mental techniques into focus and power.

Before long, Kevral could see figures on the beach. They moved erratically, unexpectedly frustrated. Apparently, the bard's music had done its job. The rest depended on Kevral and Ra-khir.

The elfin ranks broke as sand grated beneath the *Sea Seraph*'s hull. Elves darted for trees, leaving a dozen clutching swords, axes, and clubs to defend the beach. In the trees, mouths moved simultaneously; but their chant disappeared beneath the thin trickle of mandolin and bardic voice that invaded her earplugs. Kevral did not wait for the boat to fully land. She sprang over the gunwale, striking water with a splash that soaked her. Howling an echoing war cry, she charged the waiting elves with both swords drawn.

Blood lust exploded within Kevral. As the elves clustered into an offensive wave, she sprinted directly for the thickest part. The first sweep/cut combination had nearly reached its target when she belatedly remembered to turn the blade flat. Her right-hand sword battered an elf to unconsciousness. The second slapped another full in the face, sprawling him into two behind. Fire seemed to course through Kevral's veins, stoked by the memory of the envoy's Renshai, slaughtered in sleep. Killing became a raging need. She blocked three sweeps at once, ducked under an elf's guard, then hacked the ax and a finger from his grip. Renshai control struggled against Renshai battle wrath. *Don't kill! Don't kill! Don't kill!* The words cycled into meaningless syllables, but conscience kicked in where spirit failed. Kevral hacked through the elfin line without taking a single life.

The elves ceased mouthing a unison that kept dying beneath Darris' distraction. Lights assaulted Kevral, playful yet blinding. Elves dove like birds from the treetops, harrying and retreating. A savage cacophony of noises penetrated even through her earplugs. Kevral continued to fight, battle-drunk and sword-possessed. She sliced and thrashed, using hilts and flats, feet and hands, knees and head as weapons. Desires warred within her: the violent need to avenge Rantire and Randil, the urge to slaughter those who would destroy mankind and all the world, and the promise of honor she had made to Colbey's friend. That last bound her like shackles, and her war cries expressed as much frustration as joy.

Blades bit through Kevral's defense. Nails gouged her, and hurled fruit glided through her wild web of attack. She noticed none of it. Her senses retreated behind the warrior's need to dispatch enemies. Only one shred of understanding remained, that which clung to honor, that which would steal Valhalla from her death should she stoop to forsaking her vow.

Then, suddenly, a high-pitched shrill cut through the dull rumble sifting through the earplugs. The dribble of music disappeared abruptly, and a clear shout of triumph replaced it. Kevral whirled toward the *Sea Seraph*, vision clearing from the red haze of battle long enough to show her Ra-khir struggling with a staff to defend the boat from a press of elves.

"Modi!" Kevral screamed, flying toward the battle. The elves broke before her bull rush of fury. They peeled away, galloping back toward the island and leaving her a wide berth. Darris' voice returned to her ears, soft and hoarse, without the instrument's accompaniment. Kevral skidded to a halt, Ra-khir skittering out of her way.

"They broke his strings, I think," Ra-khir shouted, his voice desperately muddled. "Magic, I think. They didn't get past me."

Kevral bounced off the hull, using its stability to reverse her momentum, then raced back toward the elves. She saw their mouths simultaneously open again, though she could not hear their chant.

A presence slapped into her head with impossible clarity. It spoke with concepts rather than words, communicating a complicated strategy in an instant. Kevral caught the gist: The elves prepared a spell that would put everyone to sleep, including many of themselves. Those affected were to secure their positions so they did not fall from trees. Those left awake were to slaughter the humans before bothering to rouse their companions.

"No!" Kevral shouted as a fog seeped into her consciousness, sapping her alertness. "No!" She continued to run, calling forward the mind control of the Renshai. If the spell took her, they would all die. "No." Her shout weakened, and she felt her legs go numb, stumbling. *No.* Her mouth lost the strength to cry out.

Then another presence speared through her mind. The second held a beauty akin to Darris' music, and its ideas ruptured her concentration. She staggered to one knee as another's thoughts paraded through her mind. *Captain.* She knew without question. In a heartbeat, he questioned the very unity he had defended to Colbey. He divided the elves into factions, *lysalf* and *svartalf*, the light and the dark. He called for followers in a rousing voice that seemed to shake the heavens though it appeared only internally. Kevral's thoughts scrambled as she felt herself topple, and no one answered Captain's call to arms.

Then, suddenly, one voice responded. Others joined it, small in number yet, apparently, enough. The *jovinay arythanik* was broken. Lucidity returned to Kevral in a rush, more exciting than a second wind. She charged up the beach, swords flailing. She had taken only three strides when a figure appeared directly in front of her.

"Kevral, stop!" Tae tried to duck beneath her attack.

It was too late to pull the blow. Kevral managed to steer the left blade harmlessly upward. The other, she dropped, and the sword thumped to the sand.

Tae seized Kevral's arm. "Come on!" He ran toward the *Sea Seraph*.

Kevral left her sword in the dirt. She had dishonored it and no longer deserved to wield it. Yet the deep sense of grief and loss she expected did not come. For once, she had placed respect for a friend over that for a weapon, and she knew no guilt for that decision. As they pounded down the beach together, she watched as Rantire, Ra-khir, and Darris assisted a strange Béarnide over the rail. Then, Rantire and Ra-khir scrambled up the ladder, and Captain shoved the bow toward the sea.

Tae and Kevral quickened their run, feet gashing holes in the wet sand. They splashed through the water. Kevral scrambled up the ladder while Tae caught the rail in his left hand and hurled himself aboard. Captain swung up a moment later.

Only then did Kevral glance behind her. From amid the branches, sunlight flashed from hundreds of eyes in brilliant hues. Captain thumped aboard.

A breeze rose from nowhere, tugging the tiny craft out to sea.

EPILOGUE

Without risk, there can be no change. And, without change, the world will stagnate into an oblivion every bit as awful as Ragnarok's chaos.
                                    —*Colbey Calistinsson*

A tempest racked the *Sea Seraph,* lashing the sea to foam beneath a tarry sky that emitted no light. Captain dashed fore and aft across the bucking deck, refastening lines and jerking the tiller on occasion to snap the ship from a wild spin. Usually, he negotiated the pitching floorboards without mishap, but sometimes a sudden jolt sent him crashing to his knees. Kevral attempted to assist, but the slam of waves against wood buried his suggestions, and she heard nothing except his pleas for her to go below with the others. At length, Kevral took the tiller, holding the craft on course and freeing Captain for other tasks.

Eventually, the *Sea Seraph* floated beyond the range of the elves' spell. Cracks of light appeared in the black curtain of clouds. Slowly the darkness faded into fog, then mist. The clouds left lacy patterns, white against blue. The sun beamed down on the battered sailboat, and friendly winds filled main and jib.

Captain flopped down on his bench and reached for the tiller. A cut on his forehead trailed pink blood, and his amber eyes looked more glazed than usual.

"No need." Kevral did not relinquish her hold. "I'm enjoying myself."

The elf managed a smile. "Enjoying yourself is all well and good, but if you don't put a mite to port, we'll never make Béarn."

"Oh." Kevral surrendered the steering, unwilling to admit she had no idea which direction port was.

Captain heaved a deep sigh, and his grin broadened. "Better this way anyway. My ship's to me like a sword to a Renshai. I feel naked without a piece of her in my hands."

The captain could not have chosen a more comprehensible analogy, yet it reminded Kevral of the sword she had left lying in the sand. Once, in Matrinka's room, she had allowed a blade to slice open her hand rather than dishonor it by letting it touch the floor. Not so long ago, a piece of cold metal had meant more to her than any living creature. Moments ago, she had willingly sacrificed a sword, and she still had no regrets. Dying in glory and a place in Valhalla meant no less to her than before. Her friends had just come to matter more.

Captain looked out over the sea, the smile locked in place. "Thank you, young Renshai. I will never forget the mercy you showed my people."

Kevral hesitated, loath to admit her loyalty to her own honor, not to him, had stayed her hand from killing strokes. In truth, it did not matter. The end result was the same. "I'm the one who owes you thanks. We all do. If you hadn't disrupted that spell, we would have all died. What made you change your mind about dividing the elves?"

"It was something Darris said. Sang actually. He never stopped singing, even when he knew he could never replace his instrument in time." Captain paused thoughtfully. "He was singing about nature and its cycles, how those shortest-lived first see the need for change. Insects adapt in days, animals over years, and men through generations." Captain shook his head, the point clearly difficult. "I'd been contemplating the problem a long time, but it took that moment of realization, when the fate of the world hung in the balance, to make the decision. I only hope I chose the right path."

Kevral tried to soothe. "Unity in the cause of right is power. In the cause of wrong, it is destruction."

"Colbey Calistinsson, right?"

"No." Kevral leaned against the taffrail. "Kevral Tainharsdatter."

"I'm impressed."

Kevral drummed her fingers on the rail. "So what happens to the ones who supported you? Are they in danger?"

"I don't know," Captain admitted. "I have no fear for their lives, if that's what you mean. Killing an elf on either side means one less elf forever. Neither *lysalf* nor *svartalf* can afford that."

Kevral nodded her understanding, recognizing layers beneath Captain's words. The sea journey to Béarn would give him time to fully ponder his decision, his loyalties, and his loneliness. Kevral's dilemma of love seemed to fade in comparison, and thoughts of the turmoil waiting in Béarn crowded in. Much had changed in the lands once her home, and none of it for the better. Battles stalked the horizon. Elves and traitors would stand in their way. *But Béarn's true heir, the innocent who can salvage the world, is on his way home.*

Kevral the Confident relished the challenge.